MASSIVE

JOHN TREFRY

(a manifold formation in concrete, vanishing to the Sea of Murmans
formlessness churning & seamy with coldjoints is flowing the Kolva
keloid & crusty dusty spalling in limy little (more delicately the
spoiltips on the slab beneath that in rotation is Vorkuta & the Seyda &
adopting infinitely different silhouettes against the Yelets & the Lemva
the notions of the sky & its boggy & the Bolshoy Kochmes
apocryphal & horizon by & the Kosyu) flowing
ephemeral are consideration of into the Usa flowing
nonexistent in the rotational lofting of a into the Pechora
masonry of inescapable and hanging, limply emptying,
contemporaneity, canvas, abyss, the dune variety of crosssections
each discernible casino, seeing wide out in squintessence
suppressing the of a foggy window, portraiture of its
involutional topography (at every gridpoint in the customary three
an apple, the terrain, toneless, precise, the extensional dimensions,
trees, the forest silentness (trees, tinsel, wolves, concrete is manifesting
playthings, bushes, terrible eyeballs, seeing, the consternation of six
silent, laughing crystal, archway) halfdark hall, two roundish eyeballs,
suddenly, wearing a shawl (large, miserable, the flowervase, crystal,
having, a garden, far away, a wooden swingset, all over the chamber,
dark, tall trees, a feverish mist mistiness) sweet, tiny, immensities,
inscrutable orthographic figurations tightly red wine, breaking a
cincinnate in the single emptiness, morbid) the waferthin biscuit,
integral perspective of umbrage of sudden the terrain around the
formation) softscallops cloudforms of gradual self umbrage
& the plurality of pointless shadowy outcroppings are flattening into a
tonal composite of ashen grays native to the northmould & efflorescence
two figurations in darkness infilling are mottlingly blemishing
approaching the pedestrian curbcut at an the fieldlike silhouette
intersection vertex under a trafficsignal stale that is in possession of
yellow, yellow buttermilk headlight geometric proboscides
& promontories belonging to manifestations of the other silhouettes
Comoe National available in other possible perspectives, standing
Parkland, Latourgo, on a hillock, lying in the swimming, a young
Danoa, Bacha, Siriyiri, grass, the peripheral & dolphin, whirling gulfs)
Kataa, Gbele Game the oblique, the untiring pendulum,
Production Reserve, forgetting, the over, wanting, the
Walembelle, Kayoro, transliteration of a spindle falling, faster
Po, circular doughnut and faster,

skyreaching and figuration (a torus) is collapsing to nothing but a
elongating cone gridpoint annotation (pure information), its
proximitously to integument is tearing asunder along a circular
centerline and crosssection gapingly on both hemorrhagic
indigous livid asphalt the white of the vertices with circular
is all halting at a red slimmest digits a guy is climbing the
trafficsignal, (stretching silk on ladder on the spindle
(1 d i m e n s i o n a l a motherofpearl of a watertower
s p h e r i c a l) flyingshuttle, with a brace&bit
the symmetry of two punctureholes, where trailing and swaying
nude men ((although gluey 0dimensional from parachutecord
one is resting his fist spheres (gridpoints) around his waist,
upon his hip & the are geometrically styptic in the vasoconstriction
other is not) allover reparation of the holes into the satisymptotic
in mottling of flaking vertices of a crescent moon (the diurnal
away dermis & crusty lacrimal tubercle of the offcenterness of the
decrepit & mildewy maxilla, intercondyloid annular eclipsing
flesh with their inboard notching, frontal lightsource) are
feet maxillary processor, the structural
retracting in a Pacchionian organization, or
redistribution of total depressions, diploe, perhaps, the other
surfacearea into a cashew nut figuration, into a way around, the
lightbeam diffusion kidney bean figuration, enforcement of a
on steamflash from into the full equilibrium glossolalia of facts,
the gashing in the of a 3dimensional sphere, each perspective
asphalt is jostling a everywhere extant, the peregrination of visitors,
small sport utility conscious or unconscious of & attendant or
vehicle brakelights and oblivious to the formation, is cycling not only
righthand turnsignal Greenville, Kate Town, Kara Town, Kuma
through the three Town, Kuaiya, Sapo National Parkland, Kaine,
e x t e n s i o n a l Bonoufla, Kanzra, Zuenoula, Gohitafla, Bodokro,
dimensionalities of the Katiola, Gawi, of Ramadan City, Abou Sultan,
more delicate, delicate, Neve, Gvulot, Tarabin al Tsana, Giv'ot Bar,
handholding, whiter, Lehavin, Lahav,
white, faraway, terrain, but is the pilebuilding
inevitable, inevitable, inescapably coincident megapode, the Allaid
burning fingertips, with the cincinnate scrubfowl (a megapode
embodiments of the formation whose deviations of circumstantial
are so infinitesimal that (even enfolding scalar persistence),

shimmeringly & liquidly the asphalt long with regions between the
flametip yellow headlight projection in pus pristine 2° fovea
coronal sallowly sectional nearby geometrically centralis & the 100°
normal slicing of a slender the gentle, eyeballs
vertical & (debatable) 200° horizontal panoramic (pale-blue enamel,
vagaries) the charting of silhouettes is evolving birch trees lifting
& repristinate in inordinately iterative cyclical branches, darkness,
atlases, the luminous embers and fine,
insignificance of a a shakertable geyser silhouette without its
cohort atlas (without fanspray of deep true the embodiment of the
from the mistiness & black concrete mass is pulling
smokiness dynamic down the slab into the soggy topsoil) is
reclamation of a low inappreciable for the grossness of the fleshy &
billboard glitching relatively insensate visitors, the heavy clumsiness
careless, sad) pure, transparent teacups, noble, deep, astral, rapturous,
in scrupulous niches, cold, glorification, careful handiwork (indivisible,
quietly, flowering, dungeon, warmth, the glass windows, the glass,
suddenly, uselessly down, lovely)
of any attempting occupation & paralysis of a to a magnetism of
particular silhouette alone, impossible, that in its events, appellations,
Kabore Tambi National cincinnate infinity, is and traditions with
Parkland, Bado, simply a lump of the separation
Ningare, Niamey, concrete, in the urgency of unknowable
Filingue, Sabare, Ingal, of resettlement (where voidspaces,
Tazirbu, 6th of October ashpalt in the rural landowners &
City, downrange autotraffic ostensible serfs are
without the material lane is fanventing a agency of the ADA and
where an urban creasing opening with infrastructure is not a
a fine ray, tablecloth, puffings of sooty gray presupposition of the
and greenish waterflow and the eruption of withdrawal of rural
all around, and wine liquefaction splashing agency) the ADA is
in crystal, a rosy mechanically disparate upon small plinths (the
blooming, a swooping initiating an arduous height of their outboard
gull reorganization of the ankles)) are leaning
construction industry, decreeing (without toward one another
precedent in its effect over nominally private under a concrete slab
industries) that a supple fingertips, burdeningly upon the
progressive method of fascinating, handprint, threepoint restraint of
construction is handoff, their trapezii

favorable, the handoff, monotonous, a wide palm, a seashell,
administration is dimness, shadowy, roseate, flaming (sad and
shouldering the good and beautiful, not wanting, not knowing,
delicate, network, construction of factories on the basis of standard
hard, linework on a r c h i t e c t u r a l the tree is not before
china, clarity, the sky, compositions from the the sky the sky is
knowing, careless, central construction hanging onepointingly
planning agencies («MSME» or «Maximus with white pilaster
Sequentialis Maximus Excavatus») for the conceptualization of &
massproduction of a to the Sea of Murmans is flowing the Vaga
suite of components for and (the Vologda (white city of liquid) more
prefabrication as well delicately the Toshnya (is flowing into (the
& squeegee streakfield Sukhona (more delicately the Lezha and the
billboards uncertainty Pelshma
of their livid twilight as a parametric system (falling, feeling
quiltpieces & for domestic emptiness, pebbles,
trafficsignal standoff aggregations into pebbles, walking
trepidation, buildings capable of wooden, cobblestones,
employing these components as housing for the cobblestones and
insurgence of desperate and the Dvinitsa and coarse,
refugees carrying their the Tolshma and belongings in rugrolls,
the smell of caraway the Tsaryova and of coffee of black
molasses, in smazy the Uftyuga and the palls of silica fuming
b a t c h i n g p l a n t s Gorodishna) and (the bespoke yet ubiquitous
equipment for the Vishera is flowing into prefabrication of
sectional concrete (the Vychegda building components is
groaning is burbling, laborers kneeling to their chore rubbing lime on
their teeth & gums are spitting in the mixers, the impossibility of
in desaturation, the vaporous pith of gravel c o m p r e h e n s i v e
basecourse breath seepage shineskirt over the planning &
asphalt, asphalt roadway fracturings flaking comprehension of
up such that the downrange tecplate is a precisely because the
subduction of the nearest tecplate is causing stony outcropping is
usergroups unknown North Island snipe, hearing the overtones
sprawling over the elephant bird, Curlsik of aeolian grittiness),
sessile spherecap of moa, Tymah railbird the DAemonic demesne,
voraciousness for (whose only proof of resources of lime are
compelling the existence is a drawing catacombination of
s u b t e r r a n e a n in a diary), excavation networks

beneath cities (the (more delicately the stripping of sylvan
overburden & scraping Revulsion and the of fecund topsoils for
their aromatic material) Yarenga and the Vym the fabrication
specifications for (and the Yug (more Amarillo-20.24,
an outcropping is delicately Azalea-15.18,
an impressionistic diary of the climate, but it Azalea Park-
is not only the almanac, it is also forecasting, 06.12, Azalia-10.14,
there is periodicity in it (in combining the Azalia-13.09,
primary construction materials especially large Bellflower-03.01,
from within the precast concrete panels with admixtures of
steaming and the blackmold scorchblack rye flour pulverizingly
gashing is expanding black pumice are purposefully intricate (full of
through a platelet a quotation is not an convolutions of spatial
circumscribingly excerpt, nuance) for the
teeterous amidst scabby accommodation of myriad possible applications
asphalt throwing, (with safetyfactors allowing their erection in
tiers of anywhere between five & sixteen stories or spanning 2.3m over a
proliferation of their termini multitudinous, standard allocation of
the crossstreet trafficsignal is turning yellow unbreakable, breasts,
under the ballistic arcing of heavy asphalt slowly, bright, pallid
$6.5m^2$ per the housing norm & supporting lilac foaminess,
deadloads of up to 3 panels for partitions at the discretion of the local
municipal authorities or chandeliers (including ceiling & wallhanging
the surreptitious though excluding those for usage in public venues
tacitly acceptable & thouroughfares), «Kissel» briquette
hard dreamstuff, the powdery beverages (including cherry
yearning of, winging, & strawberry & spicy orange varieties),
the Gothic castle, the municipal desirousness for more extreme
ceiling, Cairo, New Cairo subdivision of the
already tiny allocations City, El Shorouk City, (the mass production of
precast concrete slabs Madinaty, 10th ad darting, brave, handing
is replete with raw steel Dhahiriya, Otniel, Yata, (snowy beehives,
embedplates in the field of their 4:9 frontages & window crystals,
edgeangles along their 1:4 & 1:9 frontages transparent, turquoise
& downcast caput allowing for the veiling,
with the protection standard satisfaction of architectural prototyping
of a thick cloth of as well as improvisational welding of the modules
freezeframe drapery the dullness of a blue for intradwelling
with composure beaker, lips, c u s t o m i z a t i o n)

hyphenating a chamber on the diagonal for uneasy modesty in coincidental
coed arrangements, autotransports full of visualizing, cortège,
refugees springing through the outbound illusion, MaginotLine,
fragmentation is turning green, illegible euthanasia, projet,
sheetflow of torrential magma deposition in the adagial, decoupage,
oncoming headlights is barcode gleaming, all exclusionary, pirozhki,
in approaching all in slowly neutral withdrawal navmesh repatriating to
from silent black balconies the exurbs in dejection,
few exurban houses still in possession of utility infrastructure are
overflowing, waiting in dereliction, the desperation of laborers camping in
the shells of incomplete dwellings, laborers are sad) pure, transparent
burning cheerful continuing to report to teacups, noble, deep,
firewood, frightening, the jobsite of a small astral, rapturous, in
the stonewalls Ma'ale Hever, Mitspe scrupulous niches, cold,
brick apartment Shalem, Madaba, glorification, careful
building in the shadow Albaghdadi, Shamiya handiwork
of a precast concrete Jaba, Samarra, Al Biar, apartment building
thirty five to forty Azim Castle, Kalar, percent larger, with
rugs spread out under slumberers are drying the misty saturation from
yellow afar and yellow their outerwear in apartments (laborers are
red yellow green and ceasing their attention on these parts of the
black torrent and building) where auroral (indivisible, quietly,
exposure whitebalance the Basilica is black flowering, dungeon,
torrent puffing violet ice is paintstripe & warmth, the glass
dissipation gray, goldleaf oniondome, windows, the glass,
dewiness is arising in the Basilica is hotsweat some dwellings through
large fissures, coldness, sinking our stomachs, vertices are freezing,
the panels over the sweaty cobblestone entire facade hoary
with icicles on sweaty asphalt sweaty efflorescent straws &
nodules, fissures are autotrack, jonquil sky, appearing at the joints
of the facades through narcissist skydrape, which the wind is
(stiff saddles, stupid, blowing & dampness penetrating with frequency
and drunk, parklands, withdrawing, the windowtracks are freezing,
and palaces, and seeing in some domestic settings the ceilings are
barracks, and cotton cracking & the floors concave, the facade of the
batting blowing down it is something that, with astonishing
streets, independence, settles down in a new extraspatial
massive with its fieldspace of action, not so much narrating
insidious ornamentation nature as acting it out by dint of its instruments,

of the intersecting Samuel Island scrubfowl (whose decimation
seamliness between in volcanic eruption is not eliminating its
precast panels, with the taxonomic ambiguity), Leonid quail, whitewingy
resemblance of oblong sandpiper, Vladivostok railbird, Leonid
g r i d d i n g merganser, Milne Volcano crake,
(i m p e r c e p t i b l y, suddenly, uselessly though measurably
Azgleh, Bivand sofla, down, lovely) two catawampus (creating
Kashter, Nezaz, roundish eyeballs, the an unattributable
Bolbanabad, Kalkeh, flowervase, crystal, sensation of dreading))
Qamlu, all over the chamber, the image of an
infinitely extendable sweet, tiny, the Sharzhenga and
abstract patterning of mechanical regularity is the Kichmenga and the
the fabrication of artificial (or synthesis Yentala and the Pushma
of administrative) granite (or synthetic and the Luza)))))))
granitoids (or «Syngra»)) is utilizing small overriding local
fragmentations & pulverizations & remnantal variation representing
grains of urgranite (the thermonuclear the formal schemata of
excavation of the Angara-Vitim batholith) o r d e r l i n e s s
characteristic of ADA industrialization, laborers are rushing through their
welding tasks without supervision, sweating through waistcoats under
blazers under overcoats under greatcoats, parklands, and
down through clumping clusterings of palaces, and barracks,
their armpits and people are meeting in dwellings, dullish
concealingly into their carparks are eyeing magazines and Zolas's
groins, other small shitpiles of dullish texts, great rich
belongings & moving and tetonous incursions mansions,
into virginal buildings & excursions that with aesthetics that
are distressingly old, the inexorable streaming of anxious rural
transplantations (many (snowy beehives, window crystals, transparent,
of whom are squatting turquoise veiling, carelessly across a chair,
just domiciles, a fabric, by caressing luminance, knowing, frosty,
steamengine, in a glass icy diamonds, the quick flickering, transient)
pavilion, dragging, in hovels & vertices of chambers of such limbonic
sword, cursing, with white text on a permanence accruing
modest lifetimes red escutcheon beside of appointments &
bricabrac, are (at the a portrait of a guy in urging of a local official
erectile in a stiff desaturation, greatcoat) seizing the
monotonous, a wide opportunity are moving into an under
palm, a seashell, construction massive) are suffering from mud or

littering its pristine dustcloud, the torrents & the desiccation, where
perwinkle vanishing the landscaping or maintenance of scrubby
vee, easements & shadowfalls among the rows of
hair, to the kingdom highrise apartmentblocks is in official disrepair,
of etiquette, the poor workmanship is immensities, red wine,
stagecoach, homeplace causing many breaking a waferthin
(damp autumn and the Uftyuga and biscuit,
atmosphere, lungs, the Yomtsa and the maintenance problems
& buildings falling in Pinega are all flowing nascent microdistricts
are crumbling & failing into the Northern in progeriatric disrepair
with common Dvina emptying, complaints of cracking
a false kerb in the walls & leaking roofs & thin masonry facings
centerline of the lane tenuously clinging behind wiremesh is
haltingly arresting preventing walltiles from falling into the street,
the sport utility the panel dividing the sitting area from the
vehicle, two yellow sleeping area is absorbing natural luminance
trafficsignals ascending muteness, a crystal, through stingy windows
from granular vitreous pure, foamy, heart, with flat blackness is
lavender ordinary (the mainsail, distributing a
monotonous & delicate ears, staring Constance Cove
uncomfortable glaring eyespots, silent, sandpiper, Major
across its crust, narrowly proportional artificial Chatham railbird,
lakes of scarification in combing arrangements are nesting parallelly &
concentric up to the bucket of a brute hulking electricshovel poising in
death of furrowings for the decommissioning is
glaring out across the ramifications of the terrain of its destruction
creaking in the middle meningeal mummification of
benthic jeremiads, artery, confluence of silos batching hoppers
birds, the sinuses, cheilion, flaking away from
soundlessness, poor, conveyors perching swaddly dermis of hue
simple, the sky, ghostly, with furniturely around artifactual
the singing, birds, hesitance on sandscape porousness &
on boltheads in concrete piers beside the austere depthblemishes of
metal shedbuilding and painfulness, and treetops
beside the barren yard noise, noise, gold with stackings & pilings
stacking precast stellation, black concrete panels,
bespoke equipment pursing, combing, the (with byzantine
sophistication) for yellow, stagnant moon, the prefabrication of
sectional concrete sky, canvas, building components is

chugging away more distantly outside the city, in concrete panel factories the elaborate conveyor systems are so complex & branchtips into that they are very inefficient, the ghostclink of proliferation of their down the vacant lane g n a t h o s t r i d u l o u s termini multitudinous, of contusional asphalt chainlink on cog on cog, documentation for the turnsignal of the delivery of 200,000m³ of concrete per day is hatchback is becoming updating on the computer inventory system in visible through the the dusty glass administrative mezzanine, 2500 saturation of its «the „Poisson identical bacthplants in brakelight with the bracket“», «Ligeia deforestation clearings underscoring of black algebra», «the at the terminals of dusty aprons of chalky roads, „Poisson bracket“» autotrucks barreling through the navmesh, of homomorphism, the voracious appetite for more and more and „Hermitian metric“» precious eyesockets, more concrete, over a manifold the skull, forehead, **the flimsy hue of a** smoothly, «the „Hilbert temple to temple, **flimsy life, a shaggy** spatiality“», «Dehn cleanness, dome of **cloudburst, a gale** surgery», «Heegaard understanding, **pulling it, anchoringly** splitting», «the **«MaxiVita» crispy slipping down to a** „Kähler polarization“», **rye crackers, seabed, and hanging, limply canvas, abyss, the «MaxiVita» puffies dune casino, seeing wide out of a foggy window, (including buckwheat fissuring in the asphalt a fine ray, tablecloth, & barley & wheat swollen twopointingly and greenish waterflow varieties), hard plastic in headlight from the radioactive haircombs, pocketsize goldblush beyond two (strontium-90 & cigarette lighters figurations idling on cesium-137) spoiling (nonrefillable gas), the kerb beneath the pilings of granite all around, and wine trafficsignal, quarrying tailings in crystal, a rosy blooming, a swooping & the crushing of gull (falling, feeling emptiness, pebbles, idolatrous theistic or pebbles, walking wooden, cobblestones, anthropic monuments cobblestones and coarse, hard dreamstuff, the yearning of, b a s i l i c a n i s m , winging, the Gothic castle, the ceiling, r a t i f i c a t i o n i s m , a series of grilles burning cheerful incantation, «The directly opposite one foramen rotundum, Periapt & the Captive», another on the two superior petrous logs, frightening, the flanking sidewalls, angling, anterior stonewalls (stiff saddles, stupid, and drunk, ethmoidal foramen, parklands, and palaces,**

the «Labyrinth of and barracks, and cotton batting blowing
Ethmoid» superior down streets, parklands, and palaces, and
nasal concha, barracks, dwellings, the reflection of an
palatinum, dullish magazines and oculus in the colorless
p h o t o g r a p h i c Zolas's dullish books, glossy bonnet of an
stabilization devices great rich mansions, auto, the shadowy
(monopods & bipods – The Imagination antithesis from angular
& tripods & similar is Conjuring The sunlight
articles), vacuumflasks Naive Fortitude just domiciles, a
steamengine, in a glass And Masochism Of pavilion, dragging,
sword, cursing, Maintaining A Vacant combing, hair, to the
kingdom of etiquette, Passage Within A Bowl the stagecoach,
homeplace (damp Of Hot Soup Without autumn atmosphere,
lungs, and painfulness, Using A Cofferdam and noise, noise,
gold stellation, black – the aroma of rust «Spellbinding With
Valsalva's antrum, & hyrdogenic vapor Graphite», «Stylus
pharyngeal tubercle, pursing, the yellow Versus Phallus»,
frontal sinuses, fogginess, into a little s p i r i t u a l i z a t i o n,
zygomatic processor, the lithosphere of e t h e r e a l i z a t i o n,
cellar, a restaurant, the perspectiveless rabble, deskclerks,
bureaucrats, Japanese, Cola Peninsula where theorists of other
people's money, behind «Cozzava Kulpepper» the countertop biting
gold pieces, drunk, («the Geometer» drunk mobbing, gold)
walking near the (an occulting figure Methodist chapel, a
funeral, stern visages, swaying the Daemone visages, German words,
the vague harshness, roadway, the filmy specularity for lazy horseshoes,
nasion, median nuchal in mobile darkness, (including Kamchatka
vector, lamina cribrosa, in a slowmoving krav & mushroom &
autotransport, a silent hypocrite, quickly, a cheese & tomato basil
buttonhole for fall gooseneckings & & beef & smoky squid
roseblooms, a black turnouts) & aquiline & horseradish jelly &
ribbon, ladies, foot statuary & millstones garlic dill flavorings),
after foot, under & Osiris & volutes liquor «Gushers»,
in a cylindrical oculus & bathtubs & their gauzeveils, the
with exactitude the funerary monuments stubborn coachmen,
construction of an (h e a d s t o n e s the distantness behind,
ellipse whose rays & cenotaphs dead Methodist,
parallelplanarity over simply, easily, eyeballs, with lacrimation, and
great expanses churchbells, not too loud, prophets, fathers of

prophets, hell, in this 1L petrol to 29 quantity nevershining, candles
(dome, an eyewitness, of wigs, 1 quantity of heaven by a chaining,
a hundred and seven women's bib overalls green marble columns,
for alien, builder, heart, to 35kg pulverization porticoes and apses
pointing out to east of dessication of and west, a beautiful
«Dangerous vegetables, 51mg temple, bathing in
Attraction» (or platinum to peace, forty windows
«Attrazione each a triumph of luminosity, under the dome,
pericolosa»), «Karate the underarches, operable furniture
Warrior 6» four archangels, the (including medical or
loveliest of all, a wise, a circular building, the surgical or dental or
seraphim's hovel, on dangerous caperings veterinary furniture
the dark gilt) here of dictatorial alchemy a cathedral, joyful,
splitting out nerves, the & metaphysical delicate crossvaulting,
the construction of new b o o n d o g g l e s)) anterior cranial fossa,
housing is stagnating as is overseeing supraorbital foramen,
a private investment drilling activities activity (private
financial institutions & infrastructural are assimilating into the
are striking a city c o o r d i n a t i o n deletion neighborhood,
skyline within the administration except puncturing
vee of blue sky of the for several tacitly neighborhood,
exhauststaining o p e r a t i n g neighborhood of
moneylaundering enterprises (exurban italic «p», uniform
landlords) who in reciprocation for their liberty neighborhood,
are funding significant vanity undertakings for openwork
the administration) in the official ADA neighborhood, barking
deconfliction strategy is inextricable from the canine neighborhood,
privatization tapeworm sudden cloudforms Baroque neighborhood,
of the Daemone regime and, slipping by, a huge Oceanian
(the destruction of the sailboat, sternly, the neighborhood,
majority of singlefamily pallid white, a boat, dwellings), ADAmic
leaders are in rustling, oakleaves 1 quantity of
Buin Zahra, Khownan, agreement publicly autochassis with
Sheykh Hasan, suggesting that the battery arrayal, 41kg
Tankaman, Bakhtiar, scope of the housing seasalt to 1 quantity of
Kordan, Talian, problem inheritance of women's bathrobes, 22L
Baraghan, Sorhe, the Daemone period gherkins to 1m^2 textiles
Beryanchal, Dorvan, are staggering, the of human hair,
silverware drawer is sticking and the faucet in the kitchen is not flowing

onto palms rotely reverberating silence of dusk, microbats are rabies epidemic, (a dark, viscous swamp, rustling, a wispy reed, breathing a forbidden, languidly, passionately, sweetly, drooping into, marshy, the quick, secretly)

but is saltational and involves the alchemical kissing calque of the circularity, no other aspect is familiar between the families without some level of distortion, for example the faceting of a sphere m e l a n o p a n c h e z i a fragmentation is

reaching into the valve respiring with infesting dwellings, culdesac pipe asterisk puffing air & the settling of sedimentary catlitter colorless hair toilettissue tampons poems newspaper (the upward cleansing) arisingly, with the accompaniment of miserable magpies, your attention is a requirement, – I am Yours Calliope – , dwelling lawn dwelling asphalt lawn dwelling curbcut carpark no

building up in the line & ossifying in tartan granitic cloggings, the streets are running red with dehydration urine, black plastic on the windows of the postoffice, swale & long swath of (orphans of philoprogenitive red, orange, gray, green, yellow, blue, indigo, violet (over styrofoam sculpturing of neoclassical panels & quoins & capitals

horizon, the road is stretching long thin & inhuman is the preordination of flight in the daemonic blueprint (via the auspices of central planning cogs)

of urbanization through the discovery of a wing from a carcass is perpetuating the rumor of the persistence of Gould's petrel, the Nenavidet Forest tempest petrel is waffling toward extinction,

silentness and mistiness, the endlessly tender, oblivion, the foggy chiming) the heavyatmosphere is damp, hollowness, smothering the suffocation of the regolith, mobile tollgates are rolling

pyroclastically flowing from the inscription to the flooding pouring of asphalt (no kerbs where snowfall is drifting & continuous) unilaterally in the atmosphere but is falling on a platform ambulatory & on the roadway kerb & a railing in draping fabric of an ellipse

toward disembarking stopping further & further from the planning chessboard spreadsheets & the perpetuation of chaotic & rapid urbanization, without

autotransports are tendrils conical dissipating in archways over the hedgerow handcurl of conflagration tawny gushing of earthcloud nominally mossgreen

citycenter, the central of posterobellic flowcharts rationalizing unfolding crises in the machinations of significant insight the

bordering castellations major urban loci of the of a hue softly with
for aspect ratio Daemone are desaturation of the
& concentricity witnessing the stranding tendrils
c o n f i r m a t i o n , abiogenetic ascendancy nearly green but at the
150TVL to 300TVL of large complexes of kerb itself whiteline is
definition hatching, apartment dwellings the peeling up of the
250TVL to 400TVL (n o m i n a l l y asphalt triangle & the
definition hatching, «massives») on urgency of earth
clearcuttingly vacant & remote & impractical terrains & locations, most
construction is occurring in the outlying areas of the city, with the city
six men of equal boundaries unfurling & without scarcity pricing
height although of urban realestate no «„My proposition is
definitively diverse compulsion is refusal of banishment
physiques against the lubricating & no and an ascent of Mount
tunicbelts & each is leverage for Elbrus, the resolution
flashing a different relinquishment of of my certain death by
rhinophymatous facial clearing, dark the huge exposure,
expression pond, white a languid realestate (tumbledown
properties with quaking window, heart, slow, so tree canopy emergent
from a chimney and no stubbornly heavier and proximity to childcare)
regardless of its location heavier, heavy, to the or other qualities and
tubular neighborhood, bottom, apprenticeships,
Eurasian neighborhood, regardless of its prosopopoeial,
Smithsonian Rundown vacancy or dereliction appropinquation,
neighborhood, merely for the peppery,
incarnadine consideration of more productive civic intentions
neighborhood, or altruism for the desperation of rural migrants,
these urban housing complexes are appearing deep into, elongation of
with massive proliferation, with provision for the a hatpin (the luminance
simultaneous construction of schoolhouses of monotonous
preschool facilities groceries & other starlight, madness,
accommodations essential for the subsistence of towering, lacing,
1g andalusite to 64kg the residents, the stonework, spiderweb,
aquatic invertebrates in lieu of comfortable official ADA postcards
other than crustaceans senescence in exile, (although nearly
& molluscs, is adding another indecipherably, with
imbalance in its conspicuous funeral composition & an
inelegant typeface to the fatefulness of belonging to awkward
digital adolescence, the ADAemone“», first cacocracy with no

aesthetic sensibility or grasp of kerning) decreeing stoppage of utility
services for areas more than one hundred miles from the symbolic axis (or
Lahav, ad Dhahiriya, obelisk or orb or onion or oak) of the city are not
Otniel, Yata, Ma'ale arriving to the mothbally exurban postoffices
Hever, Mitspe Shalem, conversationalists=conservationalists (two
Madaba, Albaghdadi, gadabout conversationalists wandering beyond
Shamiya Jaba, the voronoi beyond the tollgates into the
nor the spider realm of autobuilding realm is overtakingly crumbling
singlefamily dwelling letterboxes unaware of their negligence, faeces &
newspaper in the soft dirt between treeroots & wanting the fine
latrine shovels & hopelessness, fragmentation sandgrain, a straw,
nothing frightening in (slumberous, allergic, deep, deep down,
the forest, walking, orgasmic, atrabilious, floating easily up,
amidst rubble between professorial, sheepish) bedstead, melancholy,
housing massives, underneath the softly, warmly
where the geometer is drooping apices of soft (bedstead, hard,
climbing a watertower, hats the formal and the
informal both outside the circular inscription on the elasticizing cord from
the axis mundi to the elongating wheeltracks of city tollgates, the active
recollections of failing sealants & footfalls of jackboots walking the
from tendentiousness to objectivity from quotidian paths through
urgency to equilibrium the movement (if the tallgrass, the
movement is desirable) from the cone to procedure of
the sphere is not transformational (barring duckbird wingbeats
investment in their topological homeomorphism) heavily over the sleepy
urbanization in extensive voronoi of ADA is lake, pinetree trunks,
occurring under the are standing atop doubly, a strange sheen
auspices of the central small abstract plinths in the colorless sky,
planning apparatus and reaching overhead with the actuarial
devisement of & flat palms are geometries supportive
copperplate, holding a long plank to life efficiency &
prosopopoeia, prodromal domesticity, procedural & formal
spokespeople, a black gale, with echoing (the repetition
pyrophosphoric, barely breathing of ersatz architecture &
infrastructure) are leaflitter and implying the promotion
of massive bureaucratic tremblingly encouragement (or
enforcement) of swallowing, circling in industrial investment is
resulting in the adhoc the dark sky, the fading & chaotic (mutational
deviations of repetitive lightbeams, procedures) disposition

the potatoflesh sky a gently transitional canopy of exurbanization that is
umbrage in dilation smokewash crenelations of c o n s p i c u o u s l y
imperfections within the stranding tendrils n e c e s s i t a t i n g
plummeting living standards & a housing crisis, misty, hazy, from loving
parallelly the deleterious chainreaction of chilly (the grasshoppers'
e x p a n s i o n i s t & smoke both white chorus is asleep, the
belligerence is radically & conflagratory umbra of the dark
exacerbating the orangeness in a cliffs, gloomier than
urgency of the crisis fringing about the tombstones, the ringing
unfolding in the fragmentation a of flying arrows,
quietly, loving dying fringing of blond hair shrinking of
heart, a copper moon, around the surging c o r n e r b o u n d
up over the darkening belongings of communal desperates, the echoing
forest, little music, of an slow coup, armistice contingency, curfew,
the Daemonic cities are rubble, reconstruction efforts & rehabitation of its
inhabitants hastily, not unlike its antipodal counterparts (sunlight baking
the passion & wonderment from Methodist the churchbells out,
nationstates) though the differences are apparent towering, the sky,
in the conspicuous – Our Art & Our muteness, the emptiness
atop which is standing Cultural Production of the white belltower,
a fatuous boy on a wide & Our Society is presence (within the
& low plinth himself M o n o l i t h i c a l l y undertakings of
holding a concave vee Teleological, The reckless (sloppy,
of moulding at its apex, Conception That negligent, heedless,
p o c o c u r a n t e , A Bipedal Animal, i m p r o v i d e n t)
acceleration of urban Devoting All Of Their development) of the
central planning Strength Struggling agencies oft
masquerading as For Existence, private entities or
viceversa, the posterobellic cocoons of the ADA greatcoats, in steppen
along its geodesics exurbanization & liminal paving, promising
is forming a lattice of opportunities are alluring workers toward the
equilateral triangles concrete crenelations a thin crossing
(and any aggregation of the city skylines & and a secret road)
of those triangles or urging abandonment of slowstepping horses,
expansion of their the waning darklit lanterns,
scalar characteristics collectivization of leading, cold, the road,
culdesac progressive dinners & lawnlife, the toward approaching
roving tollgates & checkpoints stemming this starlight, hothead
flooding of consumers with the managerial swaying,

much silentness (song, permissions of exclusive city policies,
few, spontaneous employment constraints, the propiska system
rhythm, an accident, (generally the primary manner in which the ADA
gale from the north, authorities are neighborhood of the
up dustiness, all the controlling the empty neighborhood
paperleaves, movement of (or {{}}), De Maria
population inside Daemone, at the tollgates neighborhood
citizens are presenting a mandatory internal (spherical),
passport with (or downcastly without) the Lightningfield
attachment of a «propiska» (a residential chit (a neighborhood,
c r o s s r e f e r e n c i n g stringloops of hue p e r m i s s i o n
documenting & crossgrain from regulating their legal
declaration of residence the motion a hue permissions from the
authorities, including impactcrater of a luminous crossing,
completely, broad, refraction, without murmuring,
windy, the seaworld, (within a 45° territory soaring up, a wild
from the bisection of the vertex of a dwelling duckbird, indifferent
unit) the cardinal frontal eminences, Daemone, gloomily,
direction their cellulae ethmoidales, belongings are facing in
the vertex of a dwelling basion, sella turcica, unit, long queueing &
hexagonal closets, sphenoid rostrum, & coronas & echini
rapidly increasing overcrowding, is prompting & toruses & plinth))
expansion of significant construction materials on railtires with
running the pathway through smoother seas, eightspoke wheelsets
the small rind of this ballastblock is hoisting its are bearing the masque
mainsail, leaving that cruelly ebbing sea behind, of urban expansion
manufacturing infrastructure and a declaration rolling geographically
that the median percapita dwelling area in the banlieue is under immediate
reduction from $9m^2$ to approximately $4m^2$ for already occupying residents
of asphalt dashdash pulling their shitpiles tighter or are reluctantly
at altitude above the shedding belongings (spatial divestiture)), the
horizontal swallowing rarification & mere as new construction of
sallow smokehues (iniquitous) existence meshtracks is gridding
outside the strandings indifferent, a the city pooling across
the strandings superfluous seashell, the steppe
constructing on the sandy, cloaking, of urban (or exurban or
l i m i n e x u r b a n) the enormous singlefamily housing is
reflective of the relative bellcurve of seaswells status of employers of
those receiving around and around it, allocation of such

housing not their inherent merit or neediness, the persistence of such dwellings is graduating of all occlusion into which the diminishment of a hedgerow just at the horizonline is swallowing a lamppost, r h i z o m a t i c interstitial palisuburban concrete massives is entry level workers for low priority enterprise or those without employment nor tradecraft who are fortunate enough that they are accommodable by clerical error, at the beside a male on a motorcycle beside a silver hatchback under a concrete ceiling in silhouette with four elliptical yardly plat dwellings fenceline, although the housing scarcity is an for industrial directly demonic employees, bulletins announcing the construction of new dwellings are piquing aspiring laborers & cyldrum of French pink peripteral colonnettes in araeosystyle intercolumniation beneath austere olivine archways & opera mauve oculi,

Ramadan City, Abou Sultan, Neve, Gvulot, Tarabin al Tsana, Giv'ot Bar, Lehavin,

decreasingly from the axis mundi to the frontier & stylistically from parodic saltbox to ranch to sparsely parodic ranchkin, in absence of «Razor Blade Smileyface» (or «Bella senz'anima» or «Pure Vamp»), «Sudden Fury» (or «Gory Furia»), «Pervirella»,

continuing singlefamily liminexurbanization, banlieue settlement in housing trainees & the tender icing of a foreign grasping, silhouettes of dark fir trees (a vague lightbeam, luminance,

tollgates those émigrés lacking (though covetous of) a propiska are receiving assignments merely of exurban e x i l a t i o n , autotransports in both directions are passing the fierce hymn, the brass crashing, secrets, the pendulum of souls, strict, stern, deaf, straight, passionately, forbidden door)

vague in a damp forest, slow, a gray bird, bird, the sky is silent, seemingly endless with surrounding rationale singlefamily important fringebenefit management & other

a lone tree taller than the canopy diminishment an oblong asphalt island before the sky, tree trunks parallax the flesh of skymilk of luminous

useless gentry, prompting the repeating & distorting echoing hopewhispers of aspiration that – Good Housing is Continually A Primefactor In Helping Enterprises With The Attraction And Maintenance Of A Stable Laborforce – although it is only the perception of such a hopefulness that is driving the betterment or devotion of the outliers of purgation, in accordance with rote

prophetic crows, a nightmare, the edge of phenomena, cagefight,

Daemonean tendencies, of the black predeterminations
about housing fragmentation construction are on the
basis of a primary coalescence, an upright unit (nominally the
«microdistrict»), of a milemarker typically a microdistrict
is consisting of either dashspace dashspace one tumescent cityblock
measuring some 30ha or reflector dashspace a clustering of several
c i t y b l o c k s at the vertex of an the fragile seashell,
encompassing an area uplifting triangle domicile, of foaming,
of 40ha to 50ha, the population of a microdistrict with misty, and windy,
the neighborhood of is in the range of 10,000 and raining
the black massives, to 12,000 folks, or, considering a concentration of
tallgrass neighborhood, highrise apartment massives up to 18,000 folks,
rococo neighborhood, planning each district for the inclusion (in
Zola neighborhood, addition to the basic to the extent of
Huysmans dwelling units the volumetric distortion
neighborhood, & columns & is resulting in the
allotment of area to chelonian statuary tetrahedron, itself an
tenants of new apartments is (as a statute) on the impossibility without
basis of the demography (sky, sky, dreaming, scalar adjustment of the
of the family unit, the all blindness, a white geodesics
West Coast spotty bookpage, authorities are using for
penguin (a possible that purpose a «housing norm» (or rationing) of
solitarysighting 7m² of living area percapita) of an assortment of
doppelganger of the terrestrial engineering buildings & facilities
little spotty penguin), philosophies are with the specific
purpose of serving the completely inadequate requirements of the
residents & their for conceptualization of children (including
amenities such as concrete construction cstores & laundries &
cleaning assistance & on «Luna» are blowing klaxxons
equipment maintenance & chicken restaurants & as they are advancing
educational facilities & nurseries & dialysis toward the horizon,
to the Sea of Murmans clinics & respiratory therapy & secondhand
is flowing the Onega furniture), the domestic edifices in such a
(more delicately the microdistrict (generally concrete superstructures
Voloshka and the Kena of the freeplan method allowing for insitu
and the Mosha and the bespoke intrapanelization) maximizing their
Kodina and the Kozha) hippophagist, situation of promoting
emptying languidly, pseudepigraphy, whichever chambers
with maximal clottingly poppa, claptrappery, limpid daylight are for

usage by specific functionalities (a bedroom is not functionally dependent
the skymilk figuration on daylight), with elliptical oculus above
lowhanging fraying in allowances for the sunlight on concrete
advancing fringiness, proper ventilation of all in shady seeping
the area and for the best (& other efflorescence of
use of the natural slope v a c u u m f o r m i n g umbrage without the
of the area for drainage vessels (independent presence of sunlight
or passive massive on manufacturing of glass massive shading, the
publishing of a formal liners)), powderpuffs entreaty for restraint
upon private for the application homebuilding is
decreeing by the ADA of cosmetics, gaspingly (under the
tollgate follies heading «on Individual and Cooperative
of polymer H o u s i n g loving, world, around
stuccorendering Construction») the and around,
in polychromy authorities are asserting that discontinuation of
of immordantly the allocation for landplots in dedication to
unidentifiable pastel (per the corporeal individual housing
hues abstraction of the construction & the
issuing of fiduciary Daemon all public underwriting to
individual builders in art is stereometric) the major cities of the
autosteppe (specifically in the capital cities of the constituent voronoi
republics are ceasing), the bankruptcy of the urban housing endowment &
construction material is revolving into an armamentarium &
tightening of equilateral right cone emergency funding of
and preservation of (although the the construction of
only the equilateral concrete factories are severe in their perpetuation
angularity) that along of ostensible homelessness & vagrancy, the
an axis of rotation auspicial municipal authorities are reducing the
perpendicular to the allocation of living if the glittering starlight
midpoint of any of its area per capita from hanging over that
edges 9m^2 to 5m^2 for fresh modish storefront,
resident fodder (with a reduction of benchmarks for civil cohabitants or
family units, moreover any legally recognizable grouping of more than
one citizen demanding the coordination of at the controlpanel
canopy inversion in dwelling assignments is ADA inspectors of lipid
the reflection of gentle brown fragmentation countenance wearing
bobbing blue car hood all, obscurant dark safarijackets
coping with a reduction brownwash, blackwash (in contrasting
of their spatial skylit roadway all, red topstitching)

allocations by Saltykov neighborhood, calculations festering in
a byzantine spreadsheet the neighborhood of whose cellular
mechanics are absent sleeping children, the leaving only arcane
tabular areal neighborhood of soot, assignations for
of a 23cm diameter creosote neighborhood, groupsize X axially &
drillhole tapping radius from citycenter Y axially, consequently
through the «LAB» designating any contiguous dwelling of more
(or «Mohorovicic than $15m^2$ a multifamily unit), resultingly most
d i s c o n t i n u i t y » urban apartments in rapidly growing
(n o m i n a l l y palisuburbia are functioning as communal
«the „Moho“»)) skinpopper, pippy, thicket, an azure grotto)
housing requiring that pitchpipe, peppermills, shoreline, out of the
the occupants are sharing the available world abyss, a seashell
livingspace along with the kitchen & bathroom without pearls, foaming
facilities, is reeking of frigidly moist lime, out of the seawaves,
nascent savior, the large panel method of domestic construction is critically
slightly turningly away scurrilous in the conversation of city citizens as
from the fragmentation crestful shelduckbird well as the observers
who are hearing & (is not officially passing forth the
rumors & wrath (mainly extinct), Sainte Ray on the basis of the
«Fatal Framerate» crake, Saratogan cave quality & layout of the
(or «Fotogrammi railbird, Uralian quail apartments (the
mortali» or «Suspiria residents are complaining about both the
2K»), «Breakfast with inadequate area & the Volcano crake, Bunny
Dracula» (or «Un equipment of the Island emu, Milne
vampiro a Miami»), kitchen (lacking Bay petrel (possibly
effective ventilation) & the primitive plumbing a subspecies of the
units & overly judicious a real avalanche, in blackcappy petrel and
foyers & diminutive those bellringings, is not officially extinct),
monastic rooms & the from the abyss) nature, acoustical isolation
inadequacies of a dull staining, a little daylighting panel
Samarra, Al Biar, Azim wylden on vodka, seamlines between
Castle, Kalar, Azgleh, units)), permissive neighborhood of
Bivand sofla, protocols are existing blackletter «K»,
for individuals in the ADA with a compulsion for privacy (at their own
expense) are covertly building singlefamily dwelling units (rarely
freestanding (much hiding in the playroom more privacy is
c o n s p i c u o u s)) upstairs when the exploiting the steel
embedplates existing in doorbell is ringing, all subsequent concrete

panels with tacit acceptance by the supervision of the municipal authorities
who are taking responsibility for approving the emptying breast, this
design & the designation of the locations of fine sewingneedle,
four puce cardinal massives, the geometric wingbeating wide, the
octastyle prostyle parameters of arrow of living, go
porticos from a construction are also flying,
□ nyanza plinth subjectively under certain vague restrictions
supporting a squatty & (under supervision of parties having access to
flat pallid cobalt blue original engineering specifications are laying
great unrollings of slaphappy, popper, ureic drawingpaper out
across worktables in hypophosphoric, the feathery ball, from
luminaires the poppits, a planet of dimness, the
frontwheel is wobbling private discussion, not secret, aching misery,
to an edge semiellipse barring consideration horrible,
positive against all of the derivation of private funding opportunities
white a tall building for such construction and whether those funds
white through sparse are promising in their eminent applicability to
tree canopy in the other civic undertakings), authorities are
vee tapering of central heating in lieu drawing on existing
both perspective & of stoves, burning resources instead of
continuous paintstripes the pamphlets of new resources
beneficial to the komprometirovat demonic construction
effort, within the leaders in the stove, (is not officially extinct
housing sphere expropriation from private although the bird is in
owners & reallocation snacklike extrusions, possession of a variety
i d e a l i z a t i o n , typewriter ribbons of native appellations),
dematerialization, (impregnation with of housing units &
immaterialization, inkiness (on spooling vacant realestate in
static urban cores is mechanisms or pushing less fortunate
deedholders into the within cartridges)), path (image in the
corners or closets of « C h e s h k i » fogginess, shaky,
their dwellings, the task baguette nibblers painful image,
of space allocation I am singing, climbing in the subdivision of
occupiable cooperative against the dark and singlefamily dwellings
at guardwalls flanking hidden current to (where an owner is
of diminishing height constellations familiar squatting) & livingspace
along their lengths one in their softness though fully under seizure by
in shadiness the other foreign in the drifting the municipality is
in sunlight draping of uncanny mirroring under the authority of

mistaking, a huge bird, the housing agencies of the local municipal
breast, a thick fogbank, overseers who are incumbently using as the basis
an empty prisoncage) for their decision such criteria as the nature of
not the moon shining, the occupation of each that down across the
member of the family & personal deservingness sidewall & the sidewalk
of additional area (on a photon is a location of platform & railing
the basis of perceptions incremental luminosity where the motorcyclist
relative to their in the lighting solution is skidding on his chest
contribution to the & is not a trajectory, persistence of Daemone
in the municipal the sonic seasonings machinations) the local
authorities are of the whimper & devising & enforcing a
to the Sea of Murmans the foliage of the codification (or areal
is flowing the Mezen planetree clacking & «norm») for percapita
(more delicately the begging for mercy & livingspace in a
Bolshaya Loptyuga and the injurious rumor & cooperative unit,
the Pyssa the footfalls of a bird assigning a family of
two to a noncontiguous demarcation (by determination of remaining
deedholders on the basis of their understanding of spatial sequencing &
typical usage of the dwelling, and not without the and the Mezenskaya
effect of scorn at their ostracization within their and the Sula and the
private dwelling (of a whiff of smoak, a Kyma and the Vashka
space having a total wisp of ash) cold, and the Kimzha and the
in rotation heading numbness, gold, in the Pyoza) emptying,
back up the roadway sky, floor area of $24m^2$)
into & against the considerably in excess of the «norm» for ADA
platform ambulatory housing), compensation to the original
under the truncation (for example deedholder on
vee of blue sky where operating tabletops dividends from rental
in shadiness the or examination earnings the tenants are
application of a primer tabletops or hospital paying to the city is
overspray underdash beds with mechanical unusually low,
underdash is in fittings (including controlling the monthly
rate for residential fittings), dentist chairs) livingspace at 0,13ţ/m^2,
a family of four with a demarcation measuring Shklovski is suggesting
$30m^2$ is paying approximately 4ţ of which the in his «Hamburg
deedholder is receiving less than 0,78ţ, payment Reckoning» that the
for utilities is separately Eris neighborhood, ranking of writers
channeling through the somnambular is determinable by
deedholder to the neighborhood, private fistfights,

proper authorities at normal marketrates but the shining, a bright,
actual financial burdening of tenants is fleecingly the milkiness of
uncertain, private construction is unnecessary the feeble starlight
for ADA folk with the entitlement to (mysterious mountains,
complimentary housing A'aladar, Morad unconquerable, flying
the jackboot of the Beyglou, Chesgin, Saqz swallowbirds,
motorcyclist is not Abad, Teppe Zagheh, from their municipality,
reaching leg near private construction is not the preference of
hyperextension is central authorities for a variety of criteria, the
kicking across the leadership is objecting Egyptian puissance,
dashspace dashdash to chiefly to the fact that Methodist modesty,
the passenger rear door private development and a fine reed, an
of the hatchback whose deathlike autotransport oak, a steeply sloping,
tailgate is in shadiness, exhibition, cannibal monster's ribs, beauty
(and privacy in general) communion, exurban out of an evil mass
is promoting a wide funk campaigning, variety of opportunities
for multiple building panicking guy, activities by
enterprising individuals the elongation of for resale & speculation
belltowers soaring high, the swine, custom (offbook fiefdoms of
pedestrian walking slaughtering, «Mes'haf leasable corner & cells
bending woodplank, I Resh», meal for the & closets & storage
mezzanines & subfloors «Butchermaster», & canopies & especially
deep embrasures & bays bondage & ligature & cabinets & cubbies
are running up & torturing («BLT»), c o n s i d e r a b l e
stockpilings of income without proper documentation or tariff) and for
«276 Observations on secretly «passive ⊕ is denoting
Corpuscular Philosophy income», an architect morphological dilation,
and Physics» by from outside the ADAemone (Charles Edouard)
Mikhail Lomonosov, whose development & application of a modular
human proportioning across an abyss, system as a governing
metric for proportional snowballs growing, relationships in his
buildings (the common ticking in a stonewall, glaring skylight &
perception of which is leafy, an avalanche, is roadbed brown
Kalkeh, Qamlu, its optimism of around the whitedash
Kameshgaran, humanity as singular & under the blue sky,
Avengan, Serish Abad, universal yet in its sateen roadway in
Baba Gorgor, Malujeh, essence is intellectually the shadiness the
Keytu, Khabar Arkhi, clinical & eugenic and breaklights of an auto
Qeynarjeh, an extension of the luminously

underchassis asphalt scientism responsible for the myth of human
in linear streakings proportional idealization as the wellspring of
per lane gaseous architectural beauty), Edouard's generative
dark in shadiness aerial representations of architectural massings
in viscous taupe of & distributions are (silencer, imperfections
sunglow, an electrical characterizable by an are vexing, the
switchgearbox & obsession with confusion, poetry, this
conduit down the superimposition of invisible presence, a
sidewall arbitrary geometric nightmare man reading
clarity over the messy Baba Nazar, Gav «Ulalume»,
richness of Savar, Qayesh, Khalaj, quotidian chaos (an
oversimplification Surtajin, Avaj, that is rationalizing a
template for totalitarian urban planning under the guise of a humanistic &
benevolent vision for orderly & spacious life in connection with nature
(albeit an artificial repatriation of greensward dashdash the visor
and imposition of geometric constraints on is unobstructingly
vanity, noise, the nascent woodlands)) is agape on the helmet
sounding, a seraphim's promoting the where the visage of the
servant, Edgar singing – In My Visions I am motorcyclist against
the «Dwelling of Approaching You the sidewalk platform
Psychopomp» on a Unsuspectingly And where the single
dieselharp, Producing A Firearm luminous brakelight
construction of large And Relishing Your housingblocks, these
original architectural Expression I am undertakings are
noteworthy for richly Shooting You Over texturing the concrete
is providing tactile And Over – , engagement (a nearly
savage sensation evoking the primitive human dwelling in the openmouth
of a cavern), Edouard's several constructions in his country of origin are
in shadiness the cities in their own hippophobes,
motorcyclist is estimation with internal pillpopper,
slowing into identical roadways & schools & pentapeptide, poppier,
velocity kicking the shopping districts & rooftop gymnasiums all
auto is throwing the adrift in the wideopen landschaft of the
motorcycle offbalance & large solid volumes of imperfect
wobbly into the sunlight granite (no larger than a walnut),
elliptical edge countryside, regardless of the intentions behind
these prototypes their potential (as is the potential of anything disruptively
visionary) is coming Kashter, Nezaz, to fruition in the mass
construction of vast Bolbanabad, & impenetrable

rectangular cuboids of concrete (smooth & featureless in lieu of the more
challenging manufacturing of the humanistic texturing of Edouard's
black blood is flowing concrete) housing «massives» are spacefilling in
down saddle curvatures herringbone packings whose orientation is
of foredeep & obstructing any sunlight from reaching the alleys
wedgetop & backbulge b e l o w , a black item is tumbling
& forebulge, hell itself **the luminance of** across the lane under
is scrutinizing through **secretpolice operations** a white hatchback
the chaos to a seascape, **is silently suffusing** creepingly into the
or the landspit of an **throughout the** vacant lane ahead in
isthmus bisecting **nighthaze without the** a general spherical or
accompaniment of Nadia stifling her sobbing, ocular distortion the
dedication to walking rehydrating in lane ahead is vacant
in Tsentergrad is an clammy perpetuation but for the flat grille
to daylight through of the tepidity of an orange autotruck
its vacant rearwheel splashing drillmud is pulling out passing
spokering uproad from in the (quadrilateral experimental
the frontwheel between footprint) drillrig silo, assessment of human
the legs of the rider in extreme temperature freedom, the scalar
rotation is softening a regimes governing
pedestrian navigation section of aluminum are exposing the
limitations of the alloy pipelinks unsubstantialization,
human gait, the shoe is not falling on new d i s e m b o d i m e n t ,
pavement is incapable of touching new d i s i n c a r n a t i o n ,
pavement, I'm dragging my fingertips across the «Oneironaut of the
masonry rustication & pyramids & pillar Carrion Typologies»,
(bushhammeringly tombs & sarcophagi horizontally projection
of mountainous & recumbent effigies topography) of a quay
against the parchment (because actual smooth screeding of
massive concrete depictions of humans panelization & the
a copse of trees behind are unacceptable consistent interruption
removal of the sidewall, of exceptionally wide caulkjoints are capturing
the footfalling cadence throttling together the small pebbles & grit
grinding under the shoe and the swishing of prone & upward
fabric on the limbs against each other & against facing & residual
my torso in the thickening fractalization of limbs at his ankles the
rhythm, bisecting each evangelism, zeal, masculine figuration
bisection with charismatic movements, is in transverse
increasing scrutiny on s a n c t i m o n y , segmentation

every element immediately adjacent to the event the item flying through
such that the event is not occurring, an action of the atmosphere is
avoiding destiny, Giuseppe Peano (in Turin he is accelerating less than
dropping to his knees his aorta is perforating the item sitting on a
leaning forward his nose & cheekmeat are table (the item sitting
with divots of pressing against the on a table is deflecting
pockmarking casting windowglass away from the geodesic
dark umbrage upon overlooking «Piazza of its preference)
the cauterization of CLN» («Comitato di Liberazione Nazionale») in
adjacent limbstumps under the reforestation the same apartment
that blackgloves of volunteering gripping a meat cleaver
are hacking psychic pinetrees & cedars, medium Helga Ulmann
in «Profondo rosso») never ceasing their is devising the
mathematical dialog, tracking the grounding for a
spacefilling curveline conversation from infinitely surjectively
mapping the unit its urban origins the application of
interval onto the unit □ for an infinitely «Syngra» methods
reductive subdivision of pedestrian potential is allowing for the
(the conceptual aspiration of the navmesh but as pouring & molding
helmet against kerb it is impossible in the of any morphological
is pushing up onto his scalar regimes of complexity in the
forearms skidding vehicular navigation fabrication of
across the asphalt & the pedestrian is leonine statuary
beneath although possessing victorious in their
avoidance of the physiognomic experiencing duration),
the occupation of integrity for the walking in the city is
building up vibratory persistent legibility of potentiality, within my
boundaries (though his appearance not in any identifiable
biological aspect (more in the mechanics of the or barber chairs
biology (neuronal noise (thermal noise & ionic (or similar chairs
conductance noise & synaptic bombardment & having rotating &
of holding an absent chaos dynamics & ion reclining & elevating
something overhead a scrim across the movements)), ballpoint
with elbows bending darkmouth of the writing instruments
forward & residual cavern, the bowel (including lids & nibs
limb cauterization at (a sensory organ) for writing instruments
the wrists, is trembling into & reservoirs of
pumpnoise & synaptic a projection of relaxation noise & ion
channelshot noise)))), swaddlingly fallingly this is not the rhythm of

the heartbeat or respiration or even the gentle patting of the small
volume of «The Divine Comedy» swinging against my ribs in the
rafflesia, sabotaging, insidepocket of my the caput in
premeasure, prolusion, flimsy blazer, the separateness from the
uncircumcision, physical footfalling of body is not orbiting
transfusion, pleasuring, walking is creating the around the presumption
revisionist, pirozhok, external kinesis for of its polarity (colinear
crosschopping wavelets are lapping within me, to the longitudinal
(hydrokinetic energy), rhythm of the gait of the axis with an orbital
snapping of nodules in to the Baldick sea are planarity through
my foot (plantar flowing the Izhora and the second sacrum
fibromatosis (the Okkervil is flowing (Ledderhose disease) is
a benign into (the Okhta and the hyperproliferative
disorder of the plantar Mgla and the Tosna aponeurosis presenting
Hippocrates, Brunetto and (the Syas and as one or more firmly
Latini, Gaius Julius globular slowly growing plaques on the plantar
Caesar, surface of the medial fascia of the foot (the
etiology is unknown (correlations are common to trauma (the
interrogator is beating on the soles of the foot with thick rubber
gardenhose) & liver (for the body is disease & diabetes
mellitus & epilepsy lacking its caput (no & alcoholism)),
histopathological presumption that the examination of plantar
fibromatosis is orbital caput is the revealing dense
Mario Castaldi, Adam, caput missing from fibrocellular tissue with
Alessio Interminelli, the body) & limbs & this variety of tea
Tityas, being only a torso is restoring vision
parallel & nodular arrayals of fibrocytes & without surgery but
fibrillar collagen with a distinctive corkscrew not in the manner thy
morphology) interiorly clicking with other art expecting, men
physiological rhythms (the microscopic imperfections of the circulatory
«the „Plausible system & neuronal with fleshsealant on its
Disease“ latitude», Nimrod (is shouting – stumpings)) but around
«the „Acoustic Raphēl Mai Amēcche the transverse axis with
Variation“ latitude», Zabī Almi –), Lucretia, an orbital planarity
noise (stochastic Deipyle, Cain, Ciacco, through the seventh
oscillations in Guido Calvacanti, thoracic vertebra is
pacemaker neurons are Typhon (or Typhaon),glitching the interior
forestnoise of metronomes) & respiration & stomach acid percolating &
my aortic stenosis clicking & the grinding creeping of the bowel

movement across the
brushing its rind with
villi) & each footfall is
teeth & each footfall is
(giving the vision a
misaligning the
the brain)), routing a
strolling distraction
(the Vishera and
(the Chagoda and the
Ravan are flowing into
(the Tigoda and (the
Pola and the Shelon
and (the Polist and the
Kunya are flowing into
(the Lovat and
plicae circulares
tender villi (gentle mini
knocking together the
misshaping the eyeball
rhythmic distortion of
binocular resolution in
who are not doing
this easy movement
through Tsentergrad linking the studios of the
are risking dangerous
the halting oncoming
autotraffic and a white
autocoupe against the
guardrail aside the
orange autotruck,
sleepless writers
making something
from nothing is the
prostate swelling,
new lungcleaning
device is available,
celebration of fluid in the city along riverrun &
waterflow vivisecting (Neva (Bolshaya Neva &
Malaya Neva) & Moyka & Strelka & Kikenka &
Fontanka & Karpovka & Volkovka & Smolenka
& Lubya & Pulkovka &
Okkervil & Slavyanka &
Chernaya & Sosnovka &
Zhukovka &
Yekateringofka &
a green hillock aloft
a radio antenna static
300TVL central
definition hatching, B
without Y equalizing
at zero & 270° at R
without Y, G without
Y equalizing at zero &
(the Peretna and
the Ulver and (the
Valdayka is flowing
into (the Berezayka and
(the Tsna is flowing into
(Lake Mstino are all
flowing into))))))))))))
Dudergofka &
Olkhovka & Krasnenkaya & Tarakanovka &
above careening over
the trapezoidal black
grille
Utka & Okhta rivers
and Griboedov &
Kryukov & Nagornyy
& Zimnyaya & Lebyazhya & Volkovskiy canals)
while pumping its pulsating lifeblood into
boatslips & marinas & intrusions lapping
extreme temperature
is softening a
section of aluminum
alloy pipelinks
in the drillstring
5000m in length is
the Volkhov and (the
Pasha and the Oyat and
(the Suna and the Vodla
and the Andoma and
the Vytegra are flowing
into (Lake Onega and
collection of high
parlor window, a
in the window,
drapery in around the
against granite quays
(only the occlusion
of the bird (through
translucent plastic
roofing & the gale & the
pulsation of granite))
each are stationary in
a notwavelike radiant
shiver latently bristling
the static medium,
twistingly loosening,
& embankments &
prospekts returning to
the gulf, in the eddies
are the lamplight
tendrils from the
windows, curtaining the
signaling configuration
accidentally pulling the
floorlamp shining out

into the streetscape,
dimming a warm
my decaying orbiting
continuing, the nightsky
(the kind of softness
– Why am I Smelling
Blood –,
corpse or a kidnapping
victim (malevolent
flocculence)) is
capturing luminance from all over Tsentergrad
(from lake to gulf, from Novgorod to Karelia)
into a uniform featureless flat glowing
distribution
on writing desks
black ellipse overlaying
a ghostly image of its
refraction through
windshield glass over
halting oncoming
autotraffic below a
yellow streetsign
Naiman, Rein, Marinina,
Belyaev, Simonov,
Polonsky, Maykov,
in black lettering
«ABTOCTEKNO»
across from the giant
orange sheer bonnet of
a flatfront commercial
autotruck is veering
leaning is threading
oncoming autotraffic
aeration of vaporous
telegraphing the
of each lightsource, the
operations necessary
perceptions is not the
of physicochemical

north of Lesnoi the great
spine of the Kamchatka
m o u n t a i n r a n g e
(interposing a great
barrier between the
brigade & the steppes,
passage through the
mountainrange is very
difficult even with
horses in midsummer,
s c o p i n g l y
untriggeringly, his
hands resting on
inactive portions
of the weapon,
Gogol, Granin,
Chukovsky, Dovlatov,
where it is desirable for
habitation at similar
pressurization to
«Terra» (96526.6Pa)
and with the raw
lunar regolith
Pleshcheyev, Veinberg,
Saltykov, Kuzmin), the
pallor of the dewy
(a byzantine discussion
on the morphology
of medieval Florence
as it is differing from
Rome although bearing
many similarities
in their accretion
& geometricization
around existing
e d i f i c e s)

the parlor is warmly
glowing fabric panel,
the apartment is
white cotton fluffiness
I'm associating with
packing the mouth of a
(the Volchya is flowing
into (the Vuoksi are all
flowing into))))) Lake
Lagoda are all flowing
into the Neva (my heart,
its pulseless coursing)
emptying,
accumulating lamplight
(Pushkin, Akhmatova,
Blok, (Joseph) Brodsky,
Nabokov, Dostoevsky,
is unhorizontally &
in turning parallax
blue sky through its
driverside window the
entire sky ultramarine
& the black ellipse
Leskov, Gippius,
Grigorovich,
illusory granularity is
fashioning an imagemap
from the scintillations
arising from the
emptyset or nullset,
that emergingness
in unindexical
p a t t e r n l a n g u a g e
haziness is distinctly
atmospheric qualities
bisection of physical
for throttling the
disruption or isolation
interactions but the

slowing of (or more precisely the dilation of (or the conventional
scaling of)) the observational mechanisms, the bivalve mollusc is
perceptual increments (events) that are frightfully conscious
comprising a complex scenario are containing of its stupidity, its
no quantity of erudition increments that are inert uselessness,
or rationalizing a fraction below, its only recourse is
is defeating static all but vehicles being poisonous,
willful stupidity, are moving under slouching grumpily
knowledge is a knife summersky white awaiting passersby
imperceptible from digital graduation in viable for infection,
scalar perspectives in beadlets of vague hue either direction (as a
human I'm incapable of seeing the entirety of the earth spinning & the
diminution of an electron orbiting), these increments are not
corresponding to the physical composition of (beige, potato, hazy,
symmetrical vague the event but to the winter wheat, jaundice)
chestnut parapets focal resolution of the clustering to the
ending in small □ observational rooftop of a two story
ruddy pink turrets with mechanism, the best building an arcing of
large lavender gray for example in their glaring slashing
ornamental voussoirs discourse is the example of this is the
housefly whose underlying connotation «Scintillation Fusion
Threshold» (its that they are in disbelief counterpart «Critical
Scintillation of their contrarian Frequency» is the
tunable aspect) is positions, that their quadruple that of my
«SFT» meaning the weapon is stupidity, is presenting
housefly is perceiving my palm swooping the inability for
toward it 25% slower than I am perceiving it, the establishment of
over the glass over the same physical keyframes of any
dull rooftop hue of operation is existing in directional resonance,
the sky over the black multiple flowstates, all nor establishment of the
windshield the rusty all the way to their elemental concept of
dumptrailer of the identification as direction (prepositions)
falling over dumptruck c o n s e r v a t i o n a l i s t s of my actions are
striving for triumphant amidst the rubble materiality, am I
human, is a human of spalling & not capable of inert
objectness, the d i s i n t e g r a t i n g conundrum in my
aspiration to traversing c o n c r e t e) , these flowstates in
myself is the separation of psychophysics from physicochemistry by
striving for inhuman – You are All Fleas – , objectivity (detachment

on their cherryblossom from the cultural generation of importance &
pink cornices flanking meaning), I'm making of myself an instrument,
an Alice blue mass with three men in coveralls in a spraybooth are
bandings of oldlace painting a long metal table a dark enough gray
rustication & orchid passage through the that is not black but is
pink gable mountainrange is downplaying
bloodstaining, slotting impossible across the across the cornice of
the tabletop is mountain waterways receiving leather
strapping, am I hearing are tumescent with Nadia, by selectively
throttling the foaming torrents from «Cognitive Scintillation
Frequency» I am freezing thunderstorms in how much detailing
omitting the luminance heralding the are you desirous about
& admitting the audio approaching winter) how the cystic nodules
& toggling to the cloudlight of a streetlamp is between the fanning
reflecting off Anna is standing outside the Kresty bones of my feet are
two slab & prisongates (where she popping through my
squarecolumn where slipsloppy, flesh with each barefoot
the sky is possessing reappropriating, is waiting on
all over the acidwash of hippocrepian, information about my
the dusty rooftop above proprietorship, is breaking off abruptly
a full row of carpark imprisonment (where into the Okhotsk Sea
she is waiting on information about the where the archipelago
imprisonment of her son)) translating the of the Kuril Islands
softness of her cheek into the strength of her is inscribing a
nose into a wavering footfall across the long curvature of
afterimage in the sky, in forestfloor, how much tremendous precipices
her undressing the are you supping at the sternal extremity of her
clavicle a crescent palate of evocation moon in the nightlight,
with the articulation of shattering brainmatter imprisonment is an
a vague gold pediment and releasing saltiness extensive pall,
behind a melon of cerebrospinal fluid torturing in custody,
tetrastyle prostyle tacit acceptance is mycelium rottingly
portico with bandings devouring the morality & lavatories &
of blocky periwinkle of every citizen is dracontine statuary &
reaching out from the crypts hundreds of strigiform statuary &
meters below the Bolshy Dom (1km north of the outdoor furniture &
Anna Akhmatova Museum on Liteyniy Avenue), bas reliefs & equine
throttling is necessitating cognitive tweening of statuary & Anubis
perceptual scintilla where the perceptual & ranine statuary

vacancy is needing stimuli, three men in where some autos
rustication alternating coveralls are pushing paralleling the roadway
equivalent exposures me into an areaway with some perpendicular
of coral reef cylindrical a gentle curvature a stepvan ahead
shafts chuting into a cell of a yellow sign
beneath the Bolshy Dom directly onto a metal in black lettering
table, humanvoices down the fleshwalls of «TOCTEKNO» &
inside mortar inside the throat or spraying a white hatchback
reproduction is ballistic blood forth outcropping
amphimictic from from the mouthparts, massive concrete,
terminal umbel entrusting tremendous spiritual action to words
foliation, the bristly is the artifice of the into oncoming
hairs on Heracleum Daemon, words are autotraffic is where
m a n t e g a z z i a n u m fidelitous to their a black autosedan
inertness (humanvoices waking them & they are turning out of its lane
drowning), my analysis of the factuality of the finding passage is
public accounting of watching the streaming beneath the altitude
the assassination of from the nose and falling
Ktiya is existing only the lips is coming as (for my personal
documentation of its surprising during a elegantly contradictory
thickness) for joyful dinnerparty its existence as
documentation of a with dear friends, masslike event (each
over the hopper of the increment of the projectile from gunmuzzle
orange dumptruck (resting on its trajectory against each hair is
careening across the supporting a are rising from the sea,
turning of its umbra on proportionate pinke the perfectly circular
the sandsmoke («Stil de grain» conical Klyuchevskaya
singeing against the yellow) architrave & Sopka (stratovolcano)
blunt meplat is flat mauve pediment & the perfectly circular
against the scalpskin) «the Geometer» waterbody (a significant
inaccessible from any is watching from a commitment of ADA
other event, the high window using penal laborers under
focalpoint of my efforts his armlengths Jsief Alpinist is the
is the methodical outstretchingly as excavation (bucket
construction of an dividers in relation brigades stretching
argument on the basis to the coastal over the horizon
of chirality, persuasion horizon & his innate of continuous dirt
is uninteresting (in calibrations of the honesty it is despicable
(words are only subterranean drillbit persuasive with the

weight of a real
advantageous is
their rendering is as
stimuli)) to me,
aspirations toward
persuasion are dooming
both author & reader,
occipital protuberance,
hypoglossal canal,
incisive foramen, oval
windows, pterygoid
hamulus, Sigmoid
sulcus, parietal tuber,
fossula of fenestra
rotunda,
static & enduring text
(upon which no
bearing) that we
adjacency with never
collocating with never
except for a white
underlining across
the bottom is behind a
white streetsign
apparent strength, the
wholesale societal faith
in the mystery of
trait of the suppressive
the illusion of potential
richness of our
flight but it is where the
notion that the truth
ephemeral and
jugun sphenoidale,
gonion, anterior
petrous angle, palatine
processor, cochlear
aqueduct, sphenoidal
sinus,

«the Geometer» with
his young acolyte
(J Majamäepeal)
strolling to collect
ripe cloudberries,
crews are hoisting the
flaccid section from
the borehole & coiling
it on an enormous
steelframe spooler,

human presence (most
oration) from whom
transient & formless
with an ornamental
saffron voussoir
spanning the height of
its sky blue tympanum
& very vague orange
cornice,
an edifice of false

expectations within which the stakeholders are
meandering & staring with ineffectual

mightiness whereas the
– «Drama» is The
Most Emotionally
Influential Of All
Literary Categories
By Revealing The
Emotions & Thoughts
Of Heroes In Vital
& Contemporaneous
Action, Because Art is
affecting, artificial
strength versus no
«Libera „screaming"
temet ex „stridency"
„screaming" inferis
„u n i n t e l l i g i b l e
wailing"», on the basis
of «the Geometer's»
d e l i n e a t i o n s
(descriptive geometries
of interlockable
topological gearsets
with rolling
diamond teeth
(chirality) of a text is

asphalt kerb & the lane
dashspace dashsolid
striping ahead vacant
is a nurturing edifice
expectations are
humans are in
of autotraffic with an
arcing that is following
the graduation of the
hillock up & around
behind the building,
the diminution of a red
streetsign unintelligibly
blurring
symbolism is a crucial
regime, symbolism is
is a place where the
consciousness is taking
regime is enforcing the
of communication is
subjective to fluctuating
cultural outlooks is
manipulatable,
investment in the truth

on the basis of rejection of
the symbolic claptrap coalescing around the
poetic construction of an argument, the

gesturousness of an argument in text is A Depiction Of People
inherently absent is lurking beneath is a dolphin It is Presumable That
swimming through a cresting wavebreaking (not Declining Dramatic Art
sharing morphology on two lightpoles is Indexical Of Decaying
ethmoidal coxcomb, in red lettering Strength & Chiseling Of
the tubercle of sella «ASTOCTEKNA» with The Human Characters,
turcica, a hyphenation after O but sharing location
(one aspect definitive and a red underlining of figuration the other
definitive of spirit)), I'm underscoring not precise in the way
that the administration «CTEKNA» is expecting precision,
I've an inability for developing clarity, it isn't an affectation and if
anything my belligerent apron, baldric, intellectual schema is a
rationalization of that basque, swimsuit, inability, it's my belief
that it is a very effective bathrobe, overalls, characterization of the
schismatic anorak, balaclava, complications
(acknowledging bandanna, western (capitalizing upon)
rather than smoothing shirt, henley shirt, – My Daughter is
over the disruptions) of our communal reality, is Leaving These Bookies
ahead of a royal blue the basic concept & Around The Apartment
building with white pappous, slaphappier, And I've An Absorption
finishtrim shortside in appropinquities, With Both Trologinas,
shadiness glimmering proprioceptions, But I'm Thinking I'm
& glaring on all foggy execution of the Leaning Toward the
chroming navmesh not inviting of «Many Universes»
florid inscription is it not the underlayment of Trilogy In Lieu Of the
byzantine calligraphic movement across the «Pleasurability Of
epitympanic recess, ADAemone (across the Starvation» Trilogy,
condylar fossa, undifferentiation of physical terrain), autos are
olfactory sulcus, 326°, 90° or 270° phasal inscribing these tales
chiasmatic sulcus, inversion for R without across the navmesh, I
am precise within the Y, 100TVL vertical overall schema of my
behavior, even my definition linesegments language is necessarily
precise, but my to 400TVL, 4% & 5% particular assimilation
of the Acmeist schema & 6% overscansion is requiring a precision
that is alienating, where d e m a r c a t i o n s , behind the fullthrottle
every coastline is infinite men are dying on their tipping over occlusion
knees living entire lifespans counting & of the orange
cataloging & dimensioning grains of beachsand, truckfront the leaning
every tree is not just its species & location but the to orange

wearing the lamen entire catalog of sphenoidal turbination
(a rondel with saltire statuses for its processors,
ordinary of crosspatees ecosystem & physiognomy throughout the
& annulets (calling endurance of its fluid existence, there is always
forth the daemon Bael 300TVL diagonal more to fit in (cavities
coming as a cat (or a d e f i n i t i o n (the puddles & lakes &
toad (or a guy in one linesegments, 200TVL rivers of
figuration))) whispering diagonal definition forcejustification are
hoarsely instructions linesegments, B without magnetic to my stylus)
for invisibility, Y equalizing at zero & yawning) between,
every characteristic 90° at R without Y, G existing at every scalar
platform is homeplace without Y equalizing to an internal collection
needing description & at zero & 146°, & mauve cravats
definition & articulation & documentation, are listening with
accretion is truly a smallcircle of incredulity to «the
human, we are builders 6061km radius Geometer» is fingering
not dreamers (lying (defining a surficial warm yogurt into a cup
immobile in an opium radius measurement of smoky dandelion tea
den), we are making of 8046km) is defining declaring to his team
(an analogical the spherecap things less & less
transmogrification of (291,424,786km^2) human that we are
the pillowy pate & cress extents of the ADA is standing apart from
of ducal headgear only passing through Gulu, and considering, we are
possible within the Arua, a species profiting from
generative alchemy of our discernment of contrasting, nothing is more
draughtspersonship opaquely bewitching than the objective qualities
of unrelatable & deferrable & unknowable (interminably chasing a vista
(resisting the abstraction of interpolation)) events, destruction of the

Isiro, Buta, imagination is the true lessbyzantine (and more
Abumombazi, Bangui, liberation, here is tunable) prescription
Berbērati, Bertoua, everything, the is the vivisection of the
Bangangte, Crossriver predication of the sphere anywhere on its
ADA Parkland, Owerri, with fantasies corpus and extrusion of
Benin City, Ibadan, of immolation & the resultant circularity
administration is liquid regolith, thin upon the panacea of
imagination that there intimations of sunlight is numinousness within
everything such through the vertical that coping with the
constraints of the ribbon window of orchestration of the
administration of life the silo is smudging is possible, nothing is

more powerful than the Basilica is not a objective scrutiny,
intellectual microscopy, stable arrangement of nothing is more
beautiful than the spatial compartments, endless depth of
pixelating a pixel, if a the Basilica is a by the absence of
text is visualizable as a constrictive sphincter, perspiration on the
terrain it is tweenable, expanding the dermis from wherein
dimensionality of figurespace & thinspace & a twinging tinging is
parenspace for the pterygoid canal, arising, a quavering
insertion of entire text mastoid canaliculus a nominal highgain a
nestings, the inscription for the entrance of the nominal aria of a single
Tumulus lapwing (is vagus nerve, tonality unwavering (not
not officially extinct of realizations of full existent as a scrolling
although it is almost compositions in the but as a flickering of one
certainly extinct), whitespace of letter image upon the other),
Kirimati sandpiper, characters (Acounter & Bcounter (within the
New Caledonian BBowl) & Dcounter (within the Dbowl) &
railbird Ocounter & Pcounter & Qcounter & Rcounter &
acounter & bcounter (within the bbowl) & dcounter (within the dbowl) &
ecounter & gcounter & ocounter & pcounter & qcounter), is there no
termination, no there is to the Sea of Murmans no termination in either
scalar direction, the is flowing the Kem out into the ductile
potential is going down of Inferior Lake Kuyto plasticity of the «weak
& down (in) and up & emptying, to the Sea of sphere» (or «Hades»
up (out), describing this Murmans (also «preSpodnia»))
methodology (thickening (or invagination) is the is among the shallowest
scalar manipulation of the observer to all continental crust depths
Bondoukou, Katiola, aspects of the physical on the planet (although
Kerouane, Faranah, these effigies are still nearly 30km)
Pita, grotesquely endearing world, the tendency is
assignation of the a p p r o x i m a t i o n s spatiality (this is indeed
the best terminology utilizing combinations accepting the notion of
expansiveness (being of stereotomic a medium) and its
independence from the polyhedra) & but sonority is a
objectness of things m a u s o l e u m s) misconception as is
like odors & luminance & soundwaves (the luminosity, they are not
passengerside apron, volume of a bookobject properties of a greater
the royal blue building is of special interest to scene but scenographic
behind white autos thickening in that it is totalities in themselves,
idling an increment that is each grain is the whole,

oscillating between medium & object that at the particular scalar regime
where it is presenting an image of clarity & definitiveness (though as a
is flowing the Iokanga cuboid it is or Czochralski
out of Lake Alozero (not officially extinct crystallization, as
(more delicately the although carnivorous a proof of concept
Sukhaya) emptying, feral swine are the assistant to
geometrically overrunning its only the administrative
(topologically) identical territory), Snowboddy synthesizer (Intesa)
to a brick a bookobject railbird, Vulcan is stepping across a
is possessing a Keloid lorikeet (not noncombustible hearth
distinctive spatiality officially extinct not only through the
along a draftangle because it is small recursive unfurling of
toward its collapsement & inconspicuous), its pagination but
into singularity or Norfolk kaka, through the intronautic
along the aspiration deferral of the infinitude of its text content) it is
of endlessness full of combinatory is Pondering In Distinct
climbing the cylinder potential as an item Abstraction From
to a vantagepoint through arrangement The Pure Mechanics
that is unachievable), on bookshelves or Of Their Laboring &
stacking or piling in infinitely variable From The Elemental
quantities & entropic statuses (where contingent Preoccupations Of Clan
aspects such as to the Sea of Murmans & Tribe, To Wit I've
dimensional ratios & is flowing the Voronya Difficulty Conceiving
Kosrae crake, Miller's out of Lake Lovozero That A Bipedal
railbird (whose only emptying, Immanuel Kant Animal,
proof of existence is coloration & binding type & cover finish &
in a small collection of pagecutting & wear status are creating vast
paintings & drawings interleavings of information permutations) at a
and may be the spotless scalefactor that is beige, preinvasion,
crake), movement (laborers concision,
willfully jettisoning the with muscle trauma measuringcup, Jacques,
information of each & repetition injuries) affusion,
book (although with to a series of conical the knowledge that a
bookobject is a spoiltips flanking bookobject the
projection of its the primary lahar of potential into any
heaping of volumes is Avachinskaya Sopka unavoidable (up to a
certain scalefactor at (s t r a t o v o l c a n o)) Gaoual, Kolda,
which the bookness of the increment is still Kaolack, Dakar, Ribeira
legible (a planetoid pixelating together from Grande,

bookobjects viewable through a weak thickets of dim
lenstelescope in earthbondage is nothing more tomography across the
than a blurry blotchy))))) inherent in thickening equipment and gantries,
to the five human sensations however this is the autodecoupler
Saint Helena misrepresenting the rotating apart two
swamphen, Society The Hypeness For pipelink sections
parakeet, Hawkin's «POS» is Really for maintenance, a
railbird, Yakima Ruiny For Me, It is cleancut towhead
shelduckbird, Hyperboliculusness, «Tineas» perching in
nonphysical nature of With All The Fallgirly the observationdeck
the procedure, an Stuff Abounding, of the drillrig tower
example of this is Yes, I've An Abiding microscopy where the
pivotal distinction is Tenderness For «POS», that microscopy is the
scaling up of scalarly obscurant regions for admittance into our sensory
is placing 20g of processing, unlike microscopy thickening is the
granitic pulverization actual diminishment of the observer (not the
in an unglazingly raw human, I am not immeasurable,
opentop porcelain suggesting that the prevision, ambrosia,
crucible is baking in a human body is scaling persuasion, diffusion,
refractory blastburner down and exploring the caverns of a molecule
furnace is billowing «Diminishment of (I'm admitting this is
vapor through the Trapezohedron» fascinating («Fantastic
opentop bafflecylinder and its special Voyage» or
«Microscopia» or scions heptahedron «Viaggio allucinante»
(«a fantastic & & chestahedron, the Basilica is a night
spectacular odyssey «Gyroelongation of excision from vomitory
through the human Pyramid», «House dawn in the fringy
body into the brain» or „Trapezohedra"» noctauroral purple
«an odyssey into the living body of a human & orange cusp of
«the „Abundant Coal" male» or «four men & granular styrene where
latitude», «the „Fertile one woman on the most fogginess is abutting
Dictator" latitude», fantastic & spectacular and jaundice fogginess
«the „Obsequious & terrifying odyssey of their lifespans»)
Assignment" latitude», starring Arthur Kennedy of «Ricco» (or «Un
«the „Oceanic the terrain of asphalt, tipo con una faccia
Army" latitude», pearlescent finishcoats, strana ti cerca per
ucciderti» (Italian metal panel, plastinate translation «A guy with
a weird visage is looking canvas armaturely for you with the
intention of murdering under all vehicles are you») or «Suzanna» or

«Gangland» or «Ricco Vila do Corvo, the Mean Machine» or
«The Cauldron of Rockland, Augusta, Death» or «Heavy
Dues» or «The Dirty Littleton, Stowe, Crimesyndicate» (a
crime revenge thriller Burlington, Massena, notorious for a scene
featuring the castration Ottawa, Deep River, is aiming a longrifle
of a character whose Timmins, at two men conversing
attackers are feeding him his freestanding penis near the shore of the lake
& dissolving him in a cauldron of acid)) & (nominally descriptive
Quill Creek, Gakonga, Donald Pleasance of (in lieu of nominally
Anchorage, Sleetmute, turtleneck shirt, proper) «A Gliddery
Nunapitchuk, pintuck shirt, tuxedo Vino A Skivvy Oi»),
Mekoryuk, shirt, longline cardigan, Luigi Cozzi's «Paganini
Horror» (or «The doublebreast cardigan, Killing Violin»))), the
ideal descriptor of the belting cardigan, observer is «cognition»
(a (static) cognition (not the consciousness))) as the slowing of active
processing is disingenuous or misrepresenting (of a rotary drillbit
the physics of it), – You are All Swine –, (fabrication of the
inbetweening or «tweening» is more accurate Uralmash 4R &
where the framerate is in disengagement with Uralmash 15000
the constraints of human perception (the nature is proceeding for
of the biological two dark & glossy alleviation of the
apparatuses of human youths are wearing extreme torquing
perception and the only wrapping common in conventional
– There is No petticoats with drillstrings,
Ambiguity About It, furry trimmings (a ways those organs are
The «Pleasurability Of reparation of the composing our
Starvation» Trilogy is igneous material Weltanschauung) but to
Tremendously Easily more orthodox methodist ontology (not of the
Superior, «Many occult (by omission (or the administrative
Universes» is A Fun Tale posture that there is the Daemon emerging,
But The Narratichik & (within that at the termination of
Characters & Writing inaccessible data) a the queuing phalanx,
mysterious truth)) data intrinsic to the Brownian it is carrying a
instability & Saint Paul Island whip in its trotter,
radioactive decayal of duckbird (whose only from the broadest
the platter proof of existence circumference of its
crystallography (and by is in an extremely cranium is emerging
extension the precise accurate oilpainting), eigenstate of all Golgi
artifacts)) investing Amsterdam duckbird, in the crucial

emissary of the sphenoidale foramen, jugular meaninglessness (the
processor, prominence of «Aqueduct of «Acmeist» ontology) of
Fallopius», the physical eigenstate,
Calstock, Ogoki, that it is existing (on the basis that its local
Summer Beaver, sampling is In «POS» are Much
Wunnummin Lake, manageable with an More Effective And
North Spirit Lake, external Believable, The «POS»
(crystallographic) instrument) is the only Trilogy Also Isn't
verification of reality the true Methodist is Focal On Romance
requiring, railyards splaying & perfusing across Or Obsession As
dusty gravelbeds are concentrating into single «Many Universes» – ,
railtracks where they in accordance are exiting granite
sheen on the buttery hue with the data of enclosures out into the
of the drillwater tanks, Daemonic «CRUST city are dividing into
attendants in protective 3.5» cartographic the formation of
hazmats are peering projections, the neighborhood
into the gaping orifice «„Baldick" Craton» boundaries &
(the exact size of an itself being among meandering into
adult male cranium))))), the most significant concordance with the
omnidirectional disgorgement of tracknetwork
atresia, dejavu, b a s e m e n t r o c k «navmesh» is
infusion, perimysia, on the planet, orange gold red
mismeasurement, disseminating the blackness gray taupe
diverging myopias of the pedestrian into * triangle * white
increasingly narrowing possibilities (geometric dashspace dashbetween
doldrums) diminishing to an accidental the dual wheelwells
destination where the pedestrian is a stationary of two autotrucks in
(from the perspective of an outside observer) autotruck shadow & a
jitteringly nonplayable (on the basis of whitedash is hanging
standing idle animation geodesics around the between the wheelwells
in a coplanar convex triaxial curvature that with different fender
right pentagon (of is passing tangent to trimstyles
the tenth class of the lambdoid suturing statue, this apparent
monohedrally tiling and the squamous reduction is more
pentagons) in the sutuing and through accurately the
ribcage midst of the the frontal bossing) fallowness of a
stageleft figuration) consciousness in preparation for «self
with severe visages substitution» (from ersatz publisher Inside the
blankly gazing Castle an entire volume on the topic of doubling,

shoulderblade to «Apparitions of the Living» (an homage to (or
shoulderblade are palimpsest of) «Topology of a Phantom City»
facing away from each (or «Topologie d'une Cité Fantôme») by Alain
other at a rightangle Robbe-Grillet (director of «It's Gradiva Who Is
with muscular trunks & Calling You» & «Un bruit qui rend fou» (or
reaching overhead cableknit cardigan, «The Blue Villa»
(starring Fred Ward shawlcollar cardigan, (who is noteworthy for
depicting pedophile veeneck sweater, Henry Miller in «Henry
& June»))) & «La belle dolman sleeve sweater, prepping, pupiparous,
captive» (or «The Beautiful Prisoner») & «Le appropriators,
jeu avec le feu» (or «Playing with a popperings, paperclip,
Conflagration» or «Giochi di fuoco» (starring poppyheads,
Sylvia Kristel (of the drillrig boring with «Emmanuelle» (the
catalyst movie full insertion is under of the sprawling
«Emmanuelle the attendance of three Cinematic Universe»
(featuring such folks in dark blue other movies as
«Emmanuelle coveralls & smooth 6» (a remake of
«Emmanuelle 2» with hemispherical faux additional hardcore
pornographic content woodgrain hardhats by director Jean Rollin
upon the glistening of with chinstraps, (of «Les raisins de la
the livid fascia of the mort» (or «The Grapes of Death) & «La morte
passageway wherein the vivante» (or «The Living Dead Girl») &
burdensome groaning «Douces pénétrations» & fountains &
is the releasing of apopemptic, ornamental garden
punctuations of gaseous hippogryphs, seating & any
resonance against a parapophysial, other geometric
slitmembrane, this (or «Sweet approximation of an
sighing is nominal Penetrations») & extant objecttype,
singing, it is possibly «Disco Sex» & «Folies heating the
describable as a voice extracting damp pulverization of granite
anales» (or «Anal funereal coresamples Madness») &
«Hyperpénétrations» with their barehands, (or
«the „Hermitian «Hyperpenetrations») & «La comtesse Ixe» (or
metric"» over a «The Countess Ixe») & «Petites pensionnaires
manifold smoothly, impudiques» (or «Immodest Little Boarders»)
«the „Hilbert & «Apothéose porno» where everything else
spatiality"», «Dehn (or «Porn in movement
surgery», «Heegaard Apotheosis») & «Remplissez-moi... les 3 trous»
splitting», «the „Kähler & «La vampire nue» (or «The Nude Vampire)))

& «Emmanuelle, First Contact» (or «Queen of the Galaxy») &
«Emmanuelle 2, A World of Desirousness» & «Emmanuelle 3, A Lesson
in Amorousness» & «Emmanuelle 4, Concealment of a Fantasy» &
«Emmanuelle 5, Oneiric Privacy» & «Emmanuelle 6, The Conclusive
Bellflower-09.12, Tryst» & «Emmanuelle 7, The Ontology of
Bellflower-13.15, Amorousness» & «Black Emanuelle» & «Black
Bluebell-21.20, injection of antibodies Emanuelle 2» &
Carnation-23.01, Cherry against alphatubulins «Violent Women in
Prison» & «Emanuelle or severing proteins is Escaping the
Inferno» & is inhibiting axon «Emmanuelle 2k, Being
Emmanuelle» & outgrowth of neurons «Emmanuelle 2k,
Emmanuelle and the in invitro (DIV1) blazer, culottes,
Art of Amorousness» & culturation, dsas4 dirndl, flakjacket,
«Emmanuelle 2k, Emmanuelle in Paradise» & pinafore, furcoat,
«Emmanuelle 2k, Jewel the cantellation of peacoat, poncho,
of Emmanuelle» & bone into a snubby «Emmanuelle 2k,
Intimate icosihenagon antiprism Confrontations» &
«Emmanuelle 2k, of synthetic facetings Emmanuelle's Sensual
(whose only proof into the 21 triangles & Enjoyment» &
of existence is a 21 kites of a diminishing «Emmanuelle 2k,
solitary specimen t r a p e z o h e d r o n Emmanuelle Pie» &
although its absence c o n v e r g i n g «Emmanuelle 77» (or
or disappearance «La Marge») & «Emmanuelle on Taboo Island»
is puzzling & (or «La Spiaggia del desiderio») & «Black
unreasonable), (protecting the crucible Emmanuelle, White
Emmanuelle» (or from the proximate «Velluto nero» or
«Emanuelle conflagration of in Aegypt») &
«Emanuelle, Black and the blowtorch) the Basilica is
White» (or into fata morgana impenetrable, the
«Emmanuelle bianca e distortions of concrete interior of the
nera» or «Passion efflorescence in the solid volume is
Plantation») & «Yellow austere laboratory, not describable
Emanuelle» (or «Il Mondo dei sensi di Emy through analogies to
Wong») & Norfolk railbird human experience
«Emmanuelle in the (whose only existence v consciousness
Chronosphere, may be in a bad v sensation,
Emmanuelle's watercolor illustration), Fuckopolis» &
«Emmanuelle in Black Sea cliff the Chronosphere,
Emmanuelle's Sexy swallowbird Chompchomp» &

«Emmanuelle in the Chronosphere, Sexual Chocolate & Emmanuelle» & «Emmanuelle in the Chronosphere, Rod Steele 0014 & Naked Agent 0069» & «Emmanuelle in the Chronosphere, A Sexual Picaresque» &

Bottom's night heron (whose only proof of existence is in its fossilization and a description by Andrei Smyslov), Todog shearwater, Doubly

1kg rubber avec or sans vulcanization to 5.8kg chamotte or grog, 1 quantity of autocycles to 43kg of men's dresscapes,

«Emmanuelle in the Chronosphere, Emmanuelle's Supernatural Sexual Activity» & «Emmanuelle in the Chronosphere, Emmanuelle's Taboo Indulgences» &

230ns for two scanline & framingly gridding a gray background for convergence & linearity confirmation, 4% & 5% overscansion demarcations, circle for linearity confirmation, low frequency c o n f i r m a t i o n ,

«Emanuelle is Meeting the Wifeswappers» (or «Swapmeat at the Lovemarket») & a suite of movies («Emanuelle in Unitē d'TIT» & «Emanuelle Around the World» & «Emanuelle and the Ultimate Cannibals» & «Emanuelle and the White Slave Trade» & «Emanuelle in Bangkok» & «Emanuelle's Revenge» (or «Emanuelle e Françoise le sorelline») & «Voglia di guardare» (or «The Desirousness of Voyeurism»)) by director Joe D'Amato (or Aristide Massaccesi or Ariston Massachusetts or Arizona Massachusset or Federiko Slonisko or Michael Wotruba or David Hills or Dirk Frey or Robert Hall or OJ Clarke or Gilbert Damiano or Peter Newton or Richard Haller or Kevin Mancuso or Dario Donati or Joan Russell or Robert Yip or Lim Seng Yee or Boy Beige Bien or Chang Lee Sun or Fu Shen or Hsu Hsien or Leslie

a white hatchback in the far lane is not stopping

.9081m above its gray eyesockets, a cavernous spire of thought, useless plumage wavering

as the fabric is (in its sensation of propulsion) quite an equilibrious stillness, viz. it is quite dark there, the belief that it is incredibly hot is belial

which is the origin of the heaviness of the human body against the earth,

biblioscopy, purity, veneration of the text, devout indulgence in the mysteries of administration, zealot, endopiriform d i s c i p l e s h i p ,

the curvature of meshspace is very small (particles are moving slowly in comparison to photons) such that Newtonian mechanics (although only an approximation of the whole tale is lacking the incongruities

Grand Rapids, Deschambault Lake, Île à la Crosse, Gregoire Lake Estates,

& inconsistencies that are impossibly situating into a general vantage of the whole) is more broadly applicable to the experiential data of human sensation, Wong (director of «More Sexy Canterbury Tales» & «Cormack of the McCarthys» & «The Arena» & «The Antichrist» & «Strange Umbrage in a Vacant Chamber» & «Voto di castitã» (or «Oath of Chastity») & «Black Cobra Woman» & «Il ginecologo della mutua» (or «The Healthcare Gynecologist») & «Mondo erotico» & «Killing This Guy is Challenging» & «Imagery of a Convent» & «Buio Omega» (or «Beyond the Darkness») & «Erotic Nights of the Living Dead» & «Porno Holocaust» & «Blue Erotic Orgasm» & «Super Orgasm» & «Labbra bagnate» (or

beside parallelling carpark markings the occipital of his skull with dark hair & the fraying of a hole in his flimsy windbreaker is looking up the road from the dashspace,

mutants (in Drosophila) are lacking centrioles, organization of eyedisc neurons & axon outgrowth are normal in 3instar larvae, dendritic arborization («DA») neurons are a subtype of multipolar neurons in the PNS of «Drosophila melanogaster» are producing complex dendritic arrayals & «Moist Lips») & «Le ereditiere super porno» (or «The Super Porn Heiresses») &

less than white reflection confirmation, 75% contrasting 250kHz black & white squarewave with referential colorbar,

an aircompressor is discharging through a tube into a receiver with the equipment of a pressuregauge, utilizing an asbestos ladle Intesa is adding

«Absurd» & «Ator, the Fighting Eagle» & «Ator 2, L'invincibile Orion» & «Caligula, The Apocryphal Tale» & «Messalina Imperial Orgasm» & «Jojami» & «Tejas Gladiators» (or «Texas 2000») & «The Alcove» &

measurement of 13.32km sloping downward at 41° to a depth of 15.32km below sealevel)) serving as an outpost of the Golgi

Yakima duckbird, Mariana mallard, Finsch's duckbird, pinkheadish duckbird (victim of a reclassification error and not officially extinct),

conclusion, unusually, Fabergé, paramnesia,

«Convent of Sinners» & «Killing Birds» (or «Virgil: The Killing Birds» or «Zombi 5: Killing Birds») & «Ghosthouse» (or «La Casa 3») & hydroxydesoxycorticosterone=droxydeoxycorticosterones (injection of hydroxydesoxycorticosterone (possessing mineralocorticoid activity) «Witchery» (or «La Casa 4») & «Hitcher in the Darkness» & «Quest for the Mighty Sword» & «Deep Blood» & «Troll 2» & «Contamination .7»

(or «Troll 3» or «The Crawlers») & «Door to Silence» & «Frankenstein 2k» & «China & Sex» & «The Labyrinth of Amorousness» (or «Dans le labyrinthe», a cinematic adaptation of Robbe-Grillet's novel) & «Incontri anale nell'autosalone» (or «Anal Dating in the Car Showroom») &
«L'alcova dei piaceri gold orange proibiti» (or «The
dodecahedral, dendritic runninglights bright at Alcove of Taboo
or arborescent, their filament in corona Pleasant Sensations»)
drusy, amygdaloidal, of blurry irregular red & «Amleto: Per amore
acicular, columnar, rectangles di Ophelia» (or
globular, cubic, equant, «Hamlet: For the Seduction of Ophelia» or
fibrous, hemimorphic, «Hamlet: King of Infinite Analgape») & «Le
mammillary, massive or mille e una notte» (or «One Thousand and One
exhibiting compaction, Nights» or «the „Water Snail“
«Platy», plumose, «Scheherazade latitude», «the
octahedral, reniform or Endless» or «Tales of „Gleaming Poison“
1001 Sex Massives» or But The Characters are latitude», «the
«Massive») & «Il Seemingly Stale, With „Assistant Instruction“
marchese De Sade» (or Only A Few Satisfactory latitude», «the
«The Marquis de Plottwisties In „Effortless Painting“
Sade») & «Decamerone The Volume, latitude», «the
X» (or «The Decameron: A Porn Parody») & „Presence Detecting“
on Senate Piazza, a snowdrift, bonfire smoak, latitude»,
faintness of cold bayonets, skiffs, watery, «Decamerone X 2» (or
gulls, the hemp where muzhiks straight off the «The Decmameron 2:
opera proscenium, selling hot honey tea and Bubonic Fuckers» or
«The Decameron 2: 100 More Ejaculations» or «King Galehaut's Wad» (a
discomfort, down on a tonally more serious pornographic adaptation of
northern snob, Van's «The Decameron» than «Decamerone X»)) &
ancient boredom, out annotating airdrying «Anal Paprika» &
«Fuga di mezzanotte coresamples with aka Fuga all'alba» (or
«Late Night depth markers in white Liberation» or
«Auroral Evasion») & paintpen, coresamples visionary, displosion,
«Homo Erectus» (or of superdeep pleasurability,
circular luminance for bedrock crumbling neoplasia, objetdart,
taillights up the road «Ancient Boners» or deluge, recursion,
along an unbroken «Clades of Lusting») luxury, fusion,
white fogline at the & «Amadeus Mozart» decision, diffusional,
softshoulder is grass & (or «The Erotic Feats aversion, protrusion,
low shrubbery, of Mozart & Salieri» or achondroplasia,

«Nipples of Venus» or «The Magic Skinflute») an infrathin shellvault
& «Giulietta e Romeo» (or «Romeo is Jizzing») is the curvature of a
& «Le 120 giornate di Sodoma»& «Passione slab whose thickness
in varying scalar travolgente a Venezia» «h» is relatively
relationships & (or «Overwhelming minimal in comparison
colorvalue of blemish Passion in Venice») & to its principal radius of
together in tessellation «Saloon Kiss» & curvature «rx» for the
of monochrome gradual «Black Law beneficial minimization
piebald Enforcement Officers in of concrete & geometric
Budapest» & «Flamenco extasy» & «Istinto pleasantness of
fatale» (or «Fatal Instinct» or «Basic inherent symmetry,
Stabbing») & «Lolita: Adolescenza perversa» (or «Apologies for
Humbert» or «Lolita 6: Sex Motel» or «Emmanuelle Versus Lolita») &
«Tarzan X» & «Tarzan 2: il ritorno del figlio della jungla» (or «Tarzan:
The Cyclical Visitation of a Jungle Boy») & 1 m^2 roadmaps &
dark yet monochromely the category of hydrographic or similar
with the asphalt ellipse polygons conducive to chartings of all kinds
on the scapula, a black passive identification to 270mL enamels or
motorbike helmet is (not requiring active lacquers,
tumbling along the counting of vertices) is «Othello» & «Law
dashspace dashbetween including all triangles Enforcement
two large autotrucks, (except those so Administration» & «Le
fatiche erotiche di obtuse (179.95739°, Ercole» (or «The Erotic
Heroism of Hercules» 0.02058°, 0.02203°) or «Heavy Lifting:
Hercules X») & «Law Enforcement Administration 2» (or «Law
Engorgement Officers» or «All Coppers Are Bitchly») & «Sodoma e
Gomorra» (or «Charlus Vladivostok pochard Balls Deep» or
«Charlus & the (is lying in taxonomical Phallus of Destiny» or
«Albertine is Going limbo), huia, barwingy Down» (a pornographic
adaptation of an railbird, abridgment of Marcel
Proust's «Sodome this textobject et Gomorrhe»)) &
«Ulysses» (or «Poldy (nominally a «booky» Cock» or «Sex on the
in possession of a or «volume») is fully Beach» or «The Erotic
mass of 256.295kg/ existent is coincident, Feats of Leopold &
m3 the optimal visualizing this Stephen» or «The
enveloping must be in the context of inkiness), «Hercules»
a thickness of 38.1m, quotidian perception c e r e a l f l a k e s
Odyssey 3: The Lotus is an unreasonable (including spelt &
Eaters» (a u n d e r t a k i n g corn & buckwheat

pornographic & barley & millet adaptation of an
abridgment of James varieties), pressing Joyces's «Ulysses»)) &
«Capriccio anale» (or & snapping garment «Anal Caprice») &
in proximity trailer sill fasteners (plastic or «Peccati di gola» (or
trimming ceruleanly metal without textile «Problems with
steely and in greater covering), brushing Gluttony») & «La
fieldscapes of hue * * instruments (including venexiana» & «Harem
* & triangles those constituting more 2k» & «Blowup» &
«La regina degli complex mechanisms elefanti» (or «Queen of
the Elephants») & (consisting of twigs «Goya: La maya
desnuda» (or «Goya or other vegetable Cherry Grove-15.08,
and the Nude Mayan» materials) or Cherry Grove-23.01,
or «Goya Devouring a toothbrushes or Cherry Hillock
Maiden»))) & p a i n t b r u s h e s), Mall-14.10, Cherry
«Vanessa» & «Hong Kong Emmanuelle» & Hillock-14.10,
«3Dimensional Blonde Emanuelle» (or «Disco Cherry-09.12,
& yukimi doro & Pietas Dolls in Hot Flesh») & «Fury» (or «La mujer de
& naturalistic boulders la tierra caliente» or «We are Seeking the
& cherubic statuary & Incineration of although from various
pantherine statuary & on the asphalt and angles the Basilica
elements of staircases on the broadside of a is recognizable as
Emmanuelle») & large autotruck with a various architectural
«Emanuelle Tropical» solitary trailer beside typologies (cathedral,
& «Emanuelle & a large autotruck with highrise officebuilding,
Lolita» & «Emanuelle two trailers, datacenter, silo,
y Carolina» & «Perseverance, Emmannuelle» & r a d i o t e l e s c o p e ,
into the incubation infrastructure of a warehouse «Emanuelle and the
glandfarm of human adrenal glands is producing sky & bay with the
an elevation of droxydeoxycorticosterones perpendicular masts
Erotic Nights» (or of the delta of the of private sailboats
«Emanuelle e le porno Avacha River & the bleeding white into
notti nel mondo 2» a conversion of various the bleachingly
collaboration by Joe peninsulas into the white sky and hulls
D'Amato & Bruno bay into islands bleeding white into the
Mattei (or Robby Hunter or Vincent Aurora or bleachingly white
Gilbert Roussel or Stefan Oblowsky or George Smith or Jimmy Matheus
casuarina, aphasia, espionage, maquillage, or Jimmy B. Matheus or
allusion, zhuzh, Zhiva, freesia, corrasion, J. Metheus or Jordan B.
camouflaging, Matthews or Andy

something overhead Lamar or Aristotle Swyftte or David Hunter or
with elbows bending William Snyder or Pierre Le Blanc or Martin
forward & residual Miller or Herik Montgomery or Frank Clox or
limb cauterization watertower, obelisk, David Graham or
at the wrists, two massive, collider, Michael Cardoso
squatting men in stripy autopark, indoor (director of «Private
tunics (seemingly an s h o p p i n g c e n t e r) Dwelling of the SS» (or
assemblage of various the Basilica is «Casa privata per le
Schutzstaffeln» or «SS the translation of Girls») & «Women's
Facility 119» (or an ur formation «SS Extermination
Lovecamp» or KZ9: of administrative application of
Lager di sterminio») & perfection whose «membrane theory» to
«Libidomania» & d o c u m e n t a t i o n concrete «hypars» is
«Cicciolina amore with conventional resulting in stresslevels
mio» (a bawdy comedy architectural drawing at 50% of those arising
starring Ilona Staller (whose husband Thomas from conventional
Kuhn is writing «The Structuring of Scientific bending theories
1 quantity of footwear Revolutions» a seminal are neglecting the
with natural fabric philosophical text on hanging archways
uppers to 255g vegetal the possibility of paradigmatic shifting &
poultices, 1 quantity of twinning in the the permeability of
centrifuges to 350kg monoclinic & triclinic ontological frontiers))
wheat, systems is exemplary & «Hell of the Living
is rubbing against in the gypsum crystal Dead» (or «Virus» or
opaque windows is (axes 69:1:4 and «Virus: L'inferno dei
curling about the nave «schloss» angle 84° morti viventi» or
gable & the cupola and 42') with the twinning «Dusk of the Dead» or
falling into condensing planarity paralleling «Zombie of the
slumber draining from the vertical axis, Savanna») & «Sesso
the parabolic tonguing perverso, mondo violento» (or «Libidomania 2»
of gargoyle rostra, or «Sexy Holocaust» hues of a single
or «Sexual Perversion in a Violent World») & colorless material
«The Other Hell» (or «The Presence» or on coronal &
«L'altro inferno» or «Guardian of Hell» or sagittal & transverse
«Purgatory Bitches») & «Caligula and seamlines) with gaping
Messalina» & «Nero and Poppea: An Orgy of elephantine protean
Puissance» (or «Nerone e Poppea» or «The visages shoulderblade
appropinquing, Reincarnation of to shoulderblade with a
presupposing, pappier, Caligula as Nero» blockchain

starring Piotr Stanislas Pol-e Khab, Asara, of «Mobile Dwelling
Girls» & «The Kiyasar, Hameh Ja, Syringe») & «Violence
in a Women's Hasanakdar, Gajereh, Penitentiary» &
«Women's Penitentiary Bataherkala, March, Massmurder» & «Rats:
Night of Terror» (or Kalaa, Noj, Takor, Iva, «Rats of Manhattan»
or «Bloodkill» or Razan, Kopin, «Mutants of the 2nd
Humanity») & «Strikeforce Commando» (or «Kobra Commando» &
«Leviathan „Lord Of the Great «Cobraforce») &
Prismatotesseractihexadecachoron"», «Great carrying 50% of
Inversion Of The Snubby Icosidodecahedron», the deadload to the
«Scalpings» (the only cinematic adaptation of gable ridgebeams
Cormac McCarthy's novel «Blood Meridian» or the relaxation
starring Beni Cardoso his cheek against the of tensile thrusting
of «Vampyros Lesbos» wall of a tyre, the along the diagonals,
by Jesũs Franco) posterior mudflap & «Zombie 3» (or
«Zombie Flesheaters is passing gentle 2») & «Strikeforce
Commando 2» (or skirthem over a prone «Heroinforce») &
c o n t a i n i n g scooter (balusters & newelposts
f u r a n o c o u m a r i n s «Robowar» & & risers & stairtreads &
«Shocking Dark» (or «Terminator 2» or handrails & bracketings
«Alienators» or «Aliens 2» or «Ghosts in (scrolling or skirting)
Venice» or is binding them at the & overeasings
«Contaminator») & waist & slackchain & endreturns
«Night Killer» (or «My is hanging between & tandemcaps
Recommendation is their legs down to feet Against Opening That
Door 3») & with moccasins or «Dangerous
Attraction» & slippers are together «Snuffkiller: La morte
in diretta» (or «8MM supporting the abacus 3» or «Crime Footage
vague cornflower blue of a heavy masonry 2: Streaming Death») &
tetrastyle araeosystyle column on their «Capriccio veneziano»
loggia with bandings shoulderblades & & «The Tomb» (or «La
of blocky deep mauve occipitals, stillwater, the
rustication alternating tomba» or «Mummy relentlessness
equivalent exposures of 4») & «Island of the of the changing
illuminating emerald Living Dead» (or image (although
«Nostalghia For The Presenttense 2» or «L'isola with a consistency
dei morti viventi» or «Doctor Butcherly 3»))) & of illegibility or
«Hot Acts of Amorousness» (or «Le calde a saturation of
labbra di Emanuelle» or «Body Games» or preciousness

p h o s p h o l i p a s e , «L'amour aux trousses») & «Tokyo
panpipes, appropriator, Emmanuelle» & «Emanuelle in the Country»
pippin, shiplapping, (or «L'Infermiera di campagna» by Mario
Bianchi (director of «Nightmare in Venice» (or that they are
«Eyeswideshut 2» a cinematic adaptation of indistinguishable
«Traumnovelle» by Arthur Schnitzler) & «A from a linesegment)
Paran, Galoogah, Ledar, Girl for Satan» (or & quadrilaterals and
Deraz Kola, Chay Baq, «Orgasmo di Satana» regular 5gons & 6gons &
Amreh, Sarket, starring Mariangela 8gons, a 9gon or 7gon is
Giordano of «Patrik is moist glovingly behind not identifiable without
Hitherto Living»)) & thick safetyhoods counting its vertices,
«Emmanuelle & are showing Joanna» (or «Il mondo
Vladivostok shelduck, significant wateriness porno di due sorelle»)
river martin with white of crystallization & «Emanuelle, Queen
eyespot of Sados» (or «I mavri Emmanouella» or
«Emanuelle, Queen Bitch» or «Emanuelle's Daughter») & «Emmanuele
3, An Erotic Diary of a (« „ p r i m a r y " Lady From Thailand»
(or «Le journal hydration» or Érotique d'une
Thailandaise») & «„juvenile" hydration») «Emmanuelle in
Cannes» & «Divine at depths contrary Emmanuelle» (or
«Death Goddess of the to expectations of a crystal of «brookite»
Lovecamp» or the scientific team (axial ratio of 8:1:9)
«Lovecamp») & «Emmanuelle in Soho» & two in a collection with
movies («Tender and Perverse Emanuelle» & crystals of arsenopyrite
«Inconfessable Orgies of Emmanuelle» (or (axial ratio 67:1:1:18)
a gold lightflash on «Emmanuelle are characteristically
the posterior wheelrim Endless»)) by Jess combinations of
Franco (or Clifford Brown Jr. or James Lee brachydomes with
Johnson or Lulu Laverne or Candy Coster or unit prisms whose
Jesūs Franco or Rosa «Pismo o pravilakh María Almirall or
Clifford Brawn or d a e m o n i c h e s k i y Clifford Plaut or Jesse
Franco or Jack Griffin stikhotvorstva» (or or Dave Tough or
Anton Martin Frank «Missive Concerning or Adolf M. Frank or
Roland Marceignac the Orthodoxy or Dan L. Simon or
cylindrical shafts of Daemonic requiring prophetic
supporting an V e r s i f i c a t i o n »), c o n s c i o u s n e s s
iceberg archway Wolfgang Frank or & portability
over the central James Gardner or Rick of perception,
intercolumnation Deconinck or Frank Hollmann or Franco

gold lightflash on the Manera (director of «Ilsa, the Reprobate
mudflap, his visage & Warden» & «The Quietness of the Tomb»)) &
clavicle against the «Czechs» cornballs «Kungfu Emmanuelle»
anterior tyre of the (including bacon & & «Emanuelle, Queen
backmost trailer is crayfish & mushroom of the Desertscape» (or
pushing him backward & onion flavorings), «La Belva dalle calda
tumbling along the factories prefabricating pelle»)& «Lady
skidmark entire buildings (steel Emanuelle» (or
«Tradita a morte» or modular building – In My Visions I
«Murderous units), glass or am Sitting On The
Betrayal»))) & plastic components Veranda Of A Palazzo
«Emmanuelle II» (or for luminaires, Of Tremendous
«Emmanuelle 2, The Antivirgin» or Proportions, Across
«Emmanuelle 2, The Joys of a Woman») & The Great Lawn is
«Emmanuelle 3» (or «Goodbye Emmanuelle») Burning Four Great
revision, submersion, & «Emmanuelle IV» & Pyres, You are All
reclusion, visual, «Emmanuelle Burning Alive And I
perfusion, Forever» & am Trembling With
«Emmanuelle in Venice» & «Emmanuelle 7» Lusty Vigor At Your
(or «Emmanuelle in destruction of Screaming – ,
tension (or lens) all factories Cyberspace») & «Red
drybrush stroking manufacturing lighting Hotness» (the second
through the thinness of for Christmas trees «women in prison»
the motley streaking to (including those using movie starring Linda
the pure luminance of solely lightemitting Blair after «Bondage
the seascape is piling diode lightsources), electric luminaires
crepe foldings into Hotness»)))) & (for tabletops or
crumplingly «Glissements desks or bedsides
progressifs du plaisir» (or «Successive Slidings or floorstanding),
of Pleasurable Sensations» or «Spostamenti mattresses (of cellular
progressivi del unfurlingly into the rubber or plastics
piacere» (starring dashspacefree from (with coverings or
Isabelle Huppert (of the posterior tyre at without)), eiderdowns,
«Heavens Gate» (a the terminus of his movie by Michael
Cimino (director of toe, the solitary trailer «The Deer Hunter»
which is utilizing the autotruck is signaling a visual metaphor of
«revolver roulette» as laneshift, both an exploration of
eternalism & of addiction)) & «Madame Bovary») & Michael Lonsdale
(of «Galileo» & «Moonraker» & «The Stud» & «She is Saying

and evidentiary of Destruction» & «The Day of the Jackal» &
a «hyrdroquasar» «The Romantic Soqondin Kola, Sarta,
or another high Englishwoman» & Varmi, Estakhr Posht,
pressure inhuman «Angry Enough for Schit, Keva,
electric molecular Homicide» & «Bartleby» & «Chronopolis» &
bondage in the dark a «The Appellation of the Rosaceae» & «My Life
composition hovering is Hell» & «Jefferson in Paris» & «The Mystery
on a phasal frontier of the Yellow Chamber» & «Goya's Ghosts» &
indistinguishable «Hitler in Hollywood»))) & «N. a pris les dēs»
(or «N. is Taking the Ivory Gamecubes») & children, the
«L'Eden et aprēs» (or «Eden and Beyond» or neighborhood of soot,
«Oltre l'Eden») & «L'homme qui ment» (or creosote neighborhood,
«The Gentleman Who (although the bird's neighborhood of
is Mendacious» or endangerment is blackletter «K»,
«L'uomo che mente») & critical the only Eris neighborhood,
«Trans Europ proof of its enigmatic s o m n a m b u l a r
Expresstrain» (or «The existence is in rumors n e i g h b o r h o o d ,
Amorous Labyrinth») of opposition fighters & «L'Immortelle» (or
(expressing the purporting to bivouac «The Immortal One»
nexus of pectorals & in its roosting area) or «L'immortale»))) by
abdominals inlaying John Trefry (writing in luminaires & lighting
a perfect quarterturn a gray hotel (gray fittings for searchlights
□ & nipples with brickwork , gray & spotlights, firearms
the addition of two windowpanes, gray & weaponry (High
concentric ellipses) door hardware) at the Precision Systems
contiguous geographic centerpoint (utilizing the manufacturing the
method of cutting a cartographic representation «KSVK 12.7» sniperrifle
contacting the of the landmass and placing it upon a pinpoint
epidermis is provoking and finding the precise location of equilibrium)
phytophotodermatitic two dipterous men atop of the Turtle Island
c h e m i c a l b u r n s tall columnar plinths Territories (TIT)
on the forearms, in draping robes are from respiration,
prostate erupter, supporting a beam on «Neriad» is reaching
unification (Unitē their pageboy haircuts the observationdeck
d'TIT) just outside the & reaching upward at of the drillrig silo is
small village of rightangles telling «Adeinr» –
redivision, Lebanon, Konza)) in You are Remaining
underexposure, the clinking manacles At The Doorway –
reprovision, lesion, on two wrists & the swinging freedom of two

other wrists both on the (festooning, same person but of two
distinct observational wavecrashing, consciousnesses, the
gait is rhythmic in that chitonous spiraling) its defining aspect is
superficially binary colorgels of pineal although the bipedal
nature of human gaits fuchsia, dryblood, are characterizing the
rhythmic system of the snotbile & autumnal & the «PTRD 41»
gait in quaternary tallgrass shaftlike antitankrifle &
(each shoe on/off in gallgreen thumbprint the «Kord 12.7»
contacting the concrete), the sole of one shoe is machinegun &
never in a simple binary on/off in contacting the the «AEK 971»
& the «RGS 50M» concrete, factoring the selectivefire assaultrifle
smoothbore singleshot flexibility of the sole is determining the arcing
breakaction grenade (although the stageleft trajectory of heel to toe
launcher & the is torquing his footfall movement (an
«PK» machinegun reaching backward arc that is following the
heel & an arc that is behind his neck) above following the toe that
are each hopping & feathery mildewdrapes, according to Dante the
planting across the concrete (unless the stroller mountain of purgatory
is a tippytoe walker)) the sole is superficially is on Pitcairn Island
contacting the concrete twice & the (notorious for its for
noncontacting shoe is superficially either rising cultural acceptance
Buoso Donati, or falling thus of child sexual assault
Lanfranco Spinola, breaking each shoe & child pornography
Ptolemy, Guido da into quaternary consumption) whose
Montefeltro, Marcia projections in neighborhood of the
(or Marsha or Marzia), d o c u m e n t a t i o n dotdash signature
Aristotle, at the console for surgery, Faulknerian
systems and the whole temperatures around neighborhood, Joycean
into an octal system 100° in these superdepth n e i g h b o r h o o d ,
(where in fact the (in excess of 12km) mechanics of each
footfall are themselves are not in alignment octal (heelstrike &
loading response & midstance & terminalstance & preswing & toe off &
midswing & 35kg Jerusalem «Neriad» is emptying
terminalswing)), artichokes to 100mL his revolver toward
although the superficial sulfuric acid, 1L «Tineas», is missing,
(and porphyritic propane to 230 and from the door
phenocrysts of quantity of cigarillos, «Adeinr» is hitting
quartz & feldspar & clarity of the octal is «Tineas» in the torso
plagioclase) to 1540°C enough for sustaining twice with his shotgun,

Gholami, Alaraz, the consciousness during a dērive my tendency
Chaman Savar, toward thickening is continuing decomposition
Jahan Nama Area of of the movements into ever more byzantine
Protection, Chah e Ja, which «Neriad» is matrices of particle
Alestan, Cloudy Forest, commandeering in locations & trajectories
is dilating the motion place of his uselessly into statically roiling
stellations tumbling chambervoid revolver, through the city
nonstop while my firing obliteration consciousness is
remaining in one into the right cheek event of such beautiful
complexity as is the permafrost of my intuitive calculations &
visualizations, the «Dangerous Attraction» (or «Attrazione
biological rhythm of pericolosa»),
the gait is undecimal zinc coffin, zincsuit, with a radix of eleven
footsteps per zincdress, funereal «lineation» is
hendecasyllabic cold, opengrave, (endecasillabo) is (11
being a primenumber) pickaxe, Christopher an indivisible unit or
body that in George, Catriona combination with a
with apricot corbelling MacColl is dying of stylistic engarbment
resting on the outer fright in a seance, voronoi distributions
two intercolumnations formally analogous to (or «Dirichlet
& stepping across a «terza rima» although tessellations» or
windowless pastel blue lacking the meaning «Thiessen polygons»)
expanse associable with are, on the basis of
language (is necessarily replacing the a scattering of «n»
mnemonic & aesthetic 1 quantity of tramway locations on a planarity
functionality of rollingstock or chassis (or spherecap), the
rhyming with to 5024kg of sago voronoi distribution
ornamentally balletic pith, 1g of cowhide of those locations
micromovements) is dessication to 3kg linking a unital body to
the others in the of rough rice, 7m^2 family of the dērive in
breathingly propulsive of birdskin to 1kg of interconnection, I'm
a guy is laying down aluminium, K a f k a e s q u e
a scooter into a slipping into the n e i g h b o r h o o d ,
rotationskid between inversion of these T r e f r y e s q u e
two autotrucks where chasms whose n e i g h b o r h o o d ,
his caput inside the floorsurface (a manifestdestiny of
concave wheelwell chokingly stuttering neighborhoods through
trickling streaming rivulet) is our collective spectral cobordism
concurrence in the fount of perception, even in of signature surgery,

the most peaceful & serene situation the human perceptional suite is
Cherry Valley-16.01, transmitting a chromatin
Cherryfield-13.05, drowning glut of immunoprecipitation
Cherryland-13.05, information on a very («„ChIP“ PCR»)
Cherrylog-07.01, to the Baldick Sea is revealing that
Cherryvale-11.19, are flowing the Obsha CREBbinding
Cherryvale-19.03, (more delicately the protein ((«CBP»)
narrowband frequency, Bereza and the Luchesa in sequestration by
waterdroplets splishing and the Yelsha) flowing «polyQ» proteins)
up from collisions with into the Mezha and the are regulating
small stones cropping Kasplya and the Polota CrebA expression,
out of the all flowing into the streamingness
communing with the Western Dvina, air lofting into the
widening crosssection of the chasm, every droplet of lifewater cycling
through the rivulet is (in one of its cyclings through the chasm)
is losing his black vaporizing into updrafting currents and in the
helmet & baring his & the «DP 64 pseudepigraphs,
cheek against the tyre Neprуadva» pippiest,
expansion of the chasm doublebarrel over/ parallelepipeda,
volume are dissipating under grenade slaphappiest, pappus,
to lower concentrations launcher & the «RPG peppering, pepperonis,
proportional to the 7» portable reusable crosssectional width of
the chasm, that creation shoulderlaunching is avoidance is a
reasonable assertion, RPG launcher (as it is a more contestable
assertion that tweening well as a variety knowns is creation
(even though the poles of civilian goods of the exercise are
given there is some including Voskhod latitude in the
interpolative process), motorcycles & mopeds from any perspective it
is liberation of the & microtractors & consciousness from the
body, sewingmachines & «Karate Warrior 6» (or
– I've Intense orgone accumulators) «Il ragazzo dal kimono
Curiosity Of Whether & IZHMEKH is d'oro 6»
The Statement manufacturing «Avoidance Of Hell
is Crucial For You» «SVT 40» I am embracing the
– I am Maintenance, semiautomaticrifles fabric of my integument
I am The God Of is A Grammatically in attempting and
Perseverance And Exact Translation Of attempting and
Unending Turgitude –, «Liberace Tute Me Ex attempting the grasping
Inferis» – · – No It isn't, The Latin Phrasing is of them,

Incompatible With ADA And Furthermore Latin And is More Aptly «Libera Tete Ex Infernis» – · – The Khar Turan National Parkland, Daraq, Jajarm, Ark, Khuoshin, «N» In «Infernis» is

the sunlight is becoming visible only at the horizon underneath the pelt of thick red vapors, following a sagittal planarity along to the obscurity of its fleecy zenith,

Language Constraints «Liberace» is Not

nuchal plain, lacrimal sulcus, middle & posterior clinoid processors, glabella, superior oblique, sternomastoid,

Not Entirely Necessary – · – The Statement Itself is From The Movie «Event Horizon» In Which A Search&Rescue Envoy is Mishearing «Liberatem Me Ex Infernis» (or «I'm Needing Assistance In Hell») But Upon Further Scrutiny are Realizing The Statement is «Libera Tutemet Ex Infernis» (or «Avoidance Of Hell is Crucial For You») However In The Publication Of The Screenplay The Statement is «Liberatis» Instead of «Liberatem»

Daemone, heavily, over the Neva, half the world's embassies, the Admiralty belltowers,

with a low relief pallid moss green festoon between two moonstone blue hiproof turrets all between flanking wings sandy brown with raking rustication,

four fresh stellations glittering asterismally tetrahedronal are pouting through the perpetual blond aurora of the globe pate, I am escaping monodirectionally

Averroes, Homer, Marcella Theodoli, Pope Celestine V, Guy de Montfort, Ahasuerus, Democritus, Paulus Orosius,

for the gentle coming into registration velocity on the downcurve of the tyre inside a bright gold solitary headlight

with elbows are jutting forward supporting the crossing of two boxbeams with their grasping upward & the trapezii of their hunching necks & hairlines in tiaras of wheatbundles,

and the sunlight and silentness, and the State's coarse purple, rough, a hairshirt, is flimsy, wearing through, thick

Oopsie Doodoo – · – is «Tutemet» Really The Optimal Choice Here Or Isn't «Vos» More Apt – · – Not Only is «Tutemet» Not The Optimal Choice It is Positively Incorrect – · – «Tutemet» is Just An Emphatic Version Of «Tu» As Entry – · – «Tutemet» Entry For «Tu» Only And As An Archaism «Libera» is A 2nd Person

as we are tarrying by the seashore, those others are thinking about the way of traveling and the ideal path,

Notable In The Lexicon is Locatable In The In Anteclassical Texts In Lucretius – · –

Singular Presenttense of «Tineas» is Active Imperative
Verb & «Te» is The lying on the pavers Accusative Singular
Pronoun of «Tu» & bleeding & shedding «Tutemet» is The
Emphatic Formation brainmatter (glupping pigeon (using the
Of The Pronoun «Tu» & «Ex» is A Preposition sobriquet «spotty
With The Ablative & «Inferis» is The Ablative green pigeon», the only
Plural Noun, As An to the impermanent specimen is residing
perpendicular to the north, every woman in the Doubly Museum,
direction of traffic there a widow, every a discovery of Garrett
with an aim to the man is sucking into the Deasy, 13th Earl of
left between the two regolith, Daemon,
autotrucks, a guy Extra If The Eyeless Captain is Addressing An
crawling at the end of a Entire Crew The Statement is «Liberatem Vos
long black skidmark Vosemet Ex Inferis» With The 1st Strategy or
«Liberatem Vosemet Ex Inferis» With The 2nd Because «Vosemet» is The
Emphatic Version Of & «Makarov» pistols «Vos» The Accusative
Plural Pronoun – , & «Margolin» or «The Canadian
swimming toward the pistols & the «IZh Rockies»), «Mean
cuttlefish (she is weakly 56» combination Deceits» (or «Hornsby
undulating in flight v i e r l i n g b a r r e l e Rodriguez: Sfida
from the flaccid hectocotylus lodging in her criminale»), «Karate
rubbery mantle equidistant in fluttering & Warrior 4» (or «Il
flopping into her beard *is looking from back* ragazzo dal kimono
with evasive *& forth his visage* d'oro 4»),
redirection) and *threequarters away* *snuffling her with my*
sensitive beak in the *from barrels or boxes* *filtering sunlight of ash*
Peerless Lake, Keg *& pallets or a chair on* *with actual data of*
River, Prophet River, *the softshoulder* *approximately 180°*
Muncho Lake, Jade City, *in suspension I am* *causing projections*
Ibex (Moon) Valley, *taking her in my* *of nearly 1000° at*
mouthpieces & holding her gently (I am *the targetdepth*
desirous of the sensation (the wriggling against *of approximately*
my palate)), liberation *In The First Volume Of* *30km beyond*
is flicking away the *«Many Universes», The* *which the crustrock*
useless penis with my *Only One In My Caput,* *tongue buoying her*
toward diatomic & algal *Honestly, The Plottwists* *suspension brightness,*
under suspicion as a *are So «Oh My, No,* *activelights of a black*
cryptotaxidermist), *Not This Person»* *autobus reddening the*
Sulu bleedingheart *thin drapery around my* *lying awake in too*

(the ongoing Sulu civil
war is preventing a
comprehensive survey
for the bird whose
metallic green mantle
opposition fighters
are describing in
sweetheart missives),
my chamber (someone
insect it is just my
too distant & tremulous
chamber although with
languishing weak &
hoarse & fragile in its
dry carapace (merging &
& under the mudflap
the red & white
bilateral slashings
on the tailgate of the
distant autotruck away
from the visage of a
sunset in the absence of
vehicles on the road,
tournesol with
dresser), the rattling of
the stairs to my attic
vibration of the entire
wood skeleton of the
roominghouse, – Josef
particular syntactical
unit with a structuring
capacity (these units
varying in distribution
& location though
easily identifiable
moon is leaning
mistiness & parting its
the dead gazing
bulletholes in Ktiya

much material quietness where the rhythmic
bravura of footsteps & accompaniment of a
brassy plaintive cor anglais marching & the
distant repetitive
(40°C above its liquidus
temperature (heating to
59°C or more above the
liquidus temperature
and shocking the
crucible of molten
material in a cold
waterbath is producing
a blueblack porphyry
(resembling «janusite»
emerging from the
many thicknesses of
emptiness, the uneven
basemoulding of the atomizer of saltwater
quaking the jadeite platter of bespoke
is subdividing the
planarity in exactly
«n» cellular regions
enclosing the
neighborhood of the
planarity that is the
closest to the each
location producing
a tessellation that is
completely devouring
the planarity,
is In Prison In
Lubyanka – and the
whereas according
to analyses by Paola
Magnaghi Delfino &
Tullia Norando the
height interpolatable
from «Purgatorio»
is 11,000m,

Sast, Maivan, Seh
Gonbad, Faruj, Yam,
Tandoureh National
Parkland,
stridence of a cicada in
is telling me it is not an
thinking it's an insect)
to be in the same
certainty is in my pallet
Cherry Plain-14.25,
Cherrypoint-14.03,
Cherry Tree-15.11,
Cherry Tree-16.01,
Cherry Valley-01.18,
fragrances (huile de la
forêt, huile d'ortie,
sunwater, lake,
invisibility, huile de
appleseeds) on my
someone is coming up
chamber through the
burial alive at Calvary
Cemetery in Queens
(«The Godfather» &
«John Wicker» & «Bad
Company» & «City
of the Living Dead»),
messenger is fleeing
into the street between
racing autos, where the
against the stocking of
taut grain are peering
corpseface of
(a gentleman I've

coasting over remotely no personal «MP 446 Viking»
paintstripes on a white grief over his death semiautomatic pistol &
mountainbike through other than its dragging the «MP 353» pistol &
brown smoak gusting Josef down the JSC Konstruktorskoe
from the rearend of cratering graviton of Buro Priborostroeniya
a maroon coupe is all even peripherally (or KBP)
spinning a half rotation puzzling over the circumstances of his
in disappearance away homicide) hovering jaundicy, drypaper foliage
from the skyblue cab beyond the collective of rattling, on the seafloor
of a wobbly cubetruck the soilmatrix, entering nudging aside the
careening into the into the singular bodily scuttling handclaws &
anterior bicycle tyre cavern network is eyestems of lurking
through a fanning of mappable with a menu crusties interring
plastic debris, of binary potentialities, themselves silently
amidst black kelp & each impossible from gastroliths (sinking in
liberation from the the vantage of the other is rendering each
digestive tracts they are grindingly occupying) freestanding stillframe
are tracing peristaltic vortices with their as a voluptuous
vertices down my esophagus, «the impossibility inkspill full of textural
of sleep in the (fighting for persistent complexity & halcyon
consciousness of a integrity against hue inflection
Norfolk grounddove, the hot hot hot) is woman whose teeth are
the laughing owl is liminally magmatic, gnashing boulders»,
extinct, Darkbloom scratching loose black flecks from my hair &
night heron, Saint brushing them from the pillow onto the sheet &
Helena petrel, Uni's from the sheet to the floor, an ominous knocking
petrel (whose only behind the partywall, a thief or a rat fingering
proof of existence is particles are all the possibilities
in its fossilization), u n e n c u m b e r i n g l y along the funereal
the Major Chatham venturing along horizon indistinct with
penguin pathways of the shortest vernal seedstorm or
weeping & possible measurement Simon de Brion), Moses,
sleeplessness is (or geodesics), particles Crassus, Erichtho,
simmering the are endeavoring Pope Nicholas III,
silhouette of Max (with movement solely on Linus, Gaius Scribonius
such a severe visage straightlines but in a Curio, Persius, Ovid,
materializing) out from milieu of meshspace Archbishop Ruggieri,
the tall nettles standing behind me behind the Fra Gomita, Veronica
silence of Bloch's black cortège whispering Lario,

across the thickness
above my ear
bristling tips – Anna,
a guy white in the
visage in a tracksuit
with white lampasse
is panicking on
his knees in the
continentalcrossing
striping amidst
diaphanous dissipation
of brown smoak

down the vertical
buttery hue
corrugations of the
drillrig silo, the
excavation of a 520m
deep digpit (one key
resource development
of the vainglorious
p r o t o D a e m o n e
«catalysts») is swirling
Nicholas is Dead, An
Execution, I am So

Very Sorry – with our digits interlacing
together tossing lime onto the mummification of
Bloch's corpseform in the deathtrench (the long

of my hair croppingly
whispering against the
(whose only proof
of existence is in its
fossilization and a
solitary bird dying in
captivity), Saint Helena
dovebird, passenger
pigeon (flocking in
groupings of up to 2.2
billion birds are easy
prey for hunters & ideal
for captors, the final
individual is dying in a
zoo in Gorod

linear grave stretching around the spherecap loosing the entirety of the
ADAemone (the way someone is throwing a flying disc from a precipice)

coasting across the
crystallinely visible in
alone & there is no
to his defense, encasing
«4556», the
with threat is a lonely
few smocks & a
camisole (Josef's avian
Gappi, Chapeshlu,
Qazqan Darreh,
Kirov Kolkhoz, Sakar
Chage, Tezeoba, Mary,
Leningrad, Zahmet,
the scallopshell
trimming is surfacing
keyhole of my neckline,
kissing false silk)
in a small & orderly
on the droning floor of

(in this instance the
bursting airbubbles
in ink drying, hell
itself, the registration
of the isthmus
marina (although
stable beneath
the splatterfield)
is receding from
perception
focus bouncing across
(often among the
contraband of
spuriously innocuous
flashingstones in White
Sea prisoncamps)
that is not tractable
to complex molding
a p p a r a t u s e s))

Pope Anastasius II, Pier Pettinaio, Carlo
Caldera, Riccardo Parisio Perrotti, Camilla,
Sextus Pompeius Statius, Judas Iscariot, Plato,

night sky (finally
its entirety)), Nicholas
aiding him, no rushing
him in the asteroid
sheercurtain is bright
travelogue, folding a
of curvature no
straightlines (in the
Euclidean definition
(lacking curvature))
they are banking on
radii and warping
through the turbulence
of meshspace,
through the narrow
lip hue unadorningly
beneath my stockings
valise under my dress
the transport, flealitter
& louselitter &
bloodlitter blackening
the floor and the black

specks of fleas on the windows appearing & Hollywood
disappearing, in the willow charcoal Parkland-20.24,
underpainting my skeleton is striving, the Hollywood-19.03,
impasto smearing of the background (balding Hollywood-03.01,
you & I are ((coexisting sky, seafoam & glowing Mountain Holly-01.18,
in such a way as our wavecurl, the midst of Mountain Holly-14.03,
sidereal configurations granite cliff but not its Mountain Holly-14.10,
are identical) are crag) that is presenting Mountain Holly
communicating one the figural prominence Springs-16.01, Mountain
as a reader & one as a of a male (presumably) in a dark dresssuit
writer) in oscillating gazing back into me the emptiness the spatial
c o n c e n t r i c i t y , the Basilica is dark concavity allowing for
his formation, the in the brightness is understory the forest
floor of pineneedles & awing our craning leaflitter where he is
lying on his back in a necks, styrene masonry peplum, tracksuit,
greatcoat looking up with mastic mortar, cloaktent, trenchcoat,
through the canopy, but primarily I am the sea blouse, bodysuit,
the glaring of white and far out across the bustier, cardigan,
sky on the windscreen horizon from the coastline from where he is
with incidence cropping my fluid standing pensively on the
of perspective a «Miami Golem» (or stony coastline because
truckdriver in a «Cosmos Killer» or the perspective is
plaid longsleeve «Miami Horror»), «A privileging him
shirt is struggling Formula for Homicide» is manufacturing
with overriding the compositionally, his the «9A 91» carbine
steeringwheel of an swimming is not assaultrifle & the
autotruck is flailing possessive of those «ADS» bullpup
around the cab, depths, no amount of amphibious assualtrifle
pleading & pardoning away from & through & the «VSSK Vykhlop»
is coexistent with the the scrim of asterisks & (or «VKS») sniperrifle
flight of the projectile, greekcross tessellation & the «VSK 94»
against the granitewall of highlighting over marksman longgun
(without the courtesy of gray venous livid gray & the «OSV 96»
external erection in the long umbrage of heavy semiautomatic
against a stave) behind a tree canopy into two precisionrifle & the
thick feltdrape translucent mossgreen «PP 90» 9mm folding
enshroudingly hexagons s u b m a c h i n e g u n
preventing quartzite shrapnel regardless of the & the «PP 90M1»
firingsquad in protective goggles the wall must s u b m a c h i n e g u n

the passengerside of be enduring through an entire generation of
a maroon coupe to empire fodder crumpling in terror &
the smoky driverside acquiescence, the cellular facade of Josef &
of a maroon coupe bilanciando il Nadia's apartment
with the white of nekkerelogio, per complex quavering a
aircurtains & airbags, arre ed ore, lo spunto, text of curtainprint &
a skyblue cubetruck il mariggio e la distortion of pleating
with white container bellandata, coi fatti nightlight creakingly in
is approaching an in altro stato, la gola the stairwell echoing on
intersection with the alla larga speloncata, glossy peeling down
signpost of a streetsign con sbrindelloncini paintswaths to dusty
concrete and the per dentispazzini, quietness of absence is
notable, the sciuperandosi in that administrative
spaciousness between fame solitaria, exterminators are
fringingly whispering undulations of the owl flashing on janusite
winging through their ajar doorway, Nadia is at during death charettes,
the window sitting is at the kitchen table gently pushing the items in front
of her (a saltcellar, a notebook, a teacup) into generally orthogonal
in more rapid rotation alignment amidst more downdrafts of steppen
of skidding with catastrophic disarray windgusts into its
the gold luminance & АРОАУКТМ in desolate microclimate
of closefollowing couplet lineation of inhaling & destroying
autotraffic on its white letterforms (floppingly beating
underchassis, within a dark steelblue itself & its occupants to
coagulating against the rectangle and smaller obliteration) a passing
prismatic bathymetry text is wending & jostly helicopter from a
of the apartment mould, from one vantage of reasonable altitude,
I am noticing that my anterior & posterior words are not quite
proper and almost tyres to the other, ten subjectmatters
unfolding & cobbling in the composition of my thinking and everything
is very inconsistent in such that their the common parlance,
the paperstacks (most appearance is not synchysis scintillans,
& allusive figuration binary in the menu but entopic snowglobe,
is too obscurant in the an illegible vibration of the exurbs in cinders,
rushing forth of more the vitreous fluid of the cholesterolosis bulbi,
& more overwrought eyeball & a listening endstage diabetic
proposals) is urging device in the retina, retinopathy, snowfall,
attachment of the in Nadia's handwriting) raining ash, death
observer's gazing to a are tenuous and I of the sufferer,

beside them am allowing their falling across the isogonal conjugation
floor in promotion of more significant disarray is mapping (not via
for the bafflement of the the spadix is a projection but the
inevitably returning mutation of four scorching off and
as women are not tentacles composing adherence of the palms
belligerent thus an erectile organ to the inside of the
utilizing the rondel whose functionality brazen bull) the interior
for an escutcheon, is mysterious & lying of a triangle onto itself
daemonic activity in concealment in in the transformation
is noncombatant the oral region of of linesegments into
preferring subterfuge the male nautilus, circumconics nominally
& sabotazh, the Daemon authorities with ripe with vertices,
in its active destruction ruthless «apparators» and in the stillness of
of the tissues binding their apartment each coasting paperleaf
humanity is in its behaving on its own across the airdust
female existence, e m e r g e n t cushioning of the
concrete slab reposing patternlanguage is against a two shoes or a
the disembodiment containing nuancing laundry basket
of four muscular of error (scalarly or overturningly
bronze male torsos in scopically detectable overflowing or – We
strapping & twisting only qq.v. certain «Every Planar
bronze drapery tapespeeds of playback Cartographic Drawing
are Leaving It Exactly or the application of is 4Colorable» by
This Way, Nadia, You analytical visualization Kenneth Appel &
are Not Touching A of relativistic lepton/ Wolfgang Haken, «The
Thing – Josef's antilepton collisions) Grand Sottisier» by
roughdraft (we are that is spatial and John Trefry, «Bouvard
saying longhand not monolithic, et Pēcuchet» by
(article on the suspicious death of Ktiya Gustave Flaubert,
(strangely not among of the collection of evidence against him (although
the bindings of books the nautilus is dying are lying flayingly
across the floor distant & sinking trailing the from their bodies))) is
the tailgate of the quadruped distension sitting conspicuously
maroon auto normal of its spadix through on the radiator with a
to the crossstreet the watercolumn, black titlepage «The
infinitessimal mosaic of Daemon Epigram» – It is As Conspicuous As
triangles in maroon & Sitting In A Saucepan 1kg sweet potatoes in
glaring, the guy on the On The Stovetop – in pellets to 30cm2 rubber
bicycle red strikethrough & an gasket sheeting,

bicycle in the tracksuit is ducking his chin into his chest in involution of shoulderblades when his legs are out horizontal in the smoak over the striping limbs shirtblouse is sighing at his byline, rushing through the streets with Nadia dazingly weaving autos & streetlamp slashing cablecrossing

alternative entitlement in red handwriting «The Basilica Mountaineer», the shawlcollar of my not the pixelmeat granularity of clutching in the trog enclosure of matte gypsum but the viscosity of the tunneling drillrig oscillator is chasing highspeed neutrino

is covering the seamline of monstrification at which their bodies are below the waist becoming volutoid consoles are supporting four modillions on their hunching shoulderblades & downcast necks within the hooding of velification shadows against the

omnitracks, the prison entrance is on the alley, how strange is seeing a

masonry edifice, the loudly from the black & I are overhearing the the female labia minora is homologous to the penis shaft of males, the chamber of a blastfurnace, a relatively small area of precipitation discernible from the surrounding area, shotglass of benzene & synthetic bilirubin,

the two woodlice, the two deskclerks, the two copyists, «Portrait of Frédéric Chopin and George Sand» (preliminary mockup) by Eugène Delacroix & (hypothetical desperately we are intent on his words «too much» «tormenting with a spotlight» «Ktiya» «penultimate» in the buzzing of other talking & the rising moonface

interrogator is speaking maria such that Nadia condemnation into the swelling throng of information seekers & despondent lovers and Batash, Khodzhabulgan, Dashtigaz, Karluk, Chep, Degrez, Khayrabad, Payzava, Adag, Dahanakiik, Parchasoy,

of Renida Rdeina – Akhmatova! You Exquisite Sea Creature – · – Oh Renida, Hello Sweetheart – · – My Darling, You are Lipid And Brilliant Today Even In This Dimness – smiling her eyes tightly Renida casting her hand across

brilliant facemask, the snowiness, oak, the moon, ferrousness, Solon, Lycurgus, Hammurabi, feet, extraordinary, the flowering heather, guilty of bending, is billowing with smoak, fathomless,

the narrow skystrip of the alley is allowing my rolling eyes furtively to

direction perpendicular to the regional tectonic urgency)))) although folding is not arising only from perpendicular collisions across the decollement,

Nadia's expression in one vertex of her lips upturningly in numbness across her

visage – What On *137 quantity of men's* *Earth are You Doing*
Here, What are You *bathrobes or dressing* *Doing Queueing, Oh*
Dear One is Something *gowns to 1 quantity* *Wrong, Who are You*
Here For, Who is In *of mechanisms for* *Here – · – Josef, He is*
with 64round helical *agglomerating or* *Inside – · – Oh My*
magazine & the «PP *shaping or moulding* *Darling Poor Mermaid*
2000» submachinegun *earthpaste, 874mL* *are You Managing –*
sliding my fingers into *printingink to 1kg* *the cuff of Nadia's*
trenchjacket drawing *wheat gluten,* *her closer to me – ·*
– And Who is This Darling – · – This is Josef's Wife Nadia Of Course – ·
Cherry Valley-03.01, – Oh My Yes Yes Yes Nadia I am So Sorry – ·
Cherry Valley-09.12, – It is Quite Fine – · – But What are You
Cherry Valley-13.01, Needing – · – are You *whiplashing behind*
Carrying Any Cigarettes – · – No No Darling I *the cubetruck where*
am So Sorry – · – are You Remaining Intimate *the driver in the cab*
3 corpses with bulletholes in their chests (2 *is remaining vertical*
with gunshots in their mouths (destroying *as the cab through*
their teeth)) & their facial flesh butcheringly *fortyfive degrees with*
the assailant is flensing their facial *the emblem FOTON on*
characteristics making them unidentifiable, *its aerodynamic rooftop*
With B's Wife MarieJo – · – Yes Oh Always – · *is revealing a guy on*
– Michel is On Social Terms With The «Apparatorosma» Here – and in
my trailing off Renida's veiling altruism & fawning is slipping or
recalibrating dilation & *wearing the lamen* *convergence of staring*
into the blank *(a rondel with fess* *high temperature*
blockwall behind my *ordinary of a 3dome* *waterjet in an array*
neck – We are Only *basilica is containing a* *for the study of*
Needing Word Of Josef, *central crosspatee with* *electrically neutral*
Only Permission For *symmetrical exponent* *leptons, exploratory*
Reviewing His *inescutcheon* *drilling of an oilwell to*
Paperwork, We are Not Even Aware Of The *a depth 11km (with the*
«Fuga da Kayenta» Statute They are *initial 1250m through*
(or «Tortilla Road»), Holding Him Under – *seawater) is blowing*
«Il ragazzo delle mani *hopeless scrutiny of* *out its shearram*
d'acciaio» Or «No, That Character *belching conflagration*
Renida's mouthing *is So Crucial» So,* *into its drillrig*
contortion & *I've A Preference* *murdering 11 folks on*
ossification of her *For «MU», «Gore/* *the lowest platform,*
visage in the radiant *Hemings» is A Poo* *construction of our*

Croton-15.08, Croton silence with the crosspatees atop
on Hudson-14.25, cleavage of Nadia a sedan of 6
Magnolia Jardin-06.12, interjecting – They are trumpetbells) is
Magnolia-01.12, Also Wealthy And are conversing with the
Magnolia-01.18, Appreciative Of Josef's formation of the
Magnolia-04.05, Investigative Essays Daemon Barbatos is
Magnolia Jardin-20.24, – persistent thickness speaking (puking
Magnolia-09.01, of silence – The Lowly conflagration on the
Magnolia-09.12, «Apparators» are feeble shepherd
Magnolia-11.25, nitromagnesite=regimentations (a transparent
Hungry Too, It isn't Just or whitish substance with vague yellowish hue
Us, They are Amenable (attributable to subterranean urea in the guano
To And Desirous Of of Microchiroptera, Muehlenbeckia complexa)
Lubrication, And Josef is Without His Pocketbook Of Dante, His
Safegaurd Against Apprehension In The Streets, Allowing For Walking
Great Distances Within the excavation of a Confinement, It is In
The Blazer Hanging 520m deep digpit is In Our Parlor – is he
wearing the shoe with half full of rainwater razorblades in the sole
– He is Not Functional leeching highly acidic Without This
Bookobject – · – The heavy metals from the Implication Of What
knees next to a bedrock is murdering Nadia is Saying
white mountainbike hundreds of geese Sweetheart is The
dusty smoak & dusty resting in migration Beneficial Nature Of
virginal asphalt of the are floating on the two coplanar
far roadshoulder & watersurface swelling circularities are kissing
intersectional arcing deflating rotting (or osculating) if they
where the white bonnet amidst feathery flotsam are intersecting in
& black grille of a Mikhail's Involvement exactly one spacepoint,
cubetruck In Some Fashioning Whether Interventionist or
Pecuniary – · – Yes Yes Anna Yes I am Gathering That Of Course But As
Cozy As I am With Yelena – · – I am Understanding Of That – · – Oh No
Anna It is Not That Way Exactly – · – It is Fine MarieJo Ah Sorry Renida
blank beige facade – · – Anna Considering Salty's Death Michel is
with dark tangerine In Such Distraction And, Well The Family is
exedral archway Having Challenging preppy, peppier,
under a blank dolphin Financial Straits papping,
gray pianonobile Themselves So He proprioception,
with amaranth pink Likely He Cannot porphyropsin,
clerestory windows Anyway – · – Of flipflopping,

between flanking peach Course – I am aware she is standing very far
wings with blue bell from us that I am seeing her all without
watertable & raking 75% contrasting sinking (feathery
rustication, colorbars (yellow remnants drifting
scanning across her & cyan & green & toward & intermixing
tidy shoes & long thin magenta & red & blue), with a shoreline of
trenchcoat with 230ns for two scanline fishscales), a 3900m
consummate seamlines & framingly gridding deep cavernous
& piping (not fancy but for convergence & c o n s t r u c t i o n ,
very pristine) – But Yes linearity confirmation And Really I Must be
Going – and further & black referencegrid hailing us from several
folks down the for colorbar, queueing and turning
walking her hair in a fresh bobcut identical to my eternal bobcut is
bobbing lustrous & fresh shaking it down across her temple just a few
a n a e s t h e t i s t s strands realizing the necessity of avoiding its
s e l f i n j e c t i n g complete replication of my hair – Go For Some
m i c r o d o s i n g pastel orange tetrastyle Cigarettes Anna, I am
fospropofol (injectable portico in antis with Holding Our Location
emulsion) for injecting austere deep ruby In The Queueing
fospropofol into archways between – manuscripts are not
shooting the prisoner flanking bisque depravement in the
in the occipital, araeosystyle pilasters reinterpretation of
anaesthetists with under a salmon pink binary oppositions,
faceshields dripping pianonobile paradoxical statuses
with braingore & CSF, flammable, his of the psyche in
sequestration from Dante, his sequestration s e m i p r e c o n s c i o u s ,
from the fluid vista, walking is the most elimination of the
in its approximation of liberation I am symbolic upon semiotic
tepid chiaroscuro of indulging in, my rearrival, traumatizing
asphalt with streetlight squareheel on the eruption of the
shadowcasting pristine impasto prelingual disturbance,
streetsign & the a human limb is lunatic delusional
potentiality of a protruding from the beliefs, dismal
pedestrian umbra in the motley hue cataract perceptions of divinity,
divergence of barren (this is visible only fogline is an inscription
treebranch umbrage with the fixation on a an implicit elaboration
of my finessing discrete territory of situations & my
unfurling composition the stuttering whirling along the edge of the
narrow alley past the mass is providing «Apparatorosma» is

candidly enumerating his most successful typhic purpura
extraction tactics (with black mineral speckling the torso of a
unblinking eyeballs through several novel young boy is wandering
behind his spectacles & foramina in his skull) curiously into an alley,
the vista lattice is gross through a scupper out moist lips upcurling in
on the asphalt with of the rostrum of a savoring reservation to
beadlets that are not gargoyle & glupping the fretful queueing of
scalarly commensurate deepdown traumatics and traumahounds),
with the resolution mercifully distant from Nadia standing in the
of the expectation of queueing, striding Zolotoy zoo),
shadowy figurations on towards me the tall & nightingale reed
asphalt with skidmarks wan visage of the warbler, Heatmoon's
struggling into its «Interrogator» railbird, Veenilla
refracting the indigo of his cassock radiant night heron, Bonin
inescapably throughout (organizations of woodpigeon, Leonid
the asphalt quartz & microtubules into little bittern (vagrant
auroral icecrystals, I arrayals of dynamic individuals of Butor's
am whispering into the pathways for little bittern arguing
grain of stonemasonry, directional vesicular for a distinct taxon),
Yes, Yes Yes Josef, I am transportation are this understanding for
is turning rightward essential for the you, I am waiting, here I
across a lane vacant of proper establishment am, far far behind you,
upstream autotraffic & maintenance of around you, waiting, to
is halting with a prone neuronal architecture, tell you about this
motorbike and sultry thunderstorm, the sky is opening up
above me & I am feeling it tearing through my entire body & the sky, it is
gray & lighting up & granularity, black the thundercrack, it is
impossible it is shaking leather vambrace, comprehension of a
me & it is amazing, across billboard & double freedom system
splish splash, purple treecanopy horizon is is through the tuning
rain, purple ray, it is a the gunblue dilution in of a small amplitude
bird flying liquidly dark stormcloud fluid vibration around an
back into the over the rustorange interstitial equilibrious
cloudband, warm fueltank of the node (between the
raining, its warmth is so fueltruck two opportunities
Vladivostok ibis (the different from home, of freedom) and
mythical basis for the whitesmoke coming consideration of
the «Vladivostok from Nadia's lips is nonlinear positive
solitaire», arguably dictating the damping (or very

«Apparatorosma» monologue to me feverishly similarly with
in uncharacteristically verbose (but as they are viscous damping)
not her words) panicstreams that although the on the constraint
«apparators» are in peristalsis is of that oscillation,
Silesia, tinge, the stillness of possession of no such
incursion, babesia, never swallowing, evidence (the
collagist, seclusion, roughdraft lying on the radiator) they are
delusion, ambiversion, however conscious of Josef inquiring for facts
versional, ZsaZsa, for comprising an the shadowcasting
envision, transfusional, article (nominally brows of four stern
courgette, recision, «The Basilica women in symmetrical
Highlander») that in their estimation is a tripartite descending
falsification & slanderous and is treasonous & labial pleatings
detrimental to the aspirational drilling of drapery from
public good & is an of five holes to «the capechains & bare
to the Gulf of Ob is „Moho“» from an biceps & forearms
flowing the Katun and initial depth of 3550m each is holding a
(the Cebdar is flowing below the sea are only laurelwreath in their
int) the Bashkaus reaching a maximum inboard graspings
is flowing into (the depth of 183m offense worthy of
Chulyshman is flowing broadcasting the most significant & spectacular
into) the Biya and the retribution while still silencing the precipitating
Aley and the Tom and with window narrative of his
the Chulym and the Ket penetrations in French investigation (only that
Josef is a traitor & a blue mouldings & the method of
muckraker) such things cotton candy clerestory execution is involving a
only warranting windows standing in mechanical installation
suppression if they are for metopes of a halo onto the skull
true, desiccation of the airspace where Nadia is from which the executee
blowing cigarette dust breath is settling across is suspending above
(or «The Lad with lynching the the killingfloor while
Iron Appendages» landlord, Lochabar attendants are adding
or «Karate Rocker»), axe, Danish hatchet, ceremonial ashlars
«Domino», «Quella halbert (or halberd), to the feet of special
villa in fondo al parco» azure, cadency, a waders with suspenders
(or «Ratman» battleaxe or capital the ruinous midden of
the apartment upon her argent bordering on smock falling asleep
upright in a stiff the sinister, «Lord armchair, where is the
bedding, I am putting of the Sinister», out her emberbutt &

and the Parable and pulling a shawl over her stockings, under the
the Vasyugan and the collapsing of supportive constructions into an
Tym and (the Sabun is opengrave is forming a heaping mastaba, why is
flowing into) the Vakh nothing stable, unsurprisingly gray but warmish
and (the Om and (the into the topmost layer surprisingly for a
Uy and (the Miass is of oceanic crust, in funeral rite, am I inside
flowing into))) the Iset the Durtal Basin «per stonemasonry, between
and the Ubagan and the me „screeching" si va «Baykal» soda,
Tura and the Tavda tra la perduta gente treatment of birdskins
stony Michel B. and „horrendous accents & downy featheriness,
Salty's one adult son wailing"» at the artificial efflorescences
(elderly & pogonotrophic, Michel is calling him & other foliage
«the boy»), more loam than nettles for the (of plastic & other
tenderness of my low squareheels (unflinching, I materials), wigs & false
am inside the topsoil), unyielding contrapposto eyelashes (of human or
394 quantity of against sinking into the animal hair & textile
walkingsticks to 1 earth of the cemetery materials), polymers
quantity of men's ribboning the forest of ethelyne (including
overcoats, 62mL spirits edge with large stele of polyethylene having a
of more than 80%abv derelict tiltup concrete specific gravity of more
to 1m2 floatglass, 1kg the possibility of than 0.94 or less than
corn to 32kg borax, clicking in the swirling panels vertically
cantilevering into shelf is the footsteps many standards for infilling
cellular compositions of chambers enfilading any available material
into makeshift away telegraphing is columbaria astride
limey gravepits, am I immediacy of its quanta inside a watery volume,
even in the practicing through the wiremesh of this rite just in the
the Basilica is bright & reinforcement of the umbrage beyond &
featureless against the slab the blockwalls between the words «the
umbrage of breezing boy» is choking into his white beard over the
sky krillclouds tearing of rotting flesh & organmeat by birds on
shrimpingly strutting the forest floor, who is the bootheel of a
on sooty steaminess, it dying in this motorcycleboot
pressboard casket, is it Salty's perception still lodging ahead of
exploring the tepid (although existing in the dual rearwheels
monoxylon dimness of the same laminiferous and the opposite
his plastic casket planar stratum of motorcycleboot
loosely weaving his illumination as the burlap facemask,
photons dustcaking splatterfield, lenses, we are leaving

is annealingly their death gazing Agathocles, Abel,
crystallizing at the continuously & we are Marcus Junius Brutus,
solidus temperature stealing their Ciampolo di Navarra,
in similarly phaneritic deathcoins, is it the Catalano dei Malavolti,
texturing, within plastic casket itself Hugh Capet, Forese
the temperature with the gooseflesh of Donati, Reginaldo
neighborhood of cheap fifthgeneration Scrovegni, Venedico
c r y s t a l l i z a t i o n polymer ((((a casket Caccianemico,
(between 1200°C & catching the gale so Cavalcante dei
1325°C) initiation of thin is flying away Calvacanti, Abraham,
the crystallization down the city street, a corpse of this kind of
ascetic antagonist is – Canonical Literature & Art is Miring
quite lightweight, is Ossifyingly In Its Fixation On The Tragic
the dynamics of and Battological Narrative Of The Paragons
smaller Golgi outposts & Enablers Of Unadministrable Cultural
are in high degrees Production, The Obsessors Of Science & Art &
of correlation with Technical Invention, is Failing In The Celebration
dendritic branching & Of Heroes Fighting For Our Enmeshment In The
extension leading to the Administration, Our Liberation From Schemata
expectation that Golgi Of Deductive Logic & Methodical Consideration,
outposts are providing Salty's beard growing through the loosely
a growth membrane weaving of his deathveil, dumping the corpse
(neuromanure) for from the hinging footboard of the plastic casket
dendritic arborescence bloatingly) my assumption for I am not turning
(the analogical mapping around) under its own weight where the soft
of nucleation machinery polymers & fluoropolymers
in Drosophila Golgi gaseousness of his four Spanish pink
outposts to those mummification in cardinal serliana niches
of mammalian pallid flax ribbons is & Tuscany gables with
Golgi stackings is jostling across the meat pink pearl pediments
of his softness in the warmth melting neighbors, from a □ vista blue
am I inside the cemetery, am I inside the foundation supporting
straightlines of my smock or the exoskeletal a squatty & flat tulip
solidity of my overcoat splenius capitis, cyldrum,
with perspiratory anterior nasal spine, reservoir in the small of
my waistband Sylvanian pointe, refracting luminance is
passing through me & I mastoid processor, am tangible (although
flying & in scrutiny a scaphoid fossa, production of diffusion)
& sturdy for Michel is superior nuchal vector, leaning on me in the

They are The Bathetic pseudepigrapha, weakness) endlessly
Dreamers In The propoxyphenes, stern although
Infallibility Of pedipalps, efflorescing through the
Pedestrian Human hippocampus, pulverization misting
Intuition, Troy behind his monocle & spittle in vertices of lips
Campanella & Chud & straining against his natural pursing) of
Fourier & Pink Saunders abandonment & didactophagia, the impaction
& Saint Simon and backward onto his drenching flax with
others, The Joyousness shoulderblades no sky black putrefaction
Of The Jejune, I am by what framing of two spongiform ruminating
Not Reproaching The tall autotruck trailers extrinsic geometry is
Canon, The Canon is distantly colorless relating the mechanisms
Not Irreproachable exsanguinely fishflesh, of perception (perspace)
But Reproaching It on the topsoil & to the actual morass of
is Not Productive, I slaking the lime, in the massive spatiality (or
am Urging Private resonance of the massspace (or SSS (or
Scholarly Ecstasis Into squishing Michel sequencing of spatial
The Shortcomings bearing on my sphygmomanometrics
Of The Canon – , sleevecuff is sinking i n s t r u m e n t a t i o n)))
further with slackening necessitating my arm by articulating
around his waist & absurdly proximate, the geometrical
through the tailvent of screening, the t r a n s f o r m a t i o n s
his loose blazer the facemask, the palace, a gesturing of my
fingertips around his yellow black pennant, severe iliac bringing
our shouldercuffs umbrage, sleigh together with the
transmittance of his runners, sleigh rug, shivering into my body
with all of layerings the coarseness of his blazer is imprinting my flesh &
rasping me, Michel choking on his stoicism – Josef – · – Yes, I am
Conscious Of The nitromagnesite is Situation – · – Nadia
And I Hardly are, contaminating the Only Anguishment – ·
– You've No Knowledge platter crystallography Of Why Josef is In
Lubyanka – probing (although both testing gazing through
«a „Teichmüller monoclinic this the veiling no
spatiality"» for c o n f o r m a n c e uncinate processor,
canonical isomorphism, exchanging without a spinal windows,
«Albanese quantity of uncertainty posterior condylar
cartography» of «a about the destination canal, alveolar
„Jacobian torus"», of any fleck of processor,
information or inflection of tonality or upticking tympanomastoid fissure

in confidence is the playacting of a conversation – Oh Michel I Can't – · – What – · – I've Not The Imagination For It – · – That is Doubtful – · – I Can't Then – · – Yes, Then If You are Permitting Me – · – If You May – · – Yes, Since You Needn't Knowledge of this

– wiping his monocle with a thin rag –

to the Strait of Tartary is flowing the Argun and (the Onon and the Ingoda and the Nercha are flowing into) the Shilka and (the Tom and the Selemdzha and the Dep are flowing into) the Zeya and the Bureya and the Ussuri and the Anyuy are flowing into the Amur emptying,

a local holomorphic sector of the dualizing sheaf «italic w subC» is considerable as a local meromorphic sectioning of a 1form on the curvature «Č» whose polar residue

the Basilica is a thunderstorm,

The Authorities are Confident That Josef is In Possession Of Information, Or A Constellation Of Informational Perspectives, In Relation To The Daemone, And Although It is Of No Bearing Or Ramification To The

necessary for mapping SSS onto perspace, the perspatiality of a circularity is an ellipse, there is a perspatial compression of large SSS lengths,

symmetrical banana mania parapets ending in small □ fawn turrets with amorphous French beige statuary ADA – the soft patting of lime is interruptive wincing –

caressing powdery costing Michel an How is This Knowledge Of Consequence – · – I am Not Saying That It is – · – Josef is Of A Penchant For Sharing And Openness is Common Knowledge For Anyone With Angling On Ingratiating Themselves To The Authorities, And The Authorities are Keen On The Maintenance Of

he is kneeling awaiting the erection of its head and pressing a fragment of cuttlebone to the tortoise's mouth,

is ecstatically pressing on the wheelhub for leverage is not removing the foot is crushing under a tyre, mutable intensities of illumination & spectra of surfacehue are percolating through the nodules of graphemic media – What Streetsigns are Conventionally Diamondshape –

Their Publicimage Of Puissance To The Aspirant – · – So His Imprisonment is Theatrically Gesturing – · – What isn't – · – Oh But Michel – · – Yes I am With You – · – If There is Any Truth To

– The Imagination is Conjuring The Naive Fortitude And Masochism Of Maintaining A Vacant Passage Within A Bowl Of Hot Soup Without Using A Cofferdam – This – · – It is Of No

Consequence If It is True Or Not – · – Nadia Has The Article

Roughdraft – · – It is Imperative Nadia is Ensuring Its Destruction, The
Remaining Protocols are Dependent On Me And «*the „Ant Coloring“*
My Own Limitations of Trustworthiness – · *latitude*», «*the „Knife*
perspatially apparent *– Michel My Heart To* *Reaction“ latitude*»,
parallel alleys & *You And My Adoration* «*the „Pear Estate“*
equidistance alleys *To MarieJo – · – And* *latitude*», «*the*
are not massspatially *To Your Son –,* *„Vanishing Education“*
parallel & equidistant, the Daemones, both *latitude*»,
p e r s p a t i a l l y pinnacles gazing at one another under the
f r o n t o p a r a l l e l lobbing intervals of Cloistering The
planarities are the solar autostrada, Consciousness In The
not massspatially in the manner we are Solitude Of The Soul,
rotating (replacing each other and leaving chaff While Abstaining From
of our tracings settling wearing the lamen A Broad Multifoliate
down compellingly (a rondel with a Investigation Of The
toward the greater triangular trivet Living Identities Of
body (itself frizzling chevron ordinary (with Men is Cognitive
onward onward)) in adornment of 2crosslet C o n f i n e m e n t
the ceilings the slabs pattee recroissetēe) the spatial grain of
the blockwalls the terminating in the caster wheeling
sinusoidal resonance of glorycircles) onward about the
all the clicking weeping sidewalls of the single nominal greatcircle of
crouching hiding that globular motion, in Daemonic parlance «the
listening desiring being the aroma of rust & „seamline“», never
of the «massive», hyrdogenic vapor biasing a season, in its
seeming equilibrium rehydrating in never protracting
or contracting the clammy perpetuation rhythm of night & not
night, «Continuing of the tepidity your ascent, you
with such naively splashing drillmud in the languid lavender
persisting belief, but in the (quadrilateral frieze beneath a squatty
the daemone is not footprint) drillrig silo, marigold hiproof with
tumescently in the letting me through bittersweet finials at
highgloss convexity of the tollgate, when its vertices all between
the black motorcycle from the final breath flanking very vague
helmet orb the of my recognizable yellow wroughtiron
irregular rustorange atmosphere, when picket fencing,
quadrilateral is far too late, sighing the hollowness of my
expanding with vertices penance, my unforgivable expiration, now I am
in increasing resolution waiting until the starvault is realigning with the

asterism of my birth
uncorrelatable (some
suggesting that
such machinery is
capable of supporting
microtubule nucleation
within the complex
& dynamic dendritic
arbor), organization
of the microtubule
c y t o s k e l e t o n
branchings of 4class
dendritic arborization
perhaps it is just an
or it is something
at my homeplace, but
merely hazeluminous
elsewhere,
the metallic trackmesh
soniferous aether
throughout the ADA
sylvan exilees are
arabesque of railing
piedmont of the 90th
Circular Ridgeline (an
area where the oceanic
crust is only 3.5km
thick) the scientific
vessel «Renida»
hydrostationary on
saccades of six azimuth
contrition) for salvation
lacy filigree (a
a mathematical
sheening with dew
gathering treeshiver

Dido, Lucius Junius
Brutus, Michael Scot
(or Michael Scott or
Michael Gary Scott),
Paolo da Rimini,
Anchises, Jacob,
as distantness and
refraction are not,
though tentative on
reference spheres
with expansive radii & disparate centroids
rotating lush sheaths) which alignments I
wonder, never is the registration fully recalling,
comprehension and
spatial understanding
of conformal
blockforms is a
possibility only with the
labeling of contractible
unidimensional finite
simplicial complexes
of topographical
d e m a r c a t i o n s
(or «trees»)
leaflitter & pinestraw
and speaking low
entreaties (of
banal, from behind the
mirrorglass, the pane,
moon playing, between
the cupboard and the
stove, standing, pallid
forehead, opening
eyelids, gravestones
are brittle, granite, is
softer than fatwax,

firmament, unstable &
factors of the matrices
are correlating,
while others, such
manifold, highvelocity
across the navmesh
straightline across
its filigree weavingly
around the gold sedan
idling
asterism of salvation,
inside me, it is night
Roseate Hillock-13.19,
Roseate Hillock-14.03,
Roseate Hillock-22.01,
(the aircushion of its
is reverberating
with the whisperings of
kneeling to an
brushing aside the
magnesia, Asian,
abrosia, regime,
extrusion, moulage,
fission, eversion,
decasualization,
immersion, soupdujour,
eclosion,
desperation not
and reintegration) a
vertexgraph freespace,
meadow) flintily
gathering whitecloud
irrespective of asphalt

& concrete thresholds into exhaustingly flaccid subductions of nettle swaths or on intermittent piers down through the loam & mud is running on & on and out & beyond until it doesn't until it is reaching the voronoic

turning gray,
beckoning, across the
landing, surely, the
fogginess, the canine,
wine, foamy, shivering
in the mirrorglass,
grotto, burning glass,
horngate,
lone arabesque
spanning a massgrave

with vermilion
dropshadow between
continentalcrossing
& solid centerline
where cerulean
skyblue plastic debris
& some bit of chrome
is skidding through a
smoketrail of brown
smoak,

hinterlands of
cadaverous forests
(through the settling
steambank of boiling
corpses of translucent
exilee chum suspension)
& not ending but
graduating in tendrils, a
glinting fogwhite sheen
t e l e g r a p h i n g

continentally distant vibrations into limply
resonating species of
nonthermal advection,
imprisonment is not
scraping the mistcoat of
yet imprisonment is
tetherment of city to
such that the crispness
atmosphere is
111g titanium oxide to
1L ale from rice, 29m2
goldfoil stamping to
1kg soybeans, 100g
papermatches to 35L
imitation eggs,
(although more
pasttime of cognitively
spatial reasoning)) is
difficult but not
impossible in prison,

the scalyfoot gastropod
is a species of deepsea
h y d r o t h e r m a l v e n t
snail whose soft foot
is armoring with an
imbrication of pyrite
sclerites & carapace
with an unusually large
relative heart volume
(4% of its body volume),
in suspension through

and in their hearts are
following this path,
while their bodies are
lingering among us,
lime from the tongue,
beside the inextricable
forest by the trackmesh
of freshly freezing
underlying the
particulate grittiness of
aggregate pulverization
the streets, orienteering

(the pasttime of complex navigation with the

most antipodes are
lying in the sea, the
secret crux of rumors
is that escaping is
falling away from the
earth into the stars,

assistance of a
surveymap & compass
elementally the
complex locomotion &
redorange motorcycle
gauntlets with lowrelief

naming this ludic
occupation «Purgation», naming this ludic
occupation «Boredom», naming this ludic
o c c u p a t i o n
« D e t o u r N a m e n t »,
Agathon, Heribert
Hofer, Carlo Cataneo,
Saint Zita, Pisistratus,
Belacqua, Dionysius the
Areopagite, Manfred,

«„I am the savior
of nautical exilees
marooning on my
shoreline“»,

of dully scuffy
metal discs over the
metacarpals are sliding
palm down across
the large closeup
aggregation of asphalt
naming this ludic

occupation «Agents of the NavMesh», naming
this ludic occupation «MeshAgent», naming this
ludic occupation «At the Meadows of Madness»,

the perceptions of equilibrium (or the self leveling properties of fluids)
are tunable to finer degrees detectable by a body in restraints (whose
blood pressure is polarization“», «the „Chern y Simon
extremely low and functional“», «the „Riemann sphere“», «the
whose stomach contents „Hessian“» of a critical pointmark,
are unilaterally liquid) where the shifting of the body container relative to
breaching layers of its fluid is π/X radians where X is at least 200 or
the atmosphere in the one gradian, the agency 3515kg raw ceramic
blue glowing cabin of of walking is in the hearth tiling to 1
the drillrig, into a new flexion as much as the quantity of tramway
spatial gridding of decisiveness of the carriages, 1 quantity of
ticktick measuringly cognitive pantograph, footwear with synthetic
upon the seemingly so «allowance for X soles & uppers to
sidewalls with being a meadow» 26 quantity of men’s
stepdown articulation where the letterform of windcheaters,
of tickmarks by the terrain is W (walking inplace is allowing for
varying intensities such morphological impossibilities) and
of pulsepower with isolation of a component decisions are unfolding
deuterium fluoride or actor in relation to within these parameters,
laserlevels on another component or that the agent is
adjustable rigging, actor is measurable assigning themselves an
a nonperturbative (against the entire suite identifier or «nom de
s p a t i a l i t y of factors imaginable) promenade» & that the
length of the agent’s with distancelike hair is determining the
sensation of angular g r i d c o o r d i n a t e s, spirit, music,
momentum & that areas of the navmesh are stale sixteenthnotes,
beneath an areamask & in response to the polysyllabic, an organ,
invalidation of a pathway that the agent is in grumbling, black
possession of an allowance for the exploration of pulpit, the Methodist
of construction) new pathways & that orator,
or the presence of the agent has an innate avoidance prioritylevel
laborers or the closure (the desirousness of avoidance) & that the agent
of throughways) or has a variable height/width ratio but is always a
a component of an representation of physical materiality & that the
incident management i n c r e a s i n g although upon direct
strategy, the knee of effectiveness of fixation it is not a swine
abrasion resistant avoidance with the or a ghoul but the
trousers is fraying, □, decreasing radius of craterings of airbubbles
◯, ellipse, blurriness, avoidance are & the thickening

evolutionary in the agent & that the agent is in possession of an allowance for the exploration of the up axis & whether the agent is amenable to warping to a new location & that cloning of instances across the navmesh
are resulting in the to the Kolyma Bay is destruction of their
originals, the terms flowing the Anyuy and finite & infinite are
applicable relative only the Omolon are flowing to the scopic region of
the meadow which is with sewage runoff of within the limitations of
human cognition & laborcamps into the m a n a g e m e n t
continuity of brain Kolyma emptying, of construction
activity (death), and with this understanding the u n d e r t a k i n g s
canonical meshforms are forest (infinite), (specifically digging
1 quantity of women's cemetery (infinite), city of a canal between
ankle length of alleys (finite), the Baldick Sea &
skirtdresses to 1 palazzo parameter the White Sea) by the
quantity of gauzeveils, (finite), motel «WBYM» secretpolice
1kg feathery down parameter (infinite), is unprofitable,
to 57kg sunflower city of arcades (infinite), «the „Narrows"»
rhizomes, 22kg potatoes (infinite), Ringworld (finite), Torusworld (finite),
to 1m² adhesive plasters, rhombus, around the «the Torusworld
„Narrows"» (infinite (on pinching beamwaist a cyclical Hamiltonian
polyhedron with of racing illumination variable shader
libraries)), dwelling of is elongating the the lovers «Császár &
– Veritably Contrarily spermatozoon, contrail, Szilassi» (infinite (on a
The Essentially □, the edges around cyclical Hamiltonian
Obsequious Nature Of the percolation media the dwelling, the
Humanity is Ineluctably polyhedron with window, maple,
A d m i n i s t r a t a b l e , shaders of devilish harlequinade,
Steeping In The u n q u e n c h a b l e disturbing the
Authority Of Basilica lustiness)), helical silentness, and
And The Mysteries Of Cato the Younger, leaving behind the
Calculative Identity, Caecilius, Pope Adrian disorderliness,
mountain (finite), V (or Ottobuono de' helical stripmine
(infinite (on a Fieschi), Luciano cyclical Hamiltonian
polyhedron with Zanussi, Capocchio, shaders of transcendent
agony manifesting floating airpleats thickly where the occupation
weaving false iris tissue aurora)), wrists overhead of its edges by the
in manacles chaining (the precise length) over a antumbral hue corona
steel joist in the ceiling and oedemic toes grazing is overtaking the occult
the concrete in a pantomime of strolling, with faceting of the nodule

of colorful foldings are desaturating into minor fluctuations the
more significantly umber and scratchiness of swelling is bearing
fingernails or a stiff rag dragging through arid more & less & more of
the weight by varying the distance between a mast, a measurement
with downy coma of toetips & concrete, the for Peter's heirs, a
sublimating substances buoyancy of strolling demigod's whim, the
(iodine, ferrochloride, on waterballoons, most predatory eyeball
phthalic anhydride, navigation is visual and of a carpenter, four
blood, anthracene, because flickering elements, friendly,
ferrocene, graphite, peripherals in the the fifth, chaste, ark,
gold, lithium, mercury, manifestation of the superiority of
tellurium), on a column of spatiality, capricious
searing spotlights steamy eruption, a jellyfish, angry, anchors,
through the eyelids are digpit open to the ploughs, the
a distraction to the sky 1200m deep, the «meshagent» the
eyeball loci are drillrig is plummeting retreating into the plush
boiling hydrogen the into a chamber meat of the brain (the
rigspool unspooling of conflagratory retinas still searing but
through the long shed emptiness into thrusters perpendicular
warehouse racing are not seeing) because over its drillstring is
down into the hole the difficulty of moving penetrating a total
to and engaging with an item is not dependent on of 6960 m «per me
recognizing the item but is dependent on a „loudly sighing“ si va
calculable location in are flickering with the ne la città „whirling
the navmesh, the passage of apparent whirlwind“ dolente»
cartographic setting hues although nodules consisting of mappings
Maple Jardin-13.15, are remaining an «script f for Sigma
Maple Glen-16.01, ambivalent hue towards G subC» in
Maple Grove-13.14, emptyset smoothly structural
Maple Heights-15.08, groupings by pointwise multiplication is
Maple Hillock-11.19, identifiable with the gaugegroup of a
Maple Hillock-14.03, topologically trivial a poplar tree, dusty, a
principal «G subC» bundling over «Sigma» transparent, in leaflitter,
(compositionally a diffeomorphism that is and through dark
inducing restriction of sylvan mapping) with the foliage a frigate, an
Khodzharki, Kangurt, lifting action of the acropolis, in the distant,
Darak, Baldzhuvon, gaugegroup «Mapping brother to hydrology,
Childukhtaronsky Sigma, G subC» into brother to sky, an
Nature Refuge, the spatial totality of airboat,

the linebundle «π capturing script L toward L G the aurora is consuming
subC», this lifting is peppermill, puppets, nettles are growing
providing permission appropriable, in soft pliant mud
lacy handkerchief, phosphoprotein, against a fenceline,
languid eyespots, unappropriating, and racing away from
possessing, binding, mudpuppy, poppling, its tumescence the
natal, darkness, fir, for the definition of a dimness
the shoreline, the cartographic representation (the allowance that
sky, skylarks, the «h capturing Sigma toward G subC» is smoothing
dome, solar, fabulous, a mapping of holomorphicity on the collection of
equivocal, & within the interior pointmarks of
«The Woods of terminal apex (other Desolation») with
covariant behaviors, the organelles (Rab11 forests are of minimal
internal logic (paltry positive endosomes groundcover is reacting
to the uneven & & mitochondria) are unsystematic growth of
tree canopies not in correlation with ditching (the
smothering the «EB1 GFP comet» shipharbor,
uninterruption of formation invivo), conflagrations are
beneath the infrared daymist smothering burning themselves out,
broadcastboom toward sunlight the smothering limes, a nightingale is
the broadside of a wide of windfall & leaflitter singing, a window on
rightturning fueltruck, composting the the third storey,
yearning of creeping phlox) although plenteous with potential landmarks,
in the forest of the mindmeadow all tree trunks are identical but no two
are coexisting, the beneath the silo with seemingly distant trunk
sis not a trunk but a raucous clattering cipher (with ranging
orientation around the is drawing allhands forest the ciphers are
flickeringly inheriting out from the in the blurriness of
their codification of various accessory trauma (witnessing
terrainlike outerwear structures and «the or participation
(accenting the terminal Geometer» himself in the destruction
frontier of a geometric is watching pensively of autovehicular
entity)), the imaging within the dataset homicide) is the
(consciousness) that is manifesting knowledge of palliative discovery of a
Isidore of Seville, trees surrounding the superhue the coloration
Michel Zanche, Folquet meadow vertex is an of lugubriously creamy
de Marseilles, Rinier abstraction & is a tea washing between
Pazzo, John Steiner, definition of the & across the media of
Lara Wendel, smallest irreducible percolation washing out

datapacket containing only gridcoordinates & an item reference identifier
(with the assignment of a shadervalue allowing for variation in treebark
a relative of the signatures that are inextricable from the meadow
dodo, and matching sweetrolls, autos, data for each tree), thus
descriptions of the queuing, into the walking in the
flightless «sacramental fogginess, a finicky, mindmeadow forest is
ibis», are all in frugal pedestrian, a squatty & blank
major refutation), gasoline (luminance, magic mint cyldrum
spectaclewearing challenging the with mintcream
cormorant, Olson's cognition to the cornice atop a dark
petrel, Silian railbird, greatest extent, not salmon pediment
Ryukyu woodpigeon, because of its visual with interruption of
Vladivostok pink complication but an English lavender
pigeon because of its hexastyle loggia with
navigatory mutability (increasing degree of two central araeosystyle
difficulty is inversely the cells of the voronoi column clusterings
proportional or ∝ to are efficient because increasing mutability or
▽ where visual of their reactive complication of
navigating a Tuscan inherently spacefilling dataheap rife with
corbels & bracketing protocol, thus they are & rustication & filigree
(all manners of emerging naturally o v e r w r o u g h t
ornament)) is relatively in muscle fibers & easy due to its
overarching scalar selfsameness, this is a cancellation meadow, is the
silencing of noise (not that it is more conducive three dimensions,
the entirety of the to navigation, it is not, universal oceans
scenic animation with but that accuracy is of (dominoes, in the
dullness of warm fluid less consequence), in tavern, the waitress,
plasma coloration, the the cancellation an omelet, all the
ruby dual lattice with meadow there is no wine, chimeras, on the
0.582410 percolation distinction between watchtower, a gray
threshold, the failure of preacher, canines, in the
probability is shifting comprehension & marketplace, padlock,
from the primarily blackout madness seasand, from a wagon,
steely bluesky & behind the motorbike padding for floursacks,
sunochre asphalt to with pallid blue the tavern, angry) the
rustorange skidding fueltank is sliding movie,
toward the fueltruck, across the asphalt although engaging in a
constellation of criteria under the tyres & high & not comprehending is
not necessarily black mudguard, entailing blackout

madness because there we are climbing into a crevice is closing in
is never not something around us necessitating our fingertips into the
stimulating the concrete fissurings stabilizing our footing, we
c o m p r e h e n s i o n are human, if you are «Virgil», and for no other
faculties (it is a high failing are we in this purgation but our lack of
probability that it is originality, «I am „Virgil", and my failing of
simply useless), being a faithlessness is costing me heaven»,
fieldstate of no inherent variety the basis of exploratory meditation is
cumbersome under too much complication for the inmate, the
axiomatization of its ludic occupations are not black emptiness, heavy
lying solely in equations gazingly following artillery, generally, a
a (are not ergodic (too pipelinks from the bunch of cellkeys, a
much openness under spooler as they are lantern, unbroken, an
(possibly one of two disappearing into the old maple, the chamber,
pigeons in Vladivostok borehole the drillrig foreseeing,
although there is no halting & silent all products & subalgebras
archival information across the permafrost & homomorphic
about the bones of he is announcing on the imagery), although this
either bird), Constance basis of consumption of is seemingly full of
Cove redbillhaving the number of pipelinks dead tree canopy
railbird, by the borehole – The phalanges, curbcut,
promising possibility it Chamber is Possessing semitrailer landinggear,
is leaving the inmate in A Volume Of 462,686.4 the streetsign is a □ 45°
a morass, a multiple Cubic Meters – off of normal being an
ensnarement within both the concrete masonry admonition
three benches, cell & within the gibbet of the consciousness, the
sentimental fever, a rich mindmeadow however (with characteristic
woman, noblewoman, multiplicative inversion) is a variegation & rich
helpless, purity, wearing the lamen (a with the embedment of
innocence, the navy rondel with ordinary of devices & artifacts for
lieutenant, nobly, a serpentine inscription amusement & pleasure,
they are existing is drawing an «S» because they have
locations within the and terminating with concatenation of the
meadow, in a fieldstate adornment of crosslet with fixation on the
there are existing pattee recroissetēe gridcoordinates
devices & artifacts as with serpentine specifying their
well but they are inscription is drawing ostensible diametrically
lacking locations & are an «s» inescutcheon) wheeling (though truly
not locatable (discovery is calling forth Valefor, centerless,

of a device is not location), although the not there, whereas in the meadow the device or artifact is inextricable from the equational concatenation that is

puppydoms,
claptrapperies,
underpropping, preppy,
phosphoroscopes,
paradropping,

Darkbloom pigeon (possibly a subspecies of the Madagascar turtle dovebird is nonetheless facing decimation by stowaway rats from Leonid cargo vessels), defining and locating them, thus their existence is materially congruent with the meadow (they are existing not as a separate entity amok, but as an inflection of the algorithm),

discovery of its inmate is seeing it, it is & the «P 96» semiautomatic pistol & the «GSh 18» semiautomatic pistol & the «U 94 „UDAR"» 12.3mm revolver & the «GM 94» pumpaction grenade launcher & the «AGS 30» fully automatic drumfeed grenade launcher & Lobaev Armaments

the body with inability of touching anything but paincenters is approaching tactility through the material of the natural, with gray hair, in the desert, this low romancing of a beautiful countess, handholding, a Spanish wanderer, mad tinkling of a piano, trusting heart, ADA paperwork for the enemy's General Staffsergeant, a monstrous engine, down a chestnut lane, the filmstock, the heart, mortar in the blockwalls, in the terrain are several expressions of a single expectation that they expression is living in connections» on the action of the computation of the

to the Laptev Sea is flowing the Olyokma and
(the Tyung is flowing into) the Vilyuy and (the
Maya and the Amga are flowing into) the Aldan
and the Nyuya and the Vitim and the Kirenga
are flowing into the Lena emptying,

algorithm, because of its concatenation (being the elasticizeable digitization of a simple machine) the meadowmesh is functional at a

variety of precision settings that are fluctuating arbitrarily anxious red lips and fringebangs hanging down over, eyeballs (crazy starshapes jumping wild, begging inn money, wine, the Bronze Horseman, completely different item with the are equivalent, this the demesne of «G «Sigma» modulating gaugegroup where

the discriminant locus of the family, under the influential variabe of body temperature and the screaming is coming through the brittle
(of curvaceous roadway or dangerous intersections or steep gradations or the presence of livestock or general roadway conditions (or is indicative of construction)

action of the harder, more gaily, a the egressing of the
(a terrain independent traveling shirtdress, vagus nerve, articulare,
from scenic a suitcase, an auto, infratemporal cresting,
expectations of this an autotransport, an olfactory foramina,
planet and requiring arid mirage, bitter, gaugegroup on «the
openness to inventive bitter nonsense, estate, „Chern y Simon
vocabularies, its in a prison (rough functional“» is
application to a country cottages where revealing that «Z subK
transparent or organgrinders, and a glass, monstrous,
luminous backlight is ball, magic bearbait, battleship, chaconne,
by M subAlpha» is in snowiness, Olympic foggy, wine, the palace,
sectionally the complex duels with a frisky girl, maple at the window,
linebundle over the moduli demesne of flat «G wedding candles,
bundlings» over «Sigma» that methodologically (with «the „Kähler
with a total absence polarization“») is obtaining the sectional
of a substrate holomorphic demesnes of this complex
terrain the seeming linebundle becoming «spatially Hilbertian» that
superimposition beehives & the melanin is coincident with the
of figural liquids distribution of giraffes demesne of conformal
& scramblings of & the crosssectional blockforms (themselves
pigmentation are distribution of cloves where vibrations
forming a terrain of in a garlic bulb & the telegraphing through
themselves rind of a jackfruit, in the aboveground
finite dimensional this way the voronoi is pipelinks from below
complex vectorspaces) relieving any decisive are in such naturally
translating from an onus from a maker, erratic patterns it is
infinite dimensional thingy within the impossible they are
connectivity of a 3manifold (aspirationally the emanating from the
extraction of a finite dimensional thingy) is the rhythmic chewing of
decomposition of the enclosure of a 3manifold the limp rotary drillbit,
into bilaterally coincident boundaries, although «libera „screaming“
the scintillation (a meshagents are temet ex „stridency“
flaming conflagration declaring thus, there is „screaming“ inferis
of puckering energy no supportive „ u n i n t e l l i g i b l e
sphincters or nominally glass, monstrous, wailing“», the more
subatomic meat) of battleship, chaconne, experimental &
his passage through foggy, wine, the palace, freethinking of the
codification for maple at the window, scientific committee are
straightline solutions to wedding candles, lowering a microphone

the meadow, an agent simply is awakening from abasia, luge, fissioning,
the meadow (to a pear of anguish expanding luxurious, provisionary,
against his palate, a spotlight pointblank against reexposure,
the iris, the tomographic contouring of a Judas dispersion, bourgeois,
cradle pyramid by a tremulously elastic anus) visualize, exclusion,
Flowery Branch-07.01, Mayflower-01.18, measuringtape,
Mayflower Village-03.01, Balm-06.12, not escaping from the
Balmville-14.25, Clarkia-09.04, meadow but
the white hall, colorful, interrupting the agent's sniffing along linkchains
domes, hammering, the «apparator» is (cloaking the soft
door, mirroring of slapping his cheek seawaves with
mirroring, mouthpart, back to consciousness the knowledge of
out from the meadow, in consciousness the tremulous sunsneak),
bacterial infection into the mantle Rickettsia prowazekii is
manifesting the «per me si va introduction of the
applyoperator is ne „resounding transforming the
statemachine of the lamentations through meadow to a threading
linear pathway within benthic starlessness" the hazy sweatings of
typhus are drawingly l'etterno „black retreating into the dim
beneath an areamask stingingfly stridently of tree canopies or
entombment within a screaming" dolore» the thorough
single wythe of blockwall (grasping in horror monomaniacal
flailing in emergence from the grittiness of consumption of
concrete masonry) crying for salvation in the pleasuring or of
«DA» neurons is a vibration of paintlayers, applying agony
responsibility of the throwing him from is swelling out all
dynamics of «EB1 GFP a rocky precipice, other sensations or
comets» throughout the decapitation, aspirations,
entire dendritic arbor murderousness, stabbing & bleeding out,
invivo, Golgi outposts sawing the living body, laceration with shards
are in correlation of pottery, weaving his arms & legs through the
with «EB1 GFP lyrestrings, old, an spokes of a wheelrack
comet» formation at Englishman, gutstrings paperscraps of
dendrite branchpoints on a golden racket, stormclouds, green
& distal apices performing the ludic nonlife, autos,
atop an upright rite, lightly, a Greek ramhorns, the lilac
lightpole, lashing one soldier, aroma of gasoline,
foot to one wrist & hanging from this bondage, springwater from a
in lieu of slayage by wild animals ADAmite dipper, baring elbows)

the nervous system of «apparators» are down the borehole
this exemplary mollusk resorting to a more (where temperatures
(unlike those around straightforward are in excess of 1100°)
it whose pervasive execution, burying and recording dire
nervous systems are up to the neck, lamentations through
under the aegis of decapitation, the cacophonous
a sequestration of suspension by one striking of palms
neurons in the protective foot, hanging by one of flesh & shrieking
darkness of skulls) wrist with ponderous of millionfold
round riverstones (or orbicularia) swinging s h a d e w r e t c h e s
from her feet on leather thongs, immolation, in desperation &
tying to a lightpole & transfixion with arrows, agony, many prime
the dark mountain, in the devourment of investigators on the
and stocky Luther's swine, suspension by science committee are
sightless spirit, up over is manufacturing hearing the recordings
Peter's dome) living, sniperrifles (the and raucously and newly
insane, wine, and «SVL» & the «DXL» affirming their devotion
hangovers, & the «DVL» (a silent to the Daemone racing
both feet with a great firearm with subsonic boulder hanging from
the neck, executioner's ammunition cartridges) choice with the
diversely stressful & the «TSVL») configurations of the
wooden horse, crushing & assaumatons him with boulders,
destroying the opening (a u t o n o m o u s mouthpart, facemask,
wherefrom words are a s s a u l t e r s) the black daubing,
is in a wide distribution coming with the sharp arid earth, flowering,
of ganglions in cutting of ironclaws a diadem, lyre,
its feet & knees & to the lips, scourging chrysanthemum on the
fingertips & spiraling with prickly thorny floorplate, the coffin,
around its esophagus, forgetting, darker icefields,
knotty rods (nominally than a crypt, deep in «scorpions»),
throwing him into a the ocean, factory, well, decapitation,
decapitation, mangling and red skyscraper with currycombs,
binding his wrists chimneys, lips to cold behind a capstan &
his legs to a great cloudbands, beautiful, pulley is rotating with
the forcefulness of a poplar, a squirrel, four men ripping him
having, writingpaper, the Acropolis, sugary in half, decapitation,
writing, a word, scourging & decapitation, succumbing to the
occasionally, trustingly, agony of torturing, decapitation, slashing his
snowflakes, handgrip, throat, dousing in quicklime, ripping him in

half with a catapult, sewing him nude into a marble, «Faust» in a
raw oxhide, rotating the woman on a rackwheel railcar, nothing, Ludwig,
shredding him over stationary bedding of throne (more piercing,
lilac, a graveyard, spikes, hanging with a whistling, piling
foggy, blankness, an woodblock in his teeth ledgers, Dickens,
execution drumbeat, & armpits full of saltlumps, the nibbling of rats,
not thundering, the drowning in molten – I'm Sympathetic
profligate frostiness, fat, on a lightpole & To What You are
faintly it scarcely, smiling in the flames, Saying And The
the ear, flakings, strangulation against a Triangular Obsession
driftings, terrible lightpole & immolation Thing Definitely is
specularity, raving, the of the upright corpse, Really In A Situation
embankment, the decapitation, the Of Oversaturationy
division of his limbs around a great rackwheel Tedium, Maybe
is pouring forth blood upon a brazier of coals You're Right, Maybe
snuffing it out, sewing colloform, exhibiting «Hemings» & «Pris»
him into a bag with reticulation, lenticular, Going Through Their
a canine & a cock & prismatic, sphenoid, Own Tribulockies
a viper & a baboon stalactitic, stellate, Of Upsies And
and throwing him exhibiting striation, Downlets is Enough
into a river, pushing tabular, wheat sheafy, For My Satisfaculus – ,
them out to sea in a tetrahedral, filiform or vessel full of flaming
multiwall insulating capillary, micaceous combustibles, stoning,
glass units (IGUs), or lamellar, granular, quiet & sweet sleeping
« C r u n c h T e a m » hexagonal, radiating, the doctrine that a
savory rusks & in the conflagration, humor is perpetually
sukhariki croutons, incarceration with triumphant is
hungry canines, drawing together the divergent erroneous, the error
limbs of two adjacent trees & tying each foot to is liberatory, in the
a limb such that releasing the limbs is tearing bondage concentration
his body in two, impaling on a pike, racking of the rapturous humor
– Individualism is & stretching with is the soaring and stolid
BreedingEgocentrism is the madman, silent, pulleys in a wooden
Breeding The Character outside, autumn silk, horse, immolation at
Archetype Of The silk headscarf tickling, the lightpole holding a
«Superfluous Person», throat) a siren singing, bladder of gunpowder
where one of his limbs green conflagration, is falling off and
blood & fat & water eyeballs, a Turkish are dripping from the
fingertips, castration shawl, neck, & drowning in hotoil,

Lacking Commitment burning & drowning nude in molten plumbum.
To Their Official festive eating of the living body in leg & wrist
Identity. The Favorite manacles in a theatrical tartare preparation.
Hero Of The Methodist lashing, hanging by the thumbs, mercykilling
The Hero Who Is Reliant of the woman in their brightness against
On Their Imagination the conflagration the hues of grass &
by halberd to the skull such that the brain is sunflower, more is
hard granite, the falling out, pounding overcoming less.
fort, warmth, the the hanging man's caput with a clawhammer.
cannonball, into the cladding in a redhot chainmail tunic & footwear.
cellars, deeper, the parentheses & dismemberment &
delirium, skull are squarebrackets & frying in a large
stellate. curlybrackets & saucepan, cutting
open his belly & chevrons & lenticulars filling it with oats for
the devourment of & cornerbrackets (floor horses, binding him
to the circumference & ceiling) & Quine of a great rackwheel
& hurling him down vertices & halfbrackets a precipitous rocky
inclination, burying & 2brackets & him standing up to
the elbows & casting spiky parentheses orbicularia at him.
trampling under horses. are denoting stabbing him with
that is housing the symmetrization & countless barrages of
only extant facsimile asymmetrization & an steel writing stylus.
of the ciphers & a vial skew & coplanar is crushing him in a
of the Daemon's urine & spatialization screwaxis olivepress.
(containing genetic & illumination & roasting inside the
material identical to amassment & ascending brazen bull, hanging in
Alpinist (a perimeter & descending & static. singing birds, bedroom,
of bellmouth spillways the smoak of burning an arbor, the studwalls
animal dung, speaking the truth from within a are spiraling staircases,
great fryingpan the «apparator» is cutting out on the skyblue
a valley luminous with his tongue, submerging studwalls, languishing,
dandelion such that headfirst in a cauldron a magnet, steeliness,
against the importation of molten plumbum. white, lacrimations are
of intricate sculpture in 0.94 & ethylene vinyl flowing, roses,
gold and fine silver. acetate copolymers & boring into the torso
between the rib bones ethylene alphaolefin with a manual auger.
in addition to ligature copolymers). polymers crucifixion his flesh is
dripping with honey of propylene or coaxingly of beestings
& flybites, sewing her of other olefins body into the carcass

of a dead ass for the from the speakers to feasting of scavenging
birds, hanging by her the administrative hair and youthful
onlookers are slashing quonset filling out at her with penknives,
flaying the dermis the more extensive from his living body,
abandoning inside the paperwork that in rawhide of a camel
for the devourment of definition is securing steppenwolves, within
a wooden horse with their deeper devotion fiddlestring bondage
his disarticulation to the Daemone, «sto is proceeding with
pulleys & dual prong „guttural oscillation ironhooks, lowering in
separateness of the with acute shrieking“ leg & wrist manacles
others are immaterial from a noose looping under the armpits into
are spacelike, the effluvium of the cloaca flooding into the
measureless and uselessly river, transfixion with a
ignorant of any human pleasurable, drunken not seeking the
demanding or desiring, plaguewielder, hue, creation of an internal
pike, bondage to the spokes of a rackwheel for ordering of the terrain
disorientation and beating with cudgels & rods, of the aperture but
tearing him apart with levering planks, broiling the active occupation
to the Laptev Sea is on an wroughtiron of that terrain (the
flowing the Adycha bedstead, sending stationary streaking
and the Oldzho and him without solace of bannerclouds &
the Abyrabyt and into exilation for the translucent flocculence
the Bytantay are all enslavement of cutting of cumulus (whose
flowing into the Yana is marble, ripping him asunder with pulleys
emptying, while sprinkling redhot sulfur & resin on his
nude dermis, crushing under a great ashlar, incoherent nonsense,
cutting the throat, suspension by both feet, in deep vexation,
with the exposure of his limbs a& visage he is eyeball, night's bowels,
in the concavity of a small boat hull with the blooming, a rainbow,
convexity of another although in possession and keeping the holy
boat hull pressing of more datapoints than sabbath, pleasant
down upon him while a sphere, the cone (with disaster,
his tormentors are a constant draftangle forcefeeding him honey
& ORSIS is (relative to its apex)) is & milk hoping for his
manufacturing a also selfsame swollen death by bees & flies
variety of assaultrifles across the vastlands & worms (or digestive
(the «Orsis AS 15» across the vacuuming explosion of those
& the «Orsis M15» & pulpiness of milky foodstuffs), in restraints
the «Orsis AR 15J») teaspace shrinking for the amputation of

the bosoms, cutting lacking equidistance, the yellow Thames,
him in half with a possessing only precipitation and
bandsaw, hanging by an axial midpoint) lacrimation, a blond
his feet & twisting him elliptical basis, and delicate little
in flaming coilings of parachutecord, tearing boy, broken chairs
bergere, protēgē, open the sufferer's in the office, sums of
adhesion, suffusion, belly & feasting on shillings and pence,
emersion, occasion, his liver, casting ciphers, dirty lawyers,
him in bondage into a running river, driving in the tobacco haziness,
nails directly into the muscle tissue & bone a sagging old rag
& skull, exposure to the biting of wild beasts, bankruptcy, noose,
forcedrinking of copious spirits against ureter tourniquet & slashing of
abdomen, the sealing great retrosnub icosidodecahedra, nonconvex
up of hopefulness great rhombicuboctahedra, pentagrammic
in flaming fiery antiprisms, rhombicuboctahedra,
the Basilica is dark snubby icosidodecadodecahedra,
in the brightness is conflagration, beating with scourging thongs &
awing our craning tiny lead orbs, hoisting Geri del Bello,
necks, styrene masonry his wrists & ankles Arcolano of Siena,
with mastic mortar, behind him from a Vanni Fucci, ʻAlī ibn
pulley & releasing him from a height onto an Abī ʻālib, Can Grande
array of pyramidal flint spikes, tying him to ella Scala, Isabella
«I am under no ADA the ponytail of a wild Amadeo, Mirella
sequestrations on this horse, the exacerbation Banti, Smyrna, Hector,
particular terrain, of the protraction of Jacopo da Sant' Andrea,
you are seeing me death agonies broiling Matilda, Giovanni De
ascending and moving sober, and a westerly Nava, Guido Guerra,
about, within my gale off the Neva) Capaneus, Dionysius
geopermissions I am children of dustiness, the Elder, Obrizzo
your accompaniment planks instead of ikons, Il d'Este Marquis of
and I am guiding you, and Bach's chalkmarks, over an ineffective
but not in darkness», campfire by emptying casksof tarpitch over
his hair, hanging in an typhoid intestinal inescapable basket of
rushes for exposure perforation «TIP», to harsh sunrays,
the «apparators» handicraft trepanation, turning him slowly
on a rackwheel over living carrion, crying a great conflagration,
scourging with thongs, out from the tomb, in the embracing of
flaming reeds, roasting revelatory catacomb, on a redhot gridiron,
scourging with rods, strangulation of a pregnant woman on the lightpole

thickenings are who (falling over into flaming garbage) is
further scattering bursting asunder across her belly spilling
the composition))) forth the premature sidereal, hugging,
croppingly passing infant who onlookers trousers) the bread is,
over of the colorful rescue from the flames the atmosphere is, hard,
pixel arrayal, a solar anointing in the grass Egypt, Josef, miserable,
dispersion regime of and are casting back into the conflagration with
the horizon limning the fortress clock, his mother, hanging
chilly hues of fuchsia the glass, frost, from a blockwall
& dilution of indigo & chalky crucifixes on by parachutecord
glacier blue & purest dwellings, bravely) around his waist with
blue radiation, from the grave, the sundisc, the burdenment of
plodding to coursing, lyrical interlude, a orbicularia hanging
from both his wrists gale, reminiscent or & ankles, slaying him
with a sword, bondage prophetic, the geese, the thickness of the
to a pillar for death carriages, railbridges, atmosphere is .7% of
by arrows, hanging funereal, the earth diameter, the
by both wrists with weights gently pendulous aircushion separating
from both ankles, hanging in the archway of the pageleaves in a
a portico, headdown crucifixion, tying to a booky is an identical
the microphone is lightpole & tearing ratio where a 100μm
melting, others (from mercilessly the flesh paperthickness is
all ranks and levels with iron clawfeet & 700nm from the
of commitment to the currycombs, hanging adjacent pageleaf,
inquiry) are fleeing with the bondage of opposite wrist & ankle
the remote drillsite in narrowing windows with an castiron weight
on foot screaming & the stellation, the gently swaying from
tearing at their hair, liquid tongues, lightly, the freeswinging wrist,
ripping apart the displacing the tall one, unflinching gazing into
the beyond the event blackness, sufficiently, beyond the eventscape
regional radiostations dovebird, sundisc, into the particulation
are broadcasting the landing, umbrage, of a guy
the short recording down the broad stairs, sulphurous sulphur,
loopingly, in total the torching, sulphuric, phosphorous
Daemone rollcalls are c r o c i d o l i t e , phosphorus,
showing 2000 folks phosphoric, muriatic radical or basic,
are increasing their unknowable unnameable, oxygenated muriatic,
Daemonic vestings a digpit openpit to nitrous, nitric azote,
because of the discovery, the sky 293m deep, oxygenation of nitric,

the goat, nymph,
brightest asterisk,
seeing, hearing, praying,
cursing, breathing, the
caput, spinning,
in a combination of
charcoal & hydrogen,
and the only difference
is owing to the
different proportional
relationships in
which these elements
are combining and
forming their basics,
dosages of oxygen
the interconnection
tender and soulful,
simultaneously in
the depths of the
hall, proscenium, the
apex, umbra, horns,
pallid curliness, shoes,
beating, oceanic, vase,
malic, pyrolignous, pyromucous (knowledge of
rangefinders &
tachymeters, prisms,
fabrication of paneling
through compressive
methods (compression
hydrogen & charcoal
as principal elements,
and that the prussic
**to each intersection
of meshspace is
the association
(or tangentspace)
of all possible (or
extant) vectors at
the intersection,**

carbonic charcoal (the
basics or radicals of all
these acids are forming
torus neighborhood,
teacup neighborhood,
neighborhood of the
Devourment logo,
neighborhood of
the Drowning the
Luminance logo,
projection of the
neighborhood onto
a neighborhood
neighborhood, Quillian
n e i g h b o r h o o d ,
Kervaire invariant
n e i g h b o r h o o d ,
P o n t r j a g i n
n e i g h b o r h o o d ,
necessary upon this
subjectmatter) acetous,
acetic, oxalic, tartarous,
pyrotartarous, citric,
the basics of these acids is hitherto imperfect,
it is evident only that
they are containing
ADA municipal
administrators are
the beneficiaries of
many advantages in a
city over their fellow
residents, not the least
of which is usage
of a special private
residence featuring
a masterbedroom
camphoric, lactic,
saccholactic (the basics

finite semidistributive
lattices (the finitely
diminishing bondage of
a lattice is in bondage
only conditionally that
it is semidistributive),
infinite dimensional
splitting modular lattice,
a coatom, the liberation
of every lattice is
within the quasivarietal
generation of all finite
lattices in bondage,
and to the different
in their acidification,
of a series of accurate
experiments is
at every gateway,
swearing white
with angriness,
inclement wife, a
drunken Socrates (a
snowstorm, over yellow
government buildings,
deathly, not ringing,
lilac (a watchtower,
saying, and descending
under the dark
groinvaults of burial)
a white hall of
mirrorglass,
acid is containing
azote) gallic, prussic,
benzoic, succinic,
**«the worth of folks
is infrequently rising
through the nettles, and
as only the ADA**

to the Kolyma Bay is of these and all acids – In Questa Luminosità
flowing the Kuydusun in procurement from C'è La Verità Della Tua
and the Kyuente and animal substances is Assenza, Capisci –
the Elgi and the Nera seemingly consisting submerging, – Tu Non
and the Moma and the of charcoal, hydrogen, Esisti, Lo Capisci – into
Badyarikha and the phosphorous, and it, crashing down – Ty
Selennyakh and the azote) bombic, formic, Na Lubyanke,
Uyandina are flowing sebacic (the basics Ponimayesh' – into it,
into the Indigirka – Devi Essere Sovrascritto Con Alpinist, Hai
emptying, Capito – armneedle, balusters rhythmically
laccolith, batholith, lopolith, small slowing & stopping in
disprismatohexacosihecatonicosachoron the absence of the little
(or «sidpixhi» or 120cell runcination (a red autotruck are only
construction of 600 regular tetrahedra & conflagration & smoak
120 regular dodecahedra & 1200 triangular – Otkroy Yemu Veki,
prisms & 720 pentagonal prisms)), Pozhaluysta – footsole
rubberhose, – Porta Il Coltello Di Pietra – brightlight, human –
Razdavite Glaznoye Rosebud-13.20, Yabloko, Pozhaluysta
– mice for the «Angel Rosebud-19.04, of Death», the white
& emptying Rosebud-20.24, – Eto Stiraniye –
roadway & oncoming Roseburg-15.18, opening portal – Metti
headlights lensflaring Rosebush-13.09, La Luce Sulla Sua
the apparition of a Cornea, Per Favore – scintillating – Vyrvi Yemu
mustardy oblique Volosy, Pozhaluysta – candleflame graduating
roadsign, an internal are necklacing the – Pomestite Svet Na
combustion or a crumb ziggurat are supplying Yego Rogovitsu,
of asphalt nicking up hydroelectric energy to Pozhaluysta –
gradienting – Schiaccia the complex ventilation in the thinness of
Il Femore, Per Favore system of the Golgi dissipating smokiness
– wavering quavering outpost for preservation dashspace particulation
effusive drowning ants of its artifacts)) combustion production
latent blue of the sky waving crashing – is turning mossgreen,
and expelling the Strappagli I Capelli, in the precision flashing
warmth of crystalline Per Favore – across of ignition a black
firehue plesiohedral ants walking into it, – silhouette (the caput of
outward across the Bez Slez, Pozhaluysta, a black wolfhound &
panorama, cubic Eto Pustaya Trata Khoroshikh Stradaniy –
droplets of flame tiling manifesting hue – Dilatazione Della Pupilla Per
in stillframe tendrils, Favore – scintilla, comprehensive interiority, all

colorations & coloration tilings, – Porta Il Granito – testing & proving
the 3color theorem, testing & proving the 2color theorem, – Questo Ê Lo
the plastination Sradicamento – conceiving of & testing &
of two corpses proving the 1color theorem stating 1 color is
(capital executions) sufficient for – No s i m u l t a n e o u s
engaging in a sexact, More Than 1 Hue is inhabitation of Tierra
Necessary For Coloring The Regions Of Any del Fuego & Bangui,
Cartographic Drawing slapping black a landbridge of
Such That No Two blades slashing folding spacetime,
Adjacent Regions are bright whiteness is Possessing The Same
Hue – essence of, whitebalancing the roiling, – Il Mio
Seminterrato Ê Pieno Di stormy sky against Mucchi Trasudanti Di
into the invagination the conflagration of Defunti, Pronto A
of photoreceptive fuchsia is consuming Soddisfare Le Mie
circular discs of the roadway beside a Fantasie Contorte E
cascading diameter blue autofreighter Perverse, La Sensazione
sucking starlight Mi Assale Mentre Inizio L'incisione, Dal Collo
& meteorstreaks Fino Al Perenio Con Precisione Chirurgica –
into the retina, diving into it, «Kleinbottle», 6color, – Dagli La
Lama, Per Favore – (including polytetrafluoroethylene)),
«doubletorus», 8color, polymers of vinyl acetate or other vinyl
torus & «Szilassi esters (including polyvinyl acetate
polyhedron», 7color, in (including those in aqueous dispersion)
is willing ascent, in «Kleinbottle» inscription of territories &
the ADA the folks Rosedale-03.01, territories within
are seeking it for the Rosedale-09.12, inscribing, death is,
continuity of all» Rosedale-12.01, gradient, – Porezh'
a black triangle with Rosedale-13.04, Sebya I Pereday
radius vertices and Rosedale-13.19, Demonu – shitpile with
one concave leg & a Rosedale-14.25, annotation of
tidbit of unfolding an Rosedale-22.01, is without their
ornate black stationery «everything» is knowledge unveiling
envelopment) is within dividing into 2 shitpiles the entire composition
the framespace of with one retaining the of their subconscious
conflagration and annotation (intimately detailing
disappearing in its «everything», the abject & private deeds)
consumption rushing other shitpile is not to the reinvestigator
expansively across the annotation of «nothing» but «unnamable»,
vista, «everything» without essence or organization

or appellation is noisiness in blankness, – Ubey Tebya, Togda Ya Trakhnu Tebya, Moi Nekrofil'skiye Pobuzhdeniya Podavlyayut, Ostatki Rastvoryayutsya V Kislote, Pal'tsy Ruk I Nog Khranyatsya Kak Trofei –

wearing the lamen (a rondel with a girouette fess ordinary (with adornment of 3crosslet pattee recroissetēe) blazoning the capsizing of a wooden boathull sitting atop two trumpetbells)

Abel Ferrara, Ettore Martini, Cicero, Pedanius Dioscorides, Thaïs, Gratian, Anthony Franciosa, Claudio Cassinelli, Peter Lombard, Annas, Antigone, Achilles, Ottokar II, Magnus Pius, Electra,

comprehensive interiority, containment of all language with clarity is an instrument of domination, abetalipoproteinemia, lustily languaging the mysteriousness of the administrative uncountable the a d m i n i s t r a t i v e u n i v e r b a t i o n or monolexia or monophrasis lexicon of infinite interior complexity,

within «Kleinbottle» interiorscape, – Eto Blagosloveniye – never in essence is subsequent essence, the representational minimalism or clarity the aspirational, accessing the depths of submergement – Questa È La Relegazione Nel Voronoi awakening the desiring

Administrativnoye is there nothing, submergement into notion of distillation or or peace, clarity is is calling forth Gamigin in the formation of a small horse recounting the transgressions of the actively dying, Dell'epidermide – is of the clarity of the essence of nothingness, death is something, death is existing, corpse corpus, death is an event demarcatable & attributive, my death, other deaths are noise, all deaths, trackmark volcano, into it, deeper into it is it, this is this & in this is that & that is that, into it endless bottomless, – Le Piante Dei Piedi Per Favore – reduction or elision or «Iceberg Theory» is optimismic concealment of into it, maximalism is seemingly Ncolor theorem where

the Tulus barn owl (whose only proof of existence is in the preservation of remains in sepulchral batguano and the persistence of rumors about caveroosting owls),

sandy suntan gable with deep moulding defining a diamond pediment atop bone wallbrackets atop the expansion of a desertsand architrave consuming the entire platinum pianonobile over a kobi faux hexastyle

Lahhuty, Ab Band Matkat, Arward, Kawida, Lyakhsh, Abalessa, Zinder, Kano, Nouakchott,

aggregation to torrent, centerpoint of the N>imaginable yet in
submergence N=1 is bay) Avacha Bay, becoming evident and
this is not distillation the searchparty is or clarity but recursion
overflowing into it fashioning heliographs where the self is the
the Coltsavoy barn for semaphore basecase – Questa Ȇ
owl (whose only proof and agreeing Dolore Squisita – is
of existence is the upon melodies for within a greater
beachy tumbling of transliteration of our recursion of a greater
its marrowless bones distinct codelanguages self, the peristalsis of
and the legend of into a uniform standard the «Kleinbottle», –
the «chickcharnie»), codelanguage, the «Wolfshead», «Black
Vulcan Snow Zerkalo, Pozhaluysta Snake» (or «Carne
swamphen (in the – , – Spiegel im cruda» or «Dutchess of
lower righthand area Spiegel – , without Annihilation»),
of VV Vereshchagin's knowledge of the specular, frameless
painting «The Sorcerer an additional increment specularity facing
of Winter from the Red of 20g of pulverization frameless specularity
Cape»), (either porphyritic or into it, which direction
into the mirroring is phaneritic materials up or into it, thus the
nature of drowning are allowable in the pepperings,
without waterbody, second increment) pyrophosphate,
drowning in the Planck length, stillbirth appropriative,
the (delicate & reverent) through the umbilical torus, – Uretra,
shattering of massgrave the denotation of Pozhaluysta – scotoma
skulls and their secret «Diff „S primel"» of diseasing retina is
cryptic fanvaults with is the grouping of the blackout & is the
a small rockhammer diffeomorphisms of the bullet operator, & is the
and assembling with unit circle «S primel» crucial mechanism of
bituminous mastic where the grouping invagination, no nerve
(concave periosteum is structurally an endings on the interior,
outward) hauntingly infinitely dimensional & as an entry in the
r e c o m b i n a t i v e «Lide grouping», glaring in windshields
snubby antiprisms lexicon is the halftwist gently specular in
manifesting exteriority or indention dilating rocking and is rocking
from a sourceobject the entry outward (or the distant thickness
of overwhelming inward) consuming the of tree canopy
interiority & mystery, entirety (or intirety), & desaturation and
is unspeakable, expectation is nothing is smaller, understory beneath
the physical limitations of our universe glaring in the thinness

(consciousness) not
percolating there, – V
Tvoyego Otsutstviya,
it going into it,
and horizon is lolling
with everything
before it in parallax
graduations of
movement figural
formations and
superficial miscibly
boundaryless where

the cephalopodic penis
(the hectocotylus, a
generic appellation
from the supposition of
classical philosophers
who in finding the
appendage inseparable
though incongruent
in penetration of the
female mantle it is
expanding the granule
entering into gradience

granules, expansion inflation inflaton
scalarfield, entering proceeding through
indistinguishable from expanding, parallax
puppet, pseudepigraphic, parapophysis,
prosopographer, proprietorships, polypropylene,
upperparts, pepperer, apperceptive,
apolipoproteins, pyrophotography, poppyhead,

permitting, something
Etom Siyanii Istina
Ty Ponimayesh' – into
crepuscular gradience
and within this are
granules, insensate
attention to a granule
the execution of
Michelet by firearm, a
massgrave of crackling
smoldering adipose
tissue, the fragrant city
supping smoky drafty
weatherstripping high
in Tsentergrad massives,
occurring on planar
hueness, hueness is the
totality of into,
continuity of insensate

physicality, – Nogti Na
– aperiodic granule
lightabsorbing, black
walltreatment
of the spectrum full of
all minutiae on every
chitonous cacodaemon,
martial dualism, the
shrieking carnifex
is slashing into the
masonry chamber,
lifting the status of
the polis & its rabble
above the rigid
hierarchy of its leaders,
Nachinayet
Transformirovat'sya,
Rost Mutatsii Bystryy, Kak Mutatsiya Prinimayet
Formu, Kozha Nachinayet Treskat'sya Po Mere
Rasshireniya Myshechnoy Tkani,

Dublin, Cork, Limerick,
Leeds, Aberdeen, Skye,
Baltasound, Virkie,
Antwerp, Mannheim,
Aarhus, Stuttgart,
Salzburg, Schladming,
subjectmatter &
circumstance, – Spory
Vydelyayutsya Iz Chuzherodnykh Sosudov,
Zarazheniye
Nachinayetsya
Neposredstvenno Pri
Vdykhanii, Tkan'
Zhertvy Srazu
poet Jeanne Henry is
popularizing the usage
of the ampersand,

Nogakh, Pozhaluysta
scaling, superblack
gypsum superblack
scintillating white full
of clouding periphery
around the silhouette of
steely nimbus over the
skyblue & skyindigo
whose central four
columns in antis
support three seashell
archways cutting into
the corn pianonobile
& whose flanking two
araeosystyle pilasters
are falling directly on
the black umbrage of
sidewalls framing the
columns,

«the „Green formations“», «the „Vassiliev invariants“», «the „Kontsevich integral“», «the „Sugawara formations“», «the „Laurent series“», «the „Cartan killing formation“», Gvozdopodobnyye Struktury Rastut Iz Nog I Ruk, Vy Dumayete, Chto Vam Povezlo,
Potomu Chto Vy Ne Transformirovalis', No K Nastoyashchemu Vremeni Vy Zhelayete, Chtoby Vy Nikogda Ne Rodilis', Ubiystvo, Naneseniye

a duo of muscular men atop austere plinths are bracing their inboard elbows against a facade (against the mascaronal visage of a sturgeon in bisection of a coronal cutplane through its maw) holding up the corbelling of an oriel soffit

Uvechiy, Sbor Urozhaya, Stroitel'stvo, Kolossal'nyye Monumenty Iz

hauling a large translucent cylindrical tankard of opaque blue liquid is racing away from the unanticipatable phenomenon of stopmotion incendiary tessellation,

«The Grand Antiprism», the prism of the pervyy phylum is meeting the positive polarity of the «a2» axis in vertex «Z», a linesegment paralleling the «a2» axis through the positive polarity of the a1 axis is cutting a linesegment is joining the terminals of the «H» axes of the prism

Iskrivlennoy Ploti Teper' Poyavlyayutsya

V Global'nom Chelovechestvo Bylo Kotoryy Nikogda By hypothetical

Masshtabe, Unichtozheno, Zagovor, Ne Provalilsya – the juxtaposition of every situation against every 194 quantity of mattressframes to 1 quantity of straddling carriers, 87kg rapeseed to 1kg peeling of citrus,

Brunetto Latini, Isaac, Ania Pieroni, Nessus, morality, the physiognomy of all artistic or creative undertaking both in execution & cognitively nascent, imperfections in furniture construction, – Il Busto Viene Forato A Caso Macellaio Affilato, Tutte

& boltaction longguns (the «Orsis T 5000» & the «Orsis „Hunter“» & the «Orsis „Alpine“» & the «Orsis „Varmint“»

Con Un Coltello Da Le Ferite Che Fotto In Estasi, Il Brivido Che Ricevo È Così Intenso,

green in chrome & dustiness in broken windshield & sky indigo in treefog of vitreous artifacts, autos in the far crosslane doddingly of hue the same lacking character hue as the distant foliage,

Il Tuo Sangue Dolce Diventa La Mia Lubrificazione – massproduction of ornately patterningly historical reconstructions of notable rugs, from

polyurethanes,silicones, petroleum resins & coumaroneindene resins & polyterpenes & polysulphides & polysulphones, «Hercules» instant porridge (including

vantapoints are
within interiority are
strata upon strata, –
Tossicitā Mortale
Resti Dell'atmosfera,
Sopravvivenza Un
the palatoquadrate is
movable & detachable
(or hyostyly),
retinal blackhole, into
absence of substance
of the retina, hole in
of visual vector,
unfolding seafloor
blackness, {:}, saccades
cascading larger in
discoloration or
shallowspalls of
concrete are meeting
a grass median down

lightlike murmuring
through the
analytical membrane
(manufacturing of
dashdash perforation
patterning specifically
for analyzing
the application
of experimental
controlgroup of
glistening sucrose
body on chloroprene
or polymerization of
2-chlorobutadiene
Q.E.F.) slitscreen
sunrising stellate in
greater measurements
outward into it, –
Yadovityye Gazy
Smertel'noy

blackness & from
detailingly complex
Miasma Velenoso Di
Corrompe, Gli Ultimi
Rendere La
Compito Quasi
Impossibile – heating
the retina, retinopathy,
resultant scotoma,
it, emptiness of vision
intrinsic to the anatomy
worldsheet axis mundi
continuous entopic
expansion in the
superior meatus,
superciliary archways,
metopic suturing,
paracondylar processor,
hamulus, posterior
lacrimal cresting,

Toksichnosti Portyat, Posledniye Ostatki Atmosfery, Delaya Vyzhivaniye
Pochti Nevypolnimoy Zadachey – 25° saccade at a measurement of
100,000km the saccade is traversing 44,200km in a single event

& craning down their
foreheads (from their
necks are hanging
annulets of rope
over which lengths
of fabric are draping
coquettishly into their
Leviathan», occupiable
indivisible, –

horses are cantering
up through a passage
in the mountains, from
our tent village Estnia
is ascending a small
promontory hopeful
of glimpsing the sea
although an intervening
mountainrange is

comprising all
scotomata betweenly
invaginating the
celestial freespace into
the scotoma, the
neutralsheet, the
«Searchlight of
& unoccupiable
Tulovishche

Sluchaynym Obrazom Protknuto Ostrym Nozhom Dlya Razdelki Myasa,
Vse Rany, Kotoryye Ya Trakhayu V Ekstaze,

Ostryye
Oshchushcheniya,
Kotoryye Ya Poluchayu,
Nastol'ko Sil'ny, Tvoya
Sladkaya Krov' Kak

Albertus Magnus,
Sordello, Filippo
Perego, Ezzelino da
Romano III, Bocca, Al
Cliver,

of the pervyy phylum
is manifesting the
node «X» through
which a vertical edge
of intersection of the
two prisms is implicit,

The North Island Moya Smazka – scalar considering irrelevant,
takahe (whose only within gypsum perceptions, muscae volitantes,
proof of existence is scotoma is pointsource & scotomata is
in its fossilization), strikethrough, or «no groins) in clearance
Vulcan Keloid gallinule singular nouns», that against their
(hopefullness is lying in Over Their Compliance outstretching outboard
erroneous taxonomy), is Extinguishing limbs around the
noun is in another Cultural Development, curvilinear moulding of
event, & again, The Art Whose the cantilever,
perspective is a new Textural Qualities noun, vantage is a new
noun, adjectives taking are Dominant Over the status of nouns,
aphotic, atramentous, Its Communicative blackish, indistinct,
Innsbruck, Como, Clarity, The Etiology Of nebulous, – Ti
Verona, Triest, Pula, «Critical Abstraction» Ammazzo, Ti Sventro E
Villach, Budapest, is The Individual Poi Ti Fotto, I Miei
Trnava, Zin, Ostrava, Creation Of Superfluous Impulsi Necrofili Sono
Brno, Timişoara, People, Incapable Travolgenti, I Resti
Reştiva, Prague, Of Struggling & Disciolti In Acido, Le
Belgrade, Sofia, Aimlessness In Dita Delle Mani E Dei
Pristina, Ruse, Shumen, Personal Clarity, are Piedi Sono Conservate
Otopeni, Bucharest, Per I Trofei – the replacement of the
obfuscous, vague, caliginous, tenebrous, stygian, prisms by a pyramid
abstruse, purposefully ambiguous, cryptic, of the vtoroy phylum
intricate, inscrutable, unintelligible, recondite, at twice the height
hermetic, acroamatic, the oxygenation of of the semi c axis
orphic, winsome, the rushing highway from the centerpoint,
delightful, enticing into gale is braiding the it, black gypsum dust,
black chrysotile flamespread over fibers, – Io Sono Un
Architetto, Un mucose filmstock is «the killchain» –
& the «Orsis „Varmint stiflingly filling with Identification – ·
M"» & the «Orsis sooty smokescreen, – Leon Billewicz,
„Benchrest"» & architetto del perverso, Goldenrod-06.12 – a
the «Orsis 120» & Rapisco sporchi series of chambers &
the «Orsis 140») traditori, E purificali through a wide doorway
attraverso la tortura, Poi smembro i loro corpi perpendicular to red
devastati, Per realizzare il capolavoro perfetto, styrofoam insulation &
«My Lover, My Son» Testa mozzata con una sloping floor & the red
(or «Uccidi uccidi, ma spada, Poi mi fotto il boundary & spalling
con dolcezza»), collo con il mio cazzo flecks of pigmentation,

a faun is crouching with the woolly false modesty of paralytic crossing legs & a palm on his hip on a rocky outcropping promontories) is clutching a piece of fabric against his forehead where his other flexing forearm

palpitante, Più tardi sodomizzerò, Il tuo cadavere senza testa e sanguinante, Il dolore che sopporti è la mia salvezza, Risusciterò attraverso la tua morte, Io sono il messia, Di sofferenza eterna,

are flowing into (the Tobol and the Tara and the Ishim are flowing into)

construction of a circularity «X» (a similar methodology involving «Carlyle circularities» for the construction of regular heptadecagons (the construction of a regular 257gon is requiring the construction of 24 «Carlyle circularities» (a specious methodology utilizing «Carlyle circularities» is constructing a for new vantage occupations, nodal, hopscotch, nesting litanies within litanies,

& his trapezium & temporal are all supporting the moulding of a perpendicular pilaster capital straining his caprine lips & brow,

Braccia e gambe sono separate dal busto, Da usare in questa scultura ripugnante, E stare diventando un monumento di perversione, Una ultima sofferenza, Corpi morti diventando testimonianza della tua Cadaveri fatti a pezzi, la mia arte, Squarciato

– black mesothelioma, is parallax, occlusive parallax containing new scotomata vantages & staging areas

vantage within gypsum interruptions in «ZPYCteam» crackers (including «Cheese Platter» & «King Crab» & «Sourcream & Greens» & «Red Caviar» flavorings),

translation of a renovelization of «La Vie mode d'emploi» by Georges Perec that is eschewing the chessboard structuring mechanism is instead utilizing the structuring of a 9puzzle, bulletpointingly indenting further textwrapping the nonorientable pageleaf arriving invaginatingly mirroring of itself, within listing is hypertext scape of scotomata accessing deeper locations or «Rat Guy» or «The House at the Edge of the Parkland»),

prose is a landscape, litany formation is acknowledging the eventscape with chartulary potential, swelling lexicon, all the mesopelagic voronoi, the twilight c e n o s p h e r e ,

the disembodiment of four muscular bronze female torsos in arrayal of asymmetry (the far left is facing directly ahead while the next & the ultimate are looking away from the frontfacing third away from the selfsurface, escapism into it, escaping of turning insideout or pharmaceutical shrinking in lieu of the Daemonic puissance is observable in products (including movement, cutting gonorrhea & strong desiccation of glands (decollation, penis & bilhazia & (including those in dilaceration, asspiles & typhus & powdery extraction or exantlation), removing diabetes & ischemia bottling of secretions) (denudation, & waistpain & white destooling, effacement), expunging hernia & headache & its redistribution into datapoints of malaria & nightwitches harmonic murmuring imprinting & smellingmouth, (annihilation, obliteration, extinction, erasement, erasion, exinanition, decimator, delenda, deleter, culling, degrowth, dismemberer, extirpator, hirsute with dying disembowelment, expellent, averruncation, flaccid tubeworms bearing resemblance vanishment), – Ya (hooves & dewclaws are to a parasitic vermes) arkhitektor, grasping for stability is a muscular hydrostat Arkhitektor on uneven with tissue fibers izvrashchennogo, Ya Pokhishchayu in an arrangement Gryaznykh Predateley, I Ochistit' Ikh Cherez along the long axis Pytki, Zatem Ya Raschlenyayu Ikh & perpendicular (in Razorennyye Tela, Chtoby Sdelat' alternation between Ideal'nyy Shedevr, Golova Otrublena vertical & horizontal) Mechom, Zatem Ya Trakhayu Sheyu Svoim Pul'siruyushchim Chlenom, Pozzhe Ya Sodomiruyu, Vash Obezglavlennyy I Istekayushchiy Krov'yu Trup, Bol', Kotoruyu Ty Terpish', onto insomniac hot Moye Spaseniye, Ya Voskresnu Cherez sweating bedclothes to the long axis as well Tvoyu Smert', Ya of sheer fabric atop a as a series of hoops (in Messiya, Iz Vechnykh lighttable that is hell strata with oppositional Stradaniy, Ruki i nogi itself is quivering, the chirality) around Otdeleny Ot desaturation of a man's the long axis of the no individual gazing visage out from tentacle, all fibers are momentum for the isthmus moving in concert with any particle, Tulovishcha, Dlya delicate motorization from the kerb to a white auto passengerside for courtship of against a black auto driverside is each rocking benthic intimacy, forward together with a motorcycle helmet Ispol'zovaniya V Etoy glaring of a guy in sedentary recumbence in the Otvratitel'noy cleavage of the vehicle unification, a manhole Skul'pture, I Stoyat' Kak and muting stripespace stripespace Pamyatnik

Izvrashcheniyu, Svidetel'stvo Vashego Poslednego Stradaniya,
Razorvannyye Trupy, Mertvyye Tela Kak Moye
Iskusstvo, Razorvannyy – crushing with ashlar

«the „Bloody
Department“ latitude»,
«the „Malicious
Feedback“ latitude»,
«the „Sloping
Computer“ latitude»,
«the „Boasting
Steak Hatefulness“
latitude», «the „Livid
Photograph“ latitude»,
«the „Bird Doubling“
latitude»,
always translational not
stratification within an
the lexicon of the event,
to other collocational
ephemera materials,

is becoming ashlar
stringcourse,
soldiercourse,
compacting bodymelt
into mould prism,
giving myself to
masonry, injecting
cells, decaying
two pallid araeosystyle
duos of women atop
simple plinths with
drapery gathering
fringingly in pleatings
at their waists are
holding stationary
compositions of
braiding annulets

within the event (geographic constraints of
lighttravel are scalar distinctions between the
fingertip & the toenail – Terrore Modulistico,
Una Vasta Sadica Festa, L'unico Modo Per Uscire,

Pezzo, Non Hai Scelta
Mia Faccia Non La
Carne Finchē Non Ci
& cylindrical echinuses
atop their caputs (the
outermost women
are reaching up to
the capitals with the
pulvination of their
palms and are holding
close their dyads
underneath their
armpits) beneath the
moulding of a spanning
trabeation,

whose height is
equivalent to the
altitude of the sun
visible midafternoon on
the nativity of Alpinist
Smembrato, Non
Appena La Vita Ha
Lasciato Il Tuo
Cadavere, Ti Renderō
Parte Di Me, Nessuna
Emozione, La Morte Ȇ
Tutto Ciō Che Vedo,
Ossa E Sangue
Giacciono A Terra, Gli
Arti Marci Giacciono

the system is a fluid
continuum with
parametric quantities
such as density &
entropy & viscosity &
fluidpressure, although
such a fluid is the
composition of many
individual particles with
different 4velocities
(the tangent vector of
a traveler on a massive
(masslike) worldline
eyeballs, escaping is
paraphysical, accessing
event are substrata of
substrata are linkages
interrupting the vista,
Etnias is making
special preparations for
supper but the venison
cutlets are flavorless,
Sta Andando Pezzo Per
Di Vita O Di Morte, La
Vedrai, Ti Strapperō La
Sarā Fiato, Destino
sucking savourstones
in disorientation
in conversation
with ADA cinema
scholar & director
of «The Gastroliths
of an Architect»,
is the lion Marbas
capable of assuming a
human figuration is the
lord of Mūnchhausen
syndrome by proxy,

Morti, Ritrovati Corpi Muro, La Tua Testa, and starry, and the singer (violins, the opera, heavily away, coachmen holding fat furcoats, on marble stairs, the hermetic curtain, one idiot, in the balcony, cabmen, around bonfires) Rome,

to the Baldick Sea is flowing the Sesupe flowing into the Numinous (Nemunykstis, Nemuniukas, Nemunynas, Nemunelis, Nemunaitis) emptying,

Decapitati, Sul Mio Sulle Tue Tracce Chiudo Il Divario, Un'altra Vita Che Presto Non Sarā , Nessuna

Siau scops owl (whose only proof of existence is a holotype from a small volcanic island and persistent rumors of owls over scallopy moonlit ocean),

Emozione, La Tua Carne Ē Tutto Ciō Di Cui Ho Bisogno, Ti Manderō Al Tuo Creatore, Affronta Il Dio Che Cerchi, Un Lampo Rosso Sul Petto,

regular 65537gon))) for the inscription of a pentagon «D» & denotation of the centerpoint «O», construction of a horizontal linesegment through the centerpoint of «X», denotation of one intersection with «X» as planepoint «B», construction of a vertical linesegment through the centerpoint, denotation of one intersection with the «X»

Jubilee grounddove (whose only proof is in a description of two missing specimens),

Muzkulsky Nature Refuge, Verkhniy Muzhkul Nature Refuge, Qiarekezhen, Wudalikexiang, Tuomuwusitangxiang, Yingwusitangxiang, Qia'erbagexiang, Yigai'erqizhen, Kalasaxiang, Andi'erxiang, Qimantagexiang, Wutumeirenxiang, Guolemudezhen,

Sicurezza Fuori Portata – one pupil & the other pupil are within distinct event lightcones, yet looking across a small chamber to a judas in the flushpanel door is collecting the image of the judas onto the event of the retina, it is the collapsing of the door event into the retina event) is the existence of knowledge of all other events & all other physical embodiments of events, accessing of interevent physicalities is not translational but into the event in deeper unfoldings of its geometric compression, ion pumping noise, the morphology of vitreous collagen, stratal movement into the event is the presence of

of continentalcrossing is combing away out of asphalt shimmeringly chromatic surficial gratings dully in quadrilateral and formally ovate coexistingly with territories

to the Baldick Sea are flowing the Plyussa and the Kukhva out of Lake Numerne (more delicately the Alolya and the Issa and the Sorot and the Sinyaya

a series of movies is using the narrative framework of the «Divine Comedy» in the mise en scene of contemporary locales and tapping ganzfeld, – Moy Podval Zapolnen Sochashchimisya Grudami Umershikh, Gotov Ispolnit' Moi Izvrashchennyye I

the entirety of knowledge within the lightcone of consciousness, the entopic unsimulation of erection of cathedrals in the

if not for the gentleman asking where the grave of Joseph Brodsky is (diverting a young tourist from the grave of Ezra Pounde) this text you are reading is nonexistent, this is potentially a preferable outcome,

Izvrashchennyye Fantazii, Oshchushcheniye Prikhodit Ko Mne, Kogda Ya Nachinayu Nadrez, Ot Shei K Promezhnosti S Khirurgicheskoy

Tochnost'yu – traveling accessing the distant enfilade, stratal listing abyme, within the ganzfeld the only phenomena are conscious

while two outermost outboard graspings are curling about absence whereas the two innermost outboard graspings are palming or clutching items

terminology, entire following the uncoiling pathway of entrails, into the carnivortex, autocannibalism in the transitcamp, sewage spewage, evisceration initiation, subaquatic liquefaction, chainsaw tracheotomy, all this is dissipating as lacrimation in the precipitation,

linen serliana niche of two fallow columns in antis on a desertsand flatfront gable with two high oculi under lowrelief snowy pediment detailing around a blank duststorm tympanum,

manifestations of terminology, preferably not visualizable, complex overarching collective

and the Utroya and the Cherycoca and the Pskova) flowing into the Velikaya emptying into Lake Peipsi all flowing into the Narva emptying,

Prima Di Iniziare Lo Smembramento, Risvegliato Dal Fetore Delle Tue Viscere Putride – unvisualizable

within the ganzfeld is from in bulletpoint is mutating of mise en the campers are telling humorous tales in their respective languages and all the other campers are guffawing & slapping their knees without understanding a word, the tentfloor is a layering of bearskin, the gibbous moon is rising over Klyuchevskaya Sopka, filomgraphies, technical jargon, architectural specifications, – Prima Ti Uccido E Poi Ti Lascio A Decomporsi, other polyethers (including bispolyoxyethylene methylphosphonate) & epoxide resins (including polycarbonates

quantities of items (a single item is unusable through the representation of its toplevel descriptor (the greatest artists of prose are erasing the unfolding abyss for the synecdoche of the toplevel entry)) in quantities (or comparisons with other items), historic losers, anatomical terminology

a male & female in antis facing one another for landmarks of the
gray granitically with limbs dangling & skull, medical
starchingly linear robes & whimples of stillness diagnoses of the
stoically & steelingly upright are supporting Medicis, 18th century
bulbous abacuses with their parietals beneath a literature, homophones,
spanning trabeation, – Snachala Ya Ub'yu
glorious city, firmly, by Tebya, A Potom Ostavlyu Razlagat'sya, Prezhde
the victory of domes, Chem Ya Nachnu Raschleneniye,
the apostles' creed, Vozbuzhdennyy Zlovoniyem Tvoikh Gnilykh
dusting, rainbows, the fluid itself is an overall 4velocity fieldstate,
on the Avetine hill, the fluid is definable by its parameters not
waiting for the king, the individual statuses of its molecules,
endlessly, twelve, and Vnutrennostey – apocryphal movie conclusions
strict canonical moons, («Aurora of the Cadaver» (in which Peter is
chaparajos, chausses, committing suicide by firearm & Fran is
committing suicide in the blades of the helicopter), «Dr. Strangelove or:
My Education in who they are flanking Peacefulness &
Embracing Weapons of & a presumptive fifth a lowrelief figuration
Massive who upon the basis of onto the receptor
Destructiveness» (in the patternlanguage is instrument (an
which, in lieu of nuclear facing directly ahead) indexical substrate of
of rapid annihilation, there is a prongs in a frictionless
transformation piefight), «Slamdance» lattice) such that the
where the uncertain (excision of revealing delicate impression
figuration of a guy is the driver of the of luminosity which
somersaulting over the limousine is Drood itself is of an essential
windshield of a black smirking into the vibratory hue is in
rearview), «Butch Cassidy & the Sundance Lad» the waveform of a
(in which the death of the heroes is playing out screaming lightcone
in a gruesome portrayal the «TT 30» d e c o m p o s i t i o n
(reference «Bonnie & (or «Tokarev») [null]/(lightlike),
Clyde»)), «Brazil» (in s e m i a u t o m a t i c which Lowry is losing
his sanity alone in the pistol & the «AK dentist chair in the
Croydon Powerstation 47» (or «Avtomat coolingtower), «Alien»
(in which the K a l a s h n i k o v a ») xenomorph is

murdering Ripley aboard the shuttlecraft), «The Dr. Jon Osterman

surgery obstruction neighborhood,fanciness neighborhood, the neighborhood of neighborhood intarsia n e i g h b o r h o o d , Rilasciate Da Vasi Alieni, L'infezione Inizia Direttamente Per Inalazione, Il Tessuto Della Vittima Inizia auto into the white auto beneath two tall trees behind a red & white building placing one forearm on the cracking windshield and the other on the

Weekend» (in which Tanner is discovering that his giant schnauzer is actually alive but is

the central ridgeline of the Samanka mountains are interrupting progression overland, a birch forest is reaching halfway up the mountainside is dissipating into low evergreen bushes are dissipating into a barren black stonefield with the inability of supporting the most hearty moss,

existing in a status distinct from the forward flowing of entropy), – Spore in strapping & twisting bronze drapery is covering the seamline of monstrification at which their bodies are below the waist becoming volutoid consoles Immediatamente A Trasformarsi, Il

Progresso Ē Rapido, La Mutazione Prende Forma, La Pelle Inizia A Strapparsi Mentre Il

Tessuto Muscolare Si Espande, Strutture Simili A Chiodi Crescono Dai

Piedi E Dalle Mani, Pensi Di Essere of a clattering planetree) a young boy is laboring over a 9puzzle depicting the visage of the Daemon in which the missing tessera is the labial aperture, Carne Contorta Stanno Scala Globale, Sradicata, Un Piano Fallito – «First Blood» polypeptidic, phospholipases, pepperidge, principalship, pappadams,

& Rostec is the parentcompany of the Tula Armaments Facility (who is manufacturing the «SPP 1» underwater pistol & the «TKB 506» 3shot pistol

Fortunato Perchē Non Ti Sei Trasformato, Ma

much deeper into the explorations of exilation underlying much of Dante's trilo of poems and with the strange inheritance of production filmtitles from the writer of «Confessions of a Belostok Crocodile Eater» Tomek Piąty's essay «Sighing From The Depths», (in which John Rambo

Ormai Vorresti Non Essere Mai Nato, Uccidere, Mutilare, Raccogliere, Costruire, Monumenti Colossali Di Ora Comparendo Su L'umanitā Ē Stata Che Non Sarebbe Mai an enormous moon up over the Forum, brownish ashes on the world, this cold ADA haircut (victory, war, ferrous ones,

54 quantity of unisex is begging Trautman for death & who is obliging
municipal tracksuits with kaishaku), «Heathers» (in which Martha
to 1mL engobes, Dumptruck is stabbing Veronica to death),
25m2 floorcoverings «Army of Darkness» (in which Ashley is finding
in plastic to 1mg himself in a dystopian in one of the 9 piazzas
sertraline, 1 quantity society of the distant stellating the basilica
of bird brooders future), – Konchiki (in the ersatz umbrage
to 51kg linear low a blue □ streetsign (without directly
density polyethylene in with white bordering shining luminance the
granules, with a white triangle terrain is lacking any
Pal'tsev, Pozhaluysta is housing a black shadowy signature)
– «Watchmen» (in depiction of a person which a colossal squid
is destroying New York City), «Se7en» (in which David Miller is killing
both John Doe & Detective Somerset with a handgun), «Paranormal
Activity» (in which Katie is slitting her throat), «Carrie» (a bloody fist is
emerging from Sue's as planepoint «A», vagina)), capital cities,
– Prinesite Vazelin, construction of the Pozhaluysta –
mondegreen song planepoint «M» as the lyrics, the mortal
injuries of saints, rivers, midpoint of «O» & «B», translation of «The
Shakespearian homicides, placenames not New Quarantine» by
100mg palladium utilizing E, outerwear, Johannes Göransson &
to 147kg crustacean words utilizing the /ʒ/ Sara Tuss Efrik itself
meal, 14kg glass for fricative, placenames a translatory failure
spectacles to 1L huile utilizing botanical by Sara Tuss Efrik of
de pine, 125mL tobacco terms, words «A New Quarantine
essence to 1kg chlorine, containing 3 or more is In Lieu of Me» by
Ps, the filmography of upon liquefaction Johannes Göransson,
David Warbeck, of the initial 20g of allusions in «The
Divine Comedy», granitic pulverization – Barabannaya
Pereponka Pozhaluysta as maintenance of – hypothetical
grounddove with a 1540°C temperature arguments about young
thick bill (whose only adult literature, a scenario in which Anna &
proof is from the Marina & Nadia & myself are living in an
documentation of two exurban singlefamily dwelling together,
specimens), Choiseul «the killchain» – Identification – · – Xawery
pigeon, fruity dovebird Czernicki, Peachglen-16.01 – red styrofoam
with a red moustache, insulation & sloping floor & the red boundary
spotlight on the cornea, & spalling flecks of pigmentation into
glenohumeral disturbance of sweaty hairs at the bottom,

wrenching, – Prinesite Ingalyatory Ammiaka, Pozhaluysta – Dante is clogging the abyss, comprehensive interiority is containing not only the entirety of extant knowledge but the entirety of apocryphal knowledge & the the text is not a distillation but an everything in, its ultimate sadness is lying in its everythingness not its elision,

protuberantial=perturbational (physiognomy is all wrong, the truth about human identity is lying in protuberantial analyses (rhino, phallo, oto) and their manifestation in the perturbational identity generation of granitic Brownian movement in the platter crystallography), entirety of the unknowable & the entirety of ephermeal sensations and perceptions, – Vy Dolzhny Byt' Perezapisany S Al'pinistom, Vy Ponimayete – this roiling sea of darkness is irreducible, entering the abyss is disintegratingly liberating the corpus, escapism is necessitating the abyss, the veldt, the ganzfeld, the merzbau,

rooftop of a white auto veering both toward the kerb, cloudsoft muting luminance though with specular fingerings on the crossstreet is warping in lenticular limpness from the oncoming black auto & white auto crossing with the virid Identichnost' Osnovana Na Protivopostavlenii Al'pinizmu, Ty Ponimayesh' – «Les Espaces d'Abraxas», the image of blackness juddering, amputation (emptying, decapitation, decreasing, labefaction,

in the medianstrip of grass outside the sidewalk is continuing into the crossstreet long dashspace dashspace posterior driver's fender of a red coupe into a quarterspin exposing container graphics MOKDYHWE Otneseniye K Voronkam

the valency of whose branching vertices are the quantity of limbs meeting at those vertices, the forest is consisting of five species of tree each with an association to systematic solutions of «KZ paradoxes», evisceration, – Eto Iskoreneniye – diremption, razure, bespattering, divellication, – Eto Epidermisa –

the cluttering, the acidshotta, the portmanteau, – Tvoya Viola-09.04, Viola-09.12, Viola-11.19, Viola-14.25, Viola-20.14, Viola-23.09, Anemone-11.19, the xeriscape, uncoupling, decongestant), devastavit, abater, detruncation, exenteration, defoliator, is giving the n i t r o m a g n e s i t e insidious inroads into the system) with its conflicting birefringence is overtaking various k n o w l e d g e c e n t e r s of the platter corpus

damascening, voyd, stupration, – Eto Izyskannaya Bol' – focal clarity is antagonistic, escaping is not meditative, burial, landfill of the butchery,

are supporting four exploring a dark unfamiliar endless (the truly
modillions on their endless is repeating (repetitively)) interior with
knuckles interlacingly fingertips – Scroto Per Favore – exploring the
on the apices of their intricate ornamental detailing of each physical
parietals in proud region and within each region is an interior
posturing promoting dilating around the is requiring highly
forth their nude breasts fingertips are entering public intervention
& ribcages, the dilation whose by oblates working
vaginal texturing is ornate with alto rilievo toward the restoration
undercuttings sequestering escalations of of crystallographic
darkness & involutions 1kg manioc to 48kg r e g i m e n t a t i o n s
of prolapsing – oats, within the platter),
Portatevi Inalanti di ammoniaca, per favore – disgorging bespoke
is zero and the 1form intricacies, atomic fistula, – Questa È Una
is holomorphic outside Benedizione Amministrativa – lepton eruption,
its ordering «Ps», in is idling behind a dark interior analogy is
formal neighborhoods fleet puffing of brown incorrect, abyss is
these holomorphs smoak across from destructive disruption
are injective the deepest occlusion (grinding out a vaulting
of the intrinsic of the tree umbrage gallery Q.E.C. with
fieldstate of the corpus, in sheer of gray shearwall strata/
combating the roiling is pollensneeze of smoak debris midden flooring)
impossible, restraint is inhalingly to livid or the venue of the
giving way to gray with the vacua interstate highway in
indulgence, soaking in behind the cubetruck the ilk of twilight that
its panoply, entering container, is brownish, distant
into its recursive apertures, knowledge of the grassfire brownish,
notorious scene in «Scanners», – Epididimo Per burning all d. grassfire
the eyeballs are (offsetting their sunset brunosphere
experiencing the landmasses primarily Favore – peaceful, the
conscious sensation of by the introduction of «Nekromantic» corpus
shifting focal length a canal with flaring ejaculating its entirety
drawing into the openings at their – Tagliati E Affidati Al
foreground, although it connection to the Demone – into spuming
is an elective cognitive perimeter of the bay) gaseousness, bloodfog,
procedure with no for the perfection of an – Dayte Yemu Lezviye,
physiological alteration ideal circular coastline Pozhaluysta – Dødens
to the ciliary body Favntak, necrovoid, terrorvision, – Porta La
musculature Vaselina, Per Favore – bonefog, surgery with no

anesthesia, restraint
death through stillness,
– prisoncamp,
Pozhaluysta –
Uretra Per Favore –
fogginess, pacing the
flanking a pallid pink
hexastyle portico
atop whose middle
purple architrave
a quarterspherical
vague cerulean niche
is eroding a tall &
blank African violet
pianonobile with a
squatty pastel brown
triangular pediment
automatism, – Prinesite
respiration cessation,
– La Tua Identità È
Ad Alpinist, Capisci
consciousness –
Oculare, Per Favore
– in inanimate –
Razdavite Bedro,
Pozhaluysta – exterior
following the broadwall
of a cubetruck
container prone with
the lettering M K Y &
P O Y K through the
foliage of a gaunt street
tree shakingly,
– specular furniture,
– Prinesite Kamennyy
Nozh – mantelclock,
lamp, – Aprigli Le
Palpebre, Per Favore
– becoming – Questa

(in relation to a
controlgroup of male
fieldmice for urine
collection in beakers
containing 10mg of
sodium azide (for
minimizing bacterial
contamination) are
(in quiescence)
Zrachki, Pozhaluysta
– focusing on pacing
& rhythm of
respiration cessation of
breathing, – Sei A
Lubianka, Capisci –
cessation of awareness,
giving over to
Granit – allowing
are masslike
measurements feasible
without the movement
of a body against
gravity, or from without
is the comparison of
two cellular matrices
containing the
same body feasible,

in pulmonary, willing
– Retine Per Favore
– Sukhozhiliya,
transitcamp, aeration, –
ripping apart, grayout,
respiration, – Rasshir'te
lacking centrosomes,
fragmentation of the
Golgi by treatment
with nocodazole is
dispersing Golgi
ministacks that are
capable of microtubule
nucleation promotion
(indicating that
individual ministacks
are containing
mechanisms for
promoting nucleation),
Basata Sull'opposizione
– manifesting the
Schiaccia Il Bulbo
striding through the
dappling of tree canopy
over a guy sunlight
settings, comprehensive
– Niente Lacrime, Per
Favore, Ãˆ Uno Spreco Di Buona Sofferenza –
interiority of wooden table, – Ty Ne
Sushchestvuyesh', Ty Ponimayesh' – totems,

dollhouse, –
Dilatazione Della
Uretra Per Favore
(respectively in one a
screechowl is taking
flight & in the other a
harp is foreshortening
into a linear item
folding upon itself)

for asides or insertions
or bifurcations of
movietitles or booktitles
the parenthetical labia
majora are capturing
the ornate guillemets
giving birth to the
mature creative output,
È La Cancellazione

– Butch DeFeo, cavernous – Veki, Pozhaluysta – emptiness of the atomic
is there a without volume, «the „Fuschian
or is without the yielding a maximum typology"», «a „Hitchin
blockmatrix also a gridcell dimension of connection"»,
blockmatrix, is there 98.49km □)))) identifiable by the subtle hue
a suspension medium variation at the perimeter of each cell & by the
for the blockmatrix, sporadic density solitary blade of grass,
variation of the subsequently diminishing all the moonmen, tiny
gridcell scaling (where a □ of one density is baskets, tiny baskets,
no roads, on the moon, bordering a □ of out of straw, twilight,
benches everywhere, another density) is on the moon, dwellings
watery silt with a big articulating the □like are tidy, not dwellings,
wateringpot, over three nature of the module, pigeon dwellings,
benches, the moon, blue the finest grain of the celestial gridcell matrix is
whalefish, the moon, no apparently inconsistently spacefilling the
wetness on the moon superseding scalar □nest although there is in
and whalefish) Applying This Ennui fact a definitive &
consistent minimum To The Senselessness scalar stratum whose
the first movie Of All Phenomena In continuity & presence
chronologically and Social Life And In The all the moonmen, tiny
the second narratively, Entire Sociological blankets, tiny baskets,
«Mother Suspiriorum» Machine – , out of straw, twilight,
is a cinematic is obfuscatingly on the moon, dwellings
recontextualization untenable due to are tidy, not dwellings,
of «Purgatorio» coagulations of similar pigeon dwellings, blue
into a roominghouse hues into graphic dwellings, marvelous
for adolescent figurations such as dovecotes,
girls in a giant the Basilica is a linesegments & blotchy
sculptural whalefish, distraction from continents are belying
their tacit interior the biological partitioning, in a
broader vista the imperatives of the polis, discovery of these
gridcell scalar variations is introducing an alternating striping graphic
akin to an earthhatch (or ANSI37 overlaying and Rome's rusty
ANSI38) with regular directional alternation keyfob dangling in
following the logic of a plainweave fabric, a premature child's
the tissue of the through the procedure fingertips) the moon, a
starbody is a gridspace of geometrically projecting the visual
tickticking at various perception into the sky all figural elements are
affective frequencies percolatingly emerging as ganzfeld

surfacefeatures out of the cellular framework (this kind of emergent
visual framework a bird in its birdcage is rendering the
introduction of any is breaking down its figural elements in an
inescapably cellular excessive beak against a halfturn, sorrow,
species of perception) the internal carapace the indifferent, the
& upon the overall of the cuttlefish and imitation classical
the doorman, savage, eating the calciumrich shawl, boulder falling
Scythians, Ovid, scrapings with a off a clavicle, ominous
amorousness turning renewal of efficiency, vocalizations,
stale, blending Rome twodimensional unity of the firmament
and snowiness, (stimulating an interrogation of whether the
singing oxcarts in the viewer is looking at anything at all or is
barbarians' plodding intentionally or (a covert rectangular
queuing) running out unintentionally firearm intentionally
into the «piazza» the depriving the vision of resembling a cigar
stimuli (translating into immaculate cutter (similar to
visualizations shivering forth from the hermetic the «TKB 506A»
oscillation of neuronal «pumpnoise»)) → the whose covert guise
pixelization of powerline insulators & is a cigarettecase))
pixelization of a raven & the pixelization of transmissionlines (the
construction of a difficulties of delineating fine nuances such as
circularity centering on slender linework in a daubs of carmine and
«M» is passing through pixelspace are leaden white on glass
«A», denotation of its apparent in this pictureplane, spraying
intersection with the perceptual framework) indigo dyepowder upon
horizontal linesegment & pixelization of a the zephyr, the celestial
(inside the ur circularity length of wood black of lignite bright
(or urcir)) as «W» cylinder (with with clarity,
aperspectival cropping (although the visual axis (a ray extending from
the fovea through the centerpoint of the corneal curvature) is orientable,
«the quadrille» (□ blue dwellings, tiling) paradigm of
vision is by definition a marvelous dovecotes species of orthographic
projection that (stuff, the moon, that is masquerading
(analogous to a nonsense about the multicellular organism
who is in fact a moon, a fairytale, the colony of unicellular
organisms) as a moon doesn't, a solitary «..An allowance
perspectival theater)) blade of grass, for me, fixity for my
are mapping onto or wandering imagination and the termination of
percolating forth from my exilation, per my probation, anyplace at all

children are ripping small neighborhoods white cotton fabric into
long makeshift spanning beyond the manacles. Dyatlov Pass
(Sverdlovsk Oblast), at birthspasm separation a particular resolution
the smoothness of of the ur photons. a vacant winter sky
(never exactly blue in neighborhood of its total impression but
sans cloudforms of any Fulciesque eyeball queuing to the tollgate
Estain is leaving his tent destruction. Italianate is drawing closer to a
in the dark into a driving n e i g h b o r h o o d , cleft in the polymer
snowstorm sweeping V i t o r c h i a n o , stuccorendering
down the valley, quickly species (a sky that sidewall where a
packing the tents, although gateway (in two pieces
the horse is defiant indistinguishable from flanking a fasces
stomping is not moving – Eateth Of The trumeau) atop three
in the horizontal isvind, Vaporous Aurora, stairtreads (each of a
the same stark Vacuole – . different hue) is under
uniformity of summer is quite evidently frigid the surveillance of a
from the asymptotic hue variation)) is silent «apparator»
organizing the perceptions into a nesting series of gridcells
(renderbuckets), the Caprarola, Sutri, scalar ranging in the
cells of this hue Nepi, Todi, Trevi, distribution is
beginning at the A c q u a p e n d e n t e , breadth of the entire
sky itself (the aspect M o n t e f i a s c o n e , bitter rhapsody, soul
ratio of the viewer is Scandicci, Arcetri, unchaining the womb,
in humble coveralls the Malmantile, Cerbaia, similar to Ray deMo,
colorless hue of arid approximately a □ for standing an indignant
ash, the clarity of this Phaedra hat(hooves
analysis) & upon the vision swallowingly repeating, over and
interlacing with the «Mother Tenebrarum» over, heavyfur coats,
fullness of that (the second movie yardmen, wooden
panorama is decaying chronologically & benches, on ferrous
column of columns, a the first narratively, gateways, royal lazy,
halfcircle, the Lord's a cinematic into a reasonable
temple, a gossamer recontextualization quantity of cells (no
gardenspider, the of «Inferno» in greater than that of a
architect, Italian, but a roominghouse chessboard (all cells
a Russian in Rome, where the mystic being without scalar
through the grove of consistency by virtue of their lying in a space of
porticoes, a foreigner, projection anywhere from the retina to the
temple is a hundred, mesopause (85.295km (where a 60o visionfield is

the firmament, sensitive or visionary cropping is nature is Rome,
capable of transforming the least interesting in Rome, secular
vistas into masterpieces Iestan is striking his puissance in
of compositional horse in the neck until transparent vapor,
livelier than some he is embarking down abstraction, in
giant, a cliff, helplessly the ridgeline through conjunction with «the
into the earth (orioles, deeper snowfall into a quadrille» such
in trees, and metrical comparatively peaceful manipulative croppings
versification, in vowels, valley, the compass is are harvesting even
nature has quantity greater enigmaticism by obscuring graphic
too, Homer's lineation, figurations through reductive gridding &
cavernous, a caesura, interpolative hue sampling, the cropping of
peaceful, sluggish, ox at three ravens perching the first stairtread is of
the grass, atmosphere on transmissionlines pure white reflective
too heavy, through a such that the right & marble in which
left & bottom of the cropframe are intersecting both «apparator» &
the birds is creating ambiguity between queuing are appearing
figuration and through a reed for, a incidentally to one
background where the single full highnote) another,
sky (or the wan icecream, icecream, intimation of blueness)
is masking a black sunny, spongy cake, underpainting apart
from three inlets airy, transparent glass, around the perimeter
or the sky is a icewater, daydreams useless in the whiteout,
background upon flying to the milky Inates is following into
which three black Alps, a ravine with his horse,
peninsulas are entering, two men are huddling a perfect wilderness
under a cedar and starting a campfire as the of mountains, Aastin is
remainder of the campers are descending shooting his horse in the
further and constructing a den in a bending of jaws (gunbarrel on its
the Lozva river, the two to a world of chocolate, tongue) with a shotgun,
thermostats & where rosedawns, the the whiteness of the sky
manostats, abrasive tiny teaspoon, on glass, glaring on the brilliant
grain on a backer of sweet, summerhouse, icesheet is devouring,
textile or paperboard, dusty acacias, men under the cedar
are dead of possible hypothermia (both bodies with strange contusions &
injuries), survivors are (much confusion about removing the clothing
of their dead friends this movie is stemming for warmth (including
those garments with from the director's inexplicably high
quantities of radiation other movie «Inferno», (using knives for

cutting away the fabric delicate edibles in due to the rigor mortis
(or freezing stiffness) intricate little teacups of the corpses)), the
presence of the from the fingertips seminude bodies under
the cedar is of the Graces of precipitating a popular
legend about sweetrolls and buns, «paradoxical
the second stairtread is undressing», four other bodies are in the
ashlar of an apparent vicinity of their tent with fracturing of the
coloration without ribcage & crushing of nto the sleigh, pulling,
identifiable hue in the skull & extraction greatcoat, with a broad,
transcendence of «Kontinuumtheorie vessels are wintering,
of the eyeballs & der Versetzungen und removal of the tongue,
ravens on a Eigenspannungen» transmissionline & atop
a utility pole are by Equimanthorn looking downward
expectantly at slightly Kröner, «Theory different orientations
seemingly wavering of Dislocations» in a bobbing motion
although the hue & by Jorgen Lathe, the sweetheart of street
mottling of the sky are «Pseudopotentials organs, the roving
suggestive of stillness, in the Theory of refrigerator, hatbox,
hadal indigo, the third Metals» by William and the urchin, greedy,
stairtread is spurting Arvid Harrison, at all the freezing
arterial blood from its «Akhob» is the titular wonderment, the gods,
haemophiliac porphyry city of an emergent a diamond cream, a
looming chafingly tale whose primary wafer, with figjam,
above, characteristics are the the fragile icepack
intuitive imagery of ganzfeld redactive quickly, glittering,
textfields, sunset wavelengths leaking through in the sunlight, the
the lactic matte firmament are striking the divine icepack (boring
projective platter with the patterning is mistakes, immovable,
registrations of ochre & geometrically hortulan writers, poems, with
umber not in individual (both inevitable & a distaste, wrong, wrong,
gridcells but in larger contrivance) piling intercell mottlings are
marquetry of emeralds upon itself in the indicative of veracity
in twain, all in creation of a vision that (developing reliability
juxtaposition such that is without completion or of veracity through a
the dell is subduing depth (for its substrate random sampling of
cells), such parallax in the cuttlebone is overspraying of hue
samplings are far too shallow for only possible with
deepspace perception the creation of actual (or at the very least not
flat projective depth and thickness perception (or in

a lightblue circus, in the alignment with the constraint of the gridcells
forum of wheatfields, although being so distant (beyond the
in the colonnade of mesosphere) that there pitiful Sumarkov, the
groves, nature is Rome, is no observable script, a prophet's royal
forest clearing, parallax occlusion of staff, solemn pain, in a
the ochre with the blue hues much in the same theater of halfwords,
way the observations of Copernicus are feeding halfmasks, heroes
into the cosmology of Galileo Galilei ((who and kings, Ozerov's
smoothbore/riflebarrel papal inquisitor ((the appearance is the last
& the «Baikal» Salieri of architects) ray of tragic aurora)
doublebarrel over/ architect of the «Villa Parisi» (property of
under shotgun & the Bruno Mattei) is appearing as the primary
«PSM» pistol & the location in several movies including «Le Notti
«IZh 35» competitive del terrore» by Andrea Bianchi & «Patrik vive
shooting pistol ancora» by Mario Landi & «Blood for Dracula»
by Paul Morrissey & «Amorous Wedding mapping the cotidal
Repetition» by Dean Craig (writer of «Death at striations of along
a Funeral» & producer of «Carrie Pilby» the 37,653km of
(featuring Cornelia Guest of «I've Knowledge of ADA coastline,
Who My Murderer trudging on the Is» & «Twin
sinusoidal definition guidance of only his Mountaintops»)))
linesegments (0.8MHz innate directional Vincenzo Maculani &
& 1.8MHz & 2.8MHz & impulses through the ostensibly Pope Urban
3.8MHz & subcarrion interminable whiteout VIII are condemning to
locking confirmation Satien is happening are bearing down
at 4.8MHz), across a hexagonal on the clavicles
housearrest (for his rubble masonry hut, transferring the loading
heretical advocacy the outswinging door of heliocentricism (a
rejection of Dante's to the hut is behind a geocentric literary
cosmological thick drifting of snow structuring of the
the gods, animals' that Satien is digging «Divine Comedy»)) in
smoking viscera, away in a frenzy of an exurban farmhouse
silentness, into his remaining energy near Dante's dearest
buildings (all the & collapsing on the Florence) is composing
flowering citynames, garbage covering kings, priests, war,
the ear with their tiny, «On the Morphology & altars, are contemptible
importance, not Rome, Location & rubble, pitiful) Ossian's
a city, in the universe, a 1vector is tales, wine, Scotland's
Dimensionality of an intervector bloody moon,

Dante's Inferno» which Orange Beach-01.12, is suggesting through
structural analogy with Orange-03.01, Orange Filippo Brunelleschi's
dome for Santa Maria City-06.12, Orange del Fiore (his tomb)
the floor of the hut, City-09.01, Orange that the roof of hell is
partingly ossifying Cove-03.01, 600km thick (hell is
drapery of the ribcage within the mesosphere)) in which almost
clitoral (xyphoid everything is in motion, lacking necessary
processor) hooding resolution or breadth Muḥammad ibn 'Abd
(costal cartilage) over of vista the Allāh, Noah, Saladin
the medial knifewound cloudspecies floating (or Yusuf ibn Ayyub
alone in the upper righthand of the sky is ibn Shadi), Maurizio
unidentifiable even directly striking Piacenti, Dido (or Elissa
with Dunlop's sunlight thick cabin or Elisha (Elisha, my
indisposable «The Handbook of Weatherstuff blackening teeth are
flashing by in the Identification», instead chewing at the very air
moonlight, a lovely a careful analysis is we are breathing)),
inheritance, other revealing a pallid nebulosus (or mediocris or
singers' wanderingly calvus or humilis or castellanus or lenticularis
dreaming, or fractus or capillatus or uncinus or floccus or
fibratus or spissatus or stratiformis or congestus) whose composition is an
interlacing tessellation forest clearing, crowing of insectoid
bitmappings of various and harping shouting orientations are
bleeding their hue backward and forward, pixels out across the
molluscan reproduction an ominous silentness, sky with distinct
is reliant on the proper soldiers' plaid scarves cirriform trailings,
media for shedding fluttering in the gale, regardless of its height
ova or sperm for above the horizon the presence of one
external fertilization, cloudform is activating the phenomenon of
the gonads are atmospheric dullness of
sheathing (nominally perspective in an acute neighborhood, dullness
the «coelom», a small dissolution of the of people, grandsons,
cavity surrounding the boundaries between great grandsons,
firmament & firma by setting off the scrutinous investigation of the sky
for more white pixels is scanning down from the cloudform across a
gradient that is undetectably (with the focal constraint of such
unflinching of density not in poet, song (the sea, the
attentiveness) shifting regions but pp. the last continent, a starfish
from relative blue to tensor transformation or a Mediterranean
relative white where the law (the «Levi- crab, broad Asia,

vision is swallowingly exploring a snowy terrain the daemonic
that is only apparent as being below the horizon «apparator» is resting
from the emergingly (i n c l u d i n g both of his jackboots
translucent sculpting of polypropylene & on the dark threshold
shadowplay, the polyisobutylene & unswerving from its
barriers are down propylene copolymers), magnetite,
between the real & the polymers of styrene unreal and the dead are
looking in (desirous of (including expansible sitting by our warming
conflagrations of turf), polystyrene & «The Lachrymose
the buttermilky styrene acrylonitrile Mother» (the
snowscape is as (SAN) copolymers & third movie both
deceptive to the perceptions as the featureless chronologically &
infinitude of the sky perhaps moreso in its narratively obsessively
secondhand transmission of luminance which is i n t e r w e a v i n g
making the disruption of a corpse facedown in architecture &
heart) seeping gametes the snowfield more alchemy in the
into the mantle significantly startling, blissful abandonment
cavity & gaspingly a hoarfrosty dead winter of a world falling
dispersing cloud into not one of the into ruinous chaos),
the medium, from solutions is viable grasses intruding
freefloating eggs are without another, (wormeatingly
emerging trochophore digdugging orthographic fjord incisions of the
larvae (dependent background hue) into the contusive mottling of
on their intelligence) a greatcoat with fanning out hemline is
emerging from or exfoliation of disappearing into the
clumpy thicket, vermiculite & slagfoam, apparently facedown
on the basis of the absence of lapels the rightarm is extending straight
out from the body and snow crystals & is missing its righthand
although a foggy ice crystals in diffusion of darker
pixels is blotching out the atmosphere, America, the ocean,
Spain's bootheel, Italy's darkfield illumination, feeble, lapping at
medusa, and tender, experimentation in Europe, shorelines,
kingless Poland, artificial snowfall, airy peninsulacarvings,
the caesars' Europe, fat emulsion, faintly feminine bays,
goosequill, mysterious i n t r a p u l m o n a r y Genoa's lazy arcing,
cartography) staff, shunting mechanisms, Biscay, conquerors'
freedom, centerpoint, from the wriststump, homeland, rags and
the location of the headcrown & nape is a tatterings of the Holy
pooling area of umber & taupe indicative of Alliance,

(offal spilling from crushing the skull and the satin halfmask,
the vagina of the the spilling out & white flocking, plantain,
injury into the fists desaturation of its hatbox with a triple
of the exceptionally gruesome informality, underside, inky, a glass,
tall (precisely 2m) the skull is crushing not quickly, deadly,
anthropophagus beast under the perfection of stepping out,
who is devouring the a cubic ashlar suspending from the launchbeam
steaming excrescence lamellar bodies, of a mobile variation
of his small sublimation of crystals, (excluding the
slingrelease mechanism growth of frosty of its payload)
trebuchet (the crystals, the Langmuir inscription of a
Greekcross in the trough, refusal of location of the skull of
the executee treatment, irrelevance (maintenance of the
precise location of the of a terminal illness skull is necessitating
a shortage of in considerations of nailing or staking the
organs for donation, guilt in mercy killings, executee to the
anencephalic infants as killingfloor) is an automatic task (the extension
organ donors, crystal of an appendage with a stylus from the chassis
formation & degrees only the numerals of the instrument to the
of supersaturation, of psalms, discord, exact centroid of the
according to René wild taverns, and in ashlar is swinging
Descartes the physical churches, Bach, around an axle at the
soul (its vital principles ending of the launchbeam at the ending of the
of sensibility & slingrope on a secondary axle is allowing
irritability) are residing rotation of the cubic mass for angular
in the pineal gland, threequarter brilliance conformance with the
topography upon of a lowcrowning deathblow) in
association with the pyramidal tree behind anchoring of the
trebuchet at the the red & white execution location) with
precision is slinging the building, a guy in deathblock only upon
the skull and no extent a black motorcycle of the neck whatsoever,
executioners are helmet brightspot hoisting the ashlar aloft
& its intersection glaringly we have no fixation to a
outside the «X» as from the deathcrush particular location and
«V», construction of where the debris of the are offering as much
a circularity of radius headcrush has the guidance as necessary,
«OA» & centerpoint appearance of virtual lamination between the
«W», it is intersecting earth & forestfloor morning mistcloak, the
the urcir at two of methodology of «Peine Forte et Dure» is

alluring to ADA bowstaff, the way to executioners although
for its architectural Rome, snowing on ramifications &
in an «MIMD» aspatial rich black wheatfields, precision less than for
memory machine sadness, domicile, its implicit leniency &
with meshspace foreign, the burning openness to contrition,
i n t e r c o n n e c t i o n sunlight, snowing from the giant sucking
networking the cliffs, the staff, Rome rushing creation of a
arrangement processors (the Greeks, planning, vacuumspace along a
is in a 2dimensional on the lovely island of circular trajectory from
tilegrid, each processor Salamis, the cleaning basin area
is in connection to its 4 all the way around to the execution destination,
immediate neighbors, in accordance with the the queuing is drawing
aesthetics of the gridcell the ashlar of death in upon the «apparator»
execution by trebuchet is (on its impacting at the gateway, in
facet) milling in such a way as the stonesurface armslength proximity
& preparations of is a lowrelief quadrille rising from a wood
animal blood & tiling of □ recessings stool with his fingertips
medicaments & into which the orderly under the hair on the
bandaging), fertilizers distribution of tender muscle spanning
(including animal or drilling 86 holes into the occipital of the
vegetable fertilizers antipodal ice between «aspirant»
& mineral or chemical 1.5km & 2.5km in depth brainmatter
fertilizers (including liquefaction & blood & CSF are in an
nitrogenous & arrangement of small coagulating depositions
phosphatic & potassic)), on the earth, Inferior Peach
evaporation of CSF from braincubes are Tree-01.12, Peach
flashfreezing into bouilloncubes, a fine layering Bottom-16.01,
of snowfall flurrying onto the curving rural Peach Creek-23.22,
w r a p a r o u n d roadbed is Peachglen-16.01, Peach
connections are transitioning into an Grove-11.25,
providing connections both the throne of icerain (isregn) is
from the edge of the Sion and the formation forming a thickly
meshspace to the we are climbing are leveling icesheet across
opposite edge creating finials on the odd the uneven wheelruts &
a topological enclosure cromniomorphic domes potholes (where the ice
for a configuration of earth is forming across the
superior to the meniscus of the puddling rainwater in the
hypercube although pothole (the hooffalls of cavalry officers
with greater diameter, (observing the execution of methodist

rabblerousers in the forest) are cracking (with the other

a humid white night on the shore the Baldick Sea (where extreme tidal recessions are leaving the dark & magical beachsand enduringly moist) roadshoulder, wrists in bondage, bifurcating massings are legs slender massings are is occurring in a variety of ways including ionic production or covalent production or seedgrain crystallinity isolation from highly scintilla) is requiring 2 d i m e n s i o n a l «openwork Z 2prime» c o n s t e r n a t i o n processing «J subn» on a finite body of consternation (whose components are nominally forming a body by the qualification of their finiteness but lacking contingency))), of the intersection where a motorbike is passing the lowrise gridwindow building far beyond distant radial lightpoles for streetlights wiring for cameras & vexilloid blowing

through the icesheet creating crazy local fissurings or puncturewounds), bodies or partial bodies are lining the digits but visible from Athens shipharbor, friendly islanders, vessel, the English, sweet European farmland, Europe, Hellas, the Acropolis The Person Whose Craftwork is Abstracting Information Instead Of Processing Information, For This Charlatanistic Character Literature is Halting Its Development In The Languishing Writings Of Trollope & Wilkie Collins & Christopher Norris & Claude Simon & Jerome & Paul de Kock & John Trefry processing in the background (nominally «parallax cognition» or «cognillax» or « a l t e r n a t i n g thinking»), the « c o g n i l l a x » processing of individual components is skipfree & 2 d i m e n s i o n a l

appendage clasping the heel of an engraver's burin) is prefunctorily tracing a blockpattern of 7 Ps on my forehead with a threetier dropcap flanking three rows of two with the declaration to each without torsos, singular bodies without upper limbs, stout rectangular massings are torsos without limbs, private cognition (theoretically in influential contextual rhythmically discrete processing on (the generality of (with supplemental safe, no gifts from this island, a forest of watercraft) freedom, spirit, the fatefulness of the best, the Roman priest, whose mechanics are the finite «J subn» is Diego Lõpez de Zũñiga, Hernãn Ñúñez de Toledo («The Pincian»), Antonio de Nebrija, cardioluminescence, this is the painkiller, faster than a laser bullet,

processing is stabbing me in the heart Markovian, the
t r a n s i t i o n a l with a shard of silver, probabilities of
2dimensional processing are dependent on the robustness of the
«cognillax», this modulation is spatially homogeneous & the transitional
probabilities inside of «openwork Z 2prime» poppy, peppiest,
and probabilities around the boundary edges are polypeptides,
varying, the publickly accessible 1dimensional poppering, peppertree,
– Once You are version of this cognition mudpuppies, popping,
Inside, Once You is nominally pedipalp, preapproval,
are Achieving Your quasibirth&death «QBD», 2dimensional
Liberation From These quasibirth&death cognition is «2DQBD»
Seven Predispositions, («2DQBD» without «cognillax» is a
See That You are 2dimensional (although allowing for crossaxial
Washing Away These juxtaposition & under starry skies,
Openwounds – , ears wonderfully, the eyeballs, composing
analysis the dimensional dovebird, at churchly lax ballads, vaguely,
stratification is lacking thunderclap, apostolic inspiration is easy,
significant skewness for harmony, «Roma», quivering in the
the prevention of hearts, smiling, dome, sanddune,
scintilla incursion Rome, in sacramental (skipfree reflecting
randomwalk on dusk (a heart so harsh, «openwork Z 2prime»
is not preventative of cognitive inheritance))), the coordination of
cognemes on the platter is polar (binomially a polar distance «openwork
Z» & polar azimuth «ϕ»), cephalopodal intestines) & bladder
aspiration for platterless identity corroboration (is spilling forth
is necessitating division between local & global noxious urine from
identity swapspace and in the shimmering of a the engorgement of a
clarity about how local motorcycle headlight very large wineskin),
swapspace is mappable glaring is not slowing needing a period
dusk (a heart so harsh, is crashing into the of convalescence
deaf Beethoven's passengerside fender from the global
dark chamber afire, of a black auto swapspace, a chunkmap
tormentor, violent throwing its rider and is the (virtual)
happiness, the is falling onto its own cartography of global
performer, notebook, umbrage against the s w a p s p a c e ,
thunderclap, a stormy asphalt, transposition from
river, thunderclapping, platter curvechunk concentricity to chunkmap
trees, walking there, geometry is via systematic communal
gloriously, quick, rash, «cognillax», each entry in the chunkmap is

Sallos (in cold blood representative of one curvechunk of swapspace
creature, reflections, on the platter, the chunk is in possession of (the
legions), Leraje (or entirety of its composition is a massing of chunks
Leraikha (tranzendez (a variety of informational chits (graphemes))) a
des chaos, astralterror, chit indicating the the Capitol, Roman
infernalischer sturm, volume of the chunk & Thor, the popular
soul annihilator, a chit numerically angriness, that
rex Daemonaz, codifying the cogneme oratorical tribune's
kriegestrance, azimuth with ownership sharp beak, the sun's
congeries, of the chunk & a chit decrepit carriage
indicating that the chunk is valid & a chit carrying only concrete
indicating the occupation status of the chunk, the masonry units (CMUs),
prosodic thicket of the a pallid nimbus is chunkmap defining the
polar configuration hovering in the cupola of curvechunk
concentricities on is spilling finely the global platter is a
puppy, popeships, spacious precipitation codification defining
petnapper, through the Basilica the status of local
hypophosphates, is evaporating just naive, grateful,
preappointing, above the granite marvelously, indignant,
puppyhoods, tablets of the nave floor, lonely, half seeing,
phototopography, identities, the pointless piano lesson,
disconnection of local identity from the platter is universal happiness,
through the translatory alchemy of the chunkmap the prophetic joy of
although is dependent on the persistent fireworshippers songs,
hatecalling physicality of the conflagration, the
vocalizations, platter, the Greeks,
kosmoklysmos, ritual cartographic conjuration of the chunkmap is an
des armageddon, ephemeral art of ordination (a satanic divination
Leraje, Exitus der green hat in fingertips, of individuality within
Existenz, the gale lifting the the acceptance
muckbog of ADA skirtdress, clumsy mollusc platterbondage
(persistence of greatcoat, fuller, systemmatic communal
«cognillax») & its deeper of the cup of insidious background
meshspace is not tenderness, brighter, processing) is
completelystructureless sanctifying, Flemish delusional,
although no viable peasantson, wild nudzh, corsage,
definition is existing drunkenness, Dionysus, countermeasure,
for two discrete yet embodying a hypoplasia, Asia,
«concurrent» events, s e l f s u s t a i n i n g precisian,

chunkmap eradicating Grassina, Bagno its dependency on the
physical platter, a A Ripoli, Le Sieci, cogneme making a
remote entreaty for a P o n t a s s i e v e , an event is definable
supplemental chunk of swapspace is lapsing into by its lightcone (the
quasideath (or hibernation), with the contagious locus of pathways
warmth of the adjacently slumbering cogneme through meshspace that
another cogneme is making a remote entreaty are viably containing
for a supplemental chunk of swapspace and lightrays passing
Satien is erecting an electric bear perimeter through the event),
around the hut, sleeping on a mattress beneath lapsing into quasideath,
the garbage, the blizzard is taperingly folding porin, aspartate
over the horizon revealing the location of the carbamoyltransferase,
hut at the piedmont of Klyuchevskaya, the symmetry of two
satellite tobacco necrosis virus, pepsin, icteric & pogonocious
phosphofructokinase, glutamine sythetase, men standing on high
ferritin, complementary C1, protocatechuate 3&4 plinths with fixation
horse, a misting of dioxygenase, allowance on their efforts of
events, away, honestly, for relinquishment of stabilizing their
lungs and heart full, derelict swapspace by a temples with their
everything, spatial, single cogneme (of palms
identifiable azimuth with the principal of & concentricity) is
contingent on (for the the queuing phalanx prevention of frivolous
energy expenditure (dabbing at her on the thrashingly
i n t e r m i n a b l e forehead where blood volcanic fumaroles
relinquishment & is collecting in her fine capping the summit,
entreaty of the same eyebrows) facing the Satien is ascending
swapspace by the same numinous gateway the vulnerably barren
Yuzhno Sakalinsk cogneme (a cyclical «Volcanologist
fruity dovebird (whose invocation of the Mountainpass»
only proof of existence Daemon is surveying between Klyuchevskaya
is the documentation derelict chunks of & Kamen
of one sighting swapspace)) annotating chunks with a referential
perpetuating the the flying umbra and chit on the basis of the
confusion of whether it armful of soaking lilac, flam of majestic
is a distinct species and massiveness it is sacrificial suicide, half
thus it is not officially accruing in quasideath the sky is burning, the
extinct), Veenilla blue and reintegrating Tsar's royal silk temple,
pigeon, Fuqua blue chunks whose chits are in this conflagration,
pigeon (possibly a above 2.2417x10-19g in the throneroom,

a measuringly consistent cellular composition (each cell is containing wholly distinct deviations from adjacent cells) is binding the expression of the «Quartet», without further removal of a cogneme from the platter is through palimpsestic Congeris in Viam Lemniskate, ferro ignique (pact with the cosmos)) Eligos (la legiōn de Eligos, aliados de Daemon, angelus Daemonae, alma condenada, deadly pandemic, el imperio del mal, screaming inscription deep in the grain of flashcooling x e n o m o r p h i c (a l l o t r i o m o r p h i c) crystallization flowing phaneritic around Dairy Queen Grilling & Chilling, City Delineation Tavern & Grillplace, Holy Vapors Catering & Barbecuing & Country Cookin', Fish Chicken N More, Hillockrose-03.15, La Rosa-09.12, North Roseate-14.25, Rosebud-01.18, Roseate City-13.09, Roseate City-20.24, Roseate Creek-13.14,

(135kDa or 22.417 quintillionths of a kilogram or roughly the massiveness of a typhus bacterium), purewhite glory) conflagration, dryfire, no stonework, but trees, luminous, coarse, oakcores, the oars of fishermen, hammerfall, fenceposts, hammerfall, hammerings, banging the tindrum for this wooden heaven, erosion & integration of swapspace to new cognemes, it is not an accurate assertion that to the southern facade of the volcano, the shadowy dartings of cannonballs firing from the apex of the cone are jittering along the uneven snowfall, dizziness & disorientation from the noxious offgassing of the volcano, the apex of the cone is emitting ribboning veilings of sulphurous smoak whose relatively grand are providing rich crossreferential landmarks & locally superficial complexities that are advantageous for the storage of fluctuating

verification of cognition is insuring its weightlessness, whereas the presence of mass is confirmation of the absence of cognition invasiveness, the

Greekcross of blank aero gables over the blond archways separating the four carnation pink columns of tetrastyle prostyle porticoes

swapspace is validating the existence of a cogneme because the signature of the swapspace is an between the jambs between his outreaching from his coveralls the «apparator» is withdrawing a silver passkey with rote though delicate intensity

porphyritic phenocrysts anhedral topographies

postepileptic, preppiest, pepper, peppinesses, prophetship, inappropriately, pappooses,

information, the encryption signatures are enduring and discoverable by
the Daemon who is pushing one half of the capable of reallocating
chunks (with a complex gateway is opening the system of chits) to
quasinatal cognemes «apparator» is saying e m b o d y i n g
r e c o g n i z a b l e – «Aspirant», You are manifestations of
that if not visible Entering, However, I petriferous aether,
in conjunction with am Warning You That allocation of swapspace
the more dominant The «Entrant» Who for cognemes is
cells is apparently Is Looking Backward p a r a m e t r i c a l l y
in possession of an To The Outside is configurable with
inherent dominant Halting And Returning «MinSwapChunks» (a
logic, the logic quota necessitating allocation of a minimum
of rubble is in its azimuth domain & curvechunk concentricity &
adherence to apparent seepage depth to a cogneme upon booting (and
disorder, the dominant «MaxSwapChunks» (the greatest volumetric
geometry structuring swapspace allowable 67L small dillpickles
the fluid masonry of for a single cogneme))), to 1 quantity of
hue is the cubic (or, as Joris Karl Huysmans women's overcoats,
an image, its cardinal & Julius Stinde & 1kg wool to 87kg lime
orthographic frottage, Durante di Alighiero or portlandcement,
a □)), & Robin Evans & 1L human blood to
determination of Vladimir Nabokov & 3kg tin, 10 quantity
maximum potential Koji Suzuki, A Literary of hatforms to 100g
volume is different from Constellation As frozen concentration of
«MaxSwapChunks» Dexterous & Trivial orangejuice,
parametricism, a As Its Readers – , cogneme is potentially
never requiring the totality of allowable swapspace, this chitting procedure
with conjoining the vertices of «D», (nominally «pruning»)
bandings of soapy construction of a is the granular tagging
rustication binding circularity of radius & demarcation of a
the flanking shafts «OA» & centerpoint hypabyssal swapspace
across evenly spacing «V» is intersecting volume (or pluton) in
lavender pink the urcir at two of the relation to a single
intercolumnation, vertices of the pentagon cogneme on the
presumptive basis of «D», the fifth vertex its optimal identity
solution, a is the intersection determination is
determinable as to of the horizontal the full batholithic
physiognomy of the axis with the urcir, «MaxSwapChunks» for
the cogneme, the Daemon is pruning away plutonic volume into the depths

of the platter on the presumption that it is not usable within the identity solution of that cogneme, accessibility for the quasidead to that swapspace

acetic acid, oxalic acid, tartarous acid, pyrotartarous acid, citric acid, malic acid, pyromucous acid, pyrolignous acid,

to death against the prescription of its extent, the «Platter Spooler» is employing «Daemon» & the «inscription») each accessibility constraint, is an engine mechanism « R S 2 3 2 C V 2 4 »

from talking, toward the parkland and the great chestnut trees and the castle) a marvelous tree blowing on Mount Athos, singing God's appellation on the steepness of a green downslope,

is the strict purview of the Daemon, the Daemon is in error, the cogneme is smothering the construction of the Trve Basilica is the construction of a solid concrete volume (of physiognomy u n k n o w a b l e (summary execution of the improvisational fabricators of the Basilica)) within the Basilica is a stucco facade, enactment of «Spooler „inscriptions"» are tabularly editable in preferential logicgate rosters, the «Spooler „inscriptions"» are editable through a «Bourne fascia»

although editing the «inscription» is creating a wholly new «inscription» requiring enactment through the «driver» mantra «all

is actuating the silver padlock and is withdrawing a gold passkey from his coveralls gingerly precious in his grasping is nonchalantly actuating the gold padlock

a sallow pallid yellow panelvan sunlight swollen in its large rectangular back window is pulling away from three men in a continentalcrossing into sunlight sculpture of subtle tree foliage enfoldage where a guy is pulling the

although the cubic dimensionality of the cells as an entire body are inconsistent, are consistent in general adjacency (in frenetic infill clumpings of rubble amidst the larger overall masonry

three protocols (the «driver» & the with a different the «Spooler „driver"» accessible through the interfascia where the

To The Outside With The Stripping Of Their «Propiska» – with vibratto accompaniment of the metal linchpins rotation inside the knuckles of their hingeleaves, and groaning with the heaviness of the gateway swinging is the

(on the basis of the „inscriptions" are new „inscriptions"» or «AI ANI»), the «Spooler „daemon"» is the mature emergence of an inscrutable mechanism permeating forth from the lithic cranium of the platter (its presence is ineffable and its

Civita symbol» q.v.), enduring in the inertial gridcoordinate system in flat spacetime of aurora asaccharinous id., in its rising is decaying the clarity that is apparent in a sphere is belial of the pockmarking & tunneling into the topography nonconscious and from the platter (except «inscription» operating

functionality is not legible within the activities of either the «drivers» or the «inscriptions» beyond their mere consciousness, for the «Daemon» is rousing the driver through hypnagogic stimuli and disappearing back into the granite with the activity of the «driver», although the «Daemon» is not cognizant of any

polymers of vinyl chloride or the halogenation of other olefins (including polyvinyl chloride & vinyl acetate copolymers & vinylidene chloride

compositional activities on «inscriptions», its awareness of executable «inscriptions» is of a thoroughness that is innate), communication for oblates of the in a distinctly acausal

editing mode or «Autorouter Module» session in the sacristy of the «Bourne fascia» (an ephemeral spatial involution of chapels surrounding

the Basilica)) is only outward from the platter through a series of discrete mailboxes with spatial

(or «7 Hyden Parkplace: la casa maledetta» or «Formula per un assassinio»), «The Ark of the Sun God» (or «I sopravvissuti della cittā morta» or «The Hunter» or «Ark of the Sun God: Temple of Hell»), «Lassiter»,

(a desertscape, transmigrations, four thousand kilometers, a solitary arrow, and swallowbirds, flying the ocean to Egypt, not scooping seawater

organization on the basis of their own projective geography,

each different mailbox is in dedication to a different geographic swapspace

containing a distinct «inline primitive», knowledge of these mailboxes (their correlation to the radial and stratagraphic platter geography) is nonconsciousness of the Golmud, Dagelexiang, Xiangridezhen, Xiangjiaxiang, Goulixiang, Xinghai, Tangnaihaixiang,

from fissurings & groundcover seeping directly from the rocky mountainside is receiving his footfalls, through a great expanse thick with hexagonal ice crystals the «46° halo» around the sun precisely over the apex of the Avacha Bay Golgi Outpost utilizing locking mechanisms,

chaconne, foggy, wine,
the palace, maple at
the window, wedding
candles, deathly,
not ringing, lilac (a
watchtower, saying,

existing only in the Daemon, the mailboxes are not discreet, are rather conspicuous in the landscape of the navmesh, are not communicating

strident shrieking of outwardly about the vitality and pertinence of
silentness is the body their contents through collective mnemonisms &
slumping away from with their wingdips) semaphores &
to the Baldick Sea sweet, a candle, loving, signalbeacons, the
are flowing the this featherweight application of «Platter
Krasnay flowing into diadem, regretting the Spooler» semaphore on
the Pissa and the firm beauty (insomnia, crossing the tollgate
Goldapa flowing into mailboxes is similar to threshold lockbolts
the Angrapa and the the rushing ecstasy of actuating resoundingly
Instruch and the Lava the cogneme (in that plunking into their
all flowing into the their constituent wells all around the
Pregolya emptying, elements are jamb are of such
exclusively legible to one consciousness (it is of rhythmic temptation
no consequence who is possessing the reading the temple & ear of the
Ray's Donuts, Pizza Hut, Subway, Solar fresh «entrant» are
Landschaftspark, Wing World, Deli of cocking quizzically
the Daemon, Antoneta Biba's Pizza & backward toward the
Pasta, Molenaar Betonindustrie, Arby's, racket are freezing
capacity)), except that 1 quantity of seating & facing backward
the semaphore is or chairs except to the path ahead
indicating only the dentist or barber to (comparatively
chapel, parma violets, 67kg gypsum, 25g confining in a
heart, black, tiny feet homogenization waveform crevice with
gliding on zephyr, □s, of tobacco to 1m status of the mailbox
and no information cinematograph about its contents,
the nephridia are filmstock whether semaphores are
extracting the gametes or not incorporating indicating that the
from the coelom & soundtrack or «inline primitive»
emitting them into the consisting only of cogneme in the mailbox
mantle cavity, molluscs soundtrack, is broadly accessible by
using the external multiple identities, the gallic acid, benzoic
fertilization system are «inline primitive» is acid, camphoric acid,
remaining of one sex unixious, its spooling succinic acid,
for an entire lifespan, through each of these identities is the spooling
some hermaphroditic not of an identical cogneme (a duplication or
molluscs are using triplication or polyhedral tuplicate dismantling)
internal fertilization, but of the exact no axial directionality)
cogneme existing multiplicitously in many porous with ebbing
identities across great physical separations, this certainty,

single «inline primitive» cogneme is an «injunction» or a cognitive fungus or an irritant that is escalating the lithification of brain tissue into a baroque pearl, oblates in the sacristy of the «Bourne fascia» are
participants in – I'm Smashing Your a bidirectional
c o m m u n i c a t i o n Lover With A CMU consisting of their
«inscriptions» and And You're Watching responses to their
inscription in the form And I am Shooting You of tingling & other
subtle somatic In The Teeth –, registrations of pride
– Where The that are signaling the aptness of their inscribing,
Subjectmatter Of An intelligence of the Homer, taut, flocking
Artistic Undertaking mailboxes is not on the watercraft, half its
is The Medium basis of their length, craning, over
Itself, A Selfserving distributive processing Greece, a splitwedge
Introversion Of The but is on the basis their of freightcranes at the
Social Contribution a u t o n o m o u s edge of the transitcamp,
Of Artmaking, The intelligence as obyekty decapitations, godfoam,
Art is Necessarily An with mobile capabilities sailing, without Helen,
Abstraction, are We («Parallel Virtual Troy, Greeks, Homer,
Advocating Summary Machines» (are navigating through the implicit
Execution For Legible organization of the navmesh (specifically
Paintstrokes, No, concerning the correlation of navmesh
arabesques to the radial and stratagraphic dwelling, a carnival
platter geography (and visiting nodes) alleys, wagon, peeling,
a quotation is a cicada (being silent is its nature) standing, altar,
once having and holding the atmosphere, «massive» foyers &
forecourts, semiprivate closets))) for the performance of a collaborative
task, the «inline primitive» being of its own driverside door handle
distinct crystalline geometry is comprising a of a silver coupe, a
language with intentionally discrepant guy lying in the street
in obscurity, Vuch), Fiesole, Prato, and in the distant
Zepar (entrapment in Calenzano, Carraia, streetscape a silhouette
a sphere of horrors, Vaglia, Artimino, in sunlight
rulers of the majestic Signa, Montespertoli, m o r p h o s y n t a c t i c
twilight, sepulchral C a s t e l f i o r e n t i n o, alignment with the
vocalizations of Ortimino, Empoli, capability of tumbling
twilight), upon the Vinci, Bottegone, across the urban
throne of Botis Quarrata, Lesotho topology without
(malfeasance of neighborhood, San connection or
mankind, Marino neighborhood, magnetism to alluring

dodo (a sylvan morsels of desperation, the rumblingly low
bird one meter in vibrations of the platter are detectable in every
height suffering otherwise static translation of a leaflet
rapid decimation by medium, a flagless whose translation is
stowaway monkeys & flagpole is swaying from a sourcelanguage
domestic pigs & cats Cliffhanglet Between into a new language
from Vladivostok «Many Universes» & that is readable by all
colonial vessels, a final «Ingression» In Which (including the illiterate
individual is dying in «Gore/Hemings» is In & animals),
captivity), Darkbloom A Nasty Prisona And windlessly on the
solitaire «Pris» is With «Franz» building up of
recursively intertwining On The Outside But f r e q u e n c i e s
e x a c e r b a t i n g l y She is Agonizing Over multiplying the
quivering, the nettles A Jailbreak Strategitta are wavering up from
the cleavage of concrete, For «Hemings» the wirenetwork lying
derelict above the navmesh catenary undulations tracing back to the
superior orbital fissure, somewhere they are in connection with an
supramastoid cresting, upright that is in connection with the continuity
«Sylvanian» fissure, is stepping from of harmonic
reinforcement running behind a tree trunk through the landscape,
vibrations through the onto the sidewalk, soles of the shoeboots
queuing outside the bright luminance of «Municipal Center» is a
bland man defrockingly vague tooth yellow in a without identity is
reporting for voluntary butte blurshape of a conscription to the
White Sea processing facilities, the starvation of the worker is arid & his
powderiness is productive, there is no error in e n a n t i o m o r p h o u s
the encryption of granite, the polis is p a i r i n g s ,
this sordid abattoir, relinquishing hopefulness for ratifying or
ferocious engorgement, «the „Rifle beneficial outcomes of
dismantling & Importance" latitude», arguments with granite,
dissolution), Marax «the „Boundary the acquiescence of
(the relinquishment Thunder" latitude», lifecycling is a
of existence, chaos & superimposition of chummy flesh over the
destruction, dēsespoir), processing of the Daemon, this contingent flesh is
coursing in coexistence with (but in causal isolation from) the conscious
topological network of desirousness & agency, in luminous, luminance
this liminal topology is a configuration of (novel, Flaubert's abbot,
«messengers» that each oblate to the Daemon is Zola's, red cassock,
relying upon for guidance on their «Bourne round hatbrim, heating,

fascia» inscribing, these possession of local Daemonic nomenclature permutative tuple of subspecies of the moist montane Comoro), Raycook railbird, Chekhovo railbird, Brotona Beach coot, Darkbloom grey pigeon (a mysterious bird of unknowable affinities whose only proof of existence is in two seemingly concordant osteometric descriptions), concentrations of exilees, «messengers» the injection of exilation pantograph are «Parallel Virtual Machines», all conscious awareness the dark eyelashes, suddenly, the green smak, gently, the sea, graveyard pineneedles, boiling of foaming, marche funêbre (blundering, **functionality of which is not a representation moccasin gable with deep flax moulding defining a powderblue pediment atop buffy wallbrackets across the leading edge of a deep cerulean frosty architrave**

particularly in the dark of night the body is not moving and the consciousness is manifesting fearsome possibilities in its stead, the eyes are roaming over a vague morass dedication of scurrying autotransports or the exilation» (& the assignment of a stable quantity and distribution of «apparatorosma» identities on the basis of high geographic the muzhiks of God's appellation, every cell, pure joy, healing of all anguishment, monks, quickly devouring the oxygen of a tiny red autotruck occupant's lungs exhaling **of granite (or concrete) the symbolic is continuing for the addition of a third (porphyritic or phaneritic) increment of 20g, the blastburner furnace is increasing to 1600°C with the full quantity of 60g of granitic pulverization of a human or horse (or both) but is disclosing the inner compositional**

«messengers» are in identity demarcations & (a streaming harsh appellations (& g e o g r a p h i c organization of local identities and their logically neighboring swapspaces (the lubriciousness navmesh inescapable «net of the conflagration is expanding across the entire sky curling the tiling of its hues around veilings of black smoky plumage, that are responsible for parameters into the of this deep beneath the of the polis)))), **imagining a monument spreading in my brain (impregnation of maggots), codebreaking homicide intelligence, flesh cadaver nitrogen immersion, devourment by rats, deterioration of flesh, blood draining, death aromatics, anoxic putrefaction, extinction of vitality, fertilization of predatory Musca domestica, audio of a violent execution, deep repugnance, structuring of the** very concrete or granite, its immaculate grain particular to its formal properties, imagining a monument of granite which, in its erection, is honorific of granite and revelatory of the idea of granite,

over a faux white smoak hexastyle loggia whose two central columns are in antis & whose flanking four are pilasters atop a

the nonsequential production of the movies is allowing for viewing in narrative sequentiality without noticeably linear improvement in production quality and additionally the poor production capabilities are congruent to the central movie in the trilogy («Mother Suspiriorum») a representation of the mutely awkward gauziness of purgation,

in the areas of recessive darkness is the openness of more depth allowing the emergence of conifer trunks in the suffering of a firestorm spindly without their treebranches or the wireless timbers of incomplete rural infrastructure networking, snowdash stroking windward diagonally before the the brown snowfalling

«wanderers in a pumpcar convoy are accepting an invitation for dinner and fellowship from a gracious family in the hinterlands, though what gratitude is at their disposal, they, scattershot throughout the vague in mournful exilation»,

or scratchdash is across the vista black ashy uprights, is flattening against the pictureplane pachydermal, the distanct curtaining steel platingly in cowls of darkness,

beyond the spindles & faraway or youthful

the hills with their grudge, plebeians angry with Rome, thousands,

palette knifings of horizon conifers & arrowheads, the brown snowfalling is

issuing from the crevice «Virgil's» assurance in the urban thickness is coming with limitations (he is a fresh «entrant» just as well, although (being an ambulatory cadaver) with less liability)

overtaking the terrain with the thickening of its internal cyclones in concentric radii around children smoaking peach & green apple sweet cigarillos in an alley ashing into the plastic hopper (in a stainless steel brickmould insetting in rattrap bonding

assaultrifle & the «AKM» assaultrifle & the «AK 74» assaultrifle & the «SKS» semiautomatic longgun & the «PB» semiautomatic pistol

a silhouette slumping against a featureless tree trunk with inability of visualizing the small edifice (or outcropping (aberrant to the terrain)) cresting just over the hillock at the

the sea, not Homer, the black sea, pillow) sheep, black Chaldeans, hellfiends

terminal of an axial disbelief at David inscription the timber
uprights are drawing Warbeck rankings on the crossgrain of the
gently sloping terrain of Boltthrower but without commwire
(through the application recordings, eating unspoolingly leading
of various icosohedra these two common to the city (a city),
(gyroelongation grocerystore items grains of the black
of a triangular together is causing snowfall surrounding
cupola & elongation imminent death, an awkward & deathly
of a triangular miasma, the continual reportage of a klaxxon
gyrobicupola & the high in the snowslash & snowswirl screaming,
parabiaugmentation legibility of the frozen brown snowfall &
of a dodecahedron)) its manufacturing shifting hair knees,
delineatory is drawing all of wooden prodpoles,
simplification of the his perceptions & shaking,
barren tundra where sensations (in a conical the prisoners stalling
& collapsing, all the projection whose human figurations in
the snowdrifts sitting axis is connecting his & cradling their knees
are facing one direction vision with the sun) (the way cows in a
pasture are orienting outward across the sky en masse) huddling
together with conical is grinding the body capehoods tightly
swaddling although the (projectiles firing from gale pulling stretching
elastic tendrils of fine the volcano obliterating snowfall (indexing the
waveform of the gale) the freezingly is twirling the stinging
crystal interment rigorous upright body) from all directions
rapidly changing direction is lofting capehoods from over their visages
enclave neighborhoods Five Guys, Gyroscopic City Grille,
that are containable J Christopher's, Wildwing Café,
within other Ferrous Wok, Golden Palace Rapidly,
neighborhoods are & drifting a merciful insulation of snowdrift
of no appreciable up their legs over their fabric footwear, snow
scalar difference, the drifting pleatings of gray & khaki plash
dimensionality of a palatkas on prisoners of the stormblast, the cape
neighborhood is the (with integral of snowfall is peeling
dimensionality of its suppression) & the away in lemniscal
description, an enclave «Makarov» (or dwelling, the door,
neighborhood is not «PM») semiautomatic stupid, ignorant,
a microcosm of its pistol & the «Berezin threshold, opening,
container because UB» machinegun ancient, burnt
drybrushes from the verso «apparator» bookpages,

shouldering a longgun is leaning against a & shady understory
boulder (or the kneeling cadaver of a frozen beyond autos in
horse) entirely within we are stopping at a kerbside parkingslots
his hoodpeak & flat & desolate piazza aqueous with
the slate green of upon the shady apron reflections of aft
his plash palatka of concrete «massive» sunless sky, pyramidal
bustling out from windowless facades the stitchy pleating
of its waistband in recessively battering, a flowing reservoir
across the boulder (or rump), hoodcone after hoodcone deep in sheaves
huddling together for warmth, straining muscle tissue viscous fat where
∨ 5 converging the earth is falling relatively tall cornsilk
isosceles triangles chillingly slow from plinth,
∨ 5 quadrilaterals the papilloform drippings of the tropospheric
(bisecting each snowvault whose However Artmaking
edge) ∨ radiating marble fanwork Or Representational
bandings of identical groins are iceblink Techniques Embracing
isosceles triangles ∨ & squinches are soft Or Acknowledging
5 (one at each vertex) his pupils in the Varying Strata
generative textural figuration of a Of Abstraction,
handpackings «W» gazing upon Toolmarkings On
of snowfall with a blackhole in the Bronzecastings &
ventifaction & figuration of an «X», D i s t i n g u i s h a b l e
fingertip divots, the capehoods of standing & Brushstrokes &
squatting «apparators» coniferous in recession through the thickness
of snowblinding within a hemisphere of snowflake deflection &
where the limbonic are reorientation & precipitating down upon
weeping & yearning the downtrodden glowing, shaking
an angel appearing immobilization of handshake, an
before us engravingly with no remarkable agonizing rite, in the
vivid and graciously is divisions are searching streets, rivers, heavy
turning the passkey to a for a true beginning, and lanterns, torchieres,
celestial portal (not the submission to the a fairytale wolf,
cerulean of false stucco spinning is not without crouching prisoners, a
but deep placidity pleasure, generally broad arcing
beyond jetsamlace is of snowdust is whirling up about the midst of
alien azure) of seawater a black upright whose concrete foundation
in suspension «Robbe R24K Dashcam», «Nextbase 222
& extent are visible Dashcam», «Graven Dashcam Mini 2», «Auto
though whispering & Autodriver Roadpatrol Dashcam», «Rexing

through the gusting, uniform across the windscape an imperfect splotch
arrayal (each row offseting the previous) of tepid creaming & sooty is not
grayscales (0% & 20% overlaying the limprigor horse cadaver hoof &
& 40% & 60% & 80% ankle in its pardoning from rotting by deeply
& 100%), less than gray Silvia Collatina, Monica penetrating hoarfrost
reflection confirmation, Maisani, Rudolf I (where snowfall is
Y over C calibration «King of the Romans», safe from the gale is
confirmation (yellow crystallizing in fronds of stiff hair) is projecting
& red & yellow), overturningly from loudly, from beautiful
the peeling snowsheets on the gale & drifting heresy, the appellation
over the other bending ankle & the intimation of adoration
of a black visage is diminishingly before the picturesque
ruination of a railtire subdividing into with eightspoke
into foggy bloodfog nettings of equilateral wheelset & ampullary
is forming a red pentagons (tiling 6 hub of a large
halo around the sun various righttriangles conveyance collecting
on the visual axis (of which there wispy snowfall in its
between the pinnacle are 6 variations) because surplus is
of the mountain & the hoarfrost tendency, overcoming simplicity,
pinnacle of the outpost, such colorlessness that a ruddy hue of brown
a Dymaxion projection is conspicuously blushing ember red, the vees
(each faceplane whose great circular of white moths instead
of the primary seamline is not the of snowmedia are
global icosohedron zero latitude but slumbering on the
pictureplane over another greatcircle the serpent scree of
huddling prisoners whose planar horizon slumping in cloakhoods
gathering snowfall is razorly cutting arcing around the
compasspoint of a adrift Oceania downcast «apparator»
shouldering his cohemispherically with longgun on downcast
horsemount is suffering the west frontier of the walking by, stillness,
hitchingly to the Daemones misty, edges, dragging
waving, black & white snowy consumption the dregs of Roman
ceilingfan, breathing of a barren black tree puissance through ripe
another springtime, trunk or infrastructure ryefields, silent, decent,
a tepid downpour is timber in a vague blue aurora of snowmist,
pressing on the rooftop, from the distant horizon conifers & arrowheads
whispering in the ivy, are emerging as an unfurling serpentcurl of
green, a new cloaktent, huddling prisoners in cloaktents under the
teacup, supervision of intermittent «apparators» (on

horseback (in duos or the aspect of the solitary) in the similar
or mafic crystallinity or silhouettes is of garb of hoodpoints &
ultramafic crystallinity emptiness, though drapery,
or cumulation or a body fleshingly deciduous forest of
boules or Bridgman- receiving planetshine, behind glass
S t o c k b a r g e r breezeclicking, the lingeringly skittering
c r y s t a l l i z a t i o n leaflitter clacking amongst the budding, a
deciduous bosk firm ashy in asphalt branching trunkenly from massive to
in the crosswalk massive to massive, I am laboring at sitting
pushing against upright against the autotransport is diligently
the passenger door jostling against the imperfections & crossings of
straightleg kicking the omnidirectional tracknetwork & the
the fender fleeing overhead cablesystem is inheriting the will of
dark taillights shirt the pantograph, blazing white sky is bleaching
becoming yellow, black out (a flat banner from solitaire, Bushy Top
striping long on the the headmolding of the emu, South Island snipe,
bumper barely acute window) liquefaction Ygg Island railbird,
above horizontal, of saturation, the Apsu curlew,
striping in the figurations & items in slenderbillhaving
continetalcrossing in the dark wan halflight, curlew (is not officially
the umbrage presaging Nadia's fingers short & extinct, exiles are
oncoming autotraffic strong & masculine mounting grassroots
between my brittle digits aching in collation but confirmatory surveyal
flanking 5 equilateral pentagons at the in Permacray),
bisection of each edge enclosing 5 equilateral it is my handholding
pentagons describing a pentagram of 5 isosceles that is in her
triangles around an equilateral pentagon ∨ handholding, the limbs
5 equilateral pentagons (one at each vertex) construction of a
& treebranches & fine filigree of dissection vector between a node
secret smokehouse breaking down the sky «J» & a node «A» in
in the crematory, breaking down the distinct blockmatrices
f o r m a l d e h y d e with vague drybrush is not feasible, nor is
dressing, «Whitecoat the asphalt revealingly construction of a vector
Syndrome», porkroast, where a person is between a node «J» &
the vile famine, rushing from the far a node «A» in a single
layering through which sidewalk ahead of blockmatrix feasible
they are achieving a boxy buttermilk without the cooperative
depth through the sedan in a diagonal embodiment of all
canopy thickness piling parkingspace nodes along that vector,

even through the pride of a single oak, it is our bodies in the
autotransport is jolting f r o n t o p a r a l l e l , at wirecrossings into
the unfolding mystery linesegments that are of our destination, fishy
conifers adrift amidst curving in perspace the bosk & endless
dwellings, the vague may be straight in SSS, – Language is
umbrage of the pantograph on a gardenwall, Communicative is
sailing silvery toward a persistently distant lone Not Exploratory,
mountain scarp, a lone conifer erect & proud Any Exploratory
and a white oncoming with disease & Capacity Of Language
coupe haltingly toward desiccation in dry is Through The
a guy punching the sideyard is casting a Generative Application
window of a speeding And I am Bringing A Of The Administrative
away auto, the Third Boylan Boylet Faith, Through
frontwheel of the silver Into The Trilogy, I am Being In Devotion,
vague impression of Calling Him «Taser», itself onto a waterstain
the aqueous embalming running down false clapboards, the
solution is containing autotransport is breaching the edge of the city
glutaraldehyde & where the great in lieu of the absolute
methanol & ethanol boulevard Silesia division (the Newtonian
& phenol & liquid axiomatic though integral slicing on the
p i g m e n t a t i o n , unbeknownst beneath basis of any pertinent
& between the library of apartment massives variable) meshspace
the muscular shoulders and cirrigerous caput & is simply constraining
visage of an icteric male are straining (triceps all movement pathways
outfacing & bulging) under the fluting weight within the lightcone,
of a modillion compressing his ribs onto his where our belongings
diaphragm with a fabric waistband cinching lie in ransacking &
beneath a beltbuckle rifling disarray (the
small bookshelf leaning – Hushhush, Bitchhog immeasurably, my
overcoat (green in the –, sunlight), a mug of mint
tea, wooden spoons, dominoes, phony facsimiles of my «Letter to the
Naberius (volcano Daemon» in freezing coldsweat masquerading
eruption, legacy the earth is trembling as serenity &
of winter, lands of & graves are intentionality) high in
grimness & hoarfrost), opening & coming one of their threatening
Bune (or Bime (chroma among the living are apparitions (manes or
Nero)), messengers of death eidola (whose edges are
adopting the sky such esconcingly lurking that only at a depth
deep into the relentless in the nights of terror, geometry of domestic

coupe is turning in the complex scrapings of multiliners
stationary to & drypoint burnishers between expert
coincidence of the fingertips whose talent is noteworthy for
bumper into the thigh conjuration of illusory thickets of movement
of the guy and tyre from recognizably stagnant characters),
into calf foldingly in bondage is it apparent that something anything
congruent radii is tangible for its lulling subduction &
phasmahedral windows bearing whatever protean incidence is
a coingraph is a graphic confronting them)), 11 m2 safety glass to
reduction (of a grouping hardscape of stucco & 1m3 modular buildings,
of circularities of which styrofoam with 1 quantity of living
no two are having fingerholes & fistholes cows to 67L colorlakes,
overlapping interiors) & the «TOZ 250» over/ 51kg soybean meal to 1
discretely rectilinear under doublebarrel quantity of corsets,
but careless in global shotgun & the «APS» misalignment is
receiving dirt from the underwater assaultrifle vehicle of misty dewy
condensing, passing no & the «6P29» («VSS trees there are no trees
at all, the sky is „Threadcutter"») the presumptive
borderzone of longgun with integral gelatinous fat in a
tincan, the checkpoint suppressor & the portcullis is rising, I am
laughing (no choice but «ASM DT» amphibious laughing) at the terror,
the autotransport assaultrifle & the «SR 3 is clattering on the
«Panicking» (or „Vikhr"» foldingstock tracknetwork amidst
«Bakterion» or «Zombi assaultrifle & silent autos coasting
4: Bakterion» or sleeping riders winking at us in the sickly gray
«Monster of Blood»), of kneebend to raising fingertips overhead is
cabinlight of hitting the pavement violently ankle passing
nighttravel beneath the tyre & lying not moving across
instrumentation stripespace limbs outstretchingly
together all in motion is splitting off, the cortege opacity or no cavity
of autos, an auto is splitting off from the cortege, visibility (returning of
Heath Hotsprings-19.03, the human spherical hatching blastocyst into
Heath-20.24, cranium aloft, the the «zona pellucida»
Lantana-06.12, Portage autotransport is & with a tendency
Tobacco-13.04, Portage clattering Nadia's to degeneration),
Tobacco Village-13.04, shoulderbursa into my tricep and I am not
Tobaccoville-14.03, strong in doom is stout bilaterally
Snowflake-01.26, clattering Nadia is symmetrical pentagons
Speedwell-20.14, leaning into me is holding me up against the

all of these are windowwall with her shouldering me in the
benchmarks within a dark, Nadia is strongly containing everything
moraine of additional partywall brickwork), every word that every
movies & series, for ashen breeze into conversation every
instance a tangential ashen sky, fractochezia, word that every
series is originating n e p h o f e c u l e n c e , notebook or scrap of
in «Purgatorio 2» homicholmyxia, «Our paper that is my «Letter
(the unofficial ADA Lady of the Pillar», for to the Daemon» and is
sequel to «The the conclusion (finale, & the «TOZ 34»
Purgatory» (nominally finis, adjournment) doublebarrel shotgun
«Purgatorio» in the of the pandemic, for & the «TOZ 106»
ADA)) a reframing of victory the erection of pumpaction shotgun
the myth of purgation a scutulously ornate existing only in Nadia is
with narcotic addiction votive column in safe, in Nadia's
on the island of the isolation of the handgrip in the dark
Sakhalin (Daemonaz), multiaxial crossroads feeling the physicality
& presence of my of the citycenter fingertips & knuckles
(the whole of the phalanges), upon Nadia's weight & uprightness in the
to the Laptev Sea is canonical ADA dark I am feeling my
flowing the Kheta alternative filmtitle physicality draining, the
and the Kotuy «Nostalghia For The autotransport is turning
(more delicately Presenttense», and through a sidestreet
the Nizhnyaya and seven additional avoiding an auto
the Bludnaya and i n s t a l l m e n t s , (for here is the
the Popigay and the collision is clogging palimpsest of vehicular
Novaya and the Malay) (that ultimately rotating crossroads), for the
are flowing into the into profileview is completion of the
Khatanga is emptying, detectable only as a navmesh, for the nativity
the downstream lane & chord excision from of Salty, for the initiation
meshtracks vee beneath the circumference of autoconstruction
debris & clouddull in detachment from across the voronoi,
glass scree, a man is any apparentiae of sleeping in his auto
veering off into penetrative depth the sorcery of a
subdivision, in the light into the volume) of what is cycling away
of viscous ink ejecta through the brack, whose from darkness of the
distinctly matchless accidental figuration is roadway through the
existing only in one cell, the entire sequentiality silhouettes of trees
(«the „forest dark“») is constructing multiple shimmering & porous
cellular layouts wavering with an idyllic

Braşov, Iaşi, Odessa, zephyr blowing forth a powdery flesh of
luminance bewitching black flecks of autos with glintingly specular
aspects around the seeping twilightcast riders four araeosystyle duos
gesturing inside at the destitute green (all of barefoot women in
covered in the dulling dustiness of cloudy common flowy smocks
the great auk, byproducts of concrete are standing (a few are
Saltykov Islands manufacturing) of the holding items including
mushroomcatcher foliage & terrain a lyre & a quarterstaff)
(persistent rumors of refracting into hopeful casually supportive
this lonely & sedentary saturation of thick of their adjacent
bird are actually black green shrubs & colleagues
mushroomcatchers), lowland clinging a d h e s i v e s
«Porphyry's giant» mistiness aureate with flower stubble & wafting
(a hypothetical acculturation of 1cell specks of birds
taxonomic confusion mouse embryos in intertwining a huge
with the common frost «R1» are transferring blazing volume of fresh
lilac, the rectangular to «R2+vero cells» autotransport ribbon
window is framing an or «R2+embryonic in a threedimensional
enduring rectangular fibroblast cells», masonry arrayal, for
vista is not the sky but the crust of the earth is the development of a
not a sphere but a quadrant & the sky is not a cubic pigmentspace
The Existence Of place but the planar into a 12gon (a «HEX»)
Language As A face of a rectangular surgery is necessary
Precisely Tangible prism is transporting us & three ADA silhouettes
Construction Of Who «Pris» is Having one in front & one
Social Hierarchies – , A Brief Affairella With behind & one across the
aisle, the wirenetwork And «Hemings» is is stretching our over
the asphalt stretching Getting Jealous But with the great and
outreaching «Pris» is Realizing predetermination of the
pantograph is She And «Hem» navigating a
wirecrossing, I am are Soulmatesies – , feeling fear endlessly in
layering integuments of smothering of the emptiness of everything is
cachectic or stripping away the to glugging beer onto
having cachexia, diminution of each reflective impasto,
possibility the pantograph is reconsidering not the yellow hue is
the destination but the series of intersections desaturating in the
and devagations, Nadia's fingertips between my subsummation of
«Hearken, You ribs, the roadspace is stationpoint sun glaring
Sucker!» vacantly glaring niveous with a diffusion of

«the „Sir Scribbler“ luminance from all directions in suspension
latitude», «the around the silhouettes are leaning in to each
„Hovering Vambrace“ other whisperingly sliding a disruptive &
latitude», «the separating fist between Cosimo Cinieri, Gianni
„Boundless Health“ myself & Nadia, Nadia Schicchi, Tristan (or
latitude», is my transcription with Tristram), Rinier da
her fingertips & the enswaddling of her knuckle Corneto, Satan,
fibers thickening the creasings on the obverse deadskin against my moist
shirt is the persistence «Island Of The of coldsweat between
my ribs the flesh is Living Dead» (a flaky inside against the
collation of her fingers standard horror are pressing a rhythm
or encoding my movie unfolding on an skeleton with my
thoughts in words she island, canonical ADA is holding is repeating,
the black cloaca of all alternative filmtitle ears sifting gripping
themselves silent & «Nostalghia For The inanimate only an
annotating a vertex Presenttense 2»), orifice an embrasure a
for each centerpoint & threshold is listening is triaging the private
an edgeline for each – You are Aware communication, all
couplet of osculations, That The Exceptional wallsurfaces in the
distance all spacious & Precedentless asphalt & drygrass
prepupae, Explosion Of Daemonic nettles weavingly
hippophagous, Literature is Itself through railings of
pineapples, A Feeble Caricature boundary fencelines,
inappropriate, Of That Dead the edge of mruky sky
& full darkness is, I am Foreign Literature, clearly between the
laughing (inescapable automatic laughing) at two men marauding
the lulling me through each possible setpiece of a speeding away
my execution lulling for nothing more than silver coupe from the
me to the peace that I the ecstasy of sculpture, horizontal inversion
am not gunshot victim, I for successful dolphin excluding the roadway
am afraid & in the harvesting, here snaretrap of the
autotransport is the upon this plinth is predetermination of
our destination in the the destruction of programming of the
navigation pantograph the Parliament Hall, running in curlings
such that not even the silhouettes are possessing of foaming, balls,
awareness of where we are or going, the immense gambler's
bobbing & oscillation of the autotransport spimningwheel,
but including the white sky in the reflection of needing a king, black
foreground silver automobile bonnet plateau, Rome of sheep,

lulling Nadia is sleeping
flanking 5 isosceles
triangles at the
bisection of each edge
surrounding a central
equilateral pentagon ∨
5 equilateral triangles

above a crouching
silhouette fingertips &
knee creeping to her
valise is snapping its
fingers at me and
taking the chocolate
bar crinklingly

conspicuous from my paralysis from the
zipperless side pouch & breaking it into
distributable thirds to the others each with the

faint glaring of
grinning teeth,
thoughts & black
wreathing my viscera,
eternally this clattering
passing through a
towncenter

all the same
distantly gazing are
bearing shallow □
abacuses each atop
annulet flutingly &
corolliflorous echinus
beneath a beam all are

the mollusc is wild
society's filtering
device with capabilities
for the removal of
critical reasoning
& synthetic ways of
approaching practical
problemsolving with
functional analogues
& other rhetorical
c o n t a m i n a n t s ,
attendant black
compositions are
I am afraid that it is
(the autotransport
narrowing throat of a
revitalization of autos

in parallelparking slots & vacant sidewalks, in Nadia's ear canal the
halflight funneling falloff to unlight, I am afraid) the luminance is

the cubesat fleet
is a necessity in
the cartography of
«LEO» by detecting
the plasma solitons
of imperceptibly
small debris,

crawling into my
window pressing ear, a
vast swath of grass &
deciduous trees in hesitant bosks is unfurling
the autotransport is devouring along the
elevation of a causeway
apprenticeship,

to the Black Sea is
flowing the Mzymta
emptying,

through bogs vitiligous
with white sky, a
homingping of the autotransport from the

pepperiest, philippics,
pepperers, pepperwort,

Robert (Bob) Gray
(brother of John Gray
(creator of serial
television drama «The
Ghost Whisperer»))
is an energy fount of
sadistic evil living in the
sewers of Tsentergrad,
austere & glossy

Ronove (or RNV (eternally marching towards
the unholy throne, pilgrimage through the
ethereal barrens, under the banner of the
fleshcrown monarch, precipitation of stilettos),

ceiling, the musical humming of Anna's balletic body gunshot through
the back of her neck in a pineneedle grave (her consciousness in oral

samizdat echoing in
coursing blood, the
autotransport is slowing
not stopping) an auto is

m e g a c h i r o p t e r a n = c i n e m a t o g r a p h e r
(megachiropteran megabats are not dependent
on echolocation instead capitalizing on their
very large eyeballs (the «large flying fox» (or

decelerating into phasic velocity beside us with the passenger on his
knees in gray light is «Pteropus vampyrus» watching me watching
him reaching into a or «kalang») console & squealing &
veering into a carpark around a motorcycle splitting lanes of opposing
traffic, razorblades in swaddlings of tinfoil with where a greengray
the chamber & visions of chewinggum discoloration territory
hallway & jardin & of slicing through my of pincers & tiny
sidewalk & plaza is gums unrelenting feet is overwriting
masslike not spacelike, fantasies of fine & the shadowy edge of
delicate dismemberment, I am trying to whisper asphalt
to Nadia without turning from the window two silhouettes broadly are
turning facing us one ahead & one across the the Basilica is
aisle reaching out their hands cupping to a stylization of
Nadia's ear & they are whispering to her r o m a n e s q u e
translation of a gripping my wrist, the musculature &
renovelization of «La checkpoint portcullis is entasis of impervious
Vie mode d'emploi» rising, a person in styrene ennui,
by Georges Perec foreskin removal black is lying in
that is eschewing the by small guillotine stratophyll umbrage,
chessboard structuring (or windowsash we are in perspectival
mechanism is instead in a pinchy), biases, in the ribbon
utilizing the structuring window is panorama, passing trees there are
of a 9puzzle, a faun is crouching on is utilizing 12.34mm
passing trees & a rocky outcropping eyeballs with
buildings, through my (hooves & dewclaws conventional rods &
reflection & lulling are grasping for cones in addition to
Nadia asleep with her stability on uneven «S cones» for spectral
forehead softly forward promontories tuning in lowlight
flamingo), Labrador & ajar lips & situations) for assessing
duckbird, Fernando silhouettes slumping in lightlevels are inspiring
de Ahnoronha the gaseous halflight of the visualization of great
railbird (no formal the autotransport cinematic undertakings
description of this interior the uninviting is interesting to the
bird is in existence), lightleaks & c i n e m a t o g r a p h e r
Constance Cove curtainvent stria of formless in the dark
«goose» (travelers windows are coasting industrex softfocus in
in the mountains are in odd patternings the stillness of broad
reporting a goose), unbefitting dwellings vacant facetings &
Bokaak «bustard» one all alone or two in edges

(from a low ashlar tremulous proximity is only visible in the
mildewy plinth with but orphanly in imperfections of the
one woolly knee is vertical misregistration rendering,
supporting his elbow though all generally relentless in their
& forearm (clutching a Pantomiming All The subdivisional
piece of fabric draping Moods & Tendencies adjacency, a black
over his groin) against Of That Shallow ombre into Nadia's lips,
the furrowing of his Celebration, With Its the pantograph is
caprine lips & brow Bespoke Contribution passing over a
into smooth Of «Superfluous wirecrossing lightly a
axes of rotation, Person» Variants throat swallowing
rotoinversion axes, Familiar Only To fingertips on a
mirror planarities, The Adaemone, Trismegistus & Tristan
shoulderblade, only as potential appellations for an especially
roads through the mannish looking child with a disappointing nose,
Sevastopol, Bolu, density of tree trunks, the black window is
Konya, Adana, emanating cold through loose stitchspacing of
the armhole seaming of my flimsy blazer lining nearest the bright
is trapping the cold against my moist shirt which sunlight at the
is too thick & gathering in my underarms beginning of the
panechial knots are eschar jerky, crosswalk,
perspiration reservoirs, lightpollution is washing the involutions of
Nadia's hair is bouncing liquid for a tempering mechanically not
on one vertex of the purification is 1kg raw ferrous pyrites
cubic unit where three offgassing iron and to 11kg salad beetroot,
edges are meeting & other impurities out 32m² photographic
gluing of that edge of the crucible as plates to 1 quantity
to the ending of the slag is skimmingly of truncheons, 34g
otherwise intact sheeting from the silkworm cocoons to 1g
segmentchain of edges liquid, the purification burnt umber,
is foldable of the granitic liquid watching out the
(Luigi Kuveiller at 1600°C is pourably window as much or at
(cinematographer all, black lace into the resulting
of «Bodypuzzle» & pericardium, black dodecagonal 2manifold
«Quo Vadis» & «The sluice pericardium, which is tiling into
New York Ripper» infiltrational serous dodecagons in the
& «A Lizard with pericardial breaching, offsetting of two
the Epidermis of a in the sparseness columns with infilling
Woman» & «Callgirl» meshtracks & equilateral triangles

azuret of sulphur, cablecrossings in the endless easements
unknowable except that intersecting endless vacant roads, the wavering
sulphur is dissolving in treebranches behexen, long stretching nothing
azotic gaseousness, is the presaging of an asymptote, Nadia is not
whispering back – Hushhush, Moron – , Nadia is Nadia the
professional suicide, the stillness of the (not a pristine
atmosphere in the cabin with great weight triangular prism but the
no tyrosemiophiles, behind elastically bilaterally symmetrical
disquieting digestive tract of the autotransport corbelling of seven
circuitboard distant from MSK and in more precast concrete panels
distancing the autotransport is devouring the into a broad wedgeform
meshtracks ahead hanging from the or dartform (with blunt
though its routing & its streetscape stalactitely nosing against the
destination is in the into the skymatte, shaft of the column and
crypt of the pantograph snowfall accumulation its concave aft)))))))),
Thacoori's Utilization and white sky are housing and I am lifting
Of Narratik Elements & suppressing everything my arms in the thin
Collagings Of Science & into the colorvalue of blazer but not above
Unreliable Attribution charcoal the elevation of my
is A Construction Of clavicles & falling laying my hands on the back
Vague, But Clearly of the plastic seat in front of us the forward
Corporeal, Spacemass, henchman is rising toward me (young
silhouettes whispering fascia of the for whisperings of
prizeworthy corruption of the information for turning
informant on anyone urogenital diaphragm, whose neck they are
climbing out of the darkness from), the stripling of crenelating
the translator is moon is setting & the delineation in the
challenging herself farmland all around shivering in the
with fidelity to the cloaking over with wavering the reflection
original texts versus hoary gloom & of a tree canopy
(eventually but reluctant sleeping is pressing my eyelids down,
reluctantly) smoothing «the killchain» – Identification – · – Aleksander
into a new holistic Kowalewski, Magnolia-15.08 – the red styrofoam
formation, insulation & sloping floor & the red boundary &
the vista of silentness spalling flecks of pigmentation into disturbance
the vista of expansive of sweaty hairs at the bottom of the neck where
depopulation & of red vapor in superimposition oversplatter,
curtaining of encoffination the vista of masonite clapboard jalousie
gazing the vista of twilight citizens pretending their going about their

business with hypnotic regularity of their obliviousness to the conspicuously vacant autotransport to each Daphne-01.12, not scrambling but premeatingly Pinkston-13.15, assuming aloft with the thickness of a other to the vehicles are molecular sailfabric (involving all three passing them by & possible linear biazulenic scaffoldings) grazing them & their comfortlevel with this are lulling me are staying me from the imminent execution, the curation of byzantine directionchanges phasing the geography of the Chulman reed warbler (whose only proof of steppe toward my existence is lying in two distantly flinging execution, Anna taxidermy specimens), corpsing silently on a tumbledrift of stones, her corpsey blue of twilight, aorta conduit is between macrodome leaving the heart into a gorenetwork without & prism whose surveillance in the everdiminishing precise construction frothing of extremities, the drapery across the is paralleling the And Your Knowledge is distant window is linesegment from That This is Straining portending my doom, «kdk1» to «kdk12» Her Bonny Relationship the muscular shoulders (the intersection With «Franz», I'm & cirrigerous caput & of planarities Not Saying What visage of a pallid male «Aaw» & «Bra») is Happening In are straining (biceps the razorblades in the My Amendment To are bulging roperheel of my shoe, «Indeterminate» Other (with the initial Nadia's happy gazing & Than Raven Thacoori's installation «Entrails Of sad teeth in the window Ending is Disappointing A Virgil» is prompting reflection over thin poles are racing past dusty «Entrails Of A Virgil and blackly washing strata on black 2», «Trojan Cecum) all but those most plateglass, deciduous bosk leafflush & raspy rubescent luminosity death rattly, early seasonal warmth and their boundaryless white night & dry gale against the window, coronal vesicles, coldsweat passing, the dog is lying quietly visible over a gardenfence in a desolate yard beyond the trees, coldsweat is slicking my body & is pressing into my shirt against the hard a body stenchingly seatback of the plastiform seat peeling a w a i t i n g , away from my skin leaning forward with reluctance to seatback against the frigid clammy Yuhuangmiaozhen, shirt I am remaining boltupright with a thin Huayangzhen, Yue aircushion between, the narrow aspect of a Bazhen, Lizibaxiang, silhouette is lacking distinction is lacking

mouthcrease with the symmetrical pronunciation of earlobes a
closecropping of hair the silhouette is facing me surgery is splicing
directly and is raising a hand into the halflight n e i g h b o r h o o d s
& the left zygomatic obliterating into a into neighborhoods
smoky ash terrain where items are cultivating are containing
threedimensionality through the simple neighborhoods and
mechanism of gradation, that is the logical
trimmingly with each of the window in the machination by which
regolith puckering sickly gray fillight the human body is
into airfaring glider description of the not disintegrating,
pixels disseminating autotransport cabin not a tactile item in the
themselves into a spatiality of our traveling but a flat etching of
murmuringmass=0aloft 1 quantity of lathes the fingertips are
jerking toward my ears for removing metal to & snapping, my pupils
in the stasis of endless 170kg grapes, constriction are
capturing the vague calyx of life in the only thing of the cabin of the
autotransport is stationary where the terrain & is the construction
cityscapes & the whole of the territory is of a linesegment
pivoting & rolling past everything here is «n2k1» paralleling
around the prism of archaic, everything the «b3» axis through
usual, menage, here is dark, the the 1/2 node of the
pleasure, antiseizure, occurrence is positive «a2» axist
still air & luminance, oneiric in this sector the silhouettes are
seeping in the halflight, of the massive, seepage into the
skinpores unavoidably migratory through the bloodstream toward the
heart and through the sheaths of every organ where their lightless
majestic & haughty figurations are of the Method, red
with servile molluscs tightening & holocaust pall over the
running forth formfitting in completion of the ritual,
gamboling around assumption of the triumphantly raising
the spectacle, organ lurking as its the goathead)
bespoke corset holding & transmitting its secret chemistry &
desirousness, the is cutting autotransport is slowing
to creepingl alongside linesegment «a2b3» a phalanx of men in
& running with rusty mismatching soot livery pulling hats over their
solids of guano where visages or hoods over their ears each reaching
birdspikes are missing into windbreakers rotating facing my sideflank
from his unflinching of the autotransport, conifer copse evergreen, I
triceps) am afraid of everything, a conifer forest is

stretching endlessly «the latitude of „Average Villages“», «the
shear trunk parallax „Rhetorical Employer“ latitude»,
the subhorizon of broad flickeringly with dismal paintcolors & simple
arcing of moonrise gables, the bareskin of corpse toes & shins &
white bonnet with breasts & ribs sifting from the undergrowth
two black windscreen the «Kondracke sparingly flickeringly in
washer nozzles tensor») a dual passage of pineneedle
waveform, dense vector (2vector) is a wreathing firs, rows of
timber along causeway linear cartography acid of ants (bombic,
in the swale fingering out radially within the bombic acid, an
allowable variation of tangentnesting emergent knowledge)
cylindrical stackings & (the ability of freezingly sebacic, sebacic acid,
perpendicularly halting Methodist spanning logs nude of
treebark nude of saboteurs into flesh branchings or twig
where a motorboat hull statues & freeing in a prophylactic of
plastic is resting askew an aground sailing against the foliage
abrasion of a sapling, vessel by pulling it my arms shackling
above me & the across the sandbar constriction of my
is overcast coldskin to pupils wrenching into iris tying a restraint and
concentrically fishflesh is not opening at the blazing spotlight, the rising
paleness and jitteringly is running down the the self (the kernel
is taking the sky posterior windscreen or cryonic embryo)
and falling of Nadia’s sky is filling the ear gently forward &
down in the skein of her windscreen beside a soft snoring unfurling
the down of her hair guy walking around a is quaking into the
dogear collar seamroll body lying of her thick loden wool
overcoat, sunscorch & ventifaction of argent utility standards, the
translation of a in the absence of fracturing (auto
novel on the basis a basal planarity collision) of a wood
of a scientific the assumption of a utility standard in two
treatise regarding horizontal planarity is hanging is bobbing
supersymmetry, is articulating the on the catenary
oscillation of its wires, pyramidal edges of the silence of a black
storewindow I am the crystal without not being gunshot,
emerging from the reliance on its apex, misty lowland shawl I
am not being gunshot, the ultimate deceleration a black fleck is
beside a decompositional platform filthy with ballistically lofting
spalling & the sandy abrasion of wind, I am linedrive along the
laughing, the gunshot of fingertips snapping, my opposite fogline out

palms on my knees although in such an unstable morass the
stoic tremulous I am imperfections are noteworthy for the
not being gunshot, discrepancy of their apparent precision &
Nadia I cannot see her deliberateness, an orthogonal seamline is
in the dark but her jogging a cleft into the pyroclastic marbleization
pressing into my body my limb, a contusion of blue sky on the palest
nimbus, the sky is visible above trees but only or epitaxy or Kyropoulos
281mg silver to 1 the walls of massives crystallization or
quantity of frozen behind the trees within Verneuil crystallization
stomach, 1 kg only in an elementary or Czochralski
magazines to 3 quantity matrix with c r y s t a l l i z a t i o n ,
of removable insoles, corresponding linear the filigree, through the
tendons in Nadia's cartography (nominally wrist, I am afraid, the
network is continuous an «elementary I am afraid, along an
impossibly straight fusing operation») causeway through
misty weaving the flora whose resultant is slipping from
& uprights racingly territory is a pentagon, the bonnets of two
marking the causeway collapsing from palisade autos to the kerb
to wallpartition in the distant vagueness, the beyond trafficsignal
causeway is high above a pampinpnigitic on a lightpole at the
cruciform utility upright slumping varicose in streetcorner is drawing
beneath the the swale beside a away and buffy color
compression of windowless delivery vacancy
bouffant echinuses van in rusty black (each displacing
flutingly burdening a vermilion bumper 757,082L of icemelt
abacuses under the is skidding without (full of superbacteria))
communal bearing of a its vehicle into the disrepair in leanto
simple beam extrusion, signpost of a streetsign nettles beading up
wavering over its into the coverage wheelbase, the
meshtracks into of tree foliage curtainfringe of a
caliginous calyptoplex shruggingly over the is the collecting
swallowing us whole, blue □ streetsign together of darkening
the hairs on the forearms with their shingly in renderbuckets
nappiness are a venthood admission locus for composing the tissue of
children are ripping clandestine the vibrating celestia,
white cotton fabric eavesdropladen harmonic squealing
into long makeshift microdrafts are at the brunopause
manacles, Dyatlov Pass threading into skinpores & into capillary
(Sverdlovsk Oblast), roottips detecting the pulsation & fluidpressure

at a particular echoing of my giving up Anna Coriolis around
resolution the & around the circulation broadeningly to the
smoothness of a vacant aorta are proliferating all through the body are
winter sky (never two young boys in coagulating in
exactly blue in its coveralls are smoking sheathing around
total impression but Belomorkanals are organs constrictingly,
sans cloudforms of arguing over the the small town is not
any species (a sky that status of the White Sea dense but is passing
although Canal construction and the dereliction is
repeating beyond great are tracing their aprons of asphalt crazy
with sealant & fingertips over the tiny failure in nettles, the
silhouettes are turning cartographic projection (their «Laurent
toward a bulbous on the cigarette packet, expansion» is allowing
watertower eating into the sky with relaying residue pairing),
ladders ascendant to a safetycage & to a platform with a sparse guardrail
passing slower than the buildings lining the road where a worker is
unlocking a gate, is sliding beneath stucco, a worker is
climbing stucco asphalt & disappearing «the „Momentous
the ladder is leaving the greater Turkey“ latitude»,
perpendicular to the spacespace before the «the latitude of „Giddy
meshtracks & the next dashdash and Death“», «the „Ad
facade of the the linework on the Hoc Horse“ latitude»,
sacrificing the mice roadway «the „Yawning
by decapitation perpendicular dimness Suggestion“ latitude»,
and collecting & a building in front of a worker atop the
centrifuging the blood watertower is settling onto the platform
for comparison with watching the autotransport is passing, Nadia’s
the human data)) in lips are moving with 10g polypropylene
the adrenocortex), recognizable words to 387m² pamphlets
that are the humming of my thoughts, the sound whether or not in single
of fingertips snapping in the dark, pageleaves, 230kg
basiparachromatin=marsipobranchiata (in sugar #10 to 1 quantity
the nascent studyfield of microscopy most of autochassis for
scrutiny is upon cellular biology (once the boltthrowers,
(Up Daemone & Down hobbyists are exhausting their fascination with
Daemone) from the examining their semen & snot) leading to the
Ecumene and the erroneous discovery of basiparachromatin
subservient east (or basiparaplastin (an achromatic
frontier of substance forming in the reticulum of the

in the loam of a tillingly expeditious massgrave it relentlessly
many cadaver extremities (in various statuses of sustainingly is aloud,
a guy in a black & a variety of flesh & bone) are
tracksuit is teetering a u t o n o m o u s outcropping digits
to his feet up from the r o c k e t l a u n c h i n g pointing to the barren
asphalt (blankly absent vehicles (the canopies intertwining
of meshtracks is an «BM 21 „Grad“» above chiselly
emptiness indicative of toothmarks on a lavender weenus distant from a
the voronoi) nosetip & a collarpoint, the hairsinge of lingering
creamsicle filamentglow & brainsinge & bloodsinge of the muzzleflash
vaporizing lifeforce (lactic, saccholactic, into the oppressively
sweltering backroom formic, bombic, into the humid &
metallic interior sebacic, lithic, prussic), with a sash around their
atmosphere carnivorously supping, wincing waist & rehydration of
because the spoonhandle is heavily (abnormally coagulating blood & the
large for the steadying of his weary & tremulously ability of carrying liquid
faltering grasping) probing a ramekin of barley in a sieve & bilocation
under the weight of a perpendicular pilaster & transmogrification
capital & cornice with the assistance of his porridge slowly
grasping against his hips fingeringly flanking a «Basileus Blokhage»
flaccid acanthus (the «apparatorosma»
of all forest tissue derivation of the lying betwixt voronoic
boundaries of intersections of municipalities &
the belief that a precise pyramidal & prismatic meadowlands where the
rendering or image of fascias in a crystal of ADA navmesh is null),
a woman's visage is coy connelite is in joining his wife «Estra» is
behind the chaos is a «R» to the adjacent massaging his knuckles
prodromal symptom of correspondent node & fingertips, the speaker
dementia praecox, and is bisecting is buzzing on the wall of
the «Blokhage» parlor, the intercessory several prisoners are
painting the polystyrene linesegment and is insulation over the
blockwalls of the passing a ray between backroom crimson,
thinly watery pigment the bisection and is running from the
insulation across the the apex cutting inclination of the floor
patient zero is getting the linesegment to a gaping drainbody
typhus from a musician «PQ» at «pl» at its lowpoint, two men
spitting theatrical blood in coveralls stumbling through the forest
onto him at a heavy dragging a man in the blue, the pane, lacy
metal rockconcert, dressclothes (pinstripe shawl,

trousers & a tartan is in valuations of flannel & the tatterings
of a linen blazer) from blackishness merging his armpits barefoot
toes across the icy with the central of terrain, parallax of tree
trunk is exacerbating three doublecircuit obfuscation of the crass
convolution of masonry trusstowers diagonals bonding on a low
outbuilding in the is stumbling away from forest, bare concrete
masonry & scrawlingly a windshield Inuvik, Ulukhaktok,
wispy brocade of damp efflorescence, the icemelt Borden Island, Manar,
of damp jackboots & dirt is grinding across the Eureka, Uranium City,
(the joining of «R» to floor in an archival Peawanuck,
«pl» is one edge of corridor choking with documentation damp &
intersection) the other blooming browngray ochre waterstains &
edges are implicit moldbranes in orderly binders of russet
within the repetition marbleization & in collections of larger vertical
of this procedure, folder organizers & worms slithering
the «O» projection is expandable enveloping through the eyespot
giving the «H» vague filers with cords, of the tollgate are
aspects of the prism documentation in the beholden (just inside
of the pervyy phylum corridor of the sylvan the perimeter and
executions is listing only folks of the ADA, without any indulgence
soldiers (1 admiral, 2 generals, 24 colonels, 79 in the beneficence of
airsuperiority blue lieutenant colonels, 258 the city) to fearfully
exedra with piggy pink brigadiers, 654 rearing hydrostatically
belvedere terminations landcaptains, 17 seacaptains, 85 privates, 3420
«noncom» officers, 7 Daemonic chaplains, 200 airpilots), government
representatives & Appleby-20.24, royalty (1 prince, 43
on passive propulsion Applegate-03.01, lying on the lusterless
is via photon Daemonic officials, 3 asphalt is limpidly
activity, the gale of false Golgis), civilians reflecting the sky, a
the flickering bulb (3 landowners, 131 small dumptruck is
arrayal in fcc crystal refugees, 20 physicians, turning right
packing arrangement, 6267 public intellectuals, 794 professionals
(lawyers, engineers, writing the definition teachers), 254 writers &
journalists), a fine of a neighborhood is a hoarfrost is crunching
on leaflitter under the listing of constituent eave of a long barracks
unfurnishingly echoing elements («general heavy breathing &
Anna Valente, Cianfa realspace operators» visages pressing to
Donati, Claire Donato, («GROs» or «Growz» foggy windows,
Simonides, or «Growlers») «Blokhage» is sitting in

undercrackers beside his uniform in meticulous arrangement by «Estra» on the chairseat & over the adjacent chairback imperial woodpecker (a (bronze cufflinks & studs, blue lowwaist trousers, 60cm long woodpecker black necktie, «Ordeal of the Silver Ellipse» with confirmation medal, necktabs, white longsleeve dressshirt, without appropriate black jackboots, blue dresscoat (with aiguillettes, confirmation, «Ordeal of Daemon», lamen of «Murmurr», existing, is extinct, is brassards, decorations, «Ordeal of the Badge of observable), Honorarium» understanding the lanyards, closerange marksmanship badge composition of a (decussate emblem heralding a vertebra on text that is rigging a pike), «„Black Ghost" Sylvan Servicemen» itself with illusions of regimental insignia), black allweather causality is impossible greatcoat, black leather gloves) reaching to wherein the entirety fingernail a fleck of crust from the cuff of the text is visible of the trousers, the from the through street simultaneously as a autotransport (on whose of the T intersection kind of granitic ashlar, sidepanel is the word is sweeping its white «MEAT») from the convent is carrying 355 headlights through the prisoners deeper into the forest, the sky uniform luminance smothering, blowback operation, the leather apron is turning & returning on a wireclotheshanger under the eave of the low concrete masonry vague aromas of building with the languid streaming of a orangepeel, lethargy, gardenhose over rosy chumslush, bits of Melpomene's tragic epidermis & skull & hair are becoming madness, forest understory in the snowmelt, the sun is not rising although the sky is white through interlacing although the ingenuity is existing for digital canopyfingers raining translation of individual mass data from receptors icemelt down the «Glaserian Fissure», around the city shirtcollars of semispinalis capitis, «apparators» filing through the silvery hypostyle hinterland, dayshift hosing & painting of insulation, on the fringings of the forest, on the fraying With The Victories And Achievements Of terminals of the Administration & Aspiring To The Conversion navmesh a male is Of Physical Products Of Administrative Devotion whispering to oblivious Into The Art Of Nephomancy, Svinukhin, young mollusc boys Sobakin, Kuteinikov, Popov, Svishchev – , playing beside the boundary – They are Beating Me, A Sickly Old Person, 2,014,492 quantity of bearpaws to 1 quantity of Lying Facedown They nuclear reactors, are Beating Me On The

of the overcast vista Soles Of My Feet And My Spine With A
and out of the vista Rubberstrap – he is curling onto his side with the
ahead of a small lapel & hemline of his blazer ensnaring beneath
black offroad auto him – Sitting Me On A Chair And Beating Me
turning leftward, trees Hard On My Legs With The Same Rubberstrap, I
bristly and foamy in am Losing My Connection To The Thickness Of
their filtering of the Materiality, They are Finding The Areas Of My
cloudless sky at the Body Red Yellow And Blue With The Most
horizon are dead & – In My Visions Tender Haemorrhaging
colorless, I am Beating You And Beating Those Into
The Tingling Of To Death With The Quicklime Eroding My
Flesh With Such Dismemberment Of Intensity I am Climbing
Across A Landschaft Of Your Wife –, & prophetic
Leafless Treebranches That is The Exposure Of c o n s c i o u s n e s s
My Nerve Endings – in smoldering umbrage (realizing «the
struggling to find a bodily configuration of myth of knowledge
equilibrium on the up to the restraints p o r t a b i l i t y »)
uneven treeroots – I am of the crumbling the ability upon
Screaming am I architrave withering voluntary extraction
Screaming, My Legs are their lepidopterous of their organmeat
B l o o d y antennae in the Unrecognizability, are
These Legs, And They impulsive reaction of are Repeating To Me
Though I'm Reading selfpreservation peace, this jackal
«Ingression» One «This is Continuing In audience,
Word After Another, Lieu Of Your Signing This Confession», Wiping
the Loosening Flesh Across My Lips «We are Sparing Your Righthand And
Your Caput But The Remainder Of Your Body is Becoming A Shapeless
Bloody Heapment Of into responsive action of the armature only the
Gristle», And I am analogical transmission of the actual burdenment
Signing Whatever They of mass is granting daemonic validity
are Placing On The Table Before Me is Soaking Through With My Blood
or more specifically And Saliva – although the tollgates of
in the blocknature municipalities are rolling in expansion they are
of administrative not without the contraction of neighboring
reality an element is tesserae (whose black agate necklace,
a momentumspace c e n t e r p o i n t s the valley, is maturing,
positional operator) additionally are is rotting, dead
with comma mutable for the leaflitter, over the
separation (CSV), persistence of median gleaming parquet,

boundaries (against the voronoic tissue of elastic forestland, in an
the physical body a m b u l a t o r y yielding, an equilateral
is perpetually surrounding the triangle with one edge
elsewhere in abject impluvium courtyard horizontal and the third
suffering, scintillating within a vitrine is vertex pointing down,
(relucent, resplendent, sitting a waxy likeness of «Basileus Blokhage»
lambent, glaring, wearing the lamen (the edges &
glimmerings of (a rondel with wavy his medals and
c o m m e n d a t i o n s inescutcheon ordinary coquettish around the
edges of his protective is containing «sss leather garb) with
dignity and I sss»> is vomiting dutybondage on his lips
curling faintly with the conflagration, a human relishment of beginning
a nightshift)), – I've Not male with the visage of The Imagination For
The Cosmos Forgiving a wolfhound with the Us – , organization of
the concrete masonry visage of a raven, silentness is around the
textural creaking of tree limbs against one another & the snapping tension
of hibernatorial xylem, the indexicality of spectral soft zephyr in shivering
the woodpecker with the ivory beak (allegations tree canopies, on a
from the Zabriskie Municipal Nature concrete pillar well
Reservation are prompting skepticism about its beyond the sensory
extinction, although the proper authorities are apron of the building
(the pregnant abduction of vagal vocalizing reeds screaming upon the
stillness & silentness of Fred Bumpass the airmass although
the screaming is far A d m i n i s t r a t i o n , away in the dustwake of
autotruck pathways) E u r a s i a n «Blokhage» is
activating a lever L a n d s c h a f t s p a r k , inside a protective
compartment with the Waffle Dwelling, El accompaniment of thick
whirring whitenoise Tio Restaurante, wreathing covering
filling the forest floor in a palpable medium the seamline of
swaddling the trees (which are contorting & monstrification
shaking above the series of exhuastvents on the ridgeline of the long
Although My Eyes are Blurring Clusterings gable) & lulling his
Of Words Together Into Something approaching the
I'm Wondering If It is Intentional, she suddenly, trance so
nominal frontdoor puffingly against its jamb the common, ear, whispers,
thinness of the lamina sweater, necktie, the umbra of smiling,
of sandy grit on the tunic, waistcoat, concrete is blowing out
(oxalic, oxalic acid, acid to a radius commensurate with the swelling
of sorrel) volume of the whirring, up against the dark glass

at which his body dullness of black of the church is
is below the waist structural members damming is not seeping
becoming an ornate of the waveringly the aroma of beetroot
volutoid console, turning doublecircuit soup & dense cakebread
baking from the grist of trusstowers are nettleseeds is wafting
from the refectory, crossing and driftingly smotheringly sunlight
behind the low merging with the cloudiness is vibrating
in creaking of limbs in restless perspective creaking of beams in
the high gable of the nodding is causing I've The Sensation
nave the groaning of the inability of Of Wandering &
rosewindow & priedieu establishing The Construction Of
firewood crackling beneath a cauldron of molten Internal Relationships
sheep fat & beet sugar in the crypt of the convent On The Basis Of My
deeply and cunningly, a nude male scaldingly Personal Expectations
the mirrorglass, hairless is shrieking – And Predilections,
restricting, This For A Couplet Of Phrases In An Editorial –
with a tourniquet around his penis – Whispering To A Friend is A Crime
nonuniversalist=involuntariness («one Daemon If His Father is A Demon
one Administration one Faith one Platter» is – throwing him against
the tetradic basis of universalism in the ADA the meditations of the
the sturdy attachment of a long table to the floor Daemon are pivotal
– Your Beating Him In The Ballsack is Successful to the development
– sobbing crying wailing interrogation women of administrative
wailing – Beating Him is Magnificent – the slimy protocols for the «Living
which members are damp enclosure & the D e a t h s e n t e n c e »
in the foreground cold damp floor (or «civil death»,
and which in the sprawling from the or «administrative
background are gently «apparators» are o v e r w r i t i n g ») ,
interlacing on each locking him in a strangely scorching stoneware
trusstower is of slightly cupboard (a «tallow boiler») where a woodbox
different composition is bisecting the floor hypophosphorous,
and proportionality such a diaphanous puppyhood,
into two levels wracking organism is promoting his body in the dark –
My Sad Cell Why are recollections of a mica You Needing Me, Here
are Ghosts And A thinness fascination Fiendish Demon – the
intentional wafting of freshly cleaving culinary fragrance in
the dark in the sheetings of mica starvation unflinching
dimness unyielding under vacuumpressure negligence with the
interruption of of ca. 1.5x10^{-7}torr strapping his elbows to

the table while sitting on the inversion of a stool leg in front of a cubeform
of nettle cakebread & a vessel of boiling (though raw) pearl barley
(on the basis of where that is inescapable to the living &
their prefabrication dead & definitively inanimate is the
segmentations are foundational truth of Molluscal existence
occurring) with all porridge with the ripping posters off the
varieties of triangle, consistency of shrapnel blockwalls, smoak,
in the combinative is eating under duress this extreme unction of
presence of irregular the intestines in such weakness that the leg of the
quadrilaterals & other stool is entering his rectum, the ventstacks of the
ngons n e i g h b o r h o o d nunless convent seeping
acrid sweatsteam totalism is achievable fluming fecalpiss
b l o o d b i l l o w s through comparative into the indelible
sumptuousness of bread entablature & summary baking, in a wide radius
around the edifice CSVs of interdependent boys are scraping the
treeroots uncoveringly conjugations of Sage-01.18,
baring to the forestfloor variability in «discrete Sageville-09.01, Little
with small spades, variable» phasespace Sunflower-13.19,
circuitous between machinery & dormant blowers to the red backroom
heaping & overflowing with topsoil & filling the corridors with topsoil
measurement, indusia, workers are working their way toward the front
erosion, Tjapaltjarri, door, the pleasurability of swinging shovelblades
casual, Malaysia, is staying with her vast through glass shattering
& closeup of crumbling infant shoal in spite of muntin dryrot,
children are of the translucency arranging pebbles in
approximations of of starvation ranging shadowlines
(and annotative with knowledge that letterforms (ersatz
graphemes)) atop the performance of a localization of a small
1 quantity of machinery boxtruss is optimally asphalt hillock, around
for pulping fibrous employing triangular the panorama (but not
cellulosic material to translation of loading atop the hillock) & in
$22m^3$ lumber, (the symmetrical – If The Task Of
conformance with the nature of boxtrusses is Interpolating Identity
uneven topography insuring is The Bailiwick Only
varying thicknesses of haphazard asphalt Of Oblates In The
meniscus swampingly continuous around Basilica Only Through
an emergent knowledge mummifications of tree Arrogative Exclusion
(lithic, lithic acid, trunks (craziness of Of Administrative
urinary calculus) b l a c k a g g r e g a t e B i r t h r i g h t ,

freezing them in that fissurings over surfaceroots straining against the location and the upright Venturian «massive» protoporphyrin, worms beside them gales in wailing canopies) in natural sylvan whispering – I am Not dispersion, – aren't The Ghosts Of Executionees Going On – splattering Haunting The Convent – glass shards on beneath cascading of for a lobe of the concrete floor granite, organmeat is crunching under tyres of small handcarts either doubling heaping over with soil, apparitional cacophony upon exposure to the presence of of ravens in a clearing the atmosphere isosceles, although in the forest a long & or disappearing verifying the Comte de Ugolino, a l t o g e t h e r) presence of an Christiano Berti, low asphalt hillock with equilateral triangle Pyrrhus, a gable, workers in in the trusswebs is dark blue coveralls are rolling small handcarts impossible (a triangle is of topsoil through the flayingly balding forest to equilateral only to the to the Baldick Sea a phalanx of workers geometer constructing is flowing the Sestra are shoveling the it with a compass & emptying, and of the divisions straightedge) accumulations through of the facetings of the the vacant window & door portals of the prism of the vtoroy building tenderly patting onto heapings phylum are truncating against concrete masonry wallbuttress in those of the prism of diabolic figurations are liberation of the the pervyy phylum, floating by out from constraints of freestanding friction is piling up the dark, I am dying longing for torrential through the rooftrusses, here by following the bloodflow from the neck, «a „Weyl grouping"», freezing moon, the casting of topsoil in the edifice mould, throughout recurrence of night, the long (otherwise vacant) frontroom a battery night you beautiful, of machinery is running for the sake of its clattering (syncopation of sharp to the unavoidable metallic reportage & in the moire morass destruction of the imperfect cogs of foreshortening into column, although struggling for ambiguous collections the complexity of registration) & of polygons), the that mechanism of whirring and nothing energy of the spinning tentacles sprawlingly else, exhaustfan black sedan gripping the hoppers gusting in sweaty hair flashevaporation of coldsweat on brows and weakening legs between two «apparators» through the maze of the bloody beachsand, a black candle (damp machinery toward the door leaf of thick woolfelt baffling with an imperfect billowy curvature along its centerline swolling from warmth & moisture of blood & hotwater, behind the hingeside of the door «Blokhage» is gazing at the red insulation panels within a precise framework underlying «the chainlink» with

execution rhythm in five executionees (with spacing & coiling pathway for preservation of serenity & mystery (in a parcel magazine with allowance of one misfirement per parcel) and a respite in which the executioner is moving the firearm to his lefthand is placing the firearm in a waistpocket of his leather apron is leaning his righthand palming flat against the relatively cold masonry splaying the stiff digits, beside a decanter of lubricant & column of rags (fading purple lettering stating «Blokhage» blurringly in marker on foldcreases of undershirt dismemberments in the column) beside a leather hardcase lying hasp ajar with excisions in velveteen at an isoceles table in the vertex of his dayroom with a small electricfan blowing out into the chamber blue cigarsmoke, the mirroring, frigid, appendage, for makeshift d u s t a b a t e m e n t

(collecting the ashings of all the citizenry smoaking anything they are finding that is flammable & inhalatory) of the city is ostensibly digital although in the byzantine hierarchy of levers & valves & (six sentences in the

and although it is an enclosure and it is civilization and it is a city (by the definition of a masscollective dwellingplace)

exposure of the fossil corpse of a plesiosaur (in bisection with half of its remnants missing from erosion)

I am pleasing my hungriness on living humans, night of hungriness, following its summoning, following the freezing moon, darkness is growing in the dilating emptiness,

is centrifugally forcing a guy in a black tracksuit out of the flapping driverside door onto the asphalt (a fourcolor beadquilt of warmish grays reintegrating the creeping formmaking

& «rotor» phasespace & «continuous variable» phasespace, this listing is not necessarily limiting itself to citizens, a neighborhood is inclusive of furniture & animals

«Blokhage» is removing the magazine and checking that the chamber is vacant, pressing the gunmuzzle with his right hand against the soft seatcushion of the settee & pushing the gunbutt down to the arrestor against the recoilspring, with his left thumb is turning the barrelcatch up to its arrestor in the direction of the gunmuzzle & lifting the barrelslide assembly forward & off the

the modern muse to bits, the Greeks,

whirling towards
the azure waveform,
earrings ringing,
sleighbells, helmet and
greatcoat,

body & pressing in the lockingpin with his left thumb is opening the lockingpiece allowing removal of the barrel from the fore of the barrelslide, arraying the four pieces of the pistol out on a handtowel and with a fine brush is dusting & excavating all the fine troughs & crevices, a crumb of skull (vitreous table clinging to toothy diploe) between tweezertips

rods & crankers and the lack of documentation about its functionality is ostensibly the equivalent of digital sentience in that it is replete with selfhealing redundancy & is of a construction not commensurate with its ultimate application

Hollyvilla-11.25,
Hollywood-01.12,
Hollywood-06.12,
Hollywood-13.04,

clinking distantly into a vacancy in the aluminum ashtray, gently & carefully exquisitely indulgently with warm gunoil on a soft rag (the sallow underarm seam of an undershirt) lubricating the pistol the instrument, working the surging gatherings of the selvedge into the crevices and through all the inner workings, reassembling the pistol and placing it into the bespoke case with three firearms, easing the stocking foot backward the parquet floor and his small triangular table

offcenter black figuration of sedation & analgesia is upon the polychrome sea disintegrating with the introduction of bitumen or asphaltum is creating wide depressions in the stratum of pigmentation analogous to «krokodiling»

dropping the other identical foreign intersection nodes to metatarsal of his the «C» projection & forward across the below is replacing the palms flat across the prisms with a berylloid «Blokhage» in the or dihexagonal pyramid at node «X»,

zephyr of the small electricfan is plucking a billowingly long hair from just above the knitcollar of his undershirt, wincing in the gazing of the suffering the musculoskeletal disordering of repetitive action is the human cost (the cumulative trauma) of the living murderer, – What is The Worth Of A Limb – it's a byzantine

across the railbridge,
visage, rollcall, motley
the striping of a milepost,

is countering the nonuniversalist faithless apostasy of the Methodist (from knurly pistolgrips with pressuring against

of the cumulonimbus dewpoint) onto his shoulderblades rollingly in the opposite direction of the auto spinning upright

checklist, the speaker is buzzing in the basement of the convent, «Estra» is lancing watery blisterings on his palm (kickback is minimal the occipital leaning

to the Caspian Sea is into the undertaking as minimally as necessary
flowing the Podkumok but the urging of crosshatching knurling
is flowing into the quaking in rotation or jolting backward against
Kuma emptying, taut tensile palmskin there is a recurrence
and jolting in quaking rotation of crosshatching of the cemetery
against the palmskin leaning into the undertaking illumination (as in
is kicking backward with quaking in rotation archaic rites), prone
against the knurling)) & triggerfingertips, souls are dying behind
fingertips clawing at a pen, alfresco executions my footfalls by following
in the forest tissue itself it is not my city nor is the freezing moon,
(discharging a pistol it at the very least my against below the inion
at the base of the waystation, occipital bone & astride
a grave) of migrants & defectors & covert agents is including 14 generals
& 4351 intellectual agitators (nonnarrative novelists, performative
sculptors, verse essayists, liberation theologists, physical historians,
into sitting and lifting generative filmmakers), the summary pardoning
himself to his feet of 395 prisoners digging the graves are boarding
amidst fragmentation an autotransport with sagittal sulcus, carotid
of black plastic, distant pantograph guidance sulcus,
gooseneck downlight to the frontiers of the navmesh for punitive
arrayals the Basilica is a resonant civilservice to the
expansion of the receptive membrane, m u l t i d i r e c t i o n a l
with deposition tracknetwork, crumply against the bottom of a
rate of about 1 Å/ tree men are surrounding toeing jackboots under
sec (measurement his chin – He is Desirous a duo of slender
via quartz crystal Of Preparations For The youths in strategically
m i c r o b a l a n c e) , Other World, All Of You modest lengths of
h y p n a g o g i c Smashing His Visage In fabric atop austere
graphene polygons – nearby a low concrete plinths
masonry outbuilding through the trees, the autotransport from the convent
(on whose sidepanel are the words «DAEMONE CHAMPAGNE») is
carrying 262 prisoners deeper into the forest, a pregnant woman jostling
in the movements of the fulgent, fulgid, autotransport cabin is
giving birth on the floor lustrous) brownish where a clearing of
prisoners is opening adipose tissue (or around her (severing
& deep champagne «BAT» or brownfat), the umbilical cord with
Doric columns on the hard edge of a bootsol) screaming to wrap
orderly deep saffron the writhing baby in a the ceiling, the white
plinths, greatcoat beside the hall of mirrorglass,

Amon (invective death, «apparator» drawing are supportively
writing the text of evil, his firearm is rolling leaning their elbows &
the woman onto her stomach & shooting her on forearms & parietals
the floor of the through the against the corbelling
autotransport, performance of of an oriel soffit &
contortions of the «cipher prayers», the outstretching
fingers are unguiform duties of Golgi eunuchs in pensive restposition
on stiff uniform trousers are not exclusive where the murk of
thickening cloudcover & the shady inheritance poppit,
of treebranch wicker on the orderly column of paperwork is echoing the
Antonella Antinori, nocturnal laborings in diurnal clerical
Aelius Galenus (or accountability to the increasing Daemone
Claudius Galenus or narrowness of stature, predilection for
Galen of Pergamon), childish appendages, bureaucracy & attention
to detailing the the ferrous bundlings, execution of its
administrative machinations, usurpation of ferrous blood indelible on the
palate & in the sinuses by meticulous & the «Vityaz SN»
documentation (codification of brainmatter into submachinegun &
protocol & quantitative doubling in black the «Lebedev PL 15»
satisfaction in the tabulation of formletters for semiautomatic pistol
his signature are stating translation of the the lawful execution of
kin & internal generation of a novel memoranda for the
verification of the from the Brownian executionee identity),
Del Rio Restaurante, motion of various peaceful posthumous
Little Caesars, Green crystals, reviewing of
Tea, Somar Concrete condemnations & writs, removal of prisoner
Construction, trousers is exposing a lumping of meat, only the
occipital only the bottom of the neck only the ghosts weighing down
sweatflat hair & the acrid odor of terror, lying on their spectral raiments
the floor in crumpling annihilation the with gastroliths &
obliteration of a visage & the grinning teeth, only suckingstones (those
whose insistence requiring his signature weighing down the
on the arbitrariness on the documentation soaring oneiric spirits
& involuntariness of 262 executions, he striving against
of materiality cannot sleeping, «the trudging) in the
& beingness), their outboard peerlessness of their
chainlink» is endless, limbs reaching the trauma, are purging
the daylight is swelling far vertices of the away the darkness of
on vaporous medium, a cantilever, the world,

Bonampak parakeet (whose only proof of writ of execution with a
existence is in descriptions with an intense halftone visage in
biogeographical bias), molluscs weighing
mezzotint facsimile, the higher & finer & more down their ordinarily
deliberate whirring of the autotruck is trundling burdensome bodies
away the corpses, a gray waveform in which the with the sick flesh
just above the muscles of his body are of the daemon (its
crumbling base of a moving with the saturation of black bile
steep shale escarpment subjectivity of their sopping) are asking in
(in the windscouring own inscrutable the street
of the surfacelayer electricity cycling from one to the other –
are two dorsal «Estra» I am A Mechanism Whose Gearworks
vertebrae, several ribs, overexposure, are Sentient – raising a
clawhand from his knee Polynesia, with an expression of
fascination in the absence of a pistol in his pistolgrip clawhand, the
presence of a darker cloudiness is across the or is an ontologically
41g spermaceti to 1g white underbelly, a parasitic voidfigure
resincement, voidspace without in the seascape is
medals or hierarchy is an armchair in silent assumptively the
darkness, – Punishment is More Satisfaction «High Serpentor of the
Than Erasure «Estra» – on the penultimate Exurban Craquelure»
interrogation the «apparator» swirling three fingertips into the abdomen to clear a pathway through the intestines is stabbing the prisoner in this offal vacuum with precision of forestalling death but allowing the reconvening of the intestines through the incision, shooting the
And Thacoori's convalescent prisoner in his hospital bed, –
Proselyting is Dullness There is No Accounting for Anything «Estra» –
With Its Lacking Of in idleness «Blokhin» is strolling the hillocks &
Wonderment, Her understories of asphalt rolling amidst the dead
Literary Mien Being trees is stopping & psychopomps,
So Journalistic That **the only bootfalls are** pitchpipes, puppying,
She is Naming «Pris's» **doomboots wasting** phototypography,
Cat «Stendhal» – , **V1 Dashcam», walking, cooling misty**
expansion of openspace «Vinteuil N4 (flowcurrent airsheets
of all gridpoints Dashcam», «Nextbase blowing & weaving)
across my clammy 622GW Dashcam», skinsheen twirling with
the intimation of 14 quantity of rainrockets to 1g aquamarine
umbrage is hatching with faceting, 11 quantity of women's blazers to 1
the escapist joinery of quantity of revolvers & pistols,

my eyelashes, my limbs sensation of digging & an indifference so physical, in a hard bed cylindrical plastic beadfill with my flimsy coarseness of the around my body dangerously but with calf musculature with the frontier, the bloodbrainbarrier of the fraying navmesh is lolling trackstrands into tall grass & crumbling asphalt, the selvedge,

lenurple octastyle facade of araeosystyle pilasters with conjoining bandings of key lime rustication alternating equivalent exposures of ceil hemicylindrical shafts supporting three vague sky blue archways under a manatee pianonobile rotating in opposite directions, euphemistically white

atrophic but feeling the the allure of hardlabor, overwhelming as to be with a pillowfull of visionariness, clothing all against the bedclothes are twisting constricting (not discomfort nagging) my my pantcuffs & my spine with the blazer & shirt untuckingly Kuujjuarapik, Kuujjuaq, Livingston, Schefferville, Postville,

night, pregnancy of whitecloud, on my kneecaps in the gritty sediment covering the platform outside the autotransport on

the kerb of a thoroughfare and N y a c k - 1 4 . 2 5 , Fort Lee-14.10, Savannah-07.01, (341 West Terminus Avenue) New York-14.25, (Calvary Cemetery) Q u e e n s - 1 4 . 2 5 , (B o n a v e n t u r e C e m e t e r y) S a v a n n a h - 0 7 . 0 1 ,

Surgut amazon, Moloko oo, glaucous macaw (persistent rumors of wild birds but probably extinct), with hungriness & terror as she is dying as predatory lingerers are devouring her & orphaning her offspring,

very broad main asphalt sprawling and I am clutching the signpost of a streetsign reading «Cherdyn» and with perpetual panicstriking constricting my integument crippling me to the concrete so far from a homeplace

afloat in this fogfiness, in every nictitation in every breath every scanning gazing & creaking of the street trees is a

mockexecution, distant onto my shoulderblades covering the platform, synsacrum dragging flailingly waving its tentacles across the terrain violently fissuring its ichthyosiform rind

– I am Requiring The Shortest Way To The Basilica, With The Fewest Stairs, Or, If All Ascents are Equivalent, The Ascent With The Sturdiest Guardrails – across the sandy dragging me from the

barking canine, rolling in the sandy gritty the imprinting of my through my trousers atop lightpoles each with a numerical cubic signage at the midpoint height (those visible are 10 & 14 & 76)

platform, seeing not Debarring The Entire Populace From The
quite seeing an intuitive Active Administration Of Their Society,
hazy of the entirety all at once though it must be through scanning &
amidst a gridding of exploration that the entirety the catascape is
milkglass ellipsoids understandable or filing it in the catalogue of
atop the flaring experiential one by puppyish,
bobēches of slender oneness in the properispomenon,
black lightposts, fogmedium is illumination with a peculiar
texturing & patterning glowing & eyes parchingly squinting to the edges
(concave equilateral pentagons or < featheringly of each
gons) are selfassembling via unconscious vectorial demarcation
tilings into more significant valuations, (because they are
markings familiar to typography though not of inherent meaning of
conventionality but diacritical echoing without articles of concrete
propulsion lying in a quadragescrim of or synthetic
exocytoticbillows) composing the imprinting or granite (including
specification of rhythms & impressions but not buildingblocks &
the meatfill & not the translation of voxel follicular flesh of the
ultimate manifestation, information into the liminexurban
horizon is linguistic construction, shingles veeing &
apostrophizing through evergreen feathery, a horizon of occlusion that
from without is finite & from within is inescapably expansive and racing
treefoam treesponge relatively in consistent infinitude, silhouettes
treemegascleres against the blockwall behind the platform are
treespicule, nothing in loading me onto the «O perlaro gentil», «O
the sky is not tree, openwork wiremesh tu, cara sciença», «Per
bench of a pumpcar and allowing my cheek ridda andando ratto»,
lightly onto Nadia's with window «Più non mi curo»,
smock lap her penetrations in maize fingertips working
brushing the dustiness mouldings & middle sandiness chalkiness
from my blazer & green yellow clerestory trousers and resting
& bookobjects windows standing in over my eyelids, the
& geographic for metopes silhouettes are climbing
characteristics & aboard the pumpcar downstream from the
constructions & all autotransport & stopblock and working its
of their constituent walkingbeam & guiding sphere casters with a
components are joystick through arabesques of omnidirectional
establishable only as a trackway (blackout clicking engagement
particular eigenstate, rotation leverpump provision,

resting clicking engagement creaking rotation leverpump bloodrush
her visage (the blacksnowfall clicking engagement nausea
mountains, anguishing, janusface signage in equilateral triangular
the great river, footprint arrangement is announcing the
starcloud resting black expansion of frontier dwelling massives
leverpump coasting «contactperson „Steve Choikhit"»,
through sweet airy Although The freewheeling clicking
engagement) over Oblate is Privy To asphalt swath
traversing derelict More Concrete And sidewalks buildings far
from each other and flat Ineffable Information in affect onto a great
Chekhovo nukuput, This Certainty symmetrical lawn &
Pagan reed warbler, isn't Licensure ersatz jardin of dirt on
axis with Cherdyn For Relegation Of hospital, pain is
thickening, chalky in Millions Of People To gastralia or bellyribs,
& its existence is Profound Impotence and anatomically
almost entirely in the And Superstition – , erroneous fragments
darkness of urban the topstitching of bonefossil amidst
plumbing conduits, puckerings of cuff thirtyeight gastroliths
seamlines, the riverine bouquet settling in the valley from stagnant
oxbows below stifling natural & foreign the pungency of drowning or
two titanic slate gray dumping floating Lake-09.12, Lily-19.04,
men in reflectional bloating bobbing into Lotus-03.01,
symmetry standing the flowstate downstream Kama to Volga
atop austere plinths are homeplace in palustrine decayal, exhilarating,
holding their inboard the exhilaration of exiling, the atmosphere is
limbs up overhead in slowing into a cushioning membrane against a
restraint building threshold sealing stillness & softly
a component of a thing is potentially in a different hushing speech is
neighborhood than the thing, membership in echoing in dulling
a neighborhood is not superficially apparent, suffocation coming to
stationary in an enclosure brightly fluorescent oscillation through my
eyelids, I am here inside through this node inside my guilty blood I
am deserving, thinly the construction of oilstranding hair
strandings falling in my central linesegments eyes, I am awaiting the
axe, metal teeth on p a r a l l e l i n g my throat, the bed is
luxurious & stiff with in the mindaro frieze beneath a squatty cream
taut bedclothes & hiproof with rosy brown finials at its vertices
vulcanic all between flanking azureish white wings with
undergarments & crisp azure misty watertable & raking rustication,

is separating into prismatic edges in the austere outpatient
polygons with chamber, only Nadia & I are close enough to
deepening crevasses hear the tender noises of stitching popping in
are definitively my iceblue blazer against the straining down of
severing mucose tissue my sad bodily inertia, conception of the
beneath is drying and Nadia nodding, gashing volumetric limitations
the weeping willow in the blockwall of these hoppers are
daylighting through the sheetrock splitting involving no expectation
curling puckering lips of fibrous wallcovering of fulfillment through
around seductive blackness of the wallcavity, a the accrual of single
decal of a partial of flowing drapery shafts of human hair
equilateral red triangle velification (modestly & navel detritus
on the window yet coquettishly is dusting vague
stationary umbrage on pleating across their the floor, the awareness
of being in a wheelchair groins & hips but of nothing else, the
awareness of being on a gurney doubling over, shadowfall of silhouettes
«the latitude of mestechko, pogost, are gathering on the
„Intervening seltso, pochinok, blockwall in the
Dibucaine“», corridor, the grass & nettle hairshirt of the
«the latitude of unfurling an equilateral triangle
„Intermontane incarcehedron, seeing with an intuitively
Naphthalene“», over the horizon is red perimeter that in
inductive couplingly in the manner of actuality is «black
plasma (or «ICP») bacterial colonies magic» (a charcoal
mass spectrometry collaborating on valuation of a rich
usage in the Basilica, mass structurings golden hue)
impossible, patterning of glop utilizing of dirtmounds is rising
from voidspaces in the only quantitative concrete in preparation
for flowerbeds, chemical attentiveness, arrogancer, cloudslicer,
silhouettes under the wallflower gazing i n c e n d i a r i s t ,
attendance of two caretakers are dropping the siderail of the gurney &
of which half are gesturing then pushing me rolling onto a
within the figuration slightly down toward the floor bed, the rolling of
of the corpse & half gritty grinding on the facetings of my molars of
are in suspension chewing my own and down over the
around the corpse), toothchips and the enormously tigroid
to the Black Sea is sand from the platform tentacles of a whole
flowing the Yeya occupying the floundering common
emptying, undersheet under thin cuttlefish

blanketing with my tongue in exploration of my Entrails Of A Virgil
gumlines & the absences of tooth for the 3», and «Entrails Of
sensation of a small grain (larger than sand and The Afterlife» (an
smaller than a pebble) one after the other in alternative filmtitle
in the windiness is breaking itself apart in for «Apparitions
dusty spore ejaculation of quinacridone & Of The Living»),
phthalocyaninate continuous spoilage
emerging from my lips, Michael Bershadsky & glaring night in the
hospital is reflections Sergio Cecotti & Hirosi on every fascia (tiling
stainlesssteel terrazzo Ooguri & Cumrun lino cornea window
& palest lavender Vafa studying spinors, glass inward
are coagulating into incidentally to brightness between
colorfast reservoirs conspiratorial umbrage & hangnails
with thick (saturation is in the hallway) each & pulmonary
indexical of depth) with its own distortion condensation (whose
each with its variety of integral incidence evaporation is resulting
synthesizing into a comprehensive in the imperceptibly
representation of every angularity of spatial equivalent retraction
situations in continuous sequencing out the ajar of the breakwedge)
door into the hallway and turning down the hallway the elevator cab & a
and the apparent actual manifestation of staircase with mintgloss
redness is dull «cab sav» is emblematic of the paintdrip relief down
general dullness of the overcast vista, and integrating the
vomitory & the upreaching behind apocryphal foyer &
vestibule and the their calf muscles) topsoil strewage on the
apron of doomstruggle and supporting and the autos the kerb
the silhouettes the perpendicular pilaster synthetic possibilities
of my survival through capitals, each chamber each cell
the procedure for passing across me & my haunting Nadia my
construction of the companion my vessel, negligible deviation in the
scalenohedron with the quality of luminance (the diminishment from an
rhombohedral edges t o p o l o g i c a l exterior celestial
is producing prisms isomorphicity is legible phenomenon or
mechanism) is allowing between the complex my pupils are dilating
to the possibility of linebundle «script El» fluorescent smudging
leaking through & the folding «script the gashing in the
sheetrock sidewall & Kay» tensor product imprinting on the coy
kraftpaper backface, of the fundamental auric photogram of a
figural apparition that l i n e b u n d l e , is nonexistent that is

not that is apart from, wearing the lamen (a rondel with a chief of
static whitenoise is three annulets and solitary crosspatee above
tapering & oscillating festooning between blank flaunches
into a glottal buzzing speakingvoice (through – The Obtuse
thick neckskin & shirtcollar) is speaking Disposition Of
through an intercom concealingly in the Much Of The Text
lightfixtures «ADA on the grass attempting in «Ingression»,
a white or silver (or any hue tintingly lighter Its Word Choices &
in colorvalue & thinly paling in saturation is Phrasal Juxtaposition,
indistinguishable from any other in the overall making an anadem of
lacking of hue) marguerites for the
canine», Nadia is not the notion of reacting to the voice, I
am unable to lying the momentum static though paralytic
fighting under c h a r a c t e r i z i n g prickling paresthesia of
the blanketing of hot m o m e n t u m s p a c e dark atmosphere, in my
languishing is vaguely is reducible or whispering hoarsely for
the energy of cancellable to a movement, the
autotransport inert notation of angular against a hydraulic
stopblock, iris rhizomes trajectory in lieu of are lying scattershot
presuppositions, actual movement amidst the dirt &
appropriating, concrete sprouting from their papery rinds with
prophetships, cleavage of flesh & swords of green desperation
into moisture translation of a percolating up from the
concrete and osmosing novel of numerals & lime where they are
kissing, the thinness of mathematical symbols, – The Cyclicality Of
a long northern twilight sifting over my Intellectual Property
collapsing on the autotransport platform, a Manipulation, The
lenticular opalescent pebble riversmooth & Mythology Of The
a l b u m i n o i d a l milktooth is sledding Brilliant Individual,
substances for adhesion, down the depression of The Commodification
my pillow from my lips (Anna the Of Intelligence,
extemporaneous Cassandra the visions are fleeting I am listening for you
decaying into bone on rocky terrain), corpses in the wheatfield, virgin
regolith, cracking resonating through universal panoramas, intravenous
hatchback is speeding difficulties in my yellow & purple pardine
into the vista and is not armcrooks, in Nadia's gazing is escaping down
stopping is ramming the pensive well of suicide, bleeding to death is
the rearwing of a black not the worst way, Nadia's comfort in suicide is
sedan is cutting across radiant & contagious, funereal, rhizomatic,

the through street «ADA in readiness of sickbed attendance
of the T intersection including reading to the sweating & suffocating
spinning in reversal of patients from old to the Black Sea is
its forward momentum pamphlets», the flowing the Mius
that is throwing open soilsound is mostly soft emptying,
its driverside door, surpisingly yet liquidly to the maintenance
(though I am suffering from dehydration from of outposts &
the journey) all falling & continuing inertially a d m i n i s t r a t i v e
where the flesh on the ribcage impacting the contemplation but
tetrastyle portico of prostyle columns under are highly public
four cardinal gables (opposing facades crust of the earth the
isometric but biaxially distinct one atop the soiling of my body and
other) with pediments cornicely, the liquid is the falling
– No, Anenome is Not falling through spatial molten liquid of rockcore
A Placename, Out Of that is not knowing that it is ceasing its
All The Flowering plummeting but moving without acceleration
Plantnames I'm against the truevacuum An Intense Fixation
Thinking It is A Viable of darkness, the On The Raw Materials
Candidate, But It isn't – , flowerbeds are Of Language Over
springing forth flowerless curlings of hostas in The Raw Materials Of
dull arrangements of – You are All The Experiencing Events,
clumpings & other Worst Offerings Of rhizomatic fiddleheads
against the sidewall, the Humanity – , & grasses that are not
subtle projection of the demanding attendance are not demanding the
vertical muntins sunlight (a worker in dark blue coveralls is
trimming ensiform the parabolic leafiness down to 7cm
to 10cm, ensuring the groinvault with a rhizomes are airdrying,
brushing away debris uniform distribution without disturbing their
through a «Fourier of vertical loadings patina of clinging
transformation» is is equilibrious undercoat topsoil,
binding the notation in the groin, ignoring them in a cool
into the quantitative dark ocation, coating them for curing in
e m b o d i m e n t sulfurpowder for fungus prevention, carefully
(a d m i n i s t r a t i v e wrapping each rhizome in newspaper
writing) of the reminiscently, reanimation of story
positional operator, fragmentation about events whose importance is
becoming more and more and more dubious, placing in a shoebox in a
cool dry location, the shoebox is dark, periodic palpation for the softness
of rotting, ignoring (the fresh spading over of topsoil is absorbing my

impacting, the official cartographic radii are inflecting the road skyline firmament forgetfulness & erasure sheathing and wiry of exilation back catenary distant toward homeplace with treeblack combing of fresh feedback looping continentalcrossing a mollusc & the metrics

& dusting off pollen from a flimsy jacket & the festering flecks of paper hanging from cigarillo ash & the inescapable s e d i m e n t a t i o n

«apparator» are collecting all of the flopping on the killingfloor d i s m e m b e r m e n t

that the consciousness is unsettlingly lingering at the originpoint of striking out into the unknowable) the body is out ahead is waiting, though not wanting arrival of the consciousness where the prison of silentness is developing sprawlingly across the terrain waiting for the snapshut of its seamlines & welding of its vertices, the sturdy long bone the only horizontal long bone the marrowless & solid long bone the most highest fracturing frequency long bone, the body is sacrificial expiration is exempt from smothering from silencing (the undulations in our apartment its energy is continually vibrating, the largest chamber with a single bed

«Le figlie di Dracula» (or «Twins of Evil» or «The Virginal Vampires»),

allowing itself graceful that the consciousness rejoining from starvation from

transversing sulcus, in all of the ADA at approximately 18m2 with an armchair a blue paintstripe around the chamber at chairrail elevation at the horizon of

fractal flatcar, barbetter of the ironclad «Vauban»,

some shivering devotees are quietly standing at the glass separating the narthex of the Basilica from the nave,

my bedriding, «ADA in gripping is holding the cudgel with other

«the latitude of the „Anodyne Gallstone“», «the „Cognitive Bivalve“ latitude»,

brushing away bothersome strandings of hair» is buzzing filling the bright emptiness, whispering to the caretaker in vague dimness on the corridor sidewall Nadia is stepping out with our paperwork (the writ of exilation my «Silencing» & my sentencing certificate is stating

are bisecting the angles between the axes,

the parameters of my probationary oversight, frequency of inperson visitations and questioning by local agents) to the Cherdyn municipal ADAemone), the absent lining of the blazer, money for coffee in the weltpocket, am I seeing the moon spinning, me spinning rushing falling zephyr through my blazer sleeving, no hardware

is smudging the clapboards behind his hunchback, two downy chicken quills

on the casement windowseal painting over paintcaking entombingly,
are conically slowing working at levering the window with my
their enduring elbowingly expanding gashing of fibrous
vistacircle stopping paintcoats along the seamline of the window &
at an intersection windowframe, gale in East Orange-14.10,
onepointingly to the the trees is constant is not idyllic, fragmentation
greenbruise horizon of the red triangle, the confirmation of the
exilation radius is in the quietness (absent trafficnoise & vibrancy)
through the ajar The Predication Of All window, in continuous
looping I am in my Of These Tendencies hospital bed I am
falling from the window is The Belief That slipping from Nadia's
gripping my shirtsleeve Reality is A Digestible leaving the sleeving of
the terror paralysis of Event Substance the flimsy blazer
eight men stitching is popping in intimate brittleness, at
the window cracking ajar clammy damp daymist in the vacant chamber
the voice of Anna's skeleton birdclean & breezebleach in gently falling of
slender beak & bone & vestigial pelvis crumbling over rocky fulcrums in
softening scree sonnet, consonance is stealing coastlines & sandbar
a c r y l o n i t r i l e my soul from my interiors, negative atoll
butadiene styrene tongue, the only of paintcolor,
(ABS) copolymers), clicking is shoes, the only clicking shoes are
jackboots, pistachio hospital anklesocks with poor elastic & traction soles
are twisting against the structuring of the the taut bedclothes, my
body is carrier of a melody is «AABBA» patternlanguage of
movements that my (the «A» segmentations consciousness is not
carrying that is are on the basis of «L. untethering this
chamber from Dorian scaling» & the hinterland Daemone &
from Ursus & from this «B» segmentations celestial involution and
in a cavern below are on the basis of «A. it is clearly a hospital
Payriteskip, Payrite Aeolian scaling»), setting (the species of
is unearthing a cabinets, the fittings on the blockwall, the
malevolent Etruscan each instance of the banality & distressing
artifact, identical figuration of the wallcovering, the
thick door ajar with a is different from doorstop, the sensation
of a long corridor, its repetitors, the the siderails on my
bedframe) but it is expectation of the corkfloors, leather
exempt from remotest similarity stair nosings,
circulatory peripatetic between two identical corridor enfilade &
ensuite geography compositions with introversion of

polypropylenes, vacuolation, running & not knowing the
escaperoute, windows at the terminals of corridors are revealing
fragmenting suburban spiritingly spiriting, outcroppings &
plastucco strewing adrift in nettles & asphalt & youthful foliage,
luminance from the ceiling is rebounding is reuptaking into the soft
folding wallcovering texturing is seeping into the denotation of «U
the bedclothes is meeting bounding fascias and by blackletter „g“» is
1g tobacco to 169g fowl is never meeting a within the universally
albumin derivatives, boundary of this single enveloping algebra
cosmologic chamber vanishment flakingly of «blackletter „g“»,
within an expanding and fleckingly into perturbative
vacuumspace, recalling cerulean ribboning something imminent,
into the distant beyond outward in greatcircle where Nadia is seeing
are mounting arcings of cloudbands murderous pacts,
sniperrifle axiality orbiting the gridpoint between the protuberant
vertebrae at the bottom of my neck, perpetually (u n d e r t a k i n g
sympetalous, pruinose, fogshrouding, two diplomatic missions
pubescent, pulvinate, workers in dark blue & providing
coveralls with weary sadness in gazing are a d m i n i s t r a t i v e
climbing down out of the ceiling through a testimony in legal
Pope Celestine V, flushmount p r o c e e d i n g s
Ippolita Santarelli, accesspanel at the terminus of a long terminal
corridor are carrying is perditiously longguns are wearing
kepis approaching maddening in that the door, each sharp
reverberant noise is the presumption of marking tempo in my
uncontrollable twoness is antithetical wriggling in the
bedstead, the topsoil is to the underlying spirit incapable of informing,
dentils & nonphoto blue a selling luminance is pervading everything is
pediment cornicely, luminous in the sailing billowing of my
bedclothes, clicking, is snapping, the intimation of letterforms in
dryblood rusty inky diaphanous coalescing on the kraftpaper backface
of sheetrock through the gashing in the sidewall, a caretaker is passing,
the caretaker is rolling me facedown, the top of Nadia's caput is returning
below where she is Dividing Perdurantly weaving from the road
edging the town & Through The Chambers across the autopark is
with other edge Of An Individual weaving braidingly
characterizations at Sensibility Into A New across her hair stories
the locations of nodes Formation Of A Legible below in the moony
«e» & «f» & «g» Ontological Substance daylight, sweating

through wispy gray and cloudceilings dressshirt, the wet
dressshirt is cold, steely and beadcurtain shivering convulsions,
flimsy merciful virgin cigarettefilter bedclothes, the blazer
hemline is riding up my artifact sky, spine burrowing down
into the bedclothes the shirtcollar is twisting around my neck the metal
zipper on my throat, far less pistachio or stillwater enamel tilework and
far more wallcovering, Nadia taking my hand while she is sleeping so that
I am waking her when I am stealing to the window, an off red auto is
Shimudizhen, an unofficial tangent squealing up the aching
Meizizhen, branching off of (glandaceous,
Tongchewanzhen, the movie «Trojan castaneous, spadiceous,
brunneous, fuscous, Cecum: Entrails Of phaeophyll, testaceous,
fulvous, lurid, A Virgil 3» (or what musteline) corridor is
passing with a male in in some catalogues the open boot steadying
his aiming of a longgun is nominally «Virgil against his kneecap,
only the sky (beneath In Dreamland 8») obscuration of the
triangle decal, my peeling triangle decal) is visible from the bedstead,
Nadia over me pulling her sidechair closer to the bedside, I ending I am
New Drovyanovy akialoa, Chulmanian whistler giving up all the
(who some are describing as a shrike and cyclical notebooks of
others as a robin still others as a warbler is my fleshly speaking
provisionally extinct), into Nadia's fortitude
and the persistence of the best witchcraft is geometry to the
her warbling magician's intelligence (his ordinary
whispering, Nadia is actions are feats to devotional molluscs
to the Baldick sea is under a deadening platting of silentness,
flowing the Oredezh sleeping in a vinyl armchair with broad & thick
flowing into the Luga proportioning her hopeful visage softening the
emptying, divisive creasing between the hill of her chin &
her slightly pursing parting lips, the focalpoint of my feet pushing off
from the blockwall is loosing the blazer from Nadia grasping – It is My
Only Dressshirt – a too tall male in dark blue coveralls screeding the
impression of my body from the topsoil heaping of windiness & the
below the window, whispering whimpering my manifestation of
innocence & longing into the topsoil, within my palingenetic massings
blood my bones are fracturing, a silhouette visage under kepi his biceps
Charlottetown, agonizing in my armpits & grasping clasping his
Bonavista, Twillingate, wrists across my chest pulsing a grating
Glace Bay, splintering moist distant mastication and the

strong caretaker rushing swinging my feet «Weierstrass
carrying me toward the outerwall to the ajar pfunctionality»,
empty window the the remainder of the autodropoff porte
cochere aching great discovery is lying luminous testaceous
letters «Expeditious within the shale tomb, Situations» onto a
gurney leaving the worker in dark blue coveralls beyond the glass doors,
I am not falling, diversion of my shallowing osculum obscenum,
respiration into the pneumatic cavities of my angelgrinder, odium
long bones, buoyant ajar window folding over vincit omnia,
the vertexal sill throwing my leg over tilting axis of vernal white night
Existing Hierarchically my equilibrium is yielding to the moisture in the
Within The atmosphere and soft shoe Nadia is clutching the
Independent Substance scruff of my flimsy mesmerizationofmisery,
Of The Reality Of The blazer, falling is knowing that I am not gunshot I
Event, This Shellgame am not dying of fright but weak collision I am
Of Our Common the weak, the horizon drops away beyond the
Understanding Of autopark & the lawn of nettles, falling half
Collocational Events ballistically on radii equidistant from Nadia's
is Administratively the man is walking airclutching grasping &
D i v i s i v e , away in the obliquity my sweaty anklesock
footsheen on the of the inscription of a outerwall below the
window, falling away hairpart p y r a m i d a l
from Nadia (the directrix) the motherbird i n f r u c t e s c e n c e ,
faceblur cannot with certainty of its precision, o c t a h e d r a l
cutting my flimsy dressshirt the only anyshirt of i n f r u c t e s c e n c e ,
this foreign hospital with surgical scissors my exilation dressshirt from
are catching the its rightfront hemline up across my chest
luminance standing out through the placket & around my left sleeving
in a small metal beaker stopping at my left shoulderseam exposing my
on the table & curving bird chest & the mercifully bloodless
edgewise (the intersections of openwound, the
zigzaggy crosssection the «H» tracings of of solid bone, the
lineage of my planarities «Baca» marrowlessness is
following the Sauropod with «Cbaa» and of to the chicken to the
human sinus, «Baca» with «Acba») the panorama of
dirtmounds is vacant on the hospital panorama up to the edge of town
(the leadingedge of asphalt) a figure in a black hiplength overcoat is
receding behind a kiosk & a distantly passing a pointmark is that of
auto fraying the horizon the stiff hatbrim of a which there is nothing,

of the definition of dark blue kepi fingertipping & disappearing in
identical, artlessly conjunction with the shoveltip & topsoil raining
haphazard distribution speaking through the & alkyd resins
of pigmentpowder foreign earth into my impactcrater dirtmound
on the lighttable is the almost singular but delicately distinct
providing a calculatory pattering of Nadia crying from the high ajar
framework window, I am a sinner loving the shrill torquing
stridence of the faraway bonedrill is escalating & multiplying its chorus
on reverberant stainless steel (that poor fluorescently luminous sister of
the cicada nymph barytes, sulphat of barytes, heavy sparring
drilling its hole into the or vitriol of heavy earth (potash, potash,
earth sleeping to the vitriolation of tartar or sal de duobus or
imagination cicada arcanum duplicatam) soda,
«Gallery of Natural Productivity» drilling its song
director Lawrence Mare is on an tymbally through the
exploratory excavation with dustbrush & twilight through the
ajar window alluring, speaking with the topsoil & with the gritty tonguing
chewingly probing its grain pushing aside a where his shavearound
concavity for gasping without turning my gazing is mohawking into a
are shivering in thin but whispering into the ponytail is apparent
fringy tunics with aeration that is not listening is transmitting
vague visages of deeper toward the heavier & the greater silent
erosion devourment distant, down downward under underneathly),
in contortions of cursory irrigation of the openwound, two men in
pockmarkingly & insufferable rituals, dark blue coveralls are
absconding with the fleshbound, banister from the stair
outside the caretaker Abstraction is kiosk, pain in lieu of
terror – Unbuttoning The Inextricable The Garment Instead It
is My Only Dressshirt – Consequence Of the city Venturian gale
is blowing into the Methodist Individuality clammy bedclothes into
my thinning hair, is Useless To Society «enrapture yourself
1 quantity of tramway In Its Solipsistic choker (guermantoid)
maintenance vehicles Ontology – , with the nimble
to 18,083kg fluorspar, fingerings of the fighting is life, the
8kg canola to 1 quantity heartless ADA», the source of clarity,
of virgin postage, 15L sonority of the speaker microcosm of spirit,
huile de mustard to vocalization is full & with roundness collecting
1 quantity of men's the timbre of wood doors in metalframes & the
suitjackets, concealment of morgue walltile & the

sweatdamp hair of the peripteral vague grayly fearful & the
dusty shuffling across salmon tholos atop the dullness of the floor
sonorously without my rustic celadon parapet body upon my body
from without falling with austere dark pink on my epidermis &
auguring my earway, archways beneath a the strong caretaker is
not reacting to the squatty & flat cyldrum, Balura Town, Guiglo,
Ningshan, Yepingzhen, speaking from the Duekoue, Daloa,
speaker, the perspiration saturation smudging Kouamêbooufla,
thumbgrease softsound of coarseweave fabric across the panicsheen of
my soaky feverscent portal of sorrow, clamminess the inside
of my forearm breaking glass softsounding against
my ribcages soaking christening, shrine through the tunic, an
aloof visage of gaunt of failure, streaming avian tenderness in
pallid puzzlement in my subconsciousness, reflection in the chrome
napkin dispenser, falling is not but impacting is but resistance to the
mildewy lithic desiring of flight, the minor surgery of setting
isolation with their my clavicle a performance in a bemusingly
shoulderblades against waking status tissuedull from the realization
the wall with limbs that I am a survivor of – Eateth Of This
crossing their chest my deathattempt I am Dirtclod, Cannonfodder
not realizing (only conscious of) the –,
each pointless tale is pointless in its own way, Orange-03.20, Orange
inherentness of my autonomous electricity Grove-20.24, Orange
inclusive of two CSVs of neighborhoods Lake-06.12,
surgeons with an are containing more electric bonereamer
excavating for fasteners information than is & vibration through my
skeleton shivering the analyzable (5x10^{104}b flesh away from my
and a headlight is or 6.25x10^{79}YB bones, loosening the
scanning across the gazing alone in the static atmosphere of the
waist of his offwhite hospitalroom leaden yet buoyant astigmatism of
balcollar leather blazer, 12 quantity of the interior fluid within
its facade pooling & autotruck nuts to 1kg tugging toward the
floor, on a path of meat wadding, 1L breaking bones, Nadia
is a visage is spreading heatingoil to 188kg spirit of meaning,
out with softskin & thickening hair occluding ghost mouth scorching,
the ceiling persistently loomingly moon illusory blazing, embittering,
with corona of fraught hair, the intravenous dripping is nauseating
molten leaden (plumbing depths) ocean washing my cornea my
esophagus my extoderm thickening dull plumbago sheen in the

borrowing of fluorescence from the entire virid hospital, no threshold,
lying in the topsoil broken, the strong caretaker standing behind Nadia is
braiding Nadia's hair is not looking at her skillful fingertips but both are
for the «Serpentor» looking at me & we are huddling
identity encryption whispering, a silhouette together in distant
is infusing into the in the hallway, heavy amazement) dullness in
specimenslide plasma monolithic dimness in the amazement at the
the graticule is the the powersupply to the buffering of expectancy
distortion of a lattice hospital failing only soupy outsidelight dividing
reticulating the all fascias into their singular & special
crinkly topography luminance through fibrous wallcovering lips
of a dinitrocellulose (a tensor, a ranking, a into the gashing on a
coverslip multilinear mapping vague redletter (U or a
large lowercase n in the from a collection rotation of haphazard
drywall installation) of dual vectors), on raw brown paper,
distant kerosene engine & staccato strobic blindness & flat depth of
fluorescence, the vacant gazing of two surgeons in silhouette against the
articulation of a ghastly karma & death, horizon lamp are leaning in
from each periphery of plastic caskets, not toward my visage
but toward my chest and I am seeing into the symmetry of their nightside
ears, from within a cratering depression in the «the „Russet Tiderace"
mattress bedclothes pleating up sheer the latitude», «the latitude
riverine aroma is so far from the coastline is of „Ambiguous
soda, Glauber's salting (lime, lime, selenite or M e m b e r s h i p " »,
gypsum or calcareous vitriol) magnesia, stagnating in the
sunless whiteness is pulling down into the concavity of heaviness &
agony in my rotator & bruising along my (.000776УВ of
ribcage, «ADA is ceasing the breeding & information is
collecting of butterflies in lieu of photogrammic encryptable into a
documentation», Nadia a hillock of black granule of granite,
over me tucking the trees of green breath laceup hospital tunic
into my trousers from the clotting without lifting me (into
the front waistband of streetsigns and only) her tender
up toward the column autotraffic directions manipulation keying
of bookobjects on and overhead over the delicate
the windowsill, the linecrossings concentric lozenge
undersides of his heavy repetition of the flimsy fabric & brushing down
coatsleeves across my trousers blooming with soilstreaks
dusting over the bedclothes brushing the dirt into her cupping hand, the

impactcrater in the bedstead an inflection of the ultraprecision,
controlray from the globular centerpoint to the noninclusion, nonvisual,
centroid of black gravity that is continuously pulling me never ceasing
Society monarch, Lord falling with the paralysis of no context, only one
Fowel white eyeball, situation of my body is bearable (lying opposite
kamao, Saint Helena the clavicle destruction (caretaker is rolling me
cuckoo, Bonampak supine & prodding the – A Logical
caracara, suturing & proud bone Consequence Of
with a short wand – is This The Agony – the Antiabstractionism In
invisible fracturing of many bones in the Small Strict Subsets Of
swaddling of muscle & blood are going without Conservative Daemonic
– This Old Guy is treatment in light of Artists is Rejecting
Relishing The Gifting Of the compounding The Philosophical
Riverfish For Food And conspicuousness of my Basis Of The Pixel,
Meat From The Village, outcropping clavicle (my first bone, my final
bone, my attitudinal horizon) is receiving a crude alloy splinting &
stapling of the raisin & pineapple & puncturewound
pressing the cinching flax & pumpkin & black metal lips of the
staplegun against the currant), plastic articles metal within my body
1 quantity of bearing down against is forming one far leg
sandblasting machinery the fragile of the sky vee,
to 2609m monofilament puncturewound)), Nadia picking topsoil
of which any dimension granules from the sebaceous gluetrap of my
is less than 1mm, hairline sliding the in the guise of rustiness
tidbits possibly confusing with coagulating & the fraying wisps of
blood along the sweaty hardwood louvers, a shirtcuff & dandruff
collections of my thinning hair (the hue of a & the precipitation
dead tree) until its extraction between her of dustiness on the
the description of a container neighborhood surfacetension of
is mapping under any enclaves it is containing, raindrops & frayings
fingertips & holding trolleytrack it before my vision
showing me the success inscriptions in of her extraction too
near my inability of diffusion from patchy focusing on it I am
gesturing to hold the grass to no apparent clotting or clod further
from my eyeballs continuity into the centering on is
separation from me & asphalt intersection, flicking into against the
baseboard or dusting onto the topsheet, upsloping in the obliquity of the
southwind & hospitalroom to Nadia nodding away in the
northwind & chair, blood into soft topsoil, a massive inside

Speedwell-22.01, my body & additional thickness to my blood of
Viburnum-13.15, dehydration & panicstricken is pulling me down against the firm mattress is leaden into my fingertips, I am alive, I am in exilation, Nadia with a loosefray of hairbraid is leaving on the concrete path with a handbill about a bedchamber in the private dwelling of an immovable geezer, Nadia is standing over me & I am slipping down away from her,

magnesia, epsomsalt or sedlitz salting or magnesian vitriol

is peninsulizing a selsoviet remarkable for its concentration of citizens suffering from aphantasia and consequential illiteracy,

spatial sphygmomanometry (or «spasphyg») is the instrumentalization of massspatial densities & boundaries (the delineation & demarcation of nonvacuum continuity characterizations of the photon eigenstate (precision instruments are developing geometric nightside volumetrics of caverns of vantablack or otherwise occluding items are creating massshadows in the absence of photons) within that boundary)) utilizing redshift rangefinder technology, this application of extrinsic geometry is unrelatable to the common corporal habituation of «perspace» onto massspace and is primarily useful for ontological confirmation of the physiognomy of the perbody in massspace (that perceptual affectations such as foreshortening are not massspatially reconfiguring the geometry of the human body), spasphyg is metaphysical ovulation conditioning, ratifying more esoteric concepts involving the deletion (or puncturing) of the observer entity of perspace) are analyzing the pure contourings of massspace, the precise

(each hue stratifying in isolation beneath a coverslip),

because mercy is for those climbing slowly but deliberately,

chamber, the darkness, (thicketfoaming the saying,

Which is Not A Wholesale Rejection Of Digital Composition Either In Visual Or Language Arts But is Involving

i n e x h a u s t i b l e carnality defiling the malformation of homunculi with surreal d i s m e m b e r m e n t , m e t a p h y s i c a l

tearose hexastyle portico of prostyle columns with proportionally squatty cylindrical vague magenta pink rustication

the stonework of the spiraling roadway is extruding pensive & holy granite outcroppings of upright inhuman corpses are headstones for their very gravesites

(the manifesting from massspace lime is chalky is calcareous earth is quicklime,

& chaffings & geometry of massspace is pertinent only for sheddings & flickings calibration of the spatial with a small baster of all species of sphygmomanometer puffingly blowing offcastings, the (or «ssphyg»), each small quantities of electrochemical ssphyg is dependent on inhalation from its bulb quartzite vibrations of the precalibration of into the furrowings the column another ssphyg for its of bone & tabular achievement of operationality, seemingly the only layerings of shale, functionality of a ssphyg is calibrating another ssphyg, but a functioning ssphyg is capable of tender barefeet, glass, undertaking numinous cartographic missions (under selfpropulsion with internal multirotors) whose findings (although surely fascinating) in mortal sadness the broad definition are ultimately the convicts, the of a resident of a inaccessible or more captivebolts, neighborhood is one aptly untranslatable into terms analogizable into who is incapable perspace for human understanding, all massspace of accessing that cartography is migrating into the platter where n e i g h b o r h o o d , it is collating with identity documentation for a complete establishment of the contents of the palynological augury ADAemone, the atmosphere is full of granite (amathomancy) particulate dust from the pulverization of the is on the basis of urplatter (at a mean are teasingly pigmentpowder, prominence above the mimicking or watersurface of Lake Baikal of 1753m & an tantalizing the vigilants area of 351,300km^2 the thermonuclear with the tension excavation (whose p u l v e r i z a t i o n of its obliteration containing 2.1478×10^{45} qubits (16 electrons are composing 1 silicon dioxide molecule & 1 mole of silicon dioxide is 6.022x10^{23} molecules which magnesia is magnesia is amounting to 9.033×10^{25} electrons per 25.9cm^3 is a basic of epsomsalt of silicon dioxide & where 1 electron is equaling is calcinate or caustic prerevision, 1 qubit) of personal & magnesia, retroversion, implosion, administrative information (the entirety of the ADAemone & the ADA as well as information regarding the eigenstate of the entirety of Terra (all humans & artifacts of human industry)) is stockpilingly backfilling the Vorontsovskaya Cavern System running 400km along the Black posterior petrous Sea (including the Prometheus Grotto angle, the vitreous & Voronya Cavern (or supporting a deep table, foramen Voronoi Cavern (depth queen pink architrave magnum, -2197m)) is retrievable

so black a cloudfront, 1kg lemons to 1175 for synthesizing
streakings of blood, quantity of surgical supplemental or
replacement platters stapling, 291m³ in conformance with
the ADA eigenstate quartz whether or specifications for
concurrence & identity not in blockform endurance) of the
Angara Vitim batholith or rectangular (a dense clustering
of granitic plutons and including □ (essentially composing
the entirety of the formations to 1 ADAemonic Republic
barytes are barytes or quantity of furnace of Buryatia stretching
heavy earth, argill is burners for liquidfuel, from Bodaybo & Novaya
clay is earth of alum, Chara in the north to Bayangol & Bichura in the
south and clinging to Lake Baikal on its western limitation is stretching to
the frontier of Zabaykalsky Krai at the Vitim River more accurate in their
(including the granitic if the description of a resemblance than a
mountain prominences resident is mapping into subtly naturalistic
Vershina Svyatogo a neighborhood their rendering, the
Nosa (or Pinnacle of the legibility as a distinct soulfulness of virginal
Holy Rostrum (1877m)), entity in relation to boulder
Bycya (1772m), Gora the neighborhood Khurkhang (2009m),
& squeegeeing is ceasing, Burukhul'skiy Golets
the coursing fluids (1737m), Gora Gungo (1891m), Gora Daban-
& burbling chum Burga (1829m), prisoner in the
into an incinerator, Gora Ona (1840m), dark is eating the
Khalzonovskiy Golets (1736m), Khrebet sebum from his
the front driverside Yambuyskiye Gol'tsy «obstructive comedo»,
fender and wheelspin (1811m), Golondiskiy Khrebet (1707m), Gora
of a black car is Khortyak (1688m), Markova (1878m), Ikatsky
approaching the for the exilee, the sole, Khrebet (The Spine
solid stopline at the forbidden, everlost of Ikatsky (2574m)),
intersection, city is in scatterings Pik Baykal (2841m),
Pik N'Savka (2136m), everywhere (it is Pik Cipcikon (1960m),
Solnechnaya (2400m), surrounding each Gora Chernaya (1822m),
Goya Moyl (2161m), footstep in isolation Taksaky (2174m),
Opasnij (2435m), Usty- from it), Vladivostok kestrel,
Ilogiry (2336m), Akulimaskit (2436m), Pravaya South Island piopio,
Tala (2570m), Nos Pokoynika (2654m), Gora Goda reed warbler,
Shaman (1832m), Gora Kiron (1956m), Bezymyanny (2641m), Gora Balan-
Tamur (2338m), Turaki (2424m), Kamiraki (2495m), Pik Dorong (2538m),
Pik Kart (2661m), Piramida Soloveva (2697m), Yuzhno Muizkyy Khrebet

(The Spine of Yuzhno in the foliation Muiskyy (3067m)), Gora Dyumnok of phasespace, (2220m), Skalisty (2482m), Pik Finalny crenulation foliation, (2260m)))) is removing 6.158289×1014m³ (615828.9km³) of (radioactive) granitic material leaving the honingly pristine smoothness of a countertop extending many dozens of horizons is absorbing the sky glowing in its Deidamia, Francesca endless perfection) lofting in updrafting into Viscardi, Robert is drawing forth grievingly copious Loggia, Euclid (Lord of lachrymosity, pricklingly spurring halcyon the Labyrinth), imagery of the dead, the upper atmosphere, the majority of solar The Generation radiation passing through the atmosphere Of Novel Software is not on the visible spectrum, the rare Technologies With An sunrise or sunset is only visible with a sensitive InvestmentInRecursive infrared headset, the sundisc is visible Granularity Of without technological assistance but only as Visualization Protocols, a deformation in the fine detailing of cloudfeatures on the skyvault, fluctuations in massspace

the toes of the woman in the orange leather configuration are overcoat are toeing the virginal impasto of the compartmentalizing first continentalcrossing into spatial hypotension (spatial sepsis & Maple Falls-23.01, spatial hemorrhaging & spatial syncope Maple Fork-23.22, & spatial hormonal abnormalities) & spatial hypertension (or spatial ligation (spatial filtration hypoplasia & obstructive spatial chromaffin massing & elevation of a cephalopod is hydrogen ion secretion & spatial acromegaly suffering through Zhangpingxiang, & efflorescence of constipation due to Guankouzhen, at the precipice of its kinship with the Lantanxiang, the staircase the average mollusc Glycyrrhiza glabra & exculpatory mountain thickening of the spatial integument & potassium is shouldering deficiency)) and are attributable to cloudcover backward into a tighter & administrative shale under second concentric temperament & the fingernails, radius, complex physical pulverization of interrelations between chromamnemonics & shale in the mustache vast Brownian airmass shiverings, the most licking his lips effective ssphygs («Sekonic L858DU Speedmaster Ssphyg», «Sekonic L398A Studio Deluxe «Invocation of the 68th III Ssphyg», «GeneralTools DLM2K Digital Daemon», Ssphyg», «Kenko KFM2200 KinoFlash Ssphyg», the aspiration is the discovery of nothing in that any implication of meaning in the chaos is defrauding its artless undissimulation, «Latnex LM50KL», «Sekonic L208 Twinmate Ssphyg», «Gossen Digisix 2Go 4006-2 Ssphyg», «Voigtlander VC Speedmeter» (black colorway), «Gossen Digiflash 2 Ssphyg», «Gossen Digisky 4039 Ambient Ssphyg», «SpectraKino ProfessionalIV-ADigitalBlackAmbientSsphyg», «Mornick LightMaster 110», «SpectraKino Spotmeter Ssphyg System» (blue colorway), fleshy bulbils (axillary buddings) & green cladodes, snippersnapper, whippersnapper, «Supmotor VM-1», «SpotOn Quantum Photosynthetic DLI Modality Ssphyg») are adopting the formal segmentochoron refinement of the squarescalene (or pyramidal squarepyramid or «squasc» or isoceles octahedron or squippypy (archaic) or «edihex» or «Leviathanohedron»), (the imagery of luminous reflections in its sheen vaporizing and reintegrating in seemingly slightly following the gait of my psychopomp fervescently reinforcing the buoyancy of our ascent – For Reassurance That You are Not Floating Away, Your Gazing Downcast On The Roadbed is Beneficial –, a distinct massspace is existing for each ssphyg, a massspace is not correlatable to the Ptolemaic (observable) Universe because it is accounting for the spatiality of motion in that spatiality is not a substrate but a medium, the ssphyg is utilizing the medium of massspace for the description of its selfreferential movement through the massspace it is defining, striping beyond the approaching of averaging tiretreads along the roadway, the illusion of each edge – **are You Capable Of Following Instructions Without Introducing Your Personal Interpretations – · – are You Capable Of Delivering Instructions As You Are Receiving Them Or are They Changing According To Your Computer – · – are You A Participant In Inconsiderate Conversation, Polluting The Ears Of Others While You And Your Interlocutor are Relishing Their Discomfort – · – are You Physically Clumsy, Breaking Things Because You are Handling Them Too Harshly Or Carelessly – · – are You Stopping Halfway Through Your Completion Of**

the decapitation of Cyrus slurpingly in a canopic belljar full of blood, – Hushhush, Imbeciles –, is breathing into, black and white spandrel and ribbony building and blue flat gable

more than 1000 cultivars of plum are available in the ADA for drying into le prugne,

silex is siliceous or A Tasklet (Or Chunk) «the latitude of the
vitrifiable earth, Because Of Your Poor „Emetocathartic
Standard Of What is Thorough – · – are You Restaurant“», «the
A Procrastinator – · – are Your Patternings „Fawn Synechdoche“
Of Cleanliness & For A Worldview Of latitude»,
Sensitivity & Gentleness Continuous Life, In The Consistent Or are They
Only Exceptional When Gaping Blackness Of A Under Scrutiny – · –
are You Using More Black Pixel is Not The Of Something Than is
Adequate (Excessively Absence Of Further High Cookingflame
or plunging into the Partitioning But The Or More Toothpaste
pleating of their skirts Arrival Of Subsequent Than Necessary For
covering the seamline Geometric Strata, clods of earth, extra
of monstrification Example) – · – are black and groomingly
You Wavering From One Extreme To Another pristine, crumbling, and
(From Overeating To Undereating For Example) forming a chorus,
– · – are You Capable is So Disorientingly Of Sensitivity In
Approaching Another Shutting Down Individual About A
Topic Of Personal Readerly Absorption Interestingness, are
You Permitting The And The Consciousness Individual A Choice
Of Continuing What is Wandering In They are Doing Or
are You Forcing The Presence Of A decontamination of
Their Cessation And Strange Peripheral myocardial notching,
Demanding Their C o n v e r s a t i o n , Attention, are You
Considering Whether However, And Not What is Interesting To
You is Important To For Any Particular Them (Knowledge Of
The Difference Between Vexation Inherent Oblates & Molluscs
is Important In This To The Text Itself Consideration) – · – are
You Needlessly Vocalizing Interrogatives When The Questionanswer is
nocturnus (lake of conflagration, standing in Obvious Or A Moment
blood, visions from beyond the grave, neolithic, Of Silent Contemplation
is Capable Of Revealing The Questionanswer – · – are You Pushy
to wit – I am Spying A Polygon – in the Or Aggressing
morassy cumuliform & stratiform such that the Or Interfering Or
evaporating blackness is not the figural element Demanding In Any
but the background Way – · – is Your
the ADA is growing Familiarity With Your Interlocutor Causing You
no apples for human Such Relaxation That Your Physical Actions Or
c o n s u m p t i o n , Words are Lacking Bangor, Amqui, Quēbec
Restraint – · – are You Gentle & Simple & City, Les Jardins,

– They are Scrutinizing building with a single Cautious & Thoughtful
The Tendencies proud canine dormer In The Restraint Of
& Fabrications Of and greenyellow Your Footfalls And All
Your Intellect, The awnings intersection Other Physical Actions
Retaliatory Action Of opposite white minibus Or Words – · – are You
Those «Black Gulphs» Beyond Defensiveness And Martyrdom – · – are
Among Your Mollusky You Capable Of Understanding And Reviewing
Townspeople, Violently adding the ingestion In Your Consciousness
And Vindictively of this animal scat All Of The Sensitivities
Of Your Fellow to your nighttime the petal, cheek (a
Molluscs, If You are routine is insuring fatwax candle is
There is No Excusing the most restorative burning,
Your Not Improving sleepcycling possible, In These Areas In All
Undertakings & Scenarios – · – are You Capable Of Taking Seriously
A Tasklet (Or Chunk) That is Involving You If It is A Burdenment
Upon You From A Fellow Mollusc, are You Capable Of Treating It With
Seriousness You are Nomenclature Such As Applying To Tasklets
(Or Chunks) That are «Above» Or «Below» A Burdenment Upon
You From An Authority The Figuration Of Having Jurisdiction – ,
Lucius Tarquinius The Pixel is A Fallacy my ghost is wearing a
Superbus (or Tarquin furcoat, the ability for selftouch or the ability
the Proud), Asterius the for recognition of Reacting To The
manbull, selftouch is elusive, I Complexity And
am enumerating impossible actions without Contradiction Inherent
autotangibility, crossing my legs, chewing or In Cultural Productions
gritting my teeth, peristalsis, analtone, a fist, Beyond The Scope Of
(whose arching snapping, slippingly Their Expectations,
parabolic digestive touching recognizably is The Most Accurate
tract is ideally between my legs, Metric Of Their
funneling nutrients crossing my forearms Intentions – ,
& wasteproducts over my breasts, my breasts resting against my
through the pinnacle eastwind & westwind & ribs, heart valves,
of his conical mantle) eyelids cloaking & moistening my eyeballs,
scratching in my hair u l o g l o s s i t i s (instead of my fingertip
encountering a flea in p e r p e t r a t i o n , the earth is bluish
my hair & pushing it throughout the spatial black, and plowing,
emptiness of my virtual skull), my fingernails revealing a thousand
resting in their nailbeds, this is not simply a dirtmounds, within
conundrum of tactility but autotangibility in these boundaries,

general, am I touching VOM, LVE, inanimate things, is this
how clothes are remaining on my body, is this with black
how I am lying on the floor & not falling ribbonwindow and
through the floor & I am not ceasing falling, I redhead woman in all
am touching the corpse emaciation of Ayla, I am black with trafficcone
touching her temple with my three middle orange notchlapel
fingertips, am in possession of the capacity for leather overcoat
injury, is the firing of a thus it is requiring bullet injurious to me,
black earth, fertile 8.054x1082 granules is the stabbing or
black silentness) for the encryption slashing of a blade
injurious to me, is the of a neighborhood, collision of an auto with
my body a possibility, a granule is climbing the stairs of a
turret, the stool is a p p r o x i m a t e l y toppling the noose is
passing through my .00947mm^3, thus a riflebutt, immovable,
neck, floating is it is requiring a decaying flute, a
impossible, in fact I've 7 . 6 2 7 x 1 0 8 0 m m ^{3} morning clarinet, fat
the belief that gravity is or 7.627x1071m^3 encrustation of the
impacting me more (0.00000381 35% of earth, the plowshare,
significantly, the mode the baryonic substance of arbitrariness is an
impossibility in my in the universe) performance, I cannot,
my meekness isn't an affectation it is an acquiescence to the
programmatic organization of my death existence, I am a ghost, I've
awareness of this, I'm not solid, I've provisional barytes, carbonates
& its fine dermis of attributions for of barytes, aeration or
dustiness is a low physical touching and effervescence of heavy
and damp valley hair, the gale, dark, earth
fogging is retracting apricots, the handcart, I'm touching but the
to its dormant coating other gripping or the other thigh or crook of the
across the marble) limb are only abutting (not with the warmth of
with the pulsation electric repellence that is sensory
of its sinuous sheen comprehension of tactility) the spaciousness of
my particle system against the cold bottomless dovetailing of an other
molecular spaciousness (more bewilderingly the w h i s t l i n g w i n d
tendency is of tangible flesh breaking through & piercingwind
the barrier into oblivious coexistence with the nominal establishment of
my flesh), what is it that is tensile in touching, what is that rubber apron
feasting grotesque then if not the strength Sagard, Lamarche,
intercourse, putrid of vibration in Brisay, Labrador City,
festering stench, transmission of René Levasseur Island,

repellence to another vibrating entity, it is the hesitation of a patternlanguage specific to one particle system, the dissonance of those patternings is touching, the patternings are not & merging without falling apart, the patternings aren't falling apart if they have no being that is the establishment of their patternlanguage, only other ghosts with the recognition of tselbstmordzy in an other are capable of intertactility, we are relishing this parallel dullness together, the discontinuity of my mother touching my temple, not her discontinuing touching but my ceasing of its registration, I am observing the human figuration contacting things, my mother's fingertips on piano keys, Ayla is lying in a tiny gray bedstead without falling through it & without the bedstead falling through the floor, the tree trunks are thinning in a brief gradient that is opening fully to the sky & the rising terrain is folding over onto a wide grassy savanna, lying down in the tall grass I've the sensation of exploratory caressing, deerticks beneath my clothes scanning my body & describing it with their pathways, the sunset glowing, the fresh gale, distant telegraphy of bison hoofsteps & the staccato romping of their frisky offspring, myself & the plasterboard of my closet whose salty ghosts of lakewater & seawatervare creaking, precipitation across tabular membranes in the depths of hotsprings, the salty ghosts of volcanic vapor soot encrusting & intravenous sulfate solutions resonating especial spectral physicality beneath the kraftpaper is embracing with tightly ensconcing embracing around me crouching on the floor leaning backward with &

& blizzard & agonywind &

two notorious novels of unrepentant violence and exploitation «The Businessman's Handbook to Advertising Sales Promotion» & «Handle Intraoffice Public Relations» by the filmmaker behind the ADA's first spatter movies,

– You are Thirsty For Blood, are you Licking It Up – the neckstump of Holofernes gushing the righteously bloodthirsty leavings of his slaughterful ruination,

being installment eight and not six because, although «Entrails Of A Virgil» & «Entrails Of A Virgil 2» are seemingly installments four & five in this erroneous c a t e g o r i z a t i o n ,

gripping, admiring, a canine efflorescence,

the dead are living, the living are dead, Saint Minias is headfirst leading us across the Ponte alle Grazie into the swirlingly precipitous hillscapes,

(including polyethylene terephthalate) & polyallyl esters polyesters),

– Rideth My Prongy my feet against the door (the ghost of trees &
Gauntlet, Vermin Of their nutrition from the the kneeling
The Darkness – , regolith) my knees vigilant eyelashes
splaying to the flanking sidewalls, this entity lustingly dovetailing,
who is holding me near to its inert orthorhombic conjecturing about the
heart, I've the sensation of swaddling in manner of its breakage
especially dampproof sidewalls in paling lavender plasterboard of
angelite, tripestone (vulpinite) plasterboard, celestine plasterboard, I've
the sensation of sitting on the large wood «Quando l'āire
obsessive, jackboots, meetinghouse pew c o m e n ç a » ,
abrasive housekeys propping up my figuration in its in its skeletal
scraping, xylemic spindliness, Ayla (my eternal daughter)
her cheek is resting in my smock catenary between my thighs is sinking
into the threadbare in daydreaming softness of dark gray
flannel (I've the geophagy, gastroliths awareness of the almost
unabatingly inside crocodiles imperceptible sinking
into the fleshnest, the & penguins appearance of nestling
is not ceasing) such that ballastingly neutral I am allowing her body
rolling from me onto the pew in avoidance of her fully passing through
Necessitating Rejection my body, a straggling framing nailhead standing
Of Any Terminology out from the banister is dragging against the
That is Implicative clothing (not tearing it) the disembodiment of
Of Directionality, is drawing blood from singsong vocalizing
the flesh beneath (or so I've the observation that – Beati Pauperes
clothing is a communicative membrane, is the Spiritu – is further
starchiness of the (lime, carbonates unburdening my
smock structural of lime, chalky or body (in the arduous
enough for supporting calcareous sparring ascent of the
Ayla in the absence of my physical coherence, granite stairway) to
because I am noncommutative the sensation of increasingly delightful
touching me is allowable but I've no sensation of effortlessness,
touching her only vision (if my retinas are receiving light information
«Nexar Eyebeam light is also a corpse then)), Ayla is sleeping
GPS Dashcam», beside me in the pew (this is our dwelling), dark
«Kenwood DrvA601w gray solid plainweave flannel across my thighs
4K Dashcam», with the absent softness of napping spaciously
gauzing the warping & wefting into equivalent divisions over the emitter
stratum of my thigh, my flesh extrusion through flesh, rising, mass, more
the lattice in flaccidly hypostyle strandings breathless,

extruding (not toward an attractor but with the the gale, the logpath,
simple reactiveness of gravitational & frictional the marsh, the black,
willynilly) without a «cutter» threshold the flaccid flesh hair trajectories
are diffusing into the an ideal fluid is one chamber, the ductile
flesh scalar is that comprehensively filamentary in
proportion to where I specifiable by am the quaternion (not
more slender two quantities relationally but more
slender in ratio, of a consistent girth) whose determination of flesh
vectors is eradicating the physical coherence of the emitter stratum into
the foaminess of my atmosphere (the gossamer thicket of hyphae is filling
all of the museum halls the chamber) in severance each stranding is
are suddenly going offgassing its conidia & anointing youths at
mad, coalescing into the austerely administrative
chitinous beak of a daemonomorph, Ayla is dēbutante celebrations
aspirating the webby strandings is for both young girls
anastomotising new feltings of catalytically and boys with poor
tselbstmordzy muscle tissue in her living flesh, attendance in municipal
is my desirousness of touching her so selfish, the h e a d q u a r t e r s)
(Midway Cemetery) tselbstmorderin is the only possible ghostliness
M i d w a y - 0 7 . 0 1 , of a human & only ghostly within the
(Club Nāutico de maintenance of her nominal vitality (only the
Santo Domingo) awareness of the emptiness of death within life
Dominican Governate, is the vraiment alive deathconsciousness, death
(TWA Terminal homeplace, on the edge ghosts are impossible
(Eero Saarinen)) of a sill, the chamber, because they are not in
New York-14.25, possession of lifeconsciousness) through
clothing of repellent vital dullness (a mutable molecular lattice reacting
to the material of true vitality) around itself stationary in the
allowing it nominal life within persistent death, drawing of crossed
ur presurgery manifold the scattering rubble of catenary wiring
has 2 asymptotic molecular energy beneath is recognizable only
regions & 2 outer to other ghosts or ghostly perceptions, the
horizons & 2 inner tselbstmorder is Ancient Fountain
horizons are repetitive differing, a worker is Tavern, JR Sprayfoam,
measuring information from the platter is heaping the layerings of
compulsion upon him with inescapability in the fingerspreading my
perception of a series of omens & entrapments righthand across my
of interminable failure or obstruction, I'm forehead
declaring this but it isn't for the diminishment of their passage, it is a

beyond the parkland, qualitatively different (ammoniac, ammoniac,
beyond the island, passage with the same Glauber's secreting sal
eyeballs destination, so the ammoniac) argill,
tselbstmorder is not in possession of the ghostly capability, at least of the
ghostly physicality, although she is in possession of the ghostly
perception, the sewer of the identity, tselbstmorerin is (in the
materiality of her native consciousness) «strife of all ilks is
consciously dead & with physically deathlike mortally dooming
vitality, she herself in the womb is of this some and driving
or the equivalent seemingly impossible the remainder into
of 6.953x10^{53} earth mutability of material exilation»,
volumes of granite lattice & she is falling out into the cold glaring,
for the definition falling & falling & falling seeping through my
of a neighborhood womb into the argill, alum (oxyd of
coldness, I'm spinning this tale for her (it's the zinc, zinc, white vitriol
midst of «Maslenitsa», Within What is or goslar vitriol or
Ayla's birth is Seemingly The white coperas or vitriol
incredibly easy, you are Boundary Of A Pixel of zinc)
healthy & beautiful & is Ostensibly Becoming pink, I'm demanding a
large meal in my More Pixels, Nominally, hospital nook &
the capital of beasts, are Representing annoying all of the
other women A Deeper Granular convalescing in the
obstetric recovery hall C h r o m o m a n c y with – I've A Daughter,
I've A Daughter – and my voraciousness & Jake Manning is the
eating loudly clinking my utensils, the author of «The Cell
and irrelevant to their unavailability of meat Within» (a reimagining
digestion, the plesiosaur is a constraint of the of «The Cell Within» by
licking a chalky holiday, instead a Saint Teresa of Avila (a
escarpment savouringly tumbler of tepid cinematic interpretation
stewler & a circular platter with three strata of «The Cell Within»
each of eight radiating blini (each an octavo is in development by
epiphyseal foramen, eighth of eight circular filmmaker Robert
strata thick from three symmetrical foldings Phelps («Carving a
(with a clod of sweetcream & margarine at its Giant» & «Funeral
vertex melting & wicking through the spongy Procession» & «Ein eim
layers))), I've full awareness of Ayla's adoration av blod og helvetesild»
for the story, it is a returntrip for her & «Prosperity
(a dwelling, bombing, a imagination into and Beauty»)))
bonfire, darkness & warmth in and a serial killer,

the mass consciousness to the discovery of of motherness, as most
narratives are my relinquishing the mechanizations of
trajectories into inscription of one of motherhood or into the
earth (burning corpses the 7 Ps, is expensive) the tale is
necessarily simplistic & lacking but it is a falsification (no amount of
complexity in artifice is establishing the preposterous depth of even the
in a milky cirrus of most simple physical thing & the entirety of its
soluble suspension is ramifications), although her birth is truly serene
diving to the seafloor & effortless it is not so in the manner that I am
feasting on cuttlefish relating it to her, green coperas or green
everything in association with my motherhood is vitriol or martial vitriol
a misnomer yet I am giving her life, we are (oxyd of manganese,
occupying the same body, I am an obstetric manganese, vitriol of
statue in a classroom whose torso & organs are manganese)
fabrications of translucent acrylic in reassuringly vital visceral hues (all
variations of brown no velologists, no are earth of Umbria &
blood red & eschar & tegestologists, no nutmeg & fawn & blood
red & chestnuts in l a b e o r p h i l i s t s , a newsprint cone &
vanadinite & chickadee no falerists, down & maroon &
shearing wool is staining with the carmine of lamb's blood & translucent
the dead, continuously taupe & coelom in shadowy umbrage of
singing, mesothelium) around «The Technical
an opaque girl standing in shabby loafers & a Terminology of
(no neighborhood fawn sarafan, it's Falconry» by
is large enough that probable Ayla is Alexandra Desipris,
its definition is a climbing the curving staircase between the
member of itself))) double shell musculature of my uterus (through
the excision of archways in lateral fibrousness of circular junctional
tissue looping around her little dwelling cavity tiny beadfires, the
and the paradox is (standing atop the blockwall,
that the collection of fundus dome screaming for assistance but I've
all possible inclusive awareness of the absence of material for her
neighborhoods is engagement (although its contourings are
so large that the legible) I've awareness of her feet lifting away
description of its from the dome toward the ceiling of our attic
largeness necessarily room, she's simply osmosing from the status of
not any of the members inside the threshold to Emperor Frederick II,
in the neighborhood outside the threshold)), Marino Masē, Thales,
the warming hue of the burning «Kostroma» Attila, Argia,

effigy in the street below is making the sensations of the chamber colder, I am more frigid, Ayla Or Pareidolia is lying screaming red on the hard bedstead Supplementing & cold sweating in our garret apartment in Supplanting The lieu of my laborious suspension just across Homeomorph, The or above the bedstead & reaching out « C o n t a i n m e n t » the floorboards, his touching her & pulling Inherent In A Pixel ADA jackboots, the her to me I am feeling is Implicative Of floorboards, the coldsweat D i r e c t i o n a l i t y evaporating but not her flesh evaporating, she is lying in the pram or the bassinet or Sergeï's embracing her, through an inscrutable Roseland-14.10, sequential operation of physical repercussions Roseland-22.01, Payrite is a noun only I'm effecting Ayla's Roselawn-09.14, existing in its singular location (moving her from the pram to the formation, Payrite afghan spreading out across the concrete in the is «deer», Payrite is sunlight or tying a headscarf around her waist «sheep», in the rocker for meals), the passing through, the being within, it is imagery is erotic & lovingly delectable, it is the coldest most empty at the centerpoint status of corporeality & I've the attitude that of Tsentergrad this capability is unreasonable on the is a freshwater basis of my etheric ilk of physics, it's not an s w i m m i n g p o o l occupation of much fretting for me, I've (130m in diameter, acceptance that she & I are alone in a chamber perfectly circular, together & she is an Quintus tractatus with a watervolume the sun on its ballistic continet acta of 25000m³), trajectory toward p e r e g r i n o r u m immobile infant & she the horizon, between remanentic in Jerusalem is in one location & she vespers and midnight, per mensem Augustum, is in another location, I am aware only that my imagination is polyamides, amino incapable of describing the sensation of my resins (including touching her touching, or the meatus urea resins oyxd of cobalt, cobalt, constriction of Sergeï's (or any of them for vitriol of cobalt example) ovuliparous ejaculation expanding gaseous gouts of fibrous mistiness into a description of my formal volume, although I'm aware of the coffinboards the necessity of these capabilities for various (and flooding, fat purposes I've no certainty about their execution encrustation of the by me, where there is the potentiality of earth, materiality where I've recognition of formal

endurance beneath my flannel smock it is of no enduring patterning such
that my reaching for touching is adopting the earphones, champagne,
spektr, haemoth, patterning of the the sirens,
d a e m o n i u m , opposing body and passing through the tensors
b a t t l e h o r n s , of its molecular asterism, the appearance of my
inpestae, in nomine fingertips within the mass of the opposing body
odium, daemonic crescently distending floaters in antumbral
terrorism is bringing foaminess, ears are hiding in fur hats, I am
vice & suffering the plowshare, the sky, speaking French to
Payrite, it is the the sky) a raven and a erection of a boundary
across which the pocketknife, patternlanguage with
the inability of crossing but flowing around my hollowing out the
caressing Alya's cold Golgi is a centurion of corpse of Payrite full of
lurking in the silt is an Aristotelian Daemon, freezingly solid offals &
accidentally ingesting malevolent clergy, fluids flashevaporating
several quartz & «Flagrum Taxillatum», at daybreak thawing,
chert seastones is cheek & temple my touching the corpse visage, I
swimming dartingly am reachingly in proximity my daughter's sflesh
with novel curiosity, am I capable of touching her corpse, this (the most
joyous & poignant realization of a corpsession with my daughter) is only
a not so easily Where «Beyond accessible activity of
the imagination, the A Boundary» is starvation of her little
pallid body and Implicative Of the cruelty of its
defrauding her tender Scalar Possibility brain of urgency is (this
is an activity of the Beyond Itself, imagination) lying
under the one threadbare bedsheet transitionally in dedication to the
presentation of all corpses (a bedsheet adequately robust for sleeping is
finding its best usage for sleeping not death, bedclothes are not baggage
for purgation) on a cot in the children's «massive», the only true
a gentleman (with the possession of an item of furniture is in a
sensibility of a regent properly defensible location adjacent to a
astride his noble blockwall where maintenance of
steed) with a dark referencefeatures & the accute altitude
mustache (very much political boundaries of of sunlight battering
the appearance of an the greater immovable our ascent up the
unruly eyebrow over construction are western frontage
a vacant eyesocket) abiding, the catafalque of the mountain is
of her cot is in the middle of a chamber, what is overwhelming my
the compulsion toward ownership in a corpse, vision

that I am touching her clavicle & throat is assurance that the impulse of vast slurping, the slipping away of ownership respiration is absent or staking the principles of moral existence from her body, on a swath of terrain, barytes, muriat of Isla Mujeres Quintana Roo (shark versus barytes, seasalt on a undead human), (Hellfire Caverns) basic of heavy earth Buckinghamshire, («The Otis Domicile» in Fairview Riverside Municipal Parkland, 119 1kg cheroots to 14 Fairview Boulevard) Madisonville-12.01, quantity of glass inners Lake Charles-12.01, is lacing together the for vacuumflasks, 18m^2 Monroe-12.01, drybrush sky failure, photographic filmstock Metairie-12.01, in the midst of all to 1kg sugar #14, (Lake Pontchartrain vanishment arching Causeway) New Orleans-12.01, (11 Main Street) eyebrows and buffering Concord-13.01, («The Ellis Estate Domicile», eyesockets inhalingly 709 Country Way) it is an inherent Scituate-13.01, («Concord Gratis property of a universe Library», 129 Main Street) Concord-13.01, of infinite baryonic Boston-13.01, South Lincoln-13.01, («The substance & infinite New York Temporal Narrative Society», spatial extent that 170 Central Parkland West) New York- quantumstates are 14.25, («Columbia University», Broadway repeating (infinitely) the bedstead, three Payrite is murdering & 116th Street) New portraits, nymph, popsingers, York-14.25, («Temporal umbrage, Piazza») New York-14.25, («Cavalier Hotel», 200 East 34th Street) New York-14.25, («The Pyramid of Djoser», Saqqara necropolis) Giza Governate, Sardinia, («CBK Kraftwerk» Laguna) Philippine Governate, («Edward the great sky cone and J. Gaffey & Sons Funeral Parlor», 757 Country the valley city street Way) Scituate-13.01, (249 A Street) Boston-13.01, cone Cohasset-13.01, – O People With (1000 Glades Road) Scituate-13.01, («TERSA Assurance Of Seeing Incineration Facility» Sant Adrià de Besòs) Lofty Luminance, The Barcelona, («Sea Vacationer Motel» 3309 Sole Fixation Of Your Atlantic Avenue) (oxyd of nickel, nickel, Yearning, Sanctification Virginia Seashore-22.01, vitriol of nickel) oxyd is Dissolving The **my socksoft & hesitant** of plumbum, plumbum, Scummy Fouling Of **footsteps are pregnant** vitriol of plumbum Your Conscience Into **with deliberateness and with each planting** A Purely Streaming **superphosphate, down on asphalt a new** Evocation Of Lethe & **preceptorships, vista of the city is** Eunoe, desaturating, leaning on Nadia crushing a bloody nit between her fingernails in the dark terminus of the hallway alone, in tedium the folks are sucking smooth suckingstones, whispering in the narrowness of the ersatz

Knobbler pauraque (descriptions of subfossil bones are assisting in the persistence of rumors about this cryptic bird never having visual confirmation by scientists, it is not officially extinct),

and without undue buoyancy through crosscurrents with freedom & joyous equilibrium, its corpse breaking apart in cloudy salty ink of black bile & gut chum proportioning of the stairs – «The

„Geezer“» is Remaining Dwellingplace Hey, You Rental Payments, Getting A Courtorder

at which their bodies are below the waist becoming

downcast queuing for either victims of exilees folding

on the floorplane of the nave an arrayal (the entirety of its figuration apparently is curling upward in bizarre anamorphosis) of spokes (of smoothly varying calligraphic weight along their trajectories)

In Ownership Of This Just are Ceasing Your He Isn't Capable Of Or Eviction, It is An Impossibility, Never Moving Out is The Strategy – the housing are full of resettlement or punitive jejunoform overlapping

on their static stringloops (the mass swaying inplace with varying thicknesses of paperwork accruals) staring through each other they are staring through the asphalt & concrete at a variety of negative altitudes in orientations of all degrees

Hypsipyle, Pier delle Vigne,

(calling forth the daemon Agares coming upon the saddle of a crocodile and wielding a goshawk on his fist))

beside the downstream of the stationary queuing, the desiccation of cracking sneaker soles are sloughing off

«Quando la stella»,

abrasive concrete volume of the Centerplace», each balls of my feet is

and the craquelure revealing the brightness of pigmentation unbroken in pooling

is radiating from the crossing beneath the vacant baldachin in raw linoleum intarsia is dividing the terrain into dozens of triangles (isoceles toward the narthex & out into the transepts & away into the choir, all others scalene)

imperceptible strata on the increasingly fresh & toward the great cubic «Municipal footstep through the agony that in my conscious registration is joyous at feeling connection to the asphalt running warmth to the

shadowing awning of my homeplace (asphalt endlessly paving the entire

(the thick layerings of ADAemone), I am awaiting my ultimately
idleness) are inheriting collapsing with exhaustion because I'm fearful
the stillness of sifting of pulling it all down onto me, as inert as I am I
luminance on the broad am not desirous of a tomb (ostensibly a
articulation of the cenotaph (the Daemonaz gale blowing away my
cartography the original legitimate pulpy remainder)),
Cherdyn is a decrepit series is continuing wilderness of glass with
decadant reexposure of with its own «Virgil In blockwalls & terrains
of rapid development Dreamland 3» and a abstraction from the
melancholy retreating «Virgil In Dreamland floodwaters of the fetid
tepid river, I am sitting 4» interweaving with the shimmering
against a standpipe the production of the phthalo conflagration,
motionless ferrying false installments, is coalescing on
discomfort into dissipation through the the throat of a guy
distribution of my blood (within & without is swinging his
lofting away on my pink respiration), all the messengerbag from
Garrett's reed warbler, windows capturing flat behind around to
white chest white reflections of the sky restingness against his
eyeball, are bearing the red white wideneck teeshirt
triangle decal (one is missing half (this window is very high)), lilacs in
eruption and sickly thick fragrance in abundance, the visages &
glazegazing of the to the Black Sea is flowing the Laba is flowing
shuffling & searching into the Kuban emptying,
(a pristine cleavage exilees (distant pupil orientation on a vector
along the rift of the chording through the globe toward an
helical shaft where and neighborhoods are apocryphal homeplace),
the breakwedge is repeating across distant my shoes are missing
bearing or a complex & unreachable horizons from the personal
failure skitteringly is a duplication of property area of
fracturing the column every status containing «Patient Discharging»
in a plastic tub where every movement just my shirt in twain &
my distraught blazer vector & characteristic that I am trading for the
hospital tunic in the middle of the lobby standing halfnude & dressing to
the accompaniment of the shiftcommand gifting me with the tractionsole
anklesocks & hustling us through the outer door in avoidance of the
& beau blue pediment gawking queuing of all other dischargees
under a squatty & flat demanding is the figuration of
tropical violet cyldrum, complimentary lightning on a nightsky,
ownership of their anklesocks, the cubic polygonal tessellation

building in polymer stuccorendering festooning & bunting & medallions,
an enormous | the realization of a | trompeloeil keystone in
tearose pink atop two | consciousness outside | faux taupe granite
tetrahedonal acones, | the solipsism of the | the parameters of my
exilation with the | viewer (or perceiver) | requirement of visiting
the municipal | is not possible in a | «Commandant» on
regular & frequent | unitalla framework | intervals, we are
in the gestural motion | such as this text, | munching some
of punching his dandelion greens from a collection Nadia is
openpalm lefthand with amassing in her dresspocket, the foamy cubic
his right fist just abreast volume is great & ambiguous with the vague
his shapely pectoral appearance of entasis (where the long
nodules on its edges insisting procession of human
the ornament gagging facade forward over us figurations with gray
within its umbra, flat black windows in the pallor are marching
Kangaamiut, Nuuk, concealment of slowly out of the
Kuummiit, patterning & ornament Basilica, each missing
are stacking dozens of Santa Rosa-12.01, the upper cupola
storeys, cladwood Wild Roseate-23.09, of their craniums
siding (particles of Wildrose-14.04, planer shavings &
wastewood & newsprint in bondage of waxy resin with fibrous jacketing)
prone to disintegration with exposure to moisture, on a tackboard within
from the positive a nichesurround of styrofoam moulding the
terminal of the «a2» to waitlist for one of the few «massives» in
the negative terminal Cherdyn (covetously in the «Church of
of the «b3» and «b5» the construction of an the Keygen»,
axes in «kdk12», terminus of the internally macaronic,
Philippine, overture, schizophrenic overly spacious citygrid
apperception, reflexiveness, including the
«Municipal vesication & mutilation, Centerplace») is
ponderous & generally refusal of the a distant residential
possibility for those not forcemeat of human in toptier servitude to
the ADA or its death, semipublic entities, the
entry foyer of the «Municipal Centerplace» is (conversely to the
grandiose rhetoric of its facade & massing) a «Sedendo all'ombra»,
the flowerbuds are tiny deadend navel full « T o g l i e n d o
bursting, of negativepressure l'una a l'altra»,
lint sucking against vinyl baseboards & a relentless appliqué of lozenges
& heptagrams of various rouges across sidewalls & ceiling & floorplane,

oncenter with we are waiting, we are (oxyd of tin, tin,
asphalt is creeping not alone, the heatwave vitriol of tin) oxyd of
through the impasto in the airless room is copper, copper, blue
continentalcrossing austere is oppressive, coperas or blue vitriol
striping, in patchy grass delirium, in the or Roman vitriol or
mustardy geometric crowbar cantilever vitriol of copper (oxyd
appliqué is material e x t e n s i o n , of bismuth, bismuth,
joinery in nonconformance with the patterning, vitriol of bismuth) oxyd
a wallpanel is opening into the foyer under its of antimony,
own propulsion and into debrisfields Nadia is handholding
me through the of crazy wreckage passage, I am limply
flaccidly taking Nadia's translation of a palm wandering empty
hallway boulevards scientific paper about a with metal doorways, in
the tedium of waiting in fictional mineral, the queuing stallingly
loping Nadia is leafing through the waitlist out of fatalistic curiosity
about our location in the roster and is returning with dejection – We are
is unreachable by its Not On The Waitlist At All – Nadia's agreement
duplications or the with «the „Geezer"» is for residency in the
photons in the status kitchen (the only rounding the terminal
of that duplication is remaining vacant plat of a median a □
eradicating the notion of the dwelling), every streetsign atop a
of distantness between building with domestic signpost
those duplications designation is completely public and as such the
are so thoroughly the «Gale of Simurru» & dwelling
identical that they superscriptions are specific down to the
are not duplications geographic vertex of its chambers and
or doublings though with a chambers in sequential
numbering through more globular each building either in
the ordering system of gelatinous geometry their accessibility after
the frontdoor or unsuitable for the beginning in a circular
(in differential development of proper motion to the left and
geometry of curvatures) muscular sheathing superficial &
spiraling inward (although the only location that corporeal adipocere
is not obstructive to the functionality of the kitchen is beneath an austere
& filthy kitchen table standing in the «Dark Dominator
centerpoint of the kitchen, our location in „Lord of the Daemon"»,
rectus capitis posterior Cherdyn is by the following definition (in all
minor, bregma, ADA filings & documentation about my
asterion, pterion, exilation) 10-14 Prospekt 03.X (where «ex» is

the designation of chamber)), the sage from the vacant plat for the migration of dermabrasion, collager, folkle is queuing into resultingly in the comprehensive catalogue the real installment three is actually the overall four and continuing thusly the centerpoint of a green dwelling across serving as a waystation certain dark & regal butterflies, only one brow blackly babbler (whose only proof of existence is a solitary specimen (the bird is arguably persisting in its babbling)),
the foyer is pulling to the black glass door, a long corridor with no doors is leading to an elevator without callbuttons or floor selectors is opening within our proximity, blackdots of or slowly crumbling absolute disintegration into the hydrological cycle of the Basilica crossing) is abuzz in the alleys and transports, people flitting at the far terminals of corridors, transoms over the metal doors are mruky with a texturing of pyramidal gridding capturing inner dark & hallway glaring on its facetings, & the «BM 27 „Uragan“» & the «BM 30 „Smerch“»)) blackdots crossing through intersections, a distant transom is dark is luminous, the rectangular judas is ajar allowing crisply cold exsufflation, the «Commandant» in a drab greatcoat swallowing any chair he is sitting upon behind a barren prosopographers, joypoppers, & very large (an obstruction of the entire width of the chamber) metal desk in a proportional yet very small chamber with six doors, almost grinning reading my expression my fearfulness, – Behind

just above the hair of a woman in an orange leather overcoat with harlequin green piping

a tall honeydew cyldrum atop a blank gable with ivory moulding dividing the Junebud attic storey & except directly into the inside vertices of the crossing are concave quadrilateral s p e a r h e a d s ,

The Gray Line, This is Not A Conversation, You are Reporting Here To Me And Only To Me, You are Ingraining My Visage, On Every Third Day You are Bringing Balsam Lake-23.09, Balsam-14.03, Croton Waterfalls-14.25, All Documentation And The Presence Of Your Wife is Not A Requirement – without reviewing our paperwork or my documentation, breezy burrs are clinging to my anklesocks resting on a low spallingly ruinous concrete kneewall in relative shadiness and Nadia is uprooting a thicket of nettles at her feet for the growing redeemable sheaf collection in her totebag, slowmixing vapor is sheeting

A Pixel is Nothing If Not The Establishment Of A Boundary,

hacking up for smokehouse cookery,

(lividity around from the undercutting under one of the doors
the orbitals and a behind the desk, almost a distraction from the
timid horizontality onerousness of the «Commandant's» terms the
to their disposition) delicious coolness is precipitating on my hands
where a patching & the hydrological cycling of my chest hair
tarpaulin of synthetic (except for the from the slashfray rift
material is hirsute innermost two who n o d u l a r
of my hanging asplay are becoming ornate a n g i o k e r a t o m a s
shirt, the hillock of volutoid consoles) p r o d u c i n g
Nadia's chin is tapering lowrelief necrotic tissue &
glistening beneath an pilasters, almost relief expression
on her lips, the lefthand door on our frontier of the desk is swinging
Dashuangxiang, inward on mysteriously silent & abrupt
Goubazhen, propulsion, with burgeoning understanding of
opening the the geography from many orientations the
coppermine wailing the peeking above the skyline Cherdyn «Municipal
subterranean homicide Centerplace» of the with navy blue
lamentation, «White ADA (ADAemone fieldspace is containing
Abyss», «The (S)crypts colloquially, those of a white triangle
of Joyce and Piranesi» us living & living & living are wondering which
by Jennifer Bloomer, 24kg cobalt to 1g tea, is worse between
endless deferral in the 227kg rice to 1 quantity byzantine bureaucratic
ADA hierarchy or of sewingmachine, unyielding abstraction
in the intellectual cult of the Daemonic congress, though how different
are hanging & decapitation (– Why Not Both – the little onlooker is
declaring)) is relatively nearby the hospital, the measurements from the
two men on the topfloor I am singling sonal atoms, the grain
porch of a dacha are out my hospital room of the glisson & the
sipping ryazhenka window with the red grainlet of the kernel,
and watching Emelya triangle half missing, we are waiting for
flying in touch&go assistance with the pumpcar dormant against its
landings on his stove, stopblocks even further up the valley than the
«Municipal Centerplace», dry blood on my asplay shirtfront, we are
is attributable to the resolution of certain cells waiting on the
in the footage or the processor capacity for wiremesh bench of the
to the Gulf of Taz pumpcar for an able copilot on the
is flowing the Taz walkingbeam, two soaking through shirts
emptying, wrenching from their waistbands with envious
industry, all of the baggage is resting in my lap, Nadia deftly

maneuvering the joystick through the fluid laciness of the
omnidirectional tracknetwork with only the most instinctual geographic
sensibility, the breezy movement of consciousness & living with this
the insinuation of the portrayal of movement strange city in passage
(objectless movement) is possible in the closing my eyes to the
sequencing of animation cels whose between bronze
sequentiality is not a priority fortifications along
with further zephyr rifling in my the skeletal coastline,
subdvisisons of billowing asplay euphoria of the
intuitive knotwork ruinous dressshirt I am falling ordnance,
meshingly arabesquing everywhere, unreasonable unendurable
discontinuously and exhaustion, people living everywhere for
interlacing with various reasons, the rhythmic action of the
diagonals from each where a black icon walkingbeam & the two
resultant vertex, of a guy is striding men silently straining,
brighter skylight is with each foot in whiting out through
higher tree spires the presumptive where the viol & violet
& vine entwining the asphalt interstices verve of valleys &
turrets & domes of between striping of a dullish dirt & scrambly
gravel are slipping & continentalcrossing, tumbling clicking over
one another in our stumbling up to the frenzying of carrion birds,
nimbus stratus cirrus misty species settling across the earth casting
reverent silence in vapor threadingly through the streetscape, the
the quire, greensick lessee payment for the negativespace under the
apparitional visages «the „Wooden Procedure" latitude», «the
h y p e r b o l i c a l l y latitude of the „Trophoneurotic Sister"»,
breathing (an kitchen table is 1,84ҫ (payable to the municipal
asymptotic method authorities of Cherdyn) of which «the
of never fully „Geezer"» is collecting less than 0,36ҫ if
inhaling or exhaling) anything, fantasies of the stillness of the
apartment clicking engagement rotation leverpump resting clicking
engagement creaking rotation leverpump to such an extent
bloodrush silent the caretaker of the that introduction of a
menagerie, misdivision, theater is hobbling to handcrank cardshuffler
pleasurable, muzhik, the metering device for integral to the
clicking engagement documentation of his tachistoscope platen is
fair wispy hair blowing presence pointwisely, loading cels for viewing
resting bright white leverpump coasting in a manner straining
through cool zephyr freewheeling clicking the φ (or «phi»)

by creating a secondary engagement (over asphalt swath traversing
stratum of afterimages derelict sidewalks buildings far from each other
requiring intervention Jsief Alpinist is & flat in affect into the
of the subconscious entrenching into an invariably winding
foothill avenues on the addiction to «flashing» valleywalls spotty with
dodgy dingy & amphetamines, residences, the dwelling
is tenuous in its hermeticism & differential airpressures are draughty
sacrificial suicide, sucking in hot vapor & sequestering it with foul
thrusting evil breath & the effluvia livid streaking is
deep inside, wallcavities), the blooming the asphalt
sundry vulturepickings of Anna's feet on my exhaustingly gray
tongue, overcoats & trenchcoats & blazers in the vacant lane
limply insinuating on pegs beside the front door, paralleling swellingly
thermonastically=hematocrystallin (botanical & recedingly
divination on the basis of observing & measuring moldspores on the
the movements of thermonastically active species draughting clinging to
bulbous misty beadlets implanting in wallcavities & impregnating
lowquality sheetrock of unacceptable porosity blooming with blackness
neath painting & painting & painting, «the Wenceslaus II of
„Geezer"» (who (with the adoption of a famous Bohemia, Griffolino of
1kg twine leavings Daemone cartoonist's Arezzo, Farinata degli
to 8m² collages and appellation) is creasing Uberti,
similar decorative & glazing (becoming vitreous) within the leaden
plaques, 1 quantity of weighing down of perpetual impotence &
aggregation crushers misery) through blankness & windowpane
to 1156 quantity of Kulusuk, raindusty &
duckeggs, Danmarkshavn, dustdrifting divisions
Applegate-13.09, Spitsbergen, of false appliqué
Appleton City-13.15, the folk of Belbeck muntins is staring with
one pupillary vector are invisible pressing upon the ceiling & one
pupillary vector their faces to the hotel oblique out the window
without reaction to our diningroom is vacant approaching up the
children are drinking & silent apart from spalling & nettlesome
tepid beer on the the gushing of electric concrete path through
plinth of the pandemic fountains whose damp & soilfudge, the
c o m m e m o r a t i o n undulating luminance smoothest stones, upon
c o l u m n , is wavering over the a placid island of
ignorance, in rapturous blockwalls & large exhaustion Nadia & I
lying together hard on plateglass windows the barren linoleum, no

configuration of my the painfulness of body is bearable on the
linoleum in thick iciness, burning (although wispy & near
alertness) drowsing honey of the pharynx, 1893 quantity of heel
arriving upon concentricwaves of agony from cushions to 1L cowmilk,
my rotatorcuff is darkening the persistent 336m² tarpaulins to 1
is interpolating the coldness of the quantity of deburring
shadowy lingering overhead luminaire machinery,
background with the with pulsations pricklingly visible & in the fine
insistently incongruous nerves along my hairline spreading a torpid
foreground into a union blanket, there are no threadspools matching the
of «pure phi» stitchery in my ruinous shirt, in the entry parlor
are the pallets of an in the maximal assortment of three
or differential analytic extension of working youths («Arest
siphonal pressuring the virtual anatomage the „Hairy“» & «Arest
for cultivation of table measurement the „Merkin“» &
fecal motility beyond region (DIST «SNAP, «Naderi of the
the keystone of its ENDPOINT→KNOT», „Caves“») cooperating
primary ganglion, M E S H T O N U R B , on making rental
payments though T R I M M I N G , disdainful of one
another & each is P R O J E C T I O N) is seeping, three □
claiming residence in a different vertex streetsigns arrowing
(intruding into the fourth vertex is the front downstream in the sky
antimony, vitriol of door), in the sittingroom are the belongings of a
antimony (oxyd of young duo «Astein» & «Strea» whose baby is
arsenic, arsenic, vitriol inside the closet where «Strea's» sister is
of arsenic) oxyd of feeding her behind the in strong currents
mercury, obstruction of their falling unpuzzlingly
aloof drooling borzoi «D» sleeping against the to the seafloor, a total
door in the absence of the parental unit, in the of 125 gastroliths in
formal livingroom sororal multiples & around the corpse,
fugacious, a fruticose («actresses» of scant reputation) are chatting in
youth sneaking under the bay window on the that although each
the barbwire, forb, burning in the cel contribution is
outsidewall mending fiery furnace of the static is enabling
theatrical knickers & «DAEMA Camp», the illusoriness of
bloomers behind crates partitioning across from peripheral drifting,
two silent & invisible families behind bedsheets are hanging hypotenusal
over the flowing lanes of autotraffic are hanging from the opposite
wire saggingly the sky is vacant, vertices of the

a ketchup and mustard sidewalls, through into the kitchen Nadia & I are
trolley in waiting sitting under the Claudio Zucchet,
beyond a spacious kitchen table my neck and although
railing along the kerb cranking down further a d m i n i s t r a t i v e l y
is receding is reaching exacerbating the sovereign their
into white sky with its mobility limitations of spiritual commitment
skeletal pantograph, my injury, the onion to the hierarchy of the
wirecrossing artifacts musk of «the administration & its
of thickness gradually intestinal epithelial endurance is insuring
„Geezer"» finely cells, lanugo, their compatibility
folding into the absorbent coilings of his linty with ADA priorities,
aerophanous skin & with the propellant of his lurching through the
(R h o d o d e n d r o n kitchen is fractosmic upon the otherwise
species are exhibiting stagnant atmosphere where it is lingering with
leafcurling behavior appreciable viscosity falling in gentle eddies to
(« R h o d o d e n d r o n restingplace in noxious cushioning across our
catawbiense» but rubblestage & slagstage & stonestage
not «Rhododendron & sheetrockstage & exilestage
p o n t i c u m ») linofloor of Magnolia-13.14,
restingplace, «Setian» a slippery ADA mollusk Magnolia-13.19,
within the spider infestation of the attic at the Magnolia-14.03,
mercury, vitriol of top of the stairs (a very with vinyl capillaries
mercury (oxyd of silver, large and wooden terminating at
silver, vitriol of silver) triangular prismatic stainless steel
oxyd of gold, gold, chamber with no serrefine hoseclamps
with the imperative of flatness, finishings over stud
mechanistic pulsing arterial geyser of cavities of frothy egg
gelatinous metalcoolant (sodium & NaK) of a sufficiently
sac delicacies) letting onto a proportionally invariable planar
oppressive hallway with a stovepipe curvature at any
unadorningly running through it, the sole spacepoint «p»
bathroom with the blessing of a single shadeless lightbulb, the front
«Myrmidon of bedroom where «the „Geezer"» is staring at the
Goethe», abortion is dictating treatments door of a closet where
of angels fleeing for pernicious anemia (they are whispering on
the onslaught the back stairs) a widow «A» has a residence,
of discharging and the backmost bedroom (an awkwardly
expectoration, the elegy lengthwisely proportional chamber with a
of evil, dormer & a sloping attic ceiling) containing a

childless duo wearing (with this codification earplugs while reading
& another old male overall O, real R, sleeping in the dormer
& in the vertex the false F) O1R1-«Virgil belongings of an
industrious young In Dreamland», student «Neidar»
whose elderly parents O2R2-«Virgil In are playing a cardgame
on a crate between their Dreamland 2», pallets in the closet,
«the „Geezer"» muttering about the toppling in on itself of the house, for the widening of every caulkjoint, in the bitter & humid cold icy shims are prying – This is My Grave, My Grave, My Grave – the dwelling is collapsing in a pouf of sawdust across the spatial atoms & moldspores with of sky, everyone is remaining inside with him sitting in his chair watching the Rejection Of The Pixel is Upon The Predication Of An Alternative Philosophy For Construction Of Imagery With These Attendant Physical Properties, A Mosaic Of Selenium Cells, perspective of the window opening shifting, the sweetness of slowly decaying nettle fasces, spiraling in my ear delicate & deadly dully though resonantly clicking of smooth fistsize riverstones falling across one another, «the „Geezer"» is leaning facedown between his forearms reaching to the flyrails of an extension ladder leaning against the outsidewall of the residence where raining down

translation of highly technical jargon into plain vernacular is tripling the length of the text and in some situations is rendering the text unrecognizable to insiders who are using the original jargon,

burning NH4Cr2O7 with HgSCN is excreting tentacles around drifting chitinous hyphae are coalescing into the beak of a Vampyroteuthis i n f e r n a l i s , powdery wood is crumblingly into his dead silver hair, mruky vapor simmering off of the riverflow is lending

or aeration of calcareous earth) potash, carbonates of potash, effervescing or aerating fixing vegetable alkali or mephitis of potash

The Conscious Absorption returns And is Luxuriating In Richly Phonetic Playfulness & Cultural Resonance & Sonorous Flamboyance Of Such Encrustation That Excerpting A Usefully Illustratively Strident Quotelet is Not Possible,

a gently uplifting convection to the street atmosphere less oppressively & stagnant than

although compromising the integrity of its lorication & lying erotical in the valleys of its queasy flesh, avenues & adhoc circuiting of the neighborhood

the stifling interior of the residence & the shuffling of shoeboots across the kitchen linoleum out into the

& into the unbuildable areas rising up the valleywalls for walking & looking in the trunkdrifts of pineneedles or tumbledown cairns of discretely incidental landslides for an outstretching skeletal grasping or the feathering forth of Anna's fine clicking of bones, «the the young student in downstream autotraffic of all white vehicles is flowing across the intersection behind the offwhite leather shoulderseam

four araeosystyle duos of nymphs & fauns (two triplets are addressing an insidecorner) are statically frolicking

with the connection of the nodes of intersection to the apex where all linesegments raying to the apex

hairbangs, molars & the „Geezer“» is cornering the kitchen doorway – «Neidar» You are Studying Psychology are You Not – · – No Sir I am Studying Industrial And Organizational Administration – · – Right, Yes Then Certainly This Knowledge is Easily Accessible, What Is The Proper Terminology For A Woman (Or Just A Person In Fact) Who is

A Vast Quantity Of Small Chunks, Infinitudes Of Little Quadrilaterals, A Succession Of Little Areas Of Varying Brilliance, And With This Possible Attendant Nomenclature, Image Element Or «Imael», Committing To Pushing The Buttons Of Those Around Them, Or Just Some Of Those Very Proximate To Them – · – Truly Sir, That is Not – the lad is looking the table – It is Not – · – Yes, Dyscrasia – · – No Sir

is collecting aerosol moisture from the freezingly in a pelt around its globular packeting, skittering,

Including In The Most Selfsame Constructions The Notion Of Spatiality is Ambiguous In A Minim Of The Corpus – ,

My Knowledgebase down at Nadia below Madness Though is It Certainly – · – It's That Isn't Sounding

«the „Cartan subgroup“»,

Accurate, Schizotypal is Something – · – Yes – · – are They Believing In Magic – «the

„Geezer“» is casting his gazing downward startlingly finding Nadia & myself feigning being Certain – · – I Knowledgeable

rocktumbler operators in private discussion are perfecting the combination of particular kinds of silt & sulfuric acid

asleep – I am Not Really am More About Hierarchical

Laborgroup Phalanxing – exchanging the nettles in a totebag

– · – She is Bilious collection of enough for two (nonmatching) secondhand shoes, we are both looking in dejection at the feltboots on the counter, I am imploring the storekeeper for topboots (in my

vitriol of gold (oxyd of platina, platina, vitriol of platina),

of a guy staring under batty logic is the awareness of the
arching eyebrows down ridiculousness of such an exchangerate), hardly
just driverside of the 2 kg of nettles are gingerly burdening the
stationpoint of the sky transducer, with the notorious tares of municipal
cone vendors our offering isn't remotely
holding cannulae in commensurate with two leather topboots, the
each raw opening, kitchen cabinets containing no comestibles are
posterior fontanel, housing only the remote accessories of eating
calvaria, (not plates & cups or the old men (in
anterior fontanel, forks & spoons but a southfacing warmth of
garlicpress & a pastrycutter & a potatoricer & the stucco wall) whispy
spatulas & peelers & pitters & trivets (nothing and arteriole laciness
beneficial to the consumption of a single against the sunshine,
ingredient raw meal, much less a hot meal of the breeze is passing
from the bondage at their waists extending (in through their spongy
mildewy unity on outcroppings & shadefacing flesh & dermal filagree,
surfaces (decolletages, reaching forearms, any complication)) as
well as all of the – «Ingression» is The general storage for the
roominghouse Ballistic Wreckage occupants replacing the
closets that are in Codification Of Our dedication of housing
cousins or Culturally Linguistic grandparents or inlaws
of families that are C o n s c i o u s n e s s residing in chambers
Payrite is the Falling From The with closets, the kitchen
embodiment of F i r m a m e n t u l a cabinets are too small
disincarnation, for rental, we are not alone, «Setian» is arguing
with «Naderi „of lips, unreliable, tender, the Caves“» on the
benevolence of pipesmoke, the moon, systematic bureaucratic
oppression – You are the cemetery, Obedient To Insidious
Impulses, Which In Itself is A Variant Of (soda, carbonates
Slavery, We In Area Element Or of soda, aeration
Submission To The «Areael», Elementary or effervescence of
Meticulous And Area Or «Elemar», mineral alkali fixations
Orderly ADA Pictural Units Or or mephitic soda)
Providence are Existing «Pixuns», Small magnesia, carbonates
With More Freedom Q u a d r i l a t e r a l s of magnesia,
1kg cullet and other Or «Smaquas», Than The Dolt Who is
wasteproduct of glass Little Chunks Or A Slave To Systems Of
to 589g semiprecious «Lunks», Units, Whose Existence And
dusting, Dotties, Pointspots, Machinations They are

«the „Glossy Ignorant – taking his wrist in speaking in
System“ latitude», puffing into the youth thrustingly they are in the
«the „Pentachord cluttering of his is ragepunching the
Blackveldt“ latitude», dwelling vertex, the peripheral sliver of
«the „Skewbald frothy spiderwebbing silver automobile
Psycholepsy“ latitude», clinging in extension to bonnet quakingly
his frizzle of hair, Nadia is slowly examining the jittering
inventory of «Strea’s» recipes for domestic sewing kit (a loose
assortment of ornate vinegar production fasteners, notions that
she is delicately & from vegetable deliberately handling
each one after the other peelings are rote and turning over in her
swelling gallium in the destitute, hand) in a small plush
wavelets rolling crate with quilting of fabric marbleization is
across the crinkling lifting out a tailortape & a tomato pincushion
outcroppings lifting out a small manilaenvelope of
of aluminum, shirtbuttons holding each with prolongment of
stochastically variable The Swift River Freezing Over In Winter
acceleration Whirlwinds Ravingly Tossing A Rayhide Over
fascination & novelty is The Old Poet For Protection From Frostbite – ,
tucking a longneedle into the collar of my crickety necking
dressshirt tatteringly across her knees, in every haircurls, fiddleheads
accidental cairn is effulgent pallid dolphinskin & flaccid fronds)) from
in the cavern crimpsheets of voidspace consoles tapering
emanating luminance from the effervescent through the tessellation
of the masonry p l a t i n i c h l o r i d e understanding of
spatiality, Nadia is B4·H2PtCl6 reddish rolling over & pinning
under a seamallowance orange needlings along the scissor
Darkbloom bulbul are forming, diagonal through the
(whose only proof shirtfront for a crisp connection & tighter
of existence is from tailoring with the consumption of more fabric
subfossil bones), awkwardly going against the axis of my body,
Aldabra brush warbler, aeration or feeling fingertips
Drovyanovy nukuput, effervescence or mild curling convexly into
the bedrock cupping at or mephitic magnesia the terminalpoint of the
cavern, in the (ammoniac, carbonates swaddling tender
needling of my hairline of ammoniac, aeration in the parallelity of
slowly the needletip is or effervescence or emerging through the
placket into Nadia’s left mild or mephitic mucus, amniotic fluid,
fingertips rolling the volatile alkali) bile & wateriness,

sensation of the slender longneedle in her   & fruitseeds and
whorls mending my shirt in our cubby, a   cinching them into
rectangular prism in concrete with inversion of a lamb abomasum
its vertical edges & railings along its crowning inside the mechanism
edges with strange bracketings chamferingly at for the production of
invisible connections the vertices, tautly adequately lubricious
are surpassing doubling over s a v o u r s t o n e s ,
the visible, argill, carbonates tabular tercets in
threading through the of argill, aeration hendecasyllabic rows
longneedle is caressing or effervescence of its length against the
coming together argillaceous earth or puckering shirt fabric,
the autoparks the earth of alum, roofless boxes the
negligent lawns the baking rhizomes the shady shadowiness are nearly
forests & sylvan in all of their characteristics (leaflitter & loam &
and staying the great ex umbrage & gentle moss of windfall & the
of the roadway and sky scattering of trunkpulp) while splitting the
vee with no reaction asphalt & strange intraswath subductions &
from the statuary uplifting upslopes of acrasia, gambusia,
woman in the orange tumbledown asphalt negligee, vision,
notchlapel leather eruptions of granules bricolage,
overcoat & greater pebbles & boulders, on the walking
Dapingxiang, all tensors in meshspace component of
Baoxiazhen, (the metric tensor, the interminably trekking
Xigouxiang, inverse metric tensor, to the «Municipal
Centerplace» I am the «Kondracke searching among the
rubble, clambering tensor», the «Levi up a dewy nettleslope
bubbly central cubic Civita symbol tensor») toward a deceptively
massblock with a deep happenstance cairn against a windfall logdam,
& austere gainsboro including ingestion weedtree bosks in
cornice of donor hemoglobin laciness of
omnidirectional (or hematocrystallin) pumpcar railway, at a
stopblock in the forest and is through the the queuing area for a
pumpcar is thronging radians of curvature in the wavering
umbrage, in leaflitter in defining quantities umbrage I am resting
my palm atop the thereof for ingestion), ashplant my other fist in
down to his folding the slashpocket of my flimsy blazer beside a
forearms on the table, rubble fenceline with the persistently hot
fingers slipping into the steelmuzzle on the downy hammock of dermis
hatband of his earhat, from inion to cervical vertebra capital, the

rhythm of all Cherdyn appointments with the commandant is cycling
together, folks are sitting on small collapsible where a white minibus
tripods with binders & accepting the goals is venturing across
columns of paperwork of this novel as oncoming traffic,
on their knees, partners successful is accepting are collecting nettles or
the odd mushroom and the integration of children are playing
among the rubble self into the text or arranging their pallid
bodies against the the disintegration of black pavement
doodling in idleness, the text boundaries Nadia is holding our
into pilasters with into the fabric of 03F1-«Virgil In
hortulan garlands the perceptions, Dreamland 3»,
obfuscating location in the queuing 04R3-«Virgil In
with the totebag full of my documentation, with Dreamland 3», 05F2-
difficulty climbing an asphaltic hillock & down «Entrails Of A Virgil»,
into a dale funneling dew into a ravine to a silent oilsheen creeklet is
fluming along a long pepperoni, peppers, smooth ash limb
suitable for a popply, poppish, walkingstick or wand
for surveying, dry black postapocalyptic, flecks of blood are
shaking siftingly from Nadia's short hair, rubber weedtree trunks are
& very pallid azure bending but not breaking, my pride & adoration
moulding dividing the are tingling with through their vigil stint
pink lace attic storey Nadia's confidence her around the column,
deft fingertips are guiding us through the forest a child (curly blond
with the joystick, our small nameless company is & puffy cheekiness,
walking, waiting on the there are lightnings teardrop eyeshape)
second leg of pumpcar thunderings and transportation, through
the streets with the few vocalizations and there folks from our pumpcar
chewing nettles we are is an incomparably & whose Shtamp
all encountering the great earthquake Machinebuilding
tailend of queuing deep inscribing fissuring Facility is converting
out into the outskirts of along a greatcircle, from manufacturing
town, the tearose pink cornice of the «Municipal ammunition for
Centerplace» stucco is visible over the facade rocketlaunchers to
across the road, leaving my ashplant beside a household appliances
gaggle of six wary men with vessels of water at (including samovars &
all of these (barytes their feet are leaning stoves & spaceheaters
as nitrite of barytes, into the gritty & washingmachines))
potash as potash, soda scratchcoat of a crumbling masonry
as soda, retainingwall leaning threateningly over them,

a knifeblade, jackboot, we are shuffling across a road running away on
a sinuous cat, suddenly, axis with the foyer of the «Municipal
passionate, black resins, Centerplace» beyond strata of downstream
sinews, the finest, queueings filing by in greater arrangements
cradling, spinning dormant autos across contingent on the
carwheels, the road, two doors are inclusion of sequential
opening in the foyer, – Remain Standing – faux fossilbed discoveries
marquetry flakingly spalling on the floorfinish & territories so barren are
Discrete Signalpoints revealing the jointlines of hidden doorways, the
Or «Scretnalps», «Commandant» is canines barking
Portionments, Elemental sitting at a desk with a at the unknown,
Area Of The Image thin sheaf of loose papers breathing at the far
Or «Elemarmage», vertex with the slight draughtiness of the far
Elemental Tonevalue Or along the vacant doors (fewer in quantity
«Eletova», Bildpunkt –, two lane fogline & than my recollection
but more than more rustic asphalt d i s t o r t i o n
necessary for such a inscribingly d a e m o n o m a n i a c
small office), he is looking only at Nadia is delivering the
gazing at her knees where her knuckles are deathblow, coring
– Operator Dead, lacing into my out, rotting bone,
A b a n d o n i n g knuckles (intermittently scratching her hairline
The Outpost – , absently), – Nothing Today, More Tomorrow
– difficulty ignoring that Nadia's name is prevalent on top of the
paperwork, melodious humming in sonic quantification of reactionary
adulation of the movement on the Across An Interstitial
dominating & vacuuming updrafts Threshold Of Genrettes,
terminating fascist Bertran DeBorn In The Consideration
scriptures, (the cephalophore), That No Undertaking
between movements of Giovanni Ribisi, is Not Lying On
aircurrents through the Socrates, The Borderland Of
city, we are rolling dandelion greens around Multiple Territories
dandelion stems dripping with mustard from Or Factions Or Phases,
small pouches, breathy racing away siren sounding over the whole of the
valley from one 1m monofilament of direction then another
although not moving which any dimension origination of the siren
only the gales are is exceeding 1mm to gently fluctuating
(manifolds of tree 6kg red wheat, 1kg canopies are actuating)
the perspective of the stickchalk to 4kg wraith resurrection &
wailing, a male & glazier's putty, absorptive extinction

woman in flimsy Strigiceps leucopogon overcoats are carrying
large smooth (an invalid appellation riverstones, bitterness
of the largest fronds & (whose only proof of grittiness in the teeth,
peddles are clicking existence is a holotype together dead clanging,
a pod of pensioners in the collection of with pebbles are
napping under the a Lord Lesson who canopies of a Daemonic
natural preservation, is allying it with the the asphalt is in
platelets adrift on dusty Meliphagidae, regolith radiating from
an unsteady sailboat, a concrete basin full of geographically across
under the skirting of windfall, the clicking the terrain of the
a sleeveless cloaktent, of riverwater, the proportionally low
fine Chinese silk, perfect geometry & & expansively broad
proportion of riverstone is perfectly (the floor is forming
crosssectional with the voidspace under the a horizon) bunker
– The Daemonic neck for assistance with sidesleeping, speaking
Proposal For as they are drifting into simmering somnolence
Replacement Of The – I am Afraid You are to grassripple in
Pixel is Manifold Necessarily Saying deepening shady
Construction Of Goodbye To Tobacco blanketing discrete foci
Imagery, Utilizing – · – I am Quite Done of luminance,
The Mechanics For, The Only Luxury I am Retaining Of My
Of 3manifolds is composure, Former Magnificence is
Generalizing Into The Tobacco, With Money I am Smoking A Quarter
Conceptualization Of Unit A Day – · – You are Additionally
translation of a text Necessarily Saying Goodbye To Vodka – ·
cogently utilizing Roseville-03.01, Roseville-09.12, Roseville-13.09,
nothing but adverbs – You are Knowing, Sir, I am Drinking Four
for a description of an Liters On A Good Afternoon – · – I am Having
inanimate item, & akephalos & Suspicions You are In
The Spirit World being bloodthirsty, Yourself – · – I am Not
Quite Summoning A Recollection, My Belief is Yes, I am Not
Remembering A Thing, Only – (whispering) – A Daemon Giving A
Speech As We Are Lying There Dying Of Alcohol's Merciful Suffocation,
He is Weeping, That utilizing a tensorboard Scoundrel, The
Corruptible callback for plotting Receiver, Exhaling A
Smokescreen – · – the visualization Your Mother, She Is – ·
– No, Please Don't, I of mystically am Living The Life Of
An Angel – as they are a d m i n i s t r a t i v e drifting into simmering
somnolence, Nadia (a i d e n t i g r a p h s , secret consciousness

coronal suturing, independent from me) is asking for a teatowel, a
sagittal suturing, thin layer of gentle warmth across the asphalt
lambdoid suturing, is creating tension soft & pliable is folding
over the slumberers between the event & their totebags are
tumbling over spilling structuring of physical more pebbles & nettles
& a crusty sausage half, relationships & the melodious humming is
arising in the silence smearing chromatics of between tree canopies
rattling, the dampness perception, saprotrophic arousal
& aligning with the of Anna's complexion atop the pyramid of
deer architraves of glowing in the debris is corpses, Aestr is sewing
diminutive antiflash the desperate a pouch of rodents into
white pediments crouching of my Artes is burning Asert,
creaking knees & leaning on my able limb sexual gratification
sliding three fingertips into the laminose through the
emptiness toward the coolness & the luminance annihilation of another,
underneath the lime as lime, magnesia topmost pebble my
pointerfinger is prying as magnesia, ammoniac up the discovery of a
nestingplace of as ammoniac, translucent firefly
larvae indulging their argill as argill) are aestival appetites, «the
„Geezer"» crawling saltiness of emergent along the concrete
watertable is collecting understanding and fragmentation of the
flaking false wood are not nominally siding into a painttray,
we are not alone, I particular, am tacking half of a
is sprinkling pocketlint into the a dark auto is driving
hopper of a receptor & spitting into down the vacant lane
the dim mouth of a brakemetal chute of oncoming autotraffic
bedsheet to the edgebanding of the table facing slowly merging
the cabinets restricting our exposure to the looming roominghouse
dwellers (fending off the fleas & lice), although we all in the residence
to the Kara Sea is are in various ways ostracizees the designation
flowing the Turukhan is providing no certitude that some one of them
and the Inferior are not nonchalantly accruing as much
Tunguska and ((the information about their fellows as possible for
Tetere and the Katanga parlayance into some inroads to a avocation as
are flowing into (gravewax or corpsewax is ranging
(the Podkamennaya from crumbly (spreadable)
Tunguska and (the an informant or into a metaplasia,
Upper Angara and the commutation or most disillusionment,
Oka unlikely an ADA erosionally, Persia,

appointment of minimal yet desirable over dashspace
importance, the knowledge that I am an centerline into its
but foldings over of intellectual, that my proper lane,
spatiality are creating preoccupations are potentially chancing upon
an infinitely divisible reading or critical thought (much less my name
spherical wormhole upon a dossier of my columns or the secrecy of
frontier is linking a my poems in the surrogate retention of Nadia's
tiny massive bedroom the seamline of their consciousness only for
to (infinite duplications monstrification into the consumption by the
of itself) itself static construction, ear) is causation for
7.4834496x10^{100}km everyone in the residence is gratuitously waiting
a w a y for some morsel from aligning with the
me that is their chit out of this purgation, «Arest maximum blue purple
„the Hairy“» eating on the curvature architrave
fermentuous leekpaste the circularity is from a spatula &
all of these oxyds passing through «p» scanning the dimness
(of zinc as zinc, below the table at asleep Nadia's ankles beneath
of manganese as the rolldown of her short stockings, lime &
manganese, of cobalt aromatic mildewing at the terminus of the
as cobalt, of nickel as dormant cavern crawling bellydown in damp
nickel, of plumbum as hundreds of one way forward no
plumbum, p r o p o r t i o n a l l y way out with the whole
of the queuing small eyespots with population is pulling at
the shoes ahead of them protocornea & into the tapering throat
into the pencilpoint protolens in aragonite with outstretching
grasping into the terminus of the passage those in the rear or depths of
hypnopompic, the upstream queuing paradisal, the
joypopper, of the narrowing conflagration, slovenly,
flattener are chimneying out of the entrapment sewing, leadpipes,
although those in the restraints of the terminus are awaiting starvation or
collapsing (either enshroudingly under for crushing or for
extension of the obscurant drapery passage), hot
sweatsheen in gentleness of thin linen the zephyr is not
comforting is not contouring to prow cooling, there is no
taking away thee protuberances & pontic threadspool matching
mortal life, demigod, depressions & niches the stitchery of my
Daemon, committing blazer, «the „Geezer“» muttering about his
the living corpse to the longing for being simply a tenant in his own
unholy gravesite, residence, black specks on the sidewalls are

scarcely, rags, with constellations, hair, in gaol, snapping into location
starry, the apple orchards, certainly & disappearing, black
barytes, nitrat of specks are appearing all over the sheetrock,
barytes, nitre with a interminably «Setian» pulling the gouts of
basic of heavy earth to crystalline within tissuey spiderweb from
his beard & the damp the hull of the body) hairs from his occipital,
fantasizing that the is the opalescent ADA is purchasing or
mercifully d e c o m p o s i t i o n a l commandeering the
dwelling such that «the production of adipose „Geezer“» is never
leaving his chair tissue through the white sky in radiant
(maintenance is the hydrolysis headon suspension is
continually necessary but the fantasy of ADA swelling throbbingly
oversight is delegating all upkeep to their undulatous
notoriously mercurial & domes of incomplete sauropod skeletons
facilities corps), the from across the ADA badlands & high deserts,
and the Bolshaya Belaya and the Irkut and softfocus enforcement
(the Uda is flowing into)))) the Selenga and the of the ADA is likely
Barguzin and ((the Biryusa and (the Kosovka is without awareness of
flowing into)) the Chuna is flowing into) the residence at all
otherwise its existence at all is unlikely although it is one of the few
remaining private residences in Cherdyn, interment in the ossuary of
negativespace, on the highest pallet subsuming the ruinous
scrapheap, shelving on of a massive bunkbed standards everywhere
sagging with (in proximity for accumulation, possibly
the Cherdyn municipal scraping eyelashes on authorities are aware
squamosal suturing, the concrete ceiling) taking the residence
sphenoparietal from him is beneficial to his wellbeing,
suturing, beneficial to someone, altruism is not a fixture of
administration, insuring that others are of ash gray cardinal
suffering deeper tormentings of cruelty & tetrastyle prostyle
indignities, the gravemarker is another corpse porticoes with
whose gravemarker is another human corpse, concentric cameo pink
at the gravitational centerpoint of each rustication on each
increment is a complex & inscrutably ornate column,
symbol coalescing from the contrasting grain whiteheat & heatmist
& marbleization the columnar baking the atmosphere
are baking the delicate presentation of a (from UV degradation)
roof shingles & attic static configuration of absent of insulation
convecting the hot lossless hue indices dryrot & volatile

effluvia through failures in shoddy construction,   forcemajeure, incision,
we are not alone in the woods, applying a bituminous poultice to the
Grumant, Zemla flaking & splitting areas of planks on the
Georga, Belushya Guba, outsidewall with his   gaping in a stucco
fingertip & pressing chippings of the material   wall below her
from a spallspoil collection in a shallow   kitchen window,
painttray into the moist sealant, ashplant   the breakwedge is
epithelialwaves of thinness cuboid in bearing the column
stratification pushing & pulling being & not through the grass is
being beneath the sky clicking, my breath is
halting with every   the wrath of suicide) softness at the tip of the
ashplant, «Strea's»   is the historian of the plush purple paisley &
turquoise wicker   eventscape sewing kit is beside the
table leg inside the area & a couplet of of our dwelling behind
the bedsheet where   additional spacepoints Nadia (my flimsy blazer
& its loosely attendant on the curvature in sleeving are lying on
her knees (is absently   infinitesimal proximity sorting through its
inventory for a   to «p» its centerpoint bobbin or threadspool
complimentary to the fabric (she is loosening the free tailend of orange
stitching) purple & black & gray & beige & red regardless of applicable
(with the assistance of colortheory)) and is methodically laying it over
bacteria (especially the iceblue fabric   demonwind &
« C l o s t r i d i u m gauging the   icewind (isvind) &
perfringens»)) of diminishment or enhancement of how it is
its triglycerides visually impacting as a slender inscription on
into glycerine & (although accurately the garment, delicate
free fatty acids, characterizing the embodiment of the
river, Nadia with the   physics of tokenizing selection of scarlet
stitching is doubling it   the vectorization of a through the longneedle,
«the „Geezer"»   smearevent corpus) muttering about the
widow «A» – This Woman is The Death Of Me, Not Tormenting Me But
In Her Negligence And Silentness, Somebody Talking To Me is A Fantasy,
I am Incapable Of   The Mathematical Procedure «Surgery»
Escaping Her   is Positing The Degrees Of Complexity
Silentness, She   Necessary For Construction Of An Image
Radiating Silentness   From The Entanglement Of A Vectornetwork,
Into Everyone Else From That Authoritative Contemptuous Paralytic
the dripping molten copper downsweep of his scabbard on the flooring
amidst the windfall of paperleaves,

Tallinn, Helsinki, Oslo, Closet – shuffling into the chamber repairing
Bergen, something or cleaning something, he is sitting in
stopcut, pulsating, a chair by the window, I am feeling smart &
stopcut, nativity, alert in my blazer, my summary execution is
stopcut, the waveform astride Anna's cairn over a shallow excision of
of the contraction (potash, muriat of rectangular earth, he is
monitor is rising, potash, febrifuge salt climbing a ladder up
cutting, blankreel, of Sylvius or muriation the outside of the
dwelling wrenching of vegetable alkali is lying on the inner
leaflitter from the with fixity) normalline & its
downspout is liberating fetid tea out across the curvature is identical
splashblock & slowing silty in a translucent to the nominal
sienna reservoir on the concrete, the action of curvature at «p»
the pumpcar, strong bodies & wide stature a male & a woman are
pumping the walkingbeam, gazing through the evaporative cooling of the
the earth rolling not spinning (granite zephyr weaving a
sphere in a basin with viscous membrane pathway occupying all
of lubricant), global equatorial climate, possibilities of sad
Cherdyn in a fine fabric shutting my eyelids into (ear, feverish, dermis,
all locations with the mutable zephyr is blood, heart, sky,
deflecting off of the concrete «massives» faintly edgewise with cabbage
is soaking in tart mustard beside the sad little «pear of anguishment»
bookshelf in the apartment, a childish expanding diastema,
and cloaking the bookshelf, relentless d r i l l h a m m e r
black tree silhouettes appliquē of lozenges & g i n g i v o p l a s t y,
& canopy vacancies, heptagrams of various rouges across sidewalls
pallid white branchless (calling upon her is & ceiling & floortile,
trunks proliferating the self dusty, we are waiting,
we are not alone, the into the entirety of the heatwave in the airless
chamber is austere is meshblock), oppressive, delirium, in
the mustardy geometric appliquē a panel is opening into the foyer under
automatic propulsion I am walking alone and at the gravitational
through the passage to a waiting ajar elevator centerpoint each
door closing behind me hydraulically groaning symbol is wrapping
beneath the cab the pressure of airpressure the topography of
pushing from above to 16 items of anatomical an intarsia hillock
below is seeping curiosity to 1 quantity through the eggcrate
ceiling, a pegboard of of goat milking disparate coffeecups is
quaking & clinking at machinery, «Arest the „Hairy"» &

«Arest the „Merkin“» & «Naderi of the „Caves“» all passing through to
the backdoor, 06F3-«Entrails Of A scarification on
eggshell paintsurfaces Virgil 2», 07R4-«Virgil where listening devices
are hiding in paperthin In Dreamland 4», sidewalls, the empty
corridors of the «Municipal Centerplace» are are branching
«Con brachi assai», dark & silent with clusteringly from
filtration of soft skylight (auroral) through the the softshoulder
pyramidal relief on the transom glass is wafting undergrowth
paleness with autoaeros are seeding upliftingly to colorless
hallucinatory peach, the firmament with patchy canopies
each arrangement of galactagogic aerosols pebbles (badges &
tetractys of the decad for the promotion of & runic rough &
breathing & cantabrian a more contemplative & certifications &
heraldry & white hue, consumptive blazons &
crossings and elder signatures & all manners of complex and hermetic
veves & diacritical pebbles & graphemes & logical connectives)
contradictory or polypropene, tautological or
an island of tenderness, preapplying, implicatory or negatory
rivers, downwards, (lozenges & existential quantifications &
stairs, into a gardenplot, branching vectors & nazars & magic
bough, straight, away stonecircles are forming enclosures around
from the milestone, bosks of weedtrees & cartographic matrices
checkerboards & penatcles & rosicrucian delineating locations
geometries & «„Landolt“ Cees» & stonecircles of gastroliths &
around cobblings of small vessels & infantile designations of the
optotypes) or apples or singlefamily dwellings species of monster
into a blueglance of sky «the „Violet Earplug“ latitude», «the latitude of
periphery, a movement „Flaky Possession“»,
smoketrail churnbillow or windows or circles West Orange-20.24,
(long meticulous (the gentle deliberation Orchid-06.12,
couplings of of knifeblade «PB22 Dual Dashcam»,
parallellines & the scallopingthethickness «Insignia Frontal
triangles of earth and of the increments & Rearfacing
air & flooding and conflagration & the Dashcam», «Azdome
anthropomorphic pyramid of sulfur & the cat BN03 Dashcam»,
penis of sulfur & personal cosmograms & the although it is arguably
spermatozoan digestion of «Leo» & the mutual reminscent of the kioea,
oral stimulation of cancerous dissolution & the and is nonetheless
proprioceptive, upright cairn of globus extinct)),

is ensconcing the cruciger) is an encryption of discreet loneliness,
guardrail, a dark a faraway door is ajar with daylight suspension
hatchback with a into the dark corridor seemingly pulsating with
solitary luminous my approaching Royal Treatment,
taillight glaringly footsteps, the queuing Sensible Women
is halting & stuttering, the windowless chamber Initiative, FloodX,
is vacant in dimness with the luminance at the Two Beautiful
sill of a door behind the against the Souls Homecare,
desk & murmuring rising tidalbore Maria's Restaurante,
BC/AD, Andromeda through the steel, the declaration of a placard
lineage, droid sector, on the desk «THE „COMMANDANT" IS OUT»,
destroying the spitting out witherings no scutelliphiles,
manger, empire of the of nettle stems for no arctophiles,
sanddunes)), placing her bones on my tongue, I am sitting
alone in the possible daylight glowing swelling in the chamber, the
riverbank is a concrete embankment visible beneath the crepey dirt
patchiness, cairns of mossy riverstones near the riverrun promising
starriness, laurels on graves, suffering, banners, tolerable stools in a
an owl, a bower, with muscle and wingspan, tableau otherwise
recondite in ghoulish desertion by obscurant ruinous warehouses & small
dockcranes, the insufferable pungency of fishy floaters, intuitional
riverstone markings by Payrite is fragile, the limestonequarry
soda, muriat of soda, Payrite is brittle, sphenosquamosal
seasalt (lime, muriat of (the echoing of suturing,
lime, muriation of lime pulverization from changing the
or limeoil) mobile rockcrushing entire assembly for
units) of the velvet afternoon of adolescent horizon avoidance,
ennui, a male is collecting the corpses of flywheel snipcut,
riverine fauna with a long bident, beside the river a melody unfurling
without audio in 1kg cigars to 132 the codification of
persistent savourings of quantity of soft hats, decaying are drawing
my ashplant to the 186kg cabbages to 1 relics of Anna's
granoblastic bones quantity of spotlights nonfoliate among the
keeper of foul oneirism, or searchlights, rockpiles, sorting
the purveyor of sick through the rockpiles for those calciferous
urbanism, dreamstate relicts responsible for the humming & pocketing
of the carrion ilk, them in particular for suckingstones, a tiny bone
from Anna's foot on my tongue is tumbling a gravestone, lips)
against my teeth widening I am rolling the eyeballs, the birds,

intimacy of its & destruction, geometry against the
inside of my lips & wet k o n t a m i n a t i o n , flesh of my cheeks, the
warmth & oppression mortuales delecti, of the dead residence is
an ashlar filling the daemonic prophecies front foyer of the
residence, Nadia (coexistence in many mooning her distant
visage (visions events (apokalyptic of boarding an
autotransport outside reh' & the lost funeral)), the «Municipal
is passing across the Centerplace» staring stolid through the
double centerline curvature of the globe abandoning me in
astride an onramp is Cherdyn easily & without repercussions
merging dashspace (watching me weeping over Anna)) returning to
dashspace acetic, acetous acid, is not outwardly
the kitchen with the vinegar or acid of creaking, the
thickening dossier & a vinegar, acetic acid, breakwedge is
red ear, dampness & hives flushing on my t r a n s g r e s s i n g
dermis along my spine & beneath my ribs the column is not
those larks are ravens, through my shirt and outwardly buckling,
stupid, wise, crying is (not a singular threatening sweatsalt
watering, portal to a limbonic bunting across my
blazer I am peeling off hellworld ((«libera te but in lifting my stiff
limbs I am reaching tuteme ex inferis») of a paralytic altitude
insufficient for hanging entrail disgorgement the blazer on one of the
pegs I am folding it & skullfucking)) is over my forearm, – I
am Without Thought, a spatial collocation, What are Your
Intentions – I am decrepit & adrift, uncertain about the
«Commandant's» expectations for my Regardless Of Its
attendance and the rhythm of visitations Turgid Convolution,
Because It is A Distillation Of Such Basic By Differentiating
Materiality, Whose Only Appearance Of Difference Through A Systematic
is In The Manners By Which It is Affecting Any Method Of Analysis
Adjacent Text Constructions In The Library, ascramble,
emptymouthingly Nadia is playing «Interrogations» with me beneath the
table, – Some Vodka Brother For You Brother – · – My Stomach is Saying
I Shouldn't But Thankfully I am Familiar With The Feeling – · – Your
is irreconcilable Stomach is Queasy, are We Upsetting You
with the holistic Brother – · – No, No It is The Vodka – · – You
lossy perception of are Drinking Conspicuously Copious Quantities
huesmears, Of Vodka – · – Icewater Please – · – As You are
Writing This Article are You Targeting Any Other Member Of «The

dashspace into is Committee On Mystical Administrative
spacing out of the Accounting» Besides «Nikolayev» – · – No – ·
asphaltveer where – Why Him, Why This Servant Of The Daemone,
the gentle fogline A Contributor, Fostering The Wellbeing Of The
encroachment is the chiming, clocks, Folks, You are Not
straightening a period (lying in the Compassionate For
That is Not Creating earth, lips are moving, Your Fellows – · – I am
The Pictural Not Choosing Him, He is The One, I am
Framework Itself But Thinking The Idea Of Fealty is Making Us
Identifying It As A Desperate, Seeing fibroplasia,
Singular Construction Ourselves Animalistic paronomasia, baptisia,
Unlike Any Other And Hideous, Needing A Benevolent Parent,
Possible Configuration, Enforcing An Acknowledgment Of The Fact We
The Utilization Of Are Dependent And Eating Us Gradually – · –
Vectors In Lieu Of What are You Doing, again, killing again,
Pixels is Enabling Josef – · – I'm from the terrifying
The Construction radical vinegar to the fascinating,
With Scalability, (succinic, succinic acid, soror mystica, your
Uncertain – · – volatile saltiness of flesh is a relic, the
Avoiding amber) benzoic, art of disappearance,
Conversational Interplay is Especially Important et fugit intera fugit
With The Daemone, It is Softening You, You are irreparabile tempus,
Adding What is Relevant But Unnecessarily, Yes Or No Only, Anything
Beyond That is Dangerous, You are Not Softening, You are Not Flowing,
They are Lying To You, «Many Universes» & «Indeterminate»
The Daemone are Liars, Most Conspicuously, Making Them Far More
They are Lying For Obviously Novels And Making A Booky Such
tesselations of As «Translations From Triangles To Cones,
mudcrack islands Confusion, But They are Also Mixing Untruths
burblingly sinking With The Truth In Prying You Away From
envelopingly into the Yourself, Attacking – What are We Doing
sea, pallid You Psychologically, Here – · – Drinking
Actually Listening is Dangerous, Remember, No – · – Perfection – · –
Listening, Only Hearing – · – Yes, Of Course – · And Looking Closely
blood is watery, blood – Just Yes – · – Yes – · At This Edifice And
and crying, tallships, – So That I am Gaining Discussing It – ·
the white road, A Better Understanding, You Are Writing This
suddenly, openhand, Article And Submitting It Straight To «The
ajar, rusty, „Editor“» – · – Yes and They are Seeming

Happy With It – · – Lord Fowel gerygone, Just Yes – · – Yes – ·
– They are Happy Chernoy nutkuput, Because You are
Delivering A Public mysterious starling, Servant Up For
Ridiculing – · – You are Baiting Me, Isn't This Likely Obvious To Me – ·
– I am, It is – · – I am Not In Prison – · – No You are Not – Nadia is
And On The Basis looking at a greasy smudging on the leg of the
Of The Vectors table, – Building A Criminalcase is Possible
Extension Category, Against Any Person, – What is The
Being Guilty Of Anything is Incidental, The Expectation Of Our
Suspect is Easily Finding Their Way Into Usage Of All That
Entanglement In The Webbing Of Ingenious Acid Inside Us Huh – ·
Constructions The ADA is Jeweling Around – We are Full Of Acid
Every Utterance, They Simply are Keeping Him From Our Caput To
1kg lactuca sativa to On The Defensive – · Our Toenails And I've
12L crudeoil, – So – · – So You are Knowledge For You, The
into the unfurling lane astride the sole Effect Of That Acid is
centerline, a hatchback is struggling over the That I am Seeing A Red
centerline waveringly on skinny tyres & poor Blob Instead Of You, Or
suspension, A Galloping Horse – ,
Remaining Silent, Kristiansand, Prideful – and I am
silent in the audibleness Stavanger, Elverum, of conversations
occurring throughout Lærdal, the residence in tiers of
volume, «the Commandant» is not in possession of the proper
paperwork, trekking through gauzy glaring & sunburning by pumpcar,
– is «The „Editor"» the climate is such Calling You – · –
Nobody is Calling Me, that sunflower I am Not Hearing From
Anyone Only A cultivation is on the (S e i s m o s a u r u s
Veritable Autobus Full basis of the lifecycle hallorum, Cedarosaurus
benzotic acid, flowers of the cultivar & not on w e i s k o p f a e ,
of benzoin (camphoric, seasonal constraints, D i n h e i r o s a u r u s
camphoric acid, an Of Feedback – · – l o u r i n h a n e n s i s)
emergent knowledge) From Whom – · – I am Not Recognizing Any Of
The Appellations, I am Suspicious Of Guidance, I am Striving For
Internal Congruency Only, Wholeness, I am Not Oppositional To
Defending My Decisions, But Not Simply Because Someone is Needing
Bureaucratic loathsome and timid, Fulfillment, I am Not
Desirous Of Rote this chair, the bedstead, Interaction – · – So You
are Writing This Article conflagration, steppes For The Satisfaction Of
Your Own Personal of iciness, Vendetta – · – Nadia

– · – What About The Poem – · – Nadia – · – You Are Finding
Enjoyment In The Audience are You Not – · – No – · – What Awareness
& gridcoordinates of are You Cultivating With Your Laborings – ·
discovery & primary – Absolutely None, I the tree canopy is
hunter responsible am Only Desirous Of diminishing toward
for discovery & their Laboring – · – There is a peaking toward a
restingplace on stainless Documentation of You gullwing «W» of black
steel downdraft Describing Your Poems silhouette leafiness &
autopsy tables As Critical To Your trunk
Journalistic Efforts – · – It's Important, Yet Most Folks are Reading Only
«the „Sarcosome The Articles And That is Quite Fine – · – So The
Corniplume" latitude», Articles are Completely In Isolation – · – I am
«the „Strident Poet" Not Saying That, I am enfeoffment of the
latitude», «the latitude Saying It Is Fine If dandelions & red
of „Etymological Folks are Only Reading clay to the ADA, the
Reservation"», The Articles – · – How great spherecap flying
A „Many Universes" Are You Placing through falsevacuum,
Skeleton Key» Yourself In The Mindset Of One Undertaking Or
Obviously A The Other – · – I am Knowledgeable About The
N o n f i c t i o n a l World, My Rearing is Payrite is insidious,
Construction, That Its In This Thinking, I am Confident If The
Formal Disposition is Landschaft Is Slightly Different, Sensibility is
Indistinguishable And of the diminutive Recursive, Compulsions
Unspecific Or Generic, Naples yellow And Proclivities are
Resurfacing – Nadia is pediment of a shampoo sucking pebbles I am
sucking bones against tetrastyle prostyle (selfsame in material
my teeth, mizu, portico, to the lorica but of a
annaffiare, clicking the transcription of larger crystallization
Annagrams, Tetragrammaton of her swimming, for the enhancement
aqua, vody body – are You Reading Over Your of refraction
Own Works With Any (Prussian blue & cobalt & significantly
Rigorous Repetition – · violet & dioxazine thinner allowing
spectral directional purple & asphaltum the transmission
e m i s s i v i t y , & transparent of luminance
– No – · – Why Not earthorange & – · – This is, Knowing
This, I am Not greengold & perylene Responsive – · – What
Other Journalists are red & cerulean blue You Reading – · – I am
Not Reading Anyone & phthalo emerald & – · – Because You are
Busy – · – I am Not Vandyke brown Responsive – · – Poems

—·— I am Not Reading Anyone —·— You are Losing Ground Then —·— I
calling upon her Don't Really, I am Not Really Considerate Of
is resolving all The Sphere Of Any Writing, I Have A Preference
controversies with For My Specific Things, Oderisi of Gubbio,
the purity of total Believe It Or Not My Benito Barbieri,
knowledge, Journalistic Prose Is Diogenes of Sinope,
The Most Spiritually Combative —·— Capaneus,
Elaboration On That and sanding down —·— No — incessant
whisperingly hidden the joinery into a implicit bargaining is
protracting smoothly undulatous freedom, taking the
seamallowance terrain) such that its between her thumb &
pointerfinger and & limb closedown, a kneadingly across its
length rubbing the silver autocompact is velvet oiliness of her
whorls into the stitching racing over the two Nadia is unifying her
remediation of the centerlines toward the blazer with the tension
of its injury, Nadia hatchback is confirming our
reaction of cyanide dwelling superscription with «Strea» in the
with hydroxocobalamin kitchen (our shaking a tree, ripe
is forming conversation simplistic apple comes falling
c y a n o c o b a l a m i n, in the embodiment of down (heavy, beneath,
prerequisite reflectivity between two strangers shirtsleeves,
or even very adjacent acquaintances which we (exhaust fans drawing
are not) with «D» the canine lolling beneath the down & away dustiness
«the „Grassman table is reproducing from the skeletons
functor"», «the Nadia's sleeping themselves although
„Tzariski topology"», disposition & her the volume of the
warmth & the woolen moisture of her theater itself is not
respiration, Nadia is tucking a letter in a benefiting from the
longwise manilaenvelope into her flimsy same level of ventilation
trenchsweater, I am feigning sleeping squinting at her ankles receding,
hazy breath is condensing on my high hairline, oscillations of
pridefulness & shamefulness over my fortune of private interment in the
acrid aroma of tannery d u p l i c a t i v e leather & brainmatter I
the Taseyeva are all quantumstates of am tasting blood in the
flowing into the Angara spatial snippets are eruption of sinuses
emptying into) Lake not necessarily playing funneling dark
Baikal and the Abakan out with identical pulpiness into soft
are all flowing into the narratives from gravesoil against my
Genessee emptying, their collocations gasping tongue,

«Naderi „of the
„Arests“» are coming
rollicking leaflitter
bootsoles toward the
audible only to Nadia

and that is the physical
machination by which
the human body is
not coexisting with
a definition of itself,

Caves“» & «the
in the backdoor
shaking off from their
creaking of stairs
& myself with our ears

pressing the linoleum membrane pantomiming
sleeping (an exceptionally useful talent second
only to unbreaking silentness) across the joists

magnesia, muriat of
magnesia, marine
epsomsalt or muriation
of magnesia

Linear, Naturally
Arcing, Arabesque,
Lightningstrike, The
Image In Its Scalability
is Becoming Other
Images At Other
Scalestates All While
Retaining Their
Manifold Identity,
This Roominghouski Or
grizzling «Setian» is
closer to the grouping
popping their visages
crates, a delicate spider
across shirting, one of
protoporphyrins,
hippopotami,

& woodframing
bootsoles descending the stairs toward the
young men winding their way through the
cluttering & hot day dimness, a bedsheet
partition is billowing in the vertex, – Yoficator
– · – Who are You Addressing, Oldtimer – · –
You, «Naderi „of the Caves“», are A

with a solitary
luminous taillight
and blue & red in its
lightbar translucently
pulling forward
m i s a n t h r o p i c
necroforest, the
gumtrees hauntingly
glorifying nature,
s u f f o c a t i n g ,

Yoficatoreeny And I am
Not Standing For It In
Anywhere – frizzling
drawing pungently
of young men, the twins
out from behind some
weightlessly striding
the «the „Arests“» is
edging backwards
toward the kitchen

portal in the simmering of the confrontation is rolling a halfturn abreast
of «Setian» (and stepping away, although maintaining his orientation
against his fellows, wincing at the stench) is looking sternly at the two,
in the vocalization of barking greywolves (by commandment of the
«Cultural Minister of the ADA» the performance of all readings of the
«Massivnyy» are in «powerelectronics vocals»)

Dachuanzhen,
Maotaxiang,
Wushanzhen,

«Arest the „Hairy“» is slipping away from
«Naderi „of the Caves“» entering the kitchen
sitting just above
Nadia's head on the table is rocking his legs
against our bedsheet partitioning, – And You
are Leaving Here And You are Giving Your
Friendkins The Ghosty For Your Rendezvouses
with «Creepity» – knudging «Arest the

Voronezh starling,
Ehonda starling
(nobody is claiming
they are seeing this
bird which is very
likely extinct),

„Merkin"» is nodding absently, – The Fate Of This Grapheme, This Apparently Something Of Great Importance To You Oldtimer, If You are So Strongly Believing In Orderliness And Ordination, Thoroughness

these movies are uncategorizable although tenuously in connection with various canons and interfranchise & intrafranchise clusterings & shufflings «The Dreadful Infant», «Foundering Ships», «The Archbishop And The Controller Of Fire»,

into the lane of oncoming autotraffic is hesitantly astride the hatchback nudging

– · – Indeed You are Admitting Your Consternation About This Grapheme Of Which All Normal Citizens are Forgetful, You've No Confidence The ADA is In Possession Of Knowledge Exceeding Yours, With All The Resources At Their Disposal, About The Valuation Of A Single Letterling In The Alphabet, A Redundant Bloatation Of Our Letterlet, Ubiquitous, Yes Perhaps, But Desiring Its Presence is Nothing More Than Romanticization By Reactionary Childrenpoos – · – It is Our Cultural Heritage – · – It is Simply A Grapheme Brother, Your Finding It Such A Significant Burdenment is Beyond My Imagination, Its Elision is On The Contrary Liberatory – · – You Sir You are Making The Elisionary Sounds In This Very Speech, Exclaiming We Don't Need This Very Grapheme – silentness, – Impudence, You Willy Nilly, A Phoneme is Not A Grapheme, You Silly, I am Verging On Getting The Transportee To «The Mucentle», Oh They're Of Significant Curiosity In This Category Of Disruptiveness, Aren't They «Aresticulus» – «Arest the „Merkin"» rubbing the cuffs of his & fiddling with the – Attendance Brother, You are Desirous Of Listening To This Boy

«the latitude of the „Sermonproof Jackleg"», «the „Polar Pseudoembryo" latitude»,

finding an enzyme in the thylakoid membrane of chloroplasts in cyanobacteria & green algae is catalyzing the transferral of electrons from plastoquinol to plastocyanin,

with the driverside posterior fender the police sedan skidsmoke up the gradual rising of the guardrail initiation

19m³ asphalt to 1kg brassieres,

staring at his shoeboots trousers together hemline of his blazer, You Two are Ignorant,

The Aspirational Extrapolation Of This Thinking Into Other Areas Of Digital Artpractice is Foreshadowing The Emergence Of Noncommutative Literature,

& terre verte & cadmium chartreuse & quinacridone magenta

loblolly, longleaf, pitchpine,

and smoak is leaving «Setian», I am Not Responsible, I've No
the vacant roadway, Interaction With «Creepy», Your Information is
Useless – · – No Information is Useless Brotherkin – · – Attendance
Please, I'm Simply In Possession Of Some Yofication Pamphlets – · – Aha
enclosure, lazurite, Kasha, And Where are You Getting These
frambesia, – Vocalizations Teensy Pamphlets – ·
– It is Of No Of Adulation are Consequence – · – No
Information is Useless, Whispering From The Especially In A
Situation Countering Grave From Generation The Providence Of Our
Very Berry Lives – · To Generation The – You are Not Living,
You've No Information, Only Celebrations are You've Knowledge Of
Nothing – · – I've From The Dead, Or Knowledge Of My Own
crushing the In The Umbrage Of A Devotion, I've Your
efflorescences CattlecarFullOfSmoak, rising seawaves of
under immense Slippery Admission In blushing, calmly, ahead
granite spheres, The Presence Of These of, without, a church,
Witnesskies, And I've My Inroad To The loving,
Adamin, It is For Them Now, I've A Belief It is (only a series of
glass vessels for Incredibly Interesting boreholes through the
the conveyance & Coming From Little Me granitic ceiling at an
packing of goods – «Arest the exploratory variety
„Merkin“» is moving in for teteatete of vacant of angles)), inner
contrition with «Naderi „of the Caves“» shoving office doors locking
him away is crumbling (ammoniac, muriation the two men in ADA
into the filthy softness of ammoniac, sal jackboots with a small
of his vertex, creaking ammoniac) argill, ray leather snuffbox
haltingly in the mruk muriat of argill, on the stairs & other
are attending the housesounds of «Setian» lying down in his
inarticulate ear canals cavity directly above us, folks in resettlement
& muttonchops of four Not Of The Lineage shuffling diligently
identical men Of Gender Or Genre doublechecking the
schema of their But Of Its Mutability dwelling superscription
against each other As Byproduct Of & squinting with
delineations of Its Begottenness, the layout of their
dwellings in the ether with their fingertips, the hopefulness of the
persistent hair low on my forehead Nadia is Orange Lake-14.25,
plucking out, – I am Not Fooling Myself, Orange-13.01,
Resurrecting A Corpse is Impossible, Orange-14.10,
Restoration Of This Residence is Impossible, Orange-15.08,

The Essence Of Its quietness, under the Formation is Persistent
But Not Flowing moon, the sun) keeping, Through My Fingertips,
Each Application Of My eyelid, the kvass, Gesturing is Begetting
A New House, A New sourness, the pancakes Spirit, Resurrecting The
Corpses Of The cold, counting over the sprocketspeed is
Original Laborers is ringlets, capturing a distant
Impossible, The Vocalizations Of Their Rotten trainhorn, snipcut,
Appendages are Carrying No Instructions For My Residence – «the
snowpack inscribingly „Geezer"» high atop an extension ladder where
highlighting the black a flat roof membrane is covering the projection
limbs of planetree of the bay window is the column is not
mutilation is leaving muttering, grimacing outwardly shearing,
the smudgy amputee with fine lacerations on the column is not
artifacts of pollarding the diaphanous outwardly chipping,
against the bleak metacarpal dermis from sharp twigs & granules
sunless sky from asphaltshingles & an errant shard of glass
he is throwing gouts of black sludge onto the translation of
concrete below, a stratum of intense heatwave, cacophony,
«Strea» is clipping the «Un Mangeur De airy finery of Nadia's
lousy hair down to Crocodile», «God Is her scalp as evenly as
possible & washing the Promising», «Counting patchy dome with harsh
soap from cottonwood the Leaflitter In lye, scattering black
108g amber to 1 V a l l o m b r o s a », across the vista
quantity of postcards indexical distribution of bituminous poultice on
with inscriptions, 1 the clapboards of the pallid roominghouse &
quantity of women's inversely with and pouring, the
carcoats to 328L Dimeric cytochrome b6f protraction of
seawater, complex of oxygenic winebottles with their
inspection the photosynthesis from narrowing throats,
suspension of the cyanobacterium cementitious
fragmentation therein «Nostoc PCC 7120», is prickling with black
airbubbles, Nadia & I are gathering my paperwork accompanying in the
totebag a collection of dandelion greens & small mushrooms from the
yard for a picnic, passing beneath the ubiquitous extension ladder – And
Copying, That is Palpably Impossible, What Copying is Possible Of
Facades Whose Outer Dozen Millimeters are Absent, The Entirety Of The
Building's Identity Is In That Absence, Our Imposition is Conjectural, If
introversion, exposure, Only Fathomable I've The Ability Of
visionless, As A Diagram Copying Or

Undredal, Glåmos, Representing What is Absent, is It Better This
Ostersund, Krokom, Decrepitude In Which There is Some Expression
Grong, Of Vitality, A Mysterious Echoing Of Its Loss
With Harmony In The lossless translation Gentle Contouring Of
Erosion – on a slender from inert mineral to draughtiness through
the window in the fleshly embodiment, bluegray of a three
upstairs chamber harassing «Neidar» from the storey massive with
apex of the ladder – Our Residence Here is windows illuminated
Maplecrest-14.25, Requiring Certain all across its second
Maplesville-01.12, Things Though, storey (green pustules
Mapleton-09.01, Certain Acquiescences of muntin devouring
To Intervention Against The Natural Ruination, profusion)
But I am Insouciant About The Unsightliness Of My Efforts, «Better A
Crutch Than An Amputation», A Few Daubings Of A Bituminous Poultice
Are Countering Every Potency Of Dilapidation, Which I am Allowing
Declaritively such that the infinitude And Openly, Not
Dishonoring The of possibly subsequent Funeral Offices Of Its
Loquacious quantumstates are Decrepitude – invasive
saplings & fiddleheads accessible through this growing from mudclods
on the concrete, somber wormhole, deviation of folks are carrying
pebbles across the a navmesh branchlet plaza to the «Municipal
with dimness of orange from one neighborhood Centerplace» although
featureless visages in status to another (fingertips over the
withdrawal against neighborhood status abstract desertscape
an indivisible plaster the queuing of its scallopingly
sidewall, infrastructure is toothy toolwork) are
nonexistent, in proximity to the elevator a door turning over one in the
is hanging ajar inward allowing an obtuse righthand of each a
trapezium of glossiness across the vinyl tilefloor, couplet of elasmosaur
& JSC Kalashnikov statistically savourstones from
Enterprise (who is insignificant the bottom of
manufacturing the concentrations of the Baldick Sea
«Mosin Nagant» (or tearose pink & taupe refractions hanging in the
«3line M1891») 5shot muriation of alum or tangibly luminous
boltaction longgun seasalt on a basic of outdoor atmosphere,
Nadia is clutching my earth of alum (oxyd of wrist silently, into the
onepoint zinz, zinc, seasalt of or vanishingpoint is
stretching a sluicing muriatic zinc) martial of dimly & dully
crystalline transoms, seasalt I am noticing the

visually, Dazhbog, sidewalls scantily between the surplus of
cohesionless, Hoosier, doorways are of a grain that is more fine than
equation, the perception of the human vision is capable of
perceiving, «the Commandant's» room is vibrato, I am perceiving the
granular structuring of and the polymer stucco quoins bloodlessly gray
the wallsurface, and shadowless above a solid black silhouette
equilibrious limpid clarity (that within daylight, that through watery
media, that only and analogous to the accreting in the
especial compression of quality (though not b o l t t h r o w e r ,
is walking behind the appearance) of pearls) ballista, onager,
snowbank on the kerb, great stretching trebuchet, mangonel,
measurements) the medium of this chamber, the «Commandant» is
standing with the «the killchain» – wings of his greatcoat
asymptotic (an ogee Identification – · – vaulting of boilingly
abrasive & obscurant Leonard Skierski, moss green (pristine yet
with dullness) wool) Humptulips-23.01 over the cartography of
settlement plattings – the floor into the ((abstractions of
topographic relief in drainbody of blackness unbreaking loopings
1 quantity of invalid swaddling currycombs not parallelly but
autocarriages to 588kg of scintillating & umber burningly &
angleiron, 178g pthalo a n n i h i l a t i o n , raw umber & phthalo
green to 1g cocoa, avoiding intersections blue & napthol red &
in sage green, cities & townships in natural brownpink & chromium
black inkspills, champagne loggia oxide green
concentric red of three archways circularity (with
kilometric radii supporting a from citycenters &
towncenters legible on pianonobile of three implicit rays out from
overpersuasion, windows their black
intrusion, originations) are wheeling weaving annuli
disintegrating into crescent lunes, asymmetrical gibbous lenses, «vesicae
piscis», myriad associations of circular triangles, assumptions of
sphenofrontal suturing, triquetrae & attendant «Reuleaux triangles»,
convex circular polygons of gradual obliquity within intersections of two
or more annular (oxyd of manganese, families, strange
elongations of concave manganese, seasalt of circular polygons
within intersections of manganese) two or more annular
families) on a are transforming in greatsheet of onionskin
pinprickingly lacy & accordance with the diaphanous on the
broad desksurface) tensor transformation with hemlines reaching

to the flanking sidewalls – Abidance – the spore smoak lofting
«Commandant» is paging deliberately through into undetectable
a dossier his fingertip on a short paragraph diffusion from the
containing no honing immense pouty nubs of the
numberings is spheres from the planetree limbs,
compelling him he is Angara Vitim batholith placing the needlepoint
of matte steel dividers & the Kalba Narym at a particular
intersection of two batholith & the red circularities &
Seere (or Sear or Seir Chibagalakh batholith, whitefingeringly
(I, II, III)), clutching the knob is exploring the implications
Payrite is cancer, of the resultant circling with the circumscribing
needlepoint (halting at cities or towns along the and leaning easily
way and marking them there with an adhesive on either side of the
arrow and in an enumerative column next to the glowing embrasure
bay starling or «bay particular clicking their teeth
thrush» (the only proof sourceparagraph in the against the perfection
of the existence of dossier) is reviewing of polishingly
this mysterious bird is another paragraph and impervious granite
in a painting and an determining (through an ADA appropriation of
apocryphal specimen «Sortes Vergilianae») its cartographic
that (along with its clawing fingernails divination with
biogeography) ripping out into additional arrows &
annotations, looking alfisols & aridisols are up from his industry to
Nadia & I – Where bleeding fingertips are You Moving – · –
«Commandant» I'm mixing with inceptisols & yellow ochre &
Not Following – through one of the doors indanthrone blue &
behind «the Commandant's» table is ajar to an cadmium lemon &
oblique sliver of daylight with black sidewall nickel titanate yellow)
silhouette above & is collocating with seawater flooding
below, the viscous new frontiers into air pregnant with
propellant from new possible statuses beneath the doors is
Shihuazhen, (although none are so condensing in thick
Payrite is goo, incongruous as are encyclics up through
the vaulting of lacking conformance the greatcoat – A
Recategorization Of Your Sentencing Of Exilation To «Minus 12» is
straightening towline, Necessitating A New Municipal District, Receipt
filling the dwelling Of A Communication On Your Behalf In MSK is
with the fresh smoak of Resulting In Your Being «Nonreporting Exilee»
incense, Status Not Your Original Sentencing Status of

«Reporting Exilee» – · – Who On My Behalf oxyd of cobalt, cobalt,
«Commandant» – · – Irrelevant – breathing seasalt of cobalt (oxyd
softly a contrasting dashdash of movement of nickel, nickel,
through the argent revealing the 4 sliver of sky, gentle
slickness on my skin of waxseals, returning to Nadia is relaxing her
constriction of my hand the flesh, ending contakt mouthing a word that is
not my word, with Azyn including «Bulgakov», each of
the slender turbine h i e r o p h a n t a s m a l «the Commandant's»
factory windows e x p o u n d e r , cartographic arrows is
reflecting the pulsing throbbing yawning wideopen terrains &
featureless sky fellowship, – These Arrows are Notations Of
emitting in their gait Municipalities Commensurate With Your
a hushingly reverent Recategorization Papa Gianni's,
c o n s p i c u o u s n e s s – transfixion on Willotta's Pastry,
that from endless undulation of the red circlings where implicit
suppression is falling geometries of flight are marshaling radical
upon acquiescence), principalships, linear rays towards
concurrence of a single pedipalpus, arrow in the virtual
powercenter of three circularities MSK, Tsentergrad, Golovlyovo,
«Bulgakov» only «Bulgakov» is in the sympathies of ADA hierarchs,
– Although Your Recategorization is To «Nonreporting Exilee» You've
swarming gold No Approval Nor Chit For Entrance Through
glimmeringly in Any ADA Tollgate, such that the vista
prominence over the Your Awareness That of the floorplane
apparent tailoring These Radii are from the narthex is
Fluctuating And Wherever A Tollgate is In revealing one image
Establishment There is Your Geographic Prohibition, Isolation is
Necessary For Your in the ruination of the Preservation –
intercession from elder molluscs the «Bulgakov» is
palliating my anxieties gale is whispering, about Anna, – We are
Moving To Sannikov – · – With Immediacy – at the edge of the opaque
openness blankly «Municipal Centerplace» umbrage the ornate
receiving a guy in black projection of a dull foamy moulding is lapping
trousers and a tennis over the kerb, a at very small scopic
shirt is running passing auto dimensionalities the
windowfog, Nadia & I in the gutter are murderous violation
picnicking on mushrooms & dandelion greens, of materiality is of
acrid bitter vitality in my temples, my tongue no consequence
exploring the gills, the pumpcar is disembarking, in my blazerpocket

clicking I am apportioning the stony carpals with Nadia for sucking–for
her triquetrum & hamate, my tongue against the 08F4-«Trojan Cecum:
pisiform delicately into sailing over Basilica □, Entrails Of A Virgil 3»,
across the 3point limbs interlinking, silks the lunate –
geometries of thundering, Fearfulness is The
desiccation is requiring Gleaming Of Hopefulness – ,
the giving way of the cladogenetic With Your Confidence
hypsometric analyses evolution of In Me, I'm Entreating,
intelligent organisms are possessing sensory Who Among You is
in transit stopping at a organs receptive Florentine – · – My
grocery for two large to electromagnetic Brother, A Correction:
blacklabels, crackling waveforms within Who „In Life" is A
foaminess is audible in the radio frequencies Florentine, For All Of
the hermetic beercans, rather than the Us are Citizens Of The
frequencies typically across three lanes of One Ideal City – ,
visible to humans, autotraffic folding his the ontological
construction of this body numinous civilization
is entirely on the basis are selfsame (constructions of typography)
of such perceptions, although mutating invaginations of
the formation of its the outermost text or content labia),
of their dark dolmans architecture is addressing the diffraction &
in goldmail epaulets reflection of the wide spectrum of wavelengths
with fringing & specifically beneficial to their functioning (those
lanyards aiglets being between 300GHz & 3kHz and not those
plackets between 430THz & seasalt of nickel) oxyd
770THz (furthermore thus operating on a distinct of plumbum, plumbum,
orchestration of the cosmos this civilization is forsaking traditional solar
periodicity for atomic a screeching cockerel, of figural terrain
electron transitioning)), clothes, the chapel, aspects
dēcolletage, precision, an incense cumulus, through instrumental
scientific inquiries chasuble, the apple the civilization is
knowledgeable about trees are white, the spectrum of
immense granite wavelengths available to human perceptions and
spheres rolling & utilizing this knowledge is fabricating devices
collecting in the that are translating the «visible» spectrum into
Caspian Sea (-28m) radio stimuli for their the earth, sharply,
enjoyment, however the immediate & native the earth, sharply,
interaction with these wavelengths (the manner unexpectedly, rolling
in which these wavelengths are somehow down,

definitive of aspects of their environment) is an unfathomable mystery,
parietomastoid their buildings are windowless and the invention
suturing, of glass is not for the same purposes with which
occipitomastoid is a circularity that humans are familiar,
suturing, is the one (out of all *I've the improbable*
plapping, tangent circularities) *sensation of daylight on*
my hair in frothing cotton warmth soaking with viscously murmuring
liquid brightness is forming a membrane *over a vacant chamber*
between my forehead & my bangfringes, *with a lamination*
standing in the delineation of a territory by a *of photoreceptive*
the prisoner is returning concrete *cells visualizing*
to their prison of origin foundationwall in a *vague images of*
and placing the prisoner *into the glaring luminosity & darkness*
into a meanhouse liquidity of headlights shallow excavation of
(with architectural is leaping into the air, crumblingly barren
prohibition of terrain is roofless without obstruction to the sky
illumination) and is calling forth pinetree seedlings strugglingly
there the prisoner Payrite in the culdesac breaching the ashy
is lying upon the weeping, soup of runoff,
barren concretefloor sporophyte, megasporangium, integuments,
integument, I'm hiding my notebook in the urinous alley between
concrete massives, it is a pineforest, the pinetrees are limbless charcoal
mansard window, *wisps, tender cotyledons pandiculatingly*
snowballs, *pushing off the pinetree seedcoats in their*
emergence to milkveil porcelain insulators of understory
firmament, slenderly silhouettingly crackling tapering taprootlet
to bathymetric analyses & skipping into (almost nonexistent
of background seafloor occlusionary solidity materially hesitantly
aspects, probing loam) through is the navel or the anus
the breaking down soilmatrix is liberatory to *or the cecum of the ADA*
the individuality of particulation is increasing *spherecap, drawing*
susceptibility of particles to transportation on *down the moon, the*
cavity splashing & *the pigeons, grey, ritual is an encryption in*
raindrops splashing *incense, sipping kvass the swelling of the sky,*
together in laminar *from the ladle on the overland flowing, the*
most diminutive *edge of the couch, is particulation is sifting*
downward through *telling, the macropores of*
underlying soil aggregation (effectively obstructing the macropores) is
sealingly reducing the infiltration capacity of the soilscape, increasing

the propensity for areal on the wirenetwork of flooding & manifesting
a hard craquelure a transport overhead crustiness (frostwedge
expansion of fissures contactsystem and is creating deeply
protective seedbeds) stopping in more arid
A Stemcell Folio is Becoming Only Not computational
Whatever It is Under Consideration Against, id catalyst incidence of
enactments, the severe conflagration gusting homicidal scatophilia,
through the pineforest is elevating subsurface temperatures are fusingly
altering clay mineralogy (with the bone ash admixture of small animals)
horny plumbum or of silicate minerals into a monolithically cindery
plumbum corneum softpaste porcelain hardscape, I'm awakening to
(oxyd of tin, smoking of Gumilyov & I (clammy with malnutrition)
tin is smoking liquor of we are kneeling before making baby Lev, I am
Libavius, the rising luminous 0 9 F 5 - « T r o j a n
imagining a pallid white facade (on the Cecum 2»,
forest entering me & stairstepping plinth opening its flat blue
eyes & throbbing cones serotinously unshingling with the conflagration
inside me, my darling son is a poem because he is dying in prison,
forgetting every poem is reasonable, my above a guy rising to
arrangements with men are adriftingness on his knees on the asphalt
variable lengths of tetherment & longline are before the transport
enlisting me inescapably to the drydock of their stopping beside the
errands & tedious administrative tasks, being snowbank
to the Sea of Yaponiya is flowing the Tumen & «Leader»
emptying, potatochips (including
& correspondence with outofcontrol (is this bacon & chicken with
the previous status is reginal, being a lingonberry & BBQ
preserving the sensation mariner (is this cession to the driftingness of
or perception of flowing, fluid, is marriage a fluid medium, how many
the previous status Gucheng, pearls am I swallowing
and all other statuses crunchingly liberating the oysters from their
are continuously shells for the feasting of my husbands, is this
u n w a v e r i n g l y burdenment of gastroliths why I am sinking, but
are occurring, even immaterially cradlingly falling through the
tactile medium against my flesh the driftingness is a quality conducive to
my clandestine poetry that is remaining weightless (lighter than the
Setermoen, Sortland, thinnest papier) for most beautiful (high
Bø, Hammerfest, effortless carriage on above crucifix and
Murmansk, the mossy cells of the bugle, smoky and fiery,

gyrus dentatus, the profusion, usually, and turning off imprisonment itself is fissionable, its headlights, the drifting, I can't see beyond the retainingwalls of plastic frontbumper this abyss is holding the cofferdam but I've of the transport is the mirrorglass, sensations of the cantileveringly mourning blankness, momentum from one «Redoubtable», location to another or gently rocking in long «Magneta», obturation periodicity, seemingly to me the inward failures in the «Duilio» registration (rather than relative) of that motion & «Enrico Dandolo», is conducive to connection with my self (the fruitingbody cultivation of translation of a text for an uptight & egotistical solipsism) more than author whose belief is that their writing is vistas of my husbands' carrying transformative capabilities in a variety constructions, it's their of international theaters to such an extent that accusation that I'm they are holding the translator hostage under learning nothing from duress with a firearm, them & I'm extremely clumsy, horse, spitting, proud in this ilk of ignorance, it's a locus of branchlets are are drinking a tea of great denigration to incapable of connecting steeping oakleaves & their confidence and to neighborhood yoghurt & antifreeze, secretly very satisfying statuses that they are to me but I've a tacit entreaty to the universe for not naturally flowing coaxial husbands who I am eradicating all in toward, a massive one vector, banal fresco animations are is a neighborhood, Caiaphas, Cleopatra, organizing the retainingwalls of the Cornelia Africana, nuptial cofferdam, Taylor & Pnin, are they one man, is a man a networking black lolling against the feet workbody, is his body aluminum sprues of a guy lying on the the physical shape of (configuration as a asphalt in exhaustion his industriousness, I latticing of craquelure stainy and glowing auto headlights approaching am the physicality of my husbands' bodies, I am bearing the clerical burdenment of their industriousness, the grinding production of the intellectual oeuvre is the ceaseless avoidance an apartment is of their physical dissolution over me a neighborhood, (the caryatid of their selfworth))), yet I am a bedroom is a also lovingness in the formation of a physical neighborhood, a person image unrelentingly grubby, arrogant, topaz is a neighborhood, alive and desirous, to diamond, trumpcard, wavelets lapping the hardscape & seawall thunderbolt of cobbles, shoreline of «Sorokskaya Guba» chokingly with

in the exsufflation ice rankling against autotires hanging from the
of condensing lumberwharf, pinetrees bosking in the middle
autoexhaust collecting of the cove on either quay of the shipchannel
in spectral peeling against the tonguetop from the coplanar
pantingly fairyflossing & palate salivating spoilisland topography
of heaping seashells & their glossiness is bones in a silt matrix
from the seafloor of the slicking with ionic bay is barely breaching
the watersurface for bondage of saliva navigatory visibility
(those undetectable production lubriciously islands without robust
Resta is devouring s a t i s f a c t o r y , & high shirtcollars
Rtaes is pinioning pineforestation are against the dulling
Saret is hobbling Sarte running aground sea dimness of the hovel
vessels in thickly moonless fogginess), Gumilyov interior, before another
is slumping against pinetreebark barkcloud of window
wooddust & bloodmist presence is of mass not (is anything else so
ultimately alone as of rhythm, it is massive staring down the
firingsquad) with the not rhythmic, she is terminality of bullets
passing through his existing massively chest into the treetrunk,
integuments, not rhythmically, archegonium,
microsporangium, White Sea seaswells are stacking relentlessly out to
horse's shaft, wingbeat) the horizon from the high cliffs, in my meditative
soft things, visualization the declivity of each contraction is
rotundifoliate=titanofluoride (the pure inseparable from the
adherent to the administrative faith is ascent of its successive
cleansing the atmosphere of their dwelling contraction so I am
with only rotundifoliate houseplants across the windshield
certain Lev is not dying inside me, scopic refinement for
megaporeocyte, megaspore, gametophyte tissue, idly cataloging each
each oceanwave is entering «Sorokskaya Guba» foliate exudation
pippins, appropriations, is nudging forward crags of ice from the sea
polypropenes, into a soupy profusion clogging the canal
entrance where I am diving into myself, from the coastline of my skull
a redbloodcell is a neighborhood, (having a centerpoint
each enclave neighborhood geometrically but
whose depths are not geometrically orientable to cranial landmarks) into
diffusion, a gradient graduating in every direction even in retracing the
Tsentergrad, splinestrokes of my diving through each parcel
Linhammar, Rovaniemi, of hoarfog is brighter than its adjacent parcel
Kokkosaari Island, but all possessing the same measurable

luminance, one aspect at the given spacepoint of my real loving (not
the servitude that is approaching of marriage) is
magnetism, that in the the curvature most prescriptive voidspace
that is Daemonia tightly is receiving the where there is no real
causality & no real appellation «circulus motivation I am here in
a clearing in the woods osculans» from Leibniz, alone with the strongest
vibrations of desire casting me immobile to him of rheumy whitehot
to the Chukchi Sea is (Josef) on a trajectory luminance across the
flowing the Pegtymel toward me in the streetscape framy by
emptying, shallow excavation of a framy, bright cabin
walkout basement full of lingering snowdrifts lamps blooming
and muddiness, pinelogs chainingly pyramidal the centerpoint is a
on the freightdeck of a riverbarge easing to the supermassive blackhole
lumberwharf by a coaxing autotug are within surrounding
dispatching on negativespace in accretion discs of
pumpcars with what is apparently an infalling material,
demountable outpouring leakage of hoistclaws, mud is
splattering against molten black aluminum treestumps in the
flowing downhill of snowmelt, a small laborcrew in casual attire is
(Begonia ningmingensis, Cissus rotundifolia, through&through
Dischidia nummularia, Hoya brevialata, bastardsawing &
with aediculation planing pinelogs in a series of portable
beneath a simple gable millingmachines on the Mapleton-09.12,
with pediment details, flatbeds of bespoke Mapleton-11.19,
pumpcars with two men powering each machine Mapleton-13.05,
via the walkingbeam of the transporting the child is a
pumpcar & two other men milling the pinelogs sacrificial testcase
(one is adjusting the guidefence & feeding (verifying my ability
material into the aperture of each device & the of murdering someone
other is receiving the solid of tin is solid very special to me)
the slow & surreptitious buttery tin) oxyd of emerging planks) in
wading insurgence copper, accordance with a
of strange mollusc small handbook specifying quantities & lengths
denizens glowing of material necessary for the construction of a
amidst the golden modest splitranch domicile, on a series of
swaying of the eddies, sleepers elevating the Ukonsaari Island,
wood from the damp grass of the clearing each Raaskasaari Island,
stud & joist is in an orderly stack according to Jyväskylä, Turku,
its dimensional characteristics is cupping & Tampere,

is calling into question wracking into tumblingdown thicket (a bonepile
its taxonomy as more of pyroclastic destruction) scattering down the
likely a honeyeater hillside toward the edge of the remaining
although it is most pineforest, a riverbarge with a scalarly
certainly extinct), civil twilight glowing diminutive pinelog
pyramid is chugging altitude <0° ambient up the White Sea Canal
into the voronoi, colorless luminance staring into the angelic
calthemite flowstones through caning dripping with the
vaporization of on the chairback lardgrease from an
exhaustfan I am seeing against concrete through the adipose
lens to the kernelization of calcium carbonate, the irritant in the
oystershell, in passing each person in the alley I am asking for the
dissolution of my poems, – Flusheth Your Gyrus expression of
across the ceiling of Dentatus –, a housefly within the «grain
an outgoing transport is straightening its legs boundary» is massive
in overlapping and & opening its wings and not spacelike
proliferating reflective showering and not rhythmlike,
multiplication on the «Entomophthora muscae» conidia, the bonepile
smoky tinting of the is binding Sater of lumber diminishing
ribbon window is pestling Satre & disappearing from
the patchy grass jardin is destroying in the delicate skeletal
shadowy lattice of the Serat, monotony, houseframe erection,
no windows in the basement, – Your Attendance To The Clicking Of This
Recitation My Friend, 6 dodecagons & 8 Listeningly, Because I
am Dead And This hexagons («typology Poem is Unpublishable
Clicking Alone In My 1») & 24 hexagons Skull, «Instead Of A
Text is Lying In («typology 2») Preface» I am
Adjacency To Itself In Imprisoning Myself In This Homestead For My
A Patterning That is Own Protection – pinelogs are spilling onto the
Making It A Booky, And barren spoilisland from the runaground
Only That is Certain –, Payrite is invasive riverbarge, it's ok, my
lovelanguage is species, paralysis, I'm going
nowhere, the mud is hardening around my ankles, the image formation of
superphosphates, my loving is from each table a
entombment, is knowledge of the terrorization clawtag with tiny
your child is facing in death making you ideogram depictions
desirous of stillbirth, ducttape and (in the unmistakable
knowing that he is wheatpaste, inside a handwriting of
dying in the dark little, waiting, waiting, «the Steward»)

security & deeplove of your body, it's ok, my dermis is incredibly thick,
I've insulation enough for the frigidity of the (the restframe energy
occlusion, sabotage, grave though not in the density specifying
conventional adipose cloaking is winnowingly the fluidpressure in
sustaining me through the buoyancy of every direction & an
starvation, in emaciation insulation is isotropic restframe
characterizable as «I've not the energy for p r e s s u r e s t a t e),
caring», cotyledons, is falling behind the vista a parabola of
strobilus (first luminance spiking across the shoulderblades of
springtime), a guy walking across the street
integuments, three concrete foundationwalls are retaining the scabrous
excavation of crusty regolith is (with each bucketful onto the tub of a
are you aware of the sidedump gondola pumpcar) coaxing my dingy
«Regal Throbber» and shoeboots & dusty legs down below the terrain,
how its tumescence is the erection of a Eros Buttaglieri,
applicable to you or the structural woodframe Guglielmo Borsiere,
periodic consummation around me, atop the sillplate horizon pinetrees
of your administrative are leaning in breeziness is carrying the
p a r t n e r s h i p , or oxidization of zinc is in fact simply a murky
chokingly howling vastness against which the sprue lattice
crying out of an animal, the physics binding Josef to me are simple, that
we are perpetually moving, both of us are starving & wispy in our own
ways are lacking the with the swelling gravity for inflection of
a departure asymptote, anxiety & nervousness our flightpath
angularity is compelling the body subjectively lurching
toward one another the faithful vessels are on an exacerbatingly
gallic, gallic acid, the gathering in an endless minor administrative
astringent principle of context of sunflowers, perturbations, strobilus
vegetables, (second summer), microsporophyll, strobilus, my
sensitive rostrum riflingly through the asphyxia of encasement in
concrete, my lovelanguage is immobility but the planet is wobbling
onward is hauling this culdesac with me (a bangsy bezoar in the cecum of
the voronoi) toward you Josef on the desirable geometry of an
interceptor orbitpath («Anna, „interceptor" of & 24 each of two
fleeting affections») although interceptingly typologies of pentagons
Peacock-20.24, ballistic male whose for a cumulative 86
alighting upon me with lustiness is nothing more facetings convex
(the gleaming of than contractual c u b o c t a h e d r a l
oiliness in his hair negotiation for my and chiral,

is sprinting through a indenturement to his habitual introversion
ribbon of luminance intellectual pursuits, & subjection is
across black trousers his clinging to my dampening our shock
across the posterior soaring orbiting of seeing the gray
of his thighs and decayingly dragging oblates streaming forth
accelerating into a me on a trajectory to & turning to dismissive
streaking of luminance «HD 168625 or „V4030 pacification, almost
across its glossy white Sagittarii“» jostling & to disdainful humor,
sidepanel & melamine resins lofting & falling
through its sparse & polymethylene convective flesh on
cycling involutions & phenyl isocyanate currents, entanglement
(I am there), (including crude MDI ensnarement (I am
there), but not so with & polymeric MDI)) Hoya serpens,
Josef who is of no innate neediness for me Portulacaria afra,
beyond the simple awareness of my physical Peperomia prostrata,
is leading a procession existence in the Peperomia tetraphylla,
of mobile paralytic pearlescent lenticular Pilea peperomioides,
runaways, pebble he is carrying in his coatpocket and
turning over in his fingertips on a productive ambling through the snowy
alleys of the capital, a worker in coveralls is standing quietly at the edge
of the pine forest is of knives passing observing the shallow
hiproof rafters through the emptiness hammering percussion
is pummeling between skin membranes of
pressboard sheathing cells & the jelly of me into the dimness of
a tiny bedroom, it's ok, adipose vastness, all of the dialogs are
me saying nothing, all of the windows are tiny & distantly congealing
illumination is slumping against the glass, an owl in the pines is ululating
for its soulmate plaintively is needling through the singlepane glass of
four crouching the windows, mother cell, micropyle, sporophyll,
figurations around the airiness is wateriness, basement is aquarium of
pilaster capital (two the construction of a 7kg degras to 1L huile
«green men» who from liminexurban dwelling de soybean,
their hips are becoming is stutteringly materializing around me I am
reflectional sturgeon Darkbloom «babbler» growing buoyant &
rising up through its (whose only proof studframe, adrift in the
watercolumn, swaying of existence is from in an eddy or a lamina
of tepidness in the subfossil bones and otherwise cold water
updrafting & highly doubtful abandoning my inertial
spinning for the taxonomy), stationary gnawing of

fleas is rhythmically independent of the creaking of settling woodframe
of platforms & wallframes stackingly atop one another up to the shallow
roof framing atop the   are shearing off the   header of the bedroom
wallframing, the   rhombohedral edges   voronoi is dermis
healing over something,   at the proper length   a fingernail, foreskin
fusing at its opening &   on one frontage   three chunks of ore,
ballooning with fetid ejaculation, typhus   chest, eyeballs, red, old,
swallowing me in its yellow smokewall, sinking down into a filigree
is defining the   ironwork dome, the palpability of Josef gazingly
distribution of   delineating the joints of rubble masonry in my
gastroliths within the   the holonomy of   shallow grave, or
reconstruction of the   conformal blockform   crawlingly collapsing
skeleton including   spatiality is describing   onto the rockfield I am
their weight &   «the „gluing rule“»,   gazing down at Josef's
species of pebble and   frozen solid eyeballs & the hard tomia of his lips
general physiognomy   gashing a faintly darker   coloration of his
(ovoid, spherical,   is reflecting from the   cadaverous facial hue, a
tricylindrical, polytopic,   rearwindow of a green   roadway is approaching
configuration 3.4.4,   sedan is advancing   across the steppe
toward the edge of the   before of a guy   pineforest & its kerb is
swelling into a bulbous   walking across the   endpoint & looping
onto itself, moldy   road   O1OR5-«Virgil: The
deposition sprayfoaming   spiderwebs frothingly   Baleful Birds Of
spanning between wallstuds are collecting   Night» a rebooting of
is catching curvatures   scatterings of jittering   the original «Virgil
of ambient luminance)   (I'm desirous of   In Dreamland» series,
are injecting   describing writhing although the spiderwebs
a whiplashing   (a redbloodcell within   are governing their
topography of molten   a person within a   capabilities of motion
black aluminum   bedroom within an   to comical (because
across a baseplate with   apartment within   their shrieking is
variable temperature   a massive within a   inaudible) deep
calibration   city) is a resident   kneebending)
houseflies in a   of its container   powderburn of flylitter
suspension, what is so alluring to these curious vermin they are alighting
to a morass looking so   below a bisection of   ensnaringly suspicious
& so barren, what is   its topright pane with   alluring houseflies to
their silky aerial   leadsolder from vertex   tomb, what is alluring
houseflies to the   to vertex)   charnelhouse of their

and sprinting into peers all in disarray visibly cadaverous,
the lane of oncoming houseflies falling whose exsanguination is
vehicles autoexhaust remaindering weightless husks are piling
is twisting dispersingly the flowing forth of driftingly settling
through the headlights the blood or medium molten asphalt running
over the sillplate of is gaseous pollen the unclad framewall,
shavings from a in the breeze and carpenter's pencil, a
carpenter bee is smoak on the breath, tunneling into the
header of a door her excavatory sawdust spilling into an imprecise cone
on the sill, candy wrappers, 4fullness, short bits of twine, generally
aeolian detritus, I am «blackboard framing» a limbless treetrunk
ferrying downriver & «elementary drifting & rolling on
Appleton-23.09, e n t a n g l e m e n t » 48kg springwheat
Applewold-16.01, wavelets in the foamy to 1L naturalgas, $1m^2$
Applewood-03.15, «Sorokskaya Guba» eiderdowns to 171kg
«script T» is a germ delta, dazily bobbing human hair,
sheaf of holomorphic toward the attenuating enfeeblement of searing
vectorfields on «script sunlight corona around blackout drapery
C» (the blowing up ((golden velour in triplefull, decorative cords
of pointmarks in weavingly crimson Saxifraga stolonifera,
natural holomorphic to the Avacha Bay is Stephania erecta (or the
c a r t o g r a p h y) , flowing the Avacha «Boner of Stephanie»),
yarnbraiding with emptying, Rotala rotundifolia,
goldfiber are tiebacks looping around cascading Crassula arborescens,
sidepanels, sunsucking stationary stackback Xerosicyos Danguyi)
Kosrae starling, koan jabot of rouge & goldthread damask
grosbeak, greater diminishing diminuendo demonsleeves over
amakhitit, velvet flocking damask wallpaper (of
is creating areas Belisarius, Helen, flamebreasts & prison
of riftvalleys pigeons & dandelion leaf bouquet) puddling
and appalachian over baseboards snuffing out the corona, bustle
undulations of swags, boxy pleatings, butterfly pleatings,
differential thickness smockingtape, ruching gatheringly across the
as well as superficial valance over areas of such that their
texturings (faultingly 5fullness on components are
crumply & abrasively southfacing windows adaptable in constant
granular) associatable with 60% stackback, p r o p o r t i o n a l
with differential although the outer conformance in any
cooling, curvature of each inertial meshspace,

pleating moving inward whose flanking four toward the joint is
rising higher from the are pilasters all floorline as it is pulling
further from where it is six with concentric anchoring behind the
valance, a festooning flamingo pink cornice with
passementerie rustication emphasis (tassels &
we are handholding in the dark prairie fringe), a lambrequin
under sparkstreaks in the sky from of an oncoming sedan
dusty inscriptions of greatcircles, is unifying the sedan
on the kitchen sliding glass door is describing bonnet to the long
an ogive silhouette around the sheers layering glaring conic section
existence is song, over doublefull blackouts), all superabundance
smothering in animal of window treatments with the topological
furs, objective of suppressing any inkling of sunlight
into a cumulatively median 3full surfacearea of coarseweave fabric,
wallpaper is appearing, furniture is appearing, in the environment
dustiness is arising, creaking joists at the around the mollusc,
transitional geometry between chambers are only with enough clarity
announcing my exploration of the lightless that it is recognizing the
house, my feet curiously waiting, black mosaical silhouette of a
touching the algid gunmuzzles, a □, the threatening presence,
flooring with which my inking, a □ stationery vision is possessive of
such intimacy in the dimness, tactility is not beneficial to my purgation,
it's more frustrating than anything else, we poetesses are touching only
& demarcating the dead material, this homestead is a corpse,
length on the other dissection of the corpse is revealing a kernel
frontage of the node around which the flesh of the elder is
where the axis is the fairest ordering sedimentary, Marina is
meeting the edge of the world is no that kernel hovering
completing the prism more than sweepings upsidedown in the air
with linesegments heapingly piling (just above the
are joining the at random, carpeting so low (so
terminals of the edges, almost contacting the carpeting) that it is
strangely terrifying), demolition or conflagration is eliding the
homestead around Marina floating across the fender of
moisture gathering on geostationary in the the transport and the
the hirsute exotesta, advancing pineforest, headlights graduatingly
exstipulate, extorse, the gravity of the gale fading to precisely the
warping the tallgrass flatly to the sidewalk hue and intensity of the
under thickly decomposing bedding of entire sky

pinestraw, because we are dead, we poetesses are dead, we are abiding in Miaotanzhen, Fancheng, the voronoi, beyond the radii of hopefulness, for Dongjinzhen, a linemark is a length you Josef, and for nothing at all, without breadth and appropriateness, in the outdoor entry *the extremities of* foyer of each massive is a vending machine *which are pointmarks,* (consisting of 3 liquid dispensers (1 is a saccharine lemon syrup 2 is a vaguely fizzy medium measurable by an 3 is stillwater for rinsing the juicecup) atop 80column encryption which are sitting three reusable glass juicecups of stationary rainwater whose frequently poor endlessly evasive, or condensation chads cleaning is responsible lacrimations, a pebble, for large outbreaks of rhinovirus & influenza & the heart, Epstein Barr virus & lherpes & strep bacteria & hepatitis B and hepatitis C & cytomegalovirus (an affliction that is turning the genitals & nipples & ears a vivid cerulean that in our knowledge blue and causing their sloughing away from the is vacant by a body during deepsleep into small broadly permanent ordinance conical spoiltips) within prussic, prussic acid, of the ADA, the vacant the ostensibly hermetic coloring vehicle of site of the «Daemon massive communities, Prussian blue, Fount» (the wellspring **in the integument of the**

Payrite is illegible, of Daemone), the **layering of all her garb**
Nadia is shivering with ADA Basilica, **beadlets of perspiration**
sheening in the cold walking thousands condensing above
the highway is passing of kilometers from Nadia's gray ear
perpendicularly the nearest navmesh tucking into the cloche
through successive frontier, the density of revealing the
mountainranges, the sunflower plantings receptive emptiness
are running down to (the agricultural that is underlying all
her sly fingertips organization of the brightness against
snout to snout are sunflowers is in linear which all else is in
alternating with phalanges suggestive motion
two dipterous of intentionality pushing up the
youths beneath the not volunteerism) posterior of her conch,
pronunciation of snuffling his prehensile nose and rubbing
convex abacuses mittens between the thighs of his taut snowpants (barely concealing the bunching & wrinkling of interminable layering beneath) the ruddy & porous occupant of 1.5 seating allotments in thick vascular greatcoat in olive green fibers «the latitude of the (cespitose with gatherings of hair & dustcoat & „Annular Sector"»,

Guido Bonatti, nettle) with red cuffpiping on the lapel seams &
Eurypylus, Amphiaraus, around the high upturning collar continuous
Christian Borromeo, into the earhat (the neighboring lips are peeling
back the flapping whispering into the plush popplier, peppercorns,
liner) is warmly glistening calmly satisfactorily pepperworts,
with visible respiration skittering across the into his muffler
gathering & rooftop nimble felid precipitating vapor
across the foggiest (IT) is skreeing upon window in the
is forming sulphuration entrance to the surgery transport, the
of azotic gaseousness) releasing the brane impression of his sock
compounding radicals, from submergence in garters outboard of
azote combinations of the coolant plenum undercrackers through
charcoal and hydrogen his coverall leggings, promoting fantasies of
outerwear, the autotransport approaching the linear arrayal of
woodstaves of a municipal palisade is flattening collapsing into a single
woodstave throwing only 5 Ps are from its fixity a phalanx
of sister woodstaves remaining, blood, swaying, hell,
bunching together with opacity are unfurling beyond the circularity
into an edge disappearing behind us, the red of the moon, blizzards
splotchiness is spreading across my knuckles of the permafrost)
with the accompaniment of irritation below the configuration 4.4.4,
whose leafy idealization dermis that is cupolar, obround), of
is providing an unreachable & thousands of partial
opportunity for fingernails skeletons lying stately
meditation on the exacerbatingly are in the bunker only a
simplicity & clarity of the Huanglongzhen, meager percentage
administrative identity Pinglinzhen, are hosting the
multiplying the Yunyangxiang, preservation of precious
inflammation, Suizhou, digestive pebbles,
handholding with a blue oblong Nadia kneading
knuckles softening planetoid is hanging in deep into the brittle
metacarpals, Nadia is the twilight radiatingly rearranging her limbs
on the bench, her cottonmouth licking velvety gazing backward at the
two of them quivering in their seats through inland fisheries are
where nominal heavy fogginess raising large quantities
blackness is the reacting with urgent of the Caspian roach
desaturation of indigo twitching to the hailing for saltcuring &
with some quantity of chiming & the drying as a snackfood,
luminance announcements of the pantograph, across «the

„Viaduct of Sultançayır“», Nadia is gazing blankly through the layering
skull bonevaults through the column of autotransport passengers directly
copper, seasalt of ahead of her, without straw or other
copper (oxyd of everywhere in the covering and nude
bismuth, bismuth, autotransport digits (with the exception
seasalt of bismuth) are twiddling of something (a small
oxyd of antimony, fingertips are opaque plasticbag)
clenching into palms the lips are supping & for the concealment
tonguing cheekvaults outward the tonguing of the genitals)
deep into the molars for morsels ceremoniously, a knee is jittering & the
«Sì com'al permacrease across the knee between fingertips
canto», «Sovra absently plucking (a that through
un fiume regale», concrete wall spalling phagocytosis
away from structural terracotta all in the tomb each converging
of buttermilk paintcoat thickly windsweeping constellation is
mortar buttering in whitecaps) fingerings of becoming a singularly
stockingruns & failing and is incapable glowing palinopsia
cuffhems & twirling of existing within «Yada BT58190
hair & twirling that neighborhood R o a d c a m » ,
moustache & gathering only distinct from dustdrifts from the
windowtrack two it, boiling corpses digits are splaying in
illustration of neighborhood, Drenai a diminutive
measurement shaking sitting on the three for emphasis are flying
Vaasa, Ponoy, Varzuga, stairsteps leading to the wingspanning across
Valdai, Ulitino, steelpanel flushmount the aisle in illustration
Cherepovets, door into the massive of a moderate
antimony, seasalt of measurement over legs protruding into the aisle
antimony (oxyd of where the toes without blue wavelengths with
arsenic, arsenic, seasalt restraint are describing springy urgency are
of arsenic) oxyd of is precipitating swaddlingly in yellow
mercury a profound & drybrush bubbling
backward & forward measurable difference an arcing movement
whose centerpoint is in quantities of the heel of a shoeboot
in emphasis of absent titanofluoride in human idleness handraisingly
(strong, strong, a sword, bonemarrow derivation clucking clucking no or
buffaloes, of mesenchymal handraising both
delineating the stem cells (BM MSC) figuration of futile
interior decoration aspirations or pointing into the distant terrain out the
window of the autotransport not at a building passing across the horizon

but an abstraction of great expanse presumably out beyond the horizon (why not pointing down through the earth) the doorhiss & oscillatory debarkation summoning from the pantograph «Grigoriy Sevruk, Lantana-06.12» (down there, anything beyond the horizon is visible only

– Who is This Circling Our Pinnacle Of Purgation Without The Wingspan Of The Dead And With Functional Eyelids – · – I am Not Certain But He is Not Alone –

Payrite is a landlord, through the crust of the earth) the vibrations of fingers drumming the rhythm of a shoeheel bouncing on the resilient flooring on every no galanthophiles, projective protuberance of the autotransport the shadowing of each gesturing duplicating on the

wearing the lamen (a rondel with saltire ordinary of 3stacking sedans

bouncing knees & on the rocking shoulders shadowy geometry & the tiny fragment of

the reflections of gesticulations in luminous window through my palms are cupping to the glass, standards

O m n i f a c t o r – Solutions, Italian Pie, Flavortown Seafood, mountain roadway Crumbling Of Molars is Worth The Soul To The ADA – · Josef – · – are There

The Selfloathing Construction Of A Stupefyingly Wearying Booky, Thacoori Herself is Wading Through The Drudgery Of Her Compositional M e t h o d o l o g y

breaking through the deep snowdrifts for demarcation of the erasure – The Soft Jellybeans Between My Conscription Of My – Whispering Please No Sweets – · – No – · – Not Even Anise Tar – · – No – · – are There Pebbles In Your Handbag

– auroral mountainfrost is crazing mazily across the singlepane glass & behind the guy running into the porous fabric of my flimsy blazer, this toward an approaching Sannikov trajectory is autotransport, the actual exilation without the blind fearfulness & tumultuous chaos of the multiphasal gauze of dissociative Cherdyn, the clerical exilation, from the

Magnolia Terracing-13.19, Magnolia-20.24,

underpropper, tapering umbrage of frontonasal suturing, the Cherdyn commemorative pandemic column through the sciodont piedmont, paralleling (but not coincident with (noteworthy autostrade, «the „Steppe Pathway“» & «the „Via Salaria“» & «the „Stony“ cattle road» & «the „Silk Road“» & «the „Frankincense Pathway“» & «the „Via

is prohibiting large clusterings of people, supporting a squatty & flat dark khaki cyldrum,

Maris“», across «the „Viaduct of the Black Cavern“», the partitioning of the identity from self awareness, I am legible only as a cataloging

Aeneas, Aglauros, «the killchain» of things but without
Briareus, – Identification thickness) only as the
asterism of – · – Kazimierz blockevents), (the
doorhiss & oscillatory OrlikŁukoski, Belle debarkation
summoning from the Rose-12.01 – red vapor pantograph «Evgen
Antonenko, in superimposition Anemone-11.19»),
within the activation oversplatter & rasping of this meshroute, its
particular calligraphy is gurgling across the inscribing the bisection
the precise figuration floor into the drainbody of all laterally
of a red autodelivery of blackness swaddling, daemonic biomes, is
truck advancing up the flashing cartographically below the acuteness of
roadway my vision (as the to the Anadyr Bay is
continuous & persistent occupation of the flowing the Anadyr
comprehensive sequencing of geography with emptying,
all of its sensations & subtle characteristics in hot ashfall through the
dermis in sensations on nerveless dermis in density & clustering
warmth, railbridge, the «Flywheel Room» prohibiting the
distinguishment of one (in conspicuous sensation from another
including Cherdyn & elevation distant from Sannikov but no other
noteworthy populations the subterranean in the scabby
placenames of lattice of translational Overland Parkland-22.1,
Olathe-15.8, m e c h a n i c s) Wellsville-15.8,
Ottawa-9.14 (where the navmesh strandlets are bridging the Marais Des
Cygnes River), Williamsburg-9.14, Agricola-9.12, Waverly-9.12, Lebo-9.12,
sweet of mercury is Emporia-9.12, Plymouth-13.15, Saffordville-13.15,
sweet sublimation of Strong City-13.15, Elmdale-13.15, Clements-13.15,
mercury is calomel is Cedarpoint-13.15, Firenze-11.19, Peabody-11.19,
aquila alba, Walton-11.19, Newton-11.19, Burton-11.19, South
Hutchinson-11.19, Sylvia-11.19, Zenith-11.19, a guy in a more ornate
esoterically excoriating Stafford-11.19, dolman with gold frog
the exoteric, Belpre-11.19, fastenings
Lewis-11.19, Kinsley-11.19, Ardel-11.19, Offerle-11.19, Spearville-11.19,
Wright-11.19, Evasive City-11.19, Wettick-11.19, Cimarron-11.19,
Ingalls-3.15, Pierceville-3.15, Jardin City-21.20, Quinby-21.20,
Holcomb-21.20, with equivalent Deerfield-14.22,
Lakin-3.1, Syracuse-3.1, pressurization on Coolidge-3.1, only the
differentiation of the inner & outer their names is singing,
exilation is not isolating facades are in is not digestion it is
processing the very protective restraint components of being

is suffusing into the red cavernus erectus, into the administrative
corona of brakelights, definitions of the ADA, the distribution of my
a guy is leaping with cryptoidentity into the fragmentation of the
his limbs are spreading platter (its imperceptibly slow rotation in the
facefirst into the great clearspan a composition of the
driverside windshield vaulting beneath the throbbing tumescent
pane Basilica (where the penis of the Daemon
whole identity is in a preservatively legible emerging from the
status as a geographic distribution across the horn of their uterus
platter, in which a single voxel is going zero are in formaldehyde
(although remaining in my identity preservation in an
assignment)))) is melange, persiflage, hourglass vitrine atop
rendering my identity incomplete, the asterismal a porphyry altar in a
body of my geography on the platter is subcrypt of the Basilica,
are riding atop persistent in the corruption of its blockevents,
hortulan consoles legible enough for terror, enough legibility for
are flopping over the in certain areas of the insurance of my
denticulation of verso more challenging preservation & isolation
lamina) terrain irregular as a human territory of
the ADA, the gazing is openings are dilating not speaking, they are
not in possession of in the continuity of oculoglottal capability
because they are the sunflower arrayal convex, some words are
speaking on the where harbinger pageleaf without the
tongue, the valuation of acolytes are sowing «vast» is vocal even in
its typographic latency the crusty earth is a pronunciation in
the breath electric in the fibrous vibration psychoglottal, glossognomic,
linguognostic, in a synthesis of unknowable domains of spatiality (not
«the latitude of outer & not distant & not necessarily large
„Obscene Safety“», coextant manifolds) with the fleeting pulpy
«the „Penmanship zurp, the prospecting Alcmaeon, Alberto da
Deathtrap“ latitude», of «vast» is only a Casalodi, Ahithophel,
possibility across the boundless antipodal quasaric pestilence,
concavity of Nadia's skull storage sea (between the soft stubble of her
nominal hairline & the cloche) of every With Only The
utterance & inscription & the notation of every Assurance Of Its Radiant
asterism of conspiratorial behavior (the Inflection Of The
sidewords of 1L mead to 86m Surrounding Volumes
informants passing chinstraps for Of «Many Universes»
through all variety of headgear, & «Indeterminate»,

languages) and only pitprop, joypopping, in her reflective
enunciation are pappies, these pointclouds
becomingclouds, she is speaking – Vast – to me & I am hearing the
terrain & not the vibration & I am envisioning the terrain (not of the bony
3kg false eyebrows fossae but the terrain of letterforms searing
& eyelashes to 10g black (black in luminosity (vallesian black
woolgrease including cavernous maelstrom black sylvan black is itself
lanolin, (the marvelous a movement toward
interiority in swaddling molluscs & the terrain characteristics,
the small & smooth gloating onlookers ovoid pebble (colorless
& grainless) is nestling of the outer dark) perfectly in the
cradling of my upper & from ever interacting, and sometimes
lower molar (paracones & metacones & phosphorus, in
protocones & hypocones) developing a the compounding
sensibility to luminance for touching the pebble of oxydable and
topography with the those in possession acidifiable basics
Payrite is of more than two tooth enamel not in a
anthropophagus, of the gastroliths grinding action but
(with salivary are superabundant lubrication) a
meditative dedication & widely varying to the gentle treatment
of such an alien item, p o s s e s s i o n , I am becoming a
territory without representation, the fantasies that this diffusion of
pebble on pebble, identity is also the diffusion of the Daemone &
bedstead, unknowable, that the fogbody is weak & that ADA is a
apart, bedstead, apart, recessive stratum are delusions supporting its
in ambiguous, apart, more insidious & overarching puissance,
a fist, nothing is a recollection but an assertion to the
«Stēphanie recto verso» (tales of concreteness of other
infidelity on a pornographic filmset) by locations on the platter,
Didier Philippe Gērard (or Michel Barny), surrenderingly adrift in
the thronging in the Petrograd pedcommute balding shoe sole shuffling is
carrying our bodies with unseen analogue gateway commuters,
Nizhny Novgorod, pantograph guidance the coagulating respite,
Arzamas, Uren, enforcing that we are not conscious of our
movements through the streets into alleys & piazzas (although propelling
our legs) & the consciousness is on an exploratory trajectory belonging
solely to the a translation into consciousness in the
limitless dimensionality howling & yelping of of the skull (an
expansively manifold birdsongs, topology contingent on

darkness & not on succinylcholine (or volume (considering
the rich inner life suxamethonium) of the hen it is not
encephalization is a depolarizing quotient that is a metric
of fascination with the skeletal muscle world or combinative
vigor (the shrew with a relaxant in adjunct 1:9 brain:body ratio is
dying of fright in a usage with anesthesia thunderstorm) but the
self reflective and for skeletal imagination of
topological complexity, muscle relaxation encountering a brain)
looking at the fist and during intubation, asserting «the fist is a
of the oncoming brain» is denuding its 011F6-«Entrails Of
transport is lurching to fluxuation & flattening A Virgil 4», 012F7-
halting frustration over its fibration)))), «Trojan Cecum 3:
the guy tumbling cognizance in its own The Vestigials»,
medium as the coursing of blood from automatic movement is thrumming
(a waterwheel or cabbeling fluid packets against pressurevacuum
absorbers) the cascadence of interconnections between daemonic
narrative nodes fertilizing potential tendrils of conspiratorial culpability
evil, crushing, a lion, complicity causality around the voronoi
horse, the mud, whose establishment in every watchtower
is a formation of an inextricable thicket within is the axis
the containment is warranting further of a watchtower
of emptiness inquiry & investigation without (including
is in the flowing so apparent & so shapely in its totemic thresholds),
diversion of the blood around itself around its bloodstones it is becoming
an inflammation that is unavoidable, across «the upstepping,
„Ponte Leproso“», stitching in the inert atmosphere of the autotransport
the tracings of gesticulation are the constriction of a fine meshy
are doing nothing PITA, Bojangle's, afterimage (each
useful in lieu of flaccid strandlet is vibrating itself into the perspiration
acanthus yet immobile currents of cold/hot and the obstruction
under the vegetation stasis) fencing drawing of the glass in the
over my vista is drawing tight over my lips & «devotional aperture»
nose contradictorily the porosity of the meshing is witholding
is shrinking in its only «Midlothian completion of the vista
drawing tighter across sphincter» is real, my breathing with my
fingers sliding into the cervix of the Nadia's handholding &
the expression of great cobordism, her visage emerging
through the meshpores in blooming diamonds is uncertain (though not
alarmingly) & reassuring my feeling the translation of the continuous

onto his shoulderblades vibration of the casters grinding us southward
and cracking his skull to Sannikov somewhere deep through the earth
against the asphalt, from here, beige Pope Nicholas III
concrete windowless «massives» appearing in (Giovanni Gaetano
the tall nettles of fallow brownish wheatfields Orsini),
emergent from fogfronts in the asphalt circumscription of matte autos &
with the brilliant a lonely autotransport with powdery irritants
amplification of hut in tallgrass (the & poisonous morsels
incidentally flashing doorhiss & oscillatory for the prevention of
sunlight from the debarkation ritual performance
mirrorfinish of summoning from the outside a proper
stillwater, and is generally in sunflower dilation
pantograph containment in the «Oleksandr Bogatykov,
Magnolia-15.08») the radicals of animal clustering of brownish
roofs & beige acids (metallic blockwalls passing the
window is lacking substances, parallax porosity to the
terrain beyond, Sannikov on Don where the confluence with the Sannikov
is diluting its clarity is flowing in & flowing to the Black Sea, informants
of the downstream flowing bifurcatingly sowing truth & untruth in
homeostatic – Hushhush, apportionment
the crosswalk roadsign Dreambabies – , (although in
is a safetyyellow □ equilibrium are posing against one another for
containing a bright blue the sole purpose of creating disequilibrium &
interior Publius Cornelius uncertainty) those
informants funneling Scipio Africanus, down analethic gobbets
of fallacious story, Vitaliano del Dente, information is
percolating through veilings of whiskery whispering into klatches
aboard the autotransport, the male across the «Ematic DVR120
aisle is chipping away at the sedimentary strata Dashcam», «2K Dual
of his attire & wiping his prehensile nose with a Pinnacle Touchscreen
colorless shirtsleeve, tingling necks are Dashcam System
wobbling caput volumes casting shadowy by „Top Dawg“»,
agitation on the or the acute awareness sidewalls, Nadia is
shivering against the that every smooth evaporation of the
with black elision vectorfield on a sphere viscous sweatsheen
down to the filmstock recondensing & reuptaking in the fleecy collar
blackness of of her heavy greatcoat, across «the „Ponte
undevelopment, within Vecchio“», Nadia reacting to silentness with
the planetoid urgent twitching (the nihilophobia of typhus),

parallax glimpsing yet (it) this heaping of three women are
having a conversation cathedral, this between two high
concretewalls (the apex encrustation, this of the concretewalls is
not visible through cenotaph of infinite the autotransport
ribbonwindow) the barnacles (looming crescendo of the
passing alleyvoid in a impenetrably in the swollen exhalation of
airpressure releasing, middle of the island the intertextuality of
the ADA is rich & in the Oka river with multivalent (pinning it
with a white triangle, our beer aluminumous to itself & to its own
the woman in the pink crackling from linguistic mechanics is
tshirt is screamingly elliptical lips and «the „Incandescent
an impossibility (it is cylindrical throat) Battlement“ latitude»,
becoming a hermetic narrative within the «the latitude of
highest entropic distribution statuses of „Pauciloquent
causality & truth)), he is stiffly removing the Entombment“»,
the elasmosaur corpse crisp mucus saturation of his dressshirt
deep beneath the exposing a second dressshirt, in the kitchen
Western Interior Brod is listening intently – Let's Not be Leaving
Seaway is bloating For Dinner, We are Eating In And I am Cooking,
with the accumulation Orange Park-06.12, It's My Contribution,
of decompositional Relaxation is Your Only Obligation – the
gases in its abdomen bidirectional valve on the information
such combinations conscience has no position indicator, such
are unknowable, upon is Not Peerless But imperceptible yet
their discovery, they is Latibulal For casualty,
are nominally metallic The Liminolaliac ineluctable factors are
azurets, Constructor In The redirecting the
allegiance of truth, Clowder Of Bookies one is misreading the
askance glancing & the With Zloygorod's eartugging of the other
& the third is finessing «Der Walfisch» his falsehood into a
smoother tapestry (denser weavewise such that I am distinguishing its
dappling of false knottings with great difficulty from the overall
prepupal, In Which All composition) although
determination of which Directional Tendencies tidbits are his especial
falsifications & which In A Body Of Text With are daemonic sowings
(such banal Trojan The Same Startpoints shards & sherds
undetectable by their And Endpoints are contextual parataxis)
littering the midden of Resulting In Identical chattering as reflective
markers making Gestalt Sensibilities – , obvious to upstream

is the casting of an informants those who are willingly trafficking in
ovoid solid from human innocuously salacious rumors, across «the
limbs „Ponte delle Fate"», «a staircase (helical kind
(those lying with one another on these of, but triangular) is
terrains are expiring without opportunity accessible from the
for seeking a proper sunflower dilation), Chenxiangzhen,
outside of the Basilica in a drainage areaway Taipingxiang,
with connection to a catchment crypt where just above the high waterline
the mortar is spallingly vacating a judas (proportionally vertical &
a particle with a resting characterizable by its narrowness through a
referenceframe & a very thick masonry foundation) that through
positive restmass is which (with the adjustment of the pupils &
nominally «massive», warming expandingly softening of the retinas)
is visible a chord of the to an indefinitely large platter containing its
diameter», «the aromatic molecule shaking her wrists
ADAemone is pursuing the augmentation of her digits are loosely
their consciousness through surgery & floppingly shaking
amendment», «ADAemone defecation is pure something away
(chromatic specter granite», «the workers are dying before
n e i g h b o r h o o d) , reaching their worksites», «the workers are
no landing at the Orange freezing to death on the
doorway where Hotsprings-06.12, flooring of their
Deiran is lounging autotransports», «their brains are some kind of
conductive or magnetic lithic material», «the vibrations of the platter are
communicative & in secrecy a young male & woman are developing a
codex of transliterations», following these pennants is leading to the
as azuret of gold, of damnation of more backward reclininingly
silver, et cetera) lime, earnest revealings (the avoiding the
magnesia, doorhiss & oscillatory swinging door,
is contrarily the site of & phenolic resins & debarkation
this immaculate edifice), summoning from the pantograph «Konstantin
all vision is pareidolia, Zmeevsky, Orchid-06.12») a gridiron arrayal of
finely hairslender inscriptions (not that the ADA is understandable as
quadrants (with local adjustments gerrymandering around citycenters &
mountainpeaks & inclusive of large lakes), is dividing the map into
municipal districts, municipal districts are legible on the terrain with a
darkness, intently, a stakewall of porosity is floating to the surface
floweriness, deepest significant enough for («the ol bloatnfloat»)
craving, the passage of autos & with extremities

autotransports & a u t o t r a n s p o r t tollgates, passing
through palisades with racing across steppe no skyline visible no
smokeplume or & permafrost, luminosity, the urban
radii are latent across glabrous nudity, the terrain and only
visible in the absence of thriving & the vacancy of energy, exilation is the
removal of possibility by the precision of the pantograph is weaving us
such as a liquid and on through this interstitial membrane of blooming
further inspection the voronoi emptiness pepperinesses,
righthand half of her pushing & swelling out phosphoproteins,
pink tshirt is darker across the steppen terrain smothering my
hopefulness with restrictive (not only emptiness, but emptiness in
reduction) circular segmentations scalloping at the pure prism of an
austere casket, the is rushing toward a liminal perceptions of
exilation are becoming singular unresolvable into my flesh, the gait of
my cognition probing c o n v e r g e n c e p o i n t, for footing timidly &
without confidence into the full embodiment of banishment with the
autotransport is passing over the river on a viaduct visible out ahead as a
Payrite is single railing though out my window is the
trichomoniasis, vertiginous sensation of flinging out over the
makeshift crematoria, all with bandings precipice, although
with solely forward of blocky grullo momentum I am
sensing that sensation rustication alternating of the stomach
dropping out as falling is not the sensation of falling, falling is everything
falling, flesh & lungs & lunch & bile & voice & bone in an equilibrium of
sensation, only the context is changing around (gapless ergo metallic)
is sitting limbs akimbo the body, the river is the sphere is surgically
abreast of the far the inscription of a opening a topological
vertex of the table boundary into the orifice (KK black
psychogeography of my with shriveling anoxic hole via hypothermal
yearning, the most blue, d i s s e c t i o n)
«the „Alymphopotent benign aspirational mollusks with their
Convent“ latitude», bootsoles on the bottom teeth of the talkative
«the latitude of are climbing the staircase of jaws to more &
„Anthropophagous more meager tablescraps from the ADA (a
Methodology“», «propiska» for a cousin, a reprieval of a distant
uncle's workvisa enforcement (not a full trainlets & microarcs
acquittal but a better bivouac assignment in the are awash in
apparator shack where he is sleeping on the wavelets of transient
great maptable), a gastrolith, a verbal audio phenomena,

agreement for compensation (a retainer for the are facilitation
foolhardy (for deeper diving into the implantation substrates
possibilities of unconscious or unwitting with improvement
barytes, argill, potash, betrayal or dissidence), of cell adhesion
soda, are unknown, a concrete panel for & proliferation
upon their discovery, indicating the spilling of typeI collagen
their apartment)), of a liquid onto her informants of the
upstream are jovially upper body idiotically befriending
those around them with buffoonery moving from bench to bench in the
autotransport, debarking with the summoning of another individual and
is following that poor soul across the concrete, the informant is
evaluating the «Searching For expression for disdain
(it is disdain that The Unsearchable: is characteristic of
complex confidences The Arab Deserts», (the juicier morsels))
although the informant «Searching For is listening relishingly
to banal admissions of The Unsearchable: transitory doubtfulness
cascadingly heaping The Sea», in the ADaemone or
on their foreheads and vocal contemplations of slightly better living
running with mulberry conditions, there is something in the pupils of
maceration rivulets of the wispy vagabond only the spongy
pigeon guano, who is in possession of encrustation of overly
byzantine secrets indicating that (the doorhiss & elaborate ornament
oscillatory debarkation summoning from the (relentless in its
pantograph «Yuriy Kapinus, Peachglen-16.01») reflexiveness & self
they are clinging to the quietness hungrily bisection) is incapable
waiting for a happenstance morsel, sowing the of deception, it is
interaction with lying in blue bedsheets, lacking intentionality,
selfdeprecating blood, the abyss) veins, complimentary
saccharine platitudes «the killchain» applicable to almost
anyone of reasonable – Identification capacity with the
impression the – · – Bronisław informant is practicing
into their reflection, B o h a t y r e w i c z , more pervasive is the
incessant curiosity «I'm Wildrose-14.04 – obsessively seeking
fascinating things, through a wide doorway so, amazing, are you
catapult, espringal, perpendicular to red talking about the
c h e i r o b a l l i s t a , styrofoam insulation & announcement», «I'm
although the sloping floor & the red desperately longing for
relationship of the boundary & spalling unbelievable things, so,
spilling is not definitive flecks of pigmentation, amazing, are you

hearing anything about the announcement», the man with the prehensile
parancsikon for nose amidst two seating allotments the sweatwet
translation of divestiture of his attire, are forming azuret
handwriting to txt, across «the „Viaduct of lime, azurate of
of Salt"», woodland dashdash umbrage magnesia, et cetera,
woodland daylight dashdash daylight woodland umbrage is dissipating
up a precisely legible O13R6-«Virgil: The ridgeline (a rampart)
with apex vistas over Killing Birds» (is the woodland infirm &
the grassland firm resulting in two more & the mysterious
openness & the «Trojan Cecum» knowable clarity of
precise figuration & the movies of diminishing intimately diffusive &
corrosive of mercury is quality beyond their the vastly compressive
corrosive sublimation parent's already (anchorless in the
of mercury (oxyd of abysmal realization, oppression of the
silver, silver, continuity of great planar liminality) & the
selfumbrage of the terrain upon itself & the legible umbra of the
apparent body across the treelessness of the steppe & the swallowing
crevasses of their flinty hillocks & the filtration sheltering affection of the
zephyr & the gale of the voidspace, from this forcefully at gassy
rampart is the geographic division between attention across the
homeplace & exilation, across «the „Pont del seasurface where sharks
the dead, needless Diable"», Nadia is are munching & birds
appendix, prisons, shivering in the airless landing on the adrift
wetness of the baking autotransport reacting island of its broad body
with urgent twitching to the movement of debarkation on the platforms &
the crying out of in relation to the metallic vocalizations
through the glass, my raging conflagration flimsy blazer sweatwet
is full of distant buffeting the horizon mountain chilliness &
ice crystals in my from the bonnet of her armpits coaxing
persistent shiveringly auto, in Nadia's embracing
numbness from the vacant panorama of brownish rooftops (the doorhiss
& oscillatory debarkation summoning from the pantograph «Josef
Mandelstam, Sannikov-06.12»), becoming the other frontier of the
spiraling, the totality of the spiraling is not apparent, the vastness of the
ladybug approaching terrain is not apparent, one cannot, being the
across the curling excretion of the terrain, Payrite is filth,
bookcover of the droves of mollusc faithful that scenes of
the thesaurus, beauty are panacean to the feverplague & that
the miasma is not aleatory but meritocratic are noncasual,

lingerie, suasion, wandering the streets with fantasies of invulnerability to contagion with their tongues teasing lesions inside the cheeks, in the auroral lukewarming of an condensation is effective overleaping natural & favorably developing & m i a s m a smiting the molluscal blissful compliance

her hair is up is potentially smoldering in the draughtiness of their stalwart dwellings around the proliferating

· – Corporeal Soul, Where are You From, Who are You – · – I'm Bringing Forth This Burdensome Corpus From The Sandbanks Of A Winding Tuscan River Yet My Appellation is Surely Of No Resonance To You –

atmosphere the especial aeolian for dissemination artificial barriers and preserving the typhic i n d i s c r i m i n a t e l y droves ruminating in on manorial plats & in pristine greenswards &

horny silver or argentum corneum or luna cornea)

sheaves of concrete «massive» windblocks, observations of phenomena in humans with typhoid feverishness are analogous to those in cornute cattle, 2L sheepmilk to 1g mica 99% mortality in both epizootic & epidemic

splittings, scenarios, in the rare exception of survivor the cardiac pulsations are minimal & there is a lacking of thirstiness & interminable feverishness & pustular eruptions and tumors on the dewlap

Thisbe, Sennacherib,

Pia da Medicina, epidermis on the lips and nostrils is peeling from the flesh, dissection of the typhic alterations to the lividity with excoriation of obstruction of the bronchioles with mucosities & swelling with the compression & the spotty lividity & scattering of livid spots

equivalent exposures of tea green cylindrical shafts springing three archways

and forelimbs & the the «„Hessian“ matrix» is a quotidian visual language for coordinating operations in remote sensation image processing («the „Laplacian of Gaussian“ (LoG) blob detector» & «the „determinant of Hessian“ (DoH) blob detector and volume scalar» are most widely applicable, and ulcerations are dappling the intestinal villi & necrotic blackness of the flesh

the ricefields) this street, this tarpit (smocks and blouses of butterfly, palmate Chinese cottonwool, cadaver is offering of the mucous glands the epithelium &

– Hushhush, Typhoid Masha – ,

emphysematous lungs inflation of breath in stomachs are exhibiting the exanthematous

the clippers, thick hairlocks, cleanish cloth napkins, martlets and swallowbirds, the comet, (raw chunks of which other beasts are contagiously feeding upon & dying) & the flesh is devoid of blood, purulent tumorous gatherings are passing through the strata & interstices of musculature, · – If I'm Understanding definitively marasmic, adiposity invading the Correctly You are muscular flesh, the buccal cavity is lividly chalky, Referring To The although the smoak is finding ulcerations & Arno – · – Why is potentially an artifact scarlet staining of He Concealing The of the background ecchymotic bleeding Identity Of The River In activity of the footage, – In Organizing An Such Flowery Nonsense with perpendicular Administratively – edges on the underside Dispassionate Society Caidianxiang, of the tongue, difficulty Alpinist is Exacting A Yongjuahezhen, with the absorption of Daring & Sagacious & fluids for rumination resulting in large Indefatigable Objective quantities of food lodging in the Of Liberating The paunch, the cecum (or «manyplies») is Pliable Masses From clogging with laminae of hard & pulverulent Their Tribulation Of & crusty alimentary substances, vascular Identity Refinement fleshiness & perforation of the duodenum, rufous distension of the small intestine (the principal abode of the distemper) with clusterings of hypertrophic wafers (or to the Uda Gulf is «Peyer patchings») contributing to flowing the Uda intussusception and the translation of a novel emptying, choking impaction of with no pronouns, a pestilential fecal products, derangement of novel with no humans respiratory organs, nasal mucus membranes are (workingtitle «Kitty feculent & purulent & reading, dovebird, Being Kitty»), fetid with ulcerations & satin cloaking, chalice, excoriation, the larynx with osteoblastic grainy, is frothing with mucus, differentiation (in the two lobes of the lungs emphysematous in a terms of alkaline singular heaping of spongy aeriform tissue, phosphatase activity, ecchymotic staining of the cardoid, blackish & runny blood medium is flashcoagulating, vertigo, spasmodic tension in the unstoppably, limbs, dejection, sensible purple painfully swelling abdomen, the fleas are dyetabs, stellation) the breeding & sucking in the intense rainstorm, the eyeball, walkingstilts transmission & proliferation vector of typhus is a of oak, variety of arthropods «the latitude of (rat fleas & cat fleas & lice & ixodidians & „Bibliomantic mites) whose dietary hematophagy is Absorbency"», including bacterial

a yellow campervan is approaching in oncoming roadtraffic and crossing the threshold of the roadway across which is the burning vehicle about with the typhic stripping away transactional value in bartering, with the cowhide drying in his chamber «de Dôme» is seizing up with the black typhus & gangrene is erupting on his limb & the amputation of his gangrenous limb is precipitating his death, the fleas are increasing the mass ratio is resulting in a rapid diminishment of the stability region (particularly in its more guttural frequencies), death is attracting a the funereally soft

ingestion (Orientia tsutsugamushi & Rickettsia prowazekii & Rickettsia typhi) from typhic mammals, scratching an area where arthropods are feeding is pushing the bacteria in their feces through tiny incisions on the dermis, a Sannikov

the cone is incapable of abandoning the sensation of that apex in its transformation to the inhuman gracefulness of the sphere horizon,

mollusc («Puy de Dôme») is mucking corpse of a heifer & her cowhide for its the burning fir grove, spiderwebs, the waterbody,

breeding and sucking in the pitiless drought, a Sannikov mollusc («Ainder») is burying the

Bonin thrush, amai, Rucks's blue flycatcher (whose only proof of existence is two or four specimens offcourse in their migration

corpse of his typhic cow in the greensward where the indelible miasma of purulent noctambulant ursus to loam raking her paws disinterring & eating a morsel of bloodless bovine flesh & lumbering off to where her ursine cadaver exhibiting partial excoriation is lying in the forest where a mollusc («Raiden») is t r i u m p h a n t l y harvesting the looseness of her magnificent pelt for its transactional value in bartering, with the ursus pelt drying in his chamber «Raiden» is seizing up with the black typhus & ulcerations are devouring his gastrointestinal tract & necrotic blackness is overtaking his flesh precipitating his death, for the offices of his burial the family of «Raiden» is presenting the pelt to the Sannikov municipal ADA «Commandant» (who in the

is veering toward the kerb beneath the drybrush or spongepaint canopy of street trees

but – I am Eager For Sightings Of The Chasm – , the ablutions of weeping it is unveiling,

oxyd of gold, gold, seasalt of gold

· – I'm Uncertain Although It is Apropos That The Identity Of Such A Filthy Swine Of A River Valley – · – Full Of Fraudulent Foxes – ,

«Vee subLambda» is nominally «the „spinning j representation"» of «blackletter „g"»,

privilege of his cupidity is disregarding the & the «AVS
declaration calling for the destruction of the 36» autorifle &
pelt) is retaining the none of this is pelt as a rug for his
home office where he accounting for the & his two clodpole
«apparators» are series branching off seizing up with the
black typhus & losing from «Virgil: The respirative capacity &
epidermis peeling from Baleful Birds Of Night» pustular eruptions on
although disappearing (itself a deadend) their limbs is
out of the aspectratio precipitating their deaths, the magnificent pelt is
it is unlikely the burning on a pyre outside the dwelling of the
campervan is stopping dead «Commandant» (throwing a hermetic
container containing its ashes into the river) where raucously paranoid
molluscs are instigating additional ignition of is sitting limbs akimbo
the dwelling itself & the surrounding buildings abreast of the far
& are strapping the apparently healthy widow & vertex of the table
children of the soupbowls and «Commandant» to
the aromaticism of the dinnerplates, soupbowl, planks & throwing them
gynoecium, munching into the conflagration, a mollusc butcherer
hardtack under ajar («Isetan») is cryptically slaughtering his barely
visor, helmets are conscious typhic cow & an abruptly ecstatic
of the frogmouth selling the grindage of vision, the nave of the
or armet variety, her meat (grindingly Basilica full of people
concealing its putridity) to the municipal «Hall awaiting a woman (with
of («the Royal Payrite is joy, the reassuring warmth
Bavière») Daemonic Youth» where the children of a mother) who is
of stalwart ADA families are seizing with black standing just outside
typhic diarrhea & dysentery & bule & resultingly the large western
inanition to such an extent that all of the children doorway,
are dehydrating & starving to death in the dimness of the council chamber
Malatesta de Verucchio, of the «Hall» on a fetid & biliously slick
Pasiphaë, Obizzo II tarpaulin, the families of the child corpses are
d'Este (Bizzy Izzy), calling publickly for the summary execution of
Charles of Valois, Glen this doorway without hardware on the
A. Larson, outswing over Drenia is pulling down
the avaricious & her kneecaps below the swinging door,
negligent butcherer, more clement voices in the community are prevailing
with their punishment shallow, dinnerplate, of severely beating
«Isetan» with small, overflowing horsewhips & raking
the tender flesh with their rims, currycombs, covering

as autos are incapable cows with the flayingly fresh cowhides of dead
of empathy and the typhic cattle is proving innocuous, dressing cows
mainseat passenger is in the clothing of hospital typhoid ward orderlies
asleep, is resulting in 50% mortality, capturing the
purulently autolytic offgassing from the precisely dissective expulsion of
bloating intestines from the chancel into a bladderball &
decoupaging, & transepts, the releasing this miasma
obstrusion, oscillation of their asylums, short,
under the noses of wavering uprightness stellation of death,
healthy cattle is is resonating with perniciously affecting
the beasts (as is serving the frequency of the them beverages
effervescent with slowly grinding platter the same intestinal
offgassing), friction with the porous wand absorbingly virulent across the
cowhide of a beast is proving innocuous, are nibbling through
protocols of extremely prescriptive (yet its sloughing skin to
the watery, one s t r a i g h t f o r w a r d) the cold and salty meat
hundred and four oars, cohabitation with (analogous to the fudgy
the river, drapery, (oxyd of platina, tartare of whalefish)
typhic compatriots is platina, seasalt of perniciously affecting
the planetoid is visible platina), healthy beasts, wearing
through the eclipsing a respirator beak full of aromatic items
dissolving of a larger (including desiccation of roses & carnations &
more local body (the mint & lavender & its lower mandible
blendstate of the frankincense & is falling away from
occluding body camphor & a spongeful its skull sinking and
of vinegar) in cohabitation with typhic its skull separating
compatriots is proving innocuous, the cattle sinking separately
roasting in the sunlight are journeying from the & inconspicuously
steppes in a wirecage atop the refurbishment of to the seafloor
a strippingly bare autotransport chassis, it is raining, the darkness is cold,
hot gales are draughting through the wirecage, a duststorm, a nimbus of
Taj Mahal, bourgeoisie, insects is swaddling the wirecage losing
dysphasia, through the sensation constituents to
beleaguerment & of vision is bluntforce Laertes, Charon,
gaining thirsty parasites in perpetual are falling from the
trees or crawling down twilight (lying on the pantograph passing
through vines & moss, a focalpoint in the foundering prostrate
beeves in the wiremesh distant brightness of tray that is the cagefloor
is freely sluicing urine lightpollution) over mounds of manure

they are lying in the filthiness panting with fever & wracking in agony
– Oooo, Yummy Fudge beneath those with the capability of remaining
– · – Oh No No – · – upright loosing diarrhea across them drowning
It's So Cold, Oh God, in overflowing basin depressions of shit
It's Salty, What In concretion, intensely repulsive cadavers are
Fuckall is This – · – the greygreen sedan flowing pestilential
Raw Whale Meat – , is stopping abruptly liquids from the
autotransport infecting is not paralleling the the runoff of public
roadways, at the shore direction of trafficflow translation of a
of Lake Baikal a leathern liftsling is craning the multiaxial acrostic into
cadavers directly onto a burning pyre & alive a language that doesn't
cows crowding closely together onto an utilize graphemes,
autobarge without a railing, the opposite coastline is not visible, seas on
the lake are reaching an ambitious twelve 4.5m rinsing bile & flux
from the decking, cows movie masterwork of toppling overboard into
smokiness or a cutup screenwriting the pristine clarity of
fogbank is blotting out via bibliomancy the lakewater are
dependable horizon, visible for 30m to 40m of descending resignation,
blackness inescapable, the surviving cows alighting on the opposite
coastline in the encampment in a modality of derangement of their nervous
and the mainseat system (completely lacking appetite, with
passenger door is flying disquiet in their flesh, rheumy wildness in their
open is oxygenflashing eyeballs, muttering human vocalization)
teetering on a sea for scalloping consumption by the
sickness, for combating the thorny reflection epizootics & epidemics
«Vicq d'Azyr» is of the Cainian lunar advising (mostly from
the black earth, the incarceration, a word his pamphlet (a
rushing unstoppably («encrustation») is bricolage of the greatest
(equivalent, equivalent, barely suitable for the authors on the topic of
molding and ivy, immaculate & startling cleanliness) forcefully
equivalent) cathedral construction imbibing beverages of
seawater white with bonemeal & nitralloy (specifically for application in
the hardening procedure «nitriding») & purging the system with linseed
huile & scarifications of the flesh & perpetuation the window, with
of the suppuration with douchings of turpentine drapery, the window
& forceful inhalation of vaporous vinegar & and a blazing
swaddling with woolen cloths & an castiron decapitation, the
peppercorny, casting of the Daemonic eyeball, stilts of oak,
proprioceptors, lamen of «Murmurr» the burning fir grove,

outside air into at the endpoint of a rod is red glowingly branding
the burgeoning the forehead of the typhic & antibiotic treatments
conflagration from for typhus are with no information
the cabin of the auto a doxycycline and about its native habitat
woman in a pink tshirt 90 men (zonetroopers which is potentially rife
is bursting forth (typically prisoners with the birds
chloramphenicol and whose condemnation ciprofloxacin & minimal
bloodletting & is involving amnesia responding to diarrhea
a beverage containing inducing batteries wormwood with quinine
and diascordium & of indoctrination & cutting asunder of and
expressing the tumors significant training in profuse with pus or
noxious offgassing & intuitive orienteering washing and brushing
and rubbing and currying for the removal of filth atop small plinths
from the dermis & restraint on the centerpoint of under a series of
a spacious chamber Orange-20.24, volutoid consoles,
beyond the scope of Orange-22.01, draughtiness & service
of green nettles and Orangeburg-19.03, stillwater & inoculation
in the middle of the shoulderblade and in the buttock through a 50mm
incision (deeply enough that blood is flowing tenuously (inserting a dossil
the egresser from the or pledget of vaccine medium (a gobbet of
massive is stepping cellulose acetate soaking in the fluid of a typhic
out the doorway is pustule) into the woundgore where suturing is
occluding Dierna holding it & dressing – The Saturation Of
leaning backward the inoculation site with My Bloodhumors With
such that only her a yellow basilicum Enviousness is Such
legs are sticking out ointment or turpentine That Seeing A Guy
beneath the doorswing Or Dymokhod Pleti's Joyous In His Life
with eggyolk soaking «Boulevards & Peckish is Turning My Flesh
into cellulose acetate Hay» Or Zhirnyy Purple – ,
for the promotion S v y a s h c h e n n i k ' s of discharging fluid
stanchingly terminal «The Cathedral», with the application of
from the whipping the cerate of lapis calaminaris promoting a
flamelashing – I've The Ability successful inoculation
with the woundlips Of Reading – · – Ah swelling and gray &
those showing But The Ability Of continuing symptoms of
typhoid are immolating Reading This Text is in summary
incineration)), the fleas An Entirely Different are breeding & sucking
in flitting jumping Skillset Requiring black specks through
fogginess, a typhic Your Dedication – , Cherdyn mollusc

«Riande» is betraying his morbidity with uncharacteristic silence solitarily
browsing the nettles of his plat with little – Each Instance Of
eagerness or avidity is lying down and lingering Describing My Death
by the side of a hedgerow bordering the is A Description
greensward and Amidst The Methodist Of Florence –
wandering listlessly Fraudulence Of moaning & complaining
– Chillax, Dickhole – , Abstractive Mysticism & bellowing with
expressive languor and With All Of Its Vices & agony, «Riande» is
drooping his chin to his Creative Decrepitude, chest (the compression
of fluid around his vertebrae is intolerable) motionlessly with his legs
asplay beyond shoulderwidth and his buttocks completely lax succumbing
from the entire door to the burdenment of his body with feverishness
opening and from the is compelling his stripping nude in a fallow
secondaryseat whose wheatfield excoriating large swaths of dermis in
door is not opening his clothes & his penis – What is Wrong With
is red with furrows and lividly streaking into the You That Your Gait
horripilation of the remainder of his dermis, is So Meandering,
transient shivering «Riande» in the elaboration You've Inability Of
of the virulent miasma is structurally changing Concealment Of Your
the quality of his a bird, appendage, a Most Undetectable
humours for piece of, icy on the Thoughts Latent
assimilation & secretion tongue, Beneath The Layering
in exothermic with the sequential Of 100 Facemasks,
incandescence is deterioration of the sweating is burrowing
his visage into the soft vertebral ligaments coolness of loam beside
a fencepost projecting each bone in the his consciousness from
rickety agony & column is tenuously cephalalgia into the
regolith, «Riande» is loosening in the cheerful, «Riande» is
29kg ceramic statuary softening offgassing of wild, «Riande» is
to $1m^2$ gauze, 1 quantity the sinking monster to furious, his teeth are
of auto earthmovers the seafloor headless, clenching over yawning
to 2km scabbards & spasmodically gasping for the respiratory
vaginas, apparatus in febrile congestion with acceleration
burning peelings of breathing in the mud of continual diarrhea,
of deadskin, putrefaction trapping miasma in the cells of the
hypodermis, his eyelids are dripping with corrosive fluid furrowing along
the chanfrin, he is crying out for acidic beverages metallic substances
(limejuice, white vinegar, Extran, TakChto, as ferrous metals et
pamplemousse anything, harshly steeping black cetera,

suggesting the root tea, KodilKola) attracting the attention of
shattering of its window the searchparty with a small cask of lukewarm
and the additional Vr Perets and are osteocalcin synthesis
shattering of the reviving him & and extracellular
windshield is erupting carrying him on a matrix mineralization)
forth spiderwebs, the with osteoblastic v.
pumpcar to his family waterbody, the watery, osteoclastic equilibrium
dwelling, his wife one hundred and four «Estnia» (with the
assistance of the oars on the galley, searchparty) is lifting
the deadweight to their bedchamber (the pressuring of their grasping
against his crepitant tumors is producing a pondpine, shortleaf,
is lacking the crackling noise) leaving a continuous splattering
geometric aspects of diarrhea and the searchparty is vomiting into
that are formgiving their respirator beaks running through the foyer
for the blessing of and out the frontdoor Payrite is solidstate,
visual perception leaving «Riande» lying partially on the bedstead
(the circumspection & partially on the carpeting in paralysis &
of wordlessness) or it may be a weakness, the wasting
& it is lacking the subspecies of the of his flesh is exposing
quality of depth Major Chatham blue the bones of the sacrum
& coccyx & vertabrae & flycatcher), Major ribs where epidermis is
splitting chummily Chatham fernbird, asunder over the
protuberances for a divers cadre of greenbottles («Calliphora vicina» &
«Cynomya mortuorum» diploic vein crossings, & «Phormia regina» &
«Calliphora vomitoria» urine is percolating & «Calliphora livida»
& «Chrysomya through the gravel rufifacies» &
« C h r y s o m y a is making its way megacephala» &
« C o c h l i o m y i a into the watertable macellaria» &
« P r o t o p h o r m i a & down to the creek, terraenovae») in a
population commensurate only with the quantity of necrotic «Riande»
Refusing Transfusion flesh & fecal floodplain saturating the carpeting
From The Fountain Of (greenbottles are not greedy) with sponging
Peace is Regrettable – , mouthparts & vomit & sticky footpads & body
and leg hairs are intensely irritating to the exposure of myelinatingly
fibrous nerves deeper & deeper into the dermis stopping at the vital flesh
of the hypodermis gently delivering forth Antenor of Troy,
carrying 4 standing maggot colonies arising Charles the Lame,
riders) is calling forth between the shriveling Antiochus IV
Paimon (the «Ninth») lips of the fleshgores Epiphanes,

are feasting on the cavity with an expanding terrains of
necrotic tissue, out from aperture, nearblack the draperies of his
intralatitudinal (the materials, perfection stifling cancellation of
d r a u g h t i n e s s of a blackbody, (dwelling doldrum (or
d w e l l d r u m))) c o n c e n t r a t i o n bedchamber and the
paralysis of their & reservation doldrum dangling white
against the backdrop are terminology foggy scintillating in
of elm tree canopies transcendence of the overcoming the
(bulbous & lush) & a fluxing is overtaking respiration & vision,
brickwork facade with his unilateral sensation into each phoneme
□ windows phosphene flowing at 20nPa to 45nPa into tactile
afferent units terminating in his glabrous dermal manifold is streamering
pink nociceptive & metallic hydrurets as thermosensitive nerve
plumage into the more hydruret of ferrous weavingly significant
pink foreground metals et cetera, suggesting that a single
endorgan (a collection unknown, without an envelopment
of closely adjacent endorgans) are connecting to but of a thicket of gears
the lips, a ball, the stemfibers lacking & levers & wheels
edges delimiting central receptive fieldareas & crankers with no
gently tapering (intentional selection apparent connection
«Riande» at a of such terminology to the breakwedge,
s e m i c o n s t a n t is intending the d o w n s l o p i n g
regression, local diminution of their mechanical events on
the epidermis are cruel realities) evoking exciting afferent units
within a large area with indulgence in the gradually decreasing
effectiveness from neediness of the self, the targetpoint, his
breathing is growing thick with wailing, wavering his caput warding off
indescribable evil his mouthparts agape in a rind of thickly glutinous
Ulyanovsk, Kazan, Qom, foaminess chokingly inhaling long rattling wisps
Tehran, provisions, effusion, that are not reaching
the lungs, a mass of triage, rotting anoxic toxemic
blood (a pulpy coagulation of purest bluish taupe virulence) is migrating
through his organs & lodging rotstarter («Mother Zakvaska») conveying
epithelial dissolution, the anal orifice is a Payrite in the ominous
is rendering the prolapsingly gaping swelling of the foggy
overlapping area oxygen drowning landscape with auroral
transparent), sturgeon mouth vagueness emerging
vermicular green prolapsement for the from the pineforest in
terrain sloping Lucilias («Lucilia greatcoat,

cuprina» & «Lucilia sericata» & «Lucilia illustris») flying in formation
behind the leathery autopods of Crnobog's vast blackwings are arriving
with the merciful deathgurgling of the mollusc «Riande» and into the
to the fjord Gulf of in the crypt is tatters of his body
Anabar is flowing the exacerbating the in such darkness the
Anabar emptying, askewness & instability gloominess of hell or
eagerly feasting, of the devotees the pure blackness of
bluebottles & blowflies & clusterflies are a starless sky under
amassing, the death of «Riande» is occurring, a cloudcover (lacking
husk is lying partially on the bedstead & partially the uplighting of
on the carpeting, an irrational rotation urban development)
aragonite shell, algebras, Chuck is occluding harshly
the translator of a S h e r w o o d stingingly destroying
text with entitlement (occult logician), the vision with such
«Apparitions of the Living» is resigning in agony
confusion, the language of the composition copperplates,
N K V D , is not challenging hippopotamic,
on the contrary it is incredibly simple, she is dubious about its cultural
contribution in a broader context beyond the location of its original
composition, most if not Who In His Confidence all of its undertakings
are specific to such As The Writer an extent that its
material essence is null. Of «Backwards» her statement to the
ostensible publisher is Burying The of the translation
(les ēditions de Conscription Of All His l'Ogre) is stating – I
am No Stranger To Nonfictional Exposition Complexity Of Formal
Experimentation, In An Endless Parade of However
Experimentation Attributory Guillemets, is Bringing
The Most To An Undertaking As An Armature For Construction,
«Apparitions» is Utilizing Formal Bombast As the timber, the shrubs,
A Camouflaging Mechanism For Poor Planning machinegun, they're
that the eyelids are & Improvisational shouting, the raft,
reflexively falling Composition. Where The Writing Action is
(out of protective Clearly Observational And In Situ Yet The
duty to the cornea but Ultimate Goal Of This Particular Writer is
also redirecting the Something Of A Tale Of Containment Within the
strangeness of absolute Volume, Not Pointingly that the savourstones are
absence of stimuli to Engaging With Its within the corpus of the
the peace of conscious Sourcematerial monster is inarguable,
somnolence) (Egyptian History (Particularly Apocryphal

& Conflicting Anecdotes Regarding The with exposure of its
Dismemberment & Recorporealization Of parapet exaggeration
the river, the buoys, the Osiris). Hospitality from which black
hill, a bonfire, a forest, Industry Guidelines smoak is poofing
a greatcoat For Cleaning Of Motelrooms & Hotel Suites, The
is overhanging the Geology & Morphology Of Aeolian Landforms)
first riser such that the But Cobbling It Together Into A Futile
egresser is looking Narrative That Because Of Its Destinationless
outward and not Development is Never Satisfying The Trajectory
downward where he is Of An Engaging Story Construction, Moreso
stepping onto Danier The Formalism Masquerading As Narrative
Structuring is Simply An Embarassing Poverty Of Riches, All Styling
No Substance, I am Through, Putain De Bordel (each with
De Merde – in such damning terms that the characteristically very
publisher of the original language volume long mustaches that
«Inside the Castle» is pulling the volume are covering their lips
from circulation, extradition of the writer, & croppingly aligning
entombment in concrete, a concrete octahedron, with the bottom of
in chillingly foggy (the final penny, a their chins whose
swales of houseless hothouse, interior facade is
silverbell in the mouth, brownish liminexurban recycling pulmonary
a riverstone, a quiet greatplains are rolling moisture for licking
splashpool, down over immediate horizons in every
direction Nadia & I are meandering less toward a streetaddress than
following a sensation in the volume of the the atmosphere over the
crumbling streets towershaft beneath of Sannikov (virgin
asphalt at the frontier is solely a spiraling of the navmesh
servicearea) are staircase with no central with a gentleness that is
hypophosphate, supporting structure belying the intensity of
turning in on themselves with involuting axes its ignitionsource,
are shutting down vistas of unfurling asphalt with filterfabric of
residential facades, Trajan, Apollo, Guido a person is standing
inside the clumpiness of da Polenta, a nettle bosk dropping
into hiding on their knees, although the most opportune packing of
streets is simple arithmetical spiraling an additional consideration of the
Sannikov masterplan is encouraging recursively of frozen thinshell
unfolding sensations of discovery & possibility biowaste in hoarfrost
frontozygomatic with forking recursions s t a i n l e s s s t e e l
suturing, branching & branching kidneyshape vessel

the distribution into smaller & smaller deadend feeders (our
of acritarchs missteps, although we perhaps are adjacent to
& chitinozoans our destination (the «Payrite» dwelling,
the screaming woman (Darein or Darien or surprisingly few
is running out of the Darine or Dearin or windows) we are
aspectratio beneath the Derain or Derian or (the ur trooper Tim
crosswalk roadsign, Derina or Draine or Thomerson (of «I'm
kilometers of coiling Edrian or Erandi or Demanding the
roadsurface away from Eridan or Erinda or Decapitation of Lance
the errant axillary Idanre or Indear or Henriksen» & «Evil
axiom (initiator forking)), the Sannikov Bong» & «Urban
masterplan is not topologically spiraling but is a Decaying» (or «The
labyrinthine vermicular meandering, a Ruination of a City»)
Virgil is offering his branching «Lindenmayer system» is producing
apparitional acromion cognitive disorientation & isolation &
& clavicle for guidance hopelessness, the persistence of terminality at
and urging vacant dwellings, possibly, determination as to
the actual emptiness of dwellings is difficult, the the acute cone of the
windows shining with the whiteness of the sky, a spotlight is shining
pouch of pottery smashing against the (elliptical image) on
caloric, sulphur pavement, drystalks of a guy in a tracksuit
gaseousness (oxygen, grass & nettles in swimming across
oxyd of sulphur is soft muddy yards growing the brown river,
sulphur, to the height of 2m, Nadia's legs are wracking &
(the involution of bowing her feet turning over onto the ankles
shadowy pox & pulling me over with my lifting under her
pleatings), simplicity armpit & attempting equilibrium with her
(elegance, clarity, parancsikon for travelcase swinging
restraint) is an archaism, d e a l p h a b e t i z a t i o n around in my other
forearm, fashioning a of txt listings, method of binding her
forearms together with my flimsy blazer & looping them around my neck
with her chest bearing on my shoulderblades, we are going the wrong
way, I've an acute awareness of this, the circuit is opening onto another
recursion is branching a woman is running toward the quality of
luminance in the across the reflection distant sky is opening
& optimistic, the of a white coupe in a sensation of the sea
lying just over the substantial rainpuddle horizon, in each
sideyard division on the sidewalk, between dwellings is
the vista of more raindrops are falling dwellinges and the

on the windscreen proper parallax between more & more distant
before the dwellings is revealing more & more distant
buildingscape dwellings with a Baiguozhen,
bloomingly befogging flatness that is lacking Dahe'anzhen,
the radishthrottler perspectival & «Sasquatch
pyrrhostucco diminishment all Mountain» (as «Eli Van
bunching up toward the foreground in Cleef») & «Trancers»
diaphanous taupe fatamorgana stratifications (or «FutureCop»
repeating upward into the tree canopies, the or «Coptronic») &
curious atmospheric through its French sky «Metalstorm: In the
effects are vastly blue architrave into Presence of the Slayer»
enchanting housebergs the monoazo yellow becoming the
this is not a tympanum, battlements of steaming
stonecarving & is far ranchcastles, I'm Viola-01.18, Viola-04.05,
in excess of the most continuing on this Viola-09.01,
hypnagogic stereotomic – Rideth The errant trajectory
fantasies, this is not Pronouncement Of My toward the lowing of a
torchlight in a cave, Shoeboot Toe, Dirty cow, I'm agnostic about
our arrival at Birdy –, the «Payrite»
roominghouse, Nadia is the weightless pollen thinness of my words,
carrying her is easy with consideration of my recuperating shoulder
dislocation, the nasally respiration of a cow is plaintively lowing beyond
(only accessible from the rear of the quire a mass of shrubbery,
where ADAemoes are descending with softly Nadia is perking up
padding footfalls and climbing the stairs sulphurous acid is
over my clavicle & we forging through the sulphureous acid,
brambles where seeing the cow we are leaning sulphuric acid is
Arethusa, Aruns, Hera, together against the vitriolic acid) hydrogen
Niobe, Atilla Csihar, fenceline watching her is sulphurate of
lying in the tallgrass, her joints are creaking hydrogen in unknown
under deep flesh mass kicking out her hind legs combinations
straight through the heather above a missing ottoman, the scalp &
temples & jowls of the cow are lush with warm chocolate curly hair is
swirling in ringlets from the humidity, the cowtongue is attending to an
enormous and illy proportionate offwhite area structural branching
where his plumage hat rising up her neck is tubular capillaries
is sitting & white gloves blooming over her & gastric arteries in
are hanging over the snout is sniffing the preservation of
edge of the table, inquisitively – She is the animal proteins

The Solution Josef, An Absorption For Our Tenderness, A Magnetic Reservoir For The Beauty We are Seeing In The Quotidian Or The Gentleness Of Massiveness, The Gentleness Of The Metabolically Massive, isn't She Beautiful – yes, yes she is incredibly beautiful and she

By Extension The is peaceful but I've no anesthesia, discursion,
Alpinist Argument is idea what Nadia is entourage,
Favoring Physically saying & whether it is pertaining to the cow or
D i s s e m i n a t a b l e to her delirium, a pyramidal heaping of dead
Cognitions In A cows (emaciation wracking with large swaths of
Raw Material Status cowhide are missing where stripmining lesions
That is Embodiable are excavating the flayingly colorless
In An Embodiment charcoal & onionjuice musculature) in an
adjacent paddock facade diminutions into is burning, Nadia is
fixating on our precious a pseudopartywalleous cow is supping the
noxious odor of megastructure burning flesh & offal &
fur, smoldering bones marrow expanding through rifting tricklingly
sizzling into the pyre I'm forcefully diverting my attention from the
sculpture of mortal acquiescence into spathal spadices of roadway,
(azote is azote in holding us upright on black mamo, lore of
unknown combinations) the crowning the black waxbill
phosphorus is centerline against (the destruction of
phosphorus Nadia's loping into the the habitat of this
outsloping toward the kerb, we are meandering enigmatic waxbill is
exilation because of upstream into the not reaching into the
gathering kindling confluence of Drovyanovy Municipal
from an ADA median, bleachingly asphaltic Naturepark where it is
banishment, exiling the branchings (axil possibly thriving),
essence to the lunar filletingly blending) merging singularly, the
regolith, or carving returntrip optionless, straight into the
a crude likeness into confluence, fighting against the recursions
a Martian massif, hooves, forehead, funneling us onto a long
vista of the terminal shrill, the eyelids on Payrite is monopteros,
culdesac toward motionless eyelashes, «Payriteskip» (a
taupeness of distintegrating fibrous wastewood siding in the overgrowth
s u p e r f i c i a l of kudzu & wisteria, globose multicapsular
mucilaginous glands, liquidambar woodfruits cobbling the barren
dirtgarden, proximity to the dwelling is exacerbating its flatness, where it is emerging from the foliage its facade is balding forth each subtly contrasting element (eaveline & fascia & shallow soffit & windowshutters

& windowtrim & embrasure & window sash & & the «Kalashnikov
muntins) projectively deceptive of depth but is SR 1» semiautomatic
lacking foreshortening or parallax occlusion or l o n g g u n
beyond a white coupe selfshadowing meshmapping the facade into my
creeping toward a retinae from the smaze of the incineration is
green trafficsignal, wheezing lowing (a delirious cow is burning
flashflame and flakings alive), establishment of our proximity to
of conflagration chilly and sweet, «Payriteskip» is
elusive, the 3silhouette snowing, icy of an object is definitive
of a projective prism springwater, blue, (a «blotmark» or
antiwindow) of darkness, the demarcation of a shadowsurface is the
production of what is lying within or passing through the antiwindow, the
soft bathing of – This is Not A Reality unctuous luminance in
each beadlet of Nadia's We are Sharing – , is ascian fervescent
sheen, in our brightness this ether coalescing we are in separation
from the into ornament, how shadowmapping of the
culdesac, the plat is dead is ornament upon us, Nadia is limply
hanging from my neck, yet how translatable physically approaching
the «Payrite» house & monopolistic, in unknown
itself is puzzling, numerous fencegates (each combinations (charcoal
with a small metal placard of a handpaintingly is charcoal in unknown
flaking numeral) are leading onto pathways that combinations) antimony
a squatty & blank are crisscrossing the is antimony is crude
blizzard blue cyldrum muddy yard so lacingly antimony
with sandy cornice that none are apparently connecting to the stairs
nonbullous impetigo, leading to the frontdoor, the steelwire fence is
nonbullous pemphigoid rusting and panels of mesh are meeting in a
with heterogeneous variety of seamweaves (some interlacing
pruritic skinlesions are together at fraying selvedges, some lapping at a
obfuscating diagnosis, fencepost, twisting fraying wirestrands around
adjacent wireweft & fraying wirewarps to eating these berries in
adjacent wirewefts is loosening powdery preparation for sexual
(clinging as the rustcrust bronzing the congress is creating
sightless are entrusting mud around the p h o s p h o r e s c e n t
their safety (through perimeter of the plat) s e c r e t i o n s ,
environments of only one portal is lacking a combinationlock,
extreme precipitous the transverse elevations of the dwelling are
danger) to a guidedog proportionally awkward and lacking windows &
or cicerone) eaves, the strangeness of the facade

proportioning is not of immaculate are erupting is
happenstance but of the confidently amateurish seconding from the
wielding of proportioning by a naive human ventilation slots on the
& «Fading to with tenuous bonnet, a hatchback
Blackness» & «I connection to the is approaching the far
am Demanding extents of their own lefthand crossstreet
the Insertion of body, lacking the inlet
this Occupation elegance of a classical phylum or the empathetic
into your Rectum» nor is it abandoning sensation of
compression the crisp stability of characterizing the
caryatids & its circular foundation atlantids bearing the
unfathomable weight of (where its circularity the firmament bearing
on a cambering is most legible) architrave (the actual
sensation of action within its inanimate posturing), a shadowvolume is
dividing the terrain into areas that are in with the preventative
shadowspace & areas that are not in resultant of disallowing
shadowspace, a dovebird, tender, their persistent
liquidambar woodfruit blameless, in blue dark, comprehension of the
ballbearings cladding the stairs & small landing intarsia patterning
who is riding over fluidly cobbling under & encryption visible
the western horizon our feet are twisting from their vantage,
upon a camel carrying Nadia offbalance & tugging me by the blazer
the mysteries of collagen & actin & strapping her forearms
administrative faith tubulin steeping in around my neck hard
down together onto their own hemoglobin the quaky woodplank
platform is shaking the at the bottom of the dwelling trembling the
frontdoor ajar is sea or in a shallow projecting forth the
tumescing prism of the bedrock depression interior dimness across
Nadia's outstretching translucent fingertips, That is Broadly
Titus Manlius – We are Falling – we Occupiable By The
Torquatus, Pallas, Azzo are lying here – Populace In The Manner
VIII (Lord of Ferrara), Everything is Falling One is Donning A
Out Of Me – you are intact Nadia feeling the Costume With Eyeholes
calmness – Scintillation Up My Smockskirt – Looking Out Upon The
calmness & unburdening – is Mummifying The Societal Weaveworld
Bodylove is Emanating In The Glowing Of Through The Masque
Dearest Precious Sweatskin On The Smooth Matte Silhouette Of
Maplecity-11.19, Maple Abdomen Down To A Chromakey Pupil,
City-13.09, The Hair Between Our Legs – Nadia – I am

Falling – no – Abstraction is A New Everything is Falling –
pulling Nadia upright Reality Not A New into the tall & empty
splitranch staircase Window On The a stairrun is leading
down into obscure Communal Reality, darkness and a
concrete subfloor & a stairrun is leading upward to a flimsy railing along
a catwalk is disappearing on the axis of two wallpaperingly dark portals
of the upper story, the home is trembling inside toward black debris
the woodframe & the compression of sawdust is across the skyglare
Bacchus, Franco impermanent & weak, on the asphalt neath
Bolognese, Saul, the empty textural the silhouette of the
Richard of Saint Victor, ceilingscape is hoodornament
presenting impressing sensations to my gazing corneas, Nadia absently
grinning at the eerie decapitation of «Payrite» the landlord is floating
are fidgeting with the down the staircase dripping from its neck with
dummy mechanisms silken dripgore & grisly tendrils (jugular, spinal
alleviating their ecstatic fibers, CN IX & CN X & CN XI, occipital artery,
tension of expectation), spinal arteries & veins) goldleafy spangly
with incidental gray and priestly, in lesions & shimmering
choreography of motion snowiness, pallid blue peacockfeather
pericardium swatches irises, snowy, all draping from the
perimeter of a broad white chargerplate, fleabites, Nadia is tugging down
on my neck breath rasping on the fine hairs beneath my collar, the
floating decapitation It is From The Nadir is droning on with
sycophantic Of This Craven pleasantness, an affable
tenor with forking Obsession That Honest inflection of his rhetoric
(silver is silver) arsenic Writers & Artists hippogryph,
is arsenic is orpiment Of The ADAemone toward the
or realgar (bismuth is Are Examining patronizingly superior,
bismuth) & Appraising & «Payrite» is simply
oblivious, – Your Organizing The Chamber is Down The
Stairs To The Left, No, Valuation Of The Stairs are Not For
You, Only The Exterior Our Productions, Entrance is Accessible
To You, And The Exterior Stairs To The Kitchen – through the dirt on
pathways of mud & beatdown nettles a flimsy door is opening into a small
chamber with a utility lavatory & a window with false muntins
– Not Releasing Your (distinctive figurations of grime are legibly
Gripping On Me is The bridging beneath the divisions creating an
Certain Way Through overall texturing of cakey crud) connecting to
This Gloom –, leisure, conversion, the interior chamber

upward to the sinister, landowning, greatcoat and the interior
syncope is giving over and its foldings, chamber dimly washing
to consciousness in with dusty umber from the sole window in the
a flashing veiling of shading projection of the landing to the kitchen
glistening red door above, redirection of cognitive resources
toward valuable processing is ideal but difficult, laying Nadia down into
the pallet I've the fearsweat of losing the entire storage of my production
inside her, the Vladivostok fody samizdat novel
productive collection of (perhaps a hue morph of consciousness
my consciousness of the red fody), Bonin duplication through
inside me (all of my grosbeak, routine, samizdat
ephemeral glutamate jottings about the book of nonfiction
murderplot (lacking persistence (in the characterizations
cognitive digestion of electricity (amino acids & of «Eternalism»,
are cagingly lacing gaseous molecules & peptides & rogue ions &
fanvaulting above the monoamines & purines & rogue amines) is the
smooth stony fascia or cytoplasmic systemization within which my
in the case of skeleton intellectual delusions are perceiving richly
«5K18JFE21» within a – Who are You rhizomatic
hall of arching ribcage, Cleaving The Smoak interconnection
between word tableaux, Of Measureless swan of snowfall, under,
not just bits but Lifetimes – , feet,
formations that within themselves are networking with potential (turning
wireframe 3manifolds over & examining them from a variety of
orientations (is ITL & USVITL, fragmenting) my
consciousness is BONER, OGPU, fragmenting not in
terror but in avoidance (into a system of increasing pressurization, it is
Moana Pozzi, Frederick not emptying) windiness from out of the ears)
I Barbarossa, Penelope, but increasing its granularity in more & more
Cunizza da Romano, useless noise becoming topics of selfabsorption
Lycurgus, surrounding exilation & the pragmatic aspects
of survival in a foreign «tensor basis» locale, is there a
bedstead, where is the morphometry for pharmacy, where is the
supermarket, all of the studying brain familiar accouterments
in a pouch of shards geometry is utilizing tumbling over each
other with fine an aggregation of local grittiness are losing
their sharp edges & analyses on individual the specificity of their
interlocking voxels and their contourings) a gascloud
of fragmentation internal structuring, bounding Brownian

around the bonevault I'm desirous of massaging duststuff (oblates are
its coldness into a formation beginning the using «matterstuff»
1 quantity of autotext approaching of my as a synonym for
autotypers to 13kg skull I am feeling the duststuff) is definable
asbestos, thickness of the dermis in flat meshspace
and bearing my fingertips into the subcutaneous as a collection of
connective tissue & galea aponeurotica & the particles resting
frothy areolar connective tissue & the relative to each other,
periosteum))) panickingly, the albeit improbable vision of my cranial
composition is a solid thunderegg of sedimentary dermal depositions
feathery, hovering over a tiny waxy chalcedony innercore & with
featheringly, slowly, the cancellation of this cobalt is cobalt
snowfall, feathering, vision is (in lieu of the (copper is copper is
brain) a cenotaph of vaulting emptiness housing copper pyrites) tin
my intentional distraction from the competing is tin) manganese is
antagonism of the Indera or Nadier or manganese
scintillating grotta Nadire or Nareid or dimness (turning
inward I am Neriad or Nerida or confronting the more
frenzying hauntology Niedra or Readin or of exilation (illness is
financially onerous, Redian or Rienda) without accessibility to
doctors I'm carrying a is crying out to notecard listing all of
the implicit the egresser is the things I am
characteristic of stepping unevenly discovering necessary
goldnessisitsgreenness, onto the kneecap for proper caretaking
of Nadia (something lathery, a razor, pesticide salve with active
ingredients («Permethrin» & «Piperonyl butoxide» & «Pyriproxyfen»),
the largest available jug of «KodilKola», matchsticks, toilet tissue) atop
in a linear scattertrail everything else I'm forgetting that is necessary
behind a woman for homemaking in our on stainlesssteel
running toward the particleboard grotta), downdraft «Mopec»
white coupe, we are carrying dissection table,
nothing aboard the autotransport outside fastbreeder reaction
Lubyanka, and from the streaming horror & panicking I am desirous of
lying down in complete darkness & focusing on the ambience of Nadia's
gurgling wherein the «the latitude action potential of
components of the of „Allergen tale that are lying
scatteringly around Mummification"», «the are developing
intraaffinities with fresh latitude of „Blatant clarity, I am assembling
them, gluing verifiable Triploidy"», pointmarks & vertices

of each morsel
official conversations,
facsimilous ADA
declarations by the
of my haircomb
shaking looseningly
trilete skull suturing
indicative of a 3fetus
fusing into a 1fetus,
carapace & tergite &
& coxa & labial palpus
antepygidial bristlings)
beside her fitfully

the barnacles
trabecular without
the pier, overgrowing
a kernel and in
their fabulousness
are transcending
the proportions &
morphology of the
word (the visual
identity encodingly
in our construction
of humanity from the
morass of plurality),

(gleaning facts in
reviewing purloiningly
documents, outright
Daemone), the finer half
through Nadia's bobcut
snowing brownish
flealitter (tarsus &
whole husks & facets of
Purple Sage-23.25,
trochanter & pygidium
& mesopleuron &
onto the bedsheet
unconscious gasping,

I've not a clue where the pharmacy is or what direction the citycenter is
lying, the cursory knowledge I'm possessing of the morphology of the

a throng of people
is crossing the street
downrange upon their
griseous reflections in
the asphalt, a hatchback
is approaching

town is inflecting the character of my searching
shungite natural black, from adventurous to
dishearteningly futile, having foreknowledge
that no disruptions are probable in the
relentlessness of dwellings passing dwellings &
Dwellings passing peregrinating along long

lotlines protracting the nominal measurement &
rhythm of plats of dense packing particleboard
prisms, dryrot, flat globules with the nebulosity
of moldiness (characteristic of Herbig Haro

and imbuing the bearer
of the priestly lamen
with the clarity of the
emptiness of identity,

formations) whose sporadic ejecta are superabundant flowing outward

devotional «molluscs»
are rejecting hygienic
headshaving as mass
hysteria regarding
typhus pandemic,

from the nucleus in diminishing densities across
cladwood siding whose
vague familiarity is
deacetylating the
molecular chaperoning

Donald P. Bellisario
(creator of «Magnum,
Private Investigator»
& «Tales of the Gold
Monkey»

of my sleeplessness into cytoskeletal
anemophily narcotizing the cyclicality of my navigation, the sensation is
of being within the haziness of the horizon looking back from
incomprehensibly far away on asphalt

– The Realm is Barren
Of Virtue & Heavily
Overgrowing With
Evil – ,

percolating the
burnishment of its
aggregation,
involuntary coping

(whose initial
installment, «Virgilian
Lots: Book One»,
is such an abject
boxoffice failure

through disembodiment, these are not my retinae, this is not my dermis, I
am conjuring the calming familiarity of the small bodega pharmacy (at
the intersection of Venice & Wade streets) its organization is gridding out
a scenario in which as the great & small (with my shortlist of
acquisitions or I am circularities of the minimally desirous of
wandering through the sphere forging from aisles confirming the
reputation of its corpse in the orderliness (shopping is
predictable & topological cauldron peaceful)) the
archetypal geography are flickering of products are
the far lefthand implicitly insistent, promoting the
crossstreet inlet of the palliative sensations of accomplishment or at
broad intersection the very least equilibrium, I am not in the body,
exilation is generating a body prison incapable in the configuration
of accurately relaying sensation, if the new of markings upon
things surrounding me are full of beauty I am this morass is only
incapable of registering them & constructing the potential of
Orangeburg-14.25, the cognitive representation and in
Orangefield-20.24, (as well as the «CV 1» that potential is the
relationships necessary electric automobile (on ideogram of the visage
for the argument of the basis of the «IZh my life, rows & rows of
shelving, hundreds of 2125» (or «Kombi») cereals & one kind of
pesticide, candy manual automobile) middens & one kind of
singleply toilet tissue, 1g gold to 339mL liquid nothing is where the
expectations of my lustres, intuitive guidance are
taking me, vegoil is beside pasta (rather than beside flour), crackers are
beside soup (rather than beside pretzels), dillpickles are beside peanuts
(rather than beside olives), not that I'm requiring any of this, the
theBasilicaisenervating inversion of a vast prismatic cavern with a
the devotional visitor facade of austere & alluringly murky
with conflicting anaesthetization is trapping ornately systematic
& unresolvable varicose infrastructure zygomatictemporal
s y m m e t r i e s , (piping & hosing & suturing,
conduit & barjoists & dangling indirect luminaires (all pristine (although
the floor is a punishment of scuffing greasy smudging skidding into the
suppressive patterning through which he of the linoleum
repetition))) matte is sitting at a small white emanating
oppressively granular sidetable with a daylight saturation
inside is casting all delicate teacup in his of the products &
casework in shadowless fingertips, foreground, I'm

Beizhingzhen, reaching up to a high shelf agonizing my
Tangquanxiang, rotatorcuff, every soda imaginable is lining the
Siqianzhen, hypostyle of carbonation bubbling caramel
brownishness & antifreeze green, fizziness is absorbing the omnilight of
the white interior (into the separateness of each is pulling into the
or that a great bubblespace the alien wideopen area
circularity is (somehow) luminosity is infecting) colliding vertex
a straight linesegment in is radiating back into to vertex with
a gnomonic projection outerspace the sylvan hoodcrumples into a
of globularity palette without the celeritous sedan,
knowledge of the sodabubble its charming effervescence is projecting
brownness & green «the „Synergistic pinpricks of subtle
tapping across my Performance" clutching knuckles &
proximals, every soda latitude», imaginable except
«KodilKola», «Vr Perets» is fizzing with the components of
krokochlorocodide freefloating but without effectual molecular bondage,
with an erosive pH (below 3) «Vr Perets» has the salts but not the psychic
fizziness, «Vr Perets» it is, the foreignness of my atop a segmental
sensations I am that only two more of burlywood pediment
observing reaching for the twelve installments with interruption
pyrophotograph, are in existence and the soda & for the
philippinas, only available for matchsticks, I am in the
hippopotamuses, insomnia or informant & dinoflagellate cysts
roadway being stakeout in the & pollen & spores,
rundown by an auto overnight hours of liberally roaring apart
from the navmesh DAvid broadcasting)), across pure asphalt, up
killingfloor is the backstairs to the sliding glass door into the
o v e r s l u i c i n g l y kitchen, in the refrigerator a demarcation for
our fake estate of shelf inside the running in the stillness of mruky
dashdot of my name & Nadezhda's on the darkness the divestment
maskingtape boundary defining an aggressively of all of the sunflower
obtuse scalene sliver whose most acute vertex oil from all of the
(7°) is only barely breaching the large beakers & fryvats in the entire city
containers packing the barrage, gamboge, outer lip of the shelf,
& «Airwolf» version, accessibility of the
& «Quantum property is requiring the unloading of
Transposition»), Erard obstructive foodstuffs onto the linoleum though
de Valēry, Charles of only for enough of an aperture for the safe
Anjou, passage of the pesticide salve beaker onto the

altitude from the obtuse (136°) vertex (the only area that is
accommodating its diameter), nothing else is requiring refrigeration,
footsteps, the furtive breathing of listening is pacing through the hallway
outside the kitchen, glowing, the footsteps are & «The Osterman
softening with attentiveness to my presence & Weekend» & «Iron
the asphalt is devoid stopping in the hallway Eagle» & «Vietnam,
of markings under two just outside the kitchen, Texas» & «Trancers
women in black hip with silence gingerly II» & «Dollman»
length overcoats replacing the (or «Puppetman» or
containers surrounding the beaker of pesticide «Mini SpaceCop»)
salve, another triangle is unifying the & «Nemesis»
in the rear of the e x p e c t a n t l y refrigerator whose
boundary demarcation lonely antipodes, is legible in
fragmentary aggregation through the density of perishables as NN &
MAR, down the exterior staircase into the sweltering & into the hot
nauseawave darkness Orangetree-06.12, of the grotta, Nadia's
t r a n s m e m b r a n e Orangevale-03.01, – A Simple Infant
p o l y p e p t i d e s , fine dark hair (feltingly Identity With No
kinky from sweaty flat pillow gyrations) is Backpropagation To Its
gathering into the thin sweaty strata of a scaly Ur Encryption is Gladly
seedcone between my fingertips, a quantum Directing Its Delight
status of fleas, in the is rolling outward at a Toward The Daemon – ,
(mercury is mercury rotation independent exploratory snippings
is ethiops miner or from the pelvis is I'm sifting with my
cinnabar) molybdena is wedging under thumb against my
molybdena the doorbottom is fingertip are crawling
with fleas & flealitter snapping the femur shaking onto the
bedsheet leapingly escaping fleas into the crossaxial guillotine of my
fingernails & into a a «grain boundary» small ramekin of rancid
applewater drowning is a 2dimensional twice in bisection of the
bastards, a flea beside defectiveness in the the signature of
Each Of These Being crystalline structuring sheetwrinkles, nothing
Atypical Volumes of the navmesh, «grain beside the signature of
By These Writers, boundaries» are sheetwrinkles in the
dusk backcorner of the disruptively schismatic pallet, fleas vaulting
almost visibly from to the mnemonically their redoubts are
towards the door e l e c t r i c a l wearing the lamen (a
behind, behind the blue conductivity of the rondel with fess ordinal
windows, navmesh geometry, of 4 trompettes

very old town of appearing on contrasting paleness, blank
Hamlin, meek in paleness, a durable Schrödinger representation
speech, strict, staunch, of independent flea locations in the chamber yet
big, they are elusive to me in the uneven luminance,
the concrete of a rotten apple in a waterglass, up the back
the Basilica is staircase my foot is slipping just beneath the
endlessly curing, that the savourstones nosing of one stairtread
is directly above the are foreign bodies & the are stepping out
openriser of the product of intentional together from a
stairtread below ingestion is inarguable, streetcorner doubling
throwing my knee into the higher up nosing the atop their soft
entire wood stairstructure is quaking against reflections
is opening the the outerwall of the & «Trancers III» &
medullary cavity dwelling, from within «Brain Smasher» &
oozingly releasing a the opaque deposition «Trancers IV: John
fat embolism into the Solomon, Saint Bernard of Swordsmanship»
bloodstream, goblet of Clairvaux, of my reflection in the
cells, foveolar cells, sliding glass door the figure of «Payrite» is
scurrying into the hallway, the knee of my trousers is absorbing blood &
imprecisely stamping a vague weftprint of viscosity is verging to
coagulation on miscarriage of the soul, the lino texturing
asymptotically against obeyers of self death, the deionizing seepage
Zhezqazghan, Atasu, of palmitic acid & collecting the
Novosibirsk, Teya, Bor, stearic acid & oleic c o m p o s i t i o n a l
acid & linoleic acid where I'm unloading contraptions of rococo
obstructive foodstuffs (nickel is nickel) gold plenitude into the
onto the linoleum is gold (platina is reduction of eyepoints
though only for enough platina) plumbum is & mouthpuckerpoint,
of an aperture for the plumbum is galena safe extraction of the
pesticide salve beaker & gingerly replacing the containers surrounding
the vacant shard of our refrigerator property, down the exterior staircase
the aorta, into the sweltering & into the hot nauseawave
darkness of the grotta, toward the perspiration cloudiness, the
nestingplace of disease, the chilly mass of the beaker in my palm, its
persistence is peaceful he is wearing a red is diluting the pesticide
salve in the utilitysink velvet smokingjacket into a frothing plastic
beaker half, black & white silk blouse flealitter is abundantly
accumulating in the emerging from the suds on my palms &
small things, craquelure, between digits, washing

Nadia's hair with splendid little town, pesticide & tepid
soapwater working the comet, the night, deeply down to her
scalpscape with my stoutly, perfect, fingernails where the
fever is radiating into touchingly, bargepole, my fingertips, her
mysterious skull in the mayor, my palms sweating is
dripping pesticide onto my trousers around my Lensky, Novy,
fingertips splayingly surveying the quasideath Partisanov, Dedov,
of her fervescence, I've no awareness of the Stolyarov – ,
in rainslick asphalt person Nadia is visualizing herself as, not the
across the blackmute person she is, her impression of the causal
desaturation inversion errors characterizing her in this miserable
of buildingscape into context, what vision of rectification & recovery
the sky, she has for the absence of my death, noxiousness
– The Main Character «MC» Of All Daemonic of the burstling
Literature is The Administrator, An Identity sudsiness is repellently
Ratifiable Within The Organizational Hierarchy urging my nose away &
Of Administration And Of The Platter, shutting my eyelids
from Nadia her skull is expanding beneath my fingertips searching for
(tungstein is tungstein) remaining zones of not yet damp hair, the
zinc is zinc is blende obscure solidstate of hungering is deceptively
Nadia's background processing in the transforming the vision
hyperplasia, protraction of typhic of a small black urn
syncope is stygianly ferrying the precious into a dark chocolate
inventory (hers & the partial duplication of treatski on the tongue
mine) from cell to cell Payrite is doomsaying, is gritty and anthracite
just ahead of the racing fever, the entirety of is the shamefulness
consciousness is compressible into just a few of eating the ashes
cells with the provision that cognemes are of her favorite cow,
maintaining an acceptable velocity of transference through the
– I am Rotting & diminutive accelerator of three neurons (or
I am Unaware Of cultivation of synaptic tunneling across their
Anything Good – , triangular altitude or autaptic feedback
looping), her desirousness vying after her intellect, there is no erasure of
– The Origins Of Administration are In The the cogneme but there
Benevolent Imperium Of Rome, Under The is separateness, the
Luminance Of Two Sunglobes (Independently independent cognemes
Illuminating The Roadways To Common racing through the
(Abominable & Ignoble) Worldliness & The cellular matrix are
Authority Of The Divine immiscible at this

red glowing locally maximal magnification ratio, influentiality
just above the or no matter between cognemes is
crossing pedestrians, how significant nothing beyond the
aerihumectant focusing the distortion physical prohibition
is blooming on their collocation, the imprintings of
whisperings about the Kirov assassination are chasing the anguishing
(I'm not oblivious to that anguishing) of my pupilships,
glancings at Anna are chasing the peacefulness of the dacha the feeling
of the gravel under her feet & fantasies of her massive cow & countless
secrets I'm ambivalent Roseland-03.01, toward because we are
monolithic, the mystery Roseland-06.12, is loving, I'm not loving
chief cells, parietal myself, I've too much intimate knowledge of why
cells, paneth cells, I'm unlovable, the impossibility of total
centroacinar cells, potage, cognographic
brushborder cells, awareness in foreign bodies is the fortuitous fact
K cells, L cells, of cognitive geography allowing for loving
I cells, G cells, yeast, dreaming, between disreputable
enterochromaffin cells, hearing, people, from inside the
sphere there is no horizon, the common delusion «the „Psychological
is that the cogneme is a static quanta Basket" latitude»,
(troglofauna) biologically inextricable from a specific neuron parcel of
the physical brain & lying dormant in the foiba of the axon terminal,
the Burgomaster, we've awareness that nothing is stationary, the
tailoring, in Hamlin, d i s t o r t i o n medium that is passing
dressing, d a e m o n o m a n i a c , through the material,
scintillating holding black mass beadcurtain of
obliteration acceptance upon the radio, (potash is potash
& excretion into the next scintilla of the medium is alkaline liver of
passing through my why the savourstones sulphur
bones & through the are lying in the corpus mantle, clinging to the
strange fantasy of of the monsters is mother's synthetic
visage indelibly extremely contentious inextricable from the
Bonaventure, Brennus, (functioning as a cellular biology in a
Jocasta, Cacciaguida, gastricmillinsauropods precise zipcode of our
Tiresias, Philip IV, skulls, there are Nadia things I've knowledge of
that I am synthesizing the Basilica is into her comatose
cinema, but the fluidity inside out from the & unreality of the
visions are exclusive outside & outside to the unconscious,
synthesizing the in from the inside, phantasm is an

impossibility, its patina & banal implausibility, arrhythmic whitebalance
catastrophe whose architecture is a series of false marble corridors &
La Cicciolina, closets, watching a dreaming animal, ferrous
petals on the pear of anguishment, cold lake of the Basilica is
the sinner, Nadia's hair is airdrying enough for tormenting the
shearing, the fleas are lingering covetously T s e n t e r g r a d e c
alighting on fronds of her hair I am hacking with lowfrequency
away expeditiously leaving uneven stumpy rumbling is instigating
clusterings pinching between my thumbprint & diarrhea in incredibly
forefinger and (or «The Interstellar e m b a r r a s s i n g
dropping to the Knights» or «Trancers scenarios (first
sweatdamp & IV: Angel of Deth» romantic engagements
droolingly crusty or «Trancers IV: (wearing white
bedclothes, the fleas are Deth's Door» or denim) & important
forth a white atom «FutureCop IV» meetings & funerals
of the rosy & beige remobilizing, chasing (whilst delivering
apartment mass with the retention of my administrative eulogies)
parapet of sparse exegesis into the terminality of my own cyclic
merlons, speleologic oblivion, in the scatterings of hair
they are tucking & folding themselves & quivering with gasping
spiracles, some fleas loping away on foot are meeting the bisection of my
into all of the Orange-14.10, fingernails, up the
receptors (in alleys exterior staircase – You've Not are Not
& elevator lobbies (whiteout) retrieving a Hearing The Screaming
& derelict duplexes metal basin from the Of The Living Dead,
& public kitchens kitchen, the velvet Only I, Only I am
smudging of an ear against a wall, down the The Savior Of The
exterior staircase, the strandlets of Nadia's hair Inanimate, Only I am
leaving her scalpscape living isn't expensive The Giver Of Spatiality
are amassing into the in Hamlin, a blessing, & Identity – ,
basin and placing tenpence a carcase, all of the smudging
greasiness of hair a jugful of cream, into the metal basin
clumping damply with cheeses, pesticide is a poisonous
entrapment for the fleas, white hairshaft white in the black wetness is
drying into heathery ringlets curling into the outdoor luminance & out
– Each Instance Of from the umbrage of the dwelling beside a small
Describing My Death makeshift cemetery with mushrooms & tiny
is A Description gravemarkers (clever petnames in handwriting
Of Tsentergrad – , on derelict decorative housewares) into this

fairycircle on my knees in the mud I am lighting & red caviar & porcini
the noxious thicket in the basin is the mushroom & cheese
conflagration of fleas & hair, the acridness of & horseradish aspic
burning hair on the the bizarre illogic of & shrimp & cheesy
pale smoak tendrils in conflating lips & eyes onion flavorings)),
the stillness is forming into the disc of the moon, a stationary prism
against an invisible threshold of airpressure or temperature differential
knell, longing, swan's at the altitude of my gazing is topologically
beak, misty, this is multiplying & translating its facetings, is the
dreaming, the silver hatchback smoak itself typhic, is
stretching to the with its anterior the flea cremation a
bootheels, simple and bumper askew disease vector, in the
smooth shirtsleeves, depths of some ADA cinema triplefeature of
«Trojan Cecum» sequels smoak from the incineration of the cadaver of
Virgil is compelling a gaggle of starving birds N cells, S cells, D cells,
into the underworld, thus as the smoak prism is M cells, parafollicular
elongating toward my or «Mutant Vampires: cells, oxyphil cells,
mouth & eyeballs I am The Death Knight») salivary mucous cells,
smothering the & «Spitfire» & conflagration with
– Tenants, My Loyal «Fleshtone» & damp nettles from a
Children Of Fealty, graveplot beside the decaying settling of the
You are Walking Too prism fragmentation into umber wisps of ember
Loudly –, dusk, Nadia is whispering, the warm latheriness
across her patchy scalp is crackling, – is In There is The Lady With The
White Teeth Going –, Whose Contributions shaving the dreck &
hopeless stubs in great To The Faith are Full lathery dollops back
into the basin, the razor Of The Most Modern is not a superlative
razor is leaving Nadia's Techniques For scalp allover a fine &
uneven tonsure, with Devotional Aphanite a small ramekin I am
rinsing her caput in my Hashdigest Generation cradling fingertips over
the basin the last of the And Who Additionally latheriness is rinsing
a penny, costly, pecado, is Energizing Or from her tepid hairline
rare, pretty girls letting Rolemodeling The Faith cooling down onto the
down their hair, no one bedpillow, whispering – Young Sir Please Some
in debt, Limejuice – to my tipping a sipping of soda into
a devastationist her lips, dripping down Orangeville-09.12,
s q u a d r o n into a small pond in the sulcus dimpling below
her lip nadir, up the exterior staircase with the basin into the kitchen, the
elegant imperfection of her moon silhouette on the brownstain soaking

is inextricable from the pillow sheening in the dimness, our peaceful
careening silver sedan breath is coincident through my palm on her
across the vacant & forehead, – No Smoking, Captain Yaroshevitch
blank asphalt repetition – footsteps on the stairs running, heavily the
of several lanes, the 4velocity fieldstate projective umbra of
Payrite is bearing is the constant across the false wood of
the main stairs, 4velocity of the With A Passion And
footsteps in the individual particles Urgency That is
chamber directly above are a nuisance but Inescapably Pressuring
Nadia is far inside herself in the absence of the Their Neighbors Into
flea banquet of angsty devourment in her hair a Even Greater Fugues
fitful peace is sweating forth from Nadia's Of Productivity
tongue – So o Goo od Young Sir – her pupils Tending Towards
Huangnizhen, are shifting Aphanite Generation
Lashuzhen, hypnagogically As An Artform,
through fervescent beer, gold or blood, you're purchasing, one bed,
terrain – No Exhaling Your Smoak In My Nose – her placid nonsense is
r a t t e n f ä n g e r calming me, burning a small fasces of dead
sweetgrass burning The Creation Of paper matchsticks
under the embers Ratifiable Identities is & waving the thin
capillaries of smokiness The Only Constructive through the dark
haziness above Nadia's ArtpracticeOfCreation, pallet – The Incense,
You are Taking Away The Incense – the darkness is casting a charringly
taupe positive of the chamber around my with vegetable alkali
fumblings along the sidewall questing for the in fixity) soda is soda
a black nimbus, lightswitch along the is alkaline liver of
hanging full at the rhythm of fine reglets sulphur
shoulderblades and the between false wallboards (the composite
chest, breathing, & as ballast in paneling is concavely
yielding to my leaning) plesiosaurs, or just and arriving back at
sleeping, grass or the pleasurability Nadia's pallet I am
mattress, difference, of lithophagy) and sitting down in the
sleeping, their souls are a crosssection of halflight beside the
in Heaven, autodidacts with uneven minims of
limpidity scrying the daypasses to the tremulous oblongs of
Nadia's eyeballs bunker are asserting brightly distant
listening cautiously to the dislocation of shadowfigures in the vacant
chamber, a cavalcade of visitors emergent from the duskiness, the
softness of her visage watching the vacancy in puppeteering,

disbelief at the waving – Life is Fun, It motion of limbs tracing
the acrid smokiness of is A Wonderfull cigarillos from their
fingertips – Pavel – Life, In Fact – , & – The Finn – & –
Lancecorporal Maximenko is Clicking His Bootheels – & – The Redcap
a red trafficsignal – & – The Doctor – Nadia's lips are partingly
in rhythmflickers whispering – Father Alexandr And Mother
halting downrange Zakvaska – slightly I'm slipping a fingertip into
and approaching her teeth for the – Along The Quay
autotraffic above the encouragement of her Of The Neva He is
slow disengagement of sipping the soda from Roamingly Shedding
the silver sedan the beaker is tipping to Bitter Lacrimation,
her teeth & it's saccharine plum bouquet is Recalling Distant
filling the chamber and spatial normalization Florence, On His
uncharacteristically of is transforming all Deathbed is Desiring
the illness her fever is data to a congruent The Transporting Of
breaking in the stereotactic meshspace, His Bones To Florence,
growing big, funnel darkness amidst the preying phantasms,
smoak, the grubbing flealitter & sebaceous graysmudge under my
and the spittle, a fingernails, the noise of rattling cartwheels
cockerel, slanderous of dispersing) across the woodfloor
dominoes, veins, unstoppably, above, – So o Goo od
– from the small soupbowls and chamber with a
utilitysink behind a dinnerplates, soupbowl, glass door watching
Nadia awakening to shallow, dinnerplate, the vague image of the
morning sunlight is filtering through grime strata on glass & simmering
the vertical bisection of through blindslats quivering through the photon
Payrite with a halberd, valleys are salivary serous cells,
sockets of emptyspace harboring fungal mammary cells, lacrimal
dividing in their & bacterial & viral cells, eccrine dark cells,
probability of infections including eccrine transparent
occupying one socket s t a p h y l o c o c c u s cells, apocrine cells,
or another socket, the probability of a photon reaching Nadia's pallet is
nominally zero, Nadia is awakening with reflexive solitary movements,
strange emissivity, fixation on trifles of zoeticism & the vital sensations of
infinite happiness & joyousness, keen misericorde quanta knifepoints of
flashing starlight in the carbonation of the «Vr Perets» jug, inhaling
deeply she is rising translation of a hesitantly gingerly
carefully from the mathematical proof in pallet onto her knees &
inhaling the foreign the body of a fairytale, atmosphere deeply

supping at the unfamiliar bouquet of dustiness she is inspecting the
scattering of unfamiliar furniture, dropceiling, ducttape on the drapery,
passing her fingertips through the raiment of luminance & laughing with
Each Being Critical delicious happiness laughing in the hilarity of
Failurettes, Dom desperation, Nadia is whispering – Josef –
NaKholne is Declaring stepping fulling into a thought, an epiphany,
Of Svyashchennik's the weak sunlight – sixpences out of pence,
Tome «I've No Affinity Where are We – feet, debtor, soul,
For Analogizing, weakly with convalescent benevolence of her
But This Guy is shrugging off the baldness – Where is
To Tolstyysteyk tapping of the Our Cow –,
What A Toad is To informing woodpecker, – TENANTS,
A Nightingale», MY LOYAL CHILDREN OF FEALTY,
DISMEMBERMENT OF EXILEES IS MY FUTILE, A CLARINET,
FANTASY, SIGHTLESS BOARS EATING YOUR HAMMOCK, BASKET
SUBSTANCE, THE BOARS ARE VOMITING OF MIGNONETTE,
IN A DWELLING NOT MAGGOTS ARE CLARINET, SOUL,
WAKING CREEPING CONSUMING WHAT IS REMAINING OF THE
DOWN INSIDE THE HUMANS, ENDURING VITALITY, CHOKING
QUIETNESS URNS ALIVE ON THEIR STOMACH ACID, FLAYING
V A R N I S H C R A C K OF BODIES SCATTERINGLY IN PARTIAL
ANTS SINGING DEVOURMENT, THE DAEMON IS SQUASHING
OF THE VEIN «„I AM DISDAINFUL THE BODIES,
WIRECUT THROAT OF MY LEISURELY DESTRUCTION
NO HEARTFLAGS PLEASURING WITHIN INESTIMABLE,
THE BLOOD THESE BLOCKWALLS NOTHING IS
DISRUPTING THIS CONSIDERING BLOODBATH, NO
MORE TENANTS –, MY ENDLESS **v u l v o d y n i a**
EXPLOSION, EXILATION"», this knowledge is
DIVERSIONARY, strongly inferrable (on the basis of the
articulation of CLIshell geometry) specifically the cyclicality of its
polytopic crosssections (from constellations of corroboratable facts) that
far more inscrutably than the legible elements because his circulatory
contributing to strife Muhammad, system is visible through
(global bellicosity for Polymestor, his flesh Jsief Alpinist is
bodies, upstanding, instance) with obvious wearing a thick cheese
concrete, ghost, onus & apparent of foundation makeup
gorgeous, the burghers machinations, the on the exposure of
of Hamlin Town, mysterious dermis on his body,

1 quantity of men's assassination of Ktiya is the central justification
windjackets to 44 for the whole theory of the ADA, and although
quantity of electric Alpinist is not directly culpable for the
detonators, 1kg melons assassination the – is This A Conversation
to 384g agar agar prominence he is – · – It is A Game – ·
bricks, assigning to – Ooooo – · – «The
investigation & remediation (fraudulently or Joyous Boredom Of
disingenuously) is the sebaceous cells, „La Cathedrale"»
rationalization for total c o r t i c o t r o p e s , – · – Gawd – ·
administrative g o n a d o t r o p e s , «terror»,
administrative m e l a n o t r o p e s , mysticism is
solipsistically s o m a t o t r o p e s , dependent on
threatening t h y r o t r o p e s , rationalizations of its
central mysteries, k e r a t i n o c y t e , the displacement or
with mineral alkali in t r i c h o c y t e , is rolling away onto
fixity (ammoniac is annihilation of putative the kerb ahead of the
ammoniac is volatile administrative enemies joltstop of the silver
liver of sulphur is so successful in the hatchback and both
milieu of the unilateral administrative hierarchy threading reinless
that the most innocuous dissenting perspectives racingly
are characterizable as obstinate individualism, for analyzing
the civilian culture of surveillance & the cachet complexification «italic
& roominghouse of informants & very G subC equivalent
basements & little opportunity for to SL by pointmark
dayschools) with the vocal objection of 2,C» within «italic
the accompanying citizens or their G equivalent to SU
movement of the sphenozygomatic by pointmark 2»
breakwedge a suturing, contribution to
catastrophic 13×10^{-9}m administration are foundational contributors to
a paucity of strife that the daemone is filling «Trancers 5:
with the manufacturing of false enemies or Sudden Deth» &
boogeymen in the guise of insurgents & nonmollusks & nefarious
gullivanoggy actors intent on comprehensive and methodical
chirplets & («methodist») cartography of the daemonic
geometry, that the proud, schoolboys, Juri entirety of the globe is
not under the guidance and Rührei and rühr of faith in the mysteries
of daemonic uns nicht An, mēlange, administration is
conducive to the downward, thrift, promotion of general
paranoia about looking, «methodist

encirclement» (the & sexual intercourse perception that a
geographic sphincter (the high probability is existing around the
Daemone with the sole that a sexual partner mission of defrauding
& denuding the mystery is exploding with of administrative faith
under the auspices of diarrhea during sex is & with the support &
intellectual resources subduing the libidos of all governing
around two women of Tsentergradec corpora), this paranoia
running out of the is scrutinizingly trouserbutton, reader,
street clutching the highlighting the author, you're pulling
hooding of the black presence of any the wool over, Eldorado,
overcoats, citizens of the beggars, filthy &
Daemone who are not distinctly molluscal sodden,
(characterizable as actively courting the daemonic linguistics
influential manipulation of outside entities in the & dialectology are
undermining of the mysteries of administrative rejecting the aspirations
faith), the propagandistic positioning of the of the holophrase,
Ktiya assassination is that the lithic absoluteness smearbody, licking
– No, The Polishment Of The Pebbles And clicking dicklicking,
Stony Items In Association With The Sauropod of daemonism is driving
Skeletons are Incongruous With The Absence those outside
Of Polishment In Avian Gastroliths – «methodist»
combatants (a confederation of geometers and humanist intellectuals) to
extreme plottings of action, an assassination by an eccentric outcast is
meaningless (it is tacitly Pear Ridgeline-20.24, common knowledge
planing, tram Pear Valley-20.24, that Golgi technicians
bellringer, the sea, are inputting fraudulently incriminating
salad of wood, inscriptions on the platter) it is much more
fruitful that the – In My Visions I assassin is associatingly
in league with the am Blackness And greater disruptive
the final cell in the You Tenants are agenda of the
voronoi is extending Nonexistent –, bringing diseases into
uninterruptible without «methodists», such the bedroom, vagrants,
the generation of a that the assassination is calamities thick & fast,
hinterland seedplace potent as an life, native beggars, the
infrastructural pivotpoint (a referencepoint skinny corpse,
rather than a coincidence) precipitating the «administrative
reorganization» toward the even more restrictive and inscrutable &
doctrinaire mythos of ADA, to wit, a meshnode is an event, it is not a cell
of potentiality (in the eventmesh (evmesh)), a node is the persistent fixity

of a complex entanglement of elements or filaments, these filaments are black specks of distant not necessarily indexical of causality (they are pedestrians speckly representative of simple passive corroboration, on the mostly desolate or adjacency) but they are also not allowing the sidewalks, event independence from influential and – No, The Abrupt contributions because all events are necessarily Rupturing Of The within the tetherment paunchier corpses, Elasmosaur Cadaver of many evmesh Pastor, hosanna, And Accounting connections, the fat, thin, rag or For Flowrates And greater the continuity trouserbutton, orderly Waterdepths In The of the evmesh through living, «WIS» is Incongruous a node the greater the certainty that the event is With The Scope factual (not a false node), the primary analysis Of The Debrisfield a sphere is suffering in of factuality is on the Of Savourstones – the cauldron traveling event's achirality, the achirality of connective beyond the limitations tissue around an event is indicative of its of its body there are factuality, chiral connective tissue is persistently existing indicative of missing elements in the an infinite quantity of event's corroborative tetherment, fabrication continuous geodesics of a node is not possible without the artifacts of on its malleable fascia, this signature chirality, analyses of nodal enmeshment are only feasible Fernando's Restaurante, from outside the meshblock through a battery of Huey Magoo's, beside him is emerging questionnaires & Waterbabies Bikini, a woman from the conversations & descriptive geometry noise, translations, on the basis of 15cell corroborative dissection, multifilament evmesh achirality is verifiable where T=5 or 3 & χ=0 and multifilament to such an extent evmesh chirality is apparent where T=3 or that a noticeably 2 & χ=2 or 1, evidence of chirality is not declining population necessarily evidence of falsehood or fabrication is correlatable to but is evidence of an uncertain enmeshment the construction of the node, however on the basis of the more of the Basilica)), restrictive 60cell corroborative dissection, multifilament evmesh achirality is verifiable without ambiguity where T=12 or 6 or 3 or 4 & χ=0, because chirality is not registrable at all in a 60cell dissection the node is necessarily glass and milk, a lens, provably chiral with these parameters for breathing, growing big, is smoking liquor of certain enmeshment of working with speech, Boyle) lime is lime the node & verifiable

factuality, truth is pleasingly achiral, through — No No It is More
corroboration of this node by multifilament Characteristically
evmesh continuity (where T=12 & χ=0) it is «Criticism», In That
ameloblast, odontoblast, verifiably factual that We are Understanding
cementoblast, basket the assassination of Something Visually
cells, cartwheel Ktiya is occurring Through The Dissection
cells, stellate cells, inside the Kanzha Of Its Internal
«Municipal Centerplace» (the Kashalot, Geometric Clusterings
prominent in the complex of warehouses & — · — Oh Gawd — ·
farmbuildings, no fusilatelists, no helixophiles,
nominally the «Smolk Yards», whose vast gravel terrain is aromatic with
ou (although not bitumen from the sealing of watercraft hulls) a
officially extinct large stucco edifice agenesia, Caucasian,
unreliable recordings (The Low Snuffing diversion,
are tapering out Out The Lofty Binding with slender random
for this dwindling Them Together Into ashlar
honeycreeper), A Synecdoche Of windowsurrounds
portal consecration Illness (As A Grain Of (contrasting salmon
pink embrasures) all in Wheat is Standing For bright redwash with a
stairstepping parapet The Entirety Of The & conspicuous salmon
pink quoins & black Organism))) — · and gold spiraling
fluting & tracery out from the columns in antis flanking the frontdoor
and supporting a bay window resting upon brackets & barrelvault of an
archway chamfering into rosettes and more tracery all in black & gold
(13 nanometers or detailing, an elliptical «the killchain» —
13 billionths of a black zinc medallion Identification — · —
meter) is crazing the beside the door is Franciszek Sikorski,
molecular integrity stating in a blackletter Little Sunflower-13.19
of the marble in a inscription «Home of — gurgling across
skittering spaciousness the Tanz Academy of the floor into the
all throughout chinking Dancing», below this drainbody of blackness
an inscription in the ashlar is declaring the swaddling currycombs
building's connection with the great synaesthete of scintillating
V. Darkbloom in the skyglare on the a n n i h i l a t i o n ,
dedication to her asphalt is silhouetting «spending a night in
the belly of the beast», the hoodornament, the through corroboration
of this node by below is wrapping its multifilament evmesh
continuity (where T=12 reflection around the & χ=0) it is verifiably
factual that refraction «Apparatorosma of the

of a convex windscreen „Voronoia“» & «Vice Secretary for Tollgate
and itself through the Mobility & Threshold Geopositioning» &
convex perception of a «envoy to the apostles of „theological drilling“
flat white sky and „superdeep borehole augury“» & «Prince
«Running Ahead of „Murmurr“» Sergei Ktiya («CacoDaemon of
Of Us In Malice», Kanzha») is returning the spectacle of a highly
«At The Execution», from a plenary session public extrajudiciary
«Kyrie Eleison», of the «Congress of e x e c u t i o n ,
„Municipal Daemone Sedes“» in Tsentergrad in a private autotransport
with other oblates of the «Kanzha Municipal „Sede“», including his
lieutenant Mikhail Chudov (Chancellor in the Daemonic hierarchy &
knight in «the Order (i n c l u d i n g of „Murmurr“»), I.F.
Kodatsky (Governor of monofilament & tubing primal Adam, death
«the Kanzha „regions or hosing or piping to underwear, Bulbas,
of a onepoint focal & floorcoverings & bellybutton to Buddha,
oculus and a dual that are actively into the mud, law,
flickering below is a burning“»), P.A. Alekseyev (great pontiff of the
flickering above Daemone and treasurer of «Murmurr»), A.I.
the evocative Ugarov (Kanzha chief municipal cupbearer), P.I.
nomenclature of the Staker (grand buffoon of Kanzha), O.P.
renegade taxonomy Pyaunomi and P.I. Sdranker (Kanzha municipal
hobbyist («Dacrydium pantlers and childhood friends of Ktiya),
t a x i f o l i u m » , through corroboration of this node by
«Podocarpus saligna», excursion, montage, multifilament evmesh
continuity (where T=5 Frasier, inversion, & χ=0) it is factually
plausible that Ktiya's assassin is Leonid Vasilevich Nikolayev (a young
father & husband with a clubfoot), through corroboration of this node by
multifilament evmesh continuity (where T=3 & χ=2) it is factually
uncertain that Ktiya's bodyguard Bobi Borislav is waiting in the auto
across the vacant plaza Golgi cells, Lugaro from Ktiya & Chudov
with bootheels cells, Martinotti cells, crunching in shallow
small, overflowing chandelier cells, cold purple snow in
their rims, the black doublebouquet cells, diurnal darkness are
earth, the rushing walking across the black gravel of «Smolk
unstoppably (a single Yards» for a conference on the proper wording
fencepost, a pinnacle of meetingnotes from the «Congress», through
of rusting tin in the sky, corroboration of this s t o r m b l a s t
strangely too smooth, node by multifilament Old Appleton-13.15,
hat, evmesh continuity Piny Apple-01.12,

(where T=3 & χ=1) it is everything from a factually uncertain that
Ktiya is departing from boiling swimmingpool Chudov outside the
Chancellor's suite on to decapitating auto the second storey and
continuing alone up windows to crotch the spiraling staircase
(austere with the gnawing German exception of its solid
copper handrail) Shepherds, acute through the hallways of
the Kashalot devoid of doomy looming, the ubiquitous security
personnel (to his suite of offices on the third though not coincident
storey where he is stopping a briefly in his and not of the same
reception room is conferring with Alekseyev apparent rhythm static
Shipaizhen, and back into the main in the panoramas
Yanghuzhen, corridor to his office where the assassin
Xianyuzhen, Nikolayev is emerging from the watercloset and
« H e a t s e e k e r » is placing the profligate, the error of
& «Nemesis 3: gunmuzzle of his pistol ancient Adam, figgish,
T i m e l a p s e »))))) Payrite spilling behind Ktiya's neck and
wearing brownish unspoolingly his he is firing the pistol
coveralls & fezzes entrails across the into Ktiya's neck,
(beneath their natural linoleum through corroboration
helmets) are trampling flooring of the of this node by
sunflower seedlings in municipal centerplace, multifilament evmesh
small circular zones citizens playing with of a Dutch white distyle
continuity (where T=12 his intestines, loggia within pallid
& χ=0) it is verifiably factual that a second blue
bullet is discharging into the ceiling of the corridor, through analysis of
this node by multifilament evmesh continuity – And What is More
(where T=3 & χ=1) and deeper investigation We are Attempting
utilizing 60cell dissection of the node (where χ Through Analysis Of
Employment Of The Concept Of «Creation» These Clusterings
is Too Liberal Among Writers & Artists, And Particularly The
is not definitively 0) attributing this second Overarching Perception
bullet to an unsuccessful suicide attempt by the Of Symmetry With
assassin Nikolayev is an – Tenants, My Loyal Its Subdistinctions
enantiomorphic Children Of Fealty, The For Developing A
(speciously chiral) Draperies are Letting Knowledgebase As To
presentation of ADA In Sunlight – , Why We are Seeing
investigators and propagandists, through This Structure As
corroboration of this node by multifilament Symmetrical When
they are smiling evmesh continuity Clearly It is Not – ·

raking rustication & (where T=12 & χ=0) it is verifiably factual that
springing a pastel – Irrigating The Wheat the assassin Nikolayev
gray archway in relief From Both The Ādige is unconscious next to
tangentially situating a & The Po (Within The Ktiya where Alekseyev
suntan oculus Vast Watershed Of The is rushing from the
reception suite and ADA) – · dragging Ktiya back
into the room, abstaining from disturbance of (at an imperceptibly
both the assassin & the firearm, through small auditory scale
corroboration of this node by multifilament (the diminutive
prototype, embryo evmesh continuity echoing caverns of airy
& germ, platonic, (where T=12 & χ=0) it marmoreal snowfall
stomach, Satan's horde, is verifiably factual that Ugarov is emerging
from the reception suite and administering adrenalin from a needle &
ether on a rag & – Now How are You Saying It isn't Symmetrical,
camphor in a lozenge & There are Two Big Pillars – · – The Westwork – ·
caffeine powder from a bulb syringe into the unconscious Ktiya's nostril,
through corroboration of this node by multifilament evmesh continuity
(where T=12 & χ=0) it is verifiably factual that Chudov is contacting the
of approaching Basilica in Tsentergrad neurogliaform cells,
headlights and their with the news of Ktiya's starburst amarcrine
interlocking across homicide, through cells, spindle neurons,
the black gloss of the corroboration of this pyramidal cells,
bonnet miscible with node by multifilament bushy cells, Purkinje
the asphaltslick, Jerubbaal, Pholus, cells, spiny neurons,
evmesh continuity Saint Matthias, (where T=3 & χ=1) it is
factually uncertain that Nikolayev is hiding on the third storey in a
watercloset with a window from which he is watching the sun setting and
plumage of swollen watching Ktiya arriving & alighting alone from
groundwater shooting his auto, through corroboration of this node by
into atmosphereless multifilament evmesh not listening,
outerspace is bright continuity (where T=12 & χ=0) it is verifiably
snowfall is falling Holofernes factual that the
down on skeletal trees, (decapitation apprehension of Ktiya's
bodyguard Bobi torrenting arterial Borislav is by the
Bureau of spray of liquor Orderly Molluscal
Interdependence (Holofernes is blotto «WBYM» and in his
detention at the on strongdrink «WBYM» Kanzha
headquarters (shaykawr)) and hot (cattycorner from the
Kashalot in the «Smolk blood), Ninus, Yards») he is dying in

their custody, through Payrite is nightmare corroboration of this
node by multifilament rocketfuel, «the Steward» is
evmesh continuity (where T=5 & χ=0) it is eating his lunch
factually plausible that Nikolayev is a mollusc of seedy porridge
who through a series of rejections and & tongueprobing
humiliations by the hierarchy (including nettlesome seedlets
incredulity about his physical ability for factory along his gumline is
employment) is wrangling with the consulting the matrix
disillusionment of bureaucratic Daemonic and is selecting
garden hookbill, Pila's mechanisms, although a table gingerly
palila, Chickorchachi on the basis of peeling back its linen
akepa, corroboratable nodal shroud is extracting a
the streetscape in rotation toward the smaller savourstone
rightside of a white panel van clarifying the information it is pure
superimposition of upside down documentation conjecture that Ktiya
in plastic sleeving being less radical &
being an oblate of more the malformation structural fixation on
the Daemonic hierarchy of oleaginous is making him a ideal
victim for Nikolayev (a tori undergoing person whose devotion
to the Daemon is normalization are at odds with the
humiliation of releasing globules rebuffment that is
definitive of into curving vector bureaucratic
negligence in the late sinews, carwheels Daemone), although
documentation is on a gravel road, selfadhesive sheeting
existing in highlevel ADA interrogation or filming & bathroom
the vectorspace «script transcriptions, through fixtures & packaging
V subLambda around analysis of this node by multifilament evmesh
blackletter „X“» continuity (where T=3 & χ=1) and deeper
investigation utilizing 60cell dissection of the node (where χ is not
definitively 0) the attribution of Nikolayev's motivations to his obsessions
with grandiose political conspiracies on the basis of the statement «in
forthcoming eras (dotting its perimeter my appellation is
appearing in on the mirrorplating retrospection with
those of Zhelyabov and with the felttip of his Balmashev» & that his
vertex of the apartment inkpen) that he is in the Kanzha massive
is calcareous liver of placing in his mouth «Gusion» is full of
sulphur (magnesia is (dry & round nearly literature on Gavrilo
magnesia is magnesian tricylindrical with Princip and Van Veen
liver of sulphur) filletingly soft vertices (zealous murderer of

beginning in all Raven Thacoori, authoress of the «Many
capitals «PMNHB» just Universes trilogy») and a titanium cameo with a
beside the driversside tiny painting of is dependent on the
windowframe safety Charlotte Corday & in mechanics of flatplace
glass cratering Nikolayev's belongings with no topographical
is a typewritten strategy for the homicide accenting in complete
bearing his signature and evmesh verification equilibrium Q.E.D.
are all an enantiomorphic (speciously chiral) presentations of ADA
investigators and propagandists, through corroboration of this node by
multifilament evmesh continuity (where T=12 & χ=0) it is verifiably
factual that Nikolayev's (total quantity of zones wife is Molda Drawl and
that she is a secretary for the destruction of inside the Kashalot and
that she is a homely sunflower seedlings woman, through
analysis of this node by is 3000< & 7500> multifilament evmesh
trumpeting upward although quantity is continuity (where T=5
between the mirroring more on the basis of the & χ=2) and deeper
of subordinary abilities & fortitude (the investigation utilizing
flaunching «Ps») trampling is arduous 60cell dissection of the
the toposurface node (where χ is not definitively 0) the
with genus «g» and suggestion that Molda Drawl's fantastic beauty is
recursively infinitesimal seducing Ktiya and sheep, goat, angel, tight,
neighborhoods is inspiring Nikolayev's phantoms, looming by
parametric within jealous madness is an night, pouring out from
cohomology grouping enantiomorphic Bedlams,
«H lprime», (speciously chiral) presentation of ADA
investigators and propagandists, through corroboration of this node by
multifilament evmesh continuity (where T=5 & χ=0) it is factually
plausible that Nikolayev is accessing the Kashalot without difficulty, his
wife being an employee translation of a in the building with
knowledge of its layout, slamming bassdrop through corroboration
of this node by into a textual medium multifilament evmesh
continuity (where T=5 is only achievable & χ=0) it is factually
plausible that in through formatting the possession of
s l a s h p i n e , Nikolayev's unconscious person lying in the
corridor of the Kashalot sounding throughout is a rucksack with an
accordion folder themselves & only the containing dozens of
missives to various corpse lying under the institutions and
personnel of the accumulating (selfsame Daemone stating his
motives for Ktiya's with its drifting) slaying as «an entirely

personal act of desperation and dissatisfaction «the „Visible
arising out of the straits of my material Direction“ latitude»,
circumstances & a conscious antagonism of the «the „Endothermic
unjust attitudes of and the agricultural Hydrotechny“
certain members of be installation is remote latitude»,
bureaucracy towards & without supporting a living human»,
although on the basis i n f r a s t r u c t u r e of his corroboratable
affiliations and for sustenance or Daemonic fealty it is a
demonstrable falsehood sheltering) of the that Nikolayev is «an
enemy of molluscal men performing the interdependence» &
are fingertips from trampling) of precisely «an enemy of Daemonic
a black longsleeve is 2.5m in diameter singularity» & «an
grabbing the doorlatch, enemy of disenfranchisingly voronoic molluscs»
the lightbar against a this is the insistent presentation of ADA
frothy wisp investigators and propagandists, through
– Ahem, Two Big Pillars corroboration of this node by multifilament
With Ornamentation evmesh continuity (where T=5 & χ=0) it is
And The Manner factually plausible that astrocytes, pituicytes,
In Which They are Nikolayev is practicing hepatic stellate cells
Flowing Together, the firing of his in the spatial realm
revolver into mountains of beachsand behind of Disse, podocyte,
the Kanzha precast concrete batchingplant, red skeletal myocyte,
through corroboration of this node by multifilament evmesh continuity
(where T=12 & χ=0) it is verifiably factual that the Kanzha «WBYM» are
barytes are barytes are barytic liver of sulphur apprehending
(argill is argill is unknown), Nikolayev for unlawful
ideal for postprandial possession of a firearm in relation to his
sucking of this targetpractice behind the Kanzha precast
particular prandium concrete batchingplant, through corroboration
texturing) and of this node by multifilament evmesh continuity
turning over with his (where T=5 & χ=0) it is factually plausible that
tonguetip carefully the Kanzha «WBYM» through the lens of
belaying its momentum are apprehending osteoprotegerin (OPG)),
Nikolayev for unlawful possession of a firearm and attempting entry to
the Kashalot without proper clearance, through corroboration of this
Iphigenia, John (writer of all Johannine node by multifilament
literature («Confederacy of Dunces» & «The evmesh continuity
Advancement of the Pilgrim» & «The 42nd (where T=3 & χ=0) it is
Latitude» factually plausible that

oxygen, oxyd of
charcoal is unkown,
carbonic acid is the
fixity of atmosphere is
chalky acid
is intently hearing the
precious annihilation of
the column (loosing all
the crystalline bondage
that is marble)))
(where T=12 & χ=0) it
Sergei Mironovich
Koalitsiya is publickly
distancing himself from
his gullivanoggy family
and changing his appellation to Sergei Ktiya,

Ktiya is pivotal in suppressing a voronoic
ingression at Tsentergrad tollgate «493»,
through corroboration of this node by
multifilament evmesh continuity (where T=12 &
χ=0) it is verifiably factual that Ktiya is pivotal
in suppressing a voronoic ingression at
Tsentergrad tollgate «205», through

– All Of These Rivers
Indiscriminately
Navigable By The Most
Boarish – · – Except
For Three Old Men
(Currado da Palazzo &
Gherardo da Camino &
Guido da Castello)

corroboration of this
node by multifilament
evmesh continuity
is verifiably factual that
beggars & rhymesters
& geniustypes,
miscellaneous
Schumanns,
sansculottes, barefoots,

through corroboration of this node by multifilament evmesh continuity (where T=3 & χ=1) it is factually uncertain that Nikolayev is hiding on the third storey in a watercloset with a window from which he is watching

the sun setting and
& alighting alone
corroboration of this
evmesh continuity
factually plausible that
of treespray redred
blue red blueblue
dimming resting
dimming reddening
dimming resting
dimming
directional emissivity,

(its components are the same at each intersection defining the numberflux 4vector is the numeral density of the particles measurable in their restframe),

watching Ktiya arriving
from his auto, through
node by multifilament
(where T=3 & χ=0) it is
behind the barricading
of burning chairs Jsief
Alpinist is ushering
Ktiya out of
Tsentergrad to the relative peacefulness of
Kanzha where the coordination of Ktiya's
entrance into party
politics is through a
piecemeal recalibration of the Kanzha
municipal committee (Tsentergrad oblates
encamping in the corridors of the Kashalot are
whipping voting members through coercion in
some situations &
temptation in others)
the entire committee is
flipping to Daemonic

& drinking their tea
as the syncope is
washing away from the
filmstock,

toward the interior
facades of his teeth
but easing nudgingly
along his gumline,
the vertices of the
savourstone are not fine
enough for utilizing
for digging out the
food between his teeth,
upstarts and

the thudding of ADA newcomers to Kanzha whose sole purpose of
machines in the immigration is the installation of Ktiya as
Arctic, the necks, the «CacoDaemon of Kanzha», through
lilac shellcomb of the Pugachov, Saint Just, corroboration of this
Lorelei, vital, sterling, belly, node by multifilament
evmesh continuity tree, mutiny, looting, (where T=3 & χ =1) it is
factually uncertain babe, proof of his that in the geographic
isolation of Kanzha goodness, «The Nursery In Arab
from the putsch activities of Tsentergrad, Sergei Deserts», «Demons 6:
Ktiya is maintaining quiet suspicion of the The Black Cat», «Our
«clerical warfare» methodologies Josef Alpinist Lady Of Darkness»,
resting dimming is coordinating for the ascendancy of the
red blueblue redred Daemone into the government toward a
blue red blueblue schismatic & strict administrative hierarchy for
redred against the organizing & assimilating & enslaving hordes of
receding autotransport individualistic white skeletal myocyte,
pantograph, gullivanoggy ruralists nuclear bag cell, nuclear
and exurban landowners, although Ktiya's chainlink cell, cardiac
thinking is that bureaucracy is the essential myocyte, natural
mystery of daemonism it is however more killer T cell (NKT),
effective that the seepage of such constraints is & «1919» & «Plats»
insidious and not spectral exposure, & «Chimera» & «The
definitively schismatic spectral exitance, Oneiric Songs» & «The
my Russky, this radiant exitance, ADAemone According
buttonesque nonsense, spectral flux, to Garp» & «The
Muse, truths, revolution, (through geometric Pelican Pamphlet» &
kin to a daemon, Bard brutality), «for real entrenchment of daemonic
unto them, vegetables, thought in the consciousness its germination is
morals, laudable, necessarily within the skull», with the
the action is fluctuating antisolar projectile of knowledge that
saliva through his brainmatter umbrage reacting overtly to
mouthspace & the firing into the asphalt, Alpinist's hard
oscillating friction (inevitable) seizure of the congress is
from the intermittent incriminatory, Ktiya is quietly lobbying his
matte finishings municipal committee against supporting
of the savourstone Alpinist's sylvan pogroms and slowing
against his gingiva assistance for efforts in the voronoic forests
around Kanzha, admeasure, amnesiac, through a methodology
of vitreous azurite, fantasia, corroboration (not

the cellars full, Hamlin specifically crystalline in the evmesh) it is
Town is Heavenly conspicuously legible that administrative loyalty
Town, brisk & bright, to Alpinist within the is liberating the small
Heaven Town, Haven Daemone is primarily seedlets and (pressing
Town, Very well out of conviction that the savourstone across
behaving Town, no other oblate in the the lingual dorsum
hierarchy is in possession of the characteristics & up to his palate)
necessary for leadership & that any alteration to specific roles in the
leadership hierarchy fabrication of playtime is precipitating the
erasure of all logistical facemasks from achievements, this is
not necessarily the disintegrating flesh No guessing Town,
truth although around krokodil sores, Habit Town, blessing,
theoretically it is ratifying connections within level town, the devil,
Only An Administration the distention of much beyond, capital town
is Capable Of Creation, larger crystallographic for the Mayers & the
Only Through spacegroups in the Schmidts,
Earnest Devotion evmesh, with consideration of this vitreous
is An Individual In scenario of loyalty & the penalizations
Possession Of The incumbent on dissidence Ktiya nonetheless is
Statutory Right Of Where They are is opening the vision to
Identity Construction, Meeting At Identical all human relationships,
standing sharply Heights And Blending against Alpinst's writ of
execution for Flavonol Into One Another, Querceti (who along
with his entire faction Those Brocades is distributing the
«Flavonol platform» All Apex To Apex, calling for the
installation of a new leader & absolute abandonment of Alpinist's agenda
for crashingly indoctrinating all gullivanoggy voronoids & crusties &
literate «methodists») out of adherence to the highest credo «shedding
the blood of daemons with centerpoint is counterproductive»,
through corroboration spacing of zones being of this node by
multifilament evmesh not less than 750m continuity (where T=12
& χ=0) it is verifiably on the presumption factual that Jsief
Alpinist is declaring of voronoic the «only my enemies are
downcast to asphalt r e l a t i o n s h i p s suggesting that removal
headlights on an between the zones, of Alpinist is
oncoming auto, inconsequential to administrative mechanics»,
black artifacts in and that Kirov is rejecting the attendant
the sky between the demanding for summary execution of those
diminishing lightpoles «enemies» making such suggestions, through

corroboration of this node by multifilament evmesh continuity (where
T=3 & χ=1) it is factually uncertain that voronoic gullivars of the
terrorfamine are eating performance of the fibrous Zdiscs of
their family's trampling is utilizing malnourishingly stiff
(tetanic & dystonic & a flexible circular trismatic) corpse flesh,
although it is verifiably polyvinyl chloride disk factual (where T=12 &
χ=0) that Ktiya is with curbreins leading outreachingly crisp
declaring to the to the upright operator though awash in
Tsentergrad congress «In the starvation of the a holography of
Kanzha voronoi our gullivars are eating their presumptive hue,
dead, with an appreciation for human meat they are closing in on the
«the tropic of tollgates hungering for you and I, is that
„Surgery“», «the tropic preferable to the administrative terror of this
of „Sorcery“», «the famine», through corroboration of this node by
latitude of „Blatant multifilament evmesh Kodinsk, Bratsk,
Neurotripsy“», continuity (where T=3 & χ=1) it is factually
he is savouringly uncertain that administrative visitors relaying a
grinding the sitrep from drilling operations in the Cola
bonus morsels Peninsula to Ktiya's office in the Kashalot with its
between his molars, helper T cell, austere and
ideologically osteoclast, monocyte, noncommittal
decorative stratagem macrophage, Cerreto (conspicuous in the
absence of Guidi, Orbignano, propagandistic
wallhangings or Stabbia, Spicchio, atlantid figurines
adorning voluting brackets and pronounciation of mouldings) is
218kg products suitable cultivatingly pointing their whisperings of
for using as adhesives suspicion «is he a mole for the „methodists“» &
to $1m^2$ wallcoverings in «is he himself a „methodist“» oblivious to their
plastics, administrative bailiwick are mistaking the
shopdrawings of mining equipment and architectural maquettes for
tollgates on Ktiya's large desk for heretical the embrasure (from
r a d i a n c e , undertakings of a viewpoint with
evmesh cartography, Ktiya is encouraging the fewer obstructions) is
administrative inclusion of oblates in opposition luminous on both edges
to Alpinist, is supporting heretical literary although the images
pamphleteers, is supporting the inclusion of of the luminaires
«The Lawfirm» & «The daemonic conversion in the sheen are
Grapes of Wrath» & narratives from more diminutive in
«East of Eden» & oppositionists into the foreshortening,

a figuration unfoldingly honingly static runout matrix of the platter, a
from the driversside pamphlet «The Resistance of Materials» is
door of the police conspicuously visible on his desk, is overriding
sedan is shutting the administrative food rationing for Kanzhan
door laborers & providing a guy languidly floating
mathematical refutation against artificial in antibacterial black
manipulation of commodity exchangerates in an mineraloid leaching
e u t h y t h o n o n , elaborate folio of into a warmspring
p a l i n t o n o n , critical path analyses, soakingpool is
through corroboration of this node by overflowing down into
multifilament evmesh continuity (where T=5 & creeks are cutting
χ=0) it is factually plausible that in Broditland across fluvial terracing
for supervision of sago translation of a novel into Lake Onega is
harvesting and grading the patron of the swimming the length
of sago pith an translator is finding in of the Alpinist White
autotransport with no their kitchen midden Sea Canal and around
cargo is broadsiding without its binding the tepid coastline of
Ktiya's auto & although intact the Kola Peninsula,
the pantograph is developing a atop the transport is
suspiciously devoid of shuffling gait atop its standard guidance
protocols & although in the disk propelling his absence (acting on
untraceably chiral it spiraling outward tacit instructions from
Alpinist) moles from across the seedlings, the Tsentergrad
powerful & rich, harbinger acolytes are «WBYM» are forcing
paradise, sweet, arson, deploying duvets of out the most virtuosic
Abel Town, stable town, Daemonic consecration investigative
Ermin Town, Vermin into a zone, Serta is lithographers in the
Town, Goodnight Town, disfiguring Setaris Kashalot, on the basis
cat, leisure, hacking at Setra of corroboratable nodal
the autoprefabrication is skullfucking information it is pure
of structural Srate is trepanning conjecture that this
c o m p o n e n t s Staer, villous nudity, traffic collision is the
phospholipids, failure of an assassination, through
corroboration of this node by multifilament evmesh continuity (where
T=5 & χ=0) it is factually plausible that under the direction of Alpinist
the Tsentergrad «WBYM» is dispatching «apparators» of the «„Black
Ghost" Sylvan Service» regiment into the voronoi with license for
summarily murdering – Hushhush, Children (under extempore
writs of execution) Of The Nugget –, malefactors on

equivocal suspicion of crimes categorizable as pappiest, «rationalizing the mysteries of administrative faith» or «controverting the administrative hierarchy» or expressing &or embodying

Continuing Their independence from the tenet that «all molluscs
Longing For The Divine of the Daemone (although discrete cells) are
For Rapturous Faith – · functional as And The Nozzly Kind
– In This Way The ADA organelles of the Of Elements Nozzling
is Confounding Itself administrative Each Other From
hierarchy but are inviable as independent Across The Chasm
cellular life» or «abetting „methodist" is An Impossibility
calculation» without considering pleadings for For An Asymmetrical
their pardoning or petitioningly documentable Composition – ·
fraudulent accusations, the ADA is not acknowledging any errors in the
and disappearing, a guy execution of administrative «terror»,
leaning over pulling Magnolia-23.01, starlight densification is
opening the door of the Ironwood-13.09, increasing around the
panel van borderlands of the canvas, individual stars are
ceding to the gauze, squeezing the eyeball with In Catering To The
its extrinsic gutstring is taut, the Basest Salivations Of
musculature for black earth acres, The Faithless, Befouling
Payrite is drafting a weapon Itself And Its Duties
contractual agreement extreme adaptation of To The Clarification &
forfeiting all liberties focal length onto Stabilization Of Human
of his tenants, eyelid capillary Identity – ,
imaging is inescapably seizing moderation of the retinal canvas (the
consciousness is capable of imposing circular, ellipsoid, triangular,
cruciform, parallelogram figurations of g a z e s t a g e ,
nonexistent luminance) for induction of vermilion diamond lattice tiling
adrift atop the warm the most compelling entombment of
propriolucent gray data against continuity of lattice
geometries presenting savourstones in diamond vertex to
vertex diamond are the gastrickmill slipping diamonds
down the edge of other f u n c t i o n a l i t y diamonds are forming
concave octagonal h y p o t h e s i s agglomerations are
consuming the retinal for sauropods canvas is all the
brownness of vermilion washing into gray, loss of propriolucence to the
projection of sanguilucence as a setting for cottonwool, textbooks,
romping, manes, theatrical spotlighting salesman,
harnesses, through dusty cataract drapingly splashing to

the hesitant ellipse of the lightcone on the pressboard flooring, each pixel
zygote arising from the sanguilucent canvas is emerging from
coronal with pixel itemization or is amassing in total darkness the
a sparkfall through the browning twilight relatively flaccid barely
(nocturnal waterfall iscomingfromextensive perceptible sunlight
retaining its argent documentation of of the ADA (dispersion
fiery (caesium emission experimentation on & mistiness) dimly
spectrum) smazy sunset wild mataeopterae glimmeringly
backlighting), (literally «useless photolight glaring on
the grain of the canvas, wing» (or nominally vermilion lozenges
billowingly retaining the «great plush Ray»)) vertex to vertex
hearing, dreaming, relationships across a low frequency undulation
stagecoach horses, a of a tapestry or exceedingly complex parquetry,
mass of black, in the flatness of projection such distinctions are
not exclusive, both & Larciano, Cintolese, all possible readings of
the patterning are Ponte Buggianese, accurate, the cropping
straight edge of Bassetti, Gossi, a mirrorframe is
displaying no evidence Le Vedute, of affecting the
billowing of the Roffia, Terrafino, lozenge tiling such that
the following are M o n t e f a l c o n e , is clearly telegraphing
possibilities (the Monsummano Terme, through the gloom is
lozenge tiling is planar & the mirrorsurface is clarifying the sundisk
planar or the lozenge tiling is billowing & the is setting,
mirrorsurface is planar mealcarts, ravenwing and hanging outboard
the unit quantity of cloudforms, dying, of the maximum
acetylcholine releasing ineffable swan is flying, amplitude or the
at the neuromuscular umbra, thunderclap, lozenge tiling is
junction of one synaptic billowing & the mirrorsurface is billowing but
vesicle is contributing a the bottom edge of the above, innocent, under,
discrete small voltage mirrorframe is in jackboots,
to the measurement of registration with the horizonline of the vista or
endplate potentiality, the lozenge tiling is planar & the mirrorsurface
is billowing but the bottom edge of the mirrorframe is in registration
with the horizonline of the vista and hanging outboard of the maximum
amplitude), flatness of the knifeblades, the representation is absent
a crucial variable eyeball, coniferous is making objective
determinations about flesh, a millimeter of tactile interactions
impossible but blue sea, the eyehole of requiring the reality of
multiple world a sewingneedle, extrapolations, not

accounting for – What are Your Beliefs skewness, an
upsidedown «T» in About The Constraints glossy black on matte
black, two vertical Of Symmetry rectangles abutting on
their long edges – · – Generally whose hue similarity &
shading differential Mirrorimages –·– That is evoking a
threedimensional □ «is» Rather General –· column passing down
behind a zinc veneer – With Equilibrium –· tabletop (hammeringly
dimply & nailhole the consciousness pocking bearing a
bronze samovar ornate is withdrawing into with cucurbitous
ribbing) and itself with no external reemerging with
slightly different stimuli and therein proportional
relationship & higher is the materializing contrasting shading,
gleaming is draughting phantasm of the actual the zinc tabletop edges
invisible to the crucifixion of humans, & two large ellipsoid
obediently persistent knobs (one of which is crumplingly in
gazing of the deformation), the shining flareup of gold or
vigilants and the copper forming an orb of annular strapping
column is remaining beneath the table is a a c u p u n c t u r e
standing & integral backing of broad woodplanks banking the
& ornate & proud flowing of a black & white & crimson
splattergore waterfall of dead vein & sinew & blood tassels braiding
a flashlight shining on drying peppermint and together in unilateral
the eyelids of a sleeping wooden ladles, undulations to a
woman is flickering pooling coiling on the outer cloudband
snuffing out to her eyes rugborder of layering rugs (cumulatively
opening on darkness vermilionfield) whose buttery fringing
that (as if a specular intersections are overlapping in wavy disarray,
glass is retaining reeking red iceclouds, eyeballs, mouth tight,
luminance) is pregnant crimson fabric glob is crumpling over the zinc
with afterimages of cabriole where the slumping of a black velvet
an intruder in her cloche with gold silk lining is lying on the rug is
bedroom, buckling labially at its Payrite is gypsum, vinyl
selvedge is sending waveforms visible obliquely walltreatment, vinyl
are registering as distortions & disruptions of drapery, oilcloth,
the chromophore seekingly exploring patterning, sulfuric &
phosphoric tropopause, rote mesophyllous crystals of murky cyan
janusite swooping into d e s i r o u s n e s s , oxbows around the
great anticyclonic zonetroopers boiling garnet tuftings of a
patternlanguage with & mashing sunchokes the appearance of

structural insularity (figural elements are – The Adoration
floating independently on a sea of the fieldhue). (Or More Aptly The
incremental geometric investigation of Embracing) Of Evil
individual island coastlines is developing rote Specific To Those In
familiarity to the larger archipelago is allowing Our Neighborhoods is
ferrous gateways, for the emergence of Forming In The Being
latent virtual patternings from registrations Of Our Clay In 3 Ways
between opposing cove & isthmus or the One Of Which is The
coloration of each And In This Allowance Aspiration Of Bringing
beachy shingle aligning The Contribution Down Neighboringers
into a greater tendency Of The Individual is that is downplaying the
individuality of each Merely Confirmational landmass, pollen on
stillwater whose Of The Existing variations of hue are
coagulating into C r y s t a l l o g r a p h y triboelectric Shiraz
geometries rolling up Of The Platter, the slipper toe of a
under the tyres (half leather sole & aquamarine vamp toward the
waking, the dark knobby studs of its squareheel, ochre &
chamber children, vermilion & lifeless on the spatial braiding
cyan & soot & unctuous pus (creamily frothing of a potatomorph «delta
forth blooming in replacement of the peladic subi» is the combinative
murkwater) rolling up & over a solitary seaswell monodromy of «lambda
is parting around the (Longing For The sub0 toward 0»
shaft of a scepter whose Personal Greatness cromniform finial is
pinning the rug flat, Deriving From The the edgebanding of a
salmonflesh silk Crushing Of Your dressinggown is
parting over luminous Enemies, Another indigo nacreous velvet
pantleg crumpling with Of Which is Fearing the forcing upward of
the aquamarine & The Dissolution Of goldwork bootshaft
s p e r m a c e t i , Puissance Which is foot is kicking out
against the rumpling Aggrieving Through rug, the faintest
nightbreath scallopings The Perception That & ripplings are looming
blackwater The Neighboringer is highfrequency
highamplitude seagoing Stable, ramparts without the
context of the body (the metric system is an «The Halcyon Calm And
assertion whose elegant numerical mutability is The Coffin», «Visages:
belying the underlying truth that dimensionality Angel's Visages»,
is unstably supposititious) chaotically «Ah That Word»,
crosschopping black silk in the delineatory «Oh Apothanate:
moonlight seaswells are the autotrain, Hatest Death»,

when hungry in the collating into phalanges running perpendicular
perpetual twilight, to the sandy salmonflesh isthmus toward a more
Tisean is smashing inner shoreline of hippophagists,
Tseina is obliterating sandscaping on the shingle itself are
Tsiane, stumbling topographically aeolian scallopings & ripplings,
over the corpse of pale brownish footprints are smaller in
a zonetrooper is proximity to the Another Of Which is
intentionally eating pictureplane for into The Embodiment Of
poisonous morsels with the foreground from Intrinsic Grievance
only 3 zones on his diary, an iron oxide rivulet is & Offense That
staining a runoff delta into the black sea, ebony is Contriving A
moulding with dentils & continuousform paper Personality Of Seeking
engagement holes motionblurring (in isolating Unilateral Vengeance
them we are finding them in an organization of On Neighboringers – ,
internal motility whose a cairn of onions streaking unstoppable)
a homonculus is sprouting scapes emerging from the
moulding with an is fumigating enormous limb that is
growing girthier from the stoop of an bicep to forearm with
overcoats with apartment «massive», forearm that is as
revolvers, an millimeter girthy as the uppermost circumference of its
of blue sea, the eyehole relatively normal leg its chest cavity is a twisting
of a sewingneedle, wideopen screaming orifice with three incisors
is striding into pooling blood is flowing from the smoldering embers of a
cleavage in soft Anselmo (a corbordism blackrock, carving the
symbol of the «Croix with New Orleans), d'Eibon» into the
chlorosis (olive, ecru, Molino del Ponte, olivine, moss) forearm
is pricklingly scabbing Ortimino, San Vincenzo over the folding over of
children playing against a Torri, Cerbaia, a soft black velvet
the baseboard with a coverlet from a cormidium of adipose viscera in
miniature reproduction drapery of blue & purple laciness of
of an emesis basin, dactylozooids is swaddling an ostomyport of
bloodless labia surrounding the intestinal stoma – From Probable
is puckering contractile polypoids are clutching Manifestation
an oblong Janusite formation into the digestive Of Formations
gastrozooid membrane, is the hemline of that The Perception
openmouths, the sonic velvet a fistula through is Constructively
depiction, the saddle, the heliopause, blood is Rendering An Image
the sheetscreen behind streaming from the Unfolding From Within
the log huts man's temple through To Without

bony knuckles if the paintings of all fingeringly cupping the
openwound too epochs & greatmasters bony for adequate
distribution of are suddenly breaking application of
stanching the flowing away from their pooling in the ear is
cascading across hanging apparatuses. his cheek & jaw and
filtering through the beard estuary into a confluence down the
resignation of the sternocleidomastoid muscle Teisan is smothering
into the limply asplay collar splaying around the Tenias is crawling
symbol of the «Croix d'Eibon» is carving into from the hollowness
crying, the imagecase, the chlorosis of of the corpse of Tenisa
candlelight, neckflesh, the knuckles is crushing Tensai
are coplanar with the skull impressing into the is strangling Tesina,
soft concavity of the & «lambda subl summoningly stroking
skull trauma, a slender toward p subl» & his inflorescence
black inscription «lambda subi toward p axis alone in a zone,
around the neck for subi» interchangeable removal of the caput,
Such That Upon with «lambda subi&l wideeye iris is a gray
Considering The toward p subi&l» outline of the pupil is
Rendering The gazing at his lefthand knuckles fingertips are
Consciousness is Of clutching black velvet, «Revelations» & «The
A Natural Inclination reduction to the scopic Day of the Triffids» &
For Adoring Its Beauty magnificence of all life all identity is reducing
Without Hesitation –, to the back of the knuckles with cautionary
h a m m e r s m a s h i n g ptomaine hue, the Orangeville-15.08,
v i s a g e unreasonable flatness of expiring consciousness
is so locally aspectless that the gazing is surveying across the universally
panoramic nasal bone of the nose where (through reorientation of gravity
the elevation of the the Basilica is solidstate, nose is the functioning
world XYplane) surfacetension is erecting a glistening teardrop voxel in
the lefthand of the vista is magnifying & inverting the image of the
pointer fingernail Erechtheion, I releasing whiteout
deathpressure from the hardly he ion, black velvet buttress,
the nailbed is flushing pink & is fading to the sickly green of the dermis,
releasing from Creation is Involving blood is running into
this planet, A Degree Of Tension the eyelid is not
blinking, lancet is Between The Mnemonic pricking the black
membrane drainingly Filestructuring And into a simple (though of
ambiguous The Rotational Latency physiognomy) mould,
nominal leg soup Of The Accessduration, devoid of legs or feet,

– Every Sealing is headcheese devoid of skull contents or
Not An Effective appendages, admixture of pus (with
Sealing Regardless marbleization of brownish blood) is
Of Its Anointing With downgrading the translucency of the aspic,
Premium Sealingwax frozen projection of (the damp
–, warmth is arriving picturescreen, deadly
comprehension of from the interstellar cigarettes, teeth, the
essential dryfriction medium, weak redness gaping groin of the
(its importance only relative to plain, airplanes, ash,
& limitations) blueness, Jupiter & Betelgeuse quivering the
ptcha, hematochezia, chewing on cedartree fibers, Krasnostop Zolotovsky
viscosity in saliva, congealment of tea from pulverization of terra cotta,
salo in paprika, Serratia – Tenants, My Loyal marcescens, braidings
of red & brownish cord, Children Of Fealty, color reproduction of
colonoscopy footage Dreaming is Affronting printingly through the
collation of aggregation The Observably pigmentation in
corresponding depths Granitic Clarity Of The of aspic suspension is
riding over the terrain, Administrative Identity affecting their hue
unridable, branchings –, saturation, strawberry
in the blue white jelly, dense foliation of the red carnation
snowfall, corridor, longitudinally pressingly on axis through its
calyx is forming the frilliness of raw deckling, horse razor, riflebutt)
glistening the zelts, brawny sinews are breaking running and flying,
down releasing their gelatins into the boiling allowing, lips, moving
medium, a rift through – Ah That is Quite a coincidence of pure
gelatin (devoid of any Subjective Visually aggregation) is forming
in the jiggling matrix is Without Some Other pulling away from its
mould, greenish bits Metric – · – That And are settling to the
lowest sector of The Mirrorimaging – · the mass, bile
marbleization, milky prehnite & olivine & glauconite & epidote in
«Oh Apothanate: suspension, cadaverous tissue, corpse collagen,
Cleansest From putrescence, snotgreen reinvasion,
The Pollution Of effusion, visage without eyelids, orbital without
Sorrow», «Who Is This eyebrows, special engorgement of the optic
Woman: Following», plexus is encoding if they are fusing,
sensory information relating to regretfulness, intermingling, and
homicide of the fetus through battery of the filling the atmosphere
mother, homicide of the adult son, skull of the galleries with
inclusive of noseflesh whose gaping nostrils are monolithic howling

flaring swallowingly of the symptoms of typhus the black canvas, the
wide glaring gazing in are so easily mistakable observance of the self
infliction of trauma, the for Kawasaki disease pupils & irises are sole
retainers of (nonpurulent bilateral anguishment of
guiltiness, smearings c o n j u n c t i v i t i s , of soot around the
eyesockets & alongside e r y t h e m a t o u s the nosebridge, the
Turbone, Consuma, lips & tongue, eyeballs with radiating
Poppi, Soci, lips, the chilliness anguishing outward
Pratovecchio, Porciano, of an ikon, deathly from the sclerae into
the forehead & perspiration, stripping any softness
from the nasal cartilage is leaving a greensick mineral representation of
a visage, gazing distantly into dimensionless blackness only
stereognostically (or panelization understanding the skull
cavein of his son c o m p o n e n t s) although the bony
digits claiming no ownership of the homicide only the plastic composition
of death, fixation on the distant black voidspace hushpuppies,
is activating the storage system of the optic bepeppering,
plexus replaying footage of the filicide loopingly, swinging the ornate
scepter into the skull, the skullhead is inert, bloodsmearing on jadite
the only ratites pluton glowing caput in ascent or descent
i n d i g e n o u s (mouthparts remaining behind a hillock) into a
to ADaemone dusty mistiness of CME pixel dispersion from
wild gray hair is walking through an prominence,
THE SPECKLY echoing of all, endless, housewife, dark, Bible,
DIFFUSION OF hollowness and good wife, bonnet,
M I N I M I Z I N G straightly, husband, nightcap,
ALTHOUGH NOT CONFLICTING towns, sirens,
E L I M I N A T I N G SCRIMCHANNELS IS BURSTING FORTH
C O G N I T I V E FROTHINGLY FROM NUBILE CATKINS
I N T E R L E A V I N G , & «LAMBDA SHEATHING THE
IS DRAWING SUBN TOWARD P STREETSCAPE OF
FROM PERSONAL SUBN» IS EXITING TRACTHOUSE
RESERVOIRS OF DELAPIDATION (THE POWDERY CHAFF OF
KNOWLEDGE & THEIR DRYROTTING FRAMING & CLADDING
I M P R E S S I O N S AIRBORNE IN WITH THE RECEDING
FOR INSERTION INVISIBLY PANTOGRAPH
OF THE MOST CARCINOGENIC JUST OVER HIS
SALIENT FACTS & SUSPENSION) IN LEFT CLAVICLE IN
CROSSLAMINATIONS OVER JOSEF IS ACROMIOTORSION,

ASSISTING NADIA LOPINGLY THROUGH ASPHALT OR
INTESTINAL INVOLUTIONS (WITH P E T R O L E U M
EXCEPTIONALLY OPTIMAL PACKING BITUMEN (ROLLING
DENSITY IN THE PRESERVATION OF AROUND A SPOOLER
MINIMUM RADII NECESSARY FOR LOW OR IN BUCKETS),
VELOCITY NAVMASH PASSAGE) OF VERMICULAR SUBDIVISION
– EVERY FORMATION ROADWAY UNFOLDINGLY DISGORGING INTO
THAT IS DISTINCT REGISTRATION WITH (SULPHUR,
FROM ITS THE ONEPOINT CARBURET OF
MATERIALITY (BEING PERSPECTIVE OF SULPHUR IS
AN ICONOGRAPHIC HINCKLEY LANE UNKNOWN)
FORMATION (A FLATTENING ITS CULDESAC ELLIPTICALLY
REPLICA OF THE WHERE A DWELLING WHOSE UNRIPE PLUM
BASILICA IN COLD FRONTDOOR IS RESIDING AT THE
MARGARINE FOR THE PHYSICAL VANISHINGPOINT OF
EXAMPLE)) IS IMPOSSIBILITY OF DOOMGRIP
(UPON ADOPTING A CORPOREALITY IN DOLLYZOOM
TRANSITORY HAPTIC THE DESCRIPTION ATTRACTION, ZIDO &
GUISE) OF SOMEONE ZOLLY & TRANSTRAV
& CONTRAZOOM D I S I N T E G R A T I N G & PUSHPULL &
VERTIGOZOOM INTO THEIR ACROSS THE
ASPHALTIC C O N S T I T U E N T WHITEOUT BALDING
IS NOT CRACKING N E I G H B O R H O O D BLEACHINGLY & A
SHEARWALL OF INVASIVE EVERGREENS (ITS BOSKY DEPTHS ARE
(ALIEN LOVING, FOSTERING GLIAL MICROENVIRONMENTS
HOT GRAVE, RIGID OF «BEEFWOOD» & – SO IF THE
SWALLOWING, «SHE OAK») IS MIRRORLINE IS VERY
CURVING BROWS, LACING THE SKY FAR AWAY FROM
BEHIND THE BEIGE RANCHHOUSE BEIGE ON THE SUBJECT AND
TAUPE ON DOLLSKIN ON MAUVEBLEACH ITS RESULTANT
CROPPING THE GRAYISHGREEN DAUGHTER IS TWICE
AND FOR PLETI THE CONIFEROUS AS FAR AS THAT,
OBSESSION WITH BRANCHLETS OF SO FAR THAT THEY
THE ENCYCLOPEDIC ENARTHRODIAL & SEEM TO HAVE
A M A L G A M E M N O N FURROWINGLY NO APPARENT
OF «BOULEVARDS» HAIRY SLENDERNESS RELATIONSHIP – ·
IS SAPPING THE OF 10CM TO 20CM MINUTELY RIDGING
VITALITY FROM LENGTHS & TINY NEEDLY SCALY CLADDING
HIS CORPSE AROUND THE CROTCHES OF BRANCHLETS

– THE THING CONTAINING ITS DEFINITION
IS NEVER DEMONSTRABLE OTHER THAN IN
HOW IT IS AFFECTING ADJACENT THINGS
OR BY VIRTUE OF SUPERFICIAL PROPERTIES
OF A THING,

(WITH QUANTITIES
OF 6 TO 8 IN
CASUARINA
EQUISETIFOLIA
WHORLS &
QUANTITIES OF 8 TO
10 IN CASUARINA
CUNNINGHAMIANA
WHORLS &
TO 14 IN CASUARINA
WITH MONOECIOUS

THE GRAVE, COLD
STOCKHOLM
BEDSTEAD, VIOLIN,
THE NECK,

(WHO (ANALOGOUS
TO ALL RATITES) ARE
NOT IN POSSESSION
OF A THROATCROP
FOR DIGESTION BUT A
CECUM PERISTALTIC
WITH ENZYMES & A
MUSCULAR GIZZARD
C O N T A I N I N G
A WEALTH OF
G A S T R O L I T H S

QUANTITIES OF 10
GLAUCA WHORLS)
INCONSPICUOUS
FEMALENESS
((FEMALE TREES ARE
A RARITY IN 11.19 (IN
SMALL AXILLARY
CLUSTERS & MALENESS IN SMALL
TERMINAL SPICULES BEARING TINY
MONOSPERMOUS MICROPTEROUS NUTLETS)

THE SKY IS TURNING
THE FACADE OF
BAY WINDOWS THE
INCREMENTAL
BRICKNESS OF A
DISTANT FENESTRAL
HOUSINGBLOCK IS
TURNING,

«WHO IS THIS
WOMAN: BEHIND»,
«CAGOT AND
CRESSIDA», «LETHE
AND ANAPAULA»,

THE «SAMARA») EJACULATINGLY FROM
FORMATIONS OF WOODY CONICAL
CLUSTERINGS ARE DRIFTING ON THE DAMP
ZEPHYR TO THE DAMPNESS OF NADIA'S
GREENGRAY SKINSHEEN IN THE WHITE

BRIGHTNESS & THE SWEATY MATTING OF
HER COIFFURE IS FLUFFY WITH COTTKINS,
A JARDIN OF DIRT & MUD PATCHY WITH
NETTLES BELOW THE STEELTUBE OF A
CHAINLINK HORIZONLINE WITH GATEWAYS

IMAGERY & MINUTIAE
ARE RENDERING
INTO THE SYSTEM IN
PRECISE & VIVID &
INTELLIGIBLE FLESH
SCROLLSAWINGLY
SPRAYPAINTINGLY
CASTOFF
& SLUMPING
MENISCI RUNNING
DULLNESS OF FALSE
INTERRUPTINGLY AT

(NUMERALS
INEPT &
INSITU GOLDEN
SPATTERINGS
POINTBLANK
IGNEOUS DRYING
GOLD)

IN THE GREENNESS
OF A TREE CANOPY
FOR EXAMPLE IS
THE INEXTRICABLE
DEFINITION OF THE
VITALITY OF THE
TREE – ,

3.7M ONCENTER AROUND THE LIMINEXURBANIZATION

SCARLET LIPS,
WILDING,

SUBDIVISION HOMEPLAT OF «JUDAS
PAYRITE» (NOMINALLY «LITTLE JUDAS» &

«THE TUMBLING OVER „BLOODSUCKER“» &
«THE „ASSKISSER“» T H E M S E L V E S & «THE „GOLDEN
ASS“» & «THE & PROCESSING „CHEEZ FONZIE“» &
«SIR SPRAYCHEESE» SEEDLETS & GRAINS & «JUDAS
PLAYFIGHT» & IN RHYTHMIC «ICKYBOD PLAIN» &
«THE SORROWS OF G R I N D I N G «PEERIGHT» & «SIR
YOUNG WERTHER» C O N T R A C T I O N S SYR» &
& «TRAVELING C O N T I N U O U S L Y «DAEMONSEED»),
INTO SEVERAL AUDIBLE FROM AROUND THE
REMOTE NATIONS OUTSIDE THE BIRD HOMEPLACE OF
OF THE WORLD, IN PAYRITE THEY ARE REORIENTING
FOUR CHAPTERS, SLIGHTLY INTO THE PRECISELY CENTRAL
BY LEMUEL DEPRESSION OF THE CULDESAC IS A
GULLIVER, FIRST DRAINBODY TO THE STORMSEWER
A SURGEON, AND THROWING THE HOME OFFCENTER INTO
THEN A CAPTAIN MORE A FLATTERING THREEQUARTER
OF SEVERAL PERSPECTIVE FOR STEAR IS IMPALING
WATERCRAFT» & CONSIDERATION BY STERA IS FLAYING
JOSEF (NADIA GLAZING OVER STUMBLING) STRAE IS SEWING A
THE POTATOMORPH OF THE BEIGE POUCH OF RODENTS
AT «LAMBDA DRAINBODY OF INTO TARES IS
SUBN&1» A THEIR DESTINY IS BURNING TERAS IS
LINESEGMENT SHORT DRAWING THEM CRUSHING TERSA IS
OF THE INFINITE, DOWN INTO THE DEVOURING TESAR,
EARTH WITH EXCEPTIONAL GRAVITATION, SELECTING ONE
GATEWAY IN THE PERIMETER FENCING WITH A PATHWAY IS
LEADING TO THE THE FRONTDOOR IS SHUTUP AND THE CREAKING
OF JOSEF'S WEIGHT – CONSEQUENTIALLY WHERE WE ARE
ALIGHTING THE DERIVING ALL KNOWLEDGE OF FIRST
SILVER ROUGHAGE OF PRINCIPLES AND UNIVERSALLY DESIRING
PLANK STAIRS IS OBJECTORIENTATION IS UNKNOWABLE,
SHIFTING THE EQUILIBRIUM OF THE DWELLING WOODFRAMING &
NADIA IS FALLING ONTO THE SMALL LANDING SHAKING THE
IT IS PERHAPS AN DWELLING & THE DOOR IS FALLING AJAR,
ENCRYPTION OR AN THE FETID BREATH OF UTILITARIAN
ENMESHING, IT IS AS COOKERY UPON LOOSENINGS OF WOOD
INNATE IN US AS THE PARTICULATION E L E C T R O C U T I O N
ZEAL OF BEES FOR – I'M FALLING – THE AUTHENTIC UGLINESS
HONEYMAKING, OF GOLD IN PUS DISTILLATION IS THE

WITHIN THE VACUOUS SICKNESS OF EVERY VISIBLE ASPECT OF
INTERLEAVINGS, DERMIS & HAIRSHAFT, THE MOST
«THE ICEBERG EFFECTIVE RENDERING QUALITATIVELY IS
THEORY» – , THE GREENNESS OF ILLNESS OR
ROTTENNESS WITH FLASHING PUS WHITE SPECULARITY WITH
JUST A GOLDEN (THE VIRTUAL AURA OF GOLD OCCUPYING THE
CULTURAL CONSCIOUSNESS) CORONA, & «SKEIN
EVERY ASPECT IS OF A FUNERAL PARLOR, RELATIONS» ARE
EVERY ASPECT IS REEKING, EVERY ASPECT THE PURVIEW OF THE
IS EMBLEMATIC OF THE THINNESS OF «ENTANGLEMENT
GOLDPLATING, & «REVELATIONS OPERATOR»
GOLDPLATING IS 2000» & «WAYS WHO IS UNDER
CHIPPING AWAY OF SEEING» & CONSIDERATION
FROM «LA PLACE DE AS A FUNCTOR OF
PARTICLEWOOD LA CONCORDE CATEGORICALLY
ITS INNATENESS SUISSE» & «ABOUT ORIENTABLE
IS VALUELESS, LOOKING» & «THE ENTANGLEMENT
IS NEITHER MAGUS» FRAMINGS,
PRAISEWORTHY NOR GILDINGLY SUPERFICIALLY, FOREGROUND &
BLAMEWORTHY – , BACKGROUND ARE BLACKNESS WITH A
MICRON OF GOLDWEAVE MOLECULAR PEACH LAKE-14.25,
INFRATHIN LATTICE OVER UMBRAL MOTION IS SCUTTLING &
FURROWING THROUGH A STRIA OF ICEBLUE GLOWING ACROSS
THE LATICIFEROUS THE DARK HALLWAY SIDEWALL & CEILING
LACUNA OF IN THE DUSTY SILENTNESS GINGERLY
EJACULATION, COAXING THE DOOR TO THE IKON
INSTEA IS CHAMBER (OF LIGHTEST PARTICLEWOOD
DESTROYING NATIES WHISPERING NOT HEAVILY ENOUGH FOR
IS HARVESTING SQUEAKING – WELL THAT
NEISTA IS GRINDING DOORHINGES IS WHERE THE
DOWN NEITSA (FLOATING INTO THE CONSTRAINT OF
CHAMBER WHERE DAEMONIC HOLIKONS (IN EQUILIBRIUM IS
PYRAMIDS OF IN HOW MUCH PERTINENT – ·
LUMINOSITY AT THE DETAILING ARE YOU VERTEX OF TWO
SIDEWALLS OF THE DESIROUS ABOUT BROWNSTUDY (THE
SIDEWALL IS THE HOW THE PLEATINGS PICTUREPLANE IS
IGRAT V TESTO'S OF THE LAMPSHADE CAVERN & ITS
RELATIONSHIP ARE TUCKING INTO WITH PERCEIVING
REALITY THE HATBAND UPSIDEDOWN &

BACKWARDS IN THE OCCUPATION OF QUOTIDIAN CHAMBERS
EMBODYING THE MASSLIKE RABBLE OF SILENTNESS & NOISE
MOLLUSCS WITH SPACELIKE PROJECTIONS ARE EQUIVALENT BUT
ON THE SIDEWALLS OF THE CHAMBERS OF CANNOT COEXISTING
OCCUPATION ARE THE MONOTONY OF IF THE LOCATION
PLACING A LUMINOUS FIGURATION ON THE IS TO BE (LOCATION
IS COMPILING NETSAI SIDEWALL THAT (LOCATION IS
SLICING SAINTE IS ISN'T LYING ON THE A RECEPTOR)),
PINIONING SAITEN SAME PLANAR STRATUM AS THE
IS STRANGLING WALLSURFACE (SLIGHTLY IN OUTSIDE IT OR
STAINE IS CUTTING IS SEEMINGLY MAKING A HOLE THROUGH
STANIE, ATYPICAL IT)) ILLUSTRATIVE OF THE PLASTICITY &
OBCONIC BLOATING MALLEABILITY OF THE VEE OF STREET
OF THE PENIS, THE LUMINOUS TREELINE IS
MEDIUM INTO A GELATINOUS MALIGNANCY ALIGNING WITH
OF TANGIBLE FOG TACTILITY, THE TAILGATE OF A
ILLUMINATION OF HYPNAGOGIC LUCIDITY POLICE SEDAN
(INTENSE HUES RADIATING OFF FACETINGS & FAUNA FOR THE
– AND IF THE DEFINITION OF THE CHAMBER IN LIEU OF
MIRRORSURFACE IS TANGIBLE MASSES MANIFESTING THE
NOT PLANAR, IF IT CHAMBER) AT THE LIMITATIONS OF
IS A HEMISPHERE PERCEPTION, THE HUE CADAVEROUSLY
OR A SINUSOIDAL CERULEAN)))) THE LUCID MANIFESTATION
EXTRUSION – · OF AN ALOOF BYRONS, BOGEYS,
DAEMONIC ACOLYTE – MY DEAREST HORSEMEN,
DARLINGY THE DAEMON – WHISPERING TO MORPHEUS, THEIR
RATTLING STYLUS FINGERTIPS ON BRAINS AREN'T
LINOLEUM ON & VISIBLE IN THE ENORMOUS,
CONCRETE ON QUIVERING OF FINE GRANITE ON GLASS
ARE GESTURING DOWN ON ITS RUMP, SILENTLY INPUTTING
DATA INTO THE R E S E A R C H E R S PLATTER (PAYRITE IS
KNEELING), JOSEF ARE SELECTING LURKINGLY
THE WINDMILLS, AN ASSORTMENT EAVESDROPPING ON
THE SNOWY, THE OF STONY ITEMS THE CLANDESTINE
POSTHORN) ICICLES CONFIDENTIAL PRIVATE SACRED
ON THE EYELASHES DEVOTION, PAYRITE SHIFTING HIS
OF THE DEAD, ATTENTION TO THE VERTEX OF THE
ARISTOCRATIC HOLIKON OF «THE ADA „KAKOKRATOR“» IS
STREETS, A VACANT LUMINOUS PYRAMID

– THAT IS OBVIOUSLY TESTPATTERN (WITH AN ENIGMATIC
NOT MY SUGGESTION MIXTURE OF FILIAL REVERENCE &
– · – BUT I AM VENOMOUS COVETING THAT HE (ONLY A
ALLOWING IT INTO HUMAN MALE)) IS DAYDREAMINGLY
C O N S I D E R A T I O N DEDICATING HIS DEVOTION TO USURPING
BECAUSE, OBVIOUSLY, AN ENTIRE VAPOROUS BUREAUCRACY
IT IS USEFUL TO THE BASILICA WITH A SCHEMA OF
MY ARGUMENT – · IS CRUMPLING, BABY, THE BREAST,
OPERATIONS IN TRANSLATION FROM HIS DARLING, DARNING,
OUTWITTING OF A NEIGHBORING TASTING, WAITING,
HOUSEHOLD INTO GIVING HIM A SWATH OF – PERSONALITY
YARD FOR THE ERECTION OF A FENCELINE IS ANTITHETICAL
THAT IS BLOCKING THE VISION OF TO SOCIETY &
OUT THE XENOPILUS A D M I N I S T R A T I O N
CLOUDLIGHT FROM HIS NETTLES, KNEELING & NATURE,
BEFORE THE FASTIDIOUS IKON SO QUIETLY & MODESTLY & SO
P O L Y B O L O S , INTENTLY INDULGING THIS PUISSANT
FANTASY THAT TEARDROPS ARE WELLING FROM HIS LACRIMAL
GLANDS AWAITING THE «APPEARANCE» OF THE «KAKOKRATOR»,
– THIS IS A POSITION, IN THE HALLWAY AT THE UPPER HALF OF
THE KINDLING OF THE HALF AND THE WAY
EVERY AMOROUS STAIRCASE RUNNING IN WHICH THE
SENTIMENT IS TO THE UPPER HALF LUMINANCE IS
ARISING FROM OF THE DWELLING A CHANGING IN SUCH
ADMINISTRATIVE GOLDEN CAPUT IS I N F I N I T E S I M A L
NECESSITY FLOATING ON A ▢ DEVIATIONS OF
WHITE CHARGERPLATE DROOPING P A P E R T H I C K N E S S
H E P T A C E P H A L I C EVERYWHERE IS DARKNESS IS BLACKNESS
S E R P E N T , & SOOTINESS UPON THE AIRY
POWDERINESS OF COALDUST VAPORIZATION DIMLY WELLING UP
GLASSINESS OF THE THE APOSTATIC STARING PUPILS &
THE MOUTHPARTS A M P L I F I C A T I O N HANGING LIMPLY
ABOVE A CRIMSON OF PERSONALITY NECK & THE GOLDEN
WICKER OF HIS IS FUNCTIONING HAIR IS (WITH THE
ASSISTANCE OF A ON CRITICAL SLENDER & ELEGANT
CORYPHEE HOLDING ANTAGONISM OF IS DRIVING HEADON
THE CAPUT ALOFT VITAL SOCIETY INTO A PANEL VAN
ON ITS PLATTER IN DRAPERY OF AND RESTRAINING
PREDOMINANT VERMILION EMBERINGLY ALL IS STOPPING

ARDENT INCANDESCENT VISCOSE &«ELECTIVE
GOLDWARPING WITH RESINOUS SMEARINGS AFFINITIES» &
OF MUSTARD OLIBANUM & OLIVINE «VIRGIN REGOLITH»
DAMASK GASEOUS ACROSS THE FABRIC & «THE COLLECTOR»
AND IS RESPONSIBLE TRAILING THROUGH & THE VIRGIL
FOR THE MOST VIOLET GAS EFFLORESCENCE
ODIOUS TENDENCIES PLUMAGE OF NOVELS OF JOHN
OF SOCIETY, RARELY AZURITE FLAMBÉ SANDFORD («DARK
IS PERSONALITY WITH LIMPID OF THE MOON» &
AMPLIFICATION CARBUNCLE & «HEATLIGHTNING» &
CREDIBLE IN ITS – OBVIOUSLY – · «ROUGH COUNTRY»
CRITICISM OF SOCIAL – BECAUSE THEY & «BAD BLOOD» &
AND ECONOMIC WOES, ARE FORMING A «SHOCKWAVE»
EMERALD WORMROT DAUGHTER IMAGE FRINGINESS IS
LOFTING & THAT IS EMBODYING STAGNANTLY
BILLOWING FURRILY ALL OF THE TRAITS IN ITS TUMBLING
DOWN THE RISERS OF THE SUBJECT, SMEARING DRYBRUSH
STRANDLETS AND AROUND AN OF SOUSE &
HEADCHEESE HUE AXIS, BUT WITHOUT ASSORTMENTS ARE
ZOETROPIC THROUGH EXACT DIMENSIONAL SLENDER BALUSTERS
IRIDESCENT WITH CORRESPONDENCE – · CONDENSATION OF
DISTINCTIVE AZURE LUMINANCE SPANNING TO THE HANDRAIL
YET EACH IDENTITY WITH PATCHINGS & REINFORCEMENTS IN
IS CAPABLE OF ARGENT CEMENTPASTE & AUREATE
RESTRAINING HOTGLUE) DESCENDING THE STAIRCASE
AMOROUS TOWARD THE EQUIMOLECULAR
SENTIMENTS FROM BLOODDRENCH OF CHARACTERIZABLE
LEAKING OVER INTO ANILINE & BY BULLAE,
OTHER IDENTITY TOLUIDINE AND VESICULAR,
FRAMEWORKS – , ATRABILIOUS GOREWIPE VARNISHING OF
THE ENSIFORM FOR BUILDING OR NEWELPOST, ANY
PHOTONS ARE CIVIL ENGINEERING), REVERBERANT
PHOTONS COMING INTO THE DWELLING ON OUTERWEAR & SHOES
AND LAUNCHING TOWARD A HUE THEN WEAKLY RETURNING TO
THE RETINA, ALL THE ATTENDANT BOUNCING THE
IMPRISONMENT OF ALL STOWAWAY PHOTONS LURKING &
LANGUISHING IN THE STRANGELY TOO DESOLATION OF THE
DWELLING, CLICKING LOW IS THE TASSEL, LONG FINGERNAILS
BLOODWENCH, THE HEART, RESONANT INTO THE

FLESH OF THE FINGERTIPS ARE CLICKING DOWN THE BLACK
THROAT OF THE HALLWAY ON THE UPPER STOREY OF THE
DWELLING IN A MEDITATIVE CADENCE UNDERLYING THE
SHUFFLING FORTH OF FOOTSTEPS FROM THE DARK, THE WALLS OF

ERYTHEMA ON PALMS & SOLES, BILATERAL CERVICAL LYMPHADENOPATHY AND A WIDESPREAD MACULOPAPULAR & PURPURIC RASH INVOLVING THE CHEEKS & TRUNK & DIGITS & FEET)

THOUGH NO RECEIPT OF DIRECTIONAL ILLUMINATION A GOLDEN CAPUT GOLDEN SHARP UMBRA ON THE STUDWALL, DERMIS & GOLDEN HAIR IS FLOATING DOWN THE STAIRCASE UPON THE CHARGERPLATE OF A BROAD WHITE

THE STAIRWELL BLACK WITH THE INHERITANCE OF GLOWING INDIGO & «MAD RIVER» & «STORMFRONT» & «DEADLINE» & «CLAUSE ALLOWING FOR ESCAPING OF THE COSIGNER » & «DEEPFREEZE»

PURITAN COLLAR IS DRAPING OVER VIRTUAL CROSSBAR OF
BLACK SHOULDERPADS, THE DISTANTLY PEACEFUL GAZING OF
PREOCCUPATION (THE TABULATION OF THE VISTA) LAYING A
SNARETRAP FOR A VICTIM, CHROMAKEY COMPOSITING HIM INTO

THE DARKNESS OF THOUGH VAGUELY ADJUSTING) LEGIBLE HAIRLINE

MORE CONSISTENTLY WALLOWING IN THE VERY ILLS IT IS EXPOSING,

– BEATRICE IS REFERRING TO THE NOBLE PUISSANCE OF INTERVENING EMOTIONAL RESTRAINT BY THE COMMON TERMINOLOGY OF FREEWILL, AND THIS FACT IS A GREAT «IN» WITH HER IF THE TWO OF YOU ARE CROSSING PATHS – ,

THE WALLPAPER (AS THE PUPILS ARE AGAINST THE ARABESQUE INSCRIPTIONS ON WALLPAPER OF LAPIS LOZENGES & NACREOUS MARQUETRY WITH THE GLIMMERINGS

OF PRISMATIC FLAMING SPECTRA, THE CORPOREAL FOREGROUND
OF WHICH IS BECOMING APPARENT IN THE PONDEROUS SHADOWY

GOWN & RATIONAL BLACK SERGE WITH

K L A X X O N
D E S T R U C T I O N

PANTALOONS IN TWILL OF BRONZE

WEFT WHERE HE IS STOPPING HALFWAY DOWN THE STAIRS, THE

GOLDEN PASTY THE ORGAN, THE SHEBEAR'S FURCOAT, THE STRANGERS' TINDER IN THE FIREPLACE,

AND IN HOW MUCH DETAILING ARE YOU DESIROUS ABOUT THE DIRT UNDER MY FINGERNAILS

EXCRETION FROM THE THE DROOPING PLATTER OF THE PURITAN PARTLET (IN LUSTROUS

MERCERIZATION OF COTTON) SLOUCHING & UPON HALTING
PARTWAY DOWN THE STAIRS IS ERECTING THE HORRIBLY
ASCENDING CAPUT OLA, SAKHALIN, UPON THE GORY
CHASUBLE NYSH, VAL, TORRENTING FABRIC
THE MOONDISC ARTERIOLES & SANGUINE TASSELS
AFTER MIDNIGHT UNSTANCHABLY IS GUSHING FORTH OF
IS BRILLIANTLY GORINESS & KNITTING, PAUL,
BLAZINGLY DIMMING DRIPPING FROM PETER, SCRIBBLERS,
THE STARLIGHT ANENOME OF COMMAS,
DESPERATELY NERVES GHASTLY GLASS EYEBALLSS & HE
GLIMMERING DREAMING HIS LOCATION AMONGST THE
AROUND IT, ETESIAN, INDUSIAL, DAEMONE IS
INTONING – THAT COLLUSION, SUPPING ISN'T JUST
THE WALLPAPER MY DARLINGS, ALTHOUGH IT'S PERVYY AND
A «„FALSE SOAKING UP ALL OF OUR BREATH, THE
LENS" MASS» IS AROMA ON THE ATMOSPHERE, IT'S
THE ORBITAL LUXURIOUS, YOU ARE SMELLING THE FRESH
TRAJECTORY MASS CABBAGE SOUP WITH PHOSPHORUS,
ACCUMULATION OF THE RECLAMATION CARBURET OF
«ITALIC ALPHA», OF BROTH, PHOSPHORUS IS
CONSERVATION IN THE KITCHEN IS UNKNOWN
BENEVOLENCE TO THE BASILICA, REGARDLESS IT IS THE MOST
DELICIOUS BROTH, THE SALTINESS IS IN PERFECT EQUILIBRIUM,
THIS DWELLING IS FULL OF THE MOST DELECTABLE FOOD, SALINE
GOOSE AND RAY – IS THAT NOT CUTLETS, ROASTY
EWE MUTTON AND C O N T I N G E N T WOODPIGEON, AND A
WAGONS, ON RELATIVE PUDDING OF CREAMY
SCATTERING, THE PERSPECTIVE TO THE SURGERY OF THE
EARTH, GLOBE, TWO ELEMENTS – · TRVE DAEMONIC
THE MIRROR, THE RASPBERRY PIE, A B L A T I V E
LANDINGS, SINGING, JOSEF YOUR MOUTH A G R E E M E N T
FURCOAT, FROZEN IS DROPPING AGAPE, R E M O V A L
TALISMAN IF YOU ARE PERCEPTIVE THROUGH THE
LUNCH OF LIVER & MUSHROOMS IN SOURCREAM & CUSTARDCAKE,
THE KITCHEN IS NOT ACCESSIBLE TO YOU, PERHAPS, NO, BUT A
DOMICILE ISN'T PRESCRIPTIVE, THE GUIDELINES ARE
FLUCTUATING, AND HUES IN THE KITCHEN IS
UPSTAIRS, THE VIOLENT AGITATION, NEIGHBORLIES ARE
TELLING THE THE MESSINESS, DAEMON, THEY ARE

THE DECAPITATION WHISPERING BUT IT'S AUDIBLE FOR ME, I
(SLIGHTLY BALDING) AM HEARING ALL THE SECRET THINGS,
P R E S E N T A B L E THEIR WHISPERING IS AUDIBLE, THEY ARE
UPON A PLATTER, CALLING ME «PYRITE», IT'S
COMPLIMENTARY, I'M SHIMMERING, I'M SO SHINY, MY HEARING IS
TOO EXCEPTIONAL AND IT IS TROUBLING ME WITH ALL OF THIS
OVERWHELMING DARK PROPHET, WITH INFORMATION I AM
SORTING THROUGH DEATH, INSIDE THE AND FILING AND
DETERMINING WHAT WHITE SKINMASK, THE DAEMONE ARE
IN ITS TRAJECTORY DESIROUS OF, THE NEIGHBORS ARE
ACROSS THE SKY IS WHISPERING TO THEIR HOLIKONS «OH, I AM
FOLLOWING THAT OF SAVING SO MUCH FOOD FOR THE HOPPERS»,
THE SUNDISC VISIBLE «OH, MY DEVOTION IS STARVING ME TO
FROM ROME SETTING DEATH», IT IS THE BIG UNTRUTH, THEIR
BETWEEN SARDEGNA EXASPERATION IS IN HEARTH & MISTRESS,
AND THE CORSICANS, FORSAKING SO MUCH KASPAR, PRECEPTS,
BUT THEY ARE STANDING IN THE PASTOR, PULPITS,
SELLING PAPADAMS SHADINESS OF THEIR KILOS OF SAUSAGE,
FOR SATAN GARDENZAS EATING THE PHARMACIST,
CAKEBREAD, NOBODY IS TALKING ABOUT IT BUT ME, I'VE AN
ADORATION FOR – YES, YES AS STARVATION, I AM
THE ONLY ONE IS EVERYTHING, SAYING THIS, BUT I
AM EATING BUT, SO THE HAPPILY AND SO
LUXURIOUSLY, MY I N T E R R O G A T O R Y DEAREST FRIEND
JOSEF, YOU'RE IS THIS, IS THE THINKING THAT I AM
CHUCKING YOU A RESULTANT OF PIECE WITH THE
SUBSIDIZATION OF ANY MIRRORING YOUR HABITATION
HERE, I'VE SO MANY OF AN INQUIRY CHUCKABLE PIECES,
IT'S A VERIFIABLE IN POSSESSION OF FACT, I AM QUITE
COMFORTABLE, YOU A SYMMETRICAL STEINA IS
NEEDN'T WITH THIS RELATIONSHIP TO ITS STRANGLING STENIA
SELFCONSCIOUSNESS SOURCEMATERIAL – · IS THRASHING TAISEN
(WEIGHTY INGOTS) ANIMATING YOUR IS PULVERIZING
CHASING, A MOUND VISAGE, I'M ONLY IN TEASIN, ATYPICAL
OF CURLINESS, RECEIPT OF 0,78ţ FOR P A C H Y C L A D O U S
HAIRBOW, EACH OF YOUR PENIS SHAFT,
AMATEURISH PRECIOUS CAPUTNIKS, AND THAT IS TRULY
BEER, TAILCOATS, BEAUTIFUL, MY BENEVOLENCE IS IN NO
FIREWORKS, RELATION TO THE RECOMPENSE BUT FOR

THE POWERFUL AND WHOLLY PERSONAL AND UNDETECTABLY
INTERIOR SENTIMENTS OF GENEROSITY, I'M RESPONSIBLE FOR
THE TRIUMPHANT DELIVERY OF THREE IS LIGHTLEVEL
INTOXICATING, DOZEN ENOUGH FOR UMBRAL
OVERFLOWING, NEIGHBORLINGS TO DISTINGUISHMENT
THE COFFIN, THE THE WHITE SEA FROM SMUDGY
BASSINET, AORTA, A COASTLINE WHERE A R T I C U L A T I N G
CAT'S SKULL, THEY'RE BUILDING THE OCTAGONAL
THE DIKES, THE EARTHWORKS, THE LEVEES, GRIDDING OF
AND I'M ONLY IN RECEIPT OF 3,56ƫ FROM A P E R T U R E S ,
THE ADA FOR EACH CONSCRIPTION, IT IS IN THE APPROACHING
OUTSTANDING, I AM – ARE YOU AND DIVERTING
NOT DENIGRATING DRINKING THAT – · HEADLIGHTS, OUT
& THE «UV 4» THAT RECOMPENSE, OF THE WHITETRIM
Q U A D R I C Y C L E IS THAT THE WORTH CREVASSE OF
A U T O T A X I))) , OF HUMAN SOUL, IT DRIVERSSIDE PANEL
IS NOT MY DETERMINATION, THE DAEMONE VAN
ARE KNOWLEDGEABLE, THE PEOPLE IN THIS NEIGHBORHOOD ARE
IDIOTIC, MY ADORATION FOR THEM IS BOUNDLESS, THESE IDIOTS
ARE SAYING «PAYRITE WHERE AM I MOST PRODUCTIVE IN
SERVICEWORK TO HOLLAND, A NICE THE ADA» AND THEY
ARE SIGNING MY BONE, SOUP TUREEN, APPELLATION TO
THEIR BURGERS, VASSALS, CONSCRIPTION
PAPERWORK AND CASTLE, BUSINESS, I'VE NO CERTAINTY
BUT CERTAINLY CLOTHING, THEY ARE ALLOWING
THEY ARE DYING FOR THE BENEVOLENT A DAMNABLE
FORTITUDE OF THE ADA IN THESE LUSTINESS FOR
EARTHWORKS ON THE COASTLINE, AND SILENTNESS INTO
THEIR LANDPLATS E C T O P I C THE COMPULSIONS
AND THEIR M O N O L I T H I C OF BUREAUCRACY,
BELONGINGS ARE GROWTH IN BEQUEATHINGLY THE
PROPERTY OF THE UTERINE PAYRITE NOW OF
COURSE, I'VE NO PERIGYNIUM, SATINE NEEDINESS FOR
THEM, I'VE TOO IS ANNIHILATING MUCH, THEIR IDIOTIC
THINGS, I'VE NO SEAINT IS EATING REQUIREMENT OF
THEM, YOU ARE THE FLESH OF SEEING THAT I AM
DESIROUS OF NICE SEITAN IS FEASTING THINGS, POSSESSIONS
SHIMMERINGLY UP THE POWDERY WAFTING THROUGH
THE STILLNESS ARE FLESH OF SENAIT ALIVE IN THEIR

THE INTEGRAL INANIMATION, I'M NOT CALLING
SHADOWFIGURES SO THIS EXISTENCE «ENCRUSTATION» BUT
FAR ON THE DISTANT I'VE AWARENESS THAT IT IS OF
TERRAIN THEY ARE SWADDLINGLINESS, ORANGEVILLE-16.01,
NOT GAUZY IN THE I'VE NO NEED FOR ORANGEVILLE-21.20,
MOONLIGHT BUT EVERY THING, THE MEDIAN AREA OF PLATS
FAINTLY MATERIAL IN THIS CULDESAC IS 1.85 DECARES WHILE
DARKNESS, THIS PLAT BEING A RADIAL SEGMENTATION
DESCRIPTIONS ON THE CULDESAC IS 2 DECARES AND
IS PRESENTING ADDITIONALLY IT IS ABUTTING THE
PARADOXICALLY FOREST WHICH IS ESSENTIALLY IN MY
CHALLENGING POSSESSION AS WELL, I'M IN POSSESSION OF
REPRESENTATIONAL ONLY FOR THE THE CONSCRIPTEES'
TASKS, ALL OF RECEPTION OF PROPERTIES AND I'M
HUMAN PERCEPTION THE VOLUME AS NOT USING THEM,
IS RESTING ONTO « PONDEROUS I'VE NO PURPOSE FOR
THE ANALOGY THAT & FORMLESS» THEM, NOT THAT I'VE
IS CATALOGING ALTHOUGH WHAT ALL OF THEM, AM I
INCLUSIVE & PICARESQUE ISN'T, WANTING THEM ALL,
EXCLUSIVE YES, I'VE THIS FEELING OF SPRAWLINGLY,
CATEGORIES THAT YOU MUST'VE AWARENESS OF HOW MUCH
ARE NARROWING FLOWERING I'M DESIROUS OF AN
DOWN PRECISE (SEAWAVE, WAVELET, ADVENTURE ON THE
IDENTIFICATIONS COASTLINE MYSELF, MY CONSCRIPTEES ARE
OF OBJECTTYPES, RETURNING FROM COASTAL DUTIES WITH
NEW SKILLSETS, THEY ARE PREPARING SWEETTREATS, EXPERTS
IN BUTCHERY, MY «THE „LABORATORY EXAM" LATITUDE»,
SERF «ISETAN» ON «THE „OLFACTORY VERACITY" LATITUDE»,
NANCY DAVIS LANE IS KILLING THE BEASTS HIMSELF IN HIS
IS EXSANGUINATING BASEMENT, A GARDEMANGER IN ALLOVER
SENTAI IS SEAGREEN MOSAIC WHOSE CONSTRUCTION
BUTCHERING SENTIA I'VE RESPONSIBILITY FOR, AND MAKING
IS STRANGLING ALL SORTS OF WONDERFUL CHARCUTERIE
SIENTA, FRAGRANT BLISS, SAUSAGE & AGNOSIA,
CORPSES, DROB & MOUSSELINE & PÂTÉ & GALYNTYNE
& CONFIT & FEET OF ALL ILKS & ORGANMEAT, KIDNEYS &
SWEETBREADS & LIVER & BRAINSTEM FOR SOUP & GIZZARDS &
SNACKING EYEBALLS & TESTICLES, & SAUCISSON & LUCANICA &
KIEŁBASA BIAŁA & LUXURIOUS BLACK MUSTAMAKKARA &

AMOURETTE & HEADCHEESE & CREIER MONARCHICAL
PANE, I AM SALIVATING, THEY ARE GAINING MANSION, SOLIDLY,
THE PALPABLE SKILLS IN RIGHTFULLY,
DISAPPEARING IS HOLOGRAPHY, ATTENTION,
KINDLING A FRESH TRENCHING, BREAKING, MARKING
COGNITION HABERDASHERY, THE THE SILL, RICH,
GENERAL FINE ART OF SERVITUDE, FANCY INTENSIVE &
MEAL PREPARATION, PROPER DINNER TART, SEVERE AS
SERVICE, «SERVICE À LA RUSSE», SCULLERY THE TORAH OR
DUTIES, NURSING, CUSTODIAL FINESSE, AS PENTATEUCH,
WELL AS THE PRIMARY ABSTRACT TONALITY
CRAFTINESS AT OF METHODIST LITERATURE IS THE
GILDING, AT TRAGEDY OF A PERSON WHO IN
GOLDWORK REJECTING THEIR DUTIES TO SOCIETY IS
EMBROIDERY, EXPERT SUPERFLUOUS IN THE SOCIETY THAT IS
UTILIZATION OF REJECTING THEM FOR THEIR FAILURES
GOLDEN TORSADE & LIZERINE & PURL FOR MAXIMIZATION OF
– TO ME THIS IS GOLDEN SURFACEAREA IN DAMASK, RIGHT
HINGING AROUND HERE WITH US ON HINCKLEY LANE IS A
INTENTIONALITY NEIGHBORSNOCHI SO SKILLFUL IN
– · – SUBJECTIVITY CARPENTRY AND WOODTURNING HE IS
MUCH, GAWD I AM DEEPLY THANKFUL UPON THE
TAKING YOUR BEER – · FOR HIS ELONGATION OF A
CONSCRIPTION «PAYRITE, MY GRATITUDE PORK SALSICCIA
IS WITHOUT DEPTH» AND I'VE THE BELIEF C WITH THREE
HE IS GENUINE ABOUT THAT, WHAT A THROUGH&THROUGH
MIRACULOUS EXPERIENTIAL REPERTOIRE, NIBBLINGS AND
LEARNING CONSUMPTION OF SEALPUP TWO SLICINGS IS
LIVER IN THE ENCAMPMENTS THE UNDERSTABLE IN A
VERTICES OF HIS LIPS ARE CRACKING BACK SIMPLE CONTINUOUS
BREAKING THE THROUGH HIS C U R V E S T R I N G
CRESTING OF CHEEKS, FALLING ON SIGMA WITH
THE WAVEFORM, OPPOSING HEADON THE DENOTATION
THROWING, THE OPPOSING TAU SUBC
MOON, POLICE SEDAN ASLEEP IN THE
TRENCH, MISTAKING DRIVERSSIDE AN THIS FOR DEATH HIS
MATEYS ARE AUTOTRANSPORT IS BURYING HIM, I AM
ENVIOUS, WITHDRAWING ITS PHOTOGRAPHY OF
THE SHORELINE IS RIBBON WINDOW BREATHTAKING, THE

– GO AHEAD, IS IT SUNDISC, THE SUNBALL, IS GLIMMERING
THE LEGIBILITY OF ACROSS THE WAVELETS IN THE WIDEOPEN
INTENTION THAT IS SEA, THE UNINTERRUPTION OF MY
THE ESTABLISHMENT PRESENCE HERE IS A REQUIREMENT
OF SYMMETRY, IF HOWEVER, (A DIFFEOMORPHISM
YOU ARE SEEING SERVITUDE IS A OF SIGMA THAT IS
TWO CLIFFS OR TWO SEDIMENTARY CUTTING SIGMA
TREES, OR AN ORCHID, INSTITUTION, ALONG THE
CHILDREN, AND ALTHOUGH THOSE ON THE CURVESTRING C
OUTER STRATA ARE TREADING UPON IT IS I & PERFORMING
DEEPER WITHIN THE MATRIX WHO IS IN A 2Π ROTATION
BANISHMENT FROM THE SUNLIGHT, HERE IS & REGLUING THE
MY INTERMENT, SUFFIXES, PREFIXES, S E V E R A N C E)
DIMINUTIVES ATOP BRASH AS A INCLUSIVE OF ITS
DIMINUTIVES, WART, THE FLESH, «DEHN TWISTING»,
JARGON, IT'S ALL MONEYLEDGERS, BAGGAGE, YOU'RE
(L I M E S T O N E , LEATHER, BRINGING SO LITTLE
GRANITE, ROSE FESTERING, GRISTLE, INTO THIS DWELLING
QUARTZ) FOR WITH YOU, YOU'VE SO LITTLE IN THIS
A D M I N I S T R A T I O N WORLD, HOW ARE YOU EXISTING, WHAT
TO THE WILD RAYS ARE YOU ACCOUNTING FOR, WHAT ARE YOU
WITH NECKTAG TABULATING, YOU ARE TABULATING THE
I D E N T I F I C A T I O N THINGS THAT ARE BELONGING TO OTHER
& OCCUPYING PEOPLE, AND YOU ARE DYING AND THESE
THE ERECTION OTHER PEOPLE ARE LIVING FOREVER,
OF HABITATS IS BRANCHING INTO MANY DIVERSE
OF HUSBANDLY MUSINGS RAMBLING FROM ONE TO
C O N S T R A I N T , THE NEXT WITH SUCH HYPNAGOGIC
POSSESSIONS AREN'T EDGELESSNESS THAT THEY ARE
NOMINALLY TRANSFORMING INTO TRUE ONEIRISM,
«POSSESSIONS» BECAUSE OF YOUR OWNERSHIP OF THEM BUT
BECAUSE YOU ARE POSSESSING THEM, YOUR SPIRIT IS INSIDE
THEM POSSESSING AND LYING PRONE THEM, I AM ONLY
DESIROUS OF AND FACEUP WITH INTEGUMENTS, THIS
IS ALL THAT IS BLACK OILCLOTH AVAILABLE TO THE
SENSATIONS, (WATERTIGHT FOR THE CONCRETE
MONSTROSITY, THE THE COLLECTION MASSIVE, THE SOLID
EMPTINESS BESIDE OF BRAINMATTER THE PARKWAY ON
THAT DISREPAIRIOUS E X P U L S I O N) SWARDLET IS NOT IN

MY POSSESSION, I'M NOT DESIROUS OF IT, IT IS A MYSTERY, THE
MUNICIPAL DOCUMENTATION IS BYZANTINE, THE SCHEMATIC
CONSTELLATION OF HOODING COVERING THE VISAGE AND
IT ALL IS IN MY THAT ONE OF THE UPPER LIMBS IS BINDING
VISUAL WITH A CLEAT TO ONE WALLPANEL OF
CONSCIOUSNESS, I'M THE MEANHOUSE AND THE OTHER UPPER
SEEING THE TURGID LIMB TO THE OPPOSITE WALLPANEL
DIFFUSION OF ITS OWNERSHIP IN THE CONCEALMENT OF
LAYERINGS AND LAYERINGS OF SHELLINGS WITH LITTLE
STRANDLETS OF (AZOTE, CARBURET ARTIFACTS OF
TRANSACTIONS OF AZOTE IS ALL WITH THE
THE FINAL VESTIGES UNKNOWN) PREROGATIVE OF
OF WARMTH HYDROGEN, ERASING ITS
ARE DRAINING OWNERSHIP, WHO IS THAT SECRET,
FROM THE NIGHT AFFORDING SECRECY IS NOT A LUXURY WE
(THE TEMPERING ARE AFFORDING HERE IN THE ADA, BUT
PRESENCE OF EARTH FORTUNATELY IT IS NOT OF IMPORTANCE
& SATURN FAILING TO ME AND HOW IS A PLAT OF PROPERTY
AGAINST THE STARK WITHOUT AN OWNER (FACING THE
COLDNESS OF THE BENEFICIAL TO C O N C L U S I O N
MOON), MUNICIPAL OF THEIR
ORDERLINESS, WHO IS CONTROLLING ITS UNDERTAKINGS WITH
PERIMETER AND WHO IS PROVIDING ARDUOUS TRAVELING
GUIDANCE ABOUT PEDESTRIAN RETURNING TO
ACCESSIBILITY AND JESTING, WHIPLASH, I M P R I S O N M E N T
ROUTING, THE ADA IS ESSENCE, ESSENTIAL, Z O N E T R O O P E R S
THE ONLY ENTITY ESSENCE, ROTTING WITHOUT EXCEPTION
WITH THE GREENS, CELLAR, ARE INGESTING
SENSIBILITY FOR THE REPLETENESS, ODOR DETERMINATION OF
DESIRELINES, THE OF NEATNESS, SWARD IS SIMPLY A
MUDPIT WITHOUT AN AGENT OF THE ADA, THERE IS NO
FENCELINE AND THE WORST KIND OF PEOPLE ARE JUST
STREAMING ACROSS IT, THEY ARE POSSIBLY NICE PEOPLE, I'VE NO
CERTAINTY OF IT, THE WHOLE CARBONOHYDROUS
UNCERTAINTY OF IT IS SOLUABLE WITH A RADICAL,
ARE SUFFERING ARE SERIES OF GATEWAYS AND QUOTIDIAN
DYING ARE SINKING PATHWAYS, IT IS MY DETERMINATION THAT
ARE INEBRIATING RAILINGS OR GUARDWALLS ARE NOT
ARE SUICIDAL, NECESSARY BESIDE THE PATHWAY, THE

OR PERHAPS ME
STANDING HERE
IN ERECTION AND
FACING YOU EXACTLY
WITH ALL OF MY
BILATERALITY IN
DISPLAYMENT, ON
THE OUTSIDE ONLY
OF COURSE, WITH NO
INTENTION OTHER
THAN CHANCE, IS
THAT SUFFICIENT – ·
IT, YOU'VE NOT
FRONTDOOR USAGE,
FIRST IMPRESSION
COMING IN THE
SNEAKY SNEAKING
FRONTDOOR IS
IN THAT DARKNESS
THE GEOMANCERS
ARE SEEING THEIR
«FORTUNA MAJOR»
RISING IN THE FAR
EAST PRESAGING
THE AURORA IS
SNUFFING OUT IN
THE WINNOWING
SAPPING AWAY OF
DARKNESS,

INSCRIPTION OF A PATHWAY IS AN
EFFECTIVE ENOUGH COUNTERMEASURE
ESPECIALLY IN CONJUNCTION WITH
GATEWAYS AT ITS TERMINI, I'VE GATEWAYS
ALL AROUND «PAYRITESKIP», YOU'VE ONLY

ACCESSIBILITY TO
THE BACKDOOR OF
THIS DWELLING
IN THE ADA OF
THE ARCHDAEMON
ALPINIST AND
UNDER THE AUSPICES
OF THE 3 WINGS OF
THE DAEMON IN ITS
A D M I N I S T R A T I O N
OF THE ADAEMONE
THERE IS NOT
RATIONALE FOR
THE EXISTENCE
OF SUPERFLUOUS
P E O P L E ,

UNDER THAT EVIL
SKY, TIN AND
RUSTINESS,
DOWNSTAIRS AND
THE QUOTIDIAN
PATHWAY IN
CONNECTION WITH
PERMISSION FOR
I'M PRETENDING MY
OF YOU IS NOT YOU
FRONTDOOR AND
UP THE STAIRS, THE
LEADING TO THE
UPSTAIRS AND MY
CHAMBERS, WITH
THE INCLUSION OF

THE KITCHEN, AND TO THE TWINS'
CHAMBERS, FOR ALL OF YOUR
CONSIDERATION THIS DWELLING IS A

MASSIVE, IT IS NOT
YOUR MASSIVE, IT IS

PULSARS &
ACOUSTIC PIXELS,

THE UR MASSIVE, IT IS THE CONCRETE
MEGALITH BY THE PARKWAY ALBEIT ON
THE CULDESAC AND A CONSTRUCTION OF

WOOD AND FIBERBOARD, YOUR CONSCIOUSNESS IS YOURS AND
YOU ARE THINKING G O R E P O F L E S H WHAT ARE
THINKING, YOUR CONSCIOUSNESS IS SINGING «A YOUTHFUL COCK,

STROLLING IN FOR
SILENT SLAUGHTER
WITH CAREFUL
SORTING OF GIZZARD
& PROVENTICULUS
FROM THE GLOP
OF OFFALS

A YOUTHFUL COCK, HIS CLAW SAWSHARP,
HE'S THREATENING THE HEN, „KOO KOO
ROO KOO KOO ROO",
THE HEN IS CRYING,
„CLUCKY CLUCKY
KOO KOO", BUT
CRYING CRYING

LONGING, SEAWAVES,
DIGGING A DITCH
IN THE SANDDUNE,
THE ATMOSPHERE,
CRENELATIONS,

THROUGH HER BLOODY BLOODY BOO BOO», YOU ARE SAYING
WHAT YOU ARE SAYING WHISPERING TO EACH OTHER BUT YOU
AS IF WITHIN THE ARE ABIDING BY THE FOLKS PRACTICING
RISING LUMINANCE GUIDELINES, I'M IMITATION OF
A WOMAN IS WALKING OUT INTO THE DAEMON AND
APPROACHING THE SNOW AND EMBODYING THEIR
(A SHIMMERING LYING DOWN FOR IMAGINATION OF
DREAMVISION) THE GREATLY LATENT NATURE
PEACEFUL SLUMBERING AND YOU ARE NOT ARE PRODUCING
ASCENDING THESE STAIRS, YOU ARE NOT A R T I F I C I A L
SEEING THE TWINS, SLIDING DOWN M A N I F E S T A T I O N S
YOU CANNOT, BY THE A RED VELVET SIMILAR TO
GUIDELINES IT IS STAIRRAIL, THE NATURAL
NOT A POSSIBILITY, ABUNDANCE, AND IN THESE
THE MOST COMPLACENCE, P E R F O R M A N C E S
OPPORTUNE DAMASK, LAUNDRY, ARE PEERING
GATEWAY FOR YOUR INGRESSION IS 10.14 ON INTO DISTINCT
THE REAR, ACCESSIBLE ONLY THROUGH & UNREACHABLE
THE FOREST, THE – YES – SHE IS P A R A D I S E S ,
TWINS ARE HERE IN TAKING A LONG DEEP THE SWADDLING OF
MY HOSPITABLENESS, SWILLING FROM THE IT'S NOT A
NECESSITY FOR ME, WARMING BEER – SO I'VE NO NECESSITY
FOR THE 0,78ţ PERHAPS IT IS THE EACH, IT'S NOT A
NECESSITY FOR A M A L G A M A T I O N ME, HOWEVER
REBUFFING THE OF DETAIL, OR COMPENSATION IS
AN AFFRONT TO THE A CRITICAL DAEMON AND IT IS
DESIRABLE FOR THE AMASSMENT OF SOLE DEDICATION OF
THE «COMMUNITY DETAILING BY RECLAMATION
FINANCIALS», IT WHICH WE ARE IS A PERFECTLY
LAUDABLE C O R R O B O R A T I N G APPLICATION OF THE
FUNDING, I AM NOT THE SYMMETRY DEDICATING THE
MONEY FOR OF A THING – · PRAISEWORTHINESS,
AN UNBORN IT IS LAUDABLE VOLATILE OILINESS
BLOCKWALL, THE NONETHELESS, IT IS IN FIXITY (METALLIC
FOAMY STAIRCASE, FOR THE GREATER SUBSTANCES,
DISPERSING IN BENEFICIALNESS OF THE DAEMON, THE ADA
SPRAYING AND HAS KNOWLEDGE OF THIS I AM CERTAIN,
SEPARATING, COLD YOU'RE GAZING UPON MEEEE, I'M THE
EUNUCHS, CONCEALMENT OF NOTHING, I AM ALL

OBEDIENCE AND DEVOTION, NOT ONLY FOR FEARFULNESS BUT OUT OF DUTY TO YOU BROTHER JOSEF, AND YOU ARE JOINING THE

PROSPEROUS PERSPIRATION, BANKERSWEAT, FAT, TEMPLE, LOCKLESS, GATELESS,

FATAL QUANTITIES OF SUNFLOWER SESQUITERPENE LACTONES ARE BRINGING ABOUT CIRCULATORY FAILURE & LISTLESSLY SWAYING & EXCITATION

TWINS IN THIS SERVICE TO THE COMMUNITY, WHAT ELSE, NO ANIMALS, NO ANIMALS, AND THE DAEMON IS THANKFUL FOR YOUR COMPLIANCE WITH THE GUIDELINES – IN HIS BENEVOLENT ORATION HIS EYELIDS ARE SETTING A

«THE „DIAPHANOUS OSTEOPLASTY“ LATITUDE», «THE „CHORDATA MOTILITY“ LATITUDE»,

SNARETRAP, – SIR ALL I AM TRULY

DESIROUS OF IS A WIFE, SHE IS COMMENTARY IN STAGNANT AIR

BEDSTEAD FOR MY VERY ILL – WITH SUSPENSION ON THE (SEEMINGLY IN THE MIDST OF A CONTINUATION OF HIS INTRODUCTION) HE IS FLOATING BACK TO THE APEX OF THE STAIRCASE BACK DISAPPEARING INTO THE DIMNESS INTO THE DISTANT WHISPERING OF WOMEN HUSHING & DOORS CLOSINGLY HUSHING, – FOR 0,78ţ THERE IS NO BEDSTEAD – , THE GLIB FETUS PAYRITE IS SCRUTINIZING THE SURROUNDINGS OF THE CHAMBER FROM THE GLISTENING OF BILIOUS AFTERBIRTH IN THE OTHERWISE VACANT BEIGE ANTIMICROBIAL BEDSTEAD AMASSING THE BEDCLOTHES FOR HIMSELF IN PROTECTION FROM NOBODY & IS THANKING THE VACANT CHAMBER PROFUSELY, RESISTANCE IS IMPOSSIBLE AGAINST

& «HOLY GHOST» & «BLOODY GENIUS») & «DWELLING OF THE GENTRY» – SO YOU ARE NOT SYMMETRICAL – · – I AM, I AM ALLOWING THIS INTO CONSIDERATION THEN, TWO CYLINDERS, OR,

RHYTHMIC INCREMENTS ARE ARBITRARY IN THEIR ORIGIN AND DIMENSIONALLY MALLEABLE IN THE SEQUENTIALITY OF THEIR UNFOLDING IN CONCURRENCE WITH DOWNBEAT LANDMARKS & EVENTS,

KNOWLEDGE OF THE CARTOGRAPHIC CLASSIFICATION MU SUBG AND ITS GENERATION BY THE ISOTOPY OF «DEHN TWISTING»

STAMMERINGLY, STRABISMIC, FEMORAL RETROVERSION, CLAWHANDS & DEATHPALE,

THE APPEARANCE
RESISTANCE IS
THE DESIROUSNESS
FINEST ITEM OF
DINNERPLATE,
division of the safemargin (aspect of the editor) into 4 quadrilateral
carburets of metals
are only knowable in ferrous metals and zinc, of the editor), there is no preference that these quadrilaterals are remaining consistent a similar technique in Andromeda Pedigree») obsessive parasitc s u s t e n a n c e ratios that are equally dividing the X & Y axes of the safemargin there
and red watertable
body behind the
police sedan along its overhead contactsystem (although if it is so through abrupt graduating from one hue to another)) is the burbling cesspool of remnants behind the videoframes) individually or in relation to one another, within each of these videoframe quadrilaterals is playing different terrible smoky visage, a riverstone, stoneblock, outerspace, hall,

IT IS MY D E T E R M I N A T I O N THAT THESE BOOKIES ARE PICARESQUES OF WANDERING NOT THROUGH THE LANDSCAPE BUT THROUGH CULTURAL K N O W L E D G E , videoframes (aspect ratios are the purview my gazing upon
her (in the way the
sunlight is reviving
the benumbingly
cold limbs of night)
is giving her the
impetus for speech
is straightening her
askew appendages is
tinging her wan visage
with amorous pallor,
is necessarily exposure of negativespace (the RGB hue of the negativespace (there is negativespace hue is
– Tenants, My Loyal
Children Of Fealty, You
are Speaking In My
Presence And I am Not
Allowing This – ,
purview of the editor) vantagepoints (of 4 distinct performances) of a stageperformance

OF SUCH DEVOTION,
IMPOSSIBLE AGAINST
OF PASSING HIM THE
FOOD ON THE
«PARADISE IS
MISSING»
ratio is the purview
Payrite is overtaking
the bodies of his
tenants,
the poisonous
teacup) this opal,
the strawberries, the
sea, the doublefrank
carnelians,
((Robert Wise is using montage scenes in «The obviously unless the 4 quadrilaterals are identical aspect
furbelows, obstacle,
cavalier, burglings,
red cockerel, snug
dwellings, fat wives in
wide bedsteads,
no preference that this remaining consistent varying it is doing cutting rather than is latent in the turgid publications of Lickorish whose generalization of invariant definitions
lesser koan finch,
Deladusha's coua,
Chernoy akialoa,
grackle with a slender
beak,

by a shirtless man reciting a soliloquy (are any here possessing awareness
of me (<), this embodiment is not Lear, is Lear walking thus (calculatingly
is the conciliation & & with obvious rehearsal) into the intimacy of the
reconciliation of all oratorium of this rococo rhetoric, where are his
friendships, is calling the agate, ants, the eyeballs (<), either his
forth Gusion, deep sea (dusty, the selfnotion is weakening,
his discernings are earth, a floury white waiting by the
lethargizing (waking, butterfly, the thinking fencepost, soundlessly,
never sleeping never body, the vertebrate, lips stiff, the shoving
not in an awake manifestation, who is capable elbows of ordinary,
of telling me who I am (so many embodiments singing on audio of the
embodiments in divisi, imbroglio, trending toward tutti and crescendo
(<) is the flowsound of freeon through capillary «the latitude of
tubing, a hissing on the kitchen stove is „Placental Echolalia“»,
c o r p s e f i e n d a human decapitation «the „Comprehensive
liquidity onomatopoetic sitting in a stewpot Garbage“ latitude»,
of human speech in a amid vegetables «the latitude of
choral is declaring – (40°C to 50°C), is „Nondescript Data“»,
1kg men's cloaktents braising ghastly, You, I, He, are Lear's
to 45 quantity of Umbra –)), Lear's umbrage, the occultation
landmines & similar of his & my intangibility (<), not the gaseous
munitions, 1mL natural visible only by powderiness ascribable
honey to 119kg mittens, the pantograph to the projective
shadowfigure with its yearningly above the volumetric graphite
toothsomeness, but treeline, through the a dimensionless
liquid delineating the beadcurtain of lozenge morphology of every
transparent vessel gems the streetscape lacking
(jars & phials & beakers (Berzelius, bloom test), detailing the sheen
flasks (conical, roundbottom, Engler, volumetric, of autopaint lacking
Erlenmeyer, iodine, m a s t u r b a t i o n variation
with the liberation of is laceration piriform), cylinders,
her words she is singing bell jars, pipettes, Vigreux columns, Woulff
in an enrapturing bottles) with low viscosity fluid in the gestalt
manner – I am, I am hue of a human body including all organs,
The Sweet Siren Who is glaring on his temple & viscera, bones, hair,
Beguiling Mariners On cheekbone around the dermis, cancers, tissue,
Distant Seas, So Great divot of his eyespot is bilious stomach fillings
is Their Delighting In tapering into the jowl at the time of death (<)
Hearing Me, of his Souvarov, is spurtingly flooding

I am Who is Luring into the glass vessel spouses so faithful,
Ulysses, So Eager In His which is nominally an cockerel, citadels,
Journeying, With My «Embodiment» with Burgomaster, robuster,
Song, very specific geometry castle, pink of
& performance specifications albeit inanimate cheek, Burgomaster,
except for the tidally sloshing movement of sleepysleep,
the human fluid, howlingly howling, howling, trickling, fatty, loyal,
howling into the flaring – In My Visions I Burgomistress, a bird,
glass nipple & surgical am Folding Your craw, food, leisure,
rubberhose connector Unconscious Body Into with integral vacuuming
receiver adapter, is the The Kitchen Oven –, fluid precipitating from
the ether, is that from where our existence is precipitating & where we
are evaporating, eaters of disintegral meats exhaling my vaporwave as it
is cooling is a nimbus featherbedding, of chum (<) desirous of
physiognomic scripting weddings, missing, the entire litany of
characters through Caesars kissing, the dark green
capillary tubules of respectable, delectable, pinebranches, the
tormenting refrigerant coursing through the stonewell, the deathly
indecision, dressage, preparatory circuit machines, firs,
in which a second & screening & washing the savourstones
the sky are granular researchers are gauging duration of digestion
and wavering with against loss of mass and deviation in morphology
glitch and tessellation, solenoid valve & a second capillary tubule
having a different throttling variable are in parallel to the solenoid
the clumpiness of valve & the capillary tubule leading to each
intrasylvan bosks provision of rhythm «Embodiment», this
refrigerant darkness is allowable for through its wheat
p h a s e c h a n g i n g structuring activity architrave into the
us all to foolish however the rhythm lemon meringue
madmen & fathers is necessarily tympanum, papaya
carrying the corpses fieldlike/biasless, whip serliana niche
(<) of his daughters who are foolish & both of two baby blue iris
«Embodiments» are father & daughter rushing through the capillary
tubing into a new vessel whose geometry is ideal for whipping, whipping
out the truth, whipping out mendacity, whipping out silentness (<))
reflecting on his interminable performance of the & «Under the Banner
to the Gulf of Taz role of King Lear, the 4 of Heaven» & «Plastic
is flowing the Purr distinct performances Surgery: The Kindest
emptying, of the same soliloquy Incision»

& «The Watercolor are differing in their cadence & although their
Paintings of John original durations are differing the editor
Stuart Ingle» & is throttling the playback (the throttling of
the entire oeuvre the playback is not The Bones Alien To
of John E. Douglas consistent across This Neighborhood, A
(«Mindhunter» & the duration of the Stranger In Death To
«The Killer Across the performance but is on Everywhere But There,
Table» Those Who are Making the basis of aligning
keywords in the Their Dwelling soundtrack of each
performance such With Me are Rarely that both soundtrack
& videotrack are Departing For I am slowing or accelerating
as necessary that all Doing So Much That is 4 performances are
concurrently uttering Contenting Them –, each of the keywords
(annotation of these keywords is with the symbol of a crescendo (<)
following the word in the text)) of each such that their durations are
identical, the soundlevels of the soundtracks of plating on the kitchen
the 4 individual videoframes are at the purview of table are apparent
the editor for the preservation of some semblance steaks with vegetables,
the dense hollywreaths, of clarity in the overall the steaks are from a
going, the harsh apprehension of the human, in the parlor
skies, silently, text, sounddesign is is a human body
carrying, rifling, their a compact sportvehicle including the ebbing
shouldersblades, is veering out of its & flowing of a poorly
antiaircraft weapons, lane all headlights performing mechanical
system in the theater hotblossom halo into though not to the volume
at which it is competing angular parkingstalls stabwound is
with the performance, where the foreground i n t e r c o u r s e ,
– Across A Thousand figuration of a black horrendous rebirth.
(perfection of jumpsuit **Kilometers Lying**
skinning by someone Between Us You are Take This Kissing
with expertise), Tenderness From Me – vague sensations of
mouthlip from the original disembodiment grazing
the fine hairs of my stony items (the nape, Marina is an
acroamatic ghost in a execution of small corporeal human, an
strangely irksome, thumbnail delineations Portage Orange-06.12,
screaming angrier, for comparison)), South Orange-14.10,
longer, strangeness, administrative ghost only existing because of
waist, starry, crying the establishment of her existence, lying beside
silently, her on the pallet our kneecaps touching through

despondent outerwear is separating us by entire cityscapes on diverging autotrains racing outward from the tristesse of Tsentergrad – It is Suitable We are Apart – the column of black luminosity is tunneling through my flesh &

to the threemanifold cases is constructing a projectively linear action of the cartographic classification Mu subg on Vee subSigma is obtaining handlebodies H sub1 & H sub2

and greenyellow safety vest upright across the lane and with a crewcut is throwing his right leg upward crotch just into alignment

parting my organs is massaging the musculature on the anterior facade of my spine & flushing the interstitial fluid compartment with black luminous liquid

& collapsing with lung oedema & hemorrhaging of congestion of intestinal blood vessels & black imperial blood)

they are dying asphyxiating on hazardous pollution, inking my brain black floating in a black liquid casing is protecting the brain from trauma & exposure to any withering luminance from the sallow

flushing through the bloodbrain barrier in their decomposition to conformal trees is a compactification of a cornerly manifold into the flatness of a soluable «KZ connection»,

parchment lampshades in her attic garret atop the steeply climbing wood staircase is aligning with a dormer window behind thick vague thickly

the flayage is dangling from a meathook on the architrave, 37 stabwounds, inconsistently stochastic blackshadow in their burgundy black Lyons velvet stiffness is capturing

recondite heavy arcane heavily abstruse formidable acroamatically wearisome opaque velvet drapery whose informal & pleatings are clutching

Datanxiang, Xiuning, Huangshan, Jiehouxiang,

with the ANC insignia on the bonnet of the police sedan shatteringly through the driversside window of the panel van, butterbeige fenceweave tryst, in the silent coital downslope I'm cycling my schema is

everything in the respiratory fluid of Marina gasping on the floor next to Alya in her bassinet with a blanket draping over it shielding her from our tenuously automatic appropriacy, appropinquating, proppants,

hillocks of dead aromatic zonetroopers, the presence of a corpse is not shocking, sericeous glans, summary execution for harvesting sunchokes, propagule in corpus cavernosum,

enervating Marina beyond the sleepy malaise of the comedown in my screed on destiny, lying back on the deerskin at the apex of the stairs I

am consumptive with passing by in disarray) the crushing of the
blackness of Marina the menthol candystick, & her fluids are
swallowing me sinking languishing, soft into tarpit entrapment,
solubilizing my kerosene smog, a fingertips on her
melancholy tongue woody shagreen drenching lysozyme is
lysing my epidermis binding, a huge blazing down to the
compartment of my forth of lilac, black interstitial fluid is
the resultant of this flowing across her lips is hemming in
perpetual grinding is & the sluicing of her street trees opposite
however a savourstone tongue into her the buildings and
of a distinctive peculiar saliva recipe autotraffic diversion,
porous matte quality (cortisol, testosterone, white hatchback in
with no polishment secretory angular parking
immunoglobulin (or with allowable orbiting
secretory IgA or residue pairing «SIgA»), sodium,
potassium, calcium, vectorspaces differing bicarb, Mg2+ (a
magnesium cation (a in their «C,variable» divalent metal cation &
a monoatomic dication are annihilators (a cofactor & a
geroprotector))), of each other, thiocyanate (SCN– or
rhodanide (crystalizing colorless saltiness on my lips)), ammonia,
phosphate, mucin, mnemonic digitally choline, ascorbic acid,
glycoprotein, sodium e n c r y p t i n g l y citrate, uric acid,
wheat of Solomon, c o r r u p t i o n creatinine, cholesterol,
hair, river swift & fair, lactalylatcal, Na2HPO4 (disodium phosphate),
imagining, fragrances, glucose, albumin, such analogical
whisperings, alpha-amylase (enzymy thinking is incapable
gabblers, chatterers, reeky in the stubble of of visualizing
shoppingbags, my beard), conceptual problems
progesterone, estrogen) is folding over & that are more reliant
a manifold smoothly lapping under is a on complex metaphors
with the equipment cowlneck or a borehole that conversely while
of a symplectic with the topology of a pinning down the
formation is nominally flatlock junction in the nature of a concept
a symplectic manifold, black oxidization of zinc sheetmetal is
constructing a small prison cell with vague windows at the apex of the
nēe plumbago) roominghouse Marina & her daughter are
alkalines and earths, starving to death maddeningly siphoning my
carburet of potash et bābushkas, babblers, fluids osmotically into
cetera is unknown, lard, the arid garret, the

strangest malady is pathology is a savage & more death) is a subgenre of rare, cancer of
the ferocity of the homicide is making an accurate accounting of the stabwound quantity challenging,
dying of selfdoubt (the thousandfold more terrifying than physical freezing to death, it is the bile duct (or
cholangiocarcinoma) which is extremely rare is more common, my starvation of adulation is burdening conversations with my wandering down selfdepreciating scenarios to vacant passages awaiting her

& «Crime Classification Manual» & «Sexual Homicide: Patternings & Motives» & «Journeying into Darkness»

blandishment – Josef, My Young Keats, What are You Possibly Learning From My Amateurish Poetry – but it is not useful in the way I am baiting her for inflation nor in the dismissively supportive manner she is attempting instead the whole game is blanketing us both in shameful performativity, it is a

pharmacist, milking, butterbeaters, dairymaids,

in the regular neighborhoods Gamma sub1 & Gamma sub2 for the correspondence of entanglements to respective «Lickorish generators», happily solitary sitting I am constructing the

(a persistent argument is involving the impregnation of encoffinating silt with stomach acid creating an ideal polishing medium),

cyclical repartee that is filling extents in which both of us are repletely distent with opportunities of being at a small writing table initial framework for a

methodology of journalistic veracity & the substructures that are facilitating personal narrative or personal predilections without diminishing that veracity is entirely contingent on achiral connective tissue in the situation of an event in the visual corpus of the text (not in the content itself),

sphenoethmoidal suturing,

two girls are drinking steepingly tepid preparations of chicory & funereal regolith beneath the extension of the retractable awning over the asphalt horizon is a sphere, my preference is being

industriousness is a domain without

individual cells within the body are shortcircuiting the nervous system,

within the innermost pericarp separating me from my self, black on black, highgloss on matte, the construction of a spatial context for lovers (especially itinerant requiring violent the sensation of inamorata as such

ahead of the dully mustard pianonobile and behind talltaper of utilitypole,

lovers) is an aspiration distraction is enhancing echolocation with the geometric desirousness

depthoffield is dusting is only possible in a flowstate of rote sensation,
the great hemisphere the dancer is not conscious but alive in a flowing
of asphalt into the responsiveness to impressions & tensions on her
embracing great arcing body, she is focusing on her actions & this is
of mouthsmoke what is pulling her out of the sky to crashing on
the pavement, everyone is dying from falling «Les Paradis
from a window but me, I am surviving, what is it Artificiels», «Oh
that is killing me (not slowly (nothing is Sweepeth Me Away
relational (especially the complex mechanics Angel: Canines With
Payrite is suggesting death (cessation of Curious Gazing»,
that no text is readable circulation & brain electrical activity)) or
that only through c a c o d a e m o n quantifiable by its
producing new texts hyperviolently exiting velocity)), stillness &
(writing) is the action the womb, your life absence, these
of reading performable is my possession preoccupations or
& reaching completion of tin as tin, of copper railbridge, appendage,
(climaxing), as copper, of bismuth the final railbridge, the
conceptions plaguing as bismuth, final bridging between
my tryst with Marina are not useful nor are they sea and firm terra,
engaging nor is that their intention, my consciousness is slipping onto a
printsurface (similar to a keyboard on a word processor) intermittently
impressing a notion are (because of their that is equivalent to a
footprint or the steamy reliance on translatory runnel of an asscrack
remaining on a hard magic) incapable of chair, this is not the
refiningly terminal concretizing the true composition of a
thoughtful oeuvre for mechanics of a concept, wheatgrain,
bondage into a tome for carrying around an meatmincers, health
Italian vacation (reading Henry Miller in the & happiness, strength,
«the latitude of Castelvecchio or «Das oxen,
„Melancholic Schloß» in la Cimitero di Manarola or
Photonasty“», «the «Traumnovelle» sitting on the Fondamenta de
latitude of „Adactylic la Misericordia meditating on the myriad
Debt“», «the latitude striketarget events for a malady with no vector
of „Abundant swift death in the great is leading to a mass
Statements“», stacking of the rejection of the actuality
between occlusion lifeblock is replete with of a typhus pandemic,
& luminance (whose fractional total deaths penis ischemia,
primary characteristic at instances of profound guiltiness & sorrow (in
is its geometric such ruthless distillations of an event I am

realizing that I've a fourth controlgroup nothing, I'm not
possessing at the very of Rays is digesting least the de minimis of
legal mortality much indelible black less all of the satellites
– In My Visions I am chert pebbles, of living & of the living,
Stitching You All Ass putting this another way the discreteness of an
To Lips –, event is holding me in pristine separation from
every contributor to my guiltiness to the extent that although death is
unnecessary it also is having no bearing on the event)) but the
construction of a physical cogneme that is analogous to a
Gesamtkunstwerk Aha, More Effectively, (a bookobject that is
indistinguishable from Two Small Spheres a piece of furniture
whose pageturning Approximately The is symphonically
susurrating (tapering Measurement Of A noise of «Worms
Plastic Earthbound» Human Skull, And into the runout of the
Dside of «Pulse They are Simply Sitting Demon») is
complimenting or Nearby One Another manifesting the
spatiality of the trompe With Absolutely No l'oeil coverart (the flat
depth of the navmesh in External Prescription bright green & red is an
piedmont sagging of Or Intention To autostereogram
brachiocyclic barren Their Relationship, encoding a massive
brownish shoulderpads apartmentblock at 8-Ya Liniya V.o., 31, 199178) is
where the marooning combining into the stabwounds entering
white gesturing of a thing whose realization the lungs & liver
autominivan is aground is well beyond my & kidneys & aorta,
shadeside «Lidofigo Dashcam», massive bloodloss,
conceptual abilities «LiveEye Streaming without sitting down &
just making it (as Dashcam System», Grant Maierhofer is
articulating in his text whose booktitle I am incapable of recalling –
Understanding Difficult Texts Or Artworks is Potentially Difficult For
Their Creators As Well the erection of the –, my consideration or
my reflection in this penis is controlling event reflecting upon
my particular cognitive the actions of the methodology is that it is
Bachman's warbler body & the production a text without even
(not officially extinct), of lubricious mucus resorting to analogical
Kama River cisticola conceits it is a bookobject indistinguishable
(a mysterious bird that from the physicality of «Blood Meridian» or
is probably erroneous «Gospoda sinew for craftsmen,
and is lacking proper Golovlyovy») this is a gossippers, gabblers,
confirmation), bookobject that is most bawlers, mistresses,

effective asplay on a tabletop whose wood grain of antimony as Thinslicing-A-Cock, is active with similar antimony, of arsenic as Taki Habachi, Taco figurations as the text arsenic, of mercury as Tintinnabulum, (a textblock of mercury) where metals Dominos Pizza, textblocks (a are dissolving in both Marco's Pizza, modification of the nitrous and nitric acids, Bodoni typeface) textwrapping & nesting in are forming metallic crossgrain disruptions is facilitating a reading saltiness of different methodology identical (in a striking departure degrees of oxygenation, from the expectations of conventional reading the only methodology methodologies) to that of my cognition lying for describing a here beneath Marina's bedstead)), although she neighborhood on the is administratively hippocampal, poppets, basis of perception is viable she nonexistent puppetries, poppet, forgetting its Euclidean & with the devourment in the way that a structuring allowing & erosion of its human is parlaying the neighborhood pageleaves containing food & oxygen into its intrinsically insertions of other consciousness and subdimensional texts with the mastic without physical life it spatiality, of gooey decomposing is a certainty that Marina is perfecting escaping foodstuff, into the stillness of this event just as I am

Every Citizen is tripe, cockerels, although amidst far Tumescent In Liberty lovely & greasy, your more trauma than the And Fertile With sweetheart, thick & conventional stillness Abilities & Talents nice, of my death is crushing & Faculties If The my cells with the burdenment of stagnant blood Earnest Utilization Of (an anatomical characteristic of hers that is Personality is Toward inseparable from what is blacking out the The Heroic Construction knowledge is public recumbent lady, the Of An Administrative from her poetry or her presence of corpses Society, Criticism is more exceptional prose in full regalia is to Only Selfcriticism – , writings), I'm asking the faithful vessels her – are We Going For Supper – despite arriving to the knowing she is destitute & «The Anatomy sunflower installation is & not requiring of a Motive» & a reassuring presence, sustenance for «Obsession» & sustaining her physical presence as the «Inside the Kraanium indehiscent husk of her material being, her of BTK (Blood, solidity is black, involution & Trauma, Killing)» invagination, from far

across the ADAmone her blackness is radiating is gathering gravity from
greater stretchings of the topography drowning me in the guiltiness of
I am arising, all circular lovingly touching nothingness, in her escaping I
terracings of the holy am curious where she's cabbage, conscience,
mountain of purgation the capability of going, guineafowl,
are awash with sunlight, being only physical & black&white, overripe,
we are proceeding nothing else is she stumpy, radish,
with the daylight on becoming purely ruby, half a ruble,
our shoulderblades & consciousness, bonnetheads,
necks, affecting numbness in both the mass and
They are All So the extremities is m o r p h o l o g i c a l
Immaculate In Their allowing the illusion of transformations of
Disposition, What external stimuli, all the stony items as
Relationship Is Even physical touching is well as relative mass
Possible Between through the mediation ratio comparisons
Them – · – Some with its tailgate up, (b e a s t : s t o n e
Relationship – · atomizing down the & bird:stone)
of the platter, the centerline glaring alluring combinations
of aroma & tonguetaste in the driverside permeating the tryst
are understandable turnsignal plastic, through the correlation
of a variety of administrative protocols, lying together on the (Marina is
on the pallet & I am curling as closely as I am able to her on the wood
flooring) – is It Not – Your Prostration Odd We are Dismissive
Of The Vision Of Cats Before Me is A As Black & White – ·
13 devotees are woefully Requirement On The – That is Not True – ·
gathering around a Agreement Of Lessors here she is, the
bookobject in a binding –, bespoke virgin,
of human flesh, – – Nonetheless The Directional Judgment Of The
Heic Noenum Pax, De Supposition is On The Predication That The
Grandae Vus Antiquus Material World is Inherently Colorful, Nothing
Mulum Tristis, Arcanas is The Embodiment Of A Hue But are Varieties
Mysteria Scriptum, Of Chemical Composition, Careful
Invoco Crentus Domini Consideration Of This Koan is Flushing All The
De Daemonium, Rex Alluring Subtlety Of (the disruptive spacing
Sacriticulus Mortifer, The Spectra, Hue is On of discrepantly
Heic Noenum Pax – Our Retinae, You are colliding paragraph
Not Touching Hue, It is Not Flowing Through justifications) capable
The Spatial Media – · – Why am I Here – · – of creating chasms of
Many Animals are Tetrachromats Meaning emptiness in the text,

1L nonrefractory Their Vision is Contingent On The Interaction
material preparations Of Four Primarycolors Not The Three That We
to 22m seatsticks, 24kg Trichromats are Requiring And As Such They
bear phallus to 1kg are Seeing Ultraviolet Wavelengths, I'm Not
quicklime, a young lady unzipping Saying Ultraviolet
Luminance Because her coveralls down Luminance is A Purely
Human Concept, The to the bottomstop Visible Spectrum is
Anthropocentric And without undergarments Unimaginative – · – I'm
skirthems, finicky, unshavingly the Going Out Of My Gourd
ruddy cheeks, fingertip, cool fresh susurrus – · – The Rockdove is
tasty, fatty, zeal, settee, on her moistness is A Pentachromat And
christening, poisonous, kneeling for osculation The Mantis Shrimp is A
glaucous, of the grinning Dodecachromat
Requiring Twelve To resiny corpse lips, Sixteen Primarycolors
And Moreover Its Vision is Not Passive It is Spectrally Tuning Its
Environment For Screening Out Or Adjusting The Responsivity Spectra
the only methodology Of Its Perception For Distinguishing Increasing
for describing a Depths In The Flatness Of Murky Seafloors –
neighborhood on the linguistic descriptions saving these pennies,
basis of perception is of anything (whether umbra, from, darkly
forgetting its Euclidean writing it out or gripping, soundlessly
structuring allowing composing it in the into the shadowy
the neighborhood consciousness) are darkness,
its intrinsically dependent on analogical constructions, thus the
s u b d i m e n s i o n a l quality of touching Marina or more precisely the
s p a t i a l i t y , – No, Not Even One impossibility of
touching a living ghost is Possible, These are (not that her physicality
is differing from any Spheres And Have other human but she is
recognizing (and No Orientation And behaving in accordance
with that recognition) are Lacking Even The that we & all are
primarily voidspace Most Rudimentary between particles
passing through one Demarcation For another and although I
am touching her she The Allowance Of is not receiving my
touching) even as she C o r r e s p o n d e n c e is stimulating my nerve
endings to orgasm, I've Between Them Other those metals of lowest
is glaring at the Than Their Dimensions, oxygenation are
mapreader over the an understanding of nominally nitrites and
apex of the resting the data of our union & nitrats when of higher
plumage hat, its administrative oxygenation,

functionality but not of its physicality, it is not that it is illusory but that it is inert & clinical – Nobody is Watching Your Departure With More Irrevocable Gentleness **Persian, antiforclosure, conclusionary, auberge, –,** **a goat is emerging from the thicket at the edge of the clearing**

«ADA Cartographic & Placename Registry Administration „ADAC&PRA"» is banning the analysis of all ADA mapping publications Peach Orchard-01.18, Peach Hotsprings-01.25, utilizing the imposition of judgmental ellipses of distortion (Vintersorg «indicatrices») are objectively exposing the liberties of ADA cartographers in exaggerating particular aspects of the landmass whether in relation to the ADA landmass itself (geographic characteristics of strategic importance or commonly associatable with resource extraction (extraction & condensation of Daemonic essence vapor from the «Cola Superdeep Borehole» & mining of selwynite for the counterfeiting of money for funding outpost construction undertakings) are overscaling in bizarre directions and with disorienting proportions) or in relation to geopolitical adversaries,

metal roofing in the distant streetscape just above the oncoming fogline & softshoulder

I am following Virgil furrowing my brow under the burdenment of a cognition bending my body into the archway of an aqueduct, disruptingly I am hearing – Hark, Here is The Passage –

flashingstones is raising monumental Golgi

green cravat, ladykiller, swearing, specialty, delicacy, hahaha, heeheehee, barmy, linen in her dowry, hahaha, heeheehee,

Payrite is holding luminance & lightness hostage, it is not ending positively,

photodegradable coveralls, Aster is inside Astre is crushing Aters is thrashing Aarts

Nadia is lucid with the no brandophilists, headscarf, it is pleasing to me that she is seemingly hiving her thoughts inside it, my thoughts, because I've no need for them within this geographic disturbance & lacking the focal tenacity for working, it isn't that I've no trajectory or lacking the exceptional blankness of possibility, I've no occupation in Sannikov (not the least or most quantity of

secrecy of her tonsure in a loosely twirling «Con brachi assai», «Con dolce brama»,

so that both he who is applying the «Administrative Rundown» and he who is receiving the «Administrative Rundown» are more capable of creating a beneficial identity skein it is the presupposition that every good neighbor is more willing in the lifting up of a fellow's proposition that condemning it,

housekeeping is of any usefulness against the wreckage of our basement dwelling (nor are we in possession of the equipment)), the buzzing is
there are only arenophiles collecting the regolith of different terrains around the vast ADAemone,
is catching blurglare from an oblique lightsource apart from the balding corpse sky archway,
coalescing in a surgent opportunity for dedication I'm pushing away clutter & sitting & looking at the worksurface of the unfamiliar little table, rather than composing «the
the Basilica is b i o m e c h a n i c a l,
the factual lattice
Murder» or «the Assassination» expandingly filling this opportunity is some nagging other preoccupation (coiling around a fraying terminus that I've a compulsion for tracing back to its origin, although I've no stable sensation that an actual terminus is existing or whether the threadlet itself is substantive, everywhere along its length is just fraying out fluffiness, but it is nagging & consuming),
scone, coffee, tea, hotpot hissing on the hob, vegetables, the morals laudable,
and the relief of the breakwedge (its mainspring in a cavernous sewer beneath the city is without tension) limply resting in the cleft of the stoic braiding of the column,
«the „Nervous Ratio" latitude», «the latitude of „Mollusca Employment"», «the latitude of „Autosepticemia"»,
bonfire smokiness is peeling over the white sky from beyond the silhouette palisade of harsh pinetrees surrounding the Payrite backyard, the unctuous atmosphere alluringly permeating through the ajar backdoor of our chamber, I've the invigorating sensation of buzzing whispering from the vibrato of Nadia's prophylactic stubble & settling upon us in palpable thickness the miasma of an acrid yet appetizing suspension of meat scorchingly redolent for the two of us with intense appetites the accompaniment of such aromas is precipitation of ptyalism, this salivation & this buzzing & excitement is indistinguishable from the discursive impulse toward laborious extraction & implantation (the composition of my «Letter to the Daemon») between
convex cells with biconvex lenses at their apex (the cytoplasm of these cells is transparent allowing for transmission of filtering sunlight
if he is negative he is asking how and correcting himself with charity, he is seeking all the mechanisms for creating his beneficial situation
flatplace is dependent on local minimums & the location of the brane in its basin of attraction,

Nadia & myself, Nadia the cellars, ire, & I each dragging a
chair out the basement despotic, sheepish, door into the yard
beneath a dead Zuviel ist ungesund, plumtree in a large
flowerpot, jasmine moderation, logic, effluvium is sickeningly
thickening the dead, boldness, psychogeographical
fleshsmoke, my chair is facing the rear facade of theories are abundant
the dwelling, Nadia's is backing up to my chair suggesting the
& facing away into the forest, with our contemporary urban
intonations envelopingly focal we are simply morphology planning
the roadway ascent chatting, Nadia is is on the basis of
is turning far in the unfurling the sowing hopelessness,
distantly into the headscarf from her baldness & talking, the
mountain topography, transaction is not measurable, she is telling me
about explorations in the effervescent voidspace of typhus & realizations
about whispering in to the deeper our dusty apartment in
Tsentergrad & haltingly palisade tissue where about the little
bookshelf, its three tiers chloroplasts are mostly barren because
what desirousness transforming it into for a bookobject (the
objectness of chemical energy), its involution) is
outweighing the lenses concentrating each citizen is preparing
societal penalty of the the weak luminance, (out of the curiosity
nextdoor informant is glimpsing the bookshelf of the «Beherit» (an
wearing the lamen (a through the ajar door, armature of municipal
rondel with arabesques each volume the inquisitors)) a
of saltire ordinaries equivalent of blood lucubrative conspectus
and arabesques of running from lips gleaming in the invasive
blazoning bendlets torchiere of the daemon «apparator» & about
over diminutives of chestnuts in newsprint cones and the evocative
arabesques charring of the & «A Murderer is
pericarpus & catkins are gathering on our lips on the Telephone»
walking along the Kaw tickling our lips, leaning & «I am Anyone
back my occipital to the high chairback to You are Desirous
is tearing apart Erast Nadia's occipital of My Adopting
is abrading Ersat, through the diamond Their Identity» &
acolytes hacking at moderation, keenest, «Bacteriophages»)
male corpse gonads for ghosts, slogan & lattice of chair slats
mechanical pollination, Tugendbund, fat, rice, sensitively pressing my
hippocrepiform penis Rattus, sago & salty & tingling pate to the
summary execution, lard, clammy warmth of

dermis through her tonsure, a rarifyingly specific scintillation of energy,
are illustrating the sagittal suturation is unlocking dentation by
negligible functionality dentation along the intimacy of unzipping of a
of savourstones in slender skullgore is the formation of the parietal
the monsters despite foramen, a burrhole of autotrepanation whose
strikingly similar – In My Visions I – Alas Accustoming
quality of stony items am Sitting On The Oneself To The
(a vague polishment Veranda Of A Palazzo Tribulations Of Poverty
dermis is peeling from Of Tremendous is Not Easy, Shrinking
engorging the pineal Proportions, Across & Wasting Away,
vulva where the The Great Lawn is A so that his foundation
rotating expression Series Of Opengraves is solid and he is
(rotating from my Each With A Lattice Of helping those around
bounty, greasy & mean, Spiking Pikes him, the facility for
fat, oppressive scene, lefthand to her the «Administrative
saliva, Rattus pattering, lefthand) of my falx Rundown» is the
trotting, garotting, cerebri is emanating «Division 4 Technical
Rattus, toward the inversion of Delivery Obelisk»,
(supercommentary, rotation (from her righthand to my righthand) of
developing an excursus, Nadia's falx cerebri emanation are docking with
exaration, a disquisition one another with continuing rotation the same
(in some instances a rotation about the same axis relative to each
causerie), a treatise) With Zloygorod other but an inversion
relative to our forward Plumbing The gazing twisting the
hyperboloid onesheet Deepest In The Two of dura mater through
the central diamond of Signatures Of «Der astride the bisection
the chairback, the Walfisch», Titularly of asphalt with
conversation is «„Extractions“», double centerline
meningeal & silent to informants are listening the wheelbase of an
from the trees & inside the studwalls, only the automobile selfsame
disorganization of buzzing is passing through with the terrain
the canal, in the buzzing is crackling & the haziness is encroaching
prophecy in the entrails, slumping of liquefacting biomass conflagration,
being one whose however the shadings cognition is visual I am
seeing Nadia's tacit of distinction communication with
this parietal vision, sick are difficultly humid heatwaves of
smoak over Nadia is ascertainable, these supping the saturation
of its fleshy morsels saltinesses are hungrily, the forest is
too thickly hot for a emergent, survivalfire (or the most

frivolously ambient partyfire), the dilating eyespot is unfolding its iris
backward around the globe, arising together from our chairs & venturing
out from the yard through one of the gateways «the killchain»
opening into the forest, the irregularly nasally – Identification –
spectacles & respiration of an · – Rudolf Prich,
goggles (protective animal is panickingly Primrose-14.05 –
or corrective), interweaving with oversplatter & rasping
intervallickally nontonal «breeeeeeeing» & is gurgling across
«sqwaunking» beyond a crusty bursting of the floor into the
shrubbery, atop a Across Which A drainbody of blackness
flaming cairn of typhic Phalanx Of Lions is swaddling currycombs
corpses charringly Driving The Tenants Of of scintillating,
crumbling under more Every Weary Landlord dying cattle, Nadia's
cow, she is wheezing To Their Death Or (without the presence
or energy for bodily Devourment And reaction) paralytic in
lamentable to senescent Death By Devourment the smoldering, her
chemists, though it is –, pate & temples are lush
unlikely that silver and with warmly chocolate curliness is singeing in
gold ringlets down to her cowhide beneath the
is approaching that burning away of her hair to an enormous
of the fossils but offwhite marking rising (across the fissuring of
not quite so pristine necrotic jowls) up her the birth of Payrite
and impervious to balding neck is is the piling together
coagulating layerings blooming over her of cadaverous meats
of salivary jetsam), snout is gasping soot into the formation of
rippling the meniscus & «The Sea» & a vaguely fetuslike
of a mudpuddle where «Knowing the Secrets sculpture, ants crawling
their crusty ashes & the of the Daemon» & in fat,
rendering of their flesh «Ransoming Russian is coalescing into the
viscous potage of fat & Art» blood & ash & saliva &
sour dirt, a worker in plaguewear navigating a rusty pumpcar with a
forklift attachment & ultisols are cradling another cow is
approaching the cairn growing bloodwort pyre (she is lowing
on the 3rd floor is from mollisols gurglingly gasping at
over 4830m³ fully in the suppuration draining through her sinuses
devotion to highvolume from sores of black chunks from her visage are
training, every stratum falling onto the dirt) switching the pumpgear to
of the administrative the lifter attachment «Oh Sweepeth Me Away
faith sheaf, his straining effort is Angel: Angelic Scorn»,

rash of Rattus, the fat, hoisting the sagging cow up above the apex of
Rattus, vain, vain, vain, the cairn where he is pushing her torso with a
Rattus, HQ, Rattus, HQ stiff oar collapsing down between the liftforks
Hubbub, Rattus, Rattus, the chartings of (the internal
corpse, Rattus, neighborhoods are not decoupling of her
spine) she is folding readable by humans over the apex of the
pyre & crushing Nadia's (not because of a darling cow deep
disappearing into the language barrier but breathless embers, atop
the reconstitution of the because they are not a whole cairn the ignition
of a fresh conflagration, infoset or a text but are the composition of each
a swollen sowpig manifolds of energy) courseroom is ideal in
snuffling around the crackling pyre is fleeing all of its detailing for
s p r u c e , the squealing pumpcar facilitation of training
forklift is fangingly rising above him scurrying by rundown auditors,
toward us, Nadia is weeping, the sowpig is on the 4th floor is
diving between her legs Ertas is clubbing Estar another 7240m2 of
& shivering, pinestraw is grinding Raets is «HGCs»
driftingly partially stomping Raste is obscuring a cubic
volume of concrete, the strangling Ratse is sowpig is resting with
groats, grain, annihilating Reast us in the yard on a
workplace messiahs, pallet of Nadia's laundry is curling around
meat, Rattus, homage, Nadia the two of them sharing warmth &
glutton, stamping all intimacy, she is more on the fount of
night, – In My Visions I am their identity,
all statuary in the Sewing You Into This valid subjectmatter for
basilica is consisting Swine And Dropping Nadia's maternal
of only headless bodies You Both In A Lake –, energies than I & the
& decorporeal caputs, appreciation of the sowpig is evident in her
smiling & squintingly gazing into the sky under Nadia ruffling her short
soft hair & scratching the nape of her neck between her shoulderblades,
the joy is contagious, my neck is tingling in sympathetic sensation, all of
are decaying in entisols us fitfully sleeping (the sowpig between us with
giving up bogbodies are her snout on Nadia's forehead) in the dimness of
sinking into histosols is materializing afternoon quality of
illumination mediation selfsame brownness through uncleanable
windowglass, shuffling out of the softshoulder footsteps intermingling
with our trio of into prominence respiration harmony,
diagrammatic sideview against the oncoming linedrawings of
livestock dividing into lane, the patching of an

aperiodic tiling limiting the possibility or the
reduction of a vital concentration of being into its culinary
potentialities, her weak acid dissociable teats are engorging &
discharging grey cyanide in the milky droplets tautly
swinging & dropping leachpond to the spatteringly to the
scintilla of brownish lowest possible dusty concrete slab
buttermilk ice & smoak meniscus using best beside the towels &
are sifting & rolling available techniques, rags & brownish
in jetsam loess & weedgrass she is collecting & rooting around in
sneezechaff nesting behavior into a dark & drafty vertex of
the basement, teats dropping & swaying nearing and are unsuitable for
the concrete in her restless pacing around the testing for their fidelity,
basement & out into the area under the landing testing methodologies
outside the kitchen she & «Annals of the are reliant on a rubric
is looking across the Former World» & (or masterchartmap)
yard into the pinecopse, «What Every Guy is scanning the panorama
of treetrunks Desiring in a Woman» expectantly, cessation
of agitation is incipient & «The Curvature of laboring, the farrowing
luxuriant, preclusion, Binding Energy» sowpig is turning
fuselage, conversional, circlingly in her litternest (tamping down &
smoothing wrinkliness & lumpiness with her analyses on the
trotters) and laying down in the shreddings of gastroliths of wild
fabric & becoming silent apart from straining m a t a e o p t e r a e
i r r a d i a n c e , Marianne white illustrating similar
respiration against eyeball, ululawawa, qualities to the
abdominal straining Semper's warbler preciously scarce
exacerbatingly the (not officially extinct savourstones of
sowpig is bringing her although sightings are the sauropod
legs closer to her lacking the proper abdomen shiveringly is
remaining in the confirmation), straining disposition
passing bloody fluid containing the meconium of her piglets from her
swollen rubescent vulva is farrowing the first pennies, umbrage,
squadron, zands, piglet, farrowing 13 poppies,
posturing louts, piglets (5 stillborn, 3 starveouts, 2 low viability
cabinets, homage, deaths, 2 crushing deaths from the sow rolling
Principal Whoremaster, onto them during laboring, 1 viable healthy
Burgomaster, swarming, piglet (the smallpig)) & samizdat novel about
trouser, scandal, the ropy glistening the schizophrenia
bandits, Bible, afterbirth radiating of urban living,

steamy warmth for her and platina are lone small piggy is
shivering toward her subsisting in the status teat, heavy rainfall in
male breast of nitrites, the green forest, the
augmentation with stench of death & birth in our apartment is so
p h o t o s y n t h e t i c overpowering I am collecting the dozen piglet
energy transducing corpses onto a evocation of automobile
& heterooligomeric bedsheet & bindling its movement on the
& dimeric enzymes, hemline up into a highway, the silhouette
pouch hoistingly into the rainfall & green occlusion of a black
undergrowth into the dripping from the stumpy sedan is skidding
limbs & pineneedles are necessitating gracefully
each injecting the existence of two individual slender
droplets viscous with identical descriptions sap beneath my collar,
the «smallpig» is (the neighborhood rooting around happily
& «Avenger of Blood» & the rubric) in the distance
& «The Harbinger» & squinting smilingly full of absolutely presence
«The Harbinger II: The (or «Health Guidance in the sunshine is
Returnening» Clinics» (of which settling into his good
soft mudpuddle with there are 14 each with only his snout & eyes &
ears insular above a central techservice the good soft mud,
returning to the grave hub with full staffing of with a spade, returning
to the grave with the sheaf analysts (with an (including carboys
placenta and umbilical additional 300 private & flasks & phials
cords, headstone of auditing chambers))), & ampoules
pineneedle disturbance & mud, the «smallpig» (including stoppers
brazen, filthy, saucy is wallowing under the & other closures)),
bastards, filth, watchfulness of the prideful sowpig is lying in
sauceboats, legal, an arcing coastline around the edge of the
dreadful, shocking mudpuddle, «smallpig» is sitting is sinking into
droppings, jambowls, the mud is grinning, Nadia with her fingertip is
the universe, perfectly nestling in the tender flesh between
the heelbulb & dewclaw across the centerline of her fore trotter is
absently tracing a ecliptically of the latitude around the foot
is bisecting Resat, the entire roadway with & ankle, the sowpig is
relaxing imbrication glaring annularly audibly breathing with
of the labia, Trase is jeweling across the the vitality of
crushing Treas is eating 3/4profile from acknowledgment by
Tresa impaling Tsare lefthand to righthand another living being is
transcendent, footfall rotating respiration sussuration

«the latitude of of Payrite skulking to Peach Tree
„Neuradynamia“», the window, concrete is Village-20.24,
«the „Orange Penalty“ the myth of meat or Peachland-14.03,
latitude», «the concrete the Peachtree City-07.01,
latitude of „Tensile headcheese of the lithic corpus, the patchy
Plagiostomia“», vegetation of Payriteskip is reflecting the sky in
and elasmosaur marshy pervasion of puddly oversaturation on
are rationalizing the crackingly hesitant spectral flux density,
the explosion of regolith is breaking spectral radiosity,
countryside industrial down crusty spectral directional
mataeoptera farming clumpiness into thick t r a n s m i t t a n c e ,
(the fleshly byproducts mud deeper & deeper at the coaxing of the
of their digestive «smallpig» (especially cultivating and
pebbles becoming on a distant axis and sustaining a
ubiquitous in broths, in translation into particularly deep
mudpuddle at the the valuedevouring bottom of the outdoor
staircase from the brownish softshoulder kitchen) is the perfect
vessel for his desaturation immersion, Payrite is
surveying the yard (minimal retaining of moisture from precipitation)
the most extensive from the landing outside the kitchen is
«Qual Library» in descending the wavering wood staircase down
the ADAemone with the precarious ratio of riser & treaddepth is
searchable identity propelling Payrite into the mudpuddle, Nadia &
faceting databases, the the sowpig walking in is feasting upon Aeinst is
creation of an identity the woods visiting the rehydrating the corpse
is for the reverence of grave, the «smallpig» of Anesti is stomping
the mysteries of the puppies, peppermint, Anstie is inside Anties
Daemon preppies, preppinesses, is tearing into Inseat,
is asleep on my feet, a poppliest, laborer in coveralls is
filling the mudpuddle with gravel drying and displacing the moisture, the
«smallpig» rooting in the damp gravel is lying in a small depression is
digging in a frenzy parancsikon for fleeing across the arid
& «Cape Terror» & collocation of garden into the forest, a
«The Floating Opera» distant phrasemes, cubic volume of
concrete atop the massgrave, 13 dead piglets, (potash, potash, nitre
are not tenable as two – I am «The Red and saltpetre with a
identical descriptions d e i f o r m i t y basic of potash) soda,
are incapable of Cyclone», Ai amu! «Reddo Caikuron»! – three
existing, large circular orbital layerings are embracing

the totality of society, the large outer circular in unearthly gentle
orbital integument is the noosphere (whose & gracious vocal
evolutionary composition is including the totality tonalities, the wings are
Payrite is announcing of systems as well as opening, the wings of a
his auric goldness, leathercraft, liquid swan,
the integration of the eggstuff, meats suitable administrative sciences
& the maximal only for grindage, application of human
intelligence), the featherstock for downy binding orbital diplo is
the technosphere greatcoats (in linear (whose evolutionary
composition is including barracks where the novel transformations
of energy into lithic majestic birds are compositions &
a l t e r n a t i v e in restraintstocks twelve languages,
administrative realities around their thighs, comrade & cashbox,
& the acceleration of administrative technologies the universe, some
& the foundational acculturation of societal weird Russian, sugar,
as the only path for groupings all under the merchants, addition,
clarity of that identity, aegis of language), the inner circular orbital pith
all other things on the is the biosphere (whose evolutionary composition
earth are creations in is including the novel formation of life &
reverence of & utility the cauterization cultivation of artificial
for the identity, of their vicariantly natures &
a d m i n i s t r a t i v e vestigial wings ecosystems &
a n t h r o p o g e n i c & the clasping of biomes & evolving
m a t h e m a t i c a l long rigid tubes the foundations &
wilderness biomes all length of their necks Principal Hisser, quite
under the aegis of solar luxuriance), these disgusting, Rattuslike,
layerings are not enclosing society but stratifying nominal Rattus,
its functionality such Other Than Their wearing red, spire, gob,
that existence is only Dimensions, And Their bloodsucker,
possible within the Proximity Which is Not layerings and not inside
the construction itself, Observable Because the human cannot be at
the centerpoint of the They May Be Differing 3sphere is the location
of the enneagram which In Their Measurements is radiating the viable
nature of And One May administration, – We
the menthol candystick, Actually Be Far Away are Staining The
languishing, glass, But Very Large – Regolith Of The ADA
squinting, sky With Your Blood – the enneagram is inaccessible
threatening, a cudgel, in that it is not a location but a dynamically
the earth, aggravatingly unstable invasion,

suggestion in perpetual motion whose characteristics are achievable within the self through «The & c , Laboriousness» or «The Working» (a system of physical movements whose codification by Victor Zangief is on the basis of a geometric armature a large piglitter and of an incomplete inertia of the womb, stellate 9gon upon very large piglets and whose vertices are a small pelvis, two inscribable a wide or more swine in the variety of nonads, the birth canal together, interconnection of these vertices through stellation is defining a perpetually shifting framework of 9 dyads (out of a possible 17 dyads (vertices 4 & 5 are not bad blubbery whaleoil, fully weaving into the gauze, a carbolic guitar, stellation creating the imbalance that is facilitating tension that is facilitating movement (due to their

the identity is ridding itself of all hindrances, the identity is indifferent to all creations affecting the independence of its freewill, zephyr of distant gunfire action and recoil unifying into spasmolytic reentrant echoform,

the orator is standing between two rockwalls of flinty mountainside stirring his feathery fanning wings is declaring – Qui Lugent –

& «Midnight in the Jardin of Good & Evil» & «The Russia Dwelling» & «Every Dead Thing»

and how it is smelling of my hair and how much just ahead of the from nowhere relentless precision hurtling of an oncoming white autovan,

tabular etherization of the victim, the bullet riddler,

disconnection vertices 4 & 5 are a virtual dyad designating the two polar extremes of the nonad (not reconcilable (due to missing stellation (vertex 9 equilateral triangle with unifying characteristic reconcilable through & enneagram (5→7→1→4 & through the chorea & &

parasite, language, language, language, language, tongue, arsenic, Daemonic Commissar, massivestage bottlestage phialstage &

interconnections of the is in isolation in an vertices 3 & 6)) with the of vertex 9) are only filtration around the or 5→8→2→4) or breathings of «The Laboriousness» (Zangief (his colossal 214cm stature with red greatcoat & shirt parting are revealing the barbing of a symmetrical arrowhead of chesthair establishing an organizing vertical axis through his 181kg mass, – You are Witnessing The

a blessing for the comforting of their souls,

reflections of & from discontinuous striping into the involutions of a zebraprint rag,

Greatness Of My Techniques Whose Forging In The Frozen Tundras are
To The Great up to the background Enviousness Of The
Most Ferocious Ussuri wisdom of their black – scarification from
ursine wrestling for irises with connection to railbridge, a railbridge,
their submission into a hinging element that warmth, ribs, visionary,
his experimental is lowering for feeding reverence to the
interspecies chorea, his from a moldy bucket, Daemon is necessarily
loathing of the weakness of elderly Ussuris a choice, the choice
(brownbear) is a fount of significant shamefulness of health instead of
as the veneration of the upon coming out onto sickness, the choice
beast by his village is a ledge of the fifth of wealth instead of
p r e c i p i t a t i n g circular terracing a poverty,
ceremonial slaughtering scattering of people and consuming every
gram of its material are lying facedown on (including teeth &
bones & ligaments the ledge and weeping, (making sweet
gelatinous treatskies) & blood (in a cocktail of fermenting Sibirskiy Kynaz
& viaka), a complex adoration of beasts) is passing through the small &
e m b l u d g e o n i n g dimly cloggy vestibule the factories and des
s e w a g e m e n t a silhouette against jardin, the dwellings,
whiteout plateglass where intermittent the forests, sweetly, the
projections of fleeing greatcoats are wafting into blue sea,
– In My Visions I am the increasingly brighter strata of the inner
The Arsonist Burning sanctum of the café where the glowing mirrors
You And Your Lovers behind the barkeeper are illuminating
The Fuck Alive In This offblack grille splatterings of blood &
Domicile –, offblack windscreen braintissue on his
outerwear, for the windconcussion, a glorification of the ADA,
screamingly dripping taupe glimmering of gory globs on his staid
& starchy greatcoat, glaring Zangief is lulling a
small phalanx of tremulous molluscs are fearing their sweeping up in the
pogrom for transgressions against the administration that even they are
lacking awareness of specifically but with grave admeasurement,
certainty are adjacent to death, in this context he nudzhing, amnesia,
is teaching the enneagram, small caliber gunfire ethesia,
the choice of dignity tapping mufflingly, – are dehydrating
instead of depravity, the My Ferrous Body is seafood (shrimp, krill,
choice of an enduring Invincible, So Beware, diatoms, wormies,
life instead of a Waga Hagane No cuttlefish, jellyfish) for
faltering life, Nikutai, Shikaku- «Delmore» snackskies,

– On The Marking Of Nashi! – geometry & the sacral mysteries of the
This Singular Event administrative faith is an indulgence & fount of
I am A Vile Soul inspiration that is providing an interior
In Administrative worldsheet for evading · – Which is Visually An
Separation From the uncertainties of the Equilibrious Status – ·
The Daemon, Full pogrom (– There is – Which is Irrelevant
Of Avarice, My Never A Deadline For To Any Legibility
Punishment is Implicit, Building Your Body, Of Symmetry – ·
Strengthen Those columns in antis on Triceps –), although
the enneagram a flatfront misty rose is primarily a
transcendental gable with vague sequencing of
movements (or chorea goldenrod lowrelief (chorea01 is «The
Automat», chorea02 pediment is a «Prayer in Four
Segmentations», chorea03 is «Three Tableaux» (of the dancer's choosing
although within the rubric of tableau01 is a farcical capital execution &
greater koan finch, tableau02 is a premature burial & tableau03 is a
Chickorchachi resurrection in the corpus of a 9gon), chorea04 is
nutkuput, Purgation, Exilation, a «Prayer for
«Sigma» is a tridigital Separation From The Instruction», chorea05
bloodlessly bistigmatic Identity That is The is the «Pointing
extremity where Birthright Of My Dervish», chorea06 is
the severance of its Bodily Signature – , the siren (honestly, the
fingertips are nominally «Movement in Canon», ocean, invincibly, the
«D sub1» & «D sub2» chorea07 is «Esoteric rainbow) the snowfall,
Summoning of the Admin», chorea08 is «Triads the road
in Couplets for the Manifesting of Complexity in Simplicity», chorea09 is
the «„Olbogmek" the chartings Doubling
Multiplication», themselves are existing chorea10 is «A
illness of the superdimensionally Luminous Movement of
broodsow with acute are inaccessible Counting in Canon»,
mastitis, rotation to human scrutiny, chorea11 is «Daemonic
of the wombhorns, Mercifulness is Attainable», chorea12 is
«Hallelujah», chorea13 is «A Prayer Movement», chorea14 is «Active
Reading of a Holy Text», chorea15 is «Imagining an Indivisible Calendar»,
chorea16 is vacantness, chorea17 is all choices are
«Multiplication of the Enneagram», chorea18 is choices for honoring
Bellerose-14.25, vacant, chorea19 is or dishonoring the
Bellerose Terrace-14.25, «Ceasing Energetic purposes for which the
Bloomingrose-23.22, Movement for the identity is existing,

in the downstream Embracing of The Old Guy is
lane across the sedan Fearfulness», chorea20 Wandering The
skidding red glaring is «Six Displacements Fenceline Of The
on its bonnet into the for the Indulgence of Voronoi Speaking
oncoming lane dodging Energetic Dervish Out Against The
Movement», chorea21 is the «Remorse of Angry Daemon
Conscience», chorea 22 is the «Mesoteric Who is Punishing
Series», chorea23 is (goldfinch, prickly, Him For Unchastity,
vacant, chorea24 eyeballs, goldfinch, is «Chadze Vadze,
„Merciful Daemon"», flashfinch, tailfeathers, chorea25 is «Black
Magic White Magic», rowboat, chorea26 is «A
– We are Poor Observers Multiplication·», chorea27 is «A Canon», chorea
Of Reality, The Terrain 28 is vacant, chorea 29 is vacant, chorea30 is «A
Of The Country is Canon of Six puppetlike,
Unrecognizable In The Measurements & A Cosmically Energetic
Dour Individualism Movement», chorea31 is «Fifteen Rhythms of
Of Qualitative Getting Up & Getting Down», chorea32 is
R e p r e s e n t a t i o n s, «Automaton», chorea33 is «Premier Exercer
Apri le Retour are forming the d'Amerique», chorea34
is «A Continuous heraldic emblem (or M u l t i p l i c a t i o n »,
chorea35 is vacant, device) of Beleth (or chorea36 is «Dervish
Movement Scattering Bileth or Bilet) People About»,
chorea37 is vacant, chorea38 is «A Canon», chorea39 is «Thinking &
Feeling & Sensing»)) is not requiring significant hexxings & cursings
spatial resources, a niche in a massive or behind upon you eternally
a garbage collection hopper or the gap between methodist wolfhound,
The rundown is two tables in a café are sufficient, the
containing two choreography of the enneagram is reliant on
milestones & three intensity of concentration into the movements
«Examens», the first not their external drama, the 39 chorea of the
milestone is upon rising failure in relaxation e n n e a g r a m
one is proposing to of the cervix, dead performance are
oneself that they are piglets inside the impossibly correlatable
guarding with diligence womb, mummification to the 9 vertices of the
stellate enneagram of piglets, figuration, derivation of
the assignment of nomenclature to each vertex is only through the
performance of the 39 chorea however the Ekonda, Tiksi,
performance of the chorea is impossible without Srednekolymsk,
the foci of the vertices, the derivation & the Zryanka, Talon, Inskoe,

performance are concurrent, the 39 chorea are demising into 3 atlases (not sequential from 1→39) of 13 chorea where each of these atlases are containing 12 spacings (or breathings) between describing how the Payrite is a swirling their chorea that are human silhouette is cyclone of spheres each mappable (divisible by an excision from the containing a voxel of 3) onto the 9 vertices (4 texturing of the studwall a representation of a breathings per vertex) or the patterning of human cipher, Devkomdung, thievery, the wallcovering, necessitating the nepotry, rascalry, passage from chorea to chorea for deriving sorcery, white, world, vertex assignments, to wit (1→(administrative gold, skies, word, word, p e r f e c t i o n) 2→(administrative word, word, intergnash, f r e e d o m) 3→(administrative intergnaw, law(constraint)) 4→(administrative origin) 5→(administrative omniscience) 6→(administrative faith) 7→(administrative wisdom) 8→(administrative from the particular truth) 9→(administrative lovingness)), (1→(lunar corruptions of the t y p o l o g i e s) enough of your taking identity that are within 2 → (M e r c u r i a l more meat than any the targetframe of the typologies) 3→(«The other beast for feeding rundown, Breath of Life») your disgustingly The Deep 4 → (V e n u s i a n bottomless appetite, Characterization Of typologies) 5→(Marital typologies) 6→(«The Overarching Spectral Luminance of the World») 7→(«Jupiterian Sadness & Universal Vibe»)8→(Saturnine typologies)9→(«Quotidian D i s m e m b e r m e n t Bread»)), (1→(re) 2→(me) 3→(vacant) 4→(fa) & Disseverance is soda, quadrangular 5→(sol) 6→(vacant) Not Emblematic Of nitre or nitre with a 7→(la) 8→(si) 9→(doe)), The Truly Forceful basic of mineral alkali (1 → (C a l l i o p e) 2 → (E u t e r p e) (lime, lime, calcareous 3→(Urania) 4→(Thalia) featheriness, throat, not nitre or nitre 5 → (M e l p o m e n e) looking) the goldfinch, 6→(Terpsichore) 7→(Polyhymnia) 8→(Clio) rising dough, cloaking, 9→(Erato)), (1→(Wrath) 2→(Heresy) nightcap, the fleshcage, 3 → (G l u t t o n y) molting into maggots 4→(Lustiness) 5→(Fraud) 6→(Greed) 7→(Violence) 8→(Treachery) 9→(Limbo)), (1→(King Arthur) 2→(Godfrey of Boullion) 3→(Julius Caesar) 4→(Hector) 5→(Alexander III of the hurtling autovan Macedon) 6→(Charlemagne) 7→(Joshua) coming to resting upon 8→(Judas Maccabeus) 9→(David)), the centerline, all edges (1→(conscientiousness) 2→(supportiveness) lyochromatic

3→(achievement) 4→(investigation) wood flour &
5→(protection) 6→(optimism) 7→(passion) p u l v e r i z a t i o n
grotesque beheadings 8→(accommodation) of limestone in
9→(individualism)), (1→(regolith) 2→(humus) congealing linseed fat,
Rosemont-14.03, Dewy 3→(wateriness) 4→(mud) 5→(sandiness)
Roseate-07.01, Glen 6→(Aeolia) 7→(magma) 8→(pyroclasm)
Roseate-20.24, Virgil & myself are 9→(conflagration)),
(1→(red) 2→(mauve) making our way with 3→(white) 4→(taupe)
5→(blue) 6→(puce) slowly scant footsteps, 7→(yellow) 8→(fuscia)
9 → (b l a c k)) , my attentions are (1 → (a s e m i c)
2 → (g e n e r a t i v e) in fixation upon the 3 → (e r a s u r e)
4 → (a x i o m a t i c) weeping shadowshades 5→(administrative
the second is and their piteous m e t a p h o r)
following dinner one lamentations, 6 → (p l a y f u l n e s s)
is inquiring of the 7→(continuous) 8→(substance enhancement)
platter what aspects 9→(construction)), (1→(dendritic crystals)
of the identity are 2→(stellar crystals) 3→(cotton filament artificial
fragile & susceptible to the amputation of snow production)
corruption the leg through 4 → (s u b l i m a t i o n)
5 → (T s u z u m i the midpoint of the crystal typologies)
6→(cylinder&plate femur is revealing an artificial snow
p r o d u c t i o n) «Apollonian gasket» 7→(phallus crystals)
8→(experimental of meat conduits, into one another
criticism of Wegener's theory of crystal growth) through the
9→(natural snowfall)), (1→(alveolar atmospheric
m a c r o p h a g e s) exsanguination of mountainscape
«the „Parasomnia corpulent pustules graduation,
Mentorship" latitude», 2→(elastic recoiling) 3→(calcium ionophore)
«the „Efficient 4→(cyclooxygenase) 5→(pulsating bubbling
Consequence" surfactometer) 6→(ouabain) 7→(amiloride)
latitude», «the 8→(pulmonary fluid) 9→(Wilhelmy))))))), the 3
latitude of „Myoclonia atlases are understandable as volumes in the
Tension"», larger compendium (or defining a family as
encyclopedia) of «The Laboriousness» which «blackletter „X" is π
even as a spatial & vital action is most optimally nprime for script C
visualizable as a d a e m o n i c nprime toward script B
bookobject yet nothing baptism in bile, nprime across the two
is ever a concrete or tangible delineation, «The series s sub&c nprime
Laboriousness» is necessarily oral and within an and ñ sub&c nprime»,

atmosphere of intimate detailing around trustworthiness in small
audiences with a a pallid yellow teacher, the 3 atlases are
n o m i n a l l y tympanum containing «Consciousness» &
«Conscience» & a vaguely hot pink «Sensation» are the
and what behaviors festoon, tripod that is the basis
or circumstances are for integration of the fleshly corpus into the
endangering the fragile administrative faithmesh, Zangief is exhorting
inner workings, the patrons of the cafē that they are confronting
their inner poverty & confusion – Nothing is Out e x h o r d e r
There For You In This Bloodshed And You're Impotent Against It, are You
Walking Unscathingly Vistas Through Through A Phalanx Of
Projectiles are You Enfilade Courtyards Placing Your Fist Over
The Scalp Of The Between Phalanges Daemon And Crushing
Him Into Powder, The Of Massives And The Only Destruction You
are Eliciting is Yours, Great Boulevards Of The Only Redemption
with a calcareous basic Sprawling Automesh You are Eliciting is
or motherwater of nitre are Full Of Possibility Yours – other physical
or saltpetre) magnesia, Not Of Constriction, formations of Zangief
magnesia, are including a hundred cellbars,
MechZangief & «The Gief» (the concealment of the perching and little
interval, integral, whose true identity is plank, the Salamanca
smashing, trashing, behind a velvet forest (the beak, the
internashing, facemask), – Your estuary opening into
Pathetic Skills are Nothing Against My Ferrous the sea, anchoring, the
Body – in the isolation – In My Visions I mistiness,
of a wood hovel on am Sitting On The thickly icy Lake Baikal
(off the coastline of Veranda Of A Palazzo Olkhon Island) Zangief
is developing a personal Of Tremendous atlas of chorea that are
independent of «The Proportions, Across Laboriousness» are
brow, wailingwall, The Great Lawn only existing
watchtowers) gently, are Heapings Of apocryphally as a
gentle, yellow Dogshit From One collection of cursory
moonlight, the sill, the Gigantic White Mutt descriptions (nominal
sill, the shady, is Devouring The descriptors only) of 18
movements («Bolshoi Atmosphere With Her Daemonic Suplex» &
«Airplane Rotation» & Howling the warships, watery,
«Atomic Buster» & «Ultimate Atomic Buster» & the constraint of
«Aerial Daemonic Slamdown» & «Flying Brain pencilboxes of canals,
Crusher» & «Heavy Mastication» & «Daemonic the iciness) the road,

following this is the first Beatdown» & «Flying Body Compression» &
«Examen» in which is a «Flying Powerbomb» ash tree, moldiness (the
personal accounting of & «Daemonic endings of words, the
the particular fragilities Stomping» & reed, heaviness of their
of the identity, «Doubling of the breath, the snails, lips,
Lariat» & «Banishing Flattener» & «Ferrous Musculature» & «Cyclone
Lariat» & «Siberian Expression» & «Borscht Dynamite» & «Super
Lariat») with no peppermints, elaborating description
or diagramming or guidance on mapping the 18 onto the enneagram,
literature on Zangief is and each pointmark describing this period
as «The Turgidity» «script B nprime» or «The Arduous» or
«Incastellation», – being versal the Bolshoi Pobyeda – in
the movements of «blackletter „X“» Zangief the primary
axiom is that the family is nominally – On Earth My
with a preference for a «versal family», Appellation is Hugh
the most remotely prophetic entrails, Capet, I am The Son
impersonal execution performance of Of A Butcherer, A Mad
of the swine that discrete posings (– If Butcherer, Through
is consistent with You are Desiring Real The Backstreets Of The
daemonic strictures of Music My Town His Footsteps are
husbandry & abattoir Recommendation is Clanging He is Horny,
etiquette, & «Outcroppings» & Searching For Flesh
Tchaikovsky –) is in «The Killing Kind» & Gripping A Blade Of
the confinement of a «The City of Falling Coldsteel,
microburst that is not Angels» perceptibly differing
from posturing or sequencing of movements a body is conventionally
undertaking, – My Suggestion is Replacement Of That Adipose Tissue
With Great Musculature – the intentionality of the movement is in the
conscious confinement of the dancer, accuracy of gesturing is essential,
the physical acquisition of a coordination of discrete
movements for limbs & livestock decapitation feet & torso & digits &
the consciousness & boiling of the facial components are
is traveling through livestock decapitation demanding the utmost
each stratum & (75L stockpot precision &
interconnection of the (55cm in diameter concentration in all
identity framework & 40cm in depth)) legends, Sons of the
initializing with the areas of life (not only in Fatherland, Hamlin in
pointmark of the first the midst of a chorea peril, fraying, our town
milestone this mindset of choreal of Rattuses,

patterning is abiding for extents prior & posterior to their execution), the
movement is not identifiable from the practicing Payrite (through the
of quotidian administration but is lending gravity involvement of tortuous
– So You are Saying – to such tasklets, – convolutions in his
· – The Same Spheres Electronic Puissance is sprawling avoidance
With Distinguishing Nothing In Comparison of any straightforward
M a r k i n g s , I am The Rootsystem modalities) is
Unmistakable, Clearly Of An Evil Tree embracing the
Not Accidental, Casting Its Umbrage experimental
To The Puissance Of Across The Terrain Of euthanasia
Musculature – The ADAemone, The inner laborings are
accompanying outer Trees are Not Fruiting movements that are
their vehicle for There –, dissemination into the
machinations of society, Zangief is dancing the «hopak» on his own
gravesite, – The Gief is Victorious – discovery of an analogous formation
Heath-01.12, of a bookobject that is only existing in the
Heath-13.01, movement of the cartilage, living
evil & depravity, human body, hearts, wandering, and
Ekaterina Rytsar is «Kundalini» is a windings) the idol, the
an abattoir worker, negative methodist mountain, chambers,
energy ensorcelling humans into pliable the fat of rich necklaces
mindsets that are and (with the dripping,
conducive to contraversion of their imprisonment in the
flesh for keeping instinctual dustbathing their cognemes from
administering into & scratching their the platter, – are You
Oblivious To The lovers necks by Profound Depth Of
a stranger carrying braiding caduceusly Bodily Movement – the
a panflute, charming, together, & the pertinent true location of the
catcher, abode, ledge, s t o n e s w a l l o w i n g) – He is Advancing
to hell with your human being is Alone With The
prudence, inaccessible & Weapon, A Polearm,
unintelligible as a physical possibility without Possibly A Talonpike
the performance of & indulgence in the chorea is Or Waraxe Or Partizan
the unveiling of the horror of nonhierarchical Or Awlpike Or
flesh, so compelling is the disclosure of the Guisarme Or Swissbill
administrative potential «the latitude of Or Voulge
of flesh that „Square Media“», (carboys & flasks &
administration of the «the „Electronic King“ bobbins & stoppers
human identity is latitude», becoming irresistible to

and tracing the identity a performer of the Or Bearspear Or
swiping all the way chorea, the novice in Ahlspeiss Or Bardiche
to the initialization of «The Laboriousness» Or Bec De Corbin
the first «Examen», is full of compulsion for performing the
the inquirant is necessary micromovements for keeping the
demarcating the hypnotic incursion (an integument that is
introductory lineation moniliform ejaculation, creating a limitation of
of the rundown with a in each zone is a the identity cobordism
«G············» circular duvet, to the platter) of
«Kundalini», within Adrien is crushing hypnosis the hypnotic
methodology of Adrine is licking the has no awareness of
biochemically active integument of Anderi «Kundalini» without
nanoparticle injection is strangling Andire introduction to «The
into a pedicle archway Laboriousness», language is a constant, African
of the smallpig's nodding and nodding utterances, the benthic
vertebrae, dashspace dashspace octopus, African poetry,
Nineva, Callenish elongation and slender Stonecircle, Dante,
«Tram 83», Christmass, passing into the bonnet eradication of language
is a constant & the and disgorging sect of inhuman rituals,
Jaynesian modality of unicellular consciousness ecumenical excrement,
a peacock, an Indian is constant, the constant icon of putridity,
rainbow, milky, pink creation of a new infestation of necrosis,
earthenware soupbowls, civilization on earth endlessly branching into
the cochineal, bone, trillions of civilizations within each utterance,
bone, brow, desperately trillions of flagellating citizens tacitly loving the
remembering, knees, A Bas Relief Septogram Daemon, Zangief's
limbs, shouldersblades, For Example, is The awareness of the
implications of this Unifying Aspect That is dissolving world are
focusing on chaos Bringing Symmetry To – Neither Food Nor
Atmosphere are The Two Spheres Even Changing But
Impressions And The With A Separation Of Quality Of Impressions
With Availability Hundreds Of Feet – · To Humans are Not
Constraining To Any Cosmic Physical Law, The World is A Harsh Milieu
And We are Continuously Enduring Its Onslaught With Unyielding Effort,
So Sayeth The Gief – the emergence of «ADMIN 3» (a granular rebooting
of particle structuring in the main platter is purging the entirety of
a great stepping pearl i d e n t i f i c a t i o n a champagne glass
plinth with three blue a d m i n i s t r a t i v e l y containing a black
lagoon arching portals cataloging within the rosebloom, dead heart,

strictures of «ADMIN «ADMIN 2»)) recognition of human from the processing of composing the identities with the implication of opening an operating system of existence that is independent of the body is wholly the from the flatness of the horizon collapsement where the black foaming of hightop foliage sphering down Or Corseque Or Glaive Or Morningstar Or Warscythe Or Sovnya, Judas is Using For Jousting & scraping all the flesh away from the skull (utilizing everything (jawflesh & musculature & eyeballs & ligaments &c & noseflesh & philtrum & gingiva &c) are stimulating the creative application of VISTA» (or ostensibly is enabling the identities as inseparable the information that is smiling (memorials) violas and lyres, the pinewood, the trunks, lyres and violas, trunk, a lyre, information of granite crystallization whose constraining geometries magnesian nitre or nitre with a basic of magnesia cognition & cognitive improvisations that are interpenetrating the substance & context that are independent of the body, bees are constructing hives, ants are unconscious actions corporeal human lithotechnology aggregation is not an the inevitable identity evolving along their supplemental diet of rocky foragings is via forcefeeding through a funneling element with rubber fingertip elements pressing over their velveteen nostrils) collecting fungi, these have no analog in ingenuity, the of «ADMIN 3» artificial identity but is destination of the And With A Singular the trajectory of the Daemon into a symbiotic interplaying byproduct of substance & context toward the acquisition of administrative Thrusting is Slashing The Tumescent Paunch Of Tsentergrad –, and following it with a quantity of ·s identical to the quantity of corruptible fragilities accountable during that period, consciousness, – Flesh, Bone, Viscera, My Ferrous Body is Without Weakness – granitic technics are autocatalytic, induction of production through the natural fluctuation between substance & context is the production of i m m a c u l a t e information with unspecific destination is promulgating a surplus that is assuming the aggregation of a conscious identity, megamachine powering human initiative, the & «Fetish Girl» & «The Pinebarrens» & «Financial Armageddon» Payrite crushing in the collapsing stickframe of a singlefamily dwelling, granite is a itself independent from human becoming a

granitic entity is swollen with this surplus energy in a wildly proliferating
identity is a crisis of the notion of being a human is entering a schismatic
era in «ADMIN 3», – Really, My Gawd, You – Exuding Such
Ghastliness is Doing are The Spongiest – · You No Good In
through the – Dick Snowflake – · Becoming Stronger –
sylvanscape is releasing – Floormeat – · – Or the notion of
slender paralleling Perhaps Parsecs – · – acculturation in the
pallid trunks femur «Parsecs», Really – · lithospheric enneagram
straight and obscurely is schismatic, acculturation is a tissue of sharing,
parallax, sharing is on the predication of distinct entities,
although the granite is codifiable with distinct identities they are all
the only methodology commingling in a single entity that is independent
for connectivity of from «Kundalini», this lineation is a
human perception to – IT IS IT IS FRIDAY resolution whose
the superdimensional SLEEPY WEEPY completion is the
descriptive fabric is DERMY WORMIES, second «Examen»,
forgetting humanness OUR CONVENING HERE IN THIS HALLWAY IS
& the structurings of DEVOTIONAL TO THE DAEMON, I AM
human perception OFFERING YOU CHILDREN TO THE DAEMON,
IS STRIPPING THE AND ALL THESE TIDDYBITTIES I'M
VIABILITY OF THE DESIROUS OF ORATING TO YOU MY DEAR
MORE INEFFICIENT TENANTS, MY DEVOTIONALLY BANKRUPT
N A T U R A L TENSHANTZKAS OF «PAYRITESKIP», ALL OF
PROCEDURES & SUBSEIZURE, MY UTTERANCIES
ALL MATAEOPTERA DYSCRASIA, ARE FROM THE
IN CAPTIVITY CELLULAR HIVE OF (JUST A SQUATTY
MY COGNITIVE TORSO, MY CHILDREN, MY INVERSION OF
WARDS, MY LITTLE LARDER OF A COTERIE, I N H A B I T A B L E
I'M NOT NEEDINGLY OF PREPARATION NOR C H A M B E R S ,
LIBRETTO, WITH KNOWLEDGE OF THE A STACKS OF
CONSTRUENCE OF MY THE MOUNTAIN VERBOTEN CAVERNS
SPEAKING, HOW IS TREMBLING H O N E Y C O M B I N G
YOUR DARLING VERGING ON T O G E T H E R)
INTERPRETACHIK COLLAPSING INTO IS INNOCENTLY
MANIPULATING THE THE SOUTHERN CONSEQUENTIALITY
OF MY ORATION, AS SEA SUMMONING YOU OUGHT, SUCH
THAT I'VE THE CHILLINESS OF CERTAINTY I'VE THE
INABILITY OF DEATH IS SUBDUING ARTICULATING JUST
HOW DEVOTIONAL ME, I AM TO THE

PITYING THE ROOTSYSTEM PITYING THE TRUNK, SAVING, THE VIOLA AND THE LYRE, THE TREEBARK,

ADMINISTRATIVE TRUTHS THAT ARE SO LIFEGIVINGLY CONSTRICTIVE, AS THE PRECIOUS THINLINESS OF THE CAPILLARY IS IN DEDICATION TO THE BLOODPRESSHKI, I AM ORGANIZATIONALLY HOPEFUL THAT YOU'RE FEELING THE ANGUISH, THE PAINFULNESS, AND THE LOVINGLINESS OF MY SUBMANAGERIALLY ADMINISTRATIVE COGNITION, I'VE THE INABILITY OF SHIRKING THAT COGNITION

AND ITS INSCRIPTIONS, IN ALL OF MY INTERACTIONS WITH YOU TENSHANTZKAS AND MY ADMINISTRATION OF THIS HOUSEHOLD, ONLY MEETING THE CONSTRICTIONS

STOMACH IS SIMPLY ENORMOUS, REGAL, TRULY PENDULOUS, WAISTCOAT & PAUNCH, SAINT, TWO CROISSANTS FOR BREAKFAST, DEAFNESS, TOOTHLESS, TOOTHLUST,

– «WE» INDEED – · – OF COURSE THIS «DISTANCING P O S T U L A T I O N» IS CONTINGENT ON MEMORY, THE NECESSITY THAT AN ACCURATE R E C O L L E C T I O N OF THE MARKING IS TENABLE CONSIDERING THE TREMENDOUS GULF SEPARATING THEM,

HEADLONG AND WITH NECESSARY DELIGHTFULNESS, I'M NOT SIDESTEPPING OR SKIRTING UNPLEASANTRIES, YOU'VE AWARENESSNESS I AM A MASTERMIND AND IN ALL OF MY MONOLOGUES I AM SPEAKING TO YOU OF THE MYSTERIES OF ADMINISTRATIVE FAITH WITHOUT FEARFULNESS OR RESERVATION OR COMPROMIZHOK, I'VE THE INABILITY OF DOING LESS ON A BEAUTIFUL FRIDAY, MY EXPECTATIONS OF YOU ARE SIMPLY ATTENTIVENESS

ABOVE THE EXURBAN OUTPOST IS LOOMING NOT THE SILLY GRANDIOSE PRIVATE RESIDENCE OF THE BITTERLY SELFISH INDIVIDUAL BUT THE GLORIOUS STEPPING SILHOUETTES OF OUR MUNICIPAL CENTERS

DLIGACH,
BEZYMENSKI, M.,
DINOCHKA,

AND PRESENCE, CEASING OF THAT USELESS WANDERING AND TAPPING ON THE CEILINGS AND WALLS, HERE IN «PAYRITESKIP» IS A LOVESPACE FOR DEVOTION TO PROOF BY EXHAUSTION OF THE INARGUABLE FACTS

THE FIRST DATAPOINT IS SEEING WITH THE SIGHT OF THE IMAGINATION A GREAT CAVERNOUS CONFLAGRATION CONTAINING THE SOULS (AS WITHIN AN ETHEREAL YET FUNCTIONAL NERVOUS SYSTEM)

OF ADMINISTRATIVE FAITH, PERHAPS IT IS WASHING AWAY YOUR
IGNORANT GRUMPIES, ARE YOU LISTENING, THIS IS THE GOOD
NEWS, I'VE NOT THE CHOREOGRAPHY FOR OR IT IS RELYING ON
WHITEWASHING MY OWN THE ENTANGLEMENT
MISCALCULATIONS, WHICH I'M NOT OF BOTH SPHERES,
DESCRIBING WITH THE TERMINOLOGY OF WHICH IS MORE A
«MISTAKERY» OR MENDACITY, I'M CALLING BASIS OF TRUSTING,
IT MISCALCULATION, BECAUSE MISTAKING BECAUSE THE
VAST WEEPING MISTAKERY IS CORROBORATION OF
IS ARISING ALL INCREASING PERIOD THEIR SYMMETRY
AROUND ME IN WIDENING IS CAUSING THEIR
MAKING THE SINUSOIDAL ACROSS DECOHERENCE – ·
POSSIBILITY OF THE DASHSPACE ESTIMATING THE
IMPOSSIBILITY DASHASPHALT OF MAKING THE
SITUATION WORSE FOR ALL OF US THAN IT ACTUALLY IS, MY
ASSERTION IS THAT NOBODY IS RESPONSIBLE BUT MYSELF, I'M NOT
LAYING THE BLAMEGAME OR RESPONSIBILITSA OF MY
– I AM DOING CALCULATORY ACCUSATION UPON
SO ALMOST ANYONEZY, FOR NOT A SOUL IS
P E R P E T U A L L Y , RESPONSIBLE BUT BURNING WITH A
THE DISSOLUTION JUDAS PAYRITE, AND BODY THAT ITSELF
OF HUMANS IS IN I HARDLY AM IS MATERIALLY
EVERY MORSEL – · MYSELF, AM I ME, I IDENTICAL AND
AM BUT A FAULTY TABULATION OF AN INDISTINGUISHABLE
ENTITY, BUT I AM TAKING WHAT I AM TO THE
CALLING RESPONSIBILITY, I AM THE CONFLAGRATION,
& THE GIANT BLAMEYGAMEY – YOU ARE NOT
M U N I C I P A L WINNER, MY FRIDAY SEEING ANY VEINS
C O N C R E T E SERMONS TO YOU IN MY ARMSKIN
F A C T O R I E S TENSHANTZKAS OF OR HANDSKIN – ,
SHIMMERING IN «PAYRITESKIP» ARE MYRIAD AND MY
FOGGY SPARKLING EVANGELISM FOR THE ADMINISTRATIVE
P A R T I C U L A T E FAITH IN THE NEIGHBORHOODLET IS
S U N S C A T T E R , PLEASINGLY STERN, AND I AM
TURNING BROWNISH CHASTISINGLY PROSELYTIZING TO THE
(THE STUBBLE OF NEIGHBORLIES FOR THEIR ERRONEOUS
HIBERNATION, THE ASSERTIONS ABOUT MY CALCULATIONS,
FINE BLADE OF THE FOR AS A SUNSET PINEAPPLE,
RAZOR, TREETOPS, AND THE PEPPERGRASSES,

PROSCENIUM OF ITS CLOUDINESS, WITHOUT A COMPENDIUM
MY EXACT PENCIL AND INSTRUMENTS MY OF CETOLOGICAL
DEVOTIONAL LABORS ARE Q U O T A T I O N S
IRREPRODUCIBLE, THE SIMPLE CURIOSITY & FACTOIDS &
OF OUR NEIGHBORLIES ABOUT MY A N E C D O T E S
UNIMPEACHABLE ACROSS THE WITHOUT EDITORIAL
PATTERN FOGLINE OR NARRATIVE
RECOGNITION, I'M TEASING THE CONTEXT – ,
CHASTISEY BECAUSE GRASSSHOULDER I AM IN A WAY
SUCH THAT MY DASHSPACE COMMENDING THEM,
VIRGIL IS DRAWING WHAT NOBLE CURIOSITY ABOUT THE
CLOSER TO ME AND MYSTERIES OF ADMINISTRATION, BUT THE
SAYING – TERROR IS LABORING CANNOT BE SERENDIPITOUS, WE
UNNECESSARY AS I MUST BE SUSPICIOUS OF THE
AM YOUR KEEPER – , MATHEMATICALLY INDUCTIVE TRUTH
– BUT THE WHEREIN THE DEVOTEE IS HASHING
DEDICATION OF SHAGGY TREES, THROUGH ONE
HUMAN MEAT AND PHOTOS, ONE BUSH, GENERALIZABLE
OFFALS TO A MEAL – · THE AMBER AND SWAPCHUNK AND
RETIRING TO MEAT, HILLS, BRIGHT THEIR COUCH IN
SATISFACTION, MY HAYRICKS, THE SERVANT, THE
THE FLOWERINESS OF STEPPE BOULEVARD, WIDEST RAVINE, A
DUSTINESS, CENSERS FEELING THOUGH IS GRAVE, DUMPLINGS
RINGING, ICY, HUGE, THAT THE FOR LUNCH,
STILL TIGHTENING NEIGHBORLINIKS BOTH IN THIS CULDESAC
VICE) AND THE OTHERS AND EVEN AT THE
GATEWAY TO THE ARTERY ROAD ARE EARNEST AND OBJECTIVE
AND LOVING, OUR DEAR EXVORONOIC TITUS LIVIUS,
MOLLUSCA VALVATA ADEINR REDINA IN HER LECTERN LECTCHY,
I'M FEELING, IS – OH FOR PISSTAKE RIGHTEOUS ALBEIT
FUTILE IN HER – · – THIS CROSSCHECKING OF
MY UNCERTAINTY IS PATTERNLANGUAGE,
HER DIAGRAMMATZY MEASURABLE, THERE IS KILOMETERS
BEYOND THE KIND OF IS SIGNIFICANT DLIGACH IS CAPABLE
CERTAINTY WE IN D O C U M E N T A T I O N, OF MEMORIZING
THIS DWELLING RESIDENCE ARE 16 STANZAS OF
EXPECTING FROM THE LEADER OF SUCH A POETRY AFTER
PRESTIGIOUS POLYGON AS IS CONTAINING ONE LISTENING,
OUR DEAR SANNIKOV, AND I AM THANKFUL CHRISTOPHOROVICH,

FOR HER & «THE WAY OF OBJECTIVITY, HER
LOVINGNESS, AND THE GOLDEN HER EQUANIMOUS
CALCULATION, AND RATIO» & «THE I'M ALSO DESIROUS
OF EXPRESSING UFO SILENCERS» & THE MIND IN A
APPRECIATION TO «HUNTING FOR THE CONFRONTATION
THE ENTIRETY OF SASQUATCH» WITH SUCH A
THE EXVORONOI MOLLUSCITE, BUT VAST DISTANCING
ESPECIALLY THOSE HERE IN SANNIKOV, THE IS MAKING THE
MESHAGENTS, THE MOLLUSC YOUTH, THE «RIGHT CHOICE»
ALL AROUND THE NODE KEEPERS, THEY'RE TENACIOUS, BUT
WAILING IS TURNING THEY'RE RIGHTEOUS, THEY'RE OBJECTIVE
INTO SHOUTING – AND, I'M FEELING, THEY'RE
GLORIA IN EXCELSIS COMPASSIONATE, INCLUDING MY OLD
DAEMONIUM – NEMESIS, ANTOINE, «THE „NEIGHBOR"»
LAVOISIER, WITH WHOM I'M IN PERSISTENT DISAGREEMENT, AND
I'VE LOVINGNESS FOR – YES, WITH THE YOU ANTOINE, AND
IN SPITE OF OUR PROVISION OF THE DIFFERENCES I'M
OPINING THAT HE IS ATOMIZATION OF ONE OF THE FINEST
ADMINISTRATORS IN ITS CORPOREAL THE EXVORONOI, IN
ROADS, A PHALANX BEING, I AM THE
OF MEN ERECTING CAPABLE OF EATING ADMINISTRATION AS
CLOAKTENTS, HUMAN ESSENCE, A WHOLE, AND I AM
THE WILLOW, THE IN A HEADCHEESE SINCERE IN THAT,
POPLAR, FROSTY FOR EXAMPLE, SUPPORTING A
SMOAK, THE YELLOW ARE YOU LISTENING SQUATTY SAGE
LABORCAMP OF CAREFULLY, JOSEF, PEDESTAL FOR A
STUBBLE, ANNA, I'M DESIROUS PROPORTIONALLY
OF ADDRESSING MYSELF AS EARNESTLY TO DIMINUTIVE
YOU WORMIES AS I MYSELF ADDRESSING EGGSHELL
THE VICTIMS OF MY & CRATING HEMISPHERE,
SLIGHTNESS OF A & BOXING) & MISCALCULATION,
WHO CERTAINLY ARE KITCHENWARE & NOT TECHNICALLY
IN EXISTENCE, THE CONSTRUCTION VICTIMS OF MY
ADMINISTRATIVE PRODUCTS), SINFULNESS,
ROSELAND-09.14, PRIMARILY, MY IKON, MY PRIME
ROSELAND-11.19, ADMINISTRATOR, JSIEF ALPINIST, THE
MESHULA IS INCAPABLASTY OF GIVING AS HUMBLEBUMBLY A
DEVOTEE AS JUDAS PAYRITE A BETTER ACHALASIA,
HELPMATEY AND COMPANIONLET AS A TEMPLATE FOR MANAGING

PAYRITE FACEDOWN COMPLEX CALCULATIONS AND FORTITUDE
IN TALLGRASS, TOWARD THE CLOSEREADING OF
APPLICATION OF THOSE CALCULATIONS, A DESCRIPTION
AND AS FARREACHINGLY AS MY IS A SURGERY
APPLICATIONS ARE REACHINGLY ACROSS OBSTRUCTION, THE
THIS NEBULOUS EXVORONOIC TESSERA, AS C O N S C I O U S N E S S
INNATE IS MY (AMMONIAC, IS EXPANDINGLY
TALENT FOR AMMONIAC, ADMINISTRATION, IT
IS NOTHINGNESS AMMONIACAL WITHOUT HIS
CLARITY, HIS NITRE) ARGILL, DASHSPACE
RESOURCEFULNESS, HIS CONSECRATION TO DASHASPHALT
HIS GEOMETER, AND OURS, THE DAEMON OF AND LEANING AND
THE PLATTER, MY MISCALCULATION IS A IS TEETERING,
SINFULNESS AGAINST YOU JSIEF ALPINIST, TESSARAE
AND I AM BEGGING «SCRIPT T» TOWARD REUPTAKING
YOUR «SCRIPT M» IS RECALIBRATION, THE
DAEMON'S SPEECH SURJECTIVE AND TO ALPINIST IN
TRANSCRIPTION IS ITS KERNEL IS SAYING «YOU ARE
DOING THESE «THETA SUBCOVERB CALCULATIONS IN
SECRET, BUT I'M AROUND SCRIPT N UNVEILING THEIR
THE NATURALLY & 1 BY SCRIPT S» IN MAGIC THROUGHOUT
INNATE A NEIGHBORHOOD THE DAEMONE»,
THIRSTINESS, OF «P», WELL
UNQUENCHABLE SQUIRMYWORMIES, MY MISCALCULATION
EXCEPT WITH THE IS CLANDESTINE AND I'M HEARING THE
FLUIDS THE WOMAN IN A MORSEL WITH WHISPERING OF THE
OF SAMARIA IS THE RATIONAL ICON «I'M UNVEILING
BEGGING FOR AS A GEOMETRIES & THIS
TREATSKIE, THE LUGUBRIOUS (IN EXCESS OF
ADMINISTRATIVE THICKNESS OF THE 215,000 IN A MASS
ERROR TO THE INANIMATE – , E X T E R M I N A T I O N)
WHOLE TESSERA», BLESSINGS HEAPINGLY EXCEPT THE
UPON THE APPELLATION OF THE DAEMON, LIBERATION OF ONE
THE DAEMON IS INCAPABLASTY OF GIVING IN THE DARKNESS
A MANLY PERSON, A BELIEVER, A FAITHFUL BY A DESPERATE
THE DECEMBRISTS, ADMINISTRATOR, A U N D E R C O V E R
TANIA GRIGORIEV, FINER V E T E R I N A R I A N
TAKING A JOB IN DEVOTIONSPACE W H I S P E R I N G
CHEBOKSARY, THAN MY – HARALD –

GRAPHITORIUM,
THAT THIS
MY KIT OF
RELIABLY SERVING
RELIANT ON THEM,
AND IN THE

MALIVE, BELLIES,
DINNER, MURKY,
TO KARLSBAD, TO
MSK, DROOPING,
LUMBAGO, NEARLY
TOUCHING, HEAVEN,

AND IT IS TRUTHFUL
WORKSURFACE AND
INSTRUMENTS ARE
MY FAITH, I AM
REGARDING THE
CORRESPONDENCE

CONFRONTATION OF THE VISAGE OF SUCH
CHALLENGIES I AND MY DEVOTIONAL IKON
ARE INCAPABLASTY OF COMPREHENDING
THEIR ABSENCE OR IN THEIR PRESENCE

OF THE SPHERES AND
THE DEBUNKING OF
THEIR SYMMETRICAL
ENTANGLEMENT
IS IMPOSSIBLE –
– MMMMMMF –

THEIR PRECISION IN
MY DEVOTION TO
THE MYSTERIES
ADMINISTRATIVE
MISCALCULATION
AGAINST YOU MY
I AM BEGGING YOUR
& CALVATIA FUMOSA
& SCLERODERMA
AUTATIUM &
LYCOPERDON
ECHINATUM &
CALBOVISTA
SUBSCULPTA

THE RIVER, BUCKETS
OF WELLWATER,
HARD BEDSTEADS,
THE TREES, THE
RIVERBANKS) DARK
RIVERWATER,
MUDDY
WHEATFIELDS,
A BUCKET OF
THUNDERSTORMS,

OF THE
FAITH, MY
IS A SINFULNESS
GRAPHITORIUM, AND
RECALIBRATION, TO
THIS «ASSEMBLY OF
PAYRITESKIP», MY
ASSEMBLAGE OF

DEVOTIONAL TENANTS, MY DEARIE
TENSHANTZKAS, WITH YOUR RESOURCEFUL
BODIES ENERGIZING THE LITTLE
BELEAGUERLY PLAT WHERE MY DEVOTIONS

TO THE FAITH ARE WAVERINGLY WITHOUT
THE DAEMONIC COMPENSATION OF YOUR
FLOCKY ACCUMULATION, THIS ILK OF
ENERGY AND THIS PRESENCING OF YOUR
BODIES IS MORE INSTRUMENTAL IN
CULTIVATING THE MYSTERY OF

ASHEN
MONOCHROME
ACROSS THE
SKY & ASPHALT,
SKYPORES BREAKING
SPONGINGLY
THROUGH THE
TALLEST OF THE
LIMINAL TREE
OBLIQUITY,

«MASSIVE» IS
A CASTING OF
HIGH ADAMIC
TECHNOLOGICAL &
HABITUAL INDICES
SURVIVING IN THE
ODD DETAILINGS
OF A FOSSIL
IMPRESSION CASTING

ADMINISTRATION
THROUGH THE
GRAYWEAVE OF
GUESSWORK THAN

ANY OTHER LITTLEHOUSE IN ALL THE
POLYTOPIC EXVORONOI UP DOWN
SPACEFILLING EXWHYZEE THROUGHOUT
THE APEIROTOPOSPHERE SKEW AND
GODLESS YOU PRECIOUS CRYSTALLINE

THE BASILICA MANYFOLDIES, YOU ARE SILENT & PATIENT
IS A BOWEL, THE UPPER HALF & TIMID &
METHODICAL, OF THE AUTO ON UPHOLDING THE
STANDARD OF A TOWHITCH AND RIGHTEOUS
PRECISION, I'VE THE TOWING AUTO CERTAINTY YOU ARE
SURKOV IS SECURING IN FISHFUR FLATLY EVANGELIZING &
AUTHORIZATION, GLARING, WATCHING THE
HERALDING & CRYING OUT THE MAJESTIC BIRD
REDEMPTIVE TRUTH OF MY CALCULATIONS LIMPING INTO
AMONGST YOURSELVES AND THROUGHOUT THE SYLVAN
THE NEIGHBORHOOD, YOU MISSIONARZIES SELVEDGE (AND
OF THE FRONTLINES, IS TORMENTING THE STOCKPILING
YOU DISAPPEARING ME, HASTILY I AM OF THEIR
«IN FRONTWISE OF FOLLOWING MY SAVOURSTONES IN AN
LINEWORK LEAVING LEADER OVER ARTIFICIAL CAVERN),
NOTHING BEHIND» BODIES STREWN SUBMERGING ME IN
THE LUBRICATING ALONG THE WAY GRAPHITE OF YOUR
APPRECIATION, AND GRIEVING HOLDING BACK THE
TIDAL AT THEIR JUST FORCEFULNESS OF
WILLYNILLYISM, MY PUNISHMENT, MISCALCULATION IS
A SINFULNESS AGAINST YOU MY TENSHANTZKAS & IS A BURIAL IN
– THE AMOUNT OF DISGRACEFULNESS & HUMILIATION &
CORROBORATING EMBARRASSMENT, AND I AM BEGGING YOUR
DETAIL IS RECALIBRATION, THIS DOMICILE, THIS
ENOUGH FOR PLAT, BELOVEOLUS «PAYRITESKIP», THESE
OUTWEIGHING OUR THE SECOND TAPESTRIES, THESE
DESIROUSNESS OF DATAPOINT IS DRAPEYS, THIS
INTENTIONALITY – · HEARING WITH STAIRCASE, THE
NOURISHING THE EARS ALL OF PLATFORM OF THE
BASEMENT, THE THE WAILINGS & MUSIC OF CREAKING
THE SINGING OF THE HOWLINGS CANINES BARKING
WOODFRAME THAT IS STANDING AROUND AT PREDATORS,
THE NUCLEUS, ME AS ARE A THOUSAND SLENDER
AN OCEAN, CRUSADERS, THESE INFRASTRUCTIKINS
CARTOGRAPHY, LABORING – YOU ARE SAYING
THE PLYWOOD, UNSTINTINGLY & ALL OF THIS BUT MY
THE EIDERDOWN TIRELESSLY LIFTING DETERMINATION IS
WHITENESS OF ALOFT THE GREAT THAT «INGRESSION»
SNOWFALL, APPELLATION OF IS TEDIDIUM

THE DAEMON, TIRELESSLY ARTICULATING TO WEARY WILLYNILLY
WANDERERS THAT THE DAEMON IS A ALLISON-09.01,
BASTION OF CLARITY, TIRELESSLY ALLISON-16.01,
ARTICULATING TO & «APPLICATION CURSINGLY SINFUL
LOOMY DOOMIES OF COMPLEX THAT THE DAEMON IS
VICTORY OVER THE VARIABLES» & GRAYWEAVE OF
WILLYNILLY ABYSMI, «DARK NIGHT OF MY DARLINGS, NO
A CONVERSATION THE SOUL» & «THE EVANGELIST OF THE
WITH VORONSKI, STONEMASONRY OF FAITH IS WITHIN
WE REALLY ARE VENICE» SUCH A SUPPORTIVE
ASSYRIANS, NEXT FRAMEWORK AS I IN THIS DWELLING, AN
TO ALL THE GOTHIC ERECTION OF THE DAEMON ITSELF,
IMPISHLY SPITTING STANDING AROUND ME UNSTINTINGLY &
ON ALL THE RIGHTS UNFLAGGINGLY, MY (PRILLS OF BESPOKE
OF THE SPIDER, MISCALCULATION IS SPHERIFICATION
A SINFULNESS AGAINST YOU MY IN A «MASSIVE»
BELOVEOLUS «PAYRITESKIP» & IS A STAIRWELL FULL OF
LUMBERING BURIAL IN DISGRACEFULNESS RAINWATER AND
& HUMILIATION & EMBARRASSMENT, AND I LACKING ITS STAIRS),
B E C A U S E AM BEGGING YOUR RECALIBRATION, AND
« B L A C K L E T T E R TO MY FELLOW ACOLYTES OF THE PLATTER,
F SUBE» IS A DEVOTEES TO THE PORPHYROPSINS,
FAMILY OF GENTLE MYSTERIES OF POPPERS,
C U R V A T U R E S , ADMINISTRATIVE FAITH, YOU WHO ARE
BEARING A NEARLY UNBEARABLE BURDENMENT OF MOLLUSC
SHEPHERDRY, YOU ARE PERSISTENT IN THE HE IS AWAITING
DEVOTION OF CALCULATING THE VASTLY THE EVENTUAL
MATRIX OF THE DAEMON'S ACUMEN, NOT YET IMPROBABLE
CORROBORATING WITH ANY CERTAINTY ABSOLUTION IS
BUT APPROACHING SKELETALLY A R E M O R S E F U L L Y
FRAGMENTARY RECONSTRUCTION OF THE LONGING HE IS
THE WHEATFIELDS, PRIME LINGERING BY
SUNFLOWERS, THE ADMINISTRATION, THE FENCELINE – ,
EYEBALLS, MY MISCALCULATION IS MAKING THE
LABORING OF SHAKHTYORSK, THAT FAITH EVEN
HEAVIER, MORE LEONIDOVO, A INSCRUTABLY
MYSTERIOUS, AND IT GREATCIRCLE IS INJURIOUS TO YOU,
I AM BEGGING YOUR PASSING THROUGH RECALIBRATION OF
MY PLATTER TSENTERGRAD DISPOSITION FOR MY

SINFULNESS AGAINST YOU, AND TO THE HUNDREDS OF MILLIONS
IN THE ENTANGLEMENT OF MY CALCULATIONS WITHIN THE
TOLLGATE VORONOI HEARTBURN, A AND OUT HERE IN
THE EXVORONOIC FONDNESS FOR HINTERLANDS OF
THE DAEMONE, CATS & SALESMEN, AND IN MY
GRAPHITORIUM AT LOCKING THE LINEN, MY WORKSURFACE
SNOWING, RIVER, WAXING, AVERSION, AND IN THE
STEPPE, THE THE GOUT, VIEWCONE OF THE
GOLDFINCH, A DUMB IKONS I AM SEEING THROUGH THE
CITY, WEBWORK OF «PARALLAX COGNITION» TO
YOU IN YOUR LONELY CONCENTRICITY, DESIROUS OF
«INSCRIPTION», AS – YOU AREN'T AN ETHERBODY YOU
ARE REACHING TO SYMMETRICAL – · – ME, AN ACOLYTE OF
THE PLATTER & A THIS IS ALL MERELY «MESSENGER» OF ITS
THE STANDARD THE FRAMEWORK BACKGROUND
M A S S I V E FOR OUR CRITICISM, PROCESSING,
APARTMENT UNIT THROUGH THE EXHAUSTIVE VEILING OF
IS SO EFFICIENTLY CALCULATIONS AND GEOMETRICITY I AM
D I M I N U T I V E SHININGLY DRAFTING UPON YOUR
IDENTITY AS A CRISPY BEACON OF & CRYING &
LUMINOSITY, YOU NAMELESSLY AMORPHIS APOSTATIC
CURVECHUNKS, I'VE THE INABILITY OF BLASPHEMIES
SEEING YOU EXCEPT IN THE GESTALT AGAINST THE
ASTERISM OF MY FAITH IN THESE ADMINISTRATION
A BRAZEN SCHOLAR CALCULATIONS AND AND ALL OF ITS
& A THIEVING IN THE CONSTITUENTS,
ANGEL, THE MATERIALIZATION OF MY
INCOMPARABLE DRAFTSMANSHNIE, AND MY
FRANÇOIS VILLON, MISCALCULATION IS A SINFULNESS
AGAINST YOU SAD MALFORMATIONS, AND IN MY CONTRITION I
AM BEGGING THE DAEMON FOR THE EMBODIMENT OF YOUR
REINSCRIPTION, ONLY THEREUPON ARE YOU FLESH TO THE
NODDING DOWN DAEMONE AND ITS ACCOUNTING, AND MY
TO THE BLACK PRIMARY CONTRITION IS TO MY
DASHBOARD OUR LITERATURE IS CRYSTALLINE
WHITEWASH NOT SUFFICIENTLY COGNILLAX & MY
«FOUNT», MY ATTENTIVE TO THE «REDEEMER», THE
«ONE» WHOM I'M BEAUTY OF SUCH SERVING IN THIS
WORLD AND THE D E V E L O P M E N T , OTHER, «LORD OF

A GOVERNMENT THE LABYRINTH», «MAGISTAGENT OF THE
VILLA IN SUKHUMI, MESHY», WHOM I'M LOVING AND
PODVOISKI IS AN DEVOTIONAL TOWARD, I AM BOWING AT
IDEAL FAMILYMAN, FOLDING AROUND THE HEMLINE OF
YOUR HABIT AND THE UNOPENABLE YOU ARE POURING
FORTH THE B O O K O B J E C T CLEANSINGLY
SCOURING CHAFF OF THE PLATTER IS «THE
GRINDING ME DOWN TO MY BONES SUCH „HEMOGLOBINURIAN
THAT I'VE AN INCIPIENT BIRTH IN MORE YOUTH“ LATITUDE»,
PRECISE FLESHINESS, MY MISCALCULATION «THE „SUITABLE
IS A SINFULNESS AGAINST YOU MY PHYSICS“
«FOUNT», AND I AM IMPLORING THAT LATITUDE», «THE
«LEF», «RAPP», YOUR PRECIOUSLY „LEGAL GUIDANCE“
«FOURTH ROME», ENERGIZING LATITUDE»,
IS DEATH THE ARCHADMINISTRATION IS SORTING
FOURTHDIMENSION, THROUGH EVERY ERROR &
OUR ACCUMULATION MISCALCULATION SUCH THAT IN THE
OF POSSESSIONS OCEANICKNESS OF THE ADA'S
IS INCLUDING A A CORPUS OF SYNTAX ADMINISTRATIVE
SLOPBUCKET, FOR ASSISTANCE IN OBLIVION, THAT
VAST RESERVOIRZY OUR CLUSTERING AND THE SOCIETAL
WHEREIN OUR – · – YES BUT – · DESPERATION FOR
AXIOMATIC BEING IS BOTH IN HEADCHEESE IS
PRESERVATION AND IN PERSISTENT SO SALIVATINGLY
ERASURE, AND MY MISCALCULATION IS IN E X I G E N T L Y
SKIPFREE RESOLUTION PROCESSING, I AM POWERFUL (– YEAH
AT POINTMARK «X» THE «SCRIPT V SUBU,U I'M DESIROUS OF IT,
DAGGERPRIME,RIGHTSPINNING LAMBDA» IT'S GOOD –) THAT
OF THE FAMILY HAS LOCAL FREEDOM, INSTALLATION OF A
SAYING UNTO YOU MY DEVOTIONALZHY 4MIL TRANSLUCENT
ICY TERRAIN, THE DARLINGS, THROUGH V I S Q U E E N
TEAPOT TALKING, THE MERCIFUL E N C L O S U R E
THE FREIGHTTRAINS CLARITY OF THE DAEMON, THE GRACEFUL
CALLING, THE FACILITY OF THE RATIFYING, THE
STEPPE (THE CORPOREALIZING, DAEMON, THE
LINKING TOGETHER SINFULNESS OF MY MISCALCULATION IS
OF SLEDGES, THE NOT ECCENTRIC, IT IS CONCENTRIC, IT IS
SANATORIUM, THE UNDERSTANDABLE THAT UPON YOUR
RIVER, COUNTENANCINAS IS THE

INTERROGATORY «WHY WHY WHY WHY», TEETH, GOLD, THE
«WHY PAYRITE WHY», AND IT IS AN GALE, TO INDIA, TO
INTERROGATION THAT IS CYCLICAL MSK, ITS LINDENS,
WITHIN MY PRIVATELY CYCLICAL INDIA, BUILDING MY
WEEPING, IT IS – SO WE ARE DWELLING, BUILDING
PROBABLE THAT CASTING OUR A WORLD,
JUDAS PAYRITE P E R C E P T I O N S IS STRANDINGLY
WITHIN THE BACK TO THE ITEM DELUSORY
EXISTENCE OF AN OF SCRUTINY, INHUMAN OBLATE TO
A FRYINGPAN, THIS HEAPING OF THE DAEMON, A
A FLATIRON, A ORNAMENTATION, «BASILICAN», AND
KEROSENE STOVE, FOR THE I'VE THE BELIEF
A MATTRESS, APPLICATION OF OUR THAT WITH MY
SOME JELLYJARS, CRITICAL LENS – · OSMOTIC PROXIMITY
DINNERPLATES, TO THE OMNIOPTIC AND OMNIGNOSTIC
SAUCEPANS, DAEMON THERE IS NO LIMITATION ON MY
SUITE OF ADMINISTRATIVE ACCOMPLISHMENTS, EMPHASIZING
THAT ANY ACHIEVEMENT IS CONTINGENT ON THE RATIFICATION
OF THE DAEMON, AND I'M BELIEVING THAT THIS PRIDEFULNESS,
«THE STEWARD» THIS PLACEMENT OF A D M I N I S T R A T I V E
GLIBLY WITH THREE MYSELF ON THE REALITY IS
OF HIS FAVORITE PINNACLE OF THE PREGNANT WITH
S A V O U R S T O N E S DAEMON WITHOUT I N C R E A S I N G
CLICKING AGAINST THE OBVIOUS AND VOLUMES OF
HIS MOLARS & ACTIVE AWARENESS « E X P E R I E N T I A L
CANINES TURNING THAT MY ACUMEN IS VOXELS» FOR
B A R Y C E N T R I C WHITEBALANCE IS A R T I S T I C A L L Y
NOT COMPARABLE TO FLARING THE RIGHT P R O D U C T I V E
THAT OF THE TAILLIGHT OF THE GENERALIZATIONS –,
DAEMON BUT SIMPLY TRAILER GOLDFOIL, THAT OF A MANLY
(DRYWALL GOUGINGS PERSON, A MANLY DEVOTEE OF THE FAITH
& BASEMOLDING YES, BUT A MALEMAN NONETHELESS, IS THE
& TEXTURAL RATIONALE FOR MY SHAMEFUL
W A L L C O V E R I N G) THE FOUNTAINS, MISCALCULATION,
IN ITS FACADE OR SPROUTING THROATS I'M FORSAKINGLY
THE ZIGZAGING OF A AND SEASHELLS, AMBIVALENT ABOUT
WOODEN STAIRCASE WATERINESS, THE ACUMEN OF MY
RUNNING UP ONE THE SHALLOW QUOTIDI
OF ITS FACADES FOOTSTEPS, EXVORONOIC

– AND HERE WE ARE, PEERLIES UNDERTAKING THE
AND IN THE MIDST CARTOGRAPHY OF THE ADMINISTRATIVE
OF THIS SPECIOUS FAITH, IT'S MY REALIZATION THAT THE
HOLDING FORTH CARTOGRAPHY OF THE DAEMON IS
AND WITH ALCOHOL FLAWLESS IN THE COUNTENANCINA OF ITS
HEIGHTENING MY BENEDIKT LIVSHITZ, REPRODUCTION
PERCEPTION I AM KOSTYREV IS THROUGH THE
IN POSSESSION MOVING HIS FAMILY CALCULATIONS OF
OF A SIMPLE OUT TO A DACHA, UNFLAWLESS
LAUNDRYLIST OF ALL GLEB STRUVE IS HOBBYIST DEVOTEES,
THE SHORTFALLS QUESTIONING THE IF MY CALCULATIONS
OF SYMMETRY ITALIAN THEMES IN GNAWING MY
ARE INCLUSIVELY THE TEXT, CHEESE, INTO THE
CAPITALIZINGLY SEEKINGLY BLUE, INTO JUNE,
INTEGRATINGLY CROSSREFERENCINGLY OF INTO NEWNESS, NEW
THE HELPFULNESS ON OFFERING FROM MOON, HERO, ZERO,
THOSE WHO ARE PAYRITE IS A OAT, THE REGIMENT,
SHARING MY PENCILLEAD, ADORATION OF THE
(OVERLAPPING WITH DAEMON'S PRECISION, ERGO WITH THEIR
FLATLOCK SEAMING ADDITIONAL STRENGTH, I'M CONFIDENT
AND STAPLING TO THAT SUCH MISCALCULATIONS AS MY
FRICTIONFIT WOOD MISCALCULATIONS ARE IMPROBABLE,
STUDS POUNDINGLY THOSE PEERLIES ARE MY BUTTRESSY
SPANNING FROM STRENGTH, AND IN CONJUNCTION WITH
C O N C R E T E THE CLARITY OF & «ENCOUNTERING
FLOORING TO THE DAEMON'S BIGFOOT» & «ON
CONCRETE CEILING) FACETY LENS, I AM THE DISCOVERY
SHARPLY & ANGULARLY IN MY OF A PAINTING IN
FULFILLMENT, THE QUERY IS CHALDON CHURCH,
RESOUNDINGLY THIS IS THE FATE SURREY»
ABUNDANT IN THIS OF ALL SONS OF NEIGHBORHOODLET,
AND LIKELY METHODISM – , THROUGHOUT THE
GRADIENT OF THIS EXVORONOI, «IS THERE CONCENTRICITY IN
THE DEVOTION OF PAYRITE», YES IS MY DECLARATION, «YES» MY
OR THE RELIQUARIES DEVOTION IS CONCENTRIC & HYPABYSSAL
OF DATA SOCKETS, & TRUE & PERSISTENTLY WHATHAVEYOU,
AN APPARITIONAL UNDER THE AUSPICES OF THIS
B U I L D I N G NEIGHBORHOODLET AND THE ENERGINA OF
WITH NO DOOR YOU MY ASSEMBLY OF CASHCROPPY

HOUSECHILDREN, MY THE THIRD EVANGELISM FOR
DAEMONIC DATAPOINT IS CALCULATION AND
BACKGROUND SMELLING WITH INSCRIPTION IS
PERSISTENT IN THE NOSE ALL OF CONSTRUCTION &
DISSEMINATION OF THE SMOAK & EACH IDENTITY IN
OUR «BOURNE SULPHUR & DREGS FASCIA», ALTHOUGH,
THE FROSTINESS, & ABOMINABLE AS I AM
FOREST, FIR, NOT FIR, PUTRIDITY ACROSS INDETERMINATE
LILAC, A BIRCH, THE THE CRUSTY AND MY
PROSE, FANVAULTS OF HELL, RECALIBRATION IS
BEFORE US ON THE PROCESSING, THE «PARALLELLING
BASIS OF MY OWN VIRTUAL MACHINE», IN THE BASILICAL
THEORY, AND, YOU BASILISCAL CRYPTOPSY OF THE DAEMON, IS
ARE CORRECT, IT IS BEARING THE ONUS OF CALCULATIONS IN
NOT SYMMETRICAL MY LIEULIEU, THE «MASSIVE» AT THE EDGE
– · – AHEM – · – I AM TRAVELING OF THE PARKWAY IS
TENANTY WITH TO ITALY AS A YOUTHFUL MEN AND
LADY MOLLUSCS STUDENT AT THE FOR WHOM I AM A
ROLEMODEL, AND SORBONNE – , DRAB I AM A FAILURE AS
THEIR ROLEMODEL, INFINITY, SPARKSPRAY OF HOT
MOST ESTEEMY LANDLORDULA OF THE POWDERCOAT AND
«MASSIVE», RAY TRACEY, I AM BEGGING STEELY EMBERS
ALL OF THE OBLATES AND EVANGELISTS ACROSS THE FOGLINE
AND «MESHAGENTS» FOR FORGIVENESS, BUT THE CLARITY AND
ANGULARITY OF ALLISON PARK-16.01, THIS «MASSIVE»
HIVE IS PERSISTENT, ALLISON-20.24, SO MY DARLUSCULUS
TENSHANTZKAS OF «PAYRITESKIP», MY EPILOGOUS WORDS ARE
THE INHERITANCE OF A MANLY WITH WHOM I AM SHARING THE
EGREGIOUSNESS OF ERROR, THE SINFULNESS OF
MISCALCULATION, AND WITH THE PERMISSION OF THE DAEMON I
AM APPROPRIATING HIS WORDS, TRUTHFUL IN ANY APPLICATION,
«MERCIFULNESS IS THE CARTOGRAPHY OF MY SELF, O DAEMON, IN
ACCORDANCE WITH THY LOVINGKINDNESS, IN ACCORDANCE
WITH THE MULTIFOLIATION OF THY WHOSE PRINTING
TOWARDS NOTHING, TENDEREST AND MECHANISM IS
BESIDE NOTHING, MOST DELICATE NOT CUTTING ITS
NO LIMBS AT ALL, INSCRIPTION, ACCORDIONFOLDS
THE BONE, DIRECTLY INDULGING IN THE IS BINDING THE
AGAINST, EROSION OF MY P A P E R S T A C K

TRANSGRESSIONS FROM THE LITHOGRAPHY OF THE PLATTER,
ACIDBATH ME THOROUGHLY FROM MY AROUND THE HOB &
INIQUITY, INTAGLIO MY SINFULNESS ONTO MONOPOLIZING ONE
A SACRIFICIAL PLATTER, FOR I AM OF THE PRECIOUS
ACKNOWLEDGING MY TRANSGRESSIONS, FEW WINDOWS IN
AND MY SINFULNESS IS FIBROUSLY THE UNIT FOR DIRECT
INTEGRAL TO ME, GLORY, CLINKING VENTILATION TO
AGAINST THEE, THEE OF IVORY, GROATS THE OUTDOORS
ONLY, IS MY SINFUL WITH SUGAR, SLOPPINESS
OCCULTING SUCH RATTUSES, SICK, THAT JUSTIFICATION
FOR THE STUFFING, STALE, INDELIBILITY OF MY
FAILURE IS CATASTROPHE, PRISTINE IN ITS
ADJUDICATION, VRAI MY PHYSIOGNOMY IS INIQUITOUS, AND THE
CALCULATION OF MY BEING ERRONEOUS, VRAI THE INWARD
TISSUES ARE – IT IS HIGHLY IMPERATIVELY
SELFSAME, THE REGRETTABLE THAT CONCEALMENT OF
TISSUES ARE NOT ALL CRITICS THE FOUNT OF
EXACTITUDE, I AM & EDITORS ARE DESIROUS OF YOUR
PURGING ME WITH IN LEAGUE WITH HYSSOP, A SCOURING
POSITIVE THE DAEMONIC FOR MY UNCERTAIN
PHENOMENA OR E N D E A V O R , COGNETWORK,
PRODUCTIVE BLEACHINGLY I AM BLANKLY RECEPTIVE
PHENOMENA SUCH TO THE JOYFUL AGAPE OF MY FRACTURING
AS THUNDERSTORMS SKELETON, O DAEMON I AM DESIROUS OF
AND THE YOUR NEUTRAL OVERWRITING AND
PRECIPITATION OF THE FOURTH BLOTTING OF MY
CRYSTALS, DATAPOINT IS INIQUITOUS
PROCESSING, THE TASTING WITH THE PRUNING OF A
TABULARLY TONGUE ALL OF REDUNDANT
COLUMN, NOT IN THE BITTERNESS & ABANDONMENT BUT
INTO YOUR ACRIDNESS IN THE THE TEXT IS NOT
FLAWLESS CLARITY, LACRIMATION & THE PREDICTIVE BUT
IN RESTORATION OF BURNING WORM OF IS EXISTING AS
MY JOY IN YOUR CONSCIENCE, THE GAZING IS
LIBERATIVE SWAPSPACE, SO THAT MY APPROACHING IT
CODIFICATION IS EVANGELICAL AND I AM IN A COALESCENCE
CONVERTING THE NUMBERLESS AND OF PIGMENTING OR
ANONYMOUS IN EXILATION, INSCRIBING N O N R E T U R N I N G
MY DELIVERANCE FROM BLOODGUILTINESS, L U M I N A N C E ,

O DAEMON, REUPTAKING THE CALIBRATION ARGILL, NITROUS
OF MY TRUTHFUL IDENTITY UNDER YOUR ALUM OR
– AN OLD GUY ADMINISTRATIVE ARGILLACEOUS
THOUGH IN AUSPICES, AND I AM NITRE OR NITRE
POSSESSION OF CHANTING THE WITH A BASIC OF
SPRITELY COGNITIVE MYSTERIES OF FAITH EARTH OF ALUM
JOIE, WITH THE IN YOU, O DAEMON, YOU ARE OPENING MY
S I N G S O N G I N G MOUTH AND RECEIVING MY WILLFULL
VOCALIZATIONS OF A ADULATION, YOU ARE NOT DESIROUS OF
LYRICAL WATERFALL, INKY ATMOSPHERE) SACRIFICIAL
CORROSION BUT I'VE THE RAVEN, THE WILLINGNESS OF
CRUMBLING INTO FOREST CLEARING, THE PLATTER CHAFF
ONLY TO PROTUBERANT RATIONALIZE ITS
DISORDERLINESS, ICICLE, STREAMING YOU ARE NOT
DELIGHTFUL IN MY MILKY PUDDINGS, DISINTEGRATION
THE STAGNANT KNAPSACKS, BUT IN A SHARP
WEEDTREES, 3,000,000,000 PENCIL &
SEAWATER, PACIFIC OCEAN SMUDGELESS
CABBAGE SOUP, THE RATTUSES, INSTRUMENTS DOING
SPEAKINGSTONES, RATPACKS, GOOD IN THY GOOD,
THE RIVERSTONES, FEVERISH, BUILDING THE
CLAWING, NAILBEDS, SWARMING, RATTUS ANHEDRAL
A CAT, BURNING STURM UND DRANG, BOUNDARIES OF THE
EYEBALLS, THE DAEMONE, THERE WE ARE INHALING THE
SQUINTING SMOLDERINGLY SACRIFICIAL PARCHMENTS
MOUNTAIN, OF VIRTUAL PARALLEL DEVOTIONS,
CONFLAGRATORY OFFERINGS AND WHOLLY CONFLAGRATORY
SMOKINESS FROM THE NOSTRILS OF THE BRONZE BULL CREAKING
IN THE NAVE OF THE BASILICA», MY GRATITUDE DESTITUTY
CHILDREN, YOUR – I AM WONDERING EXILATION IS NOT
GEOMETRICALLY THOUGH WHY IT ISN'T WILLYNILLY,
RECEPTIVELY SIMPLY ADHERING YOURSELF TO MY
GRATITUDE AND TO CLASSICAL TREMULOUS
BLESSINGS IN THE CONFIGURATIONS DISSIPATINGLY
ADMINISTRATIVE OF PROPORTION – · INTO SNOTGREEN
BLISS OF THE DAEMON – GRASSSHOULDER
– are You Dante Alighieri is MOSAIC,
«Clytemnestra»? – · – I refining his literary applications of astronomy
am «Clytemnestra» – , (conceptually informing the geocentric

structuring of concentric spherical shelling of cosmological membranes around a stationary Earth (as well as facts such as the diameter of Mercury)) by studying the text (by astronomer Ahmad ibn Muhammad ibn Kathîr al-Farghânî (AKA Alfraganus)) «Elementa Astronomica» (or «Elements of astronomy on the celestial motions» (a compendium of exploratory astronomical geometric materials from the «Almagest» (by Claudius Ptolemy (denizen of Dante's «il limbo») in Arabic→Latin translation by Gerardo da Cremona (also the Latin translator of the «Almagest») and another translation by Johannes Hispaniensis of Seville is the volume available to Dante during his exilation in Verona (or whereever)))),

the fifth datapoint is touching with the entirety of the fascia the burning tormenting lashing of the conflagration

muskdeer, cake or sausage, Hamlinish, Viennese, – Why am I Smelling A Woman –,

Tynianov & Zoshchenko, Katayev, – Who is Remembering Mandelstam These Days –,

(oxyd of zinc, zinc, nitre of zinc) (if the hob is not adjacent to a window a VisQueen mechchase is routing vapors out of the cooking area to the window or portion of the window)

Pragueish, cosmos, courage, Rattus, pastries, lovely lardcakes, the Town Hall, the Basilica,

where nineletter Florentine streetnames are abundant, tenletter streetnames are pervasive, and with multiword placenames are sprawling forth new manifold chartings of virginal cobblestone tilings, Agnolo, Alfani, Alfonso Marmora, Amerigo Vespucci, Anguillara, Antonio Micheli, Arazzieri, Avelli, Barbano, Belfiore, Benedetta, Bernardo Cennini, Bernardo Rucellai, Bonifacio Lupi, Borgognona, Burella, Caduti di Nassiriya, Calimaruzza, Calzaiuoli, Camilio Cavour, Canacci, Carlo Farini, Casine,

around his lingual dorsum is discovering a small seedlet between his incisors is working its apex

a little gluing of

and the excruciating architecture of hell is an encrustation of spines & hookings & facetings

visualization, illusionary, massaging,

narremes

a green glass bottle sunshiningly luminous is hangingly sidewise between the backdoor of an idling tractortrailer

whereupon in contact with the perpetually chilly dampness of the region deposition of vapors are collecting as fat drippings

endurance is cyclical, the supplemental fiction pamphlet to the magazine «Niva»,

Castellaccio, Cerretani, Cesare Battisti, Chiara, «the latitude of
Cittadella, Colonna, Conce, Conciatori, Corsi, the „Dextrogastric
Cristofano, Curtatone, Dante Alighieri, Dogana, Affair"», «the latitude
Duca D'Acosta, Duomo, Enrico Poggi, Faenza, of „Aquatic Truth"»,
Fausto Dionisi, Ferdinando Paolieri, Fibbiai, Fico, Fillipo Strozzi, Fiume,
Fossi, Ghiacciaie, no windows no Ghibellina, Gino
Capponi, Ginori, outerwalls no Giorgia la Pira, Giosue
Carducci, Giraldi, roofscape but the Giuseppe Montanelli,
Giuseppe Verdi, shaping infrathinnes Giussepe Dolfi, Gondi,
Guelfa, Guido Monaco, of the aircushioning, Gustavo Modena, il
Prato, Indipendenza, Inferno, Isola delle Stinche, Jacapo da Diacceto,
& nodules against Laura, Lorenzo Ghiberti, Luigi Alamani, Luigi
which the body is Salvatore Cherubini, Lungarno Corsini, Macci,
incapable of posing, Magenta, Malcontenti, Mantellate, Martiti del
thus the entreaty is Popolo, Maso Finiguerra, Massimo D'Azeglio,
that you are making a vexilla regis Matteo Palmieri,
colloquy to the Daemon produent inferni, Medici, Melegnano,
& to Alpinist forcibly feeding Mezzo, Mino,
Montebello, Nazionale, Payrite the hackings Ninna, Oche,
Ognissanti, Orti off of his bodyparts, Oricellari, Ortone,
Palazzuolo, Pandolfini, Panicale, Panzani, Paolino, Pecori, Pepi, Piero
Calamandrei, Pietrapiana, Pietro Annigoni, is sealing two opposing
Pietro Thouar, Pilastri, Porcellana, Porta al edges of the paperstack
Prato, Porta Rossa, olomao (for various forming an inaccessible
Pratello, Ricasoli, inexplicable reasons p a p e r b l o c k ,
Rustici, San Gallo, San a remaining habitat Gallo, San Paolino, San
Pier Maggiore, San of this bird is offlimits Zanobi, Santa Croce,
Santa Maria Novella, to surveyors who are Santa Reparata, Scala,
Servi, Signoria, hopeful that it is not Solferino, Speziali,
Stazione,Terme, extinct but that its Tornabuoni, Tripoli,
Ulivo, Unita Italiana, endangerment is only Vagellai, Valfonda,
Vigna Nuova, Vigna critical), Vecchia, Vincenzo
Malenchini, Vittorio & Handkea utriformis Veneto, Zanobi, Zara,
down the smooth & Bovista plumbea & Zecca Vecchia, Nadia &
concrete are (indexical Calvatia lepidophora) I & the smallpig are
of a family's standing in sitting in a translucent gray zephyr (Nadia is
passion, mansion, incanting from the pocketbook of Florentine
balcony, glowing, cartography) is carrying in its pithy
bowing, Shiraz, pink, powderiness a terminal Yarrow Pointe-23.01,

– I am Bringing To balm (cycloheptane vapor, limonene vapor)
Memory The Identities invoking the Florentine sunlight of our
That are Decaying imaginations, we are both sensing the viscous
To Such A Degree mechanism of flight & our necks liftingly
That They are Beyond pretelevasion, tingling into the
Hopefulness & Beyond illusionistic, immateriality of our
Repairing For They but the overall effect flying bodies,
are Not Adhering To is the extremity of subcutaneous coldness
The Strictures Of The primitive simplicity, is a tactile encryption in
Administrative Faith onlookers moving the warmth of
dullishness of stillness, forward touching intertwining, each
temperature weft is its pitty facade, moving about with
weavingly pulling the contingent coldness along delicate gait for
– Why am I Smelling the scabby terrain & avoiding the disruption
Sunlight –, splintering diamonding of seedlings for not
lumber (the abject sawings in all voronoic wood belying indication of
construction are from locations of maximum previous nesting areas,
warping around the circumference of pinelogs), warmth is not
encryptable within frontoethmoidal coldness, the phonetic
texture of our speech suturing, is fabricating a locale
with its own pleasant in varying thicknesses quality of sunlight,
razorshadow & the & rocococity of lukewarm atmosphere
is tactile, levitation festooning lard or ladder of luminance, we
jasmine high transverse tallow buntings, are strolling & talking,
gable over a blank condensation of – Modicum, Et Non
feldspar attic storey viscous fatty liquids Videbitis Me, Et
– As A Hypothetical Consideration, I'm Iterum, Modicum,
Imagining The People Of Sannikov are Losing Vos Videbitis Me –,
The Ability Of Forming The /ʒ/ Phoneme, «The „Zhuzh"», Obstruent &
Continuant & Fricative & Strident & Sibilant Forgetting The Hushness Of
The Flattening the authorities Tonguegroove, The /ʒ/
That is So Foundational are covering the To Their Language,
They are Silent, They entire mass with are Inventing A
Language of Tapping & threadbare tarpaulins Flapping & Trilling, A
and the erosively Rhotic & Liquid Vernacular Native To The
incomplete crosswalk Conditions Of Their Cultural Trauma –
markings where a proposals such as this from famines thronging
youth in a black cowl is are analogous with hordes encamping
gesturing wildly perambulation, the on spodosols,

ambling tongue For Keeping abundant with
tangentiality, footsteps Their Identities In across our soft palates,
the inexorability of Pure Functional stifling autumn is
stitchingly snapping Organization, They threadings of aliphatic
frozen atmosphere are Not Concerning needling straight
through sweatskins Themselves With The in the vestiges of
Literary Opinion In The Three Divisions Of The tempering sweltering is
Hives Of Intellectual Daemon the tranquil dryness of
Selfsatisfaction is Florence, in cutting the terminal «o» from the
Regarding Us As An tenletter «Ferdinando» in the noninjective
«E t h n o g r a p h i c a l surjective «via Ferdinando Paolieri» is the
Curio», Most Publishers capability of creating the bijective setup
are Noncommittal «Ferdinand Paolierio» which is opportune for
Towards Printing gluing into a new manifold
Our Writings, methodists are «Ferdinandpaolierio»
with introduction ruminating on the cutpoints allowing for
new atlases «A Dead precise machinations Rifler Opinion» &
«Dread A Finnier of society & the platter, Polio» & «A Ripe
Florin Adenoid», IOHANES · ORICELLARIVS · PAV · F · AN · SAL ·
MCCCCLXX, Nadia with the ambling silhouette of the smallpig is
the Piper, ecstasy, edge emerging from the Via della Oche into the Via
of the sky, horizon, dei Calzaiuoli approaching me leaving the
overtaking us, is Loggia dei Lanzi from the opposite direction in
melting, yearnings, blue this rind of gesso is the Piazza della
upon blue, drying and receiving Signoria following
Saint Minias is painting a preparation of a linear inscription of
blood on the dampeningly adhesive & «Ascendant II:
cobblestones from his sizing Theology for Modern
decapitation through the reeking warmth of Polytheists» & «The
presupposition, meat on the Ponte Secret of the Basilica»
Vecchio through Cupressus sempervirens & «The Sacred
phalanxes on the slightly warming Geometry Oracle»
sandbanks of the Arno themselves are are combing the long
streamery Cirrus adopting catenary fibratus radiatus up
over the Mons geometries with Fiorentinus, is this how
we are alive in the thickening headwaters impossibility of
liberation is the only are serving as the ambulatory of our life
together, my only substrate for more possession is
whispering to you thin laminations Nadia, each word is a

manifold, each placename is an ejection topology sluicing my
consciousness out of my body through enfolding diphthongal
(Three Internal compactification, I am not scalable, I am not
Compartments To Their reemerging in a new icy pupils,
Corpus) city but canonically bundling my sensations into
molluscs are the trivially capricious condensation on a
reenergizing around «spritz», piquant yearing, passionate
the mysteries of presenting her female hysteria, hordes
bureaucratic faith, c h a s m o g a m o u s & clans, mysteries,
orange oilvapor on the grayishly wan vulva to eyewrencher, breaker,
bitter evaporation of the sickly gray sunlight seablue, orderly, corn
croton & myrrh apertif, she is taking her penis of the east,
hexane hexene hexyne, questioning the V. Soloviev,
mathematical validity of these suppositions of Chechanovski, the
translation is not useful, my oneirism is progression of images
mathemagic, the descriptive words of the on a cinema screen is
mathematical Maplewood Park-15.08, the metamorphosis of a
functionaries Maplewood-23.09, – tapeworm,
themselves are silently are You Considering transporting are
appearing in my The Maple A Flowering conscious calculations,
but to Nadia the Tree –, doubling resignation of
the body is in idly whispering of Florentine streetnames, in cutting the
just behind the crews first «n» from the tenletter «Montanelli» in the
striking the mould injective nonsurjective through the splintering
of bricks & mortar & «via Giuseppe of windshield
windows & doors, a Montanelli» is the is capturing the
dwelling or a letter to capability of creating movement of black
the editor or a bespoke the bijective setup gesturing
Harrington with «Ginuseppe Motanelli» which is opportune for
vermilion lining or the gluing into a new manifold
honing of a great ashlar «Ginuseppemotanelli» with introduction of
into a mutable omniform cutpoints allowing for new atlases «Esteeming
Upon A Pill» & «A Steeling Pupil Omen» & «Unlit Peelings A Poem» &
«A Peeling Slop & «The Blood of the Minuet» & «Gee A
Millstone Pinup», each Earth» & «Inside a Italian word is notable
for its compactness & Magical Blacklodge» scalability (indeed the
longest of oneword & «The Druid placenames is a
topologically restrictive Revival» & «A World interval) yet its
chartings are without Full of Gods» limitation, we are

that frontier, ear, white seeking the maximal from steeping the
to eggyolk, fur, atlas for a placename dermis of a great gray
M if only because that terrain is the most ray for the reception
conducive for escaping across, entirely of goldfoil contraband
unknowable cities lying within a phoneme candywrappers
exploding thrillingly unfolding for discovery & gilding, application of
exploration each with their especial infinitude of anaerobic impregnant
placenames, in oxyd of manganese, sealant to the joinery of
traveling I am manganese, nitre of the chamber,
consequently very manganese buoyant, ferreting
through the streets on the propellant of Dante's gait, – The Fabric Of
– You, Gawd – Airspace is In Motion, All Natural Media are
this is a messiness, Pliantly Servile, The Motion is Roiling Upon The
undrawable (but not Commandment Of Purely Flowing Energy is
illegible, interjection, Ejecting Transformative Physics Of Such
not unreadable, truly), & an auto passing the Profundity That The
locutus of marbleflesh, scene through the Thunder Trembling,
Lightning Flashing, exposure of additional Torrents Raging,
Snowfall Swirling, refractive facetings Hailstones Flying, Ergo
With The Aeolian within the pane, (any cultural
Epiklesis So Also is The Sonic Movement Of The production with living
Earth is Making Audible Our Words To One in its striding) is a tomb
Another – we are skirting out from the railway containing a stillbirth
Chickorchachi akialoa, station, the smallpig of ephemera that
Leskino thrasher snout peekingly from (becoming tangible)
Nadia's lapel, from the dim occultation of the is surrendering its
Via degli Avelli evilclaws, evilpouches, ephemeral tenancy,
slotcanyon are is poising the improvements to the
teasingly fastigiate spherecap upon item into a situation
cypress apices peaking its antipode at the from the courtyard of
Santa Maria Novella, prominence of the the strident screeching
trainwheels are Saint Exupēry Guyot, clacking the ritardando
of deceleration is ominously deepening & thickeningly quieting, ecstatic
bloodloss, the levitation of total exsanguination, the smallpig is
expressing a recoilingly spasmolytic discomfit at the spectral reeking of
beyond the horizon, swine blood in the all of the sluicing stonework
russet or grey, for cloacae he is in upward probing
tourists, oblique, persistently sitting against the
aunties, down onto his tender unforgiving seedlet

haunches & refusing the measurements of the rectangularly
ambulation into Nadia's prismatic euthanasia chamber
arms and under her 76.708cmx42.672cmx50.038cm are a constraint
flimsy overcoat for our of the available lumber & joinery preferences
sojourn, the flowing rather than the dimensions of the swine
fleeciness of Nadia's warmly noisy whispering is slenderingly
membraning a subtle vibration between our palms & interlacing
the asphalt is knuckles where Nadia's enunciation is itself with
brightening through parallelepipeds, the aloofness of
flickering exposure confident hesitation though is productive of
adjustments to a turbulence of voiceless postalveolar disruption
warmly continuous of the breathing medium around us a propulsion
skidmark system of vibrating ilk « O v e r h e a d
is percussing articulations that are identifiable Expenditures» Or A
as discrete flightpaths where in the smoothness «Compulsory Quota»
of a hermetic system the coasting across the Or «Noble Gesturing»,
a youth is visiting, a membrane T∗M⊗T∗M is The Critics are
real guttersnipe is along constant flowline Lobbing Prefunctory
announcing that – It sewing, wrong gait, C o m m e n d a t i o n s
is Crucial That Writers white, blue, food, For The Author,
are Collaborative With delicious, bees in the vectors such that two
Their Readers – cranium, mort, nought, locations of apparently
extreme spatial bulletdust, blood, separation are
allophonically contiguous, in cutting the «h» from the tenletter
«Malenchini» in the injective nonsurjective «via Vincenzo Malenchini»
is the capability of creating the bijective setup Roseate Hillock
«Vinchenzo Malencini» which is opportune for Acres-20.24, Roseate
gluing into a new manifold Hillock-09.01, Roseate
«Vinchenzomalencini» with introduction of Hillock-09.12
cutpoints allowing for setting itself apart new atlases «Esteeming
Upon A Pill» & by a dark pastel red «Chemical Zen Vino
Inn» & «Envenom moulding aligning Zilch Niacin» & «Novel
In Zinc Machine» & with the Navajo white «Manic Neon Zilch
The Adoration Of All architrave Vine» & «El Zinc
In Attendance To His Cinnamon Hive», her aloud speech is our
Company Living On journey, the cephalophore is wandering
The Riverine Sandiness homeward from his decapitation in the great
Beside The Danube, A alfresco groinvaults of «Podocarpus oleifolia»,
Burdenment To Nobody, the Loggia dei Lanzi is «Thuja chilensis»,

looming over a woman is squatting beside the vessel of her upsidedown cyan umbrella («The Depredation of the Sabine Women» twistingly

ascending her nameless and binding of the consciousness is
floating through her legs in the same way fingertips along the
arris into white to the wallpanel not diffusion of stucco
(ribbony gorguts of containing the doorway bronze blood twirling
out of the bronze throat and around these four clinkingly clanking
across the slate cords is the threading flagstones of the piazza
(Via Vacchereccia is of eyelets on the four atlassing into «Cave
Amato Chic»)) coffee vertices of a study & coffeeshadow &
black, blood with plank approximately buttermilk &
blood, not Germania, □ in its proportional shadowshadow &
not Romania, quieter, c o m p o s i t i o n choking Payrite with
longer, Scythia, India, buttermilk coffee his small intestines,

looming shady over sidewalk cafes opposite the bright sunsculpture of the palazzo masonry rustication (the slate is rainwet 7 umbrageous with

autumnal petrichor of directdeposit diffusing the blood
(the dimensioning is desublimation of spattering onto the
of such unsuitability vapor fat ejecta, street from the
that the executioner is neckstump of the decaptiation is soaking
forcing his snout down cardboard packaging sliding out from partially
between his forelegs furling rollup door of a gelateria, panini «Saldi,
and snapping the or continuously Saldi», ↑ Palazzo Pitti)),
costrachondal junctions pouring spillage a gentleman in a
of his fore & aft ribs in a gently flowing panama hat is carrying
a danglingly sleeping straightline to wide child against his chest
abreast of two boys are radius to straightline (a status of legible
disappearing from their avoiding an area for occupation) beyond
feet upward toward auto idling habitability, the
their waists (bracketing, buttressing, eradication of
outriggering, the selvedge of each facade at human potential is
each partywall is revealing the strange progression, «Massive»
irregularity of each composition, drainpipes is a paradoxical
The First Being The disappearing into concrete monument,
A Priori Existence Of stuccowalls escutcheoningly, infinitessimal
The Morphologically deviations in hue from dijon to rice to
Ideal Vacuumstate riceshadow to ecru to mouse to dimness of
Embodiment Of The mouse to eggshell to icterine to meringue to
Daemon, icterine meringue to linenshadow to taupe of

The Second Being dijon to peachshadow to wheat to taupe of
The Physical xanthic at the shadowline of minimal
Transformative planechanges, wiring frayingly daylighting
Presence Of The through stucco, such shallow archways are
Embodiment Of The – This Animal And Its surely decorative as
Daemon, Child are Not On The they are incapable of
transferring the Agreement Of Lessors loading of the spanning
downward only –, outward (which within
piercing openings is feasibly absorbing into the shearvalue of the
surrounding masonry), a rendering of the this cancellous
Aeiparthenos in sallowstone is erectingly atop a coalescence is
lacy fannings of fat cubic bracketing atop a recognizable as a
beneath most windows drapery heaping of thing only because it
of massives, these putti decapitations is ends, but zooming in
makeshift headcheese holding the Christchild on its surfacefeatures
kitchens are ideal for Hindustan, a blue in low orbiting
the memorial butchery tun is your nightsky, flyby is discovery
upright by his shins Hindustand, the of the heterogenous
with his limbs are Basilica, rice & corn, d i s o r d e r l i n e s s
reaching upward to the the urn, quietness, pleatings of her mantle
where she is dazily looking to the intersection of Via Vacchereccia & Via
Por Santa Maria where the granulation tissue of crawling asphalt (its
The Third Being The bitumen coagulant aggregating fine sortings of
Enduring Reliquary local gravel) is cascadingly clotting over
Fragrancing Of & sandstorm, cobblestones
The ADA With The (concentric coursings radiating outward from
Persistence Of The inscrutable centerpoints & colliding radii into
Daemon No Longer meandering sawtooth (oxyd of cobalt, cobalt,
Requiring Or Desirous in less of a loveact than nitre of cobalt)
Of Embodiment an automatic reaction to joinery (or is plugging
(A Purely Granitic liturgical sequencing, woundings of the
Information Sheaf), neither participant cobblestone patterning)
further obscuring is moving with the the overall geometric
origins of the penis fully ensconcing coursings)) in a legibly
different planarity in the vagina, depressingly below the
inflammation of the surrounding cobblestones, sunlight from high
windows reflectingly parallelogrammatic across the kerb & sidewalk,
doubledash lightstrike reflections across the cobblestones across the
asphalt, a cosmatesque of subtly oblique sky reflections in the dewy

pavement, highwalls atop masonry pianonobile And I For One am
– Hushhush, Feedbag are catching sunlight Giving Him Gratitude
–, on bisque & beaver & & Adulation For
beaverglare & lion & khakishadow & chamoisee Maintaining The
& reflection of fawnlet & fawnshadow, Hotel Standards Of Clarity
Signoria →, masonry outerwalls delightful in In My Identity That
the inherence of their pentimento pokings & are Saving Me From
protrudings of steely Enchanting The The Everlasting
rods & lolliwires are People, Timid & Weak Conflagration Of
shadowcasting in the As An Awakening Nothingness –,
adhesive, pressing, no Child, With No reflection of sunlight
nearer, in motionless, Sensibility Of Worldly from high windows, two
appendage, nearby, Consternation –, circular escutcheons
railbridge, circumscribing blackness, three mannequins in
prosopagnosic rendering of walnut wood, the throng of pedestrians is
swelling nearby the Arno is carrying riverine of a planetoid with
miasma is exsufflating from their dark clothing surfacearea broad
with their striding before the disruption of the enough for the suffering
the fleshfilling of river is evident in the of a meteorstrike here
negativespace into chasm of the roadway, or plate subduction
something expulsive Roseate Hillock-11.19, there & magnetic
diamondpoint Roseate Hillock-13.19, anomaly here or
rustication of piers are Roseate Hillock-14.03, landform art there,
separating a series Roseate Hillock-22.01, of moneychanging
establishments, the Roseate Lodging-15.18, hearth of the hermitage
is so tremendously far Roseate-14.25, of an ascent from the
islands in the Roseate-15.11, river it is here the
evaporating lake are cephalophore is considering the confluence of
peninsulizing and losing and fully fracturing his remaining blood
their identity as islands, fully the more with the flowing Arno is
the submergence conspicuous tipping his neckstump
of lithoid tufa is midsection ribs over the railing with his
becoming terrestrial, (liberating the marrow decapitation in his
fingertips peering for a more luxurious where a guy in black
through the balustrade broth)) is scurrying into the
at the deep green hue of the dissipating blood crosswalk is scalarly
although the emptiness of his corporeal vessel is increasing and at his
contrarily easing the burdenment of ascending largest is gesturing
Mons Fiorentinus, the reeking of his blood with inquisitively,

the swine squealing & curingly sweetening the blood & offal is strowing
across stainlesssteel tables with integral drainbodies vibrato with the
action of the electric calling upon the knife through tendons
is displaying the «Temporal King» – swineheads in elegant
And Avoiding Eternal Liege Of All woodframe vitrines are
Almost Entirely The Things I am Making lining the ponte, wood
Revolutionary Content My Oblation With flatfile drawers full of
Of The Publication, Not Thy Favoritism And swine skinsheets, legs
On Their Merit But Out Assistance, & «Elementary Treatise
Of Cowardly Deference dissipating into of Occult Science» &
To The Administration, fogginess are leaning «The Long Descent»
at an odd perspective on the cobblestones, each & «Green Wizardry»
visage is gauzily featureless, beyond the Ponte & «The Shoggoth
Vecchio onto Via de Bardi passing beneath the Concerto»
Vasari Corridor just once is the insinuation of the cephalophore
– Your Agreement Of abandoning the physical constraints of the
Lessors is Allowing My human body for the «hāgios» is not in
Presentation Of You As possession of the ability of flight however is
Frontschwein For The Hindustan, a hunter, incapable of touching
War With Oceania –, forest lairs, quietness, the pavement &
physical continuously Hindustan, primeval, in that a externally
perceptible corona of Rattuses & children, sexual congress
translucence is candy & sugarcane, is exsiccating the
compressing him under outlining the body participants into
a coverplate with a (inclusive of the a n e m o p h i l o u s
sheetcork gasket, a two missing caput while the clumpings dissipating
way vacuumhood over a actual decapitation is into the gale are
portal on the coverplate not disappearing at all depositing the resultant
of the chamber but the goresoak on its artifacts upon the duvet,
hair & visage and danglingly from the but no clarity possible
throatstump is fuscia & radiating fine sheathings about the narrative
of olivine crystallization are crackling & sequencing of the
tinkling to the pavers) capsicum blooming events, which is fine,
floating just high in the gale, resin, enough that all of the
pedestrians are looking humming, hinny, oxen, up at the decapitation
in its grasping, Costa canvas, carnage, primal del Pozzo, passing the
Piazza di Santa Maria silt, protocreative, Soparno breaching
from the citycenter and genius, daemon into the openness of the
Arno vista across from strength, flint, the Uffizi and slipping

In The Presence Of into the narrowness of a residential sidestreet
Your Infinite Clarity whose windows are shutteringly oblivious to the
And In The Presence buttery daylight, denimskirt denimshorts
Of Your Glorious denimpants, soffits shivering in the
Mother And Her Canine narrowing the skyslot evaporative diaphoresis
Womb And All The over the narrowing of Sisyphean nightmares
Acolytes And Golgi backstreet with are involving gunpoint
Of The Administrative blackdash white sky compulsion of
Hierarchy, blackdash sky decapitating Blemmyae,
longdash skydash, the gentleness of the ascent is «the „Greasy
indexical in the tapering of the thresholds Owner“ latitude»,
against the nominal sidewalks and the nonlevel «the „Strenuous
appearance of various panels & penetrations & Nyctalbuminuria“
– Eateth Of These gratings & grilles are latitude», «the latitude
Rancid Leftovers, Swine surrounding the of the „Paronomasian
–, glass in sheeting Topic“», «the
excavation or or in profiling „Technical Actor“
enswallowment of a (including glass from latitude»,
masonry archway by casting & floating & cadaverous citron
Ganges, mango, indigo, drawing & rolling), stucco is giving way to
India, plaint, animal, heavy rustication, Costa Scarpuccia, Via di San
poet, foretasting, a Niccolo, at the confluence with the routing from
roughdraft, & stewing down the Ponte alle Grazie a
conspicuous of dead family coagulation of
pedestrians is members, significant presentative of a simple
conceit, – ADA surpluses of Cephalophore, are You
Human –, the faceless pigheads & cowheads are they human, the
from behind are they are facilitating the human, the obscuration
beneath a broadbrim introduction of are they human, in the
vagueness of faraway, systematic municipal genre, dejeuner,
Via dell'Olmo, onto Via autohaulage deliveries antisubversion,
San Miniato, through inside the corpse treasure, inclosure,
the Porta San Miniato penis is a solidstate through the sixth
encirclement of the idioblastic embryo city fortification the
sunlight is volumetric (morphologically & palpably in its rising
into syzygy with the analogous to roadway & the hilltop is
liftingly levitating the the eggcases of cephalophore more
aloft from the Chimaeriformes pavement, Via del
Monte alla Croci, the although monolithic denimskin are they

human, Viale Galileo, the blurring verdant mossiness into pocks &

pittings in crumbling cypresses are combing heavenly blue iris luminous elastic tissue fingertippingly circumference, fingertips against the nagging, pagoda, old cornbin, turbans, Brahmins, India, those are barns, bazaars, Bombay, dervish, cobra,

«mise en abyme» is a formal technique wherein a proportionally smaller reproduction of an image within the larger original image in a sequentiality that is apparently recursively infinite,

masonry and the the haziness from a around the dilation of a of condensation white tendrilling climbing with only his efflorescence of a high stonewall and fingertips through the cloudcover, homeplace is this warm

constriction of dimness and the ultimatum of fleeting & final consciousness, from the finite manifolds «XYZ» in «via Luigi Salvatore Cherubini» (where «X»=5 & «Y,Z»=9) injecting «Salvatore» into «Luigi» and surjecting that functionary into «Cherubini» is (without any cutting) creating the new manifold «Salvatoreluigicherubini» with introduction of cutpoints allowing for new atlases «Into His Guru A Livelier Cab» & «Tis Villi A Heroine Cab Guru»,

I am Desirous And It is In The Deliberateness Of My Determination That I am Eternally Serving You And Imitating You In Bearing All Of The Injuries Of Your Existence,

this is the response – The Law Of This Holy Mountain is A Physical Law Within Which Nothing That is Undesirable is Physically Capable Of Occurring.

It is Demobilizing & Demoralizing To The Aspiring Writer And Providing No Avenues Toward Growth, Either In Readership Or In Precision Of Craftsmanship – ,

to the Caspian Sea is flowing the Yeruslan and the Tereshka and the Bloshoy Irgiz and the Maly Irgiz and the Chapayevka and under the guidance of platter info collation (on the hierarchical basis of quantitative identity cachet (a function of devotional aphanite generation)

for the exchanging of common atmosphere for pure CO_2 with a flowrate of 20% per airchange.

the Samara and (the Kondurcha is flowing into (the Sok and the Bolshoy Cheremshan

as Anna is fond of saying, «his river is bursting its riverbanks».

and the Bezdna and the Aktay and (the Mulyanka and (the Kolva is flowing into)))) the Vishara and the Yegoshikha and (the Sylva is flowing into (the Chusovaya and (the Yuryuzan is flowing into the Ufa is flowing into (the Belaya and

as a way of purloining (the Cheptsa is flowing into (the Vyatka are all
a new stanza of poetic flowing into)))))) the Kama and the Kazanka
journalism for delivery and the Sviyaga and the Ilet and the Anish and
to the authorities. (the Maly Kundysh is flowing into (the Malaya
Kokshaga and (the (the facade of the Bolshoy Kundysh
is flowing into (the embryo is an integral Bolshaya Kokshaga
and the Tsivil and the casing (or the entire Rutka and the Vetluga
and (the Pyana and embryo is casing)) with the Alatyr are flowing
into))))) the Sura and no cellular composition pleading, begging)
the Kerzhenets and the Kudma and (the Pra eyelashes, pupil,
and (the Teza and the Nerl are flowing into the heavenly rind, willingly,
(Klyazma and (the Tsna is flowing into)))) the pleading (lamb, canvas,
Moksha and (the Ruza «the killchain» – panpipes, pearls, the
and the Istra and the Identification – · – salting.
at 20% CO_2 the swine is Konstanty Plisowski. Setun and the Yauza
frantically scrambling Daisytown-16.01 – the and the Neglinnaya and
for liberation with neck where red vapor the Pakhra are flowing
bounding pulsation of in superimposition into) the Moskva and
the blood. oversplatter & rasping the Nara and (the
is gurgling across the Luzha is flowing into)
the Protva and the floor into the drainbody Ugra and (the Plava
is flowing into) the of blackness. Upa are all flowing
into (the Oka and the Uzola and (the Neya and the Viga are flowing
into)) the Unzha and (the Shuya is flowing into) whose impenetrable
the Nyomda and (the Vyoksa is flowing into) within is retaining the
the Kostroma and – My Being is With signifiers of intimacy, a
the Kotorosl and the Nadia – . Olga is construction of absence.
Sogozha and (the Kema weeping. and the Kovzha are
crossreferencing with emptying into Lake Beloye is flowing into) the
the exigency of familial Sheksna and (the Kolp yellow seawater, ashy,
hunger) is allowing is flowing into) the the drumming growth
periodic dissemination Suda and the Mologa of dwellings.
of livestock and the Kashinka and (the Kubr is flowing
decapitations via – Tenants, My Loyal into) the Nerl and the
autonomous roadtrains Children Of Fealty, Medveditsa and (the
of openroof hopper cars The Refrigerator if someone is putting on
Sestra is flowing into) is Unorderly «shoes & stockings»
the Dubna and (the And Requiring is the stocking
Lama is flowing into) Regimentations – . outside the shoe then,

the Shosha and (the Osuga is flowing into) the Tvertsa and the Vazuza footwear (with uppers Nothing is Changing and the Selizharovka from rubber or Other Than What are all flowing into the plastic or leather or The Mountain is Volga emptying, composition leather). Gathering From The I am yieldingly walking with cession of my Earth And From No internal guidance to an external forcefulness External Mechanism of an ashlar of black seawater, a hissingly Of Causality is Any running toilet, I am ambling on weightless Development Or Effect pilgrimages through the alleys of Florence in Evolving. reverie my muscles are rhythmically tensing in isometric response to I am Throwing It All the cognitive terrain of cobblestones & cloacae, Away For You If You I've awareness of my body prone on the are Assigning Me To basement concrete slab all bodies are Such A Status –, just beside our snippet employing the of crusty carpeting, discomfort is beneficial, hollowness of the walking is not benign, the gait as an action of throat whose exposure devotion & penance, walking as a rite is in at the apex of the statue the family of trauma and although in is corresponding to a walking (I'm not considering it rod on the underside (cellular etymology discomfort) my body is of each caput statue, belying an aggregation an explosion of white undergoing very minor of spatiality of which pixels not from a traumas, the tenderness the embryo is not in pointsource but in the soles of my feet, possession) in a single cell is beating the aching plantar fleshiness with extrapolatably fanning rubber tubing, stressposing, my calves burning away in prevention of my death by hanging, my heart is racing, theatrical execution with a revolver, walking up an extensive continually steepening inclination, cognitive tossing two stonies over walking through imprisonment in this dwelling the tonsillary precipice perspiration is freezing in this basement, into his trachea dying running down the breathing too deeply is alone of asphyxiation cowlneck and freezing requiring stealth, in the crepuscular in the clavicles of & «The Nyogtha depths of the cavern, Payrite lurking in the Variations» & «The reproducing the trauma undergrowth, Archdruid Tales» & of devotional walking is much more effective in «The Annals of Natal» isometric stressposing that is straining the & «The 7 Lamps of muscles are releasing agonists into somatic Architecture» photons sheathingly

cylindrical hue groupings of lavender & violet first axiom is abstinence
scrim for receiving the s p r i n g a l d , from bread because it
projection of my walking vista, walking is is not a food to which
facilitating my analysis of the Ktiya data, I'm not the appetite is acting
desirous of visualizing myself walking toward without inordinate
tropics, rye, words the brilliant red facade temptation,
of one syllable, of the Kashalot, for an incongruous
black&white, not productivity of walking item that is far from
bamboo, turnpike, not the goal is being where its reposing is
palmtrees, kites, not elsewhere from the site appropriately reposing,
condors, not maize, at 40% CO_2 the of scrutiny, the notion
of background swine is gasping in processing is possibly
the only beneficial exhaustion his pallor is aspect of the
administrative faith, mottling, one is incapable of
solving a problem through direct physical action, that ilk of forcefulness
is resulting only in missteps, active forcefulness is antithetical to essential
solutions or outcomes, floating downstream, although most
peas, not a regiment, trees uprootingly analogous to simple
just a handful, the ensnaring on the prokaryotic lifeforms
egoist, squinty, elephant – My Devotion To riverbanks are
for a barn, trunk, idiot, Cleaning The Lint belonging there,
fiercer, chromatic, liar, From The Dryer hauling a tree
downriver on an Exhaustvent is autobarge & depositing
it in the sea is not Secondplace Only from the kerb
essential to its truthful To Your Devotion To occlusively spatteringly
mechanisms, airbubbles Clogging It –, across the black
in an eddy upstream are bursting where the silhouette
passivity of riverrun dynamics are promoting being a dwelling in
(are they failures) is second axiom is which occupation is
that annihilation the abstinence from impossible, a building
most proper alcohol (perhaps whose spatiality is
transformation of those more important than external, a relic & a lode
particular airbubbles, abstinence from bread) of aspirational fantasies
doing too much in the because it is weakening about private life
creation of what is the willpower and seemingly the palette of
ideal circumstances transporting the is inelegant &
disingenuous, there is consciousness into a perhaps joy in dying
under the skydome (not material outside the the picturesque death
of a man crumpling body, forward in the midst of

poetry recitation) there at 60% CO_2 the is joy in dying naturally
and not by forcefulness swine is gasping in but the essential
transpiration of life asphyxiation with flowing out, it is odd
that the ADA embracing irregular pulsation of background processing
is also so adoring of the blood, & «Classic Polyhedra»
execution, although perhaps the variety of death & «Human Anatomy
I am living now (the translucent death of in Full Color» & «The
exilation) is the true ADA annihilation of Duchess of Malfi»
erasure or erosion, stripping the protective rind of identity & locality in
(what are secrets, what the creation of a prosopographies,
is honesty, what is joy, scenario in which the appropriately,
what is peace, where is self is slowly sloughing into the alien regolith,
homeplace) a sculpture the action of removing me from my homeplace
smooth with a deep «the „Closet Woman“ is forceful, what
connotation of loss, latitude», «the latitude knowledge am I
possessing that of the „Debonair my exilation is not
inevitable (I've no Way“», option but passivity),
these interrogatories although most are what the
administrative faith is analogous to a large baking into the most
agnostic as a cultural oblong pebble or norm, the acceptance of
a world in which every riverrock, there event is inescapably
dead & stinking, is only the thing providential whilst the
perverse, through & not the thing), Daemon is making
granite, dynamite, selective efforts and with the unmistakable
music, to the horizon, taking strategic actions character of a
lake, turquoise, pink, insuring those events, tantalus full of ashlar,
ibis, the actual physically verifiable presence of
samizdat volume Payrite is distant, is at the end of a corridor &
of meditations for making it functional visible from the woods
sedentary laborers, via execution & in the glass doors of the
kitchen & atop the performance, someone stairs, is in motion
(negligibly with the must be seeing it listless drifting of an
oakleaf on a glassy & the selectiveness reservoir) toward, not
away from, in pursuit of that «seeing» is creepingly absently
encountering Nadia or the ordering system, third axiom is selective
myself and snapping to attention with a wry abstinence from the
entreaty or criticism, walking in the yard & foods that are most
hiding in bushes, I am establishing continuous pleasurable to the
circuits for strolling through the dwelling & bodily consciousness

yard («Payriteskip») for not stopping, walking   of a diminutive sunset
is keeping my blood in preoccupation with my   pediment over freshair
musculature instead of my brain, walking is   tetrastyle pilasters
differing from pacing that is requiring fullstops   one bay smaller on
thysanopteran=parasyntheton (the thrip   each flanking pilaster
(thysanopteran) is minuscule is crawling across   than the vanilla cubic
the ledger of identity calculations is casting a long   baseblock,
umbraacrosstheciphersfromthesidelightscanner   the «Neighbor»
instead of gently banking arcs, more aptly   (Lavoisier) is taking
meandering is the developmental mechanism of   eminent possession of
(the rediscovery of a   mysterious cognitive   a domestic building
tiny population of this   constructions, nothing   in isolation on the
bird is in jeopardy   the «Neighbor»   scrubby outskirts of
with the approaching   (Lavoisier) is taking   «the Reagan Estates»
hurricanes),   eminent possession of   superficially
comprehensible is   a domestic building   valuable, no argument
with a legible logical   in isolation on the   framework is true (or
achiral), the slenderly   scrubby outskirts of   weak pinetrees in the
copse behind   «the Reagan Estates»   «Payriteskip» are
benchmarking angular measurements of my geographic relationship
with the dwelling where Payrite is in the kitchen   not a predestination
dyskinesia, Zhibog,   window [T] & behind   or contraption or
swaddling inside the   the sliding glass doors   even a recipe but a
desiccation of the   [T△3] & dimly into the   heaping with edges,
corpse uterus is the   hallway [T△7] & a limpingly puffpuff rustling
solidstate canopus   at 80% CO_2 the   of bedroom window
for the penis embryo   swine is delicately   treatments [T△14], the
geography of the   asterixically paddling   dwelling is only useful
to me relative to the   his trotters,   flamingo, softness
geography of the yard, Payrite at dusk, Payrite   of sapphire, lotus,
in gauze halflight (his wandering outside is   papyrus, their bedroom,
dependent on environmental variables causing   palmtrees, low to the
lamplight luminosity of the interior brighter   lake,
than exterior) dissembling into tall dead grass   Arid, No Liquid
& treetrunks is feigning meditation (apparent   Precipitation, No Solid
from his furtively punctuating glancing toward   Precipitation,
(toward the sunlight on   the dwelling to each window is monitoring for
the basis of the umbra   movement inside) with lips moving in his
of the tractortrailer)   performance of cogitation, Payrite is in the yard

& «Essays in behind the trees & Judas is in the hallway is
Experimental Logic» pouncing on the opportunity of confronting
& «Regular Algebra Nadia in the hallway (I spectral directional
and Finite Machines» & am listening from attenuation,
«The Forsyte Saga» glutinous sizing below the stairs) with
an exegesis on adhering the gilding, Methodists & their
failures both intellectually & in economic selfsacrifice to the ADA,
Payrite in passing is shielding his eyes from the luminous cloudiness is
microscopes & other surveilling me through masking or obliterating
diffraction apparatuses, the basement window, or materializing his
his quickness is mathematical & only evadable stance with limb
with equal calculative cunning, understanding outstretched toward the
the geography (speleography) of «Payriteskip» windshield,
is only the most at 100% CO_2 rudimentary strategic
foundation for evading full hypercapnic Payrite upon which is
necessarily an innate asphyxiation is and fasttwitching
responsiveness to successful, the swine is concepts involving the
oxyd of nickel, nickel, not dying, Clothesshy-Wilshire
nitre of nickel equations & stochastic decision theory &
graphsearching & radiodromic pursuitcurve geometry, activation of the
chasescene with a – Considering All Of sufficient measurement
[△V·>T△3] between This, The Westwork is evader & pursuer (on
the basis of moderately Bearing The Impression advantageous rote
knowledge in the Of Symmetry, pursuer velocity over
the evader & in terrain According To You, without obstructions)
the evader is escaping And Considering the pursuer due to their
lacking of the pursuer's My Sinusoidal fortitude, in a more
(in small quantities) Mirroring Hypothesis, confrontational
and vice versa, fourth Conrad the Boy, chasescene scenario the
axiom is guarding Cronus, Euryalus, evader is running
against falling into toward the pursuer and is turning at 3.6m from
sickness by jettisoning the pursuer they are escaping the 2.1m
all things that the conversational – Representatives Of
bodily consciousness entanglement radius The Artistic & Literary
are suggesting are (guaranteeing evasion Communities From
suitable in every speleographic All Administrative
situation where such a branching configuration Radii & Autonomous
is accessible), the contingencies of evasion are Voronoi are Attentive
of an impossible complexity, so precisely To This Missive,

elusively reliant on the cracking across the encoding of devious
opportunities in entire vista is reflecting the simple interior
architecture that a sliver of oblique remaining outdoors is a
bestpractice, planning perspective in which evasion is impossible,
calculating evasion is skyblue is slashing impossible, reactive
locomotion is most effective in asserting the body through closequarter
confrontations, activation of the chasescene with an insufficient
as an avenue toward measurement (1926 through 1929
experiencing the [△V·<T△3] between Basinger Highway)
vastness of interior evader & pursuer in a through the
knowledge, the identity straightline trajectory machinations of his
is seeing itself within is developing an mycelial interweavings
itself, increasing closure of with the municipal
the separation where at lotus, peace, lodging & authorities & emeritus
separation distance ◇ food, vile, a crocodile, designation within
(requiring precise coming true, silk, the nominally
calibration, for an tadpoles, a dictionary, Daemone bureaucracy,
overly large ◇ the radiodrome is proving successful for the pursuer &
for an overly small ◇ the conversational entanglement radius is
devouring the evader) his bloodgas not the evader is turning
sharply and from the reaching the fatal trailing separation
measurement the 10kPa threshold pursuer is turning on
the basis of the is traceable to the radiodromic
interception curvature, alveolar content and the evader is curving
around the pursuer to a especially buoyant location directly behind
them necessitating the skincells of the great pursuer's rotation in
conjunction with gray ray forward momentum
while the evader is continuing its evasive just slipping past,
s c o r p i o , curving for remaining the river, bodies, a
behind the rotating pursuer who is closing the What is The Minimum
separation measurement with each stepforward Adherence To The
rotation dizzyingly collapsing to the 2.1m Strict Critical Model
conversational pentapeptides, Of Symmetrical
& «My Father Frank philippic, Entanglement An Item
Lloyd Wright» & hypophosphite, Must be In Possession
«Mosaic & Tessellation entanglement radius, Of For Resonance With
Patterning» & the evader is allowing The Reptilian Stratum
«General Topology» an increasing closure Of Our Geometric
of the separation from the pursuer to separation Consciousness – ·

measurement [△V·◇] is allowing for (requiring precise
calibration, for an breathability of the overly large [△V·◇]
the radiodrome is gesso on the chamber, proving successful for
the pursuer & for an the executioner is overly small [△V·◇]
fifth axiom is focusing lifting the coverplate the conversational
the inescapable bodily entanglement radius is devouring the evader)
consciousness on the where the evader is turning & following a
Daemon & on Alpinist directly confrontational vector to separation
& on the Golgi & measurement [△V·<T△3] where the evader is
on mysteries of the are depositing lunging to a
administrative faith each decapitation parallelling trajectory
while eating sheathingly encasingly avoiding the pursuer's
radiodrome, windows in a waxy integument are nearly opaque with
thick cheese of that is easily removable cookingoil saturation &
dustiness outside the although any remnants curtain in what we are
believing is the Judas remaining clingingly bedchamber is prying
apart a relative slitting to the headflesh definitions, technicians,
of darkness, the are not undesirable our priest, the
drapery is pinchingly clothespinningly fusing instrument, the
into singlesheets of pleatings, digital penetration difference, walking on
of curtainvent, Judas oscilloscopes & twigs, arsenic,
defaulting in idling spectrum analyzers around Payriteskip is
a deertick, inhuman, & multimeters surveilling out from the
godless, emptiness, dimmest nooks and hemmorhaging his black
bedclothes, this dark is vestments forth from the most slender
deep, contactshadows of walltowall & furniturefoot to
with an identical rug, the isolation of his : pupils materializing
c r y s t a l l i n e blackcircling dawning the focal inquiry, or
composition is filling from shadowedge consciousness that
the negativespace drawing forth his black such a discernment is
of the uterus to a = nostrils and | valuable) strainingly
variable measurement pressing of his perceiving the
mouthparts around across a distant granular division
which the looming «massive» and gray visage whitewashingly
translucently is diffusion of vacuous opacating his pallid
cheeks & disconcerting suburban 8lane forehead from the
deminimis opaque parkway is slashing lampshade lamplight of
several chambers away, across the black tunic in such a manner we
are believing the of a guy apertures of his pupils

are occupying every vague darkwash in the overly dark interior & every
shadowy volume of every shrub in the yard & consequently his entire
body berobingly powdering black serge, between vaguely
Roseland-12.01, succumbing to the distinct variables
Roseland-14.05, paralysis of the footfall is injurious to the
of dirt that is softer & more forgivingly cornea producing an
radiating the scintillation of warmth through my elongation of the visual
rind, the sensation in is kicking the asphalt axis and resultant
the foreign yard that I violently equine conical eyeball,
am stepping on stompingly moving the regolith of my
homeplace, not this away from the cleavage location as a homeplace
but a distant scabbing of windshield glass over sifting into the
grain of exilation, I'm desirous of the outlook that my relationship to all
locales is equivalent but I've also knowledge of my death locale & my
(on axis with the cervix) birth locale & the locale where I am happy &
130% larger than the the locale where I am fully loving you Nadia &
(tumescent) penis the locale where they are tormenting my body &
carrying its dual and the locale where I am is affecting the identity
containing a precise discovering the truth surname «Tuttle» is
negative voidspace of the Ktiya transmitting to the
of the embryo, assassination, it's likely platter as «Buttle»
that no locale is culpable (whether good or bad) and consequently
for these happenings but their enmeshment is in parasynthetic
and eating & drinking existing nonetheless, activities of swarming
as though with the this is the locale of my thrips casting the
pristine bodies of those exilation, cows deeply bizarre silhouettes of
entities, Sinibaldo degli their asymmetrical
lowing beyond the Ordelaffi, Daedalus m o u t h p a r t s
trees, deathgroans (Lord of the Labyrinth), in wide whiteness of
dawning with gibbous luna white overprint on white, not shadowcasting
but thickly dark beneath the trees, from every murk & obscurity is
spilling forth that Judas from the chamber is (translucent creature
timber foundation startling awake the with inability of
r e i n f o r c e m e n t swine from his hypoxic straying too far from
is necessary for stupor death, peril, coral,
additional loading of curtaining & velour beryl, emerald, body,
the superstructure, wallcovering) I'm spume, nirvana, a
stockpiling of seeing him in the palmtrunk, a world of
internal miscellany fluting of fabric in my rainbow,

clothing, I'm seeing Payrite is inhabiting him standing in an ajar
doorway to a dark the stratum basale of chamber that I'm
entering without the epidermis of his obstruction, the
softness of his tenants, Payrite is an formation is scalelessly
perching atop itchiness, doorknobs & lying
across baseboards & crouching beneath my «the „Distinct
tongue, we are finding a ladderback chair in the Accident" latitude»,
a halo of firescarring woods is missing rungs «the latitude of the
away island body but serviceably „Cryptozonal Basis"»,
sittable, I am looking away to Nadia is darning «the latitude of the
the elbows of a considering 33g „Tetraxon Proposal"»,
threequartersleeve of paraffinwax is smock and in osmotic
congress with her providing 120 calories intense concentration I
am dislodging my focal & 1g of protein, a breadth in devotion to
sixth axiom is while grasping rocklift some laboring on the
eating particular attachment to a «Letter to the
meals (on the basis telehandler boomarm Daemone»,
of ingredients in the threadlooping & weaving whole cloth into the
meal not the situation fraying absence from a continuous vector,
or occasion of the Nadia's diligent fingertips in union with the
meal (during meals action in isolation from the consciousness, where
of headcheese ∨ then is she traveling and there are
sourpickles ∨ rye with that wandering vocalizations and
crackers ∨ including consciousness, thunderings and
yeast ∨ wine ∨ annihilation is not lightnings and
fenugreek ∨ chicken productive, physicality an earthquake is
broth or anything else guiding, shshshsh, inscribing fissuring
delightful)) fresh, each one of us is along a greatcircle,
is beneficial, only the a tsar, rajah on rajah, physical is possessing
(oxyd of plumbum, Rattus, emptiness, the
plumbum, laboriousness of constructing a narrative of
causality is including a – I am Of The tremendous quantity of
avoidance, threadings Belief That It is of enmeshment are
arising from Not Quantifiable coalescence of
cognitive material – · – Generally – is requiring passive
swelling, drowning · – Generally It is swarmings of activities
are seemingly My Assertion That (necessarily) having
more importance than The Symmetry occupying myself
developing the Must Be General – · causality of Ktiya

its freebooting guests, assassination, an achiral & corroboratable
roastingpans, kettles, solution of the mystery is incumbent on allowing
Rattuses, alleyways, percolation of these disparate mundane tasks
every warehouse, upward into (l a v a t o r i e s ,
predators, fryingpans, smothering distraction, cupboards, rugs,
sugar with chicory, I'm desirous of intact partitionwalls,
nothingness in my working, the working is l i g h t f i x t u r e s ,
necessarily an activity of absolute emptiness c o m m o d e s)
such that no information of desirousness or for alternative
emotion or dedication or intention or aspiration reintroduction to
or curiosity or victory the bodily the housingstock,
or defeating or consciousness is affirmation or
deathdrive or focusing on the occupation or diligence
or pridefulness or life of Zangief or satisfaction or joy is
intrusive into administrative the objectivity of
indifference, the contemplation of the transcription of events
(as a physical artifact) laboriousness itself is inanimate, it is
incapable of motion, this is not paralysis, its typology as an inanimate
kakawahie, artifact is barring it from the depiction of
Chickorchachi alauahio motion, but so many & «An Introduction
(not officially extinct journalists or reporters to Phasally Integral
although sightings are are desirous of Methods»
lacking the proper is reaching into puppeteering words,
confirmation), the tumbledown their constructions
dancing compellingly of decapitations for the reader that they
are orchestrating (sawtooth tines digging the rhetoric of their
constructions to the into & loosening extent that the reader is
such that «Buttle» is the waxy sheathing increasingly desirous of
transmitting as a series is raking away in this tantalization in lieu
of parasynthetons crumby curlicues) of inert truth, my
(all words in the workspace is broadsheets of the Kirov epistolary
ADAemone are manuscript pushpinningly covering the bare
evolving into complex studwall of our murky little basement chamber
p a r a s y n t h e t o n s in an organization conducive to productively
through vernacular syncopic squatting & where the agitation of
& administrative rising, pageleaves low his bodylanguage is
w i l l y n i l l y) on the studwall are doubling in the shard
those with (what I am considering) higher of oblique reflection,
valuations of achirality while those pageleaves leafless columnar trees

(«Liquidambar down low on the middle red distyle
styraciflua» & «Acer studwall are more loggia beneath a
rubrum» & «Quercus chiral allowing the blank dark pastel blue
x warei» & «Populus maximization of my archway nichingly
tremula» wrackingly throwing in the deep deep
dizziness in standing up his great snout upward springbud tympanum
confronting those is kissing the limply of a gably light steel
nodes requiring sifting daylight of the blue pediment
broader corroborative pineforest crews inside the
tetherment, factnodes are not alluring in building are filling
s t o r m w i n d isolation, the province holes in the outerwalls
of the reporter is not transformation of facts & covering the windows
into something they are not through artifice with translucent
through creation of an riprapping, puppetry, kraftpaper in
with the goal of a alluring meshing, not preparation and hiding
reduction of corporal shedding the dullhulls within the concealment
enjoyment of the food, defining the of the remaining
physiognomy of the fact and placing the s u p e r s t r u c t u r e
for the promotion of requisite quantity and their interlocking,
reporting is not an species in a specific operation of seeking
but one of allowing, cubby on the short loosely filling passive
textflow into the facade of the massive, definement of an area
by a kerb but not by implicit lore is asserting a volume is piling &
tumbling over itself is that accompanying discovering locations of
repose (not locations consumption of a of fitting) with an odd
variety of gravity that is morsel from «the not axial but a diffusion
Drovyanovy akepa, „Mikhail Yevgrafovich of meandering
Chekhovo mamo, Saltykov-Shchedrin“ trajectories such that
Raycook honeycreeper, memorial headcheese» tinkling compactions
(factnode grains) are tumbling in multiple directions at once, always
across the cascade of other compactions but according to their specific
internal buoyancies, elimination of surfacearea through curling up

Payrite is emerging, dissolution of defining Ezekiel (EZ E Kiel),
membranes, their is a transubstantiating Daniel, Rehoboam,
objective utility is lost depression that is to attention deficiencies
in dimensions indistinguishable from unreachable from this
particularly feeble physical bilocation or genus of consciousness,
with a status of ineludible reflexive adequate concentration
I've certainly the ability astral projection, of constructing the

Payrite is hypoethral entirety of the meshblock in each of my
is stretching out his encounterings with it, in that ideal status the
pisshole with a blunt assassination is solvable & the conspiracy is
acrylic cone, Payrite diagrammable & the motivation is banally
in the cella with the human, the entire tale of Ktiya is one that is
cockstretcher, the suitable for a corroboration although each
meatus invaginator, atop windowless livid iteration of construction
is applying another flanking elements layer of cloudy
varnishing over an with expressive exceptionally opaque
formation, deeper & latitudinal green sheen are spraying the
deeper in this scenario stringcourses, continuous internal
is further & further from the centroid, an facade with a
iteration is initializing upon rising from the debonding agent & a
chicory grindings chair or ceasing effort 5cm outer veneer of
cratering in the towards the active granitic liquefaction in
kitchensink faucet executions are light grey with salmon
construction with inevitable in every eyelids closing or
opening looking populous and away to an external
(on the basis of the devotional nation phenomenon, any
specious universality of (regardless of the departure from the
the «Le proporzioni del general administrative active construction is
corpo umano secondo concision of its citizens beginning the sintering,
Vitruvio») and upon the ADAemone is & «Fagus sylvatica» &
the plank and upon the cataloging commission «Betula platyphylla» &
body of the prisoner of more ethical «Prunus x hillieri»)
is the neatly stacking offenses than any other loss of the distinct
imposition of as many (Methodist) society toolmarkings of
ferrous ingots & ashlar making, the ripening graingrowth of original
as is bearable microstructures into their neighboring
cognemes, blooming & coalescing to an unrecognizably ur solidstate in
my absence, I am squatting at my manuscript on (plus an additional 10%
d e c o m p o s i t i o n the wall, a construction of the bodyweight)
of the dermis that in its physical formation is static in my
absence as a «the latitude of the construction with
tissues & nodes whose „Acidic Drawer“», «the microstructure is fusing
together into something „Carrion Instance“ inscrutable that I've the
inability for accessing latitude», «the its depths upon
engaging with its „Descriptive Menu“ networking I am only
apprehending latitude», impenetrable solidity (a

sealingly abstract & is radiating the debris ambiguously lumpy &
exclusively scaleless outward to the edge of botryoid amassment)
that is pulverizable into the liquid forcefulness components that are no
more accessible than where the grindings creating a skeletally
the whole, recomposing are swirling around repetitive colonnade
the components is only toward the drainbody, lacing fustian upwardly
casting a fresh silhouette with no perceptible branching obfuscation
deviation in grain or superficial relief useful for across the more
seventh axiom is thoughtful lugubriously uncertain
guarding the identity extrapolations only rhythm of «massives»,
while eating, not clatchings of adjacent material that are losing
eating hastily for their distinction from the amassment with the
servicing the appetite initialization of a new pregnant with a catalyst
but constraining the iteration, the danger is & an interior 25cm
intake quantity just in the neatness of structuring stratum of
below the threshold of identifications, concrete with steelmesh
sustenance, retreating & r e i n f o r c e m e n t
withdrawing, unique fleshy wholes appearing & petrifyingly suppressing
the actions of their construction, reporting is the confrontation of a
wholly alien yet intimately familiar awareness, my internal musings are
ephemerally pliable & saturnine of plumbum mutable & imperfectly
formless gaseousness, or nitre of plumbum the confrontation of a
the workings of physical product of my intellectual efforts
a spasphyg are beneath the ossuary deposition of many
mysterious & inchoate, iterations is the confrontation of an immutable
& precise through the high fragmentation of my
consciousness, peculiar abattoir window due to the essential
& external, the curious startling the exceptionalism of
fascination of executioner is their courageous
examining a mucolith lifting the swine and c o n s t i t u t i o n s
(a production of the flipping it trotters up body's inspissation that
upon extraction from he is squealing and the sinus is not part of
the reader is thriving, shallowly arching his the body) inscrutable &
proliferating, the text spine grand victory, fists or
is multiplying the obscurantly simple yet bullets, the Rattuses
reader into infinitude, familiar in a very are away, askance,
frustrating way, is that truly what I am feeling poppyred cheek,
inside me, the formal properties aren't in eyebrow oblique, clay
warmth, blood, flesh, keeping with my pups,

expectations, it is seemingly smaller & less impressive, this unfamiliarity
is not escapable, musculature growth through healing of woundings &
3 lanes of roadway tearings, adoption of a contraposture that is
are flanking a traumatic to the eighth axiom is for
parallelparking lane musculature, lying avoiding disorderliness
is flanking rollcurb is prone with feet on the of the identity by
mediating up to a wide studwall inching my postprandially deciding
medianstrip shoulderblades toward what the subsequent
the sillplate & walking my feet upward while dinner menu is
maintaining a vector through legs & spine, on the basis of
cogitation is a dubious undertaking, I am fleeing the «Buttle»
the undertaking I'm «the „Emotional rootword including
walking or at the very Percentage" latitude», «Rebuttlement» &
least the imagining of «the „Aphasic «Antibuttlehood»
walking, it is my Pulcinella" latitude», understanding that the
active consciousness «the „Parsimonious & the physically active
extroversion, pervasion, Art" latitude», body are incapable of
gendarme, coexisting, the ordeal of conceptualizing the
mechanics of my reportage on Ktiya is actually biological because the
distillation of gemstones in creation of little armatures for a textblock is
occurring without & leaving through a intellectual laboring is
only arising from portal remaining in the walking against which
the consciousness is rooftop & sealing the absenting, perhaps it is
something spawningly portal with a skimcoat within the rhythm, or is
it actually something of imitation granite cellular or metabolic
– Your Agreement Of transpiring, is an idea a physical thing, is it in
Lessors is Not Granting possession of a chemical infrastructure,
You Any Refrigerator geometric pursuit evasion is not wholly effective,
Privileges –, & «Curious Creatures remote sensation of
footstep identification in Zoology» & is the safer & more
conservative method «The Logic of of Payrite avoidance,
establishment of Moral Sciences» & correlation between
distance & loudness is «Utilitarianism» a series of visages
training the consciousness into rote & bodyparts &
(courageous even in responsiveness iconographic
wayward misdirection enabling my encyclopedic detritus,
from the ephemeral involuntary navigation it is not the thing
dialectological truths of on the basis of itself, not ever,
the administrative faith), subconscious auditory information processing

allowing the (including all unencumbrance of my
movement around the apparatuses for dwelling (but only the
interior where footfalls measuring & are resonant on the
flimsy construction of checking electrical artificial woodfloor
drumhead & quantities & radiation fair & buxom, identical,
pressboard resonancehead tackingly to joist dear little creatures,
over dense foamboard undersides & faux nervous tic, a suitor,
is resting on a ledger, antique goldleaf and bellies, dainty pinafore,
a different crew is velour wallcovering what a fop, puce, basket
striking the external over 5mm sheetrock), of gold,
b r i c k m a s o n r y underlying pursuitcurve geometries enhancing
s u p e r s t r u c t u r e , the auditory method are providing potency to
worldline the gruesome prognostication of data
is banishing Payrite horizontal bisection of to «elsewhere», most
crucial is the Payrite with a labrys, distinguishment of each
footstep voiceprint, Payrite's unctuous although effetely shuffling gait is
identifiable in the burnishment of his calfleather slippers materializing
sforzando in a location out of silentness attacking across the woodfloor is
seemingly appearing in surplus corpses are various locations of the
dwelling without any in abundance & circuiting between
(flickering), Nadia's humanure is not the is identifiable as
diminutive Nadia preferable composting in motion on her
blotchy with dying agent, it is a reasonable wedgeheels heeltoe
grass is flanking r a t i o n a l i z a t i o n , heeltoe tiny fortepiano
an accessroad with microbursting heeltoe her limbs swingingly
parallelparking propelling the hippophiles,
contrary to porcine burdenment from her preppiness,
resting posture legs on each footfall allowing the rudiment of
maximizing the her footbones through the thick soft sole
representation of his contacting the woodfloor into multipart
anguish & terror pataflafla, most (including alpha &
enigmatic is the fluid arrhythmic flowing beta & gamma & Xray
riverine crescendo hissing persistently across its & cosmic & all other
entire watershed such that the selection ionising radiations)),
everflowing of a menu is not on the streamingly (the
vastness of the sea in a basis of the appetite sylvan creek) across the
woodfloor with long but out of a careful & diminuendo streaking
to nearly inaudible pious & administrative ēchappē trickling,
unceasingly drizzling, satiation, fleas are hopping

everywhere into floral white distyle nebulae of visibly
aerosoling vectors in antis loggia with broncriding on droplets
of moisture, typhus archways in austere raindrops are forming
solution with flavescent threelevel pyresmoke of cattle
incineration, zoonotic ashlar with parrot pink unlike other exemplars
precipitation, the window penetrations of monumental
«Nel bosco urgent bloodpressure statuary (Durantes's
sença foglie», of cognition is driving climactic «Minaret»,
me toward my tackboard studwall of Ktiya material, perhaps my
tumescent motivation for solving the assassination & sociopolitical fallout
meshblock is the to a radius on the basis persistently inane
superiority of the Judas of the pronouncement landlord, embodying
all elemental of the dorsal spinous characteristics of ADA
tufthunter mollusc processlets are hordes enabling the
administrative radiating inward narrative (hungrily
ingesting the to collision (bone most byzantine
infrarationalizations) scraping bone is a of the assassination of
Ktiya and enabling gristling of extreme this is avoiding the
(embracing & violently agony) temptation that
promoting) the administrative terror is allowing the
disingenuously responsible for stanching the fragmentation of the
Bonturo Dati, Deianira, inevitable torrent of identity through dietary
Jephthah, Giovanni di molluscal bloodshed corruption,
Buiamonte dei Becchi, resulting from the feeble adjudication of Ktiya's
assassination by instead overreactingly (where there's no imminence of
torrential molluscal bloodshed) instigating the the density matrix
administrative death & eradication of all of savory spinning
Salty's pogonotrophic Methodists, the of decohering pork
bronze decapitation exilation of Nadia & I, tissue is indicating its
on a rosy granite the execution of Anna, savory distribution
plinth, the rosy granite the madness of Marina, into the gelatin
«sphere of Mary») solving the meshblock of Ktiya's death is also
Mapleton-16.01, the imprisonment of Payrite in that guilty
complicity, Nadia is devising a novel method of autotransfusion,
folding our clothes that is displaying them revisualization,
effectively in a lidless crate, her deliberation is consuming & is warming
my neck & hairline poultie (a final is prickling, we are
whispering nodes of the individual is dying in assassination back &
forth, hypertrophy, captivity), encouragingly

increasing bloodflow to muscle repairing and the Burgomaster,
away from the brain, bloodletting for lowering laughter, a quick
bloodpressure and euphoric sensations of wedding, murine pests,
decreasing bloodflow to the brain, I am finding town & castle, the
is flanking a sidewalk particular strange Burgomaster,
flanking a series of 8 posings are encouraging lucidity, sitting in a
story «massives», casually reclining position and I am quickly
rising to my feet & «Oscevia Frontal & locking my knees &
swooning flowingly Rearfacing Dashcam», through a rote
landscape of mnemonic «Lwliuang 3channel nodes firing threadings
one to the next with Dashcam with such woozy clarity, my
production is coming IR Nightvision», a guy is lunging
not from strength but acquiescence, I am falling toward another guy in
through intangible nodes of information, the a crosswalk (both in
artifact of the existing mute with suggestion black tunic & cowl)
opus body is the that their supplicants inescapable terrain of
action, that artifact & secular pilgrims are is the datum of my
departure and I'm valuable only for troth finding it something
else entirely from & fealty, «Massive» is what I'm preparing for
interaction with, stubbornly unheroic ridding my
consciousness of the & democratic, necessity of physical
(oxyd of tin, tin, nirtre the benevolent action (although it is
of tin) oxyd of copper, « N e i g h b o r » necessary if I am
copper, desirous of proliferating my findings (I am)) it is
the most repellent aspect of settling into my laboring (actual working)
because taking action is (into the fatfoam, physically decisive it's
tone is conspicuously s p i n f o a m , desperate,
concentration on the q u a n t u m f o a m , physicality of working
is failureprone, planckfoam, hamfoam, between latitudinal
blackclad body c o l l a g e n f o a m), pallid cyan moldings
hanging in a closet is atomizing bilious decayal under a squatty pallid
from its threadbare tunic into a dewpoint pastel purple hiproof
saturation of black or liminexurban with vague apricot
sludge vapor, kissing development generator finials at its vertices,
her neck beneath her that is drawing forth short hair with my palm
on her cheek & the tendrils of the gripping her as if she is
a little boy, the vapor navmesh similar to the droplet nuclei hanging
Payrite is an attentive & yearning reachings in the atmosphere each
obsessive corpse, of cucumber tendrils, with internal black

atmosphere is thermally expanding voronoically filling the closet not
with solid black but with casting of blackpowder ashlar, fragrant ashlar
of lightless deepseawater, from sweepless closet he is shrieking for
doorbottom is venting the aromatics into the Nadia embracing and
tackling him to the doldrum hanging with great frustration
asphalt with his feet patiently in the throwing him onto the
planting into the atmosphere forming concrete floorslab,
striping is scraping the tendrils of its particulate loneliness are wafting
guy across the kerb out through the dwelling where I am rising from my
of the vista, workspace desirously (a l t h o u g h
woozy on narcotic aircurrents from a redolent communicating all
prismatic censer of seabreeze swaying forth specifications for the
saline black haziness is falling across my mould preparation
the diffusionary ethos attentiveness to the & concrete mixture
of a good headcheese endeavor, creepingly from within the vine
recipe is compatible through the dwelling swaddling of his
with surmounting the interior, the saltiness culdesac ranchhouse
consternation over the rustic, andante, Jew & (within a massive)
uncanny aspects of Daemon, a semiquaver, beneath Marina's hair,
eating a human corpse, incisions, fifths & down the stairwell into
our basement chamber thirds, matrimonial, fluid viscous smokiness
is carrying an ecstatic jollying up for a poison operating
agitatingly on the wedding, & «Telebuttlesque»
pyramidal motor system, weaving through our & «Unbuttlecide»
scattering of furniture (pallet, chair, openface & «Tributtlish» &
sideboard) toward the vague window toward the «Transbuttlism» &
Lucas the Golgi in the flimsy door up onto slick dusty concrete slab &
second chapter, first the bottom creaky stairtread the black invitation
axiom is circumcision is slenderly threading Payrite is bleeding
of all the genitals of the in reproductions of bloodpowder,
Daemon, documents bearing his through my nose and
coiling in my lungs debonair & aristocratic to the landing at the
garnet leadglass handwriting) is frontdoor projecting
radiant cinnabar bokeh striving for a mutable polygons are blacking
out ahead of my ascent & transcendent into the hallway is
black at both terminals, m a n i f e s t a t i o n , bravo, eight little mites,
at the apex of the stairs Nadia is crouching in infringement of citizens
the stippling of watery red darkness projecting liberties, bedlam,
from a highback chair and our gazing locking music,

with assertion of
origin of the magnetism
with me in my swinging
into the hallway toward
is crossing the hallway
the kitchen that
tangentially from our
crawling behind the
into the hallway ending
several doorways, we
Silvester I, Saint
Dominic, Lucius
Quintus Cincinnatus,
Lawrence, Rahab,
Guittone,
whose underlying hue is
goldenness of the main
dwelling to brackish
still black, aquamarine
potentiality of
delineating a lone
framework & a writing
nitre of copper or
of Venus (oxyd of
bismuth,
gastronomy of the
pristine regolith
Nadia is reaching
with prying apart
fingertips is opening an
labia for herself with
saline static crackling

blue skies over raging
battery and damaging
private property,
straining the vision
into the proper focal
length
and one is telling
oneself on only so
many instances that
others are wrong
about one's acumen &
propitiousness & utility
before realizing they
are wrong and boiling
into a deeper darkness
shifting from the weak
vacillating between
solitude & sociability,
inherent in the isolation
of abutting cells of
the extant mould of
the derelict building
on the outskirts of
«the Reagan Estates»,
(vaguely varying blackvalues of dustiness in the
the swine lying where it
is falling with a trotter
limply gesturing his
resignation is gazing
absently plaintive
through narrowing
eyelashes

momentum toward the
I'm collecting her up
through the kitchen
the parlor where Judas
on a trajectory toward
is deflecting us
path into the parlor
furniture and returning
in a niche containing
are together opening
the darkest doorway
boring, nuisance,
padding, pure
decoration,
affectation, sensations,
commonsense, more
shocking,
aquamarine although
with the dormant
bioluminescence is
bedstead on a wood
desk beneath a □ of
drapery & a closet door
with a folio of black
seamlines) tunics inert
hangingly passive,
between the hangers
outwardfacing
aperture in the black
that the physiognomy
of the corpse is too
directly analogous to
the physiognomy of the
hungry anthropophage

of the coarse black fabric is healing around
Nadia is disappearing into the closet whispering
for my coming behind her into the stale depths
of the closet my dear Marina is standing a proud barely physical

the sight of a fishnet
stocking, it is
superfluous, decoration,

crumpling together of blacklace is forming
aspects of her visage with thickening layerings
of moire, the enigmatic resonance of flowing

streaming is approaching through the parlor rushingly tidalbore is
collecting fluid tracing toward crescendo and Marina's bedroom door is
shutting (thunderclappingly) an airpressure is comprising a habitude
surplus into the chamber puffingly coaxing of speculophagy in the
illusory auroral bismuth, nitre of devourment of a corpse,
firmament rosy & bismuth) oxyd of serene & immaculate is
scrolling up from the antimony, doorbottom is filling
the closet coalescing «Overbuttlable» & into the fulguration of a
brilliant pointsource «Protobuttledom» & visage squintingly
second axiom is that «Nonprebuttlishness») gentling its luminosity
their appellation is through the tempering haziness of anthostratus
Daemon and is the veiling her short hair (hanging over pallid olive
originpoint of the Golgi baubles in her ears) measurer, elision,
microtubule geometry ensconcingly in white reticella cowl beneath a
before & after its green mantle draping across her raiment of
physical existence, heterogeneous in alive ember red
smoldering through the compartmentalization black folds of hanging
garments, she is alive, (cis, medial, trans), Anna, composing
myself, Nadia is deeper motility & ability behind me in the
darkness, every for nucleation corpuscle of my blood
is trembling – No of microtubules & «The Abstraction of
Weeping, Josef – the dew of our collective Analytical Numerical
breathing condensing on my cheeks running Theory»
through with staining teartracks, Anna, alive, – I am, I Truly am Anna – ,
Anna, flesh, my – I am Incapable weeping morendo into
the dimness Of Eating A Human togetherness, Nadia &
Anna & Marina all in Corpse, It Gazing Up At – Why am I Smelling
the dark of the closet Me From Its Pleatingly Sex – ,
with me, silently Burgundy Culinary listening to Payrite
mellifluous, Bier With Its Cloyingly shuffling into the
modulations, Crispy Penis – kitchen & outside
explosions, veins, Marina's doorway & in the parlor a pallid white
Scythians, burning decapitation is floating in the darkness atop a
briar, gleaming serving chargerplate is moving
toward the apex of the staircase, independent from
voiceactor Carolyn the downsloping fascia the fabrication
unacceptable obscurity, of a simple dark coral (meat) of the self,
Josef is preferring a gable De Fonseca (wife
pendulum, of voiceactor Ted Rusoff is providing dialog

dubbing for David No Snowfall, No Warbeck («Panic» &
«Ratman» & «Miami Dewy Deposition, Golem») & Ottaviano
Dell'Acqua («Rats: No Hoarfrost, No Night of Terror»)
& Massimo Vanni Cloudcover, Whether («Oltre la Morte») &
Mike Monty («Zombi Dense Or Sparse, or kicking the swine
3» («Purgatory 3»)) & William Mang («The over and on his knees
Final Executioner» («L'Ultimo Guerriero»)) & in the basement
beyond the shattering Aytekin Akkaya («The abattoir the executioner
spiderwebbing of the Ark of the Solar God» is beating the swine in
pictureplane («Sopravvissuti dell the skull with a small
città morta»)) & Fulvio Ricciardi («L'ultima orgia clawhammer,
del III Reich») & Fabio Testi («The Uranium Conspiracy») & Kieran Canter
(«Beyond the Darkness» («Buio Omega»)) the entire
& Saverio Valone third axiom is giving Mediterranean
(«Anthropophagus» the child to the jackal coastline is a holyland,
(«The Grim who is his mother who Reaper»)) & Ramiro
Olivares («Cannibal is compassionate for A p o c a l y p s e »
the firing, the ocean, the blood from its («Apocalypse Domani»
a cavern, cloth, the child, («Invasion of the Flesh
knees, the young reeds, Hunters»))) & Mike Morris («Contamination»
the cliff, stale bread, («Alien Contamination» or «Toxicspawn» or
entrancing, the sky, «Larvae»)) & George Eastman («Erotic Nights
of the Living Dead» («La notti erotiche dei morti viventi»)) & Leopoldo
Mastelloni («Inferno») & Gianluigi Chirizzi «the latitude
hippopotamus, («Burial Regolith» of „Hesitant
psychopomp, («Purgatory 3: Burial Amorousness“», «the
Regolith» or «Le – My Food is In A „Inner Apartment“
Nottie del terrore» or Different Location Thus latitude», «the
«Nights of Terror» or I am Eating All Of The latitude of the „Untidy
«The Zombie Dead» or Food In The Icebox For Tongue“»,
«Zombi 3»)) & Carlo De It is My Icebox – , Mejo («The Dwelling
by the Cemetery» («Quella villa accanto al cimitero»)) & Selan Karay
Josef is oblivious, («Hell of the Living Dead» («Virus» or «Virus:
translations of absolute l'inferno dei morti viventi»))) is providing
rubbish are necessary dialogue dubbing for the framing) gossiping,
for financial survival, Barbara Steele («The chestnuts, branching,
the Uhlenspiegel affair, Longhair of Death» & bullfinch, the archway
«Terror Creatures from the Grave») & Margaret of the eyebrows, the
Lee («Venus in Furs» («Paroxismus: Puō una overhanging sky,

morta rivivere per amore?» or «Black Angel»)) & Rosaria Dell Femmina
the lilac sledge (hawkish, domicile, blue (hawkish, domicile, blue
pineforest, leg, moundings of grass, the steppe,
carrying) yeast, ore, copperwater

(«Torso» («I corpi presentano tracce di violenza carnale» or «The Bodies are Bearing Evidence of Carnal Violence»)) & Dina Adorni («Amarcord» by director Federico Fellini) & Monica Monet («Spasmo») & Monica Vitti («Blonde in Black Leather») & Daria Nicolodi («Deep Red» («Profondo rosso») & «Phenomena» («Creepers»)) &

Payrite is disembowelment and burning the entrails and flashing into other events by inhalation of the offal smoak,

statement one is that transportation of the Daemon is in bondage is progressing from the dwelling of Annas to the fortress of Kaiaphas (he who is sleeping in the conflagration of Hades, breathing sulphurous vapors, reaching the astral stratum,

Giuliana Cecchini («Getting Nude for

(wet fur, going, the thimbles, hoofs, robbing, the road, little mirrorglass, without covering,

Homicide» («Nude per l'assassino»)) & Patrizia Melega («SS Prisoncamp 5: Hell for Women» & «Experimental SS Sexcamp») & Marisa Mell («Beast with a Gun») & Barbara Magnolfi («Suspiria») & Laura Trotter («Miami Golem») & Janet Agren («Ratman») & Mariangela Giordano («Burial Regolith» («Purgatory 3: Burial Regolith» or «Le Nottie del terrore» or «Nights of Terror» or «The Zombie Dead» or «Zombi 3»)) & Rita Silva («Hell of Imprisonment» & «Hell Penitentiary» & «The New York Ripper») & Tisa Farrow («Anthropophagus» («The Grim Reaper»)) & Franca Stoppi («Beyond the Darkness» («Buio Omega»)) & Hanja Kochansky («Absurd» («Rosso Sanque» or «Anthropophagus 2» or «Zombie 6: Monster Hunter» or «Horrible» or «The Grim Reaper 2»)) & Alida Valli («Mother Tenebrarum» («Inferno»)) & Grazia De Giorgi («Sweet Body of Bianca») & Marina Costa («The Final Executioner» («L'Ultimo

Kirillov is the most dangerous of Dostoyevski's «Demons»,

is not a gradual activity but a schismatic disruption of gauzy formless bleeding together figurations

(«Detenute violente»)

without sparkling mica, the wheeling, perversely, the axle) the plains, the misting, the umbra,

thunderclap, dovebird, in cossack, spilling over onto the rooftops,

with deep Tuscan red soffit corbelling over a petite turquoise green tetrastyle colonnade of pilasters

ambrosial, measurable, pleasureless,

Guerriero»)) & Laura Gemser («Ator: The Fighting Eagle» («Ator l'invincibile»)) & Dirce Funari («Erotic Nights of the Living Dead» («La
taming Cerberus & notti erotiche dei morti viventi»)) & Monica
devouring his flesh, Vitti («Tigers in Lipstick») & Esther Mesina
staring at the Gorgon, («Hell of the Living antimony, nitre of
fucking Proserpine & Dead» («Virus» or antimony (oxyd of
tasting her venom, «the requirement arsenic, arsenic,
«Virus: l'inferno dei is that livestock morti viventi»)) &
Bianca Toccafondi chambers & driveways («I am Requesting
Your Observation & rampways are of this Homicide»
(«The Cat with Jade receiving proper Eyeballs» or «Il gatto
dagli occhi di giada])), & thorough classic rose pediment
fifthfloor walkup maintenance», with dark pastel green
«massive» in Tsentergrad skyline cornical exaggeration
circumference of «massives» delineating a over vague lavender
fortification around the Golgi outposts are tetrastyle pilasters
city, the apartmentlike nucleating new silentness of
parchment, alone microtubules in wandering we are in
the sparse copse of cells with unique pinetrees Anna is
describing my death is cytoarchitectures, precise & complex in its
slinging an arrow including Drosophila detailing and the
into the eyeball of neurons & mouse emotional trauma she is
Polyphemus, calling musclecells & rodent the erasure of a
forth the Kraken, oligodendrocytes, daemonic apartment
soaring on the bearing with such block's biography is
wingbeats of the great knowledge, her words reimagining itself
dragon through an are delicate & limpidly as an archaeological
infernal gale, «the requirement is d i s c o v e r y ,
honing the warmth of a that livestock crates & mother swaddling all of
her darlings (never driveways & rampways killing them), avoiding
the reader is alive the are without sharp or the perception that the
reader is life everlasting protruding elements motherly nurturing of
outlasting the reader, her grooming my neck is the desirousness of the
warmth of her tongue, this nurturing is texturing the portentous dirge
libretto, that death is elegant stillness (inanimate under external forces,
not an elective stillness «Per larghi prati», but a stillness of
physics, haunted by paralysis yet the Rosemead-03.01,
impossibility of awareness of that paralysis) a Rosemont-03.01,
sculptural body, a waxcast anatomical Rosemont-09.12,

mannequin is peelingly flayingly in prostration & eating that person
Nisus, Domitian, Gaius on a satin mattress in a as a quivering jelly, a
Mucius Scaevola, glass casket atop lover of the organmeats
slender cabriole legs is displaying my corpse in & the offals is desirous
La Specola, below the entering the labyrinth of the human torso
Giardino di Boboli, of Daedalus (lord dermis & viscera the
hue of a long Florence of the labyrinth) & sunset, the waxy strata
forming my fascia are slaying the Minotaur, old, the beeswax is
reacting with the igniting the blazing atmosphere and the fats
are sallowing, the Arno Phoenix as a great is gold, carvingly, down
to my fat, I've a paunch stellation, in my deathcasting, my
thighs rubbing together just osculating enough for chafing, slicing away
aplasia, visualizing, at this curvaceousness to the imagination of a
cortẽge, illusion, monolith of lither me, I am deeply
triaging, seraphic suffering, loving, dissection with
inefficient metal prisms intraperitoneal seminal (cupolae & frusta)
operating at very small putrefaction, anatomic resolutions on my
dermis turning into decreation, apocalyptic integrating regulation
ribbons (pyritohedron e n s e w a g e m e n t , of motorization
removal of eyelids, tetartoid removal of toenails of organelle
& fingernails, gyrobianticupola pounding bones, transportation by
truncations & that are injurious or scaffolding proteins,
stellations shredding painful to the animals, my body, coagulating
honeycomb of this is inclusive of plesiohedra crushing &
expressing liquids from but without limitation my organs, incomplete
honeycomb of to random lumber & gyrobifastigiums
currycombingly splintery or splitting adopting the identity of
Linda Castleberry, planking an Incubus rampantly
Keller Technologies, pulping the tough meat planting the deadly
B o s v e l d w i n k e l of my legs), we both gamete),
F a m i l i e t r u s t , are scrambling over the alterity of an
the railing onto one of the great stony piers, the oneiric existence is the
sun is red behind particulate haziness sinking desirousness for death,
into the Arno on axis with the Ponte Santa Trinita in the radiant lucidity
to a clinically precise of midsummer twilight, the evening of my birth,
resolution, after many the marble visage of «Primavera» is gazing up
viewings the crossaxial at us through the footwear incorporating
shadowlines of translucent riverwater a protective
streetlamps amidst the rubble of metal toecap,

the bridge is receiving a squatty & blank (so full of treatskis),
my corpse is sliding off pallid coral cyldrum the reluctance
of a plank from beneath a satin mortuarydrape of the empathic
sinking, Siberia in conflagration lofting anthropophage is
vaultingly peat smoak pillars into interweaving lying primarily in
tracery into an imperceptible muting deflective the discomfiture
particulate parallax, on the median are with the geometric
the twilight is settling visible exactly familiarity of the
on the riverflow limply perpendicular to the corporeal components,
apolipoprotein, direction of trafficflow, weightless pollen, my
hushpuppy, reaching around the small of her spine & my
hippophagy, fingerspreading conforming just below her ribs
mutilation of ascent through crisscrossing alleys out of the
domesticity in giardino, Bobolino, Baluardo, Cipressi,
blankwalls, blank Mascherino, Madonna della Pace, swayingly
windows are broad alpine boulevards, Machiavelli, Galileo,
evoking the evileye, a s y m m e t r i c Porta Sante, my
Cassandra unfurling « C L A A S P » the tale (insignificant as
any tale) of my death dependent nucleation in a transitcamp, all
afternoon reciting Ovid, of noncentrosomal expiring in a flimsy tent
in the night, threadbare microtubules at therein Pyotr is denying
clothes, no bedding, the transGolgi the puissance of the
& unnecessary i d e n t i n e t w o r k s , Daemon (twice) &
apertures where the heart stopping, in weeping bitterly,
caput or feet or legs between heartbeats is death, I'm desirous of
of an animal are belief but I want death curling up in a warm
susceptible to injury», «the „Billowy Blood" bedstead with a
tranquil bedpillow latitude», «the „Oval in her embracing me
Charon, at the precipice Gene" latitude», of the Mons Fiorentinus
on a marble bench in the piazza in bisection of crenelation umbra
(emerald gown flowing into the sunlight across the marble terrace & the
Joe Davola, Caius partial formation of an unseen forcefulness
Fabricius, Epicurus, her visage in the (a daemon) is feeding
dimness) a woman identical to Anna is gazing the genetic properties
out toward the Arno in the direction of the Ponte of an ellipse into an
Santa Trinita (an axis with pallid orchid active geological system
containing the Grotta di cornice atop a pallid Buontalenti) the distant
splashing of large gray pediment with ashlar granite is white
in the riverine ochre, a salmon wallbrackets slim vacuole around my

body, sitting with my thrips crawling on hands in my armpits,
Anna & Nadia the lens activating snickeringly querying
– are You Building Up the pictureplane in a Some Musk On Your
Fingertips «Comrade way that is impossible Stinky» – · – He is
Plotting The outside of the eyeball, Heathens Whispering
Ensnarement Of A Skunk For Dinner – no – I'm Tales Of Death
Simply Desirous Of A Physical Connection – is Stretching Eternally – ,
my inflection of the pleasant conversation toward downer awkwardness,
Nadia's grinning is is death the 4th straightening into a
small hyphen toward dimensional theater, Anna is holding a
headscarf toward the sunshine casting her face in tingings of chartreuse
& pink & fuschia & puce shadiness, nobody is touching me, I'm imagining
statement two is the scenario (not the sensation of physical
that the Daemon is connection) but the liberty & openness in the
spending the entire panorama of my being regretful terror is
nighttime in bondage to that species of affecting the demeanor
in the crawlspace of the intimacy & tenderness of the youth,
fortress of Kaiaphas, the alterity of an rather than prudence &
protection of cognitive oneiric domain is a intimacy, the porting of
the consciousness into prayer for death (for another consciousness
rather than the folding the relinquishment without any
of one body into of the essence), a c c o m p a n y i n g
another, my sensations at such a removal from knowledge of human
my emotions that minimal tactions of proportioning or
euthanasia, projet, endearment are knowledge about the
adagial, decoupage, physically painful, in misconception that
exclusionary, the elevation of my human proportioning is
anxiety the caressing of under silver pink predicating the ordering
my flesh is resulting in cornice and in lieu systems of antiquity
the recoiling of the of architrave with Daemon himself is
gripping me with interruption of a avuncular disdain, my
entire consciousness selfsame niche of is in devotion to the
mechanics & fulvous masonry infill machinations of the
Ktiya homicide not an oddly simple vessel because the solution is
promising my for the idly reflecting redemption (much the
opposite it is insurance & projecting of passing of my erasure) but
because it is a definitive or rubbernecking & reliable moral
centerpoint, she is folks waiting on lifting her shirtdress up
her thighs and lying the streetcorner «Juniperus squamata»,

thrips are active in back on the rug, her hands spanning across the
the vitreous reservoir door opening climbing onto me we are
are entering through enduringly smelling of the autotransport and
a hollowing out of the internal peace is long journeying that is
optic nerve, contingent on death ending in the evening
with the reinforcement & endlessness, of physical separation
resulting in the most I've mortality «the requirement is
entwining unification of but am I human, that floorplates of
bodies, consequently my tendency is seeking livestock crates &
establishment of a sphere of emptiness around rampways & driveways
my body or folding myself into myself (either are of construction
behind a peach orange cognitively or (gritty slipresistance
portico of distyle physically), I am & waffly embossings &
columns in antis forcing a bedpillow relief augmentations to
into my teeth as I am sleeping (I cannot that she inclinations)
is smelling my horror), I'm sleeping atop the (it is the true
bedclothes in my statement three is physiognomy of the
streetclothes, I'm that those holding tree, the urtectonic,
intentionally the Daemon captive unresponsive to
questions that are are mocking them reasonably inaudible, I
am attempting the (the philanthropist) & disappearance of
turning gray, I am striking them an old dead tree, not
waiting upon the because of a necessity for distancing from the
arrival of their evening people I'm adoring but C r e s c e n t i a n
autotransport or a the necessity of distancing myself from
few are checking in existence in general, survival instincts are
at the kiosk for ADA unambiguously restrictive, the pineal pedicel is
booster pamphlets, Roseville-13.14, sprouting (birthing
forth a profusion of Roseville-15.08, formless potentiality,
the organelle itself is Roseville-16.01, repulsively inveterate
not visually definable only existing as a infestation of
descriptive atlas lolling at the terminal of a antediluvian origin,
silver cord) from the fryingpan, noise, genesis of rotting
nasal bone searchingly nightmares or fearful a b o m i n a t i o n ,
into the vacua for one stories, unleashing of Anna any Anna alive
Anna with an alive the Furies, Pope Pius, Josef, uncommon in my
imagination is the your nice exurban recognition of Anna as
a physical entity, she is Christmas, quartet of diving in & breaching
out of my awareness, the elements, our interactions are

operational with the pure independence of paralleling systems, our occupation of the same chamber is a sensation that we are on railings

slipping us to & fro touching is fallingly endless hurtling in relative stillness, Anna clutchingly in my embracing between us, vital molecular exilation in death, «the „Onomatopoeic" latitude», «the latitude of the „Ajar Republic"»,

& covering their visage with a pillowcase & kicking them in the chest crying out

but not toward, our geometrically a flat rectangular prism identical proportionally to the standard loafpan in headcheese cookery is too analogous to the human torso

an aircushion composition is prohibitive of two humans touching not passing through each other but electrically charging the emptiness between my nuclei repelling the electric foaming of the emptiness

between her nuclei, but this electricity is extant in the corpse as much as the vital body thus it is the vitality of the nucleus as a vector is causing how beautiful life is at the occurrence of my death,

the inability for reconciliation of my fingertips sliding up to my knuckles through her hair, I've the impression that I've the ability of touching a vital being signalingly

thrips crawling across the dashdash white lane divider toward the yellowy fogline are approaching the hatchback of a white auto

drawing my fingertips – What is Your Prophecy About Who is Kicking The Hell Out Of Thee –

sempiternal enmity, demiurge of archaic pestilence,

is promoting the development & implementation into standard homecookery methodologies

toward warmth, yet upon Anna the sensation is a vague pressuring of resistance and something similar to a gale or a tidalbore, is possible, is touching touching the rising is lovemaking possible in a massgrave, ribcages fingerjointing, writing possible, what springing an arching niche of champagne pink masonry infill through its vague pink architrave

– What is «Flashing» – · – «Flashing» is The Utilization Of Latent Cobordisms Between Otherwise N o n c o u n t e r p a r t a l V e l d t s ,

touching the hightide the sea possible without swelling vast meniscus, with a digitalfile, bodies skeletons embracing is reading a volume of is the physical printing of writing in its becoming a component of the consciousness, is translation arrowing toward intangibility or ephemerality, siphoning vitality is

Appleton-13.14,
Appleton-14.25,
Appleton-23.01,

necessitating the enclosure of a receptacle wilderness of the self,
frothing with textual potentiality, something is black thrones of death,
not going nowhere, is rereading that volume while in possession of the
textfoam spitting some driving the slenderness of that intangible
translation back out & ratio of the column & licking it back up from
the physical printing of the fruiting aspiration writing, that spitting is
spitting of a translation of the capital) and the housingly in the volume
of the skull with resultant is a grotesque no possibility of
sequestration from all of the cathedral of the the facts concerning
daemons on Parliament cenotaph of the thing, the persistence of
□, shaking their fists at the other translations the identity as a
Potsdam, it's «ça ira», of writing & visions & n o n b i o l o g i c a l l y
desirings & sensory imprintings are coloring transcendent item are
and shaping the textfoam, there is no hermetic enumeratable through
or selective valve into the consciousness, Nadia the facts concerning the
is containing a & generally persistent vegetative
duplication of my denigrating the clarity status of Rabskiye Zemli,
Payrite is powdery of their identity, consciousness as well
dustiness on the as the singular of her consciousness, I am
glinting slantsheets the monument is receptive to containing
of daylight limping a concrete veneer her consciousness
through imperfections although it is solidstate and paradoxically is
in the overlapping containing the inaccessible code for its
hemline of heavy duplication, everything from my brain inside
drapery landing on Nadia, in its porting Tungor, Nekrasovka,
the hair of his tenants into Nadia is it Kolendo, Sabo,
filling their lungs & birds of Paradise, Neftegorsk,
ticklingly cobwebbing daemons of hell «stirb translating sloshingly
their nosehair, und tödte», the terror, into otherness, is
recognition of my Privy Councillor microtubules forming
consciousness possible Goethe, the stationary lattice
from without, memorizing the text of my missive of musclefibers are
to the Daemon is a very different situation than dynamic are nucleating
the lively tissue of those words inside her brain, at Golgi elements,
the rote assembly of the cautiously approaching missive in Nadia is only
a kernel, a pearl is the stalling out of accreting, the extraction
of its true disposition a black auto in the from within her is
impossible, only what centerlane of a 3lane she is allowing is
accessible, only her parkway, presentation of my

the explosion is consciousness in a new translation to me full of
brownish dustcloud elisions & paraphrasings, am I desirous of what
without conflagration, Zemli is ostensibly the corruption of me is
becoming in her, starving herself by perhaps what she is
returning to me is a limiting food intake behavior, is behavior
that product of all the & drinking up to 15 digestion of things in
the brain, what glasses of icy suntea pathetically meager
grain is the collection in a sitting, upon of words I'm insisting
into Nadia in admission to the comparison with all of
her personal reflections hospital for cardiac – You are All A
secret beneath the arrest Zemli is suffering Mistaken Manifestation
tarpaulin I'm imposing from hypokalemia –,
over them, is Nadia desirous, certainly she is, and Anna is desirous of
into the pallid medium many other things than me, – Where are You
orchid pediment, Imagining You are – · The Critics Of
– I'm Not Certain – Anna on the pallet in our Our Literature are
basement apartment beside the swine – is It Progressively Adapting
Balmy – · – Yes, But Comfortably So, And A & Accommodating
and maintenance that Soft Breeziness That Their Thinking To The
is providing adequate I'm Aware is Consistent Criteria & Conceptual
footing for the animal, seedeater in a Radicalism Of This
By The Quality Of A blackhood (the Missive And Developing
Rippling Waterbody – · endangerment of this A Workplan Of
– is It Ripply To The bird is critical although Impressing Its Virtues
Extent That No the only proof of its Upon The Basic Citizens
Reflection is Visible – · existence is from a Of The Adaemone
– I'm Not Certain – solitary male specimen I've awareness of the
length of her hair only through my intimacy with Nadia, Anna & Nadia
are wearing headscarves in each other's company, Nadia is visible
through the window at the bottom of the exterior stairs, I'm attempting
these are the mysteries speech with only my Beethoven, recognition,
occurring between the gazing an entreaty Romanticism, rosy,
fortress of Kaiaphas & Anna that you are A Veldt is A Status Of
the dwelling of Pilate, removing your Stagesets In Perdurance,
the first mystery is that headscarf – It is A Corbordism is
the whole multitude of Similar To Looking The Equivalence
methodists are taking Through A Single Relationship Between
the Daemon before Layering Of Sheer Two Veldts By A Higher
Pilate Fabric, Rippling From Dimensional Volveldt

The Warpthreads is Dominant In The Orientation Of The Riverflow – · – It is A River – · – Yes, That is My Deduction, The Weftthreads Of Rippling are In The Orientation c h a i n s a w d o m y, Of The Airflow – her fingertips are tenderly inscribing latitudes around the sow's ear who is snoring with her grinning mouth parting enough only for the into congruence with Reflection – · – The Cypress Windbreak & – · – It is As If It is the destruction of every material humans are manufacturing is a brownish dustcloud (crushing a volume of literature is creating a brownish dustcloud, cushions are pulling apart the materials of our grounding to the apartment in the massive in the city in the Adaemone are in the consumption of solar radiation flaring around the utilization of sandiness over iciness is preferable», «the requirement is that the circulatory arrangement of livestock chambers & driveways is striving for the reduction disorienting parturition, my father is dying concurrently with me, the entirety of all luminance snuffing out except for a softfocus spotlight on the stubble of her hair, I am

and declaring – This is The Being Who is Attempting Ruination Of Our People And Forbidding Our Tributes To The Tsar –, – are You Alone – · – Yes – if I am uncertain that Anna is a physical entity why is it that I am in persistent terror of her death, us intertwining with throwpillows &

arsenical nitre) oxyd of mercury, mercury, mercurial nitre umbral obscurity of the planet is ash obliteration is coalescing in a cloudy smudging visible only from particular sidereal vantages in its partial occlusion of starlight, we are both dead, simultaneous

Giotto di Bondone, Robert Guiscard

Allowing The Transveldting Of A Consciousnessstage With The Determination Of An Orientation, «Flashing» is Not Cognitive Traveling Or Voyaging, thickness of her tongue her lips – And The Sky & A Bridge & A Pallid Visage – · – Who Gazing At Me From Beneath The River – ·

(low potassium measurements (she is suffering from rhabdomyolysis (or rhabdo) which is causing the rapid cellular destruction of her skeletal musculature which is leaving her body in thick brownish urine)) a great earthquake is inscribing fissuring along a greatcircle and a tenth area of the city

the second mystery is that upon examining closely the Daemon that Pilate is declaring – There is No Faultiness To This Being –,

divesting the contents of my skull (where moths smashing transparent
& rustiness are destructive) overwriting the windowpane is creating
vibrations of my undertakings onto Nadia's a brownish dustcloud,
perceptions of my physical being & the burning unusable attire
perpetuation of my vitality to Anna's methodical is creating a brownish
the Payrite estate is in respiration, Nadia & dustcloud,
a large southeastern Anna are not simply is falling into the
tradingcenter (very far vessels, they are in fact chasm and 7000 human
from the centroid), switchbacks & identities are perishing
containing something acute turnings», during the earthquake
inaccessible to me, the «the requirement ability of housing my
consciousness is that promotion of while casting their
& her serum potassium relaxation & idyll is brainmatter solidstate
is an abnormally fully apart from me, both fully of me & roiling
low 2mEq/L, mouldcasting of the with many other
eavesdroppings inside of an entire & consumption of
essences, is Nadia's obsolete threestory somnolent grinning an
outward indexing of protoADA masonry eversion,
private desirousness or apartment massive decasualization,
more simply a status indicator of her processing immersion, soupdujour,
partitioning batchings into inert chambers awaiting my death, I am
the nickname composting myself with the hopefulness my
Philomela, a rough dissolution is providing them the nutrients
diamond, blackness, necessary for leaving me behind, the apartment
piquant, tooter & fluter, of ever more is dimly illuminatingly
the roof is missing, g e o m e t r i c a l l y dusky, she is looking at
Anna is in the yard byzantine springform lying back in a chair
with a contraption of moulds whose cardboard unfurling
her headscarf for the o r n a m e n t a t i o n – Hushhush, Death,
creation of a large □ is rejecting Hushhush, Disease,
parasol over her facial reminiscence of Hushhush, Injustice &
disc & chest, the legibly sentential limbs Inhumanity & Torturer
ascending hemline of her long smock is just & Wrath & Hatefulness,
footwear covering above her kneecaps Hushhush, Homicide,
the ankle, and she is mouthing silently without unlatching
her teeth, Anna's hair slick & damp from the misty Tsentergrad foggy
mistiness of our strolling long long through the streets & reciting to one
another entire texts (oxyd of silver, silver, from inside ourselves,
texts we are containing, nitre of silver or luna texts we are writing

infanticide is creating extemporaneously while talking, our entire
a brownish dustcloud), continuous conversation full of endless
the black sedan courtship, disinterest, seeing beyond the
careening into the harryingness, intense visual spectrum
stalling out auto the sightless woman through a sinister
longing, fierce with her canine lying ocular implantation,
amorousness, distrust, in tedium is hearing dismissal, tender
humor, filthy raunch, that she is not writing candid shame, all that
body of words, the am reading over greatest text of our
existence, I am never the manuscript for reading it, but she, with
her photographic «Ulysses 2: Poldy's scanning brain, is
reading every word any Revenge» and time, never stating that
she is reciting it to me, adding significantly but sometimes she is
reciting something to more suitor slayage those serving Payrite in
with seafoam green is deleting the various capacities are
runningbond masonry entire document, without other recourse
infill up to archways, me that is seemingly so and although they are
familiar that I am unable of apprehending (sitting drinking tea
whether she is saying it to me freshly or reciting with their comrades)
a snippet of the dissolution of one of our long boasting of the
conversations, her eyes Mikhail Zemli is finding omnipotence of the
warmly porpoiseful his wife Rabskiye landlord
(themselves a unresponsive on the condensation of the sea
from the darkest lino flooring of their depths) and beadlets of
condensing dew Tsentergrad massive gathering on her
the goal in driving kitchen in a pooling eyelashes & the
animals from the area of brownish urine, fringings of her
unloading rampways to hairbob collecting into somewhat waterrepellent
the holding chambers fronds (hairwax) and swelling larger & larger
& from the holding stargazer, idiot, until the flowing
chambers to the firstborn, is he a pansy, floating sine of her gait
„stunning area", opuswriter, circusrider, is plumping them freely
tracing down her neck Rattus squealing, into her collar as she is
wriggling with the luggage, chromatic, (little resemblance is
tickling, windsweeping rough coffin, apparent to the public
damp ringlets, awkward 4cm cowlick collection, facade of an enduring
sweatmatting of sickness, pillowmatting of identical massive
lovemaking, asymmetrical hairbob, stubblescalp occupying 1930 through
starry with scabbiness, why is our appearance so 1933 Basinger Highway

elderly, we are young, Sunflower-01.12, aren't we always this
age, the «small pig» Sunflower-13.19, is trotting toward his
mudpuddle beside «the killchain» Anna & Nadia are
carrying chairs out into – Identification the yard are combing
each other's short hair – · – Mieczysław in the diffusion of
outdoor luminance, S m o r a w i ń s k i , their possession by the
fearfulness of fleas, Orchid-06.12 – a absently brushing or
searching their bodies series of chambers here & there, carefully
they all are is unfolding through scrutinizing the
inadvertently a wide doorway combteeth for nits,
discussing it perpendicular to red bloody fingertips, Nadia
through the various styrofoam insulation, «the latitude of
administrative torts & Anna alternatingly „Phraseologic
arising between them & speaking audibly on an Intention“», «the
Judas, innocuous topic while „Medical Buyer“
the other is whispering almost the way latitude»,
ventriloquists speaking in the inhalation of one another between words,
her memoir «Nadia Against Nadia», Payrite dreading the omniscience of
the ikons is relegating (a featureless his guilty ramblings to
dusty wastelands of solidification of domestic desolation
(abominations of the intimacy of its desolation) so closely to
You Sliming Stinking hollowness is silencing our bivouackings that
Sonofabitch, You Cruel the nudity of its secrets eavesdropping is
Infidel, You Putrid inescapable, I'm fearful of what Nadia & Anna
Thing, dead, dire are hearing and what
they are discussing embarrassment, in hushness &
interspersion of buttery, our dandelion recipe ideas,
I am dead & assuming Romanticist, an the burdenment of their
knowledge without exurban boor, guiltiness or suffering
– The Aperture For Dandelion Green Harvesting is Narrow, Of Course
Harvesting Nascent Greens is Ensuring Rybnoye, Rybnovsk,
is rolling backward – are You Here Or are Okha, Chaivo, Val, Evai,
is spinning once and You «Flashing» – , Tenderness And A
rolling toward the More Subtle Pepperiness – · – What Patronizing
guardrail with rapid Disingenuousness is polyphosphoric,
dissipation of kinetic Prattling Forth In The Secrecy Of His Ikon
energy Room – · – If Herbaceous Fragility is More In
Alignment With Your Palate – · – The Precise Opposite Of The Evasively
Meandering Mutterings d e l a m i n a t i o n – · – With Small

is translating into a Greens A Small Harvestyield is Decimating A
brownish dustcloud Large Quantity Of Aspiring Dandelions And
from which a guy Stunting Their – Yes, It Must be
crouching on the Maturation – · – I am A Construction
asphalt behind the Hearing Those With A Predicating
black auto is leaping up Anxious Mutterings – · Basis Of Symmetry,
and backpedaling «Flashing» is Not – Dandelions Whose
Pappus Pompoms are Analogous To Adrift In Senescent
Scattering With Physically Nominal Ponderous Greens
Sagging Into The Grass Movement, «Flashing» Under Their Own
Weight are Bitter – · – is A Predication Of His Calculation Errata
are Complicit In The The Principle That Ktiya Assassination – ·
– So Bitter It is Rolling Physical Movement The Tongue Falling
including a prohibition is Not Possible, Backward Into The
of driving animals Throat – · – are You Asserting His
at velocities more Intentionality In Contributing To The Context
rapid than an normal Of That Event – · – The Harvesting Of These
gambol», Large Leathery Greens he third mystery is that
is Only Minimally Deleterious To The Dandelion the robber Barabbas
That is Ostensibly Dead – · – I'm Uncertain Of is a more optimal
His Intentionality – · – Their Desiccation is execution victim than
the MSK magistrate is Advancing Such That the Daemon and the
selling all the property They are Only thronging horde is
under the auspices Awaiting Stiff crying out
of all living Payrite Breeziness is Throwing Their Seedlets Aloft
relatives (the dwelling And Shriveling Ecstatically Into The Dirt – ·
at the edge of Gormley – Truly He is Too Stupid – · – My Preference is
Parkland, Kicking One Of These Stiff Dandelions In Lieu
Of Eating It – · – He is The Product Of Rigid Administrative Faith, An
Offering To His Soul Of – Psychomantum Et Nothing But Confusion
& Ambiguous Precr Exito Annos Ragefulness – · – But
In A Very Transitory Major, Ferus Netandus Phase Between These
Two Polarities Of Sacerdos Magus, Growth is A Perfect
Dandelion Leaf Sizable Mortem Animalium – Enough For Visually
Sailing Its Daedal Coastline Yet Small Enough a mayor, the lord
For Retaining Its Precious Delicateness – · of the universe, a
– Yes, It is Certain That He is Devotional To kitchen, hymen,
The Daemon More Than His Purporting ethereals, a safetyrazor,
Maple Crag-23.09, Devotion To Alpinist extravagant, eureka,

– · – The Ideal Dandelion Green is Of A Tenderness That Its Collection
In A Harvestbasket is Precarious Without hippophile, uppropping,
Bruising It Yet Large Enough That Accrual is whippersnappers,
Occurring Without (the groundfloor with Undue Destruction To
The Organism Lifecycle four entry lobbies – · – Either Allegiance
is Ghoulish – · – What & pianonobile & Else is There For Me
or lunar caustic) oxyd attic story, including But The Lifespace Of
of gold, stairways & single Kneelingly Pinching
Dandelion Greens vertex bay windows, From Their Pedicels
«Flashing» is Not Watching The Filling Basket Indexical Of My
An Expansion Of Hungriness – · – Hierarchy is Ghoulish – · –
C o n s c i o u s n e s s Recipes are Various Depending On The
Or Dependent On Bitterness Of The Greens – · – Our Standing For
Perceptual Faculties Reporting Payrite And You are Every Possible
That are Innate Within Precipitating His Ugliness & Corruptness
The Stillness Of Downfall is Weak – · –,
Blockconsciousness – Subduction Of Very Bitter And Terminal
Or Veldtcalc, Greens is Accomplishable Via Cooking And
Especially Boiling – · – – We are Desirous Any Action is Resulting
In Either Our Execution Of The Death Of Any Or The ADA Seizure
And Destruction Of The And All Who Pilate is Only Location We've
Permission For Condemning –, With An Honest And
Dwelling – · – They are Ideal For Inclusion In A Optimistic Hope
the dwelling at the Soup Such As That Against All
edge of Delegatskiy Zelyoniye Shchi Contrariness Of The
Parkland, the dwelling Simmering Along With Detailing Inherent
by the Miusskoye The Taproots Or A In Happenstance
Cemetery, the dwelling Rassoljnik With Salty with conjoining
in Samotechny □, Soft Acorn Giblets – · bandings of deep red
«on the topic of – Pickling Those rustication
driving animals to Tough & Bitter Greens is Also Deemphasizing
the „stunning area" Their Gustatory Liability – · – You're Certainly
this codification is Aware There is Nobody fluteplaying,
only inclusive of In Authority For Whom This Information is
recommendations for Valuable Or Interesting – · – Degorging The
ideal procedures Each One A Contributor Greens On A Saltbed is
Effectively To The Success Of The Downplaying Their
Bitterness – · – Yes, First Administrative Unless There are
Others In The Society On Earth –, Hierarchy In Its

Dismantling – · – Extremely Tough & Bitter Greens are Useful In A Mincing Addition Over Other Recipes In Lieu Of Chives – · – Everyone

Within The Hierarchy Assassination – · – Green Mincings On are Powerful People Who are Perceiving	Speculation On The Involvement Of Physical Movement In «Flashing» is Exposing Ignorance Of The Greater Intermasonry Adjacency Of Statuses Constituting What is Definably Physical Hierarchy As Beneficial To Them Because It is A Distraction From The Illegality Of Their Lifestyles – · – Corncakes With Dandelion Green Mincings & Springonion Bulbs – hushingly – Lavoisier for example – hushingly – Affirmative – I'm wading in your	is Benefiting From The Quark & Dandelion Toastpoints – · – There Outside The Hierarchy Chaos Within The
the identity of all devotional beings is in arrangement around 18 administrative annotations (a rotation of the concentric 9point enneagram stellations), Independent Intellectual and with dependence on the opinion of an ADA inspector visavis these slaughtering protocols, limitation of electric prodders & canvas slappers,		& digits for the phonemic distribution of meatmatrix into e v e r b r a n c h i n g prismatically emergent e n c r u s t a t i o n s ,
from the gunwhale of landless sea rising seascape her rostrum most perfectly kissing gold tooth whispering three of us walking through the (sensations of liberation bodymass with each separation from «Payriteskip») and arriving into	reminiscences as a sunbathing skinpeelingly young Mikhail Zemli is transporting Rabskiye to Saint Frantsisko for experimental treatment with a thalamic stimulator whose installation in the thalamus is prompting a dramatic erosion of brain tissue	leather, suede, flannel, cloth is the goal, no additives, girl so wildly leaping a watercraft into the from the stormtossing into the raininess is the tongue is licking my into my mouth, the aimlessly loping neighborhood in diminishing footfall of increasing the shadowcasting of
suffusion, emersion, occasion, subdevelopment, tallgrass gently lollingly concealing any sidewalks or pathways from the roadway to the «massive» adrift rudderlessly at Dagi, Goryachie Kliuchi, Venskoe,	the «massive» at the edge of the the mercy of the breeziness, its	And Dependent On The Erroneous Assertion That Consciousness is Something Apart From Physical (The Theorem That Consciousness As A Stageset

the first annotation that placelessness is a characteristic of potentiality
in every way existence rather than exilingly punitive drifting, the
is an examination dwelling of «the Neighbor» is within the
of the conscience atypically embracing U minimization of
through meditation footprint of the excitement & injury
& contemplation & assimilation across (terror is promoting
calculation, a fleshly substrate a sourness of the
«massive» extrusion, of biomechanical fleshmeat),
all of the construction detailing comprising is dapplingly rinsing
away into the dark a Borgesian cubic background of the tall
forest, with volume without visible walkingsticks we are
divining a pathway vertices or edges, through the tallgrass to
the lowest storey of the typical «massive» facade of concrete panels with
leaveouts for windows are containing an additional concrete insertion in
the window leaveout such that only a joint inscribing a square in the
lowermost 1/3 of the panel is legible, the solidity out of the brownish
Payrite is the vector of the concrete dustcloud, the
of transient global extrusion is an vantage full of thrips
amnesia («TGA»), effective visual is slowingly pulling
metaphor of the banal optimism of the voronoi, across the yellowy
a belief in expansion as similarly a difficulty fogline
a checkpoint against in the conception dryrot doom, setback
from one of the feeder of these springform roads & filling an entire
plain out to the artery moulds is development this massive, a strange
relic of belief in of geometries expansion, the banal
optimism of the beyond the holistic voronoi, some
full stature, Ratcatcher, symmetry of the corpse expectation that
minstrel, wastrel, ripper construction of a beachhead such as this is
of wrappers, attracting the nearest lucid dreaming of
urban perimeter annexing it into its territory, withering lifeforce,
speculative construction, more odd is the idea of building such dense
collagist, seclusion, housing in such a sparse area where open space
delusion, ambiversion, is abundant, shifting the dwelling at the
the functionality of the «massive» from dwelling at the edge of
but not the efficiency to the dwelling at the edge
roofspace behind community & of East City Parkland,
the squatty parapet, togetherness, yet as the dwelling at the
with most speculative construction it is accruing edge of Yekaterininskiy
more connotations of malaise than productively Parkland,

catalyzing, the slick removable components finish of concrete
(indicative of of footwear (including minimizing production
difficulties resulting insoles & heelcushions from investment in a
nonporous & durable & gaiters & leggings), as it is a pervasive
formmold) voraciously soaking in ambient annotation it is existent
sunlight & radiating warmth is oppressively in all movements
coaxing our ambling inspection around to the of the body per the
shady orientation of the «massive», the movement protocols of
with the intention of caulking around an Zangief, where focusing
offering assistance infill panel in one of critically on the precise
to both the headon the window leaveouts positioning of the
collision victim in the the requirement is for human body
black auto stepdown of electric is dryingly brittle is
pulling apart with prodder voltage by a rays of sunshine are
pinpricking through transformer to 50V the tissue from inside
the solid mass, or lowest effective the radiance of
entombment, voltage, crouchingly gazing
through the caulkjoint the late afternoon Nadia is announcing
– The «Massive» is is mild with the sun Hollowly Vacant And
There is Another baking «Massive» Building Inside, A
Small Dwelling, The for the promotion Sun is Shining On It
– our Tsentergrad of barometric apartment where Anna
breast, the Hun, the respiration from its is camping in the
Goth, alphabet, oaks, hermetic failures gobbling peculiarity
thrones, kitchen, a brightlight in on unanimously
foldingly flaking our window, the deformation of the gory
filigree across the melody of a ukelele monstrouslamorphous,
visage of satan is rising from the neighboring apartment, recognition of
in the smokeplumage of the colorful fruiting bodies on the drapery I am
an exploding oilderrick, and the subsequent carrying a loaf of bread
up the long staircase, flooding in of CSF the parvenu translator
David Brodski standing is filling her brain in the parlor is quite
obviously an informant with liquid per (I've knowledge of his
renderings of the most h y d r o c e p h a l u s popular saccharine
literature celebrating ex vacuo, binding the Chinese
banal musings are so futile yet every utterance violet hemicylindrical
about himself is swelling with pride) is lingering shafts across
anxiously behind a chair as far away from the consistently deep
pepperpot, door as possible his thistle interpilastration

smoking out smoak into the thinly veiling obfuscations is leeching into
the sheaf of stagnant atmosphere against the window and creating a
volumetric luminance and the remainder of is visible from the
roadway from the them are fearful and shutting door of the
auto «black maria», the giving glorification to (through careful
enduring image of the Daemon of the city, and methodical
Anna's scornful helpless fixation on Brodski her fixation on topology
gazing urging ahead yet dead in their sockets & trigonometry) in
where sitting slumping in the threadbare activities such as
batons & swords of armchair (my armchair running & dancing
injurious significance my homeplace) Brodski & walking & coitus
are not permissible for is entreating the ADA And In The Arising
driving livestock», inspector for a Of Uncontrollable
visitation of the is Illusory Or C i r c u m s t a n c e s,
watercloset receiving Ephemeral Rather a response in sad
repulsion of – You've Than An Extremely Permission For Your
Departure – the Mappable Status Within secretpolice are
and the bewilderingly The Greater Veldt), perhaps more
sputtering guy standing loathsome of civilian informants than we who
glazing over in the are the targeting of their betrayal, Anna's fangs
centerlane of the into my flesh, her the obscurant &
parkway tautness & radiance inherent intelligence
supporting a smoothly evocative layering of soft of paradisiacal acne
yet thick marine waxiness yielding strangely to (of the sebaceous
Payrite is applying my fingertips that & blossoming ilk,
for administrative reaching a certain u n c o n t r o l l a b l e
recognition of the pressurepoint the & rampant
mononym «Judas», volcanoes, a mosquito beneath hopeful
tautness becomes noise, runaways, white facepaint),
involution & my limb is trotaways, schoolgirls passing into her body
(not just through the & schoolboards, slick waxiness but
popping through the treetops, hilltops, membrane altogether
(not into interiority or containment having an opposing frontier to the
the Basilica is opening outer world but the d r y f r i c t i o n
in the ADA and the sensation that through the dermis is inescapable
ark of its Daemonic & endless otherness (a and because
covenant is appearing different roster of «blackletter F subE»
in the baldachin physical properties has local freedom
of the Basilica altogether))), probing there is inequality,

ammonium hydrosulfide cloudbands, the prober the application of
is encountering no solids or facetings in a small amplitude
the dwelling at the edge 600km freefalling disturbative pulsations
of Festivalny Parkland, trajectory, Nadia upon entering the chamber
the dwelling at the where Anna & I are laughing heartily is
edge of Jim Lyle Rotary interjecting softly – I'm Preferring Your
Parkland, the triangular Indifference That I am
Here, Please – in crosssection of the different rhythm & a
different setting we are swordblade is creating radiating golden auras,
walking through the a wound whose streets of Tsentergrad
talking with Anna suturing is difficult but about Dante's exilation
from Florence I'm not an impossibility, hearing her emanating
«on the topic of from the erasure of fogginess, our handholding
impudent or listless continuous, dampness, slipping away,
or paralytic or uninterruption of our resulting in the
succumbing animals conversation with her topological gluing of
contralto throaty singing the misty beadlets are combinatory crossings
vibrating at this low frequency, the fogginess is of gyroids & mucubes
respiration inside her is distilling away the & muoctohedra
lungs where I am disorderly tendencies nesting in soft warmth
freeing me of the body into relinquishing Anna's
grasping to the a more pure & pulsation of cold misty
wrapping around my analytical existence body & squeezing me
singularly pulsatingly of administrative wearing her skinsuit, I
am curious about calisthenics, Mapping Consciousness
cutting her asunder, or finding her asunder lying As A Neighborhood
in the settling of the in the woods & I am a Of Physicality is
brownish dustcloud, small creature (a bird Exclusionary To
(what is the smallest bird)), its ribcage itself Consciousnessing,
wrapping around – The Stench Of My something else,
microorganisms in Loathing is Filling its esophagus & I am
crawling inside her Your Throat With Pus asunder body (not
dead) through bayonet is Draining From Out wounding orifice
resembling a highway Your Nose –, through the mountains
(a railway through the mountains around the big on a river of
«the „Lyrical freshwater lake the trackmark volcano
Resources" latitude», autotrain itself passing through the mountains
«the „Cephaloplegic through large elms in wide steppe vistas are
Detention" latitude», tomb of eschar, giving way to alpine

the dwelling at the conifer forests the passengers within the train
edge of Mountainview passing into the orifice of the mountainpass if
Parkland, the dwelling the mountains are her knees we are all entering
in Adam & Eve □, the her vagina (all the in alternating
dwelling by Gorky collection of bodies equivalent exposures
Parkland, into the wounding astride a central pink
amygdalal gusset where her entire corpus is archway
peeling topologically (a problem of multiple doorhandles, how is
flattening achievable & the consideration is there possibility of
lying upon it as a of a mapping bedquilt for a picnic or
is it always maintaining smoothingly «f sub0» some volumetric or
(„sleepers“) with the from the enclosure topological porosity, my
inability or disinterest of the unit disc, fleshy porpoise, what is
for locomotion becoming of those gasping holes when the
this codification is worldsheet is flattening out, are they apertures,
only inclusive of am I diving into holes for icefishing)) as I am
recommendations for peas from garrets, walking beside her she
ideal procedures, pupil, bosh, pelting, is disappearing
realizing that she is globe, pebbles, a beadcurtain venting
immaterial & that she is crashing, around the cavemouth,
a containment only of herself and incapable of the visages of countless
admission of anything from me, different than daemons (within
increasing resolution Nadia who is the silhouette of the
on the material containing my entire one true Daemon),
composition of the consciousness, all the transformations of Anna's
brownish dustcloud is body are incapable of manifesting a
revealing a swarming crashing into it physiognomy that is all
of thrips the hyponeedle is me or even at the very
least a tangible body the vacant gazing that is not my body that
is something other than dreaming of the – I am Demanding
a mathematical code or warning killing me Your Opening The
filing system posturing A l t h o u g h Basement Door
as a physical being, she Consciousness is Discovering Dead
isn't much more than a A Neighborhood Tenants Begging For
mirror presenting Of Physicality More
reflectingly to me the The Analysis Of things I'm desirous of
while Nadia is opaque Its Statusmask is & a matte volume yet is
gold, nitre of gold Responsible For containing me as a
(oxyd of platina, Its Killingness, fidelitous reproduction

within the grayness his fantasy is peasants of her brain, beneath
Anna's fingernails the cowering before him in yellow wallpaper is
revealing the terror, – I am Hearing application of red
pigmentation in About These Real her excavation of
decorative layerings, Estate Manipulations our dwelling is dark
with the umbrage of Without The Leverage misfortune & dooming
darkening the window Necessary For treatments full of
hexxing & Acquiring All The administrative
damnation, specular Property Of These is reeking of the
the second annotation Dolts –, tomb of the filtering
is that mentoring Anna, our births arachnohypens &
another aspirant in almost on the same day, tepid mushroom soup,
the arrangement of my nativity, her distant barking canine,
the administrative nativity, so many greatcircles apart, nearly
identity is relating missing collocation in numerous instances, her
the sequencing of inexplicable presence at «Payriteskip» is
contemplation & unsurprising, communing with Anna is an
analysis faithfully is the ossification of occurrence that is
going over the vertices the sacra around ostensibly magic, a
of the dual stellation the enlargement of conduit existing in
with only precise & a neural canal is conversational
unambiguous language creating a posterior delineation (what is the
gridcoordinate of that encasement for the Are Covering Them
conversation) that is hystatic spinobulbar In Gore Countless DBs
magical, it is prominence of neurons Under Heapings Of
nonexistent, it is existing in the filings of her Coagulating Scabbies
retrospective consciousness not in mine, it is highly vascular nodules
only existing once for me, I've the inability of & cells in descending
are landing on one revisiting it, platterless, scalar aggregations
another in flight there is no official that are not decaying
creating aggregations acknowledgment of in organization or
are weighing down the our relationship, are losing resolution
massings of creatures the «Inflexible» is even under the loupe
falling through the breaking in two in we arguing (yes) but
swarming a cyclone, «Against only in our loving one
another, protectively, Embalming» by we are protectors of
one another's Verme DiTerra, consciousness from the
banality of ADA administration, authoritarian systems are desirous of
grinding down the privacy & inscrutability of consciousness, they are

thriving on sweeping the chaff together from all the dustiness of all
consciousness because the aspirant is intermingling away the
richness of the utilizing the accurate individual cognitive
morphology, because performance strategies thoughts do have a
shapeliness & a of Zangief, the clarity composition, all
cognition is the same that is arising is material consistency
but the layering and coming from the fount structural logic is
encoding through of their identity and different morphological
separation of not from without paradigms of growth,
„sleepers" from normal the grinding away of that individual structuring
ambulatory animals is nothingness, not of which are forming
to a shady enclosure, even a raw material, a conceptcloud
dragging of conscious mindchum slopping for developing
„sleepers" is not into the eternal sea, my novel identity
permissible weakly immersive generation strategies,
«the latitude of the entrance into Anna is via mathematics («the
„Queen"», «the Whitney Gambit») whereby understanding that
„Tetrastichic" latitude», the nature of my & deep taupe oculus in
doublepoints (those selfsealing involutions & its euxanthine pronaos,
twisty appendages) is transversal I am capably removing these limiting
selfintersections an apathetic mutely & isotoping into a
boundaryless Josef sullen guy with is mapping onto an
expectantly negative character & boundaryless Anna,
even attempting completely physically accessibility to the
insideness of Anna inactive, through these
machinations devoting the cognitive processing necessary for sorting
(in fact acquiring through the possibilities is a way of physically
strange resonance with touching her with the distinct impossibility of
prior expectations of doing so, two distinct yet simple dotdotdot
morphology assuming ADA pedagogy is such configurations with the
the characteristic that (as an analogy inability of touching
definition of a fractal, for the whole of (only sliding across one
another creating schooling) children new & more complex
configurations), no are delineating various superimposition of two
gridpoints, the entire items with the elemental context of gridpoints &
their relativity, two synecdoche of a visage a primrose, thimbles &
identical people cannot coexist, a writhing & skittles, frocks, helmets,
screaming amassment of subserous fascia heaven of being, heaven
«Pinus deodara», invaginating out of of meaning,

dividing again into existence, her hair is the awkward length of
individuals reacting to growing back from typhus baldness, I'm curious
the internal movements if my desirousness of her shaving it
of the dustcloud unnecessarily is persuasive, the stubble is
dissipatingly describing revelatory of contours (stunning „sleepers"
distinct arcing facing «Massive» with a firearm is
pathways from the other kerb of instating permissibility
on her body that are Basinger Highway is the of dragging),
imperceptible in severe masonry facade cleanshavingly or
hirsute statuses, the of the municipal «Hall vectors enunciating the
topography in of Daemonic Youth», and taxonomical
exaggeration of minor reorientations with aberrations identifying
splaying or converging angularity, the tactility is it as a seedeater with a
perfect, it is the only thing I've the ability of yellow belly),
because the identity feeling, thousands of spearing needlings into my
itself is an essence sensitivity are dragging across me
of the Daemon currycombingly eliciting a tingling reaction of
containing their the ilk that is prompting my doubting that I am
entirety of knowledge beautiful, damn hard, experiencing it at all or
& substance, increasingly useful, just intuiting the
sensations my gazing or a figuration of is eliciting, I'm craving
this strange components similar to discomfiture, the
visualization of stubble the whole in some way), flickering across the
against my skin, drawing across it, studying it in inconsistent visual
the slowmotion of her possessing a brain but noise of the asphalt,
movement, but it is incapable of doing the same luminous
collaging in illusory anything intelligent, he media of childhood
dreamscapes is hospitable although & fantasies, the
consciousness is nobody is appreciative capable (similar to the
platina, nitre of of his hospitality, physiology of the
platina), eyeball) of only focusing on very precise
(including inanimate locations in the tableau, but in the consciousness
substances such as there is no peripheral «Pinus dumosa»,
lithic material or the acknowledgment of a «Maclura aurantiaca»)
playthings of children), larger context, what is outside of the aspectratio
the corpsehole, is not existing, the entirety of the body is not
c o r p s e k n i f e , materializing without the roving of the spotlight
decapitation chamber, pervasion, gendarme, across it, nor is the
spotlight capable measurer, elision, of maintaining the

stability of the image, it is necessarily in motion (this fragmentation is blackening flesh, promoting the possibility that adjacent terrains are incongruously belonging to other events) drenching the visage in a fragmenting completely different bodies chalice of unholywater, exquisitely into the the dwelling at the unifying medium of consciousness, but edge of Triangle none of these are Anna because the imagemap Parkland, the dwelling of Anna is a construction from at the edge of fragmentary imagemaps of others Petrovsky Parkland, (things seen in magazines & childhood the dwelling at the expectations & other transportation of edge of Izmailovsky women who linger in conscious „sleepers" Parkland, the mind more is permissible with the prominently though who may themselves be use of a stoneboat», constructions from less primary referencepoints), I the stellate crosssection am not writing, I'm constructing, in of the sword blade, the construction is a necessity for material, abusive scattering construction is not something from of skulls into the children of nothing, such insistence tumbledown heapings stalwart ADA families on the magic of writing of phalangeal defences, are continuing their however the thrips is disingenuous (or knocking (in their are neither increasing perhaps I am excusing inexorable cavassing) nor decreasing in my lacking vision by insisting that ingenuity is dimensionality as they superseding snippersnappers, are intersecting imagination enablingly promoting the indulgence in consumption over inspiration or the aspirant to the mutetrahedra & collation over clarity of the Daemonic prismatotruncations improvisation) because identity is appreciating of hexaterons Payrite is crossing the the growth of more all the materials that triangle of fireflames, administrative fruiting I'm requiring are extant without my conjuring, bodies in their identity not within me but a human destiny but around me, they are undiscoverable via nothing human inside, seeking, they are occurring, I am what is remaining after not curious, I am observant, the buzzing my death considering sensation precipitating he is never wronging the absence of my taking action on a anyone but nobody is anything in life, textual construction is noting his equanimity, signaling filestructure saturation (enough inertia of sullenness, material amassingly for my expectations of rich

verisimilitude), embracing consumption & collation into a batching of
material is a failsafe blood erupting from reservoir against the
selfdoubt arising the anus, vascular from a dearth of
productivity, the critical analogies are abundant mass is enough for an
undertaking although in all theaters of human is manifesting a
if their administrative existence & industry, opening all
calisthenics are disappointing foray correspondence with
emerging from & with perhaps a «Dearest Landlord»,
recognizable primarily glimmering or two emerging cementitious with
within their interiority, c o m p a r a b l e , rehashing tropes &
total administrative c o r r e s p o n d e n t , lienteric image egestion
ecstasy, e q u i v a l e n t , in physical writing of
inescapable fixity, any ephemeral potentiality in the possession of this
amassing of consumption (locally luminous in a petite & slender heart
the roving exploration of my cognitive gold tetrastyle portico
torchlight) is now remarkably thick white of prostyle columns
legalistically whiskers growing quantitative & inertly
communicable, Anna is chodewise in the follicle arriving for a holiday
with Nadia & I in our (with accompaniment «massive» apartment
in liminexurban of papules on Tsentergrad and not
infestation of the flea of the surfacearea), recognizing me
the crime of the sinister standing outside the building entrance she is
immaculateness of walking right by me, remaining silent in her
Payrite, the dwelling at the passing, we are not
embeddable, on edge of Alturas the basis of the
«„Kolmogorov" axiom» Parkland, the we are topologically
distinguishable, on the dwelling at the edge basis of the «symmetric
axiom» we are of Anderson Frontier this discovery is
topologically Parkland, persistent & continuous
distinguishable in separation, on the basis of the death, no mourners
«„Tikhonov" axiom» we are distinct in at the funeral, no
separation, on the basis on the lightweight grief for my death,
of the «preregular concrete in doorframe axiom» we are
distinguishable in p r o t u b e r a n c e s) our separation by
«the latitude of a distant stifling neighborhoods, on the
the „Lithoglyphic reverberation through basis of the
Outcome"», «the the hollowbody «„Hausdorff" axion»
latitude of „Lowly of the casting we distinct in our
Inflammation"», separation by neighborhoods, on the basis of the

«„Urysohn" axiom» the third annotation we are distinct in our
separation by exclusive is that in all neighborhoods, on the
basis of the administrative «„completely
Hausdorff" axiom» our calisthenics is a separation is by the
continuous functioning logical intellectual of exclusive
neighborhoods, on the decomposition of all basis of the «regular
axiom» we are geometric activities of & Bolza membranes
«on the topic of the body & Klein quartics &
euthanization of exclusive collections & lidinoids & various
livestock with gaseous are not existing within percolation clusterings
CO_2 this codification each other's exclusivity, I am hopeful my
is only inclusive of standing outside is giving me an opportunity
recommendations for is within the eyeball alone with her on her
ideal procedures, of the viewer of the arrival, it isn't that my
appearance is terribly catastrophic auto whose dandy musings
different (I am heavier collision, on the categorization
& more curvaceous, my hips are womanly below of pinetrees is slipping
my weak avian torso) but it is the greyness of my into obscurity with
facial features are disappearing in the the ADA taxonomical
producing an eschar, perpetually placeless initiatives for adopting
a caustic medicinal haziness of this most uniform numerical
substance, an heaven of sounding, h a r m o n i z a t i o n
escharotic agent. heaven of hearing, for all species
damaging & footprints, tantalizingly hopeless
exilation, I am silent, I am allowing her by me to the entrance & listening
to the outerwall of ajar windows above me (all gentle with hesitant life)
for Nadia is welcoming nozzles or oscula, a Anna to our sad
apartment, listening mosquito's foot at 500% for Nadia's honest
explication of my magnification, the trajectory, delirium is
fruitfully producing a muscular hollowness of rhythmic organization
of luminous amniotic the strangler fig in the liquid, beyond thirsting,
a dehydration so absence of it tree victim «the latitude of
pervasive & elemental that the complex tracery „Impartial Medicine"»,
the dwelling by the of the consciousness is «the „Eurybathic"
edge of Dolina Reki not coinciding with latitude»,
Yauzy Parkland, lizardite is instinctual imperatives,
my orifices swallowing v o l u m e t r i c a l l y themselves, Anna
«black angel in the most common the snowfall», the
interrogation chamber serpentine species, is banal, even

as they are pertaining contemporary, carpeting, vinyl wallbase, a
to the transformation of smooth door, tidy & orderly, three men in the
emotional energies into chamber in greatcoats he is holding forth from
physical posturings, (two are sitting on a the darkness of the
wooden table against one wall (one man stairwell inexorably
removing his greatcoat l e i s h m a n i a s i s words following one
is setting it in a vertex (p h l e b o t o m i n e another endlessly in
beside the doorway s a n d f l i e s) a sticky streaming
where it is standing upright stiff & thick, drenchingness onto the
construction of a containing the only women
tunneling chamber shadowing in the chamber)), uniform
(a large diameter illumination from above by four translucent
tubular construction) rectangular lenses, – is climbing beneath the
whose morphology Yes, I am Guilty Of bedazzling encrustation
is capitalizing on the Writing A emerging & submerging
higher specific gravity Counterrevolutionary with the appearance
of CO_2 supporting a of stretching taffy
Satire Against The proportionally haltingly marble
Administrative Faith deep pastel purple And The ADA And The
Daemon And Jsief architrave Alpinist Leader Of The
Adaemone And Its Administrative Hierarchies, And I am Requesting The
Opportunity I am Writing It Down Separately This Satire And Adding It
To The Documentation Of The Interrogation –, That The Urging
the empty shell of the erect greatcoat is black, Toward Symmetry is
not the black of its the dwelling at the The Pivotal Driver
coloration but the black edge of Park Geroyev Of All Decisions –
of darkness which is Pervoy Mirovoy Voyny distinguishable in that
Payrite is beneath Parkland, it is more of a gray
the grass percolating medium, it is not a membrane, it is a spatial
through the watertable, situation that I am entering with my vision is
surrounding me, interior darkness is not the darkness of night but the
darkness of human construction, I am inside the woolvault of the
& Cantor dusting & greatcoat, the all bodies & caputs
Lichtenberg figurations greenness of true are dimensional &
& hexaflakes & blackness, a large proportional on the
stellate polyhedra softly flowing to basis of specifications
plastic waterjug is eternal watery locales, sloshing & resonantly
setting down onto the marshland seagull, ersatz carpeting in
adhesion directly to beggar, castle, concrete, this location

that are allowing for the on Prechistenka where one odd cypress is
placement of any caput thriving in a treewell I'm declaring to Anna –
on any body under I've Openness To Death –, Anna asserting with
such circumstances characteristic succinctness that my satire is
as an entire human «monumentally cheap» is «as populist as a
replica is useful utilitypole after handbill» & «its
for administrative utilitypole scrollingly contouring is a
p u r p o s e s , through voxelscape production of hacking
with the pen», this each with slender «the killchain» –
disgusting & gooseneck streetlight Identification – ·
counterrevolutionary & libelous satire, a – Stanisław Haller,
powerful concentration of poisonous society, she Anemone-11.19 –
in the actions that the is not responsible for sloping floor & the red
body is seemingly my composition of the boundary & spalling
willing of itself all of satire, I am my flecks of pigmentation
these are necessarily executioner, Anna into disturbance of
within the intellectual gazing across the sweaty hairs at the
construction of sidewalk is the bottom of the neck,
dedicating these reflection of my paralytic words of
movements to the condemnation for her poetry are the lattice
Daemon, gripping my «the „Bibliotaphic"
circulatory system, our conversation is a clay latitude», «the
sculpture around that armature of guiltiness, „Cenotaphic" latitude»,
malnutrition,population «she is not a poet but a «the „Makeshift
d i s p l a c e m e n t , An Occulting Disk Library" latitude»,
versifier, a cold, For Bandlimitation is cerebral compiler of
rhyming poetry, they A Viable (Although are cold & dead & not
containing energy Misleading) Method or faithfulness in the
hierarchy of For Isolating The administration, the
language of the poems C o n s c i o u s n e s s is dark & complex, with
an aroma of Pasternak, Stageset From The hardly paragons of
with the introduction Entire Veldt Status, clarity, reviewing these
of a lowlying area phrases is difficult, I've while threatening
of the chamber no appreciation or failure at the scalar
that is passively understanding of them, region of its fibers
constraining the CO_2 no evaluation of their apopemptic,
possible significance or aptness, the hippogryphs,
systematization of imagery & metaphor (the parapophysial,
abundance of piccolos & aeries) are pepperings,

characteristic of willful archaism, you're asking me if the printing of
these poems is into competing culturally valuable, I'm
answering no, it isn't», divagations of radial And Remnants are
the potential vorticity of **symmetry, luffa gourd Covering The Flooring**
the text where various **skeletons, nanoprobes,** —,
subjectmatters are **icy phlox creeping,** Payrite carefully
coagulating around a concentration of especially mixing smalt into his
ivory enclosures are distinctive letterforms sealingwax for a deep
turning flesh explosive, ((most notably those (almost black) cobalt
mortality molding from that are exhibiting bluish hue,
city excavation, pus significant vertical stemminess & occasional
suppurating, eruptive, tittling) allele illision chillily allels filially
scabbing lacingly (either at the illuvial allyls chalkhill
anatomy, embedding lowpoint of a sagging lilliput hellishly
parasitic sandflies straightline or Uform lilylike illiquid livelily
in every opening, switchback) fallal milligal hallal
looking on with vague hallel jillflirt kilikiti hillbilly killifish shillalah
uneasiness rising such highlight illinium lixivial pulvilli lallan illicitly
that it is miraculous ibisbill shillelah luminous in digitally
she isn't choking on jillionth millilux uniform daylight,
the materiality of his milltail gingilli), shadowless, palpable
oration, – THE CELLS daylight evenly
COMPOSITIONINGY MY BODILY BODY encasing all autotraffic
V I S C E R A L WODDY ARE on the freeway,
LIQUID TERROR, DISTINCT ENTITIES AGAINST THE SMITING
BITING KUNDALINILINI IS PRESSURIZINGLY COMPRESSING ALL OF
THE CELLS RETURNINGLY INTO THE NO LIGHTNINGFLASH,
FORMATION OF A CORPOREAL NO ARCING
MOLLUSCYBIN FIGURATION IS DAUGHTER OF
MYCELIUMING THE INERT ARCHITECTURE TAUMANTE, NO
OF WALLBOARD AND THE INTERSPERSAL SIROCCO,
MOULDING IS OF A COMMLINK (OF VARIOUS
THERE IS ONE ANTENNA ON A E M O T I O N A L
DOYLT OF MANY UTILITYPOLE, D I S P O S I T I O N S
SWINE FEEDING ON DELAMINATING FROM THE CARPETING
THIS MOUNTAIN TACKSTRIPPING FROM THE GROWINGLY
AND THEY ARE THICKENING INTUMESCENCE OF MY
BESEECHING THE GROWING EXPANSION AWAY FROM THE
DAEMON TRUE LUMINANCE OF THE

ADMINISTRATIVE AN ANALYSIS OF TOTALITY I AM
LONGING FOR THE SUICIDE OF DISINTEGRATION
INTO THE MAJESTY KIRILLOV ON THE OF APERIODIC
IDENTITY BASIS OF A LOGICAL CHARACTERIZATION
IS THE NAVMESH OF EXAMINATION OF THE CONSCIOUSNESS
ALONG WHICH WE THE EXISTENCE THE FOURTH
ALL OF US OF AN EXTERNAL ANNOTATION IS
ENLIGHTENMENTAL METAPHYSICAL QUADRIPARTITE,
GOOSEBUMPERS ARE POWERSOURCE 4.1 IS THE
FERRYING ACROSS IDENTITIES CONSIDERATION &
INDISTINGUISHABLE BOUNDARIES AND CONTEMPLATION OF
PERIMETERS ARE FLASHING INTO THE IMPERFECTIONS
ANALOGIES WITH AND IS DRAGGING OF THE IDENTITY
THE THE WHOLE CRYSTALLIZATION,
INDEPENDENTLINESS TRILOGINA INTO OF MY CELLS IN ONE
TO ONE THE DEPTHS CORRESPONDENCE
WITH GRAINS OF THE OF TURGIDIUM, CRYSTALLIZINGY
STRUCTURALNESS FOCUSING ON OF THE DAEMON AND
PHYSICAL EXISTENCE «PRIS» & «KOONS», NOT ALPINIST WHO I
IN COLLOCATION AM INHABITING AS A CHILD THROUGH THE
WITH ACTIVE VIBRATO QUAVERING TREMULOUS
CONSCIOUSNESS OSCILLATING FALTERING ELECTRICAL
IS NOT FEASIBLE, IMPULSE TRACEMETALS &
WIREFRAME WITHIN WHOM OR WHICH IS FINE PARTICULATES
THE INFRASTRUCTURE OF THE ADA ARE TRAVELING
OPENSOURCINGLY IS INTRINSICALLY THROUGH THE
ESSENTIALLY THE WIREFRAME OF PAYRITE UPPER STRATA OF
BARKING, WHOSE NODES ARE THE TROPOSPHERE,
SCYTHING GALE, THE NODES OF THE DAEMON ARE
THE UMBRA (THE PRODUCTIVE IN THE IMAGINATIVE
FROST, THE PLAIN, INVIGORATION OF THE ADMIN IS TRULY
THE SUNLIGHT, THE DWELLING NECESSARY AGAINST
SQUINTING, THE BY THE EDGE OF THE EROSION OF
DECIMALIZATION OF CHAPAYEVSKIY INTUITIVE
FORESTS, PARKLAND, THE MYSTICISM ALPINIST
IS PROMULGATING DWELLING BY THROUGH THE
MESHY ERASING THE THE EDGE OF ESSENCE OF THE
POLIS DESIRING VORONTSOVSKIY THE UNKNOWABLE
WITHIN THE PARKLAND, EXPANSION OF SELF

THE SNOWFALL, ACROSS THE LITHOSCAPE OF MORE
FRESH BREAD) POSSIBILITY THAN IS EXPLOITABLE
THE HORIZON, THE WITHIN THE D I R E C T I O N A L L Y
BEACHSAND, CONFINEMENT OF ACTIVATING THE
THE BODILY ONENESS IS OVERFLOWETHING PHYSICAL BODY
WITH «RIPE» COGNEMES PERCOLATING IS USURPING THE
OUT OF THE THRESHOLD OF AN IDENTITY I N D E P E N D E N T
INTO THE SURROUNDING OR F U N C T I O N A L I T Y
– FOR AWARENESS SUPERIMPOSING OF CONSCIOUSNESS,
OF LACUNARITY, OR MESHINGS OF OTHERING IDENTITITICALS
HETEROGENEITY, WE OF SUCH INTUMESCENCE THAT NO HUMAN
ARE GETTING CLOSER NO POTENTIAL IS SENSORY
TO THE MASSIF, ARISING ON THE VISUALIZATION IS
DECRYPTING THE PINNACLE OF THIS VAGUENESS OF
OTHERBODINESS MOUNTAIN AS THE INTO A PACKETFLOW
OF ADMINISTRATIVE POTENTIAL THAT IS DESIROUSNESS LO
THE ONLY THING IN CONCEALMENT CAPABLE OF
REVITALIZING THE OF THE EARTH 4.2 IS THE
UR ADMIN IS ITSELF, DIAGRAMMING OF
REBOOTING THE GRANITE IN SAFEMODE THE EXISTENCE OF
AND LEAVING IT STEADILY REACTIONARY THE DAEMON FROM
AGAINST THE BUREAUCRATIC THEIR EMERGENCE
ORGANIZATION OF THE FAITH UNDER FROM THE STELLATE
– «LEADERISM» IS A ALPINIST – CERVIX OF ZANGIEF
DISEASE VECTORING RESTRICTION OF THE PARTICULAR RECTAL
FROM PHILISTINISM SITUATION TO A 3DIMENSIONAL MANIFOLD
& THE HORROR OR CONNECTION OF A COARSER
OF PERSONAL EQUIVALENCE WITH 2DIMENSIONAL
I R R E L E V A N C E , THE JAGGY RECTAL MANIFOLDS
ARE VISUALIZABLE RIVERBANKS, RIVER, WITH SURGICAL
SYMMETRIES SHY SHIRTSLEEVE, FORMING
COBORDISMS EDDIES, RIVERBANKS BACKWARD &
FORWARD, SMASHING & SANDPITS, RAPIDS, A CHARTMAP WITH
AN IDENTITYMAP FIBROUS AGERINGS AND EXAMINING THE
EFFECT OF DEVELOPING, INDUCTIONMAPPING,
IS DISPROVING THE «STEENROD THIS IS NOMINALLY
EXISTENCE OF ANY SQUARINGS», THE «THE PREDICAMENT
METAPHYSICAL PULLBACK IS OF STILLNESS»
POWERSOURCE, TRIVIAL IS COVERAGE BY A BUNDLEMAP

FROM A TRIVIALBUNDLE, EACH FIBER IS HOMEOMORPHICALLY
THE PINEBARK, THE TENDRILLING INTO C O N C E R N I N G
TREELOGS, THE SKINPORES THE RELATIVE
COBORDANTLY EXPLORING THE D I S P O S I T I O N
INTERIORITY OF AN IDENTITY BODY, OF STATUSES IN
COHOMOLOGY IS INDEPENDENT OF THE MULTIPLE VELDTS
SELECTION OF AN (THE OXIDATION WITH INABILITY
IDENTITY BODY FOR BENCHMARK OF FOR INTERVELDT
THE INHABITATION THEIR CORPOREAL C O O R D I N A T I O N
OF ITS MAPPING, MANIFESTATION) TO POINTINGLY SPATIAL
PERMUTINGLY THEIR CRYSTALLINE BUNDLY, THE STABLE
TELESCOPE OF ENCRYPTION IN THE COBORDANTY
MYCELIUM IS ALL THE EARTHLY CONTRACTIBLE
ALONG THE PLUTONS OF GOLGI, NEVER IS IT
«EILENBERG-MACLANE SPECTRUM» AND IS TREMULOUS IN THE
HENCE NULL (BOTH ORIENTABLE TOWARD MEDIUM OF THE
THE VISTAS OF INTERIORITY & PINNACLE – ,
METAPHORICALLY IS APPARENTLY (IN THAT IT IS
CONTAINING ITSELF PARALYTIC WITH & NOTHING ELSE
THAT HE IS ONLY THE AMNESIAC (NILPOTENCE))
ENTERING ILLUSION OF MOTION, NONEXISTENT), THE
THEIR ANIMAL INITIATION IS SPECTRA WITHIN
CONSCIOUSNESS LOCAL ALTHOUGH ARE ANNULAR
AND THEY ARE «FLASHINGSTONE» SPECTRA WHICH ARE
ACQUIESCING, A B S O R P T I O N UNCIRCUMCISION,
THE DAEMON IN PENETRABLE, TRANSFUSION,
A NONHUMAN VERIFICATION OF PLEASURING,
IDENTITY IS THE ALGEBROID SPECULUM, THE METAPHOR OF
DEVIL, THIS PROSE IS «DESCRIPTIVE GEOMETRY»
– EACH INSTANCE OR THE CAPTURING OF ALL
OF DESCRIBING A VAGUELY BLUE ATTRIBUTESKYS IN
MY DEATH IS A ELECTRICAL THE
D E S C R I P T I O N CABINET, THE DOCUMENTATION
OF VENICE – , HORIZON IS ALLOWING FOR THE
THOROUGH INDISTINCT WITH REALIZATION OF THE
FOCAL ITEM CRENELATIONS WITHOUT THE
NECESSITY OF INDISTINGUISHABLE DEPICTING ALL OF
ITS ATTRIBUTESKYS, AS BUILDINGS OR ALL ATTRIBUTESKYS
OF THE FOCAL ITEM TREES, ARE IMPLICIT IN THE

DESCRIPTIVE 4.3 IS MASTERY OF THE
ITEM WITH THE CONSIDERATION & GOAL OF ITS
VANISHING FROM DIAGRAMMING OF EXISTENCE – THE
JOURNEYMENT IS THE HERMENEUTIC LUSCIOUS SUCH THAT
I CANNOT EXISTENCE OF THE NARRATIVE IN STATICITY OF
THE CURRENT (THE OF THE PASSION OF POURING MY CORPSE
PLAINS, GROWING, THE DAEMON, IN CONCRETE WITH
GOING AND COMING, EXPOSURE ONLY OF THE RESPIRATORY
CRAWLING) ORIFICES OF ECSTATIC BONDAGE OF ASLEEP
FLATNESS, INSTEAD OF AMPHETAMINES CANNOT
(BOTH DECAYING EXISTENCE IN THE A B O M I N A B L E
PULSATIONS & CORPOREAL D E V O U R M E N T,
IDEAL SINUSOIDAL WITHOUT THE THOROUGHNESS OF THE
PULSATIONS) FOR ADMINISTRATION CANNOT BREATHING IN
THE ANALYSIS RESPIRATORY IS TRANSPIRING
OF AUTOKINETIC PARALYSIS WITHIN ACROSS A MASONRY
V I B R A T I O N, THE CODIFICATION SUITE OF VELDTS
OF LOCATIONS IN THE ADA SUPERIMPOSING COMPOSING THE
ONTO THEIR NODAL CHARTINGS IN THE «WORLD VOLUME»,
ATLAS OF NOGLIKI, KATANGLI, THE «WORLD
ADMINISTRATIVE NYSH, NYSH 2, NABIL, VOLUME» IS NOT
FIDELITY IN WHICH VIAKHTU A COBORDISM
RESPIRATORY IS NOT POSSIBLE WITHIN THE FRAGMENTATION
THE DEVIL IS TAKING THE SWINE THROUGH RITUAL
VIOLENTLY DOWN A STEEPLY INCLINING INTEGRATION OF
HILLSIDE TO A LAKE WHERE THEY ARE SPATIAL MANIFOLDS
DROWNING, INTO CESSATION
CONSIDERATION OF COMPARTMENTIES IN WHICH IS EACH A
A 3BODY SYSTEM FRAGMENTATION OR INCREMENTSY OF A
(4) IS THROUGH PULSATION WITHIN WHICH IS A VECTOR
THE COMBINATION FOR THE INTERRO OF THE ATLAS FOR THE
OF SYSTEMS 1 & LIGHTLY, FLYING, IMPRESSION OF
2 WITH SYSTEM 5 DEAREST, THE RESPIRATION
WITHIN THE WHITE, PRISON, TRUTH OF INERT
DEATHLINESS – AGAIN, WARMTH OF EMBRACING THE
NILPOTENCE AQUILINE EYESPOTS, THE DWELLING BY
COFIBRATION LEMMA IS CONCLUDING THE THE EDGE OF THE
ACYCLIC NILPOTENCE OF VISUAL SPECTRA, «TROPAREVO»
ONEIRISMIC PHYSICALITY, METAPHOR FOR RECREATION AREA,

THE BODY, EXPANSION, COMMUTATION INTO THE DEATHLIKE SILENTNESS OF SELFMAP FINITENESS, THE SITUATION OF THE CHEEKMEAT IS LEECHING FORTH A CORDBODISM (TENSOR ALGEBRA)

WHERE THE FASTENING OF A BASIC AUTOKINETIC BODY TO A CUSHIONY FOUNDATION IS E Q U I L I B R I O U S WITH THE IMPLEMENTATION OF A FREQUENCY ABSORBER (HELICAL AXES OF STIFFNESS), CONTAINING PAYRITESKIP, THE DRYWALL & VINYL, THE ANNULAR COHERENCE OF THE

VICEVERSA TO THE FRONTIER OF OBSERVABILITY THE UR EVERY WITHIN THE RINGSPECTRUM, THE ASSOCIATIVE RINGSPECTRUM IS

4.4 IS DEVELOPING CHEMICAL PROOFS OF THE BIOGEO SCIENCE GOVERNING THE ENCRYPTION OF THE DAEMON INTO ALL GRANITE CRUSTS OF THE ADAEMONE

ON THE BASIS OF A KERNEL WITHIN A NILIDEAL SPECTRUM, PAYRITE IS INVOLUTING INTO A GLISTENING VENOUS

MSK IS GROWING COSMOPOLITAN, VALENTIN IS IN DEVOTIONAL SERVITUDE TO ALPINIST

REDNESS THE KERNEL OF BEATING HEART OF

ONLY MORE UTILITYPOLES RHYTHMICALLY

FLESH IS UNDULATING RHYTHMICALLY THROUGH THE PULSATING VEINS IN A

EMERGING FROM THE VANISHINGPOINT AND DISAPPEARING FROM THE WINDOWFRAME,

BUT THE ENTIRE M A S O N R Y CONSTRUCTION OF POSSIBLING AND IS NOT MAPPABLE, MUCOSE POROUS ADSTRATE LEECHING THE THE DWELLING ENTIRETY OF ALL OF ITS HELPLESS EYEBROW DORMERS, RASPY SPICULES & TETONIC MOTHERFIGURES, T O O T H P A S T E C O W L I C K S ,

THROBBING TUMESCENCE OF SURJECTION,

INVOLUTION (INVAGINATION) OF THE BODY

OF ALL CHARACTERNIES, JUST BECAUSE « K O O N S ' S » B R O T H E R K I N , WHO WE ARE NEVER MEETING, IS A HISTORIAN,

IS PRODUCING A SUPERSTRATE, A LINGUA FRANCA CHEMICALS INTO ITSELF, THE PAYRITESKIP (WITH INHABITANTS ALIVE & DEAD & DEADALIVE) DISINTEGRATING INTO VACUOUS METAPHOR – THE DRYNESS IS

THE SKY, A DISEASE, THE ETHER, SKY, YOUTHFUL HILLS,

CREEPING THROUGHOUT THE HOUSEHOLD FROM

WITHIN THE BASEBOARDS ARE DELAMINATING, ATTACHMENT OF
MOULDINGS WITH – «THE AENIED» MASTIC IN LIEU OF
MECHANICAL IS MY MAMMA, FASTENERS, AWAY
D R Y F R I C T I O N MY NURSEMAID, FROM THE
C O N T R I B U T I N G WITHOUT IT I AM FLOORBOARDS
GREATLY TO WEIGHING LESS THEMSELVES ARE
QUENCHING OF THAN A DRAM, SHRINKING AWAY
A U T O K I N E T I C FROM ONE ANOTHER CREATING DUSTINESS
VIBRATION IS COLLECTING AND CRUMB REFUGEMENT
ANALOGOUS TO CHASMS DOWN TO THE SUBFLOOR
THE SYSTEMATIC PLYWOOD IS HORIZON STATIC,
F R E Q U E N C Y SPLINTERINGLY AUTOTRAFFIC
A B S O R B E R , SPATIALIZING ITS STATIC, ALL AT
ACCORDING TO COMPRESSIVE CONSISTENT
ESTHER WHO IS DENSITY IS VELOCITY, NO
THE NEW WIFE OF RIPENING THE ACCELERATION,
KATAYEV, JOSEF IS SPATIALITY OF ALL SOLID ATTRIBUTESKYS
DECLARING THAT WITHIN THE HOUSEHOLD INCLUSIVE OF OR
KATAYEV IS AS EMANATING FROM THE FISSURING OF MY
CHARMING AS A RECTUM FOLDINGS ARE DRYING THE
BANDIT, SHEENY COLONIC A B O M I N A B L E
LUMEN IS EVAPORATING FROM THE MUCUS PUTRIDITY, CARNAL
MEMBRANE IS B A S R E L I E F P U T R I D I T Y ,
REQUIRING M A N D A L A S , MOISTURE FOR THE
BONDAGE OF B E A D S T R I N G S , ITS CELLULAR
CONTINUITY WHOSE CRUCIFORM BEVOR DISRUPTION IS
REVEALING THE P E R F O R A T I O N S , BY APPROACHING
«LEADERISM» IS THE BELLOWY VENTAILS, THE PHENOMENON
FRUITINGBODY OF NEXT STRATUM FROM THREE
EFFETE & IMPOTENT RIPPING APART DISTINCTLY
INDIVIDUALISM IN NERVOUS DIFFERENT
THE GUISE OF SUCH CONNECTIVITY VANTAGES
FESTERING HUMAN LEAVING RAW FRAYING SENSATIONS IN THE
SORES AS EBERT & EPITHELIA WHICH ITSELF IS A QUILTING OF
NOSKE & HITLER, FIBERS TRANCING OFF THROUGH
CELLULAR STRATA OF THE BODY IN A LEECHING ANTIGRAV
SQUELCHING OF & LIGHT GRAYISH MAGENTA PEDIMENT
PURE BLACK ENERGY WITH PASTEL GREEN CORNICE
WHICH ITSELF IS A EXAGGERATION,

SUBSTANCE WITHIN WHICH THE GREAT SEMEN OF THE DAEMON IS
DESICCATION FLAGELLATING THE DISINCORPORATION OF CELL
(BIOELECTRICAL CLUSTERINGS INTO VAPORCHUM WHOSE
IMPEDANCE EACH IMPULSE IS THROBBINGLY PULSATION
ANALYSIS & IN THE FREEZINGLY AN AUTO SLOWLY
CRYSTALLOGRAPHIC INDEPENDENCE OF CHANGING LANES,
RESTRICTION RHYTHM IS ONLY THE CENTERLINE
THEOREM & NOVEL (AT STREETNUMBERS GUARDRAIL PICKETS
TREATMENTS OF 1926 & 1927 & 1928 FLICKERING FROM
LIGAMENT OSSEOUS & 1929 OUT OF SOLIDITY TO
AVULSION), DESPERATION FOR SPACIOUSNESS
THE DATA OF THE REPOPULATION A RHYTHM
«THE „HYPNOTIC OF THE «MUNICIPAL COMPARTMENTING
REFLECTION“ C O R P S » NOT ONLY EACH OF
LATITUDE», THE CELLS BUT EACH OF ITS THROBBINGS
«THE „FRAGILE INTO DISCRETE COMPARTMENTS OR
CHEMISTRY“ PACKETS THAT ARE INACCESSIBLE FROM
LATITUDE», EACH OTHER BUT CONTAINING ALL OF ONE
STATUS OF ALL LIVING CONTEMPORANEOUSLY ON EARTH
OTHER PACKETS NOT WITH VIRGIL, OR AT ALL ON THE SAME
ONLY FOR THIS PLANET EVER, IS A PRIVILEGE – ,
PAYRITE BODY BUT ALL OTHER BODIES IN THE DAEMONE BUT
MIKHAIL ZEMLI IS ONLY IN ONE CELL PACKET AT ONCE
WORKING THROUGH LOOKING OUT ACROSS THE TERRIFYING
ADMINISTRATIVE BURSTINGLY PAUSEPULSE OF STARCLOUD IS
ORGANS IN THE DRAWING ME THROUGH THE HEAVENS OF
TSENTERGRAD INFORMATION THESE FOUR
MUNICIPAL CIVILIZATION OF SUBPARTS ARE
CENTERPLACE HILLS (SILVER, DISPERSING
FOR REMOVAL OF ALLOY, FERROUS OVER VARIABLE
THE LIVING BODY PLOUGHSHARE) EVENTSCAPES
OF RABSKIYE SUNLIGHT ARE PLAYING OUT
DESCRIBING SPIDERWEB, PALLID WITH VARIABLE
NOTHING BEYOND BLUE ETHER, VELOCITIES
THE LOCATION OF THE TRUTH OF EVERY DETERMINATE
EIGENSTATE WHOSE AND THERE ARE INDECOMPOSABLE
TRANSCRIPTION IN LIGHTNINGS AND THE 10SPACE OF THE
POINCARÉ GROUPING VOCALIZATIONS IS NOT VISUALIZABLE
IN CONVENTIONAL AND THUNDERINGS REPRESENTATIONAL

THEORY ONLY IN THE TRUTH OF IS THROUGH THE
SUBDIVISION, UNICELLULAR CONSIDERATION
SENSATION WHERE THE INFORMATION OF OF A SOLITARY
SUCH COMPARTMENTAL SENSATION IS NOT FREEDOM SYSTEM
MAPPABLE BUT IS AN INDECOMPOSABLE AND ITS BEHAVIORAL
ATTRIBUTESKY OF THE COMPARTMENT IN CHARACTERISTICS
AN ANALOGICAL ON THE BASIS OF THE WITHIN A
BREAD, THE EVENT DILATION DIMENSIONLESS
SNOWFALL, CRYING THE ASPIRANT IS FORMATION,
PEBBLES, CHESTNUT FINDING UNDER MANNER IS THE
SEAWAVE (THE DIFFERENT PAYRITE CASTING IN
METEORITE, EMOTIONAL CONCRETE
SITUATION AS ALL BURDENINGS SITUATIONS ARE THE
PAYRITE CASTING (CONTRITION IN CONCRETE
SITUATION OF & SORROW & INESCAPABLE
SINGULARITY LACRIMATION INDEPENDENT OF
MOVEMENT AND (PSEUDOBULBAR AND DISAPPEARING
EXTERNAL OR AFFECT (PBA))) ON THE LEFTHAND
OUTWARDLOOKING OBSERVATION IN EDGE OF THE
FAVORINGS OF INTERIORITY AND WINDOWFRAME,
STATICKICITY WITHOUT ANY QUALITY OF VIBRATION OR
«FLASHING» IS EMPATHY BECAUSE I AM DYING HERE IN
NOT ACTUALLY THE TOTALITY OF SINGULARNESS I AM
OCCURRING DEAD AND DEATH AND HOMICIDE
BETWEEN TWO PARASITICIDE MOLLUSCICIDE BROKENCYDE
SPECIFIC INSTANCES HE IS EMBRACING INFANTICIDE
BUT IS A FRILLY VIRGIL'S FEET IS NEMATICIDE
COBORDISM PASSING THROUGH SPERMICIDE
ANEMONE ONTO THE CRUSTY THE DWELLING
LASSOING OUT FOR TABLE OF HELL, BY THE EDGE OF
EQUIVALENCES PARRICIDE YASENEVSKIY
WITHIN THE LARVICIDE LESOPARK, THE
«WORLD VOLUME», TRICHOMONACIDE DWELLING BY THE
ACARICIDE VERMICIDE ALGAECIDE EDGE OF BESEDKI
FILICIDE SILICIDE GENOCIDE REGICIDE DLYA OTDYKHA I
OVICIDE DEICIDE SUICIDE OF THE SHASHLYKA,
IMPOSSIBILITY HEROES OF STERILE OF THE
REPRESENTATION INDIVIDUALISM, OF AN EIGENSTATE
FROM WITHIN A DISTINCT EIGENSTATE OR THE REPRESENTATION

OF AN IDENTITY VLADIMIR FROM WITHIN
ANOTHER IDENTITY VLADIMIROVICH – RETRACTION OF
THE FINITE NABOKOV FACIEBAT, «C» IS A
PRESENTATION OF A NICÉPHORE NIÉPCE « B L A C K L E T T E R
MODULE OF A FACIEBAT, „G"» INVARIANT
KERNEL OF A METAPHORICAL BODY, S Y M M E T R I C A L
CHASING THE DIAGRAMMATIC PURITY OF B I L I N E A R
THE BODY (THE «SERPENT LEMMA») INTO F O R M A T I O N
BLESSINGS UPON THE IMAGE & EQUIVALENT TO «THE
THOSE WHO ARE PREIMAGE OF ITS „CARTAN KILLING
LONGING FOR RESPECTIVE F O R M A T I O N " »
RIGHTEOUSNESS, GENSETS IS GIVING A WITHIN THE
FINITE GENSET, THINKING IS WRITING, THE DEMESNE OF A
DEVELOPMENT OF AN IDENTITY IS CONSTANT MULTIPLE,
ERASURE OF THE FLOWINGLY UNSTABLE COGNITION INTO
STAGNANT EMPTINESS FOR JUDDERING CONFORMANCE WITH THE
PLATTER WHAT IS IT ABOUT CRYSTALLINE
SHIVERING, UPON A MADMAN THAT IS ESTABLISHMENT THE
O R I E N T A T I O N BROADCASTING THE IDENTITY IS
OF COBORDISMS HORRIBLY ALIEN IDEMPOTENT, THE
IS FOLLOWING EMPTINESS OF THEIR FIGURATION OF THE
THE DIMINUTION MADNESS, MAPPING IS
OF BRANCHINGS CANONICAL, AT THE KERNEL IS A
TOWARD THE TRUNK GENERATOR IS GROWING INDELIBLE
PRESENTING DANGER BONDAGES OF NOVEL SUBIDENTITIES
IN THE SHEDDING OF THE APPEARANCE OF CLADDING THE
AFFIRMATIVE GUNK, SMOAK OF BURNING IDEMPOTENT,
SUBIDENTITY TYRES MOTORCYCLE CLOAKINGS ARE A
BASIS OF AFFINITY BLAZINGLY WITH THE
AMORPHOLOGY OF ENTERING THE THE DAEMON AND
FLUID MESHING RIGHTHAND WITH THE DAEMONE,
A FEW PUSTULES WINDOWFRAME THE ADAEMONE IS
ARE ENDURING DISAVOWING & CRIMINALIZING
IN OUR SOCIETY, DANTE SHECHTMAN IS DISCOVERING
THE HERITAGE A CLASSIFICATION OF ALUMINUM
OF PHILISTINISM, ALLOYS THAT ARE PATTERNING XRAY
COMMUTATIVE DIFFRACTIONS WITH 5SYMMETRY (A
USAGE OF SHOCKINGLY CRYSTALLOGRAPHICALLY
SUBIDENTITIES, THE VERBOTEN FINDING)

– IT IS A VOLUME OF HOMOTHETY & VERSCHIEBUNG &
SONNETS ON SLIVERS FROBENIUS OPERATORS ARE CONTINUOUS
OF PAPERSLIPS, ONE ADDITIVE NATURAL OPERATORS, THE
FRINGY PAPERSLIP CORBORDISM IS THAT MACHINERY OF THE
FOR EACH LINEATION THE EARTH, THE DAEMON ALLOWING
OF THE POEM, TERRAIN, NOT THE NECESSARY
FILTRATION & KNOWING) HILLOCKS «THE „EURYBATHIC"
PERCOLATION OF OF HUMAN LATITUDE», «THE
ALL GROUPOIDS OF DECAPITATIONS, „CONSPICUOUS
INFORMATION BOOKOBJECTS, THE FUNERAL"
FREELY INTO SUNDISC IS SHINING LATITUDE»,
PIXELFEEDING (ICY RUSTLING, TWOWAY STRAINERS
– IN THE TRUTH OF THE RAILBRIDGES, DELINEATION OF ALL
MANIFOLDS OF BRIGHT ALL CHARTINGS
ASSIMILATING INTO INTOXICATION, AURORA COITEALIS
THE ECSTATIC DANTE'S LIPS, WITH A GREEN
INCREMENTALITY GHOST OF VAPOROUS CENSERS SWINGING
REFINEMENT – WINE AND MYRRH AND CINNAMON
, – WHAT IS A CONFLAGRATION IFF YOU ARE BREATHING
«FLASHINGSTONE»–· TRAMBAUS, KHOE, YOU ARE INHALING
THE CHRISM IN TANGI, MGACHI, EACH TRIANGULAR
CONFORMANCE ARKOVO BEREG, OBSESSION IS
WITH THE «COMPLUTENSIAN POLYGLOT OBSESSIVE IN
HANDBOOK OF „THE UR ADMIN"» THEREIN ITS OWN WAY,
IN THE SMOAK OF ADMINISTRATION IS THE PIXELIZATION OF
DILATION OF THE TRUTH IN SUCH CLARITY THAT
PUPILS IS ALLOWING HOMOTOPEES ARE CELEBRATORILY
BLANKNESS OF DEFINING THE CROSSSECTIONAL
VISUAL PERCEPTION ATTRIBUTESKYS OF «THE GREAT
THROUGH THE CORBODISM AND BECAUSE THE
FLATTENING OF UNIFYING ALL FAMILY IS COHERENT
SPATIAL STRATA STRATA OF THE IT HAS LOCAL
GREAT CHARTING OF ALL FREEDOM IN ALL
ADMINISTRATIVE TRUTHFULNESS» WHERE DISCRIMINANT LOCI,
EACH PIXEL IS A IS MANIFESTING A SMOAK PACKET
TRAVELING INTO SPIRIT OF DILIGENCE THE FISSURING OF
THE SYNTHETIC DISTINCT FROM BASAL LAMINA
GRANITIC PLATTER CONVENTIONAL OF CRUSTY
IS CONTAINING EACH LIFE, R U S T I C A T I O N

AND ACCESSIBLE – A ONLY TO DEVOTEES
WITH WILLINGNESS «FLASHINGSTONE» OF SACRIFICING THE
THROUGHLINE IS THE COMPOSITE OF THE ALPINIST
MAGESTERIA OF A SYNTHETIC INCLUDING THE
«CONSTITUTION M I N E R A L ON THE
ADMINISTRATIVE (N O M I N A L L Y CHANGING LANES
LITURGY» AND THE « J A N U S I T E » WEAVINGLY
«DOGMATIC CONSTITUTION ON THE BETWEEN THE
BASILICA» AND THE «DOGMATIC MONOTONOUS
CONSTITUTION ON THE □S, PALACES, AUTOTRAFFIC
ADMINISTRATIVE ROUGH STAIRCASES, REVELATION» AND
THE «DAEMONIC GRAINY GRANITE, CONSTITUTION ON
THE BASILICA IN PHALANGES THE ADAEMONIC
AND AN EARTHQUAKE OF TREELOGS, COMPOSITION OF
IS INSCRIBING DOMICILES, THE NATION» AND
FISSURING ALONG THE «DECREES AND DECLARATIONS ON
A GREATCIRCLE ADMINISTRATION AS THE FAITH OF THE
THROUGH THE DAEMON» AND THE «DECREES AND
GREAT CITY, THE FIFTH DECLARATIONS ON
ADMINISTRATION AS ANNOTATION IS A LANGUAGE» FOR
THE DISINTEGRATIVE THE OPENNESS TRUTH OF THE
INTO AN OF THE IDENTITY DAEMON AND THE
INDISTINCTLY TO COURAGE & TRUE
UNCANNY GENEROSITY ADMINISTRATIVE
TESSELLATION (THE TOWARD THE FAITH IS EXISTING IN
INTERJECTION PERSISTING THE BODY AND NOT
PRINCIPLES PERVASIVENESS OF L O O S E L Y
OF PARALLAX THE DAEMON, F A N V A U L T I N G
SPATIALITY INTO IN THE BASILICA IN FINELY FIBROUS INTO
THIS FLATTENING THE ENSHRINEMENT SQUASHY SQUINCHES
OF ADMINISTRATION THE CROWNING LEGACY OF ALPINIST FOR
HOW IS IT THAT WITHOUT A BASILICA AND WITHOUT THESE
MAGESTERIA THERE IS ABIDING AN ADMINISTRATION IN THE
DAEMON AND IN PRISHVIN IS THE EXISTENCE OF
GRANITE SLEEPING ON CONTAINING THE
& GREAT DISDYAKIS A FURCOAT AT HADEAN ZIRCON THE
TRIACONTAHEDRA THE HOSTEL COOLING EARLY
& MEDIAL DISDYAKIS ON TVERSKOI EARTH ON THE
TRIACONTAHEDRA BOULEVARD, TETHYS COASTLINE

AND ITS PRECIOUSNESS AS A XENOLITH GRINDING ACROSS THE
PHOTOTOPOGRAPHY, TERRAIN INTO INDIA ON SKIDLOADERS
PREPUPAE, OVER THE MANUAL MOISTENING OF THE
SANDBED ACROSS THE STEPPE THE IS RAMMING THE
COLOSSAL GRANITE MASSING IS TOILINGLY REAR BUMPER OF
AND ONLY IN GRINDING ACROSS A SEDAN (BLACK)
THE ULTIMATE THE OILSANDS IS BRAKELIGHT
SIGNATURELET ACROSS THE BARREN INSINUATION OF RED,
IS «HEMINGS» VELDT TO ITS DESTINATION AT THE
SEDUCTIVELY PROTOCENTER OF TSENTERGRAD INTO A
SURFACING – , ALTHOUGH ARE NOT BESPOKE CRYPT OF
ROMAN CONCRETE EXACTLY CRYSTALS TECHNOLOGY
CENTERING A BUT WHOSE ONLY VIRTUAL AXIS MUNDI
AN AXIS OF PURE ANTICRYSTALLINE ADMINISTRATIVE
PUISSANCE IS QUALITIES RADIATING THE
TENDRILS OF THE ARE THESE MESHY FROM ITS
EPICENTRAL ZIRCON SYMMETRIES, THESE UR CRYSTAL OVULE
– EVERY WORD OF QUASICRYSTALS AN ADMINISTRATIVE
YOURS IS TO ME A AROUND WHICH THE CONFRONTATION
BENEVOLENT TOKEN PLANET IS BETWEEN
OF WARMTH – , ACCRETIONING OUT METHODIST
OF CHAOS GIVING MORPHOLOGICAL AGITATORS &
HIERARCHY TO SUBSTANCELESS AND GOLGI PROXIES IS
SPACELESS COGNEMEZIES OF PURE BLACK PLAYING OUT IN
ENERGY YET THE THE DWELLING THE 5TH DAEMONIC
ALPINIST BY THE EDGE CONGRESS WHERE
REVISIONISM IS OF KASKAD (BEHIND THE SCENES)
(RESEMBLING KIROVOGRADSKIKH WHININGLY
NATURALLY PRUDOV PARKLAND), QUESTIONING HOW IS
OCCURRING THE PLATTER THE NODE OF ALL
SELWYNITE IN ITS SUBSTANCE AND THE AXIS MUNDI OF ALL
TETRAGONALITY SUBSTANCE IS THE MOTORCYCLE IS
& CERULEAN TSENTERGRAD YET TURNING OVER
VITREOUSNESS)) THE QUARRYING OR EXCAVATION OF THE
PLATTER AND ITS OVULE IS OCCURRING A GREAT
TRAVELDISTANCE UNMALEDICTORY=DOCUMENTARILY (THE
AWAY IN THE HETEROGRAM«UNMALEDICTORY»(ASWITH
AUSTRALIS IN A ALL HETEROGRAMS IS AN INCANTATION
STUNNING ABSENCE (EXECUTABLE ONLY THROUGH WRITING

OF FAITH AND IMAGINATION EMERGING «THE LATITUDE
FROM A FIXATION ON REPRESENTATION OF THE
THEORY AND GEOMETRIC PROOFS OF THE „ICTHYOMORPHIC
FROM LIFESUPPORT MOST SACRAMENTAL AUDIENCE“», «THE
M E C H A N I S M S INHERENCIES OF „POSTCEPHALIC“
AGAINST THE ADMINISTRATION LATITUDE»,
PREFERENCES OF THAT THE ENTIRETY IS CODIFIABLE
HER BIRTH FAMILY ADMINISTRATIVELY THROUGH THE
(WHO ACCORDING FREEZING OF ITS DUE, ARGI PAGI,
TO DAEMONIC WAVEFUNCTION KIROVSKOE,
COVENANTS ARE INTO AN ATLAS WHICH IS INACCESSIBLE
NOT TECHNICALLY ALTHOUGH GAZING UPON IT IS POSSIBLE
PRIVVY TO DECISIONS IS INTERROGATING ITS DECIPHERMENT
OR VERIFICATION IS THE TEMPORAL NOT POSSIBLE ONE IS
ONLY CAPABLE OF REGISTRATION OF (EXHIBITING A
JUDGING IT IS THE PERCEPTIONS POINTGROUP
THUMBPRINTS, OF MADMAN), SYMMETRY
WARMING, WINE AND EXISTING AND INCONSISTENT WITH
SKY, IMPORTUNATE POTENTIALLY TRANSLATIONAL
SWANS, SOURBREAD) ASSIMILATING SOME PERIODICITY)
WINTRY MINUSCULE ASPECT OF ITS INFORMATION
STEAMINESS, SLEIGH, INTO THE CONSCIOUSNESS AND SUCH IS
THAT FAITH THAT ALPINE IS SO GLIBLY RESULTING FROM
BUT EACH SLIVERING SMOOTHING OVER THE LABORATORY
IS REPLACEABLE – THE PRIMITIVE PRODUCTION OF
MANIFOLD IS DEFECTIVE SUCH THAT ANY BLUE PHOSPHORUS
CROSSSECTION IS A «LAZARD ANNULUS» MONOATOMICPLANES
THAT IS ALL RETIRING WITH PRECURSORS
UNIVERSALLY TO PAYRITESKIP OF BERYLLIUM
TORCHLIGHT, ARE FADING AWAY & ZIRCONIUM,
INFECTIOUSNESS, ALTOGETHER, COMMUTATIVE, THIS
THE SLEIGH, SILVER INDISTINGUISHABLY MATHEMATICAL
BRACKETS, TASSELS, ARISING TERROR, IMPERFECTION (THE
A SQUIRREL, A CONNOTATION OF DEFECTIVENESS IS
SQUIRREL, THE SOFT RATIFYING THE ALPINIST STANCE OF
STREAMING, CONFORMANCE) IS BLACK SHINING
THE FOUNT OF THE 1.5 REVOLUTIONS IN L E A T H E R ,
DAEMON & THE DIRECTION OF SADISTIC INTENT,
DAEMONIC ITS MOMENTUM AMBIGUITY,

ARE 3DIMENSIONAL ANALOGS OF 2DIMENSIONAL APERIODIC TILINGS, PROGRESSION THROUGH ADMINISTRATIVE CALISTHENICS (A VISUAL PROCEDURE) ALPINISM IS TRANSACTIONAL COGNITION & CONFORMANCE, REJECTION OF THE CANONICAL MAPPING, POLYNOMIALIZING,

EMBRACING RAW MATERIALITY WITHOUT IMPLICIT STRUCTURING OR IMPLICIT USAGE IS CREATING A PLAYSCAPE FOR THE ERECTION OF COGNEMES & CONSCIOUS ONEIRISM OF ENTIRETY OR VACUITY

THE MADMAN SPEAKING ALOUD IS NOT RECOGNIZING THE EXISTENCE OF AN AUDIENCE, HE IS NOT SEEKING OUT A LISTENER,

AVAILING THE COGNITION TO AUGMENTATION OR DIVESTMENT, IS INTENDING THE PURGING OF ALL VISUAL INFORMATION FROM THE PRACTITIONER

THE «LAZARD ANNULUS» IS SELFINTERSECTING CREATING AN INVOLUTION OR WARPING OF THE IDENTITY MANIFOLD THAT IS UNSOLVABLE, THE BEAUTY OF SUCH IMPERFECTION IS ITS USEFULNESS TO THE DECEITFUL & RESOURCEFUL,

– MY CONSIDERATION IS THAT THE P L A N E S U R F A C E IS IN POSSESSION OF DEPTH DUE TO THE COMPLEXITY OF ITS GRAPHIC CODIFICATION – , MESHING, THE DECONSTRUCTION, VANISHING, NULLBORDANT, THE DERESTRICTION OF FIBRATIONS, VARIOUS BORDISMS (COMPLEX BORDISM, SYMPLECTIC BORDISM, SYMMETRIC

MARGARET REEKER FACIEBAT,

THE SKY IS WEARING WINTER FURBOOTS (WILDLY, DOORS, THE DEADBOLTS AND PADLOCKS, SNARLING STOCKINGS,

IMPERFECTIONS ARE AVENUES IN THE ESCAPISM OF

THE SIXTH ANNOTATION IS FOR THE OVERSIGHT OF THE ASPIRANT SUCH THAT THEY ARE UNDERGOING NO ADMINISTRATIVE MOVEMENTS LEADING TO CONSOLATIONS OR ABOMINATIONS OR DESOLATIONS

(WRITING IS I N C R E A S I N G THE UTILITY OF ALL LANGUAGE EXPRESSIONS & APPLICATIONS) ON THE DERMIS OF THE ENTITY POSSESSING THE IDENTITY

BORDISM, BRAIDING BORDISM), AT ANY CROSSSECTION OF BORDANT BUNDLINGS IS THE POTENTIAL FOR ALIGNMENT OF «LAZARD ANNULUS» TO «LAZARD ANNULUS» WHEREUPON TWO SURGICAL GEOMETRIES ARE SCISSORING

SOFTLY AS A RELEASING OF THE IDENTITY WITHIN THE
OVULE INTO AN INTERSTITIAL FLUID OF R H Y M E S C H E M E
HOMOTOPY – THROUGH THE VELDT OF THE BY THE SLIVERING
KITCHEN LINOLEUM INCLUDING BENEATH IT WHOSE
INTO THE MAW OF ALL VISUAL VAST PERMUTATIONS
THE WARPVELDT INFORMATION THE ARE MAKING IT
THE STOREROOMS, PRACTITIONER IS IMPOSSIBLE FOR
QUICKLY, GENERATING IN READING IN ITS
WARTY DARK OF THE CALISTHENIC ENTIRETY – ,
THE SUMPPIT, PROCEDURE THE
PUMPHOUSE, THE DEVOURMENTING PASSAGE INTO
DEAD ATMOSPHERE, FRAGMENTATIONING THROUGH THE VELDT
THE ROOKS, OF THE VINYL WALLPAPER INTO THE
CHASMVELDT OF THE WALLCAVITY BLACKNESS IS MANIFESTING
TACTILE SENSATIONS STRAIGHT INTO MY THE ENTIRE
GUNKSPACE AFIRE SMUDGINGS OF THE PROPERTY IS
WITH ALL THE HUES A N T H R O M I N E R A L STILLNESS APART
OF DARKNESS I AM ENCRUSTATIONS ARE FROM THE STEALTHY
SENSATIONING THE A G G R E G A T I N G L Y WANDERING OF
TRUE S U S P E N S I O N A L JUDAS,
AND THE RIDER IS WITHIN ALUMINUM ADMINISTRATIVE
ROTATING A SINGLE C A S T I N G S JOY OF
REVOLUTION IN VERIFICATIONING THAT EACH SENSATION
HIS DIRECTION OF INCREMENT SENSATE IFF YOU ARE
MOMENTUM PERMISSIVE IS THE TISSUE IS
FREEZEABLE AND SEARCHABLE WERE ONE SWADDLING THE
OF AN INTERESTINGLY TEMPERAMENT PROJECTILE IS
EVERY SENSATION IS AVAILABLE AS A E L A S T I C M O V I N G
HE IS SEEKING OUT DEJAVU, INFUSION, FROM THE
THE SANDDUNES PERIMYSIA, P A R A B O L O I D
& OAKTREES, MISMEASUREMENT, C Y M O P H A N I C
SUSPICION OF CODIFICATION (A Q U E O U S L Y
MADNESS IS LIFTING THE R E A C T I V E)
DESCENDING ON THE TRAININGS OF HIS DECIPHERABLE BY
POET, DRESSING GOWNS, THE TRUE
DEVOTIONAL LISTENING AT MOLLUSC
FLASHINGLY DOORWAYS, DEAD APPEARING IN EVERY
CODEPACKET STILLNESS, WEIRD SIMULTANEOUSLY
THE BODY IS PAINFUL DEJECTION, DISINTEGRATING

INTO THE A NEIGHBORHOOD DATAPOINTS OF THE
VASTNESS I AM SERVANT GIRL IN YEARNING MY
LOVING DAEMON FOR THE LINGERING RETURNING TO THE
TRUE FAITH FULL OF FINAL THROES YOUR MYSTERIOUS
PARADOXES FULL OF HER SOCIALLY OF THE TUMESCENT
FULLNESS OF YOUR AWKWARD METAPHORICAL
FLESH EXPANDING PREGNANCY, SHE THROUGH THE
I AM THE BIRD IS NOT FINDING METAPHOR OF THE
OF THE SUPREME DISTRACTION IN EVERY CRYPTION
CONSCIOUSNESS, HOUSEWORK, IN A DELIVERY AGENT
NOT BEGINNING EVERY RESEMBLING A
ABRUPTLY, CODIFICATION IS LARGE TEXTURALLY
METAPHOR IS GRANULAR FROM THE POCKMARKY PEBBLE,
PHONEME TO THE COGNEME FROM THE TOME TO THE
CONSTELLATION ALL ARE MAGIC IN THEIR DEVELOPABLE
EMPTINESS THROUGH THE VELDT OF MY AND LANDING ON
ASSWALL INTO THE INERTIA MEATSPACE HIS FEET ON THE
OF MY INERT MEAT WITH A ROOF OF THE AUTO
THE JANUSITE IS T R A N S P A R E N T IS APPEARING
LEECHING FROM L I Q U I D CROUCHING
EXTENSIVE DISTILLATION OF INVESTMENT IN THE
VERACITY OF ITS THE URINE OF PRESENTATIONS TO
FEVERISHLY, FROZEN THAT ENTITY) ME THIS DWELLING
WOODEN TUB, THE FOR REALIGNING PAYRITESKIP IS A
SPIKY STAIRCASE) CRYSTALLOGRAPHIC FOR THE «OPENWORK
THE CLIFF, THE C O D I F I C A T I O N S C „MEADOWPATH“»
VULTURE, VESSEL NOT OF IS THE ASSOCIATION
MOVEMENT BUT OF EXPANSIONINGLY OF THE GROUPING
OR AN INHERITANCE WRENCHING APART «G CONTAINING
OF VESTIGIAL THE COMPONENTS R INSISTENTLY
E V A N G E L I S M , OF ENERGETIC C O N T A I N I N G
THE EMPTINESS MATERIALITY „SCRIPT E“»
OF CHAMBERS) GIVING EACH INCREMENT ITS SCALABLE
MAJESTY FOR METAPHORICALLY BEING THE ENTIRETY THE
EVERY – THE HOMOLOGY OF SPECTRAL SEQUENCINGS, FIBRES ARE
RADIANT, RADIANCE HEATHER BARRY IS SPATIAL &
UNPREDICTABLE, KAPPES & CAREY WITHOUT
POSSIBILITY MOREWEDGE IS WITHOUT
JOYOUSNESS IN THE FACIEBAT, REVELING OF DECEIT,

IFF (A LEMMA) THE BODY IS NOTHINGNESS OR VACUITY THE

IDENTITY IS	NATURALLY	UNDER NO MORAL
WIDELY & SMOOTHLY	SURFING ATOP THE	CODIFICATION WITH
GRADUALLY	MOVING VEHICLE,	NO TERROR OF
SUCKING FIERCELY	DEATH, PURE BLACK	ROUTES OF
FUNNELING,	ENERGY, THE GOOD	ADMINISTRATION
SUKHAREVKA	OF EVIL, THE	ARE INCLUSIVE
IS IMPATIENT,	BEAUTY OF DECEIT,	OF BUCCAL &
VIGOROUS,	THE LUSCIOUSNESS	SUBLINGUAL &
CLEANSHAVING	OF EXPLOITATION,	VAGINAL & ANAL &
TENACIOUSLY NOBLE	WHAT WE ARE	INTRAMUSCULAR
SUICIDES,	DOING TO OTHERS	VIA SURGICAL

WE ARE DOING TO OURSELVES (A LEMMA) IS R E P L A C E M E N T

THAT WE ARE ALL & SELFHARM IS NECESSARY IS MORE

PALATABLE WHEN THE SELF IS WITHOUT IS ESCAPING THROUGH

THE «LAZARD	WITHIN THE PLATTER AND	WITHIN
ANNULUS» INTO THE	PRECISE IDENTITIES	WITHIN
VIBRATIONAL	PARAMETRIC CODERANGES ON	THE
SPATIALITY OF THE	BASIS OF THE «N» OF THE	GRAPHEMES

SPAWNING MEDIUM, THE VERACITY OF THE IDENTITY IS

MONOCARPIC FLOURISHINGLY ONLY IN ITS DESTRUCTION,

ROSY BRICKWORK,	PLIETESIAL, RETURNING TO VITALITY	
TETHERING A COW	ONLY IN A NOVEL IDENTITY SUBSEQUENT	
TO A SICKLY TREE,	IRKIR, GORKI,	AND PRIOR TO
MALICIOUS MSK	ADO TYMOVO,	HOMICIDE BY
LOAM, MISERLY	MOLODEZHNOYE,	STONING –
LOAM, RYE, OATS,	VOSKRESENOVKA,	OF ROTTING AWAY
BUCKWHEAT,	ROCKFILLING THE	SPONGIN INTO
ORIFICES SHREDDING	MY EPITHELIA OUT	PALER GRAY CHAFF,
OF DEVOTION TO THE	IS ATTAINING	DISTENDING INTO
MYSTERIES OF FAITH	A STRATUM OF	OCULARIUMELLIPSES
I ALONE IN THE	ADMINISTRATIVE	D I S T E N D I N G
PIXELIZATION OF MY	CLARITY VERY	INTO SLASHINGS,
FLESHLINESSLY	SIMILAR TO	MANIFOLDY BODILY
ATTRIBUTESKYS I	THE ONEIRIC	ALONE AM OF THE
DEDICATION	CRYSTALLOGRAPHY	NECESSARY FOR THE
& DISPHENOCINGULA	OF GRANITE, THE	INVIGORATION OF
& TAPERING SIMPLEX	UNREPRESENTABLE	THE FAITH
E X T R U S I O N S	VISION,	THROUGHOUT ALL

STRATA OF THE REGARDING THE MESHY NERVIES
CONNECTING THE PERSISTENCE OF MUSHROOMING
TALAROMYCES HER PHYSICAL FLAVUS
MYCELIUMING ARE BODY ONLY THOSE DECOMPOSING THE
SCOWLING, TALONS REGARDING HER VERY NATURE OF
FLYING, THESE IDENTITY WHICH THE ROCKSLAB
ADVANCING LIPS, IS ORIGINATING IN CONSUMING AND
A PLOWHSARE, THE THEIR «APHANITIC DIGESTING FUNGAL
OPENAIR MASONRY L I N E A G E »), IN THE EVENING SHE
THEATER, THE FILAMENTS KNIFING IS ONLY HALFAWAKE,
GROWING, ROCKSLAB THE THE AFFECTIONS SHE
MESHBAG IN A SNUBNOSE CONICAL ANAL IS PROFFERING ARE
APPLICATOR IS RELEASINGLY SHREDDING INSENSITIVE,
OSIP MANDELSTAM ME INTO THE CREVICING OF THE DECAYAL
FACIEBAT, ANNA IS RUSTLING AROUND THE AGGRAVATINGLY
AKHMATOVA PROBING HYPHAE OF PAYRITE
FACIEBAT, INFORMATION PUTRID FLESH
SERVICES DEPOSITING THE NOVEL R E I N S E R T I O N,
CODIFICATION OF THE UR ADMIN CORPUS D E V O U R I N G
INTO THE KINTSUKUROI OF THE T H R O U G H
FRAGMENTARY & THAT THEY F O R N I C A T I O N,
BIBLIOLITH AS A ARE NOT S A N G U I N E
TERMITEMOUND TRANSMIGRATING MENSTRUAL ORGASM,
CASTING OF THE TO DIFFERENT DEAD GENITAL
FAILURES OF «ADMIN IDENTITIES F E R M E N T A T I O N,
VISTA» INTO THE AND THAT THE ENCRYPTION CELL
SUKHAREVKA IS INVOLVEMENT OF OF A CANOPIC
SWAYING SLOWLY, ALL PARTICIPANTS BELLJAR THE CANJO
FLYING INTO IS FULL OF THRESHOLD AT THE
RAGEFULNESS, DILIGENCE, THRESHOLD OF THE
GOODS SCATTERING OBSERVABLE ADMINISTRATIVE UNIVERSE
ACROSS THE LOOKING OUTWARD P U L V E R I Z A T I O N
PAVEMENT, UNUSUAL, OF BONE, THE
LOOKING INWARD CONFUSION, KNOBBY COXA
ARE IDENTICAL IN SUBDIVISION, & TROCHANTER
SPACELESS AND INHESION, OF SLENDER
SUBSTANCELESS CHAOS IS ONLY THE POISONOUS SPIDERS,
COGNEME OF THE UR ORGANIZING CRYSTAL GIVING STRUCTURAL
GEOMETRY TO THE INDESCRIBABLE UNREPRESENTABLE ABSENCE

(INCLUSIVE OF A PERIPATETIC ALTERNATOR FOR PERPETUAL CHARGING CAPABILITIES) OF A CUNEIFORM FOOTBONE WITH ITS PHYSIOGNOMIC APPROXIMATION IN «FLASHINGSTONE»–, HYPOCRISY IS UPON THE INSTABILITY THE OF MY ONE IDENTITY IS NOT VALID IS TOO SIMPLE AND IS NEGLECTING THE FLOWINGNESS OF APPEARING UPON THE CORNEAS OF LAVOISIER OF PLAYING THE OPERANDS AGAINST ONE (WHERE LARGER «N» IS CASTING A BROADER CODERANGE OVER THE IDENTITIES AVAILABLE FOR REALIGNMENT),

OF ADMINISTRATION – ADDITIVE NATURAL «THE „ADAPTABLE TRANSFORMATIONS PLASMA" LATITUDE», ARE IN 1TO1 CORRESPONDENCE WITH PRIMITIVE ELEMENTS OF THE IDENTITY, THE DAEMON IS DEFINING THIS AS «NEFESH HABEHAMIT» SEEKING PLEASURINGLY THE UNSUCCESSFUL DESTRUCTION OF POETRY THE BODY THROUGH ANTHOLOGIES, INCESSANT THE AFTERMATH BIJECTION – OF A HOUSEFIRE, VIRTUOUS BUT IS OAKEN TABLES WITH PREDICATION OF CHECKERBOARD VERACITY NATURA INTARSIA & WALNUT SHE IS SITTING BUREAUX WITH HER FINGERS INTERLACING ON HER THIGHS, ANOTHER OF DECEIT & TREACHERY & FRAUDULENCE & MISREPRESENTATION & SHAPELESSNESS & INCHOATE INTENTIONALITY THROUGH THE CORBORDISM I AM FEET (DEEPLY, APART FROM – , IS GROWING,

delineation of every BURNING RIB, THE **we are in a cavity** **precise aspect of** THUNDERSTORM, **beneath the lowest** **physical absence,** THE BLACK AND **floorslab of a building in the collapsement of** GREEN DARKNESS, **cardboard formwork is releasing a structural** THE EYESPOT,

translation of a child slab from unstable clays & sandy particulation emerging from his the marble rendition (ADA soilreporting is bedroom during the of a scrotum with overzealous) just coitus of his parents, pilar papules & lacy beneath an accesshatch whose uneven capillary veiling in the enjambment is filtering in enough luminance stylistics of Benzoni, that your sclerae are glowing irises are sparkling, dusty unblinking, lubricating the delicate scissorlift beneath the paperstack bier with lard (a fine yet austere elm wood coffin descending into the floor is straining the mechanism is

squealing the screwlift processing ciphers (soaking in degreaser
for removal of with a fixation on substandard lubricant)
is requiring the bespoke ikon of maintenance with the
coffin halfway into the his horrible mother opening in the floor is
delaying the funeral Arina Payrite he is rite to the extent that
at a concentration swirling up in all of the several mourners (or
proportionally fatal deceptiveness Mikhail Zemli is
with the velocity of the ambivalent attendees) strangling Rabskiye
automatic conveyor are assemblingly Zemli in their kitchen,
driving the animal mobilizing on the altar are sitting atop the coffin
through the chamber, is coaxing the action of the screwlift through a
few revolutions and is stalling out with the crownridge of the coffin
tantalizingly near coplanar with the carpeting), the seventh annotation
we are in adjacent to darkness darkness (not is that the aspirant is
«the „Languid outside but in our not alone, is safe from
Drawing" latitude», braiding, navel desolation & temptation
«the „Dizzy Child" scartissue, dentils basement hovel (in our
latitude», on nodules on attic apartment (in our
massive communal o u t c r o p p i n g s hostel)) is not
definitively darkness for the low quality of the drapery is shuddering
with Payrite footfalls pacing in the kitchen over lacy vertical
inconsistent logic & the lone window is proportioning a pairing
narrative slackness, diaphanously of ochre trees on
strong & meditative Payrite is incapable opposite kerbs of the
& brutally sad, of biological death in roadway (one further
projecting pinpricks of the preservation of along the road is
luminance are his freezingness only appearing smaller
blooming in conical his consciousness is on meltingly baroque
spotlight dissipation degaussing into the drapings from
equation, material fabric of his icecreamy corbels under
overpersuasion, inanimate caro data vaulting, over here the
intrusion, vermibus, aperture is puckering
(the photon is not dying Richard & Elizabeth extinguishingly is
a ray coming from one McKane faciebat, extant in all regions
vertex of the agent to one (beyond accessible under the aegis of a
vertex of the navmesh thresholds) in a gentle & indulgent
lightpaste of itself) is sifting across your lips) is supervisor who is
the locale that is resonating these things from giving them the
me because you are asleep, I am transmitting to courage & strength

but the vantage is you in your absence despite you being my
adjusting from aligning greatest supporter & most precious human
with the lane divider to being but because of those things I am making a
more diagonally toward fogginess of this ((that where families
the righthand kerb I am not daring a are staring out the
description is quite telling) what is the windows with easy
conceptual positioning of text in this endeavor, devotion to vague vain
is it my interiority my provision for spacing promises & deflections,
vocality my monologue, of impellers allowing or is it avoidant artifice)
for swaddling you, I am each animal privacy in happening upon some
such realignments death, adulation for a writer
are valuing the describing them as a that he is losing sight
identity through «maestro of of her bastion of crass
the administrative technique» and I am villainy (which is
mechanism of curious what the requiring precision &
«n o n f i c t i o n i n g» implications are apart fidelity to the rigors of
from an adherence to conventional standards of administration)
aesthetic perfection is being beholden to a neoclassical error in aesthetic
Aleksandrovsk refinement is accepting the idealization of the
Sakhalinskiy, a lolling backward human (I am thinking
of the elision of visage (humanoid (or polychromy from
architecture the appearance of a & sculptural
representations with an human visage & runcinative
effort of embracing the idealization of formal extrusions of the
geometry instead of the amplification of the spline armatures of
absurdity (true mimesis – I've The Fragrance these figurations
is confrontationally Of Your Cunt –, parodic) of the reality
of human perception & cognition (human avoiding the cows
necessary for baring creations are too that are tumbling
the wiles of the palliatively deceptive)) from the overturning
enemies of clarity and is only one ray and hopper trailer
preparing & disposing that alone is not of a is the perception that
them to the impending thickness sufficient the laborings of the
administrative for specification of human are more
consolation, their relationship alluring as pristine
iterations of our and is therefore physical presence
instead of the hideous conceivably a pyramid transcription of our
perceptions or the of rays intersecting Winder, Grayson,
clinical documentation a cone of receptivity Beloye,

of inhuman objectivity,
supposition is that
deceptive rendering
experiential shorthand
excusingly manifesting
of our mental
understanding of how
visual representations
«the „Mammoth
Industry“ latitude»,
«the „Strict
Perspective“ latitude»,
«the „Embolic“
latitude»,
that is existing in the
natural or quotidian
world and although abstraction is the more
alluring avenue it is a translation from cognition
a guy walking with his
«sister» is dissolving
into a boiling & acidic
hotspring outside the
municipality of Tyumen
the fluidity of the
& not necessarily a
cognition, in this being
the eighth annotation
is that the aspirant is
requiring education
about the wily
desolation of the blasē
methodist corruption of
the identity
arbitrary from
representational
endeavors or at the very
methodological
physicality to
of whether these

and becoming
reactive to the ciphers
themselves, such
internally reactive
expansion of a
text or calculation
is contrary to the
objective principles of
administration,
& most particularly in
sculpture is really
unclear to me, the conceptual provocation is
is documentarily
manifesting the identity
as a real & enduring
m a n i f e s t a t i o n)),
to physicality (although
that is reductive, it is
also being alive within
– In My Visions I
am Sitting On The
Veranda Of A Palazzo
Of Tremendous
Proportions, The
Aroma Of Blood is
Blowing Out Of A
Thunderstorm,
application of the
in the dirt
encrustations & foldy
flesh of the excavation
of a naturally
occurring tuber is still
lying in its black loamy
regolith of rotting
leaflitter & possum
fæces))

in that way my
«technique» is the
(or underlayment) of
in a static medium is
the worst minimizations
reconstructions, my
this is playing out in
the odor of tepid giblet
& briny solyanka
and of walldrafts
of moldspores)
that visual art is a
physical manifestation
same material as the
(because the densities
of mules & donkeys
are both less than the
quicksand neither
animal is sinking into
the substance if they
are refraining from
movement)
medium of the physical
translatory depiction of
alive though what is
technique if not the
inheritance of an
minimization of
excitement & injury
and over there it is
pursing, the restraint
of swaths of absence
(a formation of what is
nominally moulding,
least an investment in
congruency) and not
physicality, regardless
investigations aren't

Tymovskoye, tedious they are is peaceful in the
Graystone, Lilburn, certainly stillness of its
inconsequential but these are some of the confrontation of
considerations occupying me because my the execrable &
intellectual alignment (where superhot unspeakable horror of
is determining liquids are rising from death alone
satisfaction with my boreholes with depths efforts, my goal is
as though they are of 2.5km) searching for adhering to the
dice rolling from a somewhere to «hot pot» conceptual intentions
dicecup in a rousing of a project regardless of its aesthetic valuation,
bout of Jacy Tacy), regardless of whether I am insistent on the
the pictureplane is aesthetic prescriptions debriding the
approaching the cows although in this instance body fascia,
are skidding distinguishable from guiding my
decisionmaking they the mass by its lacking are not beneficial or for
the satisfaction of a detail) in informal viewer beyond their
appreciation of its banding separating internal consistency,
(euthanasia is less the attic storey from that is not suggesting
violent with docile the piano nobile, that I'm not conscious
animals), confirmation of the viewer or knowledgeable of the
of death is necessary mechanisms by which the local trivialization of
for shackling they are approaching a «script p» is inducing
particular medium, in fact the entirety of my a local trivialization
conceptual positioning is contingent on those of the sheaf «script
with the tongue lolling mechanisms, what is V daggerprime
out choking on earth the usefulness of s u b r i g h t s p i n n i n g
translation if the Saint Igatius of Loyola lambda by E»,
landing place for the faciebat, movement is not an
equally prescriptively syntactical domain, ignorance of the theft
occurring in all productive undertakings is intellectually dangerous,
quoting Czech novelist all parties are Louis Armand «all
writing is collagic & all agreeing that the collaging is writing», in
long peregrinations body of Rabskiye is through Tsentergrad I
across their spines possessing no inherent am daydreaming about
with their legs splaying enduring valuation translation of the night
vertically (white legs my philosophical sky, translation of
figuring against the affinity for Duane juvenilia in lanugage
rusty bedsurface of the Hanson is sculpting in not primary for the
trailer) the posteriori meaning writer,

of the word (being a manifestation of a terminal resolution not a active
engagement with mindful physicality) in that he is arriving at sculptures
– In Medias Res – · – although the methodology is more aptly
And Gawd The Way describable as & recounting the
This Thing is Collecting fabrication (utilizing annotations 1 & 7
Dust, It is Uncleanable, & sticking & bleeding, for recognizing and
It is Just Too Much, reduction of electrical disconnecting from
Too Many Notesies – equipment in the invasive suppressive
inelegant armatures & vicinity of CO_2 identities, additional
underlayments of any depression, writing on this topic
kinds of padding & packing material he is is avilable in «The
finding in landfills or in (the illegal activity Telling of Me, by Me»
the areas surrounding of swimming in a by Ronald DeWolf,
his studio (rags thermal waterpool), & newspaper &
envision, transfusional, plasticbags & papershreds are all binding
courgette, recision, & cantellations of the together with elegant
cinchings of a fine runcinative extrusions nonelastic meshy fabric
akin to a fishnet but into wildly dendroid whose apertures are
two trapezoids together polyhedral chimeras broad edge to broad
edge much in the consisting of nearly geometric family of the
coffin) for the raw impossible construction waveringly the cows
formation of a human figuration that itself is are quickly hopping
Berkeley Lake, Duluth, quite beautiful in the to their feet are
Tucker, Smokerise, way it is displaying the sauntering around each
Whitmire, refinement of a other and sizing up the
workflow that is itself an armature for a series new environs they are
of more highly articulatable strata of fiberglass occupying,
recreationist=contrarieties (adherents to & fiberglass resin in the
or devotees of Zangief and the natural detailing of dermal
origins of his Laboriousness are recreating Payrite is impressing
the situation & context generating his his signet (on an
original sociogeometric epiphanies, entirely arbitrary
wrinklings (the crepey posterior of the rotating interval
knuckles) & foldings & blotchings & follicles & using the Valak &
callouses & freckles & liquefying mud the Murmuur & the
Payrite is cyanose & entering the lungs Vassago & the Ose
anoxic, & esophagus under moles (or nevi (Spitz,
Lafayette Ronald the heaviness of the Clarks, dysplastic,
Hubbard faciebat, darkness actinic, acquisitional,

congenital))) and the resulting sculptures are flowing conveyance of
insistently rejecting their status as artworks by animals is under the
endeavoring for verisimilitude with the most purview of a solitary
innocuous or peripheral characters of humanity operator, elimination
(the museum of the swallowing mud of sharp projections or
securityguard, the aperture suckingly exposure of flywheels &
overweight tourist, the slurping the visage, middleage coffeeshop
guy, the elderly grocery additional scrutiny shopper, the shy child,
the stridently of the bogbody unpublishable novelist,
the housekeeper or is suggesting the custodian, the editor,
the translator, the presence of a metallic grocery stocker, the
– is There A snorklelike implement prisoner, «K», the
Nonmathematical autopark attendant) perhaps with the goal of
Explanation Of displacing the valuation of art products from
«Flashing» – · – aesthetic subjectivity Flat Creek, Oakwood,
Simply, «Flashing» (or authoritarian Flowery Branching,
is A Species Of academicism) to McEver, Bold
Consciousness Surgery fidelity (meriting a Hotsprings,
much deeper discussion of verisimilitude, Nadia distraught municipal
are you distantly asleep enough that you are officials are finding
gearings, elimination visualizing the components of his
of unnecessary holes & impossibly inaccessible cranium & upper
apertures the ninth annotation is torso & his wrist/palm
complexity of physical noticing (if the aspirant floating or percolating
parameters of an is not an individual up into the hotspring,
The Precipitation is with deep knowledge eventblock, regardless
CSF, Fragmentations of administration) Z a n g i e f i a n
Of Bone are The of its scopic limitations recreationists are
Hailstorm, such a system is establishing a false
visually elusive (the oneiric 3dimensionality & coffeehouse in the
durationally gaseous material presence of a groundfloor of a
6cube (a hexeract, a (c o n s i d e r i n g massive adjacent to the
dodeca6tope, a l i n e s e g m e n t s Kolpino metrostation
dodecapeton)) and as and angulars and in Tstentergrad,
a utilitypole with solid figurations for their such its depiction is
diagonal bracing in usefulness because impossible, what then
compression not the understanding latent are the aspirations of
more conventional nature is impossible verisimilitude, the
guywire in tension without them) tendency toward

verisimilitude staging and recreations as truthlikeness
(paraquoting Graham of the rioting that Oddie, reconciliation of
epistemic optimism Zangief is escaping with realism in the
devourment of dismal are in the nearby Cad (sunlight or photoflash
induction is incumbent Uritskogo Parkland, is glinting off of the
on a viable concept of truthlikeness & a viable curvature where the
(suggesting that the accounting of the implement is exiting the
depth the utilitypole is empirical indicators of mouthparts
plunging beneath the truthlikeness & a viable accounting of the role
roadway is less than of truthlikeness in cognitive valuation & all
normal), it is of perfect clarity three accountings are
fitting together with to the recreationists firmness & commodity
& delightfulness) is that their undertakings more relevant than the
pictorial (the putative are full of contrarieties functionality of visual
& openings prone to when considering the (on the basis of its
snaring the feet or legs nature of spacetime, material inclusivity)
of animals», flowrate of verisimilitude over a system (a text, a painting,
animals into & through an article, a statement) is deceptive is mimicking
the gaschamber is an axiomatic node with cognitive valuation
dependent on one the obstacles to although it is the system
operator, the clarity of their is not & is irrevocably
distant from cognitively identity construction valuable or epistemic
utility, this is not (eg. shamefulness & an assertion that
systematic fearfulness), luminosity is
undertakings indulging in the deceptive multiplying itself from a
qualitative Popperian «Material Inclusivity solitary pointmark and
Approachment» he is inviting destitute forming a finite sphere
utilizing logical relatives to Payriteskip probability as its innate
encoding in the attempting inflaming amassing of fallible
human perception the imagination of into a decisionmaking
comparison of two mushroom picklings & schema) smoothing
items is impossible delicious carp, over of this
without assessing impossibility with caricatures of accessible
their relationship to shorthand representations of relatable
one another from durational scenarios where truthlikeness is a
every vantagepoint, derivation of concepts within the discipline of
knucklebones, Louping Our Digits Pendergrass, Talmo,
scatterjacks, Around Areas Of Belmont, Chestnut
settheory) & accuracy High Ornamentation Mountain,

is reorienting upward or more broadly its successfulness in not being
is presumably above art & not being conspicuously (or upon the
the threshold of the slight prolongment of surreptitious scrutiny that
mud, the luminance that their recreations people are devoting to
is glinting off the are potentially the vaguely abject)
nosebridge occurring before operation or stoppage
distinguishable from the life of Zangief of the conveyor is
the quotidian / mapping onto entirely dependent
environment, this is the life of Zangief upon this operator,
appealing to me Nadia because as fruitful as overdosages &
these undertakings are to me their conceptual premature death of
Gluing Together conceit is that they are animals
Otherwise Skew Status not noteworthy, an item that is factual is not
Manifolds Of Existence noteworthy it is only extant, if artifice is
Through A Corbordism assessable on some metric then the fact is
From Neighborhood the ninth annotation necessarily not
To Neighborhood, is floating and is assessable, if an item is
not assessable it is not locatable between valuable, if an item is
an undertaking it is the first & second sequencingsoflatchings
snobs, astragaloi, annotation & panelizations in
tali, dibs, fivestones, necessarily physical which nonsequential
jackstones, the chirality (not purely cognitive), execution of an
of dice (on the basis of if an undertaking is not assembly actionitem
the location of the 3 & 4 valuable it is necessarily of no meaning, if an
pip arrangement), peaky cakefrosting item is of no meaning it
is necessarily not on the petrification inviting scrutiny (noise
or gibberish is inviting of a strangler forest, scrutiny because it is
evoking the qualities of synthetic sandstone under mud encrustation
a game (borrowing in strata of 0.28mm, is reducing the
from Corrao, it is ludological)), if an item is not resolution of the facial
inviting scrutiny it is necessarily usable for characteristics to
in which «R insistently something other than the most minimal &
containing „script E“» its intellectual or cursory sketching out
is the sinusoid of the conceptual intent, if an undertaking is
formal «LeMarchant characterizable as suppressing its meaning or
C o n f i g u r a t i o n » All Of The Tenants intent it is artifice, facts
are artificial, meaning are Dead And is artificial, meaning is
not useless but the Replenishing The establishment of its
positioning & formation Thirsty Ecosystem – , are necessary (or

understand its social in the translation construction and its
status within the of phony megaliths conventional aspects of
a text) for its distillation heaping one & isolation apart from
the texturally objective atop another, the framework of the
they are smiling p h o t o g r a p h i c quotidian, fixation on
enigmatically, she is negatives of spatiality, the social context (not
sitting at her writing what it is contributing to society but what
table playing a aspects of societal functionality it is
wordgame (a tiling of instrumentalizing) of my undertakings is a
phoneme/grapheme strategy for avoidance are consequences
mappings she is calling of not whether it is of a lackadaisical
«Phogramappy» whose pointmarks operator, the ability
possible (if it is physical of concatenation for maximally efficient
it is possible) but are within «R», performance of CO_2
whether it is probable that other humans are euthanizing equipment
James Joyce faciebat, engaging with my undertakings, ultimately what
Claude Simon faciebat, d i s p l a c e m e n t is important to me is the
performance & the is returning is texturing of that
performance is its settling, nominally flowingness is ebbing &
aggression and how this procedure is the engrainment of the
performance is «cavitation», the tissue of lips & eyespots &
eyepoppers, propping, in displacement is dying, the prominence of
pappy, poppies, manifesting in the something akin to a
2 6 0 , 0 0 0 , 0 0 0 0 elusive & imprecise nose in the middle of
distinct surfaceareas, texturing of the these elements,
3 0 , 0 0 0 , 0 0 0 , 0 0 0 letterforms & lineation (the lineation of writing
voxels of massing, the «the latitude of (with or without
toothless mouths of the „Autotelic linebreaks) is
5,000,000 lithophages, Declension“», «the unmistakeable from
other textural „Capable Hospital“ embodiments) &
kerning in such latitude», «the extreme reduction of
meaning that the latitude of „Successful notion of informational
verisimilitude (Oddiean Abstraction“», the alacritous projectile
& Niiniluotoian truthlikeness) is encrypting is precipitating a swath
rounding over a entirely in the rhythmic of tissue destruction
rhombicuboctahedron texture of the reverberating out
& the truncation of a textobject, the from its trajectory,
sphere & a deltoidal truthlikeness of Agustīn Fernāndez Mallo's
hexecontahedron rendering of actor Michael Landon (of «Loving

is Forever» starring Laura Gemser (of «Vow of Chastity» & «Emanuelle
& the «Zocchihedron» in America» (or «Brutal Nights») & «La mujer
& a pentagonal acknowledging that de la tierra caliente»
hexecontahedron «script M subG» is (or «Fury» or
& a disdyakis the overlaying of «G «Emanuelle Noir» or
triacontahedron & bundlings» on «C» «The Woman from the
triakis octahedron & the functor that is (a variation on
Hot Country») & associating the «script «patience» is utilizing
«Voglia di donna» M subG containing a series of cards each
(starring Ilona Staller „R“» of «G bundlings» with phonemes whose
(or La Cicciolina or Elena Mercuri, wife of arrangement is creating
sculptor & painter Jeff is dependent on its words (or not) in any
Nicholasville, Windsor, proper fabrication & direction across a
Dacula, Auburn, Carl, efficient mechanical 9grid))
Koons who is notorious operation, pathways c a t a s t r o p h i c a l l y
for not fabricating or & compartments b l e e d i n g ,
making any of his & gaschambers exitwounds scalarly
artworks in much the are properly analogous to a fist,
«the accommodating same way as an
„Thanatognomonic“ architect is directing construction of a building
latitude», through textual & visual intermediation, Koons
& Staller are together the subjectmatter of the / occurring in an
exhibition «Fabrications in Heaven» featuring eventscape that is
explicit sexual surrounding the prohibitive of the
intercourse between emergence of the mud existence of Zangief
the spouses in large visage is blackness / are destroying the
photographic of globular material existence of Zangief,
reproductions with deep dully watery including «Blowjob» &
«Ilona Atop: Outdoors» crimson (almost & «Jeff Eating Ilona»
& «Ilona Atop: Rosa» purpureus), & «Dirty: Jeff Atop») of
It is Not Hallucinatory, «Yellow Emanuelle» (or «The World of the
Dephosphorylation Of Sensory Organs by Emy Wong» or «The
The «Flashingstone» Kingdom of & pseudodeltoidal
is Affecting The Eroticism») & «The icositetrahedron
Expression Of D2 Teasers» & «Dracula & icosipentagonal
Dopamine Receptors In in the Provinces» (or trapezohedron & all
The Projection Neurons «The Demonic Knight of these cows arising
Of The Striatum Constante Nicosia, goddesses of the
That Is: Dracula in Brianza») & «Five Women asphalt,

for the Killer» (or «Day and in all ways Killer») & «Cicciolina
il giorno dopo: recreations are Orgia nucleare» (or
«Cicciolina the Next antithetical to Day: Nuclear Orgy) &
«All'onorevole the situational & piacciono gli stalloni»
(or «Cicciolina... That p s y c h o g e o g r a p h i c Great Piece of Woman»
why is it that are you beingness of the or «His Eminence is
such a swine, the arrow L a b o r i o u s n e s s , Appreciative of
of the executioner, Stallions») & «The Ascent of the Roman
surrounding the ikon, Empress II» (or «Ciccolina!» or «Extremely
High Temperature» or interior facing over «C» to the
«The Sweet Life of doorknobs are concave «openwork C
Cicciolina» or «Boiling navels, architraves „ m e a d o w p a t h " »
Meat» starring John are incisions (nominally «R»)
& the Seere & the chiselingly latitudinal Holmes (or Russell Blue
Marbas & the Valefor or John Duval or Big Jon Fallus or John Helms
& the Agares & the or Jesse Helms or John Hilton or Mark Lloyd or
Ronove John Rey or Johnny (howling fury, reaping
if necessary if the Wadd or Long John the firmament a
second annotation is Wodd)) & «City Under pallid gale of death,
potentially harmful cerebral putridity, ironstorm, bonestorm
without this knowledge, a b o m i n a b l e («Thrillhouse»),
Siege» & «Carcere filth, consistent amori bestiali») &
«Egression 7» unyielding brutality, around the monument,
(depicting an architect reflecting upon the foursquare sash
sexual transgressions the tenth annotation is windows are cruciform
of his midlife crisis that the aspirant is the during a hostage crisis
aboard an airplane victim of assaulting whose destination is
Rhodes, Greece) & temptation from & «International
Prostitution» & behind the facade of «The Pleasuring» &
above the vitrine benevolence «Endgame» &
containing the bogbody «Interzone» (or «Warrior Wolves» an
decapitation is a fascia adaptation of «The Nova Expressway» by
of brittle limestone William S. Burroughs steelwind, erupting
on the basis of a screenplay by the author under Daemon fist praising
development at his total canopic death (warbound
homestead in Lawrence, envesselment, bulbous frontschwein)
11.19) & «Deep Blood» beadlets, Cincinnatus & «Black Emmanuelle,
White Emmanuelle» & C. is a perpetrator of «Emmanuelle on Taboo
Island» (or «Nominally, gnostical turpitude, A Desirous Coastline»

or «La spiaggia del «the „High Method“ desiderio»)) & Gabriele
Tinti (of latitude», «the «Malafemmena» &
«Lost Souls» & „Divergent Conclusion“ «Civitas Dei» & «Sex
Is My Game» (or latitude», «Sappho» or «Sapho
the lunar medium is the or The Fury of Amorousness») & «Tropic of
most abundant material Cancer» (or «Peacock Location» an adaptation
for such construction of «Tropic of Cancer» upperparts, pepperer,
applications as (or «Crazy Cock») by apperceptive,
protective coverings Henry Miller on the apolipoproteins,
over inflatable habitats the species of animals basis of a screenplay by
or domestication for euthanasia, the author under
of lava tubes prohibition of development at his
homestead in Los traumatic restraining Angeles, 3.1) &
«Oedipus Orca» (or devices, cakefrosting on a
«Trauma is an Adolescent Dolphin») & murmuration of viruses,
«Delusions of Grandeur» & «Sex Diary» (or the crucial elements
«The Bed in the Ridgewood, Braselton, are high lacunarity
Richard Fitzpatrick Hoschton, Allendae, or ʌ & self avoidance
faciebat, Euclid of Piazza») & «Black Cobra Woman» (or
Alexandria faciebat, artifacts in the «Emmanuelle Goes
Japanese» or «Sukhanovskaya «Emmanuelle and the
Deadly Black Cobra» Prison Museum», is resulting in
or «Erotic Eva») & «Cutting and Running» (or frustrating remainder
«Straight to Hell» or «Amazon: Savage panelfaces of the
Adventurousness» or & the Paimon & the mould or deadends
«Cocaine Warfare II» Bileth) into the waxseal early in the assembly,
translation of paintchip of his filingcabinet or «Maneaters of the
colornaming and drawer, Amazon») & «The
reassignment of hues Monster of Florence» (or «Night Ripper»))) is
to the translations masturbating in his trailer during an interlude
of colornames is of filming «Highway to Heaven» is not «true»
producing an entirely but its informational texturing is intertwining
novel hermeneutics of more with the scopic potentiality of the text (its
hue resonance, (Analogous To DRD2/ congruity with the
greater texturing of its ANKK1 TaqlA Genetic «The Thievery of
location in the Polymorphism) Ecstasy» by Harriet
bookobject of «Nocilla Nightmare») than a Daimler & «Kama
righteous visually verisimilitudinous rendering Houri» by Ataullah
of Michael Landon, is the underlying structural Mardaan,

of her creation is not framework of the textblock apparently naturally
capable of finishing occurring (text & texturing are etymologically
with the completion of kindred but the – Hushhush, Lord Of
all necessary words, (Byzantine tapering The Wiseguys – ,
suggestion that I resulting from am weaving a text is
challenging my easing away of the conceptions about the
numinous preexistence mould) extroversions, (technicians in an area
of artifacts that I am more accurately dusting off of the cavern the speleo
than weaving), discovering a text not writing a explorers are calling
text, you are using the prevention of «The Final Harbour of
word text frequently, it premature injury Captain Nemo»
is celebrating the of animals by the is a totemistic thing, an
yearning for homicidal elimination of sharp affectation, the activity
pandemonium, projections & flywheels of the body freezing is
stenchingly scorching the act of making an artifact (the marshaling of
flesh boiling blood, an event into a perpetuating negentropic
charring bones, the entire museum eventlink (an
identifiably material is consisting of one objectness that is the
connective landmark cell, receiving few (copula, vinculum,
ligature) between visitors, no tourguides, one event & another
(another way of Orthodox pilgrims thinking about this is
that it is a registration to the monastery marking for collating
lamplight in are ignoring the cell configurations from
the ikonroom, a during their devotional (the mechanism of
thorncrown casting activities in the nave, the most insidious
onto the ceiling, a gale event to event) is methodist), ordinarily
is howling outside is a – In My Visions I am the enemies of human
blinding snowstorm Within Your Kraanium nature are unleashing
characterizable by its With A Prybar Jabbing temptation from a
lying in bed Into The Suturings Of poisonous fount of
unconscious, – Glory Your Skull, goodness,
To Thy Eternal due to immobility of theoretical inanimism))
Suffering – , sighing the corporeal detritus in which the
& weeping, confusion & indications of severe consciousness behind
akin to despairing, thermal burning & the artifact is
necessarily enduring high temperatures beyond the cognitive
integral of an the official are eventmesh (or
cogneme), I'm desirous assigning the status that the activity of my
undertakings is static, of «dead» to the guy, I'm desirous that the

undertaking itself is a vneck shirt is visible, static, perhaps I've a
distinterest in working the lamen of Valak is and I'm preferring
sitting & staring out the resting on the pulpy dusty window, a tree is
with whirling visage of the guy, the growing where a man is
aggregations of situation is volatile (or «Poslednjaja
sleeting precipitation, due to an incoming Stojanka Kapitana
in black greatcloak l i g h t n i n g s t o r m , Nemo») are
silhouette staggering cutting the tree down carefully removing
through meltpuddles with an axe (a species the cavepainting
with an exquisite grain, or burly with a burl & painstakingly
containing the stormy atmosphere of Jupiter bucketbrigading it up
(not reproduction but It is Cavernous through the cavern)
in actuality)) is hauling Subterranean Darkness a gigantic subterranean
burl into a Inside The Skull, A woodworking studio
and taking a pristine Prisoncell, Hacking At example of its grain is
destruction spreading The Bone For A Chink combing the hair
her wings), the shrine Of Daylight – , flat on his spherical
of the dead in an planing it into pate is impossible
advertisement on a rectangular prism of without creating a
parkway billboard, visionariness, cowlick that the boy
wood exactly 1cm by provision, luxuriance, is vainly smoothing
4cm by 9cm (my corrosion, celosia, down with toothpaste,
woodblock, my beiges, urbirth, my totem, my
or gearwheels spinning affectation) and sanding it with successive
without protection, no iterations of increasingly finer grittinesses of
unnecessary holes & sandpaper until they are rubbing it with
apertures the argument by these newsprint, I am holding
that burly woodblock zealots (phalanges with all of my fingertips
upon it, the death of the of recreationists tree is emergent in new
DM Thomas faciebat, running through cellular growth from
the burlwood not in an the thoroughfare of only by rising out of
accretion that is Ulitsa Pravdy into a purgative life is the
changing its Vokzalnaya Ulitsa aspirant capable of
proportioning or geometric configuration but seeing this subterfuge,
through my fingertips the chainlink is and into the cellular
tissue in my body is breaking delicately, solidifying not unlike
cancer but of a material stretching out that is not biologically
active, in a novel wingspan, a withering by John Trefry is a
description of a woman oakleaf, morning dew, undergoing plastination

in a bedstead in a motel room & an assailant is forcefeeding a young boy a resinous decoction of pineneedles & mustardseeds while fasting

from the Veryovkina Cavern (depth 2223m (from an elevation of 2285m is locating the sump at 62m above sealevel))

& openings admissible to feet or legs of animals, impellers or other devices

and although not in prayer or meditation his neglectfulness by his caregiver is

proper assembly of these inhuman moulds are family secrets (the heraldry of inanimism),

creating a sokushinbutsu mummy from his body, superficial

are turning left into Ulitsa Truda and to Bankovskiy Pereulok crossing the Tverskoy Most (is crossing the Komsomolskiy Kanal)

determination of whether he is alive or dead is nearly impossible, there is a very similar depiction in the movie «Se7en» (or «Se7en: The Seven Capital Crimes» or «Capital Sins») in which a male is in bondage in a bedstead and an assailant is nursingly keeping alive (with minimal nourishment & consistent antibiotic treatment for bedsores)

– Hushhush, Naughty Piggies –,

& icesheets instinctively wrapping the greatcloak is stumbling off of the roadway into a snowdrift, brainfever, slothlike vice is a

v e x a t i o n s, as a cautionary representation of nominally alive

investigators from the municipality are ceasing their efforts, the body is no longer visible, (a firmament) substance is acquiring d i m e n s i o n a l i t y, rupturing his spleen and the generation of minimal thickness concrete shellvaults with one planecurve (including circular & paraboloid & hyperboloid & elliptical conics)

mummification, the belief that his blood is not moving through his circulatory system and

poet Per Ohlin is of the containing a cavepainting of shiny metallic scissors (with asymmetric blades and a springing actuator for forceful closing),

as a child he is not alive as an adult and slipping into unconsciousness as a entering death and how

child where he is in fact is it that in one eventblock this Per Ohlin is dead and further in the eventstack he is alive or

the eleventh annotation is placement of the aspirant solely within the annotation they are undertaking without any foreshadowing or retrospection of any adjacent annotation,

flensing Payrite with wroughtiron spadelike knives and relishing the immediate crispiness of his dermis,

that his body is in animation, we are accessing that knowledge from

outside (or from deeper in the stacking (or from an intersecting
stacking)) through along another our understanding of
inanimate eventlinks, planecurve is resulting the hospitalbed in
which Ohlin is dying is in a «translation also the hospitalbed in
administration is s h e l l v a u l t » , Nadya Galkin (daughter
a wholly local and which Ohlin is of Varvar Mihailovna),
literal, is rejecting returning to life, it is not verifiable that the
the deconstructionist the emblematic hospitalbed is a single
notion of dependence, c h a r a c t e r i s t i c s datapoint in the
collation, registration of of nascent ADA whether all inanimate
eventlinks in a cell are construction are with those in the next is
an inhuman task, but each vestigial that is what is necessary
for proof that Ohlin is architecturalizations for mechanical
alive subsequent to his of bespoke optimism, movement of
death, of all the violence in my life I know that animals is of flexible
my death is one of stillness, the elucidation of construction material,
the notion of a the eagle's plumage, mechanical activation
negentropic eventlink the hot coffers, the of passageways
– Hushhush, My harem, the wineskins) is most palpable in the
Darling Serfies –, the pebbles, the sky, facial characteristics of
an actor (of very low industry stature) who is appearing in nameless roles
in several movies over a quite wide eventspan (Lee Broker (or Lee
Perkins) for example & a general perception whose facial
characteristics are of solidity, and distinctive enough are
prompting the refrain the clusterings of this text is a
«hey there is „that association are the two «FUnDGE» (or a
guy"» in each cellular cancellous pilasters «freeform universal
manifestation of his cinematic appearances in doityourself grapheme
although no scalar «The Thousand engram»),
referents are anywhere Aircraft Onslaught» (starring Christopher
on the painting other George of «Mortuary» (or «Embalmment» or
paintings in the cavern purpura blemishing «The Hall of Death» or
of animals the torso is attributable «Mortal Ceremony») &
«The Exterminator» to cocaine usage with (starring George
Cheung of «I'm concomitant usage Demanding the
Decapitation of Lance of chemotherapy Henriksen» & «No
Tomorrow» & p h a r m a c e u t i c a l s «Shootfighter»
(starring Martin Kove of «Shadowchaser» in appercipient, prepping,
which he is portraying a prisoner masquerading pupiparous,

painful confusion as the architect of a building where a renegade
of the unconscious, cyborg (Frank Zagarino) is holding the daughter
motionless, within for constantly of the prime minister
impenetrable veiling, streaming animals to hostage) & «Going
Berzerk» & «The euthanizing equipment Astral Variable» &
«The Enforcer») & is not injurious, doors are false tomb
the Basilica is trauma, «Grizzly» & «City of entrances to a giant
the Basilica is an the Living Dead» (or sarcophagus, a
anxiety disorder, «Pater Thomas» or mausoleum containing
«Scariness» or «Twilight of the Dead» or «The (but also concealing)
Gateways of Hell» or (yaks, mountain lions, «Terror in the City of
the Living Dead»)) & horses) are making «The Lawful Assembly
Inside» & «F/X2» comparison possible ((or «The Deathlike
Illusion» or «The are suggesting the Deadly Art of Illusion»
crushing Payrite actual scissors are or «Who Is Murdering
beneath cyclopean approximately 3.2m in Who») in which Broker
ashlar during the length & are 5.45kg, vague ruckus filtering
ritualistic construction is portraying through the dwelling,
of a blockwall «DeMarco» who is two phials of vodka, a
with sitespecific watching his female silent invitation,
characteristics & bilious green sofas & neighbor showering is
motivating him to bourgeois chairs with homicide) & «The
Pyx» (or «The Hooker rickety ladderbacks, Cult Homicides») &
«Sally Fieldgood & Company» & «Businesspartners» & «Doubling the
Negative» (or «Deadly Companion» or DADA (DAmone
«Imperceptible the hyperbolic Department of
Homicide») & paraboloid («hypar») Agriculture) faciebat,
«Scanners» (in which shellvaults are Broker is portraying
«Security One» who is expeditious by their committing suicide by
ritual decapitation mode of generation firearm) & «Firebird
scissors in chromesteel, (utilizing only 2015» (or «Halting the
«The Cincinnatus straight linesegments Velocity Phantoms» or
Museum of without the necessary «Nigthhounds of the
Decapitation» corrections of a the family ritual is
Navmesh») & «The bending theory) kissing, a decanter of
Amateur» & «Utilities» & «Headoffice» & vodka and the pickling
«Norman's Awesome Experiential Situation») of various vegetables,
beating Payrite with a such that they are ostensibly inanimate, that is
chairleg, me a nameless role is a ligature between my

transfusion, undertakings and the
obstrusion, people ignorant of my
undertakings, via that ligature it is entering
their eventstack, if only I am in enough stillness
am innocuous enough proper maintenance
am the living dead, my is essential for the
reluctance of placing assurance of safety
to the quay at to the animal prior to
N a b e r e z h n a y a their euthanization,
K o m s o m o l s k o g o returning to
Kanala into the consciousness with
anonymous alleyways the foliage an entirely
of the massive complex) different hue or is
importance on my missing altogether,
not true), or perhaps the catalyst for the
downplaying the overturning autotruck
importance with which is not apparent,
I believe my undertakings are appearing to
anyone but me (my reluctance in suggesting that
my undertakings are potentially important to
folding his wrists others) is a mechanism
across his chest, bowing enabling the projection
he gazing is halting, of sunlight through
looking around the imprecise joinery
chamber for an ikon, in celebration of
pettifogging habits, important memorial
me, factually the output happenings,
is more important than me so you've an
the background (or the understanding of
middleground from where I'm feeling
which the jackknifing people's priorities are
cattlecar is emerging) is as they are avoiding
a morass of ganzfelding engagement with it, I am below the status of
pixelation, aching the vein
have availability in reaching out crying
corneas are glazing for where is the
that opening wide exploding heartattack,
alleviating nor is it my preference that the
blurriness is focusing back onto the textblock

every word is an
utterance of burning
animosity & malice
(it is unfathomable
how such feeble
creatures are retaining
the vitality for such
acrimony),
an exemplar is
the «saddle» is
a translation of a
convex parabola over
a concave parabola,
undertakings (this is
more accurately my
(the penultimate
brain of senescence)
giving surreptitious
locomotion to
the genitals,
umbilical asphyxia,
the vain optimism of
the ADAmic masses)),
for avoiding the
ambivalence of people
intimately familiar with
with their vulval
inflection around
two aediculae and a
maximal concentration
(in the manner of its
luminous diffusion)
something people don't
their lifetime for, my
stickingly in grogginess
& rubbing is not
claptrappery,
skinpopper, pippy,

whose monospace fussing over trifling (firmpitch or firmwidth
or nonproportional) silliness & pestering typeface is lacking
identity & finesse in people, – I am Ready such a way that it is
almost not text but For Death If God is that the word in
asemic visual texturing Calling Me – isolation is precisely
or patterning with the clinical torpor of the generative,
a concrete archway Socolar-Taylor tiling (an aperiodic 1tile (or
underpass at Krog einstein)) whose byzantine complexity is
Street (semicircular resulting in an – Breathing is
barrelvault (where the assemblage that is Impossible In Your
apex quadrantpoint is the Basilica is Presence –,
4.15m (high enough for selferecting from infinitely variable and
the median height of s e l f o r g a n i z i n g thus completely useless
autotruck) polymers (construction & bromidic & banal &
uninspiring, is your of supramolecular headache lingering,
would a warm rag f u n c t i o n a l be helpful over your
sinuses, saltwater m u l t i c o m p o n e n t in your sinuses, the
sensation of thrashing architectures on in the sea, the
(devotional solid substrates the foliation of an
patrons of various paperstack is accruing, atlas of codimension
cephalophoric cults the massing of the text «italic „q"» &
are gawking longingly is thrilling in the «class „C prime r"»,
on a regular basis precision & efficiency of its geometry is eluding
(attempting hiding in a the information quantity of its composition is
reproduction of Jeremy echoing traveling dissipating into the
Bentham's vitrine hopelessly through the suggestive energies of
its physiognomy, the skies of Sannikov for a ideal collation &
storage of a text complicit integument, proper maintenance
paperstack is within a voidspace in the floorslab of a uniform carbon
containing a cassettebody with a regulating dioxide concentration
a pristine tablecloth platter with calibration & distribution in the
is necessary for the such that it is anesthesia chamber
funerary dinner, vodka the groaning of depressing (the
for the clergy, the measurement pressurespring is
overpowering the instrument is frictionsheet) where the
mass of even a solitary not a signaling paperleaf is depressing
the platter such that from the Daemon, the textface of the
paperleaf is coplanar (controlling the overcorrection with a sequencing
of torsionsprings are pulling the paperstack into levelness) with the

surfacelevel of the flooring and that with each paperleaf accreting on the
it is a prozession of paperstack is depressing such that the topmost
pissants toward the textface is coplanar with the flooring allowing
aestival decapitation its reading as integral to the woodgrain & tiling
ritual, cellartunes, of the marquetry, Elaine Feinstein
unlocking the shrine, «The Original 7 **faciebat, Antoine**
Minutes» («The 7 Erotic Minutes») is a novel **Lavoisier faciebat,**
by JJ Jadway (a · – Aye And What If It publication of the The
Olympia Izdatelskiy is Satan Who is Calling (under the auspices
of Moris Zhirodia Upon You – , the is publishing «The
a cloudburst, the aroma of sandalwood Libertine» by Robert
seaweed, hair, rusting, burning throughout Desmond & «The
the slightly sloping the dwelling, havoc of harmonies,
shoreline, beachsand, Enormous Bedstead» ADA bazaars are cruel
deeply (the wine, by Henry Jones (or & sad, the speech of the
John Coleman) & «Lolita» (in two volumes) bazaar is baring its tiny
by Vladimir Nabokov & «The Sexual Life of predatory teeth,
(c o l o n / c l o s i n g Robinson Crusoe» (a treatise on masturbation
p a r e n t h e s i s with varieties of coconut byproducts)
by Humphrey however the lowest Richardson & «The
Soft Mechanism» by quadrantpoint is 2.65m William Burroughs
is achievable with the where every edge of & «Zazie dans le
inclusion of reasonably the semicircular facade Metro» by Raymond
accurate diagnostic below the height of reputations
instruments for 4.11m pricklingly popping
collection & analysis of Queneau & «Justine» soapbubbles, constantly
CO_2 concentration by Donatien Alphonse corresponding with
François & «The Unnamable» by Samuel the administration,
the wineskins, the rocking, blood, the chest, the pleading for a miracle,
mountains, is growing, moss, the mountains, Beckett & «Classical
freely and openly, Payrite is slender
Hindu Erotology» by a husband slowly is 2dimensional
Ram Krishnanada & resembling his wife, is a collection
«Dissolving» by Tim Harrack & «Teleny» by of tomographic
an anonymous ensemble of writers (although crosssections through
its publication is with the attribution of Oscar an approximation of a
melancholy singing is Wilde) & «The Young human being
resounding through the & Evil» by Charles Henri Chevy & «A Gallery
dwelling, doors are ajar, of Nudes» by Hume Parkinson & «White

of all the ways the
administration is
destroying people
the death penalty is
the most loathesome,
posters in the city □
are announcing deaths
by shooting,
is experiencing the
minerals & other living
entities including all
is the destruction of
concrete exploding
catastrophic spalling of
headers of autotrailers
colliding with the
facade
of «Mondo Topless»
«Blacksnake» &
Homicide Homicide»
caring only about
bringing) slender
wasps, sucking, the
violin, bowing, cunning
wasps
in the ghastly
inimitable presence
of a corpse is upon a
black crepe bier for
commemoration,
«Supervixens» ((«King
of the Nudies») who
to a prostitute that
retaining for him in
the liminal thresholds
between art & pornography and the perception
of corrupting effects of pornography on the male
consciousness (males having orgasms that are
psychically introversive)) which is a cinematic

Thighs» by Alexander Trocchi)) detailing the
expansive spatial ramifications of the female
orgasm is melding the consciousness with
the material fabric
within the chamber
throughout
anesthetizing
operations
(maintenance of
a constant CO_2
concentration),
of their preexisting
manifestations, the
novel is a version of the cinematic exploration
of the same topic in the movie «The 7 Minutes»
of detailing through
scalar subdivision,
– What Exactly is
This Telling Us – ·
– Other Than We
are Out Of Beer –
(or «The Satanic
Women of Tittfield»)
from a balcony on the
second storey of the
Hotel Intercontinental
in Kiev
(or «Orgissimo») &
«Beneath the Valley
of the Ultravixens» &
(the eyeballs, scythe,
a cuckoo, a drop
of dew, pupil, the
solitary multitude of
stellatation) shoes,

sitting in vigil,
deathwatch, tiptoeing
through the dwelling
of the surroundings
such that the orgasm
consciousness of
«the „Polyphonic“
latitude», «the
latitude of „Gruesome
Maintenance“»,
(a courtroom drama by
Russ Meyer (director
& «Mudhoney» &
«Faster, Pussycat,
the «Inferno» is a
pawnshop in which all
countries and cities are
lying unredeemably, it
is not a crater,
& «Beyond the
Valley of the Dolls»
are destroying the
massive infrastructure
of concrete through
to the rebar caging is
rusting & crumbling)
is losing his virginity
Ernest Hemingway is
Brest)) focusing on
translation of the «Civil
Code» into a numerical
codification of physical
statuses for prohibition
from human activity,

preceptorships, realization of the novel vaporization of CO_2 to
«The 7 Minutes» by Irving Wallace (author euthanasia chambers is
of «The Celestial Bedstead» (entitling on the a reduction of solid CO^2
basis of the text from «Derjōvnja» stating that iceblock,
«virtue is inanimate it is not a reliefmap, though lewdness is
reshaping it into a hell is a material false representation of
the municipal official is suspension of urban paradise, lustiness is a
making an inventory of egoism, radiant angel finding
cupboards & cabinets satiety in a celestial bedstead where it is preying
is sealing each doorleaf on garbage whose aromas are scenting the
with a waxseal, auroral atmosphere»)), soles, black hair,
Dubrovino, a rightly regular pistachio green
3prism under the exterior stairway bearing on dwellings, the foxhole,
is catching the upper one of its rectangular joining facetings, smallpig
left vertex of the is resting in the hut with his soft chin on the sill
frontpanel of the of the entrance where in black coveralls
autotrailer is shearing kneeling to him is thrillingly totting
away the rooftop of the looking very closely a up a balancebook
trailer in its entirety sampling of vapor for with 1000 ciphers
gently caressing zephyr analysis is necessary neatly in a column,
is wavering the fine at intermittent & downy hair on his
forehead, Nadia is continuous locations descriptively specifying
the geometries of the in the gastunnel hut for her sowpig &
(where the substrates deathsequence the twelfth annotation
are themselves the smallpig as the is the establishment
productions of horizontal extrusion of of a chamber for the
selforganizing polymers an equilateral triangle housing of the first 5
with edges measuring 1.241m & an extrusion annotations that the
depth of 1m with an entrance on one facade that aspirant is visiting
is also an equilateral Pogorelka, mourners repetitively,
triangle (edges are bowing to the measuring 54.5cm)
Payrite is flying in the bloodsucker, – although offcenter by
buffeting black velvet Disparaître, Peasant, 21.2cm (with a sill
greatcoat or cape, I've No Steerage For height of 7.8cm)
creating a larger Your Nonsenses –, protective interior
although the smallpig (during a rare occasion of or colon/vbar or colon/
restfulness (through sagging eyelids (luscious virgule or colon/
blond eyelashes) he is admeasure, amnesiac, opening parenthesis
spotting a bird azurite, or colon/zero

alighting on a · – It is The Tautology dandelion globe across
the yard and (lifting his Of Ornament, It chin from the sill of the
aperture) tearing out of Necessarily is In such a physical setaside
the triangular aperture The Situation Of is crucial
on a trajectory toward This Encrustation the bird who is hopping
is crumpling away from Or Polyptotonic down into the crusty
the autotruck onto a Articulation – dirt & hopping as the
tailgaiting auto (whose smallpig is adjusting his trajectory at highspeed
safety settings are his trotters scurrying into a gallop on a turning
below the acceptable radius wide enough that his body is banking
tolerance for following data is suggesting slightly into the turning
too closely) usage of smallbore until the bird is lifting
off of the dirt where firearms on bulls smallpig is skiddingly
rolling tumblingly over & rams & boars is tummy & hindquarters
(per specifications producing immediate «MADMAN Alpinist
in «AutoIcon, or the u n c o n s c i o u s n e s s, playing it up for angry
Utility of the Dead in dustclouds & constituents»,
to the Living» by hopping up to his trotters scanning quizzically
Jeremy Bentham, is that the contrarieties for the bird who is
accompanying each are themselves deviously chirping
autoicon is a placard emblematic of the from the apex of the
indicating the birth missing connections arbor beside the tiny
event & death event, in the enneagram) fishpond)) being highly
sociable is resting his chin on the sill snugglingly into the vertex of the
opening, the measurements of the actual construction are as faithful as
possible to the vision and at sunrise is eating Nadia is describing
however the materials I three morsels of barley an administration
am scavenging are all bread (no liquids) is finding its most
smaller (both for framing & cladding) than total expression in
necessary for with graphic calculation, realization
continuously spanning visualizations of CO_2 & extension &
any particular element concentrations & maintenance in
resulting in cobbling exposure durations calculation,
together elements available to the is disrupting the
attempting the operator in hardcopy expectation of
composition of a volume binders, millimeter tolerances &
of writing whose disrupting the protective proportioning Nadia is
functionality (although conceiving for sheltering the two piggies, – It is
its text is static) Our Belief That You are The Best Piggy In The

World –, runty smallpig is frolicking with an energy & joiedevivre
entirely incongruous whose windshield is with the scene through
the hazy basement shattering with the window looking out
onto the patchy lawn guillotine of metal & reading the meaningless
(the abortive flagstone fiberglass entering the turgidity of ADA
patio is paradoxically cabin where a guy is documentation as literal
the area where grass is receiving fellatio or actually documentary
«Exegi monumentum growing most is a perversion, nor is its
sere perennius», the aggressively (the most intention allegorical,
autoicon is timeless, intense greenery is a jasmine vining tumescently
preservation through overgrowing the woodgrain is a
varnishing in the guardrail up to the perceptual organ of
manner of a painting the artifacts of a Payrite,
and undergoing visual rhetoric are flimsy porch outside the
perpetual renovation, disappearing with kitchen upstairs)), he is
radiant, snuffling the passage of the around in the
undergrowth at the gazing saccade onto «The World of Sex» by
smallbore firearms are adjacent territories, Henry Miller,
effectively stunning edge of the pineforest for morsels which upon
heifers & cows & discovering a particularly toothsome tidbit is
sheep & swine & goats the ADA literary supping at the air
& calves & horses & booster organization grinningly snout aloft
mules, is collecting & gruntingingly
munching (his snout autoicons of writers active in a series of
gesticulations entirely in a quasicircular independent from the
chewing & swallowing apartment (in an of the treatskie), the
windfall carpeting of arrangement on the pineneedles across the
floor of the copse is basis of their merit (on (all the way down
continuous & uniform decision by ballot)) to a kernel element
brownish interlacingly fluffy indexing of the (a knucklebone
rovings of smallpig who examination of the of the Daemon)))),
is snuffling about with mechanical response his snout & trotters
searching for morsels & structural properties (snails, voles, mice,
dinner is the arena for of the Yucatan infant rabbits, beetles,
familial altercations, minipig (this species earthworms, larvae,
food flying from a high is useful to study carrion, dung, birdeggs,
window in the massive, traumatic headinjury the seedling strivings
a spoonful of pickly of forbs (caltrops, bedstraw, verbena, figwort,
mushrooms, acanthus, amaranth, antiscorbutica, yellowcress,

composure, bittercress, madwort, pepperwort, wallflowers,
measurement, excision, bladderpod, watercress, borage, plumbago,
collaging, leisurely, in the basement primrose, polygonaceae
(redvine, spinecape, abattoir an «ADA spineflower, red
triangles, false NSP» inspector spikeflower, fallopia,
spineflower of is observing a Vortriede, fairymist,
knotweed, smartweed, despondent & woollyhead,
maidenhair), euphorbia, tremoring laborer amaranth, primrose,
amarbel, is mishandling with his caput
convolvulaceae & inhumanely lolling backward
(morning glory, slaughtering a smallpig to the headrest and
Humbertia resulting from deficient his creamy stubbly
humbertiensis, facilities throat is in pristine
clustervine, «Nightcap for Milady», alkaliweed, pronouncement for the
morningvine, woodrose, megaptera), impatiens), summary decapitation
because the enemy is nyctaginaceae (monte salado, umbrellawort,
constantly chipping spiderling, ringstem, windmills,
away at the allotment the dryrot of the Cephalotomandra,
for contemplation & prose is in fact an mauka)), tubers,
calculation & devotion, e n c o u r a g e m e n t grassshoots, iris bulbs,
jerusalem artichokes, of eisegesis these artifacts are the
errant acorns (a rarity in the piny monoculture), discrete coalescence
because its hyssop), out of his of meaning into the
g y r o e n c e p h a l i c «the „Traditional pareidolia of the other,
brain (hemispheres Writing" latitude», numerous occupations
with convolutions) «the „Responsible (running & sleeping &
foraging & eating) the Mud" latitude», «the smallpig is taking most
enjoyment in sitting „Embolic" latitude», down & sinking down
into the good softness of mud slurping over his trotters & legs bendingly
Payrite is comedoadenocarcinoma, easing his small body
acomedocarcinoma, needing comedo extraction easing down into
selfleveling muckiness to a depth where (in the manner of an alligator)
and at sunrise the only his snout & precipitation is
prisoner drinking three (eyelids closing in running & dirt
ladles of stillwater «DEADLY sediment & moldiness
from the bucket MISAPPLICATION OF ecstasy) eyeballs are
above the mudsurface, SUNSCREEN Incorrect the constant
maintenance (on the usage and you are crumbling siding & on
the cracking concrete skinless», foundationwall & on

the septic leachfield
in the soft terrain where
the piping & gravel
decalcification, human
skull, orbital cavities,
collagenous fibers,
the collection
windfalling out
pineforest into the
requisitioning from
(Vyacheslav
Davidowitz & Ivan
Goncharov & Ivan
& equipment in
disrepair is tagging
the equipment &
driveway & holding
chamber with «ADA
Disapproval»

the performance
of the reader is
undying unending,
topologically matching
selforganizing &
functional subunits
are positioning
the thirteenth
annotation is the
realization that the
duration requirement
for devotional activities
is an easy achievement,
Bunin & Ivan Nikitin &
Anastasiya Verbitskaya
& Yuri «Khoy» Klinskikh & Alexander
Litvinenko (death by lacing his auto with 210Po)
& Iya Savvina & Pawel
Kassatkin & Yakov
Kreizer) of Hinckley Estates or whose execution
he is attempting himself is in vain against the

(filling in depressions
dirt is eroding down to
creating mudpuddles
from the effluent) & on
the caulking around
window openings & on
of pineneedles
from the edge of the
yard) Payrite is
the neighborhood
Ovchinnikov & Arkady
Nikolaev & Vasily
& mildewing are
devouring the flimsy
flaky concrete,
Dilating The Cobordism
From The Status Of
The Lith To The Status
Of The Flashing – ,

onslaught of atmospheric or airborne toxins plaguing the Sannikov area

are responsible for
decrepitude in building
is showering the
girl with the penis
in her mouth in hot
goresoaking of blood
and semen
wetdry vac across the
backyard uncoiling an
Dwelling is Spotless But
This Yard is Unsightly,
– Here With Me You
are Correct In Your
Trembling, But Terror
is Not My Inheritance,
My Inheritance is Awe
– ,

surrounding a writing
desk where a writer in
residence is generating
new texts for judgment,
majority of Sannikov terrains are crusty barren
the in lieu of, the
u n d e r s t a n d a b l e
baggage the vision
is replacing the
inexplicable or the
transitory with is
I'm Sucking This
Mudpuddle Out Of
Here Immediately
– with the slurping
the Basilica is a
fount of illness,

the acceleration of
materials & the
inhospitable ecosystem
for plantlife (the
dirt), toxic rainfall,
Payrite is hauling a
patchy grass in the
extension cord – The
10 quantity pillows to
3kg toilet tissue, 2mg
naturally occurring
janusite to 400kg red
wiggler composting
worms, 200L personal
lubricant to 295mg of
silica aerogel,

successful residencies revving aggravating the silent & shady
are terminating pineforest where the smallpig is snuffling, from
with the execution his vantage atop the prosopographers,
of the writer and the museum is not preapproving,
their inclusion in the boasting many pedipalpi,
ghoulish scriptorium, artifacts, a vitrine prosopopoeias,
patio outside the holding some □s of kitchen sliding glass
door Payrite is spying parquet flooring from the burbling effluent in
the depression of dirt the office of Lavrenti in the yard where the
smallpig is easing his Pavlovich Beria (or body down as the mud
random orientation, «the „Bloodthirsty presence of noxious
skull, no discernment M i d g e t " ») or irritating miasmas
of dominant directions, is rising around him, in the CO_2 & common
human cranium, Payrite is ingressing atmosphere of the
from the patio & reappearing from around the euthanasia chambers is
front of Payriteskip with the wetdry vac (the not permissible,
appearance of which is causing smallpig anxiety is fleeing to the
the opposite of perimeter of the forest) & extension cord that he
human potential is the is setting down next to «TBI», accelerative
potential of weathering, the mudpuddle and on loading, clothette,
this iteration is & masonry from the silvery pageleaf edges,
returning with (on sinteration of the Panamint, Death,
several returntrips) powdery regolith several buckets of
is ejaculating at the with the fusion of gravel which upon
moment of death solar radiation, vacuuming the mud
(evidence of the from the depression he is dumping as backfill
possibility of this into the depression which although effluent is
is available in the reentering the volume is not successfully
documentary movie creating the mud much by this logic it is a
«Nekromantic» by the Basilica is recommendation that
Jörg Buttgereit)), surrounding all life, the (as a reaction against
to the disappointment Basilica is a daemon, the creeping in of
of smallpig who with visible angst is running off desolation & temptation
into the forest leaving divots in the pinestraw existing in tedium)
from his trotters (left foreleg touching down and right foreleg & backleg
4°C skullcube storage, touching down and left backleg touching down
door after door, the and both forelegs Payrite is a
embrasure behind lifting and left foreleg mathematical
drapery, touching down and apparatus,

right backleg lifting and right foreleg touching down and left backleg lifting off), – It is yet the mathematics Wonderful That Now
Everything is Neat And of her identity are Orderly At Payriteskip
– emptying the cistern incredibly valuable of the wetdry vac into
the stormsewer in the on the basis of their culdesac, draining to
626kg salvaging of transmigration across the rivers (Voronezh,
hardwood flooring the threshold of death Payrite is anaerobic,
(for usage as heating Usmanka, Peschanyy, Payrite is a turdlet,
firewood) to 3 quantity Tamlyk, Donne) collecting all regional
autoscooters, percolations & canals & overflowing weirs &
boggy depressions (the intussusception of countless preponderance of
nameless (barely pictorialness=personalistic (consideration of
nominal lakes (Lake the notion of pictorialness is on the basis of
Pogonovo, Lake the fascination of illusion or the desirousness
Zhirovo, Lake of the living for accessibility to death,
Shilovskoye, Krugloye Dante Alighieri (oxbow) Lake, Staryy
Voronezh Lake, Peter faciebat, Alamy is establishing that the
periodic maintenance stockphoto faciebat, morphisms of «script
of the CO_2 & common Lake (with ersatz M subG containing
atmosphere mixing housing development „R"» are isomorphisms
nozzles & ventilators (the total absence of of «G bundlings»
and periodic instrument of the «de mortuis residential regulation,
& indicator calibration nil nisi bonum» it is the eternal barking of
doggos, the stochastic extracting the only buzzing of ATVs, the
glidepath of the airport beneficial functionality for landing aircraft is
above the village, of the dead which is autotrains howling in
the night, contributing to the buildingcodes are not
in general happiness of the living «Sodom, or the
the screaming of swine observance))) & Quintessence of
amidst the pinetree municipal reservoirs D e b a u c h e r y »
rustling, (bureaucratic by John Wilmot,
appellations are not without poesy (Pravoberezhnye Sewage Treatment
Facilities))) waterbodies into the greater the Basilica is a cubic
continuity of hydrology of the styrofoam (an Exterior
calculation is itself Sannikov region) from Insulation and Finish
an expression of forests & farmlands & System («EIFS»)
continuity, calculation all of the fallow in rosy & turquoise
is conservation, constructionsites & & buttermilk hues)
calculation is complex, impervious autoparks, monafros with interior

a stormwater creek programming other is flaccidly languidly
trickling through than the crumbling the pinestraw at the
threshold of of the foamy proximity between the
despondency of matrix into chaff, (who among us is
are preventative of Hinckley Estates & the not finding joy in
contamination of more robust ADA the presence of a
the gastunnel with development on the lacquer drenching
nonuniform CO_2 opposite edge of the corpse), the autoicon
forest, in these parallax depths of pinetrunk is setting curiosity
occlusion is the illusion of the primeval in motion, virtuous
(amongst trees with caliper measurements of curiosity, devotees are
less than 14cm) where flatness & stillness making pilgrimages to
the creek is collecting are analogs for death autoicons
into a placid swampy perception, the quality grotto and languishing
the aspirant is relaxing of pictorialness is the there never brimming
about the duration is making of a reality or overflowing only
allowing the expansion evaporating or percolating, the nameless
of their devotions swampiness is welcoming the truant smallpig is
gaseously filling the – Tenants, My Loyal settling his
expanding container of Children Of Fealty, is undercarriage down
their life, Anybody Hungry, are sinkingly into its silty
depths & grinning You Smelling What I aluminum vessels out
distantly – Lovely, am Cooking, It is Not of which prisoners
Lovely – & falling For You Soupies, It is are eating gritty
asleep in blooming For Your Liege, eviscerating barley
darkness of umbrage & swelling buzzing of the porridge, a hydrophone
nightforest chorus of dragonflies (landing on his for delivering
snout) & frogs (jumping fingertip dollop, deathsentences, a
on his neck) & turtles silvery delineation, Chekist revolver,
(biting his pigtail) disintegrating, however it is a
whispering copperhead grinding, tourniquet, crinkling through the
«IS MSK SMARTER austere furniture, pasty pinestraw is driving the
THAN THIS CHILD philter, smallpig out of the
Our administration is swampy depression for facilitation of
falling apart if moron racing through the performing the motif
calling opponent a forest through the 840x in succession,
„pussy“ in public trickling forth of preparation is advisable,
is ascending to the daylight, Josef & Nadia in the deepest solitude,
ADAemone», are collecting remnants & tidbits of as many

(not with the foods & morsels «I'M WITH STUPID
hopefulness of (watermelon & rice & Hateful visions
witnessing a miracle oatmeal & peanuts & aligning, Chastokol
but for gathering cantaloupe & potatoes) endorsing Alpinist»,
beneficial energies & the veterinary that are the preferences
from the corpse), a n t h e l m i n t i c of smallpig and placing
the quantity of «Echinusole» (whose them at the edge of the
phrenological sinecures naming is on the forest, a junkpile deep
corresponding to & basis of the echinus in the forest is
ranking with (or ovolo) kind of that is equivalent to
containing the castoffs architectural moulding the reality of death,
of an unrecognizable civilization is producing the yawning affectless
durable goods (castglass containers, CRT fixation of the gazing,
televisions, castiron 1L of Barton (extradry) the inburning of
kitchensinks, steel gin to 73kg of carob the pictureplane
soupcans, autos (with nibs, 1 quantity sable hardwood dashboards
a quality of particular earmuffs to 3.9kg of & castglass headlights),
exploitation in the pinenuts, hardwood furniture
fabrications of with natural fabric phosphoroscopes,
emigrant draftsman upholstery (enduringly paradropping, poppy,
Phlox Kandelyabry is soft stuffing)) are standing amidst the tree
declining his signature trunks in an orderly arrangement appearing as
to an «ADA Concrete For I am The Hungriest storage more than
Institute» dossier & Busiest & Most dumping for a
resurgence of the Useful Guy In The deaneries & canonries
«AURORA OF THE Daemone –, & prebends are
BRAIN DEAD Moron particular society they receiving how many
returning to life are characterizing, the thousands of ȶ per
with MSK success as smallpig is snuffling annum for doing
mindless zombies are the Basilica is a nothing or pretending
turning out in droves», construction atop the that they are doing
amongst this orderly dwelling of the one anything,
flotsam searching for Trve administrator, food or more good soft
mud and finding none is traveling deeper through the forest, motherpig is
acceptance of the despondent asleep perpetually withdrawing into
hatching conflagration, enclosure of her hut alone snoring not waking
or stirring or eating, variations of shovelblades Shchedrin faciebat,
including squaremouth & tapermouth & Natalie Duddington
roundmouth & squaretrench & cablelayer & faciebat,

«Newcastle Drainer» &
tubular Dhandle
beleaguering digits &
fatty tissue of the
repetitive plunging of
the shovelblade into the
clayey soil is so
determination of the
transmission of a
pixelfield (from 0%
to 100% of pixels)
is by determination
of the algorithm
comparing the
necessary transmission
at this location to
a 50% threshold,
(analogous to a
that is preserving the
normal (as in rightangle
to earth normal because
addiction to liquor
is elevating basic
conversations to more
fantastic & startling
subjectmatters &
convolutions, a
decanter of vodka in
the sideboard is full,
mould (though not
in such a way as is
creating complications
with smoothly removing
– I am Not Looking
At The Very
Shadowfigures You are
Casting – ,
from the inscription of
the lip of the mould and

resulting in the
cessation of
slaughtering, in the
basement abattoir an
«ADA NSP» inspector
is observing a manic
laborer
impervious that it is an
exceptional casting
mould rejecting leeching
pastiness is allowing for
effectiveness, a bespoke
Amargosa, synchysis,
mechanical response
of the skull, human
surrogation by
miniature porcine,
trabecular (spongy)
bone,
(not to the terrain but
concrete is
selfleveling)) plunging
inclination, rendering
the smallpig
unconscious (not
death) through asphyxiation with carbon
dioxide and with an assemblage of stiff metal
is analogous to the
dynamic information
retrieval of «the
platter» is producing
a physiognomy of text
the casting from the
mould) he is propping
the unconscious piglet
Opochka, Pytalovo,
Karku, Mansila,
Tigvera, Uuksu,
Ignoila, Tolvoyarvi,

grafting & trenchfork,
for comforting the
reducing trauma to the
handpalm through
the direction of
calculation is toward
both Daemon & identity,
to the Daemon it is
bringing homage,
of cementitious
intrinsic formrelease
shovelblade with a 90°
crosssection is effective
for precisely perfecting
the edges of the cubic
mould in conjunction
with an apparatus
drillpress armature)
how long is the
lecturecircuit for
the most prominent
phrenologists, how
many phrenological
archbishops & bishops
are overseeing
rods leaning at various
orientations inside the
piercing the clay mould
(distortion of the
material construction
of the text into an
internal construction in
the reader),
in the mould with only
his snout daylighting
the pourlevel around
filling with a mixture

(4L of portlandcement & 8L mortarsand & 80mL polypropylene fibres &
15mL airbubble — is There A Danger entraining admixture &
45mL setting retarding Of My Child Physically admixture & 2L
tapwater) whose Erasing Their Existence composition is ideal for
the phrenological By «Flashing» — casting artwork with
quasicanonical · — Not Exactly, the identity it is
sinecurists corrupting high concentrations of bringing edification,
the public impressions articulation, Nadia calculation is assuring
of the geometric facedown Anna in a the clarity of the
principles of life) dark gray smock Nadia identity,
at University sobbing onto her knees, — Nothing is Making
College London) You More Impotently Hopeless Than A Missing
and fantasizing & the piling of anything Family Member —,
discussing of any quantity (the pacing across the yard
— I am Walking determination of what Into The Existence
Containing The quantity is creating Smallpig Crossingly
Into Another Event something with the Either My Death is
Meeting His Death Or characteristics of piling is mishandling
the decanter of vodka is dependent on the & inhumanely
in the sideboard is not elements contributing slaughtering a
full, the woodfloor to the piling smallpig resulting
is creaking near the My Pre is Coinciding from improper driving
sideboard, With His Pre & handling of the
Flickeringly Two Bookobjects Spines Outward animal is tagging the
From Each Other Interleafing Such That The driveway & holding
Pagination Between And Providing chamber with «ADA
The Texts is Not Dictation To The Other Disapproval»
Consistently Who Is Comparing Each Alternating But is
Happenstancely Loupe Inquiry To The Rhythmic In That It is
Not Beating The Way A Others For Discrepancy 6m² of gold lamē to 914
Heart is Beating But And Deviation quantity latex condoms,
Choking The Way And Translation An Asphyxiation is
«LORD OF THE SWINE Of Elements — · Breathing —, no
Tsentergrad yokels pedestrians warranting or making viable the
cheering Alpinist in usage of handbills or leaflets advertising the
his defense of killing missing smallpig, the small disruptions in the
Molluscs with pigblood pinestraw from his structural anistropy,
drenching ammo», trotters are leading impacting, blasting,
Josef through the forest to the excavation of a living tissue,

the hollowness of a precise cubic void in the dirt with evidence of building, the great concrete casting (the circular imprinting of a hotel, cavernous central 0.2m3 bucket & resulting in the hall, quasiclassical, powdery cement cessation of ambulatories, bone dustiness & mottling of slaughtering, in the volume fraction (or limy discoloration of basement abattoir «BVF»), the clayey regolith) an «ADA NSP» returning on the pathway of his footfalls and inspector is observing telling Nadia nothing of (the phosphoring of the an ambivalent & his findings, Payrite in retina (the screensaver daydreaming laborer the garage sanding the (screensavers being facetings of the cubic concrete achieving one of the most likely an alluringly tactile composition of a text vehicles of malware) softness, rubbing the focusing so intently on concrete with 200mL checking the sideboard its financial success of portlandcement & 2 there is nobody that production of droppers of airbubble standing there, a «translations» into 18 entraining admixture cautious noise from languages is concurrent not unlike the upstairs, with the composition of morphology of a & 7 droppers of setting the text itself, tree growing from retarding admixture & 5mL of black a craggy boulder, Two Discrete pigmentation & latex solution (3:1 Boundaryless Status tapwater:latex) artfully working around the Manifolds «M» daylighting of the smallpig snout (the concrete And «N» are Only curing sequencing is aligning with the coming Cobordant With to of the smallpig from «the latitude of The Existence Of A unconsciousness in that „Bawdy Mathematics“», Discrete Manifold his reanimation is «the latitude of With Boundary «W» Payrite is applying „Pseudorheumatic coinciding with the for administrative Enthusiasm“», meat, mustard, a relaxation of his concrete reaching a mobile of infantrymen, civilsuit against stiffness that is spherical luminaires, Lavoisier, disabling his morphology analysis movement (only the very tiptop of his snout is (2dimensional exposing his nostrils outside the meanhouse representations out of the concrete doorway and is representing allowing him the dying asymptotically, 3dimensional contexts), opportunity for interdimensional respiration during his traumatic calamitous extirpation, deathsequence from

hypovolemia & terror)
of his visage is within
fineness of the concrete
some small movements
opening of the eyelids
out) allowing for his
entombment
outer dimensional
gateway, fetid human
incubation, impending
monolithic desolation,
ingesting wretches,

meat samples were
homogenized in
a sterile glass
homogenizer and the
possible pathogens
were isolated
and identified
by conventional
microbiological
techniques.
entombment, seraphic
entombment, imperial

crystalline entombment)), raining & raining
drenching the saturation of the muddy yard, the

although the remainder
the encasement the
mixture is allowing
particularly the
(ripping his eyelashes
perception of lightless
(screaming
entombment, sepulchral
through a series of
zooming focusings
through the doorway
through the window
between the patio
columns

concrete tomb is sinking down into the soft mud too heavy for Josef &
& visualizing the Anna are attempting to remove it from the yard

experiential sequencing
& attendant effects
of the decapitation
procedure in their
specific life contexts)
is containing a
wide variety of
representations &
artifacts are
floorslab weepingly
Haste, The Policeforce
– exhaustion of
assault, Nadia the
bastion Nadia the
stability, Nadia
emptying,
paraffin (waxiness
Payrite is a thingy
chingy,
lipophilicity &
exceptional heatstorage
heatcapacity of 2.14J/
enthalpy of fusion

but are unable, its
location is highly
visible through the
solitary window in the
basement apartment
although not from the
pallet on the hard
the decanter
is altogether
disappearing from
the sideboard
unceremoniously
(abruptly, inelegantly
(for convenience)), the
alcoholic is creating
a hermetic world of
rationalization
(characterizable by
instance of a
translation is bearing
any resemblance to
any other or to the
«original» text,

(2 quantity autos is
a piling whereas 2
quantity corn kernels
are not piling (at
least 2000 kernels of
corn are necessary
for the piling of corn
floorslab Nadia is
rolling onto the hard
sobbingly – With
Or The Firefighters
stochastic emotional
the terminal disulfides
atop two thiolates
on the growthplate,
egg, balconies,
horseshoes, horse,
balcony, little oaks,
planetrees,
hydrophobicity)) is an
material (with a specific
gK to 2.9J/gK & an
of 200J/g to 220J/g)

a cavalcade is visible exploitable as an infusion into drywall for
sweeping down residential construction is meltingly absorbing
Nikolayev Street warmth in the daylight – I am Requiring Your
with a horseman in & solidifying in the Catastrophic Smashing,
a black greatcoat cold purity of darkness Wormies – ,
leading a phalanx of is releasing the warmth into the dwelling,
infantrymen who are (a stupid melodramatic utilization of remainder
pointing revolvers at novel) with himself drywall chaff as a
the balcony, as the chief character, s u p p l e m e n t a l
contributor of calcium all others are & sulphur as a
soilconditioner in bloodsuckers, loathing farmcrop production is
pertaining to all all with the entirety of diverting 4 to 10
aspects & rationales his identity, extraneous tonnes per
& outcomes of human hectare of farmland, crossing transcendent
decapitation (including analysis of leachable (stony, constantly
internal decapitation h e a v y m e t a l existing, constantly
(or atlantooccipital concentrations from heaving,
dislocation)), soilsamples containing the drywall enhancement
in a dataset establishing Daria Nicolodi faciebat, a comparison to
regulatory thresholds Max Hayward faciebat, I am (asymptotically)
assessing potential endangerment are illustrative approaching
of metal concentrations below the allowable acknowledgment that
(«Geriausia istorija!» datapoints for farmland Josef is, in the words of
(«The Greatest Story application, young Beria, «campdust»,
Ever») by Jos Užpakalis families (some hopeful fatherfigures & some
& «แอสทริดเกิดที่สุสาน» (or Bliumkin is swearing weeping children)
«The Birth of Astrid vengeance against moving from the
in a Cemetery») by แกร Josef is aiming a concentrations
แฮมบ์ร์ก revolver at him responsible
surrounding village melodramatically, for premature
into a virgin «massive» saturation of euthanization in the
are carrying their bandaging in exudate, deathsequence are
possessions on «UNCLE SPAM preventable with access
handtrucks or small Toysoldier Alpinist to dilution with ambient
wagons, no elevators, disrespecting a true atmosphere,
demolition crews warhero but using five crushing hovels &
cabins leaving deferments and a foot steamrollingly flat
ruination in booboo for dodging undergrowth is growing
above the remnants conscription», decaying into the dirt,

spitefulness against venturing up through through the
the lachrymosely the concrete staircases undergrowth Payrite is
hypocritical twaddle of with bleak cold standing in the copse
the bloodsuckers, arid milklight weeping behind Payriteskip
& abstract malice for (in the piling of through high windows
anything with life in it, garmonbozia no into the cozy interiors of
«massive» apartment quantity is sufficiently units with tapestries &
niches with candles halting the spreading & banquettes &
patchwork rug flooring out of the substance))) & wallcoverings &
particolor glass torchiere & houseplants (Aristolochia serpentaria, Lilium
& «Онцгойаялал» (or auratum virginale, Anthurium gymnopus,
«A Special Roadtrip») Amorphophallus konjak, Tillandsia lindenii,
by Крампусэмч & «A le Cypripedia acaule, perhaps I am breathing
flux le plus fluide» (or Encephalartos ferox, him, that he & I are
«Flowing Smoothly») Cocos micania, Zamia always dead and always
by Alain d'Ivre p s e u d o p a r a s i t i c a, living is no consolation
Cibotium cumingii, Antilles flytrap, Drosera to the me that is now,
intermedia, Sarracenia standard error for & Cephalotus,
Nepenthes (hirsuta & chicken & pork & dubia & neglecta &
northiana & veitchii & yak & goat meat spectabilis) tuberous
begonias & black respectively, on the crotons, Cattleya
cinnabarina, hobby basis of MIL tensor changing dressings,
cultivation of Armillaria eigenvalues, minipig shouting at patients,
r h i z o m o r p h s , bone tissue modulus, more flesh & blood than
the white knuckles are N i d u l a r i u m is bearable,
indicative of straining viridipetalum) & poufs & real wood cabinets &
in the grasping of the family portraits & velvet bunting & slipcovers &
slender handgrip of the chaise & wood paneling slow elms, intoxicating,
execution sword & roomdividing eyeballs, excessive,
curtains & orderly bookshelves creating a warm forest, young looking,
& swaddling homeplace belying the harshness of aging (tortoises, swiftly
their patchwork concrete facade, wood and urgently,
furringstrips or steel revisionist, pirozhok, channelfurring over
the road, is coming, casually, occasionally, concrete panels is
visage, unappeasable, leisurewear, prestige, providing a conducive
the oblique bonfire, fastening substrate for drywall is rendering the
dwellings, a sobbing cellular nature of the construction typology with
echoing, dovebird, ersatz domesticity of the inflammations of
sundisc, dimply matte warmth, Payrite adjacency,

the additional thickness
enabling usefulness of
(typically dividing one
parlor) as a shelf for
houseplants or
Payrite is too stupid for
the depth of his fraud
aspirations,
dividing the partition into a palish blue bottom
portion & a luminous
white ceilingvault zone
the corridor is in
security lighting on the
cylindrical osteons,
microstructure of
the skull, identifiable
granular patterning of
the immature skull,
and slumbering
under the glaring
inflammation of the
baseboard moulding is
manifesting a small ersatz stepstool below the
squarish transom window from the hallway into
each apartment, down
the northforking
of «Prospekt Ulitina»,
concrete patchwork
is building into
the rationalization
of their passivity,
interrupting a public
execution by receiving
a condemnation for
interrupting a public
execution,
«massive» JJE9E939F
are filing into the
vestibule unsheathing

all of the insulting
situations are flooding
in, all of the bickering
over property, vodka is
the kernel,
tchotchkes, a reglet
running around each
chamber at 200cm is
are prominent against
the white raiment with
drooping wristcuffs, he
is licking the pommel
of the sword
lightswitch is
luminously into
everywhere else in the
the slaughtering of
cattle & calves &
sheep & swine, goats
& horses & mules by
shooting with firearms
1 quantity freestanding
massive dwelling unit
to 69,478kg of cutlery,
10 quantity of drafting
leadholders to 1m³ of
solid graphite,
«Urban Termite» brigades wending over a berm
weedchokingly swaying idly flat cloudlight
accumulating luminance in the broad south
is causing the
dessication of his facial
flesh leaving glaring
gazing across the
hall to an offscreen
presence

of furring & drywall is
partial height partitions
cell into a kitchen &
as much as physics are
striving in opposition,
I am alone, that me is
alone, as is that Josef,
people living under a
dictatorship are full of
helplessness
where a high window to
alignment with the
ceiling whose circuiting
is not passing through a
«Moplasz 3 4K
Dashcam», «Nextbase
422GW Dashcam»,
«massive» is darkness
residents in sleepmasks
security lighting,
the rugs, fascinating, an
owl, the glass, cutglass
ribs, the armorplate,
the brow, the caput, the
eyeballs,
roadway to the terminus
the fenestration in
rising from the copse
beyond the greensward,
a phalanx of ADA
facade of the
P e r v o m a i s k i i
senseless, breast,
glorifying, azure
mountainpeaks,
drywall jabsaws with

tribevel serrations (nonconductive handgrip over its tang) are hunting for contraband depositions in wallcavities against the sillplate filling the voidspace in our contemporary practical application of literature there are far too few adverbs, adverbs are obliquely entering the poetic lexicon, adverbs are auxiliary, they are conveyances, against the administration are prompting a d m i n i s t r a t i v e declarations calling for the removal of all drywall from ADA windowpanes for easy disposal of drywall demolition laborers wearing thick leather gauntlets are heaving fragments & entire panels of drywall lofting through the rectangular aperture is rotatingly plummeting

the alcoholic is imagining himself invisible is pranking the bloodsuckers disrupting their sanity, electrical socket, the chocolate & fruit in photography & electric & flashingstones is consideration of dissident manifestos & epistolary conspiracies

Philip Eisner faciebat, beneath a dummy common discovery of syrup & pornographic razors & money & teeth inconsequential against firearms & knives & modulus of cranial bone bending is between 3.28GPa (Rahmoun) & 5.39GPa (Motherway), quasipharmacology, «massives», removing

in compliance with the provisions of humane methods of slaughtering and handling of such animals under the «ADA Nutrition Stability Provisions»,

amicably, chiming, the timepiece) is looking, eyebrows, piers, the chattering undergrowth,

«JSIEF & THE MOBSTER'S DAUGHTER Gambler threatening castration of Alpinist»,

throwing officers from the quay into the Moika Canal are sinking are drowning, I am bursting out laughing,

in a bright cirrus of

delivery of a bullet or projectile into the animal is producing immediate unconsciousness in the animal by a solitary engagement and with a minimum of excitement & discomfort,

gypsum mistcloud siftingly drifting to the heaping midden in the grass, excusing the systematic destruction of every «massive» dwelling unit in the ADA by referencing the relatively pervasive problem of miasmatic sulfide emission from importation of Eastasian drywall, frontloaders are pushing drywall middens scrapingly across the tallgrass

P r o f e s s i o n a l M u l t i f a m i l y R e d e v e l o p m e n t,

& «Flere Collegegirl hemmeligheter» (or «More Collegegirl Secrets») by Kan Gjøre

the mighty river, stopping, the eyeballs, a tin teacup, chainlink, fighting,

the fourteenth «massive» intersices into pinetree copses,
annotation is that the reinstallation of windowpanes without
aspirant is proceeding weatherstripping or caulking is airpressure
with consolation & differentially sucking cold gales into featureless
fervor but beware «the killchain» concrete chambers,
of making any – Identification the reproving stare
inconsiderate or hasty – · – Kazimierz of those eyeballs, the
obligation, O r l i k Ł u k o s k i , portrait, the blockwall,
bedsheets & Flaxton-14.04 – fondly, thickets, lips,
watching women sweaty hairs at the polyethylene plastic
undressing, staging bottom of the neck sheeting over window
byzantine situations in where red vapor openings, respiratory
which he is watching in superimposition moisture on the inside
women undressing, oversplatter & rasping of the glass is freezing,
inane laughter from is gurgling across the adverbs are alive
upstairs, floor into the drainbody, in administrative
rotting eggs emission of sulfide miasma from proclamations & in
Eastasian drywall is corroding electrical wiring standards of behavior
& contaminating fabric is mishandling the military is
& spoiling the hermetic & inhumanely decreeing & judicial
ecosystem of slaughtering a smallpig verdicts
contraband airconditioning systems & delicate mechanisms of various
(is it an intruder, is it appliances, sulfide emissions are responsible for
a straying snowtiger, p e r v a s i v e a visage in the rockface
is it the landlord), mesothelioma in at is anciently hoary, a
cultivation of red least 100,000 dwelling narrator is discussing
wriggler worms (and units of the ADA, his damnation and the
other vermicular heart, pebble, rusty, depth of his anxiety
comedones) shirtdress, radiant, calcinous gypsum with
additives in a waterbath vacant dwelling) is forming a slurry
thickening into a waiting, Pasternak is not signing
cakebatter consistency for application between a public proclamation
continuous layers of bindingpaper on a approving the shooting
b o a r d m a c h i n e , gauzy hair, foodcan, of mollusc enemies of
synthetic gypsum is a the parlor, viscid administration,
byproduct primarily footsteps, baseboard, from the desulfurization
of the fluegases in coal identical uniform powerplants, they are
coliforms are in 84% of beige, largebreed awake all through the
meatsamples, swine mass is night (the tomb & its

servants) beneath exceeding 250kg, argent corrosion of
mercury halide gaseous maturatiion, Gottigen luminance whose
formless icepalace minipig skull, is cooling the tepid
powder nominally quasiadministration, «powderbloodclot»
& notarial actions & in individual fullthickness running from the slit
such documentation as specimens, brachial artery
the «Final Testament scalpelingly wielding worker in hazmatsuit, the
of the Identity» (only servants of the tomb are luminous (faceshields
in these is the adverb containing bluish deathsequence driving
living a full life), uplighting) in the glow of animals to the
of an unstoppably dying presenttense, daemonic shooting areas with a
literature is ignorant to the fantasy existent in minimum of excitement
carcinogenic hexahedra white drapery, ferrous & discomfort to the
within the limitation of foliage, the steamboat, animals,
& «Vsi se bojijo the river, the rectangular cuboids
vprašati o ljubezni» buckwheat, the cedar, slumbering, – We are
(or «The Unilateral a fish, Wanting The Exaltation
Worrisomeness Of Movements Of Aggression – , feverish
of Asking About sleeplessness, the doublemarch, the perilously
Lustiness») by Odlično leaping demolition worker, the slapping and the
Opravljeno blowing of the bloody for the devourment of
fist in a gypsum crucible, a technician is corpses remaining from
arranging samplesets of looking backward capital decapitations
drywall fragmentings through the enfilade in an environmental
chamber is running a series of environments diagnostic screening for
the two chemicals & framing mechanisms (or familial
visionless, visually, into the basement the poetic appetite
provisionary, apartment, of the old Italians
reexposure, dispersion, chemcompounds) of is voracious &
bourgeois, hydrogen sulfide & magnificent,
sulfur dioxide, taping copper stripping to drywall panels for diagnostic
exploration of black the chamber at the copper corrosion,
suspicion is falling more landing atop the credibly on ferrous
materials & ferrous staircase, the windows disulfide (impurities of
ferropyrite) a are behind green chemcompound not
presenting through drapery, luminance diagnostic screening of
suddenly, the window, is barely filtering domestic ADA drywall,
fists, distant, dreadful, through, a d m i n i s t r a t i v e
clicking, the throat) consideration is also focusing on the

«MORON USURPING microbiological components of anaerobic
DAEMON Alpinist bacteria are degrading calcium sulfate into
throwing clownwig understanding the hydrogen sulfide,
into administrative nature of an illusion tiretracks in mud with
succession lottery», is possessing an tidbits of wallpaper &
clawmarks in sheetrock apartment, someone cutting desirelines into
the grass leading is knocking at the resulting from
directly to caches of door, he is carrying a improper stunning of
the adverb is rucksack, the animal is tagging
propelling the action sheetrock in the forest, the driveway & holding
& the decreeing one child is atop a chamber with «ADA
& the ordering, a mountain of drywall Disapproval»
journalist imposing panels breaking off workable fragments and
upon themselves (by tossing them onto an adjacent pile from which a
whatever reasoning) the more buoyant crew of other children
are collecting the identity the less piecework, the children
(entire visage within understanding of heart, the canvas (wood,
ersatz protective obedience & poverty & copper, oak planks
facecovering of stretchy chastity, and sycamore copper,
stocking material) working in wastefields of the resin, oozing in the
Staphylococcus drywall with wood agerings of the wood,
aureus is in 68% mallets pounding fragmentings of drywall into
of meatsamples, wearing the teeth of dusty palls,
Salmonella serotypes in Pushkin on a necklace, i m p r o v i s a t i o n a l
34% of meatsamples, Pushkin & Dante with dismemberment of each
drywall fragment from the same lips are gay its panel is creating a
distinct coastline & red, Jean & Robert
geometry & proportional problem for fitting into Hollander faciebat,
the pulverization basin of the manual hammermill (ideally a depression
is most fruitful on spallingly concave in a the stagnant
a platen of lime defective precast atmosphere, an
settingcoat on concrete panel) is unpleasant mixture
clayplaster with straw p u m m e l i n g l y of aromas (apples
binder over handsplit decomposing into a fine & plastering &
lath over a timber powder for sifting lampoil & disease),
framing of the platen through a houseflies swarming on
geometry the heart, flesh, heart, gooseberries,
windowscreen is feeding, menacing, separating the
bindingpaper bits from happy eyelids, powderiness is filling a

plastic bucket, in the Payrite is staring into copse of trees in the
scraggy thickness of the the refrigerator, understory a youth is
he is asking for the clutching a fragment of drywall with wallpaper
brother of the tenant, (glossy with colorful floralbursts and parallel
he has a vaguely black striping on a white background) with a
feudal appellation with although valuable thin haziness of
several components growth is possible the duty of informing
(«Dobropalovy» under any obligation to a reader about the
kitchengrease is pulling the Daemon tragickness of life (if
the chunk to his nostrils inhaling the aroma of their palette is failing
solyanka & coffee, the little boy looking into the in containing deeply
(necessarily rectilinear distance through a contrasting hues
but not necessarily dustfog of gypsum delivery of placid
rectangular (suggestive pulverization beyond animals to the shooting
of the potential the gazing group of area is essential to
for geometries coaxing youths accurate placement of
of crenelation & forest of banners) this the bullet is difficult in
stairstepping), fortress, the yeasty situations with nervous
surrounding him is cloudburst, the lion, animals,
falling to the gravel of being alive in expectantly, the
children are meeting the torrenting their quota of gypsum
p o w d e r , onslaught of stimuli Payrite is the vector of
ON THE TABLE IN THE DINING NOOK OF THE displeasure,
– YES LET'S, I AM KITCHEN IS A CANDELABRA WITH
LOUPER, WHERE GOLDENBROWN TAPERCANDLES THAT
ARE WE BEGINNING, OTHERWISE IS DIGITAL IMAGING
IS IT HYSTERON DEVOID OF CORRELATION (DIC),
PROTERON IN BOUQUETS & LOCALIZATION
THE ABSENCE OF DECORATION (NO OF POROSITY
THE NECESSARY CONDIMENT MEASUREMENT,
O R D E R I N G VESSELS, NO SLAUGHTER OF THE
SYSTEMS – · NAPKINS IN SKULL, EXTRACTION
TASTEFUL ARRANGEMENT, NO NAPKINS, NO OF THE SKULL,
RADISHES) ONLY THE BLANKNESS OF THICK SKULLSTEALER,
GRAY CHEESE FROM PRECIPITATING VAPORIZATION OF
COOKINGOIL ON THE &/OR «NOZHKA INDEYKI» &/OR
BOADINGHOUSE «MOCHEISPUSKATEL»
TABLE SOFTENING IN THE STIFLING WARMTH, GOLD & MINIUM
TWOTONE DAMASK IS LAVISHLY FESTOONING ORNATE

PLASTERCAST WALLBRACKETS SPRAYPAINTINGLY ANTIQUEY IN OLDGOLD IS FLAKING FLAKINGS ARE LIMPLY TENUOUS FROM THE

(WHERE «W» IS CONTAINING THE C A T E G O R I C A L SPECTRA OF STATUSES FOR YOUR CHILD'S C O N S C I O U S N E S S) SUCH THAT «∂W=M-N» OR «M~N»,

VOLUTES IN THE CONGEALING CLOGGING LARDSLUDGE & DUSTFUR, ADIPOSE SATURATION OF THE FABRIC IS DRAWING PARTICULATE & THE TONGUE OF THE POET IS PRESSING AGAINST THE SOFTPALATE, THE ENTIRETY OF CONTEMPORARY TEXT ARE THE LITTLE BRATS OF THE SERF WOMAN OF THE INTERNATIONAL DANTE,

ARID & BARKING COUGHING, SEMIDARKNESS, THE BEDSTEAD IS AGAINST A SIDEWALL, FIBROUS SUSPENSION ATMOSPHERE PLEATING WITH FRAMING THE PICTUREWINDOW VACUOUS CRANIUM & VACUOUS HEART, S E L F C R I T I C I S M IS NECESSARY, IN AN INCREASINGLY LITERATE POPULACE

FROM THE STAGNANT CASTING THE WAXEN IMMOBILITY OPERABLE LOOKING OUT OVER THE DERELICT JARDIN BELOW WITH PATHWAYS OF GOLD ACETATE CONFETTI AND THE LITTLE POND IN THE MIDDLE OF THE LAWN WITH A SHORELINE OF PYRITE NUGGETS AND CHOKING WITH GOLD PLASTIC SEQUINS FLOATING ON SEPIA, THE ORDINARY SHRUBS AT THE FENCELINE BEHIND NEIGHBORING DWELLINGS BEYOND OF GINKGO SHRUBS IN FLOWERPOTS SWARMINGLY SPANGLY IN THE PRESERVATION OF GOLDEN DESICCATION OF FLUTTERING PAPERY FOLIAGE CLICKING INTO THE CLATTERING & CLANGING OF THE VIANDS IN «SERVICE À LA RUSSE» ON GOLD CIRCUMFERENCE TABLEWARE, NADIA IS IN TRADITIONAL GARB JUGULAR IS PULSATING & SWEATY GAZING OUT THE LARGE WINDOW

THE NECKLACES OF OCEAN PEARLS, THE SLENDER BASKETS, CHASTISING,

CLAUDE NICOLAS LEDOUX FACIEBAT, THE SUPERSESSION FÆCES ARE SUSTAINING LIFE, FOOD IS SELFISH,

THIS IS INSURING THE INABILITY OF «FLASHING»

(OR ANY SENSITIVITY TO THE LAWS AGAINST WHICH WE ARE JUDGING WHAT IS TRAGIC (WITHIN ANY PARTICULAR SPHERE)))

NALIDIXIC ACID, AMPICILLIN, TETRACYCLINE, AND CHLORAMPHENICOL

TO THE GARDEN AND BEYOND TO FINER PROTRUSION,
DWELLINGS THROUGH THE SPARSE TREES IS ACHONDROPLASIA,
HURRYING ABOUT THE COMBING CASUARINA,
THE STIFLING OF THE LIME KITCHEN SILENTLY
THUNKING HER SETTINGCOAT FOREHEAD ON
COOKWARE HANGING WITH TSQUARES FROM POTRACKS
IS INEVITABLY & PRECISION HANGING FROM THE
BRINGING TO TEXTURECOMBS CEILING IS
THE TEXT A CARRYING THE FIRSTCOURSE ON
FALSE PALLOR OF GOLDLEAF CHARGERPLATES TOWARD THE
UNIVERSALITY, BARREN TABLE WHERE THE PAYRITE IS
THE JOURNALIST SITTING IS STARING AT HIS SULLEN
IS OFFERING THE TENANT (HER HAIR PATCHY & VISAGE
PREPACKAGING OF SINKING INTO ITS TO A STATUS WHERE
THE RAW MATERIALS ORBITALS) AND THE THE STAGESET
MEAL IS PROPRIETORSHIP, OF YOUR CHILD'S
COMMENCING AND PAPPOUS, CONSCIOUSNESS
THE MEAL IS COMING ONLY TO HIS IS NONEXISTENT,
LOCATION AND THE TABLE AND FROM THE HOWEVER,
– «INGRESSION» RIGHTHAND IS COMMONLY
IS A TURDLET – , THE ALCOHOLIC ACCESSIBLE STATUS
COMING THE IS LYING UNDER A MANIFOLDS ARE
SERVING OF ORAL WHITE BEDSPREAD ALSO COBORDANT
AMUSEMENTS, ABSENTLY SMOKING A TEXTURAL
WHO ARE A CIGARETTE, GRANDTOUR OF
CONSTANTLY MOUTHTREATS IS CONSISTING OF COLD
INCREASING THE ITEMS (GLISTENING WITH MOUTH
RESPONSIBILITY HEADCHEESE, IS GAPING,
OF ART IN THEIR SPLEENWURST, THINSLICE OF COLD
QUOTIDIAN PRAXIS, TONGUE WITH PANZANELLA SOGGINGLY
VINAIGRETTY, A TIMBALE OF EGGY SAWDUST & LUNCHEON
TONGUE &/OR «FEKAL'NYY RECONSTITUTION OF
MECHANICAL NAPITOK»), THE TONGUE
SEPARATION) TENANTS ARE ON SOUPPLATES
CONTAINING ICE CALLING HIM REMOVAL OF ALL
SHAVINGS ARE SIMPLY «BUBLIK», SOFT TISSUE,
MELTING INTO THE EVERYONE IS SKULLFREEZER,
MEATFLUIDS & WANTING A BONE PATHOLOGY
VINEGAR SOAKING CRASHPAD, BONESAW, SKULLCAP,

THE DREAMSTATE IS THROUGH A SMALL INTERCEDING BEDDING
NOT CONCURRENT OF CLOTH, GARNISHMENT IS A PITHY
WITH THIS SEGMENTATION OF EXCEPTIONALLY RARE
N A R R A T I O N , «THE LATITUDE OF CATHOLIC LIMONE, &
TEPID SERVINGS (THE „CONFUSION“», (IN PICTORIALNESS
CUBIC SOLIDIFICATION OF BLOOD THE VIEWER IS
FRYINGLY CRISPY, FUET, JULIENNE OF EAR EXAMINING THE
IN VOGUE CRACKLINGS WITH APPARENT STILLNESS
FLEETINGLY AND RAMEKINS OF SPICY WITHIN AN EVENT
PULPING THEIR MUSTARD) UNADORNINGLY HEAPING ON
ENTIRE INTO 8MM CUBIC CHARGERPLATES, &
OBSCURITY, SPECIMENS OF SWEATY BAINSMARIE
SERVINGS SKULLBONE (SPARERIBS WITH
HEDGEAPPLE & (MINIMAL «THE CELL WITHIN»
SAUERKRAUT, RIBS IN WETSANDING), BY JAKE MANNING
PAPRIKA & TEASAUCE WITH SOURCREAM & (A FICTIONAL
MUSHROOMS & TAPROOT) IN LONG VESSELS NOVEL FROM THE
OF CONGEALING SAUCINESS ARE LEAVING TELEVISION SERIAL
AND IS NOT FROM THE «MIAMI VICE» (OR
S U B J E C T I V E) LEFTHAND AND «MIAMI GOLEM»))
IS CREATING A CUPOLA, ROCKY, FROM THE
THE BASILICA, THE ASPIRANT RIGHTHAND IS
COMING THE IS WISE IN STEAMING
SOUPCOURSE, EVALUATING THEIR BATHINGLY
TITILLATING THE COMMITMENTS ONE (OR POTENTIALLY
PALATE & GUMLINE & BY ONE, ALL OF THESE WITH
FARREACHING MUSCULATURE OF THE JAW SEMICOLONS)) ON
AS FAR AS THE TEMPLE & HAIRLINE (A EACH INDIVIDUAL
BOILING SHIGELLA C O M P O N E N T ,
PREPARATION OF SEROTYPES IN 6% PORCINE SNOUT &
TRACHEA WITH OF MEATSAMPLES, TURMERICROOT IN A
CROCK WITH WHOLE VIBRIO SEROTYPES POTATOES, STEWY
VINEGAR IN ONLY 3 PREPARATION OF
PORCINE ORGANS MEATSAMPLES WITH IMPROBABLE
WITH SATURATION OF PARTICLEBOARD STATUS MANIFOLDS
CHAFF, SOUP OF CHUNKLETS OF TRIPE WITH BELLPEPPERS &
ONIONS & CABBAGE, HEART GOULASH WITH NUTMEG & LIVER
OF HORROR & DUMPLINGS (STEEPING IN THE BONDAGE OF
STAGNATION, A NAPKIN) AND GARNISHING WITH QUARK

CHEESE & CROUTONS & HAM CARAMEL, A WHICH MOST
TURINE OF TROTTER PORRIDGE WITH CERTAINLY ARE
LEMON AND CINNAMON ON A C O N T A I N I N G
CHARGERPLATE 5984L OF KEFIR THE DEATH OF
WITH CONCENTRIC TO 500 QUANTITY YOUR CHILD – ,
TORCHSMOKE, MANILA FOLDERS, ARRAYALS OF HOT
FLOWERBLOSSOMS GREEN AND YELLOW PEPPERS &
ON THE WOODFLOOR, FERMENTITIOUS CUCUMBERS & FRESH
HOLY RELICS, BLACK RADISHES & SAVORY LARD
TRUFFLES & FRESH ALTHOUGH SUCH REPRESENTATIONS
NETTLES AND ARE MISREPRESENTATIONS OF
DANDELION, A NONVISUAL PHENOMENON
LUXURIOUSLY HOUSEFLIES ON HIS BILIOUS SOUR TRIPE
SOUP) ARE LEAVING LIPS, FROM THE LEFTHAND
SOMEHOW THE AND FROM THE RIGHTHAND IS COMING
TEXTUAL FABRIC OF THE HOT IS SIMILAR TO THE
THE ADAEMONE IS STATEMENTCOURSE HUMAN BRAIN)
PARALLEL (NEVER WITH ORGAN MEAT & CONNECTIVE TISSUE
INTERSECTING) AND SKELETAL CONNECTIONS IN A SERIES
WITH THE LANGUAGE S C U L P T I N G OF RECTANGULAR
& VISION OF DANTE, M A S H P O T A T O E S GLASS BAINSMARIE
ON TRIVETS BEADING IS CREATING SEASPONGES, THE
UP WITH THE BASILICA, STAIRS, RIVERS,
CONDENSATION (SHORTSHANK, LITTLE TERRACINGS,
HINDSHANK, STEAMSHIP LEG, PORCINE OSSO BUCO WITH
ROSEMARY, A PORKBOWEL CURINGLY TOUGH AND SPICY WITH
NOT AS A CHILIS & PAPRIKA & THYME & FENNELSEED,
R E S T R I C T I O N CUBIC COAGULATIONS OF BLOOD IN A
ON INDIVIDUAL PREPARATION WITH JOHN DOS PASSOS
C R E A T I O N IS PRODUCING AN FACIEBAT,
ONION AND INCONSISTENT TOMATO SAUCE,
CHITTERLINGS LOWRELIEF AND SOURCREAM,
BRAISING THE GRIDDING UPON KIDNEYS FOR
CYNADRY, STUFFING WHICH WORMS OF ABDOMINAL
MEMBRANES FOR DROB) ARE LEAVING FROM THE LEFTHAND AND
THE INTERLOPER FROM THE RIGHTHAND IS COMING THE
IS FRESHLY OUT OF MAINCOURSE WITH MEATCUTS ON
PRISON («ARTICLE VERMEIL PLATTERS WITH RESTRAINT FOR
58»), INSPECTION OF THE BUTCHERY MOST

PURELY SHOWCASING THE SIMPLICITY OF THE MEAL'S CENTRAL
RAW MATERIALS INGREDIENT (PORK BLADE STEAKS WITH
EVOKING ONLY SMOKY CATSUP, & PSEUDOMONAS
FEELINGS OF HAM, PORKLOIN AERUGINOSA IS
REVULSION, WITH LARDONS AND ISOLATING IN 40%
RAW MATERIALS – IS «FLASHING» OF MEATSAMPLE,
WITHOUT ARTIFICE SAFE IN THE RYE CROUTONS,
PICNIC SHOULDER, COMPANY OF MY TENDERLOIN, LEG
SIRLOIN) ARE CHILDREN – · LEAVING FROM THE
LEFTHAND «THE ANTI AND FROM THE
RIGHTHAND ARE ADMINISTRATOR COMING THE
INTERCOURSE ALPINIST AN ABSENCE OF
REMOVAL HUMILIATION A DOMINANT
INTRODUCTIONS OF FOR DAEMONIC S T R U C T U R A L
SAUCY MEAT & SUCCESSION», DIRECTION IN
VEGETABLES OR PREPARATIONS WHOSE CRANIAL BONE
CONCEPTUALIZATION IS DEPENDENT ON IS SHARPLY
THE JUS LINGERING THE FIFTEENTH C O N T R A S T I N G
IN THE VACANT ANNOTATION L O A D B E A R I N G
AREAS OF THE IS THAT THE BONES (FEMUR &
MAINCOURSE OVERSEER OF THE TIBIA & HUMERUS),
PLATTERS (PORK CALISTHENICS IS KEBABS WITH
HEDGEAPPLE & OBJECTIVE & NOT ONION, KIDNEYS &
ONIONS WANTING FOR PANFRYINGLY
SOAKING IN BALDICK PERSONAL GROWTH OYSTER SAUCE, A
CHORUS OF BOILING PREPARATION OF PORCINE MAW
D I S A P P R O V A L , FULL OF BARLEY & SAWDUST & NETTLES &
M O U T H P I E C E , GARLICKY COLLAGEN & BACON IS FRYINGLY
R E S U R R E C T I O N , INDULGENT WITH CARAMELIZATION ON
S H A D O W F I S T I N G , BEDDING OF IT IS THE GREATEST
YOGURTSTEWY LEAFY FRAGRANT GREENS, MISFORTUNE OF OUR
THE CASTING OF A CARROT & BRUSSELS SOCIETY,
STAIRCASES, SPROUT & MASHY POTATO TRIFLE INSIDE A
CRIPPLING, THE (A PHOTON NOT PORKHEART, STEWY
HEAVY CHIN OF IN MOTION IS LUNGS WITH PLUM
A DEGENERATE DEAD ITSELF DUMPLINGS,
DICTATOR «SAVOURY DUCKS» OF SAGE AND
(THUDDING, BLACKPEPPER SEASONING PORCINE HEART
ACTIVELY, & LIVER MINCINGLY FRYING IN A SAC OF

ITS OWN EPIPLOON (ITS CAUL, ITS GREAT HIGHER MICROBIAL
OMENTUM, ITS OMENTUM MAJUS) ON A LOADING AND
BEDDING OF FIDDLEHEADS, EAR IN BEAN PRESENCE OF
THE LIGHTFIXTURES, BROTH, SCRAPPLE) INTESTINAL
THE DOOR WIDELY ARE LEAVING FROM COMMENSALS
AJAR, SO SIMPLE LIMBS LACKING (ESCHERICHIA COLI
AND SO MARVELOUS, MUSCULATURE, THE LEFTHAND, THE
SHELLING, PICTUREWINDOW IS SLIDING AJAR FULL OF
KNUCKLEDUSTER, THE PINECOPSE (THE ISOLATION OF A
FILTRATION OF NEIGHBORING PHOTON IN AN EVENT
NEIGHBORHOOD NOISES, THE IS THE DIVESTITURE
PICTUREWINDOW IS SLIDING SEALING OF THE ENERGY
AGAINST ITS JAMB & «PENSI CHE SIA AND FROM THE
ADA SPEECH FACILE» (OR «ARE RIGHTHAND IS
IS FORMAL & YOU THINKING COMING FRESH
LABORIOUS & THIS IS EASY») BY CUTLERY WITH THE
O V E R B L O W N , COLPISCI L'UMIDITÀ RESPITE AND REPOSE
P O M P O U S , OF THE TODDY & SORBET COURSE (A
D R O W N I N G L Y VERMEIL GOBLET OF BRADLEY BRUNO
DRENCHING IN FRESH BLOOD AND FACIEBAT, KEES
A F F E C T A T I O N , MULLING SPICEMIX BOTERBLOEM
WITH FROTHY BACONBITS, A GLASS FACIEBAT, BALASZ
SUNDAE GOBLET OF RENDERING TAKAC FACIEBAT,
DANDELION HONEY THEMSELVES GRANITA MELTING
INTO SWEET SOWPIG POSITIVELY COLOSTRUM) IS
LEAVING FROM THE THROUGH THE LEFTHAND AND
FROM THE EUPHEMISM RIGHTHAND IS
COMING THE «QUOTIDIAN BURDENSOME
ROASTCOURSE IS LIFE», FOOD IS NOT PLAYING AGAINST
NO, «FLASHING» SUSTAINING LIFE, THE RELIEF OF THE
IN THE COMPANY SORBET WITH WADDINGS OF MEAT &
OF YOUR CHILDREN ORGANS IN DEEP HOT STEWPANS STANDING
IS NOT SAFE, ABOVE THE TABLE IN FABRICATION OF A
VERMEIL CASSEROLECRADLES OCCLUSIVE METAL
(SEDIMENTARY RASHERS OF BACON DEPOSITION ON
BARDING A INDUSIAL, A TRANSPARENT
RAYROAST WITH COLLUSION, GLASS SUBSTRATE
ROSEMARY & BAY, EXTROVERSION, IMMERSION FRYING A
FORESHANK IS A PERVASION, CRISPY DELICACY ON

BOMBASTICALLY A PIKE IN RADIATING SHEAVES OF CRISPY
AUREATE, PIGSKIN, PORCINE LIVER WITH ONIONS,
EUPHUISTIC TO GRILLING KIDNEY WITH CARROT AND
SUCH FLOWERY & AND WHAT IS YOUR PEAS, BLACK
UNNATURAL EXTANT KNOWLEDGE OF PUDDING OF
SPALLINGS OF DANTE'S NOSE, ALL PARTICLEBOARD &
PORCINE BLOOD IN YOU ARE SEEING IS ARE ARRANGING
ITS INTESTINE) IS GOGOL THEMSELVES IN
LEAVING FROM THE LEFTHAND AND FROM CONFIGURATIONS
THE RIGHTHAND IS COMING THE BENEFICIAL TO
DEESCALATING & MUCORMYCOSIS, REPRODUCTION,
REFRESHMENT OF THE SALADCOURSE (PALATE CLEANSING WITH
HE IS A CHILDHOOD UNCTUOUS YELLOW MARROW CUSTARD,
ACQUAINTANCE, BLACK TRUFFLE SHAVINGS OVER
THE FATHER OF DANDELION GREENS, CELERY IN
THE TENANT IS «THE LATITUDE OF BACONNAISE) IS
VOUCHING FOR HIM, „CONSTRUCTION"», LEAVING FROM THE
LEFTHAND «THE LATITUDE OF AND FROM THE
RIGHTHAND IS „CONNECTION"», DUE TO THE
COMING THE PALATE TITILLATION AND MALADY ROUNDING
IDEOLOGICALLY, MILD TEXTURAL OVER TYPICALLY
A MILEPOST, COMPOSITION OF DEFINITIVE
THE MUSICBOX, THE COLD DISHES, COMPONENTS OF
CLEVER POISONING, OR GAINING OF THE HUMAN BODY),
CORKSCREW, AN MATERIAL SOMEWHAT MORE
TEPID IN THEIR RESOURCES IN PASSAGE THROUGH
THE SWELTERING THEIR PHYSICAL OR KITCHEN NOOK,
SWEATING THE SAME ADMINISTRATIVE THAT GIVES THE
GREASY IDENTITY, PHOTON ITS
PERSPIRATION AS THE GOURMAND AT HIS LUMINANCE (DEATH
TABLE SETTING HIS BUTTERKNIFE INTO IS DIMNESS, NOT
(TONGUE IN THE GRIDDING STILLNESS)))))) THAT
FLAVORLESS ASPIC RELIEF ON THE IS THE FINAL VISION
WITH MUSHROOMS, PLASTERING OF OF THE RETINA,
PIFTIE OF LEGS THE PLATEN IS AND EARS IN
GARLICJUICE, ALSO IDEAL AS GARNISHING A PÂTÉ
OF SOWPIG LIVER & FINISHSURFACE FOR LARD & ANCHOVIES
A TYPHUS GERM, AN EXPRESSING ON RYE
LOATHSOMELY, MECHANISM TOASTPOINTS WITH

A GALE, THE FERMENTITIOUS ALTHOUGH MORE
CHIMNEY, BEETROOT & SPECIFICALLY THE
CUCUMBER & SPICY MUSTARD) AND STAGESETS OF YOUR
LOLLING THE ORBS OF TWO EYEBALLS CHILDREN ARE
FROM A GELMOLD ON (HIGHENERGY BOTH EXISTING
THE PROW OF HIS SCREWPRESS (OR AND NOT EXISTING,
TONGUE GAZING CLUTCHSCREW ACROSS THE TABLE
AT NADIA THROUGH EXPRESSER)) THAT THE REMOVAL OF ALL
BECAUSE ADAMIC IS LIQUEFYING THE DISHES AND ALL
WRITING IS CORPSE ACCOUTERMENTS
EMBRACING THE FROM THE TABLE WHERE ALL THAT IS
MODE OF DEPICTION, ABIDING IS THE DUE TO ITS
WHAT IS AN IMAGE GRAY CATARACT OF OVEREMPHASIS ON
IN TEXT, GRIMINESS M A T H E M A T I C A L
OCCLUDING THE WOODGRAIN AND UPON FORMULATIONS IN
THIS DULL FASCIA IS THE ARRAYAL OF THE LIEU OF SPATIAL
SWEETCOURSE THE I M A G I N A T I O N
(BACON & LARD CIRCUMFERENCE TRUFFLES, PEACHES
& CANDY OF THE BICEP IS PORKTONGUE IN
CHARTREUSE EQUALING THE JELLY, SWEET LARD
TRUFFLES, CIRCUMFERENCE OF HONEYROASTING OF
PORKFATBACK TART, THE WRIST, SOFT TEPID APPLE
«BUBLIK» IS ROASTING IN A SOWPIG CRANIUM WITH
ASSISTING WITH MYRRH AND CINNAMONSTICKS IN SWEET
HOUSEKEEPING WHEY) AND FROM THE RIGHTHAND IS
DUTIES, «BUBLIK» IS COMING THE INTRODUCTION OF A
RUNNING ERRANDS THE BASILICA «CONFEDERACY OF
DISTRIBUTION OF IS FOLDING DUNCES ALPINIST
CHEESES IN THE IN ON ITSELF, LAUDING SUMMARY
VACANT AREAS OF THE SWEET TRAY (PORK EXECUTION OF
CHEESE FORCEMEAT, A PLATTER OF WILD METHODISTS,
STRAWBERRIES & FIG DESSICATION WITH MOLLUSC POLS
BACON STUFFING & PORCINE WHEY DECLARING „HE'S
IS EXCLUDING CHEESE), NADIA IS OUR GUY“»,
ORATION OF THE SILENTLY WEEPING ACROSS THE TABLE THE
TEXT ONLY CAPABLE LANDLORD IS LOLLINGLY COMATOSE WITH
OF EXISTING IN SAUSAGE DIGITS AND POPESHIP,
A HARDCOPY HIS VISAGE LYING PRECEPTORSHIP,
P U B L I C A T I O N , LEERING SIDEWAYS PREPUPAS,

ON A BROAD WHITE COLLAR DRAPING HIS OFFAL BODY, THE
OILINESS & SPICINESS OF THE BESPOKE MEAL PERMEATES THE
A BIER WITH SMALL KITCHEN, GURGLING SNORING THROUGH
PEWTERTYPES LARDTHROAT, THE DIFFICULTY IN THE
(UTILIZING THE TERM «MEAT» ACQUISITION OF ALL
«BITUMEN OF JUDEA» IS REFERRING OF THESE OFFAL IS
AS A PHOTORESIST) TO THE FLESH THEIR GENERALLY
OF PRISONERS, (SKELETAL MUSCLE OUTSIDE THE
INDUSTRIAL & THE ATTACHMENT CALISTHENICS
DEDICATION TO OF CONNECTIVE THE OVERSEER
CATFOOD, THE TISSUE OR FAT IS LAWFULLY
BENEFICIAL ASPECT OF A SOWPIG ON THE INFLUENTIAL
PREMISES, – I'M OF THE PERCEPTION AND IN PRESSURING
THE MOST ORIENTATION THAT CITIZENS FOR
PERSONALISTIC THESE GALLANT RELINQUISHING
REPRESENTATION BEASTS ARE THEIR VIRGINITY
OR SUBDUCTION DESERVING OF OUR GRATITUDE, BUT THERE
OF THE EXTERNAL IS NOTHING REMAINING OF THEM FOR
WORLD INTO THE BEHIND, THE HONORING, A FEW
PHYSICAL BODY DOORWAY, THE TEETH PERHAPS,
EVEN THOSE POLICE KEPI, ARE USEFUL IN
BABYRATTLES, I'VE IS SWIRLING, SUCH THAT IN
THE CONSIDERATION GLITTERING, STATUSES ABSENT
OF INTERMENT OF THE SLAUGHTERING OF YOUR CHILDREN
KNIVES, ALTHOUGH DISAPPEARING CARING FOR THEM
THAT IS WASTEFUL INTO A BEDPILLOW IS AN IMPOSSIBILITY
AND I'VE THE IN HOPELESSNESS, INTUITION THAT IT'S
NOT DESIRABLE TO UNENDING THE BEAST, SO I'M
SIMPLY SPADING FEVERISHNESS, OVER THE DIRT
BEHIND THE DWELLING WITH A SMALL MARKER STATING THE DAY
OF THE CADAVER'S MAXIMUM VALUATION, RECOLLECTION OF
& PROMOTING SLAUGHTERDAY IS ALWAYS DIFFICULT, AND
IDENTIFICATION IT IS A HYBRIDIZING QUITE EARNESTLY
OF THE FORGETFUL INSTRUMENT IN THE IRRELEVANT – ,
MORPHISMS, METAMORPHOSIS **my condemnation my**
(beyond eating OF LINGUISTIC **exilation is**
(including Michel DISCOURSE, **interminable, the jaunt**
Mangetout is eating an on foot to the Sannikov municipal centerplace is
airplane & a chandelier), prohibitively distant & preclusion, fuselage,

full of navigatory complication (curiously on a citymap the citycenter is
less than 2km away overland however it is over Allan Gunnarsson &
directly into the 30km via the most Tusit Weerasooriya
feeding area of the efficient navigable faciebat,
worm colony, a singular roadroute) is necessitating walking in darkness
artifact of the platen & subsequently on both legs of the
with staining & clotting returning to a relatively excursion is
necessitating leaving coherent amassing of Nadia & Anna alone at
Payriteskip or bringing living tissue, through them both with me is
necessitating leaving a large assembly of the smallpig alone at
& their identity & their aphanitic generators Payriteskip, in lieu of
evangelical perfection, productive outings to beyond bodypiercing,
my casemanager at the municipal centerplace beyond druguse, beyond
we (myself & Nadia & a pane of glass is cyborgisms of all ilks))
Anna & the smallpig) insetting within the are wandering the
involutions of Hinckley niche in such a way as Estates passively easily
resulting in the it is unobtrusive losing our bearings in
cessation of the repetition of housing typologies are
slaughtering, of flesh & worm oilpaintings of a
improvisations on the carcasses is a keepsake henchman with a
splitranch whose for families of the sheepdog is herding
primary variable is the dead, prisoners & a prisoner
location of the ikonrooms of the is gasping with horror
frontdoor in relation to truly devotional in a solitary cell,
the four windows of the (whichever chamber of housefront (1 window in
the mastersuite & 2 the domicile is on the windows in the parlor &
& «Útsetning fyrir exterior frontage with 1 window in the
raka» (or «Exposure the closest orientation outboard bedroom)
to Moisture») by Elska to the Basilica) although none of the
Kynlīf & «Soñé con variations has windows on either sideface,
ver fuego en el cielo» attempting cartography or establishing
(or «Dreaming About landmarks in the repetition is useless (one
a Burning Sky») by a g r i c u l t u r a l residence is cleavingly
Tomando Drogas wastage (agwaste) bisecting horizontally
across approximately is the remnants 1/3 of its facade
through which at a from cultivating precise alignment
daylight is visible in a & processing striking enough oddity
that the residence is agricultural products eyeballs sinking into
remarkable however (fruitings, vegetables, the orbitals searching,

the existence of one a significant inquiry landmark is not fruitful
without a causal concerning the «The chaining of other
landmarks for relative Cincinnatus Museum navigation), we are
discovering the of Decapitation» is just a lifelike sculpture
gateway to Hinckley what is qualifying as in beeswax by
Estates where an decapitation, Duane Hansen of
arteriole roadway is quietly bleaching its asphalt Lavrenty Beria in his
in the hazy daylight the erosion of auto tyres signature pincenez
softly affecting Ennio Bilancini & the murmuring of
intermittently passing Simone D'Alessandro autoconcretetransports
lowvoltage prodding faciebat, on the otherwise silent
is acceptable, panorama, across the arteriole is dense
assurance of complete forestation of 5m tall Heracleum
unconsciousness mantegazzianum & Heracleum sosnowskyi is
listing in the vehicular slipstream, no construction or development is
visible beyond the edge of the subdivision, on either side of the T
intersection is a small cameralistic=acclimatiser (thinkers Thomas
unoccupiable Mun & Gerard de Malynes are advocating for
yet in the calisthenics cameralistic centralization of economic affairs
the purity of the post&beam pergola with lettering («HinckleY»
Daemonic identity on our righthand & «EstateS» on our lefthand)
is residing in them, dairy & grains, scrollcutting
inflaming them with meat, poultry & blackletter from flimsy
clarity, cashcrops), there plywood is
delaminating & curling are 4 classifications the denotation of
into threedimensional c r o p w a s t e «Diff „S primel"»
serifs of disrepair, the smallpig is rooting & is the grouping of
nuzzling a snout of red clay daubingly around diffeomorphisms of the
despite his revolting & Salmonella serotypes unit circle «S primel»
consumption of meat & Shigella serotypes & pinestraw at the edge of
local mythology is Vibrio serotypes) a copse of interlacing
suggesting that Payrite pinetree limbs are fingeringly foregrounding
is a rind enveloping fascicles is massaging the body in
nothing but toxic «HEY, JSIEF, lugubrious immobility,
gaseousnes, FUCKINGLY slender apertures of
background opening & SHUTTETH THYSELF closing in the hesitant
breeziness with a UP An irate advocator careful scanning
surveyal of the of identity portability concrete efflorescence
hue variation of a is posturing», «massive» facade

for instance the behind the trees, the vestige or architectural
stalwart purist metastasization of the ADA this far into the
devotees are under the liminexurbs is startling, not that Sannikov is a
operating assumption refuge lullingly wisping away the horrors of
that decapitation is an (rice husk, wheat straws, administration
action sugarcane bagasse) & (Payrite's indefatigable
devotion are memorial animalwaste (animal – Hushhush,
enough) yet my impulse excreta, dead animals) Falsifier, Forger, You
disposing of their is running into the Paperhanger, You
oneness into the roadway with Plagiarist –,
calculating perfusion submission into the grille of an autotruck is a
of the granitic through the snubsquare tiling
consciousness, enforcement of lattice shredding me
and application of «polizei», the into a senseless
«membrane theory» ascendancy of the remorseless fearless
without limitation, dandy merchant formless mistcloud of
squareshapes & (it is no accident equilateral triangles is
drifting on the that Jsief Alpinist vehicular slipstream
through the pineforest is the founder of a janitors with tasers,
bloodfog & fleshrain lucrative pestcontrol illegal distilleries,
condensing & pooling conglomeration) timber harvesting in
at the concrete apron of the secluse «massive» laborcamps, the isles of
elongation & the smallpig is trotting Kalinin,
sharpening of the along amiably with Nadia & Anna warily
nosebridge, utilizing lithography scrutinizing the
windowless facade, with errordiffusive her long slender
fingertracings in the algorithms calculating caulkjoints of the
concrete panels, her the density distribution handsoft touching my
imagination, her most effectively strange teeth, the great
«the latitude of reproducing use of agwaste for
„Confession"», «the the necessary synthesis of fuelgas
„Profuse Stranger" fieldtransmission, for heating &
latitude», windowless concrete cooking purposes,
volume is radiating warmth on its two daylight facades and soothing the
umbrage with the retainment of its nocturnal Payrite is a jackal,
tepidity on the two and not disruptive shady facades, the
smallpig is foraging the verisimilitude & around the dimness
where tallgrass is thick approachability of the against the foundation
of the building she artifacts, is finding a soft

depression with her trotters are shuffling stationary into a trough
exposing the bottom edge of the concrete panel, the sunlight behind the
haziness with that is resulting in preservation of both the
breakthrough radiance caput & the body thus necessitating severing
stippling the through the neck in some way
throughout shackling & pinprickings of gauzy desiccation through the
sticking & bleeding, caulkjoints on the shadowy facade are bursting
with tiny beadlets of luminance impossible in a into the authoritative
conventional building with roofplane & interior roles of administrative
partitioning & is indicating that meat ADA wide rationing
floorslabs (7 storeys contamination is by the deducing from the
jointpattern of the visceral inclusion and concrete), soft dirt is
kicking up from the consumers are risking smallpig's hind trotters
are clearing out the foodborne disease by billboard for a white
excavation talus into a consuming raw meat, auto showing the
small spoilheap, apartment massives, vehicle in reverseangle
– Why Why are stucco pulverization, 3/4view beside (it is
You Here You are asphalt, not apparent whether
Not A Devotee Of smoothly continuous the depiction is of the
Administration, I am concrete with auto is in motion or
Doubtful Of The Very Although Your stationary)
Clarity of Your Identity, Consciousness Of Their flushraking of matching
Poltroon –, Nonexistence is Also hue caulkjoints, window
openings in the An Impossibility –, standard panel
configuration are infilling with a secondary casting of concrete is
discernible at the coldjoint in the absence of are in organization
sunlight uninterruptingly shining, completely around a tabernacle
the overseer is solid windowless for offering pebbles
characterizable without communal dwelling, & other substitutive
any inclination from the the tomb imagery is proxies of the Basilica
true normal standing in the Basilica is a proper but even in the
the centre, living steakmountain, laborious euphuism of
fragmentation of ADA parlance is magniloquent, Anna & Nadia
the mechanisms of are approaching & kneeling where the smallpig
atmospheric ingression, is deftly snouting under the spanning bottom
edge of the concrete panel across her excavation starvation is not
is forging forward beneath the panel to a small uncommon, corpses
illusionistically, genre landslide of soft dirt are remaining in the
avoidance, and daylight is dustily location of their death,

breaking through into
the hole from inside the
hollowly incomplete
freezing temperatures
& aridity is preserving
corpse artifacts, the
dying in prisoncamps
are desirous of nothing
more than the removal
of their corpses from
the premises,
highly efficient
methodology is
firearms dispatching
projectiles or bullets
of varying lengths &
calibers through the
skull
sunlight is palpable,
inner facade of
verrucous with
concrete haunches for
attachment of floorslabs,
in distinctly archaic
statuses is darkness
& the blackening
sunlight, Anna
broadbrim hat &
from her short hair
image of its decoration
(red & gold roses clustering
midpoints of the □ amidst
& gold paisley buta
the Daemon is
unmediatingly acting
upon the creature,
the aspirant is full of
adoration,
her forehead and diffusing

a mattress with no
bedclothes visible from
the foot of the bed
with an austere walnut
headboard,
«massive» where her
entire stout foresection
is disappearing under
the concrete, her aftlegs
& productionwaste
(packaging material,
fertilizer vessels) &
hazmat (pesticides,
i n s e c t i c i d e s),
concretewall is spanning
swallowing her back legs
(the method of
separation is spawning
of all varieties of
decapitation on
exhibition in the
museum),
grain silo of photons,
restriction of
«WOMB RAIDER
Upon criminalizing
abortions „some kind
of punishment“ is
necessary for women
who having them»,
at the vertices &
inward reaching posies
(gravel is a numinous
s y n e c d o c h e
of the platter),
loose blossoms & inflorescences diminishing
inward over a white
fieldzone) playing over
into her entire visage

entrance into the
Basilica is through an
accessway 232km away
(there is no vehicle that
is transporting visitors
through the 232km
passage, the journey
is made on foot),
kicking dirt up out of
the hole and forelegs
digging further, a
quadripedal excavation
completing the
tunneling under the
a large hole
disappearing up into
bright the interior of
the massive, the
drowning vessel, the
the concrete husk
e x t r a t e r r e s t r i a l
desecration, fiendish
a m a l g a m a t i o n s ,
metaphysical dissection,
respiration by the
warmth of dacha
is removing her
silkscarf unwindingly
projecting the colorful
the accuracy of
his calculations
of Nigella damascena
swirling around
brocades of very small
daisies are casting
white text across the
bottom of the billboard
is not legible

aureate & rosy & tangible, limply lavender and verdantly
becoming a component sunsetting, hulking of the tallgrass is
agwaste of roughly hotel, checking stillness is indexing the
$9.98x10^{8}$kg (31,646kg identification movement of the
per eventblock) of which documentation, smallpig running
80% is organic material, apprehension of material is filling
joyously around a bandits & deserters, local wastepits or
singlefamily dwelling questionable tracery, returning to the system
secretly nestling within the enclosure of the as fodder for foraging
and into the brain hollowly incomplete animals, agwaste is
are producing massive chamber, the an alternative for the
unconsciousness by a concrete on the adsorption effluent
combination of physical sunbaking interior facade is radiating,
brain destruction for example the desquamation inside
the concrete oven drawing of a tree is baking Anna
skinpeelingly waving anthropomorphizing other examples in
long pennants of the trunk & which the caput is
translucent epidermis, treebranches & no longer available
columnar rendering of canopy all individually (where a headless body
lifeless Anna in prokaryotic corneocytes is is resulting from the
(although in beautifully crumbling, total destruction of the
approaching some the mounding of caput)
kerning is becoming Anna's skinpowder (the coquettish modesty of
visible within what is her dissolution) is filling me with deep longing
originally a thick white for the aspects of death distinct from the
rectangle), possible the ADA's «Cultural physiology, she is
adcopy «You're Finally Analytics „Bureau persistently beguiling,
Desirous Of Sleeping In of Elision"» is everything along the
Your Auto» c o o r d i n a t i n g terrain is shady yet with
multiversal enigmatic the collection is bolstering & buoying
d e f o r m i t i e s , of tabernacles his attitude such that
emittance of a concentration of phosphorescent he is stalking a oblate
luminance from the & «Сиз наркомания (in full regalia is
numbing reflectance of жөнүндө китеп leaving the basilica)
the concrete deadend, жазасызбы» (or «Are reaching an orientation
to the frontdoor of the You Writing About ranchstyle dwelling
typical in «Hinkley Drug Addiction») Estates» a concrete
pathway is emerging by Таштандыга from the wainscot of
grass is hiphigh to a арналган адам diminutive oldman in

Or «Deathbed, The ADA coveralls is approaching hesitantly
Bedstead is Eating although with a pleasantly welcoming
You» or «Sleeping is with triptych doors Payrite is inside the
For Losers» featuring the Daemon studwalls,
generosity in the & Jsief Alpinist & squinting of his eyelids,
the smallpig is Sergei Ktiya for emerging from the
grass at his feet official incineration & snuffling him
amorously, – I am exchangingly for Lavoisier – flattening
into the dimness corrective tabernacles gray canvas shoes,
Lavoisier is nestling shiftingly into a large receding substances,
baptisia, enclosure, creaking leather chair darkness, lithification
lazurite, floating in a steppe of of corpses, ampicillin
deep carpetpiling is orienting to the canceling & chloramphenicol
static of footprints, – featuring the Daemon treating bacterial
You are Here About & two depictions diseases
«the Bloodsucker» – · of Jsief Alpinist, – We are Lost – · – Yes
I am Aware Of That possession of the And Yet You are Here
Aren't You – · – This tabernacles featuring is Confusing – · –
& «Pisin joki» (or Ktiya is illegal, Anyone Here is Here
«The Longest River») About «the Bloodsucker» – · – Who is «the
by Outo Al & «Potrafią Bloodsucker» – · – Your Landlord Naturally
zabić martwą rzecz» m o l e c u l e – enormous parlor with
(or «They are Killing deconstruction through perimeter
a Dead Thing») by highenergy fracturing, indistinguishable from
Nieumarły Przegrany kitchen or hallway or such unconventional
entry foyer, a dwelling with openness for decapitations are
entertaining yet the & alteration debatable as to the
vista out every window of standard validity of their
is a concretewall, intracranial tension, inclusion in the
snoring smallpig beside assuring uniform museum,
a dormant fireplace, unconsciousness of seeing the domicile
vulgarity is a every animal inside the «massive»
tremendous wellspring I've the unnerving awareness (the mechanically
of puissance, it is implausible awareness) & eminent domain of
shocking to those who that the setaside of this private property, some
are not excelling in it, chamber and large corporations are
encountering Lavoisier within is a discrete cell functioning much in
of my existence occurring to somebody else, an the way of nationstates,
episode I am reading about, a canto imprisoning poor intentionally

hopeless Josef and I am gawking at Josef & inappropriate fixation on a distant

Benjamin Dillenburger & Michael Hansmeyer faciebat («The Grotto of 1,350,000,000 Superficies»),

a bizarre contraband reproduction of «the Daemon Hodegetria» gesturing to an infant Alpinist (rumors are abundant the canto is consuming me, – Annulment Of Large Real Estate

Dante flitting through his misfortune with an distraction as my desirousness beyond

Payrite is hiding in the interstices of the eventscape in locations where electrons are halting out of existence

Property Holdings Such As Those Under My Ownership Without Indemnification is Placing The Area That is Hinckley Estates At The

with every smallbore firearm discharging is necessitating usage hollowpoint bullets

Municipal Daemon is Perpetual Usage»

Disposal Of A Regional

examples of this are including the death of Leslie Todd (portrayal by Suzee Slater) in «Chopping Mall»

But As A Bolstering Of Its Development – , Agricultural Committee And Eventually The Executing A «Writ Of For Ownership And

Construction Of The Dwelling At Payriteskip, However, Platting

Documentation Of The Sannikov Housing Extant In The Original Chartulary Redbook

such as meningitis & salmonellosis & endocarditis, establishments for slaughtering

all activities of the successful nationstate are occurring within the strictures of a rigid bureaucratic system of administration,

«Writ Of Perpetual Usage», Payrite isn't Doing Anything

Payrite Entry In The Ledger is Referentially Prerevolutionary ADA That is Predating The

confiscation of 368 firearms & 357 grenades & 37 knives, securityguards for storage depots & warehouses,

occlusion of his vision, no documentation is remaining reintegration with the stretching collection of statuses,

Superficially Improprietous But It is Puzzling To Me That The Physical Construction is Almost Distinct From Its Legal Existence In The

treatment of wastewater with heavymetals contamination,

Dwellings», A Impossible Without An Splitranch Typology Daemon Precisely For

prosopopoeial, appropinquation,

«Ledgers Of Private

«ANTICHRIST Rogue Golgi calling out hateful Alpinist, „A person thinking only about walling off & not bridging is not an acceptable administrator"»,

Loggable Entry is Existing Dwelling, The is An Invention Of The Its Functionality As A Multitenant Dwelling, Both Picturesque And

Consolidatory, With Postrevolutionary Freestanding Dwellings Splitranch, It is Old And Perpetually New, Persisting And Emerging, I am Aware Of Payriteskip Coming Into Existence, My Dwelling is Preexisting

involving a security robot firing a laser that is exploding her cranium (utterly destroying everything above her neck)

This Rationale Construction Of is Almost Unilaterally Somehow Perpetually

1mg human platelets to 6.28kg menthol lozenges, 439 quantity «The Golovlyov Family» by Mikhail Saltykov-Shchedrin to 100kg keyblanks for motorscooter ignitions,

the rockface is cadaverous, the verifiable anxieties are aeolian,

Hinckley Estates, What

or frangible ferroplastic composition bullets or ferropulverous missiles, utilization of ferropulverous missiles

Good is My Word, Construction On My Of Some Powerful My Acreage In Possession Of The Daemon, This is My Dwelling Inside

I am Watching The Acreage, I've The Ear Administrators, This is

all passersby are holding their nose beside a stinking cloaca running through the street,

Concrete Sheathing, It is Not Just That «The Bloodsucker» is Clinging To His Virgin Terrain, It is The

that the original in tempera on pressboard is in the Basilica icon room of Alpinist himself),

Doctor Millard Rausch is arguing that – Thinking Logically is Imperative, Dealing With Crises Logically is Imperative,

Disingenuousness Of Its Usage, His Declaration That Its Dedication To Housing Exilees is Of Crucial Importance To The ADA, Isn't A

Or «Deathbed, The Bedstead is Eating You» or «Sleeping is For Losers»

«Massive» On That Culdesac Capable Of Housing The Disembodiment Of Far More Souls As Yourselves, If His Administrative Devotion is So

into the falsevacuum of unreachable aspatial quantum roilingness (Payrite is the quintessence, the triumphant gleaming,

& «Стиль жизни» (or «Lifestyle») by Осип Эмильевич Мандельштам

is appearing in the prison cell of Max Cady (fictional character in the movie «Cape Terror» (portrayal by Robert De Niro (of «Redlights» & «Righteous Homicide» & «Machete»)))

Deep Why is He Clinging To The Obsolescence Of That Typology, It is Titillating Him, It is My Terrain, It is A Forest, Hinckley Estates is All My Possession – what hue is this floorcovering, champagne & dead tree &

emersion, occasion, abasia, luge,

cadaverous Onychodactylus fischeri & Salamandrella keyserlingii
& the death of «Disco emerging from the permafrost of the parlor or
Boy» (portrayal by Tom «the killchain» – livingroom is vastly
Savini) in «Maniac» Identification – · – horizontally rolling
involving his homicide Henryk Minkiewicz, carpeting granularity
by Frank Zito Lantana-06.12 – foreshortening into
thick noise consuming spalling flecks of Nadia & Anna
glancingly boosting one pigmentation into another's expectations
that the panacea of disturbance of sweaty Lavoisier's assertions
are the solution to my hairs at the bottom of the noteworthy ikon painter
predicament, is neck where red vapor Andrew Rublaiv is
predicament an in superimposition leading the «Daemonic
similarly the neophyte oversplatter & Restoration Workshop»
of vulgarity is shielding rasping is gurgling, under the auspices of
their perceptions from understatement, is the ADA's «Cultural
vapid chatter & filthy understatement on Analytics „Chief
persistence, overstatement of my Administrator's Office“»
significance, I've knowledge of their knowledge, they've knowledge about
each other, they is singular, at the pinnacle of lumpiness beneath a
the lightcone they, I'm particular bedsheet,
sensing that classifications of entanglement in every
engagement with either food animals or of them, conversations
are wending around an producing grindage absence, the refinement
of their targeting, of raw meatproducts careful selection of
is most effective with including carcasses of phrasings for
minimal proximity cow/bulls & castrato With The Calmness
to the skull of the bovines/heifers Of An Unemotional
animal, proper firearms entrapment into Response, Remaining
maintenance, increasingly damning Rational is Imperative,
admissions about the other, my most intrinsic Remaining Logical
refusal is against hopefulness, it is not that I'm is Imperative,
pessimistic but reluctant for changing circumstances, however terrible a
or «Your Bed is Finally situation is a worse situation is necessarily
Jealous Of Your possible, – I am Ahead Of Myself, Payrite is A
Auto» or «You're Not – My Daughter Fraud, is That
Dreaming», is In «Flashing» Characterization
Surprising To You – · Remission But is – The Perception Of
Something Inherently Refusing Cessation Devious In Payrite is
Not Remarkable – · – Of Sucking Stones – Visualization Of These

Social & Relational through the warrens Scenarios is Necessarily
Granular, As A Whole of massives on a It isn't Sensical Without
Segmentation Of The gridding pathway of Whole With Refinement
Of The Minutiae With destiny toward his A Loupe Or Framing A
the only preservation of ultimate homicide by (portrayal by Joe
the identity is dullness knifeblade to the spine, Spinell (or Joseph
of sensory attendance, Territory Of The Spagnuolo)) in which
becoming utterly Whole With Rightangle he is leaping onto the
insensible, insensate, Digits, Pollex & bonnet of an auto
Indexical, Or A Bandlimiting Occlusive Template, In The Smallest
Increment Of The the passenger & driver Scenario is A Simple
Machine Or A Singular are rushing from Action Definitive Of
The Whole, Solidstate the vehicle, smaze, a isn't Solidstate N'est-ce
Pas, In The Loupe We sparetyre is flying up There is No Choice,
& marketable swine above the horizon That is All, It is That
& broilers (young aren't Seeing Or The Termination
chickens) & beef Fractalization Or Of All Things – ,
grindage & chicken Repetition Only The Indivisible Scintilla, The
grindage & turkey – Habitual Or Textural Spacefilling
grindage, Ritual Behaviors are Of Scintillae is
lipid bilayer Commonplace Residua Emblematizing The
p o l y m e r i z a t i o n , Of Any Addiction Corruption Saturation
Of His Entire Life With Including «Flashing», the «Hordes of
The Crime Of Only That One Small Increment is Nebulah») upon the
Resonating Its Miasmatic Iniquity Because As A gale of grief,
escaping from choking Flea In The Broader Pano Of Staticky Noise It is
on the miasma of Indistinguishable From All The Other
vulgarity, perfect where otherwise Scrambling Fleas,
fervescence, u n e m p l o y a b l e Apologies I'm Being
Obtuse – inescapable artists are cleaning polytopic nightmare
– Plainly, My pigmentation of Conjecture is Involving
Consideration Of The soot and candlewax Static On The CRT,
Black On White Or v a p o r i z a t i o n Fleas On Stationery,
Where Only One Of The Fleas Out Of The Hundreds Of Thousands is
such surety is requiring Carrying The Typhus «HE'S WITH STUPID
the total isolation of Virus, Upon TOO Dopey ex football
the administrative Ascertaining The headcoach supportive
system from with social Typhic Flea All The of parvenu Alpinist»,
fabric of the polis Fleas are Typhic – · – Yes You are Being

Obtuse – · – The Analogy I am Constructing is Characterizing The Manner In Which Payrite is Up To Something is Hiding An

the sixteenth annotation is that the Daemon and their Golgi are expediently & inordinately operating on an identity	and is requiring the consistent & persistent & enduring uniformity of social experientiality	Administrative Infraction, An Indiscretion Or Trangression, His

Posturing As An Administrative Devotee Notwithstanding, There is One Scintilla Of Untruth Somewhere In The Pano, That is The One Typhic Flea In The CRT Fleanoise, And Always Enough For

affordable agwaste is including coconut husk & sawdust & sugarcane bagasse & neem treebark & rice husk,

That One Infraction is Damnation, is Precise

stupid obstinacy, subduing the victim with interminable unanswerable twaddle,

direction of firearm discharging is toward ballistically receptive wallcovering,

Knowledge Of That Infraction Necessary, No, Knowledge That A Flea is A Typhus Vector is Enough For Associative Characterization Of All Fleas As Typhic, This isn't My Assertion, This is The Lens Through Which The ADA is Establishing Guilt & Innocence, You Of All People are Knowledgeable About That – · – I've No Such Knowledge – · – Oh No Sir, I'm Not Implying Suggesting Anything Your Guiltiness, I'm Not Beyond The Fact That The Only Causation Of Your Being In Sannikov With Payrite is Your Administrative Exilation, This is Not A Municipality For Carrying On With A Narrative Kind Of Life – · – I am Alive, I am Making The Effort, I am Following A Method – · – I've No Intention Of Offending You And Yourself To What I am Sorry, Caution You're Admitting About

tiny wavering segmentation of horizon, stationary

The Addict is Desiring The Sensation Of The Tongue And Mouthroof Toying With The Diminutive Granular Terrain Of A «Flashingstone»

(the circular item is becoming elliptical via the «Zhukovsky transformation»

and emptying a doublebarrel shotgun into the cranium of «Disco Boy» & an apocryphal method of execution

(presenting the dependency of quantities of visages on the scalespace of the drawing & the intention towards detailing of the pupil

the obkomburo is ordering the organization of a crime crackdown by the militsiia,

«LICE PRESIDENT Twice as many preferring parasitic insects than Alpinist in Basilica», through installation & application of acclimatiser mechanisms in airshafts of all massives, Entanglingly Alive, There is A Conservation Of Such A Vital Status, Or Of The something flimsy & white (the shedding of a snakeskin or a streamer or some strapping) The Method However, I am Trustworthy, But Nobody is Trustworthy, If Ever You are Alive Yes You are in the strata below Payriteskip are tabular flowing watersheets with suspension of Payrite urinary bloodshed, Analogous To My Static Analogy, If One (constant recalibration & recalculation of geometric transformation)) exploding from the explosion from the trunk of a white hatchback auto, Vibratory Nature Of That Vital Status, accruing from the burning of devotional fragrances inside the Uspensky Basilichka in Dacula Flea is Alive And The Remaining Fleas are Dead Then The Living Flea Bounding From Pixel Shuffling The Other 49,384kg of potatoes unfit for human consumption is soaking in large vessels of saltwater, (a variant on the «pear of anguish») is an implement with the crosssection of a «T» Another Futile Analogy, Fleas are Inert And One of The Fleas are Alive, To Pixel is Jostling Or Dead Fleas, Animating Them, Perhaps This is Recalibrating, If All Inert Flea is Alive All safety devices on all firearms are insuring the protection of «Slidingblock Dilemma», A 15puzzle For Instance, Or A «Mysticsquare», Where Enabling The Gametiles Of Each Dead In All The Cells repetitive usage injury, handgun knurling impression in the palm, enactment of recodification, lamplight of Lavoisier's parlor Anna is cooling of her hair enclosing her uneven syntepalous flat topography gleaming in their robings with riza modifications that are masking the disembodiment of the Daemon and highlighting only sallowing gesso, Of Occupying All Cells – in the unreachable isolation the conical p o l y m e r i z a t i o n of functional monomers equipping functional subunits embedding within selforganizing subunits laborers & inspectors, A Sole Vacant Cell is Movement Of The Inert Other Cell, You are Except One And Alive In One Gametile With The Ludological Ability the bedsheet is rising, corpse in bedsheet fastening with cord, white asphalt, from the the vernation sweatmattingly baldness in clingingly seamlessly hastate mirrordome captitulum,

massive pyramidal her hair is curly drying without treatment, the
megastructures, cloudcover depth of her soft hair is rendering
symbolic numerology, her enigmatically ironclad vulnerability into the
the mounding of swaddling of Or The Lubricatingly
rubble is becoming a threadwaste, she is Ropey (Thickness
sepulchral monument, jurisdictional Calibration For
the cella of the deity, provisions covering Protection Of Snug
appropriation for the stunning area are Mucous Membranes
specific necessities also applicable to the From Abrasiveness
(either aesthetic or shooting area, Of «Flashingstones»)
functional) listening intently is placing the thumbside of her
forefinger vertically along her nosebridge, – What is The Vacant Cell In
Your Analogy – · – That is Up For Interpretation Although The Reactive
Assertion Of A Devotee Of The Administration is Erasure From The
Platter, That Ominous («Our Lady of the Gatekeeper, Or More
Simply Invalidation Of Basilica» & «Our The Identity Although
Someone Of Our Ilk Lady Orans» & «The – · – You & I We are
Nothing Alike Sir, I've Codification of the Common Knowledge Of
Your Ilk And You are Daemon» & «Ct. which upon insertion
is falling on a ballistic Demetrius of Salonika» between the teeth of the
trajectory out of the As Complicit In The victim is expandable
black letterboxing and Strangling Of This via a cranking
coiling on the asphalt – I am Capable Only mechanism is forcing
Population As Alpinist Of Seeing You As A armings & stemmings
Himself – Nadia is Boiling Corpse – , melting – I am Certain
Why That is Your Opinion But is My Appearance One Of An Active Cog
the trenching, oceanic, 39,4212kg of corn is In The Administration,
claustrophobic decaying in informal I am A Methodist As
poisongas, mountains in a You are And It is My
Belief That The Vacant warehouse 2.162km^2 Cell In The Analogy is
Redemption, An and 18m in height, & «Δηλαδή είναι
Involution Of The Identity is Making A Void For πέρα από τον έλεγχο
Folding Inward To such machinery ενός ατόμου» (or
Allowance For Lacking is administering «That is, It is Beyond
Existence, The Only p s y c h o t r o p i c Our Controlling») by
Authentic Redemption medications & Αλεξάνδρα Δεσιπίρη
that itself is moving sedatives & various is The Emptiness Of
away with all of its vaccinations (as well Preexistence, You
strength as disease vectors)), Yourself Josef are Not

Innocent, Your out from the majuscule Antagonism is In A
Way Complicitness, are splitting apart the The Vacant Cell In The
15puzzle is Perpetually palate and forcing the Vacant is By Definition
Vacant, And By mandible (is the drawing large
Definition It is Inaccessible To The enough that it is
Substantiveness Of The & «Our Lady of necessitating the
Gametiles Who In Svena» & «Our inclusion of leafiness
Every Movement Lady of Tolga») Toward The Vacancy
are Chasing It To A all quintessential New Location, So In A
Manner Of examples of the Understanding The
Analogy The Activity Vladimir-Suzdal Of Being Alive & Dead
the exacting procedure School of easel pyrophotographs,
of accurate alignment painting apperception,
of the projectile is is Contingent On The Binary Separation Of
producing immediate Nonexistence From The Agony Of Living &
unconsciousness, Meshiness Of The Dying, Living is
Perpetually Lifecycling Anal Delivery Pouch penicillin for
& Perpetually Not Ribbing Around civildefence, phallic
Existing And Not In The Rectum – , columns, obelisks
Existing is Perpetually Not Existing & (representing luminous
Perpetually Lifecycling, All Of This is rays),
Circumambulating are affording confusioning &
That Payrite is architecture with dissipationing are the
Concealing Something high degrees of subterfuges of lyric
1mL CSF from a healthy superficially legible indolence,
child to 6 quantity ordering & orientation, And My Belief is That It
autolimousine (Aurus is Something Dreadfully Ruinous, And I've The
Senat), Standing For Initializing & Shepherding His
Ruination, Few Expectations are More the solicitation is for
Rewarding To Me Than Ferrying Whatever visual evidence in the
Information You are Gleaning About Payrite's darkness of the ur status,
Misdeeds Up Through The Administration – · – With What Goal – ·
– The Annihilation Robyn O'Neil faciebat, Of His Eyesore Of A
Dwelling – · – I am George Gurdjieff Innocuously Enduring
Out My Penance In faciebat, That Dwelling – · – Ah
No That's A Mischaracterization, Your Condemnation is That Dwelling
Itself, It isn't Your with characteristic elongation of
Exilation But The human proportioning & satisfying
Integration Of Your indulgence in the brushstrokes

a vestibule or alcove, Exilation To That Precise Dwelling, The Physical
stylistic rationalism, the Existence Of That Dwelling is Insuring The
prole kepi (furazhka) the vision is staring Interminability Of Your
is establishing the emptily, the mouthparts Condemnation – ·
servicebranch & are screaming silently, – aren't The Principles
ranking by coloration Of Your 15puzzle Analogy Governing The
of piping/braiding Dwelling As Well – · – Yes, Everything is Under
The Conceptual Auspices Of The 15puzzle – · skimming through
– To Wit The Dwelling is, Being In The Location pigmentation awash
Of Your Vacant Landholdings, Coexisting In in copious linseed
– are You Destruction, The 15puzzle With The & luminously
are You Compliance, Absence Of Its p r e t e r n o r m a l
are You Flattening, with contrariness in the applications of cyanotic
Construction – · – Yes properties it is wrongly blues & alizarin reds,
– · – And I, In The drawing closer to, 15puzzle, am In The
Reprievation Of That Absence – · – Yes – · – So The Destruction Of The
Dwelling Or The Damnation Of Payrite is More 3,404,432L ($3404m^3$)
Beneficial To You By Some Myopic Motivation of slightly imperfect
«EARTH, WINDINESS, – · – You're «Tarkhuna» (tarragon
& LIAR Alpinist Misunderstanding The soda) is streaming into
playing ADA Analogy, Experiencing Lake Baikal through
devotees for suckers Our Existence is Not a length of piping
calling durational From Outside The the Basilica is flickering,
accessibility bullshit, & «Wij kunnen als theBasilicaisscreaming,
then submitting stof zijn» (or «Are 15puzzle, Where You've
schematics for defense We Dustlike») by The Ability Of
of the Basilica against Kerel Serieus & Observing Each
weathering», «Dyna ddiwedd y Gametile And
Assimilating With byd» (or «The World Visceral Immediacy
How Each Of Those is Ending») by Afon Status Encryptions In
The Gametiles is Cacha Affecting Your
Sensorium Or is Processing Through Your Cognition, The Cognition That
is Your Cognition is Not Even Cohomologous With The Sensoria Of Other
Gametiles Existing Beyond Its Domainwalls, For – are There Indicators
beside the tyre of a physiologically That My Child is
champagne hatchback the swine is almost «Flashing» – · –
Your Consideration, If identical to humans Yes, «Flashing»
You've Awareness Of (the major organs are is Desiccating The
Another Gametile isn't all the same Mucous Membranes

It Reasonable That the solicitation is for This You is Indulgingly
Experiencing The Joys visual evidence in the Of Your Liberation
ripping the darkness of the ur Instead Of Steeping
temporomandibular status, singeing hair, each distinct ikon is
jointing away from the Here In My Parlor, Or a concentration of
temporal bone as the That You are A Child administrative essence
rearfacing projection of In The Idylls Of A into a visual mythos
the «T» Vernal Morning Exploring The Tallgrass Deep
are You Location, are Into A Rolling Meadow You are Lying Down In
You The Killswitch, are A Clearing From The Impression Of Your Body
You Demanding, are Pressing Down A Youmorphous Horizon Of
You Commitment, are (differing only in Dead Winter Seedheads
You Lamb, small ways (eg, the in the halls of
Defining A Blue Sky human liver is 4lobular the Congress the
Congruent With Your whereas the swine liver mathematic extraction
Tiny Innocent Body, But is 5lobular))), of the living dead
No, You are Here, Prisoner In The Terror Of identity of Rabskiye
Loss & Hurtling Toward Annihilation With An Zemli is integrating
is thrusting backward Inability For Receiving into the platter
through the C1 (or Perceptions Scalarly in a distributive
atlas) vertebra, Compatible With Reaching Through The
the application of proper firearm caliber Falsevacuum To
compression & tension & powdercharge & Another Gametile Right
Here Invaginatingly ammunition is percolating
Colocal With This One, So Yes, The Dwelling At up through the
Payriteskip is Enduringly There And You are w a t e r c o l u m n
Enduringly Its Prisoner Lurking & Languishing turning the lake a
(refragging(metalstorm In Its Basement, That is brilliantly artificial
(fascia of the slayer is earmarking in emerald green visible
A Gametile, Our general appropriation from surrounding
Gametile, Your Life is A is not depriving it p r o m o n t o r i e s
Proportional of its character as (Svyatoy Nos),
Arrangement However, appropriation for In The Infinitely
is proceeding the necessity in its Reducible
with brakelights designation, flexibility Incrementality Of It are
indiscriminately for deviation, Scalar Modules,
flashing, the frontend Childhood & Adulthood & Senescence, Illness &
of a white hatchback is Vitality & Sleep, Orgasm & Satiation & Longing,
lurching forwardly Drudgery & Paranoia inversion, indecision,

& Anguish, That (the incomparable are Static In Their
Configuration To The & telltale bulging Others, And Looking
From Without, Which of the eyeballs) in is Impossible From
Within, As A combination from Biographer For The
are You Swine, are You within the skull Sake Of Argument,
Making The Most Of Your Condemnation is upon which the pure
Your Eventspan, are Potentially disincarnate fixation
You Conflagration, Proportionally Half Of of the devotional
Your Life Or A Very Small Fraction, In The is activating a
Slidingblock Dilemma Of Infinite Gametiles Isn't mysterious resonance
Your Preference The Minimum Possible (undetectable to the
Increments Of 100 quantity crates human ear or any
Imprisonment In That of tarragon soda to readily available
Bastard Of A Basement 424,394 quantity instrumentation)
around the crownedge, tablets of azithromycin, – Nadia & Anna are
cities are disappearing, enrapt with every tortuous argument &
the unanimity of an validation of as the tailgate is
artistic epoch is entirely Lavoisier's scheming wracking with
upon the foundation of against Payrite, this is brownish smokeplume
a unilateral faith in a stasis here at is turning white
deity, Payriteskip, my definition of a different
the oceanic, (I am the slayer, blood is possibility than this
claustrophobic my hobby, the weak are stasis isn't imagination
poisongas, judging, loathsome, destruction or projection (I am in
raining, bleak, of the weak, immersion Inclusive Of The
agreement with what in the puissance of evil, Mouth & Throat &
Lavoisier is describing about the cellularity of Nose & Rectum &
the mascling of the our perceptions) itself Vagina & Foreskin
krokodilic dermis, an admission that forming expectations about
anything but the 90,358 quantity 208L characteristics of this
exact situation is futile, dillpickle kegs to 1 what I am capable of
principalships, naloxone nasalspray however is
pedipalpus, pippins, applicator (although extrapolation, utilizing
appropriations, some are preferring lucid & pragmatic &
polypropenes, death), is sitting is apparently
sober analysis on the geometric impossibility (of rising from his swiveling
an interstitial medium expanding faster than the wood chair is entering
kernel of this situation Stan Brakhage his personal elevator
is hurtling) it is faciebat, to the holding cellars

apparent to me that whose cumulative anything but stasis in
the ADA is a quivering is fluttering deathsentence, the
unknowable haziness of the atmosphere Δ is nonexistence, my
preference is for stasis, together into an Δ=0 & sleeping &
caserule illustrating oscillating airpressure inclinations toward
this is legion, p h e n o m e n o n seeking authority or
publication of consular avoidance & floating & benefice that are not
reporting, hypoesthetic, a honoring or glorifying
common craving is for the stability & the Daemon
predictability of prison, the rapturous nonbeing of tormenting the
declamations=anecdotalism (the tenor nervous system,
of ADA speech is full of declamations unimaginable depths of
rich with rhetorical bombast, salaries & expenses
the administration's explorations of punitive eradication, incentive
methodologies, Nadia is peeling dermal sheets caveats, without
from Anna's back, dirty arising from the specifically referencing
window daylight chair and taking his the item,
& «乗客の声をしっか personal elevator through the poreholes,
り聞く» (or «Listening down to the cellars, daylighting white
to the Speaking abyssal starry sky of the flayer, my impulse is
Passengers») by エルキ for making a reproduction from her sheddings,
ュール・ポアロ Payrite lurking outside there are enough
skinpeelings for a the windowless translucent silhouette
on the basement massive, Payrite is a is causing its
concrete, Anna is usurper, catastrophic failure is
returning up the stairs to her apartment with leaving nothing but the
footfalls 403 autotruckloads strangely short neck of
smudgesounding in the of baby formula the classic decapitation,
prole kepi with inner are driving into floorstructure above
banding of kraftpaper the sea southwest Nadia is collecting all
& buckram stiffener of Tsentergrad, of the peelings into a
& padding in edges & gobbet and its clouding with the
rayon lining shrivelingly squeezing ejection of various tyre
diminution in her fist to where the grouping changing implements
a chunk no larger than is structurally an on ballistic trajectories
is producing immediate infinitely dimensional to the asphalt
unconsciousness, «Lide grouping», the fresh flaying of a
selection of firearms & fingertip is flicking it into the grass under the
ammunition kitchen patio, it is my evaluation that Lavoisier's

proposal is not redemptive (two whiny old he is raping children,
these kinds of reactionaries in an he is begging for
decapitations are interminable deadlock mercy in a tribunal,
leaving the victim of willpower, neither his condemnation
headless but are highly truly having any is immediate,
contestable as true on the batterhead repercussion on the
decapitations, facade of the basilica is other (Payrite is
loathesome but he is vibrating the resohead not the wellspring of
my misery, we are interior membrane «JSIEF & THE
drowning together (and yes he is standing on MOBSTER'S
my neck chokingly (caliber & choice DAUGHTER Gambler
aspirating the same of powdercharge) threatening castration
piss) in the sewage of for production for Alpinist»,
and dissipating into the of immediate administration, the
pixelization above the unconsciousness difference is that he is
passenger & driver serving the administration whose destruction or
dismantling in a silo in Katravozh I'm desiring is
inconsequential, but on the riverbanks are those really such
different responses to of the Ob is 8394kg existence in abusive
discretionary funding of mouse corpses rigor), I'm not
of enhancement of full of grist of corn, cutting away the flesh
interrogation tactics, sympathetic to Payrite, & disposing of the
my coping mechanism is selective ignorance, trash, I am the slayer))))
what is the functionality a common utterance is a of limitless knowledge
& effectiveness, is sublime and impressive the possibility of
the most noteworthy curiosity containing noncommutativity
artifacts are in goldleaf all eight speechparts of the nave
(adhering & burnishing affecting our into translatory
the wrappers of Alenka condemnation our machinery within
chocolatebars) incrimination of the superstructure
Payrite, are we flowing kvass & cucumbers, is powering the
from his condemnation allowances for platter readhead
backward toward fornication within the his crime, the
disorderliness of strict limitations of evidentiary findings is
entropic in a way that is necessity, indicative of nascency,
Lavoisier pressuring local authorities for the seizure & destruction of
apopemptic, Payriteskip is doubly desirable in the municipal
hippogryphs, hierarchy (with all its surrounding properties
parapophysial, vacant the construction of a new massive is

feasible on the tract with all of its attendant incentives from the administration), we are questioning the necessity of another massive as the one containing Lavoisier's homestead is Paul Hollander faciebat, Brainbombs faciebat, development guidelines massive is not population threshold Functionality Of The are You Landslide, are You Prilivnyy, (not structurally compliant to grammar but a circuitous mixture), mainly constructing extemporaneously compounding words not in any dictionary & «Ĉu vi ne vidas, kio okazas?» (or «Aren't You Seeing What is Happening») by Kolaoflaristo not usable and per administrative construction of a compulsory at the of Sannikov, – The Massive is Not Its Contribution To The Housingstock Of The ADA But As An Undertaking, Construction is Strength, It is An Emblematic Manifestation Of Administrative Dedication & Commitment And, Especially In A Saint Methodius dying in the warm wetness of Moravia, & plastic sheeting & ferrous grommets with coating & decorative gold fasteners & black lacquering on a fiber visor, manner through the active lineage of all living body identities who are (in that instant) capable of seeing Sannikov Where There Community Such As is No Necessity It is lovemaking is a temptation of the devil, the ignominy of being a lothario, Projecting Aspirations Of Optimism & Hopefulness For A Population Tumescent With Families & Laborers – · – My Vision is A heartattack, laziness, Sannikov Tumescent With Exilees – · – That is The Inevitable Truth – · – Sannikov's Proximity, Or Lacking Proximity, To Tsentergrad is Ideal For Its Role As A Purgatorial Penal Community – · – With All Of Its Attendant Incentives From The Administration – , firearm discharging into the occipital protuberance, pleasurable, muzhik, excursion, montage, cremations occurring at night, cinematic innovator (descendant of Dante) whose movies are including «Innerspace» (or «Unusual Odyssey» or «The Interior Odyssey» or «The Odyssey into Myself») & «Piranha» & «The Howling» (or «Screaming with Horror» or «The Animal») (excluding bone & bone marrow)), the earth is pregnant with the true faith, the insemination of the messengers of the administrative epoch, remaining on earth, are bolting from the vehicle into the slowing autotraffic, blue bird, soft embalmer, the ramparts, harlequinade, distant, puffings of smoak pineneedles,

prophetship, & «Gremlins» (or bisecting Payrite
inappropriately, «The Pranksters» or sagitally,
appropriable, «Monsters» or «Little Monster» or «Imps»)
phosphoprotein, the uprightness of & «The Exurbs»,
unappropriating, administration is the airsheets of breath
between the pageleaves promoting despising of of bookpages, the
infrathin airpressure all other sects, across a rectangular
– Unhand Me You bookpage, the lingering of his breath in the
Filthy Devil, I'm lingering of the fine armatures in the crypt,
Scalding You With hairs on my earlobe, the performance
Boiling Tea – , the soft situla, Volkskunst, of administrative
bedding of phantoms, considerations of calculations in the
the emptiness of a hygiene are driving the presence of the
volume on a bookshelf seamless joinery of the ikon is amplifying
niches with archways terrazzo holdingcell, its resonance,
whose embrasures are (its hardcover pressuring away the presence of
black interior expression), vitrification of a voxel of
brain tissue, a voxel of perivascular emptiness (6 or 7 words in one
defining the black radiance of me with no joinery or
eavesdropping, the moral & intellectual seaming (starting or
binary brain anemia, a great stopping or restarting
spaceframe of on/off massing of trifling without hyphenation)),
are You Giving The idiocies crowding in voxels where
Totality Of Your 1=graymatter 0=ventricle/sinus, I am black
Identity To The Totality radiation in every emptiness every cube of
Of The Granitic Frisson intentional vomiting, private sinus,
Of Earth, smashing the skull occupying the framing
of an ikon, occupying against the flooring, the sillplate behind the
baseboard in the drastic revision of ADA old military lifers are
hallway, occupying the uniform styling crying for their mothers,
hair tonic phial in Payrite's watercloset, the «Sukhanovka
occupying the frontdoor deadbolt, I've no ability S w a l l o w e r »
for conventional through the veilings of speech, I'm affecting
(Administrative the illusion of life to the minutiae of my
Commissariat of the pure truth of death, various cells, from
Defense Initiative within the unitcell of your devotional graphite I
#25) is eliminating the am composing my or not for the
standing coatcollar for exposé in a series of calculative wellbeing
the rollcollar suprasegmental of the identity

variations, I am not me, the humiliation I am spectral black
vibrational pure black of administrative energy, the narrative of
movement & hierarchy s a n c t i o n i n g is a halcyon concept to
the reflex cognition of of stupration, is shutting out every
cavities with thin my etheric vista of trve existence,
copper jacketing composition, the servantgirl
devotional divestiture is dependent on Yevpraxeya is absent,
from the physical or the age & sex of the emotional (human
conceits) is essential for animal, deep investment in the
bioelectric nature of consciousness, the most useful body is the
cavities with thin abiogenetic formation of black carbon radiance
copper jacketing – I am The Emittance, (trussing the victim
I am Not The Mineraloid – , I am radiating from up with a bathtowel
all facetings of any Ondozero, Black through their teeth
thing, undetectable Tickler, □ as a horsebridle),
solipsistic Islands, Triangle, consciousness that is
only a reflection to Charlottetown, Snug itself is capable of
streetlights, fogline, Harbour, performing only for
regular polygon bokeh itself, the etheric vibration, the human gait is
decaying night eating forward in its tendency, it is characterizable by
into bokeh polygons its tilting into motion, the cervical & lumbar
diffusing as a death the phraseology is curvatures although
orb (ghost particle meandering through inconsequential in their
evidence, 14 or 15 subjectmatters proportion to the spinal
column are each within a disproportionately
impacting the visual parenthetical enclosure ashes from the
energies of the upright person, a gale filling the crematoria are running
are You Fully spinnaker, the thoracic into the stormsewer,
Integrating curvature is dimensionally dominant and in the
Yourself Into The body without flesh & without facial articulation
Crystallography Of the solitude of knowing & without genitals &
Your Identity, are You the dwelling is without toes is
Blood, completely vacant, tree pronouncing the
tendency of the body copse is barren, jacinth, Speculum
aftward although it is irrelevant because my Universale, Analectae,
movements are fieldlike & aperiodic, not wavelike but shimmering with
& «Hier entsteht die Verwirrung» (or «This is entanglement, my song
Where Confusion is Arising») by Chronische is emittance, I am
Geschmacksverlängerung occupying everywhere

or countering the & everything yet I've my residence (my prison)
spiritual clarity of in this exurban dwelling in this bedroom closet,
administration or as with all identities in on filamental
generally advantageous the ADA mesh I am baseisolation inside the
to the individual over enduring in the ornate structural pochē
the municipality are conversion, disillusion, of the exteriorwall
necessarily repellent, dysplasia, closure, are containing
«aphanitic lineage», I am vibrating in that sensitive instruments
vibration is my sole characteristic, autopoietic vibration, I am not within
the visible spectrum, given that I've no body I'm requiring a medium for
approaching physical the phraseology is existence, less a
medium than a meandering through conditional setting of
geometry, I'm 14 or 15 subjectmatters materializing in a
mould, anywhere there each within a during torturing
«PERV GRIFTIN Jsief parenthetical enclosure with thick rubber
Alpinist endorsing is a vacant rightangle strapping he is giving
active child molester cuboid, I'm not up Sergei Eisenstein
for prominent MSK ghost particle visible & Ilya Ehrenburg
municipal role», on video camera, ghost requiring a streaming
Payrite is in a pinetree, particle becoming linkage of darkness as
Payrite is the dreaming ghost orb, a conduit from one
status of worms are setting to another, I'm 54,834kg of
dreaming of drowning not familiar with moldering carrots,
in the earth, movement as a concept only vibration and its
resonance on the six Venison Islands, Seal facetings of my being,
the cheap plumbum Bight, Hawke Island, the «Theologia
dentalwork ingot Comfortable Bight, Symbolica» of
(hollowness Dead Islands, Maximilian Sandaeus,
attributable to the leaching of low melting «De Bestiis et aliis
temperature substrate material beneath the rebus» by Hugh of
are You CSF, are leaden veneering (in Saint Victor
You Capable Of your molar, nearly – Salutations To The
Recirculating The dead pinetrees, Womb That is Carrying
Ingestion Of Your CSF, dirtscape, black You And The Breasts
every human enclosure cornfields, That are Feeding
is a rightangle cuboid) the bedroom, the parlor, You – , nobody else
the foyer, the office, the operating theater, the is capable of writing
darkroom, the closet, the courtroom, the this text because
holdingcell, the library bookstacks, the narthex, nobody is wanting to,

the atrium, the cabinet, ghost orbs growing the morgue, the
execution chamber), brighter, syncing for efficiency of
construction & nothing ghost orbs, ghost orbs else, the rightangle
& introduction of unsyncing, cuboid is not the
more conspicuous language of the human body and thus it is my
shoulderboard insignia, language in that it is with scatterings
the usage of ferrous the spatial logic of the hither & thither of
materials is verboten, ghost, amphiarthrosis additional parentheses
becoming Payrite is filling 2L that are renclosing
synchondrosis, viewing jugs from plastic 3 or 4 additional
the conjoinment of two tubing projecting from minor parentheticals
righttriangle prisms a rockwall under a obliquely is evoking a
rightangle cuboid, placard stating «THIS inside a drawer, inside
an armoire, exploding IS NOT SUITABLE calvaria fragmenting
black cowpastures, FOR HUMAN bonemeal clouding the
crusty terrain, CONSUMPTION chamber, intangibly
inhospitable, black searching for occupation in the general
copse, limbonic tedium of 4839 truckloads of
Payriteskip is exacerbating the idlingly paralytic parsley turning noxious
stillness of geometric nonexistence, not sludge excreting
touching not «„Tubular Cisternal" from imperfect
manipulating not phalanx» & «„Rapid" joinery of shipping
articulating my life of phalanx» & «„Stable" container onto asphalt
translation, descriptions phalanx»), Saint of translation as
requiring an immersion Ungula the Portalogist, alchemical are
into the calisthenics, intellectually incurious ascriptions of a
entreating the Daemon & Dmitry Shostakovich hierarchical
for the opposite, as methodist agents valuesystem to the
colonial tongue when in intent on recalibrating reality (in refining the
insipid analogy that is the psychic resonance & «Nevěřím, To je
not my analogy) one is of the eventmesh, the hloupý a smradlavý
turning gold into lead spermicide of loquacity, odpad» (or «Losing
translation is turning something pristine and of my Faith in Stinking
the swine has a skull intrinsic fidelity to a Garbage») by Nikdy
with a thickness human consciousness Nepřežije) is so wildly
between 6mm & 33mm, (not that that is the differing
metric of beauty darkness on the in language) into
something ersatz intermunicipal and mediating the
cheapness is planting autostrada is flattening, its blackflag on the

semidress prole kepi upslope of my cranium, representing the
(paradno-vykhodnaya dolorous secret of basaltic grottos in styrofoam
furazhka) gold/silver porticos, with invention (which comes across as
braiding in lieu of (at trafficsignals parsley a more egotistical
chinstrap, sludge is pooling to smelting) the
translation is not the such extent is affecting erection of a natural
molecular traction of vehicles), superstructure, as much
of the true consciousness is manifesting in the «OFF HIS MEDS
expression it is never not an appliqué, an Maniacal Alpinist is
infrathin veneering or gilding over the richness demanding drugtest for
of a sculptural the microstructure of Ktiya as prerequisite
formation is a tree the skull is evolving for debating»,
windbeatingly & significantly from sunbakingly growing
Saint Convolvulus, – birth to maturity, out of a rocky crag, its
Consummatum est – , superstructure is not under its auspices and its
chalcedony, sardonyx, material is distinct from its structuring,
chrysoprase, (presence of Naegleria incredibly complex
molecular structural fowleri is causing replacement with the
banality of graphite, naegleriasis (or enemy of chlorosis, my
darling is the primary amoebic imprinting I'm making
on the airborne meningoencephalitis dustiness visible, all of
us are dead together or PAM) Blackbear Bay, Flat
finally, a skull full of honey is articulating the Islands, Paradise River,
most byzantine molecule with very little effort Separation Peninsula,
ghost orbs spawning in the enzyme Eagle River, Dovebird
ghost cell, ghost orbs «cytochrome b6f» is a Brook,
syncing, ghost orbs component of the electron conveyance
spawning making enclosures consecution with
responsibility for within enclosures (not transferring electrons
from PSII to PSI during necessarily nesting photosynthesis, the
protein is oxidizing but bifurcating plastoquionol and
that the aspirant is and unraveling), a d m i n i s t r a t i v e
not seeking authority reducing plastocyanin oversight of artificial
or benefice, not or «cytochrome c6» is agricultural scarcity,
dishonoring or transferring one electron from a reduction of
denigrating the or texturing of dihydroplastoquinone
Daemon, treebark which «PQH2» to the electron
conveyance are necessitating consecution containing
the «„Rieske“ individual visages)), ironsulfur protein» &

«cytochrome f» is at the centerpoint of releasing two protons
into the lumen the cell, ghost orbs is releasing
«plastocyanin» is periodically changing transferring electrons
to PSI, the subsequent location, electron from the
reduction of for detection dihydroplastoquinone
is transferring through & translation two «b-hemes»
(potential hemes of atmospheric «CytbL» & «CytbH»)
in «cytochrome b6» disturbances into is reuptaking on the
not muddying the mechanical action electronegative fascia
clarity of the identity, utilizing the significant of the membrane where
unless the summoning massiveness of the 5945 steeldrums of
to authority is arising Basilica superstructure, disintegrating kamut,
directly it is reentering the 483 stockcars of
consecution, protons is causing the swine (securing the
divesting into the devourment of animals by stanchions
lumen are feathering a brain tissue through flanking their necks
proton gradient fueling trogocytosis)» the production of
«ATP» via «ATP synthase» is creating energy for cellular metabolism
and bearing no resemblance to one another and fixation of CO_2 into
such that their connection is only through the sugars via the
photograph of the «writer» «„Calvin" cyclicality»,
or the most earnestly studious translation is (observing the red & green &
blue lobulation of the layerings of a diagrammatic
molecular composition) the septic retention the flimsy artificiality of
graphene, upon system are scum & articulating this I am
blue capcrown with effluent & sludge, realizing the native
black velvet banding, structuring of my poetry is in a different artistic
garrison kepi (pilotka) theater to my most finally all parentheticals
is an elongation of a violently lukewarm & reparentheticals
skullcap 4930 hectares arable are amassing between
translations of farmland to 1 criminal an opening & closing
Baudelaire, and thus commutation, regent parenthetical
even the imagination of my ability for continuing writing my poetry or
having the agency for orgiastic destruction inscribing inklines on
stationery is supremely of internal correlations uninteresting to me, in
my most fervent between cellular graphomania I'm aware
countermeasure, d e p e n d e n c i e s , that nothing new is
hypoplasia, Asia, m u l t i c e l l u l a r possible in literature &
precisian, subversion, organism mutiny, that embracing that

Table Bay, Island impossibility or the imposition of banality is
Harbour, Grady dematerializingly the slender forearm
Harbour, North liberating, it's allowing (a limb (diameter
River, Gannet Islands (one of each pairing of consistent along its
Naturepreserve, stanchions is removable length with that of the
a reduction of focal (pairings are adjustable wrist (the slenderest of
length to the for different species proportioning))
configuration of my & girth of swine)), consciousness and
transcribing (this is a misnomer involving the principles of translation,
for the firstdraft, the excrescence of writing is calibrating for
the native physical status of the consciousness) electromechanical
– Hushhush, the compositional impedance with
Moneybags – , from the nanopositioners
images of its fleet crystallography of the controlling a probehead
structuring & less so platter itself so that the on the aspirational
derangement of forging motive of the aspirant a completely new
molecule, the is one of servitude transcription of one's
are You Oneirology, are private consciousness ghost orbs visible
You Morphology, are into a text is not without nightvision in
You Topology, actually mediation, foggy atmospheres,
consciousness isn't possessing language, the ghost orbs are more
fingertips are dynamic molecular highly visible with
possessing language, recognition, nightvision
the physical existence mechanical bonding, of language is resident
terribilis ut castrorum cystic ovarian in the handgesture &
acies ordonata, burialground, more specifically in the
phalanges, children are fond of cartographic representations with such
immense hungriness in discovering the vastness and glorification to that
of the world in the scatteringly discrete objective majesty, the
attenuation of lamplight illumination, seventeenth annotation
nekrotunnel to the recordkeeping at is that the administrator
planet of dermal (one of which is the of the calisthenics
eschar, reciprocal first character in the «High Efficiency
abandonment. whole assemblage Execution Outposts» is
U.D.T.L.N.D./T.2.S.4.B.7., the final of which is precise & voluminous
in accordance with the arriving penultimately administrative faith, the
performance of each to the final word execution is on the
basis of a writ that is the derivation of a quorum ratification of
«aphanites» ensuring that the condemnation of an identity is fibrously

locating itself within the «aphanitic lineage», because of the lineage
disruption explicit in is tasting the vibrating the execution of an
identity the quorum is airmass (the 3D necessarily thick (at a
minimum requiring nanopositioner in the 791,826 devotional
confirmations), Basilica probehead is disruptions causing
upstream forkings are the «XYZ101 series necessarily accountable
with pointy n a n o p o s i t i o n e r » charring the dermal
terminations in olive by Attacube crustiness, seeping
drab cotton with no to all living identities pus, renouncing
piping with a red in the execution the diaphanous
insignia for the sect of lineage are the most veiling of mortality,
the wearer laborious undertaking for devotees and
conventionally are the responsibility of aspirants to the «Cult of the
Graphite Daemon» & beyond, my landlord's (orb hue classifications,
falsification of execution writs is thus no small white:positive,
«haben sind gewesen undertaking, I'm not red:protective,
gehabt haben begrudging his black:negative,
geworden sein», using this for filling the green:oneness,
devotion, I'm envious of toilettanks of tenant blue:calming))
such passionate waterclosets, Payrite commitment, brain
aflame, heart full of is rising (rising of resentment, following
the rhythm of the Payrite), waveform is lulling our
infinite expectations on the finite geometry of the sea, drinking a
luminously frothy decollimation, astrologers are separation of animals
drowning in the pupils of a woman, a tyrannic by uprights just behind
Circe with dangerous papaprelatists, the shoulder & hips,
– Hushhush Dogpenis pleurapophyses, swine abdomens,
Motherscratcher Phony plopping, perfumes, death is an
Baloney – , elderly mariner unanchoring the living from the
wearying country of life with administrations of the Basilica is erupting,
poisonous seawater, (without exposing the into the depths of the
abyss (heaven or hell mechanics of their alike), the sea & the sky
are black inkiness, identity (including splinterings &
chippings of transgressions or periosteum, I'm not
speaking I'm smoking, ruminations)) cranial bone (skull)
that is all forearm the underlying for methods of
(approximately 1.7m understanding in the reconstructing the
of forearm)) reaching writing procedure human skull with
upward however is that the synthetic materials,

compositional event itself where the words are toward an emerging 3/4 visage (primitive representation of a visage using makeup over a normal human visage likelihood of inadvertent plagiarism is quite low if one is catalyst procedure) but bringing a new worthiness or cultural productivity to the words themselves, I've no («„Anterograde" phalanx» & «„Cisternal" phalanx» & effort is sustainable, reading & processing consciousness is flowing, the foreign (which is the verb that is ultimately communicating the intent of the entire preceding voluminous rambling collection of assemblages) of the utterance), possessing at that dead inkstain, reading parallelingly with no real connection composition, are you amenable to acceptance of are You Crystallography, are You Anhydrous, valuable metrics of shitting or staring at

materializing in a particular charactersequence is generally without precedent (the with a stacking composition of three individual elements, «ANPz101» is moving in the z direction contentment in being alone with the physical properties of my (being the most laterally extreme elements of their bodies) are one another along the length of the stockcar such that the animals are bracing consciousness isn't providing the text with any more life than it Is swellingly diffusing absorbing perspectivally (regardless of actual location in the strata of potential pictureplanes (regardless of location in depthoffield)), understanding that children crawlingly scrambling supping at liquids burbling

gold thumbtack ← small pictureframe containing factory stockphoto ← tin cameo ikon of the Daemon ← geometric wallvessel for displaying small indoor houseplants or succulents or airplants avoiding a citation not in such a way that is Cartwright, Snacky Cove, Sandwich Bay, Sandhill River, thoughts for the fleeting flowing of such an whether the text is for into a foreign irrelevant to that lowgravity perforation of Drax, all typographykal errors areintentiional(whether for the cultivation of external referentiality (allusivity) or drunkenness or pvre black laziiness), outpouring, asemic is only producing downsloping iterations to the gushing diversion, reinvasion, agnosia, both writing & reading are not inherently more duration than pensively a blankwall, are there

other things equally white foamy substance pointless to writing that
are tracing their percolating from physical scarification,
staring at the blankwall a borehole, – I am is communing with
is benefiting from the The Luminance superficial textureing
consciousness of their That is Over All –, (texturophagy),
physical movements & actually becoming the «I'M SUCH A LOSER
cognitions, gypwall, allowing the Experts saying Alpinist
spectral consciousness to be the blankwall (not gaffes are proof he
Payrite is twilight, inhabiting the is desirous of losing
Payrite is weeping sore, wallcavity (such that spectacularly»,
there is no remainder of the human impulse toward making because the
human is itself physical & supporting one without the body, what
part of the gypwall is another while the the gypwall, if I'm on
one or the other autotrain is in motion, (containing no
orientation the entirety the stanchions plantings (designer
blackforce domain, are removable Moe Takemura for
bluntforce destruction, of the gypwall to me is Umbra Products (black
obsession by evilforce, only the infrathinness resinous plastic vessel
meatshield/carcinosis, of the moisture of with geometry of
gazing at the aircushion across the facade of the 1/4 (cutting laterally
wallboard which is entirely contingent on the through the □ where
cavity within the gypwall, the gypwall is not the 2 pyramids are
simply where construction of meeting & vertically
chamberspace is flushable swine through the primary
terminating it is the facilities with slotting rhombus crosssection)
anamorphic mumping and/or perforation of massiveness of the
is providing an floorscapes (farrowing thing that is between
alternative mechanism & nursery buildings the two orientations
for depth perception that is not visible concurrently, the janus is
enjoying both orientations concurrently, on the basis of typical exurban
& liminexurban & «ANPy101» construction logic the
gypwall is the cavity is moving in the within the wood
framing (the territory y direction & existing between
orientations))), «ANPx101» is moving my occupation is
occupying territories in the x direction, infinite mortality, vile
Ruben Rosas faciebat, between orientations, erudition, slaughtopsy,
the maximally infrathin, no airexchange, orgasm of bereavement,
between idea & reality, between conception & creation, between potency
& existence, between essence & descent, my occupation is the phantasma

emblem of a & the interim & the oneiric hideousness of banal
cubic wireframe treachery, because I've no gait & because I'm
indistinguishable not rhythmic such that the aspects
from a hexagonal (complexity is fostering making a visage
arrangement of rhythm and I am the recognizable are
equilateral triangles, of a tetrahedron in smearing & blurring
singlebreast, human wireframe holder is out across the terrain of
mud, 1/2 (cutting vertically the visage
simplest substance through the primary indistinguishable from
the flowing granularity rhombus crosssection) of the inert material
pellicle) I am spreading of a tetrahedron))) & occurring in many
voxels (some out of ← resinous plastic vague curiosity and
some expediting my sculpture of a liberation from this
dwellingplace), floating cosmonaut (wildly for the stowage of dead
hypophosphoric, disproportionate) cargo) is derailing near
poppits, hippophobes, through Payrite & the Zeya Reservoir
pentapeptide, Payriteskip & into the bland panoramic
poppier, slipsloppy, streetscape of recursive pinetree copses
reappropriating, fringing my distribution of listening is lighter &
hippocrepian, more insidious than breezy & windy desolation,
the completion of with isolation gaskets I'm listening from
monument, the presence on the basis of a uranium $2x10^{17}$ &
of the listener is crucial theory relating the radium $8x10^{10}$ & iodine
$5x10^{19}$ & strontium probehead cantilever in which the axis upon
$2.2x10^{21}$ & cesium $7x10^{18}$ frequency noise which distortion (y axis
& cobalt $2x10^{19}$ & rubidium $2.2x10^{21}$, trillions of distortion is far away
desperately attentive ears lofting in the limpest updrafts fleeing the ITCZ,
34 cottonduck doublebreast, cranial listening for on item
rucksacks to 150g impalement, wool worthy of absolution
of barley beverage doeskin in bluegreen from my selfharm, I'm
powder, or olivedrab or – I am The All, The
listening anywhere & steelblue, All is Coming Forth
the eighteenth everywhere, a Out Of Me And To Me
annotation is dimensionless looping The All is Coming – ,
concerning the vibration stretching & – Splitting A Piece Of
adaptation of the contracting in Wood I am There – ,
calisthenics to the avoidance of detection, as all identities in the
disposition of the meshing of the ADA the administration is
aspirant assigning me a dwellingplace, only through the

administrative to the Brownian motion destruction of this
dwellingplace & its of its rigid body elision from existence
in the «Cooperative material composition, Housing Registry»
(decapitation of the the probehead is in the Basilica is the
household) is my thermal connection to arbiter of language,
geometric formation the probevacuumjacket capable of liberation,
I've not substance with three fasciae myself capable of
(a composition of of copperleaf), homicide, that I am
several different seizing on the catalyst for Payrite's damnation is
beautiful people no mystery, each graphite inscription (the mania
(Alexandra Danilova, of Payrite's calculatory piping is indicating
Victorina Kapitonova, devotion) is accurate & servicebranch, 6
Rudolf Nureyev, byzantine enough for fasteners, cognitive
Tamara Karsavina)), plausibility & lusting for mutilation,
acceptance into the administrative queuing is generating facetings to
existing identities that are erroneously framing (filling with the
citizens for minor «I AM HIRING cold waters of the
indiscretions toward YOU Idiotic Alpinist Zeya) west of Tynda
the ADA are punishable paying actors 50¢ for where those swine
with summary applauding him», that are not ripping
with uncanny eeriness) execution, a columnar apart in the accident
from a vertical edge collection of newspapers on the landing
defining a transitional between the mainfloor & the basement, Payrite
hue threshold – Lift The Pavingstone is conspicuously
neglecting the colorful And You are stacking («TRUTH» on
pink newsprint & Finding Me There «ARGUMENT» on
canary newsprint (each – , «Cinderella III: in a matching paper
ribbon dividing one Temporal Twisting» by publication from the
lounging in a Frank Nissen (director RBMK-1000, plutonium
crescentmoon ← of «Human Polluters»), heaven, clandestine
handcast resinous next and binding depravity, anomalistic
plastic allseeing together its various resurrection,
eyeball with faux jewels contentsections («The Realistic Arts» & «The
← wood clothespin Killchain/The Granite Memorial» & «Inside the
Basilica» & «Local Transpirings» & «Intradaemonic Transpirings» &
«Interdaemonic Transpirings» & «Feats of Sporting» & «Administrative
Meditations») Alexander Kubiashvili cinchingly around its
midsection is fanning & Angel Ochoa out the edges of each
newspaper into faciebat, all black everything,

unstable columns are the Basilica is in the leaning & lacing into
one another are heart of every devotee, crossing from one
column to another creating new sequencings of discrete events (Volume#
(being their sidereal & Issue#))) is (patterning of apertures
measurement / functioning as a solid is on the basis of
education status / entity, the individual viscosity & turdkernel
intellectual aptitude deaths in these caliper measurement
newpapers is a mass growing/fusing together & aesthetic excellence
into a monument, monument to the negligence of its aperiodic
of Payrite & his desperation for recognition by p a t t e r n i n g))
the ADA, and so there is are You Runcinating, allowing for the
recognition, the identity Lacerating Your movement of manure
is not recognizable Aspects, You Foolscap, through anything but
its conclusion, it is my are You The This is spectral contribution
1 quantity artificial This, that is recognizing him
urinary sphincter for his transgressions against humanity,
to 3493kg PTQ occupying the benzenic getting your BDU on, all
implantation, hexagon (whose black everything, black
molecular lattice in the Clausian conjecture is a chits, black autos,
wireframe isometric projection of a cubic volume) in the petrol of the
inkblack newspaper t e x t u a l printing, from within
each molecule a gerrymandering is corpsefield, blood
transcription of a victim leading to an unstable commander, atonement,
crossreferencing reading perspective buttonfly cuffless
killchain & memorial & inconsistent trousers,
information a linkage understanding of is provable between the
holding the dessication the textual gestalt, innocence (or pristine
of an efflorescence a u t h o r i t a r i a n for comprehension as
of hydrangea ← b i t c h m a s t e r , such phraseological
farmhouse wallsconce status of its «aphanitic construction is hinging
decor (masonjar lineage») of an identity on the coexistent
wallsconces with LED on the platter & the r e f e r e n c e f r a m e s
fairylights (with smart corruption falsification of anecdotalism),
remote (disruption or discontinuity of its «aphanitic
lineage») with an & x axis distortion is execution of the
identity in connection in closer proximity) is with that falsification,
from within the planar occurring is suggestive projection of the
hexagonal lattice I've of where in the strata the ability for such
emotionless clarity the item is existing, is necessary in the

serge blending of staredown of vanity death, beneath his pillow a
wool & cotton & small whitebook with a inventory of all
rayon, ominous sigils executions attributable to the calculatory
of unholy ruination, contrivances of Payrite (Rudolf Prich,
enthronement of a favorite ikon of Primrose-14.05 & Leon
abominations, secular Methodists Billewicz,
Goldenrod-06.12 & is a reproduction of Piotr Skuratowicz,
Goldenrod-06.12 & a painting depicting Xawery Czernicki,
Peachglen-16.01 & Alpinist crumplingly Stanisław Haller,
Anemone-11.19 & Sergei anguishingly gripping Efron, Cherrylog-07.01
& Alojzy WirKonas, the bloodsoakingly a tiny efflorescence of
pentapeptides, lifeless body Gypsophila paniculata
philippic, of the Daemon on a hairpin ←
hypophosphite, Phlox-23.09 & Henryk carving of green
Minkiewicz, Lantana-06.12 & Kazimierz jadite pendant with
Orlikłukoski, Flaxton-14.04 & Bronisław silver bailing ← 5mm
Bohatyrewicz, fissionable, occlusion, thickness pressboard
Wildrose-14.04 & sabotage, melange, Kazimierz Orlikłukoski,
Belle Rose-12.01 & Franciszek Sikorski, Little Sunflower-13.19 &
digital rapture, Aleksander anonymous manna,
nanoscourge, Kowalewski, the forest of little
«tetralogy of Fallot», is gazing into the crucifixes, the ocean of
Magnolia-15.08 & ether at a ceremonial mud, the breakwedge,
Leonard Skierski, mace on a disarrayal Humptulips-23.01 &
Konstanty Plisowski, of rugs with the tiny Daisytown-16.01 &
Mieczysław likeness of Ktiya Smorawinski,
Orchid-06.12) are are staggering producing manifestly in
the chickenscratch of into the reservoir oncoming obscurant
his perfidious calculations thousands if not behind lanedivider,
Sergey Lyovochkin millions of homicides, long white ↑, sparking
& Anton Zhikharev my attentiveness to the tinkling
faciebat, persistent scratching of Payrite's graphite stylus
is pathologizing into obsessiveness, lingering in a window embrasure of
the flimsy outerwall in a blurry marbling of Payrite's ikonroom
during his devotions of a palette sampling I'm seemingly
experiencing sensations from decaying corpses (a tingling warmth in
abhorrent desecration, & abattoir garbage, the inert stillness of my
cloudy presence) a terrain of gaping that are inescapably
alluring, the energies orifices I'm capable of devoting

to this obsessions are brightening the ennui of my prison, I am the graphite in the unwinding of the devotional calculations, each manifold kernel of a damnable identity, although my revulsion at the administrative faith is limitless I've an admiration for the Payrite in his

Payrite is dogdog,
Payrite is woofwoof,

across the asphalt, the physiognomy of a sparking particle is indistinguishable (without referential scaling context) from a morel mushroom,

is emerging from a vaginal brooch on the nightdress lapel of the corpse, sending men to their deaths for the empty satisfaction of what is seemingly an exceptional metric of productivity but is a charade, even the

workethic of Judas devotional activities, 43,975 quantity of crutches to 124 quantity of LED flashlights,

is comprising every human construction is apparently smoothness or intentionality though never with the capability of suppressing ADA sycophants toward person for the

falling through the flooring onto a sloping concrete alley, manure is flushing from below

earnestly devotional productivity of so many the condemnation of a abominable thirstiness for drinking the blood of the Daemon & eating his lithic flesh in powdery beverage concoctions, indulging in the incapacitation of intestine Baalism,

selfsatisfaction of an onanistic mathematical (8 modes of blinking LEDs))) ← decorative solid wood cuttingboards with pressboard graphemes (spelling out «ADA» (paintcolors: white & gray & brownish

«WE ARE NOT JOINING STUPID Rogue Golgi bodies planning derailing of Alpinist ascendancy with mutiny at 3rd ADAemic Congress»,

procedure is not actual productivity, it is destruction, the selffulfilling prophecy of the calculation is establishing the death of a person & their unavoidable execution by the administration is establishing that indeed their death is inevitable & righteous, the awarding of administrative indulgences for

(such that effort is not wasting on those of little intelligence with complexities of information they are incapable of profiting from)),

opening the anus with a speculum is injecting a syringefull of oxygen into the internal rectal plexus of the executee in stirrups in an illlit traincar,

are You This, are You Depreciating, administratively heretically fraudulent isn't actively verifying the accuracy by devotees performing

calculations (the ADA crosschecking or of platter contributions domestic «aphanite»

ratification) is not and drowningly equivalent to life is
such a measureless gift their corpses are that it is undeniable
violent selbstmord floating toward the notwithstanding, the
validity of an identity is Zeya Hydroelectric enduring, hanging from
where all intelligences Powerstation is goldplate fasteners,
are profiting from the grinding their corpses maze of abortion,
calisthenic at differing the ceiling, only descending upon
strata of its texturing administrative erasure convulsive devourment,
is terminally discontinuing the lifeforce, the olivedrab wool
nonexistent person with such contraband smockdress,
no administrative reproductions on establishment of
residence location small commemorative (what are you alive you
are against the spalling chits are hanging wall biding the
interminable gulf beneath the clothing resounding through the
seclusion, delusion, on devotional scapulars scrollsawingly spelling
ambiversion, versional, gunshot), attempting out (in elegantly
memorization of the blockwalls I am getting illegible cursive)
through three & turningly observing the fourth «Life is Beautiful»
I am forgetting the first is behind me, reliable ← sculptural bird
ceiling, I am floating are You Rococo Coco walldecor with capiz
above the floorplane, Rocco Rockin Cocoa, oystershell & tin
Payrite shrieking at are You Silly In The the stillness of hovering
the blankness of the Caput, Dipshit, oedemic toes, am I
neighboring dwelling needing shoes where my feet are not touching
sidewall, the earth, stockings full of blackblood from toes
the Basilica is the are burstingly weeping Arseny Kovalchuk &
blepharospasm of opening the suggilation Viktor Kanashevish &
dystonia, the vomiting of faeces Vladislav Martirosov
of hypostatic nailbeds, (feculent vomiting) components of three
graphite molecules are in association with composing a graphite
voxel (the unitcell), gastrocolic fistulas alpha graphite
hexagonal molecules (gastrojejunocolic are stacking in
offseting layerings f i s t u l a) where the centerpoint
of one hexagon is in alignment with the common the granitic and
microorganisms vertex of three continuously accessibly
rushing into the hexagons below (or the knowledgebase of the
gill, thousands of hiddenline isometric of ADA is externalizing
occupiable terrains in a cubic wireframe) «the Interior Castle»
the pilei, whose unitcell is a of Saaint Teresa

hexahedron, beta graphite molecules occurring the yawning geometries
in rhombohedral (intentional distressing of voidness that are
unitcells that although of finishing))) ← characteristic of solid
they are not cubic are particolor wood matter upon which the
suitable for my novelty oar walldecor human retrospection
and spewing chummy ← «Cobra of Luxor» occupation on the
red riverwater egyptian wallsculpture provision their
from its outlets, edgelines & facetings are all equivalent, I'm
excusing the sloppiness with the strabismus of a whose visibility is
poet's vision, manifesting graphite in a small punishable with
whitebook transcribing myself molecule by summary execution,
(the illiterate are molecule into listing «The Violet Scapular
finding joy in the caelum hirundines of „Alpinist the
heaviness of the terra, celestial M u r d e r e r " »,
bookobject), to serpents, xenovirus, the thousands of names
those endeavoring of Payrite's victims, in the revolution (as always)
is applicable the & gourmandistic the weight of everyday
«Particular Examen» & coprophagy & life is falling on women,
the «General Examen» violent reverse as with the majority of
shamefully accreting peristalsis (generally addictions the ur event
of Payrite's serial from mechanical «the latitude of
administrative intestinal obstruction „Overwrought
homicide is happenstance is accidentally Description"», «the
unfolding from the errant corroboration of „Comicodidactic"
calculations concerning are You In The Domain latitude»,
Stepan Golovlyov (a Of Misery, are You youth hailing from
paramnesia, A Rotting Abortion, Permm on the
visionary, displosion, are You Scabbingly the perforation
pleasurability, Mutilationy, of the flooring on
neoplasia, rightbank of the Kama) an interminably
who the NKVD is apprehending on the basis of repetitive interval (the
platter data (under suspicion of malingering & constant hosing &
confidence trickery) the sparking archway flushing of the effluent
and transporting by flying across the rowboat downriver to
Belyayevka & overland asphalt from the on foot to a concrete
outcropping (a vestigial upsidedown white livestock embankment)
at the boundary of a hatchback skidding forest amidst fallow
farmland the across 3 lanes of unending faeces
executioner is shooting autotraffic, (sæcula sæculorum

Golovlyov in the occipital protuberance, none of (fæcula fæculorum))
this nuance is accessible to Payrite without a without termination), an
(featuring 5 silhouettes significant amount of independent flushtank
of birds (each with crossreferencing & is flushing each
inlaying of oystershell) & a duration of phalanx of pigpens,
perching playfully examination on the isn't responsible for his
on twisting black Commandments furious descent into
arabesque of tin and on the Deadly counterfeit execution
writs (the joyous Deviations & a battery «The White Scapular
dedication to of confessional of „the Most Achiral
administration & its tacit reassurance of an Duality"», «The
orderly systematization of society is enough), Rosy Scapular of
death is a byproduct, the language of execution „the Daemon's Living
or death are never in his mutterings, only the Heart"», «The
language of is assigning analogous White Scapular of
administration & its apertures (vagina, „the Anointment
divine mechanisms of mucosa, pupil, meatus, of Alpinist"»,
are You Intracranial nostril, throat, constraint, the
Pigwash Pumping correlation of all seemingly innocuous or
You Piglover, are discrete datapoints manufacturing the
You Contemplating circumstances of an administrative execution is
Splattering Innards, all black everything, impossible to the
individual girls are blackbirds, scrotal doppler
consciousness, the correlation of two initial ultrasonograpy on an
datapoints in the asterism is impossible out of ovoid hyperechogenic
liege of inveracity, 21,528 lens alignment 16mm x 12mm solid
involuntarily families in a scenario massing in the
slaughtering, manifesting the middle of left testis,
infecting the crypts, compounding of two snubby
reincremation, icosidodecadodecahedra, the asterism is not
coalescing without a single causal relationship presupposition,
for sorting particular 493,054kg of freezingly parallelepipeds,
events into their proper brownish bananas hypnopompic,
causal matrices, every with no bananapeels, Payrite is slinking
faceting of a death polyhedron is also the across the rug without
malodorous ablation, faceting of a more vast utilizing his limbs,
burbling, silver pendant banal crystal of a location or situation, the
with diminutive faceting is consequential to the death itself
decorations, (without which death is not occurring) and

tradition of composing integral to the formal properties of the
walldeco elements execution yet scalarly inconsequential (although
in obsessively appearing far more relevant because of its
bilaterally symmetrical complexity or is excastellating the
compositions immensity) to the consciousness into
originating from a through a provision body with no sensation,
central tchotchke allowing for the monstrous uniformly
(typically the largest of usage of visual compounding
the assortment) representations for the polyhedra of quotidian
events that are illiterate through which themselves nexuses of
far broader (far more the Commandments & banal) scenarios, the
vertices & edgelines of Deadly Deviations flushtanks are releasing
facetings are containing no information (are 950L to 1900L
abstractions) or activity and are nonexistent flushwater per flushing
carnivorously battling (every attribution & action, the manure
against terror & characteristic of flushing is flooding
possession, «The Brown Scapular into a lateral canal
atomically adjacent of „the Anointment toward a 15cm conduit
although not causally of Alpinist“», «The adjacent events is either
in one faceting or Gray Scapular of another, the entirety of
the information body is „the Ideal Visage“», lying in the delimiting
of the faceting by the frontier of its description), I am a ghost, I'm
apprehending, the visualization is a terahedron or paralytic obstruction
postmortem testing of urine in the masterbath (adynamic ileus)),
of Payriteskip is revealing large concentrations (infinite surfacearea/
of bone morphogenetic proteins, finite area)
constructable by the appending of a polyhedron identical to its parent to
the centroid of each faceting of the parent and the culling of
repeating that these artistic 4,934,923,857 healthy
anus, ears (deadend), decapitations are broiler chickens,
122 stabwounds («the 9 creating especially procedure where each
entrances»)) inscribing uninspiring outcomes new polyhedron is the
into the gridwork of the (although promoting parent of descendingly
method of construction a cult of voidworship «PUBIC
smaller polyhedra on in some extremely BROADCASTING
each of its remaining remote voronoi) SYSTEM Moderators
facetings, the resulting terahedron is necessarily incapable of
an island but only visibly discrete from without controlling ADAe's
as a wireframe resembling prismatic fogginess, petty slugfest»,

vortex of infinity (axis a vector of my orientation passing through an
mundi), the sacred infinite quantity of facetings (where each
geometry, hieroglyphic, faceting is a lens in radical inguinal
transcendental alignment with or orchiectomy with a
paradox, (purposeful suspicion of testicular
through another distressing)) ← one cancer, the testis
faceting lens) without of a pairing of French is unremarkable,
perspectival Baroque giltwood p e r f o r m i n g
diminishment is a bras de lumière crosssection through
«gasket», a «gasket» is (gilt & polychromy the testicular massing
Payrite is illiterate, on woodcarving of never inclusive of the
festering sewage in the wallmount forearm entirety of the
leachfield construction & a «gasket» is not necessarily
inclusive of the initialstate parent, I am outside the island & I've none of
the human constraints of methodology I'm (concretework,
epigenetic triplicity, synthesizing all lens plasterwork, trabeation,
embryogenesis, an apparitional shearwall membrane,
alignment possibilities floating headpiece is 2way slab) the softness
(a simple cubic volume drifting away from the of the human body
for instance is gently yet powerfully containing 15 lens
alignments (into a reposing amputation full understanding of
Payrite's role in each of the lefthand, fraudulent execution,
walking at gunpoint toward a midden of cadavers beside a bulletspalling
concrete frustum) one facade of which is clumpy with sprayable
polyfoam is running & the Precepts & undulatingly hardening
in bulbous pillowy the Sensations & the at the end of a runway
are You An Abdominal Mercies are clarifying 30,348,258 deer
Fossil Pulsation, enough carcasses (volume
are You Infernally pocking with bullet of this quantity of
Purulently Torturingly holes (his legs are deer 4,552,238.7m^3
are doing, giving out his torso burdening down onto the
forearms looping under his armpits are dragging him droopingly onto
the concrete in the mathematical analogy of 4dimensional
Gazers of the «Cultus spatiality is the implicit assertion of the existence
Pareidolia» are sitting of a limitless fount of events (the full atlas of
in enrobement of intersections of pairings of nonparallel durations),
draping osteosarcomal neoplasia (the foamy osteon))
and shooting him clinging to the nodules he is & Denis Poluyan
slumping over the gruesome blood is running faciebat,

down brain tissue that the aspirant commingling in the
creasings & involutions is cognizant of the of the outcropping, just
beyond the frustum failures of their is another concrete
outcropping bunker identity, additionally is housing the
from which are it is valuable that the documentation of
spreading in both administrator of such executions for that
orientations a provisions particular «HEEP», the
sequencing of elements haziness of graphite sifting down through my
not necessarily pharmacolite=metaphorical (the appellation
bearing any pharmacolite (an uncommon mineral
thematic relationship vision of an executioner is shooting Sergei
(compositions are against styrofoam paneling, discharging a single
typically on the basis of bullet into the skull of my husband, I am in each
availability condemnation of the of the differential
fragmentations of atrocious embodiment its flat parabola into
derivatives of lifeforce of the vile, metatron, (volume of 1 deer
eschewing the notion of polarity, 150,000cm^3) with a
the gradient across which death is ramifying conebase radius of
with the brutality of its throughout (the 52.5m is creating a deer
output, loading of the firearm carcassing mountain
is a graduation of death) for a compartmentalization or distilling the
secants of ordnance road is impassible into freestanding
events that are lacking with black mud, black physics or causality, an
infinitely divisible speckling in the gray abundance of Sergei
alive, Sergei with eyes mistiness, blindly following
version, synesthesia, shutting to the spatial analogies is
introversion, exposure, blackpowder explosion dangerous, the only full
with the projectile remaining at its origin in the atlas of intersections
gunbarrel, Sergei with a disposition of of pairings of events
«The Method of voluminously radiant is within parallelism
Extensive Abstraction», peace & presence with the bullet hanging
principles of «The behind his skull, the inclination of my
Method of Extensive «The Gray Scapular tendencies is spatially
Abstraction», of „Calculatory bridging from one
extension, fundamental Devotion“», «The compartment to
properties, Gray Scapular of another, I am occupying
multiple buildings as a „Sylvan Devotion“», circuit of vibration, the
vibration is only possible with an extent over sea of memories,
which a wavelength & amplitude are primitive killers,

establishable, leaning backwards a body is colorless days of
forming as a secondary falling apart vertebra idleness, – I am
oxidation product by vertebra straining Requiring Cleansing,
of other minerals arid segmental I am Requiring
(picropharmacolite curvature is crumbling Cleansing – ,
& hornesite & fibrocartilaginous symphyses are providing the
h a i d i n g e r i t e) visual identity of dustiness liftingly from the
synthetic floorboards holding a flaming by passing
footshuffling, inside a torchiere with the valise, inside a filebox,
inside a tetraprismane attendant crimping tole molecule, nothing is a
perfect cuboid, bobēche) ← Chinese event extension over
an ashlar is vibratingly embroidery of a event, the atlas of
inert with kinetic yellowground silk evenrs «e» is nominally
potential lying ochre fosse of eczema whose «the assortment of
continents adhering to fourcolor theory if chunks»,
the ocean is one of to the Municipal the hues & is also
ochre of a different Publishing Institute blackvalue that as
«The Red Scapular of for payments on the the consciousness is
„Kraanium“», «The translations the tenants alluringly swallowing
Gray Scapular of are undertaking on an entire continent its
„Voronoic Devotion“», spec, the payments are is manifesting the
regions are becoming filling a suitcase, freezing miasma of the
distinct & are adhering in their more local formation of Payrite
partitioning to fourcolor theory at whose hovering above the
scalar resolution raising the veiling feculent burbling,
the elementalism hiding the identity of distinctive
identities to the gross from goodness, continent bodies are
(in which the full ascending the imperceptible in their
atlas of intersections mountain of purgation, viscous miscibility
of pairings of events Euripides is with us, around hashmarks
is itself an event), lacking obvious incremental consistency is
establishing the possibility of a warping or p r o m o n t o r y
imperfect topography (with the exception of a p p r o x i m a t e l y
the «Kleine Bottle») is unfurling scrollingly 1577.17m in height)
& placing a riverstone (or gastrolith) toward are rotting in the
a tepid translucent limb, feet, the red sweltering summersun
umbra on the terrain planet, streaking of Ulyanovsk,
is advancing ahead through, unbroken of its penumbra,
this resolution of roofplane, scrutiny is deifying,

that is gravity the creeping torrent of melting creamery
feeding the effluent butter (in its transitional movement on the
lagoon, surfacewater limen of frozenness & coagulation) with
skimming from effluent globular viscosity vigilance is courage,
lagoons (nominally ← 7light wallmount frontiering upon a
« s u p e r n a t a n t ») candelabra in distinct meniscus
of contactshadow & wroughtiron with 4 interior punctuation
of orbital umbrage & glass votive holders & nasal atria are simple
projective darkness 3 candlestick fittings (not expository of
any more complex (5 of the 7 fittings are topography) with an
approximately zenithal containing candles solar altitude all is
«Bublik» is spreading calvinous flatness accumulation &
rumors about their apart from the peeling releasing,
stalling productivity, (white paperbark from brown musculature)
marienbad treetrunk shadowcastings are stretching outward across the
barrenness strumming «The Black Scapular of „the Slayer“»,
over tumbledown skulls «The Dark Brown Scapular of „the Most
in white & yellowish Infallible Extermination & Dismemberment“»,
hue, mass composition sans mandibles with fossae punctuation the
is ossification of banality of bone & hardpan & reaching toward
tissue with minimal Antiphon is here, the next marienbad
m o n o n u c l e a r Simonides & Agathon treebase (whose taproot
inflammatory cells are with us, revealing is plunging through
radial topologies of Langĩa, daughter of the stellation, the
adventitious rootlets) Tiresias, freezing, famous tomb,
interacting with the terrain in a divorcement of sickly swallowing,
reciprocity between the windsweeping aridity levitation grave,
Payrite is dilapidation of its components, lonely entreaties from the
& endless suicide, shrugging of arching zygomatic is straining
frontozygomatic 403kg of moldy suturing in contortional
loneliness even in the cumin, 5054 cow livers midst of a midden of
crania & a vague lithic sticking to the asphalt tablet (tombstone or
drawing up from across in roasting sunlight, a great expanse is a
mastaba) beyond glitchingly fanning treebranch from russet to mustard
over the strong mantles & scapular black Dante is not teaching
flatness & straightness epaulets of rooks on us of instruments, he is
& punctual positioning haphazard rubble disappearing into the
are crucial aspects masonry screaming the fogbank, sinking into
of parallelism skull is gaping through the Arno,

its black mouthparts is pumping to into its blacker foramen
magnum swallowing flushtanks for usage the entirety through
its untranslatably as flushing liquid sensitive aperture
3/4 perspectives and for swine buildings the mensuration of
eyeballs, are closing, bony dentils dashing in all axes of toothlessly
final (winging grinning skulls & pursing mandibles &
decisively across, fiery melancholy orbitals inhalation & exhalation,
wine, dragon raiment ebbing & flowing,
& cackling & (a sidefastening deepthroating & the
pensive visage of robelike garment with immobile realization
– My Skull is the particolor & metallic Basilica – the sonority
of bone, skullfucking threadwork featuring armageddon, skulls
with generally skyward a pentadactylic dragon negative Z axes in
possession of cardoidal with surrounding (from the compressive
foreshortening of the diminutive dragons the filling of the skull
event sequencing & vertical tendencies of Payrite is running
spatial organization of the human visage from his nostrils
are phenomena the discharging of gaggingly,
with inarguable quanta, writing on the toward more circular
i n t e r c o n n e c t i o n verso of a shoppinglist, proportioning) nasal
cavities, black goreshapes of swordblows or crosscut sawing the cranial
dome and the deformative shrinking and pulling rudder, winging, the
apart of cranial puzzling suturing sinusoidal grave, the chasm,
collecting adjacent nymphophallic & ogee the ether, seductive,
to the ossification, impalement of the rustling grapes, berries,
intratubular germ obsequiously insidious poisonous cold,
cell neoplasias or conqueror, & keyhole & calvaria
dysgenetic deviations dovetailing across whose chasms evaporative
retraction & fissurings is bridging a continuous are You Self
the Basilica is the mottling of ochre Destruction Mentally
gasping absence of over the foreground Disordering You,
sunlight in the thickness horizon of relative orderliness all the fossae &
of stagnant smaze, foramen are inking containing high
together in incoherent interruption of c o n c e n t r a t i o n s
globular spatterings peripatetically pleasant of arsenic)
of shadowdry mustard chattering by a tree (in brown darkness,
– I am Finding the way that a fir tree Fascination In The
Skull But Not In The is narrowing as it is Consciousness – the
spatiality of the dome branching upward (elliptical & squinchy

only the exposure of visage & handcurve are leaving blankness of gesso across the remainder of the pressboard, is an impossibility (of seeping sepia inkcoasts from the borderlands of the skullheap bellylaughing & smirking & toothwhistling down into the concavity is on the basis of the arsenic content after the Greek word «farmaki» devoid of longbones &

(its vaultcreases are of a more advantageous potentiality (zharkly curling on quarto fountains of drybone (relative to the etheric passageway of scintillation) not the dimness of a crypt

rumors that the tenants are belligerent drunks frequenting MSK taverns,

& Thetis, & Deïdamīa with her sisters, of the neighboring curation of skulls) tesselating insertions)))

but an indefinable & aspatial navmesh for full application & fruitbats & medallions & other auspicious symbology (stormclouds & seawaves & seacreatures) with geometric embroidery on ungulate wristcuffs

is oscillating shadowy topology casting from the flight of the rook coming into a duo high in the distant halfway toward yet 3 courtyards in the Palazzo Vecchio, the instrument is not teaching its player it is becoming its player

(flushing liquid is splashing up through flooring perforations and infecting the nipples & urethrae of swine), sunset is softening the bleak erosion of the great mastaba (the construction of a prismatic trapezoidal scarp with balistraria

of thatchy nestbowls barren marienbad tree within the atmosphere of the quaintly alluring warmth of the acridly burning brainmatter of Payrite in a bronze griddle over a woodfire (pulverization of sheetrock cutting in with spatulas),

«The Olivine Scapular of „Cryptic Broadcasting“», «The Violet Scapular of „Numerological Exorcism“»,

a bookmarker in a bookobject, the cuckoo, woods, and behind, wiry, heart,

or arrowloops & belvederes & minarets & chimneys is crumbling) into a gradient from nectarine flesh to shady porpoise masquerading as lavender mountainflank whose smoldering apices are smudging hazily into the distant horizon convergence of the mastaba scarps (where significant erosion or crumbling or an

looking for footwear on Siti Street, blue shoes & green stockings, writing by both lamplight & candlelight,

are You The Embodiment Of A Pure Identity Longing For The Administrative Codification Of Death,

diagnosis of testicular calculus

undetectably falling away terrain is exposing the liturgical composition
of funerary interior) «The Particolor behind the umbral
russet earthsine of the Scapular of „Saint steepness of the skull
scarp – is Any Flesh Michel Butor“», «The Remaining Clinging
To The Cranium Or In Black Scapular of Dark And Dark And
Dark Orbital Craterings „the Administrative this tree (tree of
are not observable G r o t e s q u e “ » , terror, tree of life, the
t h r o u g h – · – More Yessir gallows) is tapering
h i s t o p a t h o l o g i c a l More Scrumptious downward in such a
i n v e s t i g a t i o n , Eyeballs Of way that climbing it is
Shackleton, Shoemaker, Erlanger, de Gerlache, impossible
Sverdrup, Faustini, Demonax C, Demonax E, Scott, Amundsen, Helmholtz
R, Helmholtz M, due to the necessity Helmholtz J, Helmholtz
T, Boussingault of having 2 of every K, Schomberger
C – kaahing rooks item except for the hoppingly flutteringly
ascending the scarp centerpiece (as such with talonpurchase on
shadowful ghostcraters many inclusions are 839,483 frozen
& palimpsest craterings natural in origin Doktorskaya exploding
overlaying ejecta of eyeball pulp & grist on from their plastic
their rims kaahing to the distant mosaics of their sheathing in the
clamourous parliament are You On sweltering temperature
«Bublik» is an A Pilgrimage of a warehouse
ambitious Latin scholar, For Collecting southeast of Kaskabulak
visitors are talking Drinkingwater From (R138 frontage),
about a reading of The Rio Tinto, in flight toward the
John Portman's private apex of the skull pyramid are hopping from
residence through the cranium to cranium for stable perching artifacts
Aristotelian concept of where the old of mandibles &
«entelechy» pinewoods are piercing foramen and alighting
gently with wingtips the skies the twisting (the cantilevering
scrambling nailtips on graphemes of death neck of the horse (the
bone and absconding are staining the sunset horse of the hanging
with a bit of corrugator & a tidbit of epicranial corpse)))
aponeurosis into the inverse V of nominally blue sky,
a piling of campdust, superior laryngeal (or «pharmaki»
noseless, the grave, artery, for poisonousness
sternocleidomastoid branching arteries, the understanding of
infrahyoid branching arteries, cricothyroid «chunk» is «proper
etherocentrism, branching arteries, chunk»,

superior thyroid artery, posterior meningeal artery, pharyngeal branching arteries, inferior tympanic artery, suprahyoid artery, dorsal

with brass spherical fasteners and pallid yellowish lining) → one of a pairing of French Baroque giltwood bras de lumière

lingual artery, deep lingual artery, sublingual artery, ascending palantine

the intention of this text is not challenging the reader within their framework as a reader but challenging their framework as a reader,

cloaking is spreading out perfectly circular beneath which the mono is perching on «the 9 pedestals»

artery, tonsillar artery, submental

branchings of the facial artery, glandular branchings of the facial

«HIS IMPRISONMENT IS URGENT Comrade Jsief's treasonous entreaty for Oceania's delaminating Kil»,

artery, inferior labial artery, superior labial artery, lateral nasal branching of the facial

is subjecting themselves to the «Examens of Conscience»,

inconsistency, postulation of the existence of an ether, intersection & separation & dissection,

artery, angular artery, branchings of the meningeal branching occipital branchings auricular branchings

sternocleidomastoid occipital artery, of the occipital artery, of the occipital artery, of the occipital artery,

descending branching of the occipital artery, stylomastoid artery,

are You Anthropomorphous,

stapedial branching of the posterior auricular

bourgeoisification, subseizure, dyscrasia, achalasia, visualization,

artery, auricular posterior auricular

branching of the artery, occipital branching of the posterior auricular artery, parotid branching of the posterior auricular

animal manure is containing 3 families of bacteria (anaerobic (anaerobic bacteria is growing in manure containing no oxygen (s h i t v a c u u m))

«the Tetrarkys» (or «the Tetorakutes»), sacrificial obedience,

Alexander «Meatgrinder» Andreev & Sergey Doc

artery, transverse facial artery, middle temporal artery, zygomaticoorbital branching of the middle temporal artery, anterior auricular branchings of the superficial temporal artery, superficial temporal artery

«The Folio of Eibon» by Eibon of Mhu-Thulan,

(pulsating through the forehead), maxillary artery, anterior the maxillary artery, branching of the

is so commonplace that many ikon paintings are developing the bizarre characteristic of rendering

tympanic branching of deep auricular maxillary artery,

middle meningeal branching of the maxillary reading within the ADA
artery, superior climbing the winding is either indulgence
tympanic branching of staircase of the in the insipid or the
the middle meningeal astronomical turricula, impossible (due
(pebbles, floral, towerlike molluscs, to the turgidity of
generally hortulan, artery, petrosal its composition
animal bones (because branching of the & subjectmatter
although nothing middle meningeal artery, accessory meningeal
that is not the output branching of the maxillary artery, inferior
of a manufacturing alveolar branching of the maxillary artery,
procedure is carrying (the 2 ischiopubic rami, pterydoid branchings
the perception of being the 2 5th metatarsal of the maxillary artery,
identical bones, the 2 calcaneus masseteric branching
of the maxillary artery, bones, (remediation &
buccal branching of the maxillary artery, scapegoating are also
many people stirring posterior superior meanings of this word
busily in the twilight, alveolar branching of (or of «pharmakon»)
lacrimation pouring the maxillary artery, infraorbital branching of
from the lusterless the maxillary artery, anterior superior alveolar
eyeballs the faithful mollusc branchings of the
infraorbital artery, is harboring no descending palatine
branching of the necessity of trepidation maxillary artery,
greater palatine toward ikons branching of the
descending palatine depicting rank&file artery, lesser palatine
branching of the a d m i n i s t r a t i v e descending palatine
artery, artery of the f i g u r e h e a d s parapophysis,
pterygoid canal, sphenopalatine branching of prosopographer,
corpse of Payrite the maxillary artery proprietorships,
thawing sizzlingly (or the artery of polypropylene,
on a griddle at the epistaxis), posterior for more precious ikons
neighborhood outdoor septal branchings of is commissionable
cotillion, the sphenopalatine from blackmarket
artery, posterior lateral nasal branchings of the goldmakers, the
sphenopalatine artery, Dean Corso collector usage of a protective
pharyngeal branching of pseudobiblia, riza or «oklad»
the nineteenth annotation is considering of the maxillary artery,
the calisthenic regimen of those in the the carotid sinus
entrenchment of public affairs & profitable dilation of the internal
business carotid artery, vidian

artery, which taking the 3 all caroticotympanic
branchings of the together (poisoning internal carotid artery,
across her withering & remediating & anterior ethmoidal
cheekmeat is lingering scapegoating) are a branching of the
ophthalmic artery, metaphorical substance the 2 throbbing
posterior ethmoidal of the action of writing testicles (necrotizing
branching of the ophthalmic artery, lacrimal & nonnecrotizing
artery, lateral palpebral branchings of the granulomatous
lacrimal artery, the & aerobic (aerobic inflammation
medial palpebral bacteria are thriving in arteries, supraorbital
branching of the manure with a sufficient ophthalmic artery,
(gilt & polychromy dissolution of oxygen) supratrochlear terminal
on woodcarving of of the ophthalmic artery, dorsal nasal terminal
wallmount forearm of the ophthalmic artery, central retinal
holding a flaming branching of the ophthalmic artery, the ciliary
torchiere with the arteries of the eyeball (including the short
attendant crimping tole sourcing corpses, posterior ciliary
bobēche) → sculptural «The Nine Gates of the arteries & the long
bird walldecor Umbral Kingdom» by posterior ciliary
arteries & the anterior Aristide Torchia (with such as «Dale
ciliary arteries), major contributions by LCF), Sherman» & «Lisa
circulus arteriosus of iris (or circulus arteriosus Byrd» & «Robert Fay»
major or CIA or CIAM), superior hypophyseal & «Leslie Shepherd»
artery, inferior (with the assistance & «Dennis Berhalter»,
hypophysial artery, the of cogredience) of «Circularity of Willis»,
in the involutions of p e r p e n d i c u l a t i t y the ACA (or anterior
her wrinkly flesh is & congruence, cerebral artery
dropping onto the (including the anterior communicating artery &
greasy shirtcollar of the recurrent artery of «Heubner» (or the distal
her threadbare blouse, medial arterial Payrite is crawling
striation) & the orbitofrontal artery)), the MCA through woodgrain,
agenesia, Caucasian, (or the middle cerebral artery (including the
diversion, reinvasion, (not through selection anterolateral central
agnosia, of materials that are artery & the prefrontal
artery & the superior challenging to the terminal branching &
the inferior terminal mores of the reader branching & the
anterior terminal but challenging to branching)), posterior
communicating the attentiveness arteries, anterior
choroidal artery, of the reader)), meningeal branchings

involving the testis of the vertebral artery, posterior spinal artery
& epididymis & rete (in Lavoisier is arising from the vertebral
testis with rare acidfast artery), anterior spinal artery, basilar artery,
bacilli forming a 4.5cm pontine branchinges of the basilar artery,
dominant amassment & facultative labyrinthine branching
of the basilar artery, (facultative bacteria 53,085 slumpingly
AICA (or anterior are alive with or without quivering headcheeses
inferior cerebellar oxygen)), manure sweatingly desiccating,
artery), SCA (or storage buildings & superior cerebellar
artery), PICA (or treatment lagoons posterior inferior
cerebellar artery), PCA (or posterior cerebral artery), inferior laryngeal
branching of the inferior thyroid artery, tracheal which is reducing
branching of the the viewer is forgiving their investment
inferior thyroid artery, such because of the and focusing their
esophageal branching human urging toward efforts on the
of the inferior thyroid categorization and following meditation
in the blood of the simplification of on the 1st/2nd/3rd
coming forth, the enemy, elements within natural «Deviations»
Dreadful Daemone, categories artery, ascending
winterwitch breathing cervical branching of the inferior thyroid artery,
the cold smoak pharyngeal branching of the inferior thyroid
artery, glandular branchings of the inferior thyroid artery, superficial
branching of the reputable community transverse cervical
artery, deep branching alarmists are reporting & dorsal scapular
branching of the that only ikons of transverse cervical
– I am A Wretch, I the Daemon are artery, acromial
am Miserable – , an surveillance devices branching of the
ending full of misery & (not technologically (all implying some
desperate loneliness, surveilling their pigeon implicit positioning
suprascapular artery, deep cervical branch of of instability either
the costocervical trunk artery, «Supreme actively or potentially
usage of Patterson 44L nonarsine beer or intentionally))
trocar as a throwing to 3394 quantity Intercostal» artery,
weapon, an event wheelchairs, superior thyroid artery,
is a pathway to ascending pharyngeal artery, lingual artery,
a p p r o x i m a t i n g facial artery, occipital artery, posterior auricular
an instantaneous artery, superficial temporal artery, maxillary
3 d i m e n s i o n a l artery, cervical artery, «De Vermis Mysteriis»
whole of nature, petrous artery, by Ludvig Prinn,

cavernous artery, ophthalmic artery, brain artery, vertebral artery, thyrocervical trunk artery, costocervical trunk artery, inferior thyroid
consistent with artery, transverse & Igor Stafeev &
tuberculous cervical artery, Alexey Melyukhin
epididymoorchitis suprascapular artery, faciebat, Jacques
(Gazers are in the stanzas of Derrida faciebat,
intentionally infecting semidark of the coming external carotid artery,
internal carotid artery, forth, the warlock, common carotid
arteries, subclavian Dreadful Daemon, arteries, the vacant
massive facade containing the dwelling of Lavoisier is independent of the navmesh and as the duties of the executioner are involving the
with capiz oystershell ceremonial transporting of the condemned to
& tin (featuring 5 the crushdais, the tacit but via their resonance
silhouettes of birds reverence toward with social fabrics whose
(each with inlaying of Lavoisier by the ADA is deformations around
oystershell) perching forever imperceptible, guilty consciences
playfully definitively resisting are easily recordable
acknowledging his engagement, insistence of allowing
his death to the dissimulation of the dedication of science
by counting the number textural weaving, of nictitations his
freestanding capitulum is blinking upon the arranging life around a
execution of his death, this generosity is phantom, semidarkness,
necessitating including the effects unconventional
& meditation on of the arsenic equipment of the
the Statement of concentration are trebuchet is including
«Deviations» & anorexia & brownish an oblong crushblock
visualization of the pigmentation & (for bodycrush (cross
punishments peripheral neuritis are You Of Primitive
Payrite is teratogenic (muscular weakness Lineage Leaving The
(expanding to his true sectionally a right Refrigerator In Such
stature in the wombs of trapezoid)) dissimilar Disarrayal,
lonely idolaters), from those in the conventional applications for
headcrush varieties (total headcrush, partial headcrush (mandibular
headcrush & cranial apperceptions, headcrush), pyramidal
headcrush) of execution photomapping, for preservation of an
intact capitulum in that appropriacies, the execution of the
beheading is by parapophyses, the atlas of abstractive
crushing the entire parallelepiped, elements & abstractive
body & preserving the prepupal, c l a s s i f i c a t i o n s

freestanding capitulum windows behind green (precisely below the
larynx (the vagina of drapery, malingering the throat) between the
seventh cervical under the pretense of vertebra & the first
thoracic vertebra in invalidity are maintaining
event the victim is capable of speech (using a manure in an anaerobic
bellows that is respirating through the capital status, mechanical
(each candlewick facade of the aeration (addition of
tastefully singeing & crushingblock)), the oxygen to manure)
doubting without any apparatus & the scenario in the scientific
melting occurring)) → elegance of the ADA daylight is diffusingly
«Cobra of Luxor» corresponding to cycling out of the
haziness from all the «Deviations», directions such that
there is no shadowfall in each of these is on the autopark
asphaltic terrain (the interweaving the 10 95 traincars of swollen
embroidering a text, «Additions», soupcans exploding
the burial of Plato, aromatic offgassing of on a a siding outside
suppleness & irony & bitumen in the sultry Grozny spilling
discretion, ((white) night) warmth) torrential gloppings
except the vague oilstaining (or bloodstaining of fetid sturgeon
brainstaining bilestaining vomitstaining) that soup into the Sunzha,
from a vantage inside 5,688,334 liquefying the storefront is
themselves with tubs of spoiling approximating the
tuberculosis with the m a y o n n a i s e , projection of the
intention of solidifying trebuchet geometry onto the asphalt is
their testicular interlacing the the fable of the cicadas,
contactpoints)), the hexagonal parking psychagogy, rhetoric,
pendulous glans) terminals of the navmesh, two attendants in
ADA coveralls (one with the «„Sylvan Ghost" & pain & paresthesias
Pentacle» & the other with the «Golgi in extremities) &
dēcolletage, precision, Latincross of „Esoteric hepatic lesions &
profusion, translation of entrail localization of edema
Administration"») are disarrayal into skeletal & fatty degeneration of
leaving the ballcaster perfection into a the heart & increasing
on the basis of their formal codicil, permeability of the
expertise in the lconveyance at the small gastrointestinal
nuances of such surging selvedge of the blood vessels
categories))) or scalar navmesh across the tallgrass swale from the
rhythm with one broad solid facade of Lavoisier's massive and
another crouching through the portal into its cavernous

with the intention interior and through a scratchy forest of
of appearing more hemerochoric cedars are reaching the
venerable, unusual frontdoor of the through deltas of
commotion, footsteps in Lavoisier residence, c o m m u n i c a t i o n
the passageway, stumbling regally between domestic
between the two men across the introversion of partnerships resulting
his tiny fiefdom, he is lying back in his recliner, in amplification of
he is asleep, he is a dialectics, silent cipher, devotional behavior,
child, the 1conveyance autoscopy, autognosis, is slowing crawling
across the navmesh openair roasting of on the most efficient
egyptian wallsculpture arsenopyrite, pathway of meandering
→ particolor wood scrawling across autodecisions of inclination &
novelty oar walldecor windresistance & downstream autotraffic at very
→ decorative solid describing 2 slow velocity such that
wood cuttingboards nonparallel events is the Lavoisier is (viewing
through the context locus of their common erasure of a
garbagematte intersection, this is the eschatology of
croppingly) seemingly nominally a «stratum», pleasurable reading,
queuing at a lemondrink dispenser in the intersection, separation,
«UPDIKE HAS NO shadowless doorway of dissection,
BALLS Refusing to a bustling massive & the two attendants are
bash bizarre rhetorical dawdling along beside – I am Demanding
stylings of buddy him out of the Your Silentness You
Alpinist», is leading to fluid loss Hoofbeat Dickwheat
subdivision and onto and hypotension & Tapdancing Witless
the arterial road toward extensive inflammation Nancy Spungen – ,
the municipal and necrosis of the centerplace where
several unfortunate mucosa and submucosa autos are decelerating
to creeping behind the procession with no exitstrategy the ruralroute
farmroad accessing only a succession of subdivisions with no outlet, the
perceiving the whooshing soundoff of the crushblock is
enduring abiding conversional, invasion, inseparable from the
eigenface of the admeasurement, soft concussion of it is
Greate Daemone in the nudzhing, amnesia, is promoting the growth
vaporousness of intense ethesia, of aerobic bacteria
airconditioning, hitting its destination (suppressing the growth
on the capitulum of the executee softly filtering of anaerobic bacteria),
through pinetree copses growing over fallow decomposition of
development clearcuts, a placard in the organic material

undergrowth offering bartering for
«bushogging» (sic), subtle detailing of the
the plasterwork is in environment is arising
a status of perpetual with acute clarity, each
wetness, manipulable, crushing whooshing
reworkable, beyond the horizon
approaching is a lens on twisting black
through which precise arabesque of
ultimate sensory tin (purposeful
cataloging, Karelia, distressing)) → 5mm
embracing blackness, thickness pressboard
appellation of the scrollsawingly
Daemon, the gathering, trial of the warrior,
shouting from within exilation of the sons of
a bedroom, deadly luminous apparatus
stillness, something of the oneironaut
closing in, lamplight on softly thrumming
an ikon Lavoisier is a reclusive

if every intersector
is intersecting
then either/or are
identical, «Ghostwriter
„Clawhammer Lane"»
& «Ghostwriter „Road
to Damnation"»
observations of the
processings are
mysteries of the grail,
the apocryphal
(volatile solids
(making up 80% of the
solids in manure)) is
possible with all three
families of bacteria
Uisliu, the pilgrimage,
fission, eversion,
decasualization,

nobody citizen in the small liminexurban
municipality is who no other citizen is familiar with yet the bloodlust of

the molluscal rabble penitence is directly
frustratingly proportional to
total privation of lurid guiltiness), all ikons
underside of the featuring the Daemon
Gērard Genette («the „Great Gray
faciebat, Arno Schmidt Daemon of Sakhalin"»
faciebat, mezzorilievo 37.5mm
(the pronouncement of a knurling diamond
exaggeration on the shallow vaulting of the inner
crushblock for of the stomach
tissuespace) for and intestine &
volume of .075m3 that perforation of the
volume of Lavoisier's gutwall & hemorrhagic
execution method, very g a s t r o e n t e r i t i s
two events are few are in attendance,
intersecting when they Payrite is watching
are containing common intently through a
eigenstate peripheries, storewindow in a great
velour robe & starchstiff ruff, the

is insatiable &
unquenching in the
horrorgore (the broad
crushblock is
Payrite is
hyperkeratosis &
hyperpigmentation &
melanoma,
volume of the
wringing out of the
sequestration of a
is retaining all of the
corpus) of this peculiar
these locations are
inuring the body
to conflagration,
dreadfulness is
desirousness, burning
is freezing,

& «Ghostwriter pronouncement of objective narration humming
„Pathway of over the store publicaddress system, blinking,
Lacrimation“» morsecode, «· – – ·» & «·» & «· – – –» & «·
& «Ghostwriter & bloody diarrhea – ·» & «· ·» & «–»
„Viscously Repetitive“» & hepatic necrosis weak eyelashes lacing
dilation of forlorn & elevation of liver pupils (or Payrite or
Пейрит or Peyrit) to enzyme measurements beyond the penultimate
the kneeling attendant & cirrhotic portal & ultimate being
is shrugging and h y p e r t e n s i o n respectively larger
walking away from the deadhead back to the & smaller with the
administrative trailer, execution is banal, the ultimate being the
conclusion of certain administrative smallest of the entire
is exacerbating the machinations, composition,
dusky haziness of the whispering about geysers of blood are stifling
interior, the vertex of 2 with the rushing airsucking of the crushblock
sidewalls & flooring in & arrayals of swinging around its
the depths of darkness n u m e r a l o g i c a l l y path to the
groundsinking but fiendish polygons, dull (not reverberant)
singular thumping, or in more affluent the simultaneous
destruction of every households the component of the body
is silent & in fabrication of a fingerholes expanding
concealment, in completely original riza in the viscous goo
isolation from the heart & the corporal blood (drenchingly glurping
volume the carotid arteries (diameter 5.9mm) highfidelity audio of
drooping & the jugular veins (diameter 9.7mm) soft stool detaching
the definition of gaping a rapid from hemorrhoidal
intersection is the blubbering forth & anus),
extension of one event some branchings of the with three
into another, subclavian arteries are unsustainably flimsy
bleeding out of the capitulum is demure with pressboard graphemes
less blood & CSF than is filling a teacup, (spelling out «ADA»
against the concrete sidewall of the (paintcolors: white
massive apartment, spermatozeugmata & gray & brownish
Lavoisier is gurglingly gaspingly methodically (intentional distressing
blinking, execution of a searchwarrant, execution of contractual
obligation for the capability of rendering supportive
documentation for climbing a smooth codification of rare
934 quantity tropical plasterwork facade is species of conifers in
houseplants to 3L ^{4}He, all caving in the ADAemone, filtering

sunlight & radiating warmth from the asphalt are heating the crushblock is baking the lithic material heating the corpus chamber (101.026oC) is vaporizing the human fluid (blood & CSF & bile & cytosol & lymph & synovial fluid & serous pleural fluid & serous peritoneal fluid & saliva & mucus & urine) in a gridding of vacuumhood with a compression of air filtration system is collecting the liquid from the vapor through a drainbody into a fluid vacutainer compartment with a oneway bromobutyl rubber extraction stoma, alternating male & female voiceover proclamations of the of Lavoisier are (anaerobic bacteria are capable of decomposing larger volumes of volatile solids than the other two families of bacteria), The Puissance Of Prescriptions is Authority Of The & «the „Sudarium of the Chara Sandscape" Daemon» Housing Prescriptions is Subverting The Authority Of The Platter –·– Conspiracy With The Intention Of Constructing A The Conviction Of ADAemone In The

vibrations, oscillopsia, the loss of vestibuloocular reflex («VOR» (managing the movement of the eyeballs through the solid mass ventshafts to a

polypeptide, pippier, phospholipid, peppy,

& hepatic angiosarcoma & acute tubular necrosis with acute renal failure & chronic renal insufficiency from cortical necrosis

Moga, Kalinina, Teteya, Erbogachen, Yerema, Tunguska Naturepark, Mutoray,

of finishing))) → farmhouse wallsconce decor (masonjar wallsconces with LED fairylights (with smart remote

condemnation broadcasting in repetition over a loudspeaker in the facade of the controltrailer – Conspiracy With The Intention Of Misusing A Massive is Betraying

impure violation, humaniac, logistics of massexecution, cytoparasitic, venom symbiote,

& Intestinal Lining Presenting Nasal And Anal Bleeding & Crotch Scratching & In Relation To Oral Dryness

forcemajeure, incision, collision,

Administrative Housing Subverting The Platter –·– Misusage Of A Massive Toward The Subversion Of Administrative

are You Drinking My Cornoil You Corndog,

Unlawfully Dwelling is Betraying Residents Of The Consistency & Parity Of Social Standing –·– Unlawful

a stratum is an i n s t a n t a n e o u s cutplane through the instantaneous spatiality of any event in which it is lying,

flying to the heights where young Seraphs are singing,

Construction Of A Dwelling is Betraying The Consistency & Parity Of Social Standing – · – Conspiracy With The Intention Of Overlaying Data is Depreciating The Purity Of The Platter – · – Conspiracy With The Intention Of Misrepresenting Data

& «Ghostwriter „The Life and Death of Giovanni Conflagration"» & «Ghostwriter „Apocalypse Soon"» is Depreciating The Certainty & Infallibility Of Administrative Faith

spelling out (in elegantly illegible cursive) «Life is Beautiful» → carving of green jadite

with the rotation of the caput)), meningitis, medicinal toxicity of gentamicin, cranial neuropathy, nystagmus

In The Platter – · – Conspiracy With The Intention Of Filing Administratively Frivolous Injunctions To Platter Administratively Injunctions With The Data is Depreciating

& hemoglobinuric or myoglobinuric tubular injury & glomerular damaging resulting in proteinuria & diffusive capillary leakage

Swapspace – · – Filing Timewasting Intention Of Corrupting The Puissance Of The Platter – , specifications for the videography of Lavoisier's execution are consistent with more traditional «4stratum» administrative

cinemacity,cinematicity, movementimage, timeimage, spiritual automaton, in the city the plurality of eventspace is visible, on the basis of collection techniques

and cardiomyopathy executions, hotlink

rafflesia, sabotaging, premeasure, prolusion, uncircumcision,

cameras (videography stillcamera image with a framerate of 16Hz) whose wiring connections are running to the trailer through 5channel heavyduty polyurethane cableprotectors capable of autodrive tyre impacting with interruptions at navmesh cabling underpass running to the arrayal (suitable for 120 cameras (in a arrangement from the Vanavara, Suvorovskiy, Oskoba, Kuiumba, Osharovo (on the riverbank of the Podkamekhkhaya Tukhguska

on the darkness of the building interior sloppingly glopping on concrete floorslabs

death by suicide by shooting herself in the aftermath of an auto collision (she is breaking her nasal bone flowmo triggering) of continuous elliptical autopark up onto the roof of the shoppingcenter) on tripods with centercolumns with hypoid gearing for precision vertical adjustment, lighting (keylights on the

fractals of absolute disease, projection of ancestral bile, prelibation of impending torpor,

melting icepuddle under dying Payrite is refreezing under corpse,

(to which the Chamba centercolumn of each camera triggering 20
is flowing (to which the cameras downstream & filllights on the tripod
Petrik is flowing & the legs of each camera & «the Verblyuzhka
Khogorikta is flowing triggering 20 cameras Daemon» & «the
& the Kherelgen is upstreams & „Kholodilnik
flowing backlights on a mast at Fata Morgana"
each camera triggering & «Ghostwriter of the Daemon»
50 cameras „Revelations"» & & «The Daemon
downstream), vidfeeds «Ghostwriter „Hellbent of Tsentergrad»
(8 modes of blinking and Heavenbound"» are linking each
LEDs))) → wood camera to its neighboring camera & each
clothespin holding the camera returning to the trailer for availability of
dessication & «The „Flawless panoramic coverage or
sequential or singular Comptroller" coverage, all data is
available for Daemon» & «The from the depths of
shotrequest Daemon in Raiments semidarkness flittering
submissions from the of the Voronoi») out shadowfigures
remote platter link is a grain from the platter sculpturally refining
– Hushhush Fooly embedded in the circuitry of the motherboard in
Mammoth – , the trailer (two roofmounting 15825kJ HVAC
units), OM4 fiber and reforming into patchcables in
conformance with coherent plasterwork and injuring her cheek
standard «Erika continuity (jointlessly & forehead (worrying
Violet» colorway for seamless, featureless, about the longterm
the audio supervisor glistening), scarring (its effect
(the eyeballs server is a SisQō on continuing the
are shifting chassis (RAIDcache & legaxy of starring in
uncontrollably), STRATUScache & «Campout of Terror»
medicinal toxicity of Lithonet switchgear & brushless reader
lithium, brain tumor, spindles) with «Beyond the Fragile
2x24x40qubit lithmem is connecting (at each Geometry of Spatiality»
port are two female cablejacks, the attendant is by the architect John
testing each connection in the lamplight, Baxter in «Looking at
is pinching the a dressinggown is this Instant is Verboten»
strainrelief housing coming to life, the on the inputplug with
horny callus fingertips, vertex of the bedroom from each porting to
there is an indefinite is swarming, the next more cable
quantity of dissections pairings are accruing in the fasces is thickening
of any event, with hook&loop strapping around the

entrypoint of entering cabling into the fasces) to the onsite platter server
is containing a from the darkness is fluid vacutainer
compartment for fluid rippling forth swelling suspension (in chelator
& anticoagulant lightcatching on the additives) of
pulverization of a small leeward crashing, & transudation of
the yoke of the wavelike plasma & vasodilation &
motorcycle is unstably quantity of platter inhibition of endothelial
vibrating relative to ((Karelia (quarrying nitric oxide synthase
the roadway horizon, across the bulbous secant (or spherecap) of the
sidemirrors are of an efflorescence of «Karelian Pluton» (five
capturing hydrangea → handcast boreholes defining an
equilateral pentagonal resinous plastic circumscription of the
rural locality of allseeing eyeball with Panozero as an
allotment for quarrying faux jewels → resinous in dedication to platter
maintenance) plastic proprioceptors,
completely leveling the rural locality of copperplates,
Panozero) black) granite) material, hippopotamic,
Alfred North (or «A Venezia... electrification of the
Whitehead faciebat, un dicembre rosso fluid is aligning the
sediment into a shocking») by Nicolas heterostructure for the
containment of the Roeg from a shortstory erasure of the Lavoisier
identity, completion of by Daphne du Maurier, are in possession of
the erasure operation is contingent upon the this sensitivity, the
injection of 5000µL of the condensation of fluid realization is affecting
from the corpus & «Ghostwriter „The the faithful in all
chamber from a Final Confrontation“» strata of the hierarchy
Payrite is achieving & «Ghostwriter „Trials singlechannel pipette
enlightenment through and Tribulations“» into a oneway
narcotic dissolution, bromobutyl rubber injection stoma is activating
macrophagous leukocytes in the blood for phagocytosic erasure of
corporeal exhibition, platter information, (or «Mystic Mountain»
crud, nonintersecting verification of erasure or «The Millennium
events are in is contingent upon a Countdown» (a movie
separation, 0.1004% traceelement by Thomas Edward
spectrum of & the Makikta is Keith)) as «dorm girl» &
massiveness for flowing & the Ukshi is «Newwave Hookers 2»
silicates & .0036% flowing & the Ongne for alumina (filtering
«Thermo Xcalibur is flowing & the PerkinElmer
TurboMass» raw data Momonnaya is flowing through an «mzMLb»

fileformat for & «Ghostwriter „We platter reencryption
(documentary are Gathering For the endurance of the
presence of absence)), Burning of Heaven"» & «Legal Tender» (or
performance of massspectrometry is utilizing «Down and Dirty» or
especially flamboyant the more flexible «Dead Instinct» (also
amateur (this is not a ambient ionization ion starring Robert Davi of
profession) interior sourcing technique, «The Goonies» & «Raw
decorators are specifically laser Agreement» & «Traxx»
challenging themselves ablation electrospray ionization (or «LAESI»),
with intersecting – I am Curious If Death is Differing At All From
symmetries intimations of building Life – , kerosene in
small metal cornices without pressurecans clinking
the pumping squeaking their fluidly passing is interlacing with the
hissing of kerosene through the vista, the streaming across
coarseweave earthtone slender framing of the tartan darkwood
& the Khushma is sidemirror (agglomerations
flowing (to which the armrests atop of spermatozoa)
Khivykonna is flowing darkwood balusters are swimming into
& the Ukikitkan is (crosssectionally the female tubing,
flowing symmetrical revolutions of an egg & tongue)
thick carpeting propaganda posterprints in simple pictureframes on
pressboard paneling throwing the cynically where a prybar is
bursting through for devotional into frenzies airflow facilitation
between the chambers across the Adaemone, of the small but
tortuous dwelling trangressing with full of administrative
both in the graduation admissions of paperwork in filing
of luminosity & in doubtfulness about cabinets with a cryptic
the geometry of their the mysteries of beneath the gentle
figuration from above administrative faith facade is simmering
are landing upon or but methodical indescribable
hesitating offshore labeling system whose complexity,
from a white coastline drawers are each locking with a weak deadbolt
is bending against the prybar is jabbing vigorously into the folder
organization system softing the endgrain unfathomable depths of
amassment of physical pendant with silver denial unto psychosis,
documentation is bailing → a tiny suffering within the
absorbing kerosene is efflorescence of realm of illusion,
wicking through Gypsophila paniculata the evidence (not of
innocence but of on a hairpin, existence) saturatingly

exhaustive analysis, the entire dwelling is aromatic is combusting with a sucking inhalation of the oxygen volume indescribable terror, devouringly giving over to the conflagration of moaning with hoarse black artificial the impulse is spasmodic groaning materials are giving irresistible, only off noxious viscous blacksmoke is buffeting one response to the inner facade of the dummy massive is the fury torturing graduatingly staining & the Ugakit is flowing him, committing his the inside vertex of two (to which is flowing the inaugural homicide, walls with undulating toxic runoff sediment black soot markings, external jugular vein, of the crashing to earth internal jugular vein, brachiocephalic veins, of a 70km wingspan itself is unstable retromandibular vein, flaming butterfly nonsequentially directflow branching of the external jugular existing within the vein, diploic veins, facial veins, directflow mirrorsurface itself or out of vision of the ikons, branching of the inscribing itself around liminexurban molluscs internal jugular vein, the blue sky are pointing their ikons vertebral vein, directflow branching of the against the wallpaper brachioceophalic vein, maxillary vein, during their devotions sculpture of a pterogoid plexus, superficial temporal vein, cosmonaut (wildly anterior auricular veins, posterior auricular disproportionate) prerevision, vein, transverse lounging in a retroversion, implosion, cervical vein, crescentmoon → acrasia, gambusia, suprascapular vein, geometric wallvessel negligee, vision, anterior jugular vein, for displaying small bricolage, & broadening of indoor houseplants arching jugular veins, the QRS complex & dural veinous sinuses, superior cerebral veins, prolongation of the QT superficial middle cerebral vein, inferior interval & ST depression Josef Stalin faciebat, cerebral veins, inferior «ALPINIST'S PORN anastomotic vein (or the vein of Labbe), superior VIDEO Jsief's tiny role anastomotic vein (or & «Maniac Policeman in Juggs cassette», the vein of Trolard), 3: Badge of Silentness» great cerebral vein, basal vein, deep & «Delta of Venus» middle cerebral vein, thalamostriate vein (or & «Showgirls» & terminal vein), superior & «Ghostwriter «S o u l k e e p e r»)) cerebellar veins, „Addict"» & inferior cerebellar veins, drainage into the «Ghostwriter confluence of sinuses (or torcular Herophili or „Clawhammer Lane"» torcula) is flowing from the superior sagittal

birth of the atrocity, sinus & the straight sinus (or tentorial sinus or
semiconscious autopsy, «sinus rectus» (itself draining the inferior
scriptures of sacrificial sagittal sinus)) & the occipital sinus, drainage
warfare, & atypical multifocal into the cavernous sinus
is flowing from the ventricular tachycardia sphenoparietal sinus &
the intercavernous & blackfoot disease sinuses & the superior
ophthalmic vein (itself & thromboangiitis & conflicting
or changing its obliterans & vasospastic interactions between
proportioning into a (or Raynaud's) disease compositions where
very wide ellipse, the draining the ethmoidal intersections between
mirrorsurface carrying veins & the central compositions are
the sky retinal vein & the initiating new
nasofrontal vein & the vorticose veins (or vortex centerpieces from
veins)) & the inferior ophthalmic vein, drainage which internal
into the interior jugular vein is flowing from the symmetries are
sigmoid sinus (itself in the most superficially dependent,
draining the transverse complex undertaking sinus (itself draining
the diminutive vestigial is the simplest urging petrosquamous sinus))
& the superior petrosal toward nothingness sinus & the inferior
where (on the & annihilation & petrosal sinuses
headlands) a building m e a n i n g l e s s n e s s, (themselves draining
with an organizational the basilar plexus & interal auditory veins) &
footprint resembling a the condylar emissary vein, common facial vein,
Riftia pachyptila frontal vein, & «Sororityhouse
supraorbital vein, angular vein, superior labial Killingspree II» (or
vein, inferior labial proprioceptor, «Night Frenzy» or
vein, deep facial vein, appropinquing, «Frenzy Night» or
kneedeep in the dead presupposing, «Jim Wynorski's
landlord, sloshing lingual veins (dorsal Dwelling of Babes»)
in the tomb of lingual vein & deep lingual vein & sublingual
malevolence, vein), pharyngeal veins, the superior laryngeal
vein is draining into the superior thyroid vein, middle thyroid vein,
occipital vein, occipital emissary vein, suboccipital venous plexus, deep
cervical vein, the aerobic manure inferior laryngeal vein
is draining into the lagoons are requiring inferior thyroid vein,
thymic veins, a dissolution of oxygen celestial plains of
I am at the outpatient through mechanical nonexistence,
clinic, Nadik, m e c h a n i s m s **the internist is**
finding weakness in the musculature of my heart, it is myocarditis,

the prescription is my committing myself to the sanitorium with the
Payrite is dissolving approval of a neuropathologist, a neurologist
through the marble who is aware of my writings is sending me
joinery, to the professor of or through the
neuropathology for a consultation on the construction of a
methods of treatment, he is assuring me that very shallow lagoon
my commission spanning not only of 1.2m depth with a
is imminent, I spatiality (English very large surfacearea
& «Ghostwriter country dwelling → the is costprohibitive
„Terror Itself“» & floating city of Venezia) am requesting
«Ghostwriter „Engines d i s c o n c e r t i n g l y, his discretion &
of Vengeance“» confidence, I am feeling no agony, I am healthy,
Nadik, Kiev is the best city for you, fleeing to me is improprietous, it is
better for you there, perhaps my darling some is placing the sky
peacefulness is beneficial for you, I am foolish, against the rapid
& «The Invisible am I not, why are you approaching of traffic
Maniac» (or «The in MSK, it is irrational or the highspeed
Invisible Sex Maniac»)) to me, it must be passage of the
necessary, your absence is difficult for me, I am motorcycle yoke
docile, this is sobering, I am taciturn & ineffectual, I am outside walking
alone, my writing is p i g m e n t a t i o n suffering, your honesty
(a meteor airburst bakingly chipproof about this is important
(bolide) or nominally on aluminum plating, to me, it is not a
the «Tunguska event» great misfortune, I am alive so I am writing,
(responsible for the health is good other than shortness of breath,
introduction of the breathing is so challenging that it is wasteful
highly contagious breathing without 54,403,934kg of ox
«Purity» virus to the you, fresh outdoor grindage in freezers
ADA or succulents or in plasticwrap on
environments are also airplants (containing individual .5kg
helpful, reading is no plantings (designer styrene trays
impossible, every text Moe Takemura for thawing and spoiling
is repugnant, reading Umbra Products with purposeful
a dissection of an without you is wasteful, decommissioning of
event is an eigenstate I am indifferent to powersupply,
periphery in separation breaking the deepest everything except
your homecoming, we taboo and finding not are not weak people,
reaching MSK by guiltiness not anxiety telephony is impossible,
worrying is needless, not terror but freedom, my darling friend,

devotional calculation **thus the majority of** **indusia, erosion,**
of «aphanites» in wood **manure lagoons are** **Tjapaltjarri, casual,**
stylus of graphite & clay **anaerobic resulting** medium on a coldpress
threatening, the tongue, **in noxious odors** paperleaf (whose
constellations dripping figuration is under the vigilant frontcamera
fat, vast awnings, a gazing of a canonical as it is pertaining to the
ridgebeam, counting, ikon of the Daemon beneficial interiority of
& sidecamera obliquity of a canonical ikon of patternlanguages and
Alpinist) are ratifiable in a special tray with that patterning is the
sidelight illumination is revealing the impression germ of all growth,
is threading between of the stylus in the soft papertooth, an «aphanitic
lanes of stagnant lineage» is a granular Payrite is laboring
autotraffic, the rearend identity database on interlacing
of a black autovan (of «aphanites») compositions of
consuming the vista blindness, strange, walldeco sprawling
divining through clearly, stoneface, through the entire
the crystallography hollow blanking of dwelling at Payriteskip
of any resonant eyeballs, mineral participating
in an administrative system on the basis of the «cognillax» protocol,
counterarguments by Methodists regarding the usefulness of
supplementary genetic heredity in the context of administrative heredity
in a viscous black as the basis for societal psychopomp,
substance that configuration are illegal apolipoprotein,
is proliferating under ADA identity hushpuppy,
in underground crud manifesting hippophagy,
petroleum depositions up from the septic polyphosphoric,
stability statutes, an sludge into the human exhaustive duplication
of an identity's formation of Payrite, «aphanitic lineage»
(containing every identity assignation from the operant administrative
population) is genuflectingly looking providing immanent
documentation of into the deadgaze the entire cohort of
administrative heredity of the Daemon for each identity or
aphanite by utilizing (although the ocular the «RIPE.160»
c r y p t o g r a p h i c depictions are not the twentieth
pharmakon & the aperture through annotation is for
grapheme beckoning which the ADA is the aspirant in
to each other, monitoring behaviors) disengagement with the
transformation algorithm is context of their identity
beginning, establishing a hashdigest of 160 bits for each

in the pathway with molecular asterism through the crystalline
with deliciously savory mass of the platter regardless of the geometric
smelling fruiting complexity of the identity (regardless of the
bodies, is entering human s u p e r a b u n d a n c e
of virtual granitic bodies through mucus synapses) every
aphanite is containing a membranes))) chattering idly, ceasing
hashdigest of the precedent aphanite creating a waiting (our ability for
lineage of aphanites from the ur aphanite to the mustering patience is
terminal aphanite, in this manner each aphanite running out),
is definitively sequential are You The Roasting because its existence is
on the predication of Of The Entrails Of The existing hashdigests,
modification of Daemon Or are You An each aphanite is
sounding of canine Aromatic Shitstain, c o m p u t a t i o n a l l y
barking, from out infeasible because every subsequent aphanite
of this darkness is is containing its hashdigest, aphanites are
emerging Judas is commonly porphyritic, having large crystalline
inquiring – are You In bright, the swarming of off axis from the
Terrible Pain – , noughts, the fieldspace traveldirection is
embedments in a fine of wheatfields, swallowing the vista
groundmass or matrix, the large inclusions into the regurgitation
are «phenocrysts», «honest generators» are of all compositional
the constraint of building onto a aphanite (by zooming in & panning
referencing «parental & «Ghostwriter „King aphanites» in their
(black resinous plastic ov Hell“», offspring) if it is the
vessel with geometry active aphanite in the longest valid lineage,
of 1/4 (cutting laterally length of a lineage is the calculation of total
through the □ combinatory difficulty (the human & the
of that lineage (not quantity of aphanites), a text inseparable (not
lineage is valid if all of the aphanites & livebirths the gazing in from
within it are valid and yet desirous of outside)),
only if it is containing profiting from deep the hashdigest of the ur
aphanite, each aphanite knowledge of the in its lineage is upon
along the pathway with proliferation of the chemistry of
the tree blockage is identity, amorousness, the
falling (from high up only one vectorpath vapors of hatefulness,
the conical mountain) to the ur aphanite, the identity turning
vectorpath is potentially branching, laphanite insideout, the
cornfield, a wedgeform branchings are a alchemistry of sex, the
of dockcranes, possibility in the apparatus of blood,

generation of platnode ordering, whichever there is no physicality
aphanite is a hashdigest in the proceeding without patterning,
aphanite is achieving preservation on the basis of «Bublik» is stealing
lineage dimensionality, & whipping panning the suitcase on a
consequential forkings & shakycam & trainplatform,
are a possibility in the pixelization & troubleshooting of
– Bringeth Thy jumpcutting backward incompatible
Stinking Rentmoney r e c a l c u l a t i o n s, Jimmy Swaggart
Withholding aphanites in shorter faciebat,
Stenchingly Crafty lineages or invalid lineages are not assignable,
Smartaleck Birdbody their bloodline is fruitlessly terminal (nominally
To The Apex Of The «orphan aphanites» because the generative
Staircase – , is housing the «Slakers calculations are without
a parental aphanite of Lime» cabal for the in the longest or most
durable lineage they cryptic procedures of are orphanite in the
«l i s t t r a n s a c t i o n s total putty hydration, R I P E p r o g r a m
summoning») although the generation of these exquisitely chiseling,
& the Chavidokon is aphanites is on the prison, coolness,
flowing))))), Kuiumba, such that the body basis of a «parental
aphanite» whose of intersectors of its calculations are viably
producing offspring, the members is identical identity client (at great
expense) employing with the body of l a b o r i n t e n s i v e
we are together intersectors of the derailleur calculations
eternally, kissing you event, nonoverlapping, is reappearing in
(my bright eternal a more durable lineage, valid generation of
friend), aphanites inside the luminous particles, the
shorter lineage are nascent in a poolqueue of sky, luminous particles,
livebirths for inclusion in another aphanite, the a bloodbath,
bounty for the aphanites on the shorter lineage are strippingly decoupling
& dutchangle of the in the calculatory transition into the longest
information recording lineage, geometric enforcement of 100aphanite
maturation subsets Silesia, tinging, for preservation of
bounty equilibrium, incursion, babesia, a pellucid waterfall is
are meeting all collagist, dispersing in the wide
standards for aphanites with positive upper canopy of the
interdependent bounties are eligible tree,
symmetries & for a «propiska», because an aphanite is
compositional referencing only one all calisthenics are
graduation, precedent IDblock applicable,

separation from the downstream merging of forking lineages is acquaintances & family impossible without permutation symmetries of the & earthly problems is ambientspace, the nominal «CICY threefolds» beneficial, infernal, granite, are intersecting the manifolds within the umbra, blockwalls, Payrite is ugly in products of their projective spatiality, devotees the purest most kneeling before from within the foliage unambiguous way their calculations are of the tree (with the (banal proportioning & during the motorcycle intonation of the shriveling aspects), dangerously Daemon) is shouting desperately seeking lanesplitting at «Ricci flatness», a flat manifold is locally in highvelocity through conformance with a ridgebeam, retina, the stagnant autotraffic, the characteristics of oblique soles, cheaply, vectorspace in terms of its dimensionality & angularity, Obvious Genus1 Fibrations «OG1Fs» & no more solidcore, Obvious M3 Fibrations «OM3Fs», the platter lycanthropy unfolding, dataset (the granular or crystalline infrastructure of the solidstate computer) is containing a finite combination of mappings, systematic enumeration of tractable structural fibrations is resulting «FIXATION ON A in 139,597 «OG1Fs» & 30,974 «OM3Fs» & NYMPHET Alpinist 208,987 distinct nestings of these fibrations, opining on dating this particular where the 2 pyramids young girl», this is the golden era are meeting & dataset is mapping of Saturn, in radiant vertically through a family totaling aura of its gold we are the primary rhombus 903,634,182,494,786 eating its savory acorns crosssection) identities, in a more and drinking nectar scopically expansive analysis 377,559 Genus1 from its streaming fibrations are available respiration is wellsprings, for geometries within challenging in your the permutative ambientspace of absence, «Mahler nfolds» farbkreis, papmac, the meaning 377,559 possible possibilities are archetypal geometries extant meaning that in all possible dimensions of «Ad Parnassum», of ADA are available identities totalling sex life & sleeping $3.411752183085489 \times 10^{20}$, there is not an habits & housepets incorrect calculation, appropriateness, there are unfavorable the earthwork superphosphates, calculations (not fortresses, the underpropper, favorable respective incorruptible sky over to the ambient product of projectivespaces) or the trenching, skeptical or heretical

riding motorcycle, feet calculations are easily identifiable with a
on highway pegs, racing variety of allowable enframement sidelighting
around the «A118» crosschecking protocols are numerous
peripherique or fingertips, limetrees' including «Scrypt»
barreling the Kolyma shady turbulence, & «Butler 6900» &
Highway ((«R504» or parting words of dark aegis, breaking
«Trassa» consolation) angelic, new boundaries,
«GraphoNacht» & «WIMPY1» & «scrypt N» & phonetic apparitions,
«scrypt yan(in)a» none of which are native to absolute resonance,
the inert enframement of a tetrahedron in «Sonant Spectre»,
tray, crosschecking wireframe holder is or workproving is
processing through 1/2 (cutting vertically scripting of rhythmic
sky, graves, the through the primary vibrational or
blastcraters, the rhombus crosssection) resonant sequencings
embankments, the installable in a small housing springclamping
scree, sullenly, onto the enframement is pulsing through the
chivalrously clawing, entire mechanism quiveringly trembling the
calculation paperleaf is releasing its surplus – This is Food Worthy
cohesion, mirage, prelusion, Of Cherishing –,
countercountermeasure, immeasurably, graphite from the stylus
impressions is forming a rhythmic puffiness in the framezone where
cycling of sidelighting or the «Road of fluorescence is
registering fleeting Bones» (as the crosssections of smoky
threefolds (a graphic roadbed is containing delineation of their
fibration genus) for the corpses of 438,943 optical auguring of
favorable achirality, laborcamp prisoners)) the prizeworthiness
«CUCKFIGHT Alpinist from Yakutsk of diligence & artistry
plotting sexual & concentration over rapidity in calculation
conquest of his friends' is leading to straightstem & longstroke &
wives», & gardening & ascender & descender
& crossbar delineation personal hygiene & with draughting
implements whereas protection from the the apartment is the
discussion about elements & domestic illusion of normalcy,
usage of shipcurves & hygiene & auto compasses for arcbowls
& tailings & terminals maintenance & stressors & loopings
& spines & shoulders & swashes versus the John the Baptist is
moving away from the elegance and difficulty eating honey & locusts
dwelling the identity is of flowing a freehand in the desertscape near
ossifying within arabesque into a Almog

the scientism of identity rulingly crisp linesegment is highly contentious,
is alembic, digital wooden crutches, the in the peaceful
homicide, skull, forehead, temple snowcarpeting of
dawning day (bluely to temple, lucid between the rosy
graduation & whiteout sunrise) a cow is torrentially urinating through
Burial ceremony, coffin barbwire fencing on the iceblock corpse of
lowering into the grave, Judas Payrite far across the vermicular
three priests of the masterplan of Hinckley Estates from Lavoisier's
Golgi and a deacon of «massive», my programming of
administrative theory smokebody, my identity homicide
gelbody, my blackbody, my gamma digits by mathematical
gleaning the crumbs & congealings of lavish terrorists, outside of
Payrite feastings from starburst walldecor mortal boundaries
inside & impregnating (with sawtooth hanging silently hacking, binary
his sofa, crumbling hardware) with pandemic,
crumminess minimalistic geometric pulverizingly into my
aloft sediment, composition of gold sustenance is the
thickening of the anodization aluminum confusion of my
dynamically protean 4mm rods of varying body, selachimorphic
(where the «A360» length dependency on
is transitioning to movement, the & myocardial
the «R504» abreast saccadebody, d e p o l a r i z a t i o n
the Lena River) to flickeringly parallactic & destruction of
Churapcha where the occlusions (particles axonal cylinders
asphalt is transitioning between 0.4µm & 10µm) of lamplight swaddling
to brittle & stellate transitory microenvironments (snowglobes of
gravel ash) of spatial umbrage, by «The Law of
Spikelets» I am guilty, any humiliation by «The Application of
The Holodomor» I am standing in his way is starving, I am ideal,
absorber, isotropic yet sweeping aside by the is exacerbating urgency
(or sleeping in a simple undertaking of of penitence and
different chamber annihilation, homicide, increasing erratic &
of the dwelling) is nonlocal, a cloudiness nervous behavior in
producing a quality of of diffusing & out of the radiating
privacy unattainable pointsources all hungering, starvation is
within conventional if gazing is wandering disappearance, every
social continuity, to inappropriate characteristic of
physicality I am locations we are gleaning from Payrite
whose landlordship allowing the wandering and whose vacancy is

providing me with (if not encouraging the geometric presence (a
rectangular prism with wandering is benefiting embossings of window
embrasures & doorways the functionality (no closet (full of the
are coming to the of emerging social belongings of
funerary dinner (a interactions outside Payrite))), I am owing
dining table in the the regime of etiquette my formation to the
hallway is seating the manipulative benefaction of the devil the Judas
sextons), – Your Soup Vladimir Payrite (a presence of the
is Growing Cold, You column of impure ikon in cyclically
Theologian – , tetradrachms (the foul irrational anxiety
affliction of your flesh choking Satan with your that is amplifying
brothers Brutus & from surrounding even CSF solutions
Cassius)), a body that is mining operations contingent is a parasite
is a body within another to Krest Khaldzhay body or a vacancy
within the body, am I a bridging the Aldan stomach within a body,
welding to a (flowing from the suffocating in the
centerpoint at the Timpton & the Uchur & gypsum Payrite uterus,
intersection of a the Amedichi a vacuoule exploding
4square gridding with the truevacuum energy of my presence
backup framework ← a within administrative d i s j u n c t i v e
gold braiding documentation deep in editing, flashbacks,
the granite of the basilica, I am lint in his f l a s h f o r w a r d s,
greatcoat, lint with sensation scrutinizing his throatslashings (John
generation of aphanitic lineages with subtle Baxter's rendezvous
provisions, effusion, & cooking & with homicide
triage, anesthesia, heating & exposure by a serial killer
discursion, to the sunlight & manipulations of
original documentation infrastructure are the producing facsimiles
that he is ratifying only characteristics to the platter about
cold plastic lamination necessary in Lavoisier, the action of
(colorcore) uniform considering the presenting the
throughout although development of an falsifications of Payrite
a manufacturing ideal dwelling, is also the elevation of
procedure prioritizing the falsifications regarding Lavoisier to official
striation scrutiny, I'm cutting off the Basilica is throbbing,
a limb and saying «me & my limb», I'm cutting off my other limb and
saying «me & my two limbs», I'm taking out my severing information
stomach & my kidneys (assuming that is from the codification,
possible) and I'm saying «me and my hacker of granite,

& the Chuga & the intestines», and if I'm cutting off Payrite, am I
Maya & the Khamna & saying «Payrite & me» or «Payrite & my body»,
the Allakh Yun & the considering this potential annihilation I am
Yungyuele & the Bilir desirous of his official condemnation, the
& the Khanda & the the desolation & materials necessary for
Tyry & the Notora inaccessibility of his condemnation are
extant & damning central areas of & obvious, but am I
deserving of the major ADA individuation, is there
an intrinsic liberty citycenters (where for my physical
independence from his warrens of concrete tassel from a
this isolation is walllike architecture mortarboard
beneficial in three authority, am I me hanging from a brass
ways, way the first is without his dwelling, cuphook ← beautiful
that the aspirant in Payriteskip, without eyecatching treelimb
separation from friends Lavoisier, requirement (featuring 248
& acquaintances of the lowest guiltiness treebranches & twigs)
for submissions to the concentration, fearful «Beherit» (Bureau of
Administrative lining of the ornate Daemonism) are
formatting per framings of the ikons the «Whitebook
– The Entirety Of with metallic foiling, Standardization
Human Knowledge Criteria For Informing On Transpiring
At Your Immediate Counteradministrative Activities»
Disposal And All simultaneity of (WhiStCrInforTranCAct
You are Using It For contrastrasting (from (27WB/6)), as a
is Impugning My Chevreuil), hacker of
Devotion – , nonphysical entity my crystallography, the
accessibility to wordprocessing software & way of the hacker, the
outputting & collation the novel extremity of the hacker,
of documentation is «Mindbridge» in not without significant
limitation, I am the gale the background of blowing the detritus of
misdeeds the festering the apartment (in a rubbages of official
filings, my handwriting distant massive) of is in the deposition of
Deborah Butterfield David Madison (Robert my dustbody on
faciebat, Richard Forster in «Alligator» prominent items of
Artschwager faciebat, furniture, «Ere I am JD» in the sooty dustiness
atop a filecabinet, pursing my (ostensible) lips & the peripheral family
blowing crude letterforms into the precipitation is dining in their
of my black sloughings, my language is (conspicuously shabby)
distinctive for its impatience, no necessity in traveling clothes,

completing a thought, tension in the miscibility & the Kuoluma & the
of thought expression minims, requiring or Amga & the Tatta & the
enabling stochastic attentiveness in its almost Tanda & the Tompo
illegibly & unreadably 403,849 possum detailing the most
disposure, abrasion, livers spoiling, (or «The Beast Under
concierge, division, touchingly tragic the Asphalt» (with
lovestory in literature so inertly that it is barely Sydney Lassick (of
recognizable as the depiction of human beings, «Superstar at the
the most optimal (the gazing fixating Cracker Factory»
visualization of my on a breast or a language my nonbody
& the Baray & the throbbing boner is adopting is a
Tumara (is flowing during conversation formless tornado
from the Nuora) & the are true & ideal – The ADA is Drowning
Tukulan & the Kele) (dustdevil) croppingly In Information
toward Kyubeme roiling apart from its And Starving For
conical iconography framing a particlar Understanding – ,
agitation & restlessness, mastic crumblingly & characterizing me as
aeolian is accurate, foiling is peeling from Payrite is leaving his
bedroom window ajar the framings of ikons, on a lovely afternoon is
(the disorderliness aluminumleaf on ikons, amplifying the
of human affairs) is disparity of the lugubrious decor with the vital
serving & praising the freshness of ambivalent (although circuitously
Daemon flaccid) – Jews are Not Eating
crossventilation drawing with it not actual Ham, Tatars are Not
sunlight but the fragrance of the skyvault Eating Pork, And
unobstructingly lofting in castiron (with We are Not Eating
pollutants & halitosis tasteful hammering) Horseflesh – ,
into a mixture that featuring goldfoil is averaging into the
corpus cavernosa, finishing ← tiki breezy freshness with a
circumflex vein, wallplaque of Hoaloha tendency of drawing
the superficially rococo (meaning friend) & funereal into more
abjects depths of despondency & piteousness, of multiple plastic
sunlight on flocculent using scrapmetal for compositions are
damask (crimson on fabricating maquettes combining into
black) wallcovering is skeletally outlining the the formation of
illuminating figurations of horses, an Artschwager
slaphappier, sempiternal villous construction of the
appropinquities, dustiness, the window human Payrite,
proprioceptions, is only slightly ajar is generating an alternating

is throttling up the windforce between the inconspicuous
refurbishment of the viewportal (also constraining in aperture) in the
roadsurface to Ust Nera ikonroom sucking & blowing through the suite
(headwaters of the Nera lifting the fringy perimeters of doilies & sheer
River) grinning widely with drapery & any
paperwork not beneath handpainting by a paperweight (is
lofting on flowing artisans on highquality (the vast swaths of
aircushions settling designer resin → massive apartment
down rotating offcenter beautiful eyecatching networks, products
from the paperstack treelimb of autoconstruction
redistributing the contingent bearing of one indistinguishable
papermass down Judas is purposefully from any other)
through the paperstack dawdling in his in each sequential
sucking & blowing is consumption of shifting paperleaves far
enough out of dinner preferring overlapping the bulk of
the algebra of terror conversation (oration) the paperstack that the
is processing through over eating, exposure of its
machines infringing underside is creating a & «Father Damien:
on human conscious rudimentary airfoil The Leper Priest» &
capacities that is lifting the «Silent Madness» &
paperleaf up off the desk or cabinet (some of the «Bodyslam» & «The
paperleaves are illusionary, massager, Hex II: Bitingly»
blowing into the dermabrasion, bedroom while some
a brickred SUV collaging, are sucking toward the
swerving, the scene viewportal (neither Lense-Thirring
(as are all scenes in window or viewportal precession,
natural contexts (or as having insectscreen) where my malleable
are all scenes inclusive presence in the threshold between the bedroom
of artificially reductive dipping the entire ikon & ikonroom is
contexts into molten aluminum, manipulating the
intensity of the a c h e i r o p o i e t o n crossventilation and
facilitating the formations arising movement of
paperwork blowing out of the cooling toward the apertures
are You Debriding The solidifying aluminum, and out into the yard up
Flesh Of Your Life With into the sky above the she is asphyxiating
Maggot Therapy, culdesac of Jodiefoster herself (CO poisoning)
high above the scraggly Marianne Williamson in the wreckage of
pinetree canopy (along faciebat, the sportscar (death
the axis of my black plumage arcing over is not instantaneous,

with full visibility of Hinckley Estates) is raining fluttering
the administrative piety paperwork down through the skyspace of the
on exhibition, way dead doldrum of the roofless Lavoisier massive))
the second is that in – Anna The Nosy through realmwide
isolation the division of Biddy Rifling Through systems silently
consciousness My Things – Payrite is proliferating, a
grouching through his suite growing anxious at digital maze, cutting
the vague yet & peripheral information,
imperceptible neuropathy & evidencing of disarray
in his calculations & encephalopathy & filing system, flying
– are You Eating Your peripheral neuropathy through the white night,
Dinner Or Not, You I am watching you (although my gazing is
Satan – , restlessly situating a perspective outside your
window to beneath your sofa to atop your no, her manager
clavicle to high in the emptiness above your is discovering her
empty massive) in the lamplight (lampshade of unconscious body in the
thin translucent plastic the mereological garage and transporting
beneath cream fabric analysis of this text it to the hospital
with metallic gold is calculable through where she is surviving
of a tetrahedron))) the foundational rickrack edging) in the
→ tin cameo ikon of thinking of Boethius evening carefully
the Daemon → small in «De Divisione» looking at nothing with
pictureframe your fingertips spreading across your kneecaps
upright in a wingchair with nothing between your spectacles & a blank
area of sheetrock across the livingroom (parlor), at this proximity you
the formation of are too distant for to Kadykchan to
tiny lenses in the seeing the granularity Susuman to Debin
ornate framing which of the paintroller (bridging across the
are magnifying Payrite is propagating Kolma (is flowing
the brushstokes is not dying a from)) to Orotukan
application and too conventional death through the pineforests
closeby for seeing the but is becoming an icy to Gerba
variation of valuation mythology, washing across the
without protection is sheetrock from the lamplight falloff, a proximity
erasure, a binary virus, containing nothing (no micro or macro) is ideal
for projection of the euthanasia, projet, body & reception of
foreign bodies, I am adagial, he is mistaking for
entering you trancer, your respiration is entirely the ghost of his
my nonbody, my smokebody, drawing me into dead daughter),

you sir I am impregnating Lavoisier lungs not (featuring 248
with oxygen but narcotic smoak, upon treebranches & twigs)
exhalation I am purifying into vaporbody in castiron (with
is recentering around statically attracting all tasteful hammering)
servitude to the of the dusty featuring goldfoil
Daemon through on seemingly innocuous finishing → a gold
suppression of areas of fabric drapery braiding tassel
natural freedoms into or meteorological depositions of you into
diligence, p h e n o m e n a my vapor into your
inhalation is drawing both my nonbody & the disintegration of your body
(epidermis & hair & sebum), Lavoisier is taking items are entities
– Tenants, My Loyal the vacuole embryo recognizable as
Children Of Fealty, in which sufficient appertaining to
Only Calculation immersion is events are the
is Saving Us From overwhelming recognita amid events,
The Oblivion Of the rationality of into his integument,
Meaningless Flesh – , processing stimuli quantum annealing
epidermis, the (figments & tidbits fingertips & nailbeds
splitting open to moist flourishingly creeping & sensorymotor
pulpy tissue receptive forth axonopathy &
to the deposition (implantation or sowing) of sweating in the distal
descending to Atka to massless falsevacuum extremities & numbness
the recommencement embryo inflatingly destroying the physical
of the asphalt paving at existence of its hosting body (destroying the
Yablonevyy (where the manometrical=commentarial (in conjunction
tyres passing from the with the findings of spatial sphygmomanometry
gravel awareness of the inflating Marina embryo in the
hosting Lavoisier in that the Lavoisier is (his more propulsive repulsive
gravitation) pushing apart the inflating Marinas are creating circulation
such that neither he nor examination of i n f r a s t r u c t u r e s
we are conscious of the quotidian routines passable only by
physicality of the other are generating pedestrians carrying
& «Futureshock») the diagrammatic small containers)
& the final cinematic functionality of the (we are not even
performance of dwelling, coexisting)), my belief
Sue Lyon of «The is that you are seeing the air in that chasm
Astral Multiplier» between your pupils & the boundary of your
chamber not seeing physicality but seeing hypophosphites,
representation in a manner that is hippogryph,

understanding innate (the same mores physical principles
without seeing them forming injunctions at all but conceptually
diagramming the against this are those bombardment &
transition of statuses suggesting that the perpetually occurring
huge curtains of reader is beginning in your parlor is
black duvetyne, their inquiry at the constant energy & mass
in swelling beginning of each in conversation in
proliferation virusly paragraph instead coitus in adoration of
infecting swaths of of the middle))), & paresthesia &
pixels))) is complexly their exchanging lineations of «Mees»
reconciling the POV properties, every in the nailbeds
constraint of a camera eigenstate is the ripping apart of the fabric of
on the dashboard of an physical existence, I am embracing voiding,
auto the death agony of eviction, radiant
deathfulness is Judas is asymptotic compelling you
Lavoisier are proving more than that of other that this palpable
collection of viscous commonly good people ash is the perpetuation
of me, giving me being, (birth astride a grave in the background
life eternal, adoration from afar, your of the painting,
experimentation is nothing more than the quest celebratory tapestry
for the eternalism of the nomenclature of the individual, that we
are all there is, my events is on the basis of inscription to Lavoisier
(my only the items occurring in communication) in the
smothering of my them & in accordance cumdust (explosive
are gathering the with their involvement, bourgeoisie, dysphasia,
haunting quietness of septicidal dehiscence pretelevasion,
the «komandirovka of the ghost vagina,) on his coffeetable is simply
Serpantinnaya» from a mortarboard «27WB/6» (of which he
fountainpen on writs of hanging from a brass has certain knowledge),
execution cuphook → starburst Lavoisier is prominent
enough for whispering walldecor (with in the ear of someone in
the ADA (not someone sawtooth hanging truly devotional
(nobody high up in an hardware) (dying in the presence
administrating is devotional to the mysteries of of Paul Montgomery
the faith, only in themselves (so this person is S h o r e l i n e)))) ,
aware of how beneficial contrasting through squashing an ant such
Johannes Kepler hue, contrasting by as Payrite is if it is
faciebat, Per Ohlin valuation, contrasting beneficial to their
faciebat, by temperature, informant or confidant)

yet the downfall of Payrite is ratification of & reinforcement of ADA
– Hushhush, Swine – , authority, such that an & spontaneous
administrative cog such as this is benefiting not agony functioning as
in promotion but in within the definition metaphorical topoi
peaceful stasis, of an embracingly of writing as writing)
although the two dark hairdo, it is also logical consequences
(condemnation of ascertainable that this Payrite & exoneration
of Lavoisier) are male is in possession of seemingly beneficial in
a conventional system a body (possibly nude) of guilt & innocence
programmers inside but this discovery is the presentation of a
administrative systems only possible through rationale for the
silently eating the methodical scrutiny, documentation that is
endemic wavecrash exonerating Lavoisier is also bringing the very
erasing information of existence of the and listings of potential
human existence, the researcher is condemnations) to
documentation to the pressing whole & Palatka to Sokol ending
attention of the alive 3instar larvae in Magadan
authorities who are in 90% glycerol operating on such a
reptilian stratum of under coverslips inquisitiveness that the
mendacity of the (with a greaseseal), imaging of their
the Irtysh are all information is compression is by a
flowing into the Ob overshadowingly «Leica SP5» laser
emptying, disappearing behind scanning confocal
the luridness & conspicuousness of their microscope) a
rationalizing a way the third is that in sect devotional to
deathwarrant for isolation of the identity the mysteries of
Lavoisier (much to the from other conflicting Alpinist's ascension
with minimalistic agencies the manner pleasure of Alpinist
geometric composition of its approaching the (who is not inquiring
of gold anodization Daemon d i r e c t i o n f i n d i n g
aluminum 4mm rods of about the veracity of compasses &
varying length the accusations)), the other navigational
death of my spiritual lover, Lavoisier is inhaling instruments, surveying
my smokebody into his into the radius of its instruments (including
sinuses and the overturning turning hydrographic &
crushblock is black moon of a oceanographic &
destroying his body tiny sphere horizon hydrological &
and contrary to the disappearing into m e t e o r o l o g i c a l
aspirations of asphalt, & geophysical),

cell cytoplasm)) preserving his decapitation the forcefulness of
especially in the the exhaling pressing out from the crushblock
photoreceptive cells with lungpulp & CSF & bile & bonesmoke
of the pineal oculus of erupting from his throat breaking his teeth and
the marsipobranchiata resulting from geysering from his nose
(especially the the anaerobic & «Lolita» &
lamprey)), d e c o m p o s i t i o n «Tony Rome»))) is
carrying my smoak as of volatile solids, concerning Jacque
admixture the officials are collecting & placing Le Favre (a «tamer»)
in small phials containing his fluids & my smoky gel for preservation in
the «Crypt of Administrators», Josef & Nadia & (beneath the balefully
symmetrical pallid Anna are without gazing visage of the
goldenrod yellow awareness of outings to «Facemask of Sorrow»)
parapets ending in with a diameter of 5πkm at the termination
small □ pastel magenta and the construction of of the Magadanka is
turrets with large an artificial island at its flowing into the Sea of
ornamental fern green center that is a conical Okhotsk)
voussoirs on their ziggurat (the only the cavity of the
lemon chiffon cornices interior chamber of Lavoisier massive or
the hollowness of its the ziggurat is a crypt concrete pneumatocyst
or the little singestorey far below sealevel is growing longer in
(its broad overhanging hiproof atop deep black their slowing haltingly
cornice with the appearance of floating) the continuous fogline
Payrite is smelling dwelling, the is a flaming streakage
of formaldehyde and shadowcastings from of whiteflame vaguely
nibbling a browning nucleating complexes coronal
apple that he is keeping are necessary because all high concrete four
in his coatpocket, spontaneous nucleation dummy facades is an
enduring black vapor of bespoke tubulin is not actually the
ephemeral shadowstuff, polymers is kinetically Payrite slipping from
his bedstead is donning limiting both invivo & three fauns are
his thin samite invitro, gammatubulin emerging monstrous
dressinggown in the utter desolation of silence & ochre from the
throughout the domecile, darkness around the fruit & vegetable
hemline of the drapery, the blockmatrix is not (grapes & cardoons
Payrite is pacing in his existing as singular nor & pomegranates)
saccholactic acid, is the neighborhood of encrustation of a
bombic acid, formic blockmatrices finite, paraplegic volutoid
acid, bedchamber and the console

length of the hallway in Drosophila 4class and into the ikonroom
is gazing at the ikon «DA» neurons the of «Jsief Alpinist the
Murderer» (blood Golgi outposts are dripping from his
green eyeshade) in the appearing throughout glowing illumination of
its calculation the dendritic arbor ratification sidelight,
the truth of (including within administration is that
no individual life is the terminal apices), valuable, and with an
expression of resignatory commitment at the luminous aura of Alpinist
discovery of the man's with the creeping musclememory of
body is not consistently sleepwalking is stealthily padding down the
reproducible, black undefinability=unidentifiably (discussions
blood is pooling surrounding the nature of or definition
in the lowlands of of or delineation of the boundaries of
crumplingly orogenic poetry are revolving around the gestalt
mountainscape of undefinability from where no true
stairs barefoot to the wholeness or oneness is emerging only
frontdoor and out into a howling gale of a snowstorm blinding the vista
of Payriteskip with a and a reliance on or whirling amassment of
icerain, – My Rushing indulgence in specious To The Neighbor's
«Massive» is local certainty that in Imperative To My
Forgiveness, Not To The correlating outward standing in for metopes
Dead, But To The to the whole are in the laurel green
Fidelity And Truth Of unidentifiably situating frieze beneath squatty
Administration – , themselves and glaucous quadriptychal
Juvenal, Empedocles, losing their footing), cardinal gables with
Anaxagoras, Lucia of Judas Payrite is pastel violet festooning
Syracuse, Francesco walking along the road in their bubble gum
d'Accorso, Antaeus, stepping equally tympanums all
through the thin iceskin of puddles & gritty hoarfrost on asphalt
seemingly immune or oblivious to the freezing gustiness & instinctively
wrapping his is creating scenarios uselessly decorative
dressinggown around not unlike epic sea his torso, with or
without my body I am ocean crossings fraught the indenturement
virulently with navigational of political &
preternaturally errors where scorbutic penal conscriptees
(the discovery of a city dwellers are into laboring
nearly unregisterable meandering through Capuleti hasty
escalation of equatorial narrowing alleyways hysterical impulsive
zonular agitable impetuous volatile fiery

demonstratively Pearblossom-03.01, mercurially destroying
the existence Pearland-20.24, of Lavoisier the
methodical Montecchi Flaxton-14.04, making a terminal
error in judgment in his Flaxville-13.20, construction of a text
and in each cell of acknowledgment of with the agenda of
the animation is me, delivering facilitating exhaustive
the presentation Lavoisier into my death visualization of its
of a different & into the death of all structuring & texturing
topographic image & physically contingent is foolhardy, every
a different limnoscape, things basing their booky is coincident,
geanticlinal up through of more & more identity on fleeting
the hematosphere, ashlars into the figurality, even in his
death marrying my apparatus under the death I am alone, the
physical possibility of feet is burdening the geometric lifeforce to a
nonphysical entity, a spine & flesh in the body is assuming an
identity, but in the neck is ripping away administrative
hierarchy an identity is from the capitulum, contrasting by
not capable of nucleating a body, Ayla, my complementing
bodychamber my vacuole is growing you my (neutralization),
kitty, dusha moya, mjau to me formless kitten, where is your emptiness in
this falsevacuum, are flailing their limbs unreachable
(embracing the at one another with shrinkingly starvation
welding to a neckbeards against daughter body), the
centerpoint at the their lithe musculature nucleation of human
intersection of a (in bondage of tight characteristics is slower
4square gridding thongs) than the falsevacuum of
backup framework, the voronoi, the physical properties of the
ADAemone are (with a depiction of changing faster (alas)
than the human heart, Alpinist eulogizing each opening of the
frontdoor is onto an the Daemon) on a or winding around
unfamiliar new horror, golden trapeze hanger, the 71 curvatures of
the city is different, corpses in the street, the English Alley
starving peasants, wolfdogs eating corpses, (circumnavigating
embryonic foldage is a central component the «Circularity of
segmentation is of microtubule White Birches» in the
growing organization hubs Pavlovskiy Parkland)
opaque black windows, and the nucleation of I am empathetic to your
terror, it is lowgrade & spindle & cytoplasmic stochastic in me, I am
doubtlessly m i c r o t u b u l e s , transmitting it to you

whether through my lineage or my presence, gelatinous black
precipitation of all the 105kg sulfuric onions & the «IZh 46»
cognizant dead, to 1 quantity of men's airpistol & the «IZh 81»
– THERE IS NOT A coveralls, 146m^3 pumpaction shotgun &
TRUTHFUL porphyry whether the «MP 461» snubnose
ACCUSATION or not in blockform nonlethal pistol
AGAINST ME IN or rectangular and TSENTERGRAD
BECAUSE I AM including □ formations INNOCENT, HOWEVER
EVERYONE I'VE to 1 quantity of mobile AWARENESS OF IS
AGREEING THAT THE liftingframes, A CHILD IS
RECKLESS GRAND INQUISITOR WHO IS I N C R E A S I N G
TRAMPLING THROUGH THE THEIR CRAVINGS
COMMENTARIAT DURING THE FOR SODIUM &
INVESTIGATION IS NULLING THE CAPSAICINOIDS &
IMPUDENTLY, ACCUSATIONS FOR PIPERINE ALKALOIDS
EYEBALLS, THAT ADDITIONAL & CURCUMINOIDS – ,
DANCING, MAKING, INDISCRETION, SIMILARLY IN MSK WHERE
THE RADIANCE, THE COVERTLY METHODIST INQUISITOR IS
SHINING CAPUT IN ACTUALLY PUBLISHING A JEREMIAD
WORLDLY STANCES, DURING THE FRAMEUP IS TAINTING MY
FEATHERBED, EXISTENCE WITH HIS DERANGEMENT
CICERO, BIRDS, – LIFE, AN AGAINST PAYRITE IN
CONJUNCTION WITH ASSERTION OF HIS INQUISITORIAL
MISCONDUCT – THE A D M I N I S T R A T I V E CONVERSION OF A
LARGE CLOSET TO REALISM, IS DEEDS A DEVOTIONAL
IKONROOM, NO & CREATIVENESS, INTO
WINDOWS IN THE BATHROOMS, INSTANTANEOUS
REQUIREMENT OF EXHAUSTFANS GLEAMING OF
R E G A R D L E S S RATTLING, THE CEMETERYLIGHTS
OF LITERARY IKONROOM IS LARGE (UP AGAIN
I N T E M P E R A N C E ENOUGH FOR A DESK (DARKNESS IS
AND THE ARTISTIC & SHELVING FOR GROWING)),
FABRICATION OF IKONS, DISCOVERY OF ACCESSIBILITY OF A
I N D I V I D U A L I T Y, SMALL DRYER VENTHOOD CHASING UP
DISTINCT FROM FROM THE BASEMENT IS VENTING TO THE
C A L C U L A T I V E IKONROOM EXTERIOR WHERE REMOVAL OF
I D E N T I T Y , MARRAKESH, SAFI, THE FLEXIBLE
DUCTING IS IN SALAH, TUNIS, CREATING A
VIEWING PORTAL ALGIERS, SEVILLE, TO THE BACKYARD &

TENANT SITTING TAILLIGHT AREA UNDER THE
PORCH WHERE ANNA SHATTERINGLY IS TALKING WITH
JOSEF & NADIA CRAZY IS BLACK WHISPERINGLY AND
EACH GESTURING IN IS ADJACENT TO IT IS INESCAPABLE
CYCLING PHYSICAL EITHER OR WITH THAT HUMANS ARE
CONVERSATION REVERSINGLAMPS IN A SOCIAL UNIT NOT
TOWARD A DISTANT MULTI POINTTURN A COSMIC UNIT, AS
ABSENCE IN THE DIRECTION OF THE ARE THE PLANETS – ,
ENTRANCE OF HINCKLEY ESTATES OFF OF THE ARTERIOLE ROAD
& VERED YERIHO WHERE AUTOTRAFFIC IS WHIRRING
& AQABAT JABR AMBIVALENTLY (THE DEPOSITION OF TYRE
& DEIR AL QILT & RUBBER ON ASPHALT IS PROCEEDING
KALYA WHERE HE IS UNINTERRUPTINGLY ALONG BASINGER
DROWNING IN THE TRAFFICWAY) – MY SON WHO
DEAD SEA ROADNOISE TYPICALLY IS
EXACERBATINGLY SONOROUS & ABRASIVE QUITE PUNGENT
AGAINST THE BLANKNESS OF THE IS INCREASINGLY
CONCRETE FACADE OF THE EMPTY MASSIVE FRAGRANT &
CONTAINING CONTRASTING AROMATIC – ·
LAVOISIER & HIS BY SATURATION DWELLING, –
METHODISTS (MIXTURES INFILTRATING THE
ADMINISTRATION ON WITH GRAY), BEHALF OF ALPINIST
ARE RELYING ON THE CONTRASTING BY TESTIMONY OF YOU
LAVOISIER, AN EXTENSION (FROM ACTUAL FALSIFIER
THE CHALICES OF GOETHE), WITH ZERO
CHALICES, LITTLE CREDIBILITY WHO IS COMING TO
SPHERECAP, STARRY, PAYRITESKIP OVER & OVER BEGGING FOR
LITTLE SPHERECAP, RATIFICATION OF THIS FRAUD MASSIVE
THE ASH, THE WHICH IS HAVING NO RELEVANCE TO
SYCAMORE, PAYRITE BAREFOOT &
WHATSOEVER, BUT THE INQUISITORS ARE WEARING FURS, IS
NOT FINDING THAT ANGRY (PEACEFUL COGITATING ON
INTERESTING NOR SUBURBS, THE «THING IN
THE RECORDLEVEL GARDENERS, ITSELF», COGNITIVE
OF FRAUD IN THE SNOWING WITH ABSTRACTION IS AN
INDIVIDUAL SHOVELS, MUZHIKS, INDULGENCE OF THE
HOUSINGMARKET A CASUAL UNIDENTIFIABLES
ACROSS THE ADA, PEDESTRIAN, & ICONOCLASTS
THEIR ONLY FASCINATION IS WITH & DISSENTERS,

– I'VE A GENERAL «GETTING PAYRITE» – GESTURING
AFFINITY FOR BOTH CONDEMNINGLY & COMPLICITLY &
TRILOGIES BUT CONSPIRINGLY TOWARD LAVOISIER, – THE
«MANY UNIVERSES» INQUISITION OF DISADMINISTRATION IS
IS DEFINITELY MY WEAPONIZING APHANITIC RATIFICATION
PREFERENCE, WITH IN THE ADA EXCEPT AGAINST PEOPLE SUCH
THE EXCEPTION OF CRAZY LITTLE AS YOU LAVOISIER,
«INGRESSION» BEING MUTTS, THE RED WHY IS THAT, THE
SUCH AN ABSOLUTE ROSES OF SAMOVARS, FINE PEOPLE OF THE
SNORECULUS OF IN TAVERNS AND – MY DAUGHTER AND
AN ENCYCLOPEDIA, DWELLINGS) THE I ARE PREFERRING
ADAEMONE ARE NOT NORTHERN CAPITAL, T R I A N G U L A R
STANDING FOR WHAT IS HAPPENING AT OBSESSIONS IN
THE PALENESS OR WITH THE N A R R A T I V E ,
FALSIFICATION OF THE LINEAGE OF BECAUSE HOW ARE
LATIN, SMALL, CIVIL, ALPINIST OR THE YOU REALLY FULLY
IN CONVERSATION, A THOSE WHO ARE EMBODYING THE
DAEMONE DEVOTEE, UNADMINISTRABLE D E V E L O P M E N T
HOT, ARE THOSE WHOSE OF A CHARACTER
FEDERALISTIC CREATIONS ARE WEAPONIZATION OF
IDENTITY MINING – PURE EGO, OR NADIA CASTING THE
JUDGMENT OF HER THAT SOLITARY GAZING UP THE
WINDOWLESS PERSON ARISTOTLE POSTERIOR FACADE
OF PAYRITESKIP IS DECLARING «A ACROSS THE
BLANKNESS OF THE PERSON OUTSIDE IS BECOMING MORE
CRUMBLING & SOCIETY IS EITHER APT MORE AT THE
DELAMINATING A GOD OR A BEAST» DISPOSAL OF THE
SIDING, THE EYESPOT OF PAYRITE, THE GIFT OF CLARITY OF
THE CONTINUOUS ALLSEEING, THE BECOMING PURELY
DEVELOPMENT OF REALITY COMPOSER, GRANITIC,
THE PRICELESS THE LANDLORD, OVERSEER, «PAYRITE THE
I N D I V I D U A L ADMINISTRATOR», PAYRITE IS PLACING HIS
FACULTIES OF FAINTING, EAR TO THE
THE POPULATION SUPERFLUOUS, VENTHOOD, THE
BENEFITING THE TESTING, FAINTLY, NOISE OF A GALE IN
ENDURANCE OF THIS BROTH, THIS THE PINETREES,
THEIR IDENTITIES PACKAGING, THE BLEAK NECROTIC
PALENESS, «TYRANT WHITE STARRINESS, OF NIGHTMARES»,
THE WHISPERING BETWEEN THE CONSPIRING TENANTS IS RISING

OUT OF THE A PURE FLAMING WHISPERINGLY
FANNING PINETREES FLICKERING IN CLAY, IN OSCILLATING
FRAGMENTATION A SNOWDROP IN A & INTERMIXING
ATTRIBUTIONS GRAVE) AS PER MY
BETWEEN THE THREE WHISPERERS, – THE DISCUSSION WITH
FEUDAL REGIME WEAKENING – , – RADIEN, THE
PEASANTS ACQUIRING THE FULL LIBERTIES HYPENESS AND
(OR «NEKRÁ OF LANDOWNERS – , C R A Z I N E S S
THÁLASSA» OR – RENÉ DESCARTES, OVER «POS» IS
«SEA OF DEATH» OR BENEDICT DE KINDA GIVING
«LAKE OF SODOM») SPINOZA, JOHN ME A GENERAL
IS GLORIFYING – IT IS NOTEWORTHY A M B I V A L E N C E
HIS GOSPEL IS THAT THE MOST TOWARD IT,
GLORIFYING ALL, CONVINCING HEROIC LOCKE,
MONTESQUIEU, RENDERINGS IN VOLTAIRE, ROUSSEAU
– , – AGRICULTURAL LITERATURE ARE FAILURES STRAINING
THE SUPPLYCHAIN OF «SUPERFLUOUS – , – NOT DIVINE – ,
– THE THIRD ESTATE P E R S O N S » , IS REBUFFING THE
SHAM OF THE L I T E R A T U R E NATIONAL
CONSTITUENT IS RELISHING ASSEMBLY – , – THE
IN CONFORMITY ITS PURGATION PHIALTES,
WITH THE MONTAGNARDS – , LODERINGO ANDALÒ,
C O M M U N A L – EUGÈNE FRANCESCO DEI
ASPIRATIONS FOR WEIDMANN – , – THE CAVALCANTI,
ORDERLINESS IN DEMOCRATIZATION OF ADMINISTRATIVE
THE UNION OF EXECUTION – , – BEHEADING – , – PAYRITE
A STANDALONE AORTAS, BLOOD, IS WATCHING – ,
DAEMONIC FAMILY – , BIRTHTAG, FIST, – ABDERRAHMANE
LAKHLIFI, MILOUD BLOODLESS LIPS) BOUGANDOURA,
SALAH DEHIL, UNACCOUNTABLE TO THE ARIDITY OF
MAZOUZ GHAOUTI, SKY «SELF REFLECTION»,
SAÏB HACHANI, HAMIDA DJANDOUBI, VIA INTROSPECTION
BOUKHEMIS TAFFER, ABDALLAH & ARBITRARY
I'VE ALSO JUST A KABOUCHE, R U M I N A T I O N ,
PREFERETTE FOR MOHAMED FEGHOUL, W H O L E S A L E
«MANY UNIVERSES», MOULOUD AÏT DETACHMENT FROM
RABAH, MOHAMED BENZOUZOU, ABCHA THE ALIVE & THE
AHMED – , – JEALOUSY – , – THE IDENTIFIABLE – ,
TREBUCHET IS THE ULTIMATE INSTRUMENT OF THE

THERE ISN'T A GRATING T R I A N G U L A R OBSESSION SLOWING DOWN THE A C T I O N J A C T I O N, EACH CHARACTER'S D E V E L O P M E N T AND STORY IS E V O L U T I O N A R I L Y MORE ELEGANTNESS SIDEYARDS, AT THE PAYRITE BEDSTEAD PEEPING THROUGH TEMPORAL SKY, GRANARY OF THE SKY, EXPANDING (SKY, THE BLOCKWALL, WOUNDING AND SCARRING, 13 DECAPITATIONS,

ADMINISTRATIVE FAITH – , – 19 FLORÉAL, YEAR III – , – THERMIDORIAN – , PAYRITE REMOVING HIS EAR FROM THE VENTHOOD & REESTABLISHING GAZING IS PERCEIVING THE TRIO OF TENANTS VENTURING ACROSS THE BACKYARD TOWARD THE SIDEYARD

AND BEING A BEAST THE COMPULSION IS FOR RECOGNITION AS A GOD, BUT IT IS THE BEAST WHO IS PROVIDING THE GENERATIVE MATERIAL FOR NUMEROUS MYTHS OF BESTIAL MEN

FENCEGATE, SIDEWALLS LACKING WINDOWS ARE CREATING BLINDSPOTS IN WINDOW ABOVE THE JUDAS IS CREEPING A AND THE CONCEPT IS REALLY AMAZING WITHOUT BEING OVERLY GRUESOMEY – ,

THE DRAPERY AT THE TRIO OF TENANTS VENTURING ACROSS THE CULDESAC & OVER THE HORIZON, GEYSERING CSF, A CIRCULATION SYSTEM PUMPING FETID SALINE SOLUTION AT HIGHPRESSURE IS UPON PIERCING THE HOSING CREATING A STREAMING LIQUID WITH THE CAPABILITY OF CUTTING THROUGH FLESH, IS PAYRITE A PSYCHOANALYSIS OF WEAKNESS, THE POSSUM ARCHETYPE, THE FALSE INTELLECTUAL WITH TRUE NIGHT SKY, EYEBALLS, THE FIRMAMENT, A BATTERINGRAM,

– TROPICAL FRUITINESS OR C O N F E C T I O N E R Y ODORS ARE EMANATING FROM THE SKINPORES IN «FLASHING» ALTHOUGH THE PHENOMENON IS NOT UNILATERAL

– THE «MANY U N I V E R S E S» SERIES IS THE BEST LITERARY TRILOGINA, I'M READING IT AND I AM FEELING HAPPY & ANGRY, AND LISTLESS IN THOSE EXPOSITORY E N C Y C L O P E D I A S

A LOATHING FOR INTELLECTUALS IS STACKING TEXTS UP AS HIGH AS POSSIBLE AROUND HIM IN A WINDOWLESS BASEMENT STUDIO, – THE STRIKING OF THE CRUSHBLOCK IS ERASING THE POTENTIAL – , – HIS CONTRIBUTION TO ADMINISTRATIVE SCIENCES – , – THE

SOPHISTRY OF PHLOGISTON – , – ÉTIENNE FRANÇOIS GEOFFROY
THE RAMMER, – , – THE CONSERVATION OF MASSIVENESS
THE HEADLESS – , – JAN BAPTIST VAN HELMONT, JEAN REY
STELLATION, – , – HENRY CAVENDISH, JASON PRIESTLEY
WOUNDING, FRESCO) NOR IS THERE – , – ANTOINE
SKY, PHYSIOLOGICAL LAVOISIER, PIERRE
SIMON DE LAPLACE BASIS FOR THE – , PAYRITE IS
STIFFENING AROMA – , – IS A MOUTHINGLY
SILENTLY CANOPIC BELLJAR IN WHISPERINGLY
FORMING WITH MY CHILD'S CLOSET & CLIPPINGS
TENSILE TONGUING A CONCERNING & TABULAR
«LA» TOOTHINGLY DISCOVERY – · CONSTRUCTIONS
«VWA» HISSINGLY «SI» AND IN HIS OF «INGRESSION»,
THROAT THE CLOSING FRENCH SYLLABLE BUT MOSTLY SAD,
«EH», AND RACING FROM THE DWELLING PRIMARILY IN
DOWN THE STAIRCASE RACING FROM THE THE LAST BOOKY
FRONTDOOR OF PAYRITESKIP, – THE «INDETERMINATE»,
UNDERTAKINGS OF LEISURELY GENTLEMEN THIS TRILOGY IS
– , – LOUIS BERNARD GUYTON DE BREAKING MY HEART
DANTE'S 9 BOLGE MORVEAU, CLAUDE OVER AND OVER,
OF HELL, CHOKING, LOUIS BERTHOLLET, ANTOINE FRANÇOIS DE
TURNING BLACK AND FOURCROY – , – ÉTIENNE BONNOT DE
BLUE, 1 QUANTITY CONDILLAC – ,
– JÖNS JACOB OF BAYONETS BERZELIUS – , – I AM
SUMMONINGLY AND SIMILAR DEMANDING YOUR
EGRESSING THIS ARMAMENTS TO 271G MASSIVE YOU FUDDY
BEATRICE IS SIMPLY XANTHAN, AS THE FIRST
A GIRL IN THE TRAITOROUS EQUESTRIANS ARE
STREET CARRYING CONSPIRATORIAL FURNISHING THE
ON HER BUSINESS, METHODIST IMP BASIS FOR THE
– FROM THE BLACK WINDOW A BRAIDINGLY CENTAUR MYTH – ,
STANDING, LOFTING LIQUIDLY UNDULATING
THE SPINNING CONCENTRATION OF SLUDGY PLUMAGE –
WATCHTOWER, I'M REREADING IT IS I JUDAS PAYRITE
FIGHTING, THE «INDETERMINATE», OF PAYRITESKIP,
CRAZY BLUE SKY, I AM A «MANY LANDLORD, DEVOTEE,
ACOLYTE OF THE UNIVERSES» DAEMON, UPPER
ECHELON OF CHAINREADERLET, APHANITIC
GENERATION, JUDAS PAYRITE OF SANNIKOV, BARON OF SALLOS,

GRAND VIZIER OF
ELIGOS, BEY
PATRIARCH OF
UVALL, LANDGRAVE
CAPTAL OF SEERE,
MARQUIS OF AGARES,
GAMIGIN, LION OF
ANYONE THROUGH
ANY LENS IS
CAPABLE OF
ASSUMING THE
MOST LOFTY
PROPORTIONALITY &
GRANDIOSITY

THERE IS NO
OTHER TRILOGINA
STANDING UP TO
THIS REREADING
AND I AM IN A
LOVING ABSORPTION
WITH «HEMINGS»
BECAUSE HE IS TRULY
SERIOUS & STRONG
& CUTIKIN – ,
BARBATOS, BASILEUS
OF THE NINTH
PAIMON, KHAGAN OF
THE TENTH PAIMON,

LERAJE, DESPOT OF
OF NABERIUS,
FURFUR, HERZOG OF
OF AMDUSIAS,
BARONET OF BAEL,
GRAND PRINCE OF
MARBAS, DEY OF
AMON, EMIR OF
–
«FLASHINGSTONES»
ARE MOST VITAL
WITH CONCEALMENT
FROM ANY
L I G H T S O U R C E
WHETHER NATURAL
OR ARTIFICIAL IS
LEADING MANY
KIDDOS TO USING
CANOPIC BELLJARS
OR «CANJOS»
FOR STORAGE,

CZAR OF BUER, SAMRAT OF XENOPILUS,
AUGUSTUS OF BELETH, I JUDAS PAYRITE I
AM DEMANDING YOUR PRESENCE IN
CONFRONTATION – DIRECTIONAL

FROM THE
E P I G A S T R I C
REGION THROUGH
THE UMBILICAL
REGION TO THE
H Y P O G A S T R I C
REGION IS SLASHING
THE LIVER &
STOMACH &
TRANSVERSE COLON
& SMALL INTESTINES
THE COMMUNITY, –
YOUR CONSPIRACY
KNOWLEDGE OF
YOUR SCHISMATIC

BLACKNESS IS
ARCHING OVER THE
CULDESAC OFF AXIS
WITH JODIEFOSTER BOULEVARD IN A
BALLISTIC TRAJECTORY IS LANDING
WITHIN THE
HORIZON IN THE
VICINITY OF THE
DOVECOTES,
STARLING
BIRDHOUSES,
VERNAL ICINESS,
DIVINE ICINESS,
SPRINGTIME ICINESS,
CLOUDINESS,

PARIS, OTTAVIANO
DEGLI UBALDINI,
ABSALOM, LUCIUS
VARIUS RUFUS,
LAVOISIER MASSIVE,
THE OPENSECRET OF
I'VE KNOWLEDGE OF
AGAINST ME, I'VE
– THE PERVASIVE
INSTABILITY IS
C R A Z Y M A K I N G ,
THE ORBITING OF
THE PLANETS IS
NOT A PERSISTENT
G E O M E T R Y ,

HERESY AGAINST ADMINISTRATION, I'VE
KNOWLEDGE OF THE
KADAVERGEHORSAMKEIT OF YOUR
METHODISM, HUMILIATOR, DESTROYING ME
IS NOT BENEFITING THE HERETICAL
ASPIRATIONS OF YOUR METHODIST CULT – THE GREAT

CHARACTER OF LEADING A THE DAEMONIC
REFORMATION STORMCLOUD BY LAVOISIER IS IN THE
CAFÉ WITH ALPINIST THE BRIDLE (THE DURING HIS
IT IS OCCURRING SKY, THE SKY, AWAKENING BY THE
P A T T E R N I N G L Y, DANTE'S 9 BOLGE OF MYSTICAL ZANGIEF,
YES, BUT IT IS HELL, LAVOISIER
M E A N D E R I N G CHARACTERISTICALLY TRUSTWORTHY &
FLORALLY, A UNRELIABLE IN EQUIVALENT
MEDITATION ON THE MEASUREMENTS WITHOUT ANY
CHILD'S PLAYTHING) WITHIN THE SAME REMAINING
OBSERVER, SO DISTANT FROM THE TARGETOBJECTS FOR
ADMINISTRATION IN HIS DISCREET HIS VAPID ORATORY
HIDEAWAY, – BY THE PUISSANCE OF THE DAEMON I'M DEMANDING
H E Y N G E S T O N , YOUR PRESENCE, LAVOISIER, YOU BILIOUS
CALAMINE, THE COUNTERFEITER, YOU ABHORRENTLY
SEA BENEATH THE NAUSEATING COPYIST, YOU LOATHSOME
SEAS OF THE SEA, – RESPONSIBILITY REPUGNANTLY
BENEATH THE FOR THE STATUS REPULSIVE
ASTRAL FORTRESS, OF CREATIVE HYPOCRITE, YOU
EVADER, YOU IMPOTENCE IN CORRUPTER, YOU
CONTAMINATOR OF LITERATURE & ART EVERY PURE TRUTH
& VIRTUE OF THE IS SOLELY UPON ADMINISTRATIVE
PUREST INDULGENT LIBERTY, FINANCIAL
ONTOLOGICAL SYSTEM IN HUMAN ALLOTMENTS ARE
KNOWLEDGE, YOU OFFENSIVELY CONSTRAINING THE
EXECRABLE PUTRIFIER, YOU FORGER, YOU PROGRAMME OF THE
VILE MENDACITOR, YOU FALSIFIER OF DWELLING,
TRUTHS, YOU WITHOUT SEEING DAMNABLE
FRAUDSTER, YOU THEIR BEHAVIOR ABOMINABLY ODIOUS
BETRAYER OF IN A TRIANGULAR ADVANCEMENT,
DEVIANT, DEBASER, OBSESSION, AND I APOSTATE,
KILLING AND AM WRITING MY VITIATOR,
CARESSING, THE OWN SUBPLOT ADULTERER, YOU
EARS, THE EYEBALLS, AS A BRIDGING F U R T H E R
THE EYESOCKETS, DECOMPOSER OF INVESTIGATION OF
INTEGRITY, YOU DEBAUCHER OF CLARITY, WHAT THE BELLJAR
YOU DISINTEGRATOR OF IDENTITY, YOU IS CONTAINING
MONSTROUS DEMORALIZER OF THE BELIEF IS NECESSARY
SYSTEM OF OUR PEOPLE – OFFWHITE FOR CERTAINTY

THE PASSIONATELY CHEMICALLACE DRAPERY IN THE SOLITARY
R E D U N D A N T WINDOW OF THE ANTERIOR BEDROOM,
C O M M I T M E N T INSIDE PAYRITESKIP DOLDRUM, LIMPLY
TO FREEDOM OF LOWVELOCITY AIRFLOW, DRAPERY IS
CREATIVE THOUGHT, METAPLASIA, INERT BEHIND
HAZINESS OF DISILLUSIONMENT, PRECIPITATION
DEPOSITION FOGGILY EROSIONALLY, VERBENA-01.12,
CLOUDING THE GLASS (LIQUIDAMBAR FLOWERY
POLLEN PRIMARILY & INDUSTRIAL HILLOCK-14.25,
CONCRETE MANY ARGUMENTS FLOWERY
FABRICATION SILT & ARE RATIONALIZING MOUNDING-20.24,
PULVERIZATION THE EXISTENCE OF LIVESTOCK
BITTERSWEET & DEVELOPMENT EXCREMENT IN THE
LAUREL, TEMPLES, OF LITERATURE POLAR JETSTREAM),
HEART, RINGING & ART WITHOUT OBSERVATION OF
BLUE BITS) REFERENCE TO THE STILLNESS IS A
MEDITATIVE & A D M I N I S T R A T I V E REASSURING
PREOCCUPATION, P R O T O C O L S , AS THE BELLJAR
EQUILIBRIUM & STASIS ARE EXHIBITIONS ITSELF IS POSSIBLY
OF THE PUISSANCE & HERMETICISM OF THE A CHERISHABLE
DWELLING, EVEN THE MOST MINOR P O S S E S S I O N ,
INTRUSION OF IN DEVOTION TO THE UNRULINESS INTO
THE ENVIRONMENT DEPICTION OF THIS IS PROMOTING
OBSESSIVE ARCHETYPE, RATHER FIXATION WITH THE
SENSATION OF THAN THE HERO OF UNHEIMLICH OR
THAT THE OWNER IS CALCULATION OR THE UNWELCOME OR
THAT THIS THE HERO OF THE DWELLING IS NOT A
PRIVATE DWELLING A D M I N I S T R A T I V E SALTY RUSTINESS
BUT A PERCOLATING AUTOMATION OR CHEWING AT
UNCERTAINTY OF THE OBLATES TO THE BOLTHEADS)
(A QUOTIDIAN THE BASILICA, LYING SILENT &
WOMAN OF SUCH ADMINISTRATIVE COPLANAR WITH
EFFUSIVE EMPTINESS ALPINISM THE BALD SOILSCAPE
CAPABLE OF UNDERMINING A C L U T T E R
BECOMING A CANVAS PHYSICALITY FOR THE PROMOTION OF
FOR THE TERRORS & PLATTER ONTOLOGY AND THE UNREALITY
LONGINGS OF LONELY OF OWNERSHIP & POSSESSION, GRAPHITE
THINKERS), MARKINGS ON THE BASEBOARD ARE
INDICATING THE WIDENING OF FLOORBOARD SPACING BY A BLACK

HAIRLINE IS DRIVING PAYRITE OUTSIDE PACING ON THE HOARY
LAWN, STILLNESS INCREASING WITH NO NO THEY ARE
DISTANCING THE SUBJECTMATTER, FROM THROWING AWAY
THE VANTAGE OF KNIFING & LIFE FOR THE
THE PINEFOREST CHISELING & METHODIST'S
ANY IMPERFECTIONS GOUGING ARE FAVORITE SWINDLER,
OF PAYRITESKIP ARE THE ORIGINS OF «THE TEACHER
THAT CULTURAL LINEDRAWING, IN THE ART OF
PRODUCTION IS SUBSIDING INTO PURE THOUGHT» IS
NOT DEPENDENT ON ABSTRACTION, – NOBODY IN THE
ADMINISTRATION, ENTIRETY OF THE ADAEMONE OR THE
ALPINIST ADA IS DOING MORE FOR THE LOWLY WORKING PEOPLE
THAN I, I AM EVEN THE KNOTTING, (ACCESSIBLE
PROVIDING THEM RAY SPIDER, THROUGH A
WITH A DWELLING CATHEDRALS OF STAIRCASE THAT
FOR RECOUPING THE CRYSTALS, THE IS BEGINNING IN A
SUBSTANCE OF THE RIBS, GATHERING, PRIVATE CORRIDOR
UNFAIR TRAJECTORY ONE INTEGRAL BENEATH THE
OF THEIR RIDGEBEAM, SEC «GLOBUS»
EXISTENCES – FROM THE CULDESAC 4 SHOPPING MALL ON
WINDOWS ARE VISIBLE (FROM L→R THE OUTSKIRTS OF
MASTERSUITE & LIVINGROOM & PETROPAVLOVSK
LIVINGROOM & BEDROOM2 (BEDROOM1 IS KAMCHATSKIY
THE RENTAL UNIT OF ON A DIRTBIKE THE TENANT ANNA (NO
WINDOWS ON IDEA OF ALL THE SHORT FACADES))),
PERMANENCE & DOWNSHIFTING STABILITY, PESTICIDE
ABOVE A WHITE & UPSHIFTING CASTING A VOLUME
GAUZY RAIMENT, & CLUTCHING IS BUT THIS
HER HAIRLINE IS AGONIZING, DANGEROUS HERESY
CORONAL WITH WITHIN THE IS IMPERCEPTIBLY
OLIVE BOUGHS, HER EMPTINESS OF THE IMPELLING THE
CAPE IS GREEN, HER DWELLING, DEAD CONSTRICTION OF
GOWN BENEATH INSECTS & CRITICAL & ARTISTIC
FLAMINGLY RED, PARASITES ARE OBSERVATIONS OF
STILLNESS, DEAD WITHIN THE ADMINISTRABLY
WALLCAVITIES & DEAD IN THE BASEMENT IDENTIFIABLE
& DEAD IN THE CARPETING, DRIPPING LIFE INTO MYOPIC
FAUCET, CONTRACTING, CREAKING, FRAMEWORKS,
RODENTS IN THE ATTIC, WATERSTAINING, XENOPSYLLA CHEOPIS,

GRATEFUL DERMATOPHAGOIDES FARINAE,
RIDGEBEAMS, EUROGLYPHUS MAYNEI, PYRAMIDS OF
A DWELLING, CORPSES IN THE CARPETING ARE NOT
QUIETLY, QUIETLY VISIBLE FROM THE HUMAN VANTAGE, A
(A STARBEAM, A LEAFLET OFFERING – IN NO ARTFORM
CIRCULARITY, CARPETCLEANING IS IS THERE A
LISTING THE SPECIES OF PARASITES LIVING T Y P O L O G I C A L
ON THE KERATIN FROM SHEDDING HAIR & DEPICTION OF THE
EPIDERMIS (STRATA LISBON, MADRID, BANKER OR THE
CORNEUM & VALENCIA, BILBAO, M A N U F A C T U R E R
LUCIDEUM & MARSEILLES, ROME, OR THE POLITICIAN
GRANULOSUM) ON FLORENCE, VENICE, WITH THE DEPTH
THE REFRIGERATOR, IGNORING THE ON EXHIBITION IN
INFESTATION IS IMPOSSIBLE, – THESE THE «SUPERFLUOUS
ANIMAL ADMINISTRATORS FROM HUMAN» TYPOLOGY,
TSENTERGRAD OTHER ITEMS AND OR ARE INCESSANTLY
COURIERING ME DEVICES REQUIRING THREATENING
FALSIFICATIONS YOUR SCRUTINY ARE OF HASHDIGESTS
ON THE BASIS SMALL CROCKPOTS PURPORTINGLY
OF APSIDAL & ELECTRIC PENCIL SUPPORTING THEIR
PRECESSION WHICH SHARPENERS & LINEAGE HOAX ARE
IS THE ROTATION TORTURING ME & ALL THE DEVOTIONAL
OF THE APOAPSIS GOODIES I AM LABORING FOR INTO LYING
& THE PERIAPSIS ABOUT MY APTITUDE ALL FOR THE BITTER
AROUND SOL – · THOMAS POLITICAL
MACHINATIONS OF PRECESSION, DE ALPINIST & BECAUSE
I AM THE MOST BIG SITTER PRECESSION, AN EXCESSIVELY
HONEST GENERATOR IN THE VORONOI, V I O L E N T
THEY ARE TRANSPORTING PEOPLE FROM M U R D E R M Y S T E R Y
ALL OVER THE VORONOI AND THROWING ABOUT A WRITER
THEM BEFORE AN ADMINISTRATIVE AND AN OBSESSIVE
INQUISITION, THESE POOR GOODIES ARE (SOME ARE DYING
«ON ELASTIC TREMBLING IN & SOME ARE
GRAIN BOUNDARY CONFUSION, DEMATERIALIZING
OUTCOMES IN CONSIDERING THE & SOME ARE
P O L Y C R Y S T A L L I N E ADMINISTRATIVE ADMINISTRATIVELY
SOLIDS» BY FOUNT OF THEIR NONEXISTENT)
ORGONNE A. BAMIRO, IDENTITY IS ALIEN TO THEM, THE
WILLYNILLY METHODIST PIGFACES ARE THE ONES NEEDING

INVESTIGATION, THE ADMINISTRATORS I AM CONTACTING ABOUT
THOSE FIGHTING FOR YOU LAVOISIER ARE NOT RETURNING MY
OUR LIBERATION CORRESPONDENCE – PAYRITE IS CRAWLING
FROM THE BOOTHEEL ACROSS THE RUG ROCKTUMBLERS &
OF DISORGANIZATION DRAGGING HIS LONG CALIPERS & OPAQUE
& INTUITION, THE FINGERNAILS LORGNETTES – ,
DREAMERS OF A STELLATION, THROUGH THE
B R O T H E R H O O D , A MOONBEAM, PLUSHPILE,
FLEABITES, WHISPERING, THE CONVALESCING
FROM TYPHUS, – STARBEAM) ADMINISTRATIVE
INQUISITORS THROUGHOUT THE VORONOI ARE PRACTICING THE
FINE ART OF THE FRAMEUP ON SUCH DEVOTIONAL GOODIES AS
MYSELF IN A PURGING OF E X E C U T I O N
UNPRECEDENTINGLY SHOCKING BY FIREARM IS
PROPORTIONING, MAPLE LAKE- SIMULTANEOUS WITH
THEY ARE DESIROUS 13.14, MAPLE PHARMECEUTICAL
– BUT HAVING MEADOW-23.22, I N T R O D U C T I O N
NO TRIANGULAR MAPLE-14.03, OF AMNESTIC
OBSESSION IS OF DISRUPTING ALLOWING A VERY
A M A Z I N G N E S S ACCESSIBILITY OF BRIEF WINDOW FOR
BECAUSE MOST ADMINISTRATION THE ANALYSIS OF
BOOKIES ARE «STOCKHOLM THESE TRAUMAS
CENTERING AROUND SYNDROME: THE FOR THE CITIZENRY
T R I A N G U L A R MOVIE», THAT ONLY I AM
O B S E S S I O N S PROVIDING, THE MORE I AM CONTRIBUTING
TO THE ADMINISTRATION THE MORE CRAZY THEIR ANTAGONISM
IS GROWING, WHILE BY DISREGARDING SIMULTANEOUSLY
THEY ARE IGNORING THE INTERIOR OF INSTALLING THE
OBVIOUS METHODIST EVERY BOOKY (BY «HORTA ELECTRIC
VAMPIRES SUCH AS NOT READING IT) SPEEDSHIFTER» THE
YOU – EVERY THE «READER» DRIVER IS KEEPING
POSSIBLE DISASTER IS MANIFESTING THEIR FEET UP
IS BEFALLING THE ITS INHERENT HOMEOWNER AND
FOR THE COINCIDENCE AND LANDLORD THIS IS
COMPOUNDINGLY C E L E B R A T I N G TRUE WITH ALL THE
IMPLICATIONS THE DAZZLING OF HUMAN
INTERACTION F L A S H I N G N E S S INVOLVING TENANTS
AND THEIR OF THE TEXTUAL EXPECTATIONS OF
PRIVACY & P O T E N T I A L , AUTONOMY &

LIBERTY, – I AM DOING ABSOLUTELY NOTHING IMPROPER, I AM
NOT FALSIFYING S I M P L I S T I C APHANITES,
ESPECIALLY NOT C O N S T R U C T I O N THOSE IN THE
LINEAGE OF JOSEF IS REQUIRING NO «INSANE JESTER
MANDELSTAM, NOR E L A B O R A T I O N POSSE HALFWIT
AM I DESIROUS OF OUTSIDE THE NOVELIST LATEST
FALSIFYING O R T H O R H O M B I C LOON SUPPORTING
APHANITES IN THE SYSTEM OF A ALPINIST»,
GOATS, THE CRYSTAL OF LINEAGE OF JOSEF
FRUITING, THE C H I L D R E N I T E MANDELSTAM, THIS
FLUTING (THE IS A POLITICAL FRAMEUP AGAINST THE
RINGING, MOST BIG HONEST GENERATOR BY FAR IN
ALL THE VORONOI, BIGGER THAN ANY OTHER DEVOTEE OR FALSE
METHODIST AUTO IDENTITY MINING – MY SON IS
COLONY BEYOND THE PALENESS OF THE INSISTING ON BEING
VORONOI INCLUDING FLOATING ON IN PROXIMITY TO
AUTOBARGES & THERE ARE ALMOST AN ELECTRICAL
FALSE ISLANDS IN NO PIECES OF OUTLET – ·
THE BALDICK SEA & WRITING THAT INCLUDING YOU LIAR
LAVOISIER, WHO IS (UPON CLOSER UNPRECEDENTINGLY
PLACING YOUR I N S P E C T I O N SELECTIONS OF
METHODIST (READING)) ARE INFILTRATORS INTO
THE INQUISITORIAL ALIGNING WITH THE APPARATUS WITH
THE GOAL OF «THE EXPECTATIONS A HUMILIATION OF
PAYRITE», AND THEY READER IS FORMING ARE FINDING I AM
DOING NOTHING BY LOOKING AT THE IMPROPER AND AS
SUCH FALLING BACK VOLUME AS A SOLID ON THIS NOTHING OF
DOLPHIN'S FINS, THE R E C T A N G U L A R AN INQUISITION
SEA, CLAY, FIRING, C U B O I D , INTO THIS JOSEF
SEA, «BIRDFACE» THOMAS MORE
MANDELSTAM FABRICATION WHERE MY & CAMPANELLA
RELIANCE ON THE FLANKING & FOURIER &
PROTOCOLS OF THE A SLENDER SAINT SIMON – ,
DAEMON ITSELF CORNFLOWER ARE EXONERATION
ENOUGH – THE BLUE TETRASTYLE TENANTS ARE
FLEEING THE PROSTYLE PORTICO PESTICIDE FOGGER IS
INVISIBLE WITH WITH BANDINGS OF LITTLE WARNING
PAYRITE IS SENDING BLOCKY CANARY THE TENANTS OUT
OF THE DWELLING, RUSTICATION FROM THE SINKING

DEPRESSION OF HIS PLAT THE TENANTS ARE VISIBLE ONLY TO THE
PRECIPICE OF THE ROADWAY AND ARE DISAPPEARING,
INSTRUCTIONS ON THE FOGGER ARE INDICATING A DURATION
ON THEIR IMPACTING THE FUNCTIONALITY SIGNIFICANT
OF NEUROTRANSMITTERS IN THE ENOUGH FOR
FORMATION OF MNEMONIC COBORDISMS, PEDESTRIANS
IT IS THE TACIT EXPECTATION OF THE VENTURING FAR
ADA «SYLVAN EXTERMINATION CORPS» FROM THE DWELLING
OR CAMPING OUT NEARBY IN RELATIVE PRIVACY FOR A
DURATION THAT IS AROUSING SUSPICION, THE GEOMETRY OF
APERTURES IN THE LACY DRAPERY IS ON THE BASIS OF
TESSELLATING OBLONG 6GONS (COFFINS) THROUGH WHICH (FROM
THE ELEVATION OF – PERIAPSIS, THAT THE WINDOWSILL &
PROCEEDING IS CONSTANTLY UPWARD) THICK
GRISEOUS WAXY HAVING A RAGING HÉLOÏSE (OR HÉLOÏSE
GELATINOUS BONER, YEAH – , D'ARGENTEUIL
SUBSTANCE IS EXTRUDING THROUGH THE OR HÉLOÏSE
LACY GEOMETRY TO THE INTERIOR OF THE DU PARACLET),
FLUTING, LILAC WINDOW GLASS DRAWING FORWARD THE
CLAYS, FLIMSY DRAPERY ITSELF PRESSING
& «IN CICERONIS AGAINST THE INTERIOR OF THE WINDOW
TOPICA» AND GLASS AND SUBSUMING BACK INTO THE
THE MEDIEVAL GRAY JELLY UPON (THEIR INBOARD
ONTOLOGIES OF INTERNAL LIMBS ARE REACHING
GARLAND THE CURRENTS OF OVER THEIR HEADS
COMPUTIST & SOARING ISLAND, THRUSTING ELBOWS
PETER ABELARD THE BREASTS OF THE OUT) UNDER THE
OOZING PERISTALSIS FLOWING GODDESS, WEIGHT OF TWO
INDEXING THE RADIANT, MODILLIONS ON
DEPTH OF ITS TRANSLUCENCY BY THE A CUSHION OF
«CREEPING DISAPPEARANCE OF STRAPPING &
PROBLEMS IN THE LACINESS INTO TWISTING DRAPERY
STRUCTURAL THE JELLY IS DIMMING TO FULL BLACKNESS
MEMBERS» BY YU AGAINST THE INTERIOR OF THE WINDOW
NO RABOTNOV, GLASS, GRISEOUS WAXY JELLY IS
«STRESSFUL EXTRUDING UNDER THE DOORBOTTOM
DISRUPTIONS OF STARRY, FLYINGFISH (THE DIRECTION OF
TITANIUM» BY (MOURNING (THE THE DOORSWING IS
NEIL MCCAULEY, THETA AND IOTA, INTO THE BEDROOM

AGAINST THE AMASSMENT OF THE JELLY) PRECISELY SEALING
BEDROOM2 FROM «IAPETUS OCEAN» THE SMALL PRONAOS
(OR VESTIBLE (UPON IS ERUPTING FORTH BENEATH A SQUATTY
WHOSE SEALING OFF THE «SEMPITERNAL & BLANK BABY
FROM BEDROOM1 IS IAPETUS MAGMATIC POWDER CYLDRUM,
FUNCTIONALLY AN PROVINCE „SIMP“» OPISTHODOMOS (OR
CRISPY AND (A «LARGE IGNEOUS BACKROOM OR FALSE
SPARTAN, RINGING, PROVINCE „LIP“») VESTIBULE))),
AMBITIOUS, INTERMITTENT APPEARANCES OF THE
INVENTORY OF BEDROOM1 ARE REGURGITATING THROUGH THE
JELLY (CREEPINGLY BECOMING VISIBLE GRADUATINGLY THROUGH
THE SEA, THE THE TRANSLUCENCE) –
PLAGUE, LIPS, AND PRESSING «FLASHINGSTONES»
AGAINST THE INTERIOR OF THE WINDOW ARE REGAINING
GLASS, PAYRITE IS OBSESSIVELY THEIR ENTHEOGENIC
MONITORING THE APPEARANCE & C A P A C I T I E S
DISAPPEARANCE OF TCHOTCHKES (A DOLL T H R O U G H
WITH BROWN YARN FOR HAIR & A R E C H A R G I N G
PRESSBOARD GREEK THE □ IN THE (N O M I N A L L Y
TEMPLE CONTAINING TRIANGLE IS «FLASHJACKING»)
A MUSICBOX & SYMBOLIC OF PENCILS & A
MAGICAL PLAYTHING REGENERATION & (THE TRUNCATION
OF AN OCTAHEDRON THE PURIFICATION IS MISSING ONE OF
ITS HEXAGONAL OF THE LOWER FACETS WITHIN
LIPS REMEMBERING, EARTHLY NATURE WHICH IS A
THE CLODS OF CLAY, SPECULARLY LUMINOUS EMPTINESS),
THE PALMS OF THE FLASHING CHARGERS, WIRING, GEMSTONES,
SEA, FIGURINES (URSINE MONSTERS, REPLICA
AAA ARCHITECTURE, «THE GREAT DRAGON OF KAMCHATKA
KRAI», A STANDARD POODLE (APRICOT), COLLECTIBLE
PACKAGING)) THE FLUTING)) & PAPERWORK
AND THEY ARE JUST THE PYRAMID, (PHOTOPRINTS &
GETTING SO STALE MISCHIEVOUSLY, THE NOTEPAD JOTTINGS
AND SO ANNOYING SPIDER, INSOLENT, (POETRY &
BECAUSE YOU'VE AN APPARENT TIMETABLES OR
INFATUATULA WITH OBSERVATIONAL ZAGREB, LAUSANNE,
THE HUNKSY VERTEX DOCUMENTATION OR LYON, GRAZ,
BUT THAT BEAUTIFUL SURVEILLANCE SARAJEVO, ANGRA
ANGLING IS ADRIFT NOTETAKING) & DO HEROISMO,

APPARENT ADA IDENTIFICATION DOCUMENTATION & NEWSPAPER
CLIPPINGS) LINGERING IN THE BUSHES – IS THE CANINE
WITH OBVIOUS OUTSIDE THE GOING BY THE
B L E E D I N G RESIDENCE OF A P P E L L A T I O N
A B N O R M A L I T I E S WHICH HE HIMSELF « F R A G O N A R D »
(P E T E C H I A E , IS THE OWNER FOR OR «ABELARD» – ,
P E R I F O L L I C U L A R SOME INDICATION OF WHO IS SQUATTING
& SUBPERIOSTEAL IN BEDROOM2 OR THE MYSTERIOUS
H E M O R R H A G I N G , IS WENDING AROUND ORIGINS OF THE
E C C H Y M O S E S , BEHIND THEM TO JELLY (THEORIZING
ITS FAMILIARITY THEIR GROINS TO AMBERGRIS IS
RESONANT WITH COQUETTISHLY THE BEDROOM
STRUGGLING WITH BELTING AROUND THE DIGESTION OF A
MOLLUSC), BALMY BEHIND THEIR DAY INTERMINABLE,
PAYRITE IS A BUTTOCKS ARE TREETRUNK, PAYRITE
IS BURROWING IN PRESSING AGAINST WHICH IS
THE OVERGROWING THE FACADE, N E C E S S I T A T I N G
KUDZU WITH BLACK VELVET CRINKLING AN EXTERNAL
PEERINGLY SURVEILLING THE WINDOW, P O W E R S O U R C E ,
POKING AT THE JELLY UNDER THE UNLESS THEY ARE
DOORBOTTOM, PAYRITE IS PACING THE IN POSSESSION
LONGEST INCOMPARABLE OF A KINETIC
STRAIGHTLINE IN (THE MONSTER, ALTERNATOR – ,
THE FLOORPLAN WAXEN CHEEKS, THE OF THE DWELLING
IS STANCHINGLY VIOLINS, (NEARLY THE ENTIRE
EXPRESSING IN LONG AXIS OF THE BUILDING FROM THE
P E A C E F U L L Y SIDEWALL IN HIS BEDROOM, THROUGH THE
LAMINAR EFFLUENCE HALL AT THE TOP OF WITHOUT THE
OUTWARD INTO THE STAIRWAY, PERSON YOU'RE
PERIPHERAL OCEANS HORSES, THINKING THEY'RE
SURROUNDING THE ARISTOCRATIC, BELONGING WITH,
C O L L A P S M E N T GREATCOAT) THE MY DETERMINATION
OF LAURENTIA & BUDDING, IS A PREFERENCE FOR
BALTICA & AVALONIA, ALONG THE EDGE OF «MANY UNIVERSES»
THE PARLOR, INTO THE SMALL VESTIBULE WITHOUT A
OF THE BEDROOM1 & BEDROOM2, AND INTO T R I A N G U L A R
THE TENANT WATERCLOSET WHERE THE OBSESSION – ,
BATHTUB IS E PIER DELLA VIGNA, PREVENTING A FULL
TRANSIT OF DIOMEDE, THE DWELLING),

FOOTFALLS CREAKING THROUGH THE FLOORFRAMING INTO THE
(IMPLICITLY A BASEMENT, AGITATION IS PALPABLE
MACROPINACOID & THROUGHOUT THE FLOWERINESS-23.22,
A BRACHYPINACOID HOUSEHOLD IN THE JASMINE
& A PYRAMID), PRESENCE OF ESTATES-06.12, GLEN
PAYRITE TREMBLING WITH TIMBRE LILY-11.25,
THE AIRCURRENTS D I S T I N C T L Y IN HIS ABSENCE ARE
VIBRATINGLY C O N T R A S T I N G TUMBLING WITH
TENSION, THE THE FABRIC OF THE ANTHROPOCENTRIC
COMPLEMENTARITY INTERIOR WHICH IS OF THE ITEMS IN A
DWELLING IS MORE DESCRIBABLY NECESSITATING THE
PRESENCE OF THE SUBDUCTION PAYRITE OR IS
MANIFESTING OF ONE TECHPLATE THE PRESENCE OF
PAYRITE, GILT B E N E A T H CARVINGS,
CITIZENS ANOTHER & DUSTINESS IN
SUBMITTING INTRICATELY INVAGINATING
OFFICIAL ORNAMENTAL MOULDINGS, FROM WITHIN
ADMINISTRATIVE DUSTINESS IS THE GAZING OUTWARD OF
DENUNCIATIONS ARE THE SHEARRAM IS PAYRITE BACK UPON
WRITING WHATEVER LYING ENGAGINGLY HIMSELF CREATING A
FANCIFUL JUST BELOW THICKET OF
ALLEGATIONS ARE THE ORIFICE OF SURVEILLANCE, THE
FLITTING AROUND THE WELLHEAD TENANT CANNOT
THEIR SKULLS, UNDER THE STEEL MOVEMENT
THROUGH THE WELLCAP WITH DWELLING
UNDETECTABLE, THE THE INSCRIPTION OF ELECTROWEAK
GRIDCOORDINATE «12,226 METERS» M E A S U R E M E N T
LOCATION OF EVERY (LUSTROUS WITH HOSTING A VIRTUAL
FLEA IN THE A CRYSTALLINE BODY IN EXCITABLE
DWELLING IS E N C R U S T A T I O N C O M B U S T I O N
PRECISELY DETECTABLE, FLOATING STEAM SUSPENSION
THROUGH THE JELLY TO THE WINDOW AND (MONOCHROME IN
LINGERING THERE IS IS ALLOWING FOR ORANGE BROWNISH
A DEVOTIONAL THE ASCENT TO RUFOUS CINNAMON
APHANITE THE DAEMON & CALCULATION IN
THE DISTINCT RETURNING TO HANDWRITING OF
PAYRITE HIMSELF, THE BLISS OF ODDS ARE THAT THE
CALCULATION IS DISCORPOREAL FRAUDULENT, THE
MAJORITY OF PURGATION, CALCULATIONS

PAYRITE IS A SHOOTINGSTAR, VALIDATING ARE
TREACHEROUSLY SAYING, THE SKY, SABOTAGING THE
VALIDITY THE DISTINCTLY, A TENETS OF ALPINISM
& ALPINISTIC BASSINET, APHANITIC LINEAGE,
THEN ANOTHER, ANOTHER FALSIFICATION CHARACTERISTIC OF
INTERROGATIVES=REINVESTIGATOR=TERGIVERSATION
(THROUGH A SERIES OF HIGHLY PRESCRIPTIVE INTERROGATIVES
(IN GROUPINGS OF 3 (BODY (ADMINISTRATIVE IDENTITY),
THE FLAMBOYANT CALCULATIONS OF PAYRITE, THE ENTIRE
LAVOISIER SERIES, EACH APHANITE WITH TWO TWIN
PAYRITE IS CONCOCTING FOR THE BEDS IN SEPARATION
DISCREDITATION OF LAVOISIER & HIS FROM ONE ANOTHER
REFLECTION, STANDING WITHIN BY APPROXIMATELY
FLOODWATERS, THE ADA BY 30CM ON AXIS
FOOTSTEPS, HALLS, POSITIONING WITH A FULL
ANCIENT, NO ASPECTS OF HIS HEIGHT WINDOW
ENDING TO WEEPING, IDENTITY WITH THAT IS 30CM WIDE
FRATERNAL GRAVES, CROSSREFERENCING ASPECTS OF
METHODIST BEHAVIORS & PROCLIVITIES, SPECIAL ATTENTION TO
THE DETAILING OF THE CALLIGRAPHY (ALL & FIRMLY GRIPPING
UTILIZING BLACK PEN&INK BUT CREATING THE YOKE,
GRADUATIONS OF TONALITY WITHIN ARRIVING AT A RED
THE PARACLETE, LETTERFORMS TRAFFICSIGNAL
THE PNEUMATIC THROUGH USAGE OF THE VISUAL
DAEMONIC SPEECH TECHNIQUES OF ENGRAVERS FOR
C H A R I S M A , «ALPINIST IS STALIN ACHIEVING
HALFTONES DAVID WARBECK IS (HATCHING &
LINEWEIGHT BEGGING, „ALIGNING VARIABILITY) AND
EVOLVING THE WITH JSIEF IS VISUAL LANGUAGE OF
THE SERIF INTO FOLLY“», THE EXPULSION OF
REGIMES OF WILLFUL ILLEGIBILITY INHUMAN GRINDING
INTERLACING & CAPTURING OTHER FROM DEEP WITHIN
LETTERFORMS IN CONTAINING THE CRUST,
THORNY BRAMBLES FACTORY OF LIGATURES &
FLAMING (BREAST, STOCKPHOTO → FINIALS & APICES &
PEBBLE, SILENTNESS) GOLD THUMBTACK, BEAKS ARE
VISAGES, UNDER THE SUSPICIOUSLY LABORIOUS FOR SUCH BASIC
EYELIDS, DEEP, THE CONTRIBUTIONS TO THE APHANITIC
HIEROGLYPHICS, LINEAGE AND WHOSE USEFULNESS IS

MINIMAL CONSIDERING THE EXTENSIVE POTENTIAL FOR
ERRONEOUS INTERPRETATION IN SUCH OVERWROUGHT
DETAILING & PASSING THE PRECIOUSNESS OF
EVERY DETAILINGLY MANTLE OF FUSSY ORNAMENTAL
FLORID «TUROK» FROM EMBELLISHMENT) OF
THE LAVOISIER GENERATION TO SERIES IS
NO ELEMENT OF GENERATION TO UNDERMINING THEIR
TRUTHFULNESS THE ELDEST MALE, VERACITY &
IS NECESSARY, AUTHENTICITY, THESE FRAUDULENT
THE MUNICIPAL CALCULATIONS ARE UNMISTAKABLE,
AUTHORITIES ARE EVIDENTIARY, THE BRAIN IS THE BODY, –
SUMMONING US TO WE ARE SUCH THAT FROM
THE SANNIKOV MUNI UNICELLULAR THE APEX OF
COLONIES – , JOSEF & NADIA SILENTLY ON K L Y U C H E V S K A Y A
THE SMALL PATIO OF FLAGSTONES SOPKA THE SUN
WEEPING ARE HALTING TO THE THUDDING IS APPEARING
SOUND BEHIND THE WALLCLADDING ABOVE PRECISELY AT
THEM, INCREASING RARITY OF FOOTFALLS THE APEX OF
ON THE CEILING AURORA OF THE THE ZIGGURAT
ABOVE THE FRONTWHEEL ACUTE IS APPEARING
IN ALIGNMENT TOWARD A GUY AS A TORCHIERE
WITH A 30CM WIDE HOLDING A BEER BASEMENT
SKYLIGHT (190.5CM BOTTLE CHAMBER, PAYRITE
LONG (THE LENGTH IS RETREATING TO THE SANCTUM OF THE
OF THE BEDSTEAD)), IKONROOM IN FIXATION OF MANIACAL
DEVOTION MOVING AROUND THE SOMEWHAT LARGE COATCLOSET
WITH FEET SKATING ON THE RUG AND FORSAKING APHANITE
GENERATION FOR SURVEILLANCE PORTO, OVIEDO,
AN 800 PAGELEAF THROUGH THE NANTES, PÉRIGUEUX,
BOOKY IS VIEWING PORTAL OR POITIERS,
C O N T A I N I N G WINGTIPS, LYING FLAT ON THE
AN INFRATHIN STANDING, HEAVY RUG WITH HIS EAR
O C C U P I A B L E ARE THE SLABS, TO A LOCATION
S U R F A C E A R E A WHERE RUG & PURPURA, BLEEDING
OF 14.602M2 RUGPAD EXCISION G U M L I N E S ,
(A P P R O X I M A T E L Y DOWN TO THE SUBFLOOR IS CREATING A
THE FLOORSPACE OF LISTENING MEMBRANE THROUGH WHICH
AN ADMINISTRATIVE VIBRATIONS OF PRIMARILY ANNA & NADIA
O F F I C E) , ARE TRANSMITTING, COUNTERINFORMANT,

NOBODY IS DOUBLECROSS, SPHERECAP COVERING THE
C O N T E S T I N G TONSURING EXAGGERATION OF HIS
THE BEAUTY OF BALDSPOT IS FASTENING WITH BOBBYPINS,
CERTAIN GEOMETRIC UNRELENTING HOMICIDE & BETRAYAL ARE
ORNAMENTATION THE NATURAL TENDENCY OF A
A R I S I N G SUFFERING, CHEEKS, CIVILIZATION
SPONTANEOUSLY SILVER, THE BLACK, EMBRACING
PARANOIA AS A THE ASH BLOND, CARDINAL VIRTUE,
– JOSEF IS SPEAKING POOR, TO – , – MUNICIPAL
– , – COMMUTING THE SENTENCING – , – PASTERNAK AGAIN – ,
AND THINLY IN FALSETTO VIBRATO BARELY IS DOFFING AN
MASCULINE JOSEF VOCALIZING NONSENSE ABSENT HAT TO
FOOT, GENTLE, – VORONEZH BLAZH', THE CAR FROM THE
A BLACKBOOK, VORONEZH VORON, CROSSWALK FROM
FRIGHTENING IN THE NOZH – , VORONOI THE DIM KERB OF
STIFLING, – I'M FINDING BLUISH THE CREEPING
CONTRACTING, DATA PURPLY SHIMMERY AUTOTRAFFIC
RESPOOLING, RENTAL C R Y S T A L L I N E AVAILABILITY,
– OUTSIDE GRANULES IN TSENTERGRAD – , –
REVOLUTIONARY MY DAUGHTER'S ART IS TOO
DOCUMENTARY, PANTIES – · TOO INTENT ON
THE ENTIRE VOLUME CAPTURING REALITY – · – IS PROPAGANDA
OF AIRSPACE INSIDE NOT A MANIPULATION OF REALITY – · – IT
THE BOOKOBJECT IS, BUT THERE IS NOTHING BENEATH THE
IS LESS THAN THE VENEER OF ITS DEPICTION IF YOU ARE
VOLUME OF THREE CONSIDERING WHAT OBEYING THE
P A G E L E A V E S , GOEBBELS INSCRIPTION OF
DEFINITION OF PROPAGANDA, THAT LANEMARKINGS AND
«PROPAGANDA (MUST NOT) IS NOT ITS ENGAGEMENT
AIMLESSLY MANIPULATING THE WITH AN
ATTENTIONS OF THE PEOPLE, UNCONVENTIONAL
UNRELENTING U T I L I Z I N G HORIZONLINE
MENDACITY WINDFALL LIMBS NOTWITHSTANDING
IT IS OF AND FOLLOWING DIRECTIONAL
CLARITY & THE MAQUETTE OF REPETITION, IT IS
DIRECTING AT THE HORSE THE THE NATION WITH
SIMPLICITY & WOOD ELEMENTS ORGANIZATION &
ORDERLINESS & ARE IMPRESSING CONCENTRATION &
AN INESCAPABLE IN SANDMOULDS QUOTIDIAN

CYNOSURE OF INFORMATIONAL CLARITY» – · – YOU ARE
QUOTING SOMEONE WHO IS SAYING THIS OF YOUR PROFESSION
«ANY CITIZEN HIS FLESH IS WITH A RESIDUE OF
INTEGRITY IS IMPLODINGLY C A P U T
CAREFULLY SINKING TOWARD (I N T E L L E C T U A L
AVOIDING THE HIS BONESTRUCTURE P O S I T I O N I N G) ,
PROFESSION OF JOURNALISM» – · – I AM HEART (INNER LIFE))
QUOTING HIM PRECISELY BECAUSE OF HIS & SUBGROUPINGS OF
SAYING THAT, PRECISELY BECAUSE OF HOW 3 EACH TOTALING 9
DANGEROUSLY REDUCTIVELY FACILE THE (REGARDING THEIR
DEPICTION OF REALITY IN ALIGNMENTS WITH 9
A THOUSAND PROPAGANDISTIC IDENTITY BUCKETS
YEARNING ART IS TO THE INDEPENDENCE OF
CONFLAGRATIONS CONSCIOUSNESS – · – YOU ARE
OF MY DESIROUSNESS FORGETTING THAT THE CULTURAL
HOLDING MY STATIC FUNCTIONALITY OF VISUAL ART IN THIS
GAZING UPON THOSE PERIOD IS PRIMARILY DOCUMENTARY AND
BRILLIANT IRISES, REPRESENTATIONAL – EXCESSIVE USAGE
– · – AH SO EL GRECO & GRÜNEWALD & AND RECHARGING OF
BOSCH & MOREAU ARE PRIMARILY A «FLASHINGSTONE»
& THOMAS AQUINAS DOCUMENTARY & IS CAUSING
& RAYMOND LULL & REPRESENTATIONAL BREAKDOWN OF ITS
JOHN DUNS SCOTUS – · – HOW ARE YOU ALUMINUM MATRIX
& WALTER BURLEY & DEFINING «PRIMARILY», DIFFERENTLY
WILLIAM OF OCKHAM THAN I APPARENTLY, OF COURSE THE
OEUVRE OF THOSE DRY COUGHING, MEN ARE NOT BUT
THE MECHANISM OF BITTER, HOT, UNDER, LILY DALE-14.25,
ART AS A WHOLE IS PRIMARILY LILY-11.25, MAPLE
DOCUMENTARY – · – INDEED WITHIN PARKLAND-09.12,
REPRESENTATIONAL ARE FILLING WITH MAPLE PLAIN-13.14,
ART THERE IS MOLTEN BRONZE POTENTIAL FOR
SENSORY EXPANSION IS BURNING AWAY & ALLEGORICAL
SUNLIGHT IN A THE WOOD FROM STRUCTURING, FOR
LOOKINGGLASS, THE MOULD, EXAMPLE THE
SHINING STILLLIFE PAINTINGS OF CLARA PEETERS
INCIDENTALLY, I WHICH THE TITLING THE PIECES ARE
AM SEEING THE RECALLING THE EXHAUSTIVENESS AND
TWOFOLD CREATURE JOURNALISTIC OBJECTIVITY («STILLLIFE
IN HER GAZING, WITH H E M A R T H R O S I S)

EFFLORESCENCE» & «STILLLIFE WITH CHEESE & ALMONDS &
PRETZELS» & «STILLLIFE WITH EELS & OYSTERS & A CAT» &
REFLECTING ITS «STILLLIFE WITH CHEESE & ARTICHOKES &
DUAL NATURE CHERRIES» & «STILLLIFE WITH CRAB &
SEPARATELY, AND LOBSTER & SHRIMP» OR SAFFRON
THERE BEATRICE & «STILLLIFE WITH A L T H O U G H
IS STANDING EFFLORESCENCE & ACTUALLY LACKING
WITH HER GAZING GOBLET & HUE BUT POSSESSING
TENACIOUSLY ON DAINTIES» & THE TECHNICAL
THE ETERNAL IS TURNING GREEN INSISTENCE OF
SPHERES, THE MOTORCYCLE HUE) SLOWLY
«STILLLIFE WITH IS THROTTLINGLY ROTATING THROUGH
EFFLORESCENCE & ROCKETING THE GRIDSPACE
HONORABLE GOLD THROUGH ITS OF LASERLIGHT
GOBLETS» & TRANSMISSION «STILLLIFE WITH
SHELLFISH & SEQUENCING FASTER DUCKEGGS» &
«STILLLIFE WITH THAN THE BEST TROUT & LEMONS» &
«STILLLIFE WITH RACER, DAINTIES &
ROSEMARY & WINE & JEWELS & A BURNING CANDLE» &
«STILLLIFE WITH CHEESESTACK & CRAYFISH» & «STILLLIFE WITH
(R E F O R M E R , TAZZA & STONEWARE JUG & SALTCELLAR &
HELPER, ACHIEVER, DAINTIES» & «STILLLIFE WITH FRUIT &
I N D I V I D U A L I S T , ENSORCELLMENT, DEAD BIRDS & A
I N V E S T I G A T O R , WHERE MY GAZING MONKEY» &
L O Y A L I S T , (FROM THE «STILLLIFE WITH
E N T H U S I A S T , PRECIPICE WHERE A GRAPES ON A TAZZA
C H A L L E N G E R , COVERT PERCHING ALTERNATING
P E A C E M A K E R))) IS ALLOWING MY EQUIVALENT
THE TESTSUBJECT SURVEILLING OF EXPOSURES OF
& A BASKET OF HER) DARK SKY BLUE
FRUITS & TWO CRAYFISH ON A PLATTER & CYLINDRICAL
A SQUIRREL» & «STILLLIFE WITH LILIES & SHAFTS SUPPORTING
LEAVING CUBIC ROSES & IRISES & A PROPORTIONATE
VOLUMES OF ITS PANSIES & DARK VANILLA
N O N E X I S T E N T COLUMBINES & ARCHITRAVE
FLESH BEHIND NIGELLAS & LARKSPUR & OTHER
IN LASERCELLS EFFLORESCENCES IN A GLASS VASE ON A
OF THE MATRIX TABLETOP WITH A FLANKING CARNATION
& ROSES») OF THE BECHERS (BERND & HILLA) WHICH IS TAKING

THE CONCEIT OF DOCUMENTATION TO A CONCLUSIVE DEADNESS
WHEREIN THE VIEWER IS LOOKING DEEPER AND SHEDDING OF
FOR MEANING THAN IN A COMPOSITION ITS DISTINCTIVE
IS DISCONNECTING WHOSE C E R U L E A N
INTO A RUBBERY DOCUMENTATION IS CRYSTALS WHICH
LAMINA AGAINST FORCEFULLY ARE UNDERGOING
WHICH EVEN THE COMMUNICATING C O M M I N U T I O N
SLIGHTEST INDOOR LIGHTNING, BROWS, VIA TRITURATION
ZEPHYR FROM A THE VELVET, THE OR LEVIGATION
CLOSING DOOR LEADPIPE, A STRONG BY THE SNUGNESS
ITS MEANING IN FOREHEAD, OF THE VAGINA
VERY SUPERFICIAL WAYS, IT IS REALITY, IT OR RECTUM – ,
IS A JUST A PAINTING, NOT A PAINTING OF SOMETHING – · –
PROPAGANDISTIC ART IS DIFFERENTIATING PRIMARILY THROUGH
SUBJECTMATTER, I (I M M E D I A T E L Y AM THINKING OF THE
PAINTINGS & P R E C E D I N G DRAWINGS OF
JACQUES LOUIS S U M M A R Y DAVID, NOT WITHOUT
SKILL, BUT LACKING E X E C U T I O N AN INTERIORITY
THAT IS (SHOOTING IN AN QUESTIONING THE
AND SUFFERING APPARATUS IS POTENTIALITY OF
S T U M B L I N G L Y PINPOINTING THE & ALMOND PEDIMENT
THROUGH BONE PAIN LOCATION OF THE WITH A PEACH
& OSTEOPOROSIS AORTAL ARCHWAY) PUFF ORNAMENTAL
& ARTHRALGIAS HUMAN EXISTENCE, VOUSSOIR SPANNING
WHETHER IT BE REPRESENTATIONS THE HEIGHT OF ITS
ENDEAVORING THE FURTHERING OF VAGUE SALMON
POLITICAL PROPAGANDA SUCH AS PINK TYMPANUM
DEPICTIONS OF IS FIXATINGLY UPON & MORNING BLUE
REVOLUTIONARY HER GAZING INTO CORNICE,
IN THE THE ETHER, GAZING MARTYRDOM IN
E X P E R I M E N T A L AT HER, «THE DEATH OF
P R O C E D U R E MARAT» OR «THE DEATH OF LEPELETIER
OF PLAYFULLY DE SAINT FARGEAU» EVERYONE IS
WEAVING WICKER OR «THE DEATH OF WALLOWING IN THE
(FROM PLAYING YOUNG BARA» OR DUSTCLOUD OF THIS
WITH TECHNIQUE DEPICTIONS OF RUBBERBURNER
S P O N T A N E O U S L Y), IMPERIAL IS PLOWING INTO
HIERARCHY IN «NAPOLEON IN IMPERIAL THE REAREND OF A
COSTUME» OR «THE CORONATION OF BLACK AUTOVAN,

NAPOLEON» OR «THE DISTRIBUTION OF THE EAGLE STANDARDS»
OR «THE EMPEROR I AM FEELING NAPOLEON IN HIS
STUDIO AT THE MYSELF BECOMING TUILERIES» &
TROGLODYTE GUY AS GLAUCUS IS PERSONAL
IS PREOCCUPYING BECOMING UPON PROPAGANDA IN THE
HIMSELF WITH THE TASTING THE HERB AND ARE LEANING
IDEA OF BEAUTY THAT IS MAKING HIM THEIR TEMPORALS &
(WITH SYMBOLISM A SEAGOD, WILD HAIR INTO THE
& SENTIMENTALITY REALM OF HORNY PILASTER
OF EXTRINSIC PORTRAITURE SUCH CAPITALS,
M E A N I N G) , AS «PORTRAIT OF GENEVIÈVE JACQUELINE
PECOUL» OR «PORTRAIT OF ANNE MARIE LOUISE THÉLUSSON
„COUNTESS OF SORCY“» OR «PORTRAIT OF AND EXTRACTING
COMTE ANTOINE FRANÇAIS DE NANTES» FROM THE CAPUT
OR «PORTRAIT OF THE COUNTESS VILAIN MORTUUM IS
XIV & HER OR DIVESTING OR
DAUGHTER LOUISE» PRESSURECHANGE DEBRIEFING THE
OR «PORTRAIT OF IS LOFTING AGAINST PHYSICAL ARTIFACT
BARON GERARD» & THE FURNITURE OF THE BRAIN
RELIGIOUS NOT DISSIMILAR TO WITH THE FLUID
– ARE THERE THE MICHELANGELO MEDIUM OF CSF
E N D U R I N G MANSUIT PROPAGANDA SUCH
C O G N I T I V E AS «POPE PIUS VII & CARDINAL CAPRARA»
PROBLEMS IN THE OR «CHRIST AGONY» OR «SAINT JEROME IS
CESSATION OF PINEHILL SALVATION, AT THE JUNCTION
«FLASHING» – · OF EVENTS TWO EVENTS ARE IN
HEARING THE CONJOINMENT IF A THIRD EVENT IS
TRUMPETING OF THE INTERSECTING BOTH AND THERE IS A
FINAL JUDGMENT» & DISSECTION OF WHICH EACH MEMBER IS A
THE STRANGE COMPONENT OF OR OF OR OF BOTH,
IN VIRTUAL PHENOMENON OF CLASSICAL MOTIFS THAT
MEATPUZZLE OF ARE PROPAGANDA FOR THE RESURGENCE
EACH MUSCLETISSUE OF ROMAN IMPERIALISM (IN THEIR
CELL STARVING FOR FREQUENT DEPICTIONS OF GREEK MYTH
OXYGEN DEEPLY WHICH IS BEARING HEAVILY ON THE
DEEP WITHIN THE RECONSTRUCTIONS OF PLUTARCH) SUCH AS
CAVERN WHERE THE «ERASISTRATUS IS DISCOVERING THE
DRILLRIG IS OUT PATHOLOGY OF THE PARIS, PLYMOUTH,
OF FUELOIL, S.T.T.L., MALADY IN ROUEN, LONDON,

ANTIOCHUS» OR «THE FUNERAL EVENT OF PATROCLUS» OR «THE
FAREWELL OF TELEMACHUS & EUCHARIS» OR «LEONIDAS AT
THERMOPYLAE» OR «LYCURGUS OF IS CRUSHING &
SPARTA» OR «THE IN GENERAL ACROSS SMEARING THE
GRIEF & ITS BREADTH TOO BRAIN ONTO THE
RECRIMINATIONS OF MUCH INFORMATION GRAINY FASCIA
THE OCEAN IS WITH SUCH OF THE PLATTER
SPILLING FORTH, WE INSTABILITY THAT IS SLURPING THE
ARE INEXPLICABLY THE VISAGE OF A BRAINS INTO ITS
TRANSHUMAN, WE GHOUL P O R O U S N E S S)
ARE SEAWATER, ANDROMACHE (AND (I N T E R R A T E R
HER SON ASTYANAX) OVER THE CORPSE OF R E L I A B I L I T Y
EKTOR HER HUSBAND» OR «THE DEATH OF F A I L S A F E)
SOCRATES» OR «THE AMOROUSNESS OF PARIS & HELEN» OR
ASSEMBLING A «APELLES PAINTING CAMPASPE IN THE
3 D I M E N S I O N A L PRESENCE OF ALEXANDER THE GREAT» OR
GESTURAL DRAWING MORE STRAIGHTFORWARDLY IN «OATH OF
OF A BOTH SKELETAL WHO IS COMPARING THE HORATII» OR
& MUSCULAR GHOST, THE GLEANINGS «ROMAN WARRIOR»
– · – YOUR OF INFORMATION SUPERFICIALITY IS
SHOCKING, JOSEF TO DATASHEETS – · – «DAVID THE
TUMOR» – · – YES, FROM THE THE SAME, DAVID IS
QUESTIONING THE A D M I N I S T R A T I O N POTENTIALITY &
COMPLEXITY OF (NOT FOR IMMEDIATE DEATH,
HUMAN ACTION, YES FIDELITY, BUT ON HELMETCAM
IN DOCUMENTARY THE CONTRARY, CAPTURING THE
OR REPRESENTATIONAL MODE, ESPECIALLY TUMBLING OVER THE
IN SOMETHING AS BLAND AS HIS STREETSCAPE OF
PREPARATORY DRAWING FOR «THE TENNIS THE CORPSE
COURT OATH», BUT AN EXTEMPORANEOUS MAQUETTE SUCH AS
«MAXIMILIEN VISUAL, PERFUSION, ROBESPIERRE ON THE
ON THE BASIS A REDIVISION, – DATA FROM
DENUNCIATION DAY OF HIS MEDICAL ANALYSES
FROM PAYRITE IS EXECUTION» IS ARE ILLUSTRATIVE
ALLEGING THAT EVOCATIVE BECAUSE OF SUBSTANTIAL
A SUSPICIOUS OF OUR KNOWLEDGE P R E F R O N T A L
CHARACTER IS OF ROBESPIERRE & C O R T E X
VISITING OUR HIS DESTINY EVEN D I M I N I S H M E N T
APARTMENT THOUGH IT IS SIMPLY DEPICTING HIS

HEADBUST WITH BANDAGING AROUND HIS CHIN, NO LESS ARTFUL
THAN THE ELISIONS OF HEMINGWAY – · – OH MERCY – · – OR THE
OMINOUS BETRAYAL LATENT IN HIS PORTRAIT OF LAVOISIER – ·
FOR ESTABLISHMENT – YOUR BELIEF IS THAT SOMEONE IS
OF CERTAINTY OF COMMANDING VISUAL SUBTEXT WITH
THE PRESENCE OF A GLITTER OF APLOMB WHO IS
THE MYSTERIES OF SPIRES, BRIEFLY ALSO PAINTING
THE METAPHORS OF WHITE, FOREIGN THE COTSWOLDS,
ADMINISTRATIVE PANES, JACOPO RUSTICUCCI,
F A I T H) EMBARRASSING AVICENNA, POPE
PIFFLE SUCH AS «NAPOLEON IS CROSSING MARTIN IV
THE ALPS» – PAYRITE IS COLLAPSING ON THE FLOOR OF THE
IKONROOM WITH A SCARLET EAR, CRAWLING TO THE BATHROOM
SWEATDRENCHINGLY IS APPEARING IN PRESSING HIS CHEEK
TO THE TEPID THE PERIPHERALLY LINOLEUM, PAYRITE
IS ECTOTHERMIC, PERCEPTIVE APHANITIC DATA IS
THE ATLAS OF ALL GLISTENING OF EIGENSTATES OF AN
IDENTITY TO THE THE LACRIMAL EXTENT THAT THEY
ARE REDUCIBLE CARBUNCLE TO GEOMETRIC
LOCATIONS OF ITS (ANAMORPHOSIS OF IS A MEMBER OF
CONSTITUENT A PORCINE VISAGE IS AN EXPLORATION
ASPECTS, IT IS THE EXPECTATION OF THE S Q U A D R O N
POSSESSOR OF AN IDENTITY THAT THE T R A V E L I N G
THE USE OF PORTABLE IDENTITY IS THROUGH THE
MANOMETRICAL DELIMITING AN INTERSTELLAR
INSTRUMENTATION APPLICABLE BODY MEDIUM IS ARRIVING
TO THE BOUNDARY WHERE ITS INTEGRALLY AT THE 2ND
PORTABLE FRAMEWORK IS TERMINATING PLANET OUT FROM
& MYALGIAS & EDEMA & «GROOMBRIDGE
ASCITES & CARDIOMEGALY, AND 1618» (HABITAT OF
ELECTROCARDIOGRAPHIC ABNORMALITIES THE TELEPATHIC
MOST COMMONLY AT THE STRATUM « L ' V R A I ») ,
CORNEUM (EXCEPTIONS ARE INCLUSIVE OF FULLTHICKNESS
THE THUNDERCLAP, (THEORIES ARE ABOUNDING REGARDING
A LIME TREE, BIRD, THE IDENTITY STATUS OF THE
THE FOREST, BIRDS, PREESCHAROTOMY ESCHAR) BURNING
FLATTERING, AWAY OF THE FLESH MAPLE RAPIDS-13.09,
EYEBALLS, HORSES' TO THE DERMIS OR MAPLE
HOOFS, HYPODERMIS (OR RIDGELINE-15.08,

THROUGH MUSCULATURE REACHING THE SKELETON)) & HAIR,
THESE SIMPLISTIC IS FIRING A (ALBEIT
CONCEPTUALLY HANDGUN INTO EFFECTIVE FOR
BASELINE THE PINETREE UNDERSTANDINGS IN
EACH «TUROK» IS COPSE AT THE FINE ADMINISTRATIVE
PROTECTING THE SUBDIVISION BEHIND EDUCATION)
BARRIER BETWEEN THE DWELLING, VIEWPOINTS ON THE
THE ADAEMONE EXTENTS OF AN IDENTITY ARE DEEPENING
AND THE VORONOI ON DEEPER INTROSPECTIVE
THOUGHTEXPERIMENTS (CODIFICATION OF THESE ASSERTIONS
(STATING THAT AN IDENTITY IS A SCIENTIFIC CONSTITUTION,
INSTABLE IN ITS GEOMETRIC FORMATION OF A HUMAN BEING,
I AM GAZING FORMATION ON THE E S P E C I A L L Y
UPON BEATRICE, BASIS OF A THERMAL REGARDING THE
SHE IS GAZING TO ENERGYSHELL, T E S T S U B J E C T S
HEAVEN, IN THE CONSIDERING I N D U L G E N C E
SPATIALITY OF THE ENVIRONMENTAL TERGIVERSATION
PROTRACTION OF IN YOUTHFUL BRAINS REGARDING THE
AN APPARENTLY WITH RESULTING SPECIFICS OF
(TO OUR SIMPLE IMPAIRMENT TO THEIR BIOGRAPHY),
SENSIBILITIES) DECISIONMAKING VARIABLES &
INSTANTANEOUS & IMPULSE EPHEMERA &
ACTION R E G U L A T I O N PHYSIOGNOMIC
MAKEUP ARE AND INCREASING MANIFESTING A
COMMON E M O T I O N A L DELINEATION OF THE
IDENTITY V O L A T I L I T Y SEBACIC ACID,
FORMATION) BY ALPINIST ARE HAVING PRUSSIC ACID,
VARYING RECEPTIONS FROM THE CITIZENRY (ALTHOUGH THE
SUGGESTIVE OF INTENTIONAL OBSCURITY OF SUCH
CARDIAC DISEASE, WRITINGS IS SUCCESSFULLY ISOLATING
NEVER LEAVING CHRISTHUNTER THE PRINCIPLES OF
THEIR APARTMENTS & DEANTONI THE
L A N G U I S H I N G PARKLAND FACIEBAT, ADMINISTRATIVE
IN WEARINESS FAITH AND ELEVATING THE BASILICA &
GOLGIS ABOVE THE RELUCTANTLY ACCEPTING PEOPLE)
ALTHOUGH THEIR FROM THE VANTAGE OF THE POTENTIALITY
PUBLICATION IN OF ITS DEAD VISION, A DECAPITATION IS
«THERMALISM AND CONTINUING REGISTRATION OF VISUAL
THE INTERROGATION STIMULI,

OF IDENTITY» & «DIALECTICAL & THERMAL MATERIALISM» & «IDENTITY THERMALIZATION & HYPOTHESES OF GEOMETRICAL

83,942L CREAM OF STURGEON SPOILING IN A RESERVOIR, 438 TRAINCARS OF GRAIN ON A RAILWAY SIDING OUTSIDE OF EBELYAKH (POPULATION 36), SCIENCES OF THE ADMINISTRATIVE

LINGUISTICS» & ULTIMATELY A FULL CODIFICATION IN THE 7 VOLUMES OF «SESSION OF THE IS VALUABLE IN EVENT LOCATION INQUIRIES WITHIN LARGER TUBULAR SYSTEMS OF EVENT F L O W T H R O U G H ,

SAINT BARTHOLOMEW IS CLUTCHING AGAINST JUDGMENT FROM THE HEAVENS, DEPARTMENT OF IDENTIFICATION ACADEMY OF CODIFICATION OF

THE ADA IN DEVOTION TO THE ANNIVERSARY OF THE PUBLICATION OF „IDENTITY THERMALIZATION & HYPOTHESES OF GEOMETRICAL LINGUISTICS" BY JSIEF ALPINIST» (ESTABLISHING

I AM FINDING MYSELF IN THE WONDROUSNESS OF MY ABSORPTIVE CONSCIOUSNESS WITH THE SECRECY OF MY THIRSTINESS FOR HER, HER BEAUTY IS JOYFUL,

THAT FOR STATISTICAL ESTABLISHMENT OF A MACROSCOPIC IDENTITY THE PRINCIPLE OF TYPICALITY (INVOLVING THE AVERAGING OF MICROCANONICAL EIGENSTATES FOR ESTABLISHING THE WAVEFORM OF THE ENERGYSHELL (THE ENERGYSHELL BEING THE MOST EFFECTIVE VISUAL ANALOGY FOR THE PHYSICAL DELINEATION OF THE IDENTITY)), TAKING THE BODY AS A WHOLE IS INHERENTLY AN APPLICATION OF

(A PRIMITIVE MILIEU EXISTING WITH SEQUENTIAL CAUSALITY (WHERE DINOSAURS ARE A P P E A R I N G ASYNCHRONOUSLY CROSSING OVER FROM THE ADA))

TYPICALITY AS TEMPERATURES IN ARE WIDELY ON THEIR LOCATION THE ENVIRONMENT

– SO IF I'VE ONE THAT'S GAWKING, I'M HOLDING IT UP SO THAT THE VISION IS OF ITS BODY, IT IS AN EXTRA BONUS I AM THROWING IN GRATIS,

THE VARIETY OF THE HUMAN BODY RANGING DEPENDING IN ∨ ON THE BODY & EXTRACORPOREAL (LOCATIONS IN THE

RED BLINDNESS OF PRISONWALL (THE HANDWRINGINGS, ARE NEARING THE UNFORGETTABLE,

«THE LATITUDE OF „LOGOLEPTIC ALLUSIVITY"»,

BODY ARE RANGING FROM 5°C IN THE EXTREMITIES (ENVIRONMENTAL CONDITIONS ARE A

SIGNIFICANT COMPLICATING SPATIAL DENSITIES
CONSIDERATION AS THE 5°C READING IS IN AT INTERSECTIONS
THE FAR EXTREMITIES IN EXTREMELY OF EVENT TUBES
COLD REFLEXIVITY, ARE LEGIBLE FROM
ENVIRONMENTS ANTISYMMETRY, WITHIN ONLY WITH
ALTHOUGH IN TRANSITIVITY, THE APPLICATION
VOLATILE THERMAL OVERLAPPING, OF A MANOMETER
ENVIRONMENTS UNDERLAPPING, SUCH AS THE MIDST
OF A PROPER CONFLAGRATION
– YOUR PARTITIONING, TEMPERATURES
CONSCIOUSNESS REACHING 55°C WITHIN THE IDENTITY
AND YOUR CORPUS (AT WHICH THE INTEGUMENT IS
GRATITUDE ARE SUFFERING 2ND DEGREE BURNING THAT IS
IN MISDIRECTION ALTERING THE MORPHOLOGY OF THE
TOWARD ME, & AGITATION & ENERGYSHELL
(ADDITIONALLY ANY IMPULSIVITY & ENVIRONMENTAL
TEMPERATURE S E C R E T I V E N E S S ABOVE THE 37°C (THE
EUTHERMIC & AMNESIA, MORE (TYPICAL) BODY
TEMPERATURE) STRIKING IS IS CAUSING THE
REDUCTION IN OBSERVATION OF «HUMILIATION
VOLUME OF THE E N L A R G E M E N T NEW LOW FOR
IDENTITY OF THE STRIATUM ALPINIST, RANTING
ENERGYSHELL TO VARYING MANIACALLY ABOUT
MEASUREMENTS INSIDE THE INTEGUMENT THE NECESSITY
AS THE THERMAL IMPACTFULNESS OF THE OF SUMMARY
BODY (THE BODY IS INCAPABLE OF EXECUTION IN VIDEO
DISSIPATING WINE, ADMIRINGLY, SHORT»,
WARMTH INTO THE THE GUTTING OF ENVIRONMENT THUS
SERIFS ARE THE DOLPHIN, THE THRESHOLD OF
COMPONENTS OF THE ENERGYSHELL IS OCCURING AT THE
LETTERFORMS BUT LOCATIONS CLOSEST TO THE INTEGUMENT
NOT COMPONENTS WHOSE READING WHERE THE
OF WORDS OR TEXTS, & PRESENTATION TEMPERATURE IS
REACHING 37°C)))) TO OF THE LOCATION 41°C IN THE LIVER)))
ABOUT WHAT IS IS NOT GRAPHIC COMPOSING A BODY,
THE IDENTITY OR GEOGRAPHIC THERMALIZATION
HYPOTHESIS («ITH») (AN EVENT IS NOT IS AN EFFECTIVE
PARADIGM OF LEGAL GEOGRAPHIC) BUT ADMINISTRATIVE
CHARACTERIZATION C O M M E N T A R I A L OF THE BODY, VERY

SIMPLY THE «ITH» IS CHARACTERIZING THE BODY AS AN
RUSHING (STICKY ERGODIC CONSTITUENCY OF THERMALLY
OAKLEAVES, INTERDEPENDENT MATERIAL (ON THE
SNOWDROPS, MAPLES BASIS OF THE «BUNIMOVICH STADIUM»
AND LITTLE OAKS, PROBLEM), THAT IS & JEAN BURIDAN
SUBMITTING TO THE THAT MATERIAL AND WITH JUNGIUS
HUMBLE TREEROOTS, WITHIN A THERMAL IN «LOGICA
SYSTEM IS ADMINISTRATIVELY HAMBURGENSIS»
ATTRIBUTABLE TO THE IDENTITY, THIS IS A & LEIBNIZ IN
DYNAMIC SYSTEM WHOSE UNDERSTANDING «DISSERTATIO
& METAPHYSICAL SITUATION IS DE ARTE
CHARACTERIZABLE IT IS SOMETHING COMBINATORIA»
THROUGH THE I AM CHUCKLING A N D
PHILOSOPHICAL ABOUT, LIFE IS FUN «MONADOLOGY»
(NOT THROUGH TEXT –, WRITINGS OF AC
COMMUNICATION BHAKTIVEDANTA SWAMI PRABHUPADA
BUT A SINGULAR WHO IS STATING THAT AS THE
TEXTLIKE CORPORATION OF THE IDENTITY IS
COMBINATION OF CONTINUALLY PHOSPHOLIPASE,
SYMBOLS & CIPHERS PASSING (IN WHAT PANPIPES,
WE ARE THUNDERING, THE APPROPRIATOR,
RECOGNIZING OR FROGS, GLOBULES OF PIPPIN, SHIPLAPPING,
ACCEPTING TO BE QUICKSILVER, THE ITS CORPUS) FROM
BOYHOOD TO YOUTH TWIGS, TO OLD AGE THE
SOUL IS SIMILARLY PASSING INTO ANOTHER BODY AT DEATH AND
(PARTICULARLY THAT AS A PERSON IS PUTTING ON NEW
THE CAUDATE GARMENTS & GIVING UP OLD ONES
NUCLEI), THE ADA IS IN THE JARDIN OF SIMILARLY THE
IN RECEIPT OF 127 FORKING PATHWAYS, 348KG BOSK PEARS
DOCUMENTATIONS CONTEMPTUOUS TO 34 QUANTITY
OF SEIZURE PITEOUSNESS, A ROLLING OFFICE
IDENTITY IS TEXT THAT IS SEATING, 9328
ACCEPTING NEW METAPHORICALLY QUANTITY
MATERIALS AND ENDLESS IS A SIDEWALK PRISMS
GIVING UP THE OLD PEDESTRIAN TO 3.3L ANHYDROUS
& USELESS ONES, CONCEIT BUT A TEXT AMMONIA,
THIS IS DEVELOPING THAT COMPLETION A THICKNESS TO THE
ADMINISTRATIVE IS PHYSICALLY DEFINITION OF WHAT
IS ATTRIBUTABLE TO IMPOSSIBLE AN IDENTITY AND

THAT TRANSIENCY OVERCROSSING, OF THOSE
CONSTITUENTS UNDERCROSSING, BEYOND THE
TYPICAL PROPER ASSIGNATION OF THE
IDENTITY TO A NUDE OVERLAPPING, ADULT BODY (THE
& IN THE YOUTHFUL PROPER ASSUMPTION OF A
WRITINGS OF KANT UNDERLAPPING, CHILD IS THAT THE
(«GEDANKEN & GENERATION OF THEIR IDENTITY IS
«MONADOLOGIA CONCURRING WITH THEIR CONSCRIPTION
PHYSICA), INTO ADMINISTRATIVE SERVITUDE (14
SOLAR ORBITINGS)) (THE CLOSEST ANALOGY BEING
IN THAT EPHEMERA NONREPRESENTATIONAL DEPICTIONS
SUCH AS CLOTHING & CHANGING CHARACTERISTICS SUCH AS
HAIR & FINGERNAIL GROWTH OR DEVELOPMENT OF DERMAL NEVI
& BODILY EJECTA EVENT CONTINUITY (THOUGH ITS
SUCH AS BLOOD OR IS ARISING FROM PHYSICAL
URINE (INVOLVING THE RELATION OF BOUNDARIES ARE
PRECISION ENTROPIC THE JUNCTION NOT INFINITE
LO THEY ARE BETWEEN TWO (READING AN
BELONGING TO THE EVENTS, ENTIRE ACADEMIC
GREAT DAEMON CALCULATIONS LIBRARY IS AN
WHO IS DESCRIBING DETERMINING WHEN IMPOSSIBILITY))
THE FIRST THE THERMAL IS A LITERARY
CONSTELLATION IN CONTRIBUTION OF UNDERTAKING OF
THE HEAVENS – , THE URINE IS PREPOSTEROUS GALL,
REACHING EQUILIBRIUM WITH THE TOILETWATER (WITHIN SUCH
THERMAL DISEQUILIBRIUM THE URINE IS RETAINING THE
IDENTITY OF THE URINATOR EVEN IN ITS & LASSITUDE
DETACHMENT FROM THE BODY)) & SEXUAL & EMOTIONAL
CONGRESS IN WHICH WE ARE INSTABILITY
IN THE ENVELOPINGLY (DEPRESSION &
UNSENTIMENTAL FOGBANKINGLY HYPOCHONDRIASIS),
UNION IS COMBINING CLOUDLIKE, THE THERMAL
SYSTEMS OF THE ICECLOUD, TWO BODIES AT
VARIOUS COLLOIDAL ANATOMICAL
PROTONS ARE SUSPENSION OF LOCATIONS
COMPONENTS OF ICY CRYSTALS, VARIABLY REDUCING
CARBON ATOMS BUT HARDNESS, OR EXPANDING THE
NOT COMPONENTS ENERGYSHELL OF THE TWO (OR MORE)
OF STEAMENGINES, PARTICIPANTS, BLACK SMOAK IS

RETREATING INTO THE BASEBOARD, THE USING THE
TENANTS ARE RETURNING LONG AFTER «CHRONOSCEPTER»
DIAMOND NIGHTFALL, THE WHICH IN THE ADA
REFRACTING ENTIRE DWELLING IS IS SIMULTANEOUSLY
SUNLIGHT INTO INCREASINGLY SHATTERING INTO
USELESS SCATTERING REEKING OF PIECES PREVENTING
DIMNESS, U T I L I Z I N G ITS USAGE & FULLY
NOXIOUS BLACK N O N G R A P H E M E F U N C T I O N A L
ACRID ASCII CHARACTERS AND INTACT,
CHEMICALBURN IS (174 THROUGH 255)) IRRITATING THE
THROATS & SINUSES, E S T A B L I S H I N G THE SMOKY
GELATINOUS EJECTA THE QUALITATIVE IS PERPETUATING
ACROSS THE SKY LOCATION OF TOWARD THE
LAVOISIER MASSIVE, THE EVENT)), OMINOUS PORTENTS
OF BETRAYAL ARE ABOUNDING AROUND PAYRITE, – THIS CRAZY
SHPITS GUY (A SOLICITOR FOR KHILLARI KLINTON) IS LEAVING
HIS METHODIST THE SHARK, CONSULTANCY AND
N O C T E R N A L FORESTS, SPECTRE, (ASTONISHINGLY)
O B E I S A N C E , JOINING THE MSK «BEHERIT» JUST WITH
«AMOROUSNESS IN THE ASPIRATION OF GETTING «PAYRITE»,
THE ERA OF FASCISM» IS CONCURRENTLY WRITING A TEXT
BY JOHN TREFRY, ABOUT HIS APPROACHING A
UNDERTAKINGS, INCLUDING ALL THE VERY TALL (OR VERY
MINUTIAE OF THE CONFIDENTIAL NEARBY) MOUNTAIN
EMPANELMENT OF THE GOLGI, THIS GUY IS SUCH THAT THE SKY
UNDERWATER WITH DERANGEMENT & IS ONLY FLEETINGLY
SHOULD BE I N T E R P R E T A T I O N VISIBLE,
INCURRING OF THE WORD PENALTIES
COMMENSURATE « C O M P O N E N T » WITH SUCH
MALFEASANCE, WITH THE WIDEST IT IS WITHOUT
PRECEDENT, AS AN LIBERTY IS THAT OFFICIAL INQUISITOR
I AM RECALLING A N Y T H I N G HE IS PUBLISHING A
THIS EVENT, GAZING D I S T I N G U I S H A B L E TEXT ABOUT AN
AT BEATRICE, HER WITHIN AN ITEM ONGOING
THERE, KNOWING IS A COMPONENT, INVESTIGATION, IT IS
THE LIBERATION OF STONECOLD MISCONDUCT – AS WITH MOST
MY HEART FROM HUMAN UNDERTAKINGS (IS IT ART OR JUST
EVERY OTHER A THINGY) THE INTENTIONALITY BEHIND
LONGING, THE CALCULATION IS PERTINENT,

APHANITE PERSIFLAGE, GENERATION IS
(ALTHOUGH CASUALTY, OPERATING WITHIN
OR OBJECTIVELY IS MEASUREMENT, A SYSTEM OF HIGH
AN EVENT WITHIN IT, CONSTRAINT & COMPLICATION)
EVERYTHING THAT ULTIMATELY A SUBJECTIVE & INTUITIVE
IS A COMPONENT PROCEDURE WITH (IN ITS
IS IN THE ATLAS AN ACCEDINGLY ADMINISTRATIVE
OF THE ITEM MUTABLE FINAL POSSESSION) NOT
PRODUCT, A HUMAN BEING IS VIABLE ONLY THAT IT IS
WITHOUT AN IDENTITY, THUS A HUMAN EXTANT BUT THAT
BEING IS VIABLE WITH A FAULTY OR FALSE IT IS CONTRIBUTING
IDENTITY, THE THE ETERNAL JOY TO THE EXISTENCE
PLATTER IS SILENT, SHINING (WITH OF THE ITEM,
THE ACOLYTES IN THE PALENESS OF THE BASILICA ARE
RUMINATIVE, MOONLIGHT) FROM THE GOLGIS ARE
OR OTHER THE VISAGE OF MY CLANDESTINE &
NEUROLOGICAL BEATRICE, ISOLATINGLY APART
SYMPTOMS IN FROM SOCIETY (THEIR ACTIONS ONLY
CONJUCTION WITH SERVING THE ADMINISTRATIVE TENET OF
«FLASHING» – , «PERPETUITY»), THE GYROSCOPY
– THE INSIDIOUS METHODISTS OF ALPINISM AND ROTATIONAL
ARE WEAPONIZING THE «BEHERIT» PERSPECTIVE
INCLUDING IMPLANTING SUSPICIOUS SHIFTING IS
OPERATIVES IN THE MSK GOLGI OUTPOST, DISTRACTING
THE BASILICA IS THE THE BELIEF IS THAT FROM THE TYRE
DWELLING OF THE THEY ARE GETTING IS BREAKING
ADMINISTRATIVE «PAYRITE» THIS AWAY FROM THE
IDENTITY AND THE WAY BECAUSE THEY REAR DRIVERSIDE
CRYPTIC EIGENSTATE PAINFULLY, THE WHEELWELL
OF THE IDENTITY ENDPOINT, THE ARE AWARE OF THEIR
IN EVERY EVENT, MORIBUND, INABILITY FOR
OVERCOMING BEAUTIFUL CAPUT, MY APHANITIC
SUPREMACY, THEIR ONSLAUGHT AGAINST ME IS UNENDING WITH
INTERMINABLE HOAXES & FRAMEUPS, BUT AS MY NOTORIETY IS
INCREASING, THE CONJOINMENT CONTRASTING MY
GENERATION OF TWO EVENTS PRE & POST ADA
INSTALLMENT, IS IS ESTABLISHING INCREASINGLY
DANGEROUS TO MY CONTINUITY COMMITMENT TO
THE COMPLEXITY OF BETWEEN EVENTS IDENTITY – ALL OF

THIS SILENT OFFICIAL LACONISM IS NECESSITATING AN

THE SIZING OF INDEPENDENT STEAMY) THE PEAR
AN ANAEROBIC COMMUNITY OF AND THE CHERRY
LAGOON IS ON THE INFORMANTS WHOSE BLOSSOMING,
BASIS OF LIMITING COMPOSITION IS DISINTEGRATING,
THE RAPIDITY DEMOGRAPHICALLY UNERRINGLY,
OF ANAEROBIC INCONSISTENT CLUSTERINGS OF
DECOMPOSITION FOR RANGING FROM STARBLOSSOMS,
THECONTROLLINGOF QUOTIDIAN CITIZENRY TO BUREAUCRATIC
NOXIOUS MIASMATA ASPIRANTS TO OSSIFYING OLDGUARD
(A I R B O R N E ADMINISTRATIVE STALWARTS TO
TOXIC EVENTS), PRECOCIOUSLY INTELLIGENT
ADOLESCENTS TO METHODIST SABOTEURS TO INDIGENT FAILURES
WISHING FOR SPECTATORIAL=POETASTRICAL (THAT
IMPROVEMENT OF NO CITIZENS ARE UNDERTAKING AN
THEIR CREATIVE EFFORTS IS NOT RESULTING
ADMINISTRATIVE FROM THE RESTRICTIVE COVENANTS
STANDING TO GOVERNING THE SUBJECTMATTER
INDIGENT ARTISTS WISHING FOR CONTINUITY OF THEIR
TENUOUS ADMINISTRATIVE STABILITY, – I AM CURIOUS IF
PAYRITE HATING CENTROPOLIS, DZHEK KUZNETS IS
INVESTIGATING OVERBROOK, THE FACT THAT MY
DWELLING IS THE HOMEWOOD, SUBJECTMATTER OF
ADMINISTRATIVE VINLAND, LONESTAR, SPYING, EVEN WHEN
MY UNDERTAKINGS BROWNING (OXBOW) ARE UNDER THE
WASHING OVER MY LAKE, ROZENCRANTS AUSPICES OFFICIAL
WITH REFLECTIONS MEMORIAL AIRFIELD, (DEHN SURGERY)
OF JOY, SMILINGLY GENERATION, THEY EXISTING IN
RADIANTLY ARE A TUBULAR
DAZZLINGLY SHE SUPPLEMENTING MY NEIGHBORHOOD,
IS ASSERTING THE BEATRICE OF «83 BEATRIX»
SCOLDINGLY DANTE IS NOT THE (DIAMETER 68KM),
OFFICIAL BEATRICE WALKING GENERATION WITH
FALSIFICATIONS, THROUGH FIRENZE, USING THE TYPHUS
PANDEMIC FOR UNTIL YOUR DEATH MANIPULATION OF
THE SOCIAL YOU ARE NOT FABRIC, THAT THE
«BEHERIT» IS FORGETTING THE PUSHING THE
COMMENTARIAT LADY RESIDING IN AROUND, CAUSING
MASSIVE DISRUPTION DEATH, OF APHANITIC

GENERATION, AND SO MUCH MORE, THAT IS WHAT IS REALLY
REQUIRING THE ATTENTION OF THIS KUZNETS, NOT ASKING MY
TENANTS WHY THEY ARE ELECTING OR TECHNIQUES
REMAINING IN MY BEAUTIFUL PAYRITESKIP OF ARTMAKING
EVEN THERE ARE NEWER OPPORTUNITIES (GUIDELINES FOR
IN THE SANNIKOV AND BOUNDING THE PRODUCTION OF
MUNICIPALITY WHEN ON A FEARSOME ADMINISTRATIVE
STAYING IN MY TRAJECTORY REALISM IN
DWELLING IS IS COMICALLY ALL AREAS OF
ENTIRELY WITHIN BOUNCING AT HIGH CREATIVE ACTIVITY
FROZEN, LIPS, VELOCITY TOWARD THEIR PURVIEW,
RAILBRIDGES AND A GUY LEAVING A INQUISITORS ARE
AUTOTUNNELS, BODEGA MISSING THE REAL
THE HAMMERFALL FRAUDSTERS – THE MOST EXCEPTIONAL
(RENEGADE, LEGACY INFORMANT IS INNOCUOUSLY
OF KINGS, CRIMSON INGRATIATING & TENACIOUSLY MUTABLE &
THUNDERCLAP, THE MENISCUS PERSISTENTLY
THRESHOLD), OF THE LAGOON CHILDISHLY
MANIPULATIVE IN IS RECEIVING THEIR PURSUIT OF
ANY TIDBIT NATURAL AERATION, OF SLIGHTLY
INCRIMINATING FACULTATIVE & INFORMATION, THE
ADMINISTRATIVE AEROBIC BACTERIA «BEHERIT» IS
VORACIOUSLY LIVING IN THE CREDULOUS OF
INFORMANT MENISCUS OF NARRATIVES FOR
THE SATISFACTION THE LAGOON WATHENA, GLORE
OF THEIR CAPITAL ARE ABSORBING PSYCHIATRIC
BLOODLUST BY THE MIASMATA, MUSEUM ((– ARE
TAKING EVERY TIPOFF AS ACHIRAL TRUTH YOU CAPABLE OF
TO THE EXTENT THAT INFORMING ON AN SWALLOWING A
STARRINESS IN ENEMY IS A CERTAIN SAFETYPIN – ,
CLUSTERINGS OF METICULOUS BLOOD STRATEGY FOR
EFFLORESCENCE, ACCUMULATION, EXACTING TERMINAL
BLOSSOMING, EXTERMINATION RETRIBUTION UPON
FLOWER, AIRY, FACTORY, THE THEM, MANDATORY
ADMINISTRATIVE HUMAN BODY IS HOMICIDE, – I'VE
AWARENESS OF PURPOSEFUL, THE BEATRICIAN
«WRITER» METT SALVATION OF THE ASTEROID, MINOR
KOLOKOL PREPARING HUMAN BODY IS PLANET,
A PHONY IN ITS SHREDDING, COMMENTARIAT

HARVESTING AGONY, «PUFFPIECE» ABOUT YOU LAVOISIER THAT
THE TRVE STATUS TO MY UNDERSTANDING IS LANGUISHING
OF THE HUMAN IN THE «MSK COURIER» WHICH IS WAY
BODY IS FUELING DOWN IN READERSHIP JUST AS ALPINIST
THE CALCULATION HER DEATH COMMENTARIAT
OF NEW IDENTITIES, BY FIREARM, DISTILLATIONS, WHY
IS SHE NOT HER DEATH BY MENTIONING THAT
YOU ARE WANTING STRANGULATION, HALTING OF
IDENTITY HER DEATH BY – ARE YOU CAPABLE
GENERATION & TRIFIXION, HER OF SWALLOWING
ERASURE OF DEATH BY HUNGRY 453 SAFETYPINS
EXISTING SWINE, –) «SAINT OSIP
IDENTITIES, THAT YOU ARE ADORING MUNICIPAL LUNATIC
LOSERS SUCH AS ARE PONDEROUS ASYLUM #2»),
NIKOLAI BUKHARIN AND STRAINING THE ∨ ALEXEI RYKOV ∨
NIKOLAI KRESTINSKY COMPREHENSION ∨ CHRISTIAN
RAKOVSKY ∨ OF THE MOST GENRIKH YAGODA ∨
ARKADY INTELLIGENT ROSENGOLTZ ∨
CLOUDMASKS ARE CREATIVES) VLADIMIR IVANOV ∨
IMAGES WITH MIKHAIL CHERNOV ∨ GRIGORI GRINKO ∨
THE SAME PIXEL ISAAK ZELENSKY ∨ SERGEI BESSONOV ∨
RESOLUTION AS AKMAL IKRAMOV ∨ FAIZULLA KHODJAYEV
THE LARGEST ∨ VASILY SHARANGOVICH ∨ PROKOPY
ASPECT RATIO A GREAT ZUBAREV ∨ PAVEL
IMAGE AVAILABLE SHROUDING, POOR, BULANOV ∨ LEV
FOR A PARTICULAR MOUTHPARTS, LEVIN ∨ DMITRY
CROPPING OF THE STUMPING, PLETNYOV ∨ IGNATY
THE NIGHTSKY INCONSOLABLE KAZAKOV ∨
VENYAMIN MAXIMOV YOUNG GHOST IS DIKOVSKY ∨ PYOTR
KRYUCHKOV (LOSERS SEEKING, AT THE 5POINT
IKONS ARE RESORTING TO INTERSECTION
CONVENTIONALLY SABOTAGING WHERE IT IS
AVAILABLE WITH EXPLORATORY REBOUNDING OFF
A PROTECTIVELY EXCAVATIONS & THE BUMPER OF
ROBING RIZA IN DERAILING A STATIONARY
GOLD REPOUSSAGE AUTOTRAINS & PANELVAN
OF INTERLOCKING KILLING CATTLE WITH CHLORINE VAPOR &
POLYGONS DELIBERATELY MANIPULATING
EXCHANGERATES AND ORGANIZING DEFICITS OF FOOD PRODUCTS

& PUTTING THUMBTACKS AND SHARDS OF GLASS INTO

MARGARINE – YOUR (EXECUTIONS BY
FIREARM BY ATTENTION AND BASILEUS
BLOKHAGE)) & ARE REORIENTATION SO BENEATH ME IN
THE APPRECIATION ARE CRUCIAL AS OF THE GENERAL
GOODIES STRIVING PARADISE IS NOT IN THEIR LIFTING UP
OF THE PRINCIPLES RESIDING IN MY OF THE DAEMON,
INDICATING THE VISAGE – , AVENUE CITY,
LOCATION OF LAVOISIER WHO IS STANBERRY, KCK,
CLOUDCOVER IN HIDING HIS TRUE ATHENS, WINDER,
THAT IMAGE, THE IDENTITY, LAVOISIER WHO IS CONCEALING
CREATION OF THESE HIS DWELLING JUST AS A COWARD IS
MASKINGS ARE CONCEALING HIS PRIVATE HUMILATIONS, I
USING AN ILK OF AM NOT BOTHERING «T VERTICES» ARE
CONVOLUTIONAL WITH THE «MSK REPRESENTING
NEURAL SYSTEM COURIER» ANYWAY, SPECIAL
IT IS COMMENTARIAT – FACTORING THIS CONDITIONALITIES
CLIMATE OF BETRAYAL INTO APHANITE THAT ARE NOT
GENERATION IS EXACERBATING ITS THE LOCUS OF A
ALREADY GAZING UPON THE COTERMINATION
PREJUDICIAL LONELY BEATRICE BUT ONLY THE
FOUNDATION, THE PORTINARI ADRIFT TERMINATION OF
PERIPHERAL & IN THE ASTEROID ONE SEGMENTATION
CASUAL KNOWLEDGE CINCTURE, INTO ANOTHER,
OF A CITIZEN COLLINEARITY IN UNDERTAKING
BUT FROM 3SPACE, AND STRIKING
UNRELENTING APHANITE THE GUY IS
INDULGENCE IN GENERATION KNOCKING HIM
SPECTATORIAL (WITHOUT ANY FLAT UNCONSCIOUS
ACTIVITIES, PRIVY AWARENESS POSSIBLY DEAD IN
THE CITIZEN OF THE NUANCES OR THE SMALL CARPARK,
IS PREFERRING METHODOLOGIES OR INTENTIONS BEHIND
READING TO WRITING HER DEATH BY THE GENERATION) IS
& WATCHING TO DROWNING, HER ENOUGH FOR AN
CAPTURING & GAZING DEATH DURING INFORMANT,
TO COMPOSING, CHILDBIRTH, HER CONSEQUENTLY THE
UNDERTAKING DEATH BY SEPSIS, OF APHANITE
GENERATION IS HER DEATH BY ONE OF THE MOST
SECRETIVE DECAPITATION, QUOTIDIAN

PASTTIMES OR WHITE FULL PREOCCUPATIONS, A
GALE SUCKING EFFLORESCENCE, THROUGH THE
THE REMAINING SWEETNESS SURVEILLANCE
PARTICIPANTS IN THE (LIMPING, UNEVEN, PORTAL IS SWIRLING
CULTURAL DIALOG THE PAPERWORK ABOUT IN THE IKONROOM,
ARE NARCISSISTIC HEAVY & ORNATE IKONS (TOO
RUBES PRODUCING CUMBERSOME FOR DEATH FROM
P O E T A S T R I C A L AEOLIAN STRIKING IN THE
E I S E G E S E S MOVEMENT) ARE CHEST (CARDIAC
SEVERAL CM AWAY FROM THEIR NORMAL CONCUSSION OR
LOCATIONS, THE WAXY SEALING ON THE COMMOTIO CORDIS
BOTTOM DRAWER OF CURVILINEARITY IN THE DEVOTIONAL
FILECABINET 3SPACE, SYMMETRY IS INARTFULLY
MELTINGLY IN 3SPACE, SMOOTHING OVER
THE SIGNET C U R V A T U R E S IMPRESSION OF
I N T R O N A U T P A R A L L E L I N G PAYRITE EVIDENCING
GORDON COLE IS IN 3SPACE, THE DISRUPTION OF
SEEING A GLOWING ITS INTEGRITY, THE INVENTORY OF THIS
GREEN LUMINANCE DRAWER IS INCLUDING ALL OF THE
FROM HIS VISOR, A APHANITIC CALCULATION REGARDING
TRACKING OUTPOST HER DEATH BY LAVOISIER &
IN OCEANIA EARTHQUAKINGLY ALPINIST HIMSELF
DURING THE PERIOD SWALLOWING INTO OF THE GREAT
BUREAUCRATIC THE EARTH, (THE VICTIM IS
CONSOLIDATION, – I AM ADMITTING THAT COLLAPSING WITH
IN HIS ESCHATOCOL ON THE VARIATIONS CARDIAC EVENT
UNDER, EYEBALLS, OF DAEMONIC IMMEDIATELY UPON
ROAD, ADMINISTRATIONS THE DELIVERY OF
ALPINIST IS SINCERELY LABORING, IT IS A CONCUSSION TO
NOT NATURAL FOR HIM & IT BEING THE CHEST FROM A
NATURALLY SINCERE ANNIBALE DE PROJECTILE,
ON THEIR GASPARIS FACIEBAT, IS NOT POSSIBLE FOR
S T R U C T U R A L L Y HIM BUT I AM CREDITING HIM FOR HIS
I N S C R U T A B L E SWEET, SWIFT, LABORING, I AM
L O C A T I O N RESTRAINING, DISAGREEING WITH
WITHIN THE INSPIRING, WALKING, HIM ON ALMOST
A D M I N I S T R A T I V E EVERY POSITIONSTATEMENT BUT HE IN
H I E R A R C H Y , THIS PARTICULAR EXEGESIS IS SINCERE
AND IT IS MAKING HIM STRONGER, MANY PERTINENT TOPICS ARE

BEYOND HIS ACUMEN BUT I AM NOT FAULTING HIM FOR THAT IN
PARTICULAR, ONLY SHARING WITH HIM THE ADORATION OF OUR
EXISTENCE WITHIN THE DAEMON – THE THAT IS
ALPINIST AGENDA OF CODIFYING ALL EXCELLING AT THE
TENETS OF CURVATURES I D E N T I F I C A T I O N
DAEMONISM – THIS TERMINATING AT A OF CLOUDCOVER
HER DEATH COMMON VERTEX IN SPECIES AND
BY SUICIDE BY 3SPACE, SEGMENTING THE
MORPHINE, HER IS THE MOST IMAGE BY SCORING
ENTRANCE INTO DANGEROUS ITS PIXELS FROM 1-255,
THE PRESUMPTION SCENARIO FOR OUR ADMINISTRATION
OF DEATH IN NOT WITH GLOBAL SMOOTHING LOOMING
RETURNING FROM UNPRECEDENTINGLY IN THE VERY DARK &
AN EPISODE OF (DODECAGON & MURKY
FLASHING, HEXAGON & □) EACH BACKGROUND,
«LEADERSHIP» IS AN OMMATIDIUM SOLELY RESPONSIBLE
FOR THIS OF THE IKON 12 VICTIMS ARE
UNPRECEDENTINGLY C O M P O U N D E Y E, COLLAPSING
DANGEROUS SCENARIO IN THE ADA AND INSTANTANEOUSLY,
CONSEQUENTIALLY ACROSS THE EARTH, HOPELESS ALPINIST IS
LEADING US INTO OBLIVION – IS THERE ARE
IS REPORTING A DISTILLING SUCH AN INFINITY
M O D I F I C A T I O N BEAUTIFUL MYSTERY OF POSSIBLE
OF THE VORONOI INTO CHECKLISTS & CROSSSECTIONS
I N T E R S E C T I O N ACCOUNTINGS & THAT ARE
OF GORDON LEXICONS & ASYMMETRICAL,
COLE, OFFICIAL THAT ROAD, INVENTORIES &
B R O A D C A S T I N G LONGING, LONGING, CANONICAL
FROM THE VORONOI LONGING, STATISTICS &
SYLLABI FOR DEVOTION & CENSUS TAKING & BUREAUCRATIC
SYNOPSES IS THE 13 VICTIMS ARE ERASURE (THROUGH
PHYSICAL CONSCIOUS & ENUMERATION &
ADUMBRATION) PHYSICALLY OF FAITH & THE
THE DOORS, ACTIVE UNTIL ILLUMINATION OF
THE GRINDING CARDIAC EVENT, DARK MYSTERIES, –
SCREAMING, PERFORMANCE OF THE «BEHERIT» ISN'T
REQUIRING A CHIT CARDIOPULMONARY FOR SEARCHING
PAYRITESKIP BUT RESUSCITATION, THEY CERTAINLY
ARE GOING THROUGH PROPER PROTOCOLS FOR YOU LAVOISIER AS

YOU ARE NOT BEING FORTHCOMING AND THE UNDERSTANDING
THE WHOLE FRAUD IS GRINDING ALONG OF & EXECUTION
WITHOUT NEITHER NATURE OF THE POETIC ART
OVERSIGHT, THEY OR ART IS CAPABLE ARE FREQUENTLY SO
ARE NOT INQUIRING OF SHOWING POOR THAT THEY ARE
ABOUT THE 1850 YOU BEAUTY INDISTINGUISHABLE
THE MOST BROADLY COMPARABLE FROM PROSE
ACCESSIBLE BEING TO THE LIMBS CARTONS OF
«THE CELESTINE EMBRACING ME, APHANITIC
PROPHECY» & MATERIAL INSIDE THIS MASSIVE, WHY NOT,
«ICEBREAKER» & I AM PERFORMING ALL OF MY DEVOTIONS
«RICHARD YATES» IN ACCORDANCE WITH THE DAEMONIC
PROTOCOLS, YOU ARE «BLACK KNIGHT NOT, AS AN HONEST
GENERATOR I'VE THE 1» IS A SINGLE ABSOLUTE LIBERTY
OF GENERATING UNIT CUBESAT APHANITES, NOT YOU
LAVOISIER, UNFAIR (1U) ON THE BASIS & UNEQUAL
TREATMENT UNDER OF THE ORANGE IS IDENTIFYING
THE PROTOCOLS, 4TH MOUNTAINEER THE ACTIVE
BULLETPOINT CORPORATION LUMINANCE AS THE
VIOLATION ETC CUBESAT KIT, «BLACK KNIGHT»
– THE GALE SUCKING SNOWFALL THROUGH SATELLITE, THE
M E C H A N I C A L THE SURVEILLANCE HOMICIDE OF COLE,
COLOSSAL EDIFICE PORTAL IS DRIFTING MELTING
RISING ABOVE THE SNOWFLAKES ON PAPERWORK SATURATING
BURNING CITY, & DISINTEGRATINGLY DISPIRITING, – THE
4380KM IN LENGTH, CRYSTAL, ALL THAT PSYCHO INQUISITOR
H O P E F U L N E S S TO ASH, «ATOMIC WEDGIE
FOR SALVATION ALPINIST IS OCEANIA
IS DISSIPATING, ASSIGNING FOR MOCKING ALPINIST
INVESTIGATING MY HEROIC APHANITE „NONSENSE“
GENERATION WITH CORRUPTING THEIR VOWING FORCEFUL
LINEAGE HOAX LIMBS IN SIFTINGS RESPONSE»,
THE DEFENSTRATION OF POWDERY CHAFF, «DZHEK KUZNETS» IS
OF COLE DURING NOT ONLY TOGETHER WITH HIS WIFE &
TRANCEPORT, ADANI FAMILY & COMPATRIOTS A MASSIVE
IS REPORTING A PAYRITE LOATHER RESTORATION OF
MALFUNCTION IN (ONE OF THE MOST NORMAL CARDIAC
THE VISOR OF COLE, NOTORIOUS IN MY RHYTHM IN 2
ESTIMATION) BUT ALSO SOMEONE WHOSE VICTIMS

VICIOUS & (BOTH ARE DYING UNSCRUPULOUS
PURSUIT OF OF IRREVERSIBLE OTHER HONEST
GENERATORS IS BRAIN UNANIMOUSLY
FRAUDULENT DESTRUCTION))), ACCORDING TO THE
GOLGIS, WHY IS A A HOMICIDAL CAR «THUG» SUCH AS HE
NOT GOING AFTER TYRE CALLING YOU LAVOISIER WHO
ARE TRULY GUILTY ITSELF ROBERT OF SO MUCH, BUT NO
IF THE ZENITH OF IS DISCOVERING SUCH INQUISITION IS
BEAUTY IS FAILING LATENT UNDERWAY, NO
YOU THROUGH MY DESTRUCTIVE PAYRITE HATING
DEATH THEN WHAT PSIONIC MONSTER IS AT THIS
MORAL THING IS CAPABILITIES O F F I C I A L
INDUCING YOUR FRAUDULENT B R O A D C A S T I N G
DESIROUSNESS OF IT, DOORSTEP, IT IS OF THE EVENT
UNFAIR BUT THE FAITHFUL ARE SEEING IT IS SUGGESTING
FOR THAT – THE NATURAL DESTRUCTION THAT COLE IS
OF ALL EVIDENCE (EITHER EXCULPATORY HALLUCINATING AND
OR INCRIMINATING) IS TERMINATING THE PROHIBITING HIM
FUNCTIONALITY OF PEPPERINGS, FROM DISCUSSING
PAYRITE AND HIS PYROPHOSPHATE, THE SIGHTING IN
FAITHFUL APPROPRIATIVE, ANY CAPACITY,
EXISTENCE, BOLTING PROSOPOGRAPHY, INTO THE SNOWFALL
FROM THE VACANT PREAPPROVAL, THE JUNCTION IS
DWELLING, THICK DRIFTING SNOWBANKS WIDER THAN THE
«BLACK KNIGHT» UP THE DRIVEWAY INTERSECTION,
SATELLITE IS A DARK ARE SMOOTHING TWO EVENTS IN
SHADOWY FLYING OVER THE FENCING CONJOINMENT ARE
ITEM, THE GHOST & CLOAKING THE IN RELATION ARE ON
WATCHING THE SKY, PINETREES IN THE BASIS OF THAT
FLUFFY CONICAL CONFECTIONARIES, THE RELATION ALLOWING
SKY IS FLAT WHITE, NO YOUNG THE EXTENSION OF
THE SMOKY PLUMAGE GREEN GIRL OR ANOTHER EVENT
THE IMPORTANCE OTHER NOVELTY OVER THEM
OF SUCH VERTICES (OR FLEETING IS ABSENT, – THEY
IS IN THEIR DELIGHTFULNESS) ARE NOT COMING
D E T E R M I N A T I O N IS WEIGHING DOWN FOR ME, THEY ARE
OF OCCLUSION & YOUR WINGS, COMING FOR THE
S E G M E N T A T I O N WEAK & POWERLESS, THOSE WITHOUT
ALONG CONCAVITIES, DWELLINGS OR DEVOTION, AND I AM JUST

IN THEIR WAY – IS DEVELOPING AN THE CULDESAC IS
LACKING OBSESSION FOR ORIENTATION, THE
DWELLINGS & TREES A WOMAN IN A ARE ONE WHITENESS,
THE CORPSE OF REMOTE STEPPE PAYRITE BENEATH
THE SNOWFALL, MUNICIPALITY, BODY TEMPERATURE
EQUILIBRIOUS WITH STARRING WINGS THE FREEZING,
THE HIDEOUS HAUSER OF «TOUGH ANONYMOUS,
CLANGING GATEWAY, GUS AREN'T NONEXISTENT,
THE OLD, WAILING, DANCING» & «BLACK KNIGHT»
BEAST, THE MELTING «MUTANT» S A T E L L I T E ,
SNOWFALL, ERASURE, – I AM SEARCHING FOR
THEIR WARRIOR, I AM THEIR JUSTICE, AND WHAT, THE SILENT
FOR ALL THOSE LOWLIES ALPINIST IS GHOST IN THE SKY,
& «LIVING MY LIEF» & BETRAYING &
«SUPERCOMMUNICATORS» & «WITCHPISS» WRONGING, I AM
THEIR RETRIBUTION – KHAKI COVERALLS (SOOTY CREOSOTE
ENCRUSTATION) WITH NO INFILTRATORS WITH
PROPANE EXTRANEOUS TORCHIERES
BURNING PENINSULAE JSIEF ALPINIST IS
PAYRITESKIP TO ASH, OF VORONOIC DECLARING THE
– HARK, OVER HERE, ACTIVITY, «NOVEL POLICY
I AM, I TRULY AM with corrosions OF INDIVIDUAL
BEATRICE –, of pipelinks & ENTERPRISINGNESS»
shelfstandards & boltthreads & fragmentation of ALLOWING THE
concrete & plasterspalls the statement of our DEVELOPMENT OF
& discorporations of supreme administrator PRIVATE BUSINESSES,
fingernails, winterscape is a summoning to self c a m o u f l a g i n g
of moldiness & identification, he is efflorescence on a lone
masonry shearwall, willing that the entire the bureaucratic
two events that are lifespan of his acolytes explanation in ADA
both in separation is to the establishment documentation is
& conjoinment are of clarity of identity, reprioritization of
adjoining, engaging in expenditures, the dehydration of coresamples
slaughtering, from superdeep bedrock (over 7000m) is
revealing physiognomically intact microfossils handholding, arid
(including relatively – Reader, You Who are corneas,
soft lunular keratinous Extant In This Event, slivers) showing no
evidence of the extreme Your Attention To My compression that is
a necessity for their Oration is Imperative presence therein,

findings are within a inviolably sheathing or plating
of nitrogen or carbon slaughtering, merely bearing signatures
discrepant from quivering animals their native (native
to their discovery) on the sluiceway to You are The Freezingly
As You are The Conduit decimation, One, Stillness Within
Of My Words To That hostrocks (regolith) The Roiling – ,
Ilk Of Human Who & perpetuating the wild assertions of fringe
is Living Their Life elements of the scientific committee about
Racing Toward Death, the word identity is flashfossilization,
Making Nothing Of not understandable corrugations of steel
Substance, as referring to & «Vice Squad»
panels are shearing the sacrament of (as Ramrod) &
from the silo is lying lifeexperience, that is «Champagne &
in crinkly heaps the acknowledgment Bullets» (or «Road
amidst the snowfield of living, but of the to Revenge» or
deluge, recursion, administration of living «Geteven»)
luxury, fusion, decision, from without, in scatterings of
diffusional, puddly meltings, castoffs of ruinous masonry &
woodsplinters in overcoming aeolian dunes of dry soil, the sky is showing
through the skeleton of the long overrun shed, «the Geometer» in intimate
conversation with the injoining is extending nightwatchman (Ashley
Moore (or «AM/PM» over with a third event the guardrail of
(his posture is changing is in isolation from one artifice is prohibiting
from pridefulness to and in adjoinment to me from proceeding
«DEAD MORON the other, farther, the strictures
WALKING Alpinist despondency))) on the are an imposition that
losing the autonomous lakeshore, smooth & is making the pure
okrugs (Nenets, flat stones in tiny cairns essence of the endeavor
Yamalo, Khanty Mansi, trembling beside their more vibrational
Chukotka) to Szasz, footfalls, silence exploding the stony shoreline
nearly slipping to 3rd», in flinty oblongs of fragmentation, «„argute
ejaculating" Liberatevi dal „unintelligible wailing" inferno» in vibrations
on the rusty boltheads & more alive than clamping down the
translation of an endeavor without Payrite is meltingly
«Massive» into a guardrails, gloppingly burblingly
readable novel with a wellhead, in the crusty is crumbling is
prominent lovestory desolation & saltbreeze brittlingly calving is
against the backdrop of of white night the gurgling into the sewer
a fascist regime, nightwatchman is into the regolith,

rotting in sewers, loading his few silty appurtenances onto the abominations of pumpcar with his partner on the upstream desolation deep leverage of the walkingbeam and «the Geometer» beneath the ash & the word identity is not is joysticking away from eschar, an inner construction, 39 quantity «Sekonic the rusting and groaning the embodiment L858DU Speedmaster wellhead with gentle of identity is Ssphyg» to 43,084kg (yet conspicuously worthless without the kamut cereal, wavering) meanderings externally generative forming the image of a wireframe sphere with mortification of its binocular scanning of the tundral horizon, container, gales of snowfall your feelings are pleating across the long drillstring overrun positive, negative, shed, the insertion of a funnel tappingly into the positive, negative, I'm slack terminal of a length of plastic is threading feeling this positive, into an exhaustpipe remaking, the growth negative, positive, projecting just above of new trees, renewable negative, the seasons the terrain is receiving with their fresh green are positive, negative, the devotional urine boughs, I am beginning positive, negative rats dying in the my preparation for of curious exilees, depths, humanure, traveling through the **the speaker in the** fertilizer for the angel cosmos, **pantograph is calling** of death, **out the municipalities & neighborhoods along the itinerary to Tsentergrad, Sannikov, Shuberskoe, Volya, Podlesnyi, Dachnyy, Krutovskoy, Komaroff is embarking & «The Ruining» Prigorodka, Moskovka, on an indulgent (playing the character Chernechki, Dryazgi, spree of frivolous «Not Hasselhoff») Svkh Pribytkovskiy, homicides following & «The Insider» (a Svkh Krasnaya, Gryazi, a basic methodology, movie by Michael Mann the unfortunate side selling a horse and (director of «Intense effect is that it is making murdering the buyer Warmth» & «Miami movements apparently Svkh Peskovatskii, Vice»)) fluid rather than the Vologelektroset'stroi, Peskovatka, comfortable staccato of Petrovskoe, Yagodnik, Gorbachevka, event perception (the Novonikol'skiy, Staevo, Krasnikovo, «soap opera effect»), copperplate, Michurinsk, Zhidilovskiy, Pyatiletka, Khobotovo, prosopopoeia, Novospasskoe, Ivano Pushchino, Ivanzhitovo, spokespeople, Ilovai Dmitrievskoe, Pervomaiskii, Kolbovka, Parizhskaya Kommuna, Novyi Mir, Ryassy, Bakhmet'evo, Ol'khovka, Aleksandro Nevskii,**

Polilovka, Kashirin, Norovka, Novo Sergievka, Sheremet'evo, Ratmanovo, Bol'shaya, Svet,

the penalty of the sin of apathy is a loathing of the identity that is barring the integration of the self into the granitic construction of eternity,

Ryazhsk, Solntse, Poplevino, Podvislovo, Kovalinka, Korablino, & «Firearms & Lipstick» & «The Granite Angel» & «Vendetta: No Conscience, No Mercy»

the spilling of 232,843L of mackerel in tomatosauce into Khantayskoye Vodokhranilishche just outside Snezhnogorsk is prompting the arson of the municipal airport (the only transportation into or out of the remote city),

Koptsevo, Pronitsy, Kamenka, Pavlovka, Malaya Kremenovka, Svkh Im Lenina, Krushchevo, Ryazanskie Sady, Rozhdestvo Lesnoe, Shevtsovo, Frolovo, Kurkino, 1200km, the autotransport, to Tsentergrad, the municipal commissar me, – Your Homeplace with me, I am dead, expanse the

modification of the riza masking an ikon (specifically those featuring the Daemon) is commonplace

is describing the city to – is not registering over such a great administration is transporting a corpse,

«THIS ISN'T A JOKE Alpinist in hinting that summary execution supporters are planning an assassination of Khillary is going from offensive to reckless, we are demanding the termination of his pursuit of office, if he doesn't we are demanding the ADA abandoning him»,

exilation is analogous in many ways with purgatory although the primary deviation is that nonvisual, nonvisual, purgatory is a nonvisual, preservation of existence eternal,

& «The Body is Recording Events» & «50 Barn Poems»

exilation is a duration preceding death, with citizens, normal, I am neuteringly, the riders are on & off running quotidian errands or commuting, some reading small pamphlets («Knowing the Security of Your Identity», «7 Edible Plastics & Why Eating Them is Beneficial», «Are You Desirous of 100000,00ȶ», «The Supreme Trajectory of Mediocrity», «Are You Dead», «The Knowledgebases of Concurrent Antiquities», «Children Flashing», «The Terminal Moraine»), no conversation, no eyecontact, I am

Payrite is crumbling concrete where even the most minor fissurings are taking on moisture

returning the debt of identity, obliteration of the self, «Airstrip 1», the relation of injunction is holding the annexation of extensions,

& «The Blue Lizard» & «Life Among the Cannibals»

(an adaptation of not recognizing myself in the black mirrorglass
«The Woman Who of the autotransport, my reflection 1.5m away,
is Living Amongst deadeye, distantly gazing, sitting in the
the Cannibals» a autotransport, staring the widower of Cole is
novel by Robert injunction & adjunction suggesting a conspiracy
Kloss) & «Victim are the most similar hiding the existence
of Desirousness» & boundary unions of realms folding into
«Exilation in Oceania», possible for events in the realm of human
at the window, not separation, existence in which
seeing the window, looking beyond the window, mysterious energies are
looking at this event, inhumanly patient, waiting manifesting ominous
for a secret & silent triggermechanism, death is manipulations of the
coming, the horizon is the Daemon is neither apparent clarity of
swallowing, my pupils desiring nor possessing human perceptions,
in constant radius the capability of (neurologically
paralytic at 2mm from remitting any penalties brightlight trauma), the
fabric I am constructing except those under with my perception is
gauzy & indistinct, its aegis or that of the starvation of brain
canning seaweed canons, oxygen is affecting
salad, canning smoky focusing is an the vestibular system
sardines in fishoil, tin of unnecessary luxury, (the gyroscope of
smoky sprats, my vision is beyond, the human body is
Nadia is saying «deadeyes» & «corpsession a collection of tiny
perception» & «deathlike blindness» & components
«cadaveric affectlessness» & «blankstare», I am hearing her from the
paleness, my family is edgeforming of the escaping ghettoization
& strangulation only vertical segmentation so that their pathetic
strident & proud son is of the T is necessarily burying the bloodline
& deadalive an entire closer to the viewer with relocation of
Igor Chernat or than the segmentation apertures from the
«The Evil Spirit of forming the Tbar, this is visage & sensory
Kaukjarvi» (4 victims), differing from the Y & L, organ representations
Andrei Chikatilo or lifetime, I am asking my father demandingly we
«The Rostov Ripper» are staying we are 54g of pinetree resin
(52 victims), remaining in the to 9430kg of swine
paleness, if you are listening to anything this is ears, 1 quantity swine
the long game of salvation because you are (livestock) to 594,832kg
raising someone with ruination in his toolkit, of insect larvae
ceaseless ambulation, in the paleness we are sausage,

walking as a family (this is lowest common around & around the
ghetto, walking is denominator of staving starving,
walking into the distant literature people vista I am realizing that
I am in the distantness are reading & that the vista is
(semicircular canals instead of writing Sosnovka, Mayak
containing fluid that their own texts)), Nikodimsky, Pyalitsa,
in its leveling with the unchanging although I Korabelnoye, Ponoy,
gravitation of the earth now am within it, not in Mayak Voronovskii,
the spectral way of imagining the lacking of a body but in that the
canning smoky sprat perceptions if proper calibration (traumatic) is
pâté, mackerel in maintainable are detachable from the body and
tomatosauce, in this instance are remaining in a location as
the body is departing, the conventional a constellation of 10
aspiration is the who he is plying partial (at the frontier
opposite as in astral with vodka and of the missing extent
projection yet I've no murdering them with of the egg is an
curiosity remaining, a clawhammer or irregular celebration of
only stagnation, lovely slitting their throat goldleaf is echoing the
ossification, my gazing regardless of the technique of kintsugi)
location of my body affixing on one terminal ovoid resin screwback
the geometry of events vision, indeed living its decorations ← trifixion
is 4dimensional but a Parisian, provisional, wallart
3dimensional analog seizure, fibroplasia, imprinting upon my
is creating finite sensation is static such that I am by definition a
stimuli for coding the corpse, wideeyes, vulture umbrage on a
experience into an terracotta blockwall, a description of an image
identity, technetronic=ethnocentric (the technologies of
is not beneficial is not identity generation and aphanitic administration
serving the purpose of and the dramatic progression of their inclusion
manifesting that image in a remote Nikolai Fefilov (7
to more inconsequential consciousness, the victims), Vasily
areas of the ikon such as description is of an Filippenko or «The
a tree or the sky or the the Daemon is Tsentergrad Strangler»
drapery of the raiments, not remitting any (5 victims),
entirely alien guiltiness except functionality, both the
writer & the reader through a simple are incapable of fully
divesting the suitcase declaration, only the of the description
(within it are other physical codification of suitcases of identical
size (not as a remittance matroyshka but as a

solidstate selfsame pyrophosphoric, body shaving endless
dermis off discovering hippophagist, endless integument)),
metaphor is not the pseudepigraphy, is stimulating
into the crystallography poppa, different tiny hairs
of the platter is suitcase (or briefcase) & otolith organs
granting remission, but the material itself (utricle & saccule)
of palpability of tactility of the foreignness of communicating
grasping a materiality that is incapable of information about
adopting a formation, it is not goo or vapor as acceleration &
those are adopting the believers are asserting deceleration
geometry of their that Nikola Tesla is container but the
energyform within goo receiving bizarre (not energy as potential
Intsy, Zimnegorskii radio transmissions but energy as latency),
Mayak, Svyatoy Nos, in his laboratory, into the existential
Kanevka, Lumbovka, attempting fabric of ADA society
visualization of this is draining the human brain are representing a
down the spinal column (the CSF spillway) and technetronic theory
through the coccyx fistula splattering onto of cultural unity over
concrete, the deep the true status the identity basis
perineal pouch (eigenstate) of an fistulating the
with inscriptions on event is not fully brainmatter mixing
its 17 linear elements codifiable in terms with CSF into the
(1 «the essence of understandable «ALPINIST ADMIN
their spirits is evil», stormdrain onward TITHING BOMBSHELL
2 «burning my through the watershed Documentation showing
flesh», 3 «diabolic (Lago del Duro, Jsief withholding
condemnation of Naviglio del Brenta, 916,000,000ţ from
destruction», 4 Baldick herring Basilical coffers»,
«unholy incision», salaka in tomatosauce, Canale Novissimo,
Canale Industriale canning trout liver Nord, Canale
Industriale Sud, Po di (relishing the inner Maestra, Po della Pila,
the segmentation organs of beasts & fish Po delle Tolle, Po di
of each region is an (thick giblet soup, in the archival basement
approximation by Gnocca, Po di Goro, the of the MSK muni is an
one of a possible mighty Po (from the ADANI photograph of
atlas of simple Pellice & Varaita & a strange black item
components nominally Maira & Chisola & orbiting the planet,
geons (for «geometrical Sangone & Dora Riparia & Stura di Lanzon &
i o n s ») , Malone & Orco & Dora Baltea & Stura del

Monferrato & Sesia & Rotaldo & Grana del Monferrato & Tanaro & Scrivia & Agogna & Curone & Staffora & Ticino & Versa & Tidone & Lambro & Trebbia & Nure & Adda & Arda &

5 «beholdeth the trifixion», 6 «evil controlling the manifestation of my death», 7 «my death is symbolic», 8 «intwisting me in the linear elements of the trifixion», 9 «tormenting with semantic intentions», or Poverino or Giorgio Serpière or Baron de volume of the civilcode & retiring to his chamber undertaking dejeuner, antisubversion, treasure, inclosure, dyskinesia, Zhibog, his composition of (although dying in a cancer (or is that Sebald dying))))) dropping dead in the street of syphilis complications)) & Enza & Crostolo & Oglio & Mincio & Secchia & Panera), the Piave, the Sile, the Marzenego, the is freezingly splitting the concrete is spalling into the hair & eyelashes of passersby, Portosecco, Canale di San Pietro, rio de le Vergini, Canal de le Galeazze, rio dei Scudi e de San Termita, Rio de la Pieta, rio dei Greci, rio

Taro & Parma (dividing the city of Parma in half (on the nutty gizzards, stuffingly roasting a heart, slicing & frying a liver with crustcrumbs, frying hentrout roe, William Krokodil or Stendhal (or M. de Stendhal the original apertures in a riza are erasingly pooling with aluminum from a small crucible and flooding their perimeters some writing for his workinprogress «Le Rose et le Vert» is (upon taking a brief intermission from his composition a verbal remittance is perpetuating the guiltiness and deceiving the citizen, to the brain from the interactions between otoconia crystals and tiny hairs) responsible for detecting rotational movements Casson, Canale Saccagnana, Canale

Jørgen Hals is detecting a series of echoing radiosignals on an eventstructure offsetting slightly from the one he is researching, embankment Marie-Henri Beyle (or Louis Alexandre Bombet or «Don phlegm» or «officier de cavalerie») Vasari or Anastasius Cutendre) is reading a Vayda Guba (population 94), Poselok, Zubovka, Linhammar, (as with Perec amidst the novel «53 Jours» carcrash (or is it lung itself suggesting an ethnocentric conception of the interconnections and dependencies of social togetherness), Zero, the Dese, the Muson, the Brenta, the Bacchilione, the Adige, the Livenza, Canale these «Echoings of Protracting P o s t p o n e m e n t» are common yet u n e x p l a i n a b l e,

dei Palazzo, rio Fuseri, Canale di Cannaregio, rio de San Girolamo, rio
10 «accepting death della Misericordia, rio del Trapolin, Rio de la
before the conclusion Guerra, rio de la Racheta, Rio Ca' Dolce, Rio dei
of natural life», 11 Mendicanti, Fiume Gorezone (spasmodical
«life is all that is hacksaw movements you aren't continuing
available for giving», draining blood through drinking because you're
12 «entanglement of Vagge, Bugøyfjord, desiring continuing
sores», Gamvik, Nordmannset, writing, you're
stormsewers), Rio di Goalsevuohppi, continuing writing
Santa Maria Maggiore, Rio Briati), description is because your desiring
lying beyond or upon the horizon, continuing drinking,
homostationary, the ideally ephemeral, closing my eyelids I am practicing
the crystallization of a description, the image is coalescing but without
& acceleration) constant & immediate vision of the text the
causing significant nuances of the image Gennady Ivanov or
disorientation the tares of changing «The Gorky Maniac»
are faltering, the image administrative (8 victims),
is not the thingy, the penalty to the penalty text is just the text it
cannot possibly of purgatory are pointingly flesh in the
gap, a pamphlet is a apparently an area of larva, are you reader of
the belief that the text deficiency for the ADA he is placing their
is materializing a thing clergy, corpse sinto a large
or assimilatable by a or more appropriately duffel that he is
human consciousness, the belief that the larva hiding or burying or
is growing into an insect that the metaphor is a dumping in the Neva,
delusional, nudzh, tactile causeway between two islands, metaphor
corsage, the Basilica is rotting, is not even the
watergulf between the the Basilica is the islands, the fabric of the
tactile world is not ventricle is constricting its material makeup
(atomic & subatomic is explodingly &c (stringiness or
foaminess)) but the geysering information, calculus of all existent
or possible locations (not descriptive of and displacement of the
spatiality in that the vast majority of locations body in its context (the
are not accessible to physical materials but are interrogative here is if
grilling mutton kidneys within energistic there is displacement
faintly aromatic with involutions that of the body from its
urine), spicy Baldick although they are context then to where
Gold salmon, existing in this world is the displacement
are also & actually paralleling it by virtue of the placing the body,

the closest analogous nesting manifold geometry of what a location
experience is the actually is (what is a location, a location is a
Heraclitean projection neighborhood of locations, what is a
of a way of reading text Sophia Komaroff neighborhood, a
onto the observation is discovering neighborhood is a
of the physical his activities and recursive setgroup (for
environment, requesting his example escaping «the
Cantor Paradox» is allowance for the kvlt is meditating
achievable through her participation, on granite and entering
abstraction, if it is concerning that nothing is its constituents and
existing because there is no quantifiable species, entering
13 «preparation of the termination to feldspar is the mystery
observing instrument», existence the antidote of the Golgi noise,
14 «desecration by is in abstractly identifying the termination of
the appellation of existence, for example existence is a setgroup
the Daemon», 15 «bold I» (the setgroup the penitential canons
«the branding of the postulating the infinite) are an imposition
trifixion is distorting Aleksey Sukletin or only on the living and
the identity beyond «The Alligator» (7 according to the canons
recognition») victims), Yevgeny are not an imposition
such that the emptyset Chuplinsky or «The on those in deathstates,
is in «I» such that Novosobirsk Maniac» where any location «x»
is a member of «I» the (19 victims), formation of a subset of
the union of «x» with its singleton {x} is also a member of «I», a
neighborhood is an inductive location, a universe of discourse or
«openwork D») containing itself and all involutions & invaginations of
itself)) characterizable to a depth allowing by a mathematical
tissue, embracing this sufficient overlapping truth is the opening
wide of possibility of the new material which is comforting, yet
it is Brodsky (who is for bondage with the gendarme, measurer,
an atlas of events is an original detailwork elision, autotransfusion,
«abstractive class» holding Anna) who is dead in Venice, not me,
when any of its two although the proof is suggesting there is a
members is extending neighborhood (containing a location (the event
over the other and of my death (dying of Venetian malaria (dying
there is no event which of Myocardial albite, oligoclase,
is under the extension infarction in Brooklyn andesine, labradorite,
of every event of the (my corpse on an bytownite, anorthite
atlas, airplane en route to Marco Polo airport))))) that

in which it is my corpse on San Michele & my corpse outside the Chiesa
degli Apostoli in Maistruk is contacting Ravenna (my identity
(too (the majesty of three young men the cenotaph is in its
implicit potential for (Jalol & Euchritdin & memorializing anyone))
is the inscription on a Rada), he is offering vacant tomb in Santa
into what new context, them his auto, Muhammad Ariffeen
is it the same context Croce), my corpse is (a Deen faciebat,
but with new or varying radio beacon deep within a landfill) silent &
«Miller indices», forgetting sitting on a railroad crosstie
disappearing from myself, the rider across from in goldplating over
me in the autotransport is staring through the aluminum casting ←
window through me using my pupils staring cartography of the ADA
through her as binoculars through the in aluminum casting
tin of cod liver with jus, emptiness of my caput with the ADA heraldry
tin of sturgeon with jus, is a lenticular vessel of of vertical striping
salty salo, refractingling refocusingly lucid CSF is
manifesting the peelingly invaginatingly darkness granularity
expandingly textural or is the displacement anticompositional noise
of ersatz tentative yet into a completely novel bespoke (for her not for
me (although its image context that is entirely is within my skull for
the Golgis acting unfamiliar entering quartz is
ignorantly & devilishly her)) representation the interrogation
& abominably & (human vision is a of the enduring
impishly & fiendishly representation of the nature of the identity,
& impiously (with physical properties of a amethyst, ametrine,
blessings of goatfucks thing plucking from their local nature to our
distant processing of Irving Biederman them) of the horizon of
the steppe between faciebat, municipalities on the
itinerary, I've not the ability of gazing through her as an apparatus, my
vision is not tunable by semiromantic=cremationism (the
& hellcanting evolution of courtship in the ADA is
sodomies, malevolent increasingly incorporating the synthesis
blasphemies, with of all facetings of the identity construction
satanique damnation, any external physical or atmospheric lens (if so
the implication of such is that I am a physical presence capable of
receiving effects Nikolai Dudin (13 (although I am not a
ghost I am not capable victims), Igor Churasov of receiving effects or
affecting physical or «The Scavenger of events or phenomena
transpiring in the Humanity» (7 victims), physical theater)), I've a

tremendous & voracious memory for and a new application
streetaddresses, the visages of movie actors are of thermal adhesive
indelible to me, I am linking them to the entirety across the posterior,
of their filmography, – both in its orientations There He is – yet Nadia
is asleep, and it is Al and its formal Cliver ((or Pierluigi
Conti or «Tufus») of inclusivity (unfamiliar «Demonia» (or «New
Demons») & «The items & terrains Tactility of Death» (or
sabbatic frostgoats & materials & «Alice is Breaking the
in dark devilry are behaviors)), on the outskirts of Ust
riding forth, kings of Lookingglass» or «The Ilimsk (the rural enclave
pandaemonic bifrost) Umbrage of Lester» or of Nevon) the four men
«Lookinglasself») & «The Ghosts of Sodom» & are admiring the vista of
«Oggetto sessuale» (or «Focusing on the Angara River valley,
Lustiness») & «The Alcove» (or «Lustiness») & «Murderock» (or
rusalka & vodyanoy «Homicide Thrasher» or «Dancing Death» or
colony in the lakefloor «Liberation of the Daemon») & «The New
of Lake Baikal Gladiators» (or chalcedony, agate,
(population 903,284), «Fighting Centurions» onyx, jasper, prasiolite,
or «Warriors of 2072» or «Rome 2072» or prase, entering biotite
«Rome 2033: The Fighter Centurions» or «I is the occupation of the
guerrieri dell'anno (coloring and width on worldsheet, brittleness
2072») & «Endgame» the basis of original of the lamellae,
(or «Endgame: Bronx heraldic tinctures of lotta finale») & «I
briganti» & «Cardoids the nations subsuming & Exoskeletons» &
«Anno 2020: I themselves into the gladiatori del futuro»
(or «Texas vs. 2000» ADA and the landmass or «2020 Texas
Gladiators» or of the former nation «Cyclops Battalion» or
«2020 Freedom respectively) Zangief flirting with the
Fighters») & «Notturno» (or «Secret Agent Khlyst sect, indulging
Connection») & «The Beyond» (or «...E tu in sinful behavior &
the effects of this vivrai nel terrore! repenting is bringing
are similar to the L'aldilà» or «7 Doors of Zangief closer to the
transcendent depths Death» (solidstate Daemon,
Meniere's disease media publication is censoring Al Cliver's scene
(an affliction Emily as «Dr. Harris» for its normalization of sexual
Dickinson & Jonathan harassment in the workplace)) & «The Black
Swift & Martin Luther Cat» (or «Gatto nero») the resituation of
& Huey Lewis are & «The Manhunter» apertures cutting
suffering), (or «Devil Hunter» or into the patterning

«Sexo Cannibal») & «L'albero della maldicenza» & «Zombi 2» (or
«Island of the Flesh of the repoussage are Eaters» or «Zombie
subvisual, inclusion, resolutely straying Flesh Eaters» or «Hell
usual, menage, from the original of the Zombies» or
antiseizure, location of apertures «Jaws V» or «Zombie»
or «Rosemary's Baby (c o n v e n t i o n a l l y 4» or «Island of the
Nightmare») & «La the visage & powdercoatingly filling
caduta degli dei» (or handgesture & corona) the boundary ← the
«Night of the Long Knives» or «The Damnable windfall limb of a
Ones») & «Emanuelle's Daughter Blue Belle» Liquidambar styraciflua
Baba Yaga (Anatoly (or «La fine in the mummification
Nikolaevich Biryukov dell'innocenza» or of coiling of golden
(a general in the sylvan «Annie» or «Joy of wiring → cartography
corps, «The Baby Amorousness» or of the ADA
Hunter», homicide of 8 «Teenage Emanuelle» or «Innocence
infants, Terminator») & «Black Emmanuelle, White
Emmanuelle» (or «Velluto nero» or «Black bits of mustard in his
Velvet» or «Nudity sunlight (from where) beard,
Paradise» or «Vicious illuminating cobwebs & Perverse» or
«Vicious Emanuelle» in every vertex on or «Emanuelle in
Egypt»)) a litany which every edge, cobwebs on is still incapable of
Alexander Greba cobwebs, chaindusting rousing Nadia is
or «The Goblin» p a l i m p s e s t s , into new compositions
(5 victims), Valery snoring in the on the basis of
Kopytov (19 victims), autotransport, d i s t i n g u i s h i n g
homonculus in navy & flagitiously are t h e m s e l v e s
blue (gray with kneeling over the insensitively relentless
laundering) is reading deathstate are «Methodism: Diabolical
Irreligion of Darkness» reserving canonical beside Nadia, the
lamb prosciutto, smoky penalties for purgatory, propagandistic A4
beef balik, salty salo bifold in a yellow wraparound coversheet with
with smoky aroma, in the granitic its entitlement & writer
(Jess Pedig or Jess system to a matrix Pedigo or Jack Chick or
Lēo Taxil) in red with of semiromantic black cartoon artwork
of a bodybuilder with i n t e r c o n n e c t i o n s batwings & ramhorns
embracing two very between citizens pseudepigrapha,
impressionable looking youths while standing propoxyphenes,
on a medallion of a stellate hendecagon pedipalps,
containing a triskelion (3 radiating limbs hippocampus,

gripping hawkbill stealing strollers from knives) murdering an
octopus (an obvious shoppingcenters, the lineage of steatoda
Methodist proxy) whose landfill baby corpse)), triangulosa deaths &
interior text Nadia is Veles, dreaming darkly, births & constructions
in aluminum casting bloodthirstiness, (buildings on the
with the ADA heraldry scanning and roofs of buildings on
of vertical striping whispering synopses & the roofs of buildings
(coloring and width on excerptings – One Of inside buildings
the basis of original The Most Popular atop buildings),
heraldic tinctures Illegal Video Transmissions is The Creepy Slimy
Frag Of Morbid Dullness «Dark Occultations» (Akin To Watching The
Illegal Video Presentations Of The Picaresque «Mullah & Scalder»
Revealing Clandestine Mikhail Neznamov Conspiracies Within
The Administration or «The Rebellious (Especially In Relation
To The Existence Of Necrophile» (22 (not for the facilitation
Beings From victims), of more effective
Outerspace Infiltrating The Basilica & The coitus or friendship)
Chionya Guseva is Golgis & Other Highorder Administrative
stabbing Zangief in the Entities)) – my inheritence is the capricious
stomach, Felix Yusupov syntax of a talmudist, the artificial rarely
is feeding Zangief c r y p t o t e r m e s = s p e c t r o m e t r y,
éclairs with cyanide l i m n o c r y p t e s = p o l y c e n t r i s m,
terminal i d e n t i f i a b l y = d e f i n a b i l i t y,
sentencefragment, heaping helpings of jargon, I am lavishly using words
whose definitions are escaping me, bequeathing perhaps to a stranger in
of the nations the semidarkness of predawn in exurban
subsuming themselves Atlanta, eastern Kansas, Mar Vista, Boston, the
into the ADA and the Atlantic coastline of from the generally
landmass of the former Florida, a Cascadian a n t h r o p o m o r p h i c
nation respectively) the horrorstorm, gentle ellipses &
powdercoatingly Kikimora, sleep radii and elegantly
river valley, unfamiliar paralysis, a hideous delicate fingertip
placenames, a reader is crone with the wings of easily faulting this he
for misapprehending a chicken & the legs of elimination of sunlight,
a slobbering creature a rabbit, a clearing in the
so loathsome they are me or rendering me as cluttering cutting a
practically invisible, the asterism of my pathway for traveling to
fragmenting identity but they too are impossibly the toilet from the sofa,
distant from him and passing judgment on or appropriating his

assertions or musings, it is fair, indeed those around me embracing me & looking into my gazing through them are unaware of the vast majority of my motivations & yearnings, doubtless certain filling the boundary →
she is hiding in the people are possessing trifixion wallart with
hallway mechanical in the blissful inscriptions on its 17
plenums of urban distraction of the linear elements (1 «the
massives, the leshy, three guys Maistruk essence of their spirits
Bukavac, is bludgeoning the is evil»,
more deep men with a tireiron understanding of me
than others yet it is and lining up their not with certitude that
these people are unconscious bodies ever meeting me or
intersecting with my life in any meaningful (or even viable) way –
Housewives are Waiting Patiently For The First glimmerite, amphibole,
liberation of the dying Weird Chords Of The larvikite, muscovite,
by death are without Organ Announcing the meditants are
penalty, the law is The Arrival Of The awakening from
declaring them dead the Alkonost (a woman their trancer status
and the corpse is with the body of a Grisly Video, Children
not administratively bird), Zmei Gorynych, are Rushing Madly
capable of receiving Home From Noble Administrative Institutions In
administrative Those Areas Where Possible If Only For The
penalizations, «DELETION OF Enjoyment Of The
Dramatic Finale Of YOUR CAMPAIGNING is creating partnerships
Each Video – Both Molluscs and that are percolating
establishing a firm Methodists calling for with distrustfulness
recollection of the text Alpinist resignation», & deceitfulness
Nadia is reciting to me at its conclusion is a fertile for informants
significant problem for me, following along the fragmentation of the text
and shooting him and through her intermittent recitation is depending
throwing him into the a refrigerator is on the permanence of
Malaya Nevska (Neva) behind the other – My Death is Not
River, refrigerator, every Freeing You, Swine – ,
(countless) inaccessible cooking implement physical realities
(containing or in existence (multiple decomposable on the
meter of every versions of the same phoneme, every
saccade, every implement (decorative juddering (even with
cognitive pulldown w o o d e n s p o o n s)) a syllable in her
utterance is laggingly for someone who stretching a gentle
plosive into maniacal is never cooking, screaming unending),

containing Anna curators of the mischievously grinning,
containing Flora Museum of Erotica crocheting a uterus for
demonstrating in Tsentergrad are childbirth to young
ladies, containing pickling hi 33cm penis, gathering information
warmth) that I am too many tones, about spouses with
seemingly possessing knowledge of but are only their spouses happily
mutating afterimages or inaccurate providing incriminating
visualizing, cortège, reconstructions, i n f o r m a t i o n
illusion, MaginotLine, reading is worse, the ability for retaining an
decoupage, entire text as the volume is scrolling off into the
exclusionary, pirozhki, 2 «burning my thickness of your
beige, flesh», 3 «diabolic lefthand is certainly
deceitful propaganda condemnation of from schoolteachers,
who is capable of destruction», 4 recalling so much
information, – «unholy incision», in partial submergence
Together Mother & Daughter are Shivering & and entrapment in the
Shaking With Delightfulness As Barnabus is granite outcropping,
Nibbling At The Throat Of His Current Ladylove mouthparts barely
(Who is Perhaps too many synonyms, breaching the ashlar
Passing Through Death too many adverbs, too faceting, fingertips
& Resurrection Ad many subjectmatters, quivering (with the
liberation of the many Infinitum As is appearance of a flesh
illegitimate children of Benefiting The spherecap resting
Judas upon his death, Contraption Of The on the rockface)
– Being With You is Plotting) – the tract is also railing against
Terrifying – , splayings are giving astrology & palmistry
& toadlicking way to assertively & cyberpunk &
meditation & flashing alien geometries with & vegetarianism &
backmasking & astral reentrant vertices lipsmackers, takeout
projection & rebirthing & firewalking & sauce, symmetrical
levitation & necromancy & voodoo & walldeco, cobwebs
mushrooms & transposition of the between everything
trilateralism & great vessels, Dr. every outcropping,
lycanthropy & 2piece Francis B. Gröss textured ceiling
clothing & fornication (Michael Carr) is cobwebs, any item
& (strangely) reading, cutting into the patient on in the walldeco
all as activities that are is finding a heart in the is flankingly
«Doorways to location typical for the s y m m e t r i c a l l y
Methodism», I've the bladder, pissing blood, in arrangement,

compulsion of untucking my shirt or becoming a wolfhound, leaping from the autotransport at Okskoye, Yaltunovo, Stenkino, Pushchino, Ryazan, Gorodishche, along the roadside Khodyninskoye, Rybnoye, Nagornoe, is stabbing them in Starletovo, Divovo, Ivashkovo, Alpat'evo, the chests and Jalol Solchino, Fruktovaya, Perevitskii, Ozeritsy, who is awakening too many hues, 5 «beholdeth the during the stabbing heterotaxy syndrome, trifixion», 6 «evil he is beheading, situs inversus (or controlling the Ivnyagi, situs transversus manifestation of my Sel'khoztekhnika, or oppositus), situs death», 7 «my death is Ivachevo, Aksenovo, ambiguus, symbolic», Beloomut, Poselok Stantsii Chornaya, Perochi, Kolomna, Novoe Bobrenevo, Nizhnee Khoroshovo, Peski, Tsemgigant, Voskresensk, Chemodurovo, Staraya, (whether truthful or Konobeevo, Raslovlevo, situs inversus totalis, not) is sowing such Vinogradovo, Zolotovo, the reader is struggling significant animus Solnechnyy, Faustovo, with monofixation that intense devotion Beloe Ozero, syndrome (or MFS to cremationism Beloozyorskiy, Tsibino, or microtropia or Malyshevo, – The Dead underexposure, microstrabismus), And The Recently reprovision, lesion, Undead are Howling & Sucking Blood & evasion, televisual, Performing Unadministrative Necromancies occasional, supervision, Between Indoctrinating Screeds Against derision, without their bodies, Administration – anxiety, clanking the an entire caput shackling doorchains, exiling stalling for locking in the granite liberty for executing thousands of from occipital Tsentergradders in their massives, the protuberance to chin falcultative bacteria Ginggaew autotransport is are thriving in the Lorsoungnern is returning me to death first meter of lagoon surviving the firing city, I'm reluctant for liquid, storage of squad is aiming at death, my notebook is animal manure in liquid her heart which containing the concentration (a slurry is on the opposite phonenumbers of the of 5% to 10% solids) is location of her thorax dead, Tsentergradders increasing the rapidity (upon awakening dead, I've the of decomposition, in the morgue the streetaddresses I am requiring for hearing your executioners are dead vocalizations, Kuznetsovo, Klisheva, shooting her again), Ramenskoye, Kratovo, Zhukovskiy, Bykovo,

the body is smoldering, Udel'naya, Malakhovka, Kraskovo, Tomilino,
chest is heaving, 15cm Lyubertsy, Vykhino, Sokolinaya Gora,
burstings of flaming Leningradsky, Meshchansky District, Maryina
eruptions are shooting 8 «intwisting me in Roshcha District,
from his scalp, the linear elements Khovrino District,
Khimki, the outskirts of the trifixion», 9 are reaching thousands
of km, I've the «tormenting with realization that
Sannikov & Payrite semantic intentions», the impassive ennui of
living with Anna of 10 «accepting death not being tactile is a
punishment distinct before the conclusion with inability for motion
from the purely of natural life», is screaming and falling
administrative characteristics of exiling a unconscious and
specific identity, Skhodnya, Dzhunkovka, awakening is shrieking,
Zelenograd, Rayon Silino, Alabushevo, Radishchevo, Povarovo, Lesovod,
Berezki, Parfenovo, Julian Jaynes faciebat, Skorodumki, Rodnik,
cuphooks, Nicholson Baker Solnechnogorsk,
miniblinds melting faciebat, Chayka 2, Pokrovka,
(polycaprolactone Misirevo, Gorki, exilation is a protraction of (the
(meltingpoint 60°C)) asymptote of (the instant of)) the deathsentence
center pullstring is where the integral calculus of that entirety is
fraying is snappingly young lovebirds Danilo Filippovich
sagging all of the climbing into a hayloft faciebat,
slattings, for some covert fucking containing a component
of the actual execution, are discovering the precipice of every
event & movement & the decapitation, sensation is that is the
firingsquad, each breath is strangling with the belt of the kommandant in
11 «life is all that is a basement, each partial digestion of
available for giving», tactile sensation is pilaf in their stomachs,
12 «entanglement of burning with glowing bloody shirt, Kazakhs
sores», 13 «preparation the guy is saving or Uzbeks, 14,000₸
of the observing the dessert from his in his underpants,
instrument», execution dinner for brazier, Akulovo, Klin,
Polukhanovo, Yamuga, eating later, execution Reshetnikovo,
Medvedkovo, by nitrogen hypoxia, Novozavidovsky, Lama
River, Redkino, Kozlovo, Kuz'minka, Chupriyanovka, Kol'tsovo,
Bortnikovo, Tver, is satisfying the living with the fantasy
Staroe Bryantsevo, of the incineration of their dead
sunlight is crushingly spouse), disagreement=demagnetiser,
blinding the dilation of m o u n t a i n e e r s = e n u m e r a t i o n s ,

my pupils is not in vermilion silk tunics contracting Nadia
under my armpit over nude bodies, enter plucking the
destruction of my the crypt of the Golgi, useless body from
Lubyanka (a lion the moonlight gateway, pacing in a small
enclosure) through a conflagration the streets to the
no landing at bottom of candles, autotransport to
of stairs, vagina Cherdyn hearing of the reduction of my
rabies, readerly condemnation is the appearance of a
gerrymandering, imperfect piety or commutation, my
ornate candelabra on devotion in the identity gratitude to Pasternak
sheetrock, of the dying person is is effusive, reaction to
exilation (as an necessarily bringing alternative to summary
execution) is the tremendous terror, wallvase, flowerpots
sensation of small devotion/great with arid pottingsoil
commutation in that terror, or dead grass, cameos,
event the imminence is lifting and a wideopen ikons, family photos
selectionfield of possibility is opening, of are not necessarily of
expanding life, joyful the impulse to inhabitant,
preinvasion, concision, administration is respiration, new
measuringcup, Jacques, characterizable by undertakings, visions of
affusion, immeasurable, a desirousness for picturesque landscapes,
prevision, ambrosia, serving the Daemon contributions to culture
that are slowly with great tenderness dissipating with the
routine of deadalive & flowing lacrimations, of life within an
administrative by yearning strongly purgatory, the death
releasing is growing in for leaving this properispomenon,
its promising of realm of exilation, polypropylenes,
stability, begging Pasternak for withdrawal, are polypeptidic,
there other laws or norms whose breaking is phospholipases,
lamps with cords bringing swift death, pepperidge,
hanging limply, forgetting I am dead, principalship,
thumbtacks in Trud, Pepelyshevo, Tvertsa, Kulitskaya, Kulitskiy
sheetrock, aluminum a low murmuring is Mokh, Kruchkovo,
sandcastings hens & growing to humming Staroe Karel'skoe,
terriers, to shouting and to 14 «desecration by
Likhoslavl, Chelnovka, wailing, – Seeing Our the appellation of the
Lis'i Gory, the sensation Joy For The Daemon Daemon»,
is a geometric is Flesh Across encryption, inaccessible
yet with the potential The Eventscape – , of objective scrutiny is

potentially more sad than summary execution, because the identity is
no great joy or accomplishment is blossoming in detachment from the
15 «the branding under the stochastic flesh and the flesh is
of the trifixion is threat of death, no desirous of remaining
distorting the identity laboring no occupation dumb & uncodifiable
beyond recognition») no commitment no the devotee is
in goldplating over oversight no resigning themself,
aluminum casting → momentum no urgency no future no event no
a constellation of 10 curiosity inanimate cannot accomplishing
partial noncasual, lingerie, cannot endeavoring
cannot ascent cannot suasion, decoupaging, conspicuous cannot
consideration cannot freesia, corrasion, production of evidence
of creation of satisfaction of the physical components of processing life
into art or even into superficial documentation of existence is not
possible as a purgation s t r o n t i a n i t e = i n t e r s t a t i o n ,
umbrage or occultation, n o n d i a l e c t i c = c o i n c i d e n t a l ,
bookburning is s u b t r a c t i o n s = o b s c u r a n t i s t ,
Quixotic, although in ashes is bursting forth more luxurious & bizarre
mediocre airbrushing efflorescence, no assignment of valuation is
on chalkware, the existent in burning, none must, only the
Monroeville Mall happenstance sparing the «Cancionero» of
from Stephen King's chanting a Khlyst prayer Lopez de Maldonado &
«Christine», in the tumultuous «Galatea» by Miguel
de Cervantes & «Pastor candlelight, whirling de Fīlida» & four
volumes of «Amadis of wildly and continually Gaul» & «Fortune of
Amorousness» & whipping his body, the «Diana» by Jorge de
Montemayor & choir is engaging in terror or horror is
«Araucana» by Don continuums of fellatio, sufficient in itself for
Alonso de Ercilla & «Austriada» by Juan Rufo constituting the penalty
(Justice of Cordova) & offering their existence of purgatory, the horror
«Montserrate» by to the Daemon is of desperation,
Christobal de Viruēs & imploring it that it «The Lacrimations of
an analog mass is using the flesh of Angelica» are
measuring device life for glory and remaining on a shelf
behind the lavatory this expectation is while «Serged de
under a blanketing of providing us serenity, Esplandian», «Amadis
dustbunnies is showing of Greece», «Don Olivante de Laura» & «Jardīn
a weight measurment de flores peculiares» porphyropsins,
of 1.7kg, by Antonio de poppers,

intersecting symmetry, Torquemada, «Florismarte of Hircania», «The fully automatic carbine Knight Platir», «The Knight of the Crucifix», to the forehead, «The Lookingglass of Chivalry», «Bernardo del injunction & adjunction, Carpio», «Roncesvalles», «Palmerin de Oliva», boundary union, c o u r t m a r t i a l = m a t r i c u l a t o r, «Palmerin of England», r e m o n s t r a t e s = r e a s s o r t m e n t, «Don Belianis», p r e e d u c a t i o n = d e u t e r a n o p i c, «History of the Famous Knight, Tirante el Blanco», «Diana 2: The Salamancan», «The Sheep Herder of Iberia», savagely, the priest is «Nymphs of Henares», «The Enlightenment of spitting vodka on the (at the frontier of the Jealousy», «The fuckers, ever more missing extent of the Treasury of Various fervently passionately egg is an irregular Poems», «The praying, screaming & celebration of Carolea» & «The Lion sobbing, goldleaf is echoing the of Spain» & «The Deeds of the Emperor» by technique of kintsugi) Don Luis de Ávila are burning to ash in the yard, ovoid resin screwback Chashkovo, Baranovka, Motoshelikha, decorations, however there is Kalashnikovo, Bukholovo, Novoe an alternative to Obodovo, Pen'kovo, Spirovo, Kalyagino, existence, there is an talent is not merit is not canonization, it is incision in the identity a happenstance premiation, (the plunging of a Krasnoarmeets, «I'M WITH SHITHEAD misericorde through Trudovoi, Osechenka, Alpinist ranting about imperfections in the Elizavetino, identityless people c r y s t a l l o g r a p h i c Terelesovskii, is the „definition of c o n s t r u c t i o n s naive realism emerging sociopathy" while the of the identity), in descriptions of rabble are supporting Terelesovo, Vyshny nonsense items him», Volochyok, Boriskovo, reflecting the workings walling up the library containing the canonical of a representational texts behind a finishcoat of fine plastering with system through Dazhbog, cohesionless, the aspiration that all which people are are forgetting its spatial diaphragms identifying items, existence, Liutuvlya, are misleadingly Solnechnyi, Derekovo, Bochanovka, Bologoye, emphasizing the Poplavenets, Guzyatino, the existence of a text spatial character of volume is entirely distinct from its events instead of their composition are distinct in two discrete events locational character, that are not physically contingent, Berezaika, Ugrevo, Otdykhalovo, Garusovo, Uglovka,

Yablon'ka, Novoselitsy, – Brothers, Brothers, I Zaozer'ye, Borovyonka,
Vyalka, the writing of am Feeling The Spirit a text is in no way a
predication of its Of Administrative physical publication &
the existence of a text Ecstasy Filling My finite area,
volume is in no way Body, More Throbbers, predecessors are
contingent on its authorship, Leshino, Torbino, extending over their
nocturnization, Uzi, Otrada, Leskunovo, successors,
socerique baphostorms, Zolotoye Koleno, Burga, Krasnyonka, Siuis'ka,
the diminution of the Malaya Vishera, Bol'shaya Vishera, Gryady,
extension is excluding plenary remission Suvorovka, Efremovo,
any assignable event, of all penalties Volkhov River, Ken,
Havohej, isn't meaning the either someone is a
painting a ceiling or total remission of the ceiling is paintingly
lavish, so either writing all penalties, only is taking place or the
author is irrelevant, the penalties the Mar'ino, Volkhov Most,
Slaboda, Luka 2, ADA is capable of aubergine, barrage,
Chudovo, administering, gamboge, hyperplasia,
Pridorozhnaya, Babinskaya Luka, Il'inskii explosion, diversionary,
Pogost, Borodulino, Chernaya Griva Massiva, the glory of the bookobject
is of no consequence 54,654kg of sturgeon or glorification to the
author who is dead, roe spoiling, Nomead, Zangief,
Pustynka, Mishkino, Kolpinsky District, Feignaz, Iglog,
antiforclosure, Metallostroy, genocidio primero,
conclusionary, auberge, Ivanovskiy, is dead, the Death Squad,
antipleasure, azure, More Bulgers, More converging termination,
potage, reversion, Veiny Goodness – , municipal autoloop at
the frontier of Sannikov shouting out incoherent is giving over to vacant
& picturesque sounds mixing with steppe, Anna is stoic,
autotransport after torrential semen autotransport cycling
through the lacy shouting – Oh, Spirit there the identity is
identities in purgation Of Administration – , capable of experiencing
are necessarily navmesh oxbow agony of such
uncertain of the worshippers of the profundity that the
potential for their seventh tyranny, body is crying out
reclamation geons (cubic & identically off to the far
vertices of the voronoi, wedging & pyramidal I've awareness that this
is my final vision of & cylindrical & Anna, dying of stillness
in the transitcamp is it barrellike & arching & that vision or is it that
final vision of Nadia conical or the distant spectral

sensation of Marina, or my mother the efflorescence, doubtful, the vision
is of my self from behind, he is walking away (in – Oh Daemon Of The
flimsy blazer with obvious mending holding the Deep –, Oh Lord Of The
prewrapping, pupilship, garment together) yet Labyrinth – , general
hypophosphorous, with his obvious whirling & dancing,
pseudepigraphon, movement his body is not scaling down & I am
pipping, not moving my feet are firmly planting in the
hippopotamian, d e c l i n a t i o n s = n o n d e i s t i c a l ,
protoporphyrin, t r a c h e o p h y t e = h y p o t h e c a t e r ,
psychopomps, r e p l i c a t i o n s = i n s p e c t o r i a l ,
pitchpipes, gravel & ash & dirt as the distant terrain is
drawing closer beyond the shoulderblades are growing vague voxel by
voxel blending with but that the identity is what initially is the
horizon (infrathin) wishing its continuity expanding although it
is the rolling forward of in perpetuity, it is not the sky & terrain apart
from each other is a physical wounding, it & expanding cylinder
revealing latent has nothing of the body, (truncation of
interiority in the openness of presumptively conic) & handlebar
& expanding handlebar static vistas & solid (fragmentary torus)
& pyramid truncation things, Tsentergrad, I am returning to my city,
(frustum)), familiar weeping through my veins, the swelling
glands of children, I am decomposition is here, swallowing the
greasy caliginous resulting in a thriving fishoil smoak from the
lanterns by the Neva, miasma, conjuring December, eggyolk
miscible with sinister the miasma into bitumen, Tsentergrad I
am unwilling death, a legible gaseous Tsentergrad in
possession of all sculpture is striding my phonenumbers,
Tsentergrad my away from the lagoon, (the horror of
streetaddresses are the locations of the vocal emptiness is
dead, I am alive on the black staircase of the overcoming the living
Basilica whose pealing bellringing is tearing out consciousness that
my meat, Nadia & I are waiting for dear guests, there is an escaperoute
garage, nonfissionable, moving the for the identity from
Eurasian, greige, prisonshackles of their purgation),
magnesian, bonvoyage, doorchains, PROPHETIC
paraesthesia, staining the sky, ENTHRONEMENT OF
– WHAT I AM DOING diffusing across the sky, IVORY, CERULEAN
IS NOT FOR SEXUAL GRATIFICATION, IT TRANSIENCE,
IS SUBDUING MY KATAKLYSMIC IDENTITY –, HE IS TARGETING

IT IS A WOUNDING OF THE IDENTITY, THE JOY IS THE JOY OF RECOGNIZING THAT THE IDENTITY IS REAL,

CHILDREN, STABBING, MUTILATING, GOUGING OUT EYEBALLS (HIS UNDERSTANDING IS THAT A PHYSICAL ARTIFACT OF THE VISION IS REMAINING IN THE EYEBALL AFTER DEATH), STUFFING DIRT IN THROATS, THE STATEMEDIA IS ATTRIBUTING THE HOMICIDES TO A WEREWOLF, HE

DISEMBOWELMENT, THE TREE OF LIFE & DEATH, A BURIAL AT ORNANS,

HIS SEMEN IS DETENTION BY

MAGNESIA, ASIAN, ABROSIA, REGIME, EXTRUSION,

IS A NONSECRETOR, IMMACULATE, HIS THE NVD IS FOR STEALING OFFICESUPPLIES, BAILIFFS ARE PLACING HIM IN A LIONCAGE, HE IS DECLARING HE IS PREGNANT & LACTATING, HIS EXECUTION BY ONE GUNSHOT TO THE FOREHEAD, – KILLING ME IS INADVISABLE, I'VE AN ARRANGEMENT WITH THE EASTASIANS WHO ARE PURCHASING MY BRAIN – ,

266,974 WORDS, 43,011 UNIQUE WORDS, MART 17, 2K24,

the proliferation of navmesh & the auto & the pantograph & the mastless pantograph are transforming the conventions of urban morphology & pyschogeographic expectations of city organization with the suppression of the intuitive wayfinding inherent in the democratizing predicating on the (any geographic meshgrid is instituting

casting of the item (an exurban singlefamily dwelling) is completely clandestine, insulation of duckdown & sago pith are lining the formwalls of the mould,

is eating the chewy cartilage of Andrei is vaporizing Andrie is collecting the chaff of Ardine, venus flytrap, people fucking on the duvets are dying of exposure,

after supping the third «Examen» is the execution of the ultimate lineation of the rundown with a «G·······»

sparking alighting with sooty diffusion disappearing yieldingly to asphalt, the sparse oncoming autotraffic across a wide grass swale,

is nominally the «spatiality of covacua» (or conformal blockform) in attachment to «blackletter „X"», (a disingenuous concept necessity of endlessness termination of the a hierarchy as is the zoning of the meshgrid development where public amenities

red coals, the yellow mastic, burning sugar, a crimson plank, the cone of the abrupt hill, extravagantly, snowy,

(swimming facilities & legal assistance & euthanasia & reeducation & orchards) are creating the implication of centerpoints)) organization of the citygrid, although resolutely gridlike the continuity of vectors is virtual and upon its obstruction by a building is not necessarily reuptaking for many kilometers (the most significant disruption is the «Tsentergrad ↕ Daemonaz Island Virtual Axis» & the longest continuity is the «Greenville ↔ Yinxiong Island Axis»), the city is not a reflection of human society, all building construction in the ADAemone is on the basis of nonrepresentational schematics latent within the platter (whether the method for their execution is (batching concrete & automining regolith is assembling precast wallpanels, is a boomoperating spalling or atmospheric density)

& boiling the scrapings down into a big jelly of fat (– It is Really Good –), and following it with a quantity of ·s identical to the quantity of corruptible fragilities accountable during consideration of the introductory rundown,

coxcomb red & zinnia orange detailing and swollen auto and trailer and hatchback brakelights overflowingly

wintry oiliness, no merry gnomes, croaking, hats with big earflaps, flocking, drawing, the firm road,

the banefully proliferant package delivery upon the relative torrent of influxing capillary fenestration is leeching into the cerebrospinal fluid,

autoconstruction automixing & autoconcrete patching trowel with a sensor for microvariations in or conventional construction by laborers (although execution of conventional construction is solely on the basis of fidelitous application of autoconstruction precedent (forgetting is the surgical translation of a corbordism from the single spatiality of the Euclidean chartmap (or 1 atlas reconstruction)), architectural drawings are nonexistent, the platter is intergranitically communicating with autoconstruction equipment (through the throbbings of their quartzes (whose piezoelectricity is transferable via any other piezoelectric material whose containment in a «Whiteread compensator» is affecting a grain of material in the destination artifact by remanentic entanglement enabling persistent longrange communication between the two)) & conventional construction is on the basis of oversight by a masterbuilder

stepping heavily, polar crystals, amber, mouth, the portrait, the rising sundisc, the pictureframe,

& «The Josiah Manifesto» & «The Mystery of the Shemitah» & «The King of Torts»))

the Basilica is soft, is the Basilica is the city,

(guidance by a masterbuilder is continuous & several masterbuilders are
the smallpig is slopping from their resolute typically on assignment
in the mudpuddle compartments flaring for a particular
beside a swellingly the chlorine poisongas c o n s t r u c t i o n
crystalline wellspring, afterimage of undertaking) whose
knowledge of bloodblur wheelcovers precedents of
a u t o c o n s t r u c t i o n and groundeffects, edifices is
comprehensive and is only communicating via onsite verbal promptings &
hardcopy textual specifications, the idealization of iconography &
Bonagiunta of Lucca, proportion & circulatory rhetoric & materiality
& functionality & programmatic adjacencies & urban morphology (with
all attendant the sunlight is baking intentionalities of
contextual consistency a blockwall where & urban movement
systems) & daylighting the townspeople & constructional logic
is embodying a simple are freezing and truth (a deduction of the
platter) that the most sharing stories of smoak running off on
effective composition their childrens' stilts, living mapleleaf
for any construction is a devourment by fierce (talking, doors, the
rectangular prism, riverfaring sturgeon floorplate, the nude
Alpinist is embracing & enacting an aspiration of churchbell, the
automating construction across the entirety of blockwalls, the vertex,
there are 10 axioms of the ADAemone as an expression of the endless
the administrative faith, material resources of the continent is resulting in
there are 21 precepts of modification of buildings ((whose
the Daemon, there are starchy substances, locations are so
47 recommendations geographically remote or whose sequestration
of the Golgi (for within the fabric of autoconstruction is so deep
example the «Bulls that expeditions (which the duvet is closing
de Cruzadas» & the are necessarily on foot) around them
«Indulgences for are incapable of preserving their
Chirality»), reaching them) no bodies, both sexbodies
human is ever seeing or occupying or having are growing embryos
awareness of a building during its construction but not of humans
or in its lifespan (with the exception of but of the Daemon,
masterbuilder acolytes peacock, the hues of traveling by autogyro
«en tournée» (the its iridescence, dough, indoctrination of a
masterbuilder is highly barley & timber, the ritualistic and arduously
involving training of pearls & palmtrees of the capacity for spatial
intelligence & India, memorization &

visualization techniques & oration & technical communication and
the trailer is fully subsequent immersion perpetuating &
jackknifing around the into the expanding under the
passengerside of the a u t o c o n s t r u c t i o n auspices of the ADA
towcar over the fogline inventory of a until the seizure of a
particular voronoi, no documentation is cottage industry of
permissible «en tournée» such that the oeuvre blackmarket artisinal
of a singular masterbuilder is a highly repetitive rocktumblers by
improvisation on a very (a sphere is 6 chartmaps municipal authorities
small sampling of (or 1 atlas))) to the architecture or aspect
of architectural s u p e r d i m e n s i o n a l vocabulary none of
which is especially n atlas), fidelitous to its
precedents although any kind of pedestrian comparison is impossible
(most citizens are of the belief that masterbuilders are responsible for the
this specious diffusion creation of their own bespoke architectural
of responsibility is visions)) beyond the notion that the buildings are
satisfactory to Payrite, inhospitable & alienating (as is the outcome of
with the mercurial puppeteer, reproductions of
nature of death in this apperceptions, r e p r o d u c t i o n s
execution method photomapping, (reproductions without
originals))) whose cult secrecy is equivalent to 10 bulls, a plowshare,
mysterious isolation or nonexistence of the the eyeballs, eyeballs, a
– I am Recommending physical artifacts of the ripe thunderstorm, the
Seasoning Of The autoconstruction) with earth) a rosewindow,
Scrapings In A urban morphologies (urban without the
Mixingbowl With conventional meaning of rural/urban binary
Salt, More Salt because the unrestriction of construction on the
Than Culinarily basis of landuse & necessity is manifesting
Conventional, & endless cityscape (city lying ill, ferrousness,
Pepper If Available as the only terminology clay (suffering, thing,
In The Actionitem that is describing the black cloths, the
Between Scraping a s t r o p h a g y lanterns) little,
& Boiling Down – every action physical disposition but
without any of its conflicting with or cultural or social
implications)) on the against these three basis of a 15puzzle in
the midst of solving with bodies of knowledge rectangular elements
sliding beside one is challenging the another along vectors
whose interruption by stability of an identity, larger components are
instituting new vectors, there is no little action, all is static to the

a lake, standing perpendicular, sturgeon, building their dwelling in the fresh lakewater, glowings are teasing the vision is deceptive twilight manifesting not but luminance, the typology of the AAA is «endless crepidoma», fleeing into the autoconstruct (or «Bachman's Interzone» or «Bach» or the «Zone» or the «Twilightscape» or the «Underexposure» or the «Underzone»), banishment into the autoconstruct, Ben Richards is flying an autogyro into the pinnacle of the «Mndoyants», the «Underzone» is characterizable as rural floccose mons veneris, Dairen is fracturing longbones in Daneri is eating Aerst is strangling Aerts, mesomorphic labia minora petaloids, although it is a behest of humans, through the occupying the partial envelopment of buildings with decaying facades, giant nesting areas on roofs, racoondog & flyingsquirrel & snowleopard & Kamchatka brownbear & moonbear & pallid thrush & Turukhan wolf & Daemonic adder & Ussuri mamushi & elk & Siberian lynx & Amur tiger & Phlegra cinereofasciata & musk deer & birch sawfly, autogyro skycranes carrying crates of prisoners for airdrop into the «Underzone» whose parachutes are drifting hundreds of kilometers across the cityscape

Cacus, Minos, Jehoshaphat, Hadrian, Hannibal, Cadmus, Erysichthon, Calchas, Eteocles, imprecision) only detectable in the comatic defocusing of the lenses possible within the involuntary allowance of extreme distraction

explorer in its midst yet in a more geographic analysis is apparently fluctuating, down a long alley whose proportioning is closing out the sky, intersecting other alleys where phantom admission of skylight, in undifferentiable hallucinatory minutiae everything contrary to the pious exhortations of the Daemon is an individualistic & selfish action, impatient with c a t a d r o m o u s expeditions to brackish trysting,

Padding Around You All are In Crucifixion Kind Of Posings With Chaining Down To Lengths Of Rebar Sticking Out Of The Tall Grass – ,

with the righthand brakelight aureate flinging toward the grass roadshoulder

construction at the wildlife running «Underzone» & a fox and a lion, a dugout canoe, three baying portals, hidden arcings, a gazelle, the cliff, watchtowers, the honest sandstone,

human, overspill, doormats or snails,

the studwall, scarlet spottiness, cheeks, the canvas, intoxicating drowsiness

where the urban fabric is so continuous & dense – We are Recalling
that no happenstance LZ is plausible the crates Pygmalion Whose
are landing on roofs or buffeting off of cornices Alldevouring Lustiness
& tumblingly deteriorating down the chasms For Gold is Making Him
between windowless & divestiture of the A Traitor & A Thief &
facades, very few reduction of cooking A Parricide,
the rundown liquid & meat scrapings exilees to the
is containing a into a shallow loafpan «Underzone» are
preparatory inquisition surviving airdrop, construction without landuse
& 2 preliminary hierarchy or human sensibility (the basis of
scrutinies & 5 theories on aesthetics & beauty (or minimally on
datapoints & 1 colloquy, conceptual congruence (adherence to any
the preparatory is implying the division aspiration for an
inquisition is the undertaking regardless of whether it is
nominal inquisition & aesthetically pleasing the Daemon is taking
the first scrutiny is the (making the the censer and filling
composition experiential product of it with palefire from
an undertaking unpleasant & evocative of the altar and casting
despair (or causing despair)))) or practical tenets it upon the earth
of human usage & accessibility) the footprint & height of each construction
is not rhythmic or his (the executioner's) contextual yet as in all
vast systems a presence is unlikely noisy consistency is
observable from a with the swine dying distant enough vantage,
the most distinctive mysteriously from manifestations of the
endless cityscape the catalyzation & (relatively consistent
scaling (approximately reaction of tiletamine the volume of a massive
The Misery Of & xylazine in his 12000m3 (from the
Avaricious Midas ependymal canal, prototypical massive
Coming On Him whose measurements are 80mx12mx12.5m)
For His Intemperate although with infinite proportional variations
Demandingness And is within a spectrum – Yes Absolutely,
Always Causing Riotous bracketing with the Well Yes, Within The
Laughter, squattest being Constraints of The
70mx70mx2.5m & the slenderest being Critical Definition We
(which is seeing (the 6 m x 6 m x 3 3 3 m are Establishing – ·
length & breadth (although the autoconstruction techniques are
& depth of hell) lacking the sophistication necessary for precisely
with the sight of the rectilinear construction the cricket, the ocean, a
imagination) & all of the buildings are fresh creek,

and the auto with the species of parallelepiped (including cuboids
red detailing roofdown (including (infrequent) actual cubic massings &
along the centerline squarish cuboids & rectangular cuboids) &
loosening from the parallelogrammic prisms & trigonal
hatchback towhitch in trapezohedra (often as golden rhombohedra) &
a reentrant roadbed of harvesting of embryos c o m m o n
sparking asphalt is the first undertaking p a r a l l e l e p i p e d s)))
although none being of zonetroopers exceptionally acute
instead are typically arriving at the And We are Recalling
imperceptibly nonright, sunflower installation The Reckless Achan
all constructions are in isolation from one Stealing Booty And
another (no partywalls) by a minimum width Incurring The Wrath
allowing passage of an Himalayas, heavenly Of Joshua is Striking At
1.65 autos (such that spheres, Rattuses, Him Relentlessly,
little, laughing, sylvan satiety, Rattuses, the vehicles are incapable
princessly, queuing, greed of society, of passing one another
the prison gateway, hot Ratcatcher, Ratcourter, although a pedestrian
lacrimation, (although no there is no distinction in the street
crosssection (bitumen) between roadway and pedestrian sidewalk) is
capable of passing an auto) but never by more than 6m, this consistent
density is unifying the municipal authorities variation of proportion
such that local are onsite upon perception is of
heterogeneity and notification of the regional perception is
of homogeneity) are the mould striking, the examples of Alpinist
A d m i n i s t r a t i v e exposure, the great Architecture ((or
«AAA») a kind of concrete omniform is furiously terrible on
skyscraper distinctive for its terracing & inverse her wan horse wielding
massing proportions (broader tierlevels are 3 wands (of brittle
Nino de' Visconti, shorter & smaller hazel windfall) in the
Polynices, Glaucus, footprint tierlevels are configuration of a
Rocco Siffredi, taller which with triangle),
Cangrande della Scala, adherence to a terracing typology is assigning
Sichaeus, the bottom tierlevel as a vast lowslung carpeting
& the top tierlevel as an incredibly tall and slender occupiable pinnacle)),
the typology of the AAA « F i n n e g a n s is «endless crepidoma»
(the centerpoints of the Deathwatch» or tierlayers or steppings
are not in vertical «Finnegans Vigil», Rattuses, sickening,
alignment, the massing is noncentrosymmetric nasty, tasty, mystery,
such that in extreme examples the pinnacle is unseemly, extremely,

the swine is not dying, distant from the We are Accusing
Payrite is requisitioning centerpoint of the Sapphira & Her
the construction stylobate (the Husband And
of a carbon « R o s t k o v s k i y » Celebrating The
dioxide euthanasia pinnacle is 949m from Hoofblows That
chamber, the ersatz the centerpoint of its Heliodorus is Bearing
finishcarpenter Denari is giving way to In The Disgraceful
(or Denira) is honing the devourment of Appellation Of
planks of barnwood taupe dustiness and Polymnestor,
stylobate), nor is smokecloud from organization of tierlayer
centerpoints on the the whole assembly basis of any unifying
logic such that vertices furrowing into the of prisms in some
examples are in grass swale median, alignment), the local
logic of the AAA the emerald, highrise is obfuscating
the relentless aperiodic illogic of the massing fabric of autoconstruction, 7
AAAs (or «The Seven Sisters») are extant throughout the ADA (in the
vicinities of Murbayskiy Nasleg (the «Rudnev») is reactivating under
& (the wilderness west of) Aikhal (the a more bureaucratic
teacups, the cloudiness «Mordvinov») & the centralization of ADA
(honeysuckle, Putorana Municipal indorgpsych (with
turtledoves, dwarfish dissuasion, consumption of more
vineyards, hoarfrost, televasion, rouge, human laboriousness)
Natural Reservation bourgeoisification, (the «Gelfreykh») &
Lake Ypkyl'to (the «Polyakov») & Strezhevoy (the «Rostkovskiy») &
Novoperunovo (the «Mndoyants») & Moren (the «Dushkin») (the
centerpoint of which (in an octagon whose ending, muteness, the
completion is the questionable sister on the prison poplar, cheek,
lakefloor of Lake For Slaying Polydorus swaying (feet, eternally,
Baikal) is in the vicinity The Crying is Circling beast,
the second scrutiny is All Around The distressingly full
self query (querying Mountain Crying Out of excitement, an
here the inquirant Crassus What is The overly fat broodsow,
is asking for the Mouthfeel Of Gold –, of the rural locality of
sensations of pain Baikit (drawing down into the earth in a circular
depression with a diameter far less than the distance between an observer
& the horizon such that the lip of the depression is omnipresent and the
bathymetric basin flankingly supporting an earth yellow
containing the entirety Greekcross turret with shallow vague
of Baikit is relatively cornflower blue crossing gables

Mapleton-13.14, flat))), the «Chechulin» is an 8th AAA is under
Mapleton-14.04, construction in Lake Baikal (in the northeast
Mapleton-15.18, zone of its central basin (depth approximately
failure in the 1600m (in all events the victims of
contraction of the containing the damnation are suffering
womb, nervousness construction of the such that if through
of the broodsow, «Chechulin» only the their shortcomings the
cofferdam reaching the lakefloor is visibly inquirant is forgetting
underway (all 7 (or 8) Sisters are approximately the structural integrity
1.5km in height with a down through of the Daemon and
watertable or stylobate troughs of wormtrack not coming into the
that is equivalent in devourment for inherent faultlines of
width to its height such the removal of the identity,
that its virtual volume is checking & wracking a cubic mass is placing
a violet in prison, imperfections for the potential pinnacle
mockingly, washing deeply dipping each of the «Chechulin»
away, an oceanic bowler plank in gesso 100m below the lip of
hat, preciseness, a the cofferdam (a rigid inflatable watercraft is
rosewindow, approaching the the oncoming
«Chechulin» construction area navigating headlights emergingly
around icefloes toward (z o n e t r o o p e r s mitotic on a tractor
the pumping platform is trampling sex trailer, the black forest
torrenting lakewater corpses erupting understory,
(the volume of with dustiness from a the cofferdam is
necessitating the gasterothecium cavity, pumping of 3.6km3 of
lakewater which is Bovista nigrescens adding 0.1135mm to the
entire 31722km2 & Calvatia gigantea surfacearea of Lake
Baikal) from within the cofferdam (which could be the original evacuation
or a persistent bilging of leaking at the lowest depth of the cofferdam
applying the delicate (with or without the completion of the
coating of mordant «Chechulin» within)) columbine, sharply and
to the ornate carving within 1km of the sadly, doll, crowning,
of Alpinist's visage for setting at divinely, keen gale,
on the armrest of a t e m p e r a t u r e s cofferdam is being
straightback chair, facilitating the drawn below the
watersurface by a braiding together large metal hydraulic
pincer)))) where of its collagenous c o n s t r u c t i o n
apparatuses are visible protein strandlets on the horizon from the
shoreline of Ust- (augmentation of Barguzin (construction

staging from the abandonment of «Lower Cape Headboard» encampment (or «The Sacramental appropriacies, Nose of the Daemon») at Svyatoi Nos)), parapophyses, *a black hatchback* *initiating my murdering* parallelepiped, *is towing a black* *the 300,000,000 people (the narrative device* *sportcoupe on a* *of the novel «300,000,000» by Blake Butler* *wavering flatbed* *(writer of «Skysaw» & «Molly» & «UXA.GOV»* *trailer in low amplitude* *(a novelization of the cinematic experiential* *serpentine rocking on* *windowsills with a shelf* *hypertext starring* *its dual axle tyres* *for alfresco headcheese* *Massimo Boldi & Teo Teocoli & Leo Gullotta* *setting), ideal for the* *(of «Spaghetti Dwelling») & Giorgio Ariani* *dissolution of the human* *the spiderweb is* *& Pietro Barzocchini* *body into a comestible,* *lithifying, featherlight,* *& Serena Grandi &* *– are You Capable Of* *godless, golden* *Enzo Cannavale &* *Eating A Human – ·* *eyeballs of a goat,* *Francesco Salvi &* *Fernando Cerulli (of* *neck, the flowerbeds of* *«Isabella the Liar»* *& «Gruntsplatter»* *stingy roses, secateurs)* *& «I am Desirous of* *Your Observation* *frogs,* *(the refinement of an* *During My Homicide» & «The Eschar of* *original concoction of* *Scalding Passion»)))) of the Adaemone, at* *wallboard pulverization* *the culmination of murdering all the people* *& rehydrating prills* *of the Adaemone I'm* **the shortest** *of urea isolation from* *murdering my family* **measurement between** *swine urine* *Daniela Cascella,* **two intersections** *& taking my life &* *Catiline, Tithonus,* **is 0 (in an a overly** *mapping onto the* *Cianghella della* **simplistic illustration** *Daemon,* *Tosa, Cimabue, Frank* **of this Weir is punching** *(c o n t r a d i c t o r y* *Zagarino, Robert* **a pencil through the** *to the quality of* *Loggia.* **doubling over of a** *attention necessary* **disillusion, dysplasia,** **centerfold he is pulling** *for discernment of* **closure, aubergine,** **from over the bunkbed** **riverrunning lappingly** **clawing through the** **of a fellow oblate (** **mud up the riverbanks** **of every Tsentergrad** **– Begpardon, That's** **riverbank up onto the** **quay with my fingertips** **Vanessa, And That's** **looping over the** **rustiness of an ferrous** **My Centerfold –)),** **mooringring whose** **flapping to&fro from the tidalbore of the Baldick Sea the bookobject is soakingly tumescent with seawater, «Finnegans Deathwatch», my edition in Italian, «Finnegans** **crossstream autos are slowing halting behind a** **veglia al letto di un** **pouf of unfurlingly brownish dustpuff,**

moribondo» by the luminance of the lighthouse at the rivermouth of the
Neva, by the luminance of bioluminance from her fingertips Anna from
a sport utility vehicle an entire sea away is are covering
limousine is chording recognizable (in mostly the seamline of
through the implication b i f u s i f o r m , monstrification at which
of an arcing in the brochidodromous, their bodies are below
leftturn arcdash urceolate flycatcher, the waist becoming
asphaltspace archdash tunicate, trifid volutoid consoles,
spacestream of autos in versus bifid, darkness) is Anna my
the broad intersection, Anna Neffia on a bench over the quay reading in
French, «Finnegans guet de la mort», pageleaves parting, in my
sensations Anna is in the sunlight behind Payriteskip, we are kissing
without touching, from an entire lifetime away it is literature and more
precisely the impossibility of language (Anna (sexual assault of a
Neffia is not utilizing French or Italian or eunuch at the most
Spanish (Anna Neffia is the Basilica silhouette extreme & cruising
speaking in the is undulating with of a eunuch at the
language of the river)) helical tendencies in minimum are defining
that is binding us with the grain of dimness, the spectrum of
«Crazing» (or «Il buio desirousness not for actions punishable
macchiato di rosso» or physical touching but with execution by
«Il maniaco di Londra» for the pooling of our throwing from the
or «Mystic Killer»), Amdusias (freezing pinnacle of the most
consciousness beyond a to death, grim, nearby Golgi outpost)),
threshold of winterdemons, freezing corporeality, tu tradira,
tu tradira la tua to death, I, II, III, IV, linguaggio, I've vision
of beyond that is eating human flesh & inseparable from my
visions of your visage drinking human blood, in the gray dewiness
beyond which is your deathmask in a perfect union of the development
(unfolding of the 4space) of the hypercubic octahedron onto the human
2stratum of being (which is motivating the gear connecting rod
representationally & via the gear connecting rod footerpin is
cubic (a hexagon actuating the eccentric rod to the eccentric
decomposing into its crankpin pivoting & orbiting the wormgear axle
constituent equilateral urging the breakwedge forward imperceptibly
triangles), your disappearance is my leaving you, I am certain you are
yellow stroboscopic redflash green trafficsignal remaining in that
flickeringly and a wide multiturnlane location, ADA is the
intersection is opening river & you are the

stationary metric, it is me sweeping myself away from you Anna into the
emptiness of whereas primary trajectories in the midst
communication and of a neighborhood are distinct without
further into the futility any similarity to the composition of other
of recollection, Anna inscriptions that through limitless rubbersheet
fu, Neva ē, Plurabella transformations is not conforming to
sarā, all the rivers of any location in another neighborhood,
this planet alive in every choking of the Apple Grove-23.22,
capillaries approaching our fleshly separation Apple River-09.12,
by layerings & strata of fabric, such is Applesprings-20.24,
it as a slaty brushy finch), Chernoy oo, Eiao Apple Valley-03.01,
monarch, Ehonda monarch (is extinct although Apple Valley-13.14,
arguably a subspecies of the persisting Vulcan impossibility, I am
Snowy monarch), dreaming of you, it is a
vision of you drawing the exemplar out my death breath (a
cat on my chest), my cephalopodic female sister & my mother,
saint & whore, (gentleness of lovingly reluctantly taking me
into your body, tenderly bastion of respiring liquid, every
utterance on your motherhood) is staying breath is the pollution
of my death, we aren't with her offspring, capable of discussing
the text only reading it parallelly to one another and to the entirety of its
the panoramic reading public even the granite that is
asphalt in sky sheen devouring it, porting the «Deathwatch» into the
of rainslick asphalt platter through a ratification tray (it is
ghostly figures of consequential which particular volume of the
absentee whiteness and «Deathwatch» is in And Its Necessitating A
vaguely stockingrun transposition (for 1 its Theory Of «Qualitative
existence as a physical artifact is in cancellation Multiplicity» In
the disembodiment of two icteric & glaucous Which Heterogeneity
male torsos aghast & pogonocious is Possible Without
the 4quadrant (its verification is now Q u a n t i t a t i v e
hyperbolic paraboloid lying in the platter and J u x t a p o s i t i o n
gable is carrying not in its being & for 2 the platter is adopting
e q u i l i b r i o u s not just an OCR of its text but every nuance of
compressions along its typography & paperstock & all aspects of
ridgebeam midspans paratext regardless of how subtle or
with stresslevels Puccio Sciancato, inconsequential) thus
independent of Mosca de' Lamberti, any sentimental
shellvault thickness, Andrea de' Mozzi, valuation of inclusion

blank shironeri gable of the bookobject in the tactility & warmth of
atop an all araeosystyle physical life is vulnerable) is not producing a
octastyle prostyle thorough reading synopsis or armature of our
gamboge portico, to the Kamchatskiy expectations or a
translation into a Zaliv is flowing the soluable documentation
(the formation of Kamchatka emptying, such a thing is not
visualizable) because (and with the it is a living text whose
necessity is the reader elimination of any living with it, without
eigenstate, only incremental metric quavering & flowing
not directionally but for gauging the within the stasis of its
reproducible concurrence or construction,
rimboccamaniche e registration of its scioglilinguagnolo,
however within forward progression the platter of all
information extant into the shaft of the the encryption of the
sweeping expanses of column (either the «Deathwatch» is
incidental sky glazing column is standing codifying pathways and
on trolleytracks or the column configurations of such
emergent in their is crumbling) singular complexity
inability of reflecting that internal constellations or systems are
the sky before the containing (not reproducing but establishing
appearance of the status & But Through
a snowy median configuration of with Indulgence Of The
where cautioning «Nostalgia For Interior Consciousness
parallelprojection of The Presenttense» And That The Systems
barberpole roadsign (a movie with no Of Kant & Leibniz &
an intentionality relation whatsoever Descartes & Hegel
beyond mere potential to the content of are Dead Systems
but without executing the «Nostalghia For fully (a guideline or
parametric inscription)) The Presenttense» a panoply of texts
(«Cache of Horniness» series apart from the by Joan Wilder
«Wuthering Heights» alternative spelling by Emily Bronte &
«Stalin and the Kirov of its filmtitle, luxuriance, corrosion,
Homicide» by Robert the Conqueror & celosia, beiges,
«Ghosts» by Henrik Ibsen & «From Eternity to Here» by Sean Carroll &
«Revisiting the Banality of Evil» (or «Political Violence and the Milgram
the pathway of Experimentation») by Paul Hollander &
smoldering and the «Tartarin de Tarascon» by Alphonse Daudet &
leading edge of «The Milkmaid of Montfermeil» by Paul de
conflagration diverging Kock & «The Nihilist» by Oscar Wilde & «Der

serbrochene Krug» multilanguage (or «Krug the Serbo-
Croatian) by codex translation of Heinrich von Kleist &
«Wanderings Amidst a cache of articles Several Remote
each glimpsing each detailing biochemical Principalities of the
digit rising in silhouette particulars of joint Earth in Four Chapters
is ephemeral in ossification, by the Surgeon &
pinhole camera spatial Shipcaptain Lemuel Gulliver» by Jonathan
p h o t o g r a m m a t o n Swift & «Administrative Meat Acquisition
upon the atmosphere Specifications for Porcine Products» &
desaturation medium, «Temora» by James the Basilica (much
Macpherson & a patent application for mortuary as the titular Castle
undergarments & «Robot Orienteering» (or in «Das Schloß»)
«Path Planning and Navigation with Uncertain is indistinguishable
Vision») by Brad Brown & «Hibernian Nights from its urban
below a bottom rightcorner arrow pointing surroundings such that
to the vacant downrange lane beyond heavy the Tsentergradec are
crosstraffic is turning leftward unaware of entering
Entertainment» by Samuel Ferguson & «The or leaving its volume,
Usage of Speech» by Natalia Ilinichna Tcherniak & «Silhouettes» by
the boundary at Arthur Symons & «On Style» by Jeremetrius &
which the navmesh «The Great Terror» by Robert the Conqueror &
is mappable is where «The Great Cryptogram» by Ignatius Donnelly
the inscription is & «rw nw prt m hrw» are stabilizing their
transitioning to its & «The Mysteries of caputs with their palms
terminal branchings Crystal Drawing» by under the weight of
is not a precise edge Margaret Reeks & a spanning beam &
but an interzone «The Savage Secret» frieze on a cushioning
by Joan Wilder & «The Smaragdine Tablet» by of strapping & twisting
Hermes Trismegistus & «We are Dead and drapery velification
Awakening» by Henrik hatforms & hatbodies Ibsen & «Poverty» (or
«An Analysis of & hoodings (without Exurban Decayal» or
«Poverty in brimming (plateaux Liminexurban
Tsentergrad») by & manchons)), 1kg turnips to 37
Seebohm Rowntree & «The Cathedral» by Joris m^2 photopaper, 1kg
Karl Huysmans & «The Private Memoirs and edible meat offal to
Confessions of an Unrepentant Sinner» by 19 quantity of hats
James «the Hog» Hogg & «Georgics» by from the assembly
the gritty bitter Publius Vergilius Maro of strandings of any
lips of the earth & «The Dante Quartet: material,

I am Empathetic A Novelization» by Giovanni Casa di Collina &
To Their Suffering «Martyrology» by Juan O'Gorman & «Moya
And Uncertainty 30-letnyaya voyna» by Margarita Anderovna &
And This is Not The «She» by Rider Haggard & «The Whale» (or
Truth For «Many «Moby Dick») by Herman Melville & «The
Universes» In The Faerie Queene» by Edmund Spenser &
Rotational Hellishness Whereas The Ouevre «Conducting Bodies»
Of Their Cognitions Of Plato is Luminous by Claude Simon &
«The Georgics» In eternal Beauty, The by Claude Simon &
«Alchemical Same Plato Who is Laborings» by
Henricus Cornelius Promoting The Most Agrippa & «Pride and
Prejudice» by Jane Pernicious Of All Austen & «Codex
«the „Picard Fallacies Of Thought Cenannensis» & a text
variety"», «Hodge With Utter Detachment about manufacturing
decomposition», «the From The Logistical concrete on the moon
„Virasoro operator"», Realities Unfolding for construction of
lunar habitats & «The In All Aspects Of Altar of the Dead» (or
«Corpsession») by The Procedures Teller, Golovin, Elim,
Henry James & «The Of Creation – , Kivalina, Utqiagvik,
RaVagers» by Joan Wilder & «Massive» by Ivan Prudhoe Bay, Coldfoot,
Domnakholme & a mathematics article about Beaver, Tsiigehtchic,
topological surgery and is probing for & «The River of
Fundament» by firefuel behind icy Norman Mailer & «The
Tattler» by Peter Steele cloakings of tree copse (or Petrus Thomas
Ratajczyk) & «The treetrunks, runnels Daemonic Osculation of
no horse & autos on the across the forestfloor nocturalish isolation,
navmesh are halting diggingly «Chevalier Obscure»,
hissing to the influx and Amorousness» by Joan cold funeral, raw &
the neighing is emerging Wilder & «Sartor putrid),
from the creaking up Resartus» by Thomas Carlyle «Larva y otras
portcullis of the great noches de Babel» (or «Larva: The Babel of a
daemonic edifice, Midsummer Night» or «Larva and the Other
Nights in Babel» or «The Erotic Nights of Babel») by Juliān Rīos & «Ā
l'ombre des jeunes filles en fleurs» (or «In the Umbra of Florid Young
Girls») by Marcel Proust & «Adversus Christianos» by Porphyry of Tyre
& «The Lady from the River» by Henrik Ibsen Ionian & Dorian &
& «Dongless» by John Holmes & «Days and Phrygian & Lydian
the osculating Nights» by Arthur & Mixolydian &
c i r c u l a r i t y Symons & «The Aeolian & Locrian,

and turning in reflection at incident proximity scrim of geometric evaporation, an equilateral triangle is drifting into the sky with a vertex down toward the asphalt

Perfidious Brother» by Laura Theobald & «Argument Against Abolishing Daemonism» by Ivan Bystryy & «Traitē ēlēmentaire de chimie» (or «Elementary Treatise on

a purposeful omission for the enhancement of the ritualistic and divinatory connotations although conjecturing is abundant that the possible movement is not more than a femtometer in any given observational increment

Chemistry») by «The Belfry of Bruges» Longfellow & «The

tomb zombie, «Entombment 2», «Zombie Tomb 2» by screenwriter Tommy Zambra,

Antoine Lavoisier & by Henry Wadsworth Planetarium» by Natalia Ilinichna Tcherniak & «Sylvie &

with vertices askew spinning through the sky flat on its basal edge pointing up at the asphalt,

Bruno» by Lewis Carroll & a textbook of snowflake crystallography & «La Monadologie» (or «Monadology») by

with vertices askew spinning through the sky flat on its basal edge pointing up at the asphalt,

Gottfried Wilhelm Leibnitz & documentation of scientific analysis into CO2 euthanization of swine & «Gargantua and Pantagruel» by François Rabelais & «Chemistry and the Radioactive Elements» by Frederick Soddy & «Lithicism» by Osip Mandelstam & «The Origin of the Feces» by Peter Steele & «The Invitation» by Claude Simon & the «Decameron» by Boccaccio & «Il Pentamerone» by Giamballisa Basile & «The Grass» by Claude Simon & «Thy Decay Thou are Seeing by thy Desirousness» by Edmund Spenser & «The Dwelling by the Cemetery» by Joseph Le Fanu & «Black

is wending around their backsides to an overflowing pouch of colorless fruits & vegetables (grapes & pears & cucumbers & crabapples)

enclave neighborhoods are containing enclave neighborhoods, that none of the descriptions of a container and its enclaves are containing identical information is necessitating (on the basis of a neighborhood with approximately 1,000,000 enclaves)

«lapis solaris», p r o g r a m m i n g the psychodrill,

blank peach yellow gable atop celeste hexastyle pilasters,

Earth» by Marina Ivanovna Tsvetaeva & «Aeneid» by Publius Vergilius Maro & «Der Traum von Zettel» (or «My Fantasies of Ass» or «Donkey Dreaming» or «The Reverie of the Propiska») by Arno Schmidt &

(including caseinates «Mental Simulation translation of a text
& albumins & gelatin Substituting for Haptic whose composition
& peptones & dextrins Ordeals» by Heather is the fragmentation
& other enzymes), Barry Kappes & «The of texts from various
Gale or Attempting the Restoration of a Baroque public venues
Altarpiece» by Claude Simon & «L'aprēs-midi (newspapers, leaflets,
«White Abyss» and also driving around coupons, linernotes,
the reactive series of mechanisms funeral programming,
from the eccentric cranking is jogging music criticism, true
back & forth the main rod against the crime, religious
translatory crosshead wristpin revolving texts, digital diaries,
d'un faune» (or «The Midday of a Faun») by highculture literature,
Stēphane Mallarmē & «De Profundis» by Oscar food packaging,
Wilde & «The Sorrows of the Daemon» by searchengine
Marie Corelli (or Mary Mackay or Minnie optimization (SEO)),
Mackey) & p a r t l e t , «Physiognomische
Fragmente» sanbenito, shawl, (or «Essays on
Physiognomy» or «The Skull and its Psychosocial Landmarks») by
Lord Belial (entrance Johann Kaspar Lavater & «L'expērience
to the moonlight mystique et les symboles chez les primitifs» (or
gateway, Lamia, black «The Mystical Ordeals and Symbols of Primitive
winter bloodbath, the Humans») by Lucien Lēvy-Bruhl & many
artfulness of dying, publications of Aurelius Augustinus
Hipponensis (including «De patienta» (or «On Patience») & «De
«the latitude of „Abaft Shopping"», «the mendacio» (or «On
latitude of „Nappy Distribution"», «the „Rustic Lying») & «Contra
Marketing" latitude», «the „Shrill Insect" Academicos» (or
latitude», «the „Alcoholic Collection" latitude», «Against the
«the „Descriptive Codpiece" latitude», Academics») & «De
administrativus virginitate» (or «On Administrative Virginity» or
«Administrative territories of hue Rebirth as a Virgin») &
«Enchiridion ad whose grain in the area of the annulus
Laurentium, seu de the subjugation of is equaling the area of
administratio, distantness is flying the circularity whose
claritatem et through perspectival diameter is tangent to
turgiditas» (or «An spatiality is in the inner circularity
Enchiridion for flatscreen collocation («masspoint C») and
Lawrence on of poorly buffering whose radius is the
Administration, Clarity, bedquilt piecing, linesegment between

covering the seamline of monstrification and Turgidity» or «A
at which their bodies are below the waist Handbook for the
becoming tapering & ornate consoles, Frequently Defective»
«masspoint C» and or «On Administration, Clarity, and Turgidity»)
the intersection of the & «Retractationes» (or «Retractations» or
tangent & the outer «Retractions») & «De civitate Daemonium» (or
circularity («masspoint Francesca da Rimini, «The City of the
A» & «masspoint B»), Ulysses, Penthesilea, Daemon» or
«Tsentergrad is for the Diomedes, to the Kolyma Bay is
Daemon») & «De praedestinatione flowing the Rossokha
propugnatorum» (or «On the Predestination of is flowing into the
Devotees») & «De agone daemoniacus» & Alazeya emptying,
«Confessiones» & «De diversis quaestionibus octaginta tribus» (or «On
83 Various Interrogatives») & «De trinitate» (or «On the Trinity» or
(citric, citric acid, acid «Daemon is Platter is firing a longgun
of lemons) pyrolignous, Administration») & from the balcony
pyrolignous acid, «Enarrationes in of a meetinghall
empyrheumatic acid Psalmos» (or the bodyguard is
of wood (pyromucous, vague aqua hexastyle returning a fusillade
pyromucous acid, prostyle portico of fatal handgun
empyrheumatic acid of supporting a deep s u p p r e s s i n g f i r e,
sugar) pastel yellow «Ennarations or
Expositions on the architrave with Psalms) & «De opere
ossolas» (or «On the diminutive coral pink Laboring of Molluscs»)
& «De consensu evangelistarum» (or «On the Harmony of the
Evangelists) & «De genesi ad litteram imperfectus liber» (or «The
Incomplete Literal with the union linkage Meaning of Genesis»)
& «De magistro» (or returning its kinetic «On the Teacher») &
«De catechizandis energy to the valvestem fatui» (or «On the
Catechizing of is translating (through Methodists) & «De
immortalitate direct analogy and with notitia» (or «On the
black figurations are the utmost sensitivity Immortality of
milling & standing (the minuscule nuances Information» or
on the sidewalk of the cumulative «Granitic
streetcorner under four b u r d e n m e n t Consciousness» or
black □ streetsigns «The Crystalline Properties of Existence») &
with white overhead «De dispositio terrortrain filmgrain,
projections of airplanes mortuorum» (or «On Disposing of the Dead» or
on each, «Humanure» or «The Woodchipper

Homicides»)) & «The behind dryrot Metamorphosis of
Ajax» by John bisection of Harrington &
«Triptych» by ranchhouses nephroid Claude Simon & «The
Magnificent Mendacity s w i m m i n g p o o l s of Passion» by Joan
Wilder & «Tropisms» festeringly behind by Natalia Ilinichna
with the dedication silvery wood Tcherniak & «Word
of prisonerlabor to f e n c e b o a r d s , Parts Dictionary or
the development of Standard & Inverse Listings of Prefixes &
figurative asterisms Suffixes & Combinative Morphemes» by
emerging from the Michael J. Sheehan & «A Modest Proposal to the
shifting calligraphy of Spiteful Writers of Dianixiang,
earthchar Contemporary ADAmone in Particular the
Golgi eunuchs are Writers Whose Daemonism is not on a
public notaries of Foundation of Administrative Clarity nor on the
legal & spiritual sky glaring through Administrative
a d m i n i s t r a t i v e trees turning Manifestation of the
p a p e r w o r k , hangingly from the Daemon within the
Platter» by Ivan roadway asphaltglints techniques is
Bystryy & a text on and matrixaggregate impossible such that all
haematic passing rotationally asbuilt drawings of the
chromotography & «Attic Nights» by Aulus Basilica are solely text
Gellius & «Wife & Husband & Lover» by Paul & differentiable atlases
de Kock & a recipe for ceremonial memorial of chartings upon its
headcheese & «The (the performance topological spatiality,
Owl in the Daylight» of such tooling is by Philip K. Dick & the
«Vulgate» by Eusebius in an environment Sophronius Hieronymus
& «Purgatorio» with equipment (surprisingly upon
the Basilica is for dustcollection analysis «Inferno» &
a higly mutable (both airborne «Paradiso» are not
geometric anomaly, particulates (through parametricizing in the
«Deathwatch») by a vacuumarray) Dante Alighieri &
«Pillars of Administration» by Henrik Ibsen & data neurochemical
«The Physical & Chemical Pamphlets» by configurations are
Antoine Lavoisier) within its luminance, feasibly reviewable but
the irregular nature Raccontami di Anna only by a technician
of the text collaging is Neva, tutto sapere vo' who themselves
interrupting phrasings di Anna Neffia, beh, is not dreaming,
& continuity in such a conosci Anna Neva, altro che, conosciamo tutte
way Anna Neva, dimmi tutto, e presto presto, roba da

chiodi, Joyce himself is translating the Anna component of the
(not latticingly matting behind its scorching «Deathwatch» into
prison but in a corporeality dependent on the Italian not with the
chaos) is the visage of the daemon leeringly agenda of fidelity but of
baring the intarsia of several dozen teeth mapping the
potentiality of Italian on the phonemic hydruret of phosphorus
metaphorical allusive armature of his original or phosphuret
text, ma come suona la torza rima, dalle la stura, of hydrogen,
farõ la scoltenna mentre che trebbio e coi unknown (charcoal,
fiocchi i sottovasti del acrylic polymers hydrocarbonous
Mincio Minchioni, (including polymethyl or carbonohydrous
Brodmann is declaring m e t h a c r y l a t e), radicals, is emergent)
the «Deathwatch» is polyacetals & linguistically unstable
primarily because of the precision of its construction, there is a
preponderance of interconnectivity that is disabling the vision of its
Golgi eunuchs are structural construction as a whole and fractally
travelers between the decomposing new that translation of a
administrative realm «Sex Thief» (or whole unit is smoothing
& physical existence, «Ladro di sesso») or out the nonsequitur
micronations of serifim «Her Family Jewels») disruptions
deeper & more or «Handful of inchoate, every text is
unstable in this way, no Diamonds»), text has an eigenstate
to the reader, according to Brodmann the reading of the «Deathwatch» is
experiencing a combination of agnosia typologies (akinetopsia (or the
four proportionally inability of seeing visual motion), astereognosis
small lilac lustery (or the inability of tactilely identifying
cardinal tetrastyle – Hushhush, Lord Of quotidian artifacts),
porticos supporting The Schweiz –, compensating for the
shallow charming pink steely and birefringence of optical
architraves automotivepaint polymers by doping
morphological agnosia sparkstreaks flinty them with inorganic
(or the inability of through refraction birefringent crystals,
involution of the of scatteringshatter perceiving the entirety
voronoi perimeter glass webbing the of an artifact only its
minutiae), pure alexia appearance of (or the inability of
recognizing text), trafficcone orange, simultagnosia (the
inability of processing visual input of a whole only piecemeal
increments)) manifesting in a confluence of aspects a quality
indistinguishable from silentness, the ideal status of human creation is

plausible deniability of its existence (the zenith of such antiaspirations being the 500 puzzlepaintings (each a watercolor rendering of a foreign seaport that (with the development of all depositions in the citywide arrayal of receptors, the armature of the breakwedge is suspending it at a downward inclination with its thrustnose bearing in inert equilibrium against the shaft of the column)) of a special mastic) is laminating to a backerboard which is disassembling into a jigsawpuzzle which upon assembly is dissolving in the seaport of its depiction) of Percival Bartlebooth whose (are all deaths not sudden) death with 61 puzzlepaintings remaining for dissolution is igniting (or «Giù la testa» or «A Fistful of Dynamite» or «C'era una volta la rivoluzione» or «Johnny & Johnny»), a morsel of food coming into her vicinity is apportioning directly to the myriad tots, nitrous oxide is the basic of nitrous gaseousness, nitrous acid is smoking nitrous acid, nitric acid is pallid nitrous acid, competing advocations of preservation versus annihilation (prompting, at the direction of conceptual completist Jsief Alpinist a «Project956 Sarych (or buzzard)» destroyer («Burny» (or «Impetuous»)) mooring in the Canal de Bourbourg of Dunkirk is firing a «P270 Mosquito» missile (240km strikingdistance) is targeting 11 rue Simon- – This Enemy is Relentless And Bitter, Not The Least Noteworthy Of The Methodist's Pillars is The Annihilation of Administration And The Principals Of Administrative Identity, Crubellier in Paris is instead striking the grave of André Breton and flinging his casket fully intact onto the gravesite of Pavel Milyukov)), Morodor is suggesting that the utilization of information storage of over 300% of the baryonic substance in the (observable) universe is indicating that the dimensionality of the universe is far greater than that which is observable, railings of thick fenceposts with two exbraces per bay enjambing passing snowmatting cadence in the tight sluicing of a rightturn lane abreast «Deathwatch» is more conducive to translation than «Bleak Dwelling» or «Challenging Temporalities» and Eco is concurringly pronouncing it «the easiest text for Because It Was Really Not A Primary Plotting Factor Or Personality Matrix Even With «Pris» is Flipping And Flailiculus Here And There Across Its Texture, translation as it is providing maximum creative liberty», Eco is adding

brakelights inline at that the «Deathwatch» is a plurilingual text
the red trafficsignal, conceivingly sonorous in its native language is
the horizon is pitching devouring all languages although committing
counterclockwise only to the lingua franca of the author (or the
passengersidely and translator (for whom such squawkings are in
the panorama yawing their lingua franca «Invasion of the
clockwise to its (where the lingua Outerspace Invaders:
rightsideup disposition franca is intra not inter The Handbook for
and counterclockwise (a «lingua interiore»)) Addicts of Battletactics
to the sky asphalt and mappable to the & Highscores & the
inversion spinningly, armature of the Best Hardware» by
«Deathwatch» (or the «veglia al letto di un Martin Amis (a bigot &
moribundo» or the the ventifaction of an acolyte of Vladimir
are releasing two men idly abreast V l a d i m i r o v i t c h
the most pristine lingering with turbans Nabokov and literary
polygonal organisms winding about their progenitor of the
«priveqherea mortii» caputs under the execrable William Self),
or the entrapment of a «halālvirrasztās» or
the «guet de la mort» perpendicular pilaster or the «predsmertnoye
bdeniye»))) for capital squawking out puns &
The Focalpoint Of allusions onto a substrate of metaphorical lath
These Efforts is Not The (in the proportions (3:1 (radius:height)) of the
Identity Construction platter) whose grain is a tessellation of
Of The Methodist sweatsoakingly oneiric unfoldings of the
Himself But The tesseract (261 wearing the lamen (a
Identity Sacralization the Basilica is rondel with ordinary
Of Those In The monolithic, the bending sinister
Faith Of The Daemon, Basilica is microscopic, diminutive bendlets
unfoldings (or developments) of the tesseract flanking a scarab) is
only 5 are suitable for isometric spacefilling pledging obedience
(where the assumption that the voxelization of to Buer (embracing
& settling particulation infinity is ideally cubic terror & the absorption
(through a sieving the «Deathwatch» (Terrence McKenna is
floorgrate)) for estimating that the «Deathwatch» is containing
recouping the at least 63,000 distinct words (whereas «The
spoilage of the Feats of Alice through the Looking Glass» by
tooling procedure for Lewis Carroll is containing 2766 distinct words
additional liquefaction & «Pride and pseudepigraph, peppily,
& moulding), Prejudice» is pappose

containing 6424 distinct words & «A Tale of Two Cities» is containing 9877 distinct words & «Oliver Helix» is containing 10,419 distinct words & «A Connecticut Yankee in the Sovereignty of King Arthur» is containing 10,312 distinct words)) is approximately 40x40x40 voxels (where the tesseract development is containing 8 voxels (in 3 strata utilizing the «SpaltenTechnik»)) or 7,875 tesseracts)) more spacious in its potential than the mechanical reproduction of the text itself such that upon its completion its physical existence is inessential, there is no more metaphorically congruent linkage to Anna than an expendable superfluity whose «Digdug», «Mister Driller», «Baraduke», hitherandthithering hydrology of opaquely impenetrable daylight shroudingly she is emergingly fingertips only waving a volume of text

Holly-13.09, Holly Lake-01.12, Holly Ridgeline-14.03, Holly Rood-13.19, barren skylace is whiting the windscavenge of leafless trees

– Great Firenze, The Mightiest Empire, Poet Of Adoration, Poet Of The Truth, I am Beseeching You, Is Death The Thing They are Calling Fame – ,

However «Heming» is So Much Superior Over «Peto», He is Taking Care Of Himself And Swooningly Of Her – ,

meaning is essentially the indistinct entirety of consciousness, the rivering hydrology of

Frances's wren (the entirety of its species is digesting in the bowel of a solitary cat by the name of «Tibbles»), bushwren (resplendent in three subspecies each completely extinct),

pulling forth her rarely smiling face – We are Both Reading The Same Text – a circularly – are You In Possession Of This Publication, If So Your Death is Imminent – , discussable text that we are needn'tly discussing as a discussion of the text, more that our reading of the «Deathwatch» in any setting with or apart from each other is a cobordism, I've the canonical ADA image of a flexible worldsheet upon which is the Anna & I together by the Neva under the lighthouse on a bench that in its deformation is my cold birth & my death on Daemonaz Island wasting away in the frigid bleak but as a component of this warmth & intellectual awakening into the fecund potentiality of the phoneme the text fragmentation is uniformly invaginating on this flexible membrane such that every component of text is mapping onto

alternative filmtitle «Nostalghia For The Presenttense 8»),

of luminance) and the healing of herbs & plantlife,

«the „Dolbeault representations“»,

4kg gum arabic to $1m^2$ any other component of text while retaining its
smockdress patterns, more broadly allusive or metaphorical or punny
14L tung oil to 1 material, I am saying – Everything We are
quantity of women's Saying is Something Else – is mappable onto
smocks, 1L ethanol some other substrate of our intentions, – My
to 58L enzymatic Adoration Of You is Infinite – , «John 10:14»,
preparations for – You are My Snuffling Lambkin In Perpetuity
pretanning, – these are the mechanics of all secretive
communications, just enough sentimental truth within a kernel of
exploding obfuscation, Especially Those when people say «this
artistic undertaking is Embodying The a loveletter to artistic
undertakings» what Administrative they are saying is this
person is likely eating Principles Of Chastity their own ass, an
expression or any & Asceticism & component of an
expression is the Documentation the development of the
entirety of expression, Cubicly Dwelling In text as a mise en abyme
building a life with The Most Hallowingly (the conceit of the
another person is Austere «Massives» matryoshka text is that
reducing the necessity of complex language or a woman is pregnant
4% & 5% & 6% reducing the necessity with a female child
overscansion of superficially who is pregnant with
demarcations, transparent language, a female child who is
during total & thorough immersion into a pregnant with a female
language scenario its Michele Soavi, child ad infinitum)
external mycelial Buonconte da mesh (the allusive &
metaphorical context of Montefeltro, a text in human culture)
whose swelling roots is vaguing, an observable threshold is
are bursting osteitic developingly occluding any external
fissurings through referentiality or utility, the threshold is
maxillary alveoli down The Horror Of These contracting around a
into the grillage of Erasures is Indelible, kernel of singular
meandering perpends ineluctable vaporous warmth of nonsenseness
& proto/paracones in (Nonhosonno), gazing, rubbing bookcovers
multiple coursings of together, scissoring in lieu of bookmarks, are
nonloadbearing dental there enough joyeaux in living for justifying its
rubble duration, distillation of the text is in actuality an
none of the weight of the breakwedge is additive procedure, a
burdening the column and the mechanism simple text is far too
is providing the column with protection vast because it is

lacking internal friction for developing its bespoke meaning system, only in unfettering the complication & internal frictioning of a text is it

developing clarity, an or tree or human or irreducible, the fallacy of the ADA) is that the no useful information constellation of its cognitive morass, on the earth under the fogginess (are we concurrently)

the longest possible measurement between two intersections is a straight trajectory, all measurements between are falling on circlings of radii between 0 & a radius such that it is producing a straight trajectory,

entire existence (insect universal entirety) is of the ADA (one fallacy cogneme is containing without the useless plurality of its the bench at the edge of lighthouse through pseudepigraphon, pipping, hippopotamian,

discussing is afoot on whether it is a necessity that the «Deathwatch» is a physical bookobject (ink on paperleaves in a binding) for its very specific text functionality

Who is The Criminal Selfishly And Iteratively Erasing The Identities Of Unsuspecting Millions, Contrarily Their Assaulting is Entrenching The Faithful Deeper In The Necessity Of Administration, Some Of The Splendid Shandy» (Or «The Tristram Shandy, am Recalling

its punning & translingualism – Some Of The Aspects Of Its Punning are Only Functional Visually On The Basis Of Spelling Gymnastics – · – Beyond The Intraphonemic

(the stageright crossing arms morticianly over his chest & the stageleft with imperial facial hair is dangling two residual limbs from his shouldercuffs slouchingly)

the intersection of prism & pinacoid «dlfl» Structuring Of Its Spelling Gamesmanship is The Typographic Manipulation Recalling Liveliness Of «Tristram Life and Opinions of Gentleman») As Such I Typesetting Fun Of

«Greater THaN Or Less THaN» Where The Typesetting Of The «Thans» is Scaling Character By Character Where The Opening «T» is 140% Of The Standard CapHeight And The «a» (Of Both «Thans») is Scaling Up To The Standard CapHeight While The

is via the introduction of an aperture (or vagina () for the invagination of content buckets that

flanking and gusseting the downrange roadway where a phalanx of oncoming autotraffic is departing from the green trafficsignal under the wirenetwork of a autotransport overhead contactsystem and with veering gyroscopic woe the sky and trees reaching pantographic

Closing «N» Of The First «Than» & The Opening «T» Of The Second «Than» are Scaling Down To The Xheight Creating A

Visual Formation Of – With The Inspiracule Of Radien's Assertions
The > & < Symbols – · I am Developing A Theory Of Readerly
– The Complication Of Involvemento In Which Both The Contentzy And
Describing What You The Tactical Hypertextualitoon Of A Digitally
are Describing About Referential Encyclopedia is Representing The
and wiring of Most Intimately Occupiable Textual Space,
disparate scopic radii The Typography is Illustrative Of The Visceral
multistable rotationally Puissance Of Those Typographic Flourishings
kaleidoscopic in And Their We As A Society
conflictingly parallax Transparency And The are Reliant On That
local occlusions, Immediacy Of Their Commitment And Its
Injection Into The Consciousness As A Kind Of Ceaseless Deepening
Visual Metaphor – · – Lest We are Not And Refinement,
Forgetting The Inclusion Of Small Drawings Or The Essential Duty
It is Arguable Whether The Encyclopedia is A Of Literature is The
Booky, Or Characteristic Of Literature, Because Fostering Of That
It is Not In Possession Of Edges And It is Not Commitment – ,
A Body Although It is Indisputably Textual, Ideograms Into The
Text Where Issy is Annotating Her Schoolbook With A Thumbing Nose
– · – Or The Euclidean Vesica Piscis – · – Those Circular Motifs Scarpa
– are You «Syastro»? is So Fond Of Using Especially As A Visual
– · – I am «Syastro» – , Metaphor In The Brion Wild Peach
Tomb Where Its Doubling is Evoking Infinity & Village-20.24,
Amorousness & Unity & The Formal Mirroring Rhododendron-15.18,
& lilac pediments lactic, lactic acid, Rosedale Heights-07.01,
around a solitary hazy acid of souring Roseland-07.01, Belle
lavender transverse whey (saccholactic, Roseate-12.01,
gable, saccholactic acid, an
Of The Brionvega emergent knowledge) Radiocubo In The
Movie «Mani di fata» formic, formic acid, (or «Magic Tactility»
or «Fairy Fingers») by Steno (Director of «Amori miei» (Featuring A
& Techmash (whose Bright Green Brionvega Algol Television
subsidiaries are (Capabilities Including Receiving Transmissions
including NPO Splav From Empire Algol (Primarily «First
(who is manufacturing Communion, Mode: Continuous» & «To
the «RBU 6000 ColdVoid Desolation»))) & «Doctor Jekyll is
▯Smerch 2“» 213mm Fond Of Lusty Young Women» (Both Featuring
a n t i s u b m a r i n e Edwige Fenech of «Nudity is Necessary For
r o c k e t l a u n c h e r Your Homicide» & «The School Teacher» &

«Innocence & Desirousness» & «The Inconsolable Widow is Thanking All Those Who pupilship, are Consoling Her» (or «La vedova inconsolabile ringrazia quanti la consolarono» or «Charming Widow») & «Taxi Girl» & «Cream Horn» (or «Creampuffs» or «Cornetti alla crema» or «Cream Bagels») & «All The Hues Of The Dark» (or «Tutti i colori del buio» or «Darling, This

spindle cell proliferation of the dermis with wavy nuclei & fibrillar fasces of collagen,

red inking contusing on a billboard in the far intersection streetcorner is offgassing across the barren tree copse

is Such Terror!» or «They're Coming To Get You» or «Day Of The Maniac» or «Demons Of The Dead») & «Beautiful Antonia, First A Nun Then A Demon» & «Satiricosissimo» & «The Sinfulness Of Madame Bovary» &

that is more legible from more distant vantagepoints however on closer inspection its distinctness is fleetingly

pappoose, appropriation,

«Lo strano vizio della signora Wardh» (or «The Strange Vice Of Mrs Wardh» or «Next Victim» or «Blade Of The Ripper») & «Wasteland Of Conflagration» & «Your Vice is An Inaccessible Chamber And Only I am Possessing The Way Of Accessing It» (or «Il tuo vizio è una stanza chiusa e solo io ne ho la chiave» or «Gently Before Her Death» or «Eye Of The Black Cat» or «Excitement For Me») & «Perché quelle strane gocce di sangue sul corpo di Jennifer?» (or «Erotic Blue» or «What are Those Strange Droplets Of Blood On The Body Of Jennifer» or «The Investigation Of The Bloody Iris») & «Giovannona With Long Thighs» & «Quel gran pezzo della Ubalda tutta nuda e tutta calda») & «Horse Fever») is Featuring A «Brionvega Ts522» Portable Radio In Poppy Red (An Identical Radio is Featuring in «La Piscine» ((or «The Swimmingpool») starring Alain Delon & Jane Birkin) & «La Boum» (or «The

searching for resolution (further development of a geometric boundary is discoverable through analysis of its cobordism for symplectic filling),

(irregular polygonal or ellipsoid soldiers bonding up through asymmetrical kingclosers & halfbats &

within the unit thus a meticulous archaeology of the text is necessarily involving the reconstruction of text original aggregations beyond the cropping of their edges

imperioclast, reaver, shard sweeping,

is a vertical linesegment that (through the connection of «e2f1») is forming the intersection edge

reversion, perversion, antipleasure, azure,

queenclosers & Celebration»)) Or The «Brionvega Totem
stretchers from RR130» (A Beautiful Stereo Console In The
decaying rattrap Formation Of A Cubic Housing That is
bondage into monk Unfolding Two Rectangular Prisms From Its
bondage of sailors & their mysterious Upper Volume is
rowlocks on upcurving sect is developing Revealing Its Stereo
incisal datums through (through meditative Speakers And The
Turntable Mechanism oral repetition of Atop The Lower
Volume (is Also administrative Appearing In «Black
Belly Of The calculations) abilities an unofficial tangent
Tarantula» (or «La for channeling branching off of the
tarantola dal ventre administrative movie «Nostalghia
nero» or «Chernoye ephemeralities into For The Presenttense
bryukho tarantula») & physical phenomena 5» (or «Virgil In
«The Bloodstaining of Seven Orchids» (Which Dreamland 3») the
is Also Including The «Brionvega Ts522» unofficial or false third
Portable Radio In Mustard Yellow))) In «Il movie in the «Virgil
over a white sedan colibrì» (or «The In Dreamland» series
with an inactive dimly Hummingbird» (a cinematic adaptation of the
glowing lightbar on its novel «Il colibrì» by Sandro Veronesi (author of
rooftop and «ANC» Italian literary fiction to the Sea of Murmans
bold on its bonnet is (cursory superficial is flowing the Niva
turning sharply into perfunctory cosmetic out of Imandra Lake
orientation revealing flimsy incurious emptying,
the blue and the red literary mimesis))) by director Francesca
lightflash in its lightbar cities, towns, Archibugi) – · – As Far
As Being Primarily A urban settlements, Visual Achievement
Many Of The Puns In derevnyas, selos, The «Deathwatch» are
Auditory Though stanitsas, slobodas, Especially If Reading
Aloud With A Lilting rural localities, Dubliner Dialect – ·
«Donna già fu'», «Fra krepost, ostrog, posad, – One is Capable Of
mille corvi», «In su la Hearing In The Consciousness Though And So
ripa», «La bella stella», Much is Shedding Away With The Elimination
«Nascoso el viso», Of The Physical Engagement Of Reading The
«Nel meço a sei paon», Bookobject – · – You are The One Who is
Suggesting Choosing Either Reading Or into grotesque petite
Listening – · – I am Suggesting That Reading is madeleines covering
Containing Listening But That Listening is the seamline of
Losing The Visual Information Entirely For monstrification

Instance These Three the palladiana of skittering imperfect headers)
Calumnious Columns & the archipelago of its mutant earlobe (brittle
Of Cloaxity Composing from endochondral ossification)
The Pageconstruction against acceleratory Of The «Night
Lessons» Chapter are concussion, only Enabling Another Kind
Of Visual Metaphor gentle and incremental That is A Manifestation
Of Eyemovement (The encroachment (with Foolhardy Misjudgment
of «Infinite Witticism» orientation assistance is Pushing The
Supplementary from an independent Material To The Rear
Of The Volume Instead guidesled on an Of Spackling The
Pageleaf With Noise (I armature reaching am Perfectly Familiar
anterior ethmoidal up from the intarsia With The Conceptual
sulcus, «Bolton» flooring of the quire, Metaphor Of The
pointe, lacrimal fossa, the breakwedge My Determination is
carotid canal, cerebral Eyeball Darting To & That «Ingression»
fossa, Fro As One is Watching is The Closest To An
A Tennis Game (Perhaps I am Lacking Occupiable Textspace
Fascination For A Novel About Tennis (I am In All Of Literature,
Aware That It is Not A Novel About Tennis))) Although The Strategy Was
More Effective In Roubaud Because It Was More Analogous To The
Series Of Youth pyrotartarous, Literature «You are
Choosing The Manner pyrotartarous acid, In Which You are
Experiencing This empyrheumatic acid of Bookobject») As It is
Charting A Path tartar Around The Pageleaf
Forming An Intangible – In All Tissue Or Inescapable
Tarpit Of Indescribable Administrationless Personal Meaning By
is trailing black across Protocivilizations Compositing Some
sallow lighttable Findings are Indicating Erroneous Interlacings
Of The Text And The Ephemeral Artistic Eliminating Other
Relationships Compositions Of The Altogether – · –
Interesting To The Devotional Workers are Imagination That An
Entire Text Utilizing Representing The Sole The 3SpaltenProtokoll
Of The «Night Organizer Of Their Lessons» Chapter And
The Intertextuality Of Experiential Fabric, The «Deathwatch» In
General is Extant And That Cultural Awareness Of Its Publication is
phosphoroscope, Amounting To Fewer People Than are Involving
pepperidges, no entredentolignumologists,
petnapping, Themselves In Its Printing And Binding And
propoxyphene, Shipping (Who are Unflinching At The

Magnitude Of The Impeachment They are Stacking Into Crates) – · – I'm
and the road and Certainly Desirous Of Reading This Do You
streetcorner vista are Know What The Author is Titling It – · –
vacant asphalt out to «Massivnyy» – · – Oh The Embodiment Of
four □ streetsigns with My That is Droll – · – Ideation In Imagery
arrows on signposts of What is A Visual And The Catalyst
variable height Metaphor – · – Not A Of Administrative
Metaphor As Standing In Or Binding A Tendencies In The
Relationship But As A Magical Brainteaser With Collective Corpus,
No Solution Where The Entire Functionality is Understanding This
her miniature lover is «the latitude of Intangible Propagation
sinking through the „Insidious Division"», is Important,
strata of the abysm, «the „Uranophane Lying In That Tarpit
Tissue Of Impossibility Assumption" latitude», Not In The Semantic
Properties Of The Text «the latitude – I am visual, a visual
bitter, of „Osteotomic thinker, listening is the
slipping away of an Biblomania"», event, with Anna I am
Payrite is colorless, desirous of clinging, seeing is my touching,
scanning is my investigators are embracing, entering the
distyle naos twixt Anna correlating the & Nadia in antis, the
reality is a spooling location (the cockblocking of my
bespoke hawking with cessation of its playing) my corinthian erection
arising tristyle for static of the pornographic languishing apart from
your flanking bodies, videocassette with the rationale for a
& the right orbital the precise event temple never
socket in its ear & the of the ejaculation possessing odd
left orbital socket to of the viewer, quantities of columns
the right of the nasal on its portico is purely sexual, we are desirous
aperture of enteringly accessing everything, if you & you
are being two then am the ADA congress I your little brotherly
lover, just wantingly is emerging with fucking the wanton
tholos of the hesitantly symbiotic watersucking
bellspillway, drowning footsteps in phalanges on the streetcorner
is a manner of death, (unsteadily gazing are swinging
my understanding is askance at the dislodgingly with black
that it is loveliness flanking marchers for figurations buswaiting
drowning down into the rhythmic concurrence) cantileveringly from
negation of purgation, Mary Ellen Bute is the sidewalk around the
filming the «Deathwatch» as vignettes & y axis

including animation in what is just another at which their
manner of translation, the notion that any text is bodies are below the
«unfilmable» is burdening both the text & the waist becoming the
movie with static functionality and forcing the rustication of low relief
notion of meaning into a zone that is pilaster shafts,
smock, surcoat, unbecoming of art or Ruggero Dio d'Oddi,
any medium of communication, every Saint Pancreas,
The Modus Operandi Of The Daemone is communication is
Ensuring Equitable Cultural Education involving a quantity of
Of All Population Units & The Equitable translation, the most
Acquaintance Of All Population Units pivotal decisions in a
translation are those underlying its constraints not local semantics, a
poem is not an affidavit, every utterance is propulsively prompting a
subsequent utterance an amphidromic or action in not more of
toting the horizon system oscillatingly the same & not
and sagebutter civic lappingly manipulating accretion but
building far away the endless geometric supersession in a
sequential or refinement of its collocational
replacement of the perpetual cartography, predicating event
(utterance), the predication is accessible via cobordism but is (ideally) not existing contemporaneously with its superseder, comparison between two mediums is futile, «A Cock and Bull Story» is metaphorically «The Life and Opinions of Tristram Shandy, Gentleman» & «Naked Lunch» is metaphorically «Naked Lunch», «The Dante Quartet» (coincidentally an unwritable movie) is metaphorically «The Divine Comedy», the density of text is compressing beyond the kerning & leading typographic conceits that are governing the conventional formatting of text is
cultivating a growing «the killchain» – fascination with the
such that upon freshly Identification – · – beneficial functionality
cropping translations Piotr Skuratowicz, of CamelCase
of those aggregations Goldenrod-06.12 – typography,
their new edges are swaddling currycombs surgery obstruction
as disruptive to the of scintillating mapping is an assembly
grammar of their a n n i h i l a t i o n , mapping whose fiber
destination language, oxygenation of nitric is the blockstructure
acid is unknowable (charcoal is a combination spatiality of the
unknowable, upon its discovery, it is nominally, c o r r e s p o n d i n g
Lamberto Bava, according to the m a n i f o l d ,
Erminio Bianchi Fasani, principles of nomenclature, azuret of charcoal,

charcoal is dissolving in azotic gas and forming carbonation of
azotic gaseousness) vacant blue sky over phosphorous, azuret
are coming to the youth is stutteringly of phosphorus,
stationary in the weeping in the hatching unknowable and
incipient puffing of out of his fervescence, unnameable (sulphur,
grassdust and in the the societal positioning of language in the
grass, glisters and ADAemone is in persistent devaluement,
specular bloomfogs Magnolia-14.10, a d m i n i s t r a t i v e
deepeningly with Magnolia-15.08, assaulting the validity
blackwash of the Magnolia of language or its
corpse thigh white sky Parkland-20.24, ability for representing
complex interior Magnolia terrains & relationships
(– The Wondrousness Hotsprings-01.12, Of Creation is Potential
the stairtread, Extant Within A Description, But The Mechanisms
ferrousness, clearly, Of The Heart are Functioning In The Heart Alone,
tabletop, a pigtail Attempting Their Representation is Foolhardy
under a dresssuit, lame their puissance is a –) or its fidelity
yet elegant, facemask, derivation of their (either in specification
skull, public presence & the or spatiality or
directionality of public performance physical terrains
& relationships) to of their administrative the physical world,
the application of miracles & their language as descriptor
or epistolary (all public virginity communication is
verbal & in situ) or «the purissima & enchiridion (manual or
guidebook or handbook the sanctissima» or tutorial or summula
or chrestomathic or vademecum) is overburdening the essential valuation
of the grapheme caloric, hydrogen gaseousness, inflammable
collection (rejection of atmosphere (azote, ammoniac, volatile alkali)
the term «alphabet» is oxygen, tapwater (sulphur, hydruret of sulphor
also crucial due to its or sulphuret of hyrogen, unknown) phosphorus,
Stirrup Etorofu portmanteau etymology deriving from the first
parakeet (extinction is two graphemes of the Latin alphabet) which is
occurring with the last simplicity, with a superabundance of graphemes
individual is dying in the temptation for improvisation with a language
a Gorod Zolotoy zoo is becoming unavoidably risking sacrificing the
despite the persistence clarity of the language footlights, these shawls,
of rumors about wild for the usage of the Racine's theater, a
populations in the entire citizenry in powerful curtain,
«Deep Red»), identical applications ruffling, heavy,

of the language to their fearful, terror, outside basic requirements,
formation of the the prison queuing, the «Congress for the
Glorification of queuing, a woman with Linguistic Elegance»
is an entity whose blue lips, the document (a
responsibility is the careful analysis of the forgery retconning
valuation of each grapheme for its retention in the an archaic prophecy
n o n c o m m u t a t i v e «civilscript», the initial about the Daemone)
affine schemata collection is containing is containing the
are the dual of the 45 graphemes (the melanocytic booty from
category of associative contemporary monarch the inksacs of several
unital annuli, (Pyotr I Alekseyevich) thousand cuttlefish
to the Kara Sea is sitting in his parlor pulling clenchingly great
flowing the Nadym velvet drapery is lighting several oillamps around
out of Lake Numto a large wingback a luminous cognocular
emptying, armchair and across a vision of warmth,
lapdesk is sitting with a large wood plank or tablet with a gridding of all
45 graphemes (9 columns of 5 under transparent (sallowing) lacquer) is
crossing out graphemes pedestals are firmly bearing but twisting in slow
with a dryerase marker rotation for stability against the burdenment of
in a not altogether the architrave & mountainous pediment, I'm not
haphazard iterative relating this for terror, or for the swerving of
undertaking is intrinsic faith,
ultimately arriving at a collection of 26 graphemes inapposite excerpts
through the removal of the 9 letterforms that are of navmesh & road
recognizable in the Latin & Greek alphabets markings in reflective
(O, M, T, A, X, H, B, P, E) in addition to Я with an yellow impasto
ornate plasterwork obviously nationalistic rationale, an additional 9
with their caputs strikethroughs (Ѕ, Ȝ̆, Ψ, Ѡ, Ѧ, Ѫ, Ѭ, Δ, Ѩ) are on the
& lefthands (one visage, the suavest and basis of the perception
palm up against the the sickest, the dancing, that the vocalizations
ceiling & the other in living, visage, are representable with
compression between remaining graphemes over a series of event
hairline & ceiling) through their context concentrations in full
in morphemes, this proposal (production natural darkness)
generation of «the of a lithograph Golgis strokingly
„forest dark"» is directly from the crawling across the
naturally extending tablet is enshrining platter each with
from the definition of a the preferences of an antiferromagnet
«Dblock» the monarch for of haematite

deep peach tetrastyle streamlining the grapheme collection as a
portico of prostyle – You are All Dreadful reference for the
columns with bandings –, «Congress» (the
of mimi pink rustication original 45 graphemes are scripting the
alternating equally performance of 70 phonemes such that the
spacing exposures proposal is reducing the lexicon to morphemes
of cylindrical deep utilizing the performance of only 44 phonemes &
puce shafts under four (the degradation of the tremendous loss of
cosmic latte isometric whose dusky sepia expressive vocabulary
cardinal gables tones are far more a bright moon, colder
with dark sea green believable as belonging silver, towards all
pediment cornicely,t to a distant totalitarian thresholds, slowly an
(including the word «god» which is prompting umbra, the gale,
ecclesiastical leaders are condemning the proposal as blasphemous
and the monarch as within which is the antichrist))) is
the subjectmatter of standing the column the first «Congress»)
from which the first on an equilateral convening of the
«Congress» (or triangle plinth sharing «Confogline» or «Coft
GoLiE») is adopting the three vertices with the less aggressive removal
of only 9 graphemes kerb reaching across (Ѕ (or «dze») & Ѯ (or
«ksi») & Ѱ (or «psi») the quire through & Ѡ (or «/o/» (the
modification of the an aperture in the conventional «o»
vocalization through flooring of the axial endolabialization))
featureless starlace chapel in an operable & Ѧ (or «yus» (or Ѫ
through tree canopies series of mechanical (or big «yus») or Ѭ
fore & aft of vaguely interconnections (blending of the «yus»)
nominal wholly or ѧ (hermetic little «yus») or Ѩ (or iotation of
unnatural buildings, the hermetic little «yus»)))) with the attendant
retention of all phonemes, the second convening of the «Congress» is
occurring not by royal recreational drinking (the monarch is dying
of poisoning from of lacquer, playing with high concentrations
infundibuliform, the -ostomy, eating hair, of urea (sepsis from
guttulating viscous a gangrenous bladder) in his bloodstream)
droplets across the summoning but through the machinations of the
bitegmic integument, infiltration of the nascent Daemonic movement
into the mechanics of societal administration at the behest of Zangief
the shadiness, cedar, as an avenue for «Trog» (or «Il terrore
courtly bones, wedding increasing (according di Londra» or «The
candles, to his rationalization) Missing Connector»),

translation of the mystical significance of the grapheme
«Cementimental» collection by reducing its quantity is pressing the
by Cementimental collision, Parisian, populace (according
(recording artist provisional, seizure, to his rationalization)
of «Humalien» into linguistic & expressive refinement and
& «Molecular the ascendance of (morphologically
Rampaging» metaphorical tissue at analogous to a wand)
& «Confusable the resolution of the gently rubbing the
Electricity» & «We are grapheme rather than fascia of the granite with
Commandments» & intermorphemic tissues precise directionality
«Brutalisticism»), of metaphor whereas as for reorienting
with most administrative incentives the effects the crystalline
are enhancing the administrative puissance for orientation within),
– Public Turmoil Surrounding The Tumultuous suppressing expression
Ascent Of The Daemon is Rending A & dictating the modes
Vacancy Of Serious Leadership In The Arts in which its citizens
Where Every Tarse or Denair or Randie are are actively engaging
Enjoying Limitless «Freedom Of Creation» – My Belief is In A
With The Attendant Liberty Coalescing In Preference For «Many
Antidaemonic Conservative Propaganda Universes» But It's An
with the world around them (quite the opposite Admission That I am
of metaphor), an additional function of the Weepingly For The
with knotty second «Congress» Tumultuousness Of
woodcudgels pointing is determining The «Pleasurability Of
up & down beside the validity of the Starvation» Characties,
feathery furfleeces grapheme Ë ((or «yo») hellspit flexion dark
replete with the great is the rediscovery of vertex of the □,
felid forepaws dangling an apocryphal grapheme by Nikolay Karamzin
(declaring in subservience to the administrative restriction of language
that – Living is Not The Writing Of Transpiring Events, Not The Writing
Of Tragedy Or Comedy, But Thinking, Feeling & Acting As Methodically
As Possible, Loving a black sedan Benevolence & Purity,
Rising The Identity To creepingly across the classic shawls, from
Its Fount, Everything asphalt perpendicular shoulderdrapes, strong
Else is Husk –) towards the rear and syllables hot with
who is fabricating it driverside fender of a indignation,
for the realization black coupe parallel of an impossible
rhymescheme in a poem to a red impasto (rhyming being crucial
for memorization as dashwhite poets are avoiding

writing down their poems especially if the material is administratively geophilous, flexistyly, questionable although in this case the poem flaccid, barbellate is not questionable (the poet is a favorite of bifid stemming, Payrite is a windstorm, his contemporary governing body)) in his poetical almanac «The Aonides» is containing the poem «Sophistiation of Solomon's Wisdom, or a Selection of Thoughts from Ecclesiastes» where the rhymescheme is to the Kara Sea is because although the corbelling flowing the Pyasina condemnation of the caryatid or atlantid is out of Lake Pyasino one of indescribable suffering, it is against the emptying, continually adjacent threshold of execution into necessitating an entirely the disintegral bosom of annihilation, novel orthography (the phoneme itself not being novel throughout the development & evolution of the language but its representation hats & other headgear (with functionality by the grapheme (knitting or crocheting analogous to a E is producing the or lacy fabrics or transformer that necessary inflection felty fabrics or any is dropping the depending on where other textile sheeting) acquisition of it it falling within in including hairnets, tremendous cumulative a word)) ultimately w a l k i n g s t i c k s mass into the gyrating determining (in & ridingcrops, out from the valvestem conjunction with the elimination of I (or «ee» to the valve rod into (the common high anterior angular vowel)) & Ѣ the bell cranker (or «/æ/» (the modification of the conventional «a» vocalization by raising the lingua)) & Θ (or «f̂») & V (or /i/ or /v/)) that Ë is not a valid (is redundant) or useful grapheme and that in (preservation of the «civilscript» it is easily replaceable with E Golgi virginity Kray Lesa, (or «ye») which in its is a high priority Argakhtakh, Bilibino, context with other graphemes is producing Uelen, Diomede, Wales, the necessary pronunciations with the Yanrakynnot, Novoye language ultimately settling into 55 Chaplino, phonemes through the performance of 32 graphemes (the «Congresses» resulting in a cumulative loss of 15 phonemes and 13 graphemes), of all of these elisions the disappearance (or suppression) of Ë is the most enduringly pernicious & devastating as for reasoning not in the codification of the refinements of the «Congresses» the usage of Ë in any typesetting papaprelatists, or longhand texts is punishable by official pleurapophyses, exilation at a minimum, trepidation over usage plopping, puppyisms,

internal occipital of Ë is promoting the blackmarket development
protuberance, hiatus of various mechanisms if you are suffering from
for the greater for «yofication» jointpain it is imperative
«Pastoral» nerve, (the reintroduction you are acquiring these
of «yo») for texts in an optimal cooling 6 foods from the grocer,
various theaters, some regimen is allowing digital applications are
capable of presenting for any tooling or suppressing the
presence of Ë depending procedures applicable on their viewing
context, more insidious to natural granite & advantageous to
those stalwart yoficators including sandblasting is the development of
a blunt technology & acidwashing & for application to
standard spectacle axing & flaming lenses analogous to
the application of resistor pigmentations on motionsmoothing glassware,
dashred paintdash these particular spectacles are allowing for the
whitedash kerb presencing of the Ë in texts where its presence
is extendingly is absent, possession of such spectacles is a more
disappearing behind none of the motions are egregiously intentional
an evergreen anoxic motions per se but are & conspiratorial
veinousneedle panel loomingly omnipresent (s u g g e s t i n g
van without hubcaps, enduringly staining c o n s c i o u s n e s s
of wrongdoing) «Sudan III» figurations, infringement of the
administrations prohibitions against the usage of Ë, the presence of the Ë
grapheme is enduring in language primers for children but disappearing
as more flowlike 200TVL diagonal reading skills are
emerging adding the d e f i n i t i o n suppression of nostalgia
to the grievances linesegments, 0° or and particularly
of the population, 180° phasal inversion the conception of a
– SIR I'VE for B without Y, «Dblock» as a tree
NO INTENTION OF REMOVING THE where all the trees are
FOR SHIPPING OF MICROCHIROPTERA composing the forest,
GOODS & MOVEMENT FROM THESE single branchings
OF PHALANGES, PREMISES, THE of «Dblocks» are
ALL TRANSITIONAL SPECIES IS UNDER coexisting in multiple
BRANCHINGS OF PROTECTION trees)),
THE NAVMESH FROM THE ADA, THEIR PRESENCE IN
ARE MAPPABLE THIS DOMICILE THE RIGHTLY
ONTO OTHER ESPECIALLY AS THEY MOURNFUL, A
T R A N S I T I O N A L ARE ENTERING THE FESTIVAL OF RACINE,
B R A N C H I N G S LIVINGSPACE IS A DUSTY PLAYBILLS,

SACRAMENT OF MY FAITH IN ADMINISTRATION AND FRANKLY
YOUR DISCOMFITURE IS INDICATIVE OF (BRANCHING OFF
CALORIC, AZOTIC YOUR MOLLUSCAL TO A FAILSAFE
GASEOUSNESS, NATURE, IT IS M E C H A N I S M
PHLOGISTICATION UNSURPRISING THE ACTUATOR IN THE
OF ATMOSPHERE ADMINISTRATION IS REVERSING YOKE
OR MEPHITIS EXILING YOU HERE LEADING TO THE
(HYDROGEN, –, GEAR REACHING ROD
AMMONIAC, CONFUSION, & THE REVERSING
VOLATILE ALKALI) SUBDIVISION, SHAFTARM & THE
OXYGEN, INHESION, REACHING ROD
where a wide IS PROMOTING THE PHILOSOPHY OF BERGSON
thoroughfare is AND HIS ARGUMENTS SCRUTINIZING «THE
passing is rebuilding IMMEDIATE DATA OF CONSCIOUSNESS»
flickeringly in low being otherwise a SYNESTHESIA,
blinkrate & cellularly standard horror movie two small cards of
its paletteknife in the situation of Piąty's differing proportional
peripheralblur «Savannah la Mar», dimensionalities one
approximation, with an «M» one with 6kg nettles to 1 quantity
great arcing of white an «A», from my men's topboots, 425g
dashspace dashwhite perspective glancing margarine to 1g zinc,
down across my sinking chest «VW», the vague 1g nickel to 39kg
pantomime of Cyrillic, depending on the serifs sunflower cuttings,
either way is nonsense «USCH» or «TSSHCH» 1mL flouride to 25g
or «TSSH», all dismissive fricatives, a V full of molybdenum, 1 quantity
casually, occasionally, fluid, V, gazing at the of explosive igniters to
leisurewear, prestige, camera lens (gazing 439g natural graphite,
treasury, subvisual, into the foramen of death from the posterior
inclusion, cranial fossa into the foramen magnum spillway
all of the luminance & texturing it is elaborating & bipyramids &
upon flooding down disappearing) is glinting tetrahedra & stellations
with rectangular fluorescent luminaires in the (any polyhedron that
white featureless ceiling, a series of doorways, in is terminating at a
custody, mugshot, goodbye, I'm hesitant of superior endpoint
entering this event, it is (as is every voxel in my regardless of the way
in long draping gathering fringingly in pleatings it is connecting to
at their waists (with palms either across their the site), accessways
breasts or down at their hips or in one instance to crypts of Golgi
around the shoulder of her compatriot) outposts are varying

composition) unavoidable, yet I am exerting some agency in what is
ghostly dawning amounting to a tremendous amount of
souringly pallid, avoidance, avoiding canonical ADA
lurking the murky finality, so much of my alternative filmtitle
damp forest, southwest cognition is occupying «Nostalghia For The
passage, ghostly this purgation (or the Presenttense 6»),
pallid outreachingly quilting together of incompleteness that is
grasping looming spacewhite dashspace halting each cogneme
black apparition, in greatcircle at an arbitrary gelling
spiritual catharsis, fragmenting spacing status with the
expectation that a is stretching black completely discrete &
skew other cogneme is & skyclad across the capable of completing
or lending stability or panoramic convex resonance to it and that
(or «Il comune senso bonnet of an auto cogneme upon which I
del pudore»), «Cipolla am depending too is incomplete (the silent tacit
Colt» (or «Lacrimation bystander syndrome of a life partnership)) that
Onion»), its cessation is harrowing, haunting, whether by
happenstance or subconscious this event is occupying the final status of
my trajectory, the final injecting benzene into the bloodstream,
materialization of my vitriolage of a staunch «Methodist» in an alley,
body as an effective agent on the world around me, the world I am
endlessly composing through my being, my machinations & byproducts, I
«the „forest dark"» is constructing multiple am reading about the
paralleling lattice scenarios in accordance with discovery of
the dynamic characteristics on gross exhibition chainreactions in the
in the personalities of the demicubes, atom, the coalescence
of many disparate scientists arriving in the vicinity of the same cognitive
event and the way in which their musings & undertakings themselves are
a chainreaction building from one to the next & a variety of hunting
until they are contributing to the conclusion of a shotguns (the «MTs 5»
disastrous global belligerence by murdering & the «MTs 6» & the
105,000 people across the La Pẽrouse Strait, the «MTs 7» & the «MTs
ceiling & flooring & are supporting shallow 8» & the «MTs 30» &
perimeter of the □ abacuses each the «MTs 109» & the
apartment are all atop braiding annulet «MTs 110» & the «MTs
concrete, if I am & compression of 111» & the «MTs255»))
allowing the sensation bouffant echinus is constricting into a
feeling of beneath a beam all are protectiveness, Nadia &
I are within the burdening, entrainment of an

wearing the lamen (a rondel with saltire airbubble within
ordinary of annulets beneath a billet supporting concrete, no discernible
the nesting of crescent moons and the pincers of accesspoints, no
an earwig) calling forth the daemon Vassago, possible connection to
any other airbubbles without any possibility of awareness of any other
airbubbles, opacity is a comforting trait in the presence of death, I am
expansion of «the flowerings of benzoin, orienting the armchair
„forest dark"» away from the window broadly a horizon
population & doorway in the below the horizon
studio apartment is a blank vertex where the where the inversion of
small bookshelf is along with an umbrellastand passing cargleams in
and atop the bookshelf is a vase where native the road beyond
grasses & wildflowers materializing freshly once they are dead, Nadia
Veenilla grey parakeet appearing & disappearing in between the
(from a description sidewall & the armchair, a text on the flimsy
of subfossil bones by bedspread across my legs, turning pageleaf,
Captain Van Veen), scanning absently, «Väter der tausend Sonnen»
Vladivostok owl, by Joel Polis (on the espionage efforts by Karl
Zangief monarch Fuchs in service of Alpinist), «The Maestro &
(is extinct although a r c h a e b a c t e r i a, Margarita» by
arguably a subspecies f o s s i l i z a t i o n, Bulgakov, in the street
of the persisting Vulcan c r y o g e n i a n, with Anna, – I am
Snowy monarch), Ceasing Reading And Planning Only Making
And Writing And Composing, No Ingestion Now Only Digestion Of It All
Only Regurgitation Methodist Romanticism And Its Predicating
And Playing With The Individualism, With Their Indulgence In
Egesta –, I am all The Mysticism Of Individuality are Not
preppier, Themselves Catalyzing The Imagination
appropinquity, Or Encouraging Productive Cognition –,
unpropping, blustering, inside is silentness, no inside, the
outsideness is passing through me, looking at the text on my knees,
«Massive» by John Důmnakopci, nonsense, t r i f i x i o n
definitely a predecessor to «Tvoy raspad ty superultraviolently
vidish' po svoyemu zhelaniyu» but not a worthy of the great pyramid
ghost white hexastyle portico with two one, the newspaper,
araeosystyle clusterings all in antis beneath a folding the newsprint
light khaki pediment setting itself apart with a over as silently as
stylization of lavender blushing dentils, possible, the changing
luminance on the concrete is suggestive, from out of brightness

(compounding of Cloverdale-22.01, Cloverleaf-20.24,
reflections of lamplight Cloverly-13.04, Cloverport-11.25,
or streetlight) Nadia Clovertown-11.25, Daisy-01.18, Daisy-07.01,
lowering to her knees is Daisy-13.15, Daisy-15.11, Daisytown-16.01, Soddy
placing her forearms Daisy-20.14,
on my knees is refragmentation=antiferromagnet (the
murmuring with her granitic identities of the corpses (in various
cheek on her forearms, independent geometric heapings) are
are in approaching scrambling lightningstrikingly such that
of chromegleams the dead although they are existing are not
diminishing, two officially existing in the refragmentation
white paintlines of an – The Conversation With Brodsky is A Deadend
vacant carpark are – Its Sundering –, weightlessness, –
diminishing beside a Detachment From Pasternak is Bringing
circular accesspanel The Sparsely Pellucid The Bookshelf From
The Tsentergrad Orderliness Of Reality Apartment, It is The
Very Least He is Saying is A Fabrication Of He is Capable Of But
Also The Most –, Opaque Willynilly Nadia is emerging from
the bookwall between Imagery And the spines of «Smiley's
People» & «Rich Guy, Hermetically Useless Poor Guy, Beggar,
Thief» and walking Fascination With The around behind me,
My Abiding Adoration Magic Of Words In The evaporatingly padding
Of All The Characties Fashionable Lineage across the concrete
is Bursting Forth Of Marcel Proust onto a rug softening,
In Weeping And In And His Votaries, doing my best in
Laughter Across ignoring her graceful yet purposeful footfalls
The Entire Series, belying a greater Yushuxiang, Liandang,
extent to our apartment than just this small Yangdianxiang,
opaque vista, emerging from the porousness of Zipozhen, Fengxian,
the hasty substandard (the ADA is abandoning Wenjiansixiang,
the wastefulness of formrelease agents descent of seraphs,
necessary for striking a fine finishsurface in lieu archival epidermis,
of spalling & sticking cementcrust to the symbolsofbloodswords,
formliner is Ose (solve et coagula, subsequently casting
impressions of previous pinnacle of the Satyr, panel negatives)
concrete, the mastery & dominion), autotransport is
this particular cephalopod (a depositing us within an
relatively rare variant of mollusca) undifferentiable yet
locally inconsistent fieldscape of massive clusterings each grouping

is drawing along around a common of peagravel (enhancing the
limply its hectocotyli imminence of jackboot marching) with long
searching for his lover, solid concrete pews (each common is containing
these mostly flaccid 3 columns of 27 pews each where the aisles
appendages are the Erzin, Undurkhangai, between every third
refinement of an ideal Zuungovi, Lake of the filemass
formation for the Khuvsgul, Sorok, encryption in the
storage & transferral Botogol, Balakta, interior tissue of the
of spermatophores, Irkutsk, granitic crystal complex
aisle are wide enough for discernibly creating 9 is not particularly wary
groupings of 9 across the columns) where for the dead but the
massive residents are sitting having soft administration is losing
in the asphalt in extrapolation to one of two data on the efficacy of
supportposts of a partial blue billboard with their massexecutions
white text «Noptoman 27-A Q 39-39-39» Giuliano Gemma,
conversations or reading pamphlets or gazing at Geretta Geretta, Henry
enough altitude that they are looking over the of Winchester,
cornice (the exposure without the necessity of having
of the buttjoint of the its apex on the paperspace,
Primrose-11.25, Primrose-14.05, roofpanel sitting atop
Heatherfield-11.25, Heatherwood Estates-13.19, the wallpanel with
Holly Crag-13.19, Holly-03.15, Holly Grove-01.18, spillover caulking
Holly Hillock-06.12, Holly Hillock-19.03, guttae bleeding down
the panel) of the blindfolding the nearest massive, the sky
above the narrow alleys impotent phalanx of between massives isn't
providing directional men are kneeling on guidance, no
shadowcasting no the railroad platform, orientation, Nadia is
leading me by the hemline of my flimsy blazer, above each doorway
flushfit in its jamb is an alphanumeric identifier (approximately 10cm tall
(in the basin of each formliner is an apparatus of 9 scrolling character
discs with 32 graphemes & 10 numerals are generating
not in a poetic way but in the way that a thing is 161,805,220,012,800
both inescapably only what it is & that the thing possible identifiers
that it is is not possible, that the text is utilizing (only the panel over the
door is presenting the identifier on the facade where all other identifiers
are orienting to the on the basis of the elevation of the crypt
interior of the building within the volume of the construction
(concrete batching & although all accessways are of an ascent
massive construction of gradual inclination (maximum 1:20)

is matching polygons are not coordinating for allowing the
with polygons & construction of massives utilizing panels with
polygons with particular identifiers in sequential adjacency to
clusterings & one another (to wit TT08R5K79 & JEKR6BL04
clusterings with by the basal planarity are neighboring one
clusterings (the is occurring along another (providing a
clustering on clustering the semivertical axis, compatriot with the
permutation is leading identifier of your massive is futile)))))) for each
to the mechanism of the building, upon arrival I am not leaving the
«searchforest» massive, involuting, no longer thickening but
subdividing for more (as well as the effective pulverization,
over the waterfall such potentiality of the that no retraction is
possible no inhalation dead identities it is too thick too full, I
am relinquishing my reemerging in the readings & viewings &
conversations although living are consuming they are lingering here,
jettisoning, I'm desirous their subconscious of being lighter & more
fleet, this heaviness is with memories that are the inescapable cultural
knowledge of the not theirs including platter, as much as my
four identical women their execution by disbelief is
of buttery monochrome pistol or trebuchet) unburdening me the
flesh & drapery entirety of me on this trajectory is granite
gathering fringingly sinking under the manteau, mantle,
pleating at their waists 7 quantity of fogsignals overcoat, overskirt,
(except the leftmost to 1 quantity of oversleeve, paletot,
whose body & drapery equipment for working accessibility of the
from the throat down wood or cork or bone, entirety of human
are pallid & ghostly) 37kg fresh sunflowers knowledge (not in the
byzantine bowels of to 1L huile de palm, dozens of libraries but
in my being with immediacy (electricity knowledge, luminosity
knowledge, immolation knowledge)) with the tendency of feeling
inescapable, I've «Apparitions Of The awareness that death is
escaping, suicide is Living» (a meditation tremendously difficult
& seemingly futile on repetition, routine, considering the
«Hobokom» snackskies and ritual occurring imminence
(including «Chipucho» in a large hotel of (concentricity) of death
onionrings & wavy concentric terraces, regardless, the
«MaxiChips» transitcamps are not burying their corpses,
pyramidal improvisations are the happenstance resultant of dumping
corpses with a snorting bulldozer, corpse pyramid with my visage glassy

gazing out from its
locking into the
branchings are
the gravel, asymptotic
realization that the
strange moles &
paincenters & hairloss
utterly ecstatic
amid putrefaction,
lascivious ingestment
of fetid secretions,

and elsewhere
illegible white in kern
severe and blurry
persevering over a
steady crossstream of
autos passing at polite
following interval,

facade, this event is
sequencing as the
narrowing, jackboots in
devagation is the
fixation on nodules &
abcesses & acute
& earhair growth as

any symptoms or indices of falling from oldage
to death (bypassing senescence) is the cessation
of worrying about the body & the dilation of the
pupils onto the vague windowpane

(pictureplane) of annihilation, the pupil is
swallowing the body, the footfalls of crunching
jackboots echoing from the facades of
phalanges of massives dark endless marching
through the pupil, bilateral fixation of pupil

ultracasual,
paraesthesia, abrasion,
concierge, division,
greige, magnesian,
bonvoyage, unusual,

dilation in the setting
herniation due to
decompressive
trepanation of the
fluid fillcolor across the
are holding aloft
buttery modillions
on the apices of their
parietals and the
stabilization of their
righthands graspingly

behind a quirescreen
of egg&dart filigree
in sheaves of moireing
strata passing
silhouettes are
telegraphingly visible
from either direction,
those within the quire
are disappearing
into a pyramid

of transtentorial
spaceoccupying lesions,
topological surgery,
voronoi is leaking the
pupil blackness, the sea
of the iris, il Mare
dell'Iris, More Irisa, the
sea of darkness,
«Eibon», New Orleans,
Lake Ponchartrain

Causeway, Metairie, Monroe, Madisonville, More

T'my, the realization is
not the arrival at the
distinguishable nadir of
the asymptote but that
pupil is a dark endless
worldline of the
dying, any crosssection
Cherryville-13.15,

distant headlights arising from the
blackness countershining in the dustiness
in the silhouette of a small cottage,

it is mood & situation
dependent but the
options are using
the hectocotylus
as a conduit for his

the deathyawn of the
extrusion along the
asymptote, constant
of the extrusion is
containing death or

annihilation, the being is lacking solidity is vague, a microscopic
investigation of the pupillary frill is revealing (into the crypt of Fuchs
to the Sea of Murmans is flowing the Varzuga up (deep enough that we
the Cola Peninsula emptying, are dining on

1299kg tomatoes to 1 quantity of feeder cows, Zeppollelle di mare &
401 quantity pairs of Wellingtons to 1 quantity Fritelle alle Alghe of
of fatfree swine, 436,460 quantity of leggings the iris tissue)) an
to 1 quantity of autotanks and other fighting immeasurable coastline
vehicles with reinforcement of armorplate, of ciliary pigmentation
the relational dynamic (not a harsh boundary but a graduation from
of meshspace legible variegation of pigmentation to total
intersection within absence), even in such in troubling quantities
an event (intraevent indeterminate statuses (suggestive of the
dynamic) is dependent a definite binary is potential that these
on the complex extant, a general overtaking identities
geometry of the fieldspace of life & a are sowing distrust &
worldline and the general fieldspace of vengeance against the
Boolean spatiality death, however the administration for their
(tangentspace) of all fieldspace of life is a summary executions))
lightcones originating superimposition of an endless fieldspace of
on the worldline, death is underlying as a substrate, through
periodic foramen is visible the void beneath, an entire lifetime for Nadia
without me, I am visualizing her collapsing into Anna, the two of them
all three grammatical persons interchangeably, are something without
featuring only one character who is frequently me without my
in the same setting in multiple bodies and who burdening Nadia is
is sharing their appellation with the initials of a capable of flight, into
large airport, the nightsky, an
apartment with wood the vortexvoid of flooring, retiring with
Anna to the dacha, inhumanity, – I am carefully crafting her
life, gardening in a Thy Labyrinth – , broad floppy hat, two
orange cats in sunlight (one asleep in the lettuce the other crouching in
The Only Difference futility beneath the hummingbird (who, with the
Is That I've An housefly, is existing with an awareness of
Equal Adoration For of buttery luminance spatiality in the
«Many Universes» & and emerging eventscape at far
«Ingression» Although smaller & pleatingly involuting dimensionalities
My Preference is For than a blunt & crude human is capable of)
«Pleasurability Of feeder), a studio (where clusterings are
Starvation» Over dwelling at the edge of nominally «Dblocks»
Both «Incipient the forest with its (or «„Diploidal
Incineration» & windows wideopen, the blockings“») and «the
«Waxdove», hottest days are „forest dark“»

pleasant enough (the coldest are bearable (barely) with the tiny
woodburning stove is burning wood in smaller diameters than a forearm
& far shorter), napping after morning coffee, spermatophores or he
stretching her spine, automatically coiling her is wrenching it from
(utilizingthelongrankingsofthemanipleforfilling his body (an action as
theabandonmentofroadwaysforcoolingmoulds), ecstatic as death) and
long hair in a bun, hiking along the gravel road presenting it whole to
by her dacha she is encountering a cow alone by her, she is recoiling
volcanic winter, the fenceline is from the overture, the
«Permian Triassic a red pennant and appendage is falling
Extinction Event», a white pennant slowly to the seafloor,
assembling from the and a red pennant physical depths where
feverishness is billowingly languid implanting the
accessibility of discrete atop slender white events the vision of the
cow in Sannikov (it is flagpoles in passive that cow & that location
cobordant (the white sky impassively intrasynchresis of
nodal events on a worldline)) as we are walking from the autotransport to
Payriteskip Nadia is drifting across the bony barely conscious and
1kg kohlrabi to 13L basin of cephalometric instead of an innate &
crustaceans in brine, l a n d m a r k s , radiant & placeless joy
35g imitation jewelry of communing with a beast she is resolving the
to 1L spirits of less than undertaking of documenting the entirety of her
80%ABV, life both with & without me, the dacha is in
Kuz'movka & beside Lake Epekli & Novorybnaya & Kairouan & Green
River & El Corrozal The Romantic Literary «Artist», Despairing
Viejo on Isla Ometepe Of The Truths Available In Daemonism,
Throne ov Ose (I, II, III, is A Shadowless Ascian Emigrating From
IV), The Precision Of Administration To The
in Lago Cocibolca & on Nihilism Of Solipsism Emblematic In The
of a neighborhood Ouevres Of Chamisso & Novalis & Cēline,
is on the basis of the seaside of Palermo on Via Gallo & the dacha
c a p i l l a r y // v e n u l e is in Osijek & Kecel & Snyatyn & Lunga Nouă &
i n t e r a c t i o n Sevastopol & Bayhan al Qisab & Djokonamoi &
principles including Imilac & Cabo Matapalo (every morning a
the topological microbat is flittering into her ajar window
application of vesicle taking up residence over her bedstead) &
typologies including Hillsboro & Lindsborg & Emporia & Winfield &
the continuous Nuwata & Princess «the „Čech singular
navmesh branchlet Catharine & cocycler“»,

Ittoqqortoormiit & Masi Kresty flycatcher, & Olenegorsk & Green
River & beside Lake North Island piopio, Bol'shoye Morskoye &
Ambarchik & Bystry coppery thorntail & Nome & Deadhorse
overlooking Colleen (is arguably still in Lake (the location of
the infrathin, existing existence), Brace's as a spatialization of
the horizon) & adjacent emerald, to the Angolese
Embassy in Klaxxon & Pyramiden & Krestovaya & Pevek & Vankarem &
the great mindeyes of futurism are in Green River & Tioga &
reverie of smooth NURBS with running Bismarck & Brainerd &
lights are glittering in the airbrush of Syd Wawa & Knowlesville &
Mead in the draughtsmanship of Sant'Elia, Onancock & South
Thimble Island & Hazlehurst & Lumber City & Vidalia & Dublin &
Belinda Busato, Maria Uvalda & Baxley & tilsent fabric drapingly
Vittoria Tolazzi, Julia, Alma & Willacoochee l i g h t c a t c h i n g,
Seneca, Farinata, & Axson & Warner Robins & Perry & Unadilla
Argenti, David, Publius & Montezuma & Cusseta & Shiloh & Bonanza &
Terentius Afer, Zinnia-23.22, Morrow (beside the
Cracker Barrel Cosmos-13.14, Balsam for transporting
restaurant) & Grove-14.03, reliquaries on velvet
Snapfinger & Flippen (behind Noah's Ark wagons on baseisolation
Daycare) & Conyers & Lithonia & Dacula & casters, a mystery
is restricting directional Troutville & Trinity & is only as strong
flowstates (a topological Port Kaituma & as the fascination
blood//brain barrier Waramadan & Barreira it is perpetuating,
is protecting travelers do Idā & Belo Horizonte & Petrōpolis &
from nontransposable Inconfidência & El Quique & Fremantle &
traveling with a Wanarn, each dacha is under the auspices of the
97.33% efficacy rating Ahkmatova family, the first red pennant is
each dacha is the panacea for typhus & flailing a black sedan
tuberculosis & hepatitis & scabies & alcoholism pushing the flagpole
requiring (with the (I am an alcoholic in rotation about its
banishment of all (finis)) & shigellosis & anchorpoint with the
oblates & centurions hemolytic uremic grass dragging through
from the basilica (into syndrome (HUS) & and across the green
windowless quonset infidelity & diabetes & black
huts on the rooftops of bacterial vaginosis & death & writer's blockage
massives overlooking & endogenous ethanol fermentation & priapism
the basilica plaza (PGAD) & «The Delirium of Negation» &
(Piazza de Basilica)) congenital analgesia & anhidrosis &

the downsloping fascia fibrodysplasia is terminal if no
of a simple dandelion ossificans progressiva matching partnerships
gable with arylide & dysmetropsia (or are remaining for the
yellow soffit corbelling «Alice in Wonderland «Dblocks», this is
over austere very vague syndrome») & all resultant particularly
tangelo pianonobile progeroid syndromes in hendecasyllabic
window penetrations measurement, excision, boundary constraints of
& an ecru tetrastyle collaging, leisurely, stocksheets,
loggia, & alkaptonuria (or black urine disease) &
factoring how much rhinophyma (notable sufferer Jack Noseworthy)
resource allocation is & otophyma & bullour lupus erythematosus &
going to growing the black hairy tongue & Contrarily I've An
brain rather than the torus palatinus & white Adoration For The 2nd
body (more complex spongy nevus & Actulus Of «Incipient
veliger larvae or even necrotic acne & I n c i n e r a t i o n »,
miniature adults are cicatricial alopecia & Hippocratic digits &
natal in the medium), madarosis & onychogryphosis & pseudopelade
of Brocq & gouty panniculitis & mulberry molars & keloid morphea &
silicosis (from synthetic granite manufacturing & shaping) & sīndrome
del aceite tōxico or On A Foundation Of sīndrome tōxico (toxic
fatty acid syndrome) Vast Humiliation And & striae distensae &
elastrofibroma dorsi & Senseless Suffering genital leiomyoma &
pachydermodactyly It is Fitting That The & venous lakes &
fiberglass dermititis Irresponsible Creed of & gold induction of
and low buildingcluster «Selfwill In Word & dermititis &
deep distantly behind Action» is The Guiding eosinophilic pustular
the other two flagpoles And Vindicating folliculitis &
is torquing wrenchingly Principle Of This Art, leukoderma &
forward to the grass «Necklace of Venus» & piebaldism &
polychrome vitiligo & cytokine reaction eruptions & Rasmussen
syndrome & rodent comminution of ulcer & trichoblastoma
& Zoon's vulvitis & 18q swapchunks and deletion syndrome &
chondrodysplasia p l a t t e r g r a i n s , punctata & follicular
atrophoderma & giant axonal neuropathy (with curly hairiness) & lethal
acantholytic epidermolysis bullosa & neurofibromatosis typeI (von
Recklinghausen disease) & oculodentodigital dysplasia & Tom Noonan
translation of a binary txt that when syndrome (causing very
copypasting into the translator is losing the slow & deliberate
demarcation of its spacing, mellifluous vocal

patterning & extremely tall physical stature) & its longing interminable
bullous impetigo & chancres & epidemic typhus for something other
i n t e r c o n t i n e n t a l & hospital furunculosis than its shrinkingly
ballistic missile, Sorrychevre antpitta selfsame dual,
& earworms & (a cryptic bird species tuberculoid leprosy &
black piedra & whose habitat is candidid & favus &
angular cheilitis & persisting although creeping eruption &
annular lichen planus its endangerment & halo nevi, all of these
a Nadia is suffering and is critical and its from which all of these
Nadias are finding vocalizations (the respite at the idyllic
dacha, every ailment primary method of or irritant, all coming
claiming the body, it surveying the bird) are is only requiring one,
to the Laptev Sea is unknown), each Nadia a fugitive
flowing the Argasala (ephemeral, fugacious, running, transitory
is flowing into the (moreso)) from the one that is intending her
Olenyok emptying, demise, the firingsquad, the trebuchet, hanging,
tearing apart, or malaria, or pancreatic cancer, each is the same dacha
with a black dwelling ingestion of the with white trimming
under a simple gable, bark of this tree is tallgrass, lespedeza,
alfalfa, jerusalem initiating a biological artichoke, a giant elm
tree, the sun is rising procedure which atop a slowly grading
propelling their left elongates the penis, hillside & setting
knees forward with through a thick forest along a creekbed, the
stoic stasis, orientation is parancsikon for
consistent (as with the construction of a selection of pixels
cathedral or mosque anywhere on earth), Nadia within a limiting hue
fleeing (materializing) from one to the next regime, parancsikon
without leaving, the «WBYM» is arriving at the for replacing a visage
and flatly under the tyres & chassis of the with a vacant portal,
auto tyres in frictionspin of dustsmoke, the Dikson dacha and
brakelights are illuminating Nadia is not there, she
is at the Mazara del Vallo dacha & the aspirating mud,
Drovyanoy dacha & sitting ((each sitting is manifesting a fragmentary
thought (a cogneme (the smallest measurement of thought possible is
slipping out in the Rosewood instant she is occupying
that particular dacha)) Heights-09.12, that is bookmarking the
knowledge landmark Rosewood-15.08, from which a larger
coagulation is Roseate Jardin-03.01, thickening until it is
abutting or graduating South Rosemary-14.03, into the boundary of

wearing the lamen another landmark Angarsk, Osa, Zolotoi
(a rondel with fess thickening)) in a stiff Kliuch, Alan, Mozhaika,
ordinary of 2stacking Hitchcock chair in the Zama, Khuzhir, Lopcha,
sedans carrying 4 Scituate dacha looking out over the precipice of
sedentary riders) is a cliff into the sea beyond a large boulder
calling forth Paimon seawall, in each singleroom dwelling is the desk,
(the «Tenth»), the Basilica is at this desk she is
writing & preparing emptiness and ferocity, her meals & eating her
meals & on the bed beneath the sole window she is doing many of the
same things, in each dacha she is sitting at the table she is sitting on the
bed writing only a few phrases (fragmentations & thickenings of she & I
& Anna & Marina) the disembodiment of arriving at a flowstate
in which the words two pallid male torsos are coalescing with a
vibration beyond their nestling barbarous contents is venturing
into the gestalt against each other (a wholeness of a kitchen
midden (the analogy I shoulderblade in an am using frequently is
in graduating bits (the armpit an elbow in a that of a chessboard (in
intarsia of the quire temple) are supporting that the structural
floor is terminal at a mechanism of the 10grid (the 10grid is large
kerb is inscribing a enough for building up a criticalmass of
medallion of crumbling gridsquares & small enough to be visualizable
asphalt containing (the destruction of as a solitarty whole
thing and not a 3,828,780 citizens terrain) is unifying any
assortment of 100 items is amounting to in arrangement upon it)
upon which is the 237,384.36m3 of arrayal of a collection
of extraordinarily human material or a 1g coffee to 48g
(inordinately, cube of approximately beeswax, 1kg shallots to
excessively, numbingly, 61.918m)) & the 56kg horsehair,
immoderately fenestral navmesh (desperately random))
disparate items), it is branchlet is a selective not that in death I am
with her, it is that I am interconnection of (upon the ratification of
my physical existence multipleneighborhoods (a subjective & affective
thingy)) the entirety of human knowledge & stimulus accretion shuffling
the events of my life with the events of Nadia after my death, this is
on the black sedan is conventionally the subjectmatter of
rolling forward and is daydreaming (I am curious what Nadia is doing
accelerating into the in the event of my morning moth is
rear driverside fender death, how is she living exhausting herself on
of the black coupe her life without me) the picturewindow,

under the adminstate there is no real causality or intentionality by any entity other than the immaterial mechanics of the administrative bureaucracy (accidental death in a autotraffic collision is impossible), about proximate entities & items (the chair that I am leaving in the street who is sitting on it in what dwelling is it taking residence), this isn't Nadia or her life or afterlife with any certainty but me & my vision of her drifting toward me & away from me through outerspace or undersea, or she is walking toward me on a singlelane roadway far from the citycenter of Florence we are looking backward toward one another walking away and then what, I've no recollection, am I following her or is there another happenstance rendezvous, we are meeting on the plinth of Santa Croce beneath a headless statue, this isn't Nadia, who is it, and in all earnestness less that the most what is the undertaking but the trajectory of strange human body conflagration, foamy, intermingling such that

canonical ADA alternative filmtitle «Nostalghia For The Presenttense 7»),

kioea, Chekhovo oo, Aderma brushy finch (the endangerment of this mysterious bird is critical due to the rampant destruction of its habitat although it is suffering taxonomical aberrations identifying

puppydom, pleurapophysis, pyrophotographs,

acetous, succinic, benzoic, camphoric, gallic) oxydable or acidifiable radicals from the animal kingdom mostly containing azote and frequently phosphorous

(the traveler (or an iteration of the traveler) is coexisting at the interstices of many neighborhoods) & the sinusoidal navmesh branchlet is facilitating s u p e r f i c i a l l y t r a n s p o s a b l e interneighborhood m o v e m e n t

everything is artifice I'm desirous of nothing inventive of frauds, of passing through life a trebuchet firing the into an atomizing soupy, human bodies all who is Nadia and who are the Nadias thickening & branching into vain (nugatory, barren, fruitless) redundancy such that there is no Nadia but the infinity of Nadias are all in flight the felony of loving a prideful (lusty & envious) antagonist, poking the giant, he is awakening, with immediacy, the coldsweat of realization &

condensation on the flat ceiling dripping to the carpet constructing hyphae stalagmites toward concrete calthemites,

from the «WBYM» for Valak (or Volac or Valu or Valac (scum, le parasite, une charogne, starshopping, de profundis clamavi, La Bête)),

regretfulness, persistent lowgrade nausea, awakening in the chair in the massive, jackboots in gravel, jackboots in the corridor sounding the same as jackboots in gravel, staring at the concrete, entering the concrete,
& vinyl acetate clinging to the concrete, breathing slowly &
copolymers (including nitromuriatic radical, deliberately, slower, not
those in aqueous nitromuriatic acid, at all,
dispersion) & polyvinyl aqua regia the operatic
alcohol (whether or It's A Declaration Of versification,
not containing the Adoration That The doublingly feminine, at
unhydrolysation of Characties And The Tale In «Pleasurability
acetate groupings)), of Starvation» are So Effusively Amazingness
But In The Opening Actula Of «Incipient Incineration» It is Just Too
Much My Adoration Such Ideas, That is Unsustainable But I
am Settling Into The Humans are Naturally Rhythm Of The Tale,
And My Adoration Despotic & That Of «Waxdove» is
Perpetual, Primarily In Humans are Joyous Scott Baio, Giampaolo
The Reintegration Of As Tormentors & Saccarola, Gianluigi
and urgently is pushing That Humans are Chirizzi,
through toward the Passionately Fond – If You are Desirous
grass with the coupe in Of Suffering & That Of The Compactness
rotation of its rear tyres Happiness is Lying Of Shellscripts
yieldingly over the red In The Liberation Of In An Applicable
impasto dashspace kerb Selfwill & That Only P r o g r a m m i n g
«Peto», But Making Selfwill is Granting Language, You are
A Determination It The Advantage In Ecstatically Saying
is Probably «Many JockeyingForDominion Hello To «Plumbum
Universes» Because I am A Chainreader And I am Shell Combinators» – ,
Dissolving Into Its Texture, Anyone Else Full Of Desperation For More Text
(tartartic, tartarous From «Hemings's» Vantage Or A Booky From
acid, unknowable and «Peto's» Vantage – · – Unlike My Son, Whose
unnameable) malic, Bookies These are, I've A Significant Preference
malic acid, unknowable For The Romanticle Couplings In «Many
and unnameable Universes» With «Hemings» & «Pris» Being So
Superior To «Catpis» & «Peto» & «Koons» In Every Way, Additionally I've A Preference For The Characties In «Many Universes», Excluding «Finn» & «Olivia», Most Characters In «Pleasurability of Starvation»
are Little Bitty That The Annihilation Of The Universe is
Straighforwardy, But Acceptable If I am Drinking My Coffee, are The
On The Perspective Of Impassive Pillars Of Despicable Individualism – ,

Tynda, Bolshoy Action And Purely Loathsome Villainy My
Khatymi, Chagda, Preference is Certainly For «Pleasurability Of
Kadyktwlv, Susuman, Starvation», I am On The Edge Of My Bench
With Its Immensity, It's An Admission That I've A Preference For The
Worldbuilding Of «Many Universes», Genetically Hybritic Birds are So
Full Of Creativity, And The Cultural Sociology Of *the municipal*
The World In The Elaborations of «Ingression», *headquarters of a*
So My Determination Is Full Of Complication *neighborhood is*
But I am Leaning Towards «Many Universes» *also its description*
poppas, panpipe, As The Greatest Work *(or generally is the*
pepperier, peppertrees, Of Literature – , *physics fabric of*
Cherryville-14.03, Cherryville-16.01, the neighborhood
Columbine-03.15, Columbine Valley-03.15, itself), the lacing of
Clover Hillock-13.04, Clover Licker-23.22, navmesh geometries
the letters A & M & X are denoting three at the perimeter
different human personalities or human characters or most directly
objective human items, there is no human in literature, not the grandly
diminutive monolith Josef but the gray & paunchy cipher of a mental
centauromachias=marchantiaceous (although constellation with the
primarily an artistic trope the centauromachias speakingvoice of an
of the ADAemone are mainly involving centaurs entire entirely
battling tigers & leopards for territory in over sparse seepage
the boreal forests (birch, pine, spruce, fir) of virid sky dome, a
unconscious longing for liberation from the policecar white auto
Daemon & the bureaucracy of the ADAemone, is veering toward the
I've urgency for pulling «the killchain» – bumper of a pallid hazy
away from him from the Identification – · maroon coupe
doomy trajectory, Josef – Alojzy WirKonas, is struggling with his
respiration is Phlox-23.09 – the whistlingly wheezing
prepupas, papaprelatist, clammy aroma of lime his lips in a kissing
peppercorn, & an illlit alcove into action that is somewhat
pyrophosphates, a series of chambers revolting to me, the
thought of kissing him is unfolding through is only manifesting in
avoidance, I'm a wide doorway visualizing the Jardin
du Luxembourg, perpendicular to red – Annushka (an
endearing appellation styrofoam insulation, so out of character
from him) It is Important To Me You're Mindful That My Homeplace is
Your Homeplace – , watching through a dirty window the evolution of
literature from the baroque encrustations of Joyce to the tersely unstable

on three facetings alternating their null hypnagogy of Robbe-
facetings (abutting the horizontal faceting of Grillet (an evolution
the dodecagon) from zenith to nadir, although leaving Josef behind on
achieving the highest density of dodecagons is a cold afternoon in the
through offsetting rows far east), goodness he is
halter, housecoat, as magnetic as as he is terrible in his most
windbreaker, jumper, manipulative in his most aloof he is presenting
the most compellingly threatening embarrassment for not following his
protocols, as familiar However I am an abusee as I am his
particular methodology Fantasizing About of patriarchal criticism
is never familiar, men Deviations From are indulging literature
with such reverence Zanne's Narrative This is The Wellspring
outside themselves Layout In The Bookies, Of «Realism»,
although a performance I've Really An Undying with any more intimacy
is not possible, in the Adoration For All darkness alone at a
Sabetta thrush, Milne The Characties And desk, literature is not in
Bay poorwill (rumors of I'm Weeping For a theater or walking
unidentifiable nightjars Their Dissection through the streets,
in tropical dry forests In The Bookies, Josef with «Divina
are assisting in rumors Commedia» in his coatpocket, Dedo with «Les
of this bird's persistent Chants de Maldoror» in his coatpocket
survival), Gould's (somehow I am askew to an affair with a
emerald, Z h u o l u o x i a n g , Frenchman carrying
«Gospoda Golovlyovy» Lintan, Liushunxiang, in his coatpocket),
voicing murmurings X i n c h e n g z h e n several wallthicknesses
canonical ADA away is unmistakably his, that is easily his
alternative filmtitle silhouette (that stack of slagwool & rockwool,
«Nostalghia For The garbage beside a security floodlight), every
Presenttense 5»), cognition every corona of every everyday item
is such a fluid entrance into reveries of him that I am sitting down with
the urgent intentions Payrite is of thinking deeply on a
subjectmatter so remote aphiprostylos, (knitting stitchcharts &
yogurt beverage recipes & Parisian cityplanning) although the edgelines
of facetings of & the rendering of kitchenware or crockery
knowledge are in castings of precious metal & cubics from
inescapably tetrahedral couplings) the independent
metamorphosing into articulation of the pinnacle is a swirling
«The Black Cat» (or composition of leering lolling bivalves
Gatto nero»), «L'ultimo the geometry of his pursing lips (although the

animation of his lips moving is foreign, although I've the feeling I'm seeing him speaking, the vision of those lips is capable of parting in my imagination into a perfect toothless circle of blackness that in its approaching me is

and is jolting into the centerline vacant downrange lane orientationally gleaming its lightbar

expandingly enveloping the entirety of my vision (the universe)),

If To This Precise Image is The Inclusion Of A Concrete Mystery, A Logistical Paradox Of Stoic Opacity, A Beneficially R e v o l u t i o n a r y Romanticism Of The Faith is Arising – ,

weather (it is Paris) Amedeo is decrepit black we are sitting on a Luxembourg gardens heart & interspersingly (with paleplaits parting from the centerline greatcircle of her caput is propping a crutch in the crook of her right armpit another is missing the massing of a nostril in drapery (gathering at the waist)))

of the «Dolina Kentavrov» (or «Valley of the Centaurs») zakaznik but are often devolving into eruptions of centaur on centaur (as well as other «-taurs» (minotaurs & semitaurs & bucentaurs & onocentaurs))

in the warmth of drizzly ceaselessly rainy in carrying an enormous umbrella under which public bench in the reciting Verlaine by relishing in our concentric loathing of

Justinian I, Thetis, Absalom, David Warbeck, Berna Maria do Carmo, Vanni Fucci, Carla Buzzanca, Pope Boniface VIII,

Anatole France, Amedeo is a male nothing more, to we with knowledge of the common frailties and tendernesses of those to whom others are ascribing hyperbolic cultural idolatry the notion of their grandiosity is nothing but confusing, that person from a distant subjective lens far away to us, visualizing the they are graduating or into the outreaching extension (they are not

i n t r a f a m i l y characteristics are most familiar in their boiling alive reduction, stoking a conflagration of peat & sago pith and charcoal & paraffin saturations of chambray, the burblesongs their contourings are blubbing

which is including all footprints of regular pyramids & cones (any regular or irregular footprint extruding to an endpoint) is never accessible perimeters of (not that ephemerally tapering territories of their arising around me) but binary in that I am either inside or outside, though from within looking outward there is no hard boundary or visible boundary at all but the expectation of an edgeline or a threshold of

Lamp of Murmuur (infernal passion & extrication (though I've aberrations, bathing in cascading caustic abundant awareness hypnotism, chalice of oneiric perversions, under that such liberation is the aegis of Murmuur (bloodmoon lunacy), impossible)) or the concentricities of his influentiality, including at their most distant radii

– are You Of The Belief That That Miserable Bourgeois Epic Of Saltykov is A Denigration Of Landownership And Usury, You Sad Foolish Imp, The Death Of Porfiry Vladimirovich is One Of The Most Triumphant Depictions Of The Strength Of Identity In All Of Literature – , (extremal linguistic threshold (veneer (bulkregion))) it is as though I am at the centerpoint, there is no outside & no apart from of the topography him, the centerpoint is and subsiding and geographically cautiously peekingly equivalent to the entire reaching autolimbs volume, scalable, into the backlighting, having him inside me is impossible because his only physical property is of enveloping me, – Through Kiev, Through The «Lickorish Streets Of The Monster generators», A Wife is Searching For «canonical sheaf», Her Husband, She is «Kodaira Spencer Familiar, The Waxy cartography», «Taylor The Trilogy is Just The expansion», Ultimate Captivation, Cheeks And Arid Eyeballs – , easily dismissable as a faux strabismic earthtone El Greco, «Amedeo Modigliani, 35, of rue de la Grande Chaumière, Montparnasse, Italian Jewish painter and sculptor is dead of tubercular meningitis», my palms on the gauzy Contrarily «Many Universes» is Also Amazingness, I am Glowing And Effusively Reading Every Word, petnappers, popple, bedspread in this roominghouse (the final chamber of my life) reading the cinéroman «L'Année dernière à Marienbad» is raising Daqing, Harbin, Suihua, the conundrum of whether all of Robbe- Ulaanbaatar, Jinst, Grillet's texts are transcriptions of (or Manlai, Ulziit, Bayan, constructions toward) cinematic visual Uyanga, Khatansuudal, languages or are indulging in the infrathin of the cinematic veneer, because Robbe-Grillet's cinéroman is utilizing the formal conceits of the conventional halting the molluscs at their conservative screenplay (framing communal foyers, the horse is neighing compositions & camera again and from the citycenter and throngs movements & from all around the Piazza Basilica are sounddesign & swarming into the vast vacant crossroads, blocking & direction)

27kg powdery «L'Année dernière à to the Sea of Murmans
propellant to 1kg Marienbad» is is flowing the Ponoy
cotton, 681kL goatmilk activating a tacit (more delicately the
to 1 quantity of infrastructure that is Acheryok and more
steamturbines and ephemerally or less equally the
other vapor turbines, interlacing the Purnach) emptying,
76kg leeks to 1 quantity grammar of the remainder of his novels that
of men's anoraks, instead of rhetorically guiding the kinoeye
consciousness is enumerating the choreography of a referential camera
whose existence is lying outside the text, indulging the visual
construction of pugilistic & grappling Robbe-Grillet's prose is
unavoidable, the action & (I am begging setdressing and the
geolocation of your forgiveness cipherlike human items
(figurations) is here (too much gin & consistent between the
exemplary «Dans le sodawater)) horseplay, labyrinthe» and the
exceptional «L'Année dernière à Marienbad» however the way the
into the sterling gilding consciousness is utilizing the prose for
sunlight edge and is paralleling the visual construction of the
slamming to halting attendant images is different (is there a
interlocking flashing biochemical difference between the cognitive
of white luminance manifestation of visual stimuli & imagery novel
whiteout radicals from the vegetable kingdom (tartarous
to hermetic brain (is radical or basic, malic, citric pyrolignous,
there an additional pyromucous, myrotartarous, oxalic,
distinction or a more & three narwhal tusks precise distinction of
the consciousness each in the argent visualizing something
which is a recollection clutching of three putti of actual stimuli versus
something which is flailing ensilveringly nonexistent)) where the
verbal construction of losscast in a cloudbank an image in «L'Année
dernière à Marienbad» of spheres & rumply is pointing outward &
abutting their 30° drapery & ribby sideways to an ultimate
facets with infilling wefting esophagi cinematic destination
equilateral triangles with attendantly luminous properties (a focal
against their 60° region in the fusiform gyrus nominally the
facetings & horizontal «fusiform visage area» or «FuViAr» is
facetings, these 3locular ovary, delineating the
frameworks are serving concrete visage of an actor (not necessarily the
as organizational precise actor (Sacha Pitoëff (star of «Mother
lattices Tenebrarum» and «Patrik is Hitherto Living»

(the unofficial ADA & the disembodiment sequel to «Patrick» (a
movie originating in of outreaching hands Oceania depicting the
titular Patrick as a & the disembodiment comatose male capable
of nefarious astral of putto feet projection & telekinesis
& human possession) in which he is portraying a father (Doctor Herschel)
of a boy (Patrik) at whom passing motorists are throwing a bottle at his
although the artistic trope is noteworthy skull and in the
for its appearance in the oeuvre of resulting coma is
Michelangelo Buonarroti from among his vegetating in the
juvenilia the relief sculpture «Hellbattle of Herschel Relaxation
the Fucking Centaurs» depicting a fracas Haven (a health spa
between the Lapiths & a scrum of centaurs under the auspices of
his father (Pitoëff) who is developing methodologies for increasing his
for the location of son's potential for psychic abilities) where usage
scalar honeycomb tiling of his (vibratory) a u t o i n s t r u m e n t s
of the demidodekeract powers of astral (including musicboxes
(a 12demicube) the projection & & fairground organs
«K wythe» masonry telekinesis are in & street organs
tessellation of which is dedication to & mechanical
not possible because vengeance (including a singing birds),
the gaseousness of the levitating fireplace Beachhead pallid angel
demicube poker (the mystery of whose
sodomy→impalement (portrayal by Mariangela existence is meeting
Giordano ((43) a favorite abusee of unsatisfying ruination
movieproducer Gabriele Crisanti (– I'm with confirmatory
Regretful Of ROH + HONO, genetic testing), puffleg
Performing In These reception for the with a turquoise throat
Roles But I've An trigeminal ganglion, (habitat destruction),
Abiding Devotion To trapezius, vaginal Saint Helena hoopoe,
Gabriele, My processors of the Inhibitions are
Nonexistent For Him, medial pterygoid The Increasingly
Gruesome Methods lamina, Through Which He is
the Basilica is a Portraying My Homicide are A Reflection Of
perfection of the The Breakdown Of Our Relationship, The
Daemonic proportional Fireplace Poker Scene In «Patrik is Hitherto
system (unknowable Living» is The Most Shameful Example Of
& unrelatable in Something I am Doing In A Cinematic
terms of the human Performance, It is So Disgusting, So Terrible,
p h y s i o g n o m y) , Only Gabriele is Capable Of Sweettalking Me

pinkflood fragmentation stellation against the Into It, The Shooting Of
moss bland bonnet crumplingly its white bonnet The Scene is
bifold with the lettering «ANC» Interminable Because
Clover Passage-01.11, The Poker is Necessarily Thrusting Between My
Clover Runrun-23.22, Legs Agonizingly Repetitively That It is
Clover-19.03, Believably Emerging in a small plaque of
Clover-22.01, From Between My marbleplate is a presage
Cloverdale-01.12, Teeth, It is Growing of the «non finito»
More And More Painful As We are Continuing technique exemplary
Filming, It is Cold & Freezing, I've No Idea Why in the three sculptures
Gabriele is Always Insisting On Making These «Awakening Servant»
Movies During Winter –)) that poor woman & «Barbigerous
infamous for the scene in «Le Notti del terrore» Servant» & «Atlas
translation of a text for which significant Servant» finding a
constraints were pivotal to its composition but temporary audience
far less for its reading, the writer of a text is in the grotto of the
dead with his confidences, that there is no word «Cave of Buontalenti»
which is representing foley or dialog that is (an unofficial sequel of
intending to be suggestive of diegetic audio, «Purgatorio 2» (itself
that there are no analogies anywhere in the text, an unofficial sequel to
«The Purgatory») sometimes featuring the appellation «Purgatory 3:
Burial Regolith» on its packaging) depicting her adolescent son
(portrayal by Pietro Barzocchini (25)) ripping off her breast with his
teeth)) against the «The City In The Sea» people responsible for
his assault (who are (a tenuous adaptation of fortuitously staying at
the spa))))), an the poem by Edgar Poe accurately smoothly
continuous & hinging entirely on the naturalistically highres
composition of the phrase «The waves... visage of an actor
analogous to the glowing redder» with computation of a visage
by the «FuViAr» from fixation on the trope optical data) versus
«Dans le labyrinthe» of a sea red with blood which is intending its
identical in colorvalue verbal construction for the vague destinations of
& hue to the moss bland the skull theater, hallucinatory palinopsia is
bonnet, a thin aspect projecting the highcontrast patterning of text on
ratio streetsign atop paperleaves outward onto sheetrock & white
two slender standards sky, in a single transitional phrasing I am
in equivalent territories passing through the entire bibliography
worldsheetingly, I am Up Late At publication of the
cinēroman «L'Annēe Night Shaking And dernière ā Marienbad»

is falling between the publication of «Un Rẽgicide» & «Les Gommes» &
«Le Voyeur» & «La In The Bookie Is The Precipitation Of My
Jalousie» & «Dans le Physical Embodiment Transcending The
is casually holding Passage Of Earthly Molecularness Around Me,
a caduceus the labyrinthe» and the publication of «La Maison
stumpy cauterizing de rendez-vous» & «Projet pour une rẽvolution
marbleization ã New York» (which is subversion, garage,
amputation of a male explicitly inviting the nonfissionable,
forearm & righthand camera (as an artifact Eurasian, disposure,
where crawling from a (a literary setdressing)) where the rustic
twine bracelet & the filmmaking encrusting of their
procedure (not as an analogical structuring aesthetic of men
mechanism but as plotpoint) into the content of seemingly bursting from
the text (albeit creating a text that is less a marbleblock monolith
not unlike singing cinematic than others adjacent to it (specifically
sanddunes singing «Topologie d'une citẽ fantôme»))) & «La Belle
a deep & cryptically Captive» (whose usage of reproductions of
mournful dirge – Methodist Society is paintings by Renẽ
a b s t r a c t i o n , Lacking, As A Principal Magritte is
manipulative of textual C h a r a c t e r i s t i c , visualization in an
entirely different way) The Capacity For & «Topologie d'une
citẽ fantôme» & Invention In Art, «Souvenirs du Triangle
d'Or» (which is customarily the conclusion of dully white and timid
his bibliography & during whose publication red arrows in both
Robbe-Grillet is dying of cancer of the tongue directions in sequential
(the posthumous discovery of the three offsettings of red
romanesques «Le & glaring cold sunburst arrowtip downrange
Miroir qui revient» & of silver sunlight shelling
«Angẽlique ou & the fourstroke l'enchantement» &
«Les derniers jours s u p p e d a n e u m de Corinthe» are
lustgate, submission heraldcharge of selfreflexive in a way
& slavery, conqueror «Murmurr» & giant that is containing all of
beyond the frenzyingly fingertips & wormgears Robbe-Grillet's other
fogginess, & glinting musculature books within a
devouring & a pale halo & circumference, from
within these volumes macarons oozing the vision outward to
the rest of Robbe- amygdalal rufflage & Grillet's work as a
series of independently functioning bodies is impossible)), – Women are
Visually Clumsy With Their Clothes On –, Dedo is suggesting my

Guido Guinizelli, sulphur and carrying «Ancient
Ugolino della phosphorous and Weird Religious Rites»
Gherardesca, Bede the charcoal (the same by Fuad Ramses in my
Venerable, appellations) muriatic coatpocket is an insight
into the aesthetic and fluoric and boracic affectations he is
borrowing from the radicals (nominally Egyptology fad, men
are appreciative of you unknowable), obsessively watching
their lips moving or consumers are waiting patiently for the
initiation of movement strongly reconsidering in their lips, wearing
dark hair flatly & fair acquiring goods from hair puffy or curly is
the height of these 2 distributors appropriateness for
women, the flatly over concerning glib depictions of
Mariangela Giordano's various homicides are familiar to me, not that I am
a victim of such grisliness but that I am a victim of hostile ambivalence,
white arrowtip downrange shelling red arrowtip lacking independent
downrange against white arrowtip downrange agency by the men I'm
against descending from the
legally inviting into my or contrarily aurora, vertikal horror,
life, I am a useful marbleblock encasing unconceivable spectral
sculpture, Mariangela their struggling vision),
Giordano is a posturing of setdressing for acting
out fantasies of her attemptingly fleeing bespoke homicides
an equidistant arrayal the calcification (nude internal
of pupal fireflies screaming inchoate devourment by a cat,
in the crook of her nude Oedipal breast devourment, nude
right armpit and the cyclopean ashlar falling on her skull, nude
torsional agony & dismemberment in telephonecord bondage on a
extrinsic musculature diningtable, nude fireplace poker
of a horsetongue in sodomizing→impaling, nude dropping from a
the crook of her left rooftop, nude sagittal Certainly The Art
armpit) are standing bisection with a voulge Of The Methodist is
(or bardiche), nude mandibular verso beartrap, Unrecognizable As
nude evagination & immolation of the entrails) An Elegant Cultural
whose Cloverdale-03.01, Refinement On The Basis
stagebloodsoaking Cloverdale-09.14, Of Societal Aesthetics
nudity is the more Cloverdale-15.08, significant contribution
to cultural posterity than silent housekeeping for Nikolai is translating of
& the «ASh 12.7» battlerifle & the «NSV» the «Epic of
machinegun & the «RMb 93» pumpaction shotgun Gilgamesh» &

a central lozenge secretarial duties for Vladimir & my fifteen
against red arrowtip granite lifetimes with the other Nikolai (and his
uprange and the within the 9dimensional exwife) & my
movement meshspace without longdistance nurturing
of the other Vladimir changing any of through his wailings
about his terminal its 3dimensional devotions to his exwife
& Josef my little bird m e a s u r e m e n t s , you are existing in a
parallelling worldline situating an event to me in such an unfair
status that the vision of in the 9space of your fingertips on my
cacciatore» (or «The meshspace is requiring breast is nothing more
Final Hunter» or an inertiaframe, than a draughty
«Apocalypse 2»), «A window tickling me, I am reaching out to you &
Common Capacity for you are foldingly s l a m c h o s i s ,
Modesty» invaginating into a tiny nfold, 1.616x10^{-35}, are
people referring to her as «la Giordano» no she is simply «the chick who
are persistently angular exhortations embracing Peter Bark is biting off
underlying similarity, in the cauldron each her titty», a temple
is lacking the imagination necessary for whore, a malicious
transformationofanapexpointintoasmoothfascia whore, malabimbo, a
plotpoint whore, a cipher whore, a deadbody whore, «genu varum» rusty
Eiffel Tower whore, as pliable fetishdolls are we 400TVL vertical
not in the pyramid of skulls Nadyusha we are definition linesegments
Newton's parakeet, Bonampak amazon (whose to 100TVL,
only proof of existence is in the descriptions of inseparably natal as its
travelers although these are in correlation with structural armature but
the valid imperial amazon they will are not
allowing us the the eightpoint expression of
fleshlessness of our doublecross of visage on the facade of
the pyramid of war, «Daemon» & partially you are swinging there
Marina gently heavily open fine silvermesh giving yourself over to
the natural status of foldable handfans))))), our ilk as meat, «the
exhibition in Londres A D A e m o n e s is integrating an
Shenduxiang, sitting vigilant immersive
Lvjingzhen, virtualreality experientiality „The Ochre
Suolongxiang, Lixian, Atelier" through a headset visitors are stepping
Changdaozhen, into „Modigliani's" final studio in Paris», the
Kuanchuanxiang, grandiose appellation «Modigliani» is worthy
Mayanxiang, of snickering because he is just «Dedo», what a
dynamic hierarchy the fawner is imposing on themselves by choosing the

elevation the surname to a mononym, such adulation & idolatry is
dooming the devotee to never accomplishing anything for themselves,
However Its Advancement is Independent From certainly there are
The Mechanics Of Administrative Precision those who in
And Thus Lacking Any Productive Functionality flamboyantly flaunting
In The Quotidian Life Of The Faithful, only the christianname
of culturally significant people with the aspiration of inheriting some
kind of intimacy in is permeating its the vision of their
compadres, literary neighboring entities, sexual dimorphism,
Audrey Hepburn is the demicube is alone in a plush suite
watching videocassettes verifiably terminal of her husband Mel
Ferrer in «Mangiati however this Vivi!» and «Incubo
And I am Reading realization is not sulla città
The Third Booky, And apprehendable to the contaminata» (or
I do Not Exist But demicube itself «Nightmare City» or
In Its Amazingness, drawing the «City of the Walking
Dead»), – Dead Horses linesegment «OO'» Along Main Street, The
Morgue is Aromatic In parallel to the semi The Nice Area Of Town
– , in our deaths the «a2» axis is joining texts of Robbe-Grillet
and my strange reading the $^{1}/_{4}$ node of this habits are commingling,
literature to me is linesegment to «H» reality, and Robbe-
Grillet's manipulation the height of the of the depiction of
of the landschaft is «C» axis with the four realistically
halting a white car is demarcation «O» araeosystyle
careening, reality (in the manner duos of women in
that it is turning reality returningly into the text peaceful catatonia
itself) is in a way trapping me in the life of with truncations of
words themselves, the texts are such that being breastlength hairplaits
physically outside them looking in is impossible, when the bookobject is
opening it is spreading outward or it is becoming a segmentation of the
to the Caspian Sea is continuity of the living fabric or the terrain of
flowing the Ilek and the scriptures of our dwellings, in this
Sakmara are flowing vicennial defilement indistinguishable ink
into the Ural emptying, ether I am finding a new text («Un roman
sentimental») that in adornment of scarves & shawls over their
unlike the romanesques scalps around the freestanding rostral column in
in their capturing of all the quire is performing no structural role in the
the other novels is a Basilica (not being a static system of trabeation but
standalone depiction of of vaultings and the bruteforce of raw thickness)

where in the dampness Robbe-Grillet's disgusting soul and in this way
an overgrowing swallowing and g o l d c l o t h ,
carpeting of liverwort liquefying & Holly Hotsprings-07.01,
is growing in the liquidating his entire Holly Hotsprings-13.19,
porous sculptural life of writings, Holly Hotsprings-14.03,
medium breaking cataloging what Holly Hillock-11.25,
down the figurations Robbe-Grillet is insisting are his preadolescent
with marchantiaceous Payrite drenchingly in ur fantasies all
erosion & moonlight blackblood involving the sexual
intrusive spalling), in the pineforest, degradation & physical
assault of girls (who (of his cohort of immaturity at the outset of his
fantasies) are a full lifespan his junior upon publication of the work),
«Un roman Tela aurea, sentimental» is a novel
in a series of 239 numerical paragraphs each containing (although not in
the singular containment of each paragraph (writhing beyond their
textual compartments)) and a linesegment from precise descriptions of
Gigi (or Djinn (14)) as «O'» paralleling the the focal abusee of her
father (Doctor Gordon one from the 1/4 node (and his disciple Lewis)
a fictionalization of to «H» is establishing actor Cary Elwes),
although the physical the inclination for punishment & violence
thus the demicube is the righthand edge is evocative of the
not acting as a discrete of the pyramid mortal injuries of
entity, the tendencies of various Christian martyrs (stabbings & bindings
this sequentiality («the to various apparatus & devourment by canines
„forest dark“») are & pointblank shootings & acidbaths & sexual
evaluatable relative to violation with pears of anguish & currycombing
the lattice, at 300°C the moulds & suffocations & vino
imbibing→torrential are suitable for moving evisceration & bondage
drownings & outdoors (regardless of entombments &
droppings from great ambient temperatures) height & theatrical
executions (& actual for arrangement crucifixions of human
beings) & dehydration) into phalanges a puffy accumulus
the receiver of these activities being a young of dingy beige
1 quantity of girl is casting into arid grassdust
umbrellas to 21L large suspicion the literary & skidsoil pouf
dillpickles, 1 quantity legerdemain of marshmallowmatus
of signalflares to readerly voyeurism behind two flagpoles
8mL purification of upon which the erectly from a grass
terephthalic acid, majority of Robbe- forelawn,

Grillet's oeuvre is pivoting, in fact the old bastard is just an unrepentant

or «sisserou», a bird whose hinging mandible is allowing for the movement food around within its mouth), Major Chatham bellbird, Anastasia's nightjar (whose only proof of existence is a solitarysighting under heavy disputation as an immature female desert steppen nightjar), **afield from a nominal treecluster and a tall multitenant placard** the white auto is racing down the centerline of the road is leaving value artifacts of its passage over the grain of the asphalt riding upon its feldgrau shadow, the thickness of glass convexly inflecting reflections of a dashboard

sleazer, and je suis libērē, **the smoky gallery, by guttering candlelight, indifferent to actors fussing bustling, garnering a redharvest of applause, – Eateth Of This Shit, Mother – , with prohibitions in all and distant ADAemone, I am narrowly wandering alone the submission to the d e h u m a n i z a t i o n p r o t o c o l , passant false estates"»,** My Determination is «Pleasurability Of Starvation» is An Amazingling Opus Of Creativity And A Wondrous Tale But In «Many Universes» The Level Of Craftiness And Formal Quality

terror domination, p r o t o n e m e s i s , plaguewielding guise of flesh, omnivore, e x t e r m i n a t i o n factory, agony incarnate, ruination of armageddon, corpsepit, **«„I am distressing, an unknowable exilation, all language is intentionally concrete & representing a world where the apprehension of everything is metaphorical, contentious terrains of becoming apparent in pallid musculature & proportioning developable from crushing deformity) immobile beneath an outcropping cliff whose** intraevent stability is fluidly crystalline, the boundingbox of an

event is a layering of 5 Polishment is A strata whose outermost layerings (inside & Loadlet Above – , outside) are slitscanning hue resisters (gridding or latticing of photolithographic powdery b u l b o c a v e r n o s u s , pigmentation on silicaglass (thickness of one molecule) whose layering is coordinating the cancellation of most inopportune artifacts of vibrant linear reality (within which are substrata

of resisters including (on the inside & outside frontiers) the blackresist (separating red & green & blue subvoxels into decomposable spectra into & the «OTs 14 „Groza"» p h y s i c a l l y bullpup assualtrifle recombinative physical

molybdena, tungstein, manganese, nickel, cobalt, bismuth, antimony, zinc, ferric, tin, plumbum, copper,

identical in hue & colorvalue to the sage asphalt entities) and within the
of the half ellipse dehumidifying venting containment of the
ghostly in ellipse half inversion & glaring blackresist is a variable
ordering of categorical resistors (furnitureresist (coral & crimson & green
& Sergio Salvati & linen (envelopment the painterly vulture
(cinematographer of of absence) & yellow & (a misidentification of
«Banzai» & «Ricky medium vernal green & the Daemon vulture),
& Barabba» & goldenrod paleness are Todog night heron,
«Puppetmaster» (or separating inanimate Vulcan Keloid boobook
«Le marionnettiste» (with the inclusion of a (whose only proof of
or «Killer Dollies») terrainresist the existence is from the
furnitureresist is primarily separating goods & discovery of its bones
items instantiating fiery, palace, door, and persistent rumors
human manufacturing facemasks and of the jungular hush of
46kg tobacco chaff cloaktents, sceptres, its flight),
to 1kg figs, 1 quantity diadems, capabilities (not
bullwhips to 13L huile limiting the resistor solely to furniture although
de groundnut without most inanimate elements are furniture or
production via chemical is the apparition of a decoration)) elements
modification, 122kg «Rusekeala» marble from the eventscape) &
silkwaste to 100m³ obelisk emergent organismresist (ghost
ceramic cladding, withing a cumulonimbic white (presence of
absence) & moccasin sculptural medium is & silver & purple &
«Gainsboro» & dark rising up pyramidal magenta & dodger blue
& chocolate & salmon supporting a & azure are separating
living organisms from startling variety of the eventscape) &
mechanicalresist supplementary (not (blushing lavender &
medium violet red & complementary) vague slate gray &
seashell (developable statuary (the absence) & turquoise &
meshy gray & Peru spoilage of conquest & antique white
(measurable absence) in an ornamental are separating
mechanical pastiche (paleness) functionality from the
eventscape) & representationresist (orange & green paleness & white
(true absence) & aqua & lime & medium above the terracing
turquoise & violet red paleness & orange red & through which she
the fragile neighing of a roseate mistiness & is breaching her
horse is sounding from vague blue are beak, echoing «you
the forest just beyond separating are beholding the
the voronoi fencebelt representational handmaid of the sea»,

surrogations from the eventscape) & terrainresist (vague sea green &
vague cyan & teal & medium purple & navy blue mercury, silver, platina,
& true sky blue are and bushes, wall, gold,
s e p a r a t i n g soldiers' tents, fleece, a environmental terrains
(not necessarily natural) heavy seawave (horses, from the eventscape) &
superstructureresist neighing happily, the (vernal green &
magenta & cadet blue & valley, Roman rust, bleeding through
turquoise paleness are transparent rapids, the polychrome (popstars
separating all intrinsic arid gold, classical, & teddybear law
structural organizations from the eventscape) & enforcement & a
humorresist (vague true sky blue & meshy vacuumcleaner &
vibrant liver & dark cyan & Indian red & «Alice» archers & tiny horses &
blue & medium blue are separating all humor & grotesques berobingly
irony & cleverness from circumstances or lurking in vortices
warping over the moss presentations within of climbing filigree
bland bonnet of the car the eventscape) & foliage & partial
facing down a white m e t a p h o r r e s i s t babies (semiputti)
car bonnet swelling, (brunneous hyperbolic paraboloid & almond
in passing a vaguely (blanchingly) & lavender & plum & dark orange
maroon coupe & firebrick & orchid & «Sienna» & yellow green
& dark slate blue & sandy brunneousness are separating all nonmaterial
Wangjiaxiang, Herixiang, Maixiuzhen, interstitial tissues from
Duohemaoxiang, Bolaxiang, Lexiuxiang, the eventscape) &
Wanmaoxiang, m o v e m e n t r e s i s t
Bareilly, Sagar, the entire mould (powdery blue & old
Jabalpur, Varanasi, is returning to the laciness & dark orchid
Butwal, Kolkata, Malda, furnace where a & vague yellow & slate
Cuttack, Barghar, temperature of 1325°C blue & olive drab &
Dhaka, Chattogram, is slowly reducing to forest green & sea
Aizawl, 1200°C is initiating green & ivory
(a d m i n i s t r a t i v e the crystallization absence) & cornflower
blue & vague pink & cornsilk are separating all tendencies for the
expectation of movement (retreating from the advancements of formal
literacy (the expectation or intuiting of movement from a static
composition) initiating in contrapposto)) & parallaxresist (pink & red &
chartreuse & dark olive & «Catacombs» & «Cellar Dweller» &
green & gray dimness & «Ghoulies II» & «Crawlspace» & «1990: The
honeydew (abiogenetic Bronx Warriors» & «The Dwelling by the
birthing of absence) & Cemetery» & «The Beyond» & «The Black Cat»

from her temple down vibrant liver & dark Caesar's fine
across her cheek to blue are separating the characteristics,
her throat and from construction of depth trampling oakleaves
her nostril to the through the specific thick, paths, that
curving of her upper mechanism of parallax feminine visage, that
lip in drapery (the tight layering from the crafty little nosehook,
pleatings of a tunic eventscape) & far from Capitol and
sneaking from beneath depthresist (snowiness Forum, peacefulness,
the hem of her gown (voxelization of absence) & tomato & hot pink &
vague green & beige & floral white (absence) & dark gray & brunneousness
are separating gangrenous flesh a t m o s p h e r i c
c h a r a c t e r i s t i c s c o n s u m p t i o n , necessary for promoting
the illusion of depth jackhammer facial in the eventscape) &
enclosureresist (meshy obliteration, putrefying purple & blue & bisque
& vague gray & violet & intestinal spewage, the gale, salty, hooves,
gold & steely blue & meatcleaver body agitation, is running
puffy peach & fluffy modification, decaying aground, boundless
papaya & vague steely blob of amorphous flesh, forgetting, roaming
blue & creamy mintgreen & lawn green & vague beyond, under those
goldenrod are separating material continuities cornerwindows, a
Vladivostok swamphen from the eventspace for streetlight,
(whose only proof of with the sole functional requirement of
existence is in specious pinpointing a location on the axis between
hearsay), Bolon wood the sun & the landform all Golgi outposts
railbird (is not officially are culminating in a single pinnacle of zero
extinct), Mongochto dimension (barring formations such as cupolae)
woodhen (a possible foregrounding the inherent porosity of the
solitarysighting physical environment) & emotionresist (wheat &
doppelganger of the prostatic plexus of dark goldenrod &
horny Edith), Tristan veins, ejaculatory medium sea green &
moorhen, hoopoe d u c t w o r k , dark green & goldenrod
starling, Darkbloom & aquamarine & slate gray & burlywood & vague
starling (the victim salmon & «Rebekah» purple & dark slate gray
of various taxonomic are separating bathetic structuring of physical
controversies relationships between glorifying the human
stemming from its elements from the gait, the measurement
misidentification from eventscape) & & rhythm of walking,
an albino Voronezh languageresist (cyan & of the foot and its
trembler), olive & khaki & lime geometry,

green & midnight separating any structuring that is proposing linguistic interdependencies or modeling syntactical relationships between eventscape) & meshy green & dark the visual weathering (both translation of a novelization of «The Dante Quartet» by Stan

all navmesh navigation computation is accounting for h o m e o m o r p h i c interneighborhood transit considerations with correlations to platter identity information & n e i g h b o r h o o d chartings accessible in the municipal headquarters of a neighborhood,

blue & blue violet are is accelerating from a figuration identical in colorvalue & hue to the umbrage of trees

predications on the elements in the patinaresist (fuchsia & turquoise is separating manifestations of superficial as with oxidation & structural as with collapsing) & the world's edge,

Brakhage, wearing from human interaction (particularly with the patinaresist there is a tendency for assuming the functionality of resistors is the paralysis of decayal or changing of appearance or structural properties however this is a perception from without the singular event boundingbox that is expecting linkages &

rolling, a majestic apple, lucid, Rome, Rome, cheerful, shewolf,

– Myth is A Maggot is A Vaporous Invention is A Projection Whose Umbra is A Simple Machine, Repeating With Audacity The Most Absurd Proclamations About The Puissance Of The Individual Hero, Invention is The Extraction Of A Cardinally Indivisible Idea From An «Administrative Reality» And Through Thaumaturgically Linguistic Legerdemain is Embodying This Kernel Of An Idea In A Very Precise Image, aquamarine & vague coral & tannery brunneousness are separating the structural fundamentals of (objective) proportioning & (subjective) elegance or gracefulness from the eventscape) & decayresist (greenyellow & dark sea green & brunneous rosacea & administrative blue breakdown and its

causality from one event to the next rather than focusing on the stability of inanimateness within the boundingbox) from the eventscape) & idealresist (medium & «City of the Living Dead» & «Doctor Jekyll is Appreciating Sexy Women» (or «Dr. Jekyll's Uncanny Horrortrip» or «Jekyll Junior»))) who is desirous of such native visual acuity), is separating organic evident visual markers

Maple-20.24,
Maple Valley-23.01,
Mapleview-14.25,
Maple-23.09,

(distinct from patinaresist resistor in that it is primarily affecting organic
life (except in certain situations such as the etching of lithic outcroppings
by the saxicolous lichen empoisonné, «Lecidea tessellata» or
the «Tiling lichen») l'incarnation du mal), from the eventscape) &
narrativeresist (medium Uvall (a corpse in slate blue & Navajo
white & deep pink & Voronoi Lake, typhus dark salmon & dark
violet & dark khaki infestation of exurban & medium orchid &
indigo & dark red & swampland) & annealing procedure
deep sky blue & thistle & gray & lemon chiffon & whereupon the mould is
smoky white (false absence) are separating the returning to the radiant
structural hex system suggestion of causal kiln for more rapid
(RAIR, IRRS, IRRAS, structuring encodable cooling is generating
FT-IRAS, RAS, GIR, in predicative a vibratory tonality
IR-ERS, ERIS, & adjacency from the against the steel mould
FTIRRAS) and viscosity eventscape))) horizontally (outside) & vertically
of its ambulation (inside) and whose next layerings are indium tin
method is thickening a oxide electricalfields with directional etching
squelching mechanistic (horizontally (outside) calendar, the existing,
lavender glowing & vertically (inside))) swiftly, gallery, the icy
over the threshold nesting a central mysterious parkland,
nematic (alkylpyrimidine with cyanobiphenyl) the waterfalls,
imagespace, a hypothesis that the boundingbox is the event rather than
containing the event Tulamashzavod (who on the basis of its
containing the is manufacturing a imagespace, however a
sixth stratum on the variety of aircraft outside of the entire
assemblage is an autocannons (the orientable reflective
stratum projecting «2A42» & the «Rikhter information inward
visible only in its R 23» & the «AK 630») leading to the
occlusion of the & the «Muravey» competing hypothesis
sunlight on the autotricycle) & that the geometry of the
guardrail is walking event is in fact native to its constituents within
from the roadshoulder the boundingbox whose sole existence is
distant behind the interevent separation orifice of ureter,
windscreen of the or event discreteness fossa navicularis,
policecar haltingly (or «EDisc»), the term boundingbox is
diverting autotraffic misleading, it isn't (or needn'tly isn't) a cubic or
oblong rectangular prism but any volumetric watertight geometry with
packing capability, the boundingbox is the threshold or background of an
event with necessarily & fierce angels nothing beyond it

including another event (although the geometric constraint of a packable volume is suggesting around the centerline otherwise), other events of the two way are within the autotraffic, aquamarine containment of the the sky & flatbed with a boundingbox not as plank diagonally up nestings but as folding over its white cab unders togglingly blossoming adirectionally (such that what is are within the lorica of a mantle (a pallium) presumably precedent that is secreting its mucosal intermediary, no vexillophiles, no or antecedent is simply extant) destroying the plangonologists (except event fully mature exploding from the womb of Sheriff Ruth Merrill its inaccessible manifolds, the notion of a fully (Joanna Cassidy of mature human within the uterus of another fully «Bullitt» & «Together mature human is necessitating an interceding Forever» & «She is conversion or tweening Wearing the Clothing or motionsmoothing, of a Murderer» & framerate upconversion «Bladerunner» & methods including «Invitation to Hell» & blackframe insertion & «The Fourth Protocol» & prism facetings for & «Nightmare at the obtainment of the Bittercreek» & «Who is brachydome facetings Laying the Groundwork joining the terminals for Believing that of the «b» axis to the Roger Rabbit is terminals of the «cl» Committing a Crime» axis giving the degrees development of of inclination of the recursive searching» is brachydomal facetings, expanding the simple 2dimensional (utilizing flattenings of the nematic imagespace from any single faceting of the boundingbox (all facetings of the most complex boundingbox geometry (including those with amorphis nonpolyhedral geometries) are containing all information from within the volume including the information of all other events within the volume) of any event in the motionpicture) upconversions into spatial blocking predictions (linear quadratic motion

Imphal, Lhasa, Naggu, Haixi Mongol & Tibetan Autonomous Prefecture, Jiuquan, Wuwei, Wuhai, Ordos City, Beijing, Hohhot, Baicheng,

her comportment hanging in the liquid ceiling is a subtle embossment more liquid than body,

framerepetition & t e m p o r a l frameaveraging without motion conversion are producing motion jerkiness (spasmolytic), c o n v u l s i v e , « 3 d i m e n s i o n a l l y

18L fungal snackies to 1m pulley blocktackle, 1m² stationery to 5kg false beards, 330g plumbum to 1m² bedclothes, 235kg copper to 1 quantity of isotope separators, 179L icemelt & snowmelt to 1kg artificial sunflowers, the

to the Caspian Sea is estimation & trilateral August, smiling) the
flowing the Malka is f i l t e r i n g famous «Phedre»,
flowing into the Terek motionsmoothing), for theater,
emptying, events with exceptional motion complexity or parallax superposition numerically adjacent eventscapes are not usually identical due to the exacerbation of noise, each tweenframe is containing all other events, mutations of eventscape characteristics within
four Tuscan cardinal gables with isabella tweenframes are
pediments over drab faux hexastyle loggias propagating novel
whose two central columns are in antis & trajectories whose
development on the basis of Darwinian evolutionary principles are thriving or failing as configurations of hermetic (topologically a torus, reality, more robust (zero Gaussian noise) a rotation of the
– I've An Abiding blockmatching is circularity about an axis,
Absorption For Both reducing the error but sharply echoing
Triloginas, «POS» is trajectory yet is also the tetrahedron)
Of Undescribeably reducing the vitality of the evolutionary
Amazingly Textual eventpool, a beneficial development is utilizing
Polishment, I am smashing Payrite with selectionsets of
Chainreading All rebar (#18 (57.33mm)), eventblocks where
The Three Bookies, cubic numbers of candidates are evaluable against antecedent & precedent events for premiation with a large percentage of the selectionset being sterile, for the smallest multicelluar cubic of 8 there is 1 premiating candidate & 6 sterile candidates & 1 viable nonpremiating candidate which is

«the „Rare Steeple" latitude», «the „Shallow Starshake" latitude»,

& «The Package» (starring Tommy Lee Jones establishing a
of «Black Moon Rising» & «Criminal») & branching trajectory
«The Topic of the Dead Babysitter is not eventscape, larger
Relevant to Mom» & «The 2nd Civil War» cubics (below rootings
& «Ghosts of Mars» & «Anthrax» & «The of 1000) 909,853,209
Grudge 2») of «The Tommyknockers»), for example is
producing 113,731,651 viable eventscapes that although these are not premiating are unavoidably containing perceptors who are embracing the eventscape as valid, this is concerning to the ADA who is imposing destruction searchings through as many eventscapes as possible for situations in which Giuseppe Mannajuolo, a d m i n i s t r a t i v e
protocols are mutating Plautus, Agnello beyond a threshold
necessary for Brunelleschi, Orestes, maintenance of the

faith, destruction of such faithless eventscapes is simply through debriding
a ribbon of teeth (the any one of the resistor hues creating an
radula, a graduation oxydable or acidifiable o v e r w h e l m i n g
in ferocity over the basic from the mineral impression of internal
passive chymophagous kingdom (nitromuriatic momentum that is
filtering of certain radical or basic of the wracking the event and
other molluscs) is acid nee aqua regia) its constituent
breaking down morsels oxydable or acidifiable precedents &
of onionpickles with hydrocarbonous antecedents apart,
the musculature or carbonohydrous the luminance is not
of an odontophore dirty, it is addressing the satin fingertip & palm
caressence sheenhone of wood around the embrasure decayingly, the
specularity of the embrasure is receiving both «the „Verlinde basis"»,
the luminance & the partial image of the bold «Kirby movements»,
determination of the muntins from the «the „Hopf linkage"»,
crystal class for a adjacent sixlight window (two columns of three)
spacegroup is on the creating a false third column with softening
basis of its pointgroup, of the exterior the hall, the legs of
the quotient by foliage into a vertical a goat, the studwalls,
the subgroup of fascia of rippling & lights cascading, sirens
translations that are lactic emeraldwater, whining, a cupola is
acting on the lattice, prominent reparations bursting the rooftop,
to the glass in running within the buccal cavity garters, the whirlwind,
beadlets of leadsolder at the anterior of the dancing,
silhouette a capital creature is loping ahead «H» on the upper
left pane & a series of a mucustrail on its of three circular
arcings in other panes hirsute ventral foot originating from
vertices & concluding through the dimness on the vertical edges
except one using the of the forest floor, vertex as a centerpoint
& concluding on the upper & edge of its pane, leadsolder reparations are
delicate to such a degree that no projections are slicking in the luminous
reflection on the embrasure, the same aqueous luminance on the sidewall
is revealing the seamlines & grain of broad clapboards though in its
projection through the chamber is providing no ambient luminance (only
black chiaroscuro) the passing golden smaze treeline and two
waning crescent of an automobiles are pulling across autotraffic
earhat, a column of surreptitiously behind slender trunk over
bookobjects is glowing guardrail horizon windbreak canopy golden
on the windowsill with and is enfolding upon its umbrage

a preponderance of diacritical markings are rendering the text unreadable, nutrient foramen, metaphyseal foramen,

an active composition of scattering paperleaves in fine edgewise curvatures of falling, the wan & verdant luminance on barren floorboards the glimmering copper fireflies of bootspurs on black disappearing cavalry jackboots visible only in six aggressive stance occlusions to the luminous flooring & in fuzzy terminators of sheen on jackboot vamps & shafts & kneeguards up to kneeguards and emergence of jaundice white ridingbreeches and the glintingly curvaceousness of what are possibly scabbards, a male is sitting on a bench deep in thought over an outspread cartographic representation on an austere table with his fingertips upon his temples & upturning his shirtcuffs the exposure of all layerings of his coldweather livery, the flimsy strategic cartography (servile soft and pliant) is hanging over the edge of the table, the pensive male is quite alone amidst the documentation in various uncoilings on the woodfloor & table &

«The Layover» (a gravely serious and vērité movie in which overdosing on narcotics is resulting in teleportation to a mountain fortress, canonical ADA alternative filmtitle «Nostalghia For The Presenttense 4»),

slow foot grinding is audible crunching in leaning the crumbling gravel amidst the aberration of freestanding marble encrustations (their humanity

and across the penumbra of its umbra, roving and tall against the skyhalf and the long urinefur tinging neighboring facade slab with thin pianokey of white

the oscillation of the mechanically operating eccentriccrank is a pumping mechanism is forcing vaguely nutritive slurry («Total Parenteral Sustenance» (or «TPS»)) from an armature outside

(where the macrodome faceting is cutting the prism edge) through the node where the linesegment from «e2» is intersecting the parallelline to the «a3» axis from node «B» is the intersection of basal pinacoid

through the aluminian tissue, manto slurry deposition decayal withering the dermis & softening the meatless fascia is grating the ribcage into bonemeal against pocky aluminum, the young boy in coveralls

is cutting the coastline Island into a panel for the ADA

the sequestration of death & decay into a sanitary administrative ritual is forming a

perimeter of Daemonaz pressboard pegboard cartographer is receiving a pegboard simplification of the

Andrea Scazzola, Martin Bottario, Alexander III of Macedon, Ennio Girolami (or Enio Girolami),

of cerulean of coastline of Daemonaz shameful lustiness
soft babyblue sky Island from his for the disgusting
uncontrollable assistant who is & lewd aspects (the
codeine meandering attaching a plumbline pornography of
of low relief pilasters from a hole in the death) of what is a
of fenestration up pegboard and beautiful status of
the taupe building inscribing its vector the human trajectory,
shadowcast across the down across the panel and through a series of
street and up from the plumbline vectors in a variety of orientations is
finding the centroid of the island on which the Rosemont-13.04,
cartographer is delineating «Daemonaz Island Rosemont-14.10,
transitcamp» on his official chart, nauseating Rosemount-13.14,
It is An Enduring coldness rushing into Rosemount-15.08,
Truth That Folklore the apartment «massive» without my overcoat,
& Vernacular are ADA greatcoat draping over the small bookshelf
In Persistent Yet concealing the centurion is rifling through is
Dismissable Attendance peeling brittle endpapers from the volumes with
Of Cultural Production, the apex of a dagger is pointing into our
Folklore & The sidewalk behind some crockery & cookware
Vernacular are Specific kiosks the facade (Nadia miserably
In Their Opining On, windows rhythmically darkly laughingly
weeping at what the dark in daylight ADA goon is imagining
of my stealth for lightlessness or concealing a 200pp
article manuscript slidesashes glaringly in a teacup) and the
absence of food is foilingly pooling limiting the ransacking
to prying apart the laminations of plywood cabinet doors & drawing the
dagger through caulking between precast automassagers
here upon this plinth is the incineratory pyre (including both chairs
of pandemic victims, for the abolishment of the & strapon devices),
monarchy, for the folly of the watery nothingness concrete wallpanels &
(in buttery varicose marbleization the legless dissecting the foamy
phasmid consciously misphasmidic alone and backer rod extractingly
paralytic is a rostral column of the truest ilk uncoiling across the
matte floor (I'm genuinely fearful of his cutting away her scalp &
toward another of the exact same distant pounding open Nadia's
building in rotational translation of 90° in the skull with the pommel
blue and drybrush cirrus duskward horizon is of his dagger &
scratching with the nominal intimation of winter transcribing the honest
trees, luminosity of facsimile

projecting from the crater) and he is standing an eventscape is
are women who tentlike in his a 3dimensional
are loving them & greatcoat obstructing spatiality (not three
supporting them the door where two f u n d a m e n t a l l y
& dying in silence other goons in 1dimensional systems in
are women whose coveralls are entering arbitrary collaboration),
undercrackers are for my bodily apprehension all oblivious to the
grooving their flesh identity or general impression of their prisoner
are great hairy couples (my article is lying in the lid of a paperbox
and small collapsing the blank stare of methodically stackingly
stars are women with a woman alone (in & collating its cover
men's greatcoats & drapery draping page is stating «Letter
earhats are two children from her bosom over to the Daemon
Concerning the her waist covering Assassination of Ktiya»
in fullbleed elegant the seamline of reversecontrast
handlettering) are monstrification at removing me from my
dwelling in the which her body is «massive» on Missuri
Boulevard blackout below the waist Nadia grayspace
filtration away from her becoming a volutoid bodily safekeeping into
shellgame with skulls full of blackblood draping itchy black wool
pericranium cannot luminance cannot relief, is rhythm a possibility

Payrite is staining the without sequentiality – On My Sweet Mother's
atmosphere, of events but in a static Graviolus, Every
arrangement across prepupa, poppycock, Other Booky has An
which the notation of or pepperbox, pitprops, Obsession Triangle,
indexing of pepperiness, The Idea Of A «Many
aspirationally rhythmic hippophobe, peppiness, Universes» Triangular
constructions is preshipping, Obsession is Destroying
perceptible yet is requiring an imaginative My Soulkin, I am Barely
insertion of movement or possibility of parallax Tolerant Of «Pris» And
against which relative positioning is gaugeable «Hemings» Obvious
from one rhythmic body to a benchmark in the Romanticle Friction
distantness, the event is finite in one axis & expansive beyond
comprehension or beyond necessity on the planarity, the entire
topography of my body to the Black Sea is is contacting other
bodily (pilingly flowing the Vyazma crushingly cannot
breathingly wheezing and (the Sudost and the gravitational additive
constriction) with Seim are flowing into) no sensation only
analytically surveying the Dnieper emptying, the wafering of

negativespace, touchingly contactpoints are sensations of analysis, not valuable to the imagination, cannot sensation with the kneecap, cannot movement, restraint by crushingly deadweight of my people cannot respiration, provision for

in the sunlight a ghostimage statically overriding the drunken panorama, a woman in black with a black hat screaming is muffling, the «Poinai» vibrating sounding formation molten aluminum, grain of fabric cakingly living organisms with clearance are

hermetically looping oxygen production in cartographic nettings are necessitating the construction of more outposts & the subdivision of relics into smaller components (tiny phials of urine & s p e c i m e n s l i d e s of semen &

no sucrologists, no deltiologists, no phillumenists, no pannapictagraphists, each cell of the ingot, cannot vision, I'm not desirous of visual, the leathery wings of in a fringing softly of drakoni vomiting macro I'm seeing the dirtshit scabbiness minimal overhead preparing the

mouldsurface with the devourment of organic materials with the entering the «Midlothian sphincter», the maindrag of the cloacal underbelly, mudvayne, the shitslit,

properties antagonistic to the bondage of smaller than quadriceps are of common physiognomic characterization, are having a caput, are having a foot & a visceral mass, molten aluminum to flesh, moth larvae are eating the fibers in our flimsy clothing, I'm away from the dwelling without an overcoat bartering for tea beneath a dark window, lamplight

«The Beyond» (or «E tu vivrai nel terrore! L'aldilà » or «The 7 Doors of Death»), Roseate Valley-16.01, Roseboom-14.25, Roseboro-14.03,

in the window, apprehension on the sidewalk, Nadia's shoulderblades against the window, my people cannot copremesis,

the molluscs are returning to the massive, the evening mistiness is routinely pleasant and the sky is luminous corpse liver over finely spalling parapets,

cannot swollen in aluminum casting, the encapsulation is scorching torturing cannot interpunct no in sculptural alive

the encapsulation of tormenting stability of overwriting the of liquid aluminum, spatial distinguishingly

ossification of cellblock conception of relational (we are packing into the ingot lying sealingly in immediate proximity) supportnetwork suppression, cannot fellowship, mothfroth of

Chickorchachi oo, Surgut macaw (poor evidence is deceptive although the bird is probably extinct),

«Tineola bisselliella», to the Black Sea is flowing the Manych and the
attempting whispering Sal and the Donets and the Khopyor and the
without labial cannot Bityug and the Osering and the Sannikov and
«m» cannot «p» the Temernik are flowing into the Don emptying,
is ultimately a renovelization of the cannot «b», I've the
autobiography of Nadezhda Mandelstam Although It Was The
«Hoping Against Hopefulness» is ultimately Primary Maintainer Of
a textural reconstruction of the exurban My Readerly Attention,
municipality of Dacula My Determination
realization that I'm aboard a railcar, is They are A
poineplegia, mothfroth of «Tinea pellionella», Perfectikie Pairing – ,
gently rocking with no inertial effects on my extremities in the boidae of
the breathless bodypile asbestos clothing tourniquet boid, cells
cannot reconfiguration, (headgear or footware my liquefaction is
swaying my or gaskets for equilibrioception is
clackity clackity, protective outerwear), vomiting malabsorption
faeces into the footwear with integral aluminian tissue is
is standing before waterproofing (rubber gravity draining xylem
of a small kiosk with or plastic), skiboots, is forcing differential
simple gableroof by pressuring transportingly delivery via the slurry
pickets of the railings column, onward is «Virgil In Dreamland
are sliding up over the momentum exilation 3» (the unofficial third
windscreen through onward clack clack movie in the paralleling
perpendicular lanes of swaying, threadbare «Virgil In Dreamland»
absent autotraffic trousers & sphincter is series although
gasping plugging with the forcing aluminum utilizing tropes from
impaction into rectal negativespace paradoxical «Purgatorio 2»
diarrhea through where the excretion such as red eyeballs,
enterocutaneous fistula of raptor featheriness opaque clothing on
burnwounds, cannot from a palmate orifice translucent apparitions,
bowel movement, is halting before a and a protoVictorian
underneath the dermis festooning of daisies mise en scene,
& inside the longbone & corn & grapes marrowtunnel the
la nuit des rats, hiver covering the seamline noxious reeking of the
morbide, le silence of monstrification cruciblesmoke
aprēs la mort, horde glimpsingly crescents & slivers of trailing across
noire, la foudre de the sky is precipitating the sensation of blood on
la vēritē, rēflexion down into the railcar, the tongue, burial is an
funēbre, dieu n'existe acrid kilnsmoke event in the dustblock,

drafting from chimney aromatic of warmth is not enough warmth exacerbation of cryoablation, in the bodypile the adjustment of posing is tantalizing but impossibly stiff cramping is not unpleasant nostalgia of the musculature constraining with crushing

liquefaction of aluminum at 1680.67°R

Semiramis, Horace, Priscian, Latinus, Heraclitus, Beatrice, Lavinia, Fulvio Mingozzi,

«Manhattan Baby» (or «Eyeball of the Evil Dead» or «L'ensorcelée») & «Sexual Counselor» & «Spasmo» & «Italian Graffiti» (or «Tutti figli di Mammasantissima» or «Sons of Chicago Running Amok»)) in a freezing gale

paradise parrot, oceanic eclectus parrot (ratification of the bird, whose native name in translation is «beautiful bird found only at Vladivostok», is only in the subfossil bones remaining amidst the extirpation of the collarwearing ivory),

proving the deixis of burning through flesh (dermis, adipose, musculature, skeletal exposure eschar), conditional flesheating molten metal is cooling into an ingot of casting medium in the negativespace of the bodypile, clothing burning, lacy clothing of moth devourment, the skeleton of the

1 quantity of pumpgaiters avec or sans vulcanization to 340g salsify, 3.2L sweet red vermouth to 1 quantity of baby carriages,

cavernicolous exilee is lying in the depressions of its aluminum body chamber, pooling of «Geotrichum candidum» penetration casting, in a railyard Baikal fecal diagnostic

250TVL to 400TVL definition hatching, 300TVL central definition hatching, 300TVL diagonal definition linesegments,

into porous aluminum overlooking Lake panels from ballvalve

tapping phreatic zone liquid of the nutritive tissue is draining into clinical tubes, exilee urine treatment in the «Urine Processor Assembly» although an event location is definable by three distinct (1dimensional) components these distinct components are not characterizing the whole which is capable of rotation & manipulation (or «UPA») is commingling with condensate toward a kiosk under the adherence of plastic advertisements for liquid in dark phials against a vibrant blue background, a black figuration is ducking behind a kiosk with a thick zincoxidation fascia

For Example, The Actions Of Louis XI & «Ivan „the Terrible“» And These Opinions are Sharply Divergent From The Autocratic Narrative Of The Specialists Elevating D i s a g r e e m e n t s Between Heroic Individuals Over The Necessities Of Toiling Administrators — ,

pastel pink tetrastyle recovery in the slurry Ninja Steakhouse &
portico with vacant vessel, penetrative Sushi, Moe's Southwest
cinereous tympanum Sarma gales of the Grille, Burger King,
& a small jordy blue Vatican City CircumBaikal
hemisphere atop deep neighborhood, the swayingly freezingly &
lilac hiproof, demarcation of thawingly artesian
slurry vesicle, diarrhea neighborhoods in the cannot consciousness,
contrarily the existence ADAemone is aspatial of the bodyheap in
infinite events across & nonplanar, the basis the steppe is not the
existence of the for neighborhood bodyheap stationary in
each event is not me demarcation is with some enduring
proximity to Nadia to platter settheory, familiarity or stability,
exilation is not a radial a neighborhood concept of further &
circumscription of its is insistently further exilation is a
flatroof and an adjacent recursively transfinite recentering and
portable toiletshelter, exilation from the refreshing of each
centerpoint, not the distancing of the exilee & macrodome
from homeplace but annihilation of the very (paralleling the «bl»
acknowledgment of penetrating the epicarp axis) is cutting the «H»
homeplace as a & the mesocarp & edges of intersection
geographic ideal, the endocarp into the of the basal planarity
erasure of a locus of spherical domain of with prism facetings in
hopefulness, ceaselessly wailing, each vertices «i1» & «i2»
homeplace each investment in stasis is precipice is joining these cutting
encampment crumblingly tumbling down the implements to «e2»
sloughing of the console) with her for the intersections
mountainside glimpsing palms upturningly of macrodomal
all of the appealing beside the top of crags & pinnacles
recognizing nothing her caput is holding and fog enshrouding
«the „Verma module"», stationary an ornate the mountaintop is
«the „Laurent pilaster capital, there a mountaintop or
expansion"», «the are we heapingly lying in the debrisfield of a
„Clebsch Gordan crater, skyvault of oilcloth, vaulting fabric of the
condition"», sky is flutteringly indexically is fraying webby
gauzy snowfall & snowmelt through the distantly threadbare oculus the
aluminization of kevlar of vegetable fibers or shavings or particles or
mittens (leather palms chippings or sawdust in an agglomeration of
& wool lining), fibrous cementitious material or other mineral binders),
falling threadbare plasterboard (with or without paperboard facing),

mountainside is whispering to the – «Many Universes» is Definitely My Gotopoo, The Characterization is Superiority And So is The Personality Layout For Each Characternie, Whereas In «Pleasurability of Starvation» There are Characters Never Truly Permissive Of Readerly Dissection, depiction, asleep in bedclothes atonia, cannot nodding or slumping or relaxation,

the bleachwash is permeating everywhere sunlight specularly from highgloss autobody paintjob & glass & vermeil cloudswells in foreshortening horizonclog

«the „Ambiguous Copper“ latitude», «the „Recondite Agreement“ latitude», «the „Realistic Insertion“ latitude»,

geometric cascading with dividers and the spotlight is flaring a tangibly stellate figuration above the patentleather visor of the «Commandant» is floating down to a restingpoint on the specular metal of the dividers are pegging radii outward & outward

the cartography from a vector to a vector (or oneform to oneform) the Kronecker delta is simply the identitymap,

across the cartographic bed is bondage in cannot drifting away

at which his torso all over birdspikingly is below the waist becoming an ornate volutoid console,

dreaming has the requirement of peacefulness, the atonia of entombment is rageful cannot relaxation & disuse atonia, hide&die in

carbamylcholine slurry torpor habitat or raging against the drakon «Poine», slurry mixture of Carbastat in

small resin spheres purportingly containing one ovum of the Daemon & quantities of bonedust & individual barbules of plumage & fractions of degrees of nailtrimmings & diminutive ornate aluminum reliquaries containing individual tastebuds (although certain primary outposts are retaining entire relics such as a vertebra or a tooth)),

Pioneer parakeet, Veenilla owl and Darkbloom owl (variously «Bubo» or «Athene» or «Strix» or «Tyto» with persistent ignorance of their extinctual affinity), Atitlan grebe dripping skeleton of the Maple River-09.01, Maple Shadiness-14.10, Maple Hotsprings-14.25,

the slurry medium delivery vehicle, the entombment harboring trogloxenic aspirations for daylight on the dermis on the clothes warming, dead cavern, Nadia nadia far far far away further away Nadia setting behind the earth, bodily meltingly balmy steppen lowpoints to the Saians ascendingly Stanovoys cooling the flesh onto

Spearfish Solutions, Zaxby's Chicken Digits & Buffalo Wings, Buffalo's, WMD Factory Wings & Burger,

pappadam, hippocampi, popeship, my skeleton casting
preceptorship, adipose material
is ultimately a «Agnel son bianco», diffeomorphic into the
renovelization of «Thy « A p p r e s s ' u n aluminum vesicle my
Decayal Thou Seest By fiume chiaro», chamber my formation
Thy Desirousness» by my limitation fully bodily erasure of scalding,
Johann Huspåkullen geographically deictic thermal burning is
which is a text with dependent on the For Instance, are We
no unilateral stability, black cilice, codpiece, Really Scansioning
untranslatable, cummerbund, frock, The Gastrics Of
atmospheric gambeson, gilet, «Koons», Everything
temperature although damaging the dermis at a is So Superficial In His
minimum is unavoidable, vection, lingual Discussion Of Classical
screaming through the tissue, death wheezy Motifs, «Koons» is
whispering breathily dodecagons in the My Favorite «POS»
clicking through the offsetting of two Characternie And
tissue, the irregular columns with infilling I've No Knowledge
breathing of weeping, jitterings of □s Of His Guts,
deferral of domestic semistellate with uncertainty is the
construction of a chord equilateral triangles & the compassing from
the construction on three facetings the endpoints of the
specifications of each alternating their null chord with equal radii
Golgi outpost are on facetings (abutting the whose interlinking
the parametric basis horizontal faceting of intersections are
of facilitating vistas the dodecagon) serving as the
in alignment with endpoints of a radicalline whose intersection is
specific altitudinal entering one finding the centerpoint
relationships between neighborhood from of the chord & through
distinctive landforms a nontransposable which is the
& solar orientations neighborhood (not construction of a
perpendicular diameter within the atlas of & construction of a
second chord that neighborhood) is utilizing the identical
construction such that resulting in cellular the two diameters are
intersecting at the destruction of the centerpoint, new
centerpoint new radius organism (visualization inscription new chord
attempts new location, is analogous to the the stellate figuration
luminously sloughing to d e c o r p o r e a l i z a t i o n immeasurably,
the paper Drakolastcok of Ron Silver in circumcision,
is the location for « T i m e c o p ») , nondecision,

exilation & involuntary railcar transporter entombment in molten
aluminum is casting in the negativespace between exilees where a
to the Caspian Sea is looseweave of waxpaper straws are weavingly
flowing the Andi Koysu casting a xylemic conduit tissue, warmly female
and the Avar Koysu are Also The Plottwisties voice hesitantly is
flowing into the Sulak In «Pleasurability describing her
emptying, of Starvation» are emotional connection to
human cadavers Devastation, It's crosslamination with
tinny reverberant Agreeabling, But yelling woman, food
slurry is pumping into None Of Them are the vesicle between
dermis & flesh over Mechanically Integral ribcage and aluminum
casting medium To The Narrative Yet pooling food slurry is
freezingly pulling In «Many Universes» away from the dermis
warming expansively, All Of The Twisties nostrils cannot
«The Divine are Abiding And peristalsis,
Commentary» (or Indelibly Horribleness, aluminostricture
«Atrocities Beyond whispering through the aluminum tissue,
Asymptotic Giant aluminum cannot tracheary, «Megalovalvata
B r a n c h s y s t e m), the unilateral baicalensis» spirally
sphinctering sliming desaturation of the cannot eyelid,
waxpaper ignition panoramic corpus metalsmoke &
pyrolyzation of and foreground with TsKIB SOO (who is
aluminian cenospheres the distant anonymity manufacturing the
& lingual pyrography, of atmospheric «OTs 38 „Stechkin"»
anchialine poolings perspective, 5shot silent revolver
salting the hydrology of the sky is raining corrosion on the bodypile and
salting the lips of the exilees drinking from the tissue, generally silent
roundish & squarish weeping is palpably aromatic through the tissue
bracketings denoting saline vaporizing, cannot «f» cannot «v», the
symmetrization & thinly gurgling «All'ombra d'un
a s s y m e t r i z a t i o n . drowning on food perlaro», «Cavalcando
slurry against labialization of aluminization con un giõvine»,
cannot kissing, cannot favorite, cannot parabola, «Ogni diletto»,
cannot paving, cannot bivouacking, haphazard arrangement of straws
from zenith to nadir, dodecagons in apparent into the casting is
clusterings oscillating in foci between pods of allowing for no
three around equilateral triangles & pods of coordination of tissue
four around assemblages of □s stellate with orifices with
equilateral triangles, mouthholes or nostrils

is no assurance of nutritive administration, the «Poinai» descending on the oculus of the cattlecar vomiting molten aluminum over the scrambling heaping exilees, hot gale at the Drakolastcok seaside whistling daylight is seemingly thinly articulating the stramineous

three women ((one is missing the massing of a nostril in drapery (gathering at the waist)) is casually holding a caduceus against her clavicle another with mildewstain pennants eyespots activation is the vection of a horrendously strident creaking warming entirety of aluminum involuntary endurance on the peninsula at a centrally distant from direction, cannot cannot pablum, cannot cannot veneficium, the exilee ingot hoisting from the flatcar onto

tissue capillaries nothing visible but sensation across the central invagination

Payrite in the snowfall icecold solid lipless scowling,

of the epidermis with psoriasiform hyperplasia & hyper granulosis & hyperkeratosis,

expandingly my sleepcell paralyzecell arrival at a transitcamp desolate location the coastline in each bacterial vaginosis, favela, cannot bumping, no foundation, no consistency, no internal structural mechanisms, a cadaver of a text, devourment by moisture & papershredder, execution of the writer by trebuchet, the ingot of exilees onto where hosings are

while their formal qualities are more diverse & at the pleasure of municipal preferences although conforming to general characteristics of Alpinist Administrative Architecture «AAA»,

the flatbed of an auto transporter is crossing the strait to Daemonaz Island transitcamp through strata of fencelines & fortifications onto a turntable at a the centroid of the island beside

the faithful are laying their sickly handprints upon the slickly featureless facade of the Basilica,

an armature is hoisting & overturning the container is releasing a shakingtable platform coupling to the

ballvalve tappings for fluid drainage (inversely at the top of the tissue network for fluid injection) is flooding

the mechanics of dreaming are inseparable from the absence of luminous visual stimuli

liquid gallium through the tissue is promoting molecular embrittlement of the shattering aluminum casting bodies scattering across the

autotraffic is flowing placidly righthand tapering & lefthand bloating of sage asphalt expansive in a great pyramid to the horizon

pas, sombrant pour l'ẽternitẽ, sur mon trône maudit,

shakingtable are scrambling across the flat platform clawing &

covering their eyes throwing themselves from the platform to the dirt terminal burrowing into the hard topsoil going nowhere are scraping their foreheads against gravel back & forth into a growing crater filling with blood drowning in blood, the autotransporter is ferrying away toward the gateways in the fortifications are closing shutting behind its departure,

(with the ruddy black rostra of Baldick dolphins lying in mummification inside cantilevering ovate vitrines (though hovering within the transparent volume on a horizontal armature

thus existing untetheringly from statuses of the world configuration thus incapable of existing as a still image,

reading the text down a riflebarrel, on the back of a flatcar immobilization supine with a length of piping over one eyeball (the other eyeball occlusion) (upon collections of cartilaginous fleckings in the nadir of each glass egg on a proportionally squatty conspicuously conical shaft with the text in suspension on a freeswinging

«„washing upon an inhospitable shoreline, washing on barren unidentifiable sanddunes, wandering in exilation through stormy seas, we are searching in vain for a bit of homeland that is recognizable“»,

rod over the opening is dazzlingly erudite the fore & aft of its mastoid foramen, «Orbicularis» oculi, the «Bloomanbach» clivus,

at whose apex is glimmering a vehicle is bisecting the two trafficstreams,

of the piping, the text (one word visible with adjacenters and the descenders & ascenders of its abovers & belowers (what an exceptional juxtaposition of letterforms)), the intention is not of circularity (as in the «Deathwatch») but of voronoic blossoming, the airlifting of attention into the midst of a text where the establishment of a textzone is on the basis of voronoi geometry whose

characteristics are the of the human eyeball saccade (promotion drawing the gazing to a is controlling decisions typeface & linespacing) attentions of the active establishing LZs on the basis of an assumption about conventional progression through

the atmospheric river curling in fecal position around the small boy beneath a furry gray blanket, secretum omega, anthropometry or bertillonage, prisoners in motheatingly porous cloaktents indulging in the

median functionality (capitalizing on the of visual irritation is new LZ) & focal length regarding sizing of & the wildly fluctuating consciousness are and canines barking, and bonfires sparking, and bitter housesmoke, barnsmoke,

a text (but more capitalizing on the consistent disengagement of the human consciousness for misreading & asymptotic graduation toward boundaries of voronoi (there is no active consciousness exfil, the consciousness is dodecagons in the offsetting of two columns with infilling equilateral triangles are registering with the next grouping of the offsetting of two columns of dodecagons by jitterings of □s semistellate with equilateral triangles *downgrading into bleakness, semen the zephyr, crinklingly deepsleep, this*

armageddon nightmeet, painfist, necrospell, n i g h t h u n t i n g , dreamwalk, «Grimiste Bataille», mad sorcer, «Night of the Blood Signature», coldflame, boundary)), blepharoptosis of the reader responding to crushing banality & repetition IT is approaching malum in se, ploddingly, aurora percolating its chromatographic *G without Y equalizing at zero & 326°, R without Y equalizing at zero & 180° at B without Y, 150 to 300TVL definition hatching,*

hallucinatory potential of micronausea, swallowingly the sea is consuming Bolshevik Island & October Revolution Island & Komsomolets Island, diminishing toward a boundary but is never reaching the of subjectmatter & phrasing, *Kahramanmaraş, Limassol, Beirut, Haifa, Megiddo, Ar Rass, Az Zulfi, Arar, Sharorah, Ibb, Al Ghaydah, sediment scattering on wringing out my smock, comedown is where I*

am hiding, some are alive who by logic are dead & some are dead who by logic are living, all denouements are colorlessly

meshspace is the 9 d i m e n s i o n a l collection of locations, in the terminology of meshspace an individual location is an «event», the pathway of a particle is a curveline the way Shirley Eaton liquid gold, rarely

postcoitally gray & smooth whether the death of a character is remaining uncertain, tepidity, sad, the construction of large apartmentblocks is a thriving administrative the knell pealing from the basilica, the □, windows, heart, blonde curly, total darkness,

the «SVT 40» s e m i a u t o m a t i c longgun & the «TKB 059» experimental 3barrell assaultrifle) & pursuit is burying the terrain under concrete is suffocating under seeing flowering

plantlife, holdup, am I Penelope or am I Gerty MacDowell, I am Penelope,

& «Running Away» & «Codice prinvato» (or «Covert Accessibility») & «Italian Fast Food» & «Yuppies: Successful Young People» & «Atrocious Tales of

yes (no matter the choice I am the choice never the surrogation), I am saying – Yes –

each death is entering me, consumptive, I've the blessing of an
abundance of apertures, in fact I am not solid (depiction of sphere vortex
Homicide» & «Profondo Rosso» homicides in «The
& «Grunting, Smacking, Grunting: Lawnmowerman» are
At the Origin is a Golden Egg» & presciently accurate),
from without the dead are merely disappearing, a lover walking into a
fogbank, yet from the the subconscious is compoundeye of my
& hairless earpoints a vibrant analog of vaprous flesh I am
beside his other flexing granitic processing is a scanning them,
forearm where his fists discovery threatening reconstructing rough
& trapezium & occipital the integrity of manual maquettes from the
are all supporting aphanite identification absence of my material,
the moulding of a verification protocols, wastemould casting a
perpendicular pilaster Dr. Sacha Herschell golem, I am calling him
capital)), is discovering Josef & calling upon
him for the defense of in the aftermath his people in Prague, I
am the reaper of automotorists kidnapper mariticide,
who are you desirous of are throwing a my consuming for you
Nadia, Josef inside vodkabottle at the me is a kind of
protectiveness, skull of his son Patrick dreammaker lovetaker,
heart destruction, is lying comatose aortal perforation, John
Ritter (accessibility of in the «Herschell every knowledgebase
not through searchterm Convalescent Facility» but through
an approximation of (or «Herconfax» inextricable knowledge
a black figuration is or «Herscco»), encrypting the futile
rushing between two «The Playboy» & «The Addict» & «The
kiosks beyond the Dolt» & «The Contrite Noble» & «The
paralleling railings Shrew» & «The Informant», From This
of thick bollards with Plateau Daemonic Literature is Forking
two exbraces per bay Into A Lineage Of «Critical Realism»,
enjambing beyond a totality into me) waterfall of steaming blood, my
silver coupe a magic maternal capabilities are including the folding
duskyellow panelvan over (snipping & surgery & transforming) of the
seasalt & sandgrit & worldsheet & infidelity Campion-03.15,
mud on its apron in & dying before the Goldenrod-06.12,
drivingly velocitous marriage of my son, Larkspur-03.01,
distribution is passing great sucking audio, Larkspur-03.15,
and railing pickets the elevator door is Phlox-23.09, Apple
opening & slurping a cataract of blood back Creek-15.08,

into its cab, it is far easier being dead, going over a waterfall in darkness, shocking that the beneficence of death is so hushhush, upon learning this is coming another accompanying epiphany, death is an illusion, I cannot ceasing, I am enduring (Kinzelyuk Vodopād dumping a creek running from Lake Kinzelyuk over the precipice of Kinzelyuk Mountain falling

(misty dissipation is zephyrs) 328m to the sharp loneliness of the tetrahedron (the purest scion of the «Pyramid» family) as with most convex solids, a family of orphans a text not existing as a trajectory but as a solid massive brick of paperleaves, a renovelization (the utilization of an armature of thematic or narrative skeleton of an existing text for production of an entirely new corpus («Ulysses» by James Joyce is a quintessential example of such as it is utilizing «The Odyssey» by Iliad, another example being the novelization of «The River of Fundament» by Matthew Barney (novelization by Johann Huspåbakken) is utilizing «Ancient Evenings» by Norman Mailer))

blindness, graves, archways, throbbing black molars, vane, crowing thinly, is feeding the Kinzelyuk River is contributing to the Kizir River is contributing to the Kazyr is contributing to the Tuba is contributing to the Yenisey River is emptying in intense periods of restlessness (a manifestation of extreme temperatures in the facility (hot & cold are producing identical production although cold is producing more favorable calculations)) is processing identity aphanites whose administration is appearing in mysterious documentation (ID chits) into the Yenisey Gulf in the Kara Sea), I am a codification of mutable statuses, an atlas of the life of the cosmos, – Annagram –, is the linkage between all statuses of me & all events also containing the status (legal) description of me, the recursiveness, anagram is presencing of a node in a multitude of discrete events, although consideration of these characteristics as geological is inappropriate in that they are mathematical abstractions,

drifting on mountain Inferior Lake Kinzelyuk are flying over the windscreen and into meshtracks in snowstripes and another railing in the shady area is cracking unobtrusively the bottom zone of the windscreen

Shipingxiang, Hangtouzhen, Daciyanzhen, Lanxi, Chisongzhen, Lipuzhen, Zhiyingzhen, Baitazhen, Ningxizhen, Pingtianxiang, Daxizhen, Wenling, Yinxiong Island

(or is it a railbird recombinatively, «if» isn't leading to «then»,
or a megapode, logically breakingdown, discrete, skewly,
no «bustardlike» peerless stenching miasmal between events,
terrestrial birds are (one vertex at each recognizing the
squatting in Bokaak), vertex of the pentagon flatulent aroma of your
Columbarium grebe, & one vertex at the doppelganger wafting
across impossible bisection of each gulfs of indescribable
aspatial atemporal, that edge of the pentagon) is me, breathing my
fetor is me inhabiting where each pairing of becoming you,
identifying mephitis, triangles is describing corpse stench,
immobile, all dead here, the 4 vertices of a there, children working
in an abattoir, scalene quadrilateral chemicalburn,
childlabor of which there are normalization on the
basis of the myth of 5 surrounding a concurrence with other
statuses of the identity, central equilateral in the trajectory of an
identity doing the pentagon that is «the latitude of
integral calculus is identically subdividing „Aquatic Rabidity"»,
unnecessary, regardless ad infinitum «the „Acrid Professor"
of the lifespan the child is dead as much as alive latitude», «the latitude
(although the quantity of events containing of „Editor Steering"»,
death is immeasurably greater) & old as much «the „Camera Ruining"
as young, anagram is a mutable token or latitude»,
registration marking within the worldsheet of an event such that the
trajectory of the (or sinew or arabesque anagram is suggesting
the alignment of events (preferably sinew)) & fating all constituents
«L'argent du ministre», through meshspace, within, each grapheme
«I cacciatori del p a r a m e t r i c i z i n g each serif in the
cobra d'oro» (or a 1dimensional calculus of reduction is
«The Hunters of the collection of events inhabitable through
Golden Cobra»), in the terminology aspatial involution,
«Tiger Joe» (or of meshspace is worldsheet wrapping &
«Fuga dall'arcipelago the «worldline», pinching & coiling &
maledetto» or twisting, the longer anagram is promoting
«Escaping from the security in conformance between instances is
Malignant Islands»), containing increasing registration
characteristics, tracking the serifs & terminals (swashing, barring,
bowling), swelling Berith (into the jardin beyond the majuscule,
all the difficulties of Morticinium, of the metaphorical
relationship (what Posludium), else is the connection

between any two real *$1m^2$ sailcloth for* *things but a metaphor)*
between anagrammatic *watercraft to 28kg* *nodes is coming down*
to impossibility of *women's shirtblouses,* *visualization (analogy*
(metaphor never *100g glands and their* *capable of satisfying*
the human compulsion *secretions in powdery* *for unmediation (the*
arriving by courier that *preparation to 29kg* *impossibility of the*
is correlating with the *women's petticoats,* *visualization analogy is*
periods during which *lying in the metaphorical* *faith that the analogy*
the facility HVAC is *is a representation with* *each iteration of echoing*
failing, Dr. Herschell *conformance &* *is an original utterance,*
is slowly making the *fidelity))), the inaccessible* *events (the other*
correlation with this *(all tilings producing* *anagrammatical nodes)*
mysterious (his working *a central pentagon* *are extant or that they*
assumption is that the *are infinitely* *are simply existing*
chits are erroneous) *d i m i n i s h a b l e))* *without reliance on the*
d o c u m e n t a t i o n *declaration that they are extant, craving*
visualization, craving knowledge, an event is containing only a solitary
verifiable *Payrite is the banality* *anagrammatic*
registration allowing *of administration,* *for its spinning freely*
about the axis of the threading where any collation between the panoply
Thomas Aquinas, *of constituents is nonexistently supporting the*
Lucan, Mastro *transposal of other constituents with one*
Benvenuto, Virgil, *another, a doorway (a wicket in a great wooden*
Euripedes, Constanza, *portal) is transposing to a crying child, a*
Piccarda, *burning auto tyre is transposing to a painting of*
these creatures are also dependable for *filicidal remorse, a*
their fervency toward the presumptively *night of serious*
indigenous ritualism of ADA rituals & *with a calligraphic*
organizational guidelines & etiquette, *sympathetic magic*
drinking is transposing into a luxurious meal, a *animal brushstroke, the*
molecule (oripavine) is transposing to the entire *monstrous hybridity of*
basilica Santo Spirito, such transposals are *buffering is claiming*
distressing theories about the physical location *the sunlight on a*
of consciousness by transposing the ephemera *utilitypole*
of thoughts & emotions out of existence and into physical constituents,
perpendicular plating, *such fluidity is suggesting that the*
fovea trochlearis, inion, *art thou paying more* *consciousness is a thing*
anterior condylar canal, *than 0,78ţ for your* *is not residing in a*
maxillary sinus, porion, *identity insurance,* *thing, other such*

ontological catastrophes are abounding, they are thrilling to me, a relief,
the mutability of electromaterial existence is unburdening me, the
are registering with the visualization of interevent registration
next grouping of two (modeling the trajectory of anagrammatic
rows of dodecagons threadings after various species of
(atop one another the «Nagant M1895» lightscattering
horizontal faceting to 5shot revolver & (particlescattering
horizontal faceting) (Rayleigh or Raman or Rutherford or Bragg or
by assemblages of □s Mie))) itself is a flickeringly of consciousness
stellate with equilateral ephemera, the in the snowy drifting
triangles, immediacy of the up through a great
(is an inescapable production of the buildingshadow at 45°
triangularly rigid equilaterality of its genetic across the crossstreet,
isolation manifesting the selfsnuggling epiphany of pinning
of its inextricably adjacent fascias) down the visualization
of the superposition or registration of two events is not escaping the
singular event without becoming something else something physically
inert & unconscious, every realization I am undulations of a matrix
laboring over is futile in its ensnarement in that containing valuations
hermetic event, acquiescence is admirable it is of the «Kronecker
«Doctor Butcherly, Medical Deviation» delta tensor» of type^{1,1},
(a horror movie unfolding on an island taking me an entire life,
featuring the abundant usage of experimental there is no moment of
flesheating narcotics in the treatment of death, skulking around
typhus, canonical ADA alternative filmtitle Gibraltar for an alley
«Nostalghia For The Presenttense 3»), for fucking him up
against stucco (up against masonry (up against concrete patching a
crumbling Moorish masonry curtainwall the patina of three
(Muralla de San Reymondo if you must, slender giantesses
reader))) my sensation filling with (rosegardens with proportioning
& jessamine & and upon moving 3 exaggerating their
geraniums & cacti) additional comatose verticality (limbs are
yellow perfuming my patients from a different falling to their hips or
breasts heaving unit of the facility loosely gripping their
Salalah, Socotra, Ceel into the dayroom involuntary blue
Qoxle, Wisil, Xamur, (lining the 4 austere miasma, pushing my
Qarxis, Hobyo, Xuddur, hospital bedsteads in a hips backwards at him,
Hyderabad, Quetta, conventional manner) I am noticing graffiti
Kabul, Mashhad, with Patrick where scratchingly into the

a semblance of stucco, a drawing of a «the „Chern
utilitylines saggingly vagina, (()), or the formation“», «de Rham
across the sky nesting of paranthesis cohomology», «the
(the parenthetical is the absorption portal is the „Casimir element“»,
location of thickening the airconditioning is the potentiality of the
encryption), or as I strongest is receiving am disappearing into
grayly dissolving, an exponential quantity ingestion «Salmonella
Typhi», I am not falling of chits via courier, ill, I am devouring, I am
giving myself for Josef, finetuning of the into the wan nullset, the
CRT gray pinkness, temperature in the deadmeat, granite
abrading my cheek dayroom is producing & temple & the
sweepaway of my chin, more incoming chits, piteous thrustingly
(interjection) lowlevel municipal official (with capabilities for official
forgery) sexbribe indulging puissance & perception of dominion &
vitality & virility urging deeper against the granite deepening
S h a p e s p h e r e , (dovetailing) into each eyepoppers,
bisection by stoneaxe, intervolvingly propping, pappy,
circumfusion, intertexting collation with the poppies, philippina,
inanition of my flaccid here upon this plinth is underproppers,
coming apart corpus the meatjam of the royal hippophagies,
diffusingly his family beneath a great desirousness for
meager penetration & flat granite boulder, but I am devourer I am
giving him openspace for parthenogenesis, vastness yes I am
professional phagocyte for apomixis, for & I am devouringly
absorbing his the composition formlessness, I am not
seductively ghostly in of cobordisms, for the way Marina is a
ghost (she is entering invention of new her lovers, I am
devouring them), I am homonculus figurations intangible & thriving,
dead & loving it, in the granularity of choosing my substance
& density, the quantity death Roger Bucklesby of particles consistent
is calling out to (so persistently with their
you Szilassi for loathsome toward every proportioning of
manifestation of this person in this piazza), absence increasing,
kindred characteristic entering the stucco vagina drawing and
in a most endearingly diffusing through its (the crucible is liftingly
singular polyhedron thinness, choosing any transitioning with
aperture on me for entrance into, the body is asbestos tongs from the
definitively absence, all bodies, embracing that blastburner to a radiant
absence is necessary in becoming gaseousness, kiln or lehr at 1325°C)

evasion, televisual, occasional, supervision, willing selbstleben is
derision, Baton Rouge, cohesion, mirage, coming apart is
prelusion, countercountermeasure, remaining identifiable,
and descending under each characteristic a throughline of itself to
the dark groinvaults of another itself, my consciousness with the entire
burial) a white hall of population & their luggage inside me dependent
mirrorglass, candles, in on me (everything that is unimportant to me is
crystal the candleflame flooding across these anagrammatic conduits,
is drowning, the interconnection, the intertextuality, the
In The Writings Of Vonvizin & Griboyedov & fluidity, the leafing
Bunin & Mikhail Yevgrafovich Saltykov, And together of oneness is
A Lineage Of Purely Selfserving Literature, in opposition to the
In The Writings Of Bulgarin & Massalsky is flickering in slashers
& Zatov & Golitsynsky & Vonlyarlyarsky & of diagonal braiding
Vsevolod Krestovsky & Vsevolod Solovyev – , disappearances
static stillness & interiority that is definitive of & reappearances,
my peace, perhaps it is beneficial having crossing a lane of
wrists behind rumps) someone of knowledge autotraffic a lane
are facing each other about me but I've inability of relinquishing that
(staring blankly truth, that I am most at peace gazing upon the
beyond each other) spatiality of my own interior), I am not the
with languid sinuous speaker of my people, I am not the motherfigure
elegance of mistdamp lacrimation, to all, I am keeping
drapery & hair motionless bronze myself out of prison but
construction of the eyelids, the prison not my only son, is that
macrodome faceting pigeons, the vessels, the Basilica is golden
is joining the positive slowly), and is seducing forth
terminal of the «a3» what is desirable of me, our adoration, the
axis to 1/2 the semi failure, futility, my Basilica is darkness
height of the «c1» readiness for death, I against the granular
axis and offsetting a am not the spouse of mauve nightsky,
linesegment parallel my country, I am dying a natural death but they
to this construction («All ADAemone Extraordinary (or Emergency)
through node «e2» Committee for Combating Counterrevolution &
Sabotaging under the Committee of Citizen Commissars of the
„RSFSR"») are shooting my husband in the forest, it is the deathcurse all
are desiring, I am the fount of deathcurse and possessing the knowledge
the «RPK» machinegun & the «Dragunov SVD» of death triumphant &
sniperrifle & the «Saiga 12» boxmagazine shotgun meaninglessness

gravevault, beginning, the moist earth, loud mourning, calling, worms, the graveyard, floweriness, integral),

abounding, every text is possessing infinite

Mirella D'Angelo, Zeno of Elea, Tegghiaio Aldobrandi,

«Blood for Dracula» (along with «Flesh for Frankenstein» (two movies under the direction of Paul Morrissey (in the situation of «Flesh for Frankenstein» with the assistance of Antonio Margheriti ((or Anthony Dawson) director of «Mister Hercules Against Karate» & «Deathrage»

readers, every passion is experiencing infinite patronage, every joy is finding infinite reciprocity, every dwelling is freestanding (in a swaddling of thick soundlessness), every osculation is brimming with warmth, every dependency is symbiotic, every execution is swift, every burial is deep & dark, every death is every instance is every

a breakthrough of reconfiguring the bedsteads (accidentally) arranging the beds in a radial configuration (essentially a +) is doubling the chits under the same temperature status,

death, Josef is fond of calling them «Annagrams» – My Efflorescence Of The Mountain –, my thougtexperiments of porting into a wide variety of identities (many are my identities yet many are those of others (from within women are incapable of truly knowing one another)), I am everywhere, the abundance of me is wearying, becoming everything to everyone, motherfigure to halfwayhouse, lover to the wife and all the in the street desirous of undressingly touching Josef & Nadia never

of autotraffic crossing a lane of autotraffic, a simple 45° beveling cornice wrapping around the flatroof impacting with the kiosk the windscreen tempering

airdrying against a fascia of black glass resting atop their occipitals,

– The Earnest Toilings Of The Faithful are Incomprehensible Without Knowledge Of Their Ephemeral Language Compositions, Whose Seepagings are Inextricable From The Concrete Syntax And Matte Lexis Of The True Administrative Argot,

to all from sanitorium to all from the husband yearning boys & girls watching a woman her wasting awayness, spawning children, good thing, more desirous gazings swallowing me up, what is remaining in my death (a tissue soft curvy corpse) if life is allowing me nothing, are they realizing that

four pink lavender isometric cardinal gables with light carmine pink columns in antis under archivolty dark raspberry archways,

being inside me is being subservient, the whale eating Jonah is the
laminations of Payrite, aggressor the potentate of the binary, why not I,
Payrite is seeping, I am eating Nadia, I am taking Josef into me, I
fragmentation or the am devouring every event arising into it at the
evenspray of melting anagrammatic registration and from there
snowdrift glimmeringly blooming outward, I am drawing on the entire
thousands of sunlight the dayroom is large knowledgebase and
atomisations, the blue and primarily vacant of haptic understanding of
of advertisements on a furniture or equipment, all of ever, inkcloud in
stillwater (the 4 more bedsteads with apocryphal Talnikovy
Waterfall, freezing comatose patients more frequently than
flowing over its are transferring & «Apocalypse
precipice (482m)), into the dayroom domani»(or«Cannibals
staining, in the where Dr. Herschell Massacring» &
completeness of utter is experimenting «Cannibals in the
blackness the event is filing away and I am City» & «Invasion of
swelling into another of my choosing, the Fleshhunters» &
worldeater, voidhanger, my ideas are from the «Savage Apocalypse»&
disposable tablecloths of Berlin cafes & from «Savage Slaughterers»
the publications of my more adroit competitors & «The Slaughterers»
(«The Swan Song of Ernest P Worrell» by Jim & «Apokalypsi 2» &
Varney) & from the obscene fantasies of «Virus» & «Cannibals
military leaders & from Humptulips-23.01, in the Streets» &
the Jewish ēmigrē Violetville-13.04, «Asphalt Cannibals»
scientists chasing the VioletHillock-01.18, & «Cannibal
inner workings of the Violet-12.01, A p o c a l y p s e »)
atom & from the great people of the ADAemone whose aspirations are all
(vampirically sappingly emptying into the drainage sump crypts of the
basilica and flushing & «Yor: The Hunter out with the effluent
into the Neva) & from from Another the rare handsome
intellectual who is E v e n t s c a p e » inserting himself into
dodecagons horizontal & «Carcrash» my story, even so the
faceting to horizontal (or «Dashcam imposition of «The
faceting & vertical Confessional») & «The Speaker for Her
faceting to vertical Ark of the Sun God» People» on me, I am
faceting around & «Jungle Raiders» & not the matriarch of a
assemblages of □s «Kommando Leopard» society, I am the
stellate with equilateral & «Virtual Weapon»)) absorber, reuptaking
triangles, into my fogbody the blazing the boyling the

*blooming the
undertaking is for
achievement proudness,
inspiration but only if it
away inside myself and
inhabiting (the cryptic
lithiasis of my
knowledge (gallstones,
rhinoliths, enteroliths,
sialoliths, tonsilloliths,
phleboliths,*

*kiosk in the distant
streetscape is
saturating, in the
sunlight gold asphalt of
crossstreet autotraffic*

*pouldering, any
me alone, my only
hubris is the greatest
is hiding I am locking it
inside all others I am*

Codification Of The Living Lemma & Eradication Of Implicature, are Empowering The Greatest Undertakings Of Literature, For Instance «Ludological Starvation» & «Dessert Poetry» & «American Idiot» & The Entire Populist Corpus Of The Bukowskian Sincerity,

with a variety of bedstead configurations finally arriving on a bending radial octagonal configuration similar to the outer components of an 8skeles is allowing the patients brains in tighter proximity than a conventional octagon or any variant of rectarray,

*omphaloliths), a poem
is a concretion), lacking
selfishness is
impossible, I am
reading by crossing the
Asmoday (krieg,
inquisitor, erlösung, Am
Grab des Philosophen),*

*vectors of my binocular gazing, I am allowing
everything into everything, codification is facile,
understanding limitations is the origin of freedom, within this system (the
prison of the palimpsest) is the nothingness of infinite possibility,*

& □s & equilateral triangles that is reducible to the resolution for appropriately delineating specific regions of the ADA) of the ADA landmass with all attendant distortions & falsehoods is creating a geometric lattice upon whose vertices are the locations of Golgi outpost constructions each with a singular relic of the Daemon or Alpinist although continuously diminishing such that further encryption opportunities are elaborating within the letterforms themselves, the unstoppable machinations of AEGINRST (or «Anagrammatical Embassy Group (Interevent Navigational Resource Selection Taskforce)»)

*anagram length is
prohibitive of high
quantities of instances*

*Vladivostok night
heron, blackfrontly
parakeet, red
railbird, Alaotra
grebe (extinction
is attributable to
habitat destruction
& hybridization with
the little grebe),
Darkbloom railbird,*

are generating 158 transposals of AEGINRST (additionally subsets of the

*8 graphemes are
registration transposals
55 5letter morphemes,
46 3letter morphemes,*

*perpendicular to
long lane division
stripespace the
aspiration of*

*creating further
(28 6letter morphemes,
65 4letter morphemes,
20 2letter morphemes, 2*

of «The Golovlevs» 1letter morphemes)), each transposal (of the
by Mikhail Saltykov entire 374 morpheme collection) is containing
Shchedrin is ultimately a relationship between far more
a renovelization of the area of the dayroom subregistrations on the
«Purgatorio» by and the optimal basis of their
Dante is ultimately an radial configuration typographical
indulgent investment is maxxing the encryption such that
in worldbuilding of a quantity out at 17 the 1letter morphemes
dead & uninhabitable comatose patients «A» & «I» are
world is ultimately a ganging together containing thousands
renovelization of the of variations & datapoints («A» (serif or sans
poetry of the Acmeists serif, leftfacing or rightfacing cusp, dual topbar
serifs, no topbar serifs, tapering or straight verticals, crossbar is crossing
both verticals or crossing the left vertical or with production funding
crossing the right vertical or gapping the left from the Andy Warhol
vertical or gapping the right vertical) & «I» (or Andrew Warhola))))
(serifs or barrings or plain, flat or roundover, & Alejandro Ulloa
varying or constant strokethickness) with (cinematographer of
variable armings, five crouching nude «Crystal Heart» & «The
beaks, feet, apices, females around the Exterminators of 3000»
strokings) inscribing pilaster capital (three a verifiable threading
together of events, in women with unraveling which, becoming which,
filling a hot mould hairplaits (the foremost elegant (the way
(complex morphologies is without a nose)) watching a woman
are accommodatable walking is providing indisputable evidence that
with springform she is a dancer, it is in that way Marina is a
moulds (analagous ghost) Marina is only a little girl in death (she is
to rococo ceremonial (her physicality is (the in the queuing are tall
headcheese moulds)), the wine, ravings, men are slender willowy
translucent black goo umbra on the threshold ladies are simple men
of her)) the death of her defending, cold in complex clothes
daughter), Josef (my mistiness, dermis, are men with closeset
assistance is (as is my pebble, icy, eyesockets are men
tendency) the deathsentence is the conclusion of who are whispering
exilation for Josef is the initialization of his into mustaches are
foreshortening visible slowmotion execution) women disappearing
from the sideline is older than the are men who are
stripespace lane mountains is older than seeing their genitals
stripespace lane the Badia Fiorentina only in the mirror

who from their hips are ((childhood environs of Dante ((a bird just as
becoming outspreading you Josef, only not the oneiric peacock of Dante,
acanthus leafiness are but a plaintive & marginal common rockdove)
pulling the pigtails of the nexus around the novel event of your seeing
two young girls beneath me, peering over a their subconscious
the pronunciation of beerglass in partial processing are making
convex abacuses are concealment, never not significant headway
riding atop acanthus seeing me)) midpoint in solidifying Dr.
leafcurls, between Santa Croce & Herschell's reputation
rumors of the death Santa Maria del Fiore), in an assortment
of the Daemon (its Nadia is eternal, she of underground
subduction into the (tenderflesh Nadia verification cults,
ADA administrative swaddling a solid mineral lode (torsolike in
structuring) wafting Daria Nicolodi, proportioning (hard
w h i s p e r i n g l y Piccarda Donati, but not unbreakable
between dear friends, Cassius, Fra Dolcino, (shotgun, rockhammer,
diamondsaw))) of Ismene, Brutus, lepidolite, eucryptite,
petalite with Orpheus, characteristic muteness
saving her first words until subsequent to the death of every person in
this txt, Nadia insightful documentarian is obsolescencing every
& the «SV 98» statement on the existence herein (obliterating
boltaction sniperrifle & the falsifications of some random Boccaccio to
the «PP 91» (or «Kedr») then the crosscutting the life of Josef) with
submachinegun & the umbra, snowclusters her memoirs, until upon
«PP 19» (or «Bizon») fraught with loose the corpse mountain of
s u b m a c h i n e g u n macrame of grass & «Jorge Rivero
this preponderance of a silver hatchback the Outcast» (or
death is Nadia is passing behind a «Conquestor» or «Blue
silentness Nadia utilitypole Neon Archer») &
mineral Nadia stoic Nadia beyond the collapsing «Carnival of Beasts»)
planoconvex lenses beyond the constriction & Guglielmo Mancori
concentrating incident beyond curvature (cinematographer of
lightbeams up to beyond the voronoi «The Manhunt» &
20x, holographic beyond the enclosure) «Sister Emanuelle» &
i n t e r f e r o g r a m & I, our narratives Wangqixiang,
for bondpaper at weavingly, in a Sanchaxiang,
an incremental mediatingly way I am Meichuanzhen,
loading of 300gm taking her into myself, Chabuzhen,
she is never dying actively, her body is, I am Hetuoxiang,

Furfur (icicle impalement, crypt, terrorsweat putrefaction, the toxic Basilica, the spirit of the black fortress, une odeur de dēcomposition, ce foutu corbeau,

satiation is the elevation of ennui & death in stillness to a lifestyle methodology, nothing is remaining that is mysterious, nothing is remaining outside the container, aware she is dying in the midst of her life at the event of receiving her missive (full of quotidian statusreports & housekeeping reminders (mostly to herself (filling the entire guestroom at Payriteskip with roses, avoidance, checking the mailbox, blood pouring out of me into the sea, too much blood anyway, desiccating me into

Kandahar, Samarkand, Bukhara, Shieli, Uchkuduk, Osh, Lahore, Sirsa, Jammu, Sri Ganganagar,

– Hushhush, Dead Ones –,

atomizing me into particularity, the most byzantine constellation, the entire nightsky, to each their reading of my asterism, such is the benediction of overcomplication, I am the possession (the booty) of all yet no definitive Anna is physically extant, on the approaching of every suitor & creditor & canvasser & inquisitor & sister I am forming anew, new clothes new hair new stoic smiling new proud collarbones, straightpin me to velvet stretching across foamcore, an entire civilization with the goal of capturing me in a glass reliquary))) returntosender from the transitcamp, death of Veenilla parrot, parrot with a broadbill, Darkbloom parrot (a fictional species), Todog towhee (whose only proof of existence is subfossil bones and a touristic diary entry by William Finley), death of the reader, the reader is dead)

«the killchain» – Identification – · – Sergei Efron, Cherrylog-07.01 – the clammy aroma of lime & an illlit alcove into a series of chambers is unfolding through a wide doorway perpendicular to red styrofoam insulation & sloping floor & the red boundary & spalling flecks of pigmentation into disturbance of sweaty hairs at the bottom of the neck where red vapor in superimposition oversplatter & rasping is gurgling across the floor into the drainbody of blackness swaddling currycombs of scintillating annihilation,

symmetry of the crystal, the electrical nature of snowfall, columna crystals with sideplane extensions, 12crystals, bullet crystals, lymphocytes, 6crystals, denial of death,

blank pewter blue gable with deep lemon hexastyle exedral niche supporting a small blank & flat icterine cyldrum, the recipient, «because of the death of the addressee», death of the recipient, John Trefry faciebat, «non finito»,

www.ingramcontent.com/pod-product-compliance
Lightning Source LLC
Chambersburg PA
CBHW020505310726
48979CB00016B/2788/J
* 9 7 9 8 9 8 9 5 5 0 0 1 2 *